IN THE
SEASON
OF THE
WILD
ROSE

IN THE
SEASON
OF THE
WILD
ROSE

CLARA RISING

Villard Books New York 1986

FOR TASSIE

I was born in the season of the wild rose and the elder blossom. . . .

—John Breckinridge Castleman, *Active Service*

Library of Congress Cataloging in Publication Data
Rising, Clara.
In the season of the wild rose.
Bibliography: p.
1. Morgan, John Hunt, 1825–1864—Fiction.
2. Morgan's Raid, 1863—Fiction.   3. United States—
History—Civil War, 1861–1865—Fiction.   I. Title.
PS3568.I67I5   1986   813'.54   85-40721
ISBN 0-394-54673-3

Manufactured in the United States of America
9   8   7   6   5   4   3   2
First Edition

PREFACE

They are as remote as the Trojans, the people who are our past. More than six hundred thousand—by some estimates, because of the absence of records, almost a million—Americans died in the Civil War. That the enormity of such tragedy has been misunderstood is understandable; the ancestors of 87 percent of the present American population arrived after Gettysburg. Yet the contention and controversy over the power of the Federal government goes on. In that sense the war is still with us. Its ghosts—both gray and blue —have left us a legacy we cannot shun. To understand ourselves we must understand them. They will not go away.

They taunt us with their belief and hope, their crazy glory defying numbers. That is as it should be, for it is not through statistics that we know hope and fear, our human inheritance. This is a novel, not a history. Some characters are fictional; others are not. That, too, is as it should be, even as parts of ourselves are occasionally questionable, while the self searches for reality.

There are no heroes, as every soldier knows. And to glorify war as anything other than a necessary evil for survival is to miss the meaning of Sherman's famous definition. After 1865 the North was busy getting on with Business, railroading, the West; the South was silent from a sense of chagrin and mortification too deep for articulation, for all its brave talk of dignity in defeat. But from that silence, on both sides, we can see now what Homer saw so clearly, that wars are fought with emotion, not reason. And that some wars—the struggle for what we perceive as personal integrity and a gut-deep need to belong to ourselves—never end.

THE HUNTS

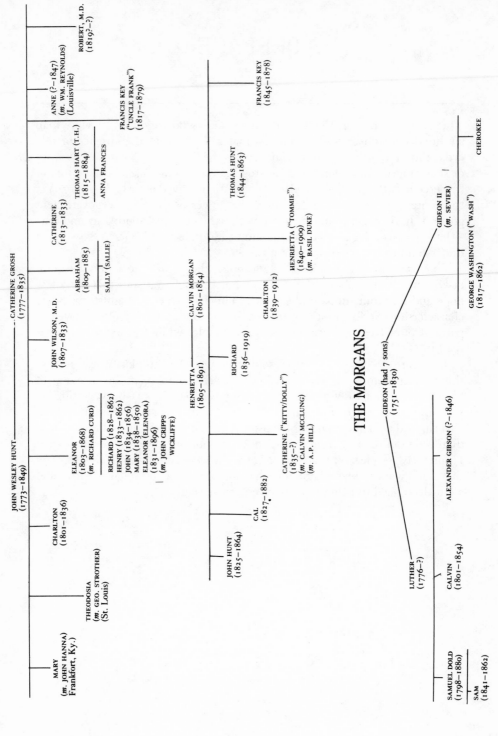

THE MORGANS

─────────── Part I ───────────

1833

1

Heaven. The word hung in the air of the little country church and over the heads of its patient congregation. Johnny Morgan sat next to his mother and looked out the window at the April fields. Under the blue Kentucky sky, dappled with clouds, gray stone fences ran like yearlings over the green swells of land. If Johnny leaned a little to the left he could see the locust tree and his mother's buggy—when she called it a *calèche* his father laughed at what he called her Frenchiness—with Uncle Simon dozing on the seat, his dusty black top hat resting on his nose as the breeze moved the leaves around him. Near the corner of the window Johnny could see Randolph, Uncle Simon's grandson—or rather Randolph's legs, for the rest of him was out of sight—laid out straight on the flat top of the fence. Johnny could just imagine his face tilted up, his head back on his arms.

Heaven.

The word drew Johnny's eyes back to the Reverend Elisha Pratt. He seemed to be struggling in his mind, standing there behind the pulpit in front of them. He slid his eyes from his congregation to the back of Miss Pamela Prichard's neck, as if he expected to find an answer there. But Miss Pamela, her eyes turned to her music, her feet on the pump and her hands poised above the organ keys, wasn't listening.

Johnny watched the preacher and instinctively drew his heels together, the way he did when he wanted to put Zennie into a gallop. *Giddup*, he wanted to say, but the preacher just stood there. *You did a mighty fine job telling us about hell*, Johnny continued his imaginary encouragement. *All those mile-high rocks laid out from here to Frankfort, with that little bird coming once a year to peck at them. Eternity . . .* The soft air came in through the window smelling of daffodils and fresh grass, and Johnny reminded himself that he hadn't believed a word.

He couldn't believe in hell because his mother was Henrietta Hunt Morgan, daughter of John Hunt, Esq., of Lexington, banker and breeder of the best horses in the Bluegrass, and he had heard her say she didn't believe in it. Furthermore, he had heard his grandfather call it Hogwash. Besides, his father was always sick with what Dr. Wolford called "weak lungs." If there was a God and if he loved everybody, why was his father always sick?

Giddup, he said to himself again, and moved closer to his mother. On the other side of her skirt Cal's stubby legs stuck out, his feet twitching. Maybe he, too, wanted the preacher to finish so they could all go home and eat Aunt Hannah's biscuits.

The Reverend Pratt must have sensed their impatience, because at that moment he looked out the window, then back at them. "HEAVEN," he said loudly into the air above their heads, "is a *Kentucky* kind of place."

Johnny breathed a thankful sigh. As he took his mother's hand he could almost feel her think, *Well, what can you expect? This is not Christ Church, but a country Baptist excuse for religion.* And if Calvin Morgan had not gone bankrupt in Alabama with those impetuous brothers of his, and if her father hadn't given them Shadeland, maybe they could be in town worshiping like proper Whigs and Episcopalians. . . .

They were near the end of the aisle and Cal, to avoid her skirts, started tripping on his shoes. Johnny let go her hand to take Cal's as the congregation bunched near the opened door. There the Reverend Pratt, acting in complete control and as if never at a loss for words, greeted each of his flock with a handshake and a quick dip of his head.

To his surprise a smiling Henrietta Morgan laid her small, neatly gloved hand on his. "Do come see us," she said, as if he had been refusing an impassioned and often repeated plea. "Calvin would so enjoy it."

She was beautiful, with wide gray eyes and dark hair and that pert, scooped-up nose that she twitched when something offended her. Yes, she was very much the banker's daughter, holding her shoulders under their green and white striped silk like a general, flanked by her two sons. But for all her severity she couldn't entirely erase the humor that played around her little-girl mouth. It was kissable, Elisha thought, aghast at himself. Did her husband appreciate that adorable short upper lip, or that little indention in her chin, as if a thumbprint had pushed into the softness? The green ribbon of her bonnet bobbed as she spoke, and Reverend Pratt watched it to keep his eyes from her mouth. She was twenty-seven, just a year younger than himself, and every time he saw her his hands shook.

"How is your dear husband, Mrs. Morgan?"

"With the springtime, he always feels better."

"Ah, yes." Reverend Pratt dared let his eyes drift to hers. "It's the winter damp which enfeebles us all," he sighed, graciously including himself in the company of those genteel enough to pamper illness.

"I thought the snow would never disappear," Henrietta answered.

"But it was a good winter for reading," the preacher countered, to prolong the moment.

She slipped her gloved hand to her parasol and raised it, twirling, its lace edge dancing a frothy halo over her head. "Papa"—Henrietta Hunt Morgan pronounced the word in the French fashion—"says Calvin reads too much Voltaire." She laughed, as if she were sharing a naughty secret.

"In that case we must give him a little dose of Saint Matthew to balance things." The Reverend smiled, turning with relief to her little boys, standing correctly beside their mama in their neat suits. Johnny looked back with his mother's wide gray eyes from a round, pensive head inherited from his grandfather.

"And how is your pony?" Reverend Pratt asked.

"He don't have a pony—he has a hoss!" shouted Cal, running after his mother, who had already started moving toward the buggy.

"Oh, fine, sir," answered Johnny, imitating that careless elegance of his father's when he sensed that someone needed to be put at ease. "He's not as tall as Cyrus, but then grandfather says Cyrus has a right to be tall, since he was king of the Persians."

"And your grandfather is quite right, Johnny. Good morning to you, Mrs. Bledsoe!" The preacher was about to turn to the lady when a planter, at his elbow, grabbed his arm with a big paw and asked through thick mustaches how his mare's split hoof was coming on.

Henrietta called Johnny and nodded to Uncle Simon to untie the reins while Randolph, awake and on his feet, helped them into the carriage. She nodded approval to him as she settled her skirts between her sons. Uncle Simon clicked the horse back, and the low *calèche* with its light, thin wheels turned easily into the pike.

"Can't I, Mama?"

"Johnny, don't beg."

"But can't I?"

"It's Sunday. Calvin, take your feet off the seat."

"But it may rain tomorrow," Johnny offered cannily.

"Your uncle Gideon and your cousin Wash are coming on this afternoon's stage."

"Not till tomorrow! They aren't coming until tomorrow!" He let his head sink into the scent and softness of her breasts. He looked up at her face glowing in the yellow light under the parasol.

"They may come today. The letter was uncertain," she said more slowly.

"I thought you said Uncle Gideon was our cousin, too," Cal piped.

"He is—your second cousin. But it's too complicated. You may call him Uncle Gideon."

"Like Uncle Simon or Uncle Isaac?"

Calvin had already learned how to irritate her, she thought. She stiffened and Johnny sat up again. She inspected the parasol lace and pulled the ends of her taffeta cape together. "No—a real uncle."

Johnny watched the rump of the swaying mare and felt with satisfaction his feet on the floor. Cal couldn't do that. But then Cal was only six. Johnny was almost eight and everybody, including his grandfather, said he was a big boy. He was almost as big as Randolph, and Randolph was twelve. Well, almost. At least his head came up to Randolph's shoulder. A new thought came to him. With one hand on the side of the carriage, Johnny slipped the other into his mother's and turned his gray eyes to hers. "Will said he needs to measure Xenophon for the saddle."

"It's Mister Webb and you know your father is not well enough to ride."

"I could take him down there."

"It's a good three miles, and past the tollgate."

"I have five cents," Johnny offered, and then immediately realized he was pushing too fast. How smooth his mother's face shone in that yellow light!

"Your father's horse is not that well trained, and I want no more argument."

"Uncle Simon . . ."

"Enough."

Uncle Simon, whose back he watched now under the black top hat, was the best horse trainer in the world and he had told Johnny that he was riding as well as his father. Xenophon was sixteen hands, a bright chestnut with a creamy mane and tail. Uncle Simon didn't like him because he only liked horses you could match for carriages, like bays. But his father had brought him home one day and they had stood, watching him run, then drop to a floating trot, and his father had said, "I'll let you ride him, Johnny!"

"Really, Father? Thank you!"

"No . . . no thanks. It's an obligation I'm giving you. An obligation to be as generous and considerate as he is." And then he laughed, thinking his son didn't understand.

And oh, that horse could fly! He so wanted Wash to see him! As if to agree, Uncle Simon snapped his whip over the carriage mare and Randolph swiveled his head and opened his round brown face into a toothy grin.

Uncle Simon never smiled. At the most, he would wink. When he was really pleased, or feeling especially friendly, he would cluck as well. In the stables he was king, and Johnny and Cal, as well as Randolph, knew better than to chase chickens or shoot their pepperboxes near the horses. He had come to them from the Randolphs, and his parents had belonged to "Marse Peter Jefferson, an' thass who Ah'm named aftah, Marse Peter, an' menny is de time Ah done wait on Marse Tommy, befo' he be Prez-si-dent. Den Ah belong to Colonel Lewis, and come heah to Marse John, yo' gran'pappy, when dat chile—yo' mama—wuz bawn'd."

"How did you get to be called Simon?"

"Marse Peter's wife, she a Randolph, an' all de Randolphs, dey know de Bible. Well, dey's daddy say, 'Dis niggah heah is *Simon* Peter, not jes' Peter.' Simon Peter wuz de name of one of Jesus's bossmen," he added authoritatively, in that solemn tone he used in dealing with religion or horses.

Cal leaned into his mother's lap, and in adjusting herself, Henrietta dropped Johnny's hand. Maybe he could get Aunt Betty on his side, Johnny thought. He pressed his feet to the floor.

Shadeland, with its four hundred acres, was a small farm by Bluegrass standards. Henrietta Morgan hated it, not because it was small but because it was too far from town. It was pretty enough, with its graveled walks and herb garden. The grove of oak and ash that gave it its name fanned out in a fifty-acre semicircle behind the house and ended on the northeast side beside a clear, meandering creek that fed a series of pastures and one large pond. But the house, a flat-faced Georgian, had no porch, and could not be compared to the columned plantation mansions that dominated their thousand-acre farms at intervals around Lexington. The house, in fact, had been built of logs, hand-hewn and chinked (with horsehair and mortar) by pioneers in 1797, and only bricked over later by more settled owners. But, to be fair, Henrietta thought, as she saw it approaching, it had been a two-story house even in its log days, and it was a comfortable house, with great flanking chimneys which provided, in the basement, a winter kitchen on one side and on the other a gathering place for the servants and sometimes even the boys, who would slip downstairs (did they think she didn't know?) for extra dessert. Bouviette, inherited from her mother to care for the children—and who considered herself a cut above the other servants—would sometimes sit by the fire downstairs in winter to tell them a story.

But then, Aunt Betty, as everybody but Henrietta called her, was family and, like family, should consider herself better than other people. Henrietta twitched her nose. Wasn't John Hunt the wealthiest, most powerful man in the West? Wasn't it even rumored that he might become—perhaps even was —the first millionaire this side of the mountains? Hadn't he hired the best architects to build Hopemont?

Hopemont! The name caught in her throat. Its fanned entrance, its rose garden and spiraling stairs, the pianoforte Papa had ordered from London. Hadn't he given each of his daughters a carriage and horses as wedding gifts —and Calvin a farm to manage when his business failed in Alabama and his lungs became weak? Hadn't he sent them all, all twelve of his children, to the best schools, Theodosia and Mary to Miss Hay's in New Jersey, Eleanor and herself to Miss Beck's Academy in Lexington? Hadn't all the boys (except Robert, still too young) gone to Transylvania? Hadn't her brother Charlton been elected Lexington's first mayor last year? And last year, too, hadn't her handsome, rowdy, loud and lovely brother Johnny returned from France with a medical degree and started practicing medicine in New Orleans? How she missed him, she thought as Uncle Simon turned the carriage toward the house. She'd never told Papa, but she had really named Johnny after him.

"Mama? We're here."

The sight of the front door reminded her of Gideon's visit. The Tennessee Morgans. There would be talk of coon dogs and cockfights. Bloodlines and bad-smelling cigars. Good, generous people—or were they just impulsive? —who could think of nothing but ride, ride, ride, shoot, shoot, shoot, fish, fish, fish. Only Calvin, of all of them, read much. She must talk to him. The boys should be going to Madame Mentelle's. It wasn't that far! The Todds went, and the Breckinridges and the Castlemans. They should be learning French and dancing—how much did they really learn at that little schoolhouse? They would be boors, like their cousin George Washington, and marry people with Indian blood, as Gideon had. Why *couldn't* they call that boy by his proper name?

They had turned into the shade of the long drive and Randolph, the first down, was holding the mare while Uncle Simon slowly and ceremoniously helped Henrietta. The boys were already running ahead through the front door, where they almost knocked Aunt Betty down. Henrietta stepped past her, starched skirts rustling, and they exchanged glances that said, Those boys, what are we going to do with them?

"Bouviette," Henrietta said, pulling off her gloves, "has Aunt Hannah braised the ham?"

"Massa Calvin say we will have fish," Aunt Betty pronounced, shaking her head as she brushed Henrietta's hat.

"You know it's too chilly yet. . . ."

Aunt Betty stored the parasol in the hall tree and nodded. "Massa Calvin wanted to get some hisseff."

"You'd better tell Aunt Hannah to finish the ham," Henrietta said emphatically, picking up her skirts and bending at the mirror to reset a pin. She still wore her hair parted carelessly and drawn back softly, as she had done before she married, with one curl behind her ear on her neck. She studied for a second the smooth skin over her high-spaced cheekbones with satisfaction. Her eyes could snap when she wanted them to. Deliberately, she did not meet them now, but tucked a stray strand of hair and turned to the window. Yes, there he was, down by the pond, without a coat, his fair hair shining in the sun. Sometimes she wished he weren't so handsome. Maybe, if he hadn't been so handsome, his lungs would have been stronger. "Nature has a way of dealing cards," Papa had said. Papa was plain, and could still, at the age of sixty, ride anything with hair.

"Calvin!"

"He can't heah you, Miss Henrietta. Ah'll go . . ."

"Send Johnny. No, I'll go myself."

"But Miss Henrietta, the mud . . ."

"It's drying. I promise—" she said with a sudden smile, her eyes teasing Bouviette's concern with a little joke they had shared since her first pregnancy: I'll be a good girl and keep my feet as dry as Noah the day the bird came back.

Johnny, in the cellar, was munching a biscuit laced with ham that Aunt Hannah had sliced and slipped between steamy dough. Cal sat cross-legged on a stool closer to the fire, where big black kettles simmered. The girl Celina, her thin face caught by a red bandanna, bent to the shirt she stitched slowly and rhythmically. A busy quietness hummed here that made Johnny feel warm inside. The sour-sweet smell of sweat mingling with thyme and bay leaves and the dusty stone floor would always be for him a remarkable, unrepeatable mixture. The Negro voices were low and even, punctuated by an occasional high, tight laugh or an incredulous question left piercing the air. This morning was special, as he could tell from the deliberate way Aunt Hannah poured, peeled, set lids, cut, tasted. Uncle Isaac, his bald head glistening, was in a rocker in the corner smoothing down the front of his black preacher suit. The starched collar at his throat chafed his bristly chin. He was in one of those steady discussions with Aunt Hannah, who, with equal determination, kept stirring and paring, lifting and wiping the flat palms of her hands against her big homespun apron.

"Lemme tell you," Uncle Isaac insisted, shaking his finger and turning his head like a turtle. "Ah 'spec sprinklin's all right fo' white folks, but it p'intedly won' do fo' de niggah."

"Hrummph."

"You know Preachah Braxton? What b'longst to de Breckinridges? He do preach mos' wunnahful, an' he sez dat niggahs mus' be 'mersed clar undah de watah so's tuh wash dey's sins clean."

"Now whym," Aunt Hannah condescended to turn to him, her spoon held high and dripping, "would dat be so?"

"And what would Wash's coming have to do with Xenophon?" Calvin Morgan dropped his hand. Johnny rubbed one toe up the shin of his leg.

"I thought—I thought I could use Zennie while Wash is here."

"There's Cyrus."

"But Cyrus is old."

"Eighteen is not old for a thoroughbred."

"No, but . . ."

"But Xenophon can run, is that it? And"—he looked back at the fields—"you want to show Wash how well you ride, eh? You're a big boy now. Well, let's see what Aunt Betty says."

If Aunt Betty agreed, they both knew Henrietta would. Johnny followed his father to the summer kitchen. The scrubbed floor shone blue from the light of the window. "So Gideon and Wash are coming," Calvin said needlessly.

"Yes," Henrietta said to an open cupboard. "On the afternoon stage."

"How will they get here from Lexington?"

"They'll hire horses, I suppose, and Uncle Simon can get their baggage tomorrow."

"Why not send Uncle Simon this afternoon to meet them?"

"Their letter *said* they would be here Sunday . . ."

"Ah, but you're not sure?"

"No, but—"

"Then can I go to Will's, Mama, please?" Johnny called out from under his father's hand, still on his head. "Aunt Hannah said the ham won't be done for hours, that we aren't eating till later. Can't I go to Will's for the saddle? Please, Mama?"

"It's *Mister* Webb," Henrietta said.

Calvin Morgan turned to his wife with a chuckle. "Did you hear that, Aunt Betty? Now how would you decide?" he asked, never taking his eyes from his wife's face. He knew he irritated her by bringing servants into conversations.

"How would you decide, Aunt Betty?" He smiled, waiting. "The boy wants to ride Xenophon down there." He pulled Johnny against his thigh and winked down at him. Aunt Betty, in spite of her mistress's frown, sensed the festive air.

"Ah'd let him go, Miss Henrietta, indeed Ah would. He's been cooped up this wet spring with those books and goin' through mud to that schoolhouse." She emphasized the word as if it were a joke, and laughed. "An' if anybody kin ride a half-trained hoss, *he* kin. . . ."

"There, so you see, it's settled," Calvin gave his son a boost out the door and his wife a kiss. He missed her cheek and plunged his nose into her hair.

"Take Randolph with you!" Henrietta called.

But Uncle Simon had other plans. He had already sent Randolph to the north field to change the yearlings' pasture, and from his look Johnny knew better than to argue. He led Xenophon from his stall and began brushing him. Uncle Simon pretended not to notice, and continued hanging up harnesses across the aisle with that official air he always used in the stable.

"Don' you wants to saddle him?"

"I'm just taking him to Will's."

"Hrrmph. He got withers lak a blade."

"Toughen me up."

"When youze get as old as me, Marse Johnny, youze'll want de mos' comfort." But Johnny could tell that his refusal of the saddle pleased something in the old man.

"Besides, I'd have two saddles to take home, if he's got the other one finished."

Uncle Simon showed his large, yellow teeth. "You know Mista Will too lazy to finish dat saddle dat quick!"

Johnny walked through the barn and legged Xenophon into a soft trot. Once past the house he squeezed him into a canter and then, leaning forward, his legs clamped under him, let him go. Oh, how nice it was, that creamy mane in his face, the wind going past Xenophon's turned-back ears! The pike stretched in front of them, level white limestone between green fields and gray stone fences. A shelf of dark clouds to the south only made the sky seem a deeper blue.

They didn't slow down until the tollgate keeper's house. Johnny retrieved a nickel from his pocket and handed it to Jake Bolton, the keeper's son. "Where's your folks?" Johnny asked, sitting back to let the stallion, out of shape from the winter, catch his breath.

"None-a *yore* business," Jake Bolton called out angrily, as if having to lift the pole were an insult. He helped his father keep five miles of road in repair. His mother, a worn-out woman who usually collected the tolls, was probably inside nursing another baby. Jake was fourteen. His muscles stood out under his dirty shirt and his eyes were squinted and cold. "Where *you* goin'?"

"None-a *yore* business!" Johnny called back with a laugh.

"Git down off'n that horse and I'll make it mine."

"Try and git me!"

He tucked his backside under his spine and Xenophon flew. He was still laughing when he pulled up at Will's. The yard was hard-packed clay, without a blade of grass, where Will's customers kept their waiting horses. Will, as usual, was working a piece of leather in the shade of his porch, his back propped against the log wall of his cabin. His only girl and oldest child, Amanda, sat on a cane-bottomed chair just inside the dogtrot, her bare toes crooked onto a rung, her liquid-green eyes wide on Johnny Morgan, her thick red hair tumbling down over her twelve-year-old breasts, which were just beginning to poke at the linsey-woolsey blouse opening at her throat.

Will Webb was a short stump of a man who had been brought to Kentucky in a saddlebag when he was eight weeks old, and always claimed that that's what had stunted his growth. He had a thatch of dry red hair that stuck out of his head like weeds. He could shake it for hours, his blue eyes intent on his work, his thoughts turned inward. He was the best storyteller as well as the best saddlemaker in Kentucky. His father had worked for Abijah Hunt,

John Hunt's cousin in Cincinnati, and had brought the first shipment of side leather and bridles down to Lexington when the Hunts were in business together in those days—1796, the year Will was born.

"Them bridles and my bornin' almost caused my daddy to miss the Battle of Fallen Timbers!"

"Fallen Timbers?"

"They called it that because there had been a great windstorm the day before an' all the trees was down."

Just a question, Johnny knew, was all Will needed when he was in the mood. The saddle wasn't finished, so he settled back for another story of the Army of the Northwest. The names buzzed like flies: Maumee and Au Glaize and Mad Anthony Wayne.

"Hell! Mad Anthony Wayne knew how to use horsemen. Mounted riflemen, he called 'em. Every fourth man a horse holder, if it come to a fight. Every bullet counted. A man cain't hit nuthin' from a hoss."

He set the leather aside and picked up a saddle tree, sighted down it, one eye closed, then started whittling.

The best trees were made of beech, split with the grain. Will would whittle and shape, kneading the wood with his palms until it was as smooth as leather. Then he would glue on canvas to prevent splitting and rivet iron plates on the head and cantle, and after that he would fasten linen webs lengthwise and across, and over that nail canvas and serge, then stuff padding between them. Johnny waited, knowing if he talked now Will might get lost and not go on.

"Them poor red devils. Them Redcoats wouldn't even let'em in or give'em help."

"I thought you didn't like the Injuns."

"Don't! But a friend ought to be a friend, even an enemy!"

The motherless Amanda, who never seemed to lift her head from the mending on her lap or the spoon bread in her mixing bowl, spoke up. Johnny had almost forgotten she was there. "I don't like Injuns, Paw. Ugh. All them scalps."

"Hush, Amanda! The Big Knife looked upon the scalps of warriors fightin' their own battles as thuh greatest trophies of war. But those scalps gotten by men fightin' fer hire he give to chillun to play with, or flung to the dogs."

The idea of dogs tearing at scalps was too much for Amanda, even if the Big Knife—her father's name for George Rogers Clark—did have an opinion on it. She picked up the bunched homespun and went inside, almost stumbling over her two brothers, Nathan and Zephaniah, who ran past her into the yard and caused Xenophon to jump sideways at the tree. "Heah, you, Zep," Will called. "Settle down, you heah?"

The boy he spoke to, as tall as Amanda and with the same thatch of red hair as his father, looked blankly from his wide-set sheep's eyes. He was the son who was "not right," as Aunt Betty said. With his bony forehead and ambling gait, Zep invited the taunts of the boys along the pike. Johnny was secretly a little afraid of him, and couldn't explain why. He made him remember a half-dead bird he'd found that had fallen out of a nest. Uncle Simon made him step on it.

"That's where my paw first saw William Henry Harrison."

"Where?"

"Fallen Timbers. He was General Wayne's lootenant."

William Henry Harrison. Will's hero. When Will was sixteen he had carried a musket to the defense of Fort Wayne and followed Harrison to Detroit that next year, all the way to Canada to the Battle of the Thames, in 1813. Nothing matched Will's telling of the Battle of the Thames or of Tecumseh. Oh, how he wished Will would tell that story again when Wash came!

A rumble of thunder from the shelf of clouds to the southwest made a low, comfortable sound, and a puff of air heavy with the scent of rain made Will look up.

"Up by the Au Glaize, above Fort Amanda, when I was with Gen'ral Harrison on the way to Detroit," Will said, still rubbing the tree, "it rained in torrents. You ain't never seen such a rain!" He stopped in awe at his own memory.

"What'd you do?"

"Tomahawks was no good against them big beech trees—we couldn't even start a fire. Lawd we was hungry! The Gen'ral stood there wrapped in his cloak and takin' the rain as it fell. I'll never fergit. He tole one of his officers to sing an Irish glee, an' we all remembered it ever afterwards, an' sang it when the goin' got tough, an' somehow we allus laughed and it made every-thing happy."

"What was it?"

> Now's—the time—for mirth—and glee
> Sing—and laugh—and dance—with me—

His shoulders shook and his face fanned sudden lines around his eyes and down his jaw. "Har! Har! Yew should'a seen 'em, Johnny! Them crazy boys, dog-tired, almost asleep on their hosses, gittin' shot at by Injuns, an' every time another shot rang out singin' to the toppa their voices, *Now's the time for mirth and glee, sing and laugh and dance with me!*' Damn fools!"

Will took a breath. "You sing that when things are down, Johnny Morgan, and I promise you you'll feel better."

When he swung himself up on Xenophon for the ride back, Johnny didn't know how soon he'd be singing that song. Before he left the yard he said suddenly, "Were you named for him, Will?"

"Who?"

"William Henry Harrison? The General?"

Will pulled at the bulb of his nose and ran his hand down his pants leg. "Mebbe."

A sudden thought struck him. "And Amanda . . . was she named for a fort?"

"Mebbe."

"Funny thing! A girl named for a fort!" But he was out of earshot, and couldn't hear what Will—or Amanda, who had just come out of the cabin —said to that.

It wasn't until he was in sight of the tollgate that he remembered he didn't have another nickel. It was a ten-dollar fine to ride around a tollgate, and besides, his father said it wasn't done. He would have to get a promise from Mrs. Bolton, if he could see her. Jake was still at the post.

"Is your mother here?" Johnny called out. Xenophon, edgy against the smell of rain, was stepping sideways, and Johnny thumped him with one leg to straighten him.

"Whut's the matter with me?"

"I . . . need to see your mother."

"She's busy in the house. Whut's the matter? Yore horse got fleas? He looks like a dog."

"I . . ." But Mrs. Bolton appeared, her left eye blackened and swollen. She was a heavy, ungainly woman, whose mind seemed folded inward by the fat on her face. She glanced briefly at him, her head turned so he couldn't see her eye.

"What is it, Johnny Morgan?"

"I . . . I've come through without another nickel, Mrs. Bolton. I can pay you tomorrow."

"Oh, it's no money now, is it?"

"Hush, Jake. Now Johnny Morgan, you can pay next time through. You lift that pole, Jake Bolton." She went inside.

Johnny waited. "Thank—" he called, but the door had closed. Jake reluctantly put his weight against the short end of the pole and watched it go up. Johnny was almost directly under it when he let it fall.

Xenophon fell first, his neck broken. His forelegs doubled under him and Johnny rolled sideways, one leg caught under. He kicked loose and only then, on his hands and knees, saw the limp neck, the glazed eyes, the feet still vaguely kicking, the head with its slender blaze twisted into mud. Before he could think, he found himself beating into the creamy mane, pounding with his fists and yelling, "Get up, Zennie! Get up! Get up!" Suddenly there was something harder under his fists, something with a tight laugh, like a sound with an iron ring around it, and he hit out at the laugh, tears of rage blurring the face of Jake Bolton. He didn't stop until the pain in his nose shot straight through his head and a black curtain dropped across everything.

The rain woke him. The pain in the back of his head and the taste of blood from his nose told him he was alive, but the muddy mound in the road, with its golden fringe blackening with water, made him roll up onto his knees. His stomach started jumping, like a thing alive and apart from his body. The throb passed to his throat: Xenophon! Beautiful Xenophon! With the softest trot in the world. And his father . . . days by the window, watching. Watching horses he couldn't ride. He crawled through the mud, buried his face in the muddy neck and rocked with sobs.

"Lookee the baby, now!" a voice jabbed behind him. "What'sa matter, baby?"

He looked up to see Jake Bolton's beady black eyes pinch shut with that laugh. Johnny dashed at him, clawing, biting, kicking, beating with torn knuckles the solid sunburned neck, the chest that held him like a clamp.

It was Tom Bolton who pulled him away, doing what his son couldn't do, the sour-sweet smell of whiskey mixing with the stench of stale sweat. Johnny fell back and threw up, his hands finding the rough bark of a tree to cling to. Behind him he heard them laugh and leave, their boots sounding like muffled shots on the porch steps, the slam of the door a final insult. He walked the three miles home in the rain, remembering only the swollen, frightened face of Mrs. Bolton on the porch, and how he had straightened, wiping his mouth with his sleeve, and stood and kept his eyes from the horse, clinging instead to the words that grew louder and louder in his head and followed him all the way home: *You are Johnny Morgan, and you don't cry. Now's the time for mirth and glee. Sing and laugh and dance . . .* But he couldn't finish it, even in his mind, and bit his lip till he tasted blood.

On the stairs he stumbled into a sleeping Aunt Betty, her haunches spread under three aprons on the landing. His stomach started jumping again. He couldn't make it quit, and then he felt his mouth spread across his face trying to keep the hot tears in.

"Hush, hush, now," Aunt Betty moaned, muffling his sobs against her. "You'll wake up yo' mama. She waited and waited, an' I tole her you prob'ly spendin' de night at Massa Will's. Lucky you done done dat befo'," she kept repeating, patting his shoulder and letting him sink to her lap. "Come on, we's gotta git outta heah." She looked meaningfully at his parents' down-stairs bedroom off the entry. He followed her, wiping his nose on a cloth she handed him. Once in his room, with the door closed, she took him in her arms and let him cry. Then she lit a candle and pulled off his muddy boots and undressed him, crooning his name and humming while she dipped a cloth in the washbasin and wiped and dried him all over.

"Ain't done dis since you wuz a baby, Massa John," she said.

From that day she stopped calling him Johnny.

He hadn't told her anything. He had only cried, but she seemed to know. With morning the telling would have to come; Aunt Betty was right. She said it couldn't wait. *You are Johnny Morgan, and you don't—*

But he did, once the words were out and he watched his father's face and his mother's open, then comprehending mouth. His father sat up in bed and swung his legs over the side, fishing for slippers. Johnny silently handed them to him and followed him into the parlor. His mother followed, with a glance at Bouviette, standing by the door.

"Aunt Betty, would you be so kind as to make us all some coffee?" his father asked. When she left he turned to his son. "Now tell me," Calvin said.

Wash came on the next day's stage. Uncle Simon didn't meet them. He was in charge of "that business up at the tollgate," as Henrietta called it.

Over his mother's protests—but encouraged by Aunt Betty and his father —Johnny went with them, the field hands and a silent Uncle Simon, more official than ever, overseeing the rigging of ropes that somehow got the bulk of Xenophon onto the low mule wagon used for hauling hemp to the drying barn. They moved slowly, Johnny on Cyrus, Randolph on the carriage mare. "Now youze sits up strit, you heah?" Uncle Simon had commanded Randolph—and, by a rolling eye, including Johnny—in the barn before they started. "This heah's a ko-tehzz, a reg'lar fun'ral. Don' nobody know the fust cit'zen uv Kentucky is allus a HOSS?"

But in spite of their efforts, the tears came, blinding, hot. Silent sobs tore at his chest at the first sight of Xenophon's still form beside the road, where he had been dragged to let traffic through. His neck looked so thin, pressed to the ground. The plate of his jawbone had been scraped across the gravel and the skin hung away like torn cloth. His legs were so still. *He was a knight of a family of knights who went up to Persia with Cyrus but his officers were murdered by Xerxes. He led his men through the wilds of Kurdistan . . . ten thousand safely. . . .*

A look from Randolph stopped him. A look and a lopsided smile that said: This is the way it is, Massa, we don't understand it, and maybe we never will. But this is the way it is . . .

He didn't know it then, but he loved Randolph from that moment, and always would.

They buried him on the mound about two hundred yards behind the stable, where Priam, his sire, and three other horses lay. Their headstones formed a semicircle, and the whole mound was enclosed by a low stone fence. They walked away separately, Randolph to the quarters, Johnny to the house.

And he wrote a book about that trip, one of the famous books of the ancient world. And about horses. Xenophon was the first—the very first to write about training horses. He said nothing should be used—nothing—harder than a man's hand on a horse's spine. Nothing, not even Uncle Simon's best brush.

Oh, Zennie . . .

Now's the time for mirth and glee . . . Come, and sing, and . . .

At the house his father waited, then insisted he have breakfast. Not a word about the Boltons, or whether the sheriff would believe it was an accident—as they both knew Jake would claim. Or whether his father would even call the sheriff. The coffee was hot and steaming, and Calvin Morgan served his son himself. It was chicory, sent by his uncle Johnny from New Orleans. It was the first time his father had let him have it without milk. He hadn't thought about that until now. Wouldn't Wash be surprised?

When Wash came riding up with Gideon at suppertime and sat over the best steaming china loaded with ham and turkey and yams and early peas from Uncle Ben's garden, Johnny couldn't eat. Aunt Hannah was always proud of Uncle Ben's garden, especially the "chilly" food, those things that came out of the ground early and you could plant again late, getting two crops. She used to brag that Uncle Ben could get "mo' food frum a piece of groun' than a wiggly wum." Her eyes asked Johnny now to try, and he did, with fresh butter puddling the plate and one of her best biscuits opening in his hand. Wash, across from him, was shoveling food with his usual gusto and pausing only long enough to hold his glass out for more wine. Tall and sixteen, Wash no longer drank "baby wine" halved with water.

The idea that the Morgans were a cut below the Hunts was one which Henrietta Hunt Morgan, try as she would, couldn't quite erase from the sound of her voice or the angle of her gestures. She paid deference enough to Gideon, a two-hundred-fifty-pound Falstaff of a man who had been a general in the War of 1812. She knew that his father, old Gideon I, had been a Minute Man in Connecticut and had moved first to New York and then to Kingston, Tennessee, where he sired seven sons, one of them Luther, Calvin's father. But when Gideon looked at her with his nearsighted eyes and paid fumbling compliments to her housekeeping or her dress, Henrietta couldn't help remembering he had married a Sevier and the Seviers had Indian blood. He had even named a daughter Cherokee! Cherokee Morgan, she thought, twitching her nose.

She steeled herself for Morgan talk. And it came: the size of a fish, the accuracy of a gun, the speed of a horse, the weight of a hog. Calvin, who could quote the whole Waterloo passage from Byron's Third Canto and read Sir Walter Scott's books by the score, who could debate with her father the pros and cons of President Jackson's hatred of the Bank or Mr. Clay's love of the tariff—her Calvin, who knew the intricacies of French politics as well as the price of hemp or horses, became another person when a Morgan arrived.

Gideon, of course, was not as bad as Alexander Gibson, Calvin's younger brother, who, after the business failure in Alabama, had followed Calvin to Kentucky and was an older version of Wash, which would always mean, in plain terms, a boy. The last time Wash was here Johnny had dampened a quart of blasting powder, made a serpent on the floor of the summer kitchen, and when Uncle Ben, coming in from the garden, discovered them, they threw the rest on the Pennsylvania fireplace, which blew up and almost burned the house down.

Calvin's third brother, Sam, had been the only one to survive the business failure successfully and lived in Nashville. Luther, their father, had moved on to Arkansas. They were an odd mixture of bravado, generosity and foolishness, with an overlay of education that never quite "took." They were, as her father said, Western.

"Lemme see where they buried him," Wash said, once they were outside.

"No."

"Aw, come on, Johnee."

"No." He bit his lip to hold back tears.

Then, sounding very much like his father, Wash said, "Tell me about it."

There was a stone springhouse on the south side of the garden, where the original settlers had lived while they built Shadeland. There was even a rectangular wooden flap near the door where they'd shot at Indians. Aunt Hannah kept the milk and cheese and eggs there, and it made a cozy place to get away from grown-ups.

Before they reached it, Cal followed. Then Tommy Cunningham, who lived on the next farm, ran up. He was a year younger than Cal, but it was Johnny he worshiped. The family called him Johnny's shadow. He watched his idol with fierce blue eyes under a mop of blond hair, his feet pumping. It was plain, from his look, that Cal had told him about Xenophon.

"Go on, Tommy Cunningham!" Johnny shouted, ashamed in front of Wash. He was anxious to get inside the secret comfort of the springhouse and sort out his confusion over Jake Bolton.

Wash sensed his need. He bet the boys a nickel they couldn't catch a fish in the pond. Cal ran up to the house for his pole. Tommy just stood there in his short pants by the lilac bush, his knees together and his arms down at his sides, those worshiping eyes still on Johnny.

The fury of grief and shame exploded. "Git out, Tommy Cunningham! You're always in the way! We don't want you!" Then Johnny lifted the iron latch, waited for Wash, and closed the door. It was almost pitch-black. He felt along the wall for the flap and pushed it up. Tommy Cunningham was still standing there.

"Git!" he yelled, and the little boy turned slowly and trudged up the hill.

Wash rolled back against the stone wall and pulled a cigar from his shirt and lit it with a sulfur splint, which he drew through a double fold of sandpaper. He put the sandpaper back in his pocket and sucked in luxuriously. Johnny coughed from the smoke.

"Well, Johnee," Wash said thoughtfully, when he'd heard the story, "Seems to me like a dool would settle it."

"A duel?"

"Yeah. You've been insulted, an' that's more than us Morgans can take. According to the Virginia rools, you need to challenge him."

The hard eyes of Jake Bolton seemed to peer at him from the dark. He stood up again and looked through the hole at Shamrock grazing in the pasture. "How do I do that?"

"It's easy. You can send your second with a note."

"My second?"

"That's me," Wash said quickly. "What kinda gun you got?"

"My pepperbox." Johnny pulled it from his pocket.

"Oh, one of them things. Can't hit the side of a barn."

"Can too!" But Johnny looked at the fat, stubby barrel for the first time distrustingly.

Wash held the little gun to the square light of the Indian hole. "You need a dooling pistol with a hair trigger. Has your daddy got one?"

"I don't know."

"Never mind. Pa has *two*. In a velvet case. We can give one to your opponent. . . ."

"But Jake's a better shot than I am!"

"That's even better."

"Better?"

"See, here's the plan. Make him fire too soon."

"How do I do that?"

"By firing too soon yourself. Only you don't *aim at him*."

"I don't aim at him!"

"Naw—that wouldn't be gentlemanly. Make him fire too soon and he'll miss."

"What if he doesn't?"

But Wash hadn't heard. Johnny followed him to the house where Uncle Ben, from the herb garden, gave them a solemn look, remembering the gunpowder. "How're yawl, Uncle Ben?" Wash called, and the old man made an uncertain smile.

"Now," said Wash, as they shut the door of Gideon's room. Downstairs in the summer kitchen, directly under them, they could hear Aunt Hannah and Celina washing dishes. Wash walked to the dresser and opened a walnut and silver case. Johnny looked inside at the pistols nesting in blue velvet.

"Ever try one of these? Well, it's about time." Wash sat on the bed with the open box on his knees. Johnny watched in silence as he measured powder, placed the patches on the ends of the barrels and rammed the balls home. "Here, you take one, and we'll practice. Stick it in your shirt so they won't see." He nudged Johnny through the door and followed him down the stairs and through the kitchen. In the woods behind the house with the setting sun making long shadows, they could just see Cal fishing, Tommy watching. Cal caught one, a wiggling iridescence at the end of his line. He grabbed at it, unhooked it and ran to the house.

"Now," said Wash. "We'll take that leaf over there. The one hanging by that little limb."

"That one?"

"Don't p'int your gun at me! Yes, that one. Now take aim like this. Hold your arm *up*. Like this!" He shot the leaf away. "Aw, I'm sorry, Johnee. Let's find another one."

"That one over there!"

"That's a respectable target. All right. Use my gun. Fire!"

Johnny missed.

"Never mind. We'll try again. Besides, you don't have to hit him. Only make him miss you."

"Wash . . ."

"Now don't *cry*. That's the rools. If he misses you five times, the dool's off."

"Does *he* know that?"

"He will. I'll write it on the parchment."

"We don't have any parchment."

"We'll call it that."

"Jake Bolton can't read."

"Don't matter. I'm your second, ain't I? Leave that responsibility to me. I'll take care of everything." He sat on his heels and picked at the grass with a stick. "Let's see. Today is Monday. Already twenty-four hours have gone since the insult." He stood up decisively. "It'll have to be tomorrow morning."

"Tomorrow morning!"

"At dawn. How far is it to his place?"

"Three miles."

"Well, we'll have to pick some place halfway."

"Reverend Pratt's church is about halfway."

"Good. Does it have a graveyard?"

"In the back."

"Good! A graveyard's the best place for a dool. More convenient-like."

"Who wrote them rools?"

"Why, Thomas Jefferson, that's who."

Johnny remembered the Declaration of Independence printed in a fancy hand on white silk in Mr. Postlethwait's tavern in Lexington. Nobody could argue about that.

"Say!" Wash grinned, throwing the stick away. "I know who can be Jake Bolton's second! Cal!"

It was full night, but with a moon, by the time they reached the tollgate. Johnny, mounted on Cyrus, held Shamrock's reins while Wash walked toward the toll house. Mrs. Bolton, her eye less swollen and with her hair up in a bun, came out and spoke to him. The moonlight cut a shadow across her face. In a minute Jake, a big boy but not as tall as Wash, was slouching against the door, a straw in his mouth, listening to Wash, whose quick hands were making jabs in the air. Jake took the straw out and spat. Shamrock fidgeted, trying to reach grass, and Johnny, turning Cyrus parallel to him to keep the reins taut, didn't see what happened next, but by the time he got the horses straightened out and looked around, Jake Bolton was on the floor of the porch rubbing his chin and Wash was walking slowly back, his hat back on his head. He took Shamrock's reins and said, "Tomorrow at dawn. Pistols at thirty paces."

Johnny didn't say anything.

"Thirty paces!" And Wash let out a war whoop as they ran back down the pike to tell Cal.

"I ain't sure," Cal said.

"Come on, Cal," Johnny whispered, using Wash's argument. "Ain't you a Morgan?"

Cal wiped his nose. "I guess I'm just as much a Morgan as you are." But he didn't sleep at all that night.

Aunt Hannah's cabin was nearest the house. "Come on!" Wash hissed the next morning, when Cal splashed into a puddle and stopped to shake water from his boot.

The stable was quiet. The soft dust of the aisle rose in clouds as they made their way to the stalls. Shamrock blew, and the carriage mare let out a little whinny. "Shut up, you loud-mouf," Randolph rasped. As official groom of the expedition, he had assumed a new-found dignity mildly reminiscent of his grandfather. He would stay behind, in case Uncle Simon gave the alarm. He was to say that Massa Calvin had ordered the horses to be let out. In the summer they were always put out at night, to be brought in during the day because of flies. In the winter it was the opposite, and in the spring and fall it depended on the flies. "Ah sho' do hope daze a shortage uv flies dis mawnin'," Randolph whined. "Whut if'n Massa Calvin fin' out?"

"He won't," Wash said, tying a rope for a rein on Shamrock's halter. Because of the plan, they couldn't take the saddles or bridles. "How is he?" he asked Johnny, not needing to explain.

"He'll stop," Randolph answered for him. "Jes' sink yo' seat in him. My gran'daddy trained him."

"Ah'm not worried about stopping," Wash laughed. "Cal, ain't you got that pony ready yet? Randolph, help him."

"Yassa! Now Massa Cal, youze knows this little filly don' like to run," he said as he helped Cal up. "Jes' keep yo' laigs back undah you, like Ah showed you. She'll do jes' fine."

Jake Bolton was already at the graveyard when they arrived. The night had been clear but now the sky to the east shone pink through a film of clouds. Low mounds of graves were catching first light. Wash dismounted, bearing the pistol case like a chalice.

"Now, gentlemen," he called out, "this headstone is about right—no graves either side and the hosses outta range. Walk fifteen paces." He handed Cal the pistol box and acted it out. "Stop about here. Turn and fire. Is it understood?"

"But—"

"Shut up, Cal."

"Lemme see that there gun," said Jake.

"It is the dooty of the second to examine the weapon first. It's the rool. Mr. Morgan, have you examined the weapon? *Cal!*"

"Yes . . . yes . . ."

"Now you must show the principal. Cal, show Jake the gun."

"Ain't nevah seen nuthin' that small," said Jake.

"It's a propah dooling pistol, made in England."

"Ah ain't usin' no baby gun," said Jake, pulling from his coat an old British horse pistol with a twelve-inch barrel.

"That ain't a propah dooling gun," objected Wash. But he seemed to think better of it and walked over to Johnny. "That horse pistol's got a *real* hair trigger," he whispered.

"What?"

"Shh—that's even better!" Aloud to Jake he said, "We are ready to begin."

Johnny looked at Jake Bolton for the first time since Wash had knocked him down. His jaw was still bruised, a purple circle that gave his face a lopsided look. Shamrock whinnied and a golden mane, blackening with rain, floated before his eyes.

"Ready!"

They stood, not touching, backs braced, Johnny's head just at Jake's shoulder. They took wide steps while Wash counted. "Fourteen. Fifteen!"

Johnny turned and felt the trigger give and heard Cal's filly snap her rope at the same instant the bullet flew past Jake and hit the fence. Something was wrong. Jake hadn't fired. Wasn't he supposed to fire and miss? Wasn't that the whole idea—to draw his fire too soon? Jake was taking aim.

"Eight—nine—TEN!" shouted Wash. Jake looked at him, puzzled.

"If'n you don't fire by ten after your oh-poh-nent, you lost your shot," said Wash.

"Whaddaya mean?"

"You wanna have this here dool good and proper or not?" At Bolton's look, Wash laughed derisively. "This here's an undertakin' for gentlemen. *Places!*"

The sun had risen full blast. Cal caught up his horse and retied her. Johnny went back to the tombstone and with trembling fingers picked up the other loaded dueling pistol.

"Ready!" Wash was calling.

"Ready for *what?*" The black figure of Reverend Pratt stood by the corner of the church, the calico skirts of his servant girl hiding behind him. The girl's great black eyes under her bandanna showed crescents of white.

"Why, fer—fer—" But Wash couldn't finish, and to Reverend Pratt's "What's this nonsense, anyway, boys? Don't you know you'll have to grow up a little first?" he flashed his cigar-smile, gathered the pistols and box and turned to his horse.

"They cheated me!" Jake whined. "They didn't lemme fire." Fiercely he turned to Johnny. "You ain't heard the last o' this! Jest wait! Boltons keep their promises!"

"Come on, Surelda," the Reverend said, holding back a chuckle. "We've got spring cleaning to do."

Wash mounted and threw Elisha a salute. He touched Shamrock into a canter, jumped the fence and was gone. Johnny and Cal followed.

How his parents found out about the duel was a puzzle to Johnny. Surely Cal hadn't said anything. Or Wash. He didn't *think* the Reverend would tell. Could Uncle Simon have found out? He asked Randolph. "No, suh, Massa Johnny, hit went off like a roostah crowin'. Uncle Simon, he din' guess a thing."

But Calvin called his son to him three days later and asked, "Now tell me about that affair in the churchyard, Johnny."

When he'd heard it all, Calvin Morgan said quietly, "Wash is from Tennessee," as if that explained everything. When the boy still looked puzzled, he added: "Kentucky is a strange place, Johnny. A special place, but strange. It belonged to Virginia. I expect Will has told you about all that."

"About the Wabash campaign," Johnny said, relieved that the conversation seemed to be taking another direction.

"Virginia was bankrupt after the Revolution," his father went on in that same tone. He was gazing past him at the fields. "Do you know how she paid her soldiers? She gave them Kentucky lands—those same lands that had been cleared and planted by Boone and Kenton and Floyd and Logan and Jim Harrod and the early settlers who thought their claims were safe under the "ancient cultivation" law of '77. But all that changed when Virginia needed to pay her soldiers.

"Besides the soldiers, there were rich younger sons of Virginia planters who needed land. So Virginia made a new law in '79, and these rich young sons brought their bright young lawyers with them and stole the land neatly and legally. Your grandfather's friend Mr. Clay was one of those bright young lawyers. They came with satchels full of fancy language and the original settlers, who had fought off Wyandottes and Shawnees and had broken their backs hauling stones and hewing trees, lost more than just their cabins and their land. They lost whole lifetimes.

"They went farther west, most of them, into Missouri or downriver. Some stayed and watched the great hemp and horse plantations grow on land they had cleared. The Boltons stayed. This was their land."

Johnny followed his father's gaze across the soft, leafy waves of hemp, the hemp of late April that would be spread, before frost, on the ground to dew rot, and then be broken and loaded onto the mule wagons to the drying barn. As Xenophon was, he thought, seeing again that muddy mound over the low, creaking wheels. He tried to say something, and choked.

"I know. I know," his father said, sighing and getting up. "There's nothing . . . almost nothing worse than the useless death of a good horse. Or of anything," he added, going to the fireplace. He rested his head on his arm against the mantel and spoke into the cloth of his sleeve. "I hope you understand about the duel." Something in his rounded shoulders made him seem smaller and Johnny feel taller. For the first time in his life Johnny Morgan chose his words carefully.

"Thank you for not being angry, Papa. Was it Reverend Pratt who told you?"

"Lucky for us the church needed a spring cleaning."

"Does Ma know?"

"Of course not! The ladies"—he grinned at his son for the first time—"don't understand these things."

Lexington in May!

"Bet you never seen a more beautiful place," Johnny called back to Wash. They were riding past Ashland, Mr. Clay's farm on the Richmond Road.

Wash laughed and pushed into a trot to catch up. "I see you don't know how to bet, Johnny Morgan. Don't evah bet on nuthin' you can't *see*."

"Well, you see it, don't you?"

The slow swells of bluegrass, broken by streams and dark woodland pastures, looked like a slumbering green sea. They had ridden out past Madame Mentelle's boarding school "to look at the girls," as Wash said, and, on the way back, to look at the donkeys Mr. Clay had imported from Spain. "Runty little things, ain't they?" Wash said.

"The donkeys or the girls?"

They trotted down Main Street, eighty feet wide and running parallel to Town Fork Creek for a mile and a quarter, flanked by footways twelve feet wide and brick stores three stories high. They passed the brick courthouse and the marketplace called Cheapside, where on Wednesdays and Saturdays you could buy anything from a traveling trunk to a field hand. There were bookstores and printing offices and nail factories and brickyards and blacksmiths and saddlers and silversmiths and even an umbrella factory. There were ropewalks and textile factories and taverns and the offices of the Lexington and Ohio Railroad, which was building a line to Frankfort to beat the steamboat trade. In the jewelry shops flashing dikes were displayed, some with gold-inlaid handles. "Let's see one of them," Wash said, and they tied their horses to iron rings on a street post and looked with respect at the sharp pointed knives, four to five inches long, with small, exquisite handles.

Inside, the jeweler met them cordially. "To be worn within a gentleman's vest," he said proudly.

"I'll tell Gideon," Wash whispered as they remounted. "Maybe he'll git me one!"

Johnny was anxious to show Wash Hopemont. He hoped he would love it as much as he did, the fan window over the double front doors, the great stairs that spiraled away past the bedrooms to the third-story schoolroom, and at the back of the house the warming room where Big Peggy served hot pies and milk.

His grandfather's butler let them in. They crossed the entry hall into the parlor, where twenty-year-old Catherine Hunt, radiant with the emotion of music, was playing the pianoforte when they entered. Wash sat politely on a small stuffed chair and listened, stunned by her beauty.

Johnny's grandmother, also a Catherine, came in then, walked over and kissed Johnny. Wash found himself tongue-tied before this regal yet relaxed lady. Her eyes were so kind, the bones in her thin, gentle face so small and fragile. She had a way of moving her eyebrows that made Wash love her instantly. She pinched one corner of her mouth, like her daughter Henrietta, but there was a softness about her that made him feel at home.

He was a little afraid of Johnny's grandfather, who looked like a bald schoolmaster and whose mouth, drawn back into his cheeks, might have just said, *And now what do you have to say for yourself, young man?*

Johnny wanted Wash to like his grandfather. He knew all about him, how he'd come to Kentucky from New Jersey to go into business with his cousin Abijah, who had a trading post in Cincinnati. Together they sold supplies to settlers pouring down the Ohio and through the mountain gaps, and to the Northwest Army. John Hunt's Philadelphia brother, Wilson, sent muslins, linens, tea and books overland to Pittsburgh by wagon, down the Ohio by flatboat and across Kentucky to Lexington. John shipped Kentucky hogs and beef, cattle, peach brandy and whiskey to Abijah, who in turn traded nails and shoes and leather from his tannery.

When Hunt imported his first thoroughbreds from the East it was Abraham Webb, Will's father, who led Royalist, bred in England by the Prince of Wales, across the mountains, the stallion Hunt had refused to buy the year before because everybody said he was vicious. Everybody except Will, who, even then, as a boy of ten in 1804, knew his horses. Two years later they brought back Dragon, sixteen hands with a star and snip, got by Woodpecker, one of the best sons of King Herod, and a brother to Diomede. . . .

After the horses and the river trade there was hemp and land and banking and all sorts of things Johnny didn't understand. He had heard people say his grandfather was fast becoming the richest man in the West. Wash, in spite of Johnny's promise that his grandfather wouldn't bite, was silenced by those shrewd eyes and glad, in spite of the good food and kindness, to mount up again.

"I saw you watching Aunt Catherine," Johnny teased when they left.

"And I saw Will's girl lookin' at you."

"Amanda? She's got *freckles!*"

"Ah sweah, Johnny Morgan. Don't you notice *nuthin'?*"

It wasn't warm enough to swim yet, but they fished and coon-hunted and spent long afternoons, when Johnny's school day was over, listening to Will while he finished Xenophon's saddle, now destined for another horse Calvin was buying.

Wash listened spellbound to Will's description of the massacre at the River Raisin.

"They got beat, huh?" Wash prompted.

"Gen'ral Winchester was captured in his drawers! Disarmed men . . . We traveled forty miles in seven hours over frozen roads so deep in snow Colonel Hukill's horse fell dead when we got there."

"How do you remember all those names?" Johnny asked.

"Sonny, when you've fought with men they become more than brothers. Now you wouldn't fergit Cal's name, would you?"

"Sometimes he wished he could," Wash joked.

Will refused to be sidetracked. He eased the pigskin and said stoutly, "Gen'ral Harrison had no truck with a standing army. He used volunteers, and volunteers from Kentucky was his favorites. He allus said you couldn't train them, though. An' he was against it, anyway. He didn't think a man had to become a slave before he become a warrior."

Amanda, her round blouse caught at the waist by an apron, offered Wash a drink of spring water. He lifted the gourd to his mouth and spilled half on his pants, and for some reason, she laughed. What's your hand shakin' for? Johnny started to ask, but didn't. Instead, they all looked at Will, who had set the saddle aside and leaned against the steps.

"Saddles, like wimmen and hosses, needs time to be shaped," he said, as he unplugged a jug of whiskey and offered the boys some. "Thet water'll rust yore pipes."

Wash took a draw, with a glance at Amanda, as if he had just done something praiseworthy and expected her approval. Instead, she tossed the weight of her red hair from her shoulders and Wash handed the jug back to Will.

"Them wuz mounted troops," Wash drawled. "Not that silly Redcoat cavalry with sabers, but mounted *riflemen*, the kind Gen'ral Wayne and George Clark used. Well, in order to take Detroit, a new plan was needed, since Winchester lost out at the Raisin. . . ."

Johnny had heard it all before but somehow never tired of it; each time it seemed new. The forts they had to build, the fight at the Thames, up in Canada. The Indian names flowed over him: White Loon and Stone Eater; Chau-be-nee, the Coalburner; Black Partridge and Tenskwatawa, the Prophet. Above all, Tecumseh.

"Who was Tecumseh?" asked Wash.

"Tecumseh? You don't know who Tecumseh was?" Will took another draw, in disbelief. "Tecumseh?"

The story came to Johnny like a dream, through Will's voice: *His name meant Shooting Star . . . thuh third baby uv triplets, an' when he come a star flashed in thuh sky. Like that! A reg'lar shower uv light, like the whole sky had gone snowflakes. . . .*

Wash looked at Johnny as if he didn't believe it, but a frown from his cousin kept him quiet. Maybe Will would tell about the Thames. Of all the battles, Johnny loved the telling of the Thames.

The warmth came again, the excitement. To impress Wash he took a swig of whiskey and watched his cousin's face as the story grew.

"Well, and did Tecumseh die?" Wash asked.

"Ah wouldn't be a-knowin'. Or a-tellin', even if Ah knew. Folks say them Shawnee expect him to return. They sneaked back on thet battlefield thuh nex' day an' buried him, but they said he would return."

"And do you believe it?" Johnny said, after a long silence.

"Mebbe."

"Can you believe *him?*" Wash whistled softly when they were back at Shadeland. "All those stories."

Johnny had never thought about not believing.

"Do you suppose *we'll* ever see anything that exciting? Do you, Johnny?"

"Naw—ain't no more Injuns in Kentucky." He burped, and wondered if he could wash his mouth out before Aunt Bet smelled him.

"Or English, either," said Wash mournfully.

"Any in Tennessee?"

"Tennessee? Hell, no!"

It was then that Johnny remembered the Dead Sea, and asked about that, too.

3

The next afternoon, after Wash left with Gideon and Calvin to visit Calvin's brother Alexander Gibson Morgan in Lexington, Henrietta called Johnny into the parlor.

"You'll have to hitch the mare to the buggy and take Uncle Ben to town," she said as she brushed Cal's hair. Cal winced, squinting past the brush at his brother. "Uncle Simon or Randolph can't go because they'll be busy with the new horse."

"New horse?"

"It's arriving this afternoon. From Woodford County."

"Aw, Ma! Why does Uncle Ben have to go to town?"

"The poor old man has a toothache and he's got to go to the dentist," she said, as if those were the last words to be spoken in the world.

Johnny found Randolph cleaning out Xenophon's stall and spreading new sawdust. Even Uncle Simon declared that Uncle Ben was in pain, so there seemed no argument. He harnessed the mare and Johnny climbed up onto the seat and led her to the quarters, where Uncle Ben was helped aboard by Aunt Hannah. "Now you bes good," she admonished him, wagging her head, "Ah don' want to heah no complainin' from you, Massa John heah bein' nice enough to take youze to town."

Uncle Ben, his head wrapped in a rag, climbed moaning into the buggy —not the *calèche* used for Sundays, but a high, square box with springs, and hardly more than a wagon. Yet it was better, in a way, for Uncle Ben had room to lie down as Aunt Hannah tucked a quilt around him. Johnny clucked to the mare and tried to avoid ruts as they swung onto the pike. At the tollgate he paid his money to Mrs. Bolton silently; with a nod of greeting and as silently she passed them on.

The fields of spring hemp, the pastures with newborn foals beside their dams. Johnny had a cozy feeling watching them. Today was Wednesday, and in spite of his pain, Uncle Ben sat up when they turned into Main Street. For years, first as a gardener for the Hunts and now in his old age helping Aunt Hannah at Shadeland, Uncle Ben had grown vegetables and sold them for "pocket change" at his own stall in the market. Everyone in Lexington knew him and he acknowledged greetings now from the back of the wagon, the "culud" folks openly, the whites always cautiously. Uncle Ben was careful to let them smile or speak first, his own eyes kept vaguely glued to an area somewhere about a foot beyond the white man's head. The white ladies never spoke.

In the spring and autumn, before planting or after crops had been paid for, coffles of slaves would converge on Lexington for sale downriver to the cotton plantations. Some—a choice stock of younger females—were sent to the dealers' upper rooms in Mechanics Alley. Most were chained and hand-cuffed in lines of forty and collected in warehouses and pens for shipment.

Johnny, like most children of the Bluegrass, had heard incomplete stories of these things, but because the Morgan servants and field hands were well cared for, he always believed that these things were happening somewhere else. Even the big three-pronged poplar tree on the courthouse lawn, where slaves caught on the streets after seven o'clock were whipped, had always been just a tree to him.

Cheapside was so crowded with men and horses and buggies that two-thirds of the street was full, and Johnny had to make a wide circle to get around a coffle of slaves, their leg irons and handcuffs connected by heavy chains to form two ranks, the men in front, the women behind. One of the women held a two-year-old girl. She, too, was handcuffed. They were all barefoot, in ill-fitting, cast-off clothes, and the stench of their sweat was overpowering.

Johnny had been in Lexington on Wednesdays before, but he had never gone down to Cheapside. His mother wouldn't let him, and now he knew why.

Uncle Ben kept his eyes on his folded ash-colored hands. The dentist's office was at the foot of Main Street, near a corner. They had three more blocks to go. Johnny flicked the whip and the mare turned the corner, and he tied her and helped Uncle Ben down. The dentist was busy. They waited on a bench trying not to hear the sounds a patient made just beyond the inner door.

"No, suh," Uncle Ben moaned, and whether he was trying to keep his own mind from the coffle of slaves or from the approaching treatment by the dentist Johnny couldn't guess. Uncle Ben held his bandaged head in his hands and said, "Why, there wuz thet Willis Barnes, de one dat done stole a ham from Massa Gratz. When yo' gran'pappy fin' out, he wouldn't whop him. No, suh. Massa John Hunt say, If'n a lifetime uv kindness warn't enuff to make Willis honest, a whoppin' wouldn't, neethuh."

"So what did he do?" The air, and the cries from the next room were making him dizzy.

"Massa John sole him, all right, ez whut rightly to do."

"What happened then?"

Uncle Ben held his head evasively, as if he realized, suddenly, that the point of his story had been lost. "Don' know, Massa John. We nevah seen Willis agin."

Uncle Ben seemed to shrink beside Johnny when they were finally admit-ted. As he unwrapped Uncle Ben's bandage, Dr. McCalla, who was under contract by both the Hunts and Morgans to care for their slaves, said kindly to Johnny, "Why don't you take a run over to Hopemont, Johnny? This may take a while. Uncle Ben here can rest on a cot in the back room when we're done, if you haven't returned yet." The smell of creosote, used to pack teeth, jabbed the air.

"Will you be all right, Uncle Ben?"

"Yassa. Massa Andrew heah, he allus take good care uv me."

The warming room at Hopemont, where food was brought up from the kitchen and which served as the children's eating area off the service hall, had never seemed cozier. The scent of baked bread replaced creosote in Johnny's nose, and Big Peggy, his grandmother's cook and Randolph's mother, was asking how Randolph was. Nicely, her helper ("She'll do nicely," they said when she was born), handed him a glass of milk and he rested against the wall and shut his eyes.

"Yo' gran'pappy in de parlor wif Marse Henry. De young peoples is upstaihs. But youze cain't use de back steps—Nicely jes' scrubbed 'em and dey's still whet. Nicely, you iron dem shirt ruffles fo' Marse John yit? Ole Miss gonna fuss at you!"

The image of his grandmother fussing at anybody made Johnny smile. Big Peggy must have been thinking the same, for she leaned against the door frame and threw her head down in silent laughter.

When Johnny crossed through the dining room on his way to the spiraling front stairway he saw his grandfather in the parlor in earnest conversation with Mr. Clay. Mr. Clay, with his long chin tucked between the white points of his collar and his sharp eyes looking out from under the inverted V's of his eyebrows, looked just like a fox. He was sipping brandy, and Johnny's grandfather was waving his plump, stubby-fingered hands in the air and didn't notice Johnny stop to listen.

He was not arguing so much as defending Judge Gratz, who sat in a corner chair by the fireplace out of Johnny's view.

"I can see Ben's point," John Hunt was saying. More reluctantly, he added, "And I can see Mr. Calhoun's."

"Mr. Calhoun's!" Henry Clay's pixie face turned red.

"You'll have to admit, Henry, this tariff you and I defend—for business reasons—is in the interest of New England."

Johnny thought Henry Clay would explode. He was saved now by Ben Gratz, who got up from his chair and came into view.

"How many Erie Canals has the South seen built from your tariff?" the thin-faced Gratz, with his Jewish humor, teased. "Or National Roads?"

"We can get that money from the sale of public lands, if Jackson will keep the price at a dollar twenty-five an acre. What I'm fighting for in the Senate" —Clay leaned closer to his host—"is ten percent of the sale price to go to the state of origin, while the lion's share would be divided among the other states."

"According to population," John Hunt reminded. "Where would that leave the South, Henry? Let's be fair."

"You claim your tariff is a national one." Gratz, standing by the window, pulled his cigar from his mouth and blew two rings. "And has raised the price of cotton . . ." He punched the first ring with a raised finger as if he were making a point in court. "And lowered the price of manufactured goods for the South." He punched the other. "If that's true, why did South Carolina hold a convention last November declaring your tariff null and void?" His mood was still jocular, but his trained lawyer's voice was tighter. "And why did President Jackson answer, not only with a warship in Charleston Harbor, but with the Force Act?"

"I don't think he'll ever use military force to collect his tariff," John Hunt interrupted, seeing his neighbor's agitation. "Besides, we all agree that Nullification's nonsense."

"Nullification's not only nonsense, it's anarchy," Gratz growled.

"You forget that my bill, just passed, will reduce the tariff by twenty-percent intervals!" Clay almost screeched in a fit of pique.

"Yes, and we'll have to wait nine years, Henry, until it gets down to twenty percent."

"The Great Pacificator strikes again," Hunt tried to joke. "A tariff Missouri Compromise." When he saw Gratz fuming, he added: "Frankly, Ben, I'm more worried about the Bank. . . ."

"And I'm more worried about our senator—or maybe even future President," Gratz said, suddenly affable again. He nodded toward the dining room. "Why don't you come in, Johnny, and settle all this? Out of the mouths of babes, eh? You look like a bright, stout lad . . ."

"Sir." Johnny sent the Judge a smile, then bowed to Mr. Clay from the waist, the way his grandfather did when he greeted guests.

"Well, speak up!" his grandfather chuckled, with a wink to Clay. "Do *you* think the President will use force to collect his tariff?"

"I wouldn't, sir."

"You wouldn't?" Clay was amused. He tucked his chin between the points of his collar and lifted his brows. "And just what would you do?"

"I'd challenge Mr. Calhoun to a duel, sir."

"A duel?" They laughed in chorus.

Johnny's face turned red. His next words, *And make him fire too soon and miss,* died on his lips. All he could feel was the blood spreading across his cheeks, and their eyes on him. He dared to look back at his grandfather's round, bald head catching the light from the window, at Judge Gratz squinting through his cigar smoke. It was Henry Clay who broke the spell, lifting his brandy glass in a flourish.

"Spoken like a true Southern gentleman." The fox smiled, the corners of his mouth tucked up, quivering. "Oversimplified, gallant, and utterly useless."

"Come now, Henry," John Hunt said, reaching out and drawing his grandson to him. "You're just jealous that the likes of Johnny here might put you out of business."

The notion of Andy Jackson dueling with John C. Calhoun seemed suddenly to take root, to spread across the face of the first millionaire west of the Alleghenies. John Hunt burst into a fit of hearty laughter. The hand on Johnny's shoulder tightened with a grip of iron. Then, as suddenly, it let go, and Johnny, under the laughter and indulgence, made his escape.

Upstairs he found his uncle Key sitting on the floor, propped by a cushion against the long Palladian window that stood directly over the fanned front doors on the first floor. This was what his grandmother called "the children's sitting room," and Johnny remembered a long afternoon in winter once, when his father lay ill downstairs and Big Peggy served them cake and milk while they waited for the doctor. Now mounds of material piled like clouds and spilled from chairs: silks and gauzy froths that seemed to float in color. An old table had been brought down from the schoolroom on the third floor and stood almost covered by opened "ladies' books." Catherine was posing in front of an oval mirror. She turned in half-circles, watching the blue embroidered muslin lift and turn, the lace "falls" on the dropped sleeves swing with the motion. Pert bows marched down the front, from the lace collar to the hem. She started humming and swirling, her fingers spread against her waist, her eyes haughty and critical of the girl she saw in the mirror, but her mouth smiling approval. Her hair came down onto her shoulders and she shook it loose with the gesture of a little girl.

Johnny had never seen anything so shining and at the same time so soft as her face. When she saw him she laughed.

"How do you like it? Look at these sleeves! Aren't they *big?* Look at this skirt! Isn't it *wide?* Won't it swing out dancing?" She picked up the tune again and held her arms out to him. "Waltz with me, Johnny! Key won't!"

She was the most beautiful lady he had ever seen and she had always been his favorite aunt. She never treated him like a little boy. She held his hands now and they circled to her counting, her brown hair lifting, falling, her pale blue dress floating away from her slim waist. When he stepped on her foot she stopped as if the music had ended and said gallantly, "You see, Johnny Morgan is the only gentleman here."

Key, the scholar of the family and already planning a law career, grinned over. "Lucky for him. That leaves me out."

"Is that Wash?" Anne's voice called from a bedroom.

"No—it's Johnny!"

"Tell him to come in here!"

"It's all right," Catherine giggled, pushing him. "She's just being finished."

He followed her into the north bedroom, with its tall, pineapple-topped four-poster and marble fireplace. A warm breeze blew from the open windows.

"Anne thinks Wash is charming," Key teased as he followed them and settled himself in one of the deep windows, the book, as before, perched on his knees.

"I do not! Ouch!"

"Keep still, Miss Anne." The mulatto seamstress, on her knees at Anne's hem, smiled at Johnny through a mouthful of pins. She had made dresses for his mother and he loved watching her quick, sure hands.

"I'm still!" defended Anne, who at sixteen always seemed to be protecting herself from her older brother. "Just because you're eighteen, Francis Key, and named after Mama's cousin."

"Well, I'd like to see you write 'The Star Spangled Banner.' "

"I think it's a stupid song."

"Now, hush," Catherine fussed, still humming. "I'm going to take this dress off and we'll all go down and see if Big Peggy has any more pudding."

She disappeared into the next room and the seamstress called after her, "Don't lose any of those pins!"

Anne laughed. "Martha Dodd Walsh Wilson O'Brien, you do love those pins."

"You would, too." The seamstress considered the list of her husbands as a catalogue of accomplishments and grinned. "They're as valuable as those beaux you talk about."

"Yankee pins," teased Anne.

"You might as well go too, now, Miss Anne," said Mrs. O'Brien, ignoring her. "That's enough for today." She began slipping pins into a little enameled box and folding the cutaway snips of extra material.

Past the garden the yells of boys playing cricket on the Transy parade ground were so loud that both Johnny and Key turned to look.

"Robert and T.H. are over there," Key said, more kindly now that the girls had left. "Why don't you go play with them?" When Johnny moved to go he added, "Go down the front stairs. Nicely's just scrubbed the back."

"I know."

At the bottom he let himself into the garden by the side door. Across the street his uncle Robert saw him and waved. He was at the wicket and Sanders Bruce was bowling. Sanders was left-handed and always tossed high. The other boys called this "baby bowling." The batman had to "give her the rush" to overcome Sanders's slow, deliberate aim.

Frank Wolford was at bat and Sam Todd at cover point. Sam called to Johnny: "We need a man at extra cover! Over here!"

Johnny slipped between Sam and Ben Bruce, Sanders's little brother, at Mid Off. The ball was wide, hitting Sam in the knees. They wore no protection and he rolled howling, but bounced up when he heard Johnny's uncle, T.H. Hunt, acting as umpire, call out "No ball!"

"His front foot was in front of the mark," T.H. said quietly.

"Was *not!*" Sanders screamed.

Johnny switched places with Frank as batman. Again, Sanders tossed wide and T.H. yelled "No ball!" In the scuffle, Johnny found himself in the dirt under Sanders, Frank and Robert.

They were stopped by the Bruce mammy, who called out loudly to Sanders from the edge of the grass. She was holding Becky, Sanders's three-year-old sister, by the hand to keep her from running. "Yo' pappy say it's time fo' suppah. Youze bettah git home, now, Massa Sanders. *Now*, you heah?"

Johnny, sweating and with one knee showing through a rip in his pants, trudged under the arm of Robert, which felt like a great log across his shoulders. "You'll make a good player when you come to Transy, Johnny!"

The table in the main dining room was set by the time they slipped in the back way and washed up. His grandmother was already supervising the serving. Mr. Clay, who was staying for dinner, was still in the parlor.

Johnny had thought to leave by the back door and unhitch the mare (who had stood patiently tied for two hours) when the usually soft-spoken voice of John Hunt called his name.

His grandfather was red with anger.

"Where's Uncle Ben?"

"At the dentist's, sir."

"You hope he is. Doctor McCalla sent a message asking where *you* were."

If Mr. Clay, with his reddish hair and pointed eyebrows looked like a fox, Johnny's grandfather, with his slightly protuberant eyes and cheeks now blown out in silent fury, pulsed just like a frog.

John Hunt misinterpreted his grandson's hesitation. "Your middle name, my son, is Hunt. And the Hunts are never humble before the haughty, nor haughty before the humble."

"Sir?"

John Hunt's inborn courtesy to guests prevented a verbal show of anger, but he couldn't keep it out of his voice as he said, "You do not treat those below you shabbily."

He was saved by his grandmother at the door. She held herself very erect under the lace fichu over her shoulders. To anybody else that little shawl would have given an air of meekness, but there was nothing fragile about her: She had raised twelve children to adulthood and, despite her sweet smile and smooth brow, an indomitable fortitude never left her face. In her presence John Hunt became the affable host, the kindly grandparent again.

"Hurry, Johnny," he said now, one small white puffy hand on the boy's shoulder. "It's almost seven. Let's hope Doctor McCalla hasn't gone home yet."

The idea of anybody in Lexington catching Uncle Ben after curfew and whipping him at the poplar tree was ridiculous, but he remembered the chained slaves and said, "Yes, sir. I'm sorry, sir . . ."

As he turned to go, the butler, behind Mrs. Hunt, apologized for the interruption. They turned to see an impeccably uniformed but agitated young lieutenant. He had stopped just inside the parlor and stood on the shining floorboards and said, "Pardon me, gentlemen, ladies . . . Lieutenant Davis, U.S. Army. Your son, sir, Mayor Charlton Hunt, sent me to be of service."

And before they could answer, he added the one word more dreaded than any on the Western frontier.

"Cholera? I don't believe it!" Catherine Hunt murmured, turning pale.

"John, go at once," John Hunt told his grandson. "Tell your mother we will leave immediately—your grandmother and the children—for the Leestown farm."

"How far is that, sir?" Lieutenant Davis asked.

"Not far. Under two miles. On the Leestown Pike, west on Main Street."

"I can escort the ladies," the Lieutenant offered.

"No need—the boys are able—our sons Rob, Key, T.H." He seemed to get some comfort from naming them.

"I'm sure Lieutenant Davis will be most helpful, John," his wife interrupted, as if, by allowing the young lieutenant to help, she was calming
him, instead of the other way around. "That will leave you to handle affairs
here." When he hesitated she added, "I should be grateful for his company.
You know how excited Anne gets in a crisis." She bent to receive the kiss
her grandson gave her as he left.

Cholera! It didn't mean anything to Johnny, but they reacted to it as if
Lieutenant Davis had brought the devil himself to Hopemont. Johnny unhitched the mare and drove down Main Street. The dentist, with Uncle Ben
beside him, was just locking his door when Johnny pulled up.

"I'm glad you came," Dr. McCalla said, not too happily. He was in a
hurry to get home; the news was everywhere. Uncle Ben climbed into the
wagon, almost falling over the sideboard.

Silently, Johnny led the mare through streets that were even more
crowded than they had been that afternoon. At Main and Walnut they
almost ran over an old black woman with a basket on her arm. She stopped
just short of the footwalk and turned to look at them, her dirty skirt dragging
in the dust. Her face was a mass of wrinkles almost hiding the two black
points of her eyes, which caught Uncle Ben's and held them. He stared back
undaunted, but in a voice hoarse with fear and urgency, told Johnny not to
look.

"Keep yo' haid turned strit. Strit ahaid, Massa. Don' look at dat woman!"
Uncle Ben held his jaw in pain.

"Why?"

"She de voodoo lady," he got out.

"Why are you looking?"

"She done made de *gris-gris* on me, an' cain't hu't me no mo'!"

The little doll with needles stuck through. Another untouchable mystery,
like the dealer's upstairs rooms with the young slave girls, or whatever
happened to Willis Barnes. Johnny clucked at the mare to move on.

"She drownz kittens an' ties 'em up in sacks an' leaves 'em on doahsteps,"
Uncle Ben mumbled, as if to exorcise her effect on him.

Uncle Ben kept mumbling and Johnny watched the quiet streets ablaze
with people in a hurry, rushing here, rushing there, some into houses, others
crying out with breathless, last-minute messages, loading wagons and the
wagons and buggies and carriages leaving town. Life itself seemed suddenly
terrifying, glorious and exciting, ominous and precious. Johnny flicked the
whip, and it wasn't until they were past the tollgate, kept up now in a state
of emergency, that he let the mare relax into a walk. Ahead of them and on
either side, for as far as they could see, the fields lay like deep, clipped velvet
in the last light.

Nobody was at the house or the cabins. Johnny had to help Uncle Ben
down and guide him, moaning, to his bed. Aunt Hannah, who heard them
drive up, ran from the kitchen with a pail of cold water and began giving
her husband orders while at the same time wetting and squeezing cloths.
She tied up his jaw with a bow at the top of his head. Johnny, under the

pretext of having to put the mare up, made his escape to the stable before he burst out laughing. Then he remembered the cholera.

Everybody at Shadeland was at the barn. The new horse had arrived, a feisty two-year-old liver-bay stallion, with a left hind sock. "Lak his daddy," Uncle Simon nodded, giggling. Then, more soberly: "Leastways he bes a bay . . . not one uv them chestnuts."

"He's sixteen hands if he's an inch, don't you think?" Calvin Morgan, his eyes almost as bright as Uncle Simon's, looked at his son.

"But American Eclipse is a chestnut, isn't he, Uncle Simon?" Johnny asked.

"He bes a chestnut, thass right enuf. It's that hind sock he got frum his daddy."

The stallion arched his neck and tossed his head and let fly a cow kick with his right hind that just missed Calvin's chest. "He got a wall eye," Uncle Simon said. "Cain't say he bes the purtiest hoss Ah evah seen. Whut's his name?"

"Sardanapalus," Calvin Morgan answered stoutly. "The last of the Assyrian kings. A man named Byron wrote a poem about him. He's got the best blood in the world," he added, still smiling. He didn't tell them that five grooms at Equiria Stud had tried to break him to halter and had failed. He hadn't moved an inch.

"Yassuh."

"Sired by American Eclipse, who was unbeaten. Never lost a race. Beat Lady Lightfoot, a daughter of Sir Archy. Beat Sir Henry, the best horse the South could produce. His daddy, Eclipse, was never beaten either, and *walked* over eight finish lines."

"He was from England," Cal offered.

"Ah knows he wuz from England," Uncle Simon answered, unconvinced.

"Sired by American Eclipse," Calvin Morgan repeated. "Out of a Dragon mare."

"He bes a dragon, all right."

It was then that the lead rope suddenly jerked Randolph off his feet as if he had been hit from behind by a locomotive. The rope left his hands, flying over the bay colt, who scattered the field hands watching at the other side of the barn, ran three times around the paddock, bucking, then jumped a fence and disappeared over a hill, the rope on his halter still flying.

Randolph started to run after him but Uncle Simon stopped him. "No need," the old man said. "No mares in dat pasture now. Let him be. Dat one . . . dat one needs to be let be."

"You'll spoil him, Uncle Simon," said Henrietta.

"No'm. Y'all jes' wait, jes' wait."

"How long?"

"Two weeks, Massa. Two weeks, at leas'. Mebbe three. Mebbe fo'."

With ultimate slowness, Uncle Simon slipped the latch shut on the new stallion's stall. It had been Xenophon's.

"Sardanapalus." Calvin Morgan smiled. "He looks like a sultan enough."

"He certainly acts like one," Henrietta conceded. She turned to Cal and

Johnny. "I want you boys to have nothing to do with him, do you hear? Absolutely nothing! Uncle Simon is in charge and you mind him. Uncle Simon, these boys will have nothing to do with that horse."

"Yassum. An' nobody else." He turned to Randolph and John Henry, a little field hand he had just taken into his charge. "Nobody." John Henry ducked his head and scampered off.

"It's time we all left and let Uncle Simon get on with his chores," Calvin said as cheerfully as he could. Even Johnny could tell he was worried about that stallion, in spite of bloodlines.

The cholera. He had to tell them about the cholera. He almost said something, but waited until they were halfway to the house. *Never upset the servants* was one of his mother's unbreakable rules.

When she heard it, Henrietta's face went pale. Johnny had never seen her so upset. When his father, to quiet her, said, "There's nothing we can do," she became more agitated. Even his "At least we can be thankful we're four miles from town" made her flash back.

"Yes . . . too far for news. What about Papa and Mama and Catherine and Anne and the boys? What if they need help? There won't be a soul riding to or from town for at least a week." Or anywhere else, she said to herself, just when Gideon had announced, just yesterday, that he planned to leave tomorrow.

"We can send someone in."

"To catch cholera?" She sent him a withering look.

"Maybe Gideon will know something."

"If Gideon spent the afternoon at your brother's, the only thing he will remember is whether Alexander Gibson beat him at poker or not."

"Did he?" Calvin asked when Gideon and Wash rode up about an hour later. And, true to form, Gideon was not perturbed by the news of cholera.

"Oh, folks runnin' around. They allus do, don't they? As a matter of fact," he chuckled, "I got Alexander this time." But he canceled his plans to leave.

Wash was glad enough of the delay when he heard about the new horse.

"Won't nobody touch him," Cal said. "Even Randolph's scared to death."

"Ah nevah seen a hoss I couldn't ride," Wash declared.

"Well, you oughta see this one," said Johnny, and then, from Wash's look, could have bitten his tongue.

That next afternoon, when Uncle Simon was busy with chores, Wash insisted on catching up Sard and riding him. The catching was bad enough, but nothing like the riding. Sard bucked once, high, then came down and rolled. But he didn't get up. He just stayed there, with Wash underneath.

"Lawd!" yelled Cal, and ran to the barn for help.

The horse rested his head against the grass and closed his eyes. Wash lifted his legs and kicked. Then the legs came down.

"God. He's dead!" screamed Johnny. "Wash is dead!"

Uncle Simon and Randolph came running. Uncle Simon raised his whip and gave Sardanapalus a mighty whack across the rump. The horse jumped and Randolph, holding the halter rope, fell backwards. Immediately he was on his feet again, after the stallion. "Let it go!" Uncle Simon yelled. When he saw that Wash was alive, he drew a breath. "Thet's whut comes from not mindin' . . ." he said so bitterly that Cal started crying. The old man turned to his grandson, who was brushing himself off. *"You"*—Uncle Simon emphasized the word—"will train him to de cart."

Randolph stopped brushing, his mouth open in disbelief.

Wash had sprained his arm and wore like a badge of honor the sling Henrietta insisted on tying around his neck. Calvin Morgan was more irate than Johnny had ever seen him.

"Now do you understand why Uncle Simon is to have absolute authority over the training of that horse?" he fumed to his sons. "Nobody but Uncle Simon must give the orders."

"He must be some horse trainer," Wash almost whispered after Johnny's father left the room.

"He used to belong to the Randolphs in Virginia," said Johnny. Cal nodded.

Wash whistled. "Still, Randolph's got a job on his hands. Wished I could watch it."

"Why can't you?"

"Pa says we leave as soon as the stage starts runnin'." To their moans he added: "Scared of the cholera, Pa is. Can you believe it?"

A week later Henrietta watched them go with a sigh. "Your relatives," she told her husband, "are interesting. I wonder," she added when the *calèche* had disappeared and they had turned to the house, "if it's in New Orleans."

Calvin walked with deliberate slowness to his favorite chair by the parlor window. From here, between the low-hanging leaves of the big oak behind the house, he could see the sun on the pond. It seemed strange to be speaking of cholera when everything out there looked so clean, so healthy. "I don't know."

"I'm so worried about Johnny."

"He'll be fine. I'm sure he's taking every precaution."

"But he's treating all those dying people . . ."

"Henrietta, I'm sure in France he learned the latest techniques. He knows how to take care of himself!"

He couldn't help smiling. When any of the servants—Celina or George or even Uncle Ben—complained of not feeling well, he would see her marching toward the quarters with a jar of quinine powder or a quart of castor oil. Often the illness would miraculously disappear before the medicine was given. "I'll not tolerate malingering," Henrietta would say.

"If you could be in charge, cholera wouldn't have a chance!"

"Come, now, Calvin." But she shivered. She went to the sideboard. "Would you like a brandy?"

"Why not? Maybe Uncle Simon will have good news when he gets back from town. Hope they don't miss the stage."

"Heavens, yes!" Henrietta laughed, and handed him a glass. "I don't find your relatives that interesting!"

4

Out of the alluvial soil near the mouths of the great rivers, in the delta of the Ganges, quiescent but no longer waiting, the Asiatic cholera reached Europe by way of Persia and Russia in 1830. It had left India in 1817, eight years before Johnny Morgan was born, and touched America just before his eighth birthday, in the spring of 1833. It had taken sixteen years, traveling the old invasion routes of man, from the south across the Plains of Turkistan to the Danube, from the north along the paths of the Khans. Now it was in the New World, traveling the paths of rivers again, crossing meadows, invading towns.

The patient collapses, sometimes without warning, and begins passing, in violent spasms, large quantities of disintegrated epithelium from the mucous membranes of the intestines. At the same time an uncontrolled vomiting of these same tissues—the surface lining of the intestines—is accompanied by agonizing cramps in the legs, feet and abdomen. The symptoms now advance rapidly. The surface of the body turns cold, the skin purple and dry and wrinkled. The features of the face become pinched and the eyes deeply sunken. There is complete suppression of the urine. The voice, a hoarse whisper, pleads for water and the mind, still clear, for something to ease the pain.

Remedies are few and futile. Mustard and turpentine are applied to the stomach as a counterirritant. Laudanum, or any form of opium, is dangerous. Toward the end there is apathy, and sometimes the patient actually seems to recover, with a lessening of diarrhea and vomiting. The end is often quick, with a complete collapse.

There is something peculiar about cholera: Almost as if reluctant to give up its victim, it lingers in the dead body in the form of fever. While other corpses cool, the dead by cholera may have a temperature that even rises a few degrees after death. Thus, from human filth and the rotting carcasses of untouchable cows, the silent invasion begins.

Henrietta had only heard such descriptions, but her slim knowledge was enough to cause sleepless nights, not so much for her children at Shadeland —they seemed so far removed—nor for her mother and younger brothers and sisters, who, Uncle Simon reported, had been removed to the Leestown farm—but for her father still at Hopemont and for her brother Johnny caring for patients in New Orleans. It was to him that her first thought flew when a young army sergeant rode into the yard and was escorted into the parlor by Uncle Ben.

He stood in the entry turning his cap in his hands and somehow Henrietta realized that Catherine hadn't gone with her mother and the others to the farm but had stayed behind at Hopemont. "I'll go with you," she said unhesitatingly. She turned to Uncle Ben. "Tell Uncle Simon to saddle Shamrock." To Calvin's objection that she take Uncle Simon and the carriage she was adamant: "Why expose our people more than we have to? Besides, you may need the carriage here. No, I can ride." She buttoned the tight waist of her riding basque and met Uncle Simon at the steps.

Johnny watched her swing into the sidesaddle and hook her knee firmly over the knob, her small black polished shoe in the tiny stirrup showing below her skirt. She had suddenly become more military than the sergeant, giving last-minute orders. Aunt Betty, importantly morose, nodded and maneuvered the boys with her hands on their shoulders to keep them out of the way of the horses as they rode off, the sergeant in the lead.

In the silence Calvin cleared his throat and suggested going fishing. To Johnny's utter surprise he heard Aunt Betty agree.

During the week of his wife's absence Calvin took his sons to the pond daily. The boys wanted to go to the stable but he wouldn't allow it. "Don't you think Uncle Simon has had quite enough of you?" Every morning he would follow his sons to the skiff and stand amused at their efforts to untie it and push off. Sometimes he would sit under the nearest tree and read his newspaper, watching them between turned pages or a sip of whiskey. It was a rare time and he wondered why they didn't spend more days like this. Was tragedy the only thing that made people see those they loved?

"What's malingering?" Johnny came up, and the shaft of his shadow cut across *The New York Sun*.

"Who said malingering?"

"Ma. When she fusses sometimes."

"It's when you pretend to be sick to get out of work."

"Was Uncle Ben pretending?"

Calvin laughed. "I hope not."

Johnny shrugged his shoulders to get rid of the shiver down his spine. He remembered thinking, when he'd seen the slaves in Lexington: What if I'd been born black instead of white? Suddenly he felt so lucky, so lucky and scared, to be Johnny Morgan with a clean bed and warm supper and people who loved him.

"Who made them slaves?"

Calvin gave his son a long look. "Well, actually, I suppose, the English."

"The Redcoats?"

"When they settled this country they forbade the colonists from freeing their slaves or from exporting—that's sending them someplace else."

"Why did they do that?"

"They needed labor to clear the fields and plant the crops. Not all of them were black. Some were white—indentured servants, they called them, serving out a term for debt."

"When will Uncle Ben?"

"Serve his time?"

The boy nodded.

"Never. We own him. Oh, don't look so sad! Let's just say we'll still take care of Uncle Ben, even if he's malingering."

"I'm glad of that," Johnny sighed, "or else how would Aunt Hannah get her veggytibbles?"

It was perfect May weather—warm but not too warm—dry with a breeze but not too dry—moist with spring and the promise of summer. In the fields the long slips of hemp were growing thicker, taller. They would, before harvest, reach twelve feet, and Calvin never stopped marveling at the way the sunlight played on the ripening tops, or listening to the sighing the wind made between the slender, leafy stalks.

With this cholera, he could expect no visitors. He read *Waverley* again, and told the boys its story, watching Johnny's gray eyes widen almost to tears at the execution of Fergus MacIvor.

"The old clans had done their duty," Calvin explained. "It was a time of change in Scotland."

"But why did they have to eks-sess-cute Fergus?" Cal asked.

"Ah, well, one day you may understand. One day you can read it for yourself." Fanny, Calvin's English spaniel, rolled over, her signal to have her stomach scratched. She was an old dog and followed him everywhere. She had a white stripe down her nose that spread around her mouth like melting snow. He rubbed her belly absentmindedly, and she scratched her back in semicircles on the grass.

Johnny was fascinated by the tales of the Border Wars, Rob Roy and Waverley and Ivanhoe. Out here under the trees he could imagine he was in the Highland forests with caves full of robbers and moors spread with chieftains, or at the lists watching the Black Knight thundering along with his ax.

"*I* think Ivanhoe was dumb not to marry Rebecca," said Johnny. "Why did he have to go and marry that old Rowena?"

"Yeah—Becca was nicer," said Cal.

Calvin Morgan's hand dropped to Fanny and massaged her ear. She stirred, settling again with her nose stretched out, her underchin rocking on her paws.

"Well, maybe it was because Rebecca was Jewish."

"What difference does that make?" asked Johnny. "Mr. Gratz is Jewish, isn't he?"

Before he could answer, Calvin Morgan saw Aunt Betty's face as she ran from the house.

"Massa Calvin, it's Miss Catherine . . . Miss Catherine, Massa Calvin! Miss Catherine is daid!"

Henrietta sat stunned in the parlor. A young officer, the same one Johnny had seen at Hopemont, was standing behind her, his back to them, his long hand steadying his saber against his leg, looking out the window. When they entered he turned his thin, concerned face to them, his eyes worn from lack of sleep. He introduced himself and explained that he had brought Mrs. Morgan home in her father's carriage. Johnny could see, through the window, his grandfather's curricle outside, with Shamrock tied and waiting patiently behind and Randolph holding one of his grandfather's bays up front.

"She was only twenty!" his mother kept sobbing. "Calvin, she was only twenty!"

"I know."

"And it was horrible! Horrible! She was conscious till the end. And so thirsty! Mr. Clay sent ice from his icehouse and we kept giving her cool . . . cool. . . ."

"I know."

"We thought she was still alive, Calvin. She was so warm, Calvin!" Henrietta stared at him through the tears that ran down her cheeks and gummed up the rice powder in sticky furrows. Johnny had never seen his mother look like this. His father's arms were around the shaking shoulders and over her head he was motioning to Aunt Betty to help him get her to the bedroom.

"Calvin, it was . . ."

"I know. I know . . ."

The parlor was quiet except for the purr and spit of the fire sending up its fringe of flame. His father came back and asked Lieutenant Davis, "You will stay?"

"I must get back."

"Nonsense. You look half dead yourself, Lieutenant. It's almost sundown now. Surely the town can get along without you for one night! Uncle Ben, see that Uncle Simon tends to Shamrock and the carriage horses." As he spoke he passed the Lieutenant a brandy, which he took in silence. He unbuckled his saber, propped it against the wall, and sank back in relief. Then Calvin went into the bedroom again and closed the door.

Johnny, stunned by the news and in awe of Lieutenant Davis's shining uniform, sat where he was, but Cal went up to him, picking at his buttons and asking questions. The idea that Aunt Catherine—beautiful Aunt Catherine who had danced with him in her new dress—was dead stung Johnny's eyes with tears. He swallowed hard and remembered again the excitement in the streets of Lexington that had sent a thrill of horror through him. There was something valuable but mysterious about life, something so deep, something that ran away the more you tried to think about it. Kicking and bucking and running away. Lashing out. Something beautiful.

"Leave the Lootenant alone," Aunt Hannah ordered Cal as she rounded the door from the summer kitchen. "You two boys, you come in heah. What we all need is a good suppah!" Lieutenant Davis, between little sips of brandy, gave her a sweet, weary smile and followed the boys into the dining room.

Calvin came in briefly and chatted with Davis, who had lived in Lexington while he attended Transylvania University, before leaving for West Point. The boys ate in silence. Aunt Betty returned.

"She askin' for you, Massa Calvin."

He left, and Aunt Betty urged Lieutenant Davis to eat a second helping of pie. "Do you good, suh. A body kin see you *fatigué, très, très.*"

Lieutenant Davis lifted his hand.

"Yo' room is right up deez stairs, ovah dis kitchun. If'n you wants anything in de night, jes' call. Tonight I'ze sleepin' right heah."

"Here?"

"Heah, Massa Johnny." Aunt Betty turned her butterscotch eyes on him. "You don' 'spec Ah could sleep a wink wif yo' mama upset? Now you boys git upstaihs to bed. . . . *Faites do-do.*"

Outside the soft evening lay golden on the grass. From his mother's bedroom the sound of sudden weeping and his father's voice made Johnny jump. Cal began pushing his fists between his knees.

"It's early yet," Lieutenant Davis said, trying to sound hearty. "Will you give us boys permission to stay up a little longer? If we promise to be good?"

Aunt Betty frowned but a smile tugged at her mouth. "Ah'll jes' he'p Aunt Hannah wif de dishes . . ."

As they walked back to the parlor Lieutenant Davis winked at the boys.

"Do you fight robber barons?" asked Johnny.

"Do you fight Injuns?" echoed Cal, crawling into his lap.

Lieutenant Davis gave a soft chuckle. "Well, you might say I've *seen* Injuns. There was one I'll always remember."

"What was his name?"

"Black Hawk."

"Was he bad?"

"He was an old man," Davis said to the fire. "He was an old man just trying to feed his people."

He waited so long Johnny was afraid he wouldn't go on. A pale light shone through the window. "Why did they call him Black Hawk?"

"Because he was proud and bold, and had coal-black hair and fierce black eyes," Lieutenant Davis told Johnny. "His father had been a medicine man, and when Black Hawk became a chief he signed a treaty with General Harrison. . . ."

"William *Henry* Harrison?" Johnny's eyelids popped up.

"The same. So now they had spoiled meat instead of deer and flimsy cloth blankets instead of buffalo robes."

Johnny leaned on his hands and held his face with his spread fingers. Will never told him General Harrison cheated the Indians! On the hearth his mother's gray cat opened its mouth with a dry sound and yawned, the whitish-pink insides looking like a snake's. Johnny watched the fire. Davis's face was twisted, talking about a massacre. Women and children on a raft.

"The whites, of course, had bayonets, and killed some in the water. The rest of the Indians went to an island covered with willows. The whites kept up the fire, dropping squaws with braves."

The cat settled again, tucking her head under her forearm.

Lieutenant Davis's eyes still kept their deadly aim at the blank space in front of him. A chill ran down Johnny's back. In the orange-blue flames licking the firewood, leaning, reaching, sinking back, hungry Indians stumbled in the willows, screamed as the bullets found them. Aunt Catherine lying in a coffin underground. Were her hands crossed, the same hands that had reached out to him: "Dance with me, Johnny!" No . . . he couldn't believe in Reverend Pratt's great boulders with their little bird! Not even for Indians!

"My job was to capture Black Hawk and bring him back. But he was caught by the Winnebagos." Davis looked up as if a spell had been broken.

Cal's head had grown heavy in the crook of his elbow. The straight blond hair fell across his sleeve, and a thumb had found its way into Cal's mouth.

"He was dressed in white deerskins that the Winnebago women made for him." Davis looked at the fire again.

"Why did they make him clothes if they captured him?"

"He was still a chief. And he was hungry and old."

Johnny held onto his cheeks.

"When he came in he stood very straight. He kept his head plucked except for a long scalp lock and his eyes were like arrows in his face. I was in charge of Black Hawk and forty prisoners." The Lieutenant shifted his legs into a more comfortable position.

"Ain't you gonna tell me the end?" yawned Cal.

"The prisoners were released. But Black Hawk was put in a cell with a ball and chain. That's where I left him."

Johnny watched the steady eyes of Lieutenant Davis. He was still looking at the fire, his interlocked fingers gripping his hands. Before Johnny could ask his question Aunt Betty stood before him with a candlestick in her hand. "Time for bed," she said with authority. "For all you boys."

Lieutenant Davis laughed. "You're right, Aunt Betty." He rose, a sudden weariness relaxing him.

Johnny followed Cal upstairs, holding Aunt Betty's hand. The sadness in her body made her arm feel heavy against him and he squeezed her fingers.

On the landing where she had waited for him the night Xenophon died she stopped and looked down and a smile softened her face. "Now tamarrah, Massa John, Ah's gwin'a need some help. You understan'?"

Johnny got in bed and pulled the covers up to his chin. He saw on the ceiling, past Aunt Betty's head, the Indian women dying on the raft, the people rushing in the streets, felt in his stomach that excitement with Uncle Ben beside him mumbling about voodoo ladies. There must be something they were rushing for. What was it? When Aunt Bet came into focus again he saw that she was staring at him through tears.

Lieutenant Davis left the next day, his spurs clinking as he went down the front steps. Then he stopped and ran back, holding onto his saber as he took the steps by twos.

"This is for you," he said to Johnny, and held out a little leather draw-purse. Inside, Johnny found a broken black feather. "I'm sorry it's broken." Lieutenant Davis was pushing his military hat down over his blond curls. "It belonged to Black Hawk. And for you, Calvin," he said with a quick grin, "here's something I made last night." From behind his back he showed Cal a wooden sword. "Now you can play soldier."

Henrietta, beside him, doing her duty as hostess, tried to smile. "You've been most kind, Lieutenant Davis." She held out her hand and allowed it to linger in appreciation but also a little pleadingly on his sleeve. Then, before he could answer she said quickly: "Will you see my father?"

"Yes, of course."

"He's . . . not given to expressing his feelings. He will keep them inside, but he will suffer like the rest of us. Will you visit him?"

It was a question, but it was given, underneath the softness, like an order.

"Yes, of course."

"Well, good-bye then." She smiled. "And thank you for the sword. I'll see that Calvin uses it with honor."

But despite the pleasantry, Henrietta's puffy face in the morning sunshine was pallid and waxen, her eyes dulled.

In Lexington fifty people died in three days. By July, five hundred people of a population of six thousand would be hauled away in death carts, the drivers' heads swathed in cloth to prevent contagion.

Henrietta's mother, with Anne and the three youngest boys—Robert, Key and T.H.—were at the farm. But her father was at Hopemont, and what of her married sisters, Eleanor in Lexington, Mary in Frankfort, Theodosia in St. Louis? And her brother Abraham in Alabama . . . but most of all, Johnny in New Orleans? In her distress she forgot that four miles is hardly enough to halt a disease that had traveled halfway around the world.

She was surprised when Aunt Betty woke her in the middle of the night.

"Miss Henrietta . . . it's Celina. She . . . she's vomitin' all ovah de place an' . . . purgin' herseff all ovah de place . . ." Aunt Betty's great Indian face shattered into unfamiliar sobs.

"I'll come," Henrietta said, throwing back the covers and reaching for her robe. "Where is she?"

"In de cabin. No'm . . . Ah din' want you tuh come!" Bouviette wrung her hands. "Jes' tell us what to do . . . Aunt Hannah and me."

"She's right, Henrietta. Stay—stay here with the boys. We—" But Calvin was cut short by a cough that took his breath. When he regained it he said deliberately and with as much determination as he could muster: "Henrietta, you are not going out there."

But she was already busily changing clothes, with Aunt Betty behind her. "And what if I don't?" she almost shouted. "First, it will be that silly Celina, who won't take her castor oil. Then it will be Aunt Hannah, then Bouviette, then Johnny or Cal, then you. . . . No, you've got to fight a disease from the beginning. If they had done as much in Lexington . . ." She almost choked, and Calvin, to divert her, admitted that she certainly knew the latest remedies.

"That's true," she said more calmly, sitting down to put on her shoes. "And I think . . ."

He watched her lovely, concerned face as she enumerated this and that, the putting on of mustard, the wrapping in blankets. She was magnificent, channeling her fear into action. How could he stop her?

"Aunt Hannah may help," she said to Bouviette. "But you will stay here in the house and watch the children, do you hear?"

The strong-willed Bouviette, who had been known to argue with her mistress like a friend—especially when she was defending the boys—said softly, "Aunt Hannah wif her now."

Henrietta poked her hair into a cloth and tied it on the top of her head, slave style. With her sleeves pushed up and one curl escaping from behind her ear, she had never been for Calvin more desirable.

"There'll be drinking only from the cistern, do you hear? *Only from the cistern.* Get some blankets," she called over her shoulder as she went through the parlor. She stopped short in the summer kitchen and Aunt Betty almost ran into her with the candle. "We'll need salt and vinegar to soak the blankets. Send Randolph. And make a bandage with cayenne pepper."

At Bouviette's raised eyebrows she said, "Yes, cayenne pepper." Her gray eyes snapped. "Mustard and turpentine. We'll need those too."

She was stopped by a brown hand, which reached out and held her arm. "Miss Henrietta," Bouviette said coolly, "it'll be all right. Ah'll do it all and you will see . . . it'll be all right!"

She didn't answer. She took an extra candle and walked down the narrow brick path to the quarters. The moon was full and a breeze blew the candle out before she'd taken a dozen steps. She could hear Celina screaming from the third cabin and see the shadow Uncle Ben's back made against the half-opened door. Between screams a thick silence seemed to mock her as she stood on the hard-packed earth shivering. She sent one look to the back of the house in the moonlight, and the boys' bedroom window upstairs. "Dear God," she whispered. "Don't let them."

The stench of vomit and feces almost took her breath when she entered. The quilt was soaked and Aunt Hannah, at the foot of the bed, was patting Celina's foot, which had escaped the covers. Presently the girl, gasping, doubled up in pain and screamed "Mah laigs! Mah laigs! Oh, Lawd, mah laigs!" But she was interrupted by a surge of vomit that spurted from her face. She almost fell out of bed trying to direct it to the floor. When she sank back a yellow-green slime covered half her face. Her bandanna had long since been pushed off and her stiff hair lay thick with sweat. "Watah, watah . . ."

"Yes, yes. Uncle Ben, go fetch Randolph. Oh, he's here. Randolph, put them over there. Did you bring the bandage?"

"Aunt Betty makin' it now. But Ah brung de vinegah an' de salt."

"Good. How many blankets?" She lifted the girl's head and tried to get a trickle of water between the cracked lips.

"Fo'."

"Good. Now Uncle Ben, you and Randolph hold her up while Aunt Hannah takes these covers off. I'll . . ." Quickly she snapped open a clean blanket and spread it on the hard cornshuck mattress, then laid another blanket crosswise and soaked the second blanket with the salt and vinegar. "Now. You can put her back now." Henrietta wiped her forehead with her sleeve. "Take those covers outside and burn them, Randolph."

Randolph took the quilt and sheet to a cleared place beyond the trees. "Need a sulfur?" a voice said behind him.

"Massa Johnny! Marse Cal! Youze bettah not let Miss Henrietta . . ."

"Here's some sandpaper." Johnny's hand came out.

"You been heah . . . ?

All the time, Johnny's nodding head said. "Hush up, Cally," he said aloud, before Cal could open his mouth.

They waited, watching the flames take hold. From the cabin Aunt Hannah's voice, cracked with fear, was asking, "Cain't Ah go get Milly?" And their mother's, irritated: "There's no need exposing more people than we need to. We've got enough. . . ."

Celina must have doubled up again. By the time Johnny and Cal reached the shadow of the tree and looked in, the spasm had subsided and their mother and Aunt Hannah by turns were bathing her face, offering her drinks from the pitcher that Uncle Ben kept filled. Behind them the glow of Randolph's fire threw fretful light on the cabin walls. "When this is over we'll lime them," Henrietta said to the walls. "Every last one of them, do you hear?"

"Yes'm."

Henrietta's eyes moved past the door, and for one heart-stopping minute Johnny thought she saw them.

"Uncle Ben, the next time you go for water get that bandage from Bouviette and tell Randolph to take your place and you go to bed." When he objected she silenced him with "I'll have no heroics here. Each one of us needs rest. Regular intervals. Do you understand? Now hurry. I need that mustard."

Randolph, who had heard, ran to the house for him, and returned with the mustard. She took it from him and drew away the girl's coarse dress and spread the mixture on a cloth, then laid it across her stomach. Celina was so weak now she merely whimpered at the burning. Her trembling, swollen lips tried to form words, but she merely looked at them in terror.

"She gon' die, Missus?" Henrietta heard Randolph ask behind her.

"Be still and give me some water." She plunged her stinging hands into the bowl, then wiped them on her apron. "I think the vomiting's stopped for a while," she said quietly.

"Miss Henrietta, youze need some rest."

"Hush! We'll take turns, Aunt Hannah. But not yet."

Outside the first cocks were crowing, although it was still dark. The moon had set long ago and that stealthy silence that deepens before dawn seemed to invade the cabin, as if the whole world were waiting for something unknown. But it was only the sun, familiar, warm and light, and when the first long shaft reached the floor boards they somehow felt better. Celina was breathing shallowly, but breathing.

Then, just as they pulled up two willow-bottomed chairs to sit down, the vomiting and diarrhea started again, punctuated by the agony of those cramps in the legs and stomach. Laudanum, thought Henrietta. How I wish I could give her laudanum! All of us laudanum. Through her fatigue she saw Randolph, taller than she remembered, supporting her.

"She be all right fo' a while, Miss Henrietta. Aunt Hannah know whut to do now. You gotta come wif me now to de house. Aunt Betty fix you some tea." She leaned on him, stumbling on the bricks. She hadn't realized how tired she was.

Celina suffered through that day and night, her dehydrated body turning a muddy purple. By dawn of the second day she lay in a stupor, and Uncle Isaac, rubbing his bald head, asked permission to see her. They stepped aside, Aunt Hannah in her vast apron, Henrietta in her robe, flung on hurriedly after a two-hour rest in the little room over the summer kitchen where Wash and Lieutenant Davis had stayed. "No, I won't hear of it," she told Calvin from a distance. "I might contaminate you all. I'll be fine here." Now, watching Uncle Isaac's uncertain step toward Celina's bed, she seemed to be watching Catherine's death all over again. Lovely Catherine! Lovely, beautiful, sweet Catherine! Already it seemed so far away, so long ago. If she thought of that she would go mad.

The old man prayed silently, occasionally letting a mumble escape his pursed mouth. His chickenboned fingers fumbled with each other at the edge of the bed. To their surprise, Celina turned her head and smiled.

"She'll live! *Of course* she'll live! She's had the best nursing in the world," Calvin laughed when Henrietta told him. He leaned over and kissed his wife's forehead, brushing her hair back. "You rest now, Henrietta. Orders from me for a change. Isn't that right, Bouviette?"

Aunt Betty, behind him, stopped folding her mistress's clothes and nodded.

"Good job well done!" Calvin blew a kiss from the door, but she was already closing her eyes.

The second the latch clicked she sat bolt upright in the bed and beat her knees with her little hands through the covers. Bouviette, alarmed, didn't dare speak. *Ah know'd she wuz too quiet*, she said to herself. *Ah know'd it!*

"Why don't they all die?" Henrietta cried, her mouth making an ugly downturned U in her face. "Why do we have to always, always take *care* of them? Where is it decreed that we have to be saddled with them?" she asked Bouviette, forgetting that Aunt Betty, too, was a slave. "I'm so tired of it! So sick of it!" She threw her head back and covered her eyes with her arm.

Bouviette drew up a chair and sat quietly, with tremendous effort not to make a sound. With a gesture like Calvin's she brushed back the curly hairline, her own eyes wet with tears.

"Miss Henrietta. Outside de birds is singin'. Lissen! Do you heah dem? Do you know whut dey's a-tellin' you? It's June fust, Miss Henrietta. Do you remember, mah *petite*, June fust? Eight yeahs ago, Miss Henrietta, Ah held you in mah ahrms when dat fust lil' baby come. You remember what I tole you? A baby bawn in de season of de wile rose, dat be a spechul baby, Miss Henrietta. Miss Henrietta—today's Massa John's burfday!"

The arm came down and Henrietta Morgan, for the first time since Catherine's death, let fly a flood of tears. Bouviette took her friend in her arms.

"An' we'll have a cake," she said as she rocked her. "To celuhbrate wif. An' . . ."

"You always spoil them," Henrietta murmured into her hand, sniffing, then giggled. "You always . . ."

"Now you get yo' res'. You as tired as Jonah when he was flung up outta dat whale."

"Can we come down now?" Cal called. Aunt Betty, obeying orders, had kept the boys in their room (or so she thought) during Celina's illness. But the danger wasn't over yet, and an isolation policy between house and cabins and cabin and cabin was maintained as much as possible. For Johnny's birthday Aunt Betty had baked a cake herself, sending Aunt Hannah to rest and Milly to watch Celina. She served it in the parlor on little blue-flaked china plates and made the boys put on their best pants and boots.

"In the middle of the afternoon?" Johnny objected, but one look at Aunt Betty hushed him. Henrietta appeared in a new flowered muslin, its wide skirt bound by two rows of ribbon, her face puffy with sleep.

"Tell him," she said to Calvin.

"Your grandfather," Calvin Morgan paused significantly until Johnny stopped biting into a piece of cake, "is giving you a horse for your birthday. . . . No, no, no!" he laughed as Johnny swarmed over him. "It won't arrive until next week. It's at the Leestown farm. . . ."

It was the best birthday Johnny could remember, even though Aunt Betty still wouldn't let them go outside. "Yo' mama's awdahs," she said.

"That's right," his father grinned. "Your mother's a Roman matron."

"Wo-man ma-twon," echoed Cal, reaching for another piece of cake.

5

Celina's was the only case of cholera at Shadeland. Gradually, the cabins came to life again. The sound of the banjo after work, women calling children and lining on Sunday mornings. It was pleasant to listen to the gentle but compelling single voice giving the line, and the answering chorus lifted in a rhythm that must have come, with their souls, out of Africa. The sound had an unbearable longing, made sadder by resignation.

And the new horse!

The new horse was a gray filly named Alice. "Now you'll have to listen to everything Uncle Simon says," Calvin Morgan warned Johnny, his sandy hair lifting in the breeze, his blue eyes caressing the top line, the flank, the angle of hock. "Look at those pasterns! I'll bet she'll float!"

"Not yet she won't, Massa," Uncle Simon said sternly. "She gots tuh be checked out fust."

"Uncle Simon!"

"Nosuh! Nobody gits on dis hoss 'till Ah kin check her out!"

"He's right, you know," Calvin told his son as they leaned on the fence watching the old man lead her in a circle.

"Will she be ready in time for the barbecue?"

"Ain't gonna be no Fo'th of Joo-ly ba'becue dis yeah, Massa Calvin say, kaze of de cholerah!"

"Can I ride her to Will's?"

"When de time kum . . ."

The old man was adamant. Johnny followed him to the stable, where Sard was now obediently in his stall. It was the talk of the farm, how Uncle Simon had handled that stallion, standing by the fence, waiting for the horse to come up. Anybody else—even Randolph—could expect those ears to flatten and a hind hoof to slash out.

"We'll put her at de end," the old man said. "Away from Big Daddy dere."

"How is he?" Johnny went to Sard's door, fascinated by danger. The stallion strained over the top, trying to bite him.

"He be fine if'n you don' tease him like dat."

"I'm only standing here."

Uncle Simon forgot to fuss, in his admiration of the big bay. "Ain't dat a nice stripe, now?"

"It's shadowed."

"Thass right. Shadowed." He stepped over to the stall and ran his finger down the narrow blaze, with its half-inch of white hairs invading the dark coat shining like polished mahogany. "Means he smart."

"I heard it means they're mean."

"Don' you believe it." The old man's voice was a caress, and the stallion's ears went up and he dipped his head to be scratched.

"Well, I'll be damned," Johnny Morgan let out, then ran before Uncle Simon could catch him.

Randolph had started Sardanapalus on the cart, back and forth and around the dirt track used for match races on the Fourth of July, when Shadeland gave its big barbecue. Uncle Simon was right. When Johnny asked his father the next morning, Calvin confirmed that there would be none that year. "But we'll have one next year," he grinned. "And by then we'll have a horse to beat any four legs in the county."

Their eyes went to the training cart, making its rounds, the stallion reaching, digging dirt with a stretchy trot. A week later Uncle Simon put him on one of the farm wagons, and the farm almost forgot that he was a stallion. After Sunday services, which had started again, the bachelor planters from the other side of the pike would drop by, joking about him. "Got you a new plow horse, Calvin?"

"Yes," said Calvin, unperturbed.

"Looks a mite weak in the gaskin."

"Might be."

"And a little sickle-hocked from here."

"Could be."

Nothing they could say ruffled him.

"How can you tolerate it? The nerve!" Henrietta slapped some mending on her lap.

With the long summer days Randolph found time to ride with the boys after supper over the fields, taking fences at a gallop to see how far each horse could jump. Alice was a dream, with her long thoroughbred barrel and perfectly balanced neck. Johnny loved the feel of sitting into her, waiting for that uplift which brought her mane close to his chest, and then the sinking back, his shoulders open, and the soft landing before the next smooth reach of shoulder, bunch of haunch. Without realizing it, he was becoming a superb rider. Not even little Tommy Cunningham next door, or Cal was better. Only Randolph, of all the neighborhood boys who came to ride with them, could keep up.

"It's a *Meesawmi!*" Will Webb said when Johnny showed him the feather. He laid it gently on the bench before him with his thick, stubby fingers.

"What's that?"

"A kinda sacred gift—with secret power bestowed by the Great Spirit."

Johnny stared at the broken feather. Cal, standing beside him, drew his lips in. "I don't see no powwah."

"Oh, it's there, all right. Mebbe not to the eye. But if you gits in a pinch, and, suddenlike, somethin' gits you *out*, you'll know." He turned to Johnny. "This here's a hawk feather."

"It was Black Hawk's!"

"Black Hawk! He was at the Thames." Will turned the feather over as if it would break.

"Why was he called Black Hawk?" Johnny asked, remembering his sudden distrust of Will when Lieutenant Davis told him about General Harrison cheating the Indians. Maybe Will hadn't seen him after all.

"Hawks don't eat dead things," Will said slowly. "Already dead, an' not that they've killed themselves." At Johnny's frown he added, "Like a man of honor don't take vengeance on a fallen foe. Gen'ral Harrison allus said that." He handed the feather back and picked up his work again.

Sometimes Amanda rode with them. Amanda was the only girl Johnny had ever seen ride like that, her red mane flying. Tommy Cunningham and Frank Wolford were good, and Randolph. But Amanda! She rode astride, her sturdy legs under her, her back straight as a pin. Sheepishly once, when Johnny talked of Amanda's riding, Frank, who was fourteen, looked at him and said, "You don't know *nuthin'*, do you, Johnny Morgan?"—and the memory of Wash stood before him. *Don't you know nuthin'?* What did they mean?

The annual July Fourth barbecue, the biggest event of the year, would be sorely missed, and as the day approached, Calvin talked Henrietta into letting the slaves substitute their own feast, since the cholera prevented a larger party. "It'll be good for the people," he said, but he was really thinking of her.

For a week the quarters buzzed with preparations. Two chestnut trees sheltered the tables and benches where the field hands ate in good weather. On one side three black iron kettles had been set up. On the other a wide trench had been dug days ago to accommodate whole carcasses of sheep, half-grown pigs, and the smoldering hickory fire that would roast them.

This was Calvin Morgan's favorite spot—besides the pond—on the whole farm. On the long tables in the shade Uncle Jacob, the cook for the bachelor field hands (really a young man and not an "uncle" at all but so good-natured the title was given), would set out great bowls of pot liquor and mounds of mustard greens and corn bread, and Calvin with his sons would find an excuse to come by for a sample. Was there anything more heavenly than Uncle Jacob's pot liquor? Calvin could always get a reaction from Henrietta to that one.

She wanted him to sell his excess field hands, but he wouldn't. It was one of the sore points between them. The hemp, which had needed labor, was no longer his main crop. He had gone into horses and livestock, and this summer he could count sixteen horses, twenty-one cows with calves, fifty hogs, and thirty-six sheep, which he watched pulling placidly at long tufts of fescue on the slopes behind the woods. Since he refused to sell surplus slaves, Calvin began hiring out his field hands once the hemp was in and the foals were weaned, and until retting and breaking time when the hemp would be taken up from the fields and stored for drying. Even George, a good carpenter, was allowed to work other places when he could be spared. The ropewalks and textile factories in Lexington always needed extra hands.

Most, though, worked close enough to return home at night and enjoy Uncle Jacob's tables, set close enough to Uncle Isaac's cabin so that he could step outside to intone long graces from his doorstep when it rained.

The weather today was perfect, and even without extra guests and a horse race, it was almost as good as a regular celebration. All day the pots bubbled, and toward sundown the real feast began, with noisy eating and jokes about consumption. Afterwards, as expected, Uncle Ben got out his banjo, his face shining, his fingers flying over the magic circle in his lap.

The banjo was special. It was so special that it alone, and not a fiddle or a harmonica, could be played in church. It was so special that not even dancing was allowed to detract from it, even when it was played on everyday occasions. If you wanted to jig or do a pigeon wing you did it to marked time by patting. When the banjo played, you listened. Only the player, if carried away, could sing. Sometimes Uncle Ben couldn't restrain himself.

> An' de possum in de 'simmon tree
>   De raccoon on de groun'
> De raccoon say, "You son-uv-a gun,
>   You bettah shake dem 'simmons down!"

In the last light, the boys were still trying to "cut the cross" on a piece of paper at sixty yards. Henrietta was wearing her green striped silk, her husband's favorite dress. Across the lawn Calvin Morgan watched her erect shoulders and the hands that had nursed Celina and smiled. She smiled back, and she had never seemed so lovely. He knew she wanted more children and regretted the ill health that prevented so much. But today, in the soft afterglow of a July day and with the smell of baking ham in his nose and the taste of good whiskey on his tongue, anything seemed possible.

When he saw his father-in-law walking down the incline from the house his first reaction was one of gratified surprise. They had never been truly friends, and Calvin knew the old entrepreneur tolerated his son-in-law as a likable failure. He helped Henrietta to her feet and they walked toward him. Johnny, under the trees and about to take his turn with his squirrel rifle, saw them stand in a tight little group, saw his mother falter and his father catch her arm. They walked to the house, sending Aunt Betty back with explanations.

John Wilson Hunt, M.D., had been killed in New Orleans in a duel.

"Over a woman!" Johnny heard his mother say through the parlor door.

"Hush! It was the honorable thing to do."

"Oh, honor! You men and those meaningless words! Johnny's gone, can't you understand? Gone!"

But there was no collapsing this time. Henrietta was more angry than grieved. Not until she returned to Shadeland after a week at Hopemont did she allow herself the luxury of seclusion.

Johnny went back to school with relief. The house was strangely quiet, quieter even than it had been after Aunt Catherine. There was no time to worry about Jake Bolton. Or at least Johnny told Randolph so.

They were sitting under a tree in front of the one-room red brick "schoolhouse"—really a cabin—about a half-mile from Shadeland. In good weather Theophile Parsons taught the boys outside. There were eight of them. Little

Cally Morgan was easily persuaded, but his brother Johnny sometimes worried the schoolmaster, with questions that cut to the core. When he'd finished telling the story of Troy, Johnny did it again. "How could Achilles be the hero if he dragged Hector's body around behind that chariot?"

"Yeah," said Cal. "That wuz a mean thing to do."

"That's true," Theophile Parsons agreed, reaching over and wiping Cal's nose. "But the Greeks had an idea that a great man was capable of great emotions in both directions—great hate and great compassion. Achilles showed great compassion when he received old Priam and gave him the body of his son."

"But he dragged him!"

"Yeah, he dwagged him!"

"Yes, and he showed great hate when he dragged him. But Achilles became great when he controlled himself, controlled the anguish and the hate. That's why he was the hero." When they still looked puzzled he added: "Well, it's as if you were as strong as a giant and you were mad at Cal, but you decided not to hit him."

Tommy Cunningham, bored with the subject, shot a rock at a robin and said, "What about the Trojan Horse?"

"Yeah," said Cal.

"Weren't the Trojans dumb to take it in?" Johnny asked, putting his finger on the central question.

"The Trojans were a religious people. They thought the horse was an offering to the gods."

"But Zeus was on the Trojans' side!"

"Zeus was, but Poseidon wasn't. And Hera, queen of the gods, hated the Trojans and wanted the Greeks to win. So she made Zeus go to sleep one day, and while he slept the fortunes of war changed. Hector was wounded by Ajax and hundreds of Trojans were slaughtered."

"But how did she make him go to sleep?" Johnny asked.

Theophile Parsons blushed and said mysteriously, "You never can tell about the gods."

"I still think they were dumb to let that horse in," Johnny said, forgetting about Hera, for which Theophile Parsons was thankful.

He soon had another pupil. It was Calvin Morgan's recurring idea that education was the only answer for an emancipation which was bound to come, if not in their lifetime, by the end of the century.

Now he looked at Randolph, Uncle Simon's bright grandson, and began to see the future hope of Kentucky. For it would surely come to pass, he told his wife, that any region containing ignorance would breed cruelty and hatred. Sometimes he thought the ultimate cruelty was ignorance. He was never, in his discussions with Henrietta's New Jersey and Pennsylvania relatives, defensive about slavery. It was a fact of life, a labor system built into the economic existence of the South. And he knew there had been for a long time a serious effort in the Kentucky legislature to enact equitable laws for the protection of slaves. Most of the people he knew treated their servants well. There was, in the back of his mind, the knowledge that it was the field

hands, those ignorant hordes shipped "downriver" ever since Louisiana became American and cotton and sugar plantations needed labor, that troubled
him. The only hope of the whole race might lie in a few bright slaves being
educated. Then the few could increase to many, and gradually. . . . He
sighed, and turned over the question in his mind again. He knew he was a
dreamer. Henrietta reminded him of that shortcoming constantly.

Nevertheless, he arranged for Theophile Parsons to take Randolph as a
pupil. Since he had never learned to read, there was no question of his
attending class with the other boys, even if Calvin had wanted him to, or if
young Parsons would agree. Calvin had no intention of stirring hostility
among his neighbors. In the quiet of a Sunday afternoon, when Henrietta
was taking a nap and the boys were fishing, he brought out his penknife and
fashioned a goose quill. "This is for you," he told Randolph. "And this is
the way you slice a quill. Shape it like this, see?" He made Randolph imitate
him, then laughed. "Be sure the words you write are true!"

Johnny was delighted. Now he could ask Randolph all those questions
about the Greeks.

With October came hog-killing. For some reason known only to the
grown-ups, the operation was in charge of the senior male cook—in this
case, Uncle Jacob—and the oldest white son. By the time Johnny reached
the quarters the immense fire of logs, blazing since daybreak, lay cradled in
its coals on piles of big rocks. Closer to the hog pen the troughs were already
filled with water. Uncle Jacob and the others were waiting for him to give
the order. With efficiency and no lost motion, the coals were scraped away
and the stones were transferred to the water, which boiled almost immediately. George, John Henry, Randolph and some of the field hands carried
the just-slaughtered carcasses for dunking and scalding until the hair could
be scraped off on the long benches set up for the purpose. Then the carcasses
were hung on stout crosspoles and disemboweled, to be taken afterwards to
the meathouse, where they would be cut into hams, chines, and sides, the
remnants into sausage. Even while the work was being done, hogs' tails and
livers were broiled on the big fire and eaten by the hands and by the young
white boys in charge of the operation, which was traditionally off-limits to
the adult white members of the household. It was here Johnny and Cal, in
the fall of the year, enjoyed the pleasures of fresh hog liver, known only to
the initiated. In anticipation of Christmas they saved the bladders, which
were hung in the top of the meathouse to dry. Filled with water and stamped
on, they made the grandest noise.

But Johnny, even though he was "boss" at hog time, liked hemp-breaking
better. Long before the first frost, which came to Shadeland about mid-
October, the tall, slender, leafy stalks of hemp were cut with short-handled
knives and spread on the ground to be softened by dew and rain. In dry
years this was done in the creek, so important was "dew rotting"—or retting
—which freed the lint on the fiber from the resin, which in turn had held
the fiber to the woody portion of the stalk. When it was time to separate the
fiber from the stalks, the field hands would go, row by row, with handmade
wooden brakes and throw the heavy levers, tossing the worthless hurds or

shives into piles. They were followed by more hands who folded and tied the fiber into long fleecy bundles, piling them high on the low mule wagon that would take them to the barn. At dusk, after the last of the crop was in, there was the firing of the shives.

A favorite braker—this year it was Edward Ross, a big, blue-black man with enormous shoulders and an even larger smile—would carry a lighted brand from pile to pile and the whole family and all the hands and house servants would come out to watch the resinous sparks send long streamers of flame into the dark November air. It was a spectacle Johnny never tired of, watching the flames, or hearing his father speculate on which navy ships would use the ropes made of Morgan hemp, or how many cotton bales would be bound by bagging made from plants grown at Shadeland. Johnny had visions of flatboats floating on the great river down to New Orleans, or even beyond—wasn't American hemp even more prized than that from Calcutta? —and watched the fires with excitement. Anybody knew a cotton bale without good hemp was unmarketable. Or that a rope not properly dew-retted couldn't hold a yearling colt, much less a ship. The fires that gathered and ballooned and shot up bolts of orange-red stars seemed to be sending all the hope and energy and sweat of a whole year as some kind of offering, some kind of appeasement, skyward.

Their eyes were turned up, naturally, when it happened. A streak of light, followed by a shower of fire from a tail . . . it stopped their breaths. The sky went "all snowflakes"—hadn't Will said that?—and Johnny shivered. Tecumseh would come again, the Shawnees said. But his father calmly noted, in his journal, that on the night of November 13, 1833, there had been a meteoric display at shive-burning time.

Randolph was getting taller, and even growing the wisp of a mustache. With his slightly slanted eyes he looked vaguely oriental. Around the house and barn Henrietta noted that his kindness and tact were genuine, a politeness that encouraged her to promote him into a kind of understudy for Uncle Ben. Although Shadeland had never been grand enough to boast a "butler," still the courtly Uncle Ben had supplied the necessary amenities. Now, more and more, Randolph, when he wasn't helping Uncle Simon, would greet guests, and when Uncle Ben needed a rest, he would take over entirely, allowing the old man to putter in his beloved herb beds.

Johnny, too, was growing taller, a fact noted by all the family at Hopemont when Calvin and Henrietta brought the boys to Lexington for Christmas. They had ignored their own birthdays—both in December—as they had ignored all but the necessary rituals since Catherine's and Johnny's deaths. Calvin hoped that this week in town, surrounded by her brothers and sisters and friends, would be a new beginning for Henrietta. He wanted to see her face flush and sparkle again. He remembered the day of the barbecue, when he watched her under the trees.

They were hardly out of the carriage before Johnny and Cal ran upstairs to find T.H., Robert and Key. Instead, they found a young artist setting up his paints before the big window in the children's parlor, and their grandmother, in a high-backed chair brought up from the dining room, posing.

"I'll look ridiculous in these butter-churn sleeves," Catherine Hunt moaned, picking at the bottle-green silk with its black velvet trim. "Does he really want me to pose in this?"

"Yes, Mama." Anne giggled. She was leaning against the stair rail and waved to the boys. "And they're not butter-churn. They're leg-of-mutton."

"That's worse! Maybe . . . maybe I could wear my lace collar. It's Mechlin lace," she defended to Henrietta, who had just come up.

"It will soften your face," Henrietta smiled.

"And my morning cap?" Her mother looked uncertainly toward the young artist, who had been arranging his easel with an eye to the light.

"Certainly, madame. Let us try it," he said, to be congenial.

He had traveled West after study in Europe and was amused, as well as surprised, by the refinement he had found in Lexington. He had expected leather leggings and oxcarts and found instead the latest Indian cashmeres and spindly carriages pulled by some of the best English bloodlines. He watched Henrietta Morgan move off in her figured chintz morning dress, with its tight, pointed bodice showing off her waist. If only she had wanted her portrait done! Or the young girl against the railing, her legs crossed in pantalettes, her tiny feet in black satin slippers. But when Henrietta returned and settled the ruffled muslin around her mother's head, it drew his attention to those fine eyes and did not, as he had feared, look too fussy. Years later, when Johnny Morgan watched his grandmother's eyes in the portrait, she came alive for him. The artist was right: No frill could subtract from that face.

"Why don't you find the boys?" she said now to Johnny, moving her eyes but keeping her head straight. "I think they're in The Bedroom wrapping presents."

Johnny opened the door behind her. It led to the large room that had housed, at one time or another, all the Hunt sons: Abraham, Charlton, Johnny, T.H., Key, Robert. Only Key and Robert used it now, since T.H., nineteen, had his own room across the back-stairs landing. The big room was reached from the back stairs by a short "children's door" which, since Key was now seventeen and taller than T.H., and Robert was fourteen and almost as tall as Key, had become a joke. "Why don't we brick it up?" John Hunt had asked his wife a dozen times. He missed the look she gave Big Peggy: It made a convenient checking place on young boys. But also, John Hunt suspected, it gave them an escape route as well.

The two beds were empty, the little door ajar. Cal pushed through and Johnny followed. They found their uncles on the side porch overlooking Second Street. It was a warm December afternoon—the snowless, almost balmy Christmas that Kentucky sometimes enjoyed. T.H. lay back in the swing with the sun on his face. Key was giving Robert lessons in blowing cigar smoke. Robert took too much and choked. When T.H. saw Johnny and Cal he rolled up and made room on the swing. Cal, fascinated by the operation, bet Robert he couldn't blow sixteen rings in a row. "He can't count to sixteen," Key called out and ducked the pillow Robert threw at him.

T.H. put his arm, in a deerskin jacket, across Johnny's shoulders.

"Where'd you get that?" Johnny examined the long fringe.

"Aunt Theo sent it to me from St. Louis."

"Yeah . . . he opened it before Christmas!" Robert called over, recovered from his latest bout with choking.

Downstairs the sounds of servants running from the cellar kitchen to the warming room and back down again made the quiet here even cozier. Johnny looked past the Bruce garden across the street at the rooftops in the slanting sunight. T.H. squeezed his shoulder and said, "What's wrong with opening presents ahead of time?" Johnny looked up at him. He was surprised to see —why hadn't he noticed before?—the fine eyes and delicate nose of his grandmother. Key and Robert had the round head and dark hair of their father. It was T.H., cheerful, always pleasant, the optimist of the family— the kind one, Aunt Betty said—who had the charm of the family, even more than his older brother, blond, good-looking Charlton.

Cal jumped down at a sound on the back stairs.

"It's Dick and John!" he yelled.

And sure enough, down on Second Street Johnny saw Aunt Eleanor and Uncle Dick Curd waving up—Aunt Eleanor a plump little woman with thick brown hair, Uncle Dick almost as short, with sandy sidewhiskers and pink cheeks and straight hair that never seemed to stay out of his eyes. Their two sons had run ahead of them and there was a great bunching on the back stairs as everybody swarmed into the warming room. Big Peggy let the boys taste her blackberry pie and nut roll, but drew the line at the great pudding, stuffed with pecans, that even now Nicely was carrying into the dining room.

Johnny was dazzled. He had never seen Hopemont look like this. Boughs of cedar, the smell of cinnamon and spices and the warm fires that sent their scents of pine and oak to mingle with the holly branches hanging from each chandelier. It was as if, after so much death, his grandmother was determined to make this the best Christmas ever.

His mother must have felt the same, because when she came down to dinner Johnny at first didn't recognize her. She was dressed in her ball gown, a low-shouldered, pale pink satin. As they took their places at the big mahogany table he saw the artist watching the chiffon roses on her shoulders and the white gauze "fall" that was nipped in at the waist by a wide satin belt. Under the gauze, with every move, the light caught the full roundness of her satin breasts. Anne had discarded her pantalettes and appeared in a frock of *gros de zane*, all blue shot with white, her square neckline not quite hiding the fact that she was becoming another beauty in the family. Catherine Hunt had escaped the leg-of-mutton sleeves and returned to a simpler dress, although of the finest cambric Edward Bennett had ever seen.

The talk was light. New York had a newspaper called *The Sun*, and the price was a penny a copy. They had heard that the dome planned for the Exchange Hotel in New Orleans would rival St. Peter's in Rome. *Tartuffe* was to be performed at Madame Mentelle's boarding school. President Jackson had ridden on a train.

"I wonder if he could tell the difference between that and his mule!" joked Charlton.

The mention of Jackson brought on talk about "pet" banks and speculators, public land and Mr. Clay's tariff, which Charlton Hunt called his "sacred cow."

"I should think . . ." Edward Bennett offered hesitantly and cleared his throat. Johnny, across the table, saw him go red. Anne watched him in fascination, Henrietta expectantly. Under their eyes the artist felt the shame of youth, the chasm of a *faux pas* opening in front of him.

". . . you would be more concerned with the abolitionist talk we hear in Boston. Even my father," he added, and cleared his throat again, "joined the Anti-Slavery Society last year."

"Oh, come now," mused Charlton Hunt, and drew his shoulders up. "No offense . . . but what can artists know of politics?"

"Yes . . . that's true," Catherine Hunt picked it up and started recounting her trip to St. Louis on a steamboat. Somewhere in the story artists and politics got lost, but there was a baby named Elizabeth, called Bibbi. "Now don't you think that's a darling name? I didn't have a nickname as a child. I do think Charlton is a little jealous since his little boy didn't walk until he was almost eighteen months. Isn't that right, Charlton? He kept asking when I returned, 'Is Bibbi walking yet?' and of course when I said yes, he didn't believe it. Now can you fathom that?"

John Hunt may be a millionaire, Edward Bennett smiled to himself, but his wife is just another aging lady with the beginning of a turkey neck quivering over grandchildren. He had watched them in Massachusetts and England and Italy talking of their families. Did they realize that half of what they said went unheard? No matter—they went on quivering and wobbling just the same.

He knew he would never paint too realistically or too unkindly the fatigue he saw in Catherine Hunt's face. Damn those collapsing tissues that robbed even the finest features of their life and form! He watched her mistaking now the concern on his face for judgment. She fell back, sat, and allowed the servant to clear her place and set before her the next course. Pheasant when in season—ham in winter, legs of lamb in spring, good bourbon and brandy all the time. Tall ceilings, warm fires. Low feminine voices and slow gestures indicating a secure power he had not observed in New England. Stamina those Boston matrons had—but of a brittle quality, more anxious than serene.

"Don't you think so, sir?"

"Eh—what?"

"I was just saying that it was Alceste and not Tartuffe who was the main character. After all, it was his need to believe that caused all the trouble."

"Ah, well, Calvin," Catherine Hunt half-whispered with a fluttering hand to calm her son-in-law, "we are all guilty of needing to believe."

John Hunt looked down the long table and said, "Gentlemen . . . I suggest a game of cards."

Edward Bennett followed his host to the parlor, tugged at his waistcoat and leaned toward Calvin Morgan. "Who is your favorite painter?" he asked suddenly, as he watched the others arranging themselves.

"Claude Lorraine."

"Precisely! I could have guessed."

Calvin smiled. "Ah, you think I'm only interested in those mystical sunsets. A deluded classicist seeking the never-never land of Arcady."

"I'm not laughing *at* you, my friend. I, too, like those golden paths and antique glades. In fact, there's a painter not very well thought of in England right now. I saw some of his watercolors and they are magnificent. And his favorite painter, I'm told, is Lorraine."

"What is his name?"

"Turner."

"Perhaps I shall see them one day," said Calvin dreamily.

Charlton Hunt was dealing.

Henrietta enjoyed her visit, and the boys were satisfied with their presents. Cal got a new pepperbox and Johnny his first really good squirrel rifle. His grandfather, when he heard he was reading Homer, gave him Mr. Pope's translation of *The Iliad*. On the way home, with a sleeping Cal on one side and Henrietta preoccupied with the scenery, Johnny asked his father again about the Trojan horse.

"That's still bothering you? You've asked me about that before! What did Mr. Parsons say?"

"That they believed it was for the gods."

"That's true."

He thought of Catherine Hunt's answer at dinner. How could he explain to an eight-year-old boy that believing in something might be the deadliest sin of all?

6

Sardanapalus became the joke of the neighborhood. Calvin Morgan's slave Randolph could be seen driving him down Tates Creek Pike on the breaking cart, a little sulky Uncle Simon built for the purpose years ago when he'd first started training the Hunt horses. As spring moved toward summer the training cart was replaced by a farm wagon, and Randolph became an expert at ignoring good-natured jeers on the streets of Lexington. "There goes Calvin Morgan's racehorse!"

Those long days on the wagon paid off. The horse's stifles, cannon bones and gaskins had developed into the working parts of a beautiful, relentless machine. When they clocked him on the mile track behind the pond Sard would roll his eye and twitch one ear, and to Randolph's "Go!" he would literally leave the ground, and Johnny saw only a whirling, digging-in whiz of legs, reach of neck. Ears up, almost smiling, back legs doubled under him, Sard came in at 1:35. Calvin tucked his watch into his pocket and called out: "That's it! That's enough for this week."

Rarely did he race a horse under four years old. If he had a strong stallion, like Sard, he would sometimes break that rule and run him at three. He knew his neighbors thought he was crazy, but putting a two-year-old to the grueling tendon-stretching, hoof-pounding demands of the track was not Calvin Morgan's idea of horsemanship. Sard was an exception, and he agreed to race him at Shadeland for the July Fourth barbecue.

"But don't tell his time," he warned. "Not even to Tommy Cunningham."

The last week in June they moved him to two miles, then three. By July he was ready for a four-mile heat.

"But kin he stan' *three* fo'-miles—mebbe *fo'*?" Uncle Simon worried. "Thass sixteen miles!"

In spite of everything they could do, the news crept out: Calvin Morgan's stallion did a four-mile in 7:54, another in 7:40 flat.

Uncle Simon needn't have worried. Sard won every race he ran that fall, even the four-milers. He hardly needed the thirty minutes' rest between heats. By November it was hard to find competition. In his first race the following April, at Dr. Warfield's racecourse in Lexington, he was so far ahead by the time he crossed the mark that Randolph could afford to pull him up.

"He walked over! He walked over! Just like his granddaddy!" Calvin Morgan was on his feet shouting like a little boy. "He walked over!"

Calvin raced Sard again that next week, a two-miler, which he won easily. Then he decided to rest him for two weeks. "I wish you could have seen him!" Johnny exulted to his mother, who was staying home that spring with what Aunt Betty called a "condition." Sard ran two more races before the season ended because of hot weather. When the next meets started again in early October, Calvin Morgan's cart horse was unbeaten and spoken of as the coming stallion of Kentucky.

Retting time found the spirits of Shadeland never higher. Sardanapalus and Calvin Morgan were congratulated in one whole column of *The Spirit of the Times*. Hog-killing had gone well: The meathouse was hanging with hams. Now a good hemp harvest was ready to be brought to the drying barn. Henrietta made a rare appearance when they burned the shives, and the whole farm gathered to watch the long flames light up the night sky.

Time, like the flames, raced by. Johnny's grandmother died, just as the October leaves were at their brightest. He watched the unmoving form on the bier in the Hopemont parlor, still dignified, with the faintest of smiles on her pale face, then rode with Cal on the dickey seat as his grandfather's curricle wheeled through the streets to an open, waiting grave. A month later Henrietta Morgan's first daughter was born. She named her Catherine. Neither Johnny nor Cal had ever seen anything so small, and when Aunt Betty at last let them into the bedroom to have a peek, it seemed the end of a long ordeal.

"She looks like a kitten!" said Cal.

"Hush, chile! She's a doll, *thass* whut she is!"

Ever after, her brothers called her Kitty, but the servants, following Aunt Betty's lead, named her Dolly. Celina sighed, washing diapers and drying them by the downstairs fireplace, that it didn't matter what they called her, so long as things would return to normal.

But they didn't. Uncle Isaac, ill since September, grew worse. He managed to get up for the banjo-playing on Christmas Eve, but they all knew it would be his last time. His bald head bent in prayer, he slumped over the edge of his bed during the first really bad snowstorm in early January. They buried him up in the old pioneer cemetery behind the woods just before the ground froze, and walked back to the house through the slushy snow of a temporary thaw, their eyes on a fresh bank of snow clouds building up to the northeast. Calvin started to say something about the weather, then stopped in midsentence. The slaves had sung spirituals down at the cabins all night. Their doomsday moaning was still in his ears.

In April Johnny's grandfather talked of Texas, of something called the Alamo, and of persuading his uncle Abraham, home from Alabama, from taking the next packet south. His uncle Abraham did go downriver that summer—but to New Orleans, into business. "Maybe that will take the wanderlust out of him," John Hunt breathed, then said to himself, but loud enough for his grandsons to hear, "Why can't they learn it's *making money* that's important?"

Will Webb was in heaven. William Henry Harrison was running for President. When the news reached Lexington that "the Gen'ral" had been defeated by Van Buren, Will stayed drunk for a week. "Ain't no help for it," said Amanda philosophically, her eyes on her brothers. "Menfolks is jest stupid. Plain stupid. How *we* put up with 'em Ah'll nevah know!" But she gave Johnny and Cal an extra helping of spoon bread and watched them wolf it down with satisfaction.

They rode out to Will's often that summer. Henrietta was busy with the baby, but they soon found out another reason for her frequent absences from the breakfast table: She was in that "condition" again. One week in mid-October when they put away the hemp for drying, another boy was born. The night they burned the shives and Henrietta appeared carrying him in a little bundle to watch the fires, all hands cheered. She called him Richard, after her sister Eleanor's husband, Dick Curd, her favorite brother-in-law.

"The Lion-Hearted," Calvin joked, then coughed. With the dampness of winter he was always worse. There was talk of sending him to Hot Springs when the roads were good enough. Or to Philadelphia, to see a famous doctor. Instead, he went to Europe, and was gone a year. Before he left, Charlton Hunt, the eldest and brightest hope of the family, died of scarlet fever, and after Calvin Morgan came back Henrietta had two more children: Charlton, born in '39, and Henrietta, born in '40.

Like Catherine-Kitty-Dolly, they didn't call the baby Henrietta long. For some reason her name changed to Tommie, and stuck.

While their father was away and their mother was busy with Kitty and the babies, Johnny and Cal rode into Lexington and spent long weeks at Hopemont. Johnny, especially, became great friends with his grandfather, riding out to the Leestown farm, watching John Hunt's latest gadgets, a horsedrawn threshing machine and a contraption (which didn't work) for planting tobacco. From his young uncles he learned all the tricks of the drawing room, how to use pomade, how to please the ladies without conde-scension and the gentlemen without deference. He loved scented soap and cool, smooth sheets and the smell of fresh linen. And because he knew who he was, his body partook of the elegance and warmth of Hopemont and turned it into a grace that was his own.

He would sit with Cal listening to Mr. Clay talk of Texas and tariffs and the slavery question. "An abstraction," his grandfather would say. "Debated by Puritan ladies and Massachusetts schoolteachers over some noxious non-alcoholic beverage—probably tea they forgot to throw overboard in Boston. Have you seen my new threshing machine?"

As grief over his wife and his son Charlton lessened, Hunt's love of the land and of horses returned. He read books on calcareous manures and sent Will Webb back East for a trotting stallion. "With better roads, that's where the money will be: good carriage horses." The old trader's eyes gleamed. "They call our Kentucky trotters 'dandy horses' back East. With no more stifles or gaskins than a sheep. Now, we can't put up with that, can we, Johnny?"

His aunt Anne married the year his father returned from Europe, and Hopemont became a man's domain, without a mistress, without babies, and away from Aunt Bet and Aunt Hannah, Johnny Morgan learned to sleep long summer mornings in the big bedroom with his uncles, who taught him to smoke cigars without coughing and swear with conviction.

He couldn't make up his mind which one he liked best: Robert, the medical student; Key, the lawyer; or T.H., who had gone into the family bagging business. He supposed, if he had to choose, it would be T.H. Or would it be Robert, who could play cards best and laughed a lot, or Key, bookish and dependable?

"If he's going to stay in there so much he might as well go to Transy," his mother said peevishly one night at Shadeland. "Johnny's fifteen, Calvin. My brothers were all going to the university at that age." She knew instinctively that her husband wanted to keep his sons around him as long as he could. She guessed that was why, using first his absence and then his health as an excuse, he was introducing Cal to the responsibility of running the farm. Half the time they would be down at the office, poring over ledgers, making plans.

When he didn't answer she went on, pretending to be interested in her needlepoint. "Of course, he isn't prepared. How could he be, out here in the country, with nobody but Theophile Parsons for a tutor? What did Mr. Bennett say when you saw him in Boston?"

"He said there was a possibility that a friend of his from Scotland might be interested."

"Oh, good! Did you tell him how much we have enjoyed his portrait of Mama?"

"I did."

When the new tutor arrived she introduced him to the family and waited, her nose twitching, daring them to react.

John McGregor Ellis McGregor arrived in kilts with three crates of fighting cocks and a parrot. "Shadeland ain't nevah seen nuthin' like *him*" was Uncle Ben's offering down at the quarters. Even more eloquent and succinct was Aunt Hannah's "Hrummph!"

Fighting cocks, Calvin reminded her, had been part of the Bluegrass since pioneer days. "I've gone to cockfights since I learned to ride horses and drink whiskey and hunt coons in Alabama."

"Hrummph! Massa Calvin, youze a *gent*'man. Thass de diffunce."

McGregor took off his kilts and settled into the routine at Shadeland, ensconcing his parrot on a perch in the little room above the summer kitchen, where Aunt Hannah endured squawking renditions of Burns.

"Cain't he shet thet bird *up?*" she hissed to Aunt Betty as she rolled biscuits. "A body cain't think! Bad enuf he has dem chickuns . . ."

He seemed oblivious to her disdain. His cocks in training must have cooked cornmeal, chopped hard-boiled eggs and raw beef. "Hrummph!" Aunt Hannah muttered after him when he gave her the instructions. "They's only *roostahs!*" As if to answer her a high squawk pierced the floorboards: *"My Heart's in the Highlands. AWKKK My Heart's in the Highlands. . . ."*

He showed Randolph how to trim wings at the slope, hackle, and rump, and how to cut the comb close to reduce the target. He asked Uncle Simon to fashion leather pads for the spurs of his trainees. He persuaded Calvin to let Randolph and George build a pit eighteen feet in diameter, with wooden walls sixteen inches high, on the other side of the spring house. Every afternoon after lessons he went there with Johnny and Cal to admire his brood.

"Aye, I prefhurr thuh Staffordshire dun. His neck's nae sa lang as his Irish brither, but frae his insides the tale will be tauld weel enuff. An' luck a' his wing!"

"How do you get them to fight?" Cal asked.

"You put 'em breast-tuh-breast."

"How do you know who wins?"

"Don't be silly," said Johnny. "The one who lives."

"Nae . . . it's nae allus a fight ta th' death," McGregor explained. "When one wants ta quit, he lifts his hackle an' shows his white fither."

"A truce flag!"

"Exactly."

"Wait till I tell Will! Is that where truce flags started?"

"I dunno. May bee."

Henrietta's early tolerance turned to dislike as summer moved into autumn. "He's arrogant and barbaric and I've heard him mouth those abolitionists' slogans," she complained to Calvin. "Slavery's a sin and we are black sinners—as if the Yankee traders had nothing to do with it! I don't trust him with the boys' education. They'll speak French with a Scot's burr."

"He's a good scholar. I fail to see—"

"A man his age in a skirt!"

"Come now, he only wears the kilt on ceremonial occasions."

"Exactly when he shouldn't, I should say."

McGregor's powerful physique, his dark, tight-curled head and massive shoulders, his hearty laugh—a man who could quote Burns and admire Byron, who could outdrink Calvin's own brother Alexander and justify it with lines from Xenophon—"When God gives thuh plants water in floods ta drink, they canna stan' up straight . . ."—why, he might have been a Border Chieftain. Besides, the boys loved him. He organized them into a secret society he called the Knights of the Silver Sword, pledged to truth, valor, and vengeance on all falsehood. How could he, Calvin Morgan, in all honesty, quarrel with that?

"A man," he said, "after a Kentuckian's heart."

At that, Henrietta gave him a sharp look. "You, my dear, are from Alabama. No Kentuckian would tolerate wasting good bourbon whiskey."

"He bathes them in it to toughen their skin."

"Hrummph!"

"They *are* getting a better education," said Calvin, turning serious. "Let's talk no more about it." The cockfight was tomorrow.

At precisely two o'clock George Cunningham and Robert Baynham, one of the bachelor planters, drove up, each with four cocks. Cunningham and Baynham used iron spurs, but McGregor's were silver, which he kept to a knife-edge point, claiming that iron was too brittle to be sharp. Calvin sat between his boys and Randolph, with his brother Alexander, Uncle Ben and Uncle Simon behind them. As usual, Alexander Morgan had wagered heavily on McGregor.

Cunningham's cocks fell out early, one bleeding so badly from the chest that Uncle Ben doubted whether he could be saved. He brought it back to the cage. Baynham's showed greater courage, especially one old Lancashire Black and Red who could lift his head over his opponent for a swift downward jab that was so fast you could hardly see it. His tail feathers were magnificent, long plumes of black iridescent silk, and there wasn't a spot on his wing slope or comb for his opponent to hold on to. McGregor's dun wore his neck feathers like a horse's mane, flat and fringed over his shoulders. His chest was enormous. When it was down to these two, a hush fell around the pit.

They sized each other up, having met before. It was as if they were remembering, and recalculating. Then the Black and Red flew, and the dun ran. In a flash, McGregor was in the ring slinging the dun above his head in tight, jerky circles. His face wore the ugliest expression Johnny had ever seen, and the shock was registered on his own. Richard, who was three and there against Aunt Betty's orders, started crying. Cal's face turned red, but Johnny sat there staring, his eyes round and unblinking. "He was a coward, Cal," he said under his breath.

His father saw his oldest son's lip quiver. "Well, we have a winner, gentlemen," he said lightly. "It looks as if you have lost your wager, Alex."

But it was McGregor's relationship with Randolph which finally caused his dismissal. Johnny and Cal would always remember that it was the day of William Henry Harrison's ball.

When General Harrison was again the Whig nominee for President and "Tippecanoe and Tyler too" won the election, Commodore, John Hunt's new trotting stallion, pulled the brougham that carried the new President from the Phoenix Hotel to the ball at the Odd Fellows Hall.

The old soldier had arrived in Lexington in a wave of bunting and cheers. John Hunt found himself one of the sponsors of a ball in his honor. His daughter Mary and her husband from Frankfort, and Anne, now married and living in Louisville, with Calvin and Henrietta and their two older boys, were due at Hopemont that afternoon.

Earlier in the day a storm had gathered to the west, and a light rain settled the dust of the road by the tollhouse. As the Morgan carriage pulled up, Jake Bolton came out to take their money. His father, weakened at last by long bouts with whiskey, spent most of his days indoors. Jake, who handled the road repairs alone now, had developed into a broad-shouldered, raw-boned man of twenty-one who seldom smiled. When he did it was with a queerly twisted mouth, as if one corner were being pulled up by a nail. "He gots the look of a hungry dog," Uncle Simon declared. "Ah don't like him."

The girls did, though. Stories reached Shadeland of the young man's conquests of the town girls, which Johnny listened to with awe. Even Amanda wasn't immune. Amanda! When they stopped at Will's to give him a ride into town and he started to climb onto the box next to Uncle Simon, Henrietta invited him to sit with them. He settled himself on the seat between Amanda and the boys. Johnny had never seen Will dressed up. He had plastered his wiry hair close to his head and wore a bottle-green broadcloth coat with a pair of dove-gray trousers. He was so excited he couldn't stop talking. Calvin, across from him, was amused. They were all in a holiday mood. "Were you at Tippecanoe, Will?"

"Tippecanoe warn't muchava battle."

Amanda was wearing one of the new straw bonnets that hugged her face ("It looks like a coal scuttle" was Will's comment), and she had to turn her head squarely to Johnny to see him. From the front, he thought, she was nothing much to look at, but when she tilted her head and the slope of her cheek caught the light beneath the curling fringe of her lashes, there was a hard smoothness about her that reminded him of the first apples in spring. Her thick red hair, escaping the bonnet, fell across the wide coat collar covering her shoulders, and when she looked at him with her green eyes, he felt a tightness in his chest that made his mouth go dry. She didn't tinkle when she talked, like the girls at Hopemont. Although she spoke softly enough, she had Will's twang, which his father found amusing.

"Them Kentucky boys warn't *always* so brave, were they, Paw?" she teased.

"Gen'ral Harrison allus said he'd take a Kentucky boy to ten of them fancy-trained soljurs, 'spite of thuh fact that them Kentucky boys was hard-headed."

Red, white and blue bunting had been strung out all along Main Street. Cheapside and the courthouse were encased in garlands. By the time they turned the corner of North Mill and Second and pulled into the carriage yard at Hopemont, Will was struck dumb with anticipation. He jumped down, snapped open the carriage steps with a clang and helped Amanda, then Henrietta, Calvin and the boys to the ground as if he were the postilion for a king.

"I've never seen him so solemn," whispered Calvin to Henrietta as they watched him walk down Second Street with Amanda on his arm.

"It's a big day for him," said Henrietta, as they went through the front door.

"For all of us," her father chuckled as he met them in the parlor with brandies. He was a Whig down to his toes, but he had wanted Henry Clay to win the nomination.

Calvin lifted his glass to his father-in-law, to smooth the rough edges he heard in his voice. "At least he beat Birney!"

"Anybody could have beaten Birney," said Henrietta curtly, pulling off her gloves. "Imagine the nerve of the abolitionists, to set up a candidate of their own!"

The next morning Johnny remembered little of the ball except girls with party dresses cut low, their shoulders framed in lace, their hair à la Grecque, bouncing when they turned their heads. And his own awkward refusals to dance.

Except once, when the refusal was refused.

McGregor arrived, resplendent in his kilt. He had walked squarely into the middle of the Breckinridges and was laughing heartily. "Ain't he a dandy?" Will wondered. "Bet he gits chilly these cool nights."

"He doesn't wear them all the time," said Johnny.

"Wal, that's a blessing!" Amanda laughed, showing her little teeth. "Why ain't you dancing, Johnny Morgan?"

"He don't go to Madame Mentelle's an' learn them Frenchy ways," Will joked, glad to have attention drawn from his own timidity. With all his talk of his "Gen'ral," he had not mustered the nerve to talk with him. "Take Johnny off'n a hoss, he has no laigs."

"Is that true, Johnny Morgan?" Amanda's green eyes laughed. "Bet you a dollah!"

He found his arm around her waist. The fullness of the skirt fell away beneath his fingers, and he felt rather than saw the close-fitting bodice that went all the way to her throat before it broke into a tiny lace collar. It revealed more than all the low-cut gowns drifting around them. They moved into a sea of muslins and silks, satin slippers and polished boots. He swung her past his uncle Alex Gibson, who had arrived with McGregor, and received an approving lifted eyebrow—the "Morgan look," Wash had called it. He saw his father's canary-yellow waistcoat flashing among the pinks and mauves and blues of the ladies, his boyish face flushed with laughter and one drink too many.

Opposite him, floating with the rhythm, Amanda's hair was a red cloud, her green eyes gazing past him at the other dancers. He squeezed her hand to make her look at him. When she did she sent him a giggle that disturbed him too much. Did she know how much she disturbed him?

It was late—almost daybreak—before he stumbled behind Cal up the stairs at Hopemont and tumbled into bed. He heard nothing until Robert nudged him for breakfast. Downstairs at the dining table Anne was still talking about the ball, and John Hunt was remonstrating over Mr. Clay, who had stayed home at Ashland after turning down the new President's offer of Secretary of State. "It'll go to Webster," John Hunt concluded. "Henry shouldn't be so puffy."

"Can you blame him? He's lost the presidency twice," Calvin reminded him.

"He could have come to the ball."

"He had a cold."

Before they could begin politics again Henrietta hustled them all into the hall. "If we leave now we'll reach Shadeland before this weather turns colder. I'm worried about the children."

Just past the tollgate Uncle Ben met them on one of the field mules. Breathlessly, the old man spurted: "De bawn! De bawn burned! All de hosses gone, 'cep two yearlin's in de shed. Sard . . . he cut up. . . . Las' night, Massa! Uncle Simon, he out dere now. De mare, she run back in. Nuthin' we could do, Massa. Jes' run back in. Sard, he run into a plow blade. Cut his ches'."

"Is the barn gone?"

"All gone, Massa. Tack, too. Don' know whut happen. We done cleaned out de manure, an' 'sides, dis time of year hit don' get hot . . ."

"Quit blaming yourself, Uncle Ben. And the house?"

"De roof wuz wet from de rain an' de spawks din't ketch."

"Ride on back. We'll be there in a while. Anybody hurt?"

"Randolph . . . he burn his arm jes' a little, tryin' to git dat mare out. We tried to bring her out. She ran back in dem flames. An' Cyrus . . . Shammy . . . Massa Cal's lil' filly . . . oh Lawd!" Uncle Ben started weeping, and the mule swiveled his long ears at the unusual sound. Uncle Ben's tears streamed down his stubby, unshaven face.

"We'll be back as quickly as we can. You go on home now."

Cyrus. Shamrock. Alice, her dapple-gray sides so smooth and gleaming. And Cal's filly. It couldn't be! But the black shell of the horse barn still smoldered and sent up an acrid plume of smoke to meet them, even before they were in sight of the house.

Randolph had moved Sard into the drying barn, and made a temporary stall at one end. A piece of meat as large as a roast hung from the horse's chest. The hole was terrifying. To everyone's surprise, Johnny took charge. He sent young field hands scurrying to Aunt Hannah for hot water and old sheets, which Randolph and Uncle Simon tore into bandages. They took turns, two-hour shifts, staying up all night, making sure the stallion didn't move. Calvin came down from the house about midnight.

"He mustn't lie down," he warned them. "On no account must he lie down. Keep him standing if you have to get under him and push."

Sardanapalus, weak from loss of blood, weaved on his feet. After their father left the barn, Cal started crying. Johnny was about to reprimand him when Uncle Ben's voice came from the corner of the stall. The old blue-black eyes were not on Johnny but on Cal, whose bent head shook with weeping, and whose "He'll . . ." broke off in fresh sobs.

"If'n as long as you don' *say* it, Massa Cal, mebbe it won' be so."

Cal nodded, still not able to look up until after he blew his nose. When he did he smiled at Uncle Ben and agreed to bed down beside Randolph across the aisle, where he lay curled up in the straw listening to the heavy breathing of the horse and Uncle Simon's soothing admonitions.

An hour later Johnny, when his turn came, couldn't sleep. The drying barn was a sieve for the chill damp air that made his hands and feet heavy with cold. He walked over to Sard and combed his mane with his fingers. Randolph got up too, shaking hay from his shoulders.

"What do you think?" he whispered, without looking up.

"He'll make it, Massa. We'll make him make it!"

Later the sky cleared and that pure, cold silence that penetrates the air before first light made Johnny instantly alert. The sound of rainwater dripping from the eaves woke Uncle Ben, who sat in the corner hugging his knees.

"Dat's de daid hosses eatin' dey grain," he hissed.

"Shh! You'll wake Uncle Simon."

"I'se awake, Massa." Uncle Simon groaned, stood up, and brushed himself. "You res' now, Massa Johnny. My turn nex'. Git some sleep."

"Can't. Uncle Simon, did you see *anybody* around the place?"

"Nobody aroun' las' night but Zep, Massa. Will's little boy. He don' do no hawm. Now why don' you go up to de house, Massa Johnny, an' git some sleep. . . ."

By the end of the fourth day, in spite of clean bandages, the stench of gangrene was so strong that Henrietta refused to let them go to the barn. "We've got to do it," she told Calvin. "We've got to do it. In the morning. Order a grave dug. Up by Xenophon."

Johnny followed Randolph and Uncle Simon, who led Sard up the hill. The bandage had come off during the night and a yellowish brown-red mass oozed across his chest. Halfway up he bucked. Randolph looked at Johnny and whispered, as if Henrietta were there: "Let's turn him out in the small pasture behind the stable. It cain't hurt nuthin', Massa. If'n he got thet much buck in him, he not ready to die."

To their surprise, Uncle Simon agreed. They watched the horse amble slowly across the small paddock to the watering trough, pulsing his ears back with each gulp. The November sun was warm on Uncle Simon's face as he looked at the sky.

"Let's hope it works," said Johnny.

"It will," answered Uncle Simon. "Let de sun git at dat soah. Jes' let it soak it up."

He followed Johnny to the house and they stopped in the summer kitchen to beg a glass of milk from Aunt Hannah, who was weaning Charlton. "Pushed out of de nes' by dat li'l old gal Tommie," was Aunt Hannah's daily comment, and her excuse for spoiling him. They hadn't taken the second swallow before they heard Calvin Morgan call sharply from the parlor.

7

"**D**on't go," he said to Uncle Simon, who was behind Johnny in the doorway. "We want you to hear this."

There was, in the deliberate way his father paused, something that scared Johnny. He waited, but Calvin didn't say anything. Instead, he turned to Jake Bolton, who was standing against the light of the window. "I want you to repeat what you just told me."

Jake shifted his feet and avoided their eyes. Then he boldly raised them to Calvin and said defiantly: "Yo' niggah Randolph set thet barn fire."

"Did you see him do it?" Henrietta stepped forward but her husband caught her arm.

"Ah did. Ah wuz goin' down the pike, returnin' a low bed wagon we done borrowed from Mista Cunningham. I seen somebody creepin' aroun' with a armful of hay."

"When was this?"

"Late. Almos' midnight."

"How could you see that well? The barn's a good three-hundred yards from the road."

"The moon warn't set yit."

"Why, it was raining that night! Besides . . . what were you doing returning Mister Cunningham's wagon so late?" Henrietta's voice made no attempt to conceal her contempt. Jake Bolton raised impassive eyes and laid a challenging look across her face.

"Paw promised him. Boltons keep their promises."

As quickly as he'd looked at Henrietta, he swung his gaze to Johnny. Johnny didn't believe, any more than his mother did, the truth of the accusation. *Boltons keep their promises.* Well, you said you'd wait awhile.

Calvin, who had taken a chair by the fire, got up slowly. He hooked a thumb in his waistcoat armhole and rested his weight on one leg. Johnny had seen him do that too often to believe he thought Jake was speaking the truth. "Thank you, Jake. We'll see that this is taken care of."

Jake didn't move. Instead, he threw his head back and allowed his twisted smile to pinch out the words: "Yeah . . . taken care of. You think you can keep this quiet. Ain't so. Paw alriddy tole the sheriff. Ain't no niggah gonna burn down white folks' property and git away with it."

"He hasn't bothered you, has he?"

Calvin Morgan was, above all things, a gentleman. But now his look pierced the dusty, unwashed youth standing before him, and his mouth turned grim. Jake looked down at his hands, folding and unfolding the greasy cap. Just at that moment, from the little room over the summer kitchen where McGregor slept, came the high squeal of *"My heart's in the Highlands. AWKKKK. My heart's in the Highlands. . . ."*

Calvin's rigid body relaxed and he held out his arm in a hospitable fashion, as if escorting a friend to the door, although he was a good six feet from Jake. "We'll certainly allow Mister Benton to do his duty. Thank you for coming, Jake. Tell your folks hello for us."

Uncle Ben, in the hallway, held the door at an extraordinarily wide angle to let him out. When he had gone Henrietta immediately sent Uncle Simon to the quarters for Randolph. "We'll get to the bottom of this," she echoed Calvin's words of a minute before.

Randolph couldn't be found. The cabin he shared with George, the carpenter, was empty; the field hands hadn't seen him and he was not in the drying barn, where John Henry was cleaning Sard's stall. "I'd tell you, Massa Johnny. I would."

"I know you would." Johnny turned from him and walked past the small paddock where Sard was grazing. Tired from his own all-night vigil, it was the first time since the barn burned that he didn't look at the stallion's chest.

Back at the house Aunt Betty was feeding Kitty and Richard. She had set up a special area in the summer kitchen with a small table and stools. Charlton was in a highchair smearing honey over his chest. Absent-mindedly, Aunt Betty, with a drooling baby Tommie hanging on her lap, leaned over to wipe it and looked at Johnny.

"Nowhere," he answered her silent question.

The sheriff called that afternoon. Mr. Benton was a big bull of a man, his half-arc of a belly caught below his waist by a belt that threatened to slip. Hat in hand, he was more than polite when Calvin received him. He wouldn't come past the entry, but stood by the front door moving his feet. "I've come for that boy of yours, Randolph. Tom Bolton's made a charge against him. He burned your barn."

"Tom Bolton says he burned the barn," Calvin corrected. "We can't find him."

Gladly Benton had lived too long in the Bluegrass to defy one of its Families, yet the Morgans had a reputation for overprotecting their own, and Tom Bolton was, after all, a white man. "Then you'd better make a mighty fine effort to try," Benton said firmly. Calvin's stiffened back made him add, more gently: "I'll be back tomorrow, Mister Morgan. Good day to you, sir."

"Good day." Calvin lifted his hand to Uncle Ben and the old man stood quietly by the half-open door. Calvin took a long time watching Benton mount his horse before he turned inside again.

After Uncle Isaac died, Uncle Simon lived alone. His cabin was the last on the row, nearest the stables. He sat on his bunk now, leaning forward on his arms, his big hands folding and unfolding, the flat tan nails making a ladder in the dusky air. Light from one window, partly covered by a dropped gunnysack, picked at the white hairs in his sideburns. "Well, now," he sighed again and leaned back. "Well, now."

Randolph, across the small room, lay back on crossed arms on Uncle

Isaac's old bunk. When he moved, the cornhusks in the thin mattress creaked. His eyes were open, his chin thrust up. He was looking at the ceiling.

"That's whut he said, Uncle Simon. That's jes' whut he said."

"Youze know," the old man answered unsteadily, still suffering from the shock of it. "Youze know thet's crazy. Why, howze you gonna run away nohow? De slave-catchers'ud git you fo' you'd git two mile outta town."

Randolph rolled over, making a pillow out of a cocked elbow. "Ah know thet, Uncle Simon."

"Then why'd youze even lissen to him, then? Man wif a skirt."

"He wuz only tryin' to help."

"He'p? He'p? Whut kinda he'p is tryin' tuh talk youze inta runnin' away fo'?"

Randolph sat up and shrugged. "That's what Ah'm wonderin', too. Ah jes' cain't figure."

"Tell you whut," Uncle Simon suddenly seemed to grasp something firm in the dim air before him and held onto it with his eyes.

"Whut?"

"Tell Massa Calvin."

"An' stir up de big house? 'Tween white folks?"

Uncle Simon's eyes strayed from the wall opposite and found Randolph's face. "Want to or not, youze got to. John Henry jes' met me outside. De sheriff done been at de house. Dey's a-lookin' fo' you. Dis din' stop wif Jake Bolton comin' heah wif his lies."

In the half-light the smooth cheek and high face bones rotated.

"No use yo' shakin' yo' haid. Kum on. If'n de sheriff is aftah you, we's gotta move. Don' you trus' Massa Calvin?"

The question settled it. They found Calvin in his office, his penknife in hand, halfheartedly trimming a quill.

"Randolph heah got somethin' tuh say," announced Uncle Simon, and disappeared.

Randolph stood uneasily and cleared his throat. Calvin waited. He folded the penknife and slipped it in a pocket on the inside of his coat. "Randolph . . . Randolph . . . come, sit down. You don't for a minute think I believe all these stories, do you? Come, tell me where you were that night so I can tell the sheriff and we can get this over with."

How could he tell his master about Maggie? He had been seeing her on the sly every chance he had, every time some errand needed doing that brought him to Mr. Cunningham's place. Calvin's hand, still in midair, half open, his slender fingers a little apart, seemed to hold a strange fascination for him.

"Ah wuz at Mista Cunnin'ham's," he told the fingers, finally.

"Mister Cunningham's? In the middle of the night?"

"Ah went ovah dere to see . . . to see Maggie, sir. You know Maggie?"

"I do. A very good girl." Calvin waited, his eyes on the slender form in the loose field clothes.

"Jake Bolton drove a wagon into de barnyard, unhitched his mule an' lef' it down behin' de stables. Den he rode off, bareback."

"When was that?"

"Jes' befo' sundown."

"Before?"

"Yassa."

"And?"

"He rode off jes' aftah that. Thass all Ah heard until de nex' mawnin'."

"When the next morning?"

"Early. Jes' aftah sunup," Randolph said sheepishly. "Ah come back befo' feedin' time . . . Gran'daddy bein' gone to town an' all. . . ."

"Didn't you notice anything the night before? Flames against the sky?"

"No, suh," Randolph answered, even more sheepishly.

"All right. Now listen carefully. You will stay in your cabin, do you understand? You will not even go to the drying barn. By the way . . . in all this I forgot. How did it go with Sardanapalus?"

Those frank eyes in that worried face. How could he tell him anything but the truth? "We . . . we put him in de paddock."

"You didn't put him down?"

"Massa. They's somethin' else."

Calvin waited.

"Marse McGregor."

"What about him?"

Uncle Simon's imploring face came before him. *Don' you trus' Massa Calvin?* "He tried to git me to run away."

"Run away?"

"Yassa."

For the first time since Randolph had known him, Calvin Morgan avoided his eyes. "He was joking, of course."

"May bee, Massa."

Calvin looked back at him, at the young, strong shoulders under the homespun. "Of course, he must have been. You didn't tell me why you put Sardanapalus in the paddock."

Randolph let his breath out. "Uncle Simon—he 'greed de sun jes' might do de trick."

"Oh, then it wasn't Uncle Simon's idea?"

"No, sir. It whur John . . . Massa Johnny's. He bucked on de way to his grave."

"Johnny?"

"Nawsuh. Sard."

Then he saw the smile on Calvin's face and laughed, too. It was a good sound, a sweet sound, and the laugh turned into a chuckle and traveled to his chest. He's a good boy, Calvin thought.

But it wouldn't be easy. He had to get to town and get some advice before Benton came back. Mr. Clay had returned to Washington City. There was Richard Curd, Eleanor's husband. A good lawyer. Without hesitation he sent for Uncle Simon. "Get me that mule from the north pasture. I'm going to Lexington."

"But he ain't trained yit, Massa Calvin."

"Then I'll train him."

"We ain't got no saddles. Dey done burn'd."

"If Jake Bolton can ride bareback so can I."

Uncle Simon seldom lost control of his face, but this was one of the times. It registered such terror that Calvin laughed. "Oh, the family honor, is it? All right, I can stop by Will's and borrow a horse and saddle. Will that satisfy you?"

"Yassa!" But he grumbled.

He found Dick Curd in his office just before noon.

"Come home with me, Calvin! Eleanor will be glad to see you. You make yourself too scarce, playing the country squire."

"Thank you, Dick. Appreciate it. Not today." He told the story, ending with the sheriff's impending return. "What can we do?" he worried. "I've thought of freeing him."

"Freeing him? No, no . . . that would be the worst thing now."

"Why?"

"As a slave, as the property of Calvin and Henrietta Hunt Morgan, and under Kentucky law, he will receive more protection as your property than he could ever expect as a freeman. A black freeman with a twelve-man white jury? Come now, Calvin. It doesn't take much imagination to predict what would happen."

"Then what?"

"Let Benton put him in jail."

"Jail an innocent man!"

"That will momentarily satisfy whoever is trying to do you in. And give us time to uncover more evidence. Now tell me again exactly where everybody was that night."

Before he left Richard Curd's office Calvin Morgan made a new will, freeing Randolph at his death. He had been thinking of it for some time. He stopped by Alexander's house on the way home.

"Aren't you working today?"

"Brother Calvin, you are living up to your name! On a fine day like this? I came home early. Wasn't it lucky that I did? Otherwise I might have missed you! Come on in, Calvin. Let's have a drink."

"One."

"One it is. Do I ever insist?"

"Never." Calvin tried a laugh.

"You are solemn."

"Randolph, I'm afraid, is going to jail. And there's damn little I can do to prevent it. But that's not why I'm here. I'm chasing clues. Did McGregor have anything to say at the ball . . . anything that would seem odd?"

"Odd? Does he say anything that's not odd?" When Alexander saw that his brother was serious he added: "He thought he had become for you one of the Border Chieftains. What could he mean by that?"

"Did he, now? How?"

"Oh, you know McGregor. Probably in a playful way. What does this have to do with the fire?"

"Maybe nothing. Maybe everything. Thanks for the whiskey, Alexander."

At the door Alex's wife, America, returning from shopping, met them on the porch. A sweet little woman with pale blond hair drawn back from equally pale eyes, she threw back her cape and offered her brother-in-law a cheek. She returned his kiss with one of her own. "Won't you stay?"

"No . . . no, I must be going." She watched him leave with worried eyes, Alexander's hand on her shoulder.

McGregor was in the little brick schoolhouse, copying out with a meticulous hand the next day's arithmetic lesson. A stack of slates stood on the corner of the desk by his elbow. "Ah, Calvin!" He rose when the tall shadow blocked the doorway. "Come to learn your two-plus-two's, I see."

"I've come to learn," said Calvin, "what you told Randolph."

"Randolph? That delightful young man who quotes Socrates?"

Calvin sat back on the top of the nearest little desk, thinking, This is where Johnny and Cal spend their days. And soon Kitty, and Richard. Suddenly he felt robbed. There was so much of his children's lives that he didn't share. Perhaps McGregor knew them better than he did. The thought did not sweeten his next question.

"Why did you urge him to run away?"

"I? Run away? Who? Whurr did you get such a ridiculous notion?"

"Didn't you know, under the circumstances, that would be the worst thing he could do?"

"I dunna unnerstan'. . . ."

"I think you do. The Boltons have charged him with arson. The sheriff is coming back this afternoon. He may go to jail for it."

"Did he do it?"

"Of course not."

"Then runnin' away doesn't seem ta bee sich a bad idea, does it now?" When he saw Calvin's anger he added quickly: "I neverr told thuh lad ta go. . . . Ye do believe me?"

"Randolph doesn't lie," Calvin managed to get out before he walked down the worn stone steps and out onto the dying grass again. The day had clouded over. There would be rain before nightfall.

"I told you so," Henrietta couldn't help saying as they watched Randolph ride off with Benton two hours later. "Your romantic ideas again! Your Border Chieftain!"

Her words were too close to McGregor's. Yes, Calvin thought, watching the drizzle that was turning into a cold autumn rain. When would he learn? He looked over at Johnny, still standing by the hall door. He had seen that look on his face only once, when McGregor killed the cock.

"He'll never get away with it," Calvin answered aloud his own question.

"It's just like Papa's hemp factory," Henrietta said emphatically, swishing her skirts. She sat by the fire, then got up again, too nervous to settle.

"The hemp factory?" Johnny seemed to wake up.

She watched him walk toward her, then stop.

"Twice it burned. The second time I was seven years old. I can still remember. Early in the morning . . . about five-thirty, people were called to put out a fire in Mister Huston's smokehouse . . . he was our saddler then . . . and the next morning at the same hour Papa's hemp factory burned. The spinning house and the store house, with eighty tons of hemp. The weaving house and the hackling house were saved. But Papa still lost about twenty thousand dollars. Two Negro boys . . . about fourteen . . . were arrested, tried and convicted. They were sentenced to be hanged."

"Hanged!"

She spoke quietly, as if to herself. Remembering seemed to calm her. "They confessed. Half-idiots they were. The whole town knew it! The day before the hanging Governor Scott pardoned them because of their age and 'some representations relative to the testimony, which were made to the governor.' Do you know who made those 'representations'? Papa. He found out a rival hemp trader who wanted him out of business paid the boys to set the fire."

Half-idiots . . . *Nobody aroun' but Zep, Massa. Will's little boy. He don' do no hawm. . . .*

"Where are you going, Johnny?"

"Do you still have Will's saddle, Father?"

"Yes."

"May I return it?"

"In this rain?"

"It will stop."

It didn't. By the time he rode the three miles to Will's both the saddle and Johnny Morgan were soaked. Luckily, Will was nowhere in sight, but Amanda was at a table in the kitchen scrubbing a pair of work pants in a tub. She pushed a strand of hair from her face and wiped one soapy wrist with her hand in her apron, then the other. "Johnny Morgan, you're a sight! Here . . ." She laid her apron back and smoothed it with her palms. "Here, we'll put this saddle in the back room. He's gone with Nathan to Richmond. Maybe it'll dry before he gits back. Do you want anythin' to eat?"

"I'm fine, Amanda. Look—I've got to know something." He stood beside her, surprisingly taller than she was. He looked down on her shining, freckled face. Her eyes were beautiful when they were solemn, two deep pools of green. Now, the little hairs at the edges of her eyebrows, damp with sweat, had brushed themselves into crazy directions. He longed to straighten them with his finger. Instead, in his embarrassment at the warm scent of her, he looked past her at the rain through the half-open door. "The sheriff came for Randolph this afternoon. Boltons say he burned our barn." Before she could say anything he took her arms in his hands and moved her down into a chair and went down on his heels so his face could be even with hers.

"What I want to know is: Do you know anything . . . anything at all, that happened the night the barn burned?"

She opened her eyes wider, her lips firm, and shook her head.

"Anything at all? Try to remember, Amanda."

She dipped her chin to the homespun blouse and made folds in the apron. Then suddenly she frowned and looked up. "Zep. Zep warn't heah for suppah. Ah remembah Paw fussin'."

"When did he come home?"

"Late."

"How late?"

She stamped her foot and got up. "How do Ah know? Do you think Zep set fire to your barn?"

"I think somebody told him to."

"Who?"

"I think you know."

The hesitation in her eyes confirmed his hunch. Even Aunt Betty had repeated the story that Jake Bolton was calling at Will's. *Ah suah do hopes Mista Will's Amanda have mo' sense den dat.*

"The sentence for arson is hanging, Amanda. Randolph could hang."

It was the old Amanda of the horseriding days who looked back at him. She stuck out her chin and her voice came to him softly and clearly, with that little lilt he remembered when she'd been ahead of him over the fences: "He went to the smokehouse. But if he's not there we'll find him."

He was in the loft of the barn, sound asleep. The day had turned colder and Johnny's wet clothes were making him shiver, but he kept his voice steady. "Zep, did you go to our place the night the barn burned?"

The dull, dark eyes looked like muddy water. For a minute Johnny thought he hadn't heard. Then Zep turned his thatch of red hair over in the hay and sat up. With a thick-lipped, slow smile he said, "Yeah. Ah went to yo' place."

"What did you do there?"

"Ah got a silvuh dollah."

"A silver dollar?"

"Who gave it to you?" demanded Amanda.

Zep smiled again. "Ah ain't gonna give it to you."

"I don't want it. Who gave it to you?"

"Jake."

"Why did he give it to you?"

"To start a fire."

Calvin, at first, couldn't believe it, although it justified his faith in Randolph. He stopped just long enough to pull on his coat. "We're going to Lexington now," he said to Henrietta. "Send Uncle Ben for the carriage. Tell him to use the mule. We'll stop by Will's. That animal will be the best trained equine in Fayette County by the time this week is out." He tried a grin, but it didn't work.

Johnny had never changed clothes so fast. The thought of Randolph in the old stone jail—what must it be like, the Negro jail? It was one of those buildings you never looked at, although you knew it was there. Iron bars. Silence. Sidestreet silence. Like the pens where the traders kept their down-river wares. Johnny shivered and his mother threatened to keep him home. "I'm not cold," he said. "Ma, I've got to . . ." He knew when he looked at her like that she could never refuse.

But they didn't go to the jail. They went to the home of old Judge Winter, who had a goatee that wiggled when he yawned, as he did now, behind his hand, when Calvin had a servant disturb him from a nap. He settled back in his chair, tasting the yawn broadly. "Hmm. Yes, yes, I see," he kept saying, first to Calvin, then to Zep, until Johnny thought he hadn't understood at all, or, if he did, had already determined to do nothing about it. To their surprise he jumped up with vigor, slapped a fist into a palm and shouted for his things. He jammed his hat on his head as they followed him down the steps and out into the street. Calvin, much to Johnny's disappointment, made them wait in the carriage while he went with the judge to the barred iron door at the side of the building. The rain had stopped, but it had turned windy again, and it was almost sundown. "We won't get home before dark," Amanda whispered to Johnny. "Paw won't know where we are."

"We'll explain," Johnny assured her, and again, although she was older than he was, he assumed a proprietary air which he found new and exciting. She gave him the same look he remembered from the ball.

His eyes went to the jail. The dark shape of Randolph emerged behind his father, followed by the Judge. They talked a moment on the sidewalk before Randolph climbed up behind Zep and Calvin untied the reins.

8

Randolph married Maggie the day after Christmas. As Henrietta walked back to the house from Uncle Jacob's burgoo tables, loaded for the occasion, she surprised her husband by agreeing that Johnny should move to Hopemont. "After all, all my brothers went to Transylvania," she said. She didn't add the thoughts she kept to herself. She had seen Johnny dancing with Will's girl at the ball, and this morning, while Reverend Pratt fumbled through the wedding ceremony, she had watched Johnny's eyes not only linger on Amanda, but connect with hers. Secretly Henrietta knew Calvin was right when he accused her of wanting to keep her firstborn home as long as possible. Yes, he was right. Even little Tommy Cunningham was going to the university. It was time Johnny associated with the right people. She deliberately forgot that she had denied Cal, who was a year older than Tommy, the same permission just a week ago.

"Don't you want Cal to be a gentleman, too?" Calvin teased.

Henrietta twitched her nose. "Next year," she said, and Calvin Morgan laughed out loud. She was always baffling him, this Roman matron, beautiful wife of his!

At Hopemont Johnny was given one of the seven bedrooms upstairs, a small one just off the backstairs landing. T.H. was married now, and ran the Hunt bagging business with his brother Abraham, who had returned to Kentucky after failing in business in New Orleans. The next room was used by Key, at twenty-five a promising lawyer whose sober bachelorhood had encouraged Henrietta's children to turn his first name, Francis, into "Uncle Frank." Across the hall Robert still slept in the big bedroom. Ever since Robert's return from Princeton, and especially now, since he was a medical student at Transy, the "big room" became the scene for much card-playing and swearing. So, in effect, Hopemont was a dormitory again. When Johnny received a note from his father with the two words, "Do well," he understood for the first time that his role as eldest son had begun.

He studied Latin, Greek mythology, the Septuagint and composition. "Uncle Frank" had talked him into joining the Adelphi Debating Society, and as he walked past the dark bricks of the Gratz house and up to the fat columns of Old Morrison he pondered the pros and cons of sprinkling versus total immersion. He chose sprinkling. Surely God didn't need an ocean to perform miracles? If a mustard seed was large enough for faith, one drop of water should suffice for salvation.

At the corner of Mill and Third he had to stop for three riders trotting toward Broadway. He watched their rhythmic backs rising and falling, felt the roll on his own thighs, the side of a horse on his lower leg. What was he doing worrying about *sprinkling*? He'd laughed at Uncle Isaac's long discussions about just such nonsense. He could still smell the wood fire and feel the warm stone hearth of Shadeland, hear Cal munching Aunt Hannah's biscuits. What was Cal doing this morning? Riding his new filly? Now Uncle Isaac was gone. Was he tasting immortality? Or were his sins still swimming around in one of de pons, trapped forever, never to reach the sea?

Immortality itself was a problem. When he'd asked, his father had answered: The Greeks didn't bother with it particularly, except for the Elysian Fields, and that was for warriors only.

Greek mythology was his favorite subject. Somehow he could never think of Latin conjugations as real—Professor Fishback, who taught both, obviously liked the myths. He had made Zeus and Poseidon and Athena real. With his small, almost emaciated frame and blazing eyes, he finally convinced Johnny Morgan that Achilles was the hero of *The Iliad*.

But the little professor really preferred Hector, and let everybody know it. And for that Johnny liked him. Strangely, this shy, soft-spoken teacher from Pennsylvania explained his father to him. Talking of Troy, Fishback said one day, "The Greeks thought the only difference between men and the gods was that men had to die."

When Johnny waited with a frown pulling at his eyes Fishback added: "But don't you see . . . that makes man better than the gods? The gods can't be tragic . . . or heroic. But man can be, because he has to cope with death."

"How can he cope?"

"By defying it," Fishback said then, looking off. "Defying it daily. Without hope. Absolutely without hope."

He took his time climbing the stairs. Would he be late for chapel again? To start every day with chapel—that was a bit holy. Even his grandfather, already riding out to his farm on the Leestown Pike to check on his horses and pigs, agreed to that. Transylvania had passed from the Episcopalians to the Presbyterians, so what could you expect? his grandfather had said. That's when he had resigned from the Board of Trustees. And now there was talk that it might go to the Methodists. Next year, John Hunt fumed, it might bottom out with the Baptists.

The chapel, to his surprise, was empty. April light through stained glass gave the air a pearly look and enhanced the silence. Johnny turned and found William Blanchard in the hall.

"Haven't you heard the news?"

"No, what?"

"President Harrison died! Pneumonia! No chapel today. Classes canceled! Let's go to my room and have a whiskey!"

"Willie . . . don't joke. Did he really die?"

"Cross my soul. Got his feet wet and caught a cold. Hey, that rhymes!"

"Will there be school tomorrow?"

"Who knows? Hey, that rhymes too!"

Johnny ran down the steps and down Mill Street, around to the side door of the warming room, grabbed a piece of newly baked lightbread from Big Peggy and with his mouth half full called out that he was riding out to Shadeland . . . the President was dead.

Will was on his porch working a piece of leather in his lap and a piece of tobacco under his cheek. His bright smile made Johnny at once feel guilty. Ever since Zep had been blamed for arson Johnny had stayed away, as if the blame had been his fault. Will had given Zep a thrashing. The Boltons had moved to run a ferry on the Kentucky River and a new family tended the tollgate. Now, Will's warm welcome made him remember all those stories about the Big Knife and Mad Anthony Wayne and "the Gen'ral." He sat carefully on the top step and leaned against the post. Inside the cabin he felt, rather than heard, the presence of Amanda. A mocker in the hitching tree went back to its endless repetitions.

"I don't think I evah heerd a critter sweeter than a mockin'bird," said Will. He switched the wad from one cheek to the other and spit wide.

"General Harrison's dead, Will."

In the silence the hands on the leather stopped. Then they started again, as if oiling this leather was the most important thing now. "He useta say 'Remember the Raisin . . .' "

"He was a great soldier, Will."

Will seemed not to hear. "But only remember it! 'Whilst yew don't have a victory,' he said. 'When yew git a victory revenge is no good.' Thet's whut he said! Thuh revenge of a soldier cain't be took out on a fallen foe. An' he nivver did." He looked up. "He nivver took revenge out on a fallen foe. He was a gentleman. Yew remember that, Johnny Morgan."

He left him, a small bent figure in a shaft of sunlight listening to the mockingbird.

He rode on to Shadeland with his news, saw his parents and Cal. Kitty was in her room being punished for sassing Aunt Betty and the babies were napping. Cal and four-year-old Richard walked with him to the stables to see Uncle Simon and Randolph. He rode back to Hopemont just in time for dinner. The talk was of death, of the President at the ball, just last year. Suddenly his arguments on sprinkling seemed silly.

All that talk of salvation really had to do with death. Some kind of insurance. Reservations for a Room Upstairs. What could keep you from it? Strong brewed beverages, Dr. Davidson, the president of the college, said every morning in chapel. Or the Depravity of Women. Amanda, who had come out on the porch with hot coffee and muffins and sat watching Will with worried eyes. How could she be Depravity? Silently, Johnny Morgan added another item to his list of Things I Can't Believe.

As soon as he could he escaped outside. To the right he could see the last of the sun through the trees in the Bruce garden. The birds had quieted, but already and unconsciously he was waiting for the first sounds of whippoor-wills. He walked down Second past his grandfather's carriage house to Broadway, down to Main and up North Mill again. Like fat white fingers pointing skyward, the columns of Old Morrison stood at the top of the street, reminding him of the debate again. His eyes went to Venus, bright against the fading sky. Venus! The Greeks had looked at that same star. The same old questions seemed to plague mankind. It might be 1841, but the President could still die of a chill.

The streets of Lexington surrounded him with their unfamiliar town smells—dank gutters mixing with warm cooking from unseen doorways. The mystery of life. The swinging skirts and trembling parasols of girls as they shopped in the stores on Main Street, or looked down at you from their sweet little box buggies, the tops folded back, a parent or servant beside them holding the reins. He'd bought a dirk once just to follow one inside a store.

What did it mean to be a man? What did it mean to trust someone as you trusted yourself—to know someone as you knew yourself? He would like to know a girl as he knew a horse—to feel that soft contact in his fingers, and the power of his own tenderness to evoke responses. There was nothing in Blanchard's bragging or Tommy Cunningham's jokes that told him they would know what he was talking about . . . if he could have mustered the courage to talk with them, which he hadn't. Fantasies of Amanda in a hayloft were as far as he had gone. They would have laughed if they had known that.

He lit a cigar and walked to Blanchard's rooms. Three of the boys were there, already on their way to feeling good. An open bottle of bourbon sat in the middle of a little table and candlewax had already spilled down two brass holders onto the wood.

"Morgan!" Blanchard squinted in the direction of the door. "Wondered when you'd come. Ain't it dandy, not having school tomorrow? Wished we had a President die every week! Do you know Martin? Sure, I forgot . . . he's in your comp class. And Harry? His father's a big fox-hunter from Clark County. Your uncle T.H. hunts, don't he?"

"All my uncles are Hunts," he joked.

"Well, a good chase is always interesting," one of the boys answered, wiggling like a girl. They all laughed and Johnny lit a cigar from the nearest candle.

He drew the smoke in and let it out slowly, and the bourbon he chased it with warmed his insides. Tomorrow was a holiday. It was past midnight by the time he left.

When he stepped up, rather uncertainly, into the back hall at Hopemont his grandfather met him with a candle in his hand and the scowl of Jehovah on his face. He didn't bother with questions. He was too furious to talk, but took his grandson by the sleeve and fairly shoved him into the warming room, sat him at the table and brought a decanter from the dining room, poured glass after glass and made him drink.

"No grandson of mine is going to get drunk," the old man fumed. "You are going to learn to hold your liquor, sir. You *will* understand that!"

He could barely make it to the washstand in the ground-floor bedroom. When he'd finished, and wanted nothing better than to find a bed somewhere, the old man was waiting, the decanter filled again. He drank his second lesson more slowly, feigning sobriety, until his grandfather was satisfied. Upstairs, he'd never been sicker in his life.

Toward noon Big Peggy appeared, breakfast in hand. He couldn't manage anything but a little coffee and a biscuit. To his surprise his grandfather walked through the door, beaming. "You've got another young gentleman on your hands, Aunt Peggy. Treat him like one."

"Yassuh."

She rolled her eyes and said nothing. It was a bachelor establishment—with bachelor hours and bachelor rules.

In spite of all Key's coaching, the debate was a disaster. Johnny had all the arguments memorized, all the possible assaults and detours, but when his turn came so did the lump in his throat and the racing heart and his mind went blank.

"Don't worry!" Key laughed at dinner. "Even Mr. Clay loses a case now and then."

But the afternoon classes didn't go well, either. He even challenged Fishback on the question of Fate. The whole day turned sour. When he saw Blanchard and some of the boys standing at the corner of Broadway and Third whistling at some girls he joined them. Their ridiculous talk and jostling acted like a breath of fresh air after the stuffy classrooms. What was Fate, anyway? Nobody really knew anything about life. Nothing made sense. Look at the flushed face of the girl across the street, trying to seem annoyed. That was all anything was . . . a big Seem. Why wasn't that one of the words they worshiped? Seem. It had a nice ring.

Blanchard was whistling at the girl and she looked at him. "Hey, Ladybug," he yelled, "how 'bout seein' you tonight? You look lonesome to me!"

"Yeah," said Eddie Marr behind Johnny. "Lonesome, that's it! Hey, lady!" Tommy Cunningham took it up: Lady, lady, lady. They made it sound lewd. Not one of them recognized her. She was the daughter of Dr. Davidson, president of the college.

If Johnny Morgan ever wondered where his grandfather would draw the line, he found out the next day.

"I've given you your head. I've let you get drunk so you could know how to hold your liquor. And I've let you stay out all night three times—yes, I knew when you came in—to indulge your growing up, hoping you would learn the distinctions which exist among the ladies. But to stand bolt upright in broad daylight and make an ass of yourself is not . . . behavior worthy of my toleration."

The argument at the tip of his tongue, that it had been only a lark, died before it was spoken. Strangely enough, his grandfather didn't speak of "using ungentlemanly language to passersby and strangers," which were the words of the official complaint, but put his finger on the core: just to win the approval of fools, John Hunt Morgan had made a fool of himself. And now faced reprimand from the university. Suddenly he wanted, more than anything in the world, his grandfather's friendship. After a few formal words, he excused himself and went upstairs.

He sat on the porch until the sun set through the trees and the afterglow lingered on the long finger of the Presbyterian Church spire. Beyond that it laid a glow over the fields toward Shadeland. Randolph was a father—a baby named James. Everybody was growing up. It was time he did, too. He could no longer bury his face in the folds of Aunt Betty's apron. Nor feel good again riding Sard over fences. Aunt Betty looked up to him now . . . he was almost a foot taller than she was . . . and Sard would never jump again. His grandfather was right. He had wanted attention, the wrong kind. And he had gotten it . . . in the wrong way.

His grandfather was wrong, however, when he thought his grandson had learned the ways of ladies. Watching the budding limbs of late April trees in the falling dark, he felt that somehow he had let him down in that area of his learning, too.

He went to his room and drew the little table he used for a desk closer to the window and lit a candle. He had a test in Latin tomorrow and needed to work on ablatives.

The rest of that school year went by with no more reprimands. Johnny Morgan breathed easier. Under the influence of guilt and the memory of his nearly lost comradeship with his grandfather, he renounced cigars and wore quiet gray suits and received approving smiles from Margaret Bruce, a strict Presbyterian, across the street. With her eleven-year-old daughter Becky in tow, she would take her daily walk under a frilly parasol and one day invited him in for cake and coffee. Even Sanders, who no longer played cricket—or even baseball, a new game the boys in his form were trying out—was civil. It was, his Uncle Alexander Gibson Morgan joked, his sober period.

But he had never been happier.

The Methodists did take over that year, and Fishback was replaced by Dr. Gladstone, a Methodist minister from North Carolina. Of the Greeks, he had but one thing to say: "Destiny is nothing but the power of our own will." At first, loyal to Fishback, Johnny disliked him. But the more he heard his melodious voice move through Cicero and read from Caesar's *Gallic Wars*, the more he realized that blaming Fate was somehow childish. Gladstone's self-sufficiency had the not-unpleasant sweetness of asceticism about it.

When fall term came, John Morgan resigned from the debating society and throughout the next school year became known as a sober young man earnestly following his grandfather's footsteps. Christmas, 1842, at Shadeland. Long talks with Cal, and Randolph a father again—this time a little girl, Annie. Uncle Simon teaching six-year-old Richard to ride. Kitty, at seven, gorging pieces of pie in the kitchen when no one was looking, then playing the demure little flirt at dinner. Charlton, three, and Tommie, two, keeping Aunt Bet on the run. The only word Tommie seemed to know was "no." Trying to talk and frustrated at her failures, she would throw herself on the floor, beat her head and hold her breath until her face turned purple. "Don' you fuss at her now, Miss Henrietta." Aunt Betty would pick her up and rock her over her mother's objections. Henrietta didn't answer. At thirty-seven, she appreciated all the help her old friend could give. There was snow the day after Christmas, and a sleigh ride and above all, Johnny carried back to Lexington with him the memory of his father laughing.

It had been a good holiday, but the world was centered now for Johnny Morgan at Hopemont, and when he walked back upstairs that first night in

January, he realized his universe had shifted. He was actually glad to get back to classes, to allow his life to sink into the schedule of assignments and obligations again. With a winter storm raging outside, Hopemont was home.

Winter passed. Spring bulbs pushed aside the rich dirt of the Hopemont garden, and before he knew it the lavender clusters of wisteria, which had been his grandmother's favorite, would send their fragrance to mix with the roses.

The house was quiet, except for the ticking of a clock somewhere. Robert had gone to the Wickliffes' to play cards; Key was courting. The flame of his candle flickered, yellowing the pages. The conjugations he understood. These cases of nouns, pronouns and adjectives came harder for him. The ablative.

When the candle had burned about a third of the way down he heard a whistle in the street. He walked out onto the porch and looked down to see Tommy Cunningham in the moonlight.

"How about comin' with me?" Tommy called up. "Come on, you need a good time. Come on, Johnny, you scared?"

"Shhhh!"

"*Shhhh!*" Tommy mimicked. "*Shhhh!*"

"You'll wake Grandfather!" Johnny leaned over the bannister.

"Oh, the bluejay, hee . . . was the first to get the worm. Oh, the—"

"Quiet!"

"Don't you like my singin'? Here, I'll try another. . . ."

"If you promise to be still I'll come down."

He reached into his room for his coat and slipped down the stairs. At the bottom he let himself out the servants' entrance and walked onto the brick passage to the carriage yard. One of the horses whinnied softly.

"Come on!" He pulled at Tommy's sleeve. Once in the street he spoke normally: "Now Tommy, I'm taking you back to your room."

"You're scared. Johnny Morgan is scared!"

"No—I'm just not foolish," he echoed his grandfather. "You're in trouble enough now."

At the corner they stopped and Johnny let go his arm. "We're going to your room. . . ."

Before he could reach out again Tommy pulled away and ran across the street. Although Johnny was strong, Tommy was a better athlete, and even the amount of whiskey that he had consumed did not blunt, but increased his determination. Since Transy had gone to the Methodists the rules were stricter. If he let Tommy go by himself he might be expelled.

He caught up with him halfway down the next block and walked with him across several streets and into an alley. They stopped by a flight of back stairs but Tommy struggled. Before Johnny could say anything he found himself on a landing waiting for someone to answer Tommy's knocks.

Tommy smoothed his hair. He became almost timid when a Spanish-looking woman opened the door. He asked for Marie. The woman was amused in a way that Johnny resented and could not have explained. She ushered them inside. The room was bare and dim and they had to wait a

few seconds before the forms of several chairs against the wall took shape in
the half-light. Then Johnny saw the woman's face: It was not her barely
suppressed grin, but the expression in the eyes—just a flicker—of contempt
that angered him. When she left he tried arguing with Tommy, then gave
up. Evidently someone had dared him.

After about ten minutes the woman came back and led them into another
room. This one was well lit, with two sofas and a row of chairs. Candles
flickered and the floor, under a worn green rug, creaked. Tommy swallowed
audibly.

Johnny realized that the Spanish-looking woman was a "high" mulatto.
His mouth went dry and he tried to swallow, too, but his tongue seemed
too big for his mouth. He didn't know what to expect. He forgot to appear
aloof, and besides, after the woman left, he had only Tommy as an audience.
His hands went cold and he jammed them in his pockets and sat down.
When three girls entered he stood again, with that automatic courtesy which
was becoming part of his anatomy. One was plump, with creamy skin and
thick lips, and little wrinkles around her eyes as if she laughed a lot. The
other two were thin, almost unhealthily so. The girls sat down and the
plump one started talking. At first the other two seemed indistinguishable,
but as Johnny watched them one seemed prettier, more demure than the
other. Her profile, with a little tilt to her nose, reminded him of his mother.
His mother!

"I'll wait for you in the other room," he said to Tommy. "Don't be long!"

"Don't be long!" Tommy tried his "man-of-the-world" laugh, but his
voice cracked. Johnny somehow found the doorknob and sat in the gloom of
the first room and stared at the bare boards. The giggle of the plump girl
flared up through the door, then disappeared. Everything was quiet, and he
wondered what the other two were doing, were thinking. He had been rude,
running out like that. The one with the nice nose and soft cheeks was sweet.
Sweet! He was getting confused. *You don't know nuthin', Johnny Morgan.*

Tommy came out at last. From somewhere the Spanish-looking woman
appeared again, and there was an exchange of money. The conversation
seemed reasonable enough, but now there was a lewd hilarity in her eyes, as
if to laugh out loud at them would be the most delicious thing in the world.

As they walked down the stairs and into the alley Tommy started singing
at the top of his voice. At the corner Dr. A. K. Woolley (elementary principles of common law, national and commercial law) met them head-on.
Beside him, returning from a late conference at the home of Dr. Thomas
Marshall (law of pleading, evidence and contract), was Dr. George Robertson (constitutional law, equity, and the law of comity). Equally brilliant.
LL.Ds all. Methodist ministers all. Johnny Morgan and Tommy Cunningham could not have met two more formidable agents of the Rules of
Discipline if they had gone to the heart of Puritan Boston. With the quickness of intuition, Johnny knew there was only one hope: They were drunk,
just a couple of wandering students. But they were too close to those back
stairs. A glance could tell the truth. Their only hope lay in the flask, and
Johnny asked loudly for it. Tommy handed it over, after taking a sip himself.

Johnny reeled, his language slurred. Deliberately, he bumped clumsily into Professor Woolley. "Oh, 'scuze me, suh. 'Scuze me. Ah beg yo' pawdon."

"John Morgan!" Dr. Woolley declaimed. "What are you doing?"

"Ish ob . . . obv . . ., ain't it, suh? Beggin' mah pawdon . . ."

"This is disgraceful," George Robertson, constitutional law, equity, and law of comity, declared. "Isn't this a relative of Robert Hunt, the medical student?"

"Hish mah uncle," Johnny smiled. "You all know him?" He let one eyelid droop.

"We certainly do." Dr. Woolley drew himself up. "And who is this young man?"

Tommy smiled and waved the flask, which he had taken from Johnny, under Woolley's nose. "Cunning . . . ham." He suppressed a burp. "At your service."

"We'll escort you," George Robertson said firmly. "Yes, indeed, we'll escort you to your rooms this instant."

"Ah lives wif mah gran'pa," Johnny whined, in Uncle Ben's best fashion. "If y'all will excuse me, gent'mens . . ." He swayed crookedly down the street in front of them. Woolley's strong hand caught him up under his arm and propelled him toward Hopemont. .

To the utter surprise of the two professors, John Hunt received the group graciously, as if he had been expecting them, suppressing a look of surprise that he let linger half a second on his face. "We will take care of the young gentlemen," he assured them. "Good night."

When the door shut he unceremoniously led them into the downstairs kitchen and dunked their heads in a basin of cold water, and nothing Johnny could do—because the passing flask had spilled liberally over his coat—could convince his grandfather that he wasn't as drunk as Tommy. Tommy slept in the girls' old bedroom with its high four-poster and Johnny, under his own covers, wished he'd never gone downstairs.

"It was a silly, boyish experience," his grandfather tried to brush off the incident the next morning after breakfast. "Surely the authorities will see it as such in the light of day."

The boys shot each other a quick look. He thought they had only been drinking! With luck, it would stay that way. But the self-righteous threats of Woolley and Robertson lingered.

Gladstone was no ascetic. Not much older than Uncle Frank, he came often to Hopemont, drank brandy in the parlor and played chess with Robert until John Hunt, an early riser, admonished his son like a nanny.

"It's all right!" Robert would call up the stairs. "We're talking about Revelations!"

"Mind you don't sleep through the Second Coming" was the gruff reply.

So he determined to ask Gladstone for help, if the incident with Tommy brought trouble. After supper he went upstairs, where Key and Robert were in a deep discussion. When he told them, Uncle Frank turned even more serious.

"If you had only gone down to Water Street, like anybody else! Old 'Babylon Block' might be the disgrace of Lexington, but it has its rules."

"I—"

"You went to the only 'house of assignation' in this town accommodating women of color, dear nephew," Key Hunt said sourly. At Johnny's stricken look he added, "Oh, I'll admit they're not very dark . . . octoroons from New Orleans. But still, decidedly not for gentlemen." When Johnny kept staring with those wide eyes Key Hunt shrugged, cleared his throat and looked at Robert.

"They cater to travelers, people without . . ." Robert Hunt broke off lamely.

Something in his face, in the way he leaned back and toyed with his watch chain, said it plainly enough: Kentucky gentlemen don't need such amusements. We thought you knew. Kentucky gentlemen can have their way with any slave they own . . . if that's what amuses them. Only transients, Yankees and foreigners visit such places. *We thought you knew.*

"This puts a distinctly different light on your behavior, Johnny." Key Hunt took up his "legal" voice again. "*Familiarity with Negroes.* The final, ultimate defamation. This, I'm afraid, will be a worse case than Robert's. Why couldn't you have just assaulted a professor?" He turned to Robert, trying to make a joke of it.

"But how can they know?" Johnny asked. "They didn't see. . . ."

"They have their ways," Robert Hunt surprised him by saying. "Who saw me punch old Cross in the nose? Served him right for publishing my name on that petition when I didn't sign it. If he wants to move the medical school to Louisville, let him. But he can't use my name. I gave him something to think about."

"I'm sure you did. Now what will you think about if they expel you?" Key asked quietly.

"I'll see them in hell first," Robert growled.

"So would I. But unfortunately that won't help your case, dear brother. Bascom, the new president, is the son of a poor man."

"What does that have to do with it?" Robert shot his glass straight up and drained it, then poured more and offered the bottle to Johnny.

"Everything. For his father it must have been the greatest occurrence in his life when Henry Bidleman Bascom became a minister in Louisville, and then, through Mr. Clay's patronage, the chaplain in the House of Representatives at Washington City, and then an agent of the American Colonization Society."

"That dream!" Robert exploded. "A cloak for abolitionists."

"Maybe. But if that's so, we're in even deeper trouble." He looked meaningfully at his nephew. "Oh, they were just a couple of skinny girls, was that it? You didn't think of them as *Negroes?*"

"I . . ."

Key laughed outright. "Two skinny girls and a fat one. It never changes. The question is: What will you do?"

He was looking at Robert again, and they began talking about Bascom, who, as the new president of the university, was as much on trial as the Methodists. "They will all be defensive—especially Bascom," Key insisted. "Our strategy is to figure him out. Just how insecure is he? How far will he go—or feel he has to go—to establish authority? That school needs funds. They don't dare allow a hint of immorality to threaten alumni funds . . . church funds . . ."

They talked on, but Key's question, "What will you do?" burned itself into Johnny's brain.

Gladstone! He would see Gladstone. He was not like the others. Gladstone would surely vouch for his character. He knew he would! He could see him now, the doughty Gladstone with his trim sidewhiskers telling them all that Johnny Morgan was an upright lad.

Before class the next day he waited for the professor to answer his knock. His office was a shambles of opened books and Latin papers. It was almost noon.

"I've heard." Gladstone stopped him before he could explain. "Sit down, John. I hope you realize the seriousness of this?" It was the same expression he used when he played chess: I hope you realize the seriousness of this? Just before he lifted the piece that could take your queen.

Why did they all assume he was never serious? Johnny thought with rising indignation. And then another thought entered: Maybe none of them know you. Even your mother. "Believe me, I know, sir." He sat down and laid his hands on his thighs and studied them. They were slender, like his father's. Gladstone was clearing his throat and leaning back in his chair. The chair creaked.

"Professor Woolley has already assembled a number of statements concerning your character. I was asked to comment." He swung around and pursed his lips. "What did you and Eddie Marr and William Blanchard do last fall when you cut classes?"

"We rode out to my grandfather's farm on the Leestown Road to see a steam sawmill. Willie wasn't with us."

"Us? Who else was with you?"

Gladstone's eyes had slid to the stack of Latin papers and back. Something in that look made John Morgan think: I'll be damned if I'll tell you. Tommy Cunningham has enough trouble without this.

Gladstone seemed to sense that he would get no answer and changed the question. "Did you have permission?"

"Yes, sir. Mr. Fishback himself gave us permission. It was a review day."

Gladstone pinched his lips and swiveled steepled fingers on thin wrists. The wrists stuck out beyond the white cuffs of his shirt. Somehow his clothes always seemed too small for him and his coat strained at the elbows.

"Fishback is gone," he said needlessly.

"Yes, sir. I . . . we . . . I was hoping you could say a word for me, sir."

Gladstone crossed his legs and kept bouncing his fingers together, watching the ends meet, leave and meet, as if he were counting their rhythm. "I'm afraid it will take more than a word, this time." He stopped watching his fingers and looked out the window. A gloomy, cold, snow-dripping January day met his gaze.

John Morgan didn't look at him but at Gladstone's reflection in the polished desk. He let his own breath out, all the way out, down to something hard at the bottom of him. He watched the reflection say: "My advice to you is: Go to classes as if nothing has happened. I might be able to do something. If so, I'll tell you after Cicero. Have you read the assignment?"

"Sir?"

"Have you read the assignment?"

"I'm afraid not, sir."

"Then do so by three o'clock."

The day was endless. It was obvious that his classmates had heard the story, but unlike the half-admiring glances his other escapades evoked, there were now sidelong looks away from him in other directions.

He had not expected, after Latin class, to find Gladstone soberly explaining, not John Morgan's dilemma, but his own.

"The college is, of course, under Methodist auspices. As a Methodist minister I have a duty to support the truth."

"Yes, sir." Still hopefully.

"But as a newcomer, any argument I propose would carry little weight. I hope you understand. And, after all, I was not a witness."

Gladstone's voice, as he went on, grew stronger, his words sharply pronounced.

Johnny could feel, flashing across his own face, the bitter smile that would one day become habitual. He was not surprised when a plump first-year boy appeared at the classroom door with the news that John Morgan was wanted in Dr. Bascom's office.

He was puzzled to find Eddie Marr and William Blanchard standing with Tommy. It was the old affair on the street corner that Bascom wanted to see them about, not the encounter with Woolley and Robertson. His mind must have been on Tommy and the larger problem, because he hadn't heard William Blanchard say that he, William, had not been on the street corner that day. When Bascom asked Johnny point-blank, he had to ask for the question to be repeated.

"Are you sober, sir?" asked Bascom, rising. "I have asked you a sober question. Were you there that day on the corner, using ungentlemanly language to a young lady?"

"Yes, sir," he said absently. It happened so long ago. What were they dragging that out again for?

"The trustees"—Bascom cleared his throat—"have suspended you for the remainder of the term." When Morgan didn't answer, he turned to the others. "As for you, Blanchard, you have received a reprimand."

Tommy, too, received a reprimand, Eddie Marr nothing. John Morgan felt that little smile again lift one side of his mouth. Eddie Marr was the biggest carouser on campus. It was he who had dared Tommy to go to the brothel. With the most imperceptible bow in the world (his grandfather would have been proud of that), he turned to go.

"Morgan . . ."

He stopped.

"You may, of course, reenter in the fall. This suspension is only for the rest of this term."

That smile again.

"Thank you, sir. I think—I shall always be grateful for what I have learned here."

Bascom watched that back, so straight, so square at the shoulder, leave the room, and wondered, indeed, at the little dramas that teachers often play in the lives of those whose development is entrusted to them.

"You mean to say that Cunningham and Blanchard get off with just a reprimand?" asked Key, unbelieving. "And Marr scot-free? If Father were still trustee . . ."

"I wouldn't want it," Johnny said. "I wouldn't want Grandfather to defend me just because . . ."

"Just because you're innocent? You are confusing bravado with bravery, Johnny."

"Maybe I don't want to go back. Don't you see how cowardly they are, for all their piety and prayers? Bascom didn't even mention where Tommy went. And Blanchard lied."

"Bascom didn't mention Tommy because it was the unmentionable. As for Eddie—didn't you know? Eddie's father is a big money-giving alumn, a big Methodist down in Alabama. Bascom took the easy way out by concentrating on the old street corner incident—almost forgotten but still in their files. But he *did* leave the way open for you . . ."

"To go back?" Johnny shook his head.

Key was holding a law book in his hands and pressed his fingers along its leather spine. "Maybe you're tired of Latin conjugations. I understand that. But the days of the pioneers are over, Johnny. The world belongs to the verbal. To people who can persuade with language. To the lawyers and politicians. Even Father, with his merchandising in the early days, sending whiskey to the army in Ohio and flour and hemp downriver, would have a harder time getting started today. This is 1843, Johnny. Not 1775. It won't be the settlers grubbing in Oregon who'll make the fortunes. They'll just fill the coffers of old John Jacob Astor in New York. No—this is the modern world. We're expanding, ocean to ocean! There's a man in town taking daguerreotypes. Latest thing from France. Why don't you get one of yourself and give it to little Emilie Todd?"

When he saw that his banter was doing little to change his nephew's mind Key turned specific again. "Look—Bascom's on a spot. He's acting president only, trying to keep the boat afloat until the Methodists get going. Wait a week or two, and then—"

"I'm not going back." His uncles wavered through tears and he shut his eyes. Damn them all with their pious talk! They mouthed so glibly words like honor and love . . . divine love, for Christ's sake! Gladstone's reflection, upside-down on the polished desk, came back. They were all reflections, and upside-down. "Damn them all to hell!" he said when he opened his eyes. He hoped it existed.

"I don't blame you," his grandfather surprised him by saying at the doorway. "Robert's going to Paris for his medical degree. And you?" He smiled. "Come." He extended his hand. "Let's ride out to the farm. I've got a proposition for you." As they were mounting in the carriage yard he added darkly, "We'll have to speak with your mother, of course. You know how women are."

He didn't, but he nodded.

9

John Hunt was, in a way, delighted that his grandson had flaunted the halls of Academia. Secretly anti-pedant, more of a shopkeeper than an intellectual, he was a man of action who distrusted abstractions. "To read Homer is one thing," he called out to his grandson ahead of him. "To ride a good mare is another."

They left Main Street and trotted up a little slope. Despite the mud from yesterday's melted snow, a drying wind had already scattered the clouds. The sky was as blue as porcelain. At the farmhouse they handed their mounts to a waiting groom, and, after a few questions to the manager about fence-mending, they walked to the barn.

"It's the perfect place," John Hunt continued, as if their conversation had not been interrupted by the ride, and Johnny realized he was talking about KMI again, the Kentucky Military Institute just started near Frankfort by a Colonel Allen "with West Point polish and discipline." "You can ride your horse and study Napoleon's campaigns. War is just chess on a larger scale. Come over here. I have something to show you." The old man paused significantly. "Well, what do you think?"

She was a bay, her black mane satin, her stockings velvet against four white pasterns. A star and snip gave her slim face a delicate elegance. John Hunt caressed her topline with his eyes. "A little lean in the flank," he conceded, to cover his admiration. "But the boys are permitted to bring along their own mounts, I imagine . . ."

"She's beautiful, Grandfather," he heard himself say. He knew his grandfather wanted a "military man" in the family. But Cal had told him Shadeland was in financial trouble, and his father was not well.

"She's yours."

"I can't take her."

"Can't take her?"

"I'm sorry, Grandfather. I know you want to send me to school. But Shadeland . . ."

There was a moment in which John Hunt allowed his eyes to remain on the mare before he turned to the boy beside him. When he did, there was a new look of respect in them.

"I think I understand, John. Of course." It was the first time he had ever called him that.

John Hunt didn't give in so easily. He waited a minute, then offered another surprise. Abraham and T.H. had made the Hunt hemp factory one of the landmarks of Lexington. Now Abraham proposed to move to Louisville, to expand the business.

"We'll need a replacement. I've already talked to T.H. about it, and he's delighted. One day it could be called the Hunt-Morgan factory," he said proudly. "And of course you'll need a horse in town."

Johnny's eyes went back to the mare.

"Even Uncle Simon can't argue with her bloodlines," Hunt laughed. "But you'd better watch out—her name's Delilah."

"Delilah!" Their eyes met, and although no word of agreement had passed between them, John Hunt shook his grandson's hand.

Thomas H. Hunt had married at twenty, declining a more formal education to follow, like his father, a mercantile career. Instead of pondering philosophical questions, he directed his intuition into outsmarting the market. And it was fun. After two years John Hunt offered him an interest in the hemp factory, and after only five years T.H. was one of the most successful young businessmen in Kentucky. The factory was on the Georgetown Road, and the day Johnny Morgan walked into it he felt at home.

He worked hard. He learned fast. Dealing with tons of hemp and problems of transportation and the hiring of extra hands for the looms were solid things, more real than ablatives. As summer moved into fall, his trips to Shadeland became fewer. When he did have an evening free he found himself in the Hopemont parlor playing chess with his grandfather or talking with his grandfather's friends, planters, tradesmen, Judge Gratz or Henry Clay, at Ashland for the summer and autumn of 1843. The first clipper ships were running. The *Rainbow* weighed 750 tons. The *Sea Witch* covered an unbelievable 358 miles in twenty-four hours, and the Hong Kong–London trip was made in only 97 days. John Hunt read *The Spirit of the Times*, but Henry's favorite was Horace Greeley's *New York Tribune*. "Have to know what the opposition's thinking," the old fox winked. The abolitionist, William Lloyd Garrison, denounced the Constitution in his *Liberator*, and threatened the secession of Massachusetts if slavery was not abolished.

"I don't understand them," John Hunt kept saying. "Don't we supply their factories with cotton and their navy with hemp?"

"You have just made the fatal distinction, Father," Key murmured over dessert. Just accepted into the faculty of Transylvania's law school and a gentleman caller to Dr. Elisha Warfield's daughter Julia, Key had, as Robert said, achieved an insufferable—and overnight—urbanity.

"What? What?"

"You said 'them.' "

Christmas at Hopemont, without womenfolk, was not Christmas at Shadeland. Johnny missed it. Outside the first snow sifted down with that lazy, zigzagging search of each flake for the ground. It made him think of the silence of the pond, of the woods, silence at all times, in the early morning waiting for the first stirrings of birds; in the night, when the moon made patterns across the floor. But Shadeland was sound, too: the sounds of babies, of children running, of falling toys and calling voices, of life.

His mind went to Amanda, the last time he'd seen her. She had lost her plumpness and had slimmed down to a willow wand, as Aunt Hannah called her, ". . . no bigger'n a stick. Ain't healthy, I say."

Will had hurt his back. "The doctor says he broke it . . ." But Amanda couldn't finish, and Johnny guessed that she was thinking he might not walk again. He wanted to tell her that she didn't have anything to worry about, that surely his grandfather, in whose service Will and Will's father had spent so many faithful years, would help. But he couldn't bring himself to speak, as if such a promise might confirm her fear. Instead, he surprised himself by bending his face close to hers and brushing her cheek with his lips.

"Then he'll be better'n ever, if you take care of him," he said gallantly. She blushed, wiped her hands, and regained her composure just before Zep came onto the porch.

"Mind you call us if you need us," he said as he untied Delilah and swung up. "You sure you don't want me to send John Henry or Randolph down to help?"

"No. Zep is a good help," she said, and slipped her arm around her brother's shoulders, which were higher now than her own. Johnny looked at them and felt a sadness descend. Nothing, as his uncle Key kept telling him, ever stayed the same. Unconsciously, every time he went to Shadeland he had started taking daguerreotypes of everything, in his mind, as if these would be the last memories of his childhood. Now, in the silence of the snow, it seemed as if the whole world was covered up, changed.

His grandfather was still in bed with a bad cough. Robert was playing cards with friends and Uncle Frank had gone to the Warfields'. Big Peggy served him supper alone in the dining room with candles gleaming on the polished table. A clock somewhere was ticking, ticking. A sudden gust of wind disturbed the windowpane and made one of the candle flames bend. He watched it recover itself, sink fatly near the wick, a blue line in the yellow pointing upward. "You want mo', Massa?" He felt, rather than saw, Big Peggy's presence behind him.

"No, thank you, Aunt Peg. That was delicious, as usual. How is Randolph?"

"Randolph, Massa? Why, fine, Ah suppose . . ."

"When have you been to see him?"

"Been to see him?"

"At the farm."

"Why, Ah ain't been to Shadeland, Massa."

Big Peggy was Randolph's mother, yet she'd never been to Shadeland and didn't see Randolph unless he came into town on an errand! There were family relationships surrounding him that he'd hardly thought about. Built into the walls, like the paint. Uncle Simon was Big Peggy's father, and yet he hadn't ever thought to tell her how he was doing, or anything about him. He suddenly felt ashamed of himself. Calvin Morgan had talked about *noblesse oblige*, that without it, we are nothing.

He sat so long at the table that Big Peggy came back and asked him if he was sho' he didn' want mo'. For the first time in his life he realized that in her own patient, soft way, Big Peggy was asking him to finish so she could do the dishes, get her own work done, and go to bed. If he had said, "No, that's all right, Aung Peg . . . leave the dishes . . . don't clean up, it can wait," her face would have fallen. He would have made what she did insignificant, and would have hurt her feelings. The world was indeed complicated.

The fire in the parlor was blazing, kept going until Key's return, or Robert's return, or whoever would be the last person to return that night. The silent hands that kept Hopemont moving. Suddenly they were all around him. Love? He'd always thought of it as such, with Aunt Bet's coondog eyes and ample bosom the essence of heaven. Or was her caring merely self-preservation? He picked up one of his grandfather's discarded newspapers and tried to read. Only then, remembering his father's admonition again, did he realize the cause of his discontent.

Winter moved imperceptibly toward spring. Henrietta Morgan was expecting a baby in May. Robert Hunt would leave for Paris in April. Johnny rode to Shadeland when he saw the first daffodils.

The house was abuzz not only with Henrietta's announcement and Robert's leaving but also with the possibility that Henry Clay would run for President again. "I hope he makes it this time," Calvin said, smiling over his whiskey. Henrietta had never looked more beautiful. He had never felt better. And now, with Johnny doing well in the business, Shadeland's shaky finances would look up. "Clay for President! Let's drink to it!" He grinned, lifting his glass.

"He'll have his hands full!" Alexander Gibson blurted. He had come out from Lexington with his wife and little boy to enjoy the good weather. "The settlers have formed their own government out there and have asked Congress to make them a territory. What a grand land it must be!"

"Where did they get that name? And doesn't the land belong to England?" asked Henrietta.

"Nobody knows," Alexander answered, "It may be a Spanish name, or French, or even Indian."

"It sounds more French," said Calvin. "Ore . . . gon . . ."

"Could be. As for England, I know the forty-ninth parallel was agreed upon, but '54°–40' or fight'—you watch, that'll be the slogan for the campaign next year. There's talk of going to war if—"

"Oh, war." His wife, America, stopped him, and tried to laugh. "Alexander, you are like a little boy playing with toys. Can't you ever be serious?"

"Yes . . . as serious as he was when he almost went to Texas back in '37," Henrietta teased, but to her dismay her brother-in-law looked hurt and sulked. He really is a little boy, she said to herself. Toy guns. "Come now, Alex," she said aloud. "We all admired your desire to help the Texans in their dilemma. But see, it's turned out all right. They are free and independent. . . ."

"Not for long. Maybe not for long," grumbled Alexander, not to be appeased. "England is sitting like a vulture ready to gobble her up . . . and the Mexicans are camped on her borders ready to pounce any minute."

"Speaking of gobbling," interrupted Calvin, whose illness had made him sensitive to any melancholy note in those around him, "I'm starved for some of Aunt Hannah's goodies."

"Mr. Clay is bound to be the Whig candidate again," Alexander kept up, reluctant to abandon his point. "Maybe he can make a stand. I only wish he weren't so wobbly about Texas. That just may lose him the election. . . ."

Johnny, following him into the dining room, thought some things didn't change so fast, after all.

In May Henrietta Morgan was delivered of a fine baby boy.

"T.H. never thought I loved him as much as my other brothers." Henrietta smiled as Johnny, by her bedroom door, watched Aunt Betty fondling the baby. "We'll call him Tom. Thomas Hunt Morgan instead of Thomas Hart, though. But the initials will be the same." She smiled, then held out her arms, and he walked over for her kiss.

All the news at Shadeland was not good. Cal brought him to the farm office and talked about the accounts. Their father seemed distracted. It was as if, since his trip to Europe, he had divorced himself from problems. The price of hemp or horses didn't interest him. Since Sard had been injured and retired to stud, even the races failed to excite him. Calvin Morgan had become a country squire, depending on Randolph and Cal, and Cal was scared.

Outside, the May breeze moved the oak leaves. It was 1844. In another month Johnny would be nineteen. As he stood there watching Cal's worried face, he felt his own role slip imperceptibly from that of son to that of the head of a family.

He began going to Shadeland on a regular basis. In August Maggie had another son, Jesse. Now more than ever, Johnny appreciated Randolph's good sense with figures. The hemp harvest was good. On the surface, Shadeland hadn't changed.

The world was changing, though, as T.H. kept reminding him. Summer moved into fall. Although the telegraph had been invented, it was the New York mail, arriving on the ten P.M. stage, that brought the news to Henry Clay of James Polk's election. He was attending a wedding in Lexington and turned to John Hunt with a grim smile. "This will mean low tariffs, lavish land policies, Texas, and war."

Hunt grinned back. "Don't fret, Henry. When Texas becomes a state, maybe the South can enjoy a justly deserved piece of the political pie."

"And Mexico?"

"A country of half-breeds and Indians? Why, my grandson Johnny could pick off a dozen without aiming."

"Let's hope he won't have to."

That Henry Clay had been defeated for President again, and by a dark horse from Tennessee that nobody had ever heard of, was a joke turned sour. "I like horse-racing," said John Hunt, "but this is ridiculous."

When the truth came out—and, as usual in politics, too late to change the outcome—even the Yankee press was shocked at immigrants being herded into the naturalization rooms to be "citizenized" *en masse*, then led like cattle to the ballot boxes.

"To vote Democratic." Hunt folded the paper in disbelief.

"Believe it!" Dick Curd laughed bitterly. "One judge naturalized twenty-five hundred at one swoop. In Albany, seven thousand fraudulent votes were cast. In New Orleans people were loaded onto packets and plied up and down the river to vote more than once. One landing that had never polled more than three hundred forty votes gave Polk a majority of close to a thousand!"

"Like runnin' a donkey against a thoroughbred" the old Whigs had laughed, but now they regretted their optimism, and the fact that Henry had been so wishy-washy over Texas. One of the last acts Tyler accomplished before he left office was the annexation of Texas—a Mexican province whose independence the United States had never acknowledged—by a joint resolution of Congress rather than by a treaty.

"You'll have to give him credit," Key Hunt grinned. "A treaty would have required a two-thirds vote of the Senate. The old boy was smarter than we thought."

"You goin'?" Nathan, who now towered over his father, asked Will.

"Where? Oregon?"

"No, Paw, Texas."

"Hadn't thought to. Why, yew?"

The boy looked around, at the few acres and patch of garden, where Zep's bent back rose and fell.

"Got to."

Will followed his gaze. Hadn't his own father come to Kentucky when it was a wilderness? Hadn't he inherited that itch to move on, and sometimes hadn't he wondered, after his time in the army, if he had been right to accept the Hunts' kindness—first old Abijah's in Cincinnati and then old John's down here. It wasn't that he didn't like the place. But there were times when Will heard the words *Oregon* and *Texas* and even *California* with a pang in his chest. The night before the boy left he gave him his best saddle and blanket and watched him trot away with wet eyes.

John Morgan heard of it when he rode out to Shadeland in January. But Will's news faded before his father's: Henrietta was expecting a baby again. Calvin sat in the farm office and slowly put the ends of his fingers against his thumb. "August," he said. Joy and worry made a strange mixture on his face. Henrietta would be forty; this was their eighth child. Henry Clay had already buried two girls from childbirth, Henry, Jr.'s wife and his daughter Anne.

"She'll be fine, Father," Calvin heard his son say.

It was a mild winter, and Delilah would be four that spring. John Hunt was anxious to supervise her finished training. Despite gout and a recent bout with winter fever, he insisted on riding out to Shadeland at least once a week beginning in February. Johnny was twenty, a good rider, but he had things to learn.

"You don't *squeeze* a horse into a canter," the old man said, trying to keep testiness from his voice. "You *touch*. Here, let me show you."

John Morgan watched his grandfather swing up and settle, wait a minute, collect, and, with an imperceptible tensing of his inner calf, start Delilah in a walk. Almost by magic—for Johnny couldn't see the motion—the old man rounded his lower back and Delilah floated into a trot. John Hunt sat so erect it was as if his head were suspended from an invisible ceiling, his heels reaching for the ground. Then the outside leg drew back and the inside one touched the girth, and before his eyes Johnny saw Delilah pick up the canter and the old man, his seat and thighs glued to the saddle, undulate over the fields like a centaur, one with the horse. *He's seventy-two* kept running through Johnny's head. Then, with the softest closing of the fingers, his grandfather brought her back into the trot and walk and finally halt. "That's how you do it," John Hunt said, dropped the reins and dismounted.

He looked at his grandson and cleared his throat. "You have a friend. If your friend is afraid, you reassure her. If your friend lacks confidence, you supply it. She depends on you. You depend on each other." He stopped and then held Johnny's eyes. "You may need a friend if you go to war."

Without another word, he walked to the house to see his daughter.

"My, my, ain't that a ridin' gent'mens?" Uncle Simon asked admiringly. Then, abruptly, as if some of old John's determination had rubbed off on him: "We's got *wukk* to do, Massa."

Delilah learned quickly—everything but overcoming a fear of crossing puddles. Uncle Simon had the field hands build a mound in the center of the back paddock, then flood it. Twice a day John Henry waded out with feed and watched Delilah, after missing three meals, dash through the water to eat. "She won't cause you no trouble 'bout watah, Massa. You could lead her through the Rivah Jordan aftah dis."

"You may have to, if we go to war," Calvin Morgan said behind him.

"You must have been talking with Grandfather," his son grinned.

March turned cold again, but April bloomed with all the promise of spring, and before they knew it the wisteria was out and it was summer, with warm nights and fireflies.

"Here. Have a brandy."

"Thank you, sir."

Over chess, John Hunt let his hand stop in midair. "Have you heard about Cassius?"

"No, sir. What's he done now?" Henry Clay's cousin, who had gone north to Yale and came back an abolitionist, was the butt of good-natured jokes. Nobody took him seriously.

His grandfather's hand came down and he moved his bishop. "He's started a newspaper. Calls it *The True American*. His type's been stolen. While Cash was flat on his back upstairs with typhoid. Robert went by this afternoon and there he was, his shotgun useless by his bed. But you know what the ole rascal did?"

There was no need to answer. His grandfather would tell him anyway.

"He'd set up two cannon in the hallway—you know, those little things a little over a foot long—and rigged some wire so he could fire them from his bed!"

"And did he?"

"Damned if they didn't fail to go off. I can just hear what he must have said. So now there he lies, his type shipped off to Cincinnati. I like Cassius. But it may get serious." His eyes wandered from his grandson's queen to his face.

It was true. Like a slow-boiling kettle, the slavery "question" was heating up. The Methodist Church had split over it and the North saw the annexation of Texas, settled mostly by Southerners, as a political threat.

"Checkmate," John Hunt said quietly.

"They have more to fear from Polk," Calvin Morgan told his son one afternoon after a workout. They watched Delilah grazing in the center grass of the track across the pond. It had been a fresh July morning; they both knew the afternoon would be too humid to ride. Henrietta was now in her eighth month, weary of the heat and irritable. The menfolk, puzzled and helpless, stayed out of her way. Even Aunt Hannah had received some gunfire. Only Bouviette could communicate with her, calm her, make her comfortable. Calvin and Johnny felt safer talking about real gunfire. That they could understand.

"Yes, we'd better fear Polk," Calvin repeated.

"Grandfather and T.H. admire him."

"Your grandfather is an old man and won't have to fight. T.H. has always been a hothead."

That summer, Polk sent Zachary Taylor with 3,500 regulars—almost the whole American army—to the Rio Grande, a boundary claimed by Texans but never acknowledged by Mexico, which had drawn the line at the Nueces. Not satisfied with that invasion, Polk ordered Commodore Sloat to seize California.

"But I thought only Congress had power to declare war."

Calvin Morgan gave his son a look. "Polk was a dark horse elected on the promise to reoccupy Oregon and reannex Texas, remember. In spite of the fact that we've got a treaty with England and know as well as the Mexicans where that Texas border is."

"In other words . . ."

"In other words he's taken the reins in his own hands."

"But that's—"

"Illegal? I'm afraid you'll learn, Johnny, that legality depends on who's doing the defining."

In August, two days before Charlton's sixth birthday, Henrietta took to her bed, and Aunt Hannah's birthday cake-baking was interrupted by calls for more hot water, more tea, more clean linen. John Henry ran back and forth and Maggie kept the younger children outside playing games. Only once in two days did Aunt Betty's worried face appear at the kitchen door, asking for cold milk. Aunt Hannah tried to make her sit down, but she took the glass without answering and left. On August 23, Charlton's birthday, Aunt Hannah was determined to have a party. She arranged a table down by the pond, away from the cries from the downstairs bedroom, and carried out a cake lit with candles. Johnny and Cal politely sat with the children and were relieved, before Charlton opened his presents, to see their father come from the house to join them. "How is she?" Cal whispered.

"It will be soon." He smiled at Kitty, but spoke so low she couldn't hear. It was over his objections that the girls were kept at Shadeland and not sent into Lexington to their Aunt Eleanor's. "I want them with me," Henrietta insisted, in a new fit of anxiety, and her frightened eyes made him comply.

That night was hot and humid, with clouds covering the stars. Johnny went outside, to get away from those anguished cries. In his mind he could see his mother's sweat-streaked face turning on the pillow. Fireflies blinked syncopation in the thick fog that had settled over the pastures. Through the faint, last light he could make out the silhouettes of horses in the south field, where the old barn had burned. The cries stopped, and a new crying came.

His name, Calvin announced to his family in the parlor the next morning, was Key. There was something in the way Henrietta received her children by her bedside that told Johnny this would be her last baby.

"Imagine . . ." Calvin cleared his throat. "Two boys with the same birthday." And Uncle Ben, his twisted, arthritic hands grasping the doorframe, echoed: "Eeemagine dat, two boy babies wif de same burfday!" And they laughed, and the children, Kitty and Tommie first, were allowed to kiss their new brother.

In town, the talk was glum. Not only T.H., but John Hunt believed there would be war. "If only Henry had been elected . . ." the old man would say, and then immediately recover himself. It had never been his policy, in business or in private life, to regret. "If it comes to that, it comes to that." Already volunteers from Fayette County were signing up. The office at the Hunt hemp factory, which had served in earlier days as John Hunt's job center for the unemployed, now became a meetingplace for would-be recruits. A regular messenger service sprang up between the Phoenix Hotel, where the stage came in, and T.H.'s desk. "Wish we'd get a telegraph station," he said impatiently. "Washington City's got one."

"We're in the backwash, T.H.," Johnny laughed. He was on his way out and left fast enough to dodge the wad of rope his uncle threw not too playfully after him.

"Under it all," he told his father at Shadeland that afternoon, "T.H. is serious. And Grandfather. What do you think?"

They were drinking coffee on a bench under the oak in a patch of sunshine. Around him the shadows of the overhanging leaves made patterns on the grass as the breeze moved. He'd turned Delilah out into the back pasture and on the way toward the house passed Uncle Ben working his garden. He had recruited Maggie to help him, and she was swinging a flat basket against her skirts and humming. When she saw Johnny she stopped, self-consciously dipping her head away from him when he called out a greeting. His father laid aside his book when he came up. "No, don't move," Johnny said, sinking to the ground on folded legs.

"You'll dirty your trousers."

"No . . . the grass here is dry."

They fell silent now, watching the pond sparkle in the wind.

"It's so peaceful here," Calvin said, reading his son's mind.

"I miss it. I didn't know how much."

"So you think they're serious?" Calvin asked, afraid of the tone he heard in Johnny's voice. His own deepening periods of melancholy, caused partly by his illness, partly by the worsening financial condition of the farm, made him cautious in the presence of sadness, even the mildest nostalgia. Calvin knew his son's weaknesses, for they were too close to his own. Generous to a fault, Henrietta said. Too sensitive. "He'll never make a farm manager. Cal is more level-headed. You'd better depend on Cal," she had said. Johnny's voice came in again.

"In Lexington all they talk about is war. It's funny to hear them hold up Henry as a peacemaker. He was really a warmonger in 1812. We didn't have to fight that war."

"We don't have to fight most wars," Calvin sighed. "I think maybe Mr. Clay has learned his lesson."

"We have more reason to go to war now than we had then."

"Tell that to Will," Calvin chuckled as he rose to his feet when he saw his wife walk toward them.

As for Texas, Mexico took no action. President Polk offered to buy California for twenty-five million and New Mexico for five. With an American army refusing to withdraw from Mexican soil on the north bank of the Rio Grande, Mexico said No. On April 23 the Mexicans captured a small body of American dragoons. Hearing of this ambush President Polk declared, on May 11, that Mexico had invaded the United States, that America's patience was at an end, and asked Congress for ten million dollars, fifty thousand men, and a declaration of war. Point Isabel, General Zachary Taylor's port of supply, was shelled; Major Brown was killed, and six thousand Mexican soldiers formed across the plain of Palo Alto. The Mexican losses were six hundred, mostly wounded; nine Americans died and forty-four were wounded. In Washington City war was formally declared on May 13, even before the news of Palo Alto reached the capital.

Colonel Kearney marched from Fort Leavenworth to Santa Fe, captured the old town and declared all of New Mexico to be part of the United States. He then set out to capture California, but Kit Carson stopped him only a few miles from Sacramento with the news that Commodore Sloat had landed and the Stars and Stripes were already floating over the town. On May 18, Taylor crossed the Rio Grande.

At Shadeland, with Calvin talking politics with his brother Alexander, Henrietta withdrew more and more inside herself. It was enough to stretch the budget and maintain a decent level of entertaining without trying to make them hear her views, which they wouldn't understand anyway.

Only with Johnny did she seem to retain some of her old self. He adored her, and she basked in his approval. But even her Johnny was, she feared, too much of a Morgan. All this swashbuckling he brought home from town. All this drinking late with T.H. and Alexander Gibson, talking war. Alexander's wife was right. Little boys. She had hoped that Johnny would help with the accounts, that Shadeland could show a profit. When she read more war news in a copy of Mr. Greeley's *Tribune* all her pent-up frustration exploded. She confronted her husband as if he were a child who had just stolen cookies.

"What is this?" she stormed, waving the paper. "American soil? The boundary was never at the Rio Grande. What were we doing down there anyway? How can they justify war? You are just children!" she shouted, no longer trying to keep the contempt from her voice. "Children who'll stay home and send babies . . . boys like Johnny or Cal or even Richard or Charlton if they were old enough, to do your fighting for you. It's ridiculous!"

"It's Manifest Destiny," her father told her in the parlor of Hopemont, the day after she learned Johnny had joined the volunteers.

"It's insanity!" she moaned, but all the fight had gone out of her. John Hunt tentatively reached his arm around her bent shoulders and patted the air an inch above her dress.

"There, there, Henrietta. He's an excellent shot. And he can ride like the wind."

"He'll have to have someone look after him," she sobbed. "You know how he takes chances. And dares. He lets anybody dare him to do anything. Cal will have to go with him."

"Of course! What a capital idea!" John Hunt declared, looking at her in amazement. To save one son she would offer two. He would never understand Henrietta. She would always be a wonderment to him.

"But we're going to have the biggest barbecue ever," she said to Cal, distractedly brushing a tear from her cheek and looking away from him when she returned. She had gone into Hopemont alone, and was pulling off her gloves by the hall table. "And you're going to take mosquito veils with you, and there'll be no arguing." The other children, a tiered audience, stuck stacked heads around the door.

"Can we have a match race?" Richard, in the middle of the pile, almost yelled.

"We can. And we will."

"And ices and pudding and yam pie?"

"Oh, Charlton, you're always thinking of your stomach," Kitty cut in.

"Well, don't you?" Richard extracted himself to defend his brother. "You're always pretending to be such a little lady at Grandfather's, but I see you sneaking off—"

"Hush! Hush now, or Johnny won't have to go to Mexico to find a war."

When the children left and she was alone with Calvin for the first time since they'd heard the news, she turned to him and asked: "Are you all right?"

"Perfectly fine. You're worried about them, aren't you?"

"Cal's so like you. You know those colds he gets. . . . Maybe . . ."

"They'll be perfectly fine. I'm sending John Henry as a body servant."

"John Henry? That boy hasn't a brain in his toe."

"It's not in his toe that he needs one." Calvin Morgan leaned over and felt her scented hair brush his face as she left him.

It was the biggest barbecue ever. Even Key, not yet a year old and wiggling out of Aunt Betty's arms, seemed to catch the excitement. There was a match race, too, and Delilah, her hind legs digging turf, her forehand reaching, reaching, won. At seven o'clock the next morning Johnny rode with Cal, whose own big dun was dependable, down the pike toward town. Henrietta and Calvin and all the children except little Tom and Key would follow in the carriage in the afternoon. When they left, Aunt Betty, holding the baby, waved to them from the front door. "You be good, you!" Tommie was sticking out her tongue before Charlton, behind her, pulled her back. Henrietta stood bolt upright and motionless, and Maggie, standing a little behind her, set Tom down and waved his arm also.

"I will! I will!" But the sound of horseshoes on gravel as they turned onto the pike covered Johnny's words. He was hearing, instead, the cries at that rally in Lexington:

> *FAYETTE VOLUNTEERS! Remember your glorious history, be worthy of your immortal ancestry.* . . . The cheers! The insane cheers! *You are hereby commanded to parade on the grounds of Transylvania University.* . . . *You are hereby commanded to assemble on Thursday next at one-thirty o'clock, punctually, to take up the line of march to Louisville . . . by order of the Executive Department. Cassius Marcellus Clay, Captain.* . . .

If even that hotheaded abolitionist, Cash Clay, could join, it must be serious! Hail, Columbia! Yankee Doodle! For Mexico, fall in! Hadn't Tennessee raised thirty thousand men when the call came for only three thousand? Kentucky would not be out-volunteered: Within four days it had two regiments of infantry and one of cavalry—its quota filled. Two of the cavalry companies were from Lexington, one led by Clay and the other, Company K, by Captain Beard.

Now, as Johnny and Cal rode into North Mill Street, young ladies of the Female Bible Society were distributing New Testaments to the soldiers gathered on the Transy parade ground. The Morgan boys were in Captain Beard's company of the First Kentucky Cavalry, in Colonel Humphrey Marshall's regiment. As volunteers, they were not issued uniforms; Johnny wore his best boots and a wide-brimmed hat, and Cal was in something as military as possible. But the banners and brass band more than made up for the lack of regimental attire. Boys threw shoulders back and chests out and compensated for wavering drill lines by the intensity of their "military" stares. If the Mexican Army had been lined up across the street the war would have been over before it started. "If looks could kill," Cal joked, arms crossed, legs apart in an appraising attitude.

Amanda had ridden in early and stood now, under her best bonnet, with Zep across the square. At last she caught sight of Johnny. Their eyes met and his eyes held hers as if he would never let go. Suddenly she didn't want him to let go . . . Johnny Morgan. Johnny, Johnny Morgan . . . why hadn't she known? But he lived at Shadeland, and she . . . But in the circle of this moment, with his eyes on her through the missed notes of a trombone, nothing else seemed to matter. . . .

Then a flag, drooping in the humid heat of the July morning, tipped down as a boy on horseback allowed his pole to falter, and Johnny's face was gone behind the flag and then, again, it did matter. And it always will, she said to herself, feeling the tears well up. She sniffed and laughed, and when she saw his face again he was watching the Hunts and Morgans lined up in front of Hopemont. Even Reverend Pratt and Miss Pamela (it was strange to see her without her organ) stood waving tiny flags. Reverend Goodman, on a platform, prepared to give a blessing. Suddenly Amanda saw a man break from the crowd on the sidewalk and run over to Johnny and then to Captain Beard, waving his arms.

It was Alexander Gibson Morgan, who could stand it no longer. When a sudden downpour reduced Reverend Goodman's sermon to a quick prayer for their safety, Alexander ran back to his wife and son, kissed them, and ran back after Johnny, who had already started Delilah toward the stock-yards, where they would pick up more recruits. Alexander was yelling, "Wait for me! Wait for me!" When Johnny stopped, smiling, his uncle added: "I'm the best shot in Fayette County. Maybe in all Kentucky. Want to bet I'll kill more Mexicans than you do?"

It was a strange way to go to war. Johnny looked back at the crowd, scattered by the rain into doorways. Uncle Frank and T.H., his grandfather, his mother and father, his father with one hand raised in farewell, his other hand on ten-year-old Richard's shoulder. Only one figure, in a straw bonnet and blue homespun dress, stood firm against the limp and dripping trees.

10

They marched down the Frankfort Pike, Tommy Cunningham on his big gray gelding, Cal on his dun, and John Henry with a young but level-headed trotting filly. Johnny stayed behind at the stockyards and when his uncle arrived with a hurriedly packed knapsack strapped behind his saddle they cantered smartly past the last houses, carbines riding across their backs, on their way to Louisville.

Before the company boarded the steamer *Bunker Hill* for Memphis, in a little ceremony by the wharf, John Hunt Morgan was elected first lieutenant. "Lieutenant John Morgan," Alexander Gibson said proudly. "Guess I can't call you Little John any more."

At Memphis the troops disembarked for the march overland to Texas. The Mississippi lay like a flat sheet of brown iron in the heat. "More like a pond full of snakes," said Cal, pointing to the moving eddies curling just under the surface.

"Don't let it fool you, boys," a sergeant said, pausing in his inspection of the unloading. "That river's lots faster than she looks."

Colonel Marshall rode by. A heavy man whose capacity for whiskey was already the joke of the regiment, he sat his horse sluggishly and watched the proceedings with undisguised disinterest. Already, he was wishing he was back on his front porch in Kentucky. Not a breeze stirred.

Alexander Gibson, like Cal, was a private. Somehow he was glad he'd refused a commission and had hired on as a soldier. Maybe in the back of his mind he kept some notion that as an enlisted man he could more easily drop out of that twelve-month promise and go home.

He might have known better. Disaster and disease, not patriotism, made him stay. He couldn't abandon Johnny and Cal to the stupidity of Marshall. Ill armed—of the ten companies only four had rifles—without enough clothes, tents or rations, such an army couldn't hope to keep its men well. As for pay—they'd seen none, and even before the trek through the marshes of Arkansas had taken its toll too many had traded the few good coats and shoes they had for whiskey and potatoes, anything to replace the buggy flour and rancid meat that passed for food. Before they reached the Washita one-fourth of the men suffered from dysentery, measles or fever. The rest pushed on to San Antonio for orders to reach Zach Taylor's army down on the Rio Grande.

Cal was first, then Johnny. Alexander, ignoring their pleas that he should go on, stayed behind to nurse them. "It will be only a few days. Time to enjoy the scenery," he joked. "Besides, we joined this war to kill Mexicans. Morgans don't die of *disease*."

And, after a week in Little Rock, they did seem to get better. They didn't want to miss the war! It might be over before they got there! They talked him into moving on. He'd been a damn fool to listen. The weather fell apart. The Red River was a surly, swollen lake. Drenched, they swam their horses and rode the last twenty miles through a downpour. They were lucky to find a cabin with kind people who knew the perils of the frontier. For two days he watched the red, puffy face of Johnny sweating under the frayed blanket, and Cally, sleeping now on his side—Cal better, thank God. Gently he moved Johnny's hand under the net, then slapped a mosquito on his own arm. The boy stirred.

"Rest, Johnny, rest. . . ."

The boy's eyes opened and he lifted his chin. The action made a stream of sweat run off his forehead into his ear. "I wish Wash wuz here."

"Ain't I Morgan enough for you?" his uncle frowned, and wrung dry the dripping cloth he had just pulled from a basin. "Here." He slipped the cloth under the net and packed it around Johnny's neck, under his chin. "This'll help." He set the basin aside and sank into a chair with a sigh.

But the fever soared. Then, miraculously, the next day, he was better, swallowing in gulps the watery oatmeal that the farmer's wife gave him. Alexander fed him the last of it and sank back.

"You do look weary," the woman told him. She had just returned from the barn with a pail of milk. "You need some rest, or the nurse will be the patient."

"I'm fine, ma'am." Alexander flashed her his winning smile.

"I'm putting you to bed," she said with determination, wiping her hands on her apron. "But before I do there's one thing I want to do and another I want to show you. The first is, I want to wash those poor worn-out pants and the second . . ." She reached out, grabbed his hand and pulled him to his feet as if he were a little boy. Grinning, he followed her to the porch.

"See there?" She wiped her hand again and lifted it toward the setting sun. "That's Texas.

"That's Texas," she said almost menacingly, in her desire for him to see what she felt. "And don't you ever forget it."

He followed her gaze. The sun, resting on the top of a low hill, had broken into a star of light. It was gone in a second and a broad shelf of clouds, its underbelly ruffled lumps of gold, turned orange in the afterglow. Like a funnel, it drew the eye to a pale expanse of sky at the horizon, which could have been a clear, bottomless sea. Below this, and stretching as far as Alexander could see, undulating land flowed with prairie grass and turned in the wind.

It was six hundred miles to Camargo, as the crow flew, and it was already the 5th of August. Even if they could travel thirty miles a day—which in the heat and with Johnny's condition might be unlikely—it would take them twenty days. They left a week later.

The first night out the Texas dark fell like a thunderclap. Johnny thought he had never seen such stars. Night sounds, sharp but far off—the high wail of a coyote, the short, sharp squawk of a bird—made solitude deeper, almost tangible. As the nights passed he drew in great gulps of the clean, cool air, and felt stronger. Tomorrow would be oven-hot again, each breath like a wad of cotton stuck in his throat. Only the wind made the sun bearable. The wind was crisp and pure, glinting sunshine off the moving heads of prairie grass until all around them as they rode seemed a sea of gold. And the sky was so big! The sky in Kentucky had been merely blue, a place for clouds. Here it dominated, and vast as the land was, it lay under that expanse and waited, prostrate, for the sky to decide its fate. . . . One night he had just fallen asleep when the rain broke, lashing the tent until the canvas gave way. They finished the night under a rock ledge.

Two hundred miles later they crossed the Brazos—the uncle, his two nephews and the boy John Henry. They watched clapboard cabins give way to adobe houses, their rounded edges soft in the vertical sun. Deep in seed-tufted prairie grass flights of wild geese and curlews settled in shallow pools drying hourly under the steady heat. Jackrabbits the size of small dogs crashed ahead of the horses.

They saw no buffalo and that, Alexander Gibson said, was good: Where there were no buffalo, there would be no Comanches. But there were wolves howling at sunset and antelope bounding, their little turned-back horns and wide eyes breaking a path through grass so high it brushed the horses' bellies as they waded south. Alexander killed one at two hundred paces, hitting the white spot on the chest, and John Henry roasted rump steaks over the fire. The land rose into dry, mustard-colored cliffs and the ground, bristling with cactus and broken by sudden ravines, hardened into cracked clay and shriveled clumps of sagegrass. One morning the horizon turned black and started moving . . . buffalo! With their great shaggy heads and lumbering gait, their tails stiff in the air as they ran. . . .

They hobbled their horses at night, letting them graze in the morning while they broke camp, until a rattler scared one and they dashed off, plunging like rabbits. One of the extra horses broke his leg. It was a serious loss; after that, they drove pickets into the ground and stood guard. They reached the little fort at Bastrop exhausted, the horses needing shoes. Alexander Gibson wanted to stay an extra day, but the boys voted to push on to San Antonio, where orders might be waiting.

Orders had indeed been waiting. Most of Colonel Marshall's stragglers had left for the Rio Grande more than a week ago. Alexander Gibson found a dozen men from the original detachment and decided to wait four days for others to arrive to make up a party, with Sergeant Joe Havens as escort. An old-time frontiersman who had seen service at San Jacinto, Havens was sanguine about their efforts against the Mexicans but cynical about the results. "Oh, yew fellers'll do," he said, rubbing a grimy finger across a scar that folded one cheek. Then he added, before he let fly a stream of tobacco: "But hit won't make a rabbit's print in last year's snow a hundret years frum now."

Some of the party voted to wait a week; the others vacillated. Alexander Morgan, livid with disappointment, swore he would go alone. To Johnny's surprise, the unconcerned Havens agreed.

"Some fellers'ud wait till their bones bleached. A'skeered of Injins, Ah reckon," he said, and spat.

They moved out early, Havens with a torn buffalo robe belted at his waist, a Springfield carbine across his back and a rifle on his pommel. Two Indians, their mouths like saber cuts in their grim faces, sat in the dust watching the departure.

"Kiowa," Havens said derisively.

Another, in white man's clothes, his long hair in braids under a tall felt hat, nodded as they filed by.

"Osage scout," Havens threw back to Cal. "Knew him up on the Arkansas. But yew ain't seen an Injun till you meet a Comanche." He thumped his mule into a trot.

Brants, herons, cranes, ducks and even a few gulls cut the air as the riders swung closer to the border. Prairie dogs sat in front of their burrows squeaking a high yelp. A tarantula in the road reared, as if he would defy the horses. Texas!

"It means friend," Joe Havens said. He lifted one side of his lip to reveal a broken tooth. He had dropped back from scouting ahead, but his eyes were on low hills to the west. "*Tejas*. How the Mexicans hate that word!"

The muscle in his jaw, under the stubble, tightened. His eyes looked off. Without glancing down, he slipped one hand under his rifle to feel if it had rubbed his mule. "I lost a brother with Fannin's men. Killed by Injins hired by the Mexicans." He kept his eyes on the horizon.

Three heads, then three ponies rose from the nearest hill, their silhouettes dark against the sky. Havens swiveled his head and held up an arm, a signal for the others to stop. Johnny closed his fingers on Delilah's reins and, with Cal and John Henry, watched Havens jog his mule to within thirty feet of the Indians. The one in the middle raised his palm and nodded, his single feather bobbing. Havens came back and drew up next to Johnny, a grin tugging at his mouth. The Indians galloped down the hill, yelling at the tops of their voices, circled the four halted riders at a dead run, leaning parallel past their ponies' manes as if they would use their mounts as shields, then disappeared over the hill, still yelling. Johnny was speechless, then swore in admiration.

"Yew're right!" Havens spit. "Them bastards is *riders* . . . Comanche. Now yew kin say yew've seen Injins."

Prairie gave way to *brasada*, the brush country, the sere grass and the cactus. Yucca bloomed like creamy, thick candelabra and *paisano* birds ran on their toes like ballet dancers. A boy without sandals waved at them from his burro, his smile all teeth, but most of the people they saw sat in front of their hovels watching old women make bread. Once at night Johnny and Cal lay terrified, listening to a stumbling sound that seemed to be about twenty feet away. Johnny slowly, under his bedroll, reached for his gun. He could hear Cal's uneven breathing, and thought: I'll take care of you, Cally. I promised Ma. He sat up and pulled the trigger and, instead of hearing the groan of a wounded man, Joe's shrill laugh.

"Hit's an armadillo!" Havens said. "Yew remember thet the next time yew get a-scairt," he said. "Most things air toothless, jest like this critter, an' thinkin' more on their own business than yours!"

Five miles from Camargo they halted and Alexander insisted that the party freshen up. "For our entrance," he winked to Johnny from his stance before a shaving mirror hanging from a tree. He drew out a new shirt, saved for the occasion, and directed John Henry's attention to Johnny's "uniform." "And Cal, you're hopeless," he fussed. "Why do you always look like a feather pillow?"

"Because he has feathers for brains," Johnny teased, and ducked Cal's swing. But underneath their horseplay the excitement of actually *joining the army of General Zachary Taylor* made their fingers tingle as they buttoned and smoothed and polished. Finally, after watering their horses and resting for almost two hours in the shade of some cottonwoods, Havens declared the party ready to proceed. From somewhere Alexander Gibson Morgan produced a plume, folded his hat on one side and stuck it in. With a military swagger he led them into Camargo single-file, parade-style. It was September 11; they'd made it in less than a month. They felt like conquering heroes.

The sleepy village slept on. It was the siesta hour and except for three Mexicans dozing under sombreros, no one noticed them. About a hundred yards beyond the village a flagpole told them where the Americans were. As they rode into camp a few shouts rang out from boys lounging in the sparse shade of some bushes, trying to cope with 112-degree heat. Cal recognized a boy he hadn't seen since Memphis, but the military reception Alexander Gibson hoped for was nonexistent.

Camargo was below sea level, on the San Juan River upstream from its entrance to the Rio Grande. The American camp was behind high rock walls, where no breeze stirred. Hoping for a cool breath of air, the volunteers had pitched their tents near the river. They had been here since July: The contaminated water supply sent dysentery, fever and measles through the ranks. Fifteen hundred deaths filled the graveyard; the coffin makers, having used up wood from gunboxes and flour barrels, wrapped the corpses in blankets and joked that the dead needed them more than the living, anyway.

Riding into the compound was like riding into hot glue. Alexander and his nephews dismounted, slipped their reins under their stirrups, uncoiled the hitching ropes and tied their mounts to the rail in front of a hut that looked as if it might be headquarters. John Henry grinned toward a leather-faced youth, his cheeks gray with dust and his lips cracked from the heat, who ran toward them. Johnny couldn't believe his eyes. It was Tommy Cunningham. "Hey! Johnny! Cally! John Henry, that you? And Mr. Morgan!" Tommy pulled off his cap and showed them his shaved head. "Lice," he said proudly. He turned to Johnny. "Ain't you got none yet?"

Johnny held out his hand, but Tommy ignored it, as if such niceties had been left behind. "Where is Captain Beard?" Johnny asked. "We'd like to report," he said, he hoped not too formally. The contrast between his jacket and the dirty shawl Tommy had draped over one bare shoulder was painful.

Tommy caught his eye. "Hey! This here's a serape. You need to find one.

It's a great blanket at night and if you prop it with a stick you can make some shade. . . . Aw, my horse is all right, and around here that's all that counts. We eat pretty well. Better'n the Mexicans, though that's not sayin' much. Captain Beard is off lookin' for stragglers. But shucks, that's a waste of time. If he'd just wait a bit they'd come in from hunger or fear of rattlers." As if he thought he's said too much, he looked away.

"And Colonel Marshall?" Alexander asked.

Tommy made a pantomine of a bottle tipped in the air. "All the time."

"Well, and General Taylor?"

"In there." Tommy pointed to the building in front of them with tent flaps for windows and half-adobe, half-timbered walls. A soldier, presumably on guard, sat on the sill of the doorway. "Hey, I'll see you later," Tommy called out. "I left a good hand of cards. We're over there. . . ." He pointed to a group under a tree. From somewhere came the aromatic woodsmoke of a piñon fire, making Cal hungry. "Tell you what," said Tommy. "After you get done here, come on over to the boys and we'll get some grub."

Inside headquarters, once past the suddenly alert guard, all was dim and remarkably cool. A little air found its way through the flaps and dried the sweat on their faces. In the gloom they found "Old Rough and Ready" in his shirtsleeves, shaving. Under a thatch of unruly hair the deepset eyes never left the business at hand, but Johnny was conscious of being watched. Zach Taylor's weathered face obeyed the pull from two stubby fingers as they stretched one cheek level to the blade. He stuck out his heavy jaw and pushed the soap downward, leaving a clean swath over the deep laugh lines that framed a wide mouth. It was the face, Johnny's grandfather would have said, of a soldier's soldier. The unkempt eyebrows rose just slightly as the General allowed his eyes to drift toward his visitors. Alexander began the introductions when Taylor half-turned to him and said bluntly: "I suppose you want a champagne reception! Complete with ladies in laces."

"Well, no, sir, I . . ."

"And crossed sabers."

"Sir, I . . ."

"And banners flying."

Alexander Gibson Morgan drew himself to his full height and bowed silently, prepared to turn on his heel and leave. General Taylor reached out a great paw and grabbed him by the shoulder and swung him around. "Well now, boy, I'm glad to see you." The paw became a pumping handshake, and Zachary Taylor guffawed out loud when a blob of shaving foam landed on Alexander's "uniform." Carefully, with small jabs of a towel that hung around his neck, the General removed it.

"There. Be good as new." He grinned as he turned to Cal and Johnny. "Welcome to the 'Army of Observation,' as our good President calls us. But first," he said seriously, licking his lips. "I'm sure you Kentucky boys will want a taste of home."

The whiskey was good. Then they got down to business.

"Supplying ammunition is *one* of our problems," Taylor growled. "And your horses?"

"Good shape."

"Extra?"

"Two."

The General indicated some maps spread on a camp table. "With luck, we'll finish this business down here and get home before the snow flies."

Alexander Morgan took the hint and rose, his nephews following his example.

"Have you found your unit?" the General asked. "If you need anything . . ."

Outside, the whiskey made the sun seem hotter, the glare blinding. Tommy Cunningham's card game had broken up and disappeared, evidently toward the piñon fire and food. Only one outfit seemed alive, a group drilling under the energetic directions of a blond officer, tan as a jackrabbit.

"Don't we know him?" Alexander asked in awe. "That colonel . . . I seem to remember him from somewhere."

Memory stirred in Johnny too.

"It's Lieutenant Davis!" his uncle said.

Johnny couldn't wait for the drill to end and the men to be dismissed before he ran up and introduced himself. Colonel Davis suppressed a smile as he gave the final order and turned on the balls of his feet, ramrod-straight, and returned the salute of Alexander, who had come up behind his nephews. Nothing in the casual atmosphere at "headquarters" prepared them for the military precision of Jeff Davis's men.

"You mustn't judge the General by appearances," Davis answered Alexander's remarks as they walked toward Davis's tent. "He's a very fine tactician. We're lucky to have him." He held the tent flap, then followed them in. "And this is Cal!" he beamed, unbuttoning his collar and making himself comfortable. "Did you bring your wooden sword?"

Cal was embarrassed. He didn't want to say he didn't know what Davis was talking about. Moreover, he couldn't quite accept the loose-jointed, grinning man before him as the awesome disciplinarian of the drill ground.

"Well," Davis laughed, "I hope not. We'll need more than toys here."

As Johnny's eyes grew accustomed to the light he noticed a great mound of a man asleep on a bunk in the back of the tent. The mound emerged as a big, rawboned frame with piercing blue eyes who, when he sat up, almost brushed the sloping roof. The skin across his cheekbones was paper-thin and cracking, as if he had felt too much Texas wind. His mustache and bushy eyebrows and hair were a sandy blond, and there was something about him—a languidness veiling tension—that made Johnny think of the prairie.

"This is Al," said Davis, with no apology for the love in his voice. "Al Johnston."

Johnston slapped a mosquito on his neck, wiped his hand on his pants and extended his arm to each of them with a slight bow and a dip of his head. He was bare from the waist up and gleamed with sweat. "Pardon my attire, gentlemen. My uniform, alas, succumbed to the sea water at Point Isabel. So you're just from Kentucky? I'm from"—he let out a sudden laugh—"a long way from Mason County myself. Our Mr. Clay made a brilliant speech in favor of Texas. Too bad he didn't mean a word of it."

"Ah, well, don't be too hard on him, Al," Davis said, motioning Alexander into the only chair. Johnston moved over on the bunk to allow Johnny to sit and Cal perched, legs swung back under him, on an overturned keg by the door. "Clay's walking a tightwire right now. Congress is playing with an idea called 'the Wilmot Proviso.' It promises that no new territory acquired from Mexico will be open to slavery."

Johnston said slowly, "Isn't that just like them, to start carving the bird before it's cooked?" That sudden laugh again. "And now we're here all roasting together. All except my disbanded regiment!" His laugh turned bitter and he shook his head. "I can't believe it! One man! I talked exactly one man into changing his vote! Hell of an orator I am!"

Davis explained that Johnston's six-months' volunteers had asked to be disbanded rather than reenlist. Johnston appealed to them in what he thought were ringing tones, but only one man changed his mind. Johnston, chagrined but determined to see his own six months out, was waiting for word from Taylor.

"What do you think he'll give you?" Alexander asked.

"I'll be a paper soldier," Johnston said, and stuck his chin out. "When the old boy knows I want troops. . . ."

"You'll get your marbles, Al," David said reassuringly. "They're just buried."

Alexander raised his eyebrows. Davis grinned. "When Al was a kid he was the best marble player around. Beat everybody. He won so many marbles he decided he'd own all the marbles in town . . . in the state . . . in the world! He put them in a jar and buried them, keeping out only enough to invest, so to speak. Well . . . all his rivals fell except one, who seemed to have an inexhaustible supply. . . ."

"Did he beat him, too?" asked Cal.

"Finally. Then, when Al dug up his jar he found out where all those marbles he'd won came from. . . ."

When the laughter died Davis cleared his throat. "Old Zach needs every good man he can get, Al. In whatever capacity."

It's like Priam's tent on the plains of Troy, thought Johnny and suddenly Captain Beard and the drunken Colonel Marshall and the Kentucky volunteers were amateurs beside the casual, tight-lipped Johnston and the disciplined drillmaster Davis. It was Davis, not the reticent Johnston, who told most of Johnston's story. "He joined the Texas army as a private and left it as a commanding general, to become Secretary of War for the Republic of Texas."

Johnston tried to minimize Davis's adulation by saying to his whiskey, "All that's in the past. For six years now I've been nothing but a Texas dirt farmer."

"What are you now?" asked Johnny.

Johnston grinned. "A Texas dirt farmer."

At that moment Taylor's orderly, a thin-faced boy with a stammer, came in and asked Johnston to follow him to headquarters. Johnston donned a red flannel shirt and followed, sticking it into his jeans as he stepped over Cal's legs and went out the door. Ten minutes later he returned, stood as erect as he could under the low ceiling and gave them all a snappy salute. "Colonel Albert Sidney Johnston, Inspector-General of field division of volunteers, under Major-General Butler's division reporting, sirs."

They cheered, and received Johnston's look of sarcastic resignation. "You got here none too soon," he said glumly. "We move out tomorrow, first light."

Colonel Marshall's Kentuckians marched behind Davis's Mississippians, and Johnny couldn't help but be surprised when he saw Albert Sidney Johnston on horseback. Davis rode a smart little gray Arabian named Tartar, but it was Johnston, straight as a board in work jeans and a red shirt, with a torn checked coat and "wide-awake" hat, who couldn't have looked more like a general if he'd been covered with braid. General Taylor led them, not much better clad, and from the tone with which the men spoke of him it was clear they considered his sloppiness a badge of honor.

"Ain't never seen him in full uniform," Joe Havens beamed. "Most of the time he's got so much dirt on him he runs thuh risk of bein' auctioned off as real estate!"

The army moved from Camargo and concentrated at Cerralvo on the 12th of September. To the southeast, across the rough cacti and rock-strewn terrain, where Sergeant Havens swore only lizards and the iguana could live, they could see the Sierra Madres rising like a black citadel against the sky. They met angry stares but no resistance from the few people who ventured out. A turkey herder with a dozen birds weaved past the regiment, controlling their direction by tossing out handfuls of shelled corn ahead of them. Burros with bundles of firewood three times their size jerked down the dirt-choking road after the horses had passed. Then thorny thickets of chaparral gave way to pines on the upper elevations. But no amount of altitude could get rid of the insects, the fleas, ticks, mosquitoes and gnats that almost blinded the horses and made Johnny wish he had shaved his head like Tommy. At a place called Marin they regrouped on the 17th and arrived at the forest of Santo Domingo, three miles from Monterrey, on the 19th. It was two days' hard riding, but at last they felt the cooling winds from Cerro de la Silla, Saddle Mountain, at the foot of whose rocky pommel the old city of Monterrey lay.

The 19th and 20th were spent in reconnoitering the enemy's defenses. Johnny rode with his uncle and a detachment from General Worth's division. He couldn't help admiring the rich valley of the Santa Catarina River at the foot of Saddle Mountain and Miter Mountain—Cerro de la Mitra. The city, almost surrounded by these peaks and protected from the chill northern winds by the still higher Sierra Madre range to the east, was itself high enough—more than a mile—to enjoy year-round springtime. But the colonels who rode ahead seemed oblivious of the tiered rooflines and iron-grilled doorways they watched through their field glasses. They were more concerned with the fortified bishop's palace on a commanding elevation at the western edge of town, and with a massive stone structure called La Teneria, protected by a redoubt and heavy artillery. If they could take La Teneria they could block communications with Mexico City. But the place of greatest resistance would come, they all knew, from the admirable and powerful system of defenses at the lower end of the city, where heavy artillery and ten thousand Mexicans under General Ampudia awaited Taylor's army of six thousand.

Late into the night of the 20th and most of the morning of the 21st Zachary Taylor, surrounded by his staff, laid their plans. General Worth's division would occupy the gorge of the mountain above the city on the Saltillo road and would commence the attack, move on the bishop's palace with infantry and dismounted Texans and along the streets with light artillery. Twigg's division, supported by Butler's men, would tackle La Teneria. The Louisville Legion, detached temporarily from Butler, would assist a mortar throwing shells into a fort at the upper end of town.

The night of the 22nd Johnny Morgan couldn't sleep. Mexico! Monterrey! La Teneria! Excitement almost suffocated him. The idea of advancing, of galloping Delilah under fire, with banners flying, his comrades on either side —he could almost see their laughing, eager faces. Would he meet the test?

He got up and wandered about the camp. Other men, too, were restless. The volunteers nervously asked surreptitious questions of the regulars. Texas Rangers, not daring to admit the fear at the core of their own unrest, answered gruffly. Instead of turning back to his own bedroll Johnny walked out to the picket lines where the horseholders, muleskinners and blacksmiths were gathered around a little fire and a black pot of bubbling beans. There was a quarter moon, but the night was cloudy. In the half-light he easily recognized Cal's dun. He knew Delilah and his uncle's horse and John Henry's trotting filly would not be far. He found John Henry asleep against a tree, the three lead ropes in his limp hand, although the horses were tied. He stepped softly over to Delilah and buried his face in her mane, taking deep breaths of home. Shadeland came back: Xenophon and Shamrock and the fields, Randolph and Uncle Ben and Aunt Betty and his mother, Richard and Charl, little Tom and Key, just a baby—and his sisters, Kitty and Tommie, who cried when he went away. He swallowed a lump that rose to choke him and sniffed back tears. My God, he thought. After all the battles you've read and talked about. After all the guns you've fired. His hands were sweaty, his lips cold. My God, don't get scared! Wouldn't *Wash* laugh at him?

One of the men at the campfire moved over to give him room. He hadn't intended to sit down, but he did, and held out his hands to the warmth from the coals and breathed deeply of the fragrant woodsmoke. The man's courtesy had been an unconscious reaction to another body close to him; his whole attention was on the problem they were discussing.

"I tell you it ain't the bullets," a thin-lipped boy with a button nose across the firelight kept saying. "It ain't the bullets."

"What is it then?" the man next to Johnny asked.

"It's them lances. And them bayonets. I tell you there's something about lances and bayonets that makes me squirm."

"Aw," drawled a third soldier, with the insignia of the First Ohio. "Come on now. It ain't dyin' you're a-feered of, now is it?"

"Naw, it ain't dyin'. It's doin' whatever I have to do to die that worries me." The boy broke a stick and threw a piece into the fire and stared as it flared up.

In the light Johnny saw he belonged to the Fourth Infantry and felt sorry for him. A man on horseback always had a better chance. "And those lancers," the boy said to the fire. "Those damned Mexicans kin ride."

"It's hurtin' that bothers you," the Ohio man said.

"Well, all right. It's hurtin', then. Them lances and bayonets. I sure wouldn't like the *feel* of them."

The Ohio man ignored a chuckle in the background and asked: "What's the difference?"

"Well, a bullet's . . . a bullet's clean. You know what I mean?" The boy appealed to the man beside Johnny, who would give him no help, but leaned back on crossed arms, a straw in his teeth, which he moved back and forth across his lips with the tip of his tongue.

At last the man said, spitting the straw away from him and sitting up, "It's artillery shells I'm afraid of, and that's a fact."

The others nodded and avoided each other's eyes, and fell silent. It was as if a truth had to be considered.

They were talking, not of death as Reverend Pratt discussed it, with speculations about a hereafter or the payment of sin, but of *dying*—and the chill Johnny felt deepened and returned and he remembered the stench of a dead mouse, caught in the wall at the landing of the stairs at home, and how it lasted for days and kept him awake at night. Suddenly he was conscious of his body, each part of his body, his arms, his legs, the backs of his heels, his chest, as if they were living, precious things to be protected, to be saved . . . to be saved at any . . . But at the same time *to meet the test*. To face death and meet . . . And then the voice that had chuckled in the background cut through the silence with a laugh.

"I tell you, hit won't make a rabbit's print in last year's snow a hundret years from now!"

11

"**A**nd I'll tell yew something else, sonny," Sergeant Havens said jovially, his arm around Johnny as they walked back to camp. "There's not a man amongst 'em—generals, colonels an' all—who are gittin' what yew could call a good night's sleep this night."

Johnny learned that he would be in the second day's fighting, not the first. All day he waited in camp for the news of General Worth's success, which came in at sundown. Everything was running smoothly, according to Alexander Gibson, dirty but happy. He splashed water on his face and wiped his eyes with a towel as if that clean cloth were the most sensuous, rewarding thing in the world. But wounded were brought in, groaning under the trees, and cloth-covered mounds awaited burial. The smell of the mouse returned. Johnny Morgan pushed it away.

Worse than the waiting was the news that he would be fighting dismounted. All those turns-in-place! How he wanted to feel the charge of Delilah under him! His condescending sympathy for the infantry boy by the campfire came back to taunt him.

The next morning he found himself moving carefully down a dusty street, its buildings seemingly bare of inhabitants, its stones ringing too loud with every footfall. Earlier that day the Americans had been so bloodily repulsed by the Mexicans entrenched in La Teneria that a new flag had been run up to cheers from within the fort. Under a galling fire of grape, a third of the Fourth Infantry fell. In his mind, Johnny could see them: squeezing together in a funnel of smoke and stumbling bodies. Now Colonel Marshall's regiment, with Captain Beard's company in the advance, was assisting the second assault.

Johnny steadied his own gun, a little topheavy with the unfamiliar weight of a bayonet, and slipped into the shadowed recess of a doorway. Snipers on the flat rooftops across the street kept up a steady peppering that kicked up dust and tore plaster from the edges of windows. La Teneria loomed ahead, with its fresh flag and protective redoubt. The Mexican artillery waited there, ominously quiet. Johnny let out a shallow breath. There was an invisible line, somewhere out on that street, which marked the difference between his own army and theirs. It seemed silly now to think in terms of armies. There were only the black half-circles of snipers' heads against the sky, a man in a Texas Ranger's uniform in a doorway (he could just see the bottom of a pants leg) and boys like Cal, who had boasted nervously over a breakfast none of them could eat that he would kill more Mexicans than Tommy Cunningham. Mexicans weren't turkeys! Or quail or deer! Those heads against the sky were probably laying their own bets. *Where was Cal?*

A sudden firing from behind made him jump. The Tennesseans and

Mississippians had moved up, the first to the left of the redoubt, the second on the right and in front. The firing was American, and the Mexican musketeers lining the breastwork between pieces of artillery began answering with a broken, cracking *zat! zat!* followed by silence. Over their heads and behind them in La Teneria, more musketeers in large numbers were shooting into the masses of troops now moving relentlessly past Johnny's door. He moved out among them, automatically, unthinking, raised his gun and fired.

Through the smoke he couldn't tell if the man fell; if he did, another took his place. He pulled the fishtail lever of his Hall, bit off a cartridge and dropped it in the chamber, running and ramrodding all the while. He stopped, took aim, and fired again. Someone pushed him from behind and he went sprawling, his gun rolling from him. A hand reached out, pulled him up and he ran on, gunless, yelling insanely with the rest. The whole regiment, the whole street, which seemed now a monster alive with frenzied bodies, rushed forward. It's crazy, came the thought: We're outside the range of our rifles, but downhill and within range of theirs! Lost in smoke, he stumbled again and felt a groaning body fall against him. Without looking at the face, he let it fall, caught at the rifle, and pushing his way to the wall of a building, found a cartridge and loaded. The boom of the artillery and the sharp clatter of bullets seemed normal now. He took a breath and saw to his disbelief American uniforms storming the redoubt. Somebody was waving a pistol and yelling, "Tombigbee boys, follow me!" A whole regiment scrambled over the breastwork, chasing running Mexicans to a stone building in the rear. Without knowing how he got there, Johnny felt the rough stones of the fort tearing at his fingernails. By the time he reached the top a colonel and a lieutenant had forced the main door open and the Mexicans surrendered, the officer in command advancing and delivering his sword.

It had all happened so fast! So this was war! He looked around and took a deep breath of acrid smoke. He was alive.

But he wasn't through. After La Teneria there was Fort El Diablo. He ran on, with a glance at Tommy Cunningham, who had been put in charge of some prisoners. Their eyes met, unrecognizing. At El Diablo he almost collided with Colonel Davis. Elated, flushed with victory, Jeff Davis's eyes glittered like a madman's. He had assaulted La Teneria without orders; his men were merely to clear the snipers, secure the streets. But once in the street something had happened. It was as if they had been picked up and carried, beyond reason, and by some collective will outside themselves, to an inevitable fate. And unreasonably, they had won. Davis, sweating and grinning, turned to an orderly who had just come up. The boy handed him orders from General Quitman, the brigade commander, to retire.

"Retire!"

Johnny saw the struggle in Davis's face. That furious desire to go on and on and on, to lead his men, who had accomplished the impossible and were ready to climb to the skies if need be, made war on his face with all the training of the disciplinarian.

They were behind a long wall near a street corner and under crossfire from the Mexican artillery still operating to the left. Davis walked over to a grimy horseman in a torn red shirt, whose smoke-blackened face looked down and broke into a smile. What could he be smiling about at a time like this? Johnny thought, and then he recognized Al Johnston. "We are uselessly exposed," Davis was saying.

Johnston answered: "*If we can't get any orders*, and if you'll move your regiment to the *right place* the rest *may just follow.*"

It was Davis's turn to grin, and Johnny followed them, knowing full well they were acting against orders, but knowing also that these men were soldiers to the core and that sometimes instinct was more trustworthy than protocol. With a crowd of men behind, they crossed a small stream and passed through a cornfield to the front of a *tête-de-pont*, a small fort in front of a bridge. Captain Field, with a company of infantry and Colonel Mansfield, of the engineers, held the bridge, and a plan was devised for an immediate attack. Johnny heard from somewhere that General Butler had been wounded and that General Hamer was in charge.

General Hamer came up with his command and, in a voice loud enough for the men on the bridge to hear, ordered Davis to retire.

From where he was, beside the *tête-de-pont*, Johnny could see a discussion, and guessed that Davis was arguing. His men had been withdrawn from their assigned posts and were advancing; they had gone too far to return. But Hamer won, and Davis and Field withdrew across the field.

Captain Field, walking just ahead of Davis, was hit by fire from the fort. He was dead before he fell.

Johnny ran now into the cornfield, enclosed by a high fence of chaparral beaten down between upright posts, as solid as a stone wall. Men were climbing over it wildly and running through the corn, which snapped and cracked under the artillery barrage.

Davis's men had gone some distance to the rear when the Mexican Lancers, seeing the retreat, found a place low enough in the fence, jumped their horses into the field and began cutting down stragglers and the wounded who couldn't run.

This was the first time Johnny had seen them, the feared Mexican Lancers aflame with bright uniforms. Men had talked of them in muffled tones ever since Camargo. Yet they looked like nothing more than boys dressed up on horseback out for a ride, except for the lances, with pennons flying.

He stood horrified as one man, hopping under a momentum that he couldn't control, kept running for about ten feet across the field on one leg, his other cut away behind him. He fell beneath the first lancer's horse. Johnny would have been cut down himself if the second lancer's horse hadn't tripped in a hole, throwing the Mexican to the ground at Johnny's feet. There was no time to load—he couldn't remember if his gun was loaded, anyway. Reflexively, without thinking, Johnny Morgan stuck his bayonet through the Mexican's uniform as hard as he could.

It was soft! As soft as a feather tick! The man—he couldn't have been much older than Cal—looked at him with amazement, as if Johnny had just insulted him. This look of surprise was followed almost instantly by one of disbelief as the brown eyes widened and the mouth opened in a cry of silent outrage. No sound emerged, no sound at all. Johnny pulled his blade out and the man fell, spouting blood.

Through smoke and dust Johnny pushed down a sudden nausea and saw Davis's men, who had regrouped at the far end of the field, drive the lancers back. Joe Havens's face flashed, mouth open, but his yell was swallowed up in the din. Johnny turned and ran with them, his legs pumping, conscious of nothing but the rushing back of the man ahead of him and his own sweat, which ran down his face and almost blinded him.

Somehow, the Americans scrambled over the chaparral fence and toward camp again.

The streets were deserted. Fallen men in strange positions, some doubled under, some on their sides as if they were sleeping, lay in doorways and in the streets. One still moved. Already medics from the hospital unit were running, turning over, bending down, lifting. The unshapely humps of dead horses, their legs looking uncommonly small, their necks pressed to the ground, were already drawing flies.

Where was Cal? Back at his own "camp," an area where they had spread bedrolls and a few tents under trees, Johnny walked among the weary groups, some passed out with fatigue, face-down in the grass. "Cal Morgan? He that little plump kid with the light brown hair? No, I ain't seen him since . . ." "He your brother? No, sonny, don't recollect seein' him since the march from Camargo." "Have you checked the wounded wagon?"

Frantically, Johnny moved among the bloodstained bandages, the moans, the faces too dazed, the eyes too bewildered to answer. The busy surgeon, his smock covered with blood, advised him impatiently to go to headquarters for news.

Hitched horses, dozing in the shade by the tent Zachary Taylor and his staff called headquarters, stirred as Johnny approached the sentinel. Before he finished his question Alexander Gibson emerged, one sleeve dangling from his jacket from a saber slash, his face still gray with dust. "Johnny!"

Cal was safe, getting a hot meal at Colonel Marshall's regimental headquarters, the obvious place for Johnny to have looked. Colonel Marshall, with the rest of the staff, was inside conferring with the generals. Alexander had just learned that General Quitman would order Colonel Davis, with four companies, to make a sortie into town at dawn. Although just a private, Alexander had volunteered, with picked men of his own, to make up part of the party. Without asking, by his uncle's grin, Johnny knew he would be one of the volunteers.

But the nausea came again, and the memory of the brown eyes with their disbelief, the open, raw mouth. Was this what heroism meant? Mounds of fly-covered horses, twisted bodies, and under it all the memory of a rotting mouse. He *had* survived. Wasn't that what he wanted? He had killed a man, but the man would have killed him . . . and wasn't that what war was all about? The frenzied elation of Jeff Davis's face after they had taken La Teneria, the indomitable determination which made him lead his men over that cornfield—yes, there were reasons to be proud and to want to try again.

"Come on," his uncle said with a laugh, "we've got to make ourselves presentable for tomorrow! Fine soldier you are!" Alexander tossed his plume, which miraculously still stood intact. Johnny ran a hand across his cheek and looked at the black streak of smoke and sweat. "Now that's no way for a Kentucky gentleman, is it?" Alexander Gibson prodded. "Let's go for a wash and supper. We've got to get up early."

"Is . . ."

"Cal's coming with us. We stay together from now on. I promised your mother I'd look after you boys, and I'd rather fight the Mexicans than contend with her when we get back."

When they advanced into the town just after daylight they found Mexican artillery in the bishop's palace trained on the main plaza, where the cathedral had been turned into an arsenal.

Beyond La Tenería snipers were again posted on the flat roofs, and the first job was the clearing of this obstacle. Ahead of Johnny and Cal, Alexander Gibson ran into a house and onto the roof and killed a sniper before the boys got there. Two other snipers leaped easily onto a balcony of the next house. Johnny missed the second one by inches. Before he could reload, Cal's shot cracked out and the man fell to the narrow alley. There was no time to think. Alexander pulled a wooden box, which the snipers had used for cover, to the corner of the building and the three of them became snipers themselves, directing their fire onto the rooflines down the street.

Johnny could see Colonel Davis waving his arms and running in serpentines, back and forth, directing his men. When it seemed he would succeed in gaining a still higher house where his men could silence the fire pouring from the windows across the street, orders came again to retire. Johnny couldn't hear Davis's reply, but Alexander Gibson's, next to him, was unprintable.

"They've done it to him again," he fumed.

Davis regrouped his men, but by now the situation was critical. Mexican cannon were trained on the street by which they had to make their way back. Every few minutes fire raked the cobblestones. After the first three volleys they could almost count the intervals while the Mexicans reloaded. In those intervals Davis ordered his men to run in groups of two or three under cover of the smoke.

But the Mexican snipers were good. They would rise up, stand a second with elbow out, head bent, taking careful aim. Eight Americans fell. A cannon blast killed one. The one was Tommy Cunningham.

Once back in camp, Johnny couldn't believe it. He wouldn't believe it. Against his uncle's orders he went to the morgue, where John Henry and some of the horseholders had been assigned. "Where is he?" he begged a chaplain, standing to one side. Rude coffins, hastily put together, had not yet been closed. "Don't . . ." the chaplain said, but it was too late. Johnny pulled back the cloth on the first one, then the second. The third was Tommy. Half his face was gone.

Johnny wheeled and ran into the trees, down the road toward the town.

A sentry caught him and demanded roughly, "Hey, what're you doin', boy?" Two soldiers pinned his arms and marched him to headquarters.

"This here feller's out of his head," one of the soldiers told the orderly. "Better tell the adjutant, or else he'll cause a rout."

Behind his desk Albert Sidney Johnston pushed aside papers and came forward. "You can let him go now, boys. I'll see to it." In the fresh air behind the tent he held the boy, doubled, while he retched. "It's all right, Johnny. It's all right. Nothing to be ashamed of."

Shame! That had nothing to do with Tommy's face. It wasn't himself he was concerned for. Didn't Al Johnston know that? Didn't anybody know anything?

The next day, September 24, 1846, after General Worth's division had secured the heights and captured the bishop's palace, the Mexican General Ampudia sent a flag of truce asking for a parley. A committee of three, Colonel Davis, General Worth and Major-General Henderson, the governor of Texas, were to negotiate the Mexican surrender. Some considered the terms too liberal, but General Taylor, ever a practical man, thought more of saving lives than of political plaudits back home. General Ampudia was to evacuate the city by ten o'clock the following morning. The Mexican Army, however, would be allowed to retire below Saltillo, forty miles to the south. An armistice of eight weeks would be declared, time enough for further instructions from both governments.

"It won't work," a colonel mumbled. "The Mexicans will just regroup at Saltillo. They've never been known to honor a truce yet."

Colonel Davis argued that with less than half the force of the enemy and no heavy artillery, it would be folly to demand unconditional surrender. "We are lucky, with our numbers, to have come this far. But for the fortitude of our troops we would all be lying dead at the foot of La Teneria."

A general at one end of the table, with tight black waves held down by thick pomade—the scent reached even Alexander Morgan, at the edge of the group—uncrossed his legs, raised up on his elbows, and leaned across the table toward Zachary Taylor, who was lounging back picking at his nails with a penknife. With the happy look of a schoolboy who expects to receive top prize for his answers, the General enumerated on one uplifted finger after another his reasons for demanding more. The Mexicans are cowards. He glanced around. As stupid as they are, even they must know when they are beaten. He glanced around again. If we allow their army to escape, we will only have to fight rested troops rejuvenated by the six weeks or more it will take instructions to come from President Polk. He nodded at his audience, receiving their silence as agreement. He delivered his final volley: "In the meantime we could be in Mexico City."

Zachary Taylor looked up from his nails, his eyes squinting, as if to register accurately and for future memory the General's face.

"In the meantime, sir, we could all be in hell."

He went back to his nails.

General Worth, across the table, watched the plain, blunt face of Zachary

Taylor, the lines that dropped from the sides of his nose to the corners of his mouth like two fishhooks. It was a fatherly face, a face given to laxness, like his clothes. Taylor had been one of those volunteers who had joined the army and stayed on. Now, those slapdash tactics that had so often caused jokes among the staff—and which Worth considered dangerous—had given way to caution. He was glad to see Old Rough and Ready getting some sense. Worth agreed with Davis. He hoped, when the insecure government in Mexico City heard of the fall of Monterrey, it would sue for peace.

The agreed-upon terms of capitulation were written in English and Spanish—Al Johnston's knowledge being adequate for the challenge—and delivered by Davis, who left Mexican headquarters with Ampudia's promise that the document, with his signature, would be ready "as early as he should call for it in the morning."

By evening the whole camp knew that the next day would tell the tale. Alexander had John Henry wake them early and rode with his nephews and a dozen or so others the three miles to town. At the edge of the street leading to the Grand Plaza they dismounted and waited in full view of the armed infantry lining the flat roofs while Davis and Johnston, in his red flannel shirt, walked their horses slowly toward the square. The air was thick with silence. Davis's Arabian pranced a little as they approached a barricade, its gunners in place. Johnston raised a white handkerchief, and Johnny could see them stop and Davis say something to the artillery captain. A soldier was sent inside.

No one, not even Cal, made a sound. Behind them a horse, shaking off a fly, jingled his bridle, and his owner caught up the reins and held them firmer. Delilah stood like a statue, as if she understood the breathlessness of the moment.

A second messenger was sent in. He, too, did not return. A third was sent. Davis and Johnston were between the end of the barricade and the wall of a house, an area just wide enough for one horse to pass. While they were waiting, a woman in the house opposite saw Johnston's floppy hat, leaned out, and yelled derisively, *"Tejano!"* A crowd came up and they were blocked from view.

"What are they doing?" Cal whispered.

"Let's hope nothing," his uncle replied, reaching unconsciously for his revolver, then returned his hand to his wounded arm and the sling that hugged his chest as if to keep in the tension. Through a break in the crowd Johnny could see a Mexican officer on horseback in the narrow passage and Johnston turning his own horse deftly to block him.

"What's going on?" Cal asked again.

"Shhhh!"

After half an hour Johnston and Davis returned. The crowd made way for them. When they reached the end of the street the Americans silently closed ranks around them, still unspeaking. Once past the last houses they broke into a canter and dismounted, their throats tight with questions. They knew Davis and Johnston would have to report to Taylor before they could get news, but that didn't make the waiting any easier.

On Friday, the 25th of September, the Mexicans marched from their impregnable citadel and the Americans marched in, playing "Yankee Doodle" to the booming of twenty-eight guns from the bishop's palace. By the 28th the last Mexican soldier had gone; in three days Zachary Taylor had won a battle more significant than any in American history, said Davis, since Yorktown.

"Until the next one," Alexander Morgan murmured. Where was the boyish calling out, the eager "Wait for me!" at Transy? Tommy Cunningham was dead, who loved a coon hunt almost as much as hot biscuits. Alexander said again, to nobody in particular: "Until the next one."

The coffins were removed to wagons to await the trip back to the Rio Grande and the boat to Point Isabel and home. That night Johnny dreamed of turning wheels, so feeble they seemed against the rocky earth downhill.

In Washington City the news of the fall of Monterrey was received with wild enthusiasm. By all but the Democratic administration. That Zachary Taylor, a Whig, should be the national hero was repugnant—if not dangerous—to the political ambitions of those who hoped to keep a Democrat in the White House. President Polk was careful, then reluctant with his praise. Kentucky's Senator Crittenden defended Taylor on the floor of the Senate, reminding his colleagues that the Americans had been outnumbered and ill-supplied, had negotiated the best peace possible under the circumstances. Saving American lives in the face of a better equipped, larger enemy was no small feat. But his colleagues chose to be censorious. The truce was terminated a few days before its expiration.

Davis was in gloom. Taylor wrote in his own defense that "it was thought it would be judicious to act with magnanimity towards a prostrate foe particularly as the President of the United States had offered to settle all differences between the two countries by negotiation." Not to mention, he said privately to his adjutant, by outright purchase of the land under dispute. Johnston, as bitter as Davis, said nothing.

The squabble in Congress over Texas, which had kept up ever since the annexation debates, led John Quincy Adams to declare that the whole Texas revolution was only a scheme to establish a new slave market. John C. Calhoun insisted that annexation was necessary for the protection of Southern interests. And now, with California and New Mexico added to the ante, the North had produced the Wilmot Proviso, closing former Mexican lands to slavery. The card game for political power was in full swing again. Taylor called his orderly for a fresh bottle of whiskey and toasted his adjutant, and then himself. "Old Rough and Ready, was it?" he said aloud. And under his breath he added, "I may have been rough in my time, but I was not ready for this."

He must have been more ready than he realized, because he was not even surprised when he received the new battle plan: His army would be depleted in favor of General Winfield Scott, who would march on Mexico City through Veracruz. Eighty percent of Taylor's troops were to accompany Scott to the capital.

"Eighty percent!" Taylor stormed to Davis. "What do they expect us to do, kill Mexicans with tortillas?"

"If we wait, that might just happen anyway," Davis grinned, trying to make a joke of it.

The sight of Davis seemed to awaken Zachary Taylor from a sleep. "Oh, yes," he said. "Sit down. There's a personal matter that came in the same dispatch. The government is refusing to pay Al Johnston for his service as adjutant-general, on the ground that his assignment by a commanding general gave him no legal status. This, even after Butler and I recommended his promotion to brigadier after Monterrey. Now I don't want to lose him. What do you think I should do? Can you talk to him?"

"Nobody changes Al's mind," Davis replied wryly. "Especially if he feels his honor's been involved."

He was right. Colonel Johnston left for his Texas plantation, near Galveston, with an invitation to Alexander Morgan and his nephews to visit him if they could. They watched him mount his big bay gelding and trot north, a straight-backed man in a torn checked coat, with the frayed brim of his hat flopping around him.

"You'll not see the likes of him for a long time," Alexander murmured behind them, and Johnny heard, once again, love for another in a man's voice.

Among those they watched depart for Point Isabel, where a boat would take them to Veracruz, were Sergeant Havens and the button-nosed boy from the campfire. So he's alive, thought Johnny. And a warmth that would have surprised him a month ago rose in his chest for this stranger. But there were no strangers now, especially among those who were left. He would miss Joe Havens. They had been abandoned, reduced by more than half, and half of those were raw recruits. But raw or not, Taylor refused to wait with them at Monterrey as ordered. He had no intention of giving up hardwon territory, or of retreating to the Rio Grande to become a supply depot for Winfield Scott. He moved his army twenty miles farther into Mexico, to Agua Nueva.

It was, as Taylor wrote in his official report, a beautiful and healthy position high on the Mexican tablelands at the foot of the Sierra Madre—and, he added to his staff, it was completely boring.

The Mexicans had disappeared into thin air.

They waited, played cards, and waited. Almost daily, "Old Rough and Ready" rode Whitey out into the surrounding countryside, as if he were taking a morning constitutional. His absence became so habitual his staff never expected him to ride up until after breakfast. The "Regulars," who at first took some interest and pride in showing off to the volunteers, stopped drill. Only Colonel Davis kept up discipline. Colonel Marshall drank.

The political maneuverings which had depleted Zachary Taylor's army had also given permission to an old enemy, Antonio Lopez de Santa Anna, scourge of the Alamo, captured by Sam Houston at San Jacinto but seven times the chief executive of Mexico and now an exile in Cuba, to pass through the American blockade so that he might "stop the war." Santa Anna promised his friends in Washington City "a good American peace . . . after the Mexicans have been slightly chastised for their misdeeds." Maybe, Polk thought, he could still buy Texas and California and New Mexico—as Jefferson had gotten Louisiana. That would surely squash Taylor's popularity and ensure a second term!

The Mexicans promptly made Santa Anna, the hero of Mexican independence who had lost a leg fighting the French, their commander-in-chief. At San Luis Potosí he gathered an army of twenty thousand and started north in a carriage drawn by six dove-colored mules. Sad-eyed but resplendent in his elaborate uniform, he was supremely confident. With his leg propped up he turned to his gamecocks, in cages behind him, and crooned softly, "Do not worry, my little darlings. We shall show these Americans what valor is! We shall show them our talons and give no quarter!" And his body servant, whom Santa Anna had ordered to play "Adios" on his guitar, strummed louder, his eyes never leaving the Generalissimo's brown, sweating face.

On February 21 a scout brought the news to Taylor: Santa Anna's cavalry were less than a day's march away.

Zachary Taylor opened his chest and rose to his feet. When he strode from his tent he seemed much taller than any of his soldiers remembered. As if by magic, an energy snapped through the troops. Within an hour, tents came down, supplies were packed, stores too heavy to carry were fired, as well as the wagons, and a double-quick march brought them to a narrow pass close to a ranch called Buena Vista.

Outnumbered four to one, the Americans waited. Santa Anna had a reputation for being shrewd, but Taylor had so arranged his men in deep gullies backed by hills that their situation was, even in Davis's view, a strong one. Those early morning rides on Whitey had paid off.

"I hope so," said Alexander Gibson, checking his revolver.

It was Washington's birthday, and the watchword was "Honor to Washington." Taylor himself, once his men were safely in the ravines of the ranch, had trotted off on another morning ride. On his way back he was greeted by the sight of twenty-five hundred Mexican horsemen charging down the valley toward his troops.

Unaccountably, the Mexicans stopped just beyond the rifle range of the Americans. Taylor made it back to the ravine, where he soon learned why: Under a white flag Santa Anna had sent a message demanding surrender.

Brevet Major William Bliss, a West Pointer on Taylor's staff and engaged to Taylor's youngest daughter, cleared his throat and watched his future father-in-law. "A formal reply . . . that's the best way to gain time," he said.

The old man grunted, but agreed. While Santa Anna's messenger waited, Bliss, fluent in Spanish, wrote swiftly, and handed Taylor a paper to sign. Taylor read it with distaste.

"Obedient servant, indeed," the old man mumbled as he scratched his name.

Santa Anna attacked that afternoon, when the sun was hottest. Before nightfall he gained a ridge and the Americans fell back to a plain at the foot of that rise. Stalemate and a sleepless night: cold and starless. Knowing that guns were trained up there in the dark didn't help the effort to get some rest, although they knew they would need it desperately. "Sleep, boys." Alexander Gibson tried to keep his voice light. "There'll be time enough to keep awake tomorrow."

At daybreak the shooting started, and the Mexicans began moving in three columns. The American left gave way and started running.

It was then they saw him: Zachary Taylor on Whitey, in full view. He had ridden that horse, an indisputable target, where his troops—and the Mexicans—could see him. The left regrouped, and when they saw Davis's Mississippi Rifles, with two extra companies, move off under heavy fire toward a strong position held by General Ampudia, memories of Monterrey made some of them set up old Injun yells and run, headlong, to help. The fire was blistering, and the Indiana volunteers fled pell-mell downhill. Davis pleaded with them, and with his confidence they marched back to the relief of the others. It was in that interval, when Davis stopped his horse and stood long enough for a Mexican musketeer to take aim, that a ball found his foot. Brass splinters from his spur dug into his flesh, the shot shattering a bone. He rode on, and from where he watched, Johnny could detect no slackening of the attack.

They were busy enough themselves, for the Mexican artillery started a barrage and Colonel Marshall, sober for once, directed Captain Beard's company to a protected gully just behind a row of chaparral. The hiss and whine of artillery—at no measured interval, but punctuated by short, sometimes long pauses, to explode suddenly, unexpectedly—kept heads down. There was no way to tell where the Mexicans were, or how well the Americans were doing. Marshall's orders were to hold their ground. Between volleys horses whinnied in the distance; Johnny worried over Delilah. Then they heard yelling, and couldn't tell at first whether the shouts were joyous or fearful.

It wasn't over yet. Santa Anna's cavalry appeared on the left, determined to capture Taylor's artillery. Over the rim of their relatively safe gully Captain Beard's men watched Davis's regiments form a deep V, its ends fanning out to either end of the ravine, to receive the advancing lancers. Johnny couldn't help admiring the Mexican riders, and Cal, by his side, whistled. Both horses and men were covered with ornament, the men in braid, the horses jaunty with tassels jigging from their blankets. They came in beautiful order, so close they looked like some giant insect with upright tentacles. The Americans in the V waited, and still on the lancers came until, more and more crowded, canters became trots, jogs became walks. They seemed almost to halt within eighty or a hundred yards of the Mississippi rifles, which opened up in one thunderous volley that sent smoke swirling among the jumbled mass of fallen horses and screaming men. That such a parade of polish could explode into seared flesh in an instant was a memory John Morgan would always hold in his brain. Again and again he would remember it, and even though they were the enemy, those horsemen, like their horses, were magnificent.

"What stupidity!" his uncle was murmuring beside him, but there was elation rather than sympathy in his voice. Johnny set aside his own pity for the victims of that senseless slaughter. They should have taken a lesson from Will: They should have dismounted, thrown away those cumbersome lances —and the tradition that went with them—and fought for their lives.

It was then that Colonel Marshall ordered his regiment to mount. With Bragg's artillery and Davis's rifles, they were to attack the enemy at the base of the mountain. Johnny's throat was dry with fear and anticipation. He mounted Delilah and put all memory of those Mexican lancers out of his mind. Fools! He would save himself and his horse if he could, his honor if he couldn't. No marching into traps for him. He looked over at Davis's men, plodding parallel to his own company. Taylor, ahead and giving orders, halted the columns and the Mississippians scattered for cover. They didn't have long to wait before Santa Anna sent the brunt of his attack to the right.

Broken ground and boulders kept the action from view, but the crack of muskets told the direction. Captain Beard's company dismounted and joined some of Davis's men to support the crumbling line. Once over the rocks and after running about two hundred yards, they saw through the smoke the Mexican infantry marching on Bragg's battery, which, in the rout, had been left unprotected. Bragg stood there, ordering shell after shell, oblivious of his silhouette against the sky. The men around Johnny and Cal gave a yell, stumbling over the rocky plain. They took aim when the Mexicans were within a hundred yards of Bragg's guns. A terrible explosion on all sides broke out: Johnny had never been in the middle of a rifle volley before. When the smoke cleared the Mexicans were gone.

All that afternoon skirmishes flared on all sides. Once, when his men were trapped hopelessly, Santa Anna sent a flag of truce, and while Taylor waited, expecting negotiations, the Mexicans maneuvered to safer ground and Taylor had new cause to swear. "So he's a swamp rat just like I am," Old Rough and Ready rasped. "Very well. So now we know each other, for all his fancy respects. I wonder who he got to write his letter for him? Some renegade American?" With renewed fury, Taylor ordered the Illinois and Kentucky volunteers to charge Perez's corps of lancers, which outnumbered the Americans six to one. Even from this distance Johnny could see them standing four deep, their horses' chests swelling under breastplates, the pennons on their lances fluttering—a wall of horses and men, waiting.

Henry Clay, Jr., was one of the volunteers, and called over to Alexander Morgan as they rode off, but the sound of hoofbeats covered his words. Instead, he flashed a smile and waved his sword. Johnny drew his legs back, turned his toes out and felt Delilah's instant response as his spurs touched her sides. Sweat ran under his hat and matted his hair, and Delilah's shoulders, bunching with her plunging reach, smoothed out into a gallop under him. This was what he had waited for, to ride like the wind! Ahead he saw a line of Mexican uniforms and a blur of lances catching the sun. Before he knew what was happening, Delilah brought him into the midst of onrushing horsemen and between two lancers. His legs hugged Delilah. A lance slashed the air above his head. He threw himself down past her mane, as he had seen the Comanches do, dug his legs in her sides and spurted between the two horses at a full gallop, then turned, fired and missed. *Ain't I tole you, Will's* voice came, *nobody kin aim right from a hoss?* The next time he got a chance, though, he didn't miss. Will would have been proud of him.

But the air seemed full of sabers, lances, the bent backs of uniforms, the flashing of braid. Choking with dust and not believing his eyes, Johnny saw three lancers bearing down on Alexander Gibson. Yelling at the top of his voice he saw his uncle grab his chest and fall, his body turning over and over under the horses that went on, his own horse stumbling off streaming with blood. He was about to ride over when a sound behind him sent shivers down his spine: the unmistakable jingling of Mexican horse trappings. Johnny didn't even look, but sent Delilah into a dead run. All around, the Americans were flying as fast as they could back to their own lines. Mexican Lancers might have been packed useless in Davis's trap; here on an open plain they were death with five legs, and the fifth leg a shaft of Spanish steel.

Men and horses lay everywhere. Afterwards, tacticians would say that Taylor's orders for that charge had been foolhardy, a risk only a volunteer would have tried. Its failure seemed to clear the old general's head. As calmly as any West Pointer full of charts, he gave new orders. Serene on Whitey, he sat while bullets slit through his shirt and ripped open his coat. Relentlessly, the American batteries kept up a murderous fire. Through gut-busting fatigue the men on the ground loaded, reloaded, fired and fired again. At about five o'clock the Mexicans retreated from the field.

Back in "camp"—that gully which had taken on the coziness of home— Johnny collapsed. Cal and John Henry came in later, and they sat huddled together in the unreality that Alexander Gibson Morgan, that encouraging optimist who had nursed them like a mother and had ridden with them through the mosquitoes of Arkansas and the dust of Texas, was gone. That brother of his father whom his mother looked down on—as she had looked down on Wash and old Gideon and most of the Morgans—for his gambling and his boyish ways. He had been a man today, Johnny thought grimly. How would they get his body home? He would have to be buried in the Bluegrass. Johnny couldn't think of him in this hostile land.

"Pardon me, Massa," John Henry said with native practicality. "But we's bettah think of gettin' home ourseffs. This heah war ain't ovah yit."

"I'll go see Colonel Davis," Johnny told them. He was, now, the only old friend they had left. Then another fear shot through him: the memory of Davis's wound. But he had ridden on. Perhaps it wasn't so bad after all.

He wasn't at the headquarters tent, where Taylor's staff had settled down for a night of uncertainty. Brevit Major Bliss sent Johnny to the hospital wagon, a covered affair from which the wounded were emerging, some on stretchers, from the makeshift operating room. That day's casualties had been over six hundred—counted so far, a distracted surgeon told him. He would have to search for himself. Johnny found Davis on a low bed in a tent that had been set up to receive the more seriously wounded. His boot, before he had finished the charge up the ridge, had filled with blood, and splinters from the brass spur were threatening blood poisoning. But it wasn't for himself that Davis moaned. Henry Clay, Jr., had not returned from what they all silently called, to themselves, Taylor's folly.

"I didn't see him," Johnny said, full of his own sad news, which he couldn't put into words. *If'n as long as you don' say it, mebbe it won' be so. . . .*

But it was and he knew it, and before Davis could comfort him a fresh wave of pain broke on the Colonel's face and sank his body back on the bed. General Taylor, who had been told Davis was dead, appeared. "I told them I didn't believe it," he said gruffly. "My poor boy," he muttered helplessly. And then, as the old soldier of Black Hawk days took over, he added: "But I do wish you had been hit in the body. You would have had a better chance of recovering. I don't like wounds in the hands and feet. They *cripple* a soldier so . . . he can't run." The old man's concern was such that he didn't notice the grin that came on Davis's face, even through the pain.

That night was endless. When will they be able to get his body? Johnny thought. And then the horror that every man felt after a battle, when he saw a buddy fall: Suppose he's not dead. Suppose he's out there now, passing out and waking up, passing out and waking, getting weaker, in pain? From the gully they could see the reflections of Mexican campfires. What would the next day bring?

John Henry woke them early. Johnny, surprised that he had slept, spread a wet cloth across his face and handed it back to John Henry, who squeezed it out in the inch of muddy water in the basin and handed it ceremoniously to Cal. Cal scrubbed his neck and hands, and as the memory of his uncle returned, his morning cheerfulness faded. He swallowed hard. Would they live to see another sunset?

When Zachary Taylor's soldiers emerged from their gullies and ravines on that February morning on the ranch known as the Beautiful View, they received a better vista than any of them could have wished: The army of Santa Anna had disappeared.

12

Sergeant Joe Havens had never been so thirsty or hot. The nine miles from the old camp at Camargo down the sluggish Rio Grande to Brazos Island had been bad enough. Now there was this infernal waiting. It was tolerable when he had gone on down, after leaving General Taylor, and joined Scott's siege of Veracruz. That had been three weeks of action, all right! But when Scott's army went inland, following Cortez's old route to Mexico City, he was kept at Veracruz and then sent back north to Brazos to protect supplies. He heard of Scott's victory at Cerro Gordo as the first river boats with the boys from Buena Vista came in. He ran down to the dock looking for buddies.

Overhead a lone buzzard circled slowly, casting lumpy shadows over the baggage, horses, and men who were unloading. A line of pine coffins waited in the sun. He found Johnny and Cal standing disconsolately to one side, watching them. He'd heard of Henry Clay's son being killed, and General Butler's wound. The absence of Alexander Gibson worried him. Maybe he's supervising the unloading of the horses, he thought. He never did trust John Henry around them horses.

His worst fears were realized when he saw Johnny's face. Even after almost three months, disbelief and a refusal to accept the truth stamped a sadness across his eyes.

"How's that mare of yours?" Havens asked, by way of greeting. "Good thing she didn't come with us to Veracruz. What a rough time we had on that there open water. If'n I ever get back to the hills of Tennessee, I'm never leavin'."

He was relieved to see Johnny's sweet smile, although the eyes remained remote. Cal, as always, was more talkative, and as they walked to the area where the horses were stepping reluctantly down a ramp from the river boat onto dry land Cal recounted their march from Monterrey to Agua Nueva and the situation after most of the troops left. When it came to the cavalry charge against the lancers, he fell silent, and it was Johnny who told Joe about their uncle.

Joe Havens screwed his eyes to the blazing sky and down again. "He was a fine man, he was. You boys kin be proud of him. . . ."

Havens's worn, leathery face came into focus again and Johnny told him about the others: what had happened to Colonel Johnston, and that Colonel Davis was wounded and on the boat with them. Joe, as if showing his own hand of cards, offered news about Cerro Gordo, how Santa Anna had placed thirteen thousand Mexicans across Scott's path, but how Scott, with ten thousand, had outflanked him. Then Havens remembered Tommy.

"Say, I'm sorry about yore friend."

"Tommy? I'm sorry, too" was all Johnny could say. He was so sick of death. He wanted life. He wanted to gulp it down in great throatfuls and they had to wait two weeks in the heat of Brazos Island, cleaning gear, getting horses ready for the boat trip to New Orleans. When they could, they watched seagulls.

The morning Delilah's turn came to transfer from the lighter which took them to open water and the waiting steamboat, Johnny, for the first time, came close to despair. She stood on the large open barge that was rolling in the waves, her hooves threatening to slide on wet boards, her head thrown back, her eyes rolling. She could panic and break a leg, he thought. Or even worse . . . go overboard. He surprised himself by his own trembling. How he loved her. She had taken him through all that firing, waiting patiently for him. And he could still feel her sides against his spurs when he ran through the lancers. If she hadn't obeyed him then, he could be in one of those boxes now.

General Taylor's Old Whitey, veteran that he was, made the transition from the barge to the steamship in good form, taking the intervening space as if it were a log in a pasture. Delilah was next. When a soldier struck her on her rump to make her follow she began snorting and rearing, her right hind dangerously close to the edge. When she came down it was with such force that the lighter sank in the water on that side and a film of water puddled around her, making the boards even more slippery. John Henry yelled and almost felled the man with his fists. The soldier, afraid of being trampled or thrown overboard himself, sank back. John Henry retrieved the lead rope and began an inarticulate, soft baby-talk that calmed her enough for Joe Havens and Johnny, on the steamboat, to coax her toward the edge. Then Johnny, holding a second rope, called her gently. Delilah crouched, and for an instant he thought she would rear again, but she was evidently waiting for the lighter and the steamboat to reach the same level. Then she made her move, a smooth, flat arc that landed her safely on the other side. Joe Havens looked down at the water and let out a whistle.

Eleven days later they arrived in New Orleans. Zachary Taylor was hailed as a national hero, and Colonel Davis, on crutches, his face occasionally shot with pain, heard his name linked with Lafayette and Andy Jackson. They were the first returnees from a war that had all the trappings of a carnival: ill-equipped volunteers who had marched off to do battle with a foreign, treacherous foe. To hear the crowds at the Place d'Armes you would have thought the war was over, when in truth General Scott was at that moment crossing the Valley of Mexico with an inadequate force to face Santa Anna on his home ground, in the streets of Mexico City. Blaring bands, firing cannon, weeping women and inexhaustible orators filled the humid Louisiana air with more noise, Cal whispered, than they had heard in the cornfield.

But what did it matter to these people that soldiers were still sweating in Mexico? They needed heroes, and the ladies in their chemisettes of white muslin and their tiny parasols looked down from lacy balconies or across to the stolid Cabildo and watched the line of horses and carriages that passed before the cathedral and threw handfuls of gardenia blossoms as the procession wound its way through the Vieux Carré.

Almost as soon as they landed, the Morgan boys were sought out by old business friends of their grandfather and of the young doctor who had died in a duel. "John Wilson Hunt. I knew him well. Tragic end. But for love and honor. And I see you boys have upheld the family name." A packet of letters from home awaited them, with a sizable bank draft from John Hunt, and Johnny guessed that his grandfather had written ahead and arranged for these invitations to stay at palatial homes in the Garden District. He declined, for himself and Cal, and took a room at the St. Louis Hotel, where Colonel Davis and some of the others were staying, until steamboat passage upriver could take them to Louisville. It was as if the silent coffins which accompanied them—the news of Henry Clay, Jr.'s death had reached New Orleans by carrier pigeon and aroused much concern—required their services until the inevitable leavetaking occurred. Jeff Davis was in charge of Clay's remains and, because of his wound, anxious to get home. He chartered a steamboat which would stop at the smaller landings; three days after he arrived in New Orleans with his Mississippi volunteers, he made his farewells.

The night before he left a great ball was given in their honor. Neither Johnny nor Cal had ever seen anything like it. The marble-paved octagonal rotunda of the Exchange Hotel, with its great dome 185 feet high, overflowed with people, and if excitement had been combustible, would have exploded. Cal, who at twenty was now sporting a mustache, endured his brother's teasing. They were both tired from the day's parades and speeches, the blaring horns and the handshakes. Secretly, Johnny wished he could be with John Henry, taking care of the horses down at the docks. "You like dem?" Cal mimicked. "You wand one fo' yo' own? Dad kin be haranged."

It was true Johnny had never heard language spoken as if it were savored, like the taste of a good cigar. Aunt Betty's broken bits of French, sandwiched between the shakings of her forefinger, were pristine Parisian beside the patois they heard all around them. "Yo' wand disserd?" the waiter at the St. Louis had asked. And Cal, who had caught on easily to the slurring, easy talk, answered, "Hof coze. Fedge me zum."

The ballroom buzzed and sparkled. Candles in crystal chandeliers cast spangled light over the moving splendor of lace and embroidery, of crepe capotes falling away to reveal jeweled necklines and bare arms and open bodices filled with the froth of muslin and ribbons. The gentlemen were no less wonderful than the ladies, and Johnny's broadcloth "best," worn out from dust and grime, had been replaced by a replica, bought the day before in one of the fashionable shops in the Rue Royale. It was there he met again the friend of his uncle Johnny. He was himself a doctor, a Monsieur Le-Breton, whose wife and niece, across the ballroom, descended on the Kentucky boys when they were pointed out to them. "You muz visit wid us, Captain Morgan," Madame insisted. "We hav' one off de bez 'ouzes in de Faubourg Sainte Marie. You will kum?"

Cal answered for them, his mustache concealing his grin. "Hof coze . . ." And then, under Johnny's frown, he dropped the clowning: "Of course, Madame, we would be delighted."

"An' now," the lady continued, before her husband could speak. "Whad bisniz do I have, keepin' deeze brev zhent'men frum hinjoyin' demselves? Kum," she said, almost as an afterthought, "May I hintrodooze you to mah neeze, Eugenie?"

Cal redeemed himself by asking Madame LeBreton to dance, while Johnny, under the smiling permission of the doctor, guided Eugenie Villard onto the floor.

She was dark, her black hair caught back and shining, her face long and tan, not the tan from the sun, but an inner gold that seemed to come, as the brown of her eyes, from some hidden source. Her mouth was soft and solemn, but when she laughed her teeth flashed, small and even, in that otherwise boyish face. Her slender waist, caught tight in silk, slipped under his hand. He had to hold harder, and she took the added squeeze as a little joke, to be enjoyed secretly between them. His apology died on his lips. This wasn't, her perfume kept saying, Kentucky; here other rules, unspoken and old and European and undying, operated. Her bare round arms lifted to his shoulders as they started the waltz, and he regretted lessons never taken at Madame Mentelle's. It had been too long since he'd felt lighthearted. But his fumbling only seemed to amuse her, and after he stepped on her satin slippers for the third time, she took his hand and led him, running in mock desperation, into a side room. It proved to be a smoking room where four gentlemen were playing cards and filling the air with fumes from their Havanas. Pretending to be modestly offended by their masculine activity, Eugenie rolled her eyes and sighed heavily, waving her hand in front of her face as if she would faint. They laughed, taking her pantomine as a compliment, and she, in turn, used it as an excuse to open the tall leaves of a French window and drag Johnny onto a balcony. He closed the window behind them and they found themselves confronted by the city, strangely silent after the din inside.

A dim fog had settled over the river and from somewhere the smell of baking bread lingered through her perfume. The awkwardness of the dance floor left him and he leaned back against the rough brick of the building, his shoulder touching hers, as they looked over the iron railing at the sleeping town.

"An' whad does your name mean, this Morrgan?" she asked, so seriously that he almost laughed.

"Why, I hadn't thought. Nothing, I guess."

"Hmmmm. French names usually men someting. LeBreton mens de one from Brittany."

"What does yours mean?"

"Vee-yarr? Id wuz once Vieillard, old man . . . *les vieillards*, old pepple."

"You will never be old," he ventured.

She surprised him by jumping away from the wall and turning to him, pressing cool fingers on his lips. "Don' say dad! I wan' to be old. . . . You are crezzie, you Americains! I wan' to, *Dieu sait*, grow verry old." Her eyes fell to his mouth and her face, close now, blurred.

"You will always be young, inside."

"Where, inside?"

"Here." He laid a tentative finger on the white chemisette.

"No . . . here." She moved his hand lower, to one side, and cupped it. Even in the half-light, she could see his blush.

She laughed out loud, a little girl's laugh, and he thought of his sister Kitty, who at twelve was the family flirt. But Eugenie was more than a flirt. She was mischievous, startling, insanely startling, startlingly insane. And above all, alive. She had been with him half an hour, and already he felt as if they had known each other always. It was as if she were playing a game, openly, invitingly, one by one, laying out her cards. First the perfume, then the slippery silk, then the eyes, and the soft mouth concealing sudden laughter and then, with little purses of her lips, giving him her thoughts with that silken-soft language. It was delightful. He was in another world, here on this balcony, in the dark. No, in no world at all . . . He found it hard to breathe. She wouldn't help him, but looked again at his mouth, waiting. Then she lifted her eyes to his. "Are you brev?" she asked. She had divined his secret.

"Are you?" he asked her in turn, the next morning, propping himself on one elbow and tracing with his finger the full curve of her mouth. She had led him, down some side stairs, to a town house in Toulouse Street that her father kept for business in the city. The maid, a plump mulatto, had admitted them, and accepted the arrangement that Mademoiselle would spend the night.

"I still can' billiv you . . ." she said, then laughed aloud, throwing her head back on the pillow, spilling her hair around her like a shawl. It only partially covered her bare shoulder, which he covered now with the sheet, kissing her neck as he did so.

"Belliv it," he murmured.

"Bud you are . . ."

"Twenty-two," he moaned against her throat.

She held him away from her. "You are yo' mama's boy. Thad's why," she said. "Otherwise, for the rez . . ." She slipped her hand down his chest. ". . . Doze Kentuckee girls don' know whad dey haf missed."

"Ah, well, mebee dey do," he grinned back.

She turned instantly serious, and frowned, pursing her lips. "It goes so *fai-fai*, Johnee. Lif'. *Mysterieuse. Fai-fai.* I wand to ketch it wid bof han's . . ." She held them up and he caught them for her and brought them to his lips.

He tried not to think of Tommy. Had he ever loved a girl?

"I know it goes fast," he said. "Believe me, I do."

"Whad do you wan' from life, Johnee?"

Why was it she couldn't talk small talk, like the girls in Lexington or his Aunt Anne? She was probing, probing. "Everything," he answered.

She nodded and sat up. The fringed black shawl of her hair covered her breasts, from which one pink nipple shone like a rose. *"Tou' c'ose,"* she whispered, as if to herself. "Yez. Everyting."

Her look was so sad that he said loudly, sitting up himself and throwing back the covers, "Say, I'm hungry enough to eat burgoo."

"Burgoo?" She laughed. *"Qui ci ça?"*

"Kee See Sah?" he mimicked.

"Whad is dad?"

"Oh," he said, rising and pulling on his clothes. *"Dieu sait, ma cere,"* he said mysteriously, *"Dieu sait."*

"And whad will you do?" Eugenie Villard asked, once they had dressed and finished breakfast, served by the mulatto, in the courtyard. A breeze picked up damp air through the carriageway and blew spray from the fountain in the center of a flowerbed.

Before he could answer, three young men about his own age spilled down small wooden stairs from a wing of the house he hadn't noticed before. It was the *garçonnière*, she explained, a section reserved for the young men of the family, and these were her brothers. "You mean . . ." Johnny started, but their laughter finished his question.

"Hof coze," Julien, the youngest, laughed, reaching for coffee. "We had to kum to de ball. An' when did you gid hom'?" he asked his sister, but before she could answer he called out to the maid, who was watching them from the kitchen doorway, "Fedge me some mo' *café*, plez, Jou-Jou." To Johnny's questioning look, he added: "We call her dad . . . for so long now we forgod her name."

"Jou-Jou iz bebbe talk fo' 'play-ting,' " Eugenie explained. "Bud," she insisted, leaning on her elbows and crisscrossing her fingers and resting her chin on her joined hands in a very businesslike fashion, "whad will you do?"

"Till I'm mustered out? Stay at the hotel, I suppose."

A chorus of protests rang out. No, no! He would visit their father's sugar plantation on the river road. Their mother, an invalid, would delight in another young man to entertain . . . Oh, well, then his brother was *hof coze* welcome, moz welcome . . . They would arrange it. Johnny left them still lounging in the shadowed sunshine dappling the old round stones and the fountain, drifting now with oleander blossoms that had fallen when Julien, in his haste to reach for the coffee, had shaken it.

Cal, dead asleep on his stomach, smelled of whiskey and moaned when he shook him. It was already after noon. Colonel Davis's chartered steamboat was due to leave about midday. Johnny had seen him briefly and only from a distance last night at the ball, propping himself painfully on his crutches and putting on a considerate smile. Johnny went to his room but there was no answer, and the clerk at the desk informed him that Colonel Davis with his party had already left. At the dock the Mississippi heaved like a breathing animal. There was much activity: Boats creaked as they pulled against their moorings; stevedores shouted, men hauled ropes, black backs sweated in the humidity. To his question one steamboat captain, himself ready to run up a gangplank, lifted an outstretched arm. The speck he pointed to, just going out of sight beyond a bend, was the slowly churning paddlewheel of Davis's boat.

A sense of loss hit Johnny low in the stomach. He never knew, until he watched that shadow blend with the shore willows and the sandbars, how much he loved those men: Al Johnston and Jeff Davis and the boy with the bumpy nose. Where was Joe Havens?

He turned and walked along the Rue du Canal, then into the Vieux Carré, down the Rue Dauphine all the way to Esplanade, then back again. Behind the cathedral, on St. Ann Street, some colored nuns nodded to him in their starched headdresses. The smell of damp alleyways and baking bread was everywhere. In the market, open stalls seemed to have spilled out the wealth of the sea: oysters, shrimp, crabs, fish of all kinds, their sides gleaming silver against green melons and caged parrots. Three Indians, folded in long dirty blankets, offered him a live songbird—*"Grit bon-bon,"* the oldest said through ashen wrinkles—or something that Johnny took to mean "Great good." He declined with a raised arm and stopped to buy a cup of chicory, feeling its warmth revive him. He went back to the hotel room and crawled in with Cal. He could sleep for a week.

Cal woke him that afternoon rattling the pages of the *Picayune*.

"What could be so interesting that you have to make so much noise?" he grumbled.

"Well, for one thing, news of our friend Sergeant Havens," Cal answered with a chuckle.

Johnny sat up.

"Want to hear?"

"Don't tease me, Cally. I've got a headache."

Cal grinned. "What was her name?"

"Whose?"

"The owner of the scented handkerchief in your pocket."

"Oh,"

"I'll tell you if you tell me."

But he wasn't quick enough for Johnny's hand, which had reached out and grabbed the paper. "It's on page three," Cal said, relenting. "But I'd still like to know her name."

"Eugenie," said Johnny. "And it's all very . . . *gentile.*"

"Is it, now?"

"We've been invited to her home . . . plantation on the river."

"Oh, it's gone that far, has it?"

But Johnny had found the article and bit his lip in thought, then threw his head back and laughed. Brawling, drunken soldiers had been thrown in jail. When questioned, they said all they wanted to do was to go back to Kentucky so they could fight in peace.

"I'll bet Joe was one of them."

"He's from Tennessee."

"No matter. How much do you wanna bet?"

The question was so natural, so like their uncle Alex, that both of them sobered. "I think we should accept your friend's invitation," said Cal off-handedly, turning his face down in an effort to button his waistcoat. "Do us good, after Mexico."

It was said that a Louisiana sugar plantation was worth ten cotton ones in the Delta, and maybe fifteen or twenty hemp farms in the Bluegrass. When Johnny saw Oak Allée he could believe it. A long avenue of arching live oaks, planted more than a century before by the first Villards from France, led from the river to broad, squatty columns whose width belied their height, for they reached the full two stories and enveloped all four sides of a substantial mansion. Boxwood-bordered brick paths were everywhere. Eugenie, with her three brothers, greeted them on the deep porch. "Let me introdooz you," Eugenie said to Cal, smiling at each of her brothers in turn, Olivier, Edouard, and Julien. "Now you muz meet Mama," she said, taking their hands and leading them up broad stairs to an upstairs bedroom. From its windows her mother, ensconced in a huge four-poster, could watch the river winding off in the distance.

"I count seventy, sometimes eighty steamboats in a day," she said unceremoniously to them, as if she had known them all their lives. But she spoke in French, and Johnny tried to respond.

"I've been told my French is abominable," he said falteringly.

"Monsieur, with those eyes and that smile, you have no need of language," she surprised him by answering in flawless English.

It was true. Madame Villard was Boston-born and educated, as it turned out, at the same school for young ladies in New Jersey where his aunts Mary and Theodosia Hunt had gone. "It was a horrible school," the lady sighed, "full of rude girls trying to get polished." Then she laughed, and he saw again Eugenie's delightful smile. "But that is where I learned French. And if I hadn't wanted to practice my French, I would never have come to Louisiana, and I might not have met your father," she said, turning to the girl at the foot of the bed, who smiled back.

"She fell from a horse after Julien was born," Eugenie explained without embarrassment, as the boys took Cal to show him the stables and Johnny sat beside her in the garden. "That's why she won't let me ride sidesaddle."

"You ride?"

"I am the shocking example for the whole neighborhood," she laughed. "Astride . . ." She leaned to him, mimicking astonishment.

Where can we? his eyes asked. And hers answered: Not here. Perhaps later. I'll let you know.

"I admired your mare as you rode up," she said aloud.

"She's steady," he answered.

"You rode her in the war?"

"Yes. In the war."

"What was Mexico like?"

"Mexico." He looked at her, sitting on the bench in her morning dress, a printed cotton high at the throat, where a small flat collar of lace primly framed her neck. He remembered kissing it, the scent of her, and he wanted her again, that instant.

"You said once you wanted . . . everything," he said, looking off toward the low-reaching, moss-draped limbs of the old oaks.

"*Tou' c'ose*," she corrected.

"*Tou' c'ose.*"

"Yo' French iz gidding bedder," she smiled. "It iz rilly *tout chose* and I know bedder." She tossed her thick hair, closed her eyes and sighed. "*Mais mo pas capabe mague . . .*" Then she remembered him and switched to English, as surprisingly good as her mother's: "But I cannot make life boring. Id iz too briff," she lapsed into her patois again and smiled.

"Wad you wand?" he grinned. "You wand dis crezzie Americain to cud his troad?" And he made a slashing movement with the side of his hand. She caught it and held it, then dropped it and unbuttoned the high collar of her dress, drawing out a gaudy picture of the Sacred Heart, framed in crochet. She untied the ribbon, slipped the scapular off and pressed it in his hand.

"Keep dis," she said.

"What for?"

"Good lug. *Dieu sait, ma cere, mo pas conne. . . .*"

"What don't you know?" her fourth and oldest brother Etienne, who had not yet met Johnny, laughed. "Don't look so serious, Gennie. Or are we interrupting a tryst?"

His Aunt Anne would have flown at him, dissolved in tears. Eugenie just laughed, stuck out her tongue and with a wave of her arm presented Johnny. "Eel ay *sans peur*," she said stoutly. "An' dat is mo' den Ah kin say fo' *youz. . . .*"

It was true. A Louisiana sugar plantation did outrank a Bluegrass farm by many acres. Their grandfather, even at the height of the hemp business, had never worked more than eighty slaves at his looms or in his ropewalks. At Oak Allée more than two hundred hands moved in fields of cane. There was a brick factory, a gunshop, a blacksmith shop and the sugar mill, a rambling cypress building with presses turned by mules, which could have contained three ropewalks.

Eugenie changed clothes and gave them a tour, showing them the vast copper-lined vats and black kettles, each with a name—"grande," "flambeau," "syrup," "battery"—and the furnaces for each set of four kettles which consumed sixteen cords of wood a day. She said it all matter-of-factly, leading them to the cypress cooler tanks, and then to the draining room where the hogsheads would gradually leak into big molasses cisterns underneath. It was all quiet now, waiting for the October harvest. The quarters looked like a small village, with neat, crushed oyster-shell streets shining white between rows of cabins. Eugenie rode down them on a small gray Arabian as easily as her brothers, and looked like them in her black broadcloth trousers. Johnny had never seen a girl ride so well—unless it was Amanda. But Amanda never sat a horse as if she were following a waltz.

They did meet again at the house in Toulouse Street. While Cal rode with her brothers and her mother thought she was visiting her aunt. A mockingbird drank from the fountain, then perched on the oleander and jumped up and down, up and down, as if in some ritual dance. "He is calling fo' his made," Eugenie said, rustling the covers as she gathered them in front of her. She leaned out the window watching him.

Over her shoulder he could see the river.

"You love it, don' you, Johnee?" Without turning her head, she sensed that he was looking off.

"What?"

"Dad Kentuckee."

"Yes." He thought a minute. "Yes."

"Mo' den anyting." She tucked her knees under her chin and hugged her legs.

"Yes. Yes . . . I suppose I do. How did you know?"

"You talk in yo' sleeb."

"I do?"

"So!" She jumped up, suddenly full of energy. "I muz see Madame Dubois today. She iz mekkin' me a new drezz. Dere iz a ball nex' munss. . . ."

He caught her arm and turned her to him, wiping the tears at the corners of her eyes. "And what will you do?" he asked seriously.

"*Moi? Ma courri c'ez moin,*" she said in patois. "I will go home . . . I will marry some crezzie planter's son. . . . Papa, I think, has already chosen one. . . ."

"But . . ."

"Here, kum, kum. Why don' you get a wardrobe while you are here? Monsieur Hebert in the Rue Bienville. He is de one. He can mague you a splahndeed suit. . . ."

"Splahn-deed?"

"Like no ting you will see in dad Kentuckee," she said vehemently, and he guessed it wasn't clothes she was thinking of.

"I'll never see anyone—anywhere—like you, Eugenie."

But she was already slipping on her underthings, a square-necked chemise with little ribbons running through the straps, and pantalettes caught below the knee with bands of silk roses. The gathered waist made a soft white pillow of her bottom as she raised her hands to do her hair. She looked back at him through the triangle of her arm. "You will for-ged me . . ." She snapped her fingers over her head. "Like dad."

"I will never forget you, Eugenie."

He wanted her again, but she unclasped his arms from her waist and walked to the armoire, flipped through hanging dresses and then, to ease his disappointment, turned and threw him a kiss.

"Go down an' see if Jou-Jou kin mague you brekkfass. Ah muss feenee mah toilette." She smiled and let her eyes drift to his. "Aftaire all, eef Ah am going to be seen wif a splahndeed zhent'man. . . ."

She wiggled into her skirt, tying it in front, and reached for her bodice. It was of the finest fabric he had ever seen. If it had been any thinner it would have been a spider's web. He watched her dress as he would have watched a dancer.

"*Allez*," she said, knowing he was watching her and pretending not to like it. She arched one foot and then the other into her slippers.

He dressed and waited a moment at the door. She was already looking in the mirror, tilting her head and tracing an eyebrow with a dampened finger. The tip of her tongue, which had just touched the finger, still showed in the corner of her mouth, where she bit it in concentration.

He went downstairs, to the little table under the oleander. It was a scene that had become so familiar he felt at home. Jou-Jou served him hot coffee and *beignets*, and he watched the fountain while he waited for her.

"Kum," she said after they ate. She held both arms out stiffly, the way children do when they play.

So with the maid Jou-Jou trailing like the wake of a ship, they shopped, Eugenie perching on tailors' stools or watching him try on beaver hats and canary-yellow waistcoats. "Dad is jus' right," she would nod like a matron over a child. "He will take it," she told the proprietor peremptorily, and off they would go to another shop. Within a week Monsieur Hebert's cadre of seamstresses had completed a soft woolen dove-gray coat and two suits with three splahndeed waistcoats.

"Now," said Eugenie when they arrived and were fitted to her satisfaction. "You may go back to the hotel and get your brother and take me to the concert tonight. A violinist . . . is here and they say he is better than Paganini."

Her flawless English worried him. Whenever she used it she was preoccupied, thinking of other things. But he knew it would do no good to ask.

Cal was furious. "Where've you been? Some friends of Grandfather's called and invited us to dine. . . ."

"I thought you were busy riding."

"I can't ride all the time. And John Henry's sick." At Johnny's stricken look he added: "Well, not very. Ate too much good food. You know John Henry."

It was then Cal noticed the clothes, and the boxes on the bed.

"There's a concert tonight," Johnny said as an excuse. His eyes met Cal's and they both laughed.

"Well I must say she has you around her finger like a thread." Then he sent a right hook into his brother's shoulder and they fell down wrestling, laughing until they were exhausted. "Hey!" Cal let out a muffled yell. "It's too hot for this. Besides, I'll wrinkle your fancy new shirt."

The violinist may well have been as good as Paganini. Johnny wouldn't have known. He hardly heard a note. Eugenie had obtained the services of her Aunt Mathilde and that lady, recognizing Johnny from the night of the ball, wagged her chins and spread her fat little hands, which had been squeezed into black lace gloves, across her skirt, patting its folds as if she were petting a kitten. "Well, now," she breathed, turning from one boy to the other, who flanked her on either side. "An' have you been hinjoyin' yo'seffs in New Aw-lins?"

Eugenie, beside him listening to the yearning music of the violin, had every right to act like royalty. Her father had business interests not only in

Paris and London but in South America. Etienne had gone to school at Montpelier, before deciding that he "did not prefer" medicine after all. How Henrietta Morgan, who enjoyed fine things, would have loved strolling through the gardens of Oak Allée! Hints of financial worries at Shadeland had come in her letters, and bothered him momentarily, but he set them aside with the thought that he would straighten out everything when he got back. Got back? He looked from the chandeliers to the red brocade of the concert hall to the creamy shoulders of the girl beside him and felt the aura of her perfume caress his insides. Yes, he might love dad Kentuckee mo' dan anyting, but he never wanted to leave.

Cal was full of surprises. He turned courtier with "the aunt," as he called her, leaving Madame LeBreton beaming with pleasure as the boys deposited the ladies at the broad doorway of the house in the Faubourg Sainte Marie. They declined further use of the family carriage and walked back to the hotel, singing as they crossed Canal Street, unbuttoning their coats to the riverwind, breathing deeply of the scent of marsh grass and, once into the Rue St. Louis, of the ever-present aroma of baking bread that pervaded the Vieux Carré.

But it was Eugenie's perfume that lingered on Johnny's skin, and he hesitated over the porcelain basin the next morning to wash it off. He unfolded for the fifteenth time the little note she had pressed into his hand as they said good night. She would meet him again in the Rue Toulouse that next afternoon.

All the way—which was short, but which seemed forever—from the hotel to the grilled gates of the Villard courtyard, Johnny Morgan whistled. Where it would end he had no way of knowing. The late June morning was glorious. He would be early, and perhaps she would not be there yet. Or perhaps she would, and would greet him in the upstairs room, which had become for him so familiar that he could see, as he walked, the great mahogany armoire gleaming like some giant doorway in the corner. Between buildings seagulls soared and pigeons cooed under ledges as they picked at soft mortar. Pink bricks, blue sky—the smell of a perfume shop. He stopped and bought flowers from a vendor at the corner, the last corner before her house. He could see it from here, as he tucked the flowers under his arm and walked the last few steps to her door.

Jou-Jou met him, hesitantly. Instantly, he knew something was wrong. She took the flowers with a slow nod and ushered him into the little front room, used by Paul Villard as an office. The contrast of the furniture here —all no-nonsense oak desks and upright chairs—was a world away from the room which he would always think of as hers. To his questions Jou-Jou handed him a small blue envelope.

Her father had returned, and she would not be seeing him again.

He went to the river, past crowds in the market, and climbed the levee. From here he could see the square and the cathedral and the ten blocks which had become known as the Vieux Carré—the old square—extending from the river to Rampart Street, from Canal to the Avenue d'Esplanade. Esplanade—in Spanish the same as *Champs Elysées*—those Elysian Fields

where the Greeks said warriors went when they died. He turned his back
on it and looked upriver, to the flat expanse of water, like hot, moving oil,
shining bronze in the sun. He had watched Colonel Davis disappear around
that bend. He would go back too, where he belonged. That's where warriors
went. There was no other place.

Before they left, Cal wanted to see a quadroon ball. And there were
invitations from his grandfather's business friends to be answered. He and
Cal accepted, and sat in stuffy parlors smiling over Sèvres cups, making
proper answers, being polite to plump daughters whose American twang
twisted in Johnny's mind like rapiers. Where was she now? Was she thinking
of him?

"I say," came the kindly voice of an old man who had known John Hunt
in the early days, "I did sympathize with your uncle. It was over a girl, you
know. Miss Carleton. Your uncle had every right to take to the field to
protect his honor, given the circumstances. He had been insulted by his rival
—imagine, to insinuate that Dr. Hunt had used language unbecoming a
gentleman! And, of course, when a young lady was involved—well, there
was no question. But I suppose it is difficult to understand. . . ."

"No," said Johnny so quickly that he shook the tiny cup in his hand and
the lady of the house looked at him inquiringly.

"No," he answered less loudly. "No, it is not difficult to understand.
And," he added, because the lady kept her eyebrows raised, "I am sure that
my grandfather—our whole family—sympathized."

"Dueling is not so well thought of as previously," the old man said,
allowing his voice to take a neutral tone. "England has already outlawed it.
But I still consider a challenge the proper method for settling differences
between gentlemen."

He saw her only once again, a block away, alighting from her father's
phaeton in a dress full of flounces. Would it have been one of those M.
Villard brought back from Paris? The idea that he would never know seemed
more important than the fact that he and Cal had received their mustering-
out orders that morning and were scheduled to leave in three days. He ran,
but they had disappeared, and he looked into so many shops so quickly that
the proprietors became alarmed, and one threatened him with the police.

The night before they left, Cal saw his quadroon ball. "It's in the Orleans
Theater, just behind the cathedral," he said. "Can't you hurry up? Joe
Havens told me . . ."

"You've seen Joe?"

"Yes . . . while you were busy in Toulouse Street," Cal said meaningfully, buttoning his shirt. "He said to wish you good luck. He's on his way
up the Trace, back to Tennessee."

The Orleans Theater was a strange place. Not far from the cathedral
garden, it had been a dance hall, and then an opera house, and then a mixture
of opera-theater house, until the better class of patrons were lured away to
the St. Louis Hotel and other entertainments. Now it was known for its
"quadroon" balls, where people of mixed heritage could mingle freely under
the anonymity of masks. A little reluctantly Johnny let his mind drift to the

question that had hammered all day: Where was Eugenie? She hadn't answered the note he left with Jou-Jou.

He followed Cal through the doors. The air was blue with smoke, but under the masks the laughter was strained. Painted faces leered at him, and Spanish, West Indian, Choctaw and Louisiana French shouted advice, crooned invitations. An upstairs room in a Lexington brothel came back, the contemptuous eyes of a woman at the door leading Tommy Cunningham into the room with the skinny girls. . . . Johnny Morgan had perhaps had enough of New Orleans. He was glad they would be mustered out the next day. In the Place d'Armes, where they had paraded almost a month before, they were formally thanked for their services to the U.S. Army.

On the way to the steamboat Cal heard loud music and dragged him off to investigate. It was a Negro funeral, and the mourners, dressed in white, were dancing a kind of twisting, shuffling, spiraling column down the Rue Conti, across Bourbon and out to the old ramparts. One boy's body was consumed with rhythm, his face one sweating, blissful smile caught up in the beat. He moved as if in a trance. It was the one last memory John Morgan would keep of New Orleans, this joy in life by defying death . . . no, by accepting it. He hoped, at Shadeland and Hopemont, they could do the same.

Part II

1847-1861

13

They were all there: his mother in the doorway surrounded by her children, little Tom pulling at her skirts, Aunt Betty holding Key, who was sucking his thumb. They were all, unbelievably, there, and for the first time Johnny Morgan realized how much the fear of never seeing them again had taken hold.

Then pandemonium broke loose.

"Marse Johnny! Massa Cal! You home? You home?"

"My darlings! My dear, dear darlings!"

"Tell us about the Mexicans! Did you kill lots?"

"Wanna play some baseball? Papa bought Charl a mitt. . . ."

"An' John Henry! My, ain't you growed!"

Aunt Betty set Key down. He ran on stubby legs into Tom and they fell, rolling. Kitty pulled them up, then sank on her heels in a froth of muslin, looking at each in turn. "You act like gentlemen today, you hear? Johnny and Cal are back!"

"You've gained weight, Calvin!"

"Have I, Ma?" But Cal hardly had time to speak. Richard and Charlton were hanging from his neck, hugging and pounding.

"I'll be eight next month!" yelled Charlton. "Papa says I'm big enough to ride Sard!"

"I'll bet you are!"

"Wanna play some baseball?" Richard repeated, suddenly shy.

"Later," Cal laughed. "We've got to see Pa first. . . ."

"He's down at the office," Henrietta told him, taking Johnny's arm. With Richard and Charlton still asking questions, they walked through the dining room and summer kitchen. Aunt Hannah, in the herb beds, straightened and threw her arms over her head.

"Lawsa mercy! Lawsa mercy!"

Johnny's look asked the question.

"Uncle Ben died during the winter," his mother answered. "Pneumonia. We buried him next to Uncle Isaac. . . ."

Beyond the quarters the trees rippled in the slanting light of afternoon. Just this morning they had arrived in Lexington by train from Frankfort, pushing through the glad, happy crowds to a ceremony at the Court House Square. His grandfather had been there, short and solid in his impeccable frock coat. The coffins would arrive the next day; the funerals were scheduled for the day after. He and Cal bypassed some of the festivities and rode home. Now Uncle Ben, who had been Aunt Hannah's husband for forty years.

"That parsley looks good."

Aunt Hannah's face brightened. "Ah ain't fo'got how much you boys likes it," she smiled. Her thumb rubbed the handle of Uncle Ben's trowel slowly. Then she seemed to wake up. "Lawsey! You boys bettah git yo'seffs downta de office! Marse Calvin down dere!"

"We'll wait here," Henrietta said suddenly, a shake of her head sending a message to Kitty and the boys. "You go alone. Johnny, Cal. Surprise him!" she whispered archly, her head high.

"Ma . . ."

"Go, now!"

They walked down the brick walk to the little office, built on a rise of ground to catch the breeze. Calvin Morgan sat over his accounts in an old pair of corduroy farmer's pants and a homespun shirt open at the neck. He was stirring the air in front of his face with one of the woven willow fans the ladies used in church. Randolph, his shirtsleeves tied back at the elbows with twine, was rearranging ledgers on a shelf. Cal entered first, and there was much back-slapping, scraping of chairs, rustling of papers to make room. "You sure it's safe to come in here? You know how much work disagrees with me!"

"You're back! You're back! I can't believe it!" Their father leaned forward with both hands, taking each of theirs in turn.

"Father . . ."

"Pa . . ."

"Randolph!" But Calvin Morgan didn't finish. Randolph disappeared into the back room, returning with whiskey and water. Gingerly, he poured the gentlemen their drinks. "Randolph." Calvin looked up at him. "You have the finesse of a Greek courtesan."

"Massa?"

"To the returning heroes!" Calvin Morgan held his glass high.

"Hear, hear!"

"You are looking well." The even, toneless words lay across the air.

"We should be!" Cal blurted. "All that good food in New Orleans."

"You received my letter?"

Cal and Johnny looked at each other.

"Well, it's just as well." Calvin Morgan turned the glass in his hand.

"We met some friends of grandfather's," Johnny said too lightly, to put off the inevitable questions. Cal was quick to take it up, with his own version of their New Orleans reception. Their father's eyes, quietly waiting, stopped them. The easy smile below those eyes could not conceal a gentleness that was somehow for Johnny alarming. A red flag of fear went up. Was it the gentleness of grief or of physical weakness? Randolph treated him with a careful, almost courtly delicacy. Randolph's eyes moved to Johnny and Johnny laughed to cover his own confusion. As Calvin Morgan's favorite servant, Randolph's care was only natural. But it wasn't that. There was something new, a conciliatory caution, the air of a nurse at a deathbed. Standing there against the light of the doorway with his massive shoulders, his body a controlled spring, pantherlike in its polite waiting, Randolph had become something more. Johnny caught his eye. It was only a moment. Then Randolph smiled.

"You would have been proud of him," Cal said, and cleared his throat. It was then that Calvin Morgan asked his sons the particulars, and listened, the low sun etching new lines of weariness on his face. Then he lifted his head, visibly setting aside his grief.

He picked up his glass. "To valor," he said into Cal's eyes, then looked at Johnny.

"To valor," they echoed.

Calvin Morgan let the silence settle. "He was my favorite brother."

"He knew that, Pa," said Cal.

"You think so?"

"I know so."

"You came home none too soon," Calvin Morgan took up a new tone and looked toward the door. "Randolph will be a father again. . . . What will you name this one, Randolph? You've got a James, a Jesse, and an Annie."

"Simon, Massa. Simon."

"And if it's a girl?"

"It bes a boy, Massa. Simon."

As if in answer, a horse whinnied. Suddenly Cal could wait no longer. "How's that rascal Sard?"

They walked into the dimness of the barn. Uncle Simon, at the far end, had just heard the news from John Henry. Still, he stared, unbelieving.

"Massa Cal! Marse John! Youze be back! Be back!"

"How are you, Uncle Simon?"

"Fine, suh. . . ."

"How's ole Sard?" Cal asked. He went to the stall door. The stallion strained over the top, trying to bite him.

"He'll be fine if'n you don' fuss him like dat."

Calvin Morgan, his arm around Cal, walked toward the barn door with Johnny. "What would you think about breeding Delilah to him in the spring?" His eyes went from Johnny to the long line of walnut trees that climbed the hill. A single cloud drifted, frayed, was gone. Tomorrow the whole family would meet at Hopemont, then go to the Episcopal graveyard for the funerals.

They had stopped, and the sun on his father's face made Johnny realize how much he had aged. "That would be wonderful, Father. She could have something really special."

Calvin's eyes kept a steady gaze on the sky. "Yes she could, couldn't she?"

Tommy Cunningham's was first. Johnny and Cal as pallbearers kept pace, then took their places by the graveside with crossed hands and bowed heads while the burial service flowed past them. Young Sid Cunningham's face, red as a beet from crying, looked straight ahead. A bird nearby was singing his heart out in the full flush of summer. Green everywhere—in the trees, bushes. Everywhere except in the mound of brown earth waiting.

Johnny tried to concentrate but couldn't. Tommy with his laugh and screwed-up eyes when they used to race horses. On days like this. Tommy fishing, that summer they'd had the duel with Jake Bolton. Tommy with his dirty serape, greeting them at Camargo. . . . Uncle Alex with his plume. It all seemed so long ago, and yet the war wasn't over.

People in Lexington acted as if it were. That reception when they'd arrived, girls in bonnets waving little flags, old men bragging about their own youth. As if they knew about lice and sweat and dust in your throat, and fear. A brown-skinned man, his mouth open with a cry that would never come, a man who had done him no harm. Where had he been buried? What Mexican woman was weeping over him, as Tommy's mother now was?

The war. The war was Tommy's poor face inside that closed box and the thumping, broken body of Alexander Gibson Morgan rolling under legs of horses on the ground.

America Morgan and her son stood a little apart from the Hunts at her husband's service. Only old John Hunt, with his usual reserve, went over, as if silently communicating his appreciation of her husband's sacrifice. Despite their differences, he'd always admired Alexander's dash.

Johnny left the graveside dazed. He didn't want to hear the loose dirt hitting the coffins. He walked past the old stones of the Episcopal churchyard, realizing for the first time that Alexander was gone. What a nurse he had been in Arkansas! *Ain't I Morgan enough for you?*

Yes, you were, Johnny answered silently to a mockingbird who hopped in a tree at the edge of the lane. The others hadn't come up yet and he stood and watched the bird as if its antics held the secret of the universe.

At Shadeland, Henrietta took charge. Her father, T.H. and Robert, just returned from Paris with a medical degree, rode out with them. T.H., whose nine-year-old Mary had died in February, sat with Calvin in the parlor. Alexander had often ridden with him on fox hunts, and his quiet voice talking of those times seemed to help Calvin more than all the condolences he had heard at Hopemont.

Food. Johnny watched them seek refuge in it. As if the body could stand no more, and the stomach would become an avenue toward acceptance, toward living in the world again. Or was it, as his father would have said, that women, with their animal instincts, were simply burying their dead with chicken livers and gravy? Johnny mumbled a polite excuse and walked outside.

He went to the pond and stood throwing pebbles at the water, watching the slow circles move out. Tommy. Tommy fishing, right over there, half asleep under a straw hat, and then almost pulled in by a sudden jerk on his line. And he'd never told his grandfather about the brothel. Now he never could.

He took a deep breath of the soft air. The sun had already started to swing toward the distant hills. *You love dad Kentuckee, don' you?*

If things had been different, maybe he could have explained. With his grandfather's help he might have finished Transy. He might have gone on to study law or medicine. Or to West Point. Now all he seemed to have were the graves of Alexander Gibson and Tommy. Were they to be forgotten, covered over by mud and food? Down in the stores they were selling Buena Vista and Cerro Gordo hats . . . "light enough for summer wear." Young Dick Curd had one. A Buena Vista hat!

If they only knew what they had named that stupid hat for. Zach Taylor on Old Whitey and that foolish charge. Alexander Gibson, the lancers . . . and then the cruelest blow of all, at Hopemont this morning.

Everybody was in the parlor. He had stepped into his grandfather's office to get away from talk. There was the no-nonsense desk, the ledgers, the accounts in neat rows. On the shelves, day books from years past: how much flour to the Spaniards in New Orleans, or whiskey to the army, or hemp, or horses. The China trade, the bank, and now land in Kansas. Busy-ness. Where was life? On the shelf he recognized a book of his grandmother's. He picked it up and let the pages fall. It was Milton's *Paradise Lost*. He read a passage marked by Catherine Hunt's small hand:

> *God made thee perfect, not immutable;*
> *And good he made thee, but to persevere*
> *He left it in thy power. . . .*

Am I changeable? And to persevere in what? Behind him in the hall he heard his mother's voice—irritable—and his grandfather's consoling.

"Alexander Gibson was Calvin without bad lungs. . . . I can't, I can't forgive him for encouraging my sons to go off to war like that!"

"Yes, yes. Calvin, too, would have been as impetuous. . . ."

He was glad his grandfather's office had a door to the street. He walked out into the air, taking great gulps of it, and only then allowed himself to cry.

Cal walked up, then squatted, poking a stick at the grass. He looked across the pond. "You helped him, Johnny. Tommy wouldn't want . . ."

"No, no, I didn't. I gave him shame."

"How?"

"He graduated. I dropped out. He couldn't speak to me after that. That's why, in Mexico, he stayed away from us. You didn't notice?"

"Hey, we were pretty busy, remember? We'd hardly gotten into Camargo . . . we moved out the next day."

Johnny didn't hear him. Inside, he was reliving a vision of that lonesome kid, angry and rejected and sad, standing there with his knobby knees by that lilac bush. He couldn't tell Cal that. Then he couldn't help telling him, to purge himself.

"You remember, it was the day Wash bet you you couldn't catch a fish. We were in the springhouse."

But Cal had forgotten.

"I yelled at him. I . . ."

"He wouldn't want you to—"

"No, I know."

Cal waited, then said quietly, "I saw Sid this morning."

Johnny said nothing.

"I mean . . . to talk to. He told me the government's requisitioned two regiments of infantry from Kentucky . . ."

"Sid! He's just a kid. He can't be fifteen."

"He's almost seventeen. Like Tommy, he's tall for his age."

"But what would Sid Cunningham do in an infantry company?"

"That's what he said."

Johnny looked at his brother.

Cal cleared his throat. "He wondered if you'd be interested in starting a volunteer cavalry company. Round up some of the veterans from Monterrey . . ."

Johnny stared in disbelief. "What did you say?"

"You know how I feel about going off to war again—Mexico or anywhere. I've had enough, thank you. But I thought you'd like to know."

"Oh, yes. . . . Well, I'll have to thank him for his confidence."

A dog barked down at the barn.

"It wasn't entirely Sid's confidence," Cal was saying. "Tommy wrote home from Mexico. I guess he said some pretty nice things about you."

A breeze stirred the heavy tops of cattails and sped across the surface of the water like a fan. "Tommy . . ."

"I know. It's crazy, isn't it? Who would want to get shot at again?"

The memory of an old red shirt, a floppy hat, a gray Arabian's slow walk under the trained eyes of Santa Anna's sharpshooters. Two men who had lived in the vortex and had survived. Would he ever see the likes of them again?

"Yes . . ." he said absently. "Who would?"

At Will's, nothing had changed. Zep ran out to meet them. Will, slightly drunk, sat against a post on his porch running his fingers up a dog's back. When he discovered a tick he pulled it out and snapped it between his nails, then flipped it to the ground.

"Hey, Amanda!" he croaked. "Come out here an' see this here fancy ridin'."

"I seen all thet fancy ridin'," she complained from the dogtrot, but her face was rosy with a grin. Johnny's eyes traveled over the outlines of her body. She sensed his appreciation and met his eyes with a laugh. *You know, now, don't you?* her eyes said. And his answered: *You know I do.*

But a restraint—the restraint of class, of the knowledge that an abyss separated Will's log cabin from the big house at Shadeland—held back her inclination to welcome him physically. She must have felt his disappointment: She reached out and touched his arm briefly as he dismounted, then let her hand drop—not demurely, as a Lexington girl would have done, but with a quiet sort of resignation. Her arm, tan below the pushed-up sleeve, fell limply into the folds of her skirt. He smiled and she answered with that tilt of her head which caught, as he had remembered in a hundred dreams on the plains of Texas, the golden light of a Kentucky afternoon on the flat, smooth skin of her face. Freckles still sprinkled her nose, and her dimples were deep enough, as Will joked, to drink coffee from.

"Amanda, fetch us thet jug uv whiskey. These here boys cain't go off ta war with dry gullets! Lemme see yore gun, boy."

"They ain't goin' off ta war, Paw. They's just been."

Cal handed over his Colt Paterson. "See, Will," Cal said to cover his embarrassment, "it's got a flask with five nozzles, so you can load all five shots at once!"

"Well, I never. And you, Johnny?"

"The same. We've got a pair."

"Well, I never! Ain't like them flintlocks that 'ud hang fire and hafta be reprimed." He aimed the gun at Cal, who ducked.

Johnny accepted his cup from Amanda's tan hands, her eyes avoiding his. He drank in silence, hearing the old man ramble on, Amanda's presence still disturbing. The whiskey stung his throat. How could he joke about Mexico? It wasn't a cockfight. The Mexican lancer had been brave, and Tommy, and Alexander Gibson, but Fate had wrung their necks, just the same. Eugenie was gone from him forever. He looked at Delilah, her back dappled in shade. There was only one thing that seemed to matter, the memory of real valor. . . . Davis and Johnston walking up that death-quiet street in Monterrey, the woman yelling *"Tejano!"* and the mouth of a Mexican twelve-pounder looking down. . . . God, nothing here—money or talk of horses or "What will Johnny do with himself now?" (unsaid but on all their faces at Hopemont)—nothing mattered against that comradeship, that almost holy alliance of men bound together in a knowledge of death and the meaning of life. Maybe Sid was right. Maybe he should try for a cavalry company. He looked up to find Amanda watching him, her eyes soft, her face serious.

"So what will you do?" she asked, echoing his family.

"Pick up the pieces," he said, suddenly embarrassed. Of all the people he knew, he wanted most to talk with her. The irony was, that of all the people he knew, she was the least equipped to understand.

The barbecue was set for August 4. It was to be a "festival to do honor to our heroes." Calvin Morgan was busy for a week organizing the parade of fire companies and a military band—his assignment as a committee member. With Henrietta, Richard, Charlton and Kitty, he rode into town in the carriage; Cal and Johnny would ride in later.

The streets of Lexington were packed. Where had all these people come from? There was an air of carnival. When they saw two boys in uniform, a cheer went up. Johnny and Cal pushed through a knot of carriages and wagons at Cheapside and had just enough time to hitch their horses in the carriage yard at Hopemont before they found their places in the group of veterans forming on Main Street.

A militia band was first, their horns held straight from their faces. Then the fire companies passed in review. The files of volunteers, answering the cheers of the crowd with chests thrust out and faces beaming, brought up the rear. James West, Bill Messick, John Sisson, Van Buren Sellers, Alex

Tribble—men from Fayette, Bourbon, Scott, Clark and Montgomery counties who had shared the dirt and grime of Mexico now shared the glory. It was impossible not to feel proud.

The closer they got to the Transylvania parade ground the thicker the crowd bunched, spilling over into North Mill Street. As the veterans marched up, the human wave parted, broke and bunched again around the tables, arranged in a square a hundred yards on each side. Great cauldrons of burgoo were bubbling, and kegs of whiskey and rum stood on sawhorses with their spigots handy. On a platform draped in bunting Johnny saw his father, his grandfather and his uncles T.H. and Key Hunt. Suddenly he was in a circle of his own: boys who had been with him in Memphis and Camargo, and others, like young Sid Cunningham and John "Cripps" Wickliffe, from Bardstown, who wished they had.

"Say, have you heard the latest?" James West grinned. "Ole General Trigg's been given the Medal of Honor for his part in the Battle of Monterrey!"

A roar went up from the veterans. They knew he wasn't there.

"Where was he, then?" young Dick Curd asked.

"He was in his tent . . . with the results of a laxative," Cal giggled.

The disbelief on Dick's face made Johnny laugh out loud.

"You don't believe me!" said Cal. "I tell you, Dick, most soldiers don't worry about diarrhea. They're scared shitless!"

It was the wrong thing to say. Dick turned away. He was wearing his Buena Vista hat.

"*Their gallantry . . . beyond the call of duty,*" came a voice from the speaker's stand. "*Truly SPARTANS OF THE REPUBLIC!*"

Ruffled parasols twirled. When the toasts—fifteen in all—were over, the girls turned their attention to the heroes. Johnny had been standing, his foot against a tree, his arms folded across his chest. He uncrossed them as Emilie Todd, with three of her schoolmates from Madame Mentelle's boarding school, came by.

"Ah understand you might raise a cavalry company," Emilie said as she examined her glove, before she raised her eyes to his.

Unconsciously, with an air of self-assurance that they evidently found irresistible, Johnny Morgan straightened. Emilie was wearing something silky and embroidered with little red roses that rustled when she moved. Behind her, a girl with shining blond curls bouncing on her neck pinned him with her gaze. The band struck up again and he had to raise his voice to answer. "Yes, I've heard. . . ." The music stopped and he looked around at the eager faces. "There's been some talk of raising a cavalry company."

"Oh, you will do it, won't you, Johnny Morgan?" the blond pleaded. A fan came out, opened, fluttered.

"Sam says he'll reenlist if you get one." Emilie's eyes sparkled.

"Tell your brother to get his horse ready," Johnny joked.

"Do you mean it? Do you really mean it?" they squealed.

When they left Cal turned to him. "You can't be serious."

"Why not? It wasn't so bad, was it?"

"That depends on whether you're insane or not."

"No, seriously . . . the war will end any day. If we can get a company formed and attached to one of those regiments, we could get commissions. . . ."

"We? *Shheee*," breathed Cal, just like Aunt Betty.

Johnny hadn't heard him. His eyes went back to the platform, where his father was standing, shaking hands. Suddenly tears stung his eyes. They were doing this for Alexander Gibson. Getting a company together didn't seem so silly after all. What would he do here, anyway? Run the farm? With Cal back, his father had plenty of help for that. Help Uncle T.H. in the bagging factory again? The Hunts didn't need him. His grandfather had said often enough that they should have a military man in the family. Why not?

Before they rode back to Shadeland, John Morgan had signed on fifteen would-be volunteers. By the end of the month he had enough to present a muster roll to Colonel Manlius Thompson.

"But we have no quota for cavalry," the Colonel said, after expressing his thanks.

"Perhaps special authorization can be given, sir. . . ."

The Colonel looked at the eager face. "Perhaps . . ."

Just in case, Johnny penned a letter to the War Department, applying for a commission in the regular army.

On his next trip to Hopemont, his grandfather surprised him by offering his office as "headquarters" for the recruiting. "It should prove convenient. You could have your rolls filled in no time." The eyes were kind. "There is no neutrality," the old man added. "In war or in business. I had to choose, as you have to choose. I sometimes think it's nobler to choose the military. A battlefield is at least honest. Makes life simpler."

So you will help me? Johnny's eyes asked.

"I have a friend . . . in the Treasury Department." John Hunt lowered his cigar and patted the ashes in a dish. "A small connection, but perhaps he could help."

That Hunt condescension again. Still, he needed help fast. He hadn't told anybody, but some of the men were already talking about withdrawing, especially the veterans. It was already the first of September, and Thompson's Third Kentucky Regiment was due to rendezvous at Louisville. No authorization had come from Washington. Johnny nodded.

"I'll see what I can do," his grandfather said.

On September 14, General Winfield Scott captured Mexico City. The war was over.

14

"**W**hat?"

"I said I'm going anyway, if I can."

"That's crazy," Cal moaned. "Why go anywhere? Hey, Uncle T.H. needs help running the factory. I heard him say so myself. You helped him before. . . ."

Johnny shook his head. "Only as a temporary thing, after I was kicked out of Transy. No, don't you see, Cal?"

His eyes sent the message silently: *I've got to find my own life and live it.*

Cal's round face suddenly broke into a grin. "All right, Johnny. But prepare yourself. Your first battle will be with Ma."

By October 5 John Morgan's cavalry company had disbanded.

"I doubt if another can be recruited," he wrote his grandfather's connection in Washington. "But I am still very desirous, sir, of obtaining a commission in the regular army. I am, at present, engaged in no business; waiting to hear from the seat of Government. Could you not obtain for me an immediate answer from the President? Are not the letters of recommendation which I've sent sufficient? If they are not I'll send more."

He read it over and almost tore it up. Begging. Downright begging. What the hell. He mailed it anyway.

The work at Shadeland moved imperceptibly through its seasons. He helped Cal in the office and realized again the slim margin with which they operated. Cotton prices had dropped, which meant a lower price for bagging. But the price of labor remained the same.

"The Cunninghams are trying tobacco," Johnny offered.

"But tobacco takes even more hands—the setting, the stripping. . . . Besides, we would need a larger drying barn."

"Well, what about mules? Mr. Clay has done well with mules. Those cotton farmers never were any good at raising their own livestock." He smiled, but Cal missed the joke.

"You may be right," Cal said. "I'll think about it."

In the middle of hemp harvest Maggie had a baby boy. He lived two days. They named him Simon.

"It may be a blessing in disguise," Henrietta said as they walked back from the burial.

"Henrietta, how can you say that?" Calvin Morgan looked at his wife's clear gray eyes, her broad brow. She thought, sometimes, too much like her father.

"Well, what are we going to do with them? Shadeland is not Mount Brilliant, or Castleton, or even as large as Papa's other farms. We simply can't produce enough income for all our people. We need to sell some of them."

"We're doing all right."

"Now. But what about next year, and the next? I've heard Papa talk."

He knew she was speaking the truth. "I'll think about it. When . . . if the time comes."

They had reached the house. Henrietta pulled off her shawl. The others had not come up yet. She laid it on a chair by the fireplace. "I didn't tell you," she said. "Everyone was so busy. We've had an offer to buy John Henry."

Her voice was firm, and he waited a minute before he could trust his own. "Who?"

"Jake Bolton. Since his father died, he needs a hand with the ferry."

Her father, Calvin knew, would not have hesitated. By law, Kentucky could no longer import slaves for the downriver market. That encouraged exportation. It had always been discreet. But this summer, for the first time, a trader named Robards advertised in *The Lexington Observer and Reporter*. Calvin had seen the list:

> Jesse, 45 years old, a piece off one of his ears, a scar on one side of his forehead, and his right shoulder bone broken.

> Mose, a stout black boy, who has a burn on his buttock from a hot iron in the shape of an X, his back much scarred from the whip.

> Alex, who has had his ears cropped and has been shot in the hind parts of his legs.

> A negro girl called Callie . . .

For sale. Down at Magowan's slave jail. He knew, once John Henry sold, Henrietta might want to sell others. He couldn't do it.

Besides, Robards was continually in litigation. It was well known that his agents kidnapped free Negroes near the Ohio River. He had so much "stock" that he'd had to lease a jail from old man Pullman and set up slave coops in the yard. They were plainly visible along Mechanics Alley in Lexington, fetid, stinking cages. The moans and coughs could be heard all the way to Broadway.

"I know all that" was Henrietta's objection when her husband worried out loud. "But can we reform the world? We would be careful. We would choose the purchaser."

"Would we?" Calvin answered more than asked. He was still watching Aunt Betty, with Charlton and Kitty, walking back from the graveyard. "And would we know who the next purchaser was, and the next?"

"We don't know about your horses."

"As much as I love horses, Henrietta, people are not horses."

And for the first time in their married life, Calvin Morgan stalked out of the room away from his wife.

Am I to blame? she thought. It's like a web, a trap. We are locked into this insane system. Some of them are good—Bouviette is priceless. Some of them are worthless. Most of them are worthless! Made even more worthless by Yankee talk.

They have an inexhaustible flow of new labor with the Irish and now the Germans, she argued with Calvin, listening now in her mind. *And if they don't work they can fire them. Can you fire John Henry when he sleeps in the middle of the day?*

If you want to be really *practical, Henrietta, John Henry does more work than Uncle Simon. Would you sell Uncle Simon?*

Of course not! Do you think I'm heartless?

But it was an imagined conversation, for there was no Calvin there.

He had tramped out to the pond, where Johnny found him casting pebbles at the water. A shimmering green dragonfly hovered, then spun away. Wind parted the cattails and threw their upside-down images onto the swaying surface.

"You know about the offer for John Henry?" Calvin asked.

"This morning. I haven't had a chance—"

"I don't want you to think I'm refusing the sale because it's Jake Bolton." Plunk.

Why not? Johnny wanted to ask, but kept quiet. His father's face, sad enough at the burial, had darkened even more.

"It's not because it's Jake Bolton that I'm refusing to sell John Henry," Calvin Morgan said harshly. "Although Lord knows I'd hate to see him own anybody. It's because your mother has spoken abut selling some of the children. A sale for John Henry might just start something." He picked up another stone.

"You wouldn't sell them, would you, Father?"

"The children? No." Plunk.

A black and tan pup with its nose to the sky and a turtle in its mouth trotted up. Pawing tentatively, looking off self-consciously as if half expecting to be reprimanded or interrupted, the pup laid the turtle down and jumped back, dipped his chest to the ground and gave out a cracked yelp. Calvin Morgan watched it, then chuckled softly, his eyes on the fields. "The hemp will hold us for a while," he said.

Christmas came with a dusting of snow. The family gathered at Hopemont. John Hunt, as paterfamilias, had never presided over his brood with more aplomb. The English had just invented a power loom for weaving cotton.

"We could be the Massachusetts of the West!" he said for the third time.

Johnny smiled. His grandfather was always getting excited about new inventions. In '38 it had been a horse-drawn threshing machine. In '43 it was a steam sawmill. Last year it had been a newfangled "sewing machine."

John Hunt saw the smile and waited. I won't, my boy, give up so easily, he thought. "You'll agree, won't you, Johnny, that T.H. has made the Hunt bagging factory a landmark in Lexington? Well, now, with Abraham doing well in Louisville . . .

"T.H. needs help," John Hunt went on quickly. "I've already talked to him about it, and he's delighted. With this new loom—yes, I've already ordered three—and that new machine for sewing, we can go into the manufacture of jeans. Good, sturdy work clothes for the West!

"Look"—he warmed to his subject—"we have a chance to get into some real manufacturing. Last year Kentucky exported twenty thousand yards of bagging per loom. . . . That's four hundred yards per week, over ten million yards for five hundred looms! *Now* you see why I'm excited about a power loom? Just think what a steam engine could do! We've got to get onto this bandwagon. We've got to get away from bagging and rope and produce clothing. We can call this operation the Hunt-Morgan factory," he said significantly. "Well, my boy, how about it?"

Johnny felt the letter in his pocket, written just yesterday, to be sent today from Lexington, another request to Washington for a commission.

"You'll need another horse, of course, if you breed Delilah," his grandfather bribed. "Well, now! You don't have to make up your mind this minute. Here come the ladies."

The Curds arrived also, Eleanor with her soft voice and Dick, his sandy porkchop whiskers making a frame for his cheeks, pink from the cold. He brushed back his straight brown hair from his eyes and gave them each a smile. It was too cold, thank God, for young Richard's Buena Vista hat. His brother John went immediately in search of the girls, and Henry, fourteen, tagged behind Cal for more war stories. Their sisters, Mary and Eleanor, scampered to the warming room. Of all the family, Johnny Morgan trusted his uncle Dick's opinions. After the huge meal, the ladies retired and a card game started in the parlor. It was the perfect excuse to talk.

As it turned out, Abraham Hunt, six years older than T.H. and full of a recent trip to Scottish textile mills, dominated the conversation, assuming the air of a world traveler. He had learned a lot since his business failure in New Orleans in the panic of '37.

"As long as Kentucky ties itself to the lower South it must suffer the consequences," he said pompously. He blew cigar smoke. "You know as well as I do, T.H., the Southern planter operates on a one percent margin, drawing on his payment even before his goods arrive in England. When he starts playing that game, some speculator gets the profit. There he sits, with his land and more often than not his next crop mortgaged. It doesn't take a gambler to guess what the next few years will bring."

It was nothing new. Johnny pulled on his own cigar and was about to let his thoughts drift when he heard a touch of scorn in the otherwise calm voice of T.H.

"Meanwhile," T.H. breathed as he picked up his cards, "they watch Mr. Clay and the Whigs support a tariff to protect New England and forget that the lower South needs free trade."

"But Grandfather's a Whig." Johnny softened the reminder with a smile. His cigar had gone out.

"Our father," said T.H. slowly, nodding for approval from his brother, "thinks only a gentleman votes Whig. But he hopes, like the rest of us, to lower the tariff, just the same."

"I still can't see. . . . Wouldn't a tariff help us, if we go into manufacturing?" Johnny asked distractedly, his mind on his hand.

"It will never be lowered anyway," Abraham Hunt said, suddenly excited. "Not as long as we're stepchildren in Congress. Taxation without representation."

"Surely the sugar plantations . . . ?"

"The sugar planters are the worst of the lot. With the rising cost of labor it's a losing game. . . . If they have daughters pretty or bold enough, they sometimes combine their fortunes . . . or misfortunes. . . ."

I will marry some crezzie planter's son . . .

"So you see," T.H. smiled sourly, "our Kentucky downriver trade in mules and hemp is only part of a far gloomier picture."

"And Shadeland? What about Shadeland?" Johnny couldn't help asking.

T.H. waited a minute. He slipped a ten of hearts into its place, then fanned the cards with his thumb. "In another year, maybe less, Shadeland may have to be sold."

After the others left he tore up the letter to Washington and dropped it in the little wastebasket in his grandfather's office. He rode back to Shadeland with his parents in the carriage and watched the leafless forms of trees against the sky. When Aunt Betty greeted them, and Aunt Hannah, and Celina . . . when he went to the stables to see Delilah and Uncle Simon, every gesture, every word slowed into new meaning.

He would have told his father then, but Calvin Morgan took to his bed with a chill. Then, three days after Christmas, Anne Hunt Reynolds died in childbirth. Calvin would be unable to travel, but Henrietta took the stage to Louisville. When she returned he told them.

"Well, I must say they'll need you, with Abraham gone," she said, not even trying to hide her elation.

John Hunt exulted when he received the news at Hopemont. "Rope and bagging and jeans! There's no end in sight, my boy! I wasn't joking! Kentucky can be the Massachusetts of the West! Look at the settlers going into Kansas and Nebraska, and now that Oregon is a territory. . . . Ah, the work is ahead of you, John. How I envy you! If I were a young man now!" He looked through the parlor window at the garden drifting in snow. "Why, when I came here the cow pastures started right over there, right beyond Transylvania's parade ground. Can you imagine? I was a young man not much older than you. Henry was a young man. But don't mind me." He leaned over and poked the fire. "Go see T.H. Remind him to check on the looms. They're supposed to arrive in sixty days."

At the Hunt hemp factory Johnny hitched Delilah and let her drink deeply from the stone trough before he entered. T.H. was in his shirtsleeves, caught below the elbows by rubber bands to keep the cuffs clean. One of the richest young men in Kentucky didn't mind looking like a clerk. He raised his head from the papers before him with an expansive smile. "John! So good to see you!"

"I've taken Grandfather up on his offer."

"You have? That's excellent news!" T.H. rose and extended his hand across the desk. "Welcome aboard . . . ! We'll have a million things to talk about." Then, with a brief twinge of embarrassment crossing his face, he dipped his head toward a young lady holding out her hands to the warmth of a potbellied stove. "You know Betty Wickliffe, of course."

"Old Duke" Robert Wickliffe was the largest slaveholder—and dealer— in Kentucky, and his daughters were notoriously beautiful. Blond, blue-eyed, with smiles to match the electrifying energy that they seemed to cast out from them like nets, they knew the power of their charm.

"Why, Johnny Morgan," Betty said now, extending her hand for a kiss. "It's so sad you couldn't get your cavalry company! Cousin Cripps was ready to ride anywhere with you. . . ." Her eyes flickered from his face, then back again. "Now he's gone back to Bardstown, in a sulk, you may be sure! I've just been asking your uncle here for some advice, but now that you've arrived, maybe you will help."

"Glad to, ma'am." He let go her hand reluctantly.

"I have a suitor who positively *won't* leave me alone. I'd thought of mar-ryin' him just to get rid of him, but T.H. here will *not* give me any advice."

"Get rid of him, ma'am?"

"Oh, don't look so puzzled. You know how husbands neglect their wives once the honeymoon is over! Look at T.H., now. He pores over these books day and night."

T.H., who, as his sister Henrietta often joked, was "the most married man in Kentucky," cleared his throat and shook his head at the question he saw on his nephew's face.

"Now surely, Miss Betty"—T.H. allowed a mock-pleading note to enter his voice, as if he were speaking to a child—"you understand that you ladies couldn't buy those nice ribbons and parasols if we gentlemen didn't tend to our business. . . ."

She moved to the door, conscious that the light played with the blond curls at her neck. "One would think you were blind, never taking the time to notice those very ribbons."

"Oh, don't leave so soon, Miss Betty." T.H. cleared his throat again and rose to his feet.

"I just came by with that order from Papa. He's so glad you've decided to expand into the clothing business. Did you talk him into that, Johnny?"

"No, I'm afraid. . . ."

"It's a capital idea, Papa says. It's about time we emancipated ourselves from those Yankee factories. Besides, the trousers they make fall apart."

"I'm afraid we plan on something much more lowly, Miss Betty. Sturdy work jeans . . ."

"Anything you would produce would have style." She twirled her parasol under T.H.'s chin. "And you know it."

When she left they both stared at the closed door for a full minute. "Does your wife know?" Johnny finally got out.

"There's nothing to know. That's the joke of it," T.H. sighed in pretended disappointment. "Betty's like that with everybody. Have you ever seen a woman more captivating?"

Johnny didn't answer. His uncle stiffened, and when their eyes met, Johnny knew his silence had been misinterpreted: Old Man Wickliffe was a slave trader. How could his daughter be a lady, no matter how much money she had?

"I was thinking of someone else," he said, so seriously that his uncle looked up. "Now what about the looms?" he added quickly, with sudden energy. At his question, T.H. motioned him into a seat, sat down before his papers again, and outlined his ideas.

At Hopemont Johnny was given his old bedroom off the back stairs landing that he had used in his Transy days. Robert now occupied the room with the big four-poster overlooking the garden. Key—Uncle Frank—had the largest room, lined with his law books, but would leave it soon—he had just become betrothed to Julia Warfield. Her father had already promised them some acreage of his plantation as a wedding present, and Key was busy with house plans. Aunt Peggy and Nicely were the only females in the house. Often, with Robert out seeing patients and Uncle Frank busy at his office, the house hummed with silence.

That first week in January the thermometer stood at minus-fifteen three nights in a row. Johnny was glad he had left Delilah at Shadeland. She would be bred to Sard in February. Then the looms arrived and he had no time to think. T.H. would convert part of the long ropewalk into a jeans factory; Johnny would be in charge there, while T.H. managed the bagging operation farther out the Georgetown Road. In the interim, T.H. would help his nephew hire hands and oversee setting up the cutting room. The sewing machines arrived the day the cutting room was ready. These were a new 1846 version of the old lock-stitch machine, using two threads. They could not sew a curve, only a straight line. "Never mind," T.H. laughed. "We'll cut the pattern without curves."

"We'll all be walking around with corners sticking from our bottoms!" Cal joked when he rode in one day, but he was obviously impressed.

The earth churned into March mud and it was May almost before they knew it. He sent for Delilah, and Randolph brought her into town. When the weather warmed into the seventies and the bluebirds returned, Johnny could stand it no longer. He rode to Shadeland. He walked Delilah to the barn where Randolph helped Johnny unsaddle and brush her, laughing at her eager sprint for the pasture when they turned her out.

"She doesn't like town any more than I do," Johnny said as they walked to Sard's door. The stallion was standing quietly, munching hay.

"Do you remember when he used to plaster his ears back and lash out with one of those hind feet?" Johnny asked, his voice seeming loud in the quiet of the barn.

"Only Granddaddy could handle him," Randolph mused.

"Until he let you take over. That was quite a compliment."

"Mebbe it means Ah wuz crazy." Randolph smiled.

Johnny looked at him, this friend of his childhood, the father of three children who was still grieving over little Simon. They walked to the big doors, open to the air.

In the slanting light of sunset they could see, at the far end of the pasture, Delilah grazing. With a little sidewise jerk of her head she tore off a tuft of grass, then slowly, delicately lifted a foreleg as she bit off another, setting the hoof down softly, rearranging her haunches as she ambled to the next chosen morsel. She would graze here in the moonlight, with the fireflies, all night. A breeze stirred her mane. Johnny felt rather than heard the breathing of Randolph beside him. He knew Randolph loved the land as much as he did. And worried over its survival . . . they had both heard Cal's ominous figures often enough. I've got to save it, Johnny thought, any way I can.

He told Randolph good night and walked to the house. Its windows were yellow squares of candlelight. Maybe I should get married, too. Ma hints as much. Find me a rich planter's daughter . . .

It would certainly not ever be Amanda. When he came out here today he had stopped by Will's. The afternoon had been Kentucky-hot. He had discarded his coat and was riding with the sleeves tied around his waist when he saw her. The prospect of a cool drink was inviting. Amanda was on the porch, shelling peas. Will was asleep, Zep was hunting rabbits. Without speaking, Johnny tied Delilah to the grooming tree and sat on the step in the shade, his coat crooked in a finger over his shoulder. Pop, pop. He watched her with a grin. Pop, pop.

"You do that so fast," he said.

"All you have to do is push the rounded part on the back side," she said.

"Let me see." He moved to her chair and leaned over.

"Like this."

"Show me again."

"Like this." She held his fingers over a pea, her thumb on the curve at the lower end.

"Why it works!"

"Of course it does!" She set her basket down. "Now what may I serve you, Johnny Morgan? A cool drink of spring water, or whiskey?"

She rose but he hadn't moved, and they stood facing each other, very close. Suddenly her eyes flooded with tears. What had he done? What had he said? *She's got dimples deep enough to drink coffee from.* John Morgan steadied her chin with his finger and kissed her. She gave him a slap that stung him even after he mounted and rode away. "To my dying day," he told Delilah, "I'll never understand women."

Remembering that slap, he had a frown on his face when he walked into the parlor and greeted his parents.

"Our Johnny is unhappy," Henrietta told her husband after they went to bed.

"Well, there's nothing like a horse race to fix that," Calvin moaned complacently, half asleep. "Just wait until tomorrow. . . ."

But they did not go to the races. That night John Henry ran away.

Cal avoided the real consequences when he told Johnny of it. The panic would spread. The ever-present, senseless fear of insurrection would make the slave-hunters even more vigilant. "Already a posse's forming," Cal added.

Yes, Johnny could see it: the gathering, as for a squirrel hunt. Within the hour the clopping of hooves sounded on the pike. "They're heading for the Ohio River!" a man yelled through the front door. As Johnny closed it he turned to Cal. "They? I thought it was only John Henry?"

"It is . . . but you know how these things get exaggerated. They'll expect us to join them."

Johnny laid a hand on Cal's shoulder. "He's not very bright. Both of us know that. But he's got a good heart. Do you want to go?"

Cal shook his head. As he watched his brother ride back to town, the trace of a smile pushed at his mouth. "I hope he makes it," he whispered.

The posse caught him in a field near Cynthiana the next day at first light. Cal took the back stairs at Hopemont in twos. Johnny pulled on his clothes. A light drizzle had started. "Let's get T.H.," he told Cal.

"And Uncle Dick," Cal added.

The Lexington Observer and Reporter warned of "abolitionists in our midst—emissaries whose business it is to tamper with and run off with our slaves. . . . there is not the shadow of doubt."

Dick Curd nodded, his blue eyes calm. "Yes, but he still belongs to Calvin. He will be returned to his owner. It will be up to Calvin. All this"—his finger tapped the paper—"is sensationalism."

Henrietta was adamant: John Henry must be sold. If not to the Boltons, who probably didn't want him now—besides, she heard they had sold the ferry and moved to Louisville—then to someone else. The price would certainly have to be lower. But he had to go. Even Cal agreed. Calvin Morgan gave in. Ned Baynham had watched the young man handle horses. He could use him on his farm.

"I'm more worried about Johnny," Henrietta said irritably in bed that night.

"Johnny?"

"You don't see anything, you men." She twitched her nose. "It's unhealthy, all this business, business and horse-racing. It will breed sadness. Lord knows, we have enough of that."

Calvin was silent. When his wife's mind seemed to go in circles, he knew it also had affinities with the travels of a bee. He lay on his back, made a pillow out of a cocked elbow and watched the ceiling. He let his own thoughts drift, his wife's voice a purring in the background.

"Most of the girls have gone to the spas," Henrietta was saying with unabashed emphasis. What in the world was she talking about? Calvin chose his words carefully.

"Does Kitty . . . ?"

"Kitty . . . ! Where have you been, Calvin? I've been talking about Johnny. He's unhappy, anybody can see that. A good trip to a spa would do us all good."

Oh, she's only matchmaking! he thought. Well, that's normal enough. With a sigh, he rolled on his side, drew his knees up and allowed himself to drift to sleep.

15

The spas of Kentucky were famous. Louisiana planters and cotton merchants from Memphis and Natchez, bankers from St. Louis and Mobile came to escape "the fever"—that general term which meant malaria. "I strongly advise you to come North this summer, dear Sister," Kentucky relatives would write their downriver cousins. They came to Blue Lick on the Licking River, to Crab Orchard Springs and Olympian Springs, springs with mineral baths and racecourses, hotels with ballrooms and spacious lawns and old trees by streams where children could splash in the shade.

But above all there was Graham Springs near Harrodsburg, the "Saratoga of the West," the most fashionable spa of them all. Its main building had a piazza across the front that could accommodate a thousand guests. Kentucky River packets named *Blue Wing*, *Sea Gull*, *Spread Eagle*, *Jenny Lind*, *Plough Boy* —and of course, now, *Monterrey*—met the Mississippi-Ohio steamboats at Louisville and deposited their passengers at landings along the river. Guests arrived with extensive wardrobes and retinues of servants, who would work with the staff to provide all the amenities. Belles of the day could display the latest fashions: Sally Ward (who would one day marry Dr. Robert Hunt) and Fanny Smith from Louisville, Alice Carneal from Cincinnati, the widow Shelby, the Preston and Wickliffe girls from Lexington and the Poignard daughters from St. Louis. Judge John Rowan's daughters came, and George M. Bibb's granddaughters. New Orleans ladies with small waists paraded under parasols; the more regimented joined walking parties to see the sunrise. Breakfast was served at eight, followed by billiards or impromptu concerts around the piano in the parlors. Moore's melodies might float across the veranda: "When the Stars Are in the Quiet Skies" or "Love's Dream." Dinner was served at one, followed by a nap before the arrival of the stage, where one might greet more friends. Supper at seven, dancing at eight, with an occasional Grand Fancy Masquerade Ball to keep things lively. Reinbolt's Brass Band would provide music guaranteed to reward all comers with "an infinite amount of fun and amusement."

Henrietta read the announcement to her husband the next morning from *The Kentucky Statesman*. "I really do think we should go," she said. "This summer has been miserable. The heat and then that John Henry business. You need the waters."

"I think we should take Johnny with us," he said craftily, waiting for her reaction. "He needs diversion."

"Do you really think so?"

"I do."

"Then I'll write for reservations," she said, ignoring his smile.

After he left, as she dipped her pen at the little writing table in her bedroom, Henrietta Morgan let her mind fly ahead of the words on paper. She was going over a list of eligible girls for Johnny. Emilie Todd: engaged to the Helm boy. Mary Cunningham: away at school. The Breckinridge girls: either too old or too young. The Castlemans: too flighty. Little Becky Bruce: She had been ogling Johnny often enough. A bit too prim, Henrietta thought, and downright skinny, reflecting with distaste on the girl's chest. Then, almost as soon as she thought that, she worried in the other direction; the Morgan men were so . . . she couldn't find a word and ended with "impetuous," when she was really thinking how much they—even old Gideon—had an eye for the ladies. Perhaps a nice flat-chested girl might be best after all. . . .

And Johnny was so handsome! The fact that he didn't realize his charm made him even more irresistible. Cal, in truth, was just as attractive, but Johnny, her firstborn, worried her. There was always something special about him. She remembered how she—yes, how she had fallen in love with the first sight of her first baby. How she had marveled that such a creature had come from her body. She was still, even after seven more children, enthralled by the memory of that first sight of her first baby. She could never tell the others—how could they understand?—that Johnny, the first, was special because he was the one remaining, living link to her girlhood. When she saw him ride or laugh or move across a room she saw her own life as it once was—it didn't matter that he was a boy—she saw herself in him and then, as Cal or Charlton or Richard or Kitty or Tommie or Tom or little Key would appear, she would have pangs about this secret narcissism of hers. Unconsciously she determined to pick a wife for him.

The Bruces, who lived on the corner of North Mill and Second opposite Hopemont, were Presbyterian but prosperous. Hemp, horses and land— the same combination that had proved so successful for her father had made them comfortable. Not wealthy, but respectable. Sanders, the older boy, had gone into the crockery business. The crockery business, she thought, forgetting that her father had started with a store. "And too competitive . . ." she said aloud, forgetting her father again. Older than Johnny but not as old as her brother Robert, who was twenty-eight now, Sanders had always drawn comparisons between his accomplishments and theirs. She thought he was actually elated when first Robert (who actually punched a professor!) and then Johnny was suspended from Transy. *He* had never this, *he* had never that. His father was even worse. The mother was neutral. If her son could have a reasonable mother-in-law, Henrietta could handle her.

She needn't have worried. Of all the girls Johnny met at Graham Springs, Rebecca Bruce was for him the most charming. Others were more vivacious, more forward in their flirtations. But he had drunk champagne on Toulouse Street. Nothing could ever compare with that. Becky's fresh little-girl slimness, her pale face and large molasses-colored eyes were like sips of cool spring water in the hot sun. He was, although he could not have analyzed it at the time, reacting from too much adventure. She was almost like a sister. He had known her all her life.

Now she was a "lady" of seventeen and he remembered her, in bonnet and gloves, standing sedately in the crowd when he went away to Mexico last year. She had changed, with a new, deliciously unconscious coquetry, sweet and pure and ten times more effective than the others. His attentions seemed to generate an excitability that flushed her cheeks. She would watch him with adoring eyes, then laugh a high, lilting, liquid sound, and shake her head in mock disbelief until her brown hair would slip away from her little ears.

"She has no jaw," Calvin complained to himself, half-hoping his wife would hear. "And her mouth's too small. Never trust a girl with a small mouth. They get petulant."

"How would you know?" Henrietta asked him.

He fell silent, pulled on his pipe—a new habit, recommended by Dr. Wolford to replace cigars—and opened his book again.

Picnics at the springs, although organized, were the only activity affording any opportunity for budding romances to blossom unattended by chaperones. Becky, who loved wildflowers, led Johnny away from the group to one clump, then another, naming them: heal-all, starry campion, virgin's bower, bouncing bet, yellow passion-flower. There were the tall spikes of purple false dragonhead, and all the asters: the wavy-leaf, the crooked stem, the calico. The violets and trillium of early spring and the daisies of June might be gone, but she delighted in these late-blooming varieties and made him see more than he had ever known existed, hidden in thickets, under grass, at the edge of woods.

"It's so fragile," she said.

"Yes."

"And the wonder is, they have no one to take care of them. Yet they come up year after year, after winter snows and rains you'd think would wash them all away."

"Yes."

She held a tiny primrose in her hand. "I have Mama and Papa to take care of me. But this one . . ."

He surprised himself by saying, after Mexico: "Maybe God takes care of everything."

She looked at him in mild surprise. "Do you believe in God, Johnny?"

"I do when I look at you."

It was hot. They had wandered so far from the others he had lost all sense of time. They welcomed the shade of a tree by a stream, where he spread a cloth for the basket of food he had been carrying for an hour. She had packed fried chicken, fresh bread and peaches her servant Ellie had gotten from the hotel kitchen. He bit into a peach, feeling the fuzzy skin break and the cool flesh on his tongue. "Have you ever tasted anything better in the whole world?" He tilted his head back, closing his eyes.

She smiled at his question, busy with setting their "table."

"Just think," she said. "The stage will be coming. People back at the hotel will be buzzing around the steps, getting news. Here it seems so peaceful."

"Here it is."

He accepted a piece of chicken and rested against the tree, stretching his legs. She bent her head daintily to her piece and he was amazed at the clean, smooth line of the part in her hair. "How do you get it so straight?" he asked.

"What?"

"Your part. Mine is always all over the place."

Her eyes were soft and level on his as she leaned forward and ran her fingers through his hair.

But he wasn't ready for that, and joked, "Hey, use your napkin!"

She drew her hand away with such a hurt look that he grabbed it and brought it to his lips.

"I didn't mean that, Becky. I . . ."

It was their first physical contact. They finished eating in silence, but it was a silence full of the sounds of their own thoughts. Clouds rolled up, but they didn't seem to notice. After they put the things away he found himself with his head on her lap, in the folds of muslin smelling of lavender. He closed his eyes and a fainter scent—she must use the same soap as Kitty— made him think of home. He stirred, pretending to sleep, and she traced his eyebrows ever so lightly with the tip of her finger, thinking he wouldn't know. He opened his eyes suddenly, to catch her face close to his, and before she could move away, tilted his mouth to hers.

After that, it seemed natural that they should be seen everywhere together. She was so . . . so light, like a doll. He found her frailty somehow flattering. When she leaned on his arm as they followed the "walking party" at dawn—the early hour gave her eyelashes a gossamer look—or fluttered her fan after a waltz, her dependence on his decisions gave him the odd, pleasant feeling of being in charge. With the women in his life—his mother, Aunt Betty, and . . . and especially Eugenie—*he* had been the one listening, following. Now he led for a change. Becky would never be a wife to interfere with him, in business matters or otherwise. (What he meant by "otherwise" he couldn't say.)

Once, the sight of a dress full of flounces almost stopped his heart. The girl turned, and a blond with blue eyes met his gaze. He blushed and Becky, by his side, interpreted his reaction as interest in the girl, who had arrived from Frankfort on the afternoon packet, and he did not tell her differently.

Three weeks later, on her eighteenth birthday, they were engaged.

The day Zachary Taylor was elected President of the United States, Becky Bruce stood in her bedroom for the final fitting of her wedding gown.

As she had done so many times before, Mrs. Martha Dodd Walsh Wilson O'Brien talked with pins in her mouth. She eyed Becky's dress appreciatively. Brussels lace, showing just the hint of crinoline.

"Oh, they make a dress sit so beautifully," she mumbled through the pins to Mrs. Bruce's objections. She took the last pin out as she fluffed the gathered hem to make it fall. "They never crease or get out of form."

"They look drafty," Margaret Bruce repeated.

"Oh, you're always too practical, Mama." Rebecca laughed. "Why, I'll wager even you might wear one next year."

"Wager?" What kind of language is that?"

"*Morgan* talk," her daughter answered impetuously, bending from her waist, her elbows out. She swung around the room. "How do I look?"

Her mother melted. "Absolutely beautiful."

It was true. She had often worried about her frail little girl who couldn't seem to hold onto weight. Now, in the bloom of young womanhood, a new energy infused her. Margaret Bruce set aside her husband's fears, that such energy had perhaps too much excitement in it. "Excitement is not good for young girls, especially of Rebecca's temperament," he had said mournfully, after a dance at the Springs.

"Nonsense," answered his wife, relieved that Becky had shown some interest in young men. "Maybe marriage is just what she needs. The calming influence of a regular routine. . . ." She started to say "in a home of her own" but stopped, knowing instinctively that her husband dreaded the loss of Becky . . . little Becky, who had always been his favorite. And she couldn't deny that she, too, had wished for a better match. Unconsciously, from Becky's sixteenth birthday, Margaret Bruce had daydreamed of one of the Breckinridges, or perhaps a Crittenden, or some young law professor at Transylvania. The Bruce house was almost opposite Henry Clay's law office on North Mill. She had watched Henry come and go over the years, building the estate at Ashland. She could see her daughter in a similar setting, ordering her servants, her life, strolling under big trees.

It was with some consternation, then, that she watched the romance with young Morgan blossom. His father had not the best business reputation around. Although she admired generosity and a certain style—still, one had to be practical. The grandfather's connections were the best, of course. On that score she mollified both herself and her husband. "You couldn't find a more substantial family," she told him.

"And Mister Hunt has taken John into the business," she added, careful to keep her eyes on her embroidery. "There's not a morning goes by I don't see him going to the factory. I must say, you can set your watch by his coming and going."

She had tended, of late, to say only those things for which there could be no argument. Especially to her older son. It was true, Sanders didn't like Johnny, but Sanders sometimes tended to be overly critical, judging people the way he did horses. Margaret Bruce wondered, secretly, if some of his competitiveness wasn't a kind of defense against his own shortcomings. Sometimes she didn't like Sanders so much herself.

So, by degrees, she let John Hunt Morgan's sweet smile and winning ways soothe her fears. He seemed, above all, to be most concerned for Becky's welfare, and she almost fell in love with him herself when he agreed that Becky should not take on just yet the cares of a household.

But where would they live? With a young girl's impatience, Becky wanted to be married *right away*. To her mother's objections she had ready answers. A suitable length to the engagement? "But I've known him all my life, Mama!" John won't have time to build a house. "But Papa says he wants us to live here!" You'll need a trousseau. "But aren't you always saying I have more clothes than I can possibly wear?"

Becky couldn't tell her mother the real reason she wanted to be married in November: She was afraid she would lose him. He was so handsome! She had seen how the girls at Graham Springs had watched him. Who else, who else in the whole world had been as kind to her as John Morgan? She felt so comfortable, so free with him! Freer than she had ever been in her life! And so important! He made her feel so important!

When Margaret Bruce watched her daughter's radiant face, she capitulated.

Now, with the wedding dress finished, the guest lists completed, there remained only some last minute instructions for the ceremony itself, to be held in the Presbyterian Church across the street. But Becky adamantly refused a rehearsal. "I want him all to myself, Mama! I don't want anybody —anybody at all—to share that holy moment, even if it's only a rehearsal!" So the minister came to the Bruce parlor, where they met with John to go over the details.

Stand here, John. No, a little to the left. When the music starts . . . Repeat after me . . . John, you'll hold the ring in this hand. John . . .

Ah, well, he thought to himself as he left them, it had to come sooner or later. He couldn't be Johnny forever.

He crossed the street to Hopemont and found Cal in the parlor reading a letter. He had come to town for supplies, and a little crippled boy named Adam, John Henry's replacement, was waiting with the wagon in the carriage yard. The letter had been sent to Hopemont. Johnny picked up the envelope and sniffed.

"My, Cal, you've been keeping secrets from me! Where did you meet her?"

"Come on, Johnny, now . . ." But Cal wasn't quick enough to save the first page. His brother held it out, leaning back in a chair by the window, a breeze from the garden moving the curtain.

" 'Oh, how often do I think of my trip home. 'Tis one of the sunny spots in my life, and the *evening* spent in your company will not be forgotten. . . .' Wow, Cal, which evening was *that?*"

Cal reached for the letter, but Johnny was too quick.

" 'There is to me a peculiar pleasure in chatting with the silent tongue of the pen. . . . The fair forms and pleasant countenances of the dear ones we address are ever floating before our imagination. . . .' " He held it high, out of reach. " '. . . and we almost fancy ourselves beside them (on a *steamboat* for instance). . . .' Is that where you met her, Cal?"

"You were so busy mooning at the riverbank you didn't notice? She got on at Natchez, bound for Louisville."

"Natchez to Louisville! Wow, over a year ago and she remembers it! You must have had some sunny spots and evenings. . . ." But before Cal could grab the page he went on: " '. . . listening to the soft music of their voice and gazing into their soul-speaking eyes. . . .' "

Cal chased him around the room.

"I didn't know your eyes were soul-speaking, Cal. Let me see them. What do they say?"

"More than yours do. Damn. Now give me the letter."

Johnny relinquished it. He had seen that flicker of eyelid and guessed his brother's thoughts. He had seen the same look on his father's face. And T.H.'s. But what did they know?

"She's a nice girl," he said defensively.

"*Hof coze* she's a nice girl." Cal caught himself. "I'm sorry, Johnny. I didn't mean . . ."

"That's all right."

His conversations with Cal, and even with his father, always seemed to end like this. Did he have to convince them of his love for Becky? He was betrothed to her, after all—wasn't that proof enough? When he'd brought up the subject with his father just yesterday, Calvin Morgan looked at his son for a moment and then said slowly, "Do you? Do you have to convince yourself?"

They didn't know, he thought, what she represented: the order and peace his life needed after Mexico. And would need, with the uncertain financial times ahead. Secretly, he realized his irritation with their remarks came from the same source—doubt that he was doing the right thing. Did he love her, really love her? It didn't seem to matter. He had already made his decision. He had given up his own dreams, had settled for going into business with T.H. He had vowed to save Shadeland. He left Cal sitting at his grandmother's writing desk trying to compose an answer to his letter.

He found his grandfather in the garden, sitting on a bench in the deep shade of the magnolia. Its thick leaves, like enameled pieces of wood, clicked in the breeze.

"Did you ever see a tree to match the magnolia?" his grandfather asked. Then, abruptly, his mind switched to business. "How are the looms working?"

"Fine."

John Hunt leaned back, spreading his arms along the wrought iron roses. "We should get more. I can envision thirty thousand dollars capital. Twelve looms doing the work of twenty horses—three hundred spindles! I've calculated that you could produce over 250,000 yards of jeans cloth—linsey-woolsey, if you can get good wool. I've heard there's wool to be had from New Mexico. . . ."

Keep on top of things! Make your money work for you! Find the opportunities, then pull out when the ship leaks! When the frontier roads replaced mud trails, John Hunt went into carriage horses. When Whitney's gin made baling cotton possible, and each bale needed fifteen pounds of hemp, he went into the bagging business. When Napoleon's wars caused a drop in exports he went into the China trade. Gradually he closed most of his hemp operations, handing over his factory to T.H., and started handling other people's shipments on commission and credit, via his Philadelphia and New Jersey relatives. Payments for debts conceived with depreciated western paper could be politely refused "until more acceptable currency could be obtained"; his Philadelphia connections could buy Kentucky bank notes in Pennsylvania at a discount, send them to Hunt for sale at full value west of the mountains. By 1818 John Hunt was president of a bank that cannily rode out the panic that next year. He invested heavily in the Bank of the United States, and when Andrew Jackson declared war on it, withdrew—unscathed—to become a director of one of Jackson's "pet" banks, the new Bank of Kentucky. He was president of a life and marine insurance company, president of the yet unfinished railroad to Frankfort. Now, with gold discovered in California and Oregon opened to settlers, he was buying land in Kansas and making jeans.

He knew the tonnage and times of all the clipper ships on the Hong Kong–London run. He mentioned one now. "That must have been some race around the Horn," he was saying, his eyes wide in wonder.

Johnny looked at him. The old man was actually seeing those vast sails spread, feeling those surging troughs of water under his feet. He was indeed a remarkable man. He was seventy-five. He rose and walked into the house with the step of a thirty-year-old.

The garden was quiet, except for the falling of an occasional leaf.

Money. What was it, anyway? It seemed incredible that so much of life was devoted to it. Money. It was one of those words like war or love, with the power to make life miserable. The autumn sun lay like candlelight at his feet. Bare limbs of trees outlined themselves against a mother-of-pearl sky. In some ways he liked this time of year best. Those leafless skeletons, like hard ironwork, would do battle with the winds of winter. Down with the worms and in the dirt, next year's leaves were already a possibility. Life with all its mystery did go on, and if money made it turn, what was wrong with that? Money was better than the void he felt when he thought of Tommy or Uncle Alex. It gave some momentary purpose to life, even if momentary. No, it gave more, as his grandfather knew: It gave freedom of choice. That was the power of money, the power to choose. It had built the hemp business, it had built Hopemont and Shadeland. Not money, but the power it allowed. With it, the idea of having to sell Shadeland's children would be unthinkable. Without it . . . but John Morgan determined never to be without it.

When he saw Becky walking slowly down the aisle toward him a week later all in white with little silk lilies of the valley outlining her veil and satin ribbons floating from the bouquet in her hand, nothing else seemed so important after all . . . money, hemp, even Shadeland, beside this frail sweetness with the glowing eyes and timid, yet certain smile.

All the Hunts who could come were there. Aunt Dee from New Jersey, Uncle Abraham and his wife, Ellen, with their daughter Sallie, flirting openly with Cal's friends. The whole Morgan clan came up from Tennessee. Gideon was seventy-one now, and Wash thirty-one and still a bachelor. He had been a colonel in the Mexican War, with General Scott at Veracruz and Mexico City, and had been presented with a matched pair of Whitneyville Hartford Dragoons, the grips overlaid with silver and engraved with "Honor to the Brave, For Gallantry and High Military Bearing." Sheepishly but proudly Wash showed them. "Some different from that pepperbox you used to have. Well, say, one of them is yours . . . wedding present, sort of."

"Wash! Wash, I . . . it's fine! I . . ."

"Jes' don' git inta any dools with it now, ya heah?" Wash said in the old way, grinning.

Samuel Dold Morgan, Calvin's third brother, a merchant in Nashville, had arrived with his son Sam Junior two weeks before the wedding, and now the big day was here. It was one of those warm late November mornings. Little Sam was playing in the garden with Mary Curd, tall for her age at ten, and considered too big to be a flower girl. That honor went to her eight-year-old sister Eleanor, who, with Tommie Morgan, also eight, was upstairs getting "prissied up." "I don't care!" Mary said as she bit into a cupcake Sam had just sneaked from the kitchen. "With their ribbons and tussie-mussies. Who wants to go around holding a tussie-mussie anyway? They make me sneeze."

"You can't eat it," agreed Sam, and basked in the smile she sent him.

In the parlor the gentlemen were arguing about slavery in the new territories. "Why, sir, it's the manifest destiny of this country to extend its borders from coast to coast." Gideon's round eyes swelled.

"Those lands won't support slavery," Henry Clay declared as firmly as he could. "The climate's not right. You're not dealing with the Mississippi delta, but with arid plains short on rainfall."

"Rainfall be damned! It's the principle of the thing!"

"Come, come, gentlemen!" John Hunt smiled. "It's a day of festival, of pleasure. Our Johnny is being married within the hour, and Hopemont will see a reception worthy of Lexington! Where are those boys, anyway?"

"Upstairs, outside, in the carriage yard," Calvin Morgan answered from the doorway. They stopped to look at him and he read their faces. Did he look that poorly? Then Henrietta's insistence that he take naps was wasted. "I've been preserving my stamina for this day," he answered their unspoken question, "and don't intend to be disappointed."

"Johnny?"

"He spent the night at Shadeland and will ride in any minute."

"I hope so!" John Hunt held up his glass to the sunlight. "Time for another one, gentlemen, and then the ladies can take over, as they usually do."

In the big upstairs bedroom where her brothers had slept when they were children Henrietta, with Aunt Betty at her side, was pulling down over Kitty's head the latest creation in tulle and embroidery of Mrs. Dodd Walsh Wilson O'Brien.

"My, my, Miss Martha done outdone herseff dis time," murmured Bouviette in appreciation as she fussed the gathers at the back of Kitty's waist.

"Thanks to the pins Aunt Dee brought!" Kitty said graciously toward Aunt Dee, still suffering from her "overland ordeal," as she called her trip from Trenton.

"A man can make a hundred thousand in eleven hours, using the new machine," Aunt Dee clipped out proudly.

"How horrible for him," Henrietta said brightly, standing back to admire her daughter. "Now, Bouviette, what do you think about that hem? Does it sag to the left?"

Kitty, at thirteen, was becoming a little beauty and knew it. "Oh, Mama, we've measured that hem seventy-seven times! It's all right, isn't it, Aunt Bet? Say so!" She reached out slim embroidered arms to catch Aunt Betty's shoulders. Bouviette shook with laughter and Henrietta, watching Kitty swirl the skirt this way and that, had to agree.

"I suppose," she said, not to concede but not to argue either, "we can't expect perfection on this earth. Tommie, quit scratching at your pantaloons!"

"But Mama, they itch!"

"Hush, chile. Ain't no chiggahs in Novembah."

"Richard, will you help Charlton with his boots? Have they been polished? Tom, how did you get your face so dirty? Where's Key?"

Aunt Dee smoothed her own costume in front of the mirror and said smartly, "Little Key, Big Key; Little Richard, Big Richard; Little Tom, Big Tom. My goodness, Henrietta, can't the Kentucky Hunts find some new names?"

"They are *family* names," Henrietta answered, more hotly than the subject demanded. She sensed the Hunts saying behind her back that Calvin was a failure and that Johnny had been set up in business by her father. Or, if they hadn't said it, let it lie under their smiles and shrugs and infinitely patient looks. Because she wanted to defend her men she became extra sensitive about other things, and adept at letting fly her own cutting remarks. As she had done this morning at breakfast, when "the family," in their molasses-thick comfort, with talk of New Jersey business deals and Philadelphia mercantile successes, had stirred a hot lump that rose to her throat and made her sit a little straighter, her ankles crossed at the most proper angle, even though they couldn't be seen—more proper because they couldn't be seen—and all the while her smile most gracious as she spoke to this same Aunt Dee's complaint about lax discipline in a Trenton Sunday-school class and her determination "not to put up with" all that because, after all, she was a volunteer, doing "it all" for nothing.

"Would it make any difference if you were taking money?" Henrietta heard her own sweet question cut the air like a knife in soft butter. "Or are your feelings for sale?" She remembered making her hand linger purposefully over her coffee cup before she lifted it gently to her mouth. "What a Yankee idea!"

It was then that her mother's gaze, as always, caught her from its portrait above the sideboard. It said so eloquently, as it always had, I patiently bore the appellation "orphan," knowing that true aristocracy comes from within. I patiently waded through hours of uncertain waiting while John, your father, stayed away on business trips or spent long hours, first at his store, then with his hemp, then with his horses and politicians and bankers. I tolerated inept servants, taught clumsy maids the art of serving, of making a bed properly, of cleaning a child, a cupboard, a candlestick, a floor, a piece of furniture. I kept accounts, of social visits, of dinner obligations, of sugar, flour, yards of cloth and ribbon. I supervised candle-making, bread-baking, peach-preserving, mediating the talk of Wilkinson or Burr or Napoleon or the latest man-crazed idea over the mountains at Washington City as carefully as I blended spices into a Christmas turkey. I nursed hurt feelings and bruised knees and sick servants as you, too, Henrietta, have done and I know it and for that I thank you as a mother thanks a daughter. But self-possession is the first hallmark of aristocracy and we are the new aristocracy across the mountains of the West and to lose self-control is the first sin of an unconscious rebellion, a resistance to one's destiny. I say all this with the soft, crooked smile under the furrowed brow that even the artist didn't—didn't want to—erase and under my lace morning cap that you used to laugh at but which gave me a sense of protection—not only from the dust and dew but from exposing myself too much. That is something you will have to learn, Henrietta, the art of not exposing yourself too much.

And her mother looked down from the portrait, from a life complicated by grief but undaunted by failure, a handsome, beautiful woman, in contrast with the flat-faced New Jersey Hunts. . . . The real looks of the family had come from her, as the real looks in her own children had come from Calvin. She looked at him now, dear, handsome Calvin—his smile could still stop her breath—Calvin, with his foolish, impulsive relatives, Alexander Gibson throwing himself away in a boy's war, Wash, swashbuckling, silly, "gallant" Wash, and even old fish-eyed Gideon—they had their charm. Calvin caught her look and she returned it with a smile, her own eyes saying *Don't you know I'm defending you?* but hearing to one side in her mind Bouviette's reproach, as she had reproached her so often when she was a girl: *Hush, Miss Henrietta. What would Ole Miss say?*

Luckily, she thought at breakfast and now watching Kitty hooking behind her neck with excited fingers her own pearls which she had lent her daughter for this occasion, neither Mama nor Bouviette heard my rudeness. And she tried, for the rest of the day and through Johnny's wedding ceremony and the reception afterwards, to be civil.

None of them knew, not even Calvin, that deeper than her concern over the Hunts' hinted judgment of her husband was the worry that the Bruces might think the same of her Johnny. Stiff-backed Presbyterians who attended meetings of the American Colonization Society (she conveniently forgot that Henry Clay had once been its president) with their high-minded ideas of shipping freed slaves to Africa (while owning their own share of servants), they belonged to that increasingly large number of Kentuckians who wanted it both ways. *"Well, you can't have it,"* she said fiercely to herself, but loud enough for the New Jersey aunt to hear and misinterpret the remark as relating to herself. Without bothering to ask questions, Aunt Dee left the room.

"Oh, where are Cal and Johnny and Wash?" Henrietta asked the air above Bouviette's head in anguish. "He'll be late for his own wedding." To herself she added: And what will the Bruces have to say to *that?*

Still green in spite of several frosts, the grass curled wetly from an early morning rain, which had disappeared now and left the trees gleaming. Wash was ahead, posting smartly. Cal was behind, and then his uncle Robert, with his cousins Dick, John and Henry Curd. Even Uncle Frank had taken a holiday from teaching his law students to ride out to Shadeland with them. Last night had been grand. They drank and laughed and romped like boys, with Johnny being thrown into the pond and then, one by one, the others following. Henry, fifteen, was there only because he had promised he wouldn't drink too much that night. Henry had held his liquor better than any of them, and was unanimously appointed as an emissary to Aunt Hannah for hot baths and toddies. She scolded, but sent Randolph with a tray of midnight snacks.

"Stay," said Johnny. "You never could pass up Aunt Hannah's apple cake."

"That's Maggie's apple cake." Randolph grinned.

"That's right!" yelled Wash, rubbing his head with a towel. He flipped it out like a fencing foil and did a little sidestep. "Randolph's an old married man! Give Johnny here some advice!"

"Nawsuh, Mista Wash, Ah cain't do dat. . . ." For the briefest second, Randolph's eyes met Johnny's and he laughed again and accepted the piece of cake Henry Curd handed him. "Thank you, Marse Henry. Sho' is a big evenin'! Sho' is!"

If only he hadn't laughed like that, Johnny thought. Behind those bright eyes he's a sphinx. Why is he talking like a field hand? Nawsuh. He'd never heard Randolph say that in his life. The glow that three hours of whiskey had given Johnny vanished with that "Sho' is!" and a hollow in the pit of his stomach opened. He felt like someone on a sinking ship watching the water rise. Watching Randolph, who had been like a brother, vanish before his eyes. Like his life, like everything that had gone before. Was this what getting married did to people?

Now as they rode past the old tollgate, the new keepers waved. At Will's Johnny called a halt. Will, he knew, wouldn't be coming. For some reason, this morning, he had to see him.

He was in the cabin by a low wood fire, in spite of the warm day.

"He's had a chill," Amanda explained. The others waited outside, still mounted. Amanda stood by the door while he spoke with her father.

"So my boy is getting married." Will looked up and Johnny was shocked at the age on his face. The old back injury had taken its toll.

"I'm afraid so."

"Well, yew have a good life, boy." The leathered face broke into a laugh. "Thanks for stopping."

Amanda, at the door, tossed her mane and grinned. "Ain't you gonna give me a good-bye kiss?"

He bowed, he hoped gallantly. "Of course, ma'am. If you don't reward me the same way as—"

But she caught him around the neck with both arms and kissed him full on the mouth, kept kissing him, turning his head to one side, bending her own under his until he felt the bone of her cheek pressing into his shoulder.

"Don't smother the boy!" Will called out.

He rode the rest of the way into town under a shower of envious taunts. "Let me in on your secret," Wash called back over his shoulder. "Ah'm a bachelor yet, remembah. Wouldn't mind visitin' that little lady myself. . . ."

He didn't tell them that he was more surprised than anybody.

An hour later he stood in the church on wooden legs and forgot not only Amanda but most of the ceremony. From somewhere he heard a voice that he vaguely recognized as his own make responses, and before he knew what had happened, he was kissing Becky and standing in the parlor at Hopemont accepting congratulations.

At the reception, while he waited impatiently for Becky to change for the stage to Frankfort, Margaret Bruce drew him aside. "You *know*, of course, Rebecca's delicate condition," the lady intoned. Her eyes, behind puffy lids, glinted like two beads.

"Ma'am?"

"I *know* you will be *most* considerate of Becky, John. She is of delicate health, and her father insists, absolutely *insists* . . ."

He waited, puzzled.

"That she not bear children until she becomes stronger," the lady got out.

"Of course, of course, Mrs. Bruce, I . . ."

"I *knew* you would understand," she smiled, nodding to a guest across the room as if they had been discussing nothing more than the flower arrangements.

16

Not until a giggling Becky settled on the stage beside him and they felt the first sway of the carriage on its springs did the unreal day fade like a dream.

They spent the first night with the Hannas in Frankfort—John and Mary, his mother's oldest sister. Their house sat on a bluff overlooking the Kentucky River, and Becky, who had never been farther west than Versailles, was full of talk about the rest of their journey.

"Down the Ohio to Cairo, then up the Mississippi to St. Louis! Johnny's Aunt Theodosia has been so kind as to invite us to stay with her," Becky told Mary Hanna breathlessly.

"It's on the frontier," John Hanna teased. "Won't you be afraid of Indians?" It was awkward talking to this little bride. She made him think of his own wedding night and wonder where the years had gone. But Mary Hunt had been more robust, more . . . This one was a mere chit, he said to himself. A weanling, he mumbled as he crawled into bed with his wife.

"Well, you know what you always say." His wife smiled.

"No, what?"

"You've got to wean them before you can train them."

"Go on with you, Mary Hunt! What a scandalous thing to say!"

"Well . . ." She arched her brows. "Would you say I'm trained?"

"You're your father's daughter," her husband pretended to grumble, then sank back on his pillow, his arms under his head, looking at the ceiling. "Still, it does make you wonder, doesn't it?"

"What?"

"Where life went."

The packet to Cairo was named the *Blue Gull* and was not the spacious steamboat Johnny had described. But the dining room on the sternwheeler they boarded at Cairo, although not as large as some of the more famous Mississippi boats, was formal and allowed Becky to wear some of the best dresses from her trousseau to dinner—the white India muslin lined with pale blue silk that had been her mother's favorite, the crinoline petticoat that Mrs. O'Brien had insisted on making to let it "stand out." At Cape Giradeau it was cool enough for a new wrap called a Cornelia, made of cashmere with no seam at the shoulder, which could be gathered up on the arms like a shawl. She felt absolutely elegant in it. But her favorite was a Kasaveck jacket imported from Russia and sent as a present from Judge Gratz's sister Rebecca in Philadelphia, for whom Becky was named. It was close-fitting, with wide, braided sleeves, and wadded.

"I like it, too," said Johnny, pulling her closer to him as if to warm her from the wind.

"Johnny!"

He looked around. "Well, we're married, aren't we? Who cares whether they look or not?"

"They're"—and she nodded significantly toward two ladies at the rail not far from them—"not looking at me."

"Aren't they?"

"No, and you know it." She smiled mischievously. When she did that the points of her mouth turned up like a little girl's. "They can't keep their eyes off *you*."

He looked their way just to tease her. "Oh, can't they, now?"

"You know they can't. With those eyes of yours, John Morgan. How do you manage to puff the undersides when you look at someone? When you really look at someone?"

"Do I?" he laughed. "I didn't notice."

His aunt Theodosia, a widow, lived in the most fashionable section of St. Louis, and had planned a number of "evenings" for them. The ladies who came, wrapped in rich mantles (the Second Republic was the rage in France), toyed with chains of beads and tossed ostrich feathers in languid circles.

"They're called Josephines," Becky whispered.

"What?"

"The capes. I wonder where they get all these styles?"

The memory of a ball, with pink silks and roses. "New Orleans, I imagine. Maybe even Paris. Look like Frenchy clothes to me. . . . But you see, they need them. They're not as pretty as you."

Nor, I hope, as complicated. The truth was, he was confronted by a peculiar rejection: the fear of a virgin. Nobody would have believed that after a week their marriage had not been "consummated." When it was, the event was painful, tearful, and heavy with guilt.

When they returned to Lexington there was a great flurry at both Hopemont and the Bruce house, with servants running back and forth across the street with trunks. Margaret Bruce had arranged a homecoming dinner with mounds of food, and afterwards discreetly let the newlyweds "find their way" upstairs.

Becky had completely redone her room in blue, her favorite color, and Sanders's old bedroom next door was now part of a suite separated by double doors. In effect, they had the whole back of the house overlooking the garden to the west.

"We'll be able to watch the sunset," Becky said wistfully, holding back the lace curtain.

Behind her, he fit his body to hers and nibbled at her neck. "You can watch the sunset." He turned her around and held her face in his hands. He took her hand from the curtain and led her to the bed, but she held on to the post and resisted his pull. He let go and fell back, luxuriating in the softness.

"John! What will Ellie say?"

"Ellie?"

"She takes *hours* smoothing that feather tick. With a broomstick!"

"With a broomstick!" His head went back with laughing.

"That's what the daybed's for—resting in the day, so you won't disturb—"

He sat up. "Are you serious?"

At his look she giggled, and let him pull her on top of him. "Well, for once," she murmured against his chest, "Ellie can fuss."

"I guess she can. Poor ole Ellie."

But she had been more serious than he guessed. They did "rest," more often than not, during those afternoons he stole from the office, on the curved-back sofa that stood demurely between the windows. "Not disturbing Ellie's feather tick" became a joke and later an irritant, especially when the weather turned cold. After Christmas John Morgan found himself spending more afternoons at the office, and Becky more afternoons at tea and sewing parties with her young married friends. Sometimes the parlor would be fairly clicking with needles and snapping with threads and girlish laughter —marriage seemed to have given Becky a new dimension, but one he couldn't share.

When her parents were present she became more reserved, tucking her chin into her chest and keeping her eyes averted whenever they were in the parlor or at the polished mahogany table. Ben, studying to become a doctor, tried to make medical jokes but her father sat opposite his new son-in-law in a pose stiff enough for a daguerreotype. *I know you will be most considerate . . . her father absolutely insists . . .*

Suddenly, he felt like an intruder. Only in the garden, where Becky planned a bed of wildflowers for the spring, did she seem herself. But with the first snow in January, when activity moved indoors, she turned to stone again. When a warm spell came he mused ironically that he hoped the snow wouldn't be the only thing to thaw. At first she merely turned over. By morning she lay near the edge of the bed, her arms crossed across her chest, her knees drawn up. What had he done?

In the office, in the middle of calculations and plans, T.H. laid down his papers and looked straight at his nephew. "Tell me about it," he said.

"There's nothing to tell."

"That's precisely your problem."

"Uncle Tom . . ."

"I'm not that much older than you are, Johnny. I have no idea how much . . . experience you have had with the ladies," he got out. "How much . . . you have had to encourage those you may have known. But these little sheltered girls . . . Have you frightened her?" he finally blurted.

"I don't think so. . . ."

"Well"—his uncle breathed easier—"if you don't think so, then perhaps you haven't. But be careful, Johnny. Early impressions in a marriage can set a tone. . . . Now," he said brightly, "let's get to work."

As enthusiastic as Johnny might be about the new looms and plans, his mind was at Shadeland, waiting for the excitement of Delilah's foal. The sudden thaw had left mud and half-melted snow mushing the fields. He had never breathed air so pure. He took great gulps of it that next morning as he rode one of his grandfather's trotting horses to the office. When he got there he couldn't resist telling T.H. he needed the day off. T.H. understood. He shook his head in empathy as he watched his nephew remount and ride away.

He was too late. She had foaled during the night, and already the whole family had gathered in the barn to watch Uncle Simon feed her warm mash and brush her down while she ate. A fawn-colored colt the size of a small deer wobbled on absurdly long legs, his mane a stiff brush that stuck straight up along his neck from his ears to his withers.

"Ain't he got long ears?" Randolph worried.

"Shows intelligence. Can hear better." Calvin Morgan grinned.

"He's bone-lazy. Look at him," Randolph drawled. "Most times, a colt will be already moving out. He jes' stays by his mammy."

"Smart fella." Calvin would not be perturbed and looked over at Cal. "Remember how feisty Sard was, and your grandfather said that if he'd been his he would have either castrated or shot him, preferably the latter?"

"Yeah, but Sard turned out all right." Cal leaned on the stall door. Charlton, Kitty and Tommie, holding onto Tom's hand, had not taken their eyes off Uncle Simon, who kept brushing, in spite of the fact that the colt had dipped his head under Delilah's stomach and was punching her unmercifully.

"Well, at least he knows where his grub is," Uncle Simon sighed. "An' dis one won' need no cart."

"Mebbe a buggy whip to git him goin'." Randolph could not keep the disappointment from his voice.

Uncle Simon, with the easiest, slowest motion in the world, had walked around the back of the mare, bent from the waist, and slipped a halter on the colt before he knew what happened. He backed up, bounded once, all fours off the ground, then sank into a shuffling walk, circled, and found his mama again.

"I tole you he wuz bone-lazy," Randolph said.

"Thass it fo' today, folks," Uncle Simon declared when he closed the stall door. "Let 'em settle. Dey's had a long night."

"What will you call him?" Calvin asked his son on the way back to the house.

John Morgan looked across the fields, at the swells of land and the line of trees reaching bare limbs to the sky. "Shadeland," he said.

He was the pet of the farm. He had an endearing, quizzical expression and a positive fascination for hawks that, as winter moved into May, came looking for rabbits in the spring woods. If a hawk swooped into a brushpile anywhere near his paddock, Shadeland would race across to investigate. Before he was weaned he had learned to untie the rope at his stall door. "Jes' lak his daddy," Uncle Simon fussed. "Wal, so long's he don' git inta de cawn," the old man added, reaching over and scratching his ear.

The business went well. They ordered more sewing machines. "They should come before Christmas," John Hunt beamed, and a new frontier gleamed before his eyes.

Spring blossomed into summer. Blue chicory waved again in the fields. In the Bruce garden, Becky's wildflower beds were sporting crisp daisies and purple heads of phlox. There was, of course, no house yet. Talk of it faded as even Ben joined the general family conclusion that Rebecca was indeed too delicate to manage a household of her own.

That would have been fine. John Morgan could have accepted that. But not Becky's receding from him. As if, when he reached out, she automatically withdrew. An image in a mirror. A shadow on water. He tried to find an hour every evening to be alone with her, to sit with her in the garden watching the stars and the fireflies against the dark. "I wonder if we can have one," he mused.

"What?"

The word was sharp.

"An oleander."

He could hear her breathe out.

"No . . . it's much too far north for that. Besides, they are poison, I hear."

"Poison?"

"The leaves. When you burn them."

"Why would you want to burn them?"

"They need trimming. Otherwise they grow too tall. And the blossoms are messy. They get all over the place."

"Yes, I suppose they do."

He fell silent, thinking again about the sharpness of her question. He knew she had misunderstood. And she knew he knew. Had her mother, like his, been asking questions? He knew they both expected—perhaps hers feared—grandchildren. "Rebecca is so delicate" rang in his ears. He had, to the best of his Morgan ability, left her alone or found alternatives, which would include her. But pumping himself against her body . . . that was not acceptance.

"I suppose it is," he said, not knowing to what he referred.

"We could have a mimosa," she offered, sensing his thoughts.

He reached over and patted her hand. In the dark he could see her wide eyes, the softness of her mouth. He lifted her hand to his lips and felt the rosewater on her handkerchief brush his face like a breeze. "You are the only blossom I need in this garden, Becky. Only you."

"John, I . . ."

He waited, thinking, for some reason, of Tommy Cunningham. He hadn't thought of him in months.

"I know you . . . want . . ." She took her hand away and bent her face into the handkerchief and twisted it in her fingers.

He started to call her name. From somewhere a dog barked. It was a solitary sound.

"No. Don't touch me or I can't go on. I know you . . . want . . . love," she got out.

"I have that."

The dog barked again.

"No. You know what I mean."

"Becky . . . Dr. Wolford says—"

"I know what Dr. Wolford says. And Mother. And Father. I'm not help-less!" She caught her breath. "Don't you love me?"

"You know I love you." He laid his hand on her shoulder, spreading his fingers. "That's why—"

"That's why you hold yourself away from me, why you go out to Shade-land all the time, why you . . ."

He drew her to his lap and rocked her back and forth, feeling the lightness of her body, like a child's, against him. "I go to Shadeland to see the new colt. You would love him! Let's take your father's gig and go see him tomor-row."

She shook her head against his chest.

"I'm only trying to take care of you until you get stronger," he said more soberly, dropping the festive tone. "I promised . . ." He cut himself short.

She stiffened and sat up. "You promised who? Who?"

"Myself," he lied. "That we would wait until we had a house of our own and you were strong and would enjoy your first child as you should . . . with no worry about anything."

"Anything?"

"We could . . . be alone."

She jumped up and stood in front of him. "Oh, you think Mother and Father interfere too much, is that it? After they have given us their home to live in while you get established? Sometimes I think you are the most self-centered, selfish man in the world, John Morgan! Sometimes I think Father is—"

"Why don't you finish?" he asked, puzzled at her sudden change. Hadn't she just been blaming them for making her helpless? "Why don't you say 'right'? That's what you meant to say, wasn't it? That I'm a failure like my father, like all the Morgans, and I have to depend on their generosity to provide for my wife? Is that it?"

He hadn't meant for this hour to end like this. They had been married eight months and they had not had one night's real lovemaking since the honeymoon. What had happened? From the time they had returned to Lex-ington Becky became a different person. Her father talked of his little girl's bad heart, the fear of "phthisic." It became a favorite word, uttered with relish. The promise her mother had extracted from him was, he felt sure, more of the father's making than hers, for Margaret Bruce had developed, he thought, some sympathy for him. So had Ben. Sanders, who had rented a house for himself shortly before they moved in, was cool almost to hostil-ity. Betrothed now himself, he no longer attempted to conceal his contempt at what he considered a less than favorable marriage. *I hope with all my heart you succeed just to show Sanders* the mother's look often said. Becky never discussed finances with him. He spent more and more time with T.H. hiring and buying hands, poring over the drawings for a new building. And with Cal, who came in from Shadeland on a regular basis now, with his ledgers, for advice. He would show them. He would show them all.

"Let's . . . let's go to bed now" was all he managed to say.

He was busy during the rest of July—in humid, stifling heat with no breeze to remind him that this was Kentucky and not the middle of a boiling kettle. The cholera had come again. It started with the death of an old Irishman who worked at the stone quarry. Within forty-eight hours as many people died, and an exodus began. From her upstairs window Becky Morgan watched the wagons and buggies leave, and shivered. Margaret Bruce ordered all windows closed, all shutters drawn. The house was stifling, and only Ellie was allowed to go out, and then only for absolute necessities. The number of doorways draped in crepe multiplied, and the number of houses that stood silent and empty. After sundown the death carts could be heard making their rounds, picking up bodies. A new cemetery was opened.

But this time Lexington fought back. The city poorhouse was turned into a hospital, and all inmates of the workhouse were released to nurse the sick. Outlying farms sent in fresh milk, eggs and smoked meat. Dudley and Carty, and then W. K. Higgins opened their wholesale grocery stores to the destitute, free of charge. The medical faculty of Transylvania requested that fieldpieces be brought from the armory and stationed at strategic crossroads in the city to be fired at regular intervals to "disturb the atmosphere." One was at North Mill and Main, and kept up its infernal booming day and night. The Bruce windows rattled at every salvo. Sour kitchen smells and the musty odors of unaired rooms made the August heat insufferable.

"Can't they have a breath of air?" Morgan said aloud to himself. Across the street, Hopemont with its cool garden and long opened windows seemed an oasis. Inside, he knew his grandfather would be sitting, wine glass in hand, reading the newspapers, hatching new financial schemes. The *Sea Witch* had made it from New York to San Francisco in eighty-nine days, fourteen hours. Garibaldi was fighting in Italy. Louis Napoleon was the new President of France. He could see the folded *Tribune*, delivered fresh by steamboat and stage. From the Bruce house, Hopemont looked like an avenue to the world. It took tragedy in stride, not hiding behind shutters. If there was physical weakness, it was taken in stride, too, not pampered. Life went on.

"I'm going to ask Robert if that infernal barrage is necessary," he said with so much vehemence that Becky looked alarmed.

"But if the doctors . . ."

"Hah, the doctors!" He watched her carefully replace a needle in her pincushion. She kept her sewing box by the bed at night, like a talisman, and squinted in the candlelight.

He walked across the street to his grandfather's carriage yard and let himself in by the side door, into the service entry. Big Peggy, at this hour, would be sleeping in the servants' wing at the back of the house, but the sweet pie-baking smell of her would still linger in the warming room. He walked through the dining room to the front parlor where, indeed, John Hunt had fallen asleep sitting bolt upright, a newspaper spread on his knees.

"Grandfather . . ."

"Hmm? Yes? Why, it's Johnny. Yes. Come. Sit. Have a brandy?"

"Thanks. Yes, I will. Where's Uncle Robert?"

"Playing cards at the Wickliffes'. Doctor Wolford can handle his patients for a few hours. He needs diversion. Why don't you join them?"

"Speaking of the Wickliffes," John Morgan said, pouring himself a drink, "we've hired some Wickliffe hands."

"Oh?"

"Cheaper than buying right now. We needed girls. They are much better at the machines. More reliable. Although we've gotten some good men, too."

"Have you seen your father lately?"

"Not for a few days. Is he all right?"

"Fine, fine. He came in this morning, while you were at the factory. Had to get back. Something about the hemp."

"You don't sound too certain."

"Fine, physically. And Henrietta's right, to avoid town just now. But Shadeland . . ."

They both fell silent.

"What would *you* do, if it were yours?"

"I'd sell," his grandfather replied.

"Sell! Yes, I suppose so, from a business point of view."

"What other point is there?"

"Gentlemen, gentlemen," J.C. Robards crooned. He fanned his hand, then snapped the cards together. He leaned back and tongued his cigar from one corner of his mouth to the other, pulling at it first with his lips and then with his fingers as he made gestures in the air with its smoking end jabbing at the chandelier above his head. "Let us continue to play. Enough talk!"

Cripps Wickliffe leaned back and gave Robert Hunt a quick look. What have you got? the look said. I'm bluffing and you know it. His glance slid to his cousin Betty, then to Ned Baynham, who had dropped out and now stood behind Robert's chair.

They waited for Robert Hunt. But bluff as he would, Robert lost again. His pair of fives waited on the table like two orphans for the onslaught of Robards's straight, laid out with a little flick, one by one. Johnny, with a hopeless hand, dropped also, and mumbled something about the late hour. Above Robards's objections they excused themselves with murmurs of early business appointments and a joke about Cripps's need to study for Uncle Frank's exam at the law school tomorrow. Robert, with ill patients, needed no excuse: The regular explosion of the cannon on Main Street was reminder enough. They made their way through the wide front door and down the generous, shallow steps onto the street. Baynham left them at the corner after some remarks about John Henry and horses. Robert stopped to light a cigar, flipping the match into the gutter. The night had clouded over a fitful moon, but humid heat still lay thick and stifling. The low sky seemed to be sending the insane booming down on them, as if the guns were up there, and not down here.

"Remember the old sulfur splints that you had to draw through sand-paper?" Robert said. It would be another hour before the air turned cool.

Only if it rained or the temperature dropped would the artillery stop. At his nephew's silence he continued: "Pshaw. I don't guess you do."

"Yes, I do," Morgan answered. The solid wall of air threw his own breath back at him. "We used them in Mexico."

But his uncle hadn't heard him over the nearest salvo. He stepped across the street, walking quickly. "I remember smoking cornhusks. And hemp. Have you ever tried hemp, Johnny?"

"It made me too groggy."

"Maybe that's the answer."

"The answer?"

"To all this." Robert waved his arms at the street, where some of the black ribbons tied to doorknobs were already frayed and bleaching. The cannon boomed again, a stupid salute to nothing.

"To all this," Robert waved his arms again. "To life. To cholera and catarrh and nigger consumption. To all the money-grubbing and hours of human suffering. What do most people want, anyway?" he asked the shuttered houses. "To be the richest man in the cemetery?" He looked away. "I've seen too much death, Johnny, to know what life's all about. Maybe it's simple, so simple we miss it. Maybe just staying groggy is the answer."

Hopemont, on the corner, was already visible, its fan window over the double front doors catching the street light like a half-closed eye.

"I can't think that."

"You mean you won't think that."

They walked past the Gratz house and let themselves into the garden. Through the downstairs windows they could see T.H. talking with his father. The thought came again to Johnny that T.H. was more like old John Hunt than any of them. He rose early and worked harder than any of his slaves. He had visions of business expansion. And yet T.H. was different: gentle, fun-loving. The looms were humming as they spun out more yardage every day. And the new sewing machines. My God, what his grandmother could have done with one! He could still remember her supervising her servants in the sewing room, five girls surrounding her, her own fingers flying as fast as the brown ones with their pink, flat nails, her own knuckles angled purposefully, her wrists turning, her fingers gathering under, letting go, gathering under again, her lower arms twisting in that unconscious, no-nonsense female rhythm that produced, produced, for children and men and servants and the world. That was *after* the thread had been spun, the cloth loomed by hand! Now he and T.H. could watch the yardage reel off, flat and even and falling in curving folds. They were making the best jeans in the West, guaranteed to wear well. Already the orders were coming in from as far away as Kansas City. Lexington, as John Hunt had dreamed, would be another Massachusetts. . . .

The night sounds of crickets and an occasional dog barking in the distance gave to the garden an intimate feeling, the lighted window the air of a stage. They watched the gestures of the two men for some minutes.

"She has an extraordinary bosom," Robert said.

"Who?"

"Miss Betty, of course!"

"Maybe *that's* the meaning of life."

Poor Becky, he could hear the other young ladies think as they glanced at "the little married Bruce girl" at church socials and meetings of the Readers' Guild. Poor Becky with her chicken breast and timid chin and that soft mouth always a little open, as if prepared for a surprise.

"Well, I've got to go," Robert said wearily, crushing his cigar on the bricks. "I'm dead-tired. Enjoyed that game. But it's back to saving humanity."

"How's the cholera?"

"Abating somewhat. Bad enough, though." He rose and stretched his arms. "Don't stay out too late. And don't mind what I say about getting groggy. Work's the only answer. Take care of yourself." He screwed his face into a yawn. "I think I'll take my own medicine."

Morgan watched him let himself in the garden door, which led to the spiral stairs. Two minutes later a lamp shone in Robert's bedroom, then went out. *Take care of yourself.* Celina. Celina in the cabin, screaming. And Aunt Catherine. He hadn't seen his aunt Catherine. Was she covered with that reeking vomit, her bed filled with excrement, her body twisted in pain? The cholera. He was eight when Aunt Catherine died. He could still remember standing with Randolph, watching his mother nurse Celina. He looked up through the trees at a dark night sky refusing to show itself. What was it he missed from the old days at Shadeland? What? The whippoorwills. Yes, it was as simple as that. In town you didn't hear the whippoorwills.

He saw T.H. stand up and gesture broadly. He pushed himself up from the bench and walked across the street to the Bruce house, up the stairs to Becky's room. Why had he never thought of it as their room?

He found her on the bed, curled on her side, sleeping. He lit a candle and lay down behind her, his arm lightly on her waist, letting his mind drift from the cannon to his marriage, thinking how whenever he tried to talk— or make love—Becky scurried away into the corners of her own little-girl world, playing dolls with her thoughts. He had given up trying to intrude. When he did, the soft corners of her mouth drew back and the irises of her eyes became two black, glinting points. But there was still her little-girl body, and his own need. And the cholera, the sense of death all around, the sense of urgency. The question came back: What was life, anyway? He let his fingers drift over the soft froth of her gown. She stirred, and pushed him away with her upper arm. "What?" he murmured into her back.

She sat up, and for the first time he noticed something red and crushed in her hand. "This is what," she said flatly, opening her fingers. It was the scapular. So. She hadn't been asleep, after all.

"I found it in your shirts, when I was putting some sachet . . ."

He had never seen her eyes so dead. Her chin quivered in an effort to hold back tears. "Becky, I can explain . . ."

"Oh, I know, I know!" she cried. "This bit of Popish junk . . ." She threw it from her hand and it landed just beyond the rug, on the floor in front of the armoire. "Like all the Morgans, you have an explanation for everything!"

"What is that supposed to mean?"

"Nothing," she said, and then: "Anything you want it to mean," even more fiercely.

He leaned over his long legs, stretched beyond the edge of the bed. Eugenie. *Hof coze*. The oleander. The café au lait and the low sky red with morning over the river. How could he explain? That had been a world ago, beyond Graham Springs and a girl naming wildflowers. How could he tell her that her slender body had been like a sanctuary after the scorching Mexican dust, the fear, the gratitude of being home again? How much she had represented that return to his own life, to himself, to all the values he had believed in? Without those . . . His uncle's empty questions cried out again.

Or had he merely assigned to her those values? It was amazing that he had ever found her dependence charming. His mother, his grandmother, Eugenie—all the women he had ever known, even Kitty and Tommie—had opinions of their own. The Bruce women didn't. Margaret Bruce was a sponge. And Becky wasn't a child, in spite of the fact that her parents wanted her to remain one. Remorse turned to irritation.

"The scapular was given to me by a friend. For good luck."

"Oh, a friend, was it."

"For good luck."

"Was her name Amanda?"

"No. Of course not."

"Why of course not?"

"Because Amanda . . . How did you know about Amanda?"

"Never mind. Then it must have been that other one. Geenee?"

"Eugenie. But how . . ."

"You talk in your sleep, John Morgan. Or didn't you know? It's the only time you bother to talk to me."

"That's not so," he managed quietly. He took her hands and she tried to draw them away but he wouldn't let go. "That's not so," he repeated, thinking *I'm getting to be like her mother.*

He let her hands go. She folded them into little fists and pounded the bed on either side of her, sobbing silently. There was something in the downward bend of her shoulders that repelled him. He jumped up and walked back and forth. With a vicious thrust, more energetically than he had intended, he tore open the shutters and the waited-for breeze billowed the curtains inward and blew out the candle. "You live like a trapped animal in a cage. No daylight, no fresh air."

"You know as well as I do, it's the cholera," she said more evenly, her lip still quivering. He didn't answer. She waited, as if trying to get her breath. "Was it Betty Wickliffe, then?"

"Betty Wickliffe?"

"Who gave you the picture."

"I think"—he paused—"I think, if you don't mind, Becky, I'll sleep at Hopemont tonight. Robert's dead-tired and may need some help."

Her silence as he pulled on his clothes was the cruelest remark he had ever heard from anybody.

Cool night sounds. Quiet house sounds. A clock ticking. A cat in the warming room, stretching on the bench. Somewhere, his grandfather snoring. He went to his old bedroom off the back landing and crawled into bed and watched the moon shafting through passing clouds, falling across his body in a silver wave.

Big Peggy woke him with coffee on a breakfast tray. "Nicely done tole me we has annuvah custamah. When you come in?" Then, before he could answer she said quickly: "Ain't no need gittin' up early today. Too hot. Ain't nevah seen it so hot."

"But T.H. . . ."

"You rest. Yo' uncle Tom done sent word he warn't even openin' de factory today. De cholera, hit got dis town by de troat. Drink yo' coffee. You like dat biscuit?"

"Where's Robert?"

"Long gone. Dat boy eckscapes fastah den a coon frum a tree."

"What do you know about coon-hunting, Big Peggy?"

"Plenty." She rolled her eyes. "You don' think Ah've been old *all* mah life, does you? Now eat yo' biscuits. Dey's aigs downstaihs waitin'. Gittin' cold," she said emphatically, pulling the sheet from him with a great flourish. "Lawd knows," she said, when she discovered he had been sleeping nude.

He dressed and found eggs waiting on the little round table in the warming room where the Hunt children had taken their suppers in the old days. He wolfed down more biscuits and coffee, spreading strawberry jam from a little blue dish. "That's perfect," he said as he leaned back, rubbing his middle. Through the window the bricks of the courtyard looked cool. The day hadn't stoked up yet. He looked at the clearing morning fog and the rooftops past the Bruce house. Becky would be sleeping under that roof, but he tried to bring his mind to other things. "Where's Grandfather?"

"Still restin'."

"That's strange."

"Not a-tall. Dat man, he still de workin'es' man Ah evah done seen. Did you know he he'p Marse Robert wif a patient las' week?"

"No. It's dangerous."

"Dat's whut Ah tole him. But would he lissen?"

"Maybe I should help, too."

"Now whut good would dat do? Ain't it enuf to have Massa Robert riskin' his life fo' white trash?"

"Cholera knows no class," he said unsmiling.

"Don't Ah know dat? Who you think you are, lecturin' me?"

She was so serious, with her lower lip stuck out and her eyes bulging, that he had to laugh. She was Randolph's mother, and he had seen that same look on Randolph's face often enough. He bowed pertly.

"Oh, go on wif yo' Frenchy ways . . ." But she was smiling as she turned to go.

He couldn't find Robert. The town was dead, as it had been that time when he had taken Uncle Ben to the dentist. He had a longing to see Shadeland, to take his mother in his arms. Aunt Betty. Dearest Bet! And Kitty and little Tom, and tomboy Tommie, and Cal. What was all this business about proving himself to the Bruces, anyway? Under the big oak in Hopemont's carriage yard he saddled up. The empty houses down Main Street stood like foreboding, hollow echoes. He legged the horse into a trot, then flexed him, but John Hunt's roan had a plungy canter and he settled him back into a trot and patted his neck as he looked up at the sky. With fields on either side, not even the heat of August could limit that sense of freedom. He had known another kind of freedom once, in a New Orleans garden. That memory was his and had nothing to do with Becky. Remembering Eugenie gave him a feeling of reality. He couldn't quite explain it, even to himself. How could he expect to explain it to anyone else?

At this time of year, with the trees in leaf, Will's cabin wasn't visible from the road. He hadn't planned to stop but Amanda, in gum boots and a wide hat, called to him from the lane. What was she doing working the fields? In the garden, to the right of the house, he could see Zep hoeing, his back bent into a flat V of sweat between his suspenders.

"Git down." She smiled. "Stop a spell."

"Can't. How's Will?"

"Paw's gone to California."

"California!"

"To hunt gold," she said flatly, then laughed.

"What will you do?"

She shrugged, but he could see a defiance building up.

"And that no-good Nathan's still in Texas. Who knows? He may meet Paw in California, for all I know. On some mountain digging rocks."

"You can stay here."

"Stay here?" She turned on him in all her fury. "We are *tenants*, Johnny Morgan. We don't own this land. Don't you know that?"

"But Grandfather . . ."

"But Grandfather," she mimicked, ugly now in anger, "has gotten his rent all these years. You don't know nuthin', Johnny Morgan. . . ."

"Where will you go?"

"To Louisville," she snapped. "We got relatives, too, Johnny Morgan."

"That ain't all she got in Loo-uh-vull," said Zep. "Ain't you heard?" He came up, rubbing his nose. "Amanda's done got her a fella. Gonna git marrid."

Little clouds had come together and were flowing across the fields, their shadows lumpy and spreading like dark waves, a silent ripple chased by sunshine. He waited until the sun picked out a fence again before he said "Who?"

"Jake Bolton."

The roan threw back his ears at the sudden squeeze on the rein and stepped sideways nervously.

"Whose horse is that?"

"My grandfather's."

"Puny, ain't he?" Zep spit.

He laughed, and was surprised at the sound. He kept his eyes from Amanda. Well, what had he expected? The world doesn't stand still. Did he think he could come here forever, as he had to Aunt Bet's aproned lap, for spoon bread and those long looks under a tossed red mane? Or listen to Will tell Injun tales? *Now's the time for mirth and glee* . . . He looked up and held her eyes with his. Then she turned and went back down the lane.

He paid his nickel to the broad-faced German woman at the tollgate and let the roan pick up a trot. Jake Bolton. He couldn't believe it. Then, where the road dipped, behind its trees, he could see Shadeland.

Adam, now under Uncle Simon's tutelage, ran out with his lurching gait to hold the bridle.

"Adam! How are you, boy? He needs a drink."

"Fine, Massa John. Jes' fine. Yassa, Ah sees he be thirsty."

"How's Sard?"

"Feisty as evah."

"And Delilah?"

"Fine, fine. But dat colt a' hers is de messines' hoss Ah evah seen. Allus chasin' dem crows."

"Crows? Well, he's only seven months. Give him time. Maybe one day he'll chase records."

"Yassa . . ." But Adam didn't seem too sure.

Henrietta met him in the entry. She took his hand and made him sit in the parlor by the window. He could see, down at the pond, Richard and Charlton fishing.

"So," she said, and twitched her nose.

"So you've been well, Ma?"

"Yes."

"And Father?"

"You know how he hates extreme heat. But it's cooler in the office."

"Cal and the boys, and Kitty and Tommie?"

"Everybody's fine. Randolph's been extremely helpful."

His eyebrows went up. She never spoke of Randolph in that tone. "In what way?"

"Oh, with the accounts. It hasn't been a good year, as Cal probably told you. Although I never understand those things," she lied. She looked off. "You'll find them down there. Cal might be there, too." She stood by the door and watched her son walk under the trees, his hands in his pockets.

Calvin Morgan made room for him by moving a ledger from a chair. "So. And how are things in town?"

"Fine, fine." He told them about the business, the new looms, the fact that Robert thought the cholera had been contained.

"It's my theory that rain would do the trick," his father said. "It's been too hot, too dry, too long."

Just as he spoke a low roll of thunder came to them with a sudden puff of breeze through the windows.

"That's your answer." Cal laughed.

"I hope so."

It was all there the next morning—the soft sheets and sunshine, the children's building blocks on the stairs, the bowls of peaches and baskets of beans, the smell of herbs simmering for winter medicine, the bunches of thyme and rosemary gathered for drying and hanging from the rafters. The heavy, oily scent of hot tallow told him that his mother was already up, supervising the candle-making. He surprised her in the coolness of the winter kitchen, downstairs by the fireplace showing one of the younger maids how to dip so that the wax would gather evenly.

"Good morning, Ma."

His arms were around her, squeezing the waist that was getting plumper, holding the shoulders that were rounding more every time he saw her. Were they rounding from all this medicine-making, candle-dipping, children-watching and servant-instructing? Only since the looms did he realize how much he had taken cloth for granted, the cloth that his mother and grandmother had patiently woven from thread spun out on those wheels that were as much a part of a house as its windows and floors—from the lowliest cabin to Shadeland's parlor. Standing tall above her, her shoulders in the arc of his arms, he felt indeed of a new generation. He and T.H. would change all that. Progress. His grandfather was right. And with progress would come the funds to help Shadeland.

"Your father isn't . . . well."

Her remark, muffled into his shirt, cut like a rapier.

"Tell me. Tell me everything, Ma."

"Not here!" She laughed, a shrill little sound that caused the servant to tip the holder sideways. But her mistress had already turned to the stairs. Was it really here, he thought, giving the girl an encouraging smile as she dipped the candles again, that Uncle Isaac used to tell his warped versions of Bible stories? Now Joshua, you see, he had de biggest banjo evah wuz, an' when he strummed hit, dem walls. . . . De devil tole Jesus if'n he would kum wif him he would give him all de chickens he could eat. . . .

Yet when he saw his father again at the breakfast table Calvin didn't fit the unhealthy description Henrietta reported. Perhaps she had sensed something else, some giving in, that was elusive to casual observation. There was, if one watched, a worry in his father's eyes. If only they could hold off a little, Johnny prayed, he could save Shadeland. He determined to talk with his grandfather about a loan.

In the stable the old smells of sweet hay and oiled leather made him breathe easier. Uncle Simon was in the tack room rubbing sour milk into a bridle. Two saddles, already drying, sat on sawhorses in the corner.

"At it still, Uncle Simon? Now don't you go rubbing that throat latch out of sight."

The old man's gray eyebrows flew up and he laughed hoarsely.

"How's Shadeland?"

"Sassy as evah. De hosses still out. Ain't put 'em up yit."

Johnny walked to the light at the far end of the barn and stood in the wide doorway watching the colt paddle along the fence beside Delilah.

"Ain't nevah seen a lazier hoss," Uncle Simon mumbled behind him. "An' still a runt. Won' make fifteen han's. Yo' granddaddy gonna put him down?"

"He was joking."

"Hrummph! You know as well as Ah does, Marse John Hunt don' joke."

"Well, don't you worry. He's mine, and I won't let him."

The morning sky, studded with little puffy clouds and veils of cirrus drifting high before an unseen wind, seemed to communicate a new urgency. Even as he watched, the little puffs were already drifting together. He wanted to cry out *Now*. Beyond the paddock the long line of black walnuts that his father had planted when they'd first moved from Alabama were standing tall and full, like troops marching toward the pond. Life. It seemed that he had to grasp it, anywhere, in any form.

When he trotted away they were all standing by the front door, waving.

This may be the last time I see them like that, he thought. There had to be a way. Find that, and so much else would fall into place. Money! He tried to shake away that worry with a good gallop, but the roan was still rough. When you get a horse that goes downhill, give him lots of leg, his grandfather had said. "Well," he answered out loud as he pulled back to a walk, "I don't feel like giving much this morning."

His apologies to Becky, carefully rehearsed to the roan's cadenced trot, were never spoken. When he let himself into the side door of the Bruce house Becky's mother met him with such a stricken face that he started to dash for the stairs.

"No, no, it's not Becky . . . thank God. Your grandfather, my dear boy. My dear, dear boy. Your uncles are over there now," she called after him as he spun away from her.

He found Robert and Key and T.H. in the parlor. Dick Curd was just leaving. "Have to get back to Eleanor. She didn't want me to come. The children, you know."

"How is he?" he asked Robert.

"Bad, I'm afraid, Johnny. Doctor Wolford was just here. He agrees, he's much weaker. It seemed to work on him fast. He's not a young man, you know."

"He's strong as an ox."

Key Hunt's raised eyebrows and drawn-back mouth disagreed eloquently.

Robert was more communicative. Rubbing his face, puffy from loss of sleep, he said gruffly, "It came suddenly. I've never seen anybody go down so fast."

"Do you think . . . ?"

"There's always a chance."

"May I see him?"

"Johnny, I wouldn't."

"I must!"

Robert looked at T.H. and shrugged his shoulders. *You've got to think of Becky* was the unspoken thought on all their faces. But he had to see him.

The usual blankets, plasters, poultices, calomel and rhubarb were there, underlining but not overcoming the stench of vomit. John Hunt was propped against damp pillows, his thinning hair matted against his head, showing the shape of his skull. A basin half-full of yellowish-green mucus had not yet been cleared away. In a corner of the hot, dark room Morgan could discern the form of Big Peggy weeping, drying her eyes with a corner of her apron. He asked her to empty the basin and she came forward as if he had paid her a compliment, glad to do something useful. She, too, hadn't slept. Poor old soul, he thought. She's been with him since he married. She has seen all his children born.

Suddenly the man on the bed jerked up in agonizing pain, cried out, then dropped back, rolling his head from side to side. His grandson dipped a clean cloth in a basin of water, squeezed it out and laid it across his forehead.

"Grandfather, can you hear me?"

Weakly, the man on the bed nodded. A line of spittle found the deep wrinkle from the corner of his mouth past his chin and his grandson wiped it. The old man grabbed his hand and looked at him wildly. The force of the grip surprised him, the terror in his face. He seemed to be looking past his grandson, over his shoulder, toward the ceiling, past the ceiling at some dreaded horizon.

"Rest now," he heard himself say, trying to take his arm away to pat the shoulder. Finally, the fingers let go and he rearranged the pillows. Big Peggy came back with a clean basin, followed by Robert and T.H., then Key. Silently they passed each other in the doorway, and Morgan entered the parlor as if it were another world. It was like rising from the dead, to come into that room with its long, sunny windows and spinet and portrait of Byron.

"We've sent word to Shadeland," Key Hunt said in that testy, professorish way he had. "I'm surprised you didn't meet Bob on your way back. Robert sent him with the news as soon as we knew. . . ."

Morgan sat down, his head in his hands. He rubbed them through his hair and threw his head back against the chair, closing his eyes and sighing. "So alive" was all he could say. "So alive. All those years. Those schemes of his, those endless schemes." His eyes went to the sideboard in the dining room, to the China vases with their ridiculous log houses, painted like palisades because the Chinese artist had never seen a log house. How disappointed his grandmother had been! He felt a bitter smile on his mouth.

"What . . . ?"

"Nothing, Uncle Frank."

By the time Henrietta arrived to see her father the voice had dropped to a whisper pleading for water. Diarrhea had stopped, and even the vomiting had lessened. But the patient now seemed in a state of total apathy. Her father no longer recognized her.

They sat up all night. Ellie brought ice from the Bruces' icehouse, extra bed linen. "Miss Becky, she understan's," the girl said. "She say to stay an' take keer of yo'seff."

Toward morning there seemed to be a change for the better. When he followed his mother into the sickroom, Morgan was surprised that his grandfather was propped up in bed. Freshly washed and seemingly without fever, he grinned a bit sheepishly at his daughter. "Thought they had me that time, Hen?" To Johnny he joked: "Tell Bob to saddle up the horses. We'll just go out to the Leestown farm this afternoon to check those yearlings."

"Yes, sir!" Well, he thought, maybe the old boy has pulled it off after all. He walked across the street, told the Bruces the news and collapsed on his bed. At sundown he felt a soft hand shaking him. It was his mother-in-law.

"Come downstairs," she whispered. "Come downstairs. We've had news of your grandfather. One of the servants came over. We've had news of your grandfather."

"It was his age," Henrietta said tearfully, when he finally got her calm enough to speak. She was wiping her eyes with a wet handkerchief, her chin trembling to keep back the sobs. "We thought he was fine!" She broke down, then forced herself to continue, not allowing him to comfort her. She had to work this out for herself. *You Ole Miss now, Miss Henrietta.* Oh, Aunt Peg . . .

"We thought he was fine," she said more evenly. "Then, about noon . . . it must have been about one o'clock, he seemed to get worse. There was no energy left. He just sank back, and the fever rose and rose and rose."

Why didn't you call me sooner? But he didn't let it get to his voice. Instead, they talked of details, as if the measurement of time, of fever, of words passing from the dead man's lips could matter now. But that was all they had to cling to, because the truth, the reality of a larger void behind those details, was too deep for examining. They ignored the void and concentrated on the minutiae, and talked as if death could have been avoided. The what-if's and the if-I-had-done-such-and-such started, and it was then that he had to surround her shoulders with his arms and let her cry it out.

It seemed only natural that Henrietta should move her family into Hopemont after her father's death. All his other children were well situated, and she had an ailing husband for whom the responsibilities of a farm were burdensome, if not physically dangerous. To a man, her brothers T.H., Robert, Key and Abraham and her sisters Eleanor Curd, Mary Hanna and Theodosia agreed. Robert, the only remaining bachelor since Key married, graciously decided he needed to buy a house on Broadway with a front room which could be used as an office.

Calvin had lost weight, and as John Morgan watched his father standing by the long parlor windows after the last visitor had repeated his sympathies and left, he thought suddenly of Alexander Gibson, and then let his eyes move to Byron and the uncanny resemblance: that same handsomeness, that same slight pout about the mouth and clarity of the eyes. Emotional faces, impulsive people. No wonder Henrietta had chosen, defensively, to stay a Hunt. In her heart she had never left Hopemont. Now she was home.

She fixed up the downstairs bedroom behind the parlor and off the backstairs foyer for Calvin and herself. The children were upstairs, spread throughout the bedrooms, with the old schoolroom on the third floor, where her own sisters and brothers had learned their letters, reopened for the younger ones. Aunt Hannah, Bouviette and Celina, who had graduated to seamstress, moved into the servant wing. Bob, her father's groom, would go to Robert, whose medical practice needed a buggy at the ready at all times. The inevitable friction between Aunt Hannah and Big Peggy was settled by selling Big Peggy to Key, whose wife, Julia, could use an excellent cook. "It's only moving a few blocks away," Henrietta reassured her. "Until their new house is built. And they have one of those new cooking stoves. I know you'll love it." But still, there was a catch in her throat as she watched Big Peggy leave.

Kitty, now fourteen, and Richard, a year younger, enrolled in Dr. Ward's Academy. Charlton went to Van Doren's Institute for Lads and Young Gentlemen, and nine-year-old Tommie, with the "babies," Tom, six, and Key, five, studied upstairs with an Episcopalian student of theology from Transylvania who boarded at Hopemont in return for his tutoring. Kitty also attended Madame Blaique's Dancing Academy and before she knew a Circassian Circle from a waltz, was begging her mother for a ball gown. Cal, now twenty-two, would stay at Shadeland to manage the farm.

The only one who worried her was Johnny. Every day she watched him walk across the street to the Bruce house. She knew he worked hard. And she knew what he was up to: He would save Shadeland if he could. But was it worth it? Like her father she was a survivor.

She couldn't know that as the weeks passed her talk of selling Shadeland no longer seemed to John Morgan a betrayal, but a continuation of his grandfather's ability to swing with the tide, and almost, now, an inevitability. When he agreed with Richard Curd and Uncle Frank, both astute lawyers, that he should accept Sanders Bruce's offer, even Cal, almost tearful at first, was persuaded. Shadeland had been one of John Hunt's farms to begin with; it had proved a haven for Calvin Morgan when the Alabama business went broke, had given his children a home for almost twenty years. It was time to move on.

Still, it was painful for Johnny to break the news to Randolph and the others. And there would be the moving and the memories. The horses would go to the Leestown farm. The springhouse, the pond, the summer kitchen with its room above, where Lieutenant Davis had clanked his sword and McGregor's parrot had chortled Burns. And down the road, the little brick schoolhouse where Theophile Parsons had taught him how to spell and Cal had skinned his knees on the steps. The window in the parlor where his father had spent so many afternoons watching the seasons pass. The track, the stable. It was all there, like a dream he remembered, but more real for the remembering, for the dreaming. He wondered if Sanders could love it as much.

And the horses! Shamrock and Cyrus and Xenophon. Xenophon falling . . . who was to blame? He didn't know anymore, and yet it had seemed so clear then. And Amanda marrying Jake Bolton! Sard trotting, tail up in the spring, ready to breed. Delilah with her sweet, learning ways. And now her bone-lazy colt.

He walked to the stables, past Uncle Ben's herb garden, to look for Uncle Simon. At this time of day the horses would be in the barn and Uncle Simon might be in the tack room.

Unaccountably, the barn was empty. He went to the other end and saw the horses still grazing in the paddocks. He called out: no answer. The quiet of the place, the smells seemed to contain his whole life: the scurry of a kitten, the buzz of a fly, the faint, salty scent of horse sweat. Sunny mornings over fences, the new-mown fields in their noses, following Randolph or Cal or Amanda, the feel of wind or mist or moonlight against your eyelids, the sure rhythm of a three-beat canter under your seat . . . it was all here in this silent aisle between the empty stalls. Again, a sudden worry: It was feeding time; the horses should have been inside. Where was Uncle Simon?

He found him in the tack room, face-down, with a bridle still in his hand. A chill ran down John Morgan's back. Henrietta had sent word just that morning about the sale. Was there such a thing as a broken heart? He walked outside and leaned on a fence, watching the fields. They blazed green in the afternoon sun. "Well, you couldn't have left it anyway," he said softly. "Now you won't have to."

They buried him in the pioneer cemetery, beside Uncle Ben. Reverend Pratt, who had a church in town now, came out for the ceremony. "Two noble old men," he said afterwards to Johnny and Randolph. "You know as well as I do, Johnny, that if there's a heaven, they are there."

"Looks like we both lost gran'pappys, Massa John." Randolph said it simply, then smiled and looked away. John Morgan would always remember how his old friend placed his hand on his wife's shoulder as a signal that it was time to go. Maggie was pregnant again. James, eight, and Annie, seven, walked ahead. Five-year-old Jesse solemnly took his father's free hand.

Henrietta, to his surprise, was heartbroken. Only the presence of Aunt Betty sustained her. If Bouviette should go now, he thought, it will be the end of her. The end of all of us.

He had little worry. Aunt Betty proved to be a rock. He had never appreciated or loved her more.

Nor Randolph. A quiet, sweet-voiced Randolph eased Calvin over the rough edges. "He's a gem," Richard Curd, who was taking care of most of the finances, told him.

"Without Randolph," Key Hunt said frankly, "Calvin simply couldn't manage."

Maggie had her baby the first day of November. Morgan, who had gone out to Shadeland to supervise the moving, went down to the quarters as soon as he heard the news. It was a balmy day. They were outside, Maggie seated in the shade of the big tree by their cabin. Randolph, standing beside her, crooned to the bundle in his arms.

"Billy," he said with a big smile as Morgan came up. "He bes Billy."

Why not Simon? Morgan almost asked, then saw Randolph's face.

"Billy's a good name. May I hold him?"

Randolph stood erect in his homespun shirt as he handed the baby over. His thin beard and high cheekbones under that broad brow still gave his face an oriental look. Morgan looked past him down the long lines of trees to the pond. Randolph, then Maggie, followed his gaze. It was as if, in that moment, they were saying good-bye. Just then the baby's hand escaped the blanket and grabbed Morgan's finger. "He's a strong boy!" he said, and cleared his throat.

"Yassuh, he is," Randolph murmured, his voice cracking on the last word. "Mebbe we kin teach him to ride a hoss!"

As for Hopemont, it was a strange arrangement. The house, lot and slaves were part of the estate. In reality, Henrietta and Calvin owned nothing but the money from the sale of Shadeland, and debts ate into that. The rest of the Hunt servants, including Nicely, went to T.H. The Leestown farm, although part of the estate, had been left to Henrietta's management. Now, with Shadeland gone, Randolph and his family would move there. The Brewers, who had managed the place for thirty years, had finally saved enough to buy a river farm near Cincinnati. T.H. hated to see them go, but Johnny's confidence in Randolph assuaged his fears. "He'll be as good or better," he predicted. "He knows all of Uncle Simon's tricks with horses, and not even Cal can keep better books." Adam replaced Bob as coachman-butler. Things seemed almost back to normal that Christmas when Kitty, now the prize pupil at Madame Blaique's, announced her first ball. Calvin, in John Hunt's old office off the front hall where he had set up his library, laughed out loud when she begged him to escort her. "I'm too old for Monsieur Giron's fancy parties," he grinned. "Ask Richard."

"But Richard is a baby."

"He's only a year younger than you. . . ."

Kitty stopped her father with a look. With her hair parted in the middle and drawn back over her ears, to explode in little bouncing curls at the back of her neck, she was indeed a young lady. Her sharp tongue, he reminded himself, was often like her mother's. But she had a smile that she knew could devastate the men of the family, and she turned from her father to Johnny and used it now.

"Why can't you take me?"

"Me?"

"I'm sure Rebecca wouldn't mind."

She did, but he had a good time anyway.

The winter was mild. Shadeland was weaned and grew big and ate hay, and life seemed to settle again. Abraham Hunt's Louisville branch was thriving. Henrietta became Mrs. Calvin Morgan, a Lexington matron who attended lyceums and concerts with Mrs. Gratz, the Bruces, Mrs. Todd and the sisters of the governor. Kitty took pianoforte lessons, and Tommie went around the house conjugating French verbs. Henrietta especially liked to see Johnny ride out the Leestown Road to confer with Randolph and the Shadeland field hands they had managed to save from the sale, who were fencing and plowing old pastures, preparing the change from a horse-breeding operation to tobacco. "We'll have enough hands to make the switch," she told Calvin confidently. "Vice, as Papa said, is always a staple crop."

She avoided political talk. She wept over Fredrika Bremer's novels of simple Swedish life, served cakes and chocolates at sewing circles and reading guilds, and borrowed copies of *The Quarterly Review* to study the latest Godey fashion plates while Calvin read *The New York Sun* or Mr. Greeley's *Tribune* or *The Lexington Observer and Reporter*. Early in February Henry Clay introduced his "Omnibus" bill, which would be known as the Compromise of 1850.

"It won't work," T.H. complained. "Seems as if Henry's given up California without a fight, in exchange for slave trade in the District of Columbia —an area not much bigger than Fayette County! As for the fugitive law, they don't obey it now. Does he think they'll obey an even stiffer one?"

For ten weeks the great debate raged in Congress, and the Hopemont parlor became a forum spread with New York and Kentucky newspapers. Henrietta didn't mind; it gave Calvin something to do. She was amused that Hank Clay, the Old Coon of the early cartoons, had become the venerated Prince of Politics. The gentlemen in her parlor took it all so seriously: the Wilmot Proviso—the idea that anybody in his right mind would want to move to New Mexico! They sympathized with old John C. Calhoun, on the verge of death, who had to ask James Mason to read his last speech in Congress, a lament over this new talk of disunion, which Calhoun blamed on the changing character of the Central Government.

"He's right," the gentlemen echoed. "The Central Government is only interested in power. The Great Wet Nurse!" Privately, when the ladies couldn't hear, they added: "What do they want, a nation of head-nodders? What next will they control? How much we piss? Or fill our chamber pots?"

They eagerly read the speeches of Douglas and Webster, and quoted Jefferson Davis, now a senator from Mississippi. "He says disunion will be inevitable unless a balance of power is maintained."

"Amen!" someone said.

"With California in as a free state, that can't be," muttered T.H.

They all looked at him in alarm. It was a fear they all shared, but had never allowed to surface. Southern politicians planned a meeting in Nashville for what they called the Resistance Movement. The pot, as T.H. kept warning them, was heating up. Nowhere, thought Johnny, could you escape the infernal debate. The Bruce house, normally nonpolitical, was no exception.

Margaret Bruce had the irritating habit of saying almost everything twice. "Can you get that ball of yarn for me, Rebecca? Can you get it for me, the ball of yarn?" When they heard that Mr. Clay's Compromise had indeed passed Congress with more Democrats than Whigs supporting him, she was delighted that the conciliatory spirit of Douglas and Webster had prevailed. "You see, we won't have trouble after all, in spite of everything that some people say. In spite of what some people say, we won't have trouble after all."

The "some people," Morgan knew, were the Hunts and Morgans, although he had certainly not joined the argument one way or the other. Even his father, who loved a debate, had remained aloof. There will always be people on the bottom, Calvin Morgan had said. What difference does it make what we call them? The more important question is whether they are taken care of or left to shift for themselves. Isn't it better that they are cared for? He smiled at his wife. Isn't that right, Hen? *Noblesse oblige.*

And because of the cough that followed, John Morgan remembered that his mother did not argue, but turned the talk to other things.

Margaret Bruce, with her black hair plastered back, came into focus. I can't blame her, Morgan thought. Maybe she says everything twice because she is afraid of being interrupted. Yesterday in the Bruce parlor, a stuffy room with plump little chairs holding their upcurving seats like so many pincushions, he sat balancing a teacup on his thigh, the tiniest of napkins making a predictably unsuccessful effort to catch any spills that might occur. At that moment his father-in-law was exploding.

"Mr. Clay's famous Compromise is no guarantee that we won't have trouble, my dear," John Bruce grumbled. "As long as there are hotheads who go about clamoring for their 'Constitutional rights.' "

"I thought that's what we based our whole government on, sir. Constitutional rights." He surprised himself by the loudness of his voice.

"Rights, rights! Have you read the document recently? And that bunch of fools down at Nashville—have they read it? Do they know that the writers of it and the signers of it were not Hebrew prophets by a long shot, but politicians like themselves. . . . That libertine Franklin. That blustering Patrick Henry. And Sam Adams! God help us. *Rights!*"

They had come together, he reminded himself, to discuss Becky's health. The new furnace they had installed would certainly help. But it was the summer they were worried about. She had received another invitation from Rebecca Gratz for a visit to Philadelphia. It could coincide with his own trip east, to settle some business in New York and Boston. For weeks he had looked forward to it. Should she go with him? Or with her mother, and meet him in Philadelphia later? She had enjoyed herself so much at Graham Springs, and returned feeling stronger. A trip would do her good.

"Yes, I remember."

Yes, I remember her at Graham Springs, laughing in wildflowers. And now they were talking of her as if she were a child, or an idiot incapable of thinking for herself. She was upstairs, dutifully upstairs, and her brother Sanders had been brought in as added ammunition for their cause. Sanders had ridden in from Shadeland and sat on one of the needlepointed chairs, legs crossed at the knee, swinging his foot. "I don't see that there's much to discuss," he said, looking levelly at his brother-in-law as if he were lining him up in the sight of a gun. Something in the way he turned his head, turtlelike, made the blood rise to John Morgan's face. He had actually put a buffalo rug in the parlor! "I wonder if he left the head on," Kitty said when she heard of it.

Margaret Bruce saw her son-in-law's flushed look and quickly called out across the room: "Why, of course there is, Sanders!" She tried a laugh and looked at her daughter's husband. "John just wants what's best for Becky. He thinks a change would do her good."

Does he now? the look on Sanders's face said. His usually dour expression stretched into a grin. Or would the arrangement of separate travel be convenient for other activities having nothing to do with medical considerations?

Wouldn't they be surprised if they knew that, contrary to rumors, nothing has happened with Miss Betty Wickliffe? That John Morgan, so-called libertine and womanizer, is really more chaste, more shy than they suppose? That card games and late hours and whiskey were substitutes for trust? His own unanswered questions brought that little crooked smile to his mouth. He crossed his own legs, swung his own foot, and infuriated Sanders with his silence.

"Rights," John Bruce repeated distastefully. He lingered on the word as if satisfied that his antislavery views would irritate his son-in-law sufficiently. The upstart had even offered to help him make out manumission papers for the Bruce servants!

John Morgan looked toward his mother-in-law as his only ally. On the stairs, just this morning, she had agreed with him that Becky should go. If she stayed here she would just get weaker, sitting in the heat day after day, doing that damned needlepoint, making those little square sachets. Puffed up like the cushions. Stuffed with dried-out life.

Margaret Bruce avoided his eyes and looked instead at her husband, leaning back now in his straight-backed chair, a limp-wristed, slight little man with a mass of dark hair that made his face seem thinner. Many people had been fooled by those limp wrists and that seemingly hesitant smile. The wrists were limp not from weakness but from having spent a lifetime getting what he wanted, from his mother, from his wife, and now from Becky.

When Rebecca was a child and he spoke to her alone it was always with a bantering tone, as if he would badger her into some rebellious remark, which he would find delightful and could report as an amusing anecdote to his friends. When, at about the age of twelve, she began realizing unconsciously that his jokes were really a kind of patronizing sarcasm, she began meeting them with a wide-eyed reticence that he interpreted as innocence. He was puzzled, then irritated, by her smiling silences. He would have been dumbfounded if he had known her acquiescence was merely the clever caution of self-preservation. Because he didn't understand her he put her at a distance, like a doll on a shelf, and gradually stopped bragging about her to his friends. His revenge—as unconscious as her growing distrust and fear of him—was to replace her impertinence with infirmity. He simply made an invalid of her. The fact that his son-in-law suspected this, and the fact that he suspected his son-in-law suspected this, made the presence of the young man in his household intolerable. As for his wife, Margaret had long ago made her own compromises.

Now, as he waited in a shaft of dust motes by his parlor window, John Bruce wanted agreement. The sun shot two dots from the glass of his spectacles. He pulled them off and swung them in a circle. There was nothing indecisive in the action. Becky would stay home.

Morgan canceled his own trip.

A patent for a machine which could sew curves came out and T.H. ordered a half dozen. On the 9th of July Zachary Taylor died.

Morgan was sitting in the Bruce garden when Kitty brought him the news that the President, who had drunk cold milk under the blistering sun at a Fourth of July celebration in Washington City, had died within a week. Surrounded by Becky's wildflowers, he read the account of the funeral again after she left. Webster and Clay were pallbearers, and Old Whitey, stepping in tempo with the booming cannon, followed the procession, inverted spurs swinging from his stirrups. The memory of a red-faced man with a shaving towel circling his thick soldier's neck came back . . . the stern look followed by the surprisingly easy laugh, the sudden warmth and deep concern of Zach Taylor. Monterrey. Old Rough and Ready and the boys at Buena Vista. Could it have been so long ago?

And now Shadeland, too, was gone.

He turned, instinctively, to the business, as if making money, building a secure future would somehow be a tribute to all the effort that old John Hunt had given the family. Shadeland had been part of that. To preserve and build that inheritance became a driving force. Because his father was, that Christmas and winter of 1850–51, less and less active, Morgan came to think of himself as the head of the family. Unconsciously, "home" meant not the rooms he shared with Becky at the back of the Bruce house, but Hopemont. Frequently he missed meals and felt less and less the need to apologize. For Christmas he made Charlton a model ship at a table in Sanders's old bedroom—now their "morning room"—cutting and glueing pieces. Becky worked on her needlepoint. They would spend hours not speaking.

Cal joined the business, and T.H. became an older brother for both of them. When two of the spinners showed up one morning with a bottle of corn whiskey, T.H. marshaled them to the police station with the force of his voice, disdaining the pistol Cal offered. John Morgan had never seen, even in his Mexican days, a sterner look on a man. "What a general he would have made!" he half-joked. Cal, standing beside him and watching the procession march off, the two black men with T.H. striding behind, said softly, "You've forgotten Al Johnston. But I agree. T.H. is quite a fella."

Spring came early. Redbud and wild plum and dogwood. Key Hunt finished Loudon, his neo-Gothic house on land Dr. Warfield, his father-in-law, had given him as a wedding present, and talked about running for the Kentucky legislature. The Lexington-to-Frankfort railroad was finished and challenged the stage: The stage won. Will came back from California.

"I ain't seen no gold," he said sheepishly, more than a little drunk. Henrietta, in spite of some misgivings, agreed to let him live at the Leestown farm. There were saddles to be mended, and his knowledge of blacksmithing would help Randolph, whose time could be used more profitably with the field hands. Sard was moved to the old log barn to give Will a workroom and it became routine, as May moved into summer, that the older boys, Richard and Charlton, would ride out there with Johnny. Shadeland's training had started and Charlton, especially, had inherited his father's passion for horses. His own mare, a little liver chestnut he called Lucy, was nursing a foal and Henrietta let them take the *calèche* as often as weather permitted. When Richard, like the town boys, started calling it a barouche, she threatened to make him walk.

As John Morgan watched twelve-year-old Charlton take fences, his own days with Cal and Amanda came back. But when Charlton wanted to try Shadeland, his brother was adamant. "How old is Shadeland? Two. He needs a year at least on the flat. No jumping."

"He'd be too lazy anyway."

"Look here, Charl. Red Man here jumps because he wants to. Shadeland is smart. Why should he jump—or do anything—if he's smart? You've got to win his confidence. You do that by being honest. Honest with him, honest with yourself. You're not good enough for Shadeland."

"I know, I know," Charlton lashed out. "Only Randolph is good enough. Randolph, Randolph, Randolph. . . ."

"See here, young man, Shadeland is business. Business, do you hear? He's not just a horse. If he races well, we can retire him to stud. Your mother needs all the money she can get. . . ."

But he wasn't being quite honest himself. The business had gone well, and his mother's financial outlook had improved. Still, the boy had to learn.

After supper, when he let himself into the front door of Hopemont for his usual nightly visit with Henrietta, Cal called him into the stairwell and closed the door. He drew him down onto the second step of the curving stairs. The door to the garden was open and he got up and closed that, too, then settled again. They were alone at the bottom of the great well, with the stairs spiraling above them.

"What's this all about?"

"I'll tell you," Cal said softly, glancing up the stairs to make certain the younger boys were not awake. He waited a minute, and when there was no sound he said more evenly, "You've got more to worry about than training horses."

"Well, tell me."

"Shush! Not so loud!" He looked at his hands, then up again. "Richard's gone insane."

John Morgan leaned back and almost laughed. "Come now, Cal, don't be stupid."

"It's true. He wants to go with the Crittenden boy to Cuba."

"Cuba! Whatever for?"

"With a man named Lopez, who's recruited volunteers to free Cuba from the Spanish."

"Well, I agree with you. That *is* insane. He's only fifteen!"

"How did you think when *you* were fifteen?"

He remembered Wash. "Maybe you're right. This could be serious. We'll have a talk. . . ."

"I'm afraid that's what we don't want to do. You know Richard. He'd do it then to spite us."

"You're right. Then let's talk with Bill Crittenden."

The Crittenden house was one of the most sumptuous in Lexington, and William Crittenden, twenty-one, reflected the blond good looks of the family. He greeted John Morgan graciously and spoke of the expedition as a lark, a holiday which would make Cuba into another state.

"That may be all fine and eventually commendable," Morgan said quietly, feeling older than his twenty-six years as he watched this boy full of enthusiasm for the dust and blood and pain no young man thought of when flags waved and bands blared. Especially when an expedition was secret, enthusiasm could enjoy an element of passion. He would have to argue carefully, remembering his own state of mind before Mexico. How exciting it had all seemed! And he returned with two coffins.

Discreetly, he maneuvered young Crittenden into promising that he would leave Richard behind for further recruiting "when the situation was stabilized and men would be needed to solidify the gains."

"Yes, yes . . . that sounds good. Perhaps you, sir, would care to join our efforts?"

"Unfortunately"—he tried to smile—"I've had my fill of Latin expeditions. Not that I don't wish you the best of luck, mind. Be careful." He shook William's hand at the door of the drawing room. "Don't bother seeing me out. I can find my way. And good luck again."

Richard, disappointed, bought himself a Buena Vista hat for his future visit to the tropics. Then they received the news that Lopez had abandoned fifty-five volunteers on the beach while he went inland. When he didn't return they took to small boats and were promised the status of prisoners of war by the captain of the Spanish warship which picked them up an hour later. They were not treated as prisoners of war; they were lined up against a wall and shot.

Yes, I can see them, Morgan thought. And the waste of life was appalling. Was he getting old? He was only five years older than Crittenden, whose illustrious uncle John J., the ex-governor of Kentucky, was now President Fillmore's Attorney-General. When Willie's body was returned, the whole town turned out for his funeral. Morgan stood beside his brothers and tried to console Richard, whose sobs were audible in the thick summer air under the trees.

John J. Crittenden came back to Kentucky for the ceremony. He needed to see Henry Clay, who was ill. There was talk of promoting the Whig candidacy of General Winfield Scott for President. Yankee Whigs would support the General, but the Southern faction was suspicious of Scott's free-soil leanings. "We've got to make sure that Henry's Compromise stands," they murmured. Crittenden, on the other hand, regarded Fillmore as vital to their wishes. Only a moderate, he argued, and not an old war horse like Scott, could prevent the reopening of the slavery controversy.

"Why would they want Scott, anyway?" Morgan asked, remembering how bitterly old Zach Taylor had watched half his army leave for Veracruz.

"The question is why would they want Seward and the other Northern extremists who are behind Scott?" T.H. answered bitterly. "Seward has already declared that there's a higher law than the Constitution. That's dangerous talk."

As winter turned to spring and the political conventions of 1852 moved closer, the speculations in Henrietta's parlor heated to the boiling point. "Hopemont has become a convention hall itself!" Henrietta wailed, but only half-heartedly. She enjoyed the give-and-take of ideas. She was not surprised to receive a note from a Mr. Gordon Niles, a newspaperman from New York, who had met her brother Abraham on his trip through New England. Niles was staying at the Phoenix Hotel and would be pleased to meet her.

That did surprise her. "Why me?" she asked, and twitched her nose. "And whatever for?" She looked at her sons. They knew her opinion of Yankees.

Cal shrugged. "Probably wants to sample some of Aunt Hannah's cookin', Ma. Uncle Abe's always braggin' about it."

Gordon Niles was a clean-shaven young man with fine sandy hair that fell into his blue eyes. Eager, pink-cheeked, with a quick smile, he sported a checked suit and a red tie. A real dandy, her brother T.H. would have said, but Johnny liked him and brought him around to Hopemont shortly after his note arrived. Henrietta received him in the parlor, ensconced between the windows in an armchair. Niles sent her a boyish laugh as he stood before her, his feet on the polished floor.

"Yes, ma'am. I met your brother, Mister Abraham Hunt, in Massachusetts."

"Indeed?" Henrietta asked in her most imperial tone.

"Mister Hunt made the South sound so interesting that I asked for an assignment and *The New York Times* has commissioned me to write a . . . a kind of travelogue of the South."

"Oh?"

"I intend to call it *A Journey into the Middle South*."

"Indeed? It sounds like something Mr. Swift might have written," Henrietta said icily. "Are we to be the Lilliputians or the larger specimens from Brobdingnag?"

"Come now," said Calvin, "won't you have a seat, Mr. Niles?"

The young man sank onto the chair and looked cheerfully toward his hostess.

"Neither, my dear lady. I know what your opinion of the Northern press must be. But the *Times* is a new paper, and hopes to present a more objective view than the sometimes overly critical ones of Mr. Greeley's *Tribune*. And I'm going to surprise you by saying that it was in England, of all places, that I determined to defend the South."

"Defend?"

"The English have no conception about life here. They get everything from the abolitionists' papers . . . and Mrs. Stowe."

"But you hadn't visited the South then, had you?" Calvin put in.

"Only briefly—to a relative in Charleston. Then I determined, if given the chance, to bring the powers of honest observation to a subject too long shrouded in misunderstanding—and now fanned into fantasy by William Lloyd Garrison. . . . Do you know that they actually believe the South wants Cuba as a state—and even Mexico, so slavery can expand endlessly?"

"They can't possibly believe that vile book," said Henrietta, still thinking of Mrs. Stowe. "I should think England would have more to think of just now."

And so the talk turned to the Crimea, the Cossacks and their horses, Kentucky thoroughbreds and Kansas.

"It's too bad your Mr. Clay isn't running again. He should have been our President in '44. Maybe we would have avoided that trouble with Mexico and all this squabbling over territories!"

Calvin cleared his throat. "Henry would have made a good one. You can't say he didn't try!"

Henrietta took her oldest son by the arm. "John, you've got to entertain him. He is a gentleman, but your father is getting too tired with all this talk. Ask Robert, or T.H. . . . You'll know what to do. If only it were later in the year, you could take him fox-hunting!"

"I'll find something, Ma."

He didn't have far to look. A political barbecue was scheduled at Mount Brilliant, at which Cassius Clay would speak.

"It will be Kentucky at its worst," Cal groaned. "Count me out."

Cal had reason to expect violence. "Cash" Clay, although Henry's cousin, was the local abolitionist—vitriolic, theatrical, some said hysterical. His bloodlines made his outbursts amusing, passed off as the results of a bad Yankee education. But sometimes his views were a downright embarrassment.

"I've heard," Cal said, "that some of Cash's enemies have paid a hired gun to come up from New Orleans. Man named Brown. Forty fights and never lost a battle."

"You can take my place at the factory." Morgan grinned. "Be good experience. Robert wants to go."

"Uncle Robert's going for the burgoo."

Two days later John Morgan sat between young Niles and Robert Hunt in the doctor's gig, with the top down. Ahead of them, on its hill, they saw the white portico of Mount Brilliant. A rolling lawn swept down to a natural amphitheater which was already filling with people. Robert parked the gig at the end of the driveway, behind a row of carriages. "Some people take Cash too seriously," Robert said to Niles as they walked across the grass toward the crowd. "And that suits him just fine." He laughed. "You wait and see."

Brown was easy to spot—a big man who took little trouble to conceal a six-shooter. He'd let it be known that if Clay opened his mouth he would "blow his damned brains out." Everyone's eyes were on the speaker, a pro-slavery candidate for Congress. He had just quoted a denunciation of Clay, not bothering to notice that some of his listeners, forewarned of his tactics, held handbills proclaiming the quotation to be false. Clay, at the edge of the crowd, reminded the candidate of the denial. Almost at once, Brown was on his feet.

"That's a damned lie!" he yelled.

"You lie," Niles heard Cassius say quietly, but loud enough. The word was barely out of his mouth when a gang of men who had come with Brown jumped Clay with clubs.

"Let me at him," Brown shouted, and Niles saw Clay in a cleared circle, with Brown not fifteen feet away, leveling his six-shooter.

Clay turned his body sideways and with the only weapon he had—his bowie knife—advanced to within arm's reach of Brown before the pistol fired. Clay grabbed his side; he knew that with five more shots, Brown would kill him now unless he made his move. With a flash the knife came up and then down, into Brown's skull and across an ear, digging out an eye in the process. Before Brown's stunned helpers could intervene, Clay had tossed him over a low stone wall and down into the creek.

"Some barbecue," murmured Niles in shock.

"Just Kentucky politics," Morgan answered.

"Is there a doctor? Is there a doctor?" someone yelled. Dr. Cross, the Transylvania professor that Robert had once punched in the nose, immediately went to Brown, Dr. Wolford to Clay. Miraculously, the ball had struck the silver-lined scabbard of the bowie knife and deflected, lodging in the back of Clay's coat. The only mark he had on him, besides the lump on his head from the club, was a spot of blood over his heart.

"Well, have you had enough excitement for one day?" Robert asked Niles as he picked up the reins again and turned the gig toward town.

"What do you think will happen?"

"Any jury in this county will be proslavery and anti-Cassius," Robert said decisively. "He hasn't a prayer . . . unless Henry defends him."

"Will he?"

Morgan grinned at Niles's innocence. "Ill as he has been, you can bet Henry Clay won't miss a chance to perform in court! You've got to stay for the trial, sir. It will be spectacular, I promise!"

"I'm sorry, John. If I had known . . . some people in Tennessee are expecting me. Friends of my father's. . . ." He looked back at Mount Brilliant receding in the last light of the warm afternoon. "Believe me, if all this were mine, I should never go away."

"Well, at any rate, you've now been thoroughly introduced to Kentucky," Robert Hunt laughed when they pulled up to the hotel.

Niles stuck out his hand to each in turn. The grip was warm, the blue eyes intense.

"I've enjoyed knowing you, Mr. Morgan. Maybe one day we shall meet again."

Morgan laughed. "That's not likely . . . but if . . . I'll be delighted!"

As predicted, Henry Clay's defense of his cousin was brilliant, ending in an appeal to family honor which put the jury on trial more than Cassius. Cassius was not only acquitted, but even the most adamant proslavery citizens of Lexington toasted Henry's oratory and loyalty to kin.

It would be Henry Clay's last victory in court. Ill and dying, he watched his Compromise ignored by Northern Whigs, who nominated General Winfield Scott for President. When the Democrats found a man named Franklin Pierce, old Whigs resurrected a slogan from the Clay-Polk campaign of '44: "It's like running a blood horse against a donkey."

Scott's antislavery stance would be, Calvin Morgan predicted, the end of the Whig party. When they heard of Henry Clay's death on June 29, they were not surprised. "At least he won't live to see it," T.H. agreed. "A worn-out old man who tried to save so much."

"The town won't be the same" was heard on all sides. Lexington gave her Old Coon a funeral fit for a king.

"This year I'm going."

"There's no reason why not."

"Now that the weather's cooled off . . ."

"Your father seems more agreeable."

"And Mother."

"And your mother."

"And you?"

He almost laughed, then managed a quiet smile. "I have to stay with the business this time."

"Don't you always?"

He still avoided her eyes.

"I'll try to see the Philadelphia Hunts," she said, folding linens, bustling about.

"That would be interesting. How long will you be gone?"

"Does it matter?" Becky turned to him. "Kitty's seventeen and you've got to screen her beaux. Richard doesn't want to go to Transy and you're worried about him. Charlton—how old is he, thirteen?—needs a father and you ride with him out the Leestown Pike every chance you get, to sit around and teach him how to smoke cigars with Randolph. When will you start with Tom and little Key?"

He kept telling himself, as he watched the soft bun of her hair turn from him, that in all fairness, she was right. His father, little by little, had abdicated his role as the head of the family, and even Henrietta's strong will could not manage the rough-and-tumble adolescence of young tomboys— Tommie not the least among them. Yes, he supposed Becky was right: He was the head of a family. When she returned, he promised himself, he would be fair to her. He would defy her parents and give her what he knew she wanted. He would build a house in the spring, and they would start a family of their own.

He pored over house plans. He became a member of the school board, a captain in the fire department, a city councilman. He sat in the Hunt pew in Christ Church almost every Sunday. He contributed to the alumni fund at Transylvania University.

"A regular pillar of the community while Becky's away," Robert Hunt joked, then sobered. "Then you haven't heard. No, you couldn't have. You've been out at the farm."

"What?"

"Caroline Turner's on the rampage again."

Caroline Turner was the notorious, Boston-born wife of wealthy old Judge Fielding Turner, whose big house, not far from the Todds', overflowed with servants. It was common knowledge that she beat them in fits of such violence that Judge Turner had spoken to Robert Hunt about it, worrying that she had been the direct cause of at least six deaths and asking his advice about declaring her insane. Now, this afternoon about four o'clock, she had thrown a small black boy from an upstairs window onto the stone flagging of her courtyard. Besides a broken arm and leg, his spine was injured.

"How badly, Doctor Wolford can't tell right now," Robert said, sitting down by the fire and leaning forward on his knees. "I called him for his opinion." He held his head in his hands and sighed. He took the drink Johnny handed him and gulped it down without tasting it. He looked back at the fire. "She's done things before, but nothing like this. He may not walk again." Robert rubbed his palms together, his dark head bent so that a curl of hair obscured his eyes. "She won't get away with it this time. The whole town's enraged."

The doctor was right about the rage. But the old judge had his wife

forcibly removed to the lunatic asylum the next morning, and Caroline
Turner never came to trial, despite the report from the commissioners of the
asylum, who "found no evidence of mental derangement." The jury was
discharged and the matter dropped.

It was as if, in a way, Brown had found his target. It was Lexington's
answer to Cassius Clay and emancipation.

Becky Morgan came back radiant just before Christmas, full of health and
news from Philadelphia. "You'll never believe . . ." But her husband
stopped her with a kiss. Two months had been too long. "And I actually
saw one lady wearing Mrs. Bloomer's outfit. . . ."

"You are beautiful. Did I ever tell you? Did you do something to your
hair?"

"No."

"It's beautiful." Why had he ever thought her dull? Her little face was
rounder than he remembered, her smile sweeter. He had missed her more
than he knew.

In January Rebecca Bruce Morgan was "in a delicate condition."

"Of course you must have rest," her mother told her.

"Mama, I've never felt better."

"Just the same, you mustn't be overdoing. Let Ellie help you more."

"Poor old Ellie. She can hardly get around herself."

"Just the same . . ."

Her mother's admonitions passed lightly through the air. Becky had never
been happier.

18

February was brutal. Sleet slashed through a north wind that fairly cut into the brick walls of the Bruce house and made Becky shiver in spite of all the quilts they could find. In the midst of his worry over her, Morgan received word from Randolph that Sard was down.

By the time he arrived they had walked him for three hours. But he kept stumbling.

"It's not colic," Morgan said.

"No, Massa," Randolph agreed.

"It may be pneumonia. That wind last night through that old log barn. It's not even chinked."

"We thought it would be a good winter, Massa."

It wasn't Randolph's fault. He should have ordered the chinking last fall. Becky's coming home, his own joy . . . he had neglected coming out. "Get some ropes. Four. Throw them over the rafters. And some canvas. We'll hoist him up."

"Hoist him, Massa?"

"And stuff those open places between the logs with anything you can find. Straw. Feed sacks. Rags. Anything."

Will, behind him, had already started stripping a side of leather for padding.

"And once he's up, I want his legs massaged." Sard, weak and trembling, had already broken out in a sweat. His shivering sides ballooned the canvas cradle as they hauled him off the floor. He was a pitiful bundle, this once great horse.

"He'll be great again," John Morgan promised, hardly believing his words. Nobody else did either, but they all pretended. Sardanapalus! That crazy colt, rolling on Wash . . . bucking on the way to his grave . . . how the neighbors had laughed when his father put him on the cart! How he had surprised them all! Dear old Sard!

Calvin came out the next day. The stallion was still hanging there, his legs a foot off the ground, with Randolph's James, now a lad of twelve, rubbing, rubbing, "He won' eat," James kept saying. "If'n he would eat . . ."

"Here, let me try." Calvin took a bucket of grain and sent James to the house for molasses. They mixed it, a sloppy, gooey mess, and Calvin held it up to the stallion's muzzle. His mouth twitched, then opened. Charlton and Randolph, behind him, gave a cheer. Calvin left orders for the mixture to be offered three times a day, plus water.

"Keep up the rubbing," John Morgan said to James. "Maybe we'll get the old boy on his feet yet."

But during the night the ropes broke, and when Randolph came into the stable the next morning he found Sard dead in the stall, his body splashed with blood.

"He beat hisseff to death," Randolph said as they watched him, Maggie weeping. "He tried to git up, an' beat hisseff to death."

"He was a fighter to the end," Morgan said quietly when James brought the news. They all put away from them the vision of what had happened: the flailing legs, the head thumping against the wall, that superb last effort to rise, against all odds, and the final giving in, in the pool of blood.

"Nobody has beat his time yet. You remember that 1:35 we kept secret?"

Calvin Morgan's eyes traveled from the fireplace to the window. In his mind, he was in that old log stable again, his hands numb with cold, feeding Sard grain.

"I know. We kept the secret," Cal answered. To Johnny his eyes sent a silent worry: He looks awful; this is more than grief over a horse.

As winter moved into spring, the gray colt Shadeland was their hope and joy. Nine-year-old Tom loved to go out to the farm and play with Jesse, who was his own age, while Johnny talked business with Randolph. Once, Morgan found them by Shadeland's stall. They had gone up to the barn to find Will, but he had gone to town.

"You're not getting any ideas about mounting?"

Tom shook his head. Jesse dug his toe in the dust and studied his foot.

"Then what?"

"Do you think, Brother Johnny, you can see someone in his eye?" Tom asked seriously, and looked up at the gray head hanging over the door.

"In his eye?"

"Like he's looking at us from a long way away . . . ?"

"A long way away?"

"Like, well, like he knows a lot more than we do. . . ."

Morgan looked from Tom and Jesse to the soft brown eyes of the colt. "I'm sure he does, at that," he said quietly. "Now, do you want to see the new baby? Jesse here has a new brother . . ." He followed them to the house. They scampered ahead, skipping in jerks, their arms flailing.

"What's his name?" Tom asked. The baby was already two months old. Maggie bounced him on her lap and looked away. Annie stood by her mother twisting her skirt.

"Massa. . . ." Randolph stopped, letting worried eyes drift to Morgan's face, then down to his hands again.

"Why don't you and Jesse go down to the pasture, Tom, and ask James to catch Delilah up? You can ride her, and we'll work Shadeland at halter before we go home," Morgan said cheerfully.

Randolph watched them run off before he cleared his throat.

"Massa, you don' suppose they bes . . . they bes anything wrong in namin' him Simon? I knows we had one thet died. But Ah sho' would lak a boy named Simon, Massa."

Morgan watched the baby's round, fat arms reach for his mother's hair.

Soon Becky, too, would be holding a child close. "Lots of folks have two sons with the same name. I think Simon would do just fine."

Randolph's face brightened.

"Now, will you promise me one thing?"

"Massa?" He caught up four-year-old Billy in the crook of his arm.

"You'll help me name mine when he gets here in September?"

Becky, so far, was fine, thank God. It was his father who worried them all. Not even Kitty's engagement to Colonel McClung, from Louisville, nor Shadeland's training—and he was good, that lazy colt, when he was asked —removed the lethargy which seemed to drop over Calvin Morgan like a cloak.

The office seemed to be the only place where the talk didn't turn on health, but it was no less tense. T.H. excitedly reported the activities of a new political party.

"But why are they calling themselves Know-Nothings?" Morgan asked. "Seems to me that's an insult."

"They consider it a badge of honor. When they first organized they met in secret and gave that answer to any busybody wanting to know what they were about."

"What *are* they about?"

"Saving the country from the immigrants."

"Immigrants? You can't be serious."

"I think they're crazy, too," T.H. said without humor. "They're a bunch of bigots. But can't you see the abolitionists recruiting those thousands of foreigners for their own purposes? *Those* are the poor souls who know nothing."

"I thought you agreed with Henry Clay's plan for gradual emancipation for Kentucky."

"I did. I do. But that's a far cry from immediate freedom, with no preparation for jobs or education. It would destroy the economy of the South. Of the nation. Of us. John, are you listening?"

"Yes . . . yes, I'm listening."

Did I hurt you? My God, if I hurt you . . .

No, no, it was beautiful.

No, no, I hurt you.

Silly boy. It was beautiful, I tell you. You're getting worse than Father.

I want to be your father and your brother and everything.

Outside their window her wildflowers were blazing in the May sunshine. By September . . . by September this delicate girl would give him a child. It was incredible! He saw T.H. watching him and grinned. "Come now, T.H.! The sun is shining! Did you ever see a more glorious day? Or smell one?"

"I forgot," T.H. said, rubbing his nose and putting his handkerchief back in his pocket. "You're counting months now, aren't you? The birth of a firstborn son is more important than all this nonsense." He was not, essentially, a political man.

"How do you know it will be a son?"

"Your mother says so. The ladies have a way of knowing these things."
T.H. frowned. "By the way. Not to spoil your day, but . . ."

"But?"

"Ned Baynham's had some very bad luck with cards. A game in Bardstown. Lost everything. His slaves have been auctioned off. John Henry's
gone to Caroline Turner."

Shortly after his wife's release from the asylum, Judge Turner died, leaving a will which gave his slaves to his children. None of them, he wrote,
were to go "to the said Caroline for it would be to doom them to misery in
life and a speedy death." But Caroline, through her lawyers, renounced the
will and kept most of her slaves. Now she had John Henry.

That summer Morgan saw him driving the Turner buggy around Lexington, his round face breaking into an easy smile when he saw him. He was
good with the horses.

For a while he forgot about John Henry. In June little ten-year-old T.H.,
Jr. died. How can they stand it? Morgan thought as he watched T.H.'s wife
Mary at the cemetery, this quiet, sweet woman who had buried three babies
early in her marriage, and nine-year-old Mary while he was away in Mexico.
Now, little T.H. It seemed too much. Yet she could smile and talk of a
merciful God. Morgan made a point, that summer, of visiting them often.

Their lives were now immersed in their children. Catherine was nine,
Anna Frances—"Nannie"—was seven, and little Tilford five. He never
came empty-handed.

"You spoil them so, John."

"Do you mind?"

Mary Hunt smiled. "You know I don't. In fact, you provide quite a threat.
All I have to do is tell Nannie that if she isn't good, Uncle Johnny won't
come by . . . and you should see her mind!"

T.H. came in. His face was still haggard, lax with grief. Tilford ran to
him and his father swung him around in circles.

"You smell like a barnyard." Mary held out her cheek.

He set the boy down and sent him off with a pat on his bottom, then
kissed his wife. "I've been out to see the hounds."

He looked at Johnny with his gaunt, gallant smile.

In August Margaret Bruce directed Ellie and the other maids in the preparation of "the coming event." The room was scrubbed from ceiling to floor,
unnecessary items of furniture were removed, curtains, bedclothes washed
and ironed. Becky, in her own burst of energy, arranged and rearranged the
baby clothes in a chest in the morning room. Morgan had never seen such
tiny shirts. "Mrs. O'Brien and her daughters have made enough for an army.
Will he really need so many clothes?" She laughed, and he pretended to be
more ignorant than he was, if that gave her pleasure.

"Look," she said. "Isn't this little gown adorable? Delphine—Mrs.
O'Brien's girl—did it. Look at that stitching! Have you ever seen anything
so lovely?"

"Yes," he murmured, kissing her shoulder.

"John, do go to the races tomorrow. I know you want to. Don't stay with me. I'm fine! And I know your father is looking forward to it."

Morgan hummed assent, remembering the enthusiasm on Calvin's face. For the first time in months he'd seemed alive again. "He is that!"

"Then it's settled."

"Who does Sanders think will win?"

"Darley, of course. Doctor Wolford's colt by Boston. Have you seen Sanders's latest notebook? He has piles of names. It will be the beginning of an American stud book, Father says."

"Sanders has the heart of a bibliographer."

She looked up at the sarcasm in his voice.

He should say nothing to spoil her day, he reminded himself, and Sanders's scribbling was valuable. Even Calvin Morgan said so. But Shadeland, that 15.2 compact little gray colt, would win.

"I think I will," he said.

It promised to be the race of the year. Richard and Charlton were already at the racecourse when he went to pick up his parents, the girls, Tom and Key. It had rained for two days and the turf was pastern-deep in mud. "You know how his mama hated de watah," Randolph worried.

They sat on the gallery of Dr. Warfield's The Meadows, overlooking six hundred acres and the track where Sard and Randolph had made history walking over the line. Now Shadeland. Morgan felt a terrifying delight almost take his breath. Could they do it again? To the north he could see the tower of Uncle Frank's and Aunt Julia's Loudon, just over a rise of ground. The view was excellent and Calvin was flushed with excitement as he talked with Julia's father about the horses.

"I hope it's not too much for him," Henrietta worried to her two oldest sons.

"You sound like Randolph," laughed Cal.

Still, they were all worried, and though they did not acknowledge fear, they all knew it: Calvin Morgan was in a decline. A horse race had never yet failed to revive his spirits. There were a dozen horses entered. It would be a good day.

Just before the start, a hawk flew over. Shadeland saw it and took off. He was followed by Madonna and Garrett Davis; all three horses ran two and a half miles before they could be pulled up. Garrett Davis appeared to be in great distress, limping back, and was withdrawn by order of the judges. Madonna trotted up smartly to the starting line. Shadeland loped back, swinging his head.

"What's the matter with him?" Calvin asked, and insisted on going down to the paddock.

"His right eye, Massa. Might have stuck some brush in it, in dat field ovah dere," Randolph said, fingering the reins to keep the stallion straight.

"Should we withdraw him? Johnny, hold that lid while I look." Calvin pulled the lower lid down, looking for a speck of bark or leaf. The eye was watering, but he saw nothing.

"I honestly think he'll be all right," John Morgan said reluctantly. How he would hate to spoil his father's day. "He cantered back in good form."

"He did that, Massa," said Randolph, still aboard.

But the best two miles out of three? Morgan looked at the eye, and the quivering lid. "Well, let's try it."

Calvin's feet were soaked, and Morgan insisted that they return to the house. They were lucky. They were settled again on the veranda before the single drumbeat announced the start.

Darley flashed to the front, and was never headed. He won the first heat in 1:55½, distancing all but three others.

"What's distancing?" asked Tom.

"Going for Sweeny," said Charlton disdainfully. "Don't you know that?"

"In a mile heat," their father explained, "if a horse falls behind the leader more than forty yards he's eliminated . . . distanced. In a four-mile it's eighty yards."

"Why? And why do they call it going for Sweeny?"

Calvin Morgan laughed. "Nobody knows. Maybe there was a rider called Sweeny who just galloped along to save his horse for later heats. That wouldn't be playing fair."

"Oh."

What Calvin didn't explain was that Richard Ten Broeck, owner of most of the stock in the Metairie Course in New Orleans, was there that day on the lookout for horses to run in the Great State Post Stakes, a race he was promoting to draw the best horses from each state, with the greatest purse ever raced for. Darley had now won the first heat. Would Shadeland win the second and third? And maybe represent Kentucky in the Great Stakes?

They broke, with a Boston filly, Midway, in the lead. On the backstretch Darley headed her, then Shadeland came from nowhere and the three of them ran as a team. Even at the turn, it was anybody's guess, until, digging in the mud with water flying, Shadeland plunged home two lengths ahead. Calvin was on his feet, cheering wildly. Even Henrietta, who had become immune to her husband's "turf madness," as she called it, cried out, her arms waving.

They waited for the third heat, which would tell the tale. The anxiety was almost suffocating. The horses lined up, Midway fidgeting, and Darley, a strapping bay with a blaze and four white stockings, nervous as a warhorse. Shadeland seemed unconcerned: Was he excited enough? They broke, with Darley in the lead. He led them to the wire and there was never any question which horse would represent Kentucky in New Orleans.

"But he wasn't distanced," Calvin Morgan kept saying, between coughs. Henrietta's look said: *Let's get him home.* Although the sun had come out the wind was up, and the water-sogged ground out to the carriage was, as Kitty kept saying, soup.

John and Cal, with Richard and Charlton, walked down to the stables. Randolph and James were brushing Shadeland down. The eye was closed. Cal adjusted the blanket and stood with his brothers watching Randolph walk him out. "We'll get Abe Buford to look at him," Cal heard Johnny say, but tears choked his throat and he swallowed back his answer, which would have served no purpose, anyway.

"I've got to get back to Becky," Morgan said slowly, hating to leave.

"We'll take care of everything," Cal got out. "Don't worry."

A week later it was confirmed: Shadeland had lost an eye.

"He can still race. Did you see him go? And he was in pain. What if he didn't have pain? Hell, he can see with one eye." So all the Morgans said, in one form or another. "And we can breed him. We can find the best damned mares this side of England and breed him."

"His times have been nothing to be ashamed of," Calvin said.

"We will," John Morgan told Randolph as they stood watching Shadeland in his stall at the Leestown farm. "We will find the best damned mares."

"Yassuh!"

One balmy evening in early September, at his mother's urging, he stayed at Hopemont for supper and talked until almost midnight with his father and brothers. Calvin Morgan was in a festive mood, and it was so good to see him enjoying himself that no one wanted to stop talking. The Curds came over and they played poker.

Becky was already in bed when he came in. Toward morning he felt a grip on his arm and heard her breathing, hard and fast, a gasping that garbled her words, but she had no need for words. He roused her mother and sent for Dr. Wolford. Afterwards, there were the hours spent in the parlor being "informed." Toward noon the bustle and running back and forth subsided, and he met Dr. Wolford at the foot of the stairs. "Things have settled a bit, my boy," he said, laying a hand on his shoulder. "Sometimes it's that way. We must wait for Mother Nature. It's early, you know. Almost a month. The pains have subsided. You may see her now."

He had forgotten how small she could look in bed, like a child with a great pillow for a stomach. He had watched it grow, in awe, felt her attempts during the long nights of this last month trying to get comfortable, throwing one leg over a folded sheet to prop up the weight pulling at her sides.

"It's early anyway, the doctor says," he said. "Maybe it's a false alarm . . ."

"It's no false alarm." The harsh fear in her voice startled him. "It's in a bad position, Ellie says. She's seen many babies born."

"What can we do?"

"Nothing . . . that's the thing of it!"

She started crying and turned her head from him. The action made her hair stick to her neck, wet from tears and the cold cloths which her mother kept dabbing her with. Margaret Bruce, in a chair by the bed, gave him a long look, her finger to her lips. He nodded and she left them, satisfied. His hand began stroking the soft brown head, and became a thing apart from his body. Back and forth, across her hairline: lift, smooth, lift, smooth. Her eyelashes rested like a baby's on her cheek. She was a beautiful girl and he loved her more than anything in the world. Didn't she know that? He pushed aside the thought: Did she care?

She slept, her breathing barely lifting the white muslin at her throat. He let his hand lift away, and sat watching her until the light grew dim.

"Come heah, Massa John!"

It was Ellie at the door.

"De suppah's gittin' cold! Miss Margaret, she say to kum downstaihs now."

The others had eaten. Margaret Bruce took his place by the bedside while he wolfed down chicken and lightbread. A bottle of port waited in the parlor. Marse Bruce, the butler told him, had retired. The room was quiet, the air through the window sweet with the faint first smell of autumn.

He didn't know when he slept. The butler was shaking him by the shoulder and he immediately looked toward the stairs. It wasn't Becky but Reverend Pratt, who wanted him.

"He won' kum in, Massa. Say he mus' see you. He outside, Massa."

"Good evening, Reverend Pratt. Won't you come in?"

The little man declined. "John . . ." He cast his eyes to the threshold, then back at John Morgan's face. "John, I have a favor to ask."

"Surely. Surely, of course. Ask it."

Reverend Pratt looked down at his thin-fingered hands turning his hat in circles. "You know the seamstress . . . Mrs. O'Brien?"

Morgan chuckled, relieved. Reverend Pratt had a reputation for being overly anxious. Probably more baby clothes. "Doesn't everybody in Lexington?"

"Yes. Well. Could we speak in private?"

He looked around. "Aren't we alone?"

"I guess so."

"Would you like to come inside?"

"No, no . . . The fact is . . ."

He stopped, unable to go on.

"Perhaps you would like a walk? Just a minute." Morgan turned, said a word to the butler, who was still waiting, and returned. He took the preacher by the elbow and they stepped across the street, up North Mill toward Transy. The night was pure September: restless cumulus clouds passing a waning moon. As they walked, shadows sped before them up the slight incline of the parade ground and over the columned façade of Old Morrison. They walked onto the clipped lawn of the campus and found a bench. "Now tell me," Morgan said. "It can't be as bad as all that. . . ."

"I'm afraid it is." Sitting down seemed to calm the preacher and he laid his hands firmly on his knees, palms down, and began tapping his fingers. "You know that Mrs. O'Brien is an octoroon? Has Negro blood?"

"Somewhere, I suppose, I'd heard it. But it's been long ago forgotten, hasn't it? She's an institution in town."

One of the hands came up impatiently and swatted the air. "She may be an institution, but about eighteen years ago she had twin girls by one of her paramours." The word sat oddly on Reverend Elisha Pratt's lips, and he hurried on. "Who was half-Negro himself, I understand. Anyway, the girls have somehow lost their free papers."

"That could easily be corrected. Judge Gratz . . ."

"I'm afraid not. They are at this moment in Robards's upper rooms about to be sold."

"That can't be. Who would buy them? Everybody knows Mrs. O'Brien . . ."

"Cripps Wickliffe told me. There's a trader from Louisville who is making up a shipment for Natchez."

"Tell me, Reverend. Why did you come to me?"

"If your grandfather were alive, I would have gone to him, Johnny. I thought of you . . . and the Wickliffe boy agreed. He said if you would bid, he would bid against you, and maybe prevent the agent from Louisville from . . ."

In 1849 Kentucky had repealed the Non-Importation Act of 1833 and had become a slave mart again. Not only were southbound riverboats loaded with field hands, but no person freed after 1849 could remain in the state. Lewis Robards had been quick to take advantage of the situation. As soon as slaves could be imported, Robards had leased the old Lexington Theater on Short Street and expanded his operations. He had built a high stone wall across the yard in the back, where his "lots" waited to be led inside and paraded across the stage. Now, four years later, he had added a two-story brick house next door to the theater and was using the ground floor as a marketing office. It was a large, bare room with a bar on one side and several tables in the middle where traders could loaf and talk shop over whiskey or cards. Morgan had been there several times with T.H. to buy hands, but never upstairs, where Robards kept his "choice stock," quadroon and octoroon girls, educated seamstresses with genteel manners who were, before the consummation of a deal, taken to the "inspection" room in the ell of the house to be stripped to the skin for the purpose of confirming Robards's "warranty of soundness." Just the idea of Mrs. O'Brien's girls being led there made Reverend Pratt shiver.

John Morgan looked at the delicate little man in his long, ill-fitting linen duster and saw courage. They both knew that if those girls were sold, they could go downriver.

"Will you do it?"

Morgan bent courteously forward, but somehow the movement became one with the upward swing of his body. He took the preacher by the arm and they walked toward the Robards establishment. The moon had completely disappeared and they had to make their way by an occasional street lamp and the light from houses set close to the walk. There was only one coal-oil lamp burning in the Robards office; all the activity was upstairs.

They were surprised at the elegance of the rooms, the comfortable sofas and clean carpets. New gaslights gave out an acrid smell. Gentlemen holding drinks or smoking cigars stood about in groups. Except for Johnny Morgan's memory of a knowing leer on a Spanish-looking woman's face, it might have been an after-dinner gathering in any parlor in the county. Cripps Wickliffe caught sight of them and nodded slightly.

"Glad you got here," he said in an undertone to Pratt. "They are next, I understand." He looked toward the back wall, where two girls, about eighteen (Kitty's age!), were nervously holding hands. Delphine bore a stoic calm, but Kate O'Brien had that short, hectic cough called "nigger fever," a consumption which ran rampant throughout slave jails but which did not deter unscrupulous traders from making quick deals.

"They go as a pair," Wickliffe said. "Take one, take both. And it's not because old Robards has family feeling, believe me. I'm wondering just how long the thin one can survive."

"She needs a doctor's care!" Pratt almost blurted.

Wickliffe gave him a look, then moved to an empty corner by the door.

From where they stood Pratt and Morgan could not see the girls' faces, only their bent heads as they conferred in whispers. Presently the agent for a Louisville trader walked through the central door at the opposite side of the room. It was Jake Bolton.

For some unaccountable reason which he couldn't explain even to himself, John Morgan bent one knee and rested his foot flat against the wall. He crossed his arms, leaned back against his shoulder blades and felt a grim smile tug at the corners of his mouth.

"How much am I offered for the wenches?" Robards called out, his hand on Delphine's arm, pulling her forward. Kate, shrinking, stayed where she was. "Well trained, both of them. Educated to sewing and skilled in all the household arts . . . if you git my meaning, gentlemen!" He turned the girl around, to show the profile of her body. "She's been appraised at seventeen hundred dollars, her sister at fourteen hundred. That's, if you count, over three thousand dollars, gentlemen! But I'll tell you right now I won't take less than twenty-five hundred for the pair, so we can start there."

No one thought it odd that Cripps Wickliffe, as an agent for his uncle, made the first signal that $2,500 was agreeable with him. Nor, apparently, when Robards jerked Delphine's blouse back to reveal her bare shoulder and breast. "Look here, gentlemen! Here's a wench fit to be the mistress of the wealthiest man here!"

Bolton, acting the shocked stranger, made sarcastic remarks about Lexington's appreciation of quality and upped the bid to $2,700. Morgan motioned $2,800. When Bolton added another hundred, Wickliffe went to three thousand.

"Come, come, gentlemen! We are bidding for two!" Robards yanked Kate forward and she stood shaking beside Delphine, who was trying to hold her torn blouse together.

"Three thousand five hundred," Jake Bolton called out.

Robards pretended to be offended. "Thirty-five hundred for two wenches, sir? Both with poise and education? And this?" He shot his cane to the hem of Delphine's skirt, lifted it and exposed her from her waist to her toes. "This, gentlemen—" he let the skirt fall like a curtain—"should certainly be useful to any man here worthy of that definition!"

A thick-necked Frenchman from Natchez called out "Forty-six," but was hardly heard through the guffaws.

"Forty-six?" Robards said as if in surprise. "For this swarthy queen of Egypt? Fit to be . . ."

"Five thousand," Cripps Wickliffe rang out.

"Fifty-five, monsieur," the Frenchman glared.

"Fifty-five," Robards repeated. He raised his hammer, let it fall, raised it again. Before he could lower it the final time a cotton broker from Memphis entered the bidding.

"Fifty-seven," the man from Memphis, with a white beaver hat, called out cautiously.

"Did I hear six thousand?" Robards asked the Frenchman. "Very well, then. Five thousand seven hundred once. Twice. Do I hear more? Three . . ."

Before the gavel fell the Frenchman made it six.

"Six thousand dollars." Robards rolled the words around his mouth like a cigar.

Six thousand dollars was exactly the amount Morgan had set aside for Kitty's dowry. Her sparkling blue eyes came before him, her smile, her delicious smile. How happy she was! He felt Robards watching him expectantly. He caught Wick's eye, which told him this could go on all night, that evidently they were up against a Frenchman who wouldn't quit. Jake Bolton's voice cut the air like a challenge: "Sixty-five hundred."

John Hunt Morgan heard his own voice say, as he took his foot from the wall and planted it on the floor under him, "Seven thousand dollars." Through the tumult he heard Robards's gavel pound three times.

"I'll help you!" Wickliffe offered, once they were downstairs.

Morgan declined. "I'm just glad we could save them," he said quietly. Suddenly he was inordinately tired. He'd been up all night with Becky and he needed to get home. Elisha Pratt came down the stairs with the girls and they told Wickliffe good night, then walked to Pratt's house, where Mrs. O'Brien was waiting. After the tears and hugging subsided, Morgan spoke to her about free papers. "I'll see Judge Gratz tomorrow."

She looked at him with grateful eyes and he kept himself from assuring her of more. They both knew a move from the state was imminent once freedom was obtained. How could he offer her hope of staying? He'd overheard too many of Uncle Frank's observations. Short of some kind of dispensation from the governor—he knew little of these matters—they would leave Kentucky.

He told her again as he left that he would see Judge Gratz first thing in the morning, but as he walked down North Mill, the gaslight in the Judge's study was still burning. He let the knocker slip from his fingers twice. The Judge himself let him in and courteously listened to the story. "Well, now that you own them, free papers can be easily drawn up. Now don't worry. Have a brandy?"

"That's not quite the trouble, Judge. They'll have to leave the state, won't they?"

The Judge cleared his throat. "Yes . . . yes. That's understood. . . ."

"What I want to know is . . . is there any way. Some special order from the governor, I don't know . . ."

Ben Gratz pursed his lips and hunched his shoulders. He was a short man, an old Jew much respected not only for his knowledge of the law but for his humanity. When he looked up there was a pained look in his pale gray eyes. "The mother can stay, of course. The girls, as newly freed persons, may have to go."

The night was still overcast, and outside the window Morgan saw a light rain falling on the Transy parade ground across the street. It had been a long day. "Yes, sir. Well, thank you." Ben Gratz followed him to the door and stood a moment, his hand on his neighbor's shoulder.

"Now don't go frettin', Johnny. Maybe we can fix it. It would have been easier, of course, if that courthouse upstate hadn't burned."

"I wonder if Robards knew that."

"Of course he did. You have to get up early to outsmart those fellows." The old man frowned, then lifted heavy brows. "But what they don't know is that both of us have had plenty of practice getting up early, eh, John?"

It was past midnight when he let himself in. All was quiet upstairs and the only sign of life came from candles in the dining room, where Sanders sat staring at the reflection on the polished table in front of him.

"What—" But he didn't finish.

"Where were you? My God, man, where were you? Rebecca . . ."

Sanders's swollen eyes stared across the candles. The look pierced him like a sword.

"*Becky* . . ." He wheeled toward the door.

"Becky's all right, no thanks to you," Sanders got out. "The baby's dead," he said bluntly. "There's nothing you can do. In fact, you've done enough already. Quite enough. With your gambling and carousing. It's one thing to be the grandson of a millionaire and another to earn enough money to support a wife. . . ."

All the training his family had given him, all the notions of a gentleman's conduct drove back the rage that almost choked him. "I'll ask you to retract those statements, and judge them to be spoken by emotion . . . which has warped your reason."

"Wastrel! Profligate! Slaver!" Sanders sneered, satisfied that he had found the ultimate insult. "The Morgans and the Hunts have earned their bread from the sweat of slaves and pretend to be high and mighty! The Hunts—"

Morgan's hand at his throat choked off the next word. He lifted Sanders to his feet and calmly, but with precision, felled him with a blow of his right fist.

Upstairs, John Bruce met him at the door of Becky's room. "She doesn't want to see you," he said.

"She has to want to see me!"

"Why should she?" Bruce stiffened. "You've made her life—all our lives —miserable since you came here. . . ."

He pushed the older man aside and went in. Margaret, in an upright chair by the bed, was bent over, her hand brushing Becky's head. In the little room where the chest of baby clothes and the cradle stood, Ellie was bending over a bundle and weeping.

"Becky!"

She opened her eyes and looked at him from far away. Without answering she closed them again. He longed to push the mother away and take her in his arms, but he turned to Ellie instead and saw his son, a beautiful child with long blond lashes resting on his cheeks.

"You're wrong! He's alive! He can't be . . ." He reached down, but Ellie's strong hand clamped around his wrist and held firm.

"He bes daid, Massa John."

Her voice was fierce above the trembling he felt through her fingers.

They buried the baby, unnamed, in the Bruce lot. He did not go to the funeral. He was not wanted, John Bruce told him. When he looked at Becky for confirmation of that decision, she turned her face away.

19

Calvin Morgan never quite recovered from the chill he got that day at the races. The rest of the summer and fall his strength seemed to ebb. But even stronger than her concern for her husband was Henrietta's fear for Johnny.

After the baby's funeral he drank for a week. When he finally succumbed to sleep, she had Cal and Robert bundle him off to the Leestown farm. He awoke looking into the faces of Randolph and Maggie, with the tom-toms of the worst headache he could remember hammering behind his eyes.

"Massa Cal and Massa Robert . . . dey brought you heah," Randolph was saying in his quiet way. "Say, no use you spendin' mo' time in town. An' Miss Betty Wickliffe, she sent you dese." He handed him three notes, with Betty's scent still faintly clinging between the pages. All efforts by Judge Gratz to allow the O'Brien girls to stay in Kentucky had failed. Their mother had chosen to go with them, and Cripps accompanied them himself to Cincinnati, where some family connections would help them resettle. As for his own recent loss, Betty sent her warmest thoughts and sympathy. . . .

His stomach felt tramped on by a hundred horses. He laid the letters down and went outside and sat under a tree, taking great gulps of air. Dr. Wolford had said the baby was in a bad position, that there was nothing anyone could have done, that his being there or not being there wouldn't have made the slightest difference. And yet it had. His not being there had made all the difference. And Dr. Wolford had said something else: Rebecca Morgan should have no more children.

The money for Kitty's dowry was gone. She said it didn't matter, but he knew better.

He did what he always did when he was troubled, when he had to think. He rode. Randolph saddled Delilah and he rode. He rode the fencelines of the farm, then down a lane which connected Leestown Pike with the road to Frankfort, trotting under overhanging trees. Some of the leaves were already falling. Where had he been when she needed him? Tears finally blurred the road ahead, and he had to stop the horse. When he returned to the farm, Will's stories seemed no longer droll or amusing. Without a place of his own or real work to do, Will hadn't made a saddle since he'd come back from California, and mending tack left too much time for drinking. Amanda didn't need him; after she'd married, Zep had run off.

"You know how it is, Johnny?"

You're an old man who can't see I've got troubles of my own, Morgan wanted to say. You still think I'm Johnny, and that your tall tales of the Long Knife and Mad Anthony Wayne are important. You're mad yourself. Maybe we all are.

He went back to Lexington. The Bruces were polite. He slept at Hopemont.

"Forget it, John," Dick Curd said for the third time. "Sanders has always been a hothead. It was said in grief. Don't do anything now to upset Becky. She has to regain her strength."

His father agreed. "It will all turn out all right, you'll see," Calvin assured him. He looked so tired that his son said nothing.

But Becky did not regain her strength. Her right leg was swollen painfully and she remained in bed.

"I know you're always trying to be kind."

When he tried to answer she kept pleating and repleating a corner of her cover, her eyes nervously away from him. "Maybe it is best you stay for a while at Hopemont. That sofa in the sitting room is hardly comfortable."

"I'll stay if you want."

"No. You'll be more comfortable there." Her lips trembled and she looked up at him with her wide-apart, soft eyes. "But don't you see how Fate has played its trick on me?"

"What do you mean?"

"Father always wanted me to be an invalid. Now maybe he'll get his wish."

He was shocked. Did she realize the cruelty of that remark? At twenty-three she was no longer an innocent girl. Was she also, in her own way, telling him how guilty he was? But she was right about Hopemont. What a haven it would be. And she was getting the best of care. Even if he had stayed, a visit twice a day from him was all Dr. Wolford would allow. *She has to regain her strength. . . .*

Colonel McClung actually laughed at the idea of a dowry. "We certainly don't need it." He smiled. "Your lovely daughter," he told Henrietta, "is reward enough for a king." A practical man, he actually seemed relieved that they would have a quiet autumn wedding.

Handsome in his Regular Army uniform, young, vibrant, ramrod-straight, Calvin McClung would take his bride to Jefferson Barracks, St. Louis. Kitty had met him in Louisville six months before, and theirs had been a whirlwind courtship. "Kitty could never do anything at a normal pace," Henrietta beamed, only half apologetically, to her family. She saw the old Morgan impulsiveness in her daughter, and wondered if Kitty had ever known how much she loved her. She was the first child to leave home.

Full autumn. The crunch of leaves. Overhead, and in the distance, yellow, gold, apricot, peach, red trees shimmering in the sun. Between branches, blue sky. God, had John Morgan ever seen such a blue sky? And then, the morning-balmy smell of rain. Mother-of-pearl clouds drifting, the nip of frost, the pang of Indian summer. With November, the passion of fox-hunting. They were all glad when T.H. said he would ride out to Clark County with his old riding buddies.

"It will do him good. Why don't you come for supper tonight, John?"

Mary Hunt's eyes hovered for just an instant on his own. In that awkward pause, he felt her sympathy; the family knew that Dr. Wolford had strictly forbidden another pregnancy for Becky.

Christmas, with snow and a sleigh ride, the Morgan children giggling, the Hunt uncles and aunts amused, and even Calvin, tucked under shawls in the parlor, sending them all his old brilliant, heartbreaking smile.

Becky was sweetly distant the day he sent Adam for his winter clothes. "Of course!" she said. He stood before her in the little room which would have been the nursery. The chest and cradle were gone, and Becky was sitting in the cane-backed rocker tying little bundles of sachet. The room was fragrant with dried leaves and powders from her garden. Her fingers moved quickly, snipping squares of cloth, tying ribbon. "It's all *right*, John," she said, her eyes bright and dry. "Dr. Wolford says perhaps this is best for a while. That my . . . that I regain strength. . . . Are you comfortable?"

Didn't she know? Didn't she know she could never . . . they could never . . . "Quite comfortable."

"Sanders has decided to plant tobacco." She set another little square of cloth on her lap and slipped the scissors under the edge. "Can you see him as a farmer?" She tried to laugh. Snip. "I can't. Imagine Sanders getting up at dawn, going out into the fields to inspect the latest crop. . . .

"Here," she said, handing him a little puffed-out square of cloth. "Put this in your shirts. With the . . . what's it called?"

He refused to say it. What was she doing, still clinging to her old anger? He'd forgotten the scapular . . . didn't know where it was. If she wouldn't grow up, maybe he could do it for her. His silence made her look up. "We were foolish," he said.

"I suppose . . . we were." She sighed and looked away.

"Let's not fight again. Get well." He kissed her lightly and left.

Her parents were still distant. He knew what they said. Kitty was selfish, Cal a fool, Richard lazy, Charlton a spoiled brat. His father a malingerer. They buzzed about Tommie's riding astride and playing ball with the boys. A young lady of thirteen! Only Tom and Key escaped their wrath, until the day Tom broke a parlor window and Key's dog overturned their trash and spread it over Becky's flowerbeds.

For Christmas he had given her an inlaid music box he had ordered from Paris. It stood on slender legs and played something light and tripping.

"Do you know what it is?"

"No."

"It's Mozart, silly," she said, laughing with that little gasp he had once found so delightful. She was still "convalescent," in her mother's words. But when he saw the purple, swollen leg he could agree. They spoke of going to spas, of cures, of changing doctors.

"Dat dere's a milk laig," Aunt Hannah said authoritatively. "Po' chile."

Margaret Bruce pretended that her daughter's marital problems were trivial, and her son-in-law's removal across the street temporary. At dinner, she would look hesitantly toward her husband and say carefully, "The boy is working hard to get our Rebecca a home."

"Let's hope so," John Bruce said. "We both know, however, that he has assumed obligations across the street that may postpone that indefinitely."

"Would that be so bad?" she asked craftily, sensing that he secretly wanted that postponement. "Other families live peaceably together. . . ."

"My dear, you know as well as I do, living peaceably with a Morgan is a trick beyond even your powers. We are not magicians."

He folded his napkin and laid it on the table and left. She sat playing with her spoon and watched the church spire across the street. Pigeons were circling. When the last one settled, she sighed. Ah, well, maybe he was right. She dreaded, as much as he did, losing their only daughter to a round of household cares and the possibility of children. It was, under the circumstances, unthinkable. At least, she said to herself, he has left her alone thus far. . . . Maybe her husband was right. John Morgan could continue on forever at Hopemont if it meant Becky's health.

"Hogwash!" Morgan heard his mother's voice as he laid his hat and gloves on the table in the front hall. Even from here he could hear the others gasp. What could they be talking about, Cal and T.H. and Uncle Frank, to bring out a remark like that? When he walked into the parlor he knew without being told: They had been talking about him. Maybe it was true that he hadn't tried enough to make his marriage work. He looked at his mother but couldn't ask the question. Whose side was she on, anyway?

He poured himself a whiskey at the sideboard and looked up at his grandmother. "Did Becky like her Christmas present?" Henrietta called over. Through the false cheerfulness he knew she was asking his forgiveness. "Yes," he said to the portrait, and drank. He turned the glass in his hand. "Yes, she did," he said with the same cheerfulness, and turned to them.

Incredibly, T.H. and Mary Hunt buried two more children before spring could warm the cold ground of winter.

"How can they stand it!" Tommie cried. "Little Catherine . . . and Tilford! So sweet!"

Brain fever. Convulsions, then coma, and the final, tossing fit. Buried a month apart. Now two fresh graves lay beside those of Mary, who had died in '47, T.H., Jr., who had died just last year, and the three babies from the early years of their marriage. T.H., that gentle man, seemed to sink into grief. Only the necessity of cheering his wife seemed to keep him alive. Morgan felt so helpless. He sat with them in the gloom of a March afternoon after Tilford's funeral, then walked back to Hopemont through a cold night mist, but couldn't sleep. He stepped into the garden. A sudden longing for Becky, for his own dead son almost took his breath. He needed to pick up the pieces of his life. Through the window he could see his father in the downstairs bedroom, so wasted himself, propped on his pillows, and a chill passed through his chest. Calvin Morgan, his once good looks fading before his eyes. He looked up. The sky was sodden with stars. They swam together like sparks of sunlight on water.

April came, cold and damp. Rain flattened the daffodils. Calvin Morgan, over his wife's protests, rode out to the Leestown farm to see the horses. He was drenched when he came back. Shivering, he allowed Henrietta to put him to bed, but insisted on seeing Dick Curd. "It's important."

"It can't be that important."

Fear of upsetting him made her relent. She sent for Dick, who stayed in Calvin's bedroom, behind closed doors, for an hour.

"It's his will, isn't it?" she asked when he came out.

"Everybody needs one."

Not the Morgans! she wanted to cry out. They've never cared about such things! Only then, when she realized Dick might be serious, did she allow herself to really worry.

Calvin slept for two days.

"He just may not recover," Dr. Wolford told John Morgan privately in the parlor of Hopemont a week later. "I don't want to alarm your mother, but . . ."

"But . . . ?"

"But you may have to expect the worst." At Morgan's look he added, "Surely you've seen it coming on for some months now?" When there was no reply the doctor added, "Well, we'll do the best we can. He's had a good life, a good family. We must remember that. Calvin has had fifty-three good years."

John Morgan shook his head to bring the doctor into focus. "Fifty-three. Fifty-three," he repeated, dazed. "Too young to die!"

The doctor laid his hand on the young man's arm. "It is always, at whatever age, my son, too soon to die. Don't bother the servants. I can see myself out."

Morgan went into the darkened room, redolent with scented soap and rose water. Aunt Betty was just clearing away a basin from the morning bath. His father lay on the pillows, a faint smile on his face as he turned his head to his son. "Johnny." He held out a hand. "Come here."

The fingers groped and he noticed how frail the wrist had become.

"I'll ask Robert to see you, as soon as he gets back from Louisville. Another opinion . . ."

"You'll take care of your mother. Promise."

The fingers took a firmer hold.

"Promise? Nonsense, Father. You'll be—"

"Don't play games, Johnny. You know, since Christmas—" He was interrupted by a violent cough and let go. His son held a bowl for the spitting that came almost every time now.

"Don't talk. Just rest." He patted the sick man awkwardly on the shoulder, avoiding looking at the blood in the bowl as he handed it to Aunt Betty. "You know I'll take care of Ma . . ." He couldn't go on, but closed his eyes and felt the thin fingers close again and give an answering squeeze.

Dull, dull. His mind and body went numb. He couldn't think. He wouldn't allow himself to feel. He went about the house bumping into things until Aunt Hannah moved the china vases out of his way. Henrietta suggested he go back to the office. *There's nothing to be done. Keep him comfortable.* Attention to details: the temperature, the covers. Nourishing food. It was all useless and they knew it, and yet they kept up this round of remarks and small tasks as if the world revolved around fresh soup and the amount taken, as if saying he looked better this morning made it so. Cal took turns going to the office to help T.H. Richard, who would be eighteen in October, was beginning to take an interest in the business, and began to spell them. Randolph came in from the farm and spent a week in the servant wing, then had to go back to keep up with chores. Old friends visited: the Breckinridges, the Buckners, Judge Gratz. Eleanor and Dick Curd came by every afternoon. The day Calvin's brother Sam arrived from Nashville even the most sanguine visitors grew doubtful.

And yet the end, when it came, was peaceful. They were all in the room: Robert, T.H., and Mary; Uncle Frank and Julia; Henrietta and Kitty, who had come with her husband from St. Louis; Richard, Charlton, Johnny, Cal, Tommie, Tom, and eight-year-old Key. Aunt Betty, as usual, was the cornerstone of their sanity. It was morning, about ten o'clock, the 1st of May, and raining. A steady drum of water from the gutters splashed on the brick wall just outside Calvin's window. Low thunder complained in the distance and made the sick man open his eyes. Henrietta bent toward him and he smiled, sighed, and sank away from them. It was as quiet as that. Kitty's sobbing and Tommie's sudden gasp were the sounds John Morgan would remember. That and the song of a cardinal in the garden. The rain stopped.

Calvin Cogswell Morgan, Dec. 16, 1801–May 1, 1854. That was all. So little to tell, so much forgotten so fast. His stone, set on a circle which, when filled, would girdle the tall spire of John and Catherine Hunt's grave like a miniature stonehenge. Charlton Hunt, who had died of scarlet fever at twenty-seven; Dr. Johnny, dead from a duel at twenty-six; Catherine, from cholera at twenty. And across the way, the row of T.H.'s children on the other side of the monument, two graves so fresh the grass hadn't started yet. Like children waiting to be told a story. Like retainers surrounding their king. And across the lane in the Bruce lot, a silent, small grave with no name. *Infant son of J. H. and R. B. Morgan, Sept., 1853.* Not a year ago.

When Calvin's will was read, it was discovered that he had freed Randolph. "What will happen to the Leestown farm?" was Henrietta's first reaction. "What will happen to Maggie and the children? He'll have to leave!" She looked at Dick, who, as lawyer for the estate, was still in the room. "It will go on as before," she said evenly, drawing her shoulders up. "We'll find a way."

"But—"

She turned on her eldest son in a small fury. "But what? How can I free his family, too? That's what you expect, isn't it? So they can go with him? You know our finances as well as I do. I can't afford to find anybody else. I own nothing, after the debts are paid, except a few household servants. If I let Randolph go, it would mean giving up the vegetables and chickens and meat from the farm. I can't do it."

"Ma . . ."

But she was trembling. Confronted with this valiant bout with grief, which amazed them all, her son was silent.

"We could possibly postpone . . ." Dick Curd said, stacking papers. "If Randolph wants to stay—and I think he will—I can just put his manumission papers in safekeeping, to be used at a future date. If I file them now, as you know, the law would make him leave the state. I don't think he'll want to leave his family. You and I and he will know he's free, and that's all that counts right now."

"Tell Eleanor to come see me," Henrietta sniffed. "When she can."

"Indeed, she will. She only wanted to wait . . ."

"Tell her I am fine," Henrietta said, offering her hand.

Richard would not go to Princeton. Randolph, as predicted, would not leave his family, and stayed on to manage the farm. Henrietta refused financial help from her brothers Key and Robert. She was, Richard Curd reflected as he left her, her father's daughter.

As the weather warmed, the Bruces decided that Becky should accept Kitty Morgan's invitation to try the waters at the Hot Springs in Arkansas, where Colonel McClung was presently stationed.

"We have to do something to restore the poor child's health," Margaret Bruce told her son-in-law as he held Becky's hand in the aisle of the car. Becky, already settled by the window, lifted her face to his kiss. The inevitable pillow was under her legs, propped on the opposite seat and covered by a light shawl. His eyes caught hers, and for a moment a chill of fear crossed his heart. Would he ever see her again, this child-bride-mother he knew so little? Their marriage had hardly had a chance. He promised himself, as he bent for her kiss, that they would work it all out when she came back.

"Don't let Father worry too much. And tell Sanders I'm sorry he couldn't come, but that I'll bring him a present."

He dropped her hand.

"I won't. I will."

From the platform he watched the train pull away, belching sparks and steam. Why hadn't he gone with her? There was no reason to stay . . . a month's absence from the business would hurt nothing. Except, he answered his own question. Except, as he watched the wheels pick up speed and the caboose with its flat little cupola move away, except that she no longer belongs to me. If she ever did.

He went back to the office. T.H. was at his desk in his shirtsleeves. "Thank goodness the rain stopped. What a summer it's been!"

"Why can't we?" Morgan asked.

"Can't we what?"

"Hire free hands."

T.H. set down the papers he had been shuffling on his desk. "Look here, John, I tried that a long time ago. Only had trouble."

"But you'll admit we'll need good hands."

"I'll admit. But all the free hands worth a damn already have jobs . . . or have gone into business on their own. And since that damned law, the more recently freed have to leave the state. That leaves the old codgers, the shiftless, or those prone to whiskey."

"Cal and I have sent for that New Mexico wool. Two hundred thousand pounds of it."

T.H. set the paper down. "So you're serious about going into linsey-woolsey with Cal?"

"Two hundred thousand pounds serious. It's uncleaned, of course. And we'll have to freight it overland. But if we order now, maybe we can get it by this fall. . . ." *And hire whatever damned hands we please*, his look said. T.H. saw the look and grinned.

"Right now I'd be satisfied if you'd take these drafts to the bank. And there's some bank notes in this envelope—ten thousand dollars' worth. Needs depositing. With good weather the contractors will be ready to start on the new building. Oh . . . and if you see Cal, tell him Wilson and Dyer are expecting that shipment."

John Morgan walked toward Main Street, his head bent, watching for puddles. Before he reached the corner he was almost run over by a buggy.

"Amanda!"

"So." She pointed her parasol tip against his shoulder and smiled.

"What are you doing in Lexington?"

"Haven't you heard? Robards went bankrupt . . . land speculation in Kansas. Jake and his partner bought him out. He's building me a fine house on the Versailles Road. Want to come see it? I'm going out to check on things." Behind her he noticed a new carriage, a light phaeton swung low to the ground with a rumble seat where a young black boy, decked out in livery, grinned. She was driving, her skirts spread out, a restless gray prancing under her hands. There seemed no reason to refuse.

"If you'll wait till I go to the bank."

She crinkled her nose. "For that I'll wait." She gathered her skirts to allow him to climb up. They said nothing as the mare trotted around the corner, her gray back silken under the harness. With an expert's eye Amanda parked parallel to the walk and watched him jump down and go through the door. Ten minutes later, feeling the floorboards sway with his weight as he got in beside her, she looked ahead as if their conversation had not been interrupted. "The house will be Italianate," she said, flicking the reins. Her red mane, caught in a bun against her lace collar, shone under her bonnet.

"Will it, now?" He grinned.

"You're laughing at me."

"No, I'm not." The horse settled into a floating trot. His grin submerged into a smile. "Why should I laugh at you?" They turned right into High Street. "When I don't have a house myself . . . even an Italianate one?" he added.

"Johnny . . ."

Silence was so good with her. He had almost forgotten. As the town fell away, he watched passing fields.

Her house stood behind trees, a half-finished monster already crying "money." He looked at it and she turned enthusiastic again, to cover her confusion at his silence.

"Red brick with a three-story tower trimmed in white stone. To look crenelated. Like a battlement," she added, turning to him with a smile, as if he needed an explanation. When he couldn't help grinning at her new vocabulary, she went on: "Louisville's quite a city. We're getting any number of architects with new ideas." They stopped at the top of what would be a curving drive and he helped her down, handing up the reins to the groom, who had scrambled, still grinning, onto the leather seat. She pretended hesitation across the planks, spread to make a temporary sidewalk, and he took her arm.

"We're certainly backwoodsy here," he sighed, keeping his eyes turned up at the tower as his hand lingered on her arm. "We can use all the culture we can get."

Her silence made him turn, and they burst out laughing. When Amanda almost fell he caught her close. They stood, unable to move, her eyes on his mouth, his eyes roving her face until he made her lift her eyes to his.

"Amanda . . ."

She stiffened and held his sleeve with a gloved hand. "My, you are the gentleman now. That's what a lady needs. A gentleman to steady her . . ." From the other side of an unfinished wall two carpenters, hammers in hand, caught her glance and went back to work.

"So, I see you've discovered the new Mrs. Bolton," Cal smiled to himself, bent over the accounts.

"How did you know?"

"You almost ran over me as you turned into High Street. Didn't you notice?" Then he hissed in mock terror, "Better not let Ma see you!"

"Aren't you coming home to eat?"

Cal shook his head. "Be by later. When I finish these." His pen was already scratching more numbers when Morgan shut the door.

Before he reached Cheapside he saw Robert Hunt's buggy careening down Main Street, the doctor himself at the whip.

"Johnny!" His hands, busy with the reins, held the horse. "Get in. Something's happened." He was out of breath. "Caroline Turner's dead."

Morgan must have looked unconcerned.

"She's been murdered. They think John Henry did it."

"The evidence is irrefutable," Dick Curd said quietly, when they found him in his office.

"What evidence? I can't believe . . ."

She had ordered John Henry to be shackled in the back yard for a beating from her own hand.

"With her usual zest," said Robert. Dick Curd, across the room by the window, nodded. "And when he had had enough, he broke the chains and strangled her."

Morgan said nothing. He could almost feel her hard, thin throat under his own fingers. The little boy she had crippled years ago still limped around Lexington. Good for John Henry!

"He's been arrested and is in jail, of course," Curd said evenly.

"They can't hang him," said Morgan. "Isn't there that law you quoted when Cassius cut up that hired gun from New Orleans? Something about sudden passion?"

"For white men, yes. Black men are not supposed to have passions . . . at least any protected by law. Especially since that runaway incident they'll think it would never do to allow an upstart slave to attack a master . . . under any circumstances."

Morgan went with his uncle to the arraignment. John Henry's black eyes were glazed as he heard the charge. He seemed not to hear or understand that he had "acted against the peace and dignity of the Commonwealth of Kentucky." Two weeks later he was led into the courtroom, went through the formality of a trial, and was led again, a week later, to the jailyard, where, at precisely eleven o'clock on a Saturday morning, he plunged, feet first, through a narrow trap door.

"I didn't go to see him. I could have gone to see him. I never thought . . ." John Morgan murmured when Dick Curd came around to Hopemont with the news.

"Any other time it might have been . . . different," Dick kept saying, his hand on a glass of whiskey, his eyes on the clock. It was a German clock that Calvin Morgan had brought back from Europe. It had fat little wooden men with green hats who came out on a track with hammers to strike the hour. One of them had lost his arm but the hammer still stuck up beyond his shoulder on a wire. Dick drank the whiskey at a gulp.

When Becky stepped off the train her husband had never seen her more beautiful, her large soft eyes on his, lingering an instant before her head turned to her father. He could feel himself blush and the palms of his hands go wet. He followed them into the new brougham which John Bruce had bought. Sanders was there also to meet his sister, standing on the ground and calling up to the coachman. As the door closed Morgan leaned back against the fringe of Becky's shawl and accidentally pulled a thread.

"Oh, John!" She smoothed it quickly. "It's Tunisian silk . . . and goat's hair. Mama bought it for me in Memphis. How do you like this?" She thrust her chin up to show him a locket hanging from a gold chain. "Kitty gave it to me. And guess what's in it?"

"Ah . . ."

"A picture of Sanders, with a lock of his hair. You wouldn't believe Arkansas . . ."

Maybe I would. I've seen it before, remember? But what she knew of his life seemed dim. Why was he surprised? Ordinarily he didn't mind. He took out a soft monogrammed handkerchief, wiped his hands and put it back in his pocket. Tommie had embroidered it for his birthday. He almost told her about Amanda. Instead he felt a little half-smile twist his mouth and looked down Main Street, wondering if it would rain for the start of the new building.

They turned into North Mill, and as he helped her from the carriage the weight of her body against him suddenly made his hands go cold again. He followed her into the Bruce parlor. When she took off her bonnet he noticed that she was doing her hair in a neat bun. He longed to find the little point of hair he knew lay at the back of her neck and kiss it; instead, he found himself answering his mother-in-law's pleasant, vacuous questions. They got around to his business, finally. He told them about the new building, but his enthusiasm was gone. Becky had certainly gained strength.

"And some weight," her father beamed. They stared at her openly and she, in turn, sent them a smile. Her cheeks were like two round little sachets on either side of her nose, folding lines to the corners of her mouth. They gave her face a petulant, pushed-in look, as if she were drawing her chin in, about to complain. He saw she would look like her mother when she grew older. Ah, but what was the matter with him? She was sweet and her eyes were soft, and how could he expect her to be excited about business? She had been away. It would take a few hours for the circles of their lives to converge.

When would her parents leave the room? When would they go upstairs? How had he ever thought of the little lace-curtained room as anything other than charming? He felt like a bridegroom. He had been good, working hard. At last the Bruces left. He hadn't even seen Betty Wickliffe since May.

"How many times have you seen her since I've been gone?"

He jumped at the question. Was she reading his mind? He heard himself say, "I don't know what you are talking about."

Her lips trembled with the beginnings of anger and the lines from her nose to her mouth deepened. "Oh, come now, John. We're grown people, not children. Sanders wrote me about your rides around town with that slave-trader's wife. Amanda Bolton . . ."

Sanders! So it was Sanders again!

She went on breathlessly, as if she hadn't noticed his reaction. "How nauseating! Absolutely nauseating! But what did I expect? I've heard you often enough returning from your card games. Is that all you play at . . . cards? Or life?"

It was a question he had been asking himself too often lately. He looked at her in amazement.

She got up and walked around the room, unconsciously dusting the needlepoint seats with her gloves. She dropped them on the table and stood in front of the window with the curtained light framing her silhouette against the Presbyterian Church across the street. She seemed determined to pick a fight and waited for his answer.

"I only know I have missed you very much," he said softly.

He couldn't see the tears of frustration in her eyes as she watched his tall, neatly dressed body walk away from her into the hall, through the front door to Hopemont.

That year, with England at war in the Crimea, wheat jumped from 30 cents to $1.70 a bushel. The Missouri Compromise was repealed. Massachusetts had a Know-Nothing governor and Miss Betty Wickliffe bought herself a hoop skirt.

There was another new political party that year, called Republican, which T.H. said would come to nothing. "It's too radical."

That next spring, in March 1855, five thousand "Border Ruffians" crossed over the Kansas line from Missouri and elected a proslavery legislature; as a counteraction, free-soilers held a convention in Topeka, ratified their own constitution and sought admission of the territory as a free state. With two rival, fraudulent governments, Kansas focused the nation's attention on slavery again.

Know Nothings carried Kentucky, electing its governor over his Democratic rival by more than four thousand votes. In Louisville there were riots, with Democrats blaming Know Nothings, Know Nothings blaming Democrats. T.H. read the newspapers and wondered out loud at his nephew's disinterest, as John Morgan wondered at his uncle's concern over politics, the outcome of which seemed as remote as the moon. Still, if such interests removed T.H. one step more from grief, he wouldn't argue.

Becky's health improved, and yet John Morgan stayed on at Hopemont. He joined the Masons because T.H. did. He almost joined the Know Nothings because T.H. did, but when he heard that local Know Nothings planned to burn St. Peter's Catholic Church, he didn't hesitate to ask T.H. to help him stop them. With Cal and Richard and Sid Cunningham they pulled a small cannon from the armory and set it up on the corner of North Limestone. Reinforced by T.H.'s fox-hunting friends, who brought their rifles and horse pistols, they waited with their eyes and guns trained on the church door. When nothing happened, T.H., relieved, was surprised to hear young Richard Morgan express disappointment. "If we could only have winged one of the sons-of-bitches," Richard said.

"Then what?" John Morgan demanded.

When Richard saw his brother's fury he sobered. Without looking back, Morgan walked away.

Winged one of the sons-of-bitches! What could Richard know of killing? It wasn't a fox hunt! He would have to give him more responsibility at the factory. They had to get the new building completed before bad weather. A man named Isaac Singer had patented a sewing machine motor, and they had ordered a dozen machines. . . .

Almost before he knew it, another Christmas had come and gone, another spring. It was May again, and he was busy in the front office when Tom and Charlton dashed in with the news.

"Haven't you heard? *He's* going to be in Lexington for May and June. What a chance! What a chance, Brother Johnny!" Tom was out of breath.

"Slow down! Who? Why?"

"Lecomte," Charlton answered.

T.H. and Morgan looked at each other. There was no need to explain, but Charlton did: Lecomte, son of Boston, undefeated in five straight races, and considered the fastest horse in the South. Last year, too, he raced against his half-brother, another son of Boston, the great Lexington. Lecomte won by six lengths; his time: 7:26 for four miles, beating by 6½ seconds the record set by Fashion when she defeated Boston twelve years earlier. He had an effortless, floating stride, the most beautifully gaited runner seen in forty years or more. . . .

Charlton ended his encomium with a gasp: "If you could breed Delilah!"

"You'll have a foal born after May first," T.H. warned. In the South a horse's birthday was counted from May first. That would mean a two-year-old might have to run as a three-year-old, carrying extra weight.

"A small consideration." Morgan grinned. Lecomte! He couldn't believe it.

"He's being shipped to England from here," said Charlton, then worried: "I hope he isn't booked."

"He won't be," said T.H., frowning. He handed Morgan a newspaper. "I hate to change the subject, but look at this."

Morgan scanned the headlines: FIVE BRUTAL MURDERS OF PROSLAVERY KAN-SAS SETTLERS.

"You gentlemen are stirred by children's tales," Henrietta scolded in the parlor of Hopemont. She folded the scattered newspapers. Morgan watched her. She had worn her grief well. Her figure, with her perspective, had broadened. The girl-mother he remembered was turning into the Lexington matron. All the servants called her Ole Miss now, and she didn't seem to mind, presiding as she did over the "salon" of her brothers and their friends.

John Brown was never prosecuted for the Kansas murders. Several hundred proslavery men attacked Brown and his sons at Osawatomie. One son was killed and Brown went east.

"I hope that's the last we hear of him," Henrietta breathed, her fingers picking at the shawl she was drawing over her shoulders.

"Ma, it's too hot to wear that."

"I'm going out, John Morgan. Ladies do not appear on the streets unless they are properly clothed."

She was Ole Miss, indeed.

Before Lecomte left for England, Morgan bred Delilah. "Seems like old times, Massa," Randolph said. "What you bet she has a filly? Won't that be fine?"

The nostalgia of turning leaves came before they knew it. One Indian summer evening at the Wickliffes' only made Morgan long for Becky as he remembered her. He looked up. Miss Betty was in the dining room, fussing with flowers. "You *will* stay for supper, John? You never accept my invitations. I do believe you don't like our company."

"I do, Miss Betty, I assure you."

"We're getting a little game up later," Cripps said. "Robert's promised to come over."

"Well, what do you say, John, will you stay?" Wickliffe's blond hair, in neat waves, made a Greek's head on his shoulders. He bent it to the decanter, poured two drinks and handed him one. Cripps had lost so much money at cards that he had cultivated an aura of wistful underdog that was appealing, especially to his cousin. "It's true, what Betty says. You've been neglecting us lately. I hear you bred to Lecomte. Now that was a horse on a backstretch. . . ."

Comfortable. That was the word. From the cool gray tones of the Wickliffe parlor, and later, the crystal gaslights, the steaming food on gleaming mahogany. Miss Betty's bosom almost spilling from soft muslin. Horses, politics, money. But here, even money became a game, like all life, a game of chance. Robert Hunt came in, and the cards came out.

They talked of Robert's design for a new house, now that he planned to marry. Robert spread his hand, pulled a card and slipped it into place, contemplating the new arrangement.

"When are *you* building a house, Johnny?" Miss Betty teased, as she watched them.

"Johnny doesn't need a house," Cripps murmured around his cigar, lipping it to one corner of his mouth. General laughter, and more whiskey all around.

Robert Hunt looked at his nephew, but saw the frown had passed. "What does T.H. think about the rope and bagging business, now with peace in Crimea?"

"He's expecting a crash on Wall Street." With his thumb Morgan spread his cards. "But honestly, he's more interested in my starting a drill team."

"A drill team? How delightful!" Miss Betty sighed behind Morgan's chair. He could feel her arm resting on his shoulder. "Will you be its captain, Johnny? You look so splendid in uniform!"

"I might, at that."

The truth was, he couldn't keep his mind on anything they said. When *are* you building a house? When, indeed, Becky . . .

Better not, John. Oh, John, really . . .

No, he would put all that behind him.

Then other voices: *That's John Morgan, whose wife's the little invalid. Pretty little thing. Damn shame. For which one? For Becky,* the ladies demurred. *For John,* the gentlemen winked. *But I understand he enjoys solace in a very fine manner* . . .

Damn them all to hell.

He found T.H. in the front hall of Hopemont, pulling on his coat, Cal and Richard behind him. "I've been thinking of your suggestion," he said so solemnly T.H. thought he was talking about business.

"About that twenty-horse?"

"No . . . about the drill team."

T.H. grinned. "I think that would be splendid, splendid, Johnny! You'd join, wouldn't you, Cal? And Richard?"

Morgan winked at Cal. "Richard's too much of a businessman, now that he's given up Cuban expeditions."

"Not a bad thing to be," T.H. retorted, but pleased. "Not a bad thing at all. Well, when will you start recruiting?"

Business intervened. T.H.'s predicted crash on Wall Street came in April. In mid-May Delilah had a filly. Before he was sent to England Lecomte was raced lame and was beaten by Lexington. That once great horse would never be the same again. To right that wrong, somehow, Morgan named the foal Miss Lexington. As he watched Delilah with her he was a boy again in another May, before Mexico.

20

"**C**areenin' aroun' on a hoss like a TOMboy."

He could hear Aunt Betty even here in the parlor and let his eyes drift to his mother's face, but that imperial lady remained adamant: Tommie would *not* ride with his drill team. "Imagine," she kept saying. "A young lady of seventeen careening around on a horse."

Did she know she was imitating Aunt Betty upstairs? Her son laughed out loud. He was flattered; the whole town was talking. They would use a room above the armory for meetings and practice on the Transy parade grounds, opposite Hopemont. He wasn't unaware of the fact that Becky would be able to see the activity diagonally across the corner from the Bruce house. Deep down, he wanted to cut a dashing figure.

Within two weeks the muster numbered some of the best riders in the county.

"Nothing sloppy. Nothing sloppy," he said that first morning, unconsciously using his grandfather's tone. "We are following an unseen pattern on the ground, a form. To be accurate we must always keep that form in our minds." He handed out copies of the formations. Little ovals with tiny squares to represent horses' heads marched across the paper in twos, fours, and eights.

"Abreast, we align leg to leg. That means we'll have to rate our horses, not just follow the man ahead. Now it's obvious that to execute this one"— his finger pointed to a figure at the top of a page—"Cal and Castleman will have to go double speed; Kennett and I, in front, will fall to half speed. When the last two men of the eight catch up and we approach the corner, the inside man will have to give a good inside leg at the girth with an indirect left rein to avoid a flat corner and reduce speed almost to a turn in place. The outside man, too, can't afford to cut the corner, but he'll have to go faster. Can anybody tell me how much faster?"

Tom, who was now thirteen and had begged his brother to be an alternate, stood behind him listening quietly and said, "Eight times faster?"

His brother looked around appreciatively. "Right! Now you see how important it is to be able to rate your horse accurately."

"What if the indirect rein isn't enough to get into the corner?" Richard asked.

"You can try a very light indirect on the outside, in front of the withers. Something like the outside rein used for a turn on the haunch. Only very light, very light. . . ." At Tom's nod he went on: "Anybody have a horse that bites or kicks?"

Sid Cunningham raised his hand. "Ole Tobe likes to cowkick to the left."

"We'll put him on the inside then, going left. No use trying to reform old-timers. But you can minimize the problem by tightening pressure on that left rein and make him carry his head to the left. Then he won't be able to get that left hind in action. Or let's hope so. Now, does everybody here understand what I mean by a cadenced trot?"

An hour later, after they had marched around the room above the armory, pretending to be on horseback to memorize the formations, some of the boys giggling, they agreed to meet at the parade grounds the next day by six-thirty. "I want everybody up and ready to go by seven," Morgan called out. "It's too hot to ride after nine, and I want two good hours every day this first week."

"What will we wear?" someone asked.

Morgan pursed his lips, looking around. "Cal, could we produce a uniform?"

"We could."

"If you don't mind, gentlemen, I will detain you a little longer."

They decided on a color: green, to be enlivened by gold braid and brass buttons. Richard would draw the design, to be voted on at the next meeting. The Lexington Rifles were born.

"Foolishness, all this male preening and prancing," Henrietta said, but smiled to herself when her son didn't notice. She hadn't seen him so happy since Shadeland. The gloom which had descended after the baby died was at last being replaced by the old Johnny she loved, the sweet smile, the bright eyes. She stood with Tommie and watched the practice during those June mornings, the sunlight filtering through the trees of the garden. Later, Johnny and Charlton, or Cal and Richard and Tom would come reining up, their horses still prancing a little, Tom swooping off his hat in cavalier fashion. Every night for weeks they talked over dinner of extension and collection, of two tracks and setting up cavalletti and taking them in twos and fours, without reins, arms extended, or with hands on hips, no stirrups.

"Whatever in the world are 'cavalletti'?" Tommie asked, shaking her curls.

"You'll see," said Tom mysteriously.

"And 'two tracks'?"

"The horse moves in two directions at once, sidewise and forward." Morgan smiled. "It's really not as complicated as it sounds."

Amanda Bolton parked her phaeton just past the Gratz house so she could get a good view.

"That's cavalletti," a voice from the sidewalk said proudly. Amanda looked down to see the younger Morgan girl, her brown curls swinging on her shoulders. Everybody thought the blond Kitty was prettier, but Amanda knew better. Just wait.

"Those poles on the ground? Whatever for?"

"To cause collection."

"Collection? Isn't that something that happens in church?"

"Well, not exactly . . . If you'll let me sit up there," said Tommie, "I'll explain. . . . I've been standing here over an hour."

"Why, sure, sure . . ." Amanda gathered her skirts. She was wearing a black beaver hat with plumes, and the plumes shook as she made room.

"That's my brother. And my other brothers." Tommie's finger pointed, but her eyes went back to a dark-haired boy with a square chin who sat bolt upright on a horse that wanted to jog despite everything he could do. His efforts to control it were turning his face red, although they were more effective than his joshing companions would admit.

"It's obvious who's your favorite brother," said Amanda, giggling.

"Is it?" Tommie laughed, then blushed. "Well, what if it is? I suppose you want to know his name."

"I'm dying to know."

"John Morgan."

"And the dark-haired boy?"

"Which one?"

"The one sitting so straight and pretending not to know you're watching him."

Something in the lady's laugh made Tommie look at her more closely.

"Amanda!"

"I was waiting for you to recognize me."

"Amanda! I feel so foolish. . . . You're . . . different." Her eyes went to the plumes.

"You still haven't told me his name."

"Well, if you mean *that* one, it's Basil Duke. From Scott County."

"He's handling that horse well," Amanda said slowly, with the cautious praise of one good rider to another. She pursed her lips and Tommie noticed the cameo on her ample bosom, the perfume and the rouge on her cheeks. Mama never let her use even rice powder. She leaned forward.

"He was your favorite, too, wasn't he?"

For just an instant, the lady's eyelashes fluttered in confusion.

"I'm a married matron, Tommie Morgan, I'll have you know!" Amanda giggled again.

"And I'm the best darned rider in Lexington," "Little Henrietta" retorted, lifting her head and addressing the air beyond Amanda's parasol.

"Are you now? Well, I'm the best darned rider in Fayette County!"

"Are you now?" Tommie's eyes were laughing but her voice was firm.

Oh, she is a Morgan all right. "I'll show you tomorrow morning, Tommie Morgan."

"Very well. Where?"

"Right here, over your cav . . ."

"Cavalletti. And I accept your challenge, Mrs. . . ."

"Bolton," Amanda said, still delighted and a little amazed. "Bolton, Miss Tommie Morgan."

"Bolton! Can you imagine Amanda marrying that nasty Bolton boy?"

"Hrummph. White trash," breathed Aunt Betty, pulling at Tommie's stays. "Now don' you be late for suppah agin'. An' when you git downstaihs, send Tom and Key to be washed off. Ole Miss fussin' 'nuf 'bout all dis horse sweat."

"They're not babies anymore, Aunt Bet."

"Horse sweat is horse sweat. Mah nose cain't count."

"Will you lend me your horse tomorrow?" Tommie whispered to Tom at dinner.

"What for?"

"In the morning. I want to ride on the parade grounds."

"Hey!" He turned to Key, but she stopped him.

"Shh! It's a secret."

"Better get yourself plenty of soap afterwards or it won't be a secret long."

"Tom!"

"Or you won't have any skin left after Aunt Betty's through."

"Will you do it?"

"Henrietta, what are you whispering about? It's not polite."

"Sorry, Mama . . . *Will you do it?*"

Amanda was early, in a black riding habit showing off her figure. When Tommie trotted up on Tom's bay she saluted smartly. Amanda was riding sidesaddle, her skirts spread across her horse's side. "See?" she laughed. "I'm even giving you the advantage."

But there was no need. Tommie had never seen anybody ride like that, not even her brothers. Amanda sat perfectly balanced, taking the poles at an even pace at the jog, and then at the faster trot. "Want to raise them?" she called out, and Tommie nodded. Amanda ordered her groom, waiting by the sidewalk with the carriage, to turn the ends over. "Space them about two feet more apart." He did so, slowly, while the ladies waited. "There!" Amanda said with satisfaction. "Now we'll canter through, no reins!" Without waiting for Tommie's answer she turned her horse into a canter, made a circle, and headed for the row of cavalletti, her arms straight out from her shoulders.

"Lak a bird, Miss Mandy! Lak a bird!" the groom called out, laughing.

"Like a fool," John Morgan said loudly behind them. "Amanda, do you want to break your neck?" But the lady had reached the end of the row, picked up her reins, and trotted up to him, saluting.

"I can do that."

Before he could stop her, his sister squeezed the bay into a trot, then cantered a half-circle and dropped her reins on the horse's neck as she spread the fingers of her outstretched hands in a mock wave. Halfway down the row the reins fell forward as the horse looked down, then dangled an instant in front of the lifting hooves before they tangled. The bay stumbled. Tommie, her attention on her audience, fell forward on the horse's neck. The forelegs folded and the horse rolled on its side. Tommie fell clear and lay motionless. John Morgan and Amanda ran to her. Before the hand on her shoulder could turn her over Tommie sat up, laughing, more angry than hurt.

"You don't suppose a few little poles on the ground could hurt me, do you, Brother Johnny?" But she was furious when he wouldn't let her try again.

"Come on, Tommie. You lost your bet. That's gambling." When she shrugged away from him he said, more sternly: "You're *not* to try this again."

"Who do you think you are, John Morgan? My—"

The almost-said word stopped her.

"No, but we both know what he would have said," her brother said soberly. "Basil likes you too much to see you hurt."

"Does he? Does he, Brother Johnny?" Her anger was gone.

"Of course! Didn't you know? Now come on and get cleaned up before Ma sees you." He grinned as he watched her walk across the street toward Hopemont.

"Like her brother," Amanda said behind him. "Stubborn, obstinate, delightful."

Delightful. Was it another fancy word she had learned in Louisville? "She's a handful."

"No . . . not yet," Amanda murmured just low enough so the groom couldn't hear. "But she will be," she smiled when he turned and looked at her. "Don't you think? Sam, tie this horse to the carriage and drive me home."

"Yassum."

In August of '58 the Rifles were invited to perform at Crab Orchard Springs. Tommie, carefully assuming the air of a young lady, succeeded in getting her mother to promise that she could go.

"Brother's absolutely a handsome creature!" Tommie exulted as she walked across the veranda of the hotel.

"Which one?" Cal teased. "You've got five others, you know." He blew his nose.

"Oh, Cal, you know. Everybody says so! Even the Lexington paper. Did you see that article?"

"Oh, that piece about esprit de corps and decorous deportment?"

"You know very well what I mean. No, their warning to all young ladies 'lest they lose their hearts among this handsome group.' "

"Well," said Cal, straightening his jacket and sniffing a runny nose, "that must include me!" Without warning he picked his sister up and swung her around. "And which one of the handsome group are you losing your heart to, as if I didn't know? If you marry him, will you be a duchess? Hey, don't! You'll tear my braid . . . or ruin your parasol!" He ducked, laughing, and ran to his waiting horse. The exhibition was about to begin.

Ah, well, it certainly was splendid, Tommie thought, watching them swirl and turn and trot and halt, all in perfect rhythm. How did they manage to keep the horses moving at exactly the same pace? They planted their front hooves as if they were pulled taut by the same string. Try as she would she couldn't keep her eyes from Basil Duke. Well, why should she? There he was, sitting his mount with such an easy, upright grace, while the others— even Johnny—let their horses mill about while they waited for the long-winded politicians to stop whining at each other: Beriah Magoffin, with his endless talk of Southern Rights, and old Senator Crittenden, with his cheek bulging with tobacco. Kansas, Kansas, Kansas! She wanted some pink lemonade.

The stage trip home seemed endless. Tommie raced into her mother's bedroom.

"Oh, Mama, they were glorious! Simply glorious!" She untied her bonnet ribbons and shook her hair free. "You should have seen them! Too bad you stayed home with Charlton's grippe! Aunt Bet could have nursed him!"

"Hush, Henrietta!"

"You should have seen the girls going wild over Johnny!"

"Hush, Henrietta!"

"Well, they did! And rightly so, too! I never saw a more disciplined, decorously deported group of handsome young men."

"Henrietta, quit teasing me. I read the papers, too."

"Well, they're right! But it's not the young ladies who'd better watch out for their hearts."

"What do you mean by that?"

"Johnny's a man, Mama. . . ."

"Henrietta!"

"I don't care! And some of those young ladies are not so young that they don't know what they're doing. Don't you think you'd better talk to Rebecca?"

Henrietta stiffened. "It's not my place to lecture my son's wife. Now run along and see if Aunt Hannah has any supper left."

Once alone, Henrietta Morgan admitted to herself that perhaps she was not too unlike Margaret Bruce across the street; she would keep her children with her as long as she could.

The next morning, with a pang of guilt, that same thought burned through the blue ink scrawl of Kitty's letter as Henrietta read the news of Colonel McClung's death. The idea flashed: Now Kitty will be home again. She called her children into the parlor.

"An inflammation. Such a young man! And Kitty. Poor Kitty . . . our lovely, vivacious Kitty, a widow at twenty-three! She must come home, of course. Some intestinal trouble . . . and fever. Can you imagine? He was such a robust, healthy man!"

Henrietta waited for Kitty's arrival with more impatience than Bouviette could remember. The thought of her Kitty—her vivacious, flirty Kitty—condemned to a "decent period of mourning" was too much. Even if she didn't want to go out, she could receive friends. Hopemont needed her. Her mother needed her. With all the boys (she included Tommie with them when she thought this) careening around on horses, Henrietta would appreciate the company of her oldest daughter, who was more like her than any of them. Bouviette, seeing her mistress's face light up when her Dolly arrived, agreed.

But Kitty wasn't inconsolable. A little subdued, and quiet, but hardly heartbroken. She insisted on riding out to the farm with her brothers and hearing all the latest gossip. She missed her family and spoke of going to Frankfort to visit Aunt Mary, to Louisville to see Uncle Abraham. Fourteen-year-old Tom followed her around as if she were a queen. Key followed

Tom. When Margaret Bruce made her "call," Kitty was glad to leave the older women in the parlor and stroll in the garden with Becky.

"But even *she* looks at me with those owl's eyes," Kitty groaned, staring through the circles of her thumbs and forefingers and turning her head so slowly that her mother burst out laughing. "What am I, anyway, some kind of freak?"

"They are only trying to be considerate of your feelings," Henrietta said, after she caught her breath. "Thanks, Bouviette. That's just what we need. Here, have some tea."

"You see, Mother? Even you are doing it. What I need is a whiskey. What I need is a ball!"

"Would a horse race do?" Johnny asked.

She turned to her oldest brother with a brilliant smile. "You always did understand me, didn't you, Johnny?"

Six months later she met a dashing Virginian with a red beard who had been a lieutenant in Mexico and a captain of artillery in the Seminole war, and was now with the U.S. Coast Survey in Washington. In the spring they were betrothed.

"That means you'll move East," Henrietta said quietly.

"We've set the wedding for July." Kitty stretched her arms over her head and twisted her skirts into a swirl. "Just think! You can come visit us at Washington City!"

"Hrummph! When I have a better city here?"

The summer of 1859 was torrid in Kentucky. Temperatures in the high nineties were not uncommon, and Henrietta, with some reluctance, accepted her son's invitation to watch the Rifles perform at Blue Lick for the Fourth of July.

"It will be cooler there, Ma."

"Did you know the last battle of the Revolution was fought at Blue Lick Springs?" Richard asked her as Adam bumped the Hunt carriage to a halt before the hotel. "And Daniel Boone's son was killed?"

"And ole Dan'l himself captured by the Indians?" added Charlton, not to be outdone. "Wasn't he captured by the Indians?"

"Why do men measure everything by gain or loss?" Henrietta asked, but their excitement was catching. Johnny, too, seemed more animated than usual, and for that she was glad.

He had good reason. Miss Lexington had her daddy's stamina, and at two could challenge any three-year-old, as she would today. As he watched her now he had only one regret: Becky had refused to come.

Shining chestnut, Miss Lexington stood sixteen hands and had perfectly matched stockings on her back legs. When she ran they became a white blur in the morning mist. Henrietta had stood often enough between her boys and watched Randolph's James, now eighteen, sweet-talk the filly into the final spurt, the ultimate generosity. "She hates spit almos' as much as de whup, dat hoss does," James would tell them after a workout, with Miss Lexington pushing against him and rubbing her mouth on his trousers.

"But she'll be as fas' as her daddy, you wait and see," Randolph added, his eyes proudly on his sons. Jesse, now fifteen, was the official "groom" of the Rifles, and little Billy, nine, was his "assistant."

She was, John Morgan had to admit, the sleekest racer he had ever seen. She would stroll out of her stall like a lazy clown, knowing that she had unlatched the door hours earlier and had chosen, of her own accord, to wait for James to open it. When she reached the end of the aisle she would stop, also of her own accord, and be tacked up as if she were a girl getting her hair brushed for a party and bored with the whole operation. At the gate of the track she would stop again, again without being told, and wait for James to settle on her back as if she were bestowing a royal favor, never once taking so much as a step until she received a pat on her neck, her signal that it was time to go to work. And go to work she did. My, how she did!

"Remember, Randolph, what Uncle Simon used to say?"

"He said a lot, Massa."

"Stop calling me Massa. You're a free man."

"It's jus' a word, Massa. Free is in yo' mind, yo' daddy said."

Their eyes went back to James, using all of Uncle Simon's wisdom, filtered down.

"He would be proud," John Morgan said, not bothering to explain.

"He sho' would," Randolph answered, knowing they both understood.

Every chance he got, every hour he could spare from the business and the Rifles, Morgan had gone out to the farm to watch the filly's progress. Now, at Blue Lick, it all seemed to come together: The Rifles would perform at nine o'clock, just before Miss Lexington's first race. There were ten horses entered. Sanders Bruce's black stallion, Warrior, was the favorite. Cripps Wickliffe had a dark bay gelding with a long neck and speed. But secretly, Morgan thought Miss Lexington had better legs. Even at rest, or just walking down the aisle of a barn, there was something languidly powerful about her haunches, something understated about the reach of her hinds. The great undercurve of her chest told of a reservoir of wind for the long stretch. There was a quality, however, that just looking at her could never uncover: You had to know her to realize the depth of her heart. That was her real secret, the giving when asked. Not demanded. Asked. James seemed to have a magic touch, an almost mystical communication. Even Randolph, used to the miracles produced by Uncle Simon, was spellbound.

"She'll do it," Randolph kept saying. But because she was born after May first, she would be carrying the three-year-old weight of eighty-six pounds instead of seventy. "She'll do it," he murmured again. It was a prayer.

Stallions are stronger. Everybody knows that. And Warrior was a big horse. Still, Morgan thought there was something uncertain in the way he handled his right shoulder. It was known that he drifted. Or did Sanders's jockey deliberately eliminate competition that way?

"No, no, Brother, you're just keyed up," Cal kept saying as they mounted for the drill. "Sanders may be an abolitionist, but he's a gentleman. Did you hear he's starting his own drill team, to be called the Chasseurs? Can you imagine that?"

But the announcer was calling for the Lexington Rifles to make their appearance, and their show began.

Twos, fours, eights. Pair to three, three to pair, pair to four. Double speed, eight abreast in the turn, interlocking flank turn at the trot, oblique turn, dividing pairs. Half-circles, double circles. The heart, the spiral. Then the finale: the great star, really a double wheel, with the outside horse cantering while the pilot horse walked. And above the brushed, shining flanks and ramrod-straight green-uniformed backs, the upright staffs and fluttering pennons of the Lexington Rifles. Was anything—*anything*—asked Tommie, clapping her gloved hands, prettier?

Afterwards, the crowd bunched, then wandered. It was the silent signal that all attention was now on the racecourse, a mile-and-a-quarter oval of sand laid against the green grass of July. Morgan left his horse with Jesse and walked over to the fence with Cal and Richard. Charlton, who, at twenty, had his father's unruly blond hair and good looks, came running up with Tom and Key.

"How did we do, how did we do, Brother?"

Tom's face, too, was radiant. "I held her back, didn't I? Did you see me in the wheel? I was practically *crawling* to keep pace. How'd I do?"

He wanted to do so well, and actually there had been some mistakes, undiscernible to the unknowing eye. But he's just fifteen, Morgan reflected, and ran his hand through his brother's hair, pulling him to him. "Just fine, Tom. You did just fine! Now if Miss Lexington can do as well . . ."

"She will, she will!" yelled Key behind them. Something in his exuberance made Morgan wish again that Becky could share this day.

Girls came up, twirling parasols, smiling at him, calling over, openly inviting. Richard, at twenty-three, as openly received their admiration, although he knew Brother Johnny was the center of attraction.

Girls were forgotten, though, when the race began.

Silently, he was with Randolph and James, those mornings at the farm.

How do you do it?

Ah jes' lissen to her, Massa. Jes' lissen.

She broke well, but came off the mark sixth. At the back turn she was fifth, on the outside, with an Ohio horse first and Sanders's Warrior second. A Madison County horse was third, and then on the backstretch Morgan saw James make his move. Fifth. Fourth. Third. The Ohio horse fell back to second, but there was hardly a length between them as they rounded into the stretch. Four horses were bunched, dust flying. James bent forward, his hands together on her neck, his face lifted to the wind between her ears. And then it happened. Warrior drifted and Sanders's jockey raised his whip and hit the filly in the face. She swerved, and for an instant it seemed impossible that James could stay on.

But stay he did, recovering the stride. For the first time in his life he gave her the whip, and she finished second.

"It's not fair!" Cal was yelling, with Richard and Charlton moaning behind him.

"That's horse-racing." John Morgan tried to sound philosophical.

"That's plain thievery and you know it!" Tommie fumed.

"Match race! Match race!" the crowd was yelling.

"Why don't you?" T.H. asked. "Go ahead. Talk to him. Make him prove it, by God!"

Sanders was surrounded by admirers, accepting their adulation with as much graciousness as his own satisfaction would allow. His expression froze on his face when he saw John Morgan step up.

He was even more astounded when Morgan held out his hand. "I congratulate you, sir." The eyes were soft, but the twisted smile made Sanders uneasy.

"Why, thank you . . ."

Always, always, grandson, put yourself in the horse's place.

"Warrior is a fine horse, fine specimen."

Sanders straightened and cast a glance around to his friends. "We think so."

"And a fine rider on his back."

Learn to think the way the horse does . . .

Sanders didn't answer.

And you'll be able to think like your enemies also.

"I would imagine that horse and rider are the finest in the country, hereabouts," Morgan said, as if reluctantly admitting a point.

"Well, he just proved it, didn't he?" Sanders answered, looking around at his friends for their expected confirmation, which they gave.

"Who?" Morgan asked with a look of endearing innocence.

"The horse, of course."

"Oh, I thought you were speaking of the jockey."

"Oh, well, both. It takes both."

"Then it's not entirely the horse. Wouldn't you agree?"

"See here," Sanders said impatiently, "how can you have a horse race without a rider?"

Morgan pursed his lips and pretended to think a minute. "No, I suppose you're right. I suppose not." He looked up suddenly. "Then you'll agree to a match race with different jockeys, just to prove your point?" He smiled sweetly.

"See here . . ."

"But surely it would be a test of the *horses'* ability?"

The men behind Sanders mumbled, some nodding among themselves. Sanders was not unconscious of their reaction.

"If you are challenging me, sir . . ."

"I'm not challenging anybody." Morgan laughed quietly, as if amused, but the eyes were no longer soft, and the laugh ended in that little twisted smile.

"Come on, Bruce," someone said behind him. "You know you've got the best horse. Take him on!"

Sanders waited a minute, frowning.

"Come on!"

"Very well, then."

"You name the time," Morgan said.

"At three o'clock, after the political speeches. The best three out of four four-mile heats."

Morgan lifted his eyebrows, then calmly said, "At three o'clock, after the political speeches." He offered his hand, and Sanders Bruce took it reluctantly, noting sourly how ramrod-straight his brother-in-law's back was, under that green uniform, as he moved away.

"She'll be all right, boss." It was a term James had picked up around the track from some Yankee trainers, and Morgan smiled. The mare shifted her back legs, stuck up her tail and urinated. James watched the heavy yellow stream and grinned. "She'll be all right."

When Morgan told James of the arrangements, his face fell. "Who'll ride her, Massa? Ain't nobody kin make her run like Ah does . . ."

Morgan cleared his throat and looked at Randolph.

"Me, Massa? Nah, not me. Look at mah size! Ah ain't been on a hoss to race since Shadeland . . . six years ago now, Massa!"

"Then it's settled."

"Jesse, Massa?"

Morgan shook his head.

"*You*, Massa? Ah, no . . . Nah, now—why, Massa? Nah, no. You cain't go out deah an' ride like—"

"Like what?" Morgan seemed amused. "Like 'ordinary folks'?"

"Ah, now, Massa." James, who had been cooling the filly down, squeezed the sponge in his hand and listened to the water splash in the bucket between his legs. He tried to laugh.

"So, you fellows don't think I can ride!" Morgan pretended disappointment.

"Naw, Massa, we din't . . ."

"Sho' not, boss . . ."

"Well, then, it's settled. The race is right after the politicians' speeches. I know you boys will get her ready. In the meantime, I feel the need of some refreshment."

"Yassuh, Massa."

They said it in unison, scrapers and sponges in midair, watching him walk away from them.

"Sho' hope he carries a whup," said Adam, who had come up.

"Hesh up," said James, with the authority of a freedman's son to a slave, although Adam was older. "Cap'n Morgan knows whut tuh do wif a *hoss*."

"If de ladies don' gits to him firs'."

"Hesh up and fetch me dem cloths. Gots to git dis heah hoss dry 'fo' she gits a chill."

"Chill? You been too long talkin' to dem Yankee ridahs. Dis ain't de Nawth. Ain't no chill in Kentucky in *Jooly*."

The spa at Blue Lick, with its three-story frame hotel, airy galleries, and boating on the Licking River, was almost, in its own way, as grand as Graham Springs. When John Morgan walked up the porch steps and into

the large dining room, where long, linen-covered tables formed a giant U of
food at one end, he was hardly noticed, and yet everyone knew he was there.

He drifted into a sea of muslin and summer suits. Tommie, near the
desserts, was talking with Basil Duke. Kitty, as usual, was surrounded by
admirers. Henrietta was gesturing to her lady friends, who were no doubt
discussing *The Idylls of the King* or *The Virginians* or some fashion from Philadelphia. Snippets of conversations floated by. Someone had heard Adelina
Patti sing; someone had just come from St. Louis. Underneath the guffaws
and drifting cigar smoke coming from one of the three parlors at the back of
the dining room, political empires were being built on jokes and promises.
He helped himself to a piece of very thin, pinkish roast beef.

"Ain't you gon' have mo' den dat, Marse John?" asked the waiter tending
that part of the table.

"Not today. Got too much to do."

"What have you got to do?"

It was Amanda, her own plate rounded with ham and dressing and biscuits. She moved her shoulders so that her bodice, which had crept up,
settled again. When she saw his eyes linger appreciatively on her low-cut
neckline, she laughed. "Maybe you're not eating much because you're in
love. They say love will take your appetite."

"Yours seems safe," he joked.

"Let's sit over heah," she drawled to cover her embarrassment. "At this
little table by the window. Did you evah feel such heat?"

"There's a breeze."

When he spread his napkin he looked up to find her staring at him. "Sorry
about the race," she said. "That cheating Sanders. Everybody saw it."

"We'll recover."

Her green eyes went to the speaker's platform, draped in bunting, just
past the porch, and beyond, to the track. "When?"

"Right after Magoffin speaks."

"It'll be moonlight at hign noon and the Licking River'll run dry by the
time that ole windbag finishes."

"Oh, you don't like him? I thought Jake . . ."

"Oh, Jake," she said, and bit a biscuit.

"May I get you more lemonade?"

She reached out and held his wrist. "No. Don't move."

He fully expected, when he turned, to see Jake, but it was only his
mother's Reading Guild, watching them as if with one pair of eyes. He
laughed out loud.

Jake did emerge, his cigar still in his face, with a group of men who
bunched themselves around the governor-elect as he made his way to the
gallery. The diners followed.

"Let's stay here," Amanda said. "We can see from here."

"Not if folks stand on the porch."

Her look said, It won't matter. Behind them the suddenly emptied dining
room had a deserted air; the only sound was the discreet clink of silver on

china as servants cleared the tables. He leaned back and stretched his long legs sideways, to avoid her skirt.

"You look tired, Johnny." He had closed his eyes.

"No . . . no. Just thinking."

A ponderous voice came to them, introducing the speaker. Morgan thought he recognized one of T.H.'s friends. Magoffin cleared his throat and bellowed: It was the South which supplied the bulk of American exports. It was the South which bought the bulk of goods imported from abroad. But it was the NAWTH which enjoyed the profits. . . .

"I was thinking . . . how nice it would be," Amanda said expectantly, looking away, "if you could come out to the house again sometime. . . ."

"*We must frrreeee ourselves from this subservience! New AWlins must supersede New YAWK as the port of the nation!*"

She looked over to see his eyes closed again, a little twisted smile on his face. She sank back, watching him, the line of his cheek, his mouth, his eyelids.

"*We of the South have been hewers of wood and drawers of water for those who fatten on our prosperity . . .*"

Oh, Johnny! When you were away and I thought I'd never see you again . . .

"*. . . while they rejoice at our misfortune . . .*"

Then I went away. But I'm here. I'm here, Johnny . . .

"*Gamblers and money changers in New YAWK, thieves and swindlers in BAWston. . . .*"

She leaned over. The ruffled sleeve slipped up her round arm as she reached for his hand. He jumped and she laughed out loud. "You were asleep, Johnny Morgan."

"I was? What time is it?"

She looked at a grandfather clock ticking across the room. "Two o'clock. Why?"

"*. . . sport with men's fortunes as children with toys.*"

"Will you excuse me?"

"*The South must suffah because the NAWTH panics . . .*"

"It's time to go." He stood up and stretched.

"*Ah tell you, ladies and gentlemen, it is time we free ourselves of this vassalage! It is time we throw off this thralldom!*"

"I thought we'd watch the race together."

"Can't," he said. "See you later . . ." he almost shouted as he left her, through the cheering of the crowd as Magoffin finished. She went to the porch and made her way to the railing. He had walked to the edge of the track and she could see him talking to Cal. A semicircle of green uniforms surrounded them, but Miss Lexington had been led out and saddled. Closer, and nearer the edge of the hotel lawn, Sanders's black stallion was standing and ready to go. A jockey wearing colors she recognized as one of the Ohio stables had mounted him and leaned down for instructions. John Morgan took off his coat and handed it to Cal.

"Who's going to ride the Morgan filly?" a voice behind her asked.

She saw the white shirt and dark head swing up.

"Why, it's Morgan himself!" the man shouted. "Morgan's riding his filly himself!"

21

He couldn't believe it. He had ridden many horses, but he had never felt one like this. Even when he'd tried her on the farm, she had been easy. Now she sensed the challenge and turned on the power in her haunches. But it was an effortless, floating stride under him, her croup dipping, her shoulders reaching, reaching. He drew himself forward and down and she became an arrow, hardly touching the ground. He could only imagine how her hooves were digging back the turf. Her nose lifted toward some unseen goal straight ahead. For his part, he had to count the number of turns around the track. One mile. Two. Three. Four. She finished a full six lengths beyond the stallion. As Morgan settled back and closed his fingers, he heard Warrior puffing behind them. Already he was planning what he would do in the thirty-minute rest period before the next heat.

Randolph quickly took charge. Morgan hopped down, handed the reins over and followed James, Cal and Richard to the stable area. Tom and Key came running up, Charlton and Tommie following. He gulped the water Cal handed him, spilling some from the gourd as Richard kept pounding him on the back. While the others worked, he sat on a stool in a blaze of congratulations, admonitions and advice. Miss Lexington, walking in circles, seemed unconcerned. Before they knew it, the thirty minutes were up.

Again, that give and reach and feel. And then, on the backstretch, in the second mile, something went wrong. It wasn't a stumble so much as a sudden sinking. She almost fell before he pulled her up. The stallion flashed by.

Randolph and James and Cal appeared from nowhere.

"What happened?"

Morgan jumped down. They walked her back. He ran his hand down the cannon bone of the right fore. There was the heat, the unmistakable bulge. The leg pulled away at his touch.

"Bowed tendon."

Cal groaned. "When . . . ?"

Randolph shook his head. "You know as well as I do, Massa. From the looks of it, with rest, at least two months. Maybe mo'."

Sanders was magnanimous. He had won this time, of course, but offered a match race, any horse, any jockey. They settled on the first week in September. With luck, she would be ready.

As they led her back, Randolph shook his head and clucked to himself. "Maybe she was gittin' it and we din' know," he worried. "Maybe thass why she kept refusin' the right lead lately. Favorin' it . . ." He looked at Morgan and they both looked back at the horse. Even if the tendon healed by September, a race so soon after an injury could cause serious lameness. Morgan knew horsemen who wouldn't have let that stop them, but he had inherited a tradition from Uncle Simon and his father and old John Hunt.

"Her sire raced lame, and it finished him," he said grimly. "We've got only one horse with stamina enough to do it."

"Shadeland, Massa? Naw, he's ten years old now, Massa. 'Sides, his eye —he bes *blind*, Massa . . ."

"He runs around home, doesn't he?"

" 'Roun' home, yassuh, but thass anothah mattah. Ain't no race," Randolph muttered.

"Haven't you said that with one eye he's better than most with three? We'll do it. We've got six weeks."

"Massa?"

Randolph watched that old Johnny Morgan smile, and he was with Aunt Hannah in the winter kitchen at Shadeland after Johnny had gotten his way again. *Mm, mmm. Dat boy could sweet-talk de stink outta a skunk.*

"You kin, too, Massa."

"Not this time. You'll ride him."

"Me? Naw. With all this weight, from Maggie's cookin'? Naw. Now, James . . ."

"James? Well, maybe you're right. Yes, you're right. James."

When they told him, James beamed and replaced the brush with his hand as he patted Miss Lexington's shoulder.

"Do you notice how it almost always at least *threatens* to rain in July?" Henrietta fretted when he came into the parlor at Hopemont the next morning. She turned her gaze from a darkening garden to her oldest son, who was already stretching out his long legs in front of the sofa. His spurs dug at the carpet, but she did not admonish him this time; a look of sadness on his face stopped her. "How are the Rifles?" she asked. "How is old Tobe? Still kicking left?"

"We switched horses," he said absently. "Tom's riding in place of Sid."

"Tom's riding again? Well, he'll be pleased!"

But they both knew they were asking and answering questions, under their words, about Becky. He had not, after all, moved back across the street after Becky returned from Arkansas. Quietly and almost unconsciously, he had made a decision. His life would henceforth shift its center from one corner of North Mill to the other. He looked at his mother and smiled.

"I don't like it," she murmured to Aunt Betty, her only confidante. "Bouviette, he's unhappy. Our Johnny's unhappy."

"He sho' likes them Rifles."

"He does, doesn't he?"

"Yes'm. An' he'll be happy agin across de street. Jes' you watch."

She did, but there was no change—and, with Kitty's wedding just two weeks away, no time to think. The whole house was bustling, fairly bristling, with starched muslins, laces and linens, and the smells of special cooking, for Captain Hill was due from Washington City any day.

Who couldn't like Powell Hill? With his red beard and snapping eyes and ready wit, he carried with a flair the easy grace of his ancestors. For once,

Henrietta was thoroughly pleased, and almost fell in love with him herself. One of his forebears had been a captain of horse in the army of Charles II— a Cavalier, of course—and after the Cromwell nonsense, when his family left England and settled in Virginia, Powell's grandfather had served as a colonel under Light Horse Harry Lee. As for Powell, a bout with yellow fever in Florida, where he had served with the army, left him with sudden spells of recurring fatigue. But his energy and happy disposition more than overcame any concern his future mother-in-law might have for his health.

Powell's mother, too, was descended from Cavaliers, but had, unfortunately, left the Episcopal Church for the fanaticism of the Baptist "new light." Evidently Powell had survived that, too, for he kept in his pocket a lucky hambone his mother had given him in her saner days when he went off to the war in Mexico. He showed it to her jokingly the night before the wedding. Thank the Lord, the boy's superstitious! Henrietta thought. He would never turn sour, like little Becky Bruce. He was a pagan after Henrietta's own heart.

The ceremony took place in the parlor at Hopemont, with servants peeping around doors and a brilliant July garden splashing color against the windows. Captain A. P. Hill, erect and utterly charming in his uniform, flashed an endearing smile past his bride at his mother-in-law.

"You take care of him, now," she told Kitty when they left.

"Mama! Isn't he supposed to take care of me?"

"*That* would be impossible, even for a capable man like Captain Hill," Henrietta smiled as she stood between her brothers Robert and T.H. They watched the newlyweds run toward the carriage.

T.H. saw little of his nephew during the rest of July and August. Almost every day Morgan rode to the Leestown farm to watch the action. With Cal and now Richard working at the factory, T.H. could get on without him for a few days. Richard was even talking about starting a jeans factory of his own. One night at Hopemont, over cards, he outlined his plans.

"I think you're wise, Richard, to start planning now," Dick Curd told him. "With Oregon a state and California growing, Kentucky will be, as she always was, the road leading west. Only more so." He laid his cards down and grinned. "I'm out."

"I fold, too," T.H. sighed, and reached for his whiskey.

Charlton gave them his shy smile, then laid his ten, jack, and queen of hearts in a row. Johnny, who had joined the game late, looked down at his own hand and chuckled. "Well, Charl, looks like you've got me this time."

It was one of the few times he hadn't kept his mind on the game. Richard stretched his legs, raised his arms high over his head and groaned.

"Hard day at the office?"

"Too much courting," Charlton answered for his brother, with a grin.

"There's never too much courting, gentlemen." T. H. settled himself on the sofa and smiled. Catherine Hunt's sweetness lingered around his mouth, almost lost in the salt-and-pepper beard that covered his face. How much he has become a father to us, John Morgan thought. Tragedy has made him gentle, and able to savor every moment. It was obvious how much he loved his sister's family. "You are all so exuberant," he had said more than once. He was the last man anyone wanted to hurt, simply because betrayal hurt him so much. When he spoke quietly, as he did now, everyone listened.

"Courting—how gracious it is! What a lovely custom. We must cling to all our lovely customs."

"You sound sad, T.H," Dick Curd murmured.

"No, not sad. Well, maybe sad."

"Why?"

"Why? Well, the important things are going. You read Seward's speech last fall—all that talk about 'irrepressible conflict.' "

"That's nonsense," Dick sighed. "The Constitution guarantees the protection of property. Most Northerners understand. That's politicians' talk."

"What frightens me," T.H. said, "is that Seward is a conservative."

"Then the Lord protect us from the radicals!" John Morgan poured himself a drink.

T.H. smiled over at him. "Have you heard that the governor may be asking private and municipal units to join the State Guard?"

"Whatever for?"

They all looked at him.

"My nephew is not political, gentlemen," T.H. said kindly, but a little uncomfortably.

"What about Miss Lexington?" Charlton asked, to get the talk away from politics.

Morgan leaned back. "I'm not racing her."

"Then you'll forfeit?" Curd raised his brows.

"No . . . the bet was on any horse, any jockey. We're using Shadeland."

"Shadeland?"

"He's only ten. Boston raced at ten, Uncle Dick. You wait. He'll show you."

"I only hope he shows that brother-in-law of yours," Dick Curd said as Aunt Hannah set another decanter of whiskey on the little table by his elbow. He waited until her back had disappeared before he added: "Any man who reads that damned *Impending Crisis* and believes it—! The very idea, trying to get non-slave-owning whites to rise up and free the darkies! Can't they see our only hope is with the Union? The abolitionists are as bad as the states' righters." He was glad that his sister-in-law preferred candles to coal-oil lamps. They smelled, Henrietta said. Candlelight gave bourbon the proper glow.

"The answer, it seems to me"—Dick added more calmly as he stared over the candles—"is a third party."

"We tried that." T.H. sounded sour, remembering the Know-Nothings.

"Maybe the Vice-President will run," Richard offered. "Breckinridge has influence in the North."

"He's been too tied to Buchanan, unfortunately. No, I think Crittenden's the man . . ." Dick Curd said.

"You are all wrong, gentlemen," Henrietta announced from the doorway.

Behind her they saw Basil Duke, in his Lexington Rifles uniform from the afternoon's practice, with his shako still under his arm. "*This* is the man." Holding his hand was radiant, nineteen-year-old Tommie. They were betrothed.

"Pray he don't see no hawks," Randolph joked as they led Shadeland from his stall for grooming. Randolph himself would ride him the six miles from the Leestown farm to the racecourse at Dr. Warfield's plantation. There he would be stabled for two days before the meet, James sleeping in an adjoining tack room. Every morning Morgan and Randolph came out to watch the workout. Loping easily, reaching under and out, neck balanced, Shadeland was everything they wanted. They didn't push, but his time was adequate. The eye, as Morgan had predicted, seemed to make no difference. The afternoon before the race, when Warrior was led to his stall, there was general joking between the grooms. Only the trainers, Randolph, and the Ohio stablehand whom Sanders had retained for this race, were tense and talked of pace and laps. Shadeland's bad eye, like a glazed white marble, defied jesting when he flowed across the track.

A sizable crowd gathered by the fences the next morning, more than Morgan had expected. A long line of carriages was parked up the curving drive to Dr. Warfield's house. Watching Shadeland being tacked up, hearing Randolph's last-minute instructions to James as he mounted, Morgan stood apart remembering how Delilah's bone-lazy colt had run after a hawk and lost his first race and a good right eye. Shining silver and sleek, he seemed to embody his name—that lovely, lost land. His win today might redeem, in some strange way, a need too deep for words.

In the first heat the gray stallion confirmed their faith. Drawing the inside, James sent him off at a rattling pace, with Warrior laying up within two lengths down the backstretch on the first mile. But that was as close as Sanders's stallion ever got. Shadeland drew off and came loping across the finish line hardly lathered, a good five lengths ahead. When they unsaddled and sponged him down, he was barely puffing. He was in the best shape they had ever seen him, trim but muscled, rested but ready. And he had given the younger Warrior eleven pounds. Even the extra weight didn't bother him. "He's the warhorse," Randolph kept saying. They rubbed him down, brushed him off, and he was ready to go again. James was ecstatic. It only seemed a matter of doing it.

In the second heat Shadeland held a three-length lead for the first two miles, then the Ohio rider gathered Warrior and collared Shadeland at the half-mile pole on the third lap. With that black head pumping and that mane flying almost in their faces, James wisely gave Shadeland a breather and let the Bruce horse gain a length. Then, at the last turn, he leaned up on the gray's neck and whispered "Git!" as his father had taught him. Shadeland bunched and spread, reached under and flew past the finish a neck ahead.

"Too close for comfort," Randolph grumbled, but John Morgan was all grins. "Three out of four," he kept saying. "That's all we need—one more."

The stallion was beginning to tire. They massaged his legs and learned from his time that a new world record had been set. When the news spread, the crowd rushed forward as toward a magnet. No fences, only low hedges, separated them from the track. As the horses came down to the wire some of the more intent spectators ran out. Races had been lost because horses couldn't find a lane through the crowds. Randolph worried, but James only grinned. "We'll fly over if we have to," he said. "Like a hawk!"

Time was called. The two horses, black and gray, cantered to their places, Warrior nervously sidestepping and resenting the restraining hand his rider had to use to keep him straight.

"A steam engine in disguise," an admirer said behind them.

"Runnin' outta steam," Randolph chuckled under his breath, sensing the black's stubbornness under all that fidgeting. *A great horse has heart*, Uncle Simon had said. *He'll give all you ask. Watch out when they jump around too much—sign of stinginess.* "Be as stingy as you like," Randolph said aloud.

But the Ohio rider knew what he was doing, and closed Shadeland's four-length lead to two by the end of the first mile. On the backstretch of the second, it was nose to nose. The crowd was already pushing through the bushes and standing on the course when they came thundering past, Shadeland ahead by a neck. Then, for some inexplicable reason, they saw James actually pull him up on the last curve before the homestretch of the third mile.

"What's he doing?" Randolph yelled. With one voice, the crowd chanted, "Go on! Go on! Keep it up! It's not over yet!" James, realizing his mistake, gave Shadeland the whip and they surged forward. But they had lost so much ground they finished just within the distancing line, at seventy yards. Once started, Shadeland went so fast that James could hardly stop him. He raced past the stallion, but beyond the finish line.

"What did you do?" Randolph finally got out. Morgan thought Randolph would kill him on the spot.

"Oh. Ah . . . lost count . . . thought it wuz fo' mile already, Paw, not three. We been aroun' thet track so menny times, Paw. Ah'm sorry . . ."

"Sorry!"

"That's all right," Morgan said. "We've got two out of three. We've still got a chance. Win the next and we're in."

"We gots to win the nex'."

"We will."

Those standing by the fence and up on Dr. Warfield's porch said they had never watched a heat like it. Shadeland took the lead from the beginning and never relinquished it, sailing so easily around the last turn that James actually pulled him up and loped over the finish line. In the drawing room toasts and congratulations flowed freely. Morgan longed to be at the stables, but politely accepted breeding offers and plans for next year's crop. "Ole One-Eye" was declared as good as Sard, his sire. American Eclipse, Boston, Diomed, Sir Archy—they were magic names, and now Shadeland was spoken of in the same awed tones. Chatting near the steps, Morgan could see, across the long lines of rooftops, the brick walls of Hopemont. He shook Sanders's hand and something seemed vindicated, but he didn't know what.

How he wished his father could have been here this day. No tiresome politics. No talk or doubt about whether anybody loved anybody or not. Just a horse race, the pure act of intelligence and will and spirit giving everything. Until now Shadeland had not had the best mares sent to him. Maybe now he could prove himself, as Morgan always knew he could. Already the owners of twelve mares had spoken about next spring.

Henrietta did hear of John Brown again.

After the Kansas murders, Brown, with three of his sons, went to Canada and solicited money "for secret service and no questions asked." Even Brown was surprised by the response.

His plan was simple: His group would invade the South, teach its slaves to bash in the heads of their masters, burn plantations and take to the mountains, where they would resist any attempt to overcome their "revolution." In the second week of October 1859, with twenty-one men, including his three sons and five Negroes, Brown set up camp on the Maryland side of the Potomac. Pikes, pistols and carbines were stored in a barn, ready for the attack on the Federal arsenal at Harpers Ferry. Sunday night was chosen. It was almost too easy.

The first person killed was a free Negro on his way to work as baggageman at the little station. It was one-thirty in the morning. Brown took possession of the arsenal, armory, and rifle factory. He took hostages and raided a plantation and killed half a dozen citizens, including the mayor. The engineer of the early morning train—probably finding the dead baggageman—gave the alarm. Colonel Robert E. Lee, with Lieutenant J. E. B. Stuart and a detachment of Marines, were dispatched by a special train from Washington and demanded surrender. Brown refused. Lee gave the order to break in the door. In a quarter of an hour it was all over. Brown was captured; one son was dead, another mortally wounded, the third escaped. Ralph Waldo Emerson compared Brown's "glorious scaffold to the cross" when he was hanged in December, and in the North towns were draped with black, bells tolled, cannons fired and prayers went up for the new martyr.

"Thus this madman who has hacked to death settlers in Kansas and left a freeman to bleed to death on his way to work is the new Christ of the North," T.H. groaned. "And they call Southerners sadists."

"Don't they know Simon Legree was a *Yankee*?" Tommie asked her uncle indignantly.

"They'll remember what they want to remember."

Henrietta had never been so mortified. "And a 'glorious scaffold,' indeed! I'll never read another of Mr. Emerson's essays again."

When she heard that Reverend Elisha Pratt had asked his congregation to pray for the good people of the North who needed guidance in this time of crisis she was beside herself. "The idea! Expecting us to forgive insanity! It was the Yankees who hanged him, remember, not us! Even they have better sense than to let a madman run loose. . . ."

John Morgan didn't bother to remind his mother that Reverend Pratt hadn't asked his congregation to forgive John Brown but merely to pray for the good sense they all needed.

Christmas, for Henrietta, was miserable, with all this talk of trouble, and it was followed by the worst winter anybody could remember. Now, with spring and another election in the fall, she knew the men would be full of nothing but more nonsense, all summer until November. With the Republicans tied more and more to the abolitionists, the Democratic Party seemed the only hope for saving the Union. But it was badly split. People now talked of Southern Democrats who would rally around Breckinridge, Northern Democrats around Douglas. Richard Curd was more convinced than ever that the time for a third party had come. Just after the holidays he went to Washington to join Crittenden's staff. He was back in Lexington in February to test, as he said, the atmosphere for a third party. "For the Union and the Constitution," he said. "So we've named it the Constitutional Union Party. I'm holding a meeting at the Odd Fellows Hall to call a state convention for ratification of the platform. North Carolina, Virginia, Massachusetts and Pennsylvania are all enthusiastic. In Boston there was a big meeting at Faneuil Hall; eight hundred delegates recommended the Crittenden-Everett ticket."

Henrietta was amused. She had never seen her brother-in-law so agitated. He denounced Jeff Davis as a firebrand who would ruin the country. "With his nit-picking theories," he fumed.

Her favorite cat, with hair like black silk and enormous eyes, perched in the sunshine on the window sill and swiveled its head like an owl. "And Mr. Crittenden?" Henrietta asked.

"Crittenden's got a plan. . . . He wants to restore the Missouri Compromise. Extend it to California. When a territory becomes a state, then it can choose."

Henrietta started to say something, but the worried look on her brother-in-law's face stopped her. She looked at the cat, settled now on tucked-in paws, its great jade-green eyes staring placidly.

As the weeks went by she began taking politics seriously. More and more she talked with Dick, who, more than her brothers, held on to objectivity.

"We all know Seward has the Republican nomination sewed up," she confided to him one morning. "But with his talk of an 'irrepressible conflict' who would vote for him?" She bent her head to a sampler she was making for Tommie. It read *Earth Hath No Sorrow That Heaven Cannot Cure*. She didn't like it. In fact, she thought it stupid, but the colors were nice.

"Don't be so sure," Curd said quietly. "Have you heard that Cassius Clay is stumping for Lincoln?"

"Cassius is a peasant."

"Cash went to Yale."

"That explains it," Henrietta said, biting off a thread.

"In January the House of Representatives refused to let him speak at Frankfort," her brother-in-law chuckled. "He did anyway, on the street."

"I told you he was a peasant."

"He plans to speak at Richmond this week—in fact, tomorrow."

Henrietta threaded her needle and twisted the thread end deftly into a knot. "If the people of Madison County want to waste their time, I suppose it's their business."

"They want John and the Rifles to show up to keep the peace."

The needle stopped in midair.

He didn't tell her, as he had told Johnny and Cal, that the proslavery forces had planted a cannon in the public square, or that he'd sent an anonymous note trying to dissuade them from violence.

"And so they want John to do their swaggering for them."

"Yes, you could put it that way."

"He has a school board meeting."

Henrietta's cat jumped at the sound of her voice. Dick Curd, too, knew better than to argue.

As it turned out, the Rifles did go to Richmond, and watched Cash Clay hold down the papers of his speech with two navy revolvers and a bowie knife. He denounced slavery with that backhanded wit the crowd understood, just as they tolerated his insults because he was a Clay, and vilified him good-naturedly with shouts of "Shoot him through the head!" because he was Henry's cousin, not meaning a word of it.

The Rifles, mounted and just within earshot, kept a collective eye on rainclouds gathering to the southwest. It was a good twenty miles back to Lexington, after they crossed the Kentucky River on the ferry. If Clay talked much longer, it would be midnight before they got home. To their delight, Cash ended quickly and sat down.

Colonel Oliver Anderson, a Democrat, was next. He was introduced by a heavyset man whose surly face was well suited to the insults he now flung at his audience. There was a burly quality to his muscles which even the broadcloth frock coat couldn't conceal. Morgan leaned on the pommel of his saddle. Yes, it was Jake! Since he'd bought out Robards he'd gone into tagging behind politicians, introducing them when he could, endorsing them —sometimes to their embarrassment—when he couldn't. But there was a strange vigor about Jake that you had to admire. It was the vitality of the barbarian.

"I repeat," Jake bellowed, "all that I have said about Cash Clay and his friend Robert Todd, and can prove it. Who constituted a majority of the committee that nominated Robert Todd? Emancipationists! Who almost— if not entirely—conducted the proceedings of the meeting that nominated him? Emancipationists!"

Morgan smiled. Jake, like Amanda, had picked up some "language" along the way. You had to give him credit. Jake had also learned the rhythm of political rhetoric. With repetition and emphasis in all the right places, he was pretending puzzlement that anybody in his right mind would condemn slavery, since the Good Book itself supported it.

Cassius Clay was on his feet.

"We are here, gentlemen, for the purpose of selecting a representative to the Congress of the United States, not to listen to this perversion of religion.

. . . I have always suspected that when a man starts quoting Scriptures he's either a coward or a liar," Clay shouted.

"Would you help a runaway slave?" Squire Turner, a rawboned Anderson supporter, yelled from the crowd.

"That would depend upon which way he was running," Clay called back, and the crowd roared.

"Nigger thief!"

It was Cyrus Turner, the Squire's eldest son. Before anybody knew what happened, Clay, no small man himself, jumped off the platform and struck Cyrus a staggering blow with his fist. Cyrus hadn't landed on the ground before a dozen Turner kinsmen surrounded Clay. One man had a club, and before Cassius could draw his bowie knife it was jerked from his hand and the club found its mark. Morgan was about to give a signal to charge the crowd when Tom Turner, Cyrus's brother, stuck a six-barrel into Cassius's face. To move now would be instant death. But miraculously the caps failed to fire—three times. Dazed and reeling, but taking advantage of the momentary confusion of his opponent, Cash lurched out and grabbed his knife, blade out. In the scuffle he was stabbed in the left breast, over the heart. With his hands cut to the bone, but with the knife in his possession again, Clay buried it to the hilt in the stomach of Cyrus Turner.

By the time the Rifles rode into the crowd and dispersed the curious, both men had been carried into a nearby house. A half-hour later word came that Clay was dead and Turner was dying. The crowd, sheepishly satisfied, withdrew. There seemed no more use for the Lexington Rifles at Richmond that day.

It was past midnight before they trotted into Lexington. Talk buzzed as they waited for the ferry, then died again as they watched the river. Cash was dead, and although they may not have agreed with him, he was a gentleman of their own kind, a man not afraid to stand up for what he believed. The rain had passed and, mounted again, they watched the road ahead dip and rise, a strange mauve-white between the hills.

A mist had settled in the hollows. Across its shifting surface the crests of the hills looked like islands dotting the landscape for as far as they could see. Someone started singing, and the creak of leather and hooffalls marked time until they reached town and, one by one, the Rifles dropped off toward their homes. When Morgan called out his last good night and saw Hopemont, sedate and solid on its corner, it was with a surprise he would always remember. There it was, like an anchor, containing all its memories, its special sounds, surrounded by its walks and gardens, where those sounds still seemed to linger—the voice of his father, of his grandmother and his Aunt Catherine. Of Tommy Cunningham and Alexander Gibson, even of old Henry Clay, who had hated the war that killed them. Now people were talking of war again. It was as unreal as the night, with its floating islands.

22

"What are you doing walking, Johnny Morgan?"

It struck him that so few people called him that these days. He stepped across to her phaeton, with its little rumble seat for a groom. No groom was with her today.

"Playing grown-up."

"Isn't it funny?" Amanda said as he sat beside her. "When we're little we want to be big. When we're big . . . So when was the last time you rode like a banshee across a field? Come now, tell me. I'll bet you can't remember."

"To tell you the truth I can't."

"I read all about Shadeland. Quite a race. I'll bet Sanders was furious!"

"Has it been that long since I've seen you?"

"It's been longer than that. I hear Kitty has a baby!"

"Yes. A little girl."

"What did she name her?"

"Henrietta."

"So now you're an uncle."

"Yes."

"Aren't you going to ask how Jake is doing?"

"How is Jake doing?"

"Jake is in Frankfort playing politics."

"And Will?"

"He's still in Cincinnati. Ever since he went to California, it seems he can't settle. Found some of his old soldier buddies up there."

"I didn't know he'd gone."

"There's lots you don't know, Johnny Morgan."

Because he was looking serious she said quickly, "I hear you and Richard are going into wool."

"Who told you that?"

"Never mind. Have you thought about making uniforms?"

"Uniforms?"

"Everybody's talking about war. If I were a man I'd make uniforms."

She turned the carriage with the ease of an expert, the top down to the sunshine. Watching the reins in her hands, he thought, Yes, she would, too. She had the same stamina as his mother. Pioneer women. Wouldn't Henrietta Hunt Morgan have puffed up at that?

"What are you smiling about?"

"Was I smiling?"

"It's good to see you smile."

He looked at her but her eyes were already back on the horse. They were maneuvering down Main Street.

"I forgot—have to get off at the bank—something to deliver."

"I'll wait. That is, if you want me to."

From the street he looked up at her. "Yes, do. I do."

"You haven't been to the house in ages," she said when he swung up again. He didn't answer, busy bowing deliberately to a friend of his mother's, a member of the Reading Guild, who was passing in another buggy. It was Amanda's turn to laugh, and the sound was deep in her throat. "You're still the same Johnny, in spite of what people say."

"What do people say?"

For the first time she seemed confused and paid attention to her driving.

"Here, let me take the reins. Even though you think you're better with a horse than I am."

She relinquished them and watched him with her wide green eyes. "How is Tommie?"

"Excited about getting married. The house is filling up with linen. Hopemont has become Hopechest."

"You don't sound too happy about it."

"Oh . . . I am. Basil is a gallant, courageous gentleman. She couldn't have found—"

"And you?" she asked bluntly.

He was glad he had the reins. He flipped them and clucked.

"And you?" she insisted.

Why did he always talk with women who got to the point? *Tou' c'ose* . . . He determined to beat her at her own game. "And you?"

"I asked first."

"I, too, am a gallant and courageous gentleman."

"How courageous?" It was a flirtatious challenge, but the smile on her mouth did not reach her eyes.

"I'd hardly be a gentleman if I refused, now, would I? Besides, Warren Viley has a stallion I'm interested in. Been thinking about riding out your way to talk with him about it . . . may breed Miss Lexington in the spring."

"Paw was right," she said, pretending to be hurt.

"And what was that?"

"You're too much like your mama."

Ahead of them the Versailles Road spun out under the blue sky like a limestone ribbon. The fresh green of June fields sped by. Beyond a fence festooned with wild roses a pond caught the sun and broke it into a million pieces. The smell of honeysuckle and flowering locust was everywhere. He talked of going with the Lexington Rifles to Louisville, where Simon Bolivar Buckner, the man the governor had asked to train the State Guard, was conducting a training camp.

"How long will you be gone?"

"Not long . . . two weeks."

Before he realized they were there, the brick towers of her Italianate house stood above young ash trees down the long circular drive. It had a brazen elegance. A groom took the horse at the marble steps, and Morgan followed Amanda into the parlor. Slanting sunshine from tall windows fell across curved-back sofas and deep carpets. Fat, baroque cherubs had been carved into the wooden posts that supported the mantel. Oversized Ionic columns flanked a single step leading to an extension of the parlor—a poor imitation, his mother would have said, of a ballroom. But the sun came in there, too, and a pair of wing chairs facing a low marble-topped table had been placed by a bay window. Amanda sat in one and arranged her skirts, looking up expectantly. He sat across from her and watched her ask her butler for whiskeys.

"You don't mind, do you? You always liked whiskey."

He grinned. "Of course not. I always take what the ladies offer."

Her green eyes opened wide, and for the first time since his wedding day he remembered the pressure of her head against his shoulder when she'd kissed him. Was she trying to tell him something, even then? Like T.H., and Cal, and his father? He wondered now, sitting in this awful house, with its oversized, overdecorated, overelegant everything, why he hadn't listened to them. Even here, no amount of false architecture or bad taste could deflect the honesty of the eyes that searched his for an answer. The thought crossed his mind that he could be happier here, even with those stupid cherubs, than in the very proper Bruce parlor, or in the little ruffle-and-lace bedroom with its sewing box by the bed and its long-neglected sofa between the windows. When had he slept with Becky? He couldn't remember. Since before the baby. Seven years ago. She had gone to those "cures" in Arkansas, but no amount of hot springs seemed to remedy the swollen legs or "spells" with her heart that plagued her. In a flood of remorse at his thoughts, he looked down at his hands. It wasn't her fault, after all, that she'd been ill. And then, almost as suddenly, her repulsion of him came back, the scenes, the chill. Sanders called him a Tin Soldier.

"This is good," he said. He had been silent so long that the old black man had served them and then just as quietly withdrew. "Do you have good servants?"

"With Jake's business we get quite a selection."

"Ah. Yes."

"I'm sorry about Cash Clay. Even abolitionists are human," she said seriously, setting her own glass down, already half gone. She had inherited Will's capacity, but it didn't show. "At least he lived."

"Yes, that's not the first time they thought they'd killed him. Grandfather would have said, like some horses, Cash has staying power."

"Warren Viley's plantation is just over the hill."

"I know."

"Which of his stallions are you interested in?"

He crossed his legs and leaned back, letting one arm rest on the chair. "King Alfonso. Good bloodlines."

"You think a lot about bloodlines. That's where you're just like Sanders. I hear he's taking down names and dates from everybody."

"He'll have an American Stud Book before he's done. It's needed."

"It's good to know you've done something in your life that's needed, even if your name is Sanders Bruce." She drained the bourbon from her glass. Her red mane, tamed into its bun, escaped into little curls around her ears and he had the irresistible urge to kiss her neck. Didn't Jake make her feel needed? He looked around the room. The floors shone like glass. At Hopemont, boards were pockmarked from spurs, from those many long legs stretched out in talk, ankles crossed. He could vaguely remember his grandmother rushing with footstools, then giving up. Hopemont, unlike the other big houses he'd known, had no "gentlemen's withdrawing room" where the men retreated with brandies and cigars after dinner. The women of Hopemont partook of thought and business as much as the men. Catherine Hunt could hold her own when Henry Clay argued for his tariff. Her daughter Henrietta was even better, and half the time Tommie could be found in Calvin Morgan's library reading Aeschylus or Sophocles. In some ways Tommie was more like their father than any of them. Now she was getting married. Sometimes, from the door of that little office off the entry hall he had watched Becky alighting from a carriage—on Sundays, usually, helped down by her father. He closed his eyes and pushed back the idea that life was insane.

"Are you all right, Johnny?"

"Of course! How long have you lived here?"

"Here? Why, let's see. Five years."

Plenty of time for spur marks. Those floors worried him. For the first time, he wondered what she did with herself. She was not accepted by the society of Lexington. She had no children.

"Do you still ride much?"

"Every morning. I've got a mare that's pure sugah clear through."

"I'd like to see her."

"You can. You can even ride her if you like. And I'll tell you that's a compliment, Johnny Morgan. I'm the only one's ever been on her back."

"I'd love to." He made a motion as if to leave.

"Oh, I forgot," she said, looking away from him. "I got a letter from Paw. He's been to the Chicago convention." She jumped up and ran to a little desk in the parlor, behind one of the columns. "That feller Lincoln," she called out, gathering up her skirt over the single step as if it were a mud puddle. The action was unconsciously graceful, as delightful as the crinkles she sent across her freckles when she laughed. From the way she moved, he could tell she must be as athletic as a girl under those crinolines. He had just turned thirty-five, and Amanda was four years older. Childless and beautifully mature at thirty-nine, this girl whose body was born to create life. How strangely their lives had turned out. He, too, was childless. Cal not married. Even Wash was still a bachelor. The Morgans were drying up.

"What does Will say?"

"Here, read it if you can. Only promise not to laugh. He may not spell right, but you know what he says."

"Give me a man," he smiled, "who knows what he says. Plenty of folks know how to spell right."

But he was not prepared for Will's brand of language. He grinned, and at times couldn't help laughing out loud.

dear dotter,

I hop you are well I am in good helth now but lean from Cough. Went to Ag Fare with G. Talbutt, you never new him, he was with us up at the Maumee. We had a good tim drinkin to the Genull. The Ag Fare was up at Chigauger and we met some men who'd kum up from Illinoise, be pade to kum by thet Linkun feller.to pollitick.

They sed we kud make sum too if we stuck with them. Talbutt went. They got fresh printed tickitts an five dollars appees fur showin up at the hall next mornin, fiv o'clock, befor the doars open.

I declared to Talbutt's fase I wuldnt be no sham dellagate but he went and tole me how they crowded into thet hall and wuldnt let the reel dellagates in. Thet's how thet feller Linkun got nominated, like a Rober. I no this fur a fack. If it dos not suit you to tell Jake, that is fin, but you mite tell J. Morgan if you see him. Tell him we got a reel fit on our hans, a skunk playin possum.

You no I deel in trooth not lis. I don need no muny now. I mad sum by tamin a hoss fur a feller. Theys lots of fellers up here dont no nuthin about hosses. Talbutt sez he mite stay to, we kud go aroun the kuntry traynin hosses fur folks. So dont wurry bout me nun. Take kare of yoreseff, dotter.

yore paw

Morgan laughed, handing her the letter. "I'll bet he'll give them some sweet cake."

"Just like Uncle Simon." Amanda smiled, folding the paper. "What was in it, now?"

"Twelve hours of fasting, one pound of oatmeal, one quarter pound of honey . . ."

"And plenty of sweet talk, if I remember right."

"Yes. Plenty of sweet talk."

"Uncle Simon. He was one in a million, wasn't he? Remember how he fussed at us in the stable?" She pushed out her lips and scowled until he laughed. Then she said seriously, with sudden tears in her eyes, "I guess we all needed that."

"What? His scolding?"

"No. His sweet talk." Before he could answer she said quickly, "He always treated his hosses better'n us, though. Always pattin' an' rubbin' an' talkin'."

She had dropped her Louisville twang and slipped back into the soft sounds he remembered. She got up to return the letter to the desk, but he stood and stopped her, his body close to hers.

"Let's not talk anymore," he said.

"It's true," Dick Curd told him. "I'm a Union man down to my toes, but these Republicans will split it asunder faster than Breckinridge ever could."

"I can't believe it."

They were in the office of the bagging factory on the Georgetown Road. Cal worked here, while Richard spent more time at the jeans business and ropewalk closer to West Main.

"Your friend Will was right," Dick said, so agitated he forgot to light his cigar. "Three hundred strangers were in Chicago that night. Came up from southern Illinois on cheap excursion tickets provided by Lincoln. A man named Lamon met them. Long after midnight he was signing them up, giving them bogus delegate passes. And the next morning they filled the hall."

"Honest Abe."

"It was masterful, I assure you."

"I'll bet it was."

They were interrupted by two free hands, Amos Jackson and his son Moses, a shy and somewhat slow boy of sixteen. They were good workers, and polite.

"Excuse me," said Morgan. He walked into the storage room and shut the door. "How are you doing, Amos?"

"Jes' fine, Marse John."

"I see Moses has learned to use that steam loom."

"Yassuh. He bes good wif machinerry. Yass he be." Amos wiped his bald head and frowned.

"Mister Cal tells me he's doing thirty yards an hour."

"Yassuh."

They were talking about the boy as if he weren't there, but out of kindness for his shyness. Moses beamed. One of his front teeth was missing and the gap only made his smile more expansive.

"We're making bagging for three cents a yard. That's five or six cents cheaper than those old hand looms used to do it," Morgan went on, implying that they were more responsible for the profit than the new equipment.

"Yassuh."

Morgan waited, knowing they would tell him in their own good time.

"Massa John, hit's Silas."

"Silas?"

"Mah oldes' boy. He wuz workin' down at Mistah Beard's stable . . ."

"I've seen him. A good farrier."

"Yassuh. Wal, he wuz helpin' out wif Miz Mary Witt's tabacca . . ."

"An' fell frum de roof of de bawn," Moses spoke up.

For the first time, Morgan could see, under their decorum, how worried they were. "Where is he?"

"Home, Massa."

"Can he be moved?"

Father and son looked at each other.

"Tell you what—I'll send my uncle Robert around. Do you think he's broken any bones?"

Amos rolled his eyes. "He bes *swollen*, Marse John."

Morgan laid a hand on Moses's shoulder. "How fast can you run?"

"Fas' . . ."

"You know the house on Broadway, near the corner of West Fourth Street, two doors north? It's a brick—"

"Yassuh," Amos answered for his son.

"Ask for Doctor Hunt." He was pulling a paper from his coat and scribbling a note. "Give him this."

"Yassuh!"

"And hurry!"

When Morgan returned to the office, Dick Curd was still holding an unlit cigar. "Here, let me light that for you!"

"Thanks." Dick took quick puffs. "I plan on going to Washington to join Crittenden. I tell you we've got to get this third party going. That's our only hope."

"You may be right." John Morgan looked out the window to where the Georgetown Road met the Newtown Pike in a **Y**. Beyond, the spires of Lexington shone in the autumn sun. He raised his hands in mock surrender. "You've got my vote!"

It broke the spell. Dick rested back in his chair and sighed. "I guess I do get steamed up." He puffed again.

"Not at all. I guess you have a right to. I'm just sorry the Democrats are splitting up. I'd like two horses on the track instead of four."

"Ah, well, to you it's a game. You never were political, John. One day you will be, when everything you ever owned or loved is threatened."

His face was so serious that Morgan asked, "You're accepting Kitty's invitation?"

"Yes . . . and Eleanor is delighted. The ladies can visit with friends while I'm busy, and I won't feel so guilty."

"Kitty is the perfect companion, then. I can't imagine anyone feeling neglected when she's around."

Curd laughed. "Nor can I."

"She'll know everybody in Washington City by now."

"I'm glad she married again. She's too young to bury herself in widow's weeds."

"Aren't we all?"

After checking with Richard he stopped by Robert Hunt's before going on to Hopemont. Bob, his grandfather's old groom, bowed him in, his white hair a tight wool cap above the raised eyebrows. "Massa John!"

"I can't stay. Is Marse Robert at home?"

"Nosuh. He not bes back yit. Done gone wif yo' boy frum de fakterry."

"Well, that's fine. I was just checking. Ask him to send me word and any bill that's connected with it."

"Ah wills, Massa."

Before he reached the street Robert's gig pulled up. "Just some ribs," Robert said, tying the reins. "He isn't one of your boys, is he?"

"A son of one of the spinners."

"Well, you do spoil them, John. Come in for a drink?"

"Not now. I'm on my way to see Warren about his stallion."

"Oh, well, if it's horses, don't let me stop you!"

It was not, he had to admit to himself, Warren Viley he wanted to see. Jake might be gone, involved in the congressional election, and after all, her house was on the way to Viley's . . .

Jake was in Frankfort, and he rode her mare, and it was "pure sugah." And afterwards, from upstairs, he looked through the long windows across the fields and wondered why such a strange loneliness kept pulling at his insides. He should feel on top of the world. He was successful; he had at long last taken care of his mother's family. Kitty was married, Tommie betrothed, Cal and Richard in business. He represented the Second Ward on the town council. He was a member of the school board, a respected, prosperous citizen. And he could have, if he wanted, the best mistress south of the river, and he knew it. He sat on the big bed with the soft light of a Kentucky afternoon falling across his knees and pulled off his boots. The scent of her, the wantingness—he had never felt anything like it. And yet something was missing, and she knew. Behind him, her beautiful mouth grew soft with thought. "When do you go to Louisville?"

"Tomorrow."

"How long do you stay?"

"Oh—two weeks. Just long enough for the governor to organize the Guard. T.H. has raised a company. He'll be on Buckner's staff, as a matter of fact."

"Will you miss me?"

"You know I will."

"No, you won't."

"How do you know?"

"From the corner of your mouth. You could never lie, Johnny Morgan. You're itching to prance around and show everybody how well you can sit a horse. All those—what are they? Turns on the haunch?"

He was still sitting sidesaddle on the edge of the bed, one knee drawn up. He fell sideways, but she wouldn't let him find her mouth. She unbuttoned his shirt with the care of a mother for a child, chiding him with soft, caressing clucks.

"I'm only interested in one turn-on-the-haunch," he said, looking down at her.

"You're all alike. Impatient . . ."

But he caught her off guard, opened her mouth with his lips. Her breasts were unbelievable. Will, and all those stories about the Indians. Now he knew why he'd gone by Will's so much. Even when he was eight and she was twelve, with those little budding nipples under her rough blouses. *You don't know nuthin', Johnny Morgan.* She loved him even then, as he loved her now.

To T.H.'s consternation, he hired two more free hands before he left. They were good workers, in their forties, and had come highly recommended.

"I promise you, T.H., they'll work out. You'll see. I know you had bad luck before, but absolutely no whiskey's allowed on the premises . . . outside the office, that is!" Richard, left to hold the business together, gave him a look, and promised he would try.

Kentucky's militia was all but defunct following the Mexican War. But Brown's raid at Harpers Ferry and the vigorous anti-South hate campaign in the Northern press alarmed Kentucky into action. Governor Magoffin warned his legislature that training an "active, ardent, reliable, patriotic, well-disciplined, and thoroughly organized" Kentucky militia was now indispensable. In March the legislature called for every man of sound mind and body between the ages of eighteen and forty-five to join. From their numbers would come an elite corps of volunteers, the State Guard. Simon Bolivar Buckner, breveted for bravery in Mexico and instructor of infantry tactics at West Point before he resigned to become a lawyer in Louisville, was picked for the job of training and equipping nothing less than a small army. Tall, darkly handsome, thirty-seven, with a broad forehead, deep-set eyes and a well-trained, wide mustache, he looked every inch a soldier. Seated, he seemed easygoing enough, but when he stood before his troops with that barreled chest thrust forward from his six-foot-plus frame and added the quiet authority of a voice which would brook no argument, Buckner could be awesome. Morgan liked him immediately.

From the first, the new commander concentrated on picked cavalry units as the nucleus of his Guard, and had asked a dozen or more companies to gather at the state fairgrounds in Louisville for training. Young Tom Morgan, who still hoped his mother would let him go to KMI in the fall, was ecstatic. He would have a leg up on all the other cadets!

If he had known how far Henrietta's mind was from his concerns at that moment, he would have been crushed.

She was waiting for a visit from Becky. It was Sunday afternoon, shortly after the Rifles left for Louisville. Becky arrived in her church-going clothes, a prim brown dress with little waves of cream lace at her wrists. Her crinoline was not exaggerated, and only stood out enough to give the gathered skirt a graceful circle at her feet. Henrietta wondered if the leg was still swollen. Rebecca Bruce sat in the Hopemont parlor in the heat of that summer afternoon, a shy, troubled but determined girl, and Henrietta Hunt Morgan remembered long afterwards that all she could think was Why doesn't she use her fan? The poor girl is sweltering in that outfit. Why doesn't she fan herself? But the fan, like Becky's hands, lay limp and immobile in her lap. Her face, too, would have been immobile except for the little twitch that pushed the corners of her mouth deeper into her cheeks. It gave Henrietta the same feeling that Cal's runny noses used to send through her fingers when she would try to wipe them and he would twist his face away. She lifted her own short upper lip, which, she knew, had once been considered "pert" and which, she suspected, intimidated some people even now. It was not her intent to intimidate the girl, but her eyes, she knew, despite everything she could do, were saying unmistakably, *You didn't want him when you could have had him, and now that other women want him, you come to me. . . .*

"It's a little like war," she said aloud, when Becky confessed, in an oblique, implied way, her problem.

"I hardly ever see him, Mrs. Morgan," Becky said, her lips trembling.

It was easy to see that the girl despised herself for that single instant of weakness. Henrietta could guess at the secret hours of rehearsal for this interview, the determination to appear dignified blown away by one choked-back sob, and the silent self-recrimination that was even at this moment going through her guest's head.

"Love is a little like war," Henrietta repeated.

"How is that?" Becky opened her fan and closed it instantly, as if she had committed an indiscretion.

"It isn't won. It's . . ."

They were interrupted by Aunt Hannah serving tea. The clatter and activity of the tray, the silver, the cups on saucers. The handing-outs and thank-yous brought a different rhythm into the room, and made their voices, when they resumed, seem crisper, more distant. Henrietta crossed her legs under her skirts as she leaned forward for a tiny square of lightbread spread with butter and cheese.

"It's all in understanding yourself—and your opponent," she said, tasting the cheese and feeling clever. Did the butter have too much salt? She must speak to Celina.

"And Johnny? I must understand Johnny?" Rebecca Bruce said with a trace of desperation. "I'm afraid it's not that simple."

"Why not?" The teacup halted an imperceptible moment in midair before Henrietta set it back softly. A breeze cooled the perspiration on her forehead and she was thankful for it. She hated to disturb her powder with a hand-kerchief.

"He's a man," Rebecca said simply. "And although I have two brothers, I can't understand how a man thinks. You, Mrs. Morgan, have had six sons. You have seen them grow from little babies . . ." She went steadily on, determined not to think about her own buried son. "I know him to be sweet and kind and considerate and loyal to what he believes in. It's what he believes in that puzzles me. If I could understand that . . ."

Henrietta opened her gray eyes wide and picked up her cup. She could hear Key running around upstairs. He knew better! Where was Bouviette? She sat up straighter, absently fingering the handle. "What he believes in? What we all do, I suppose. Family . . ."

"That's just it, Mrs. Morgan. Whose family? Yours? John forgets . . ." But she couldn't go on.

Henrietta bristled. "He's very loyal. Surely that's a good trait." Where was Bouviette? That boy will break the floorboards!

"Loyal?" A laugh broke from the girl's mouth.

"Yes, loyal. Men have different tastes, different needs . . ."

"I don't believe that, Mrs. Morgan." It was a simple statement, but before Henrietta could answer, she went on: "I don't believe that running off on a horse or to a card game or"—she stopped, unable to articulate the words *other women*—"or worse, I don't believe that's being loyal."

The surge of anger that made her stays hurt and her breath come short was easily controlled when Henrietta saw the genuine anguish on the girl's face. After all, she had known her from the days when she had toddled next to Ellie watching ballgames on the parade ground. She remembered picking her up once when she fell and hurt her arm. The little girl's tears were gritty and left a smudge on her favorite striped green dress, but the weight of the bent head in her lap had left the memory of a pang in Henrietta's heart. Poor little girl! Who wouldn't be frail and skinny with John Bruce as a father and that ninny Margaret for a mother? She thought of her own daughters, the flirt Kitty and the tomboy Tommie. And then, as instantly as that same frailty had aroused pity, the memory of it caused an upsurge of resentment. It was you, little girl, who changed my Johnny. Who made him unhappy and withdrawn, who, more than Betty Wickliffe or Amanda Bolton, took him from me.

One day this girl might understand why her mother-in-law seems so distant. Or would she? Could anyone understand? There was once a girl named Henrietta Hunt who started out with such fine hopes: Calvin in business with his brothers, that handsome house in Huntsville. Oh, it isn't a fine house which makes a marriage, my girl. You reproach my Johnny for not giving you a house! Little do you know how fortunes can change your life. Or illnesses that steal in like thieves in the night, to rob your handsome gentleman of his strength . . . but not his ability to add to his responsibilities. As for that, you're lucky and don't know it. Hasn't he left you alone? Isn't that what you wanted? No, I guess not. You want it both ways. Well, I can tell you have a lot to learn about being a woman. Already, in your own mind, as your own defense, you've set me up as the ogre. Have you done so yet in Johnny's mind? No, from his eyes and his smile I can tell you haven't. And you won't. By God you won't!

"I know John loves you," she said more evenly, gingerly laying out, like a poker player, the card of encouragement, which might prevent future envy and more competition. "When he speaks of you, my dear, his face lights up. Oh, my, if you could only see how his face lights up!"

"Does he? Does it?"

"Of course. Now let's look at the situation. Since your baby died, of course you've been convalescent . . ."

"But I'm stronger!"

"And John has been busy building up the business, so he will be able to build a house . . ."

"Does he say that? Does he?"

"Every man wants a home," Henrietta said evasively. The footsteps ceased and Bouviette's scolding sang out.

"Of course! Of course! That's what Mama says. He's getting established."

"Massa Key! What you stompin' aroun' fo'?"

"There are times when we must be patient."

"Like a hoss, thass whut you is! Jes' wait till Ole Miss . . ."

"Of course!" The girl snapped her fan open and laid it across her chest.

"In my own life . . ." But it was Henrietta's turn to be embarrassed. Quiet had descended from upstairs and Calvin's illness, which had exasperated her all those years, now seemed like a missed opportunity at understanding. "Try one of these little cakes," she offered, hoping it didn't sound like an order. "Aunt Hannah's special."

A sudden breeze made some leaves on a tree in the garden break away and twirl downward on the grass.

"Sanders says we'll have an early fall," the girl announced.

"Well, there are signs. The summer's been so dry."

They both watched the leaves, like women fascinated by the antics of favorite children.

"It's going to be an early fall, Hen! Uncle Ben says so! His herbs are drying faster than usual. Don't you love the autumn, Hen? It's Greek, absolutely Greek. What are you laughing at? Of course it's Greek, this feeling of Fate as the earth shifts in its orbit, as the air changes. Don't you feel it, Hen? As if the earth has a life of its own and it's trying to tell us something."

"It's trying to tell us it's time to get that hemp spread for retting before the first frost."

"Oh, Hen, you're so practical . . ."

His eyes, his eyes were still with her. And his beautiful smile. It's been six years, she said to herself. And the image of his face, so wasted at the end, his eyes turned so pleadingly to her, the grip of his hand slipping as he sank away from her to become a strange, still emptiness on the pillow. She could still remember the shock of knowing that this ghastly thing before her, already cold as stone, had been her Calvin. *How quickly they get cold!* That magnificent man. That warm, magnificent man. She looked at the girl more kindly as she walked her to the door. It's all so short, she thought to herself. We know so little. About them, about ourselves. And then they are gone.

"It does seem as if it's getting a little cooler. Fall is just around the corner!" she said brightly, wondering how many momentous conversations ended with talk about the weather.

23

The camp had a festive air. The Lexington Rifles, the officers with their shakos, the men in French kepis, looked no less ridiculous than other companies with tricorns and cockades. To a man, they would have felt at home in the glitter before Waterloo. With the enthusiasm of a barbecue and the fervor of a camp meeting, the boys took to drill as if their lives depended on the approval of their sergeants, but the ice cream vendors who stood watching at the edge of the parade grounds and the fiddle music some boys made when they rested made circus win out over ceremony.

Only once in the two weeks did the real world seem to intrude, the afternoon some of the Rifles went into Louisville to hear Crittenden introduce Bell. Old Whigs were the backbone of the new Constitutional Union Party, and Morgan recognized many of his grandfather's friends.

"I've heard the Douglas forces have offered to combine with Crittenden if the Republicans look likely to win," someone behind him said.

"Let's go back to camp. I don't even see any good-lookin' wimmen here," a voice piped up. "I've got some special whiskey I haven't opened yet." The boys cheered and the candidate looked their way and gave them a smile, thinking his latest sally was appreciated.

T.H., with his infantry company recruited mainly from friends, proved so able a leader that Buckner promoted him to colonel in the Guard and gave him one of the two regiments to be formed and the job of recruiting more. When the two weeks were over and they rode home on the train, Morgan joked with his uncle about his new-found glory, but Charlton, at twenty-one, was clearly impressed by so many brass buttons and gilt braid. It was Colonel Thomas H. Hunt—only the family called him T.H.—who could discuss military tactics with authority. Henrietta was not surprised. Under that fatherly beard, she always knew her brother had enough valor and bravery for them all.

The next day two carriages were parked at the end of the curving drive off Versailles Road, but Morgan tied his horse at the post and walked up the marble steps. He was about to knock when he saw Amanda in the garden by the sundial. She was in a trim gray riding habit with a standing collar and blue silk necktie. A veil of blue tulle had been pushed back from her black felt hat.

"I thought you never rode sidesaddle," he teased.

She jumped and turned to him. "I didn't hear you come up."

"You *are* riding sidesaddle!" he said, eyeing her skirt.

"I'm playing lady." She crinkled her nose and looked at the house. "Some planters from Alabama."

He moved closer.

"Not here, Johnny! My, you're getting brave! You always come on auction day. . . ."

"I couldn't wait. Aren't you glad to see me?"

"If you'll come back. They won't be long. I think they're about to leave. I've got to go in to see them off. Will you come back?"

"What if I say no?"

She looked at him and he laughed so loud she put her hand over his mouth. "Shh! They'll hear you."

"Are you really afraid for me?"

She pretended to hit him with her crop.

"I'll ride down to Stonewall and see how King Alfonso is doing. I'll tell him there's at least one lady around who's interested enough not to wait."

When he got back the carriages were gone, and the old black manservant at the door bowed and told him she was upstairs. She had changed into a cashmere robe and turned to him from the long mirror, the brush still in her hand. Her red hair fell to her waist and when he took her in his arms he wondered how he could have thought marching around Louisville was a pleasure. She laid the brush quietly on a table behind her without letting her lips leave his.

Her big mahogany bed had always reminded him of a ship. As she moved over, waiting for him, ripples spread on the lace-edged sheets. From the foam of pillows Amanda's lovely thin-wristed arms reached up to him. The room was drenched with sun. He pulled the drapes and the light turned pink and warm. It was hard to wait, but he knew it delighted her when he took his time. He sat on the bed and pulled off his boots, conscious of her knee against his back. He took off his clothes slowly, talking needlessly of the past weeks, what he'd done, the grand fellows he'd met. He knew she hadn't heard a word. When he turned to her, her smile put all talk to an end.

"Well, are you going to breed her?" she asked. Her arm was behind his neck, her fingers fondling his hair. "Do you know your hair is getting thin? You'll be bald like your grandfather."

"Yes, I'm going to breed her. And will you love me when I'm as bald as my grandfather?"

"You didn't race this spring," she said, ignoring his question. Her fingers kept up their slow motion and he pushed his chest against hers.

"I was busy. The weather was horrible and we were trying to build onto the factory."

"I'd like to see it."

"I'll show it to you."

She sat up suddenly, leaning over him. "And Miss Lexington? Can we go out to see her, too?"

"Of course . . ."

But she broke away from the arms that would pull her down.

"When?"

"Tomorrow, if you like . . ."

"Promise?"

"Of course. That is, if you're not going with those Alabama gentlemen."

"Now why would I be going anywhere with those Alabama gentlemen?" She turned slowly and her hair made a tent over his face when she kissed him.

Henrietta surprised them all by being less opposed to the idea of Tom's going to KMI than they had feared. She had known all along that Tom wanted to go away to school. The Kentucky Military Institute, only thirty miles away, was preferable to Maryland or New Jersey, where most of her friends sent their sons. Besides, it was good to see some happiness on Johnny's face again. She never rode herself, but if prancing around made him feel good, she wouldn't argue.

Tom left in a flurry of packing, just in time for the fall term. Aunt Betty loaded him down with dried peaches, candy, and a bottle of Dr. Hart's Vegetable Extract. He was, after all, her first baby to go away to school. They went with him to the depot and stood waving long after the cars rounded the curve and the baggageman cleared the platform.

"I'll write him every day," said Tommie on the way home, but she didn't. Basil Duke came for a visit and stayed through the fall racing season. When she wasn't taking long carriage drives with him, she was at Hopemont reveling in showing off her beau. Best of all, Tommie thought, Johnny liked him. Johnny had never seemed happier. The factory was running smoothly, the Bruces were friendly—and if her betrothal to Basil was the excuse for their treating Johnny better, she didn't mind—and Miss Lexington won six of her seven starts.

Basil left for St. Louis and his law practice. They would be married next summer. "Why do I have to wait?" Tommie fretted. "Eleanor's not waiting! She's getting married next month!"

"Hush, chile," crooned Aunt Betty. "Marse Cripps done got hisseff a practice. . . ."

Cripps Wickliffe had joined his father's law firm in Bardstown. When his wedding to Eleanor Curd was set for November, he asked Morgan to be his best man.

"You see?" John Bruce asked his wife. "That shows you, if nothing else can, which side our beloved son-in-law is on. Slave dealers!"

Margaret studied her embroidery. Keeping amicable relations just short of animosity was more delicate—and irritating—than avoiding a hole with a French knot. Cripps would be leaving Lexington. That should stop some of the card-playing, at least. Now if his cousin Betty would just go away! She punched her needle through and kept her thoughts to herself.

Across the street, Henrietta Morgan was doing much the same.

"You will go, won't you, Mama?"

"How can I, Tommie?" Henrietta whined, tucking a hair. "You and Cal —or Uncle T.H. or Uncle Frank—will have to do the family honors."

"T.H. is too busy. You know as well as I do that Uncle Frank is campaigning for Breckinridge. I'll ask Uncle Robert."

But Robert Hunt, too, declined. "I'll send along a present." Cal, as it turned out, had one of his bad autumn colds and a fever, and at the last minute Tommie started sneezing and complained of a chill. So, in the end, because the Curds had left a week early to enjoy a visit with their future in-laws, John Morgan rode to Cripps's wedding alone.

Wickland, the Wickliffe estate at Bardstown, was beyond belief. A stair-case three stories high rose from the entry hall, and the double drawing room was flanked by pier mirrors that, if you stood between them, reflected endless avenues of chandeliers. Cripps's sisters, Roanne and Sallie, were, as Cal would have said, "real knockouts," and Eleanor Curd was the same pretty, sweet girl she had always been. "Do you remember when I was your flower girl?" she whispered when she met him. Now, as Morgan watched her walk toward them, her arm in her father's, he had never seen her lovelier, or Dick Curd happier.

When he left them two days later, with Eleanor's nuptial vows still ringing in his ears and the memory of Sallie Wickliffe's appreciative smile sending soft messages as he bowed his good-bye, he knew, somehow, that he wouldn't be able to resist seeing Amanda again.

Amanda, he thought that next night at Hopemont, as he poured himself a whiskey from the Waterford decanter on the sideboard and heard his mother and brothers in the parlor. Candlelight caught the cut crystal as he set the decanter down. He looked up to find the steady eyes of Catherine Hunt on him. You wouldn't blame me, would you, Grandmother? In your morning cap? You were a lady, but you had twelve children. Funny I've never thought of that. Grandfather was industrious in more ways than one . . . and maybe you were pretty efficient yourself. The lady looked back from her portrait, noncommittal, keeping her own secrets.

Amanda. He couldn't get her out of his mind.

Just after noon the next day Cal saw the Bolton carriage outside the office. "Well, well," he said.

"I'm going out to the farm to see Randolph."

"Of course. Did I say anything?"

"You said 'Well, well!' "

"And that, as they say, is a deep subject." When he saw his brother wasn't smiling Cal called after him, "If you ride, jump a fence for me!"

Randolph had grown a mustache that summer and looked older by ten years. He was complaining about the state of the tobacco.

"We had such a wet spring, an' de summah has been mighty dry. Hope we git some rain befo' we stick it, else it'll nevah come inta case."

"We will. What do the old-timers say? Dry August, wet November."

"Randolph always did worry too much," Amanda said behind him. Her summer dress, the filmiest of muslins billowing from her waist to the hooped circle at her feet, did not prevent beads of sweat from lining her forehead. She turned her parasol slowly.

"It's coolah down by de stable, Massa," Randolph said diplomatically.

"How is she?"

"Fine, fine. James been workin' her ev'ry mornin'. She's clockin' a mile in undah two fo' the past month."

"And four?"

"Fo' in seven-thirty. Onc't in seven-twenty-six. An' Jesse—Ah've started him ridin'. Not Miss Lexington, a'course—Delilah. He does fine on Delilah."

"How old is Delilah now?" Amanda asked.

"Eighteen," Morgan answered, then turned to Randolph. "And Jesse?"

"Sixteen, Massa. Las' month."

Morgan took Amanda's arm and the three of them watched Miss Lexington lazing in her stall. It seemed incredible, looking at her now, that she could move so fast. Shadeland was at the end of the barn. He had proved a magnificent sire, producing some notable stakes winners. Morgan asked Randolph to lead him out, and they spent some time in the aisle petting him. The stallion perked his ears and let Amanda scratch him under the chin. His coat was clotted with mud.

"Hawd to keep a gray hoss clean," Randolph apologized. When he met Morgan's eyes he added, "But Ah'll git Jesse right on it, soon's you leave."

The old log barn where Sard died was downhill. You could see it through the door. Still unchinked, it made a good hanging barn for extra tobacco. Randolph had followed scrupulously Morgan's orders that no horse would ever spend a night there.

"I'll be out next week. Do you need more hands for the tobacco? Let me know."

Before they left, Maggie ordered Annie to serve coffee. Ten-year-old Billy and his little brother Simon, now seven, watched the white folks with big eyes from a corner. Randolph, obviously pleased with the visit, still regretted James's absence in the fields. They were waving from the porch as the phaeton spun away. Amanda looked back the longest, and then turned to him under her parasol with tears in her eyes. "It's been a nice day, Johnny. I won't forget it."

"Why should we?" he asked. "Forget anything? We've had good lives, on the whole . . ."

She was silent. He watched the dimples appearing and disappearing in the mare's rump as she strained against the traces. Over the crushing sound of the limestone road he heard himself say, "I don't really have that much to do this afternoon . . ."

"No, no . . . there's some things," she said too quickly. "Jake's bringin' out some people. Have some shoppin' . . ."

He alighted at the office under, he felt, the eyes of the whole town.

"It's not so," his mother told him when he came in with a bolt of cloth she'd ordered from one of the shops on his way.

"What?"

"That you've had the nerve to openly ride about with that Bolton woman. That the town is talking about you."

"Whatever for?"

She answered his question by telling him that Cal had been by. "He's worried," she said, then squared her shoulders and twitched her nose. "But he needn't be. This town will not talk about a Hunt."

"I'm a Morgan, Ma."

"You're a Hunt, and don't forget it. As you've seemed to do lately."

"You didn't object when I visited the Wickliffes."

"The Wickliffes are old Kentucky."

He could feel the blood pulsing in his throat. "The Boltons and the Webbs are older Kentucky and you know it! What you're really saying is that the Wickliffes have more money. You choose to forget they get it from the same source."

The truth only made her turn from imperious to imperial. "I don't presume to dictate your manners, John. It is you who are choosing to forget—who I am and who you are. That's all I have to say," she pronounced frostily, and like all women when they say they are through, went on to say more.

"Look at him. That's all I ask you to do. Just look at him. What woman with any delicacy at all would have anything to do with him, much less—"

"Ladies don't talk like that. . . ."

"I'm not speaking of a lady, so the usual rules don't apply. Or is that your excuse? No . . . let me finish. I haven't told you. Becky has been here, trying for a reconciliation. As we all are. It's a disgrace."

"What . . . ?"

"I'm fifty-five years old, and my sons have given me no grandchildren. Who will carry on your father's name?"

He sank in a chair and stared at his feet.

"Don't dig your heels into the carpet."

"Sorry."

"Is that all you have to say?"

"No. I think you're being extremely unfair." Had she forgotten that all the doctors said Becky should never try again? What was he supposed to do? He looked up.

"Don't try those tactics on me, John. They worked for Calvin, but they won't for you."

I'm too healthy, is that it? I've been the surrogate father, the mainstay of this family . . . maybe if I had a cough I would get more consideration. Can't you see I'm only trying . . .

For the first time in his life John Morgan left his mother without a word.

Versailles Road was endless. At last the ridiculous crenelated towers rose above the ash trees. He rang the bell and waited. To his surprise, Amanda herself, and not the old black manservant, opened the door. She wore a low-necked gown more suitable for a ball than for a hot August afternoon. The deep, soft shadow between her breasts drew his eyes away from the diamond pendant at her throat.

"Johnny! What a pleasant surprise!" Her confusion told him someone was in the parlor.

He started to speak, but a pleasant-faced, frock-coated man in his fifties strode forward, hand extended, introducing himself. "Well, Mrs. Bolton," he said urbanely, "since your husband is not at home, I shall call back tomorrow." He bowed slightly, revealing a bald spot on the top of his head.

"At least you're consistent," Morgan said when the gentleman left.

"What do you mean?"

It was clear she was prepared for a fight. Her breath was short and the diamond sparkled.

"You like men with thinning hair."

"Would you marry me, Johnny Morgan?" she flung at him. "Even if you could? No, I see it in your face. You could never lie, remember?"

"A man—"

"But we love each other? Plenty of people love lots of things they can never have. You loved Shadeland. God, how you loved Shadeland! And Paw loved Nathan. And I love you," she ended bitterly. She knew he could never stand tears and fought them back. But her quivering lip and shaking shoulders were too much. He took her in his arms.

"You have me," he told her hair.

She pushed him from her, sniffing. He offered her a handkerchief and she blew her nose.

"No, I don't. The least we can be is honest. I've never had you. Hopemont has you. And your Mama and Charlton and Richard and Kitty and Tommie and Key and Tom . . ."

"You forgot Cal," he said, trying to make her smile, but his joke only made her furious.

"Why don't you challenge him? He's not nearly as good a shot as you are. Or is it that you don't really want the lady?"

The idea of meeting Jake in another "dool" almost made him laugh. But he saw that she was determined to be irascible, and anything he said would only fuel her anger. Yet perversely, unreasonably he goaded her. Did she think he had no pride?

"And the gentleman we just met? Does he want the lady? Would he marry the lady?"

Before the look on her face could turn ugly and confirm everything his mother had said, he turned and left her, walking slowly and deliberately down the steps, aware that she was watching him. He untied the reins and mounted just as slowly, letting his leg swing over and settle in the stirrup before he leaned into a turn and legged his horse into a trot. On the way he hummed, and didn't realize until he reached the carriage yard and handed Adam the reins that it was Will's old glee.

The news reached Lexington the morning after the worst November rain anybody could remember. Lincoln had won.

At the hemp factory T.H. and Cal sent for Richard and Johnny. Within the hour Key Hunt and Richard Curd came by.

"It means war," said Key.

"Maybe not," Curd answered quickly. His straight brown hair, as soft as a girl's, kept falling into his eyes. He brushed it back and leaned toward them. "Look here. Have you seen the figures? It's not as bad as we think. The popular vote for Lincoln was 1,858,200. For Douglas, 1,276,780. For Breckinridge, 812,500. The Democrats actually outvoted him by over two hundred thousand votes."

T.H. looked at him. "But he won, Dick," he groaned.

"By electoral vote, and only in the North, except New Jersey," Curd answered excitedly, not to be disheartened. "Don't you see? Kentucky was solid Bell, which shows we want compromise. Bell and Douglas together exceeded Breckinridge's vote in the slave states by almost a hundred thousand . . . which shows that the 'solid South' is no more 'solid' than the North, which also voted heavily for Breckinridge, just as many in the South voted for Douglas."

"So? I fail to see—" T.H. began, but Key stopped him.

"I do. Dick is saying that Lincoln is actually a minority President."

"Correct." Curd looked appreciatively at Key. "And the way I see it—he pushed his hair back again—"this election shows a definite desire for common sense. Lincoln was rejected by a unanimous vote in ten states. Ten states, mind you, out of thirty-three, with a majority in only five! I would wager that those folks who voted for him never intended their votes to mean war."

"Maybe it's time for your Mr. Crittenden," T.H. conceded.

"You're right!" Dick slapped his thigh. "I've delayed going to Washington City long enough. I'm leaving next week. Crittenden has asked me to help him draft a compromise. . . . The Republicans are still outnumbered in Congress. . . ." He stopped long enough to draw a deep breath. "I tell you this talk has heartened me, gentlemen."

T.H. nodded and followed him out, his hand on Dick's shoulder. He left him at his house and walked on to the telegraph office to send a message to Buckner, asking for instructions. As he wrote it, T.H. prayed he wouldn't need them.

"I don't like it," Key Hunt muttered, watching them leave. "All these numbers mean that the election of Lincoln has been strictly sectional. It will be taken by some hotheads as a declaration of war against the South. This just proves what an imbalance of population can do."

"Your vulgar majority? But isn't that what elections are all about—numbers?" When his uncle, who had just lost his seat in the Kentucky legislature, frowned, Morgan quickly added: "It's too confusing for me, Uncle Frank. Surely it will turn out all right, if that many people want it to?"

His mother was frantic. "What about Kitty? Washington will be dangerous. Black Republicans," she fumed. "And what would the abolitionists do with our 'freed' population, pray tell? Turn them loose . . . but not to go North. Did you hear that Yankee senator quoted in yesterday's paper? That he didn't give a d——n what the South did with its niggers as long as they kept them home?"

"Ma!"

"It's true. I'll show it to you." She searched through a pile. "It was even in a Yankee paper—"

"Never mind, Ma. I think I saw it."

"You don't care, do you?" she let fly, not at Johnny, but at Cal, unlucky enough to have just come in. "You stroll around, you men, bringing us all to the edge of insanity, playing with your words . . ."

"I'm not a senator, Ma!" said Cal with a mock whine. "I only want to run a hemp mill, and with the best hands I can find, free or slave. Ask Johnny. It doesn't matter . . ."

But she left the room in tears. Maybe Dick Curd was right, Morgan thought. His mother, like the country, was ready for compromise, from Crittenden or anybody else. He waited until he thought she had calmed down, and tapped on her door. Her "Come in" was steady enough. She was sitting in her sewing rocker by the window. Outside, the November garden looked drab and matted.

"I wish Uncle Ben were here," she said unexpectedly. "If Uncle Ben were here, that garden wouldn't look like that."

"Do you want me to have—?"

"Oh, Adam's all right, but he's not Uncle Ben."

"No." He waited a minute before he said, "Ma, I think you should talk to Dick. He thinks all this panic is foolish. And when you look at it, maybe he's right. A President elected by less than forty percent of the people— we've got to remember that Congress has the power to make laws, and the Republicans still lack a majority there."

The word seemed to infuriate her again. She twitched her nose. "Black Republicans! At least New Jersey didn't vote for him!"

"That's right! Cousin Pearson arrives tomorrow, doesn't he? I'd forgotten."

"Be nice to him."

"Why shouldn't I be nice to him? I've never met him!"

"He's the favorite son of Papa's oldest brother, and owns the largest factory in Trenton. You may not know it—maybe T.H. hasn't told you— but it was Pearson who helped finance T.H. in the bagging business. We owe a good deal of our bread and butter to Pearson."

"Then of course I'll be kind to him!" He kissed her lightly on the cheek, but she missed the irony. It must be no coincidence, he thought, that his grandfather named his sons after his other brothers—Robert, Abraham, Wilson—but not one was named Pearson. When he met Pearson, Jr., he knew why.

Pearson Hunt, Jr., strolled into the Hopemont parlor the next morning as if he were slumming. He looked around and sniffed through his long, pale nose. "What *is* that smell, Henrietta?"

"Aunt Hannah is boiling some herbs. For the grippe."

"Ah, yes, I suppose you do have to do that sort of thing on the frontier." Pearson pinched his thin lips shut.

"Have you seen T.H.?" Henrietta asked cheerfully.

"At the factory. Just been there." Pearson drew out his watch. "He said he would be by in a half-hour."

"Have a whiskey," Morgan offered. "He'll be around in a little."

"How is Uncle Wilson?" Henrietta looked from the fire back to him. She picked up some embroidery, then set it down.

"I don't get down to Philadelphia," Pearson said, and fell silent. He allowed John Morgan to hand him a whiskey and stared at it, then through the window. "Your garden isn't much," he said.

"No . . . this time of year . . . we lost our best gardener."

"Run away, did he? I shouldn't wonder, the way you pamper them."

"Uncle Ben died," she said stiffly.

"So how's Trenton?" Morgan asked brightly.

"The business is fine. Booming, in fact! Since we got rid of our slave labor about five years ago. Good profit, too . . . man in South Carolina."

"But they weren't field hands!" Henrietta bit her lip at the sharpness of her tongue, which had often enough been a subject of conversation among her Yankee relatives.

"They are now!" said Pearson, and leaned back. "We replaced them with Irish immigrants. That famine was the best thing that ever happened to us."

"The Lord works in mysterious ways."

Morgan couldn't resist it, and Henrietta shot her son a look.

"Glad you see it that way, Johnny! You'll go far!"

They heard T.H. exchanging soft pleasantries with Aunt Betty in the entry. His short, hesitant step gave his slight body a bounce as he walked into the room. "Cousin Pearson!" He held out his hand.

"We've talked all morning," Pearson said, keeping his hand to himself.

"Indeed we have! And how are you, Henrietta? Hmm . . . I smell the smellies. Runny noses won't have a chance in this house, come January! Well, I suppose you have had a chance to catch up on family gossip? Are you planning to visit Abraham in Louisville while you're west of the mountains?"

"Lexington is quite far west enough."

"Oh, it's only the beginning, Pearson! We're buying wool from New Mexico, can you believe that? New Mexico!"

"I've told you what I think of that venture," Pearson Hunt said dryly. "With the South running headlong over a cliff, she will have no more money to buy pants than she will to bale cotton."

"There's still plenty of cotton to be baled," T.H. smiled sweetly.

"Perhaps."

An hour later, when T.H. got up to leave, Pearson Hunt suddenly became magnanimous. He held out his hand. "You worry me, T.H. You look wild in the eye. I'll pray for you."

"You do that," said T.H. He looked beyond Pearson and threw a kiss to his sister. The fan window over the front door rattled as he left.

Cousin Pearson journeyed the next day to Maysville, then up the Ohio and home. There would be no more support from the Trenton side of the family. "We'll make it, Ma," Morgan told Henrietta.

"Of course we will!" she said fiercely. "He was happy enough when his investment made four hundred cents on the dollar!" Then, as if her son had challenged her, she turned to him and glared. "Whoever said we wouldn't?"

The next morning at the office John Morgan looked up into Amanda's shining green eyes and was automatically, instinctively on his feet.

"Amanda! Here, may I get you a seat?" He reached for another, more comfortable chair. "I'm afraid our accommodations are rather—"

She laid a gloved hand on his arm. "Don't bother, Johnny. I'm heah on business."

"Yes, of course."

She handed him a paper. "Jake wants these. Overalls for the field hands, some jeans for the overseer. The sizes are here . . ." She laid the paper on the desk and they bent over it, their heads almost touching. The scent of her came to him and he straightened.

"We'll have it ready as soon as possible."

"When is that?"

He looked at the list again. "We have most of these in stock. By Friday, at the latest."

"You don't usually sell retail."

"No." He returned her look and one corner of his mouth turned up. "But you are a special customer, wouldn't you say?" She hesitated a moment and touched his arm again. Their eyes met and held, but he moved his away first, and she let her hand drop to the handle of her parasol.

She let him open the door and he watched her pick up her skirts and allow her groom to help her into the carriage. He closed the door and watched them drive away. The carriage turned the corner and a wedge of crinoline moved out of sight. He knew he only had to ask. Ah, like an Alabama "gentleman" asked?

With autumn moving into the drizzle of December, and with the Curds in Washington, Morgan was trying to get as much done as he could before the January snow. His eye turned from Amanda's phaeton to Charlton walking down the sidewalk with the mail. At twenty-one Charl hadn't, as old John Hunt would have said, "settled" yet, but there was a special, happy-go-lucky air about him which was delightful, and prophesied success. He was fair and good-looking, like Kitty, like his father—maybe, with the exception of Tom, the best-looking of them all, including the girls (wouldn't Kitty kill him!).

"Hi!" Charlton said as he closed the door, shaking rain from his hat. He caught it on a rung of the coat rack and gave a mock shiver. "It's started again—and getting colder! Here's the mail, Brother Johnny."

A letter near the bottom of the pile had a return address that surprised him. It was a brief note from Gordon Niles. "You may not remember me," it said. "I visited your charming family that summer when your father was ill. I heard the news of his death after returning to New York. The *Times*, alas, did not approve of my Southern 'observations.' For the past few years I have been with Mr. Greeley's *Tribune*. I am writing now to let you know that I have left the *Tribune* and have started a paper of my own, upstate. Nothing big, but at least I can live honestly. The part Mr. Greeley played in getting Lincoln elected is, to my mind, unconscionable. *Now* Greeley wants to retract, and play the part of peacemaker. I refer you to the enclosed editorial. . . ." A folded column of newsprint had slipped to the floor and

Morgan picked it up. The last sentence Niles had underlined in ink: *"We hope never to live in a Republic whereof one section is pinned to another by bayonets."*

When he showed the clipping to Charlton the boy burst out, "Well, he won't. He won't have the chance, for we'll leave it first!"

The stab of excitement in his own chest surprised him.

"You know what Grandfather always said," Charlton said more quietly. "He didn't go after people, but by God he didn't budge, either."

Before Morgan had a chance to answer they both saw T.H. running toward them in the rain. The news had just reached Lexington: South Carolina, by a vote of its convention, had seceded from the Union.

24

"It will ruin Christmas," Henrietta fretted. "Why couldn't they have waited just five or six more days?"

"It may still blow over."

"Oh, Johnny, you sound like Eleanor's husband." Dick Curd became "Eleanor's husband" whenever Henrietta disagreed with him.

"Well, even Horace Greeley says the South has as good a right to secede from the Union as the colonies had to secede from England."

"I don't believe it."

"Here, I have a copy of the editorial here. And you'll never believe who sent it."

"Who?"

"Gordon Niles, the newspaperman from New York. You remember . . ."

"Oh, yes, I remember. A gentleman . . ."

"A gentleman?" Morgan laughed. "You could hardly stand him, Ma. Remember?"

"I have enough to remember," she said bluntly. "Before I forget, Margaret Bruce called this afternoon. They want you for dinner tonight."

"Tonight? I thought—"

"I know. You thought you would talk more politics with Key or T.H., and drink the cellar dry of brandy."

"I don't talk politics, Ma."

"I know. You don't say much of anything to anybody. You worry me, Johnny," she said more kindly. "For once . . ."

It was unlike her to be cautious. He knew she was avoiding the word, to spare him insult, so he used it for her.

"For once accept their transparent attempts at a reconciliation? Is that what you wanted to say? *I* was rejected, remember."

"A gentleman—"

"That seems to be a broad category with you lately, Ma." Almost as soon as the words were out he regretted them, but she was distracted and hadn't heard—or diplomatically pretended not to. She was following some thought of her own, and probably, he thought resentfully, medical. In another minute she would be prescribing a laxative.

"Are you worried about Becky?"

Her question caught him off guard.

"I lost that battle a long time ago."

"Men!" She raised her arms and slapped the apron on her lap. She rose and twitched her nose. "Why do you always put things in terms of war?"

"Because we're warriors, Ma," he said lightly, and kissed her cheek. "You raised us that way." He watched her leave the room with that step of a general, which told him she was satisfied he would obey.

Like an obedient child he had been summoned. And like an obedient child he would go. The irony was, they were the ones who had wanted him to leave her alone. Now "reconciliation." What did that mean but sleeping with their daughter and making a proper wife of her? But did she want it? A clock somewhere chimed the hour. Suddenly he felt tired, his body heavy. The fire felt good. He looked across the room at Byron, still holding court above the spinet. "Well, you renegade," he said aloud. "You had your problems with women, too, didn't you?" He would have just enough time to go upstairs, bathe and dress. On his way he sent Celina for hot water and fresh towels.

He dressed carefully. At thirty-five his body was still muscular and hard, the muscles toned from riding. Only the hint of a paunch—almost mechanically he drew his stomach in as he glanced down—from too much good eating. He carefully trimmed the mustache he'd started and pulled at the budding beard. What would Becky think of it? In a flash, and unfairly, he compared her with Amanda. Becky had never, even in the best times, welcomed his ardor. It had always been something endured, with the candles blown out, like her monthlies, which well-bred little girls never talked about.

He had, for a while, during that first year, felt almost ashamed of his need. Maybe he was, as her look all too often told him, too demanding. Yet when he obliged her and demanded less, she turned peevish and proper, and wore her femininity like a coat of mail. Only after her return from Philadelphia, in those months before the baby came, could their relationship have been called normal. If he had only asked himself why, he could have understood that, pregnant, she felt protected from him; pregnancy had replaced propriety as a hedge against his sexual vitality. Then, after the baby, had come the invalidism. Now what? A new effort at reconciliation, his mother said. Deep down, he loved her still, although more now like a sister. Had she sensed that . . . less threatening need? And would she be more comfortable with him now? Instinctively he squared his shoulders, pulled on his underclothes, a clean shirt. Yes, the mirror told him, his hair in front was getting thin. Maybe, as Amanda predicted, he would look like his grandfather.

He walked briskly across the street, swinging the tails of his frock coat. He hadn't been joking with his mother. She had raised them to fight. That was why they still had Hopemont, why he had—with T.H.'s help, to be sure—salvaged the family fortunes. He had done that much, anyway.

The Bruce parlor was decorated with garlands of Christmas greenery that sent a piney smell all the way to the front door. Becky met him herself, a still ethereal Becky in spite of the spreading hips her hoop skirt couldn't quite conceal. She reached toward him with arms tightly bound in taffeta, the froth of lace at her wrist scratching his nose as he kissed her hand.

"You're growing a beard!"

"Yes."

"A little pointed beard! You'll look like Shakespeare."

He, too, was a little bald in the front? Ah, well . . . He followed her hand, still holding his, as she tugged him toward the parlor. She was gay, almost mildly frantic, in a little-girl way. They were alone, although he heard Sanders's voice and the high trembling laugh of Sanders's wife at the back of the house. "They're checking on the pudding," Becky giggled. "We're going to have a feast tonight!" Then she went on about his beard, sticking out her chin and clasping her hands in that child's stance he had once found refreshing. But her repartee failed to stir desire. He was, he thought with some surprise, almost as chaste as she was.

She sat now in front of him, her skirt, looped with festoons, spreading like a tent. She wore her hair in what Kitty would call a "waterfall," but it only made her cheeks seem puffy and her brow too pale. Her little mouth had kept its ability to tremble, giving her a self-pitying look that might have been charming when she was twelve. How old was she? He had to count back. Eighteen when she married, twenty-three when the baby died seven years ago. Seven years. Where had they gone? In some ways she didn't look thirty, but in others she seemed older, with the dry, drawn-in look of a recluse. At her throat she wore a black velvet band with a gold locket on it that he had given her on their first anniversary. It had his picture in it. He wondered what he looked like and what had happened to the one she'd brought back from Arkansas, with a lock of Sanders's hair. Maybe she was wearing this one as a signal?

With a twinge of incomprehensible anger he noticed that the velvet on either side of the locket had slipped into the folds of her neck. Where was the slim-waisted girl lying back on grass, surrounded by wildflowers? Had she ever existed? He sat amazed at his own deception, looking at this plump, too-young matron and wondering at her little histrionics. Had she learned them from fulfilling the role her father had ordained for her? He looked past the quivering lips and round eyes to the bottom of her soul: She was alone. She, too. Only she was no longer groping. He caught himself up. How could he know that, simply because he still was? How do you know anything about anybody?

"There's a Christmas cotillion at the Odd Fellows Hall," she was saying.

"I was hoping to take everybody for a sleigh ride."

" 'Everybody' means your brothers and sister, I suppose." But before he could answer she said quickly: "Everybody says we won't have snow for Christmas."

There it was again, the fencing. The I want–you want. He tried to master a rising resentment. From the first, she had rejected him, had tried to turn him into something else. A safe, dispassionate father surrogate. And now what game was she playing? He longed to burst out in rancor: Where is my life that losing your love cost me? And why? I watched your illness become a refuge, like some garden with a magic gate shutting me out, compelling me to live in my "male domain," as you call it, forcing me to move to Hopemont and become the father of my own family, and now to stand before you calling out with every pore of my body: What do you want, Becky? An escort at a cotillion? A bespectacled businessman? Ah, but you forget that's what you are, he told himself, without the spectacles. He was powerless to stop the bitter grin that tugged at his mouth. She took it to mean that he was thinking ill of her and became confused, her eyes going even rounder. The thought came for the first time that maybe she was actually afraid of him. It was so ridiculous that he laughed out loud and she smiled uncertainly.

The entrance of her parents and Sanders covered her confusion. John Bruce was friendly. Margaret viewed her daughter's husband with a maternal coquetry that spared him neither appraisal nor curiosity. He bowed stiffly from the waist, like a courtier, and she smiled as if there were some secret understanding between them. Sanders was sticking out his hand in a hearty greeting. A prosperous marriage had made him less surly.

Behind him, his wife was checking her ankles in the petticoat table in the hall. She was a tall, big-boned woman who wore Garibaldi blouses and little round hats with rolled brims trimmed with drooping feathers. They were called "jockey hats." Morgan knew because Amanda had one. This was the first time he had seen Sanders's wife without a hat. He had the insane desire to ask her Where's your hat? Sanders misunderstood his look as admiration and let his hand extend into an arc that fell just short of patting Johnny on the shoulder. "How are you, John? And your horses? How are your horses?"

Ben—jolly Ben—interrupted them with the flurry of his entry. Shaking off his coat as if it were covered with snowflakes, he dropped it on the hall tree and strode into the room with the healthy reek of whiskey and wheat flour. He still joked about giving up the practice of medicine for the grocery business. "I eat better," he kept saying, rubbing his hands together over the fire, although his mother reminded him it wasn't really cold outside. "It must be these Christmas decorations," he said. "Makes things cozy."

Dinner was, as Becky promised, superb. Morgan took her in on his arm and seated her as if she were a queen, and she looked sweetly up at him over her shoulder in appreciation. The decorum of the table saved him from controversy. The conversation was bland. "I've always noticed," he said as a compliment, "how talk expires in direct proportion to the excellence of the food. And we all are remarkably quiet."

John Bruce took his remark as a criticism. He sat up straighter and said something about the politics of the time. His wife tried to smooth things over by murmuring, "John's only telling me he likes the meal, dear." She smiled as if to direct attention from Sanders, who was an audible eater.

Sanders is going to fat, she thought. In another ten years he will be called, with kindness, portly. Somehow his small eyes didn't match his large jaw. Toward dessert he slowed down and started talking about the possibility of war. He looked at his fork, loaded with pie, then placed it in his mouth and chewed.

"War?" said John Bruce, his eyeglasses catching the candles and sending a little shower of sparks down the table. "I think it's all talk." He looked uneasily at his son-in-law.

"Have you heard from Richard Curd?" Margaret Bruce asked.

"Only briefly. He's busy working with Crittenden."

"I do hope he comes up with something," John Bruce breathed. "Critten-den is a smart man. And we can be proud of Dick. A real Union man." He cleared his throat.

"We're in need of all the good men we can get," Morgan said politely.

Was politeness his way of escape? Was thinking of oneself as a gentleman merely another never-never land where one crawled to avoid emotion? But on the heels of that thought came another: Being boorish was just as much an escape. Maybe everything was. Underneath, Sanders and he had the same goal: financial security. Only Sanders didn't wear his so well. He could give himself that much credit.

He was the only one there who had seen war. They used the word so lightly. Even the color of Becky's petticoat (he had glimpsed the edge of it under her gray dress) was called Solferino. Didn't they know that purplish red represented blood? He became quieter as the meal wound down, like a top wobbling. You knew it would fall, and yet you waited. He left about an hour later, pleading an early morning appointment. He kissed Becky's hand and said something about the cotillion: Of course he would take her.

Outside the night air came in great fresh gulps down his throat. He looked up at budding stars between the two buildings, the Bruce house and Hope-mont. For a moment he stood in the middle of the street, as if his life hung there, under that sky, between those two houses. So much had kept him from Becky—the business, his mother's family, and now the Rifles. So much had taken her place.

The warm, musty smells of drying herbs came to him from the warming room. On the table by the back stairs stood the row of candlesticks that his grandmother, and now his mother, kept there ready for taking to bed. Some things never changed. It was only after closing the door of his own room that he remembered, with some surprise, that he hadn't listed Amanda as one of the usurping interests of his life. Had he forgotten her, too?

There was enough, during January and February, to make him forget everything. On January 9, Mississippi seceded. The next day, Florida. The next day, Alabama. Then John Morgan received a letter from Louisville:

Jan. 17, 1861

Sir,

I am directed by Maj.-Gen. S. B. Buckner to say to you that you having been appointed to muster in a company of cavalry of which James B. Clay and others are members. You have his authority to fill the blank of judges of said election and to designate the exact time and place of holding said election.

I am Sir
Your Obt Sevt.
Alexander Casseday
Major and Asst. Adj. Gen.

On January 19, the Lexington Rifles were mustered into the State Guard. "Why do you want to get mixed up in all this?" Henrietta fumed.

"You know as well as I do, Ma, what's happening in Charleston."

"Games. Games men play. So the President sends some boat to a silly island and it gets turned back—what has that to do with you? I've seen too many Hunts and Morgans get excited about other people's troubles."

"I see that Seward has made a strong speech for moderation," he said quietly.

"Seward! After all he's done to wreck the country! Here, do you want to know about Seward?" She pulled a letter from the drawer of the little table by the sofa. "Let Kitty tell you about Seward."

"Do you mean she's writing about anything besides balls and the baby?"

She had crossed the room on her way to the kitchen, and stopped in the doorway. "A little cotillion wouldn't do you any harm, either, Johnny Morgan!"

Seward had refused to back down from the Republican platform against slavery in the new territories. "Uncle Dick says the Republicans are all insane to 'beat a dead horse,' " Kitty wrote. "That popular sovereignty in the territories is working, and anyway who would want to take slaves out there to die in the desert? But *that's their platform* and they'd rather see the country fall apart than back away from it.

"I bought the sweetest hat yesterday when Aunt Eleanor and I went visiting. We were invited . . ."

In late December Crittenden's proposals had been put to death in a Senate committee of thirteen, and although Dick blamed the five radicals on the committee, it was, as everyone knew, the strangely silent President-elect who was calling the shots from Springfield. "This country lawyer," Dick wrote, "with the flimsy jests of a harlequin, the vulgarity of a Yankee tavern-keeper, is pulling the strings. He's made puppets of his henchmen."

Dick's letter was prophetic: on January 15, Crittenden's resolution was sidetracked for a railroad bill, then killed by a vote of twenty-five to twenty-three, all twenty-five being Republican.

Crittenden wasn't through. He called for a plebiscite, to bring the vote to the people, and Dick agreed. "You have no idea, Johnny, how many petitions we've received. The people of the North *do not want war*—which is what disunion will bring. In Philadelphia, six thousand workmen came to Independence Square at night in a snowstorm and voted unanimously for the proposal. We have petitions from all over Pennsylvania: Harrisburg, Lehigh County, Easton, Monongahela County—more than I can name. From Maryland, Delaware, Michigan, Illinois, Ohio, Minnesota, Wisconsin, New Jersey, Kentucky, Maine. It took four pages in the Senate Journal to list them all. Even Seward walked into Crit's office with a petition from New York with almost forty thousand names. On Lincoln's birthday we had petitions from 182 cities and towns of Massachusetts—twenty-two thousand signatures. Now even Greeley thinks only a very few more Republicans are needed to secure the passage of the plebiscite. Hope and pray with us. I know you are not a Union man. But we are all Kentucky gentlemen, I hope. The time has not yet arrived when we can say all this will come out right in the end."

But the clock was ticking. Georgia pulled out on the 19th, Louisiana on the 26th, and by the 1st of February Texas joined them, to bring the number of seceded states to seven.

"The Pleiades," laughed Key Hunt.

"But I thought—"

"I am a States' Rights man, John. But I don't think, when the chips are down, the South will fight." Key played with his watch chain, running his thumb over the links. "Why should they? According to the census, ninety-five percent of Southern whites own no slaves at all. Of the five percent who do, only one percent own a hundred or more. So slavery is not the issue. What is? Tariffs? No. Representation in Congress? Hardly enough reason to go to war! And look. . . ." He dropped the chain and pointed to a map of the United States under the glass on Morgan's desk. Over the sound of the steam-powered looms—Morgan finally had to shut the office door—his uncle pointed to Kentucky and Tennessee. "They are like two fingers pointing west, where the development of this country lies. It is not in our interest, at this time, to consider leaving the Union, although I have no particular love for this administration. Let's not forget," Key added in his best law school voice, "the Republicans do not enjoy a majority in Congress. At least they don't now. With these seven states out, they may. Don't you see? Our only hope for correcting the situation is to work within the system, not abandon it."

"It is the system, gentlemen, if you'll pardon me, which has abandoned us, by abandoning the Constitution," T.H. said in his quiet way behind them. He closed the door, but Morgan noticed his hand on the knob was shaking. "It seems," T.H. went on, "that our Southern sisters have met in Montgomery and nominated Jefferson Davis for the presidency of a new confederacy."

To their shocked faces he added: "And Buckner has asked me to establish a camp on the Salt River near Shepherdsville. For recruiting and instruction."

"And are you?"

When T.H. declined to acknowledge Key's question, Morgan asked, "How long will you be gone?"

"As long as it will take," his uncle answered with a strange new calmness.

"Let me go with him!" Charlton almost yelled. "Now's the time to show our colors. You don't want to sit idly by and let the Yankees run all over us, do you?"

He was Richard, going to Cuba. No, not exactly; Morgan's own heart was pounding. Simon Bolivar Buckner . . . the Guards! The camaraderie, the sense of purpose. His breath came short and he deliberately turned to his desk so they wouldn't notice his agitation. On the top of a pile of papers, skewered by a holder, lay an order from a known Southern sympathizer in Bowling Green. T.H. had sent two shipments down there already, which were shipped at once farther south. It would take three days, four at the most. If he sent Charl, maybe it would give that anxious little brother of his enough activity to keep him from doing something foolish. His promise to his mother that they "wouldn't get mixed up in all this" rankled like a vague betrayal as he proposed the trip to Charl and watched his elation. At breakfast the next morning, after she'd received the news that Charlton was going to Bowling Green, she had to hold her coffee cup with both hands.

"Give him something to think about," he said brightly. "Otherwise . . ."

"Otherwise?" She set her cup down and took a long time buttering a biscuit.

"He wants to join the Guard."

"Guard!" Before she could explode he stopped her with the information that her brother was leaving to help Buckner.

"T.H. is too emotional for all this."

"I don't think so, Ma. Think a minute. T.H. is a Hunt, down to his toes. It's just plain good business to resist any disruption of the economy right now. Hold the line. Reason over rage. Grandfather would have agreed. In a few months the Yankees and the seceded states will come to their senses. You'll see."

She wanted to believe him, and looked up to see the blond head of her handsome Charlton come around the door. "Here," she said. "Aunt Hannah's made this special omelette. You'll need something substantial for your journey."

When two weeks passed and they heard nothing, she panicked. Morgan sent Cal and Henry Curd to Bowling Green to investigate. They came back with the incredible news that Charlton had been captured.

"*Captured?*"

To his mother Morgan tried to make a joke of it. "Seems there are Union sympathizers down there, too."

"What can we do, Johnny?" She sat a little straighter. "Bribe somebody? Surely . . ."

"I'll see what can be done, Ma."

The next afternoon Charlton showed up on a borrowed mule, and his "trip South" became a lark, something to elicit the admiration of Lexington girls. Henrietta fumed. To ease her fears Morgan laughed out loud at Charlton's version of his escape, and she somehow caught the pride in his laugh and let her mouth relax into a little hidden smile. But alone with Charlton later that night, Morgan heaved a sigh and made him promise that he would wait.

Charlton held his face perfectly still, but his eyes shone. "For?"

"When the time comes. When the time comes, Charl." The hard excitement in his own voice surprised him. Was he waiting, too?

For days they moved like people holding their breaths. T.H.'s absence worked on them like an omen. Then a letter from Dick Curd seemed to calm things down again. Virginia had called a peace conference, inviting all thirty-three states, including those that had seceded. "Some of the delegates are already arriving, and I have the honor of serving as one of the advisers for Kentucky."

But Kitty's letter in the next mail threw a pall again. "I've never seen such preparations," she wrote. "Positively frantic. Old General Scott, who loves to parade around, has set troops and cannon in 'strategic' locations. What do they think these peace delegates are, an invading army? The town is rank with rumor . . . there are plots to poison the military horses! I heard an otherwise sane woman say yesterday, as if she were quoting the Scriptures, that a Southern army would occupy Washington City before the inauguration. *What* Southern army? But the absolutely choicest joke of all happened last week when an artillery company sounded reveille and people rushed into the street thinking the war was on! Then a few days later, when there was a salute to honor the new state of Kansas, another panic. . . . Oh, by the way, I may come home soon to show you your namesake . . ."

She really means, thought Morgan, that if Virginia secedes and A.P. goes south, she'll come home for safety's sake. Yes, in the midst of fire, pestilence and sword, the ladies would survive. His father was right.

And maybe Dick also, with his quiet fight for reason. On February 26, Congress passed, by a vote of 133 to 65, a constitutional amendment prohibiting any amendment to the Constitution giving Congress the power to interfere with slavery. It was Crittenden's idea. The sixty-five nay votes were Republican, but Lincoln, it is said, had approved it, to appease the Southern states still in the Union.

John Morgan's own compromise with the Bruces was less happy. He had planned to take Becky to the Christmas Eve cotillion, but the day after he saw her, she came down with a terrible cold and couldn't go. He sent her notes and brought her fruit, but she seemed to have withdrawn again, requesting that he "not come upstairs." Then, when she was better, she greeted him from the day sofa, brought down to the parlor for the purpose.

"It's her heart, Doctor Wolford says," Margaret Bruce whispered to him in the hall. They had had their first real snow of the season. It was bitterly cold, and although he had stamped his feet outside, flakes of frost fell from his coat as she took it from him.

Becky was paler than he had ever seen her, and a sudden pang of fear almost took his breath. She held out her arm and let a limp hand hang from its wrist for him to kiss. He sat gingerly on one of the stuffed seats. Outside, a March wind was beating against the window, and the bare limbs of a tree sent wild shadows across the blanket that covered her. She drew her shawl closer and looked at him with her round eyes.

"Tell me everything," she said.

"Everything?" One of the shadows cut across her face.

"Yes. All the news. I hear Sanders and Father talking, but it's all so confusing."

He smiled at her and crossed his legs. "Then you are with the rest of us. It's confusing for everybody." The seat creaked.

"Oh, don't go brushing me off, John! I want to *know*. Everybody always brushes me off," she said so impatiently that a little color came to her cheek.

His fear for her heart made him uncross his legs and lean forward on his arms. "You know Kentucky. Why, without it there practically would have been no Union. At least in the West. We were the finger pointing—"

"Sanders says Kentucky wants to eat its cake and have it too." She coughed and he reached for a glass of water. She accepted it, sipping delicately, swallowing as she nodded. Somebody—probably Ellie—had lit a candle beside her for reading, and the light made her upraised hand seem almost transparent.

"Don't talk. Just rest."

"No, I—"

"Then I'll talk. You mean the Union Convention in Louisville? Well, yes, that was childish. They didn't want to secede, but they threatened to form *another* separate Confederacy unless the Constitution was amended!"

She blew her nose and folded the lace-edged handkerchief in a neat square, smoothing it under her thumb. The bones of her fingers, he thought, were as fragile as a bird's. She studied the operation as if a solution for all their troubles lay in that square of cloth.

"They're all the same. After their own security and comfort. They don't mind breaking up the Union, only they want to do it their way."

The bitterness of her tone, even more than the shrewdness of her observation, made him look at her admiringly.

"And that special session of the state legislature that Sanders told me about, the one Governor Magoffin called last month. They wouldn't call a state convention, but they want to call a national convention to revise the Constitution!"

"They were afraid that a state convention might provoke secession," he said. "That's been the first step in other states."

"They're afraid . . . they're afraid . . ." Her color rose again and she sat up halfway, still clutching the edges of the shawl and the folded handkerchief.

"They did say that if certain Northern states sent force to subdue the South, Kentucky would resist such invasion," he said to quiet her.

"Does that mean *you* would fight?"

"Me? I . . ." It had started snowing again. He looked out the window and watched one crazy snowflake, lifted by the wind, go up, not down. For a second it hung there before it fell with the others.

"You are part of the State Guard, aren't you? The Rifles? Like Sanders, with his Chasseurs? You would fight, wouldn't you?"

For the first time he saw his mother in her and knew she loved him. If only he could reach across that gulf of shawls, blankets, doctor's orders, recriminations, misunderstandings. Another if.

"You're tired," he said softly. "No, I'll never leave you, Becky, if that's what you're asking."

" 'Never' is a long word." But she stifled a yawn with the back of her hand. The fire had warmed the room and in another five minutes he, too, would be sleepy. That Bruce fear of fresh air, he thought, but before it became an irritation he kissed the top of her head and left.

On his bedside table lay the Adams and Deane pistol Uncle Frank had given him for Christmas. It was decorated with rubies and silver, with an inscription: CAPT. J. H. MORGAN. He picked it up and turned it in his hand.

A .50-caliber, five-shot double action. A beautiful gun. A work of art. "Too fine to take to war," Tom had said jokingly. Sweet Tom. Christmas, and that high, clear voice that rose above the others in Christ Church, singing hymns. Sweet, sweet Tom. No, he might better take Wash's old Mexican War Dragoon, if he went. Wash! Yes, he would be just the type, if Tennessee . . . Ah, but Tennessee, too, pointed west, and hadn't seceded. From his window he could see the gaslight in Becky's room go out. The wind was still howling and his sheets felt cool. He curled up on his side and buried his cheek in his pillow. No, I won't leave you, Becky. But Wash! I wonder what Wash will do?

A. P. Hill resigned from the federal service in March and became a colonel in the Thirteenth Virginia Volunteers; Kitty would come home with the Curds, who planned to leave Washington City after the Inauguration. Dick sent one last letter home describing the last days of the Thirty-sixth Congress. It had been the longest, most grueling weekend of his life, long hours of debate and sidetracking, with Northern Republicans insisting on "a little bloodletting" and Crittenden watching the last hours of the session wind down to oblivion, taking with it any hope that the new amendment would be ratified. For three months they had argued, and now they were about to adjourn. They had accomplished nothing. The Senate of the United States, facing the real possibility of civil war, had done nothing. Had allowed party to override country, personal pride to outweigh sanity, like a man watching his house burn down, hoping the fire will stop.

"But it won't stop," Tommie said when she read it. "A chill goes down my spine right into my heels, in spite of everything Uncle Dick says."

25

"**Y**ou won't be chilled for long," Cal laughed, and she threw a book at him, then giggled.

It was true: Tommie was getting prettier by the minute, under the teasing. "It's only three months away!" she would say, bouncing down the stairs.

"Wedding, wedding, wedding," Aunt Betty grumbled, her eyes sparkling, waiting for Tommie's explosion, then allowing a chuckle to spread across her face at Tommie's stuck-out tongue, her pretense at hauteur.

Kitty, as planned, came home with the Curds, with Baby Henrietta, and the house was thrown into turmoil again. Tom, home for the week-long Easter holiday, sang lullabies at the top of his voice and Aunt Betty forgot to shush him, in her joy at rocking a baby again.

"Let's send word to the office," said Key.

"No, let's surprise them," Kitty smiled.

"*Won't* they be surprised?" Tommie laughed, holding out her arms to take the baby.

"They're late! What's taking them so long?" her mother grumbled, after an hour in the parlor watching a misting spring drizzle dampen the garden.

"They'll be around in a minute," said Cal, who had just come in. "Won't they be surprised?" he said, echoing Tommie. "Tell me all your news. . . . How is Uncle Dick? And Washington City? How is our new President?"

"The Yankees have really done themselves in this time," Kitty answered, pinching the corners of her mouth. "And a coward, to boot! Can you imagine *anybody* sneaking into town disguised as an invalid . . . changing trains, afraid the people of Baltimore would kill him?" She took the baby from Tommie.

"Well, what can you expect?" Her mother, lifting a needle from her embroidery hoop, pushed it through and twitched her nose.

"But to parade poor Mary Todd around!" Kitty swayed, little Henrietta's head bobbing. "Overdressed as usual. She was a public exhibition, Mama. He kept introducing her to crowds as 'the little woman.' Ugh! You can't imagine how stupid they are, Mama. They are supposed to be so smart, those Yankees. They actually believed the rumor that Lincoln would be shot at the Inauguration by an air-gun—in the hands of a Secessionist, of course."

"Did you see the Inaugural?"

"Heavens, no." Kitty wiped the baby's nose and flopped her, stomach down, across her lap and began patting her unmercifully. "And neither did anybody else. Even *that man* . . . as tall as he is . . . was hidden by cavalry as they escorted him like a prisoner up Pennsylvania Avenue! Artillery and infantry companies were posted all over the city—I never saw so many soldiers! And that silly General Scott was going around thanking God that things were going peacefully. What else did he expect?"

Johnny came in then. The picture of blond, beautiful Kitty with her baby, against the first signs of spring beyond the window, held him in the doorway.

His mother, her back to him, was not aware of his presence. "It didn't surprise me to hear Lincoln refused to see the Southern peace delegates. So Senator Crittenden, I hear, has come home to 'educate Kentucky to loyalty.' " She snipped a thread.

"He'd certainly have a job on his hands in this room!" Morgan laughed at Kitty's gasp when she saw him.

"Johnny? Oh, Johnny!"

"Loyalty! The nerve!" Henrietta balled up the cloth and plumped it beside her. "Heavens, let me take that baby, Kitty! You'll pound her to death!"

Kitty handed little Henrietta up and ran to Johnny and hugged him.

"Don't you want to hear about A.P., Mama?" she giggled into his coat.

"The dear boy. The dear, dear boy," Henrietta crooned, rocking back and forth with the baby draped expertly across her shoulder.

Kitty sank back into the circle of Johnny's arm. "He'll be here for the wedding! He's asking for leave . . ."

"Oh, Kitty!" Tommie danced to the window, where she sat on the sill and drew her knees up and hugged her ankles. "I can't believe all this is happening! I think I'm so happy I could die!" She jumped down and sat at her mother's feet.

"You won't, love," Kitty laughed. She squeezed Johnny's hand as she moved away.

Over her grandmother's shoulder little Henrietta looked up at him with her tongue hanging out, wobbling her head. She had A.P.'s thin face and red hair . . . hair? Little sprigs of silk that fell in all directions, mostly over her ears—but Kitty's big blue eyes. They looked at him now, round as buttons. With her mouth open she looked stupid, but when he made a face and waved his hands, a sudden blurpy giggle sent a shower of wrinkles across her nose.

"May I have her?" he asked. She smelled of powder and soap. "She's so small!"

She was an ugly little monkey, and yet when he tickled her and she opened her mouth in that soundless laugh—a laugh so wide it closed her eyes—she became breathtakingly beautiful. And when she opened her eyes again she looked as if she were seeing the world for the first time and found it delightful. Then she looked straight at him, as if they shared a secret. Would he ever hold a baby of his own in his arms? His palm cradled the back of her head. She stretched, sighed, and wet his pants.

He lifted her imploringly and everyone laughed. The nurse that Kitty had brought from Washington appeared at the door and he handed her over gladly.

The next day Dick Curd started on his tour of the state in support of Crittenden's plea for neutrality, and T.H. came home on a brief leave for Easter.

"Neutrality?" T.H. moaned when he heard of it. "Poor Dick—he's ignoring the obvious. It always beats me how a good lawyer can be blind when he wants to be."

"Blind . . ." Key Hunt walked to the sideboard, poured himself a whiskey, and walked back into the parlor. Last night they had had quite a party in honor of Kitty's return. The ladies were upstairs napping. He hoped his brother wouldn't get excited and raise his voice. T.H. was sometimes too exuberant.

"Who do you think he was talking about when he said he opposed any amendments to the Constitution 'originated by others'?"

"Who is 'he,' T.H.?" Cal blew cigar smoke at the window. Daffodils were blooming by the fence. A cardinal dropped to pick through the leaves.

"Lincoln, of course. 'Others . . . not especially chosen for the purpose' were the exact words in the Inaugural. That has to be Crittenden. Nobody else! And then that threat, that there need be no bloodshed . . . *unless it be forced upon the national authority.*' The fool! It's a damned challenge, that's what it is."

"I don't like the man any more than you do," Key Hunt murmured. "But let's be fair. He also said there will be no invasion."

"No invasion! Who the hell does he think he is? I'm surprised at you, Frank. You're as bad as Dick. You're a lawyer, but you missed the point. The inaugural reads *'beyond what may be necessary,* there will be no invasion.' I tell you, he's spoiling for a fight. I tell you, Kentucky needs to secede before it's too late."

Morgan watched the blood rise in T.H.'s face. He leaned forward and threw his own burned-out cigar into the empty fireplace. The curtains billowed with a fresh breeze. Morgan smiled. "Didn't Uncle Frank tell us that ninety-five percent of Southern whites don't own slaves? I can't see them fighting. Besides, immediate emancipation would only put our people out of work. I can't see how destroying the economy of half the country could possibly benefit the other half. . . ."

"That's precisely my point," Key Hunt said, getting up to go. "Neutrality may be our only answer. As long as Virginia on our eastern border and Tennessee on our southern stay in the Union—and neither has made a move yet—it would be suicide to isolate ourselves. We would be a pocket of rebellion surrounded by loyalty!"

T.H. rose too, pulling on his coat. "I don't see that situation lasting much longer."

"Well, until it changes, Crittenden will try to talk Kentucky into some sense," Key said at the door as he let himself out.

"You know, Johnny," T.H. murmured, "I secretly hope he's right."

"Let's all hope so," Morgan breathed. He held out his hand in a formal way that made T.H. stop, his fingers on the top button of his coat. "Anyway, it's April. That's something to be thankful for."

On the 12th of April, at half-past-four in the morning, the shelling of Fort Sumter in Charleston harbor began.

When Hopemont heard the news Henrietta agreed to let Charlton join the State Guard. John Morgan, excitement rising in his chest, telegraphed Jefferson Davis in Montgomery: CAN RAISE 20,000 TROOPS FOR SOUTHERN LIBERTY.

"He must be busy," he told Cal when no answer came.

Reaction to Sumter was swift in Kentucky. When Lincoln issued a call for seventy-five thousand troops and asked the governor of Kentucky "by tonight's mail" for four regiments of militia, Magoffin's answer was swift and unequivocal: "Kentucky would furnish no troops for the wicked purpose of subduing her sister Southern states." Yet the Kentucky legislature was too timid to provide its own troops with enough funds to operate effectively. Union men in the legislature distrusted the State Guard, which was openly sympathetic with the South, and since the States' Rights Convention, held in March, had accomplished nothing, they felt secure enough, when Buckner presented his estimates for $3.5 million for the year 1861, to reduce that figure to $20,000. Yet, even with that amount, Buckner was determined to protect his state's neutrality. Few of his officers knew he had turned down a full Confederate generalship, nor did they know of Lincoln's matching offer of the same rank, when the State Guard met for spring training at KMI.

The Guard numbered almost five thousand well-trained men, now thoroughly organized. Even the U.S. Army was only a little more than twice that size. "I venture to say," T.H., now on Buckner's staff, laughed before he left Lexington, "Lincoln would like to get his hands on our little army." The Lexington Rifles would leave the next day.

The grounds of the Kentucky Military Institute—a plantation-turned-spa-turned-military school near Frankfort—lay dappled under big trees. But all tranquillity faded once Morgan stepped past the front door. Buckner's office, in a book-lined library to the left off a wide hall, was the scene of intense activity. Young men, in all manner of home-designed garb representing their different outfits, scurried back and forth with messages.

Buckner was no less energetic. "It's been a while since our little 'camp' at Louisville, eh?" He shook Morgan's hand across his cluttered desk.

John Morgan received his orders and walked down the central hall to the back of the house, where a veranda overlooked a small court, now a parade ground with Old Glory snapping from a staff in the middle. Across the way the annex, which had accommodated three hundred guests in the old spa days, was now a barracks noisy with KMI students and the first-day excitement of young recruits. Tom Morgan was in his glory, showing his big brother around as if he owned the place: his room, the mess hall, the drill field. When Morgan assembled his men for the first time they broke out into "Cheer, Boys, Cheer!," Tom's clear tenor ringing above the rest. The songs, the sights, the sounds of those boys that summer. Would he ever forget them? He soon had his men settled into the routine and learned the details of Buckner's new organization. Tom Crittenden was also on Buckner's staff, and Emilie Todd's husband, Ben Helm. Ben lent him his copy of *Hardee's Tactics*.

"But that's infantry."

"Don't worry. You'll know infantry, artillery, cavalry, and the logistical mysteries of the quartermaster before you leave here. Buckner's very thorough."

Morgan thought he had never met a kinder, more gentle man in his life. He liked Helm immediately. His fellow officers were equally appealing, in different ways. He sank into the ease and comfort of their company as if he were coming home.

He felt even more at home with his Rifles. Their appreciation bordered on adoration. He defended himself against it. The more they admired him the more reticent he became, until he was known as the most modest commander there.

Inside, though, he was prancing. His men were the best riders in the Guard and they knew it, and he knew it, and the other companies soon knew it. And he was the most daring, the most precise, and the most demanding company commander, and if he depended less on discipline than the others, he relied more on love.

After dinner one night, over brandy and cigars, looking out onto the parade ground where some of the boys were lounging, writing letters or reading some from home, Morgan had a sense of history. There they were, the sons of the Bluegrass—aristocrats most of them—due to inherit the richest, the most beautiful land on earth. A sudden chill passed over him. What if the Greeks were right to believe in their three Fates? Were they all blind, or just the one who carried "the abhorrèd shears" and cut the thread at death? He couldn't remember. It was bad enough that the one with the scissors couldn't see.

Buckner was still struggling to arm his Guard, and they all knew it. Most of the men had come with their own squirrel rifles, shotguns, and even dueling pistols. A few had old smoothbore flintlocks which refused to fire in the rain. Supplying ammunition became a nightmare. When the legislature proved adamant, Buckner went North, and Governor Magoffin even sent agents to the Confederacy for support. Nothing came of it, and the men shouldered empty weapons. A common joke around the barracks was that only the sentiments were loaded.

It was true. Tom Crittenden had already announced his loyalty to the Union, while Nuckols's Glasgow men from Barren County actually paraded openly under Confederate colors. A dozen left in disgust for Virginia. Morgan sat up all night talking Charlton into staying home, repeating all of their uncle Dick's arguments.

"You don't believe them yourself," his brother told him.

Just before their time at KMI was over, they heard the news: The legislature, by a flagrantly unconstitutional act, had transferred all military power from the governor to a committee of five—mostly Union men. The committee immediately set up a rival militia, the Home Guards, *not subject to the governor's orders*. As for Buckner's State Guards, they were ordered to take the oath of allegiance to the Union.

Amid the grumbling, T.H. was cheerful.

"Where are their guns?" he asked Johnny. Uncle and nephew looked at each other, then burst out laughing.

Their feeling of security was short-lived. Within ten days five thousand muskets were delivered to the new "Guards" by Lincoln, and another five thousand followed three weeks later. When the Rifles returned to Lexington, talk of these impertinent "Lincoln guns" was everywhere. The only hope for sanity seemed to be a convention of border states, to be held in May.

When it met, only a handful of delegates appeared.

Meanwhile, Lexington's three militia companies—until now almost social organizations—trained in earnest. In tail coats and braided trousers and fancy headgear, like so many toy soldiers, Sanders Bruce's "Chasseurs" drilled at Cheapside; John Morgan's "Rifles," with headquarters in the armory building not far from Hopemont, took turns practicing on Transy's parade ground, sharing it with Captain S. W. Price's "Old Infantry." By May 20 there were six militia companies of the Bluegrass camped at the old trotting track, now renamed Camp Buckner and under the command of Colonel Roger Hanson, a large, round-shouldered Mexican War veteran with a limp from a duel, a broad-faced man with a menacing look (Cal called it "an Irish face trying to look German") that exploded into laughter. His men called him "Ole Bench-leg," and in a few weeks he was "their man."

T.H. Hunt, his temporary military assignment over, returned to Lexington in time to see the first shipment of "Lincoln guns" arrive. They were sent to David Sayre, a staunch Unionist who kept them in the private office at his bank on Mill and Short, opposite the telegraph office. From there they were distributed to a company of Home Guards, who practiced in secret until they were sure their drilling would not be laughed at. Just two days before Tommie's wedding they made their first public appearance at Cheapside. Reverend Elisha Pratt had joined them, much to Tommie's amusement.

"Your sister's tongue is getting sharper every day," T.H. said with a grin.

"She's practicing for marriage," Cal quipped, then pressed his mouth shut when Tommie passed by.

May was beautiful and crackling with almost as many rumors as Tommie, who, in the excitement of love, had become a Confederate patriot par excellence. In April the governor of Missouri had sent Basil and another Southern sympathizer to Montgomery to ask President Davis for guns. His hair-raising escapades up the Mississippi through Federally-held Cairo and New Madrid were by now household lore.

Kitty troubled them more. Under her motherly smiles she was terrified for A.P.'s safety. And she had good cause. He was at Harpers Ferry facing a massing of troops calling itself the Grand Army, the largest concentration of manpower, according to the Yankee papers, the continent had ever seen.

But of them all, Kitty had stamina. She had inherited from her mother a tight-lipped toughness that had already seen her through widowhood and the loss of a baby she never talked about. She covered her worry with wit. "The Flat Rock Grays," she laughed. "And the Bourbon Rangers. The Governor's Guard. My, they do find high-soundin' names."

"They're high-soundin' men," her brother teased.

"And you, Johnny," she said more seriously, her blue eyes growing dark. "What will you do?"

It was a question he had asked himself too many times. As long as T.H. held on, he would stay, hoping with Dick and the others for neutrality. God, he couldn't imagine the fields of Kentucky covered with blood. No, to be honest with himself, there was a deeper reason. Since February, Becky had not been well. She had succumbed to another of her "conditions"—this time a frightening shortness of breath that curtailed physical activity. She still puttered in the garden, but her mother already talked of the summer heat with dread. Sending her to Philadelphia or Arkansas was unthinkable now, with all the uncertainty, and she had no inclination or stamina to go to a spa. She spent whole days in bed behind those drawn curtains at the back of the house. He visited almost every afternoon, but sometimes his activities upset her too much, and often, if he couldn't tell her of the Rifles or of the latest rumors, he found he didn't have much to talk about. He was in her room when a wild cheering came through to them from Main Street. Tennessee had left the Union on the sixth of June, and the first Confederate volunteers were marching through Lexington on their way to Camp Boone, a recruiting center near the state line. He must have looked impatient, for she lifted a hand to his arm and said softly, "Go. I know you want to. You want to stand on the sidewalk watching them."

"No, no . . . it's not important!" But with every fiber of his body he strained to hear the cheers.

Richard and Cal, interrupted by Charlton, Tom, and Key, in that order, told him the details. T.H., in recognition of the recruits, ran up a Confederate flag over his factory. The next day one of Sanders's Chasseurs took it down, and the next day T.H. ran up another. When that one disappeared, T.H. ran up another. This kept up for a week, until T.H. won. "And it's lucky, too. I was having a hard time finding any more red cloth!" He might laugh at Tommie's pro-Southern rumors—that Washington City had already fallen to the Confederates; that Lincoln, drunk since the election, dared not leave the White House for fear of assassination—but in his quiet way, T.H. was more of a Confederate than any of them.

Richard talked Johnny into selling retail as a general practice, to reduce their stock, "in case."

"In case what?"

But Richard didn't answer, reading from his latest advertisement in the *Observer:* "Blue flannels and gray jeans priced to suit the times."

"True neutrality," Richard added with a grin, and read again: "In view of the distressing conditions of affairs, our goods will be sold for cash and cash only."

They felt lucky to be still in business. All around, partnerships were being dissolved, livestock and land were offered for sale at reduced prices.

"I wonder what Grandfather would have done," Morgan mused.

"Grandfather would have made the most if it," Richard said without emotion. "He would have made a fortune."

"You think so?"

"He was a Yankee at heart."

"But what if they get nasty?"

"Hopemont belongs to Ma, and the Hunt name will protect it. The Feds want to keep Kentucky, and they'll woo it with every trick they can think of. Don't worry about Ma, Johnny, she'll be safe. Besides, can you see a Yankee officer marching in there and telling her what to do?"

The vision was so ridiculous they both laughed.

Still, it had been a sobering conversation. John Morgan looked on Richard with new respect. He wasn't just a bookkeeper, after all. Methodical, level-headed, he might make a better soldier than Cal or Charlton. Unconsciously, he was measuring everybody that way these days.

He wasn't surprised when Dick Curd dropped by the house with a request that he talk to Henrietta alone. "You stay, too, John," Dick said, and cleared his throat. He patted his lips with his fist as he followed them into John Hunt's little office. They took their seats and waited for him to stop frowning. Morgan thought he would speak of Hopemont and the possibility of some Federal move to confiscate property if Kentucky seceded, but instead he talked of Randolph.

"The time may come," he said, "when he may need them."

"I don't see why," said Henrietta. "Of course, he can have them any time he wants. He knows that. You explained that to him after Calvin died."

"I know. But times have changed. You don't seem to understand the gravity of the situation, Henrietta. President Lincoln has suspended the writ of *habeas corpus*. In Maryland, blank arrest warrants have been issued. The time may come when a man will have to prove his freedom. If property is confiscated—not Hopemont—I don't want to alarm you . . . but labor—"

"They wouldn't dare!"

"They would," Curd said after a pause. It was the first time Morgan had heard his uncle speak against the Federals.

"Are you serious?"

"I've never been more serious in my life, John. General Butler has de-clared slaves of Southern sympathizers contraband. I pray to God Kentucky stays neutral, but even if she does . . ."

"Even if she does? What are you trying to say? That even if she does they won't abide by the Constitution and protect our property?" Henrietta was on her feet, and she was formidable on her feet. Dick rose too, out of unconscious courtesy, but the fact that he stood two inches shorter than his sister-in-law did not give him confidence. He folded his fingers together in front of him, as if for support.

"It's best he has his free papers. It's safer."

She threw her head back and studied the ceiling in a theatrical gesture which told her son she would agree, then leveled a look at Dick. "All this to worry about! With the wedding, the fittings, and all this marching . . . Celina and Bouviette can hardly keep up with the uniforms. And now this!"

They both knew that the louder she complained, the more she would comply. When she was silent she was dangerous. "I'll take care of it, Ma," Morgan told her.

"Now where is Eleanor?" Dick asked, as if some bridge had been crossed. He let out a long-held breath. "Are the ladies through talking about tea cakes and crinolines?"

"Oh, pardon me, Dick, I haven't even offered you a brandy. . . ." Henrietta was a hostess once more, and they followed her into the parlor, where T.H., Key, and Robert were lounging in a June breeze billowing the curtains. She had assembled her troops just in case, Morgan thought as he watched her leave the room. *I was wrong. She, not Richard, would make the better soldier.*

"So, how's the neutrality coming?" Key Hunt reached for candy from a tray. His animosity toward Lincoln was academic and had nothing to do with Southern sympathy. Even though he believed in neutrality, he had remained aloof, refusing Dick's repeated invitations to get involved. His voice held a professorish, sarcastic edge over that classroom calm which infuriated Curd. Dick's face, under its cap of soft brown hair, turned red. He was on his short legs instantly, his chest thrust out. For a second Morgan thought Dick would hit him. Only the entrance of his wife, Eleanor, holding over her arms an elaborate cloud of tulle and lace—Tommie's wedding dress —broke the tension.

From his corner of the sofa T.H. uncrossed his legs and said softly, "Well, gentlemen!" And instinctively every man in the room fell into a leisurely pose. The ladies, after all, shouldn't be concerned.

All politics were forgotten as the great day approached. Basil Duke arrived from Missouri and stood self-consciously beside Tommie in the Hopemont parlor, accepting congratulations from a stream of visitors. A.P. Hill was promised a five-day leave, but had not yet arrived. It was already the sixteenth of June and the wedding was scheduled for the nineteenth, only three days away. Kitty was beside herself, but Basil tried to reassure her. "He'll be here," he said. "He's all right."

That night Morgan listened in silent envy to Basil's stories: his mission to President Davis for guns, his trip to New Orleans to smuggle them into Missouri, and the loss of the guns to the Yankees after all. Basil told it now almost as a joke, with a hint of glad terror at his lucky delivery from danger. There was in his talk a breathless fascination with uncertainty, not of war but of all the future, of Basil's life with Tommie opening up, of unseen adventures and opportunities for gallantry and valor, of testing courage, of defending honor. To Morgan it seemed a glimpse into another world, forbidden to him because of what? Because of Becky, ill again, and his duty to his mother's family? Suddenly, sitting in the parlor looking out at summer roses just beginning to reach their full bloom in the garden, he realized how much his own prancing around with his Rifles had been child's play, a sponge for his frustration, a mere toy. Basil's antics at least had a purpose. Even if he'd lost those guns.

He left them with brief apologies and walked across the street. He would try again to get his in-laws to let Robert Hunt examine Becky. Robert had become one of the best "heart doctors" in Kentucky, but so far his politics had prevented the Bruces from allowing him to examine their daughter. Dr. Wolford, whose Union sentiments coincided with their own, was a good doctor, no doubt about it. But Morgan would have been better satisfied if Robert could see her.

It was a brilliant June day. He was, after all, to be Basil's best man. A.P. was due any day. Little Tommie's wedding at Hopemont! Surely Becky's problem was the same old succumbing to her father's encouragement. If he could only . . . Then his vision of a healthy, laughing Becky faded before the reality of her plump form on its pillows.

Her parents talked of Dr. Wolford's decrees as if they were Scripture. His own suggestions seemed intrusive, if not absurd. Then the parents monopolized the conversation, as if neither he nor Becky were there. He looked across at her and she gave him a weak smile, which struck at his heart. Perhaps she wasn't malingering? His fingers, on the arms of his chair, turned cold. She did seem so pale. He was her husband, after all. If he wanted Robert Hunt to examine his wife he would do so, he heard himself say bluntly and too loudly. It wasn't as if holding Southern sympathies made Robert a killer. He was a qualified doctor. . . .

Reluctantly, they agreed. He went straight to his uncle's house and was admitted into the large drawing room. "Of course I'll see Becky," Robert said.

"When?"

"In the morning, first thing."

He left much relieved, delivered the message to Margaret Bruce, then crossed the street to Hopemont just as news of A.P. Hill's arrival reached them.

A.P. devoted every minute to the baby and to Kitty, gazing at her, holding her hand. He called her Dolly. After the ladies retired, he sat up until almost dawn with his brothers-in-law, speculating about the war.

He talked about Harpers Ferry and a VMI professor named Jackson "who sits his horse like a sack of laundry." But his most glowing account was saved for the dashing exploits of "Beauty" Stuart, not yet twenty-eight, who was in charge of Joe Johnston's cavalry.

"Those three hundred men," A.P. said with wonder, "were in charge of picketing the whole Potomac line from Point of Rocks east of the Blue Ridge to Berkeley. Johnston calls Stuart his 'yellow jacket'—no sooner brushed off than he lights again."

Basil nodded. "The eyes and ears of the army."

"That's right. The cavalry. Can't do without them." Hill grinned. "I tell you there's scarcely a school in Virginia left with a student! They laid down textbooks and took up muskets, and their fathers joined them. Not caring about rank—you'll find ex-state senators enlisting as privates! No complaining, even after hard marches in mud or days in the saddle. One purpose. What a glorious lot they are!"

He pulled at his whiskey and his eyes misted with emotion. The war news, too, had been good. At Bethel, down on the peninsula just north of Hampton, 1,800 Confederates beat back a Federal force of more than four thousand. But it was Powell Hill's own story they were eager to hear, and he returned to it. "Anyway, we checked the advance, and when we fired the railroad bridge across the Potomac and headed South, I left my command to come here."

"Where are they now?" Richard asked.

"At a place called Bunker Hill on the Winchester-Martinsburg turnpike. The plan is to move on to Winchester, where I'll meet them. There they can control five roads, like the fingers of your hand, reaching out to all of Northern Virginia."

The words *advance, beat back, fired*. The poetry and the rhythm of the sound of "Northern Virginia." It must be grand, Morgan thought, riding at dawn, outsmarting the enemy. He could do it! But immediately the vision of his doing it faded before the reality of Hopemont, his mother, Becky.

"Come, let's get some rest." He smiled. "After all, if I'm going to be your best man tomorrow, Basil, I'll need to be awake!"

He dreamed that night of riding over hills that became clouds, and landing in a bed of wildflowers. Charlton, already half-dressed, woke him. "You'll be late for your sister's wedding," he laughed.

Downstairs the excitement was intense. Only Kitty seemed to have her head on securely. And she, he thought, of all of them, should have been most upset. A.P. had to report back to Virginia immediately, with a major battle shaping up. She was inordinately calm, and went around as if saying "Steady!" to everybody. "Kitty's a brick," Robert Hunt laughed, and Johnny saw again his mother in her. Tom sang a wedding march in his sweet tenor, and his oldest brother watched him as from a dream. How quickly it was over, this moment that hung in time, that would change these four lives! He etched them in his memory: the brusque-looking but gentle A.P. Hill in his gray Confederate uniform beside Kitty, her blond hair caught softly under lace; Basil—dear, excitable, but dependable Basil—not in uniform (he had not been sworn into Confederate service yet), but wearing a frock coat, erect as a soldier listening to the words, attentive to the responses. And Tommie with her freckles and brown hair and penetrating eyes, who seemed to know already that their brief "honeymoon" at the Dukes' Georgetown plantation might be all they would have, for Basil would be gone, too, in a few days, back to Missouri, where he didn't know what to expect.

The war. It stood like an uninvited guest, unseen but almost tangible as Reverend Dupree intoned the half-heard promises.

The war. It had kept Becky away. Even more than her illness. Her mother had implied as much. How could she expect her husband and sons to stand there, with *those uniforms* in the same room? A.P.'s was the only one, but it would do no good to argue. The groom kissed his bride, and then the feasting began.

The food was pure Kentucky, with an overlay of Gallic cuisine that was Aunt Hannah's specialty. Ducks in wine sauce, cool slabs of sliced turkey, smoked ham with beans and yams, cakes and pastries. Sitting by the parlor window afterwards, watching the guests, Morgan had a heavy feeling of futility—not from too much eating but from a sadness, as if he were watching all this for the last time. When he could, he slipped out the garden door and walked around the house and across the street.

Becky was in her room, writing a letter. The windows were open to a breeze that moved the lace curtains with the sun-washed air of June. "It's so beautiful out," he said. "You've got the windows open!"

"Yes, isn't it! I hope the Hills are nice people," she said suddenly.

"I'm sure they are."

"That's what Mama says, in spite . . ."

She covered her confusion by closing the inkwell and putting her pen down.

"I'm sure they are," he repeated. "Everybody was disappointed that you couldn't come."

"Were they?"

"How do you feel?"

"I'm fine. Doctor Wolford says just to rest . . ."

"Robert will see you again if you want him to."

"Papa says . . . No, Doctor Wolford is just fine."

I'm fine, Dr. Wolford's fine, everything's fine. She wasn't stupid, but he felt as if he were talking to a girl in a mirror. He bent to her and brushed her forehead with his lips. Her hairline was moist with perspiration. "Are you sure?" he whispered. She looked up, half laughing, and told him again he worried too much.

"Go have a good time before they miss you. You were Tommie's best man, remember?"

"Basil's."

"Well, yes."

Her parents were out visiting. The house was quiet, except for the sound of birds in the garden. He left her, feeling unreal, heavy and unreal. At Hopemont he avoided the front door, or even the side entrance, where kitchen activity would be at its height. He walked around to the garden door. It was ajar, and the door to the front hall was closed. He sat at the bottom of the spiral stairs and wondered at his sadness. When they were children they used to call this stairwell the "tower room." Kitty was usually the princess imprisoned at the top, Cal the page, and Johnny the knight in armor. The stairs still spun upward, without support, an architectural wonder, like their dreams.

Laughter and the tinkling of glasses came to him. It was here that Cal had told him of Richard's wild scheme to go to Cuba with young Crittenden. How lucky they'd been that Richard hadn't gone. Were they as foolish now?

Maybe the Bruces were right. But underneath that thought, like a cat crouching in a corner of his mind, a restlessness stirred, a contained energy longing to burst its bonds. He looked up to find Kitty staring down at him, and made room for her on the step. She slipped her arm through his and laid her head on his shoulder. "What are you thinking?" she said.

"Of Richard. That time he wanted to go to Cuba."

"Do you think the Confederacy is another Cuba?" She straightened when he didn't answer, waiting, her blue eyes unrelenting.

"No."

Her head rested again and she moved her cheek against the roughness of his coat. "Neither do I. I don't think I could stand it if I thought it would be just another 'expedition.' " She laid her hand on his and the palm was cold. He caught her fingers and rubbed them.

"Are you all right?"

She laughed, her face turning pink above her soft mouth. "You always knew me better than anybody else, didn't you Johnny? No. I'm scared to death, as a matter of fact."

His silence seemed to soothe her.

"After it's over," she said as if he had spoken aloud, "I'm going to Richmond."

"Does Ma know?"

"No. I'll write some friends there. Maybe they can find us rooms to rent. I have to be with him, Johnny."

"Of course."

"I'll write."

"I'll answer."

She shook her head. "You're a horrible correspondent, and you know it. You didn't write me a line while I was away. When will you go?"

Not if, but when.

"I won't."

"Yes, you will." She managed a smile over the tears that had already begun to sparkle in the corners of her eyes. "Wait and see. For now, come with me. You don't want to deprive the ladies of your company, do you?"

Two days later, when A.P. Hill left, Richard went with him, the first of Henrietta Morgan's sons to join the Confederacy. Her face was a mixture of pride and worry, and she bustled around the house with the residue of wedding presents and guests as an excuse not to think. Aunt Betty assumed a magisterial attitude among the servants, and Aunt Hannah rolled her eyes, whispering to herself, "We's got anuthah Ole Miss on our han's. Sure do."

Kitty rode with Morgan to the farm. As the carriage turned into the drive, children and chickens scampered. Randolph, with some confusion, took his free papers, and Maggie promised to keep them in a safe place. "Kin you all stay fo' suppah?" she asked timidly.

"No, I'm afraid we can't, Maggie." When Kitty saw her face fall she added, "But I'd love a glass of your good buttermilk."

Maggie sent Jesse to the springhouse.

"So James takes care of the stables now," Kitty said to Randolph.

"Yes, Miss Kitty. He's almost another Uncle Simon."

"Uncle Simon," Kitty said slowly, and they were silent. "You know I'm taking Celina to Virginia?"

"No'm."

"That means Aunt Hannah will need a hand at Hopemont. Do you suppose Annie could help out?"

"Annie?" Randolph frowned, then let his face fall into a smile.

"She shy, Miss Kitty," Maggie said hesitantly.

"How old is she now?"

"Nineteen, Miss Kitty . . ."

Kitty smiled. "She'll do just *fine*. She'll learn all those Frenchy dishes you used to like."

"Ah still does," Randolph grinned.

James showed them a new crop of yearlings and Miss Lexington, in foal.

"It's too bad you bred her," Kitty said bluntly to her brother in the cool, musty air of the barn.

"Why?"

"Who will you ride South?"

"You still think I'm going, don't you?"

She didn't answer.

On the way back—they were in Henrietta's light *calèche*—he remembered Gordon Niles looking around at the Kentucky countryside when they'd come back from Mount Brilliant. *If all this were mine, I should never go away.*

The house seemed enormous with absence when they returned. Tommie was still with the Dukes in Georgetown. Cal was at the hemp mill and Charlton at the factory, and Key and Tom were out riding. Henrietta had gone to her room for a nap. "Don't leave me yet," Kitty pleaded. "Let's walk in the garden just a bit."

They strolled past the wisteria and turned into a walk bordered by roses. She slipped her arm through his and squeezed it to her upper body in a feminine gesture that was at once protective and asking for protection. He had always enjoyed Kitty, her blond good looks, her blue eyes that looked right through you. He could well imagine that she had been the belle of Washington.

"Did you ever notice how much like Queen Victoria Mama is getting to be?" she asked, kicking the leaves from the walk.

He laughed. "No. No, I suppose not."

"She'll have puffy cheeks when she gets older, and wear her hair parted in the middle, and get dumpy."

"Come now, Kitty . . ."

"It's true!"

He said nothing as they followed the narrow brick path. He was aware of the swing of her legs under her skirts beside him. Kitty was a beautiful woman, totally unlike her mother in looks. But underneath she was more like Henrietta Morgan than any of them. Even more than Tommie, who looked more like their mother but who was, on the inside, Calvin all over again, from her feats on horseback to her love of reading. He doubted whether Kitty had ever read a book from cover to cover in her life, and yet she seemed to have all the wisdom she would ever need.

"I'm so proud of you, Johnny." They were at the wisteria arbor again, and she surprised him by blinking back tears.

"Me? Why?"

"You're the one . . ." She stopped and looked back at the house, waving an upturned palm in an arc . . . "who has held all this together." When he started to speak she held cool fingers to his lips. "No, let me finish. I know how worried you are about Becky, and I know your trouble with the Bruces. Remember what Tommie used to say when we played the princess game on the stairs, and Cal wanted to be the knight?"

"Tommie is too much like Ma," he lied.

"No, she isn't, and you know it. I'm too much like Mama. That's why we don't get along."

"Oh, come now, you do get along . . ."

"Superficially. But you're evading the question. What did Tommie say?"

"I honestly don't remember."

" 'There are some people who are born knights, and others who are just pages. And that's that.' " She pulled him down onto the garden seat under the wisteria, whose blossoms hung like a thick shawl. She laid her hand in his. She was one of those women who had to touch you before she said anything important. It betrayed an outgoingness, but also a need for reassurance which, he imagined, had rarely been refused.

"Look at it, Johnny," she almost whispered, her eyes still on the house. "Hopemont may not ever be the same. Everything that matters about it may be gone one day."

"Oh, Dolly," he said to cheer her. "It can't be as serious as that."

But her blue eyes stopped him, as he guessed they had stopped more discerning gentlemen than he. When they walked to the house Kitty leaned against him suddenly, squeezing his arm to her in that way women have when they say good-bye.

26

Henrietta was frantic with fear for Richard. The Yankees were not gentlemen. They had heard all the stories. How, at one place, under a flag of truce to bury their dead, the Yankees had left their dead and used the white flag to set up batteries, which they turned on the people who had just given them respite in a common grief. How, at another fight in Arkansas, they unfurled a Confederate flag, then under false identity and cries of "Don't shoot! We're friends!" fired and fled.

But there were stories right here in Kentucky, excited accounts of midnight arrests, military courts, people hustled away to Northern prisons for nothing more than criticism of the Lincoln government. A banker taken from his house in Louisville. A lawyer in Frankfort, an old friend of Dick Curd's (and a Union man), shipped North on suspicion of Southern sympathies. By July, even the most faithful Unionists had to admit that neutrality was dead. The Federal government opened a recruiting camp twenty-six miles from Lexington, and some of the soldiers had even encouraged a few slaves to run away. When one old Garrard County resident, with two house servants, went there in search of one of them, he was tied to a post and given twenty-five lashes on his bare back.

"I can't believe that, Ma," Morgan said quietly. "General Nelson may be called 'Bull' for his size and his temper, but after all, he is an officer and a gentleman."

Her eyes said: *You would tell me he is even if he isn't . . . How many other things do you keep from me? You and your* code d'honneur *that I hate because I fear it so. . . .* "Gentleman! How can you say such a thing? Besides, maybe he doesn't know everything that goes on in his camp."

When a detachment of Union recruits marched through town she watched them with a sour expression and surprised her family by going to Main Street and standing on the sidewalk to cheer the next group of volunteers marching south. "They're marching to real independence," she declared. It was the Fourth of July.

"And we?"

"We? We are coping," she said as she dropped her thin summer shawl on a chair and smoothed back her hair. Well, one thing was clear, he thought: *Her* neutrality was dead.

On the twelfth, Sanders Bruce was made Inspector General of the new Home Guards, a position comparable to that held by Buckner with the State Guards. "What did you expect?" Henrietta said in her new bitter, sarcastic tone. "Money-grabbers."

Morgan wasn't really surprised when he received a note from T.H. to-

ward the middle of the month. T.H. was already in the parlor, holding back
the curtain and looking out the long window at Hopemont's garden when
Morgan came downstairs. Morgan stopped briefly at the door. His uncle
looked tired. In that instant before T.H. turned to him, as he watched that
gentle face drawn in thought, he knew something momentous was about to
happen.

"Another leave, T.H.? Either you're so successful you can afford to take
time off or else you've come to recruit your relatives!" He chuckled at his
own joke and was relieved to see his uncle's sweet smile as answer.

"No—nothing like that, Johnny." The smile faded. "I came to tell you of
my decision. I've sold the bagging factory. If I don't, they will take it
anyway."

"Has it come to that?"

"It has. Even Dick admits they are confiscating property of Southern
sympathizers in Missouri. Everybody knows where my sympathies lie,
John. Well, I might as well follow those sympathies. I'm going south."

"But—"

"But you thought I'd wait for Buckner? Poor Buckner, sending the Guards
to Columbus, to be attacked by McClellan's volunteers—another broken
promise." He sighed. "I'm afraid I don't have that kind of patience."

"Aunt Mary and Nannie?"

"They'll stay here. Until I can send for them."

"Don't worry . . . the Yankees won't bother women and children. After
all, they want Kentucky's cooperation, not resistance."

"It's their need I'm counting on to produce their goodwill," T.H. said
grimly. He looked up and added, "Did you know Buckner met with Lincoln
on the tenth?"

"I knew he had gone to Washington."

T.H. shook his head. "Lincoln wrote a statement saying he has no 'present
plans' for sending armed force into Kentucky, but would make no promise
that would 'bind his future course' . . . as he put it. Then he refused to sign
the statement!"

So that's why you're leaving, Morgan thought. The handwriting on the
wall. Suddenly he asked, "When did you see Buckner last?"

"When he returned, last night. Also Hanson. Ole Bench-leg sends you his
regards."

Something in the way he said it made Morgan know that Hanson was
leaving and T.H. was going with him. But he said nothing.

"Be careful, Johnny."

"You, too."

"I can't believe he's doing it," said Eleanor Curd.

"I can," Henrietta sniffed, her eyes shining. She cried and embraced him
as if he were her only hope in the world. When she found out that Tom
intended to go with him she exploded. "*Seventeen!*" she wailed. "He's only
seventeen!"

"Joe Breckinridge is going, and he's seventeen!" Tom defended.

"Joe! Does his father know?" Henrietta looked at her son as if he were insane.

When it was obvious that Tom was adamant, his oldest brother, as spokesman, persuaded her that if he must go, it was best for him to go with someone like T.H., who could look after him.

"I'll bet I'm mustered in before Richard!" Tom laughed that night as Aunt Betty packed his things. "Camp Boone's closer'n Virginia!" He gave them all bear hugs and they stood numb in the front hall.

The house seemed empty after they left. That night Tommie tapped timidly on her brother's door.

"Johnny! Oh, Johnny. Just the thought—not to hear his sweet voice again!"

"You will, you will," Morgan murmured, his arm around her shivering shoulders. "Come now, get some sleep. T.H. will take care of him. The war will probably be over before he can fire a shot. You know how Tom loves a uniform." He found a handkerchief and dried her face with a corner of it. "Come now, what would Basil say?"

He went back to his duties at the factory, wondering how important the making of money was in the face of the excitement that invaded every conversation, every thought that underlay each business transaction, however minor. Old customers, Union men, withdrew orders. Even some of his friends crossed the street to avoid him. Frank Wolford had joined the Federal Army, but his father remained the same, treating the sore throats and fevers of his "Southern" patients as carefully as those of his "loyalists." But his nonpartisanship was rare.

In the Northern press since Sumter, editors boasted that the rebellion would be put down in a month, that the rebels were just bands of bums. *Jeff. Davis & Co. will be swinging from the battlements at Washington, at least, by the 4th of July . . . Illinois can whip the South by herself . . .* What really sickened him was the recruitment of New York "roughs" from the gutters and jails, and the adulation by the press of the notorious Billy Wilson, who boasted that when his "regiment" moved south, there wouldn't be a thief left in New York City. They marched up Broadway yelling brutal promises, and a New York newspaper called them "gallant souls."

In a fit of remorse, anger, and frustration, Morgan ran up a Confederate flag of his own. It billowed and snapped over the jeans factory. Cal came out of the office and they stood in the middle of the street watching it. "Just let them try to take it down," Morgan breathed.

Two days later, news of the Confederate defeat at Rich Mountain, in western Virginia, reached the bar at the Phoenix Hotel.

"If they'd only had more cavalry," Warren Viley groaned. "But still, it's a wonder they escaped annihilation. Imagine that little army of three thousand surrounded by McClellan's twenty thousand, marching for sixty hours, without food or horses . . ."

Greeley's *Tribune* reported the battle as the end of the Confederacy. Cal was furious. Charlton swore that if he'd been there . . . Morgan listened to them as if from the distance of a dream. How like blond Tommy Cunningham Charlton was! Those flashing blue eyes! Tommy would never again turn a horse smartly. But oh, how he wished he could lead young men like them all!

Their concern and frustrated enthusiasm were catching. Even Key Hunt moved a notch South in his academic neutrality. He studied the finances of the two sides. "The North is not in as good a situation as they would have you think," he said one afternoon in the Hopemont parlor. "The ordinary expenditures of the whole Federal government for the fiscal year ending June 30, 1862, are estimated at eighty million. Yet Lincoln has asked Congress for four *hundred* millions! Chase has admitted receiving only five million per quarter from the tariff. At that rate you have a government with twenty million a year contemplating an outlay of almost five hundred millions!"

"Where will they get it?" asked Cal.

"They plan on taxing property and selling more public lands. Whereas the South can, for the first time, sell all its cotton directly to Europe. Last year almost four million bales were exported. I read not too long ago that cotton represents a capital investment of around nine hundred million dollars. *Nine hundred millions,*" he repeated, to impress them. "And with cotton going for three hundred dollars a bale—in gold, I tell you—cotton is still king, gentlemen. The South furnishes five-sevenths of the cotton used by the entire world. If England will guarantee loans on next year's crop . . . I tell you, things aren't as bleak as they seem."

"With Tennessee and Virginia out of the Union, I see no reason for Kentucky to wait," Charlton said.

They looked at each other, refraining from reminding him that in the last state elections Union sympathizers had won hands down.

But all their minds were on Virginia, and Richard, now A.P. Hill's assistant adjutant. The North had left nothing undone to increase and prepare its "Grand Army." It faced a Confederate force armed with shotguns and old flintlock muskets which had seen duty in 1812 or earlier, reworked to accommodate percussion caps. It seemed a pitiably uneven contest, but Cal and Charlton were enthusiastic. "Just you wait," they kept saying. "Southern boys can outshoot and outride Yankees any day." Kitty would leave the room.

News of Bull Run reached Lexington on July 19 by telegraph the day after the battle. Three thousand Federals assaulted twelve hundred Confederates, who had not one yard of entrenchment or one rifle pit for protection. Yet miraculously the charge was turned back—twice. Under a shower of shells Longstreet changed the placement of his guns and the Federals fled. For two hours the Morgans and Hunts relived every detail. Henrietta and Kitty were frantic with worry, but Henrietta's sons had only one thought: They wished they could have been with Richard and Powell Hill. If only Kentucky would show what it could do! At the jeans factory, Charlton, who had taken Richard's place, held an informal council of war after each telegraph message, each arrival of a newspaper. John J. Crittenden's son George resigned his commission in the Federal Army and was now a brigadier-general with the Confederates.

"I hope they have enough whiskey to keep George happy!"

"We'll have to send him some."

"What about Tom?"

"Tom's a Union brigadier-general."

"Poor old Crit."

"Well, he tried for neutrality. Maybe his sons are just applying it."

They were still sitting around the office smoking cigars and planning imaginary campaigns when Adam appeared at the door, breathless, hat in hand. "Massa John . . . Miss Becky . . ."

He was on his feet and out the door before the others could ask a question. He leaped onto his horse and leaned into the gallop, almost running down two men with a cart on West Main. Becky . . . Becky . . . Her name swelled in his head and shut out everything else. Time, each second, took on eternal importance. He ran through the front door of the Bruce house and up the stairs, scattering servants and relatives as he went. Ben, at the bedroom door, tried to say something, but he pushed him aside.

She was gone by the time he got there. A strange, empty bundle lying heavy on the bed, as if the gravity of the earth were already pulling her down. They had closed her eyes and smoothed her hair, and her small mouth, with its full lower lip ending in a soft shadowed corner, looked as if she would at any second open her eyes and smile. He reached for her shoulders to shake her, but Margaret Bruce caught his arms.

"John . . ."

He let his fingers linger on her forehead at her hairline. The face was already cold. This was Becky? Where was Becky? He turned wild eyes to the woman by the bed. *Where was Becky?*

A chill passed down his spine. The world would go on, forgetting she had ever existed. He looked back at that peaceful face surrounded by its dark hair spread across the pillow. No. As long as she had laughed, had tied bonnets or delighted in a new ribbon or a wildflower. These things would live. They were somewhere . . . had to be somewhere . . .

Where? The hand on his arm, gently insisting, blinded him with tears. The bed swam before his eyes. *Nowhere*, the tears said. She's as dead as Pharaoh and you had your chance to make her happy and you failed. Bonnets and wildflowers! They are gone as she is gone, do you understand that?

Gone.

Failed, failed.

Even Kitty's worn face couldn't bring him back to life. She was sick with worry; A.P. had been at Bull Run. Or had he? She hadn't heard.

The day they buried Becky they had the news of an even bigger battle at Manassas Junction.

Morgan stood hatless in the July heat under the trees of the Lexington Cemetery and watched a polished coffin lowered beside the tiny grave of his son. The Presbyterian minister stood like a black column, the breeze moving

his hair as he bent his head over the limp, open book tipping forward on his
palm. A thumb clamped the rustling, gilt-edged pages, but through the
monotone of a psalm John Morgan heard only a girl's smooth voice:

> *Soft blows the breath of morning*
> *In my own valley fair*
> *For it's there the opening roses*
> *With fragrance scent the air . . .*

Where had they been when she'd sung that? At Graham Springs. One
morning early, so long ago.

He clung to details. Then a trapdoor at the bottom of his mind opened
and he fell through, where no details mattered.

After the funeral he stood by a window in the Bruce parlor and received
the expected condolences as if he were watching a procession in a dream.
Becky's young married female friends, girls she had gone to school with—
he had always secretly thought them a little silly, but now their soft eyes
blurred with tears and their little hands in his were cold with grief. The
voice of Sanders's wife came in to him. "She was *truly* a Christian lady.
With the grace of *forbearance* and *long*-suffering." In her stiff white blouse.
Was there just a hint of recrimination in that "*long*-suffering"?

Sanders's Chasseurs stepped a little awkwardly forward. They had called
him a Secesh, and who knew but the one offering his sympathy now was
the one who had taken down one of T.H.'s flags? But what did it all matter?
When he searched down into the middle of himself he found nothing. He
could not even stir resentment.

For four days he sat in the garden, his hands folded between his knees.
Nothing seemed important. He tried to shut out kitchen sounds, Annie's
giggles and Aunt Hannah's remonstrances. He could guess what she was
saying: *Now, don' you make too much noise, heah. Massa John. . . .* And they
would roll their eyes only a little less than Aunt Bet. His mother, for the
first time in my memory, seemed powerless to help him. Worry over Tom
and Richard and "what will become of us all" deepened the lines between
her eyes. Tommie had thrown her arms around him when they came home
from the cemetery, but then, in a strange fit of awkwardness, avoided him.
Kitty, withdrawn in her own concern over A.P., was unusually sweet. All
their efforts failed.

A blue jay argued in the tree above, sending out a squawk that sounded
more like a crazy laugh. He looked up to see the sun making patterns on a
sycamore across the street. Something in the pattern stirred him, the way
the gray paper-thin bark clung to the bone-white trunk. He had never realized how beautiful a sycamore could be.

Adam seemed surprised but pleased when he wanted the chestnut saddled. He was a good gelding, about twelve years old, an animal his grandfather would have called "serviceable"—indicating thereby the slightest
shading of disdain. Well, maybe Miss Lexington would have a rare one in
the spring. He rode out to the farm.

The heat was breathtaking. He took off his jacket and laid it across the horse's withers. As he rode he could see James, with Jesse, just leaving the stable. He walked over, swung off, and James took the reins and tied the gelding to a ringed post. "How is she?"

They walked into the gloom of the stable, and the smell of dry hay and oiled leather met him like a balm. "So you keep her up in the daytime, away from the flies?"

"Yassuh. Jes' like Uncle Simon. Away frum dem Joo-ly flies."

Morgan rubbed the mare's forelock and let his hand drift down her nose and cup her muzzle. A soft tongue caressed his palm. "Dem Joo-ly flies," he repeated, and then smiled weakly. "Yes, dem Joo-ly flies."

Randolph and Maggie were not surprised when he accepted their invitation to spend the night and ride over the farm with Randolph the next morning. Phlox were blooming down by the stream, great heads of lavender and pink. Purple milkweed spotted the pastures. Talk turned to the cattle, tobacco, the fertilizing that spring. Overhead the sky was one deep expanse of blue, without a cloud. They stopped on a rise to look back. It was good to be alive.

When he returned to Hopemont he found the house in turmoil. Kitty had just received a telegram from A.P. telling her both he and Richard were safe. Ironically, A.P. hadn't been in the fight at all. It was Beauregard's battle, jealously guarded by "Little Napoleon." Powell Hill's regiment, assigned to Joe Johnston, was ordered to a reserve position on the Confederate right flank. But a letter from Gordon Niles described with flair the battle at Manassas Junction. They saw through Niles's eyes the sensation-seeking crowds from Washington City, senators' wives in carriages and idlers on horseback anxious to watch the Grand Army beat the Rebels into submission. Instead, that Sunday at Manassas, the carriages—with thousands of frenzied, running men, caissons, riderless horses and overturned wagons—formed part of the rout that crowded the roads back to the capital.

"If the South will just follow up this great victory," Niles wrote, "it will win the war now, before more lives are lost. Washington is in total panic. Some of those Federal officers kept running all the way to Pennsylvania. The city is defenseless. Where are Joe Johnston and Beauregard?" He sent his address. "I will be here until September, when I will return to New York. If I don't join the Confederates before then."

His enthusiasm made Morgan smile. *"If you could have seen them . . .* on that hill when the firing was at its height. The roar of artillery shook the ground like thunder. Then the whole valley was one boiling cauldron of dust and smoke. But louder than the guns was that bloodcurdling, high, hoarse, shrill shout that the Yankees are calling the 'Rebel yell.'

"It must be something they learned from the Indians . . ." Niles's hurried scribble ran off the page. "Or maybe your fox-hunting friends, but I tell you it sounds as if all the devils in hell have been let loose."

And there it was, this spectacle, with the Blue Ridge against the sky: "Through my field glasses I thought I could see two generals in plain view with their troops under fire, and the Rebel cavalry with plumes in their hats everywhere. My God, how they fought, dashing headlong, never better than when their left flank had been fairly overpowered. Defeat seemed to inspire them to a kind of frenzied, supreme effort. My God, when I think of it . . . don't be surprised if my next letter is postmarked from Richmond."

Things in Missouri weren't going so well. There had been small victories in a few skirmishes, but the big prize, St. Louis, still lay unchallenged in Federal hands. Would Southern forces succeed in taking it? Tommie hadn't heard from Basil. She became religious and then morbid. She grabbed each new issue of *The Lexington Observer and Reporter* or the pro-Southern *Statesman* and turned to the obituary page, running her eyes down the lists of Confederate dead. "What number of souls have been launched into eternity!" she would mumble. "The mourning hearts and desolate firesides created within one short week! The lamentations will equal those of Rachel! Mothers mourning their sons, wives their husbands . . ."

"Come now, Miss Tommie."

For the first time in his life, John Morgan saw Aunt Betty embarrassed.

"Wheah's mah lil' tomboy? Whyn't you go ridin' wif Marse Cal?"

"I'll ride with you!" cried Key, but his sister's reproving look hushed him.

"No one to comfort them," she said, stubbornly refusing to be interrupted. "Because their loved ones are gone—passed away." She sighed.

"Is she . . . ?" Morgan asked his mother when he could.

"John!"

"Well . . ."

"She's merely expressing what we all feel!" Henrietta closed her eyes and sniffed. "Those poor, dear, brave boys!"

A.P. wrote Kitty a long letter from Richmond. Tom Jackson, the VMI professor, was now known as Stonewall, and J.E.B. Stuart's name was in every other sentence. As for Manassas, the rout and the panic were complete. "But we couldn't hear them for the cheers and yells from our own lines. It was a day, dear Kitty, which will live . . ."

As he handed back the letter, her eyes were on him.

"You will go," he said.

"Yes."

"When?"

"As soon as I can pack. Fact is, Brother Johnny, I'm having another child." At his open-mouthed surprise she laughed out loud. "It must have happened just before I left Washington. Another little Confederate to give Abe Lincoln a fit." She reached toward him suddenly and squeezed his hand. Nothing could have told him more eloquently how frightened she was.

"Does Powell know?"

"Luckily, no. He thought I'd been eating too much of Aunt Hannah's pecan pie! Besides, he wouldn't want me to travel . . ."

"Does Ma know?"

"Now, there's no need to start another war, is there?"

There was no dissuading her, and he couldn't help but think how lucky Powell Hill was.

Matter-of-factly, the next morning, they discussed the danger. The easiest and quickest way—without a war, of course—would have been by rail from Cincinnati to Baltimore. Now that was out of the question. He looked again at the map under his fingers. The South was a patchwork of railroad spurs. The only main lines north and south were those of the Louisville & Nashville to Memphis and Corinth, branching at Bowling Green. The Memphis & Charleston, passing through Corinth, could take her to Chattanooga, where she could catch the Virginia & Tennessee on to Richmond.

"You could visit Uncle Sam in Nashville. That would give you a rest before you went on. There's a branch line to Stevenson, Alabama, where you could take the Corinth line for Chattanooga . . ."

"Why doesn't the South have railroads?" She closed her eyes and clutched her fists. "How do they expect to fight a war without railroads?"

She was busy folding shawls and chemises. He had to move the map on her dresser to give her room. She pushed in a drawer so suddenly that a bottle of perfume overturned and there was a flurry of handkerchiefs mopping it up. Celina, her head and shoulders buried in the armoire, came up for air with three dresses on her arm.

"No, not those. The blue one, with the velvet trim. And let's not forget that cloak I gave you last winter. You'll need it. . . .

"NASHVILLE?" she said, finally catching his meaning. "It seems you are sending me around the world, Brother."

"But getting to Richmond from Washington . . ."

"I have friends there." She frowned at a skirt, flung it on the bed and clapped her hands to her cheeks in excitement. "Do *go*, Brother dear. I can't think. Celina, should I take this?"

Robert came by that afternoon and spent an hour with her in the parlor. To Morgan's surprise, after he left, she offered no argument when the Nashville visit was mentioned again.

"That would be pleasant, after all. I haven't seen Uncle Sam and little Sam since they were up for your wedding. Maybe I can find a new dress . . . freshen up for the rest of the trip. . . . It's just too bad the train doesn't go all the way to Louisville."

She left the next day on the Frankfort stage in a pouring rain, with her Washington nurse carrying the baby, and Celina in tow.

"Didn't you notice how her crinolines fluffed out?" Tommie giggled.

"No . . ."

"She had Celina sew packets of morphine in the hem. Uncle Robert brought them."

The August heat was insufferable. He tried to sleep without a sheet and stripped to the waist waiting for a breeze, thinking of Richard and A.P., and of Kitty on the train to Nashville with child and with morphine in her hem. And of little Henrietta and her soundless laugh of joy. He walked out onto the porch and watched the Presbyterian Church spire in the light of the moon. Across the street there were no lights in the Bruce house. He looked back to the church to avoid the little window over the garden. His mother, Kitty, the boys, and Tommie had all been so kind. It was strange to remember that T.H. and Tom didn't know Becky was dead.

Tommie's spirits rose the next week when she received a long letter from Basil, now officially in Confederate uniform and serving under General Hardee in his move on St. Louis. Morgan left her still reading the letter and walked into the warming room. He opened a biscuit and spread butter. There were eggs and ham, pork chops and hash browns, if you wanted them. It was a Hopemont breakfast. He was still savoring it when he heard Key slam the children's door off the back stairs. He heard his smooth, impatient steps as he raced down. His scrubbed, shining face turned the corner and he sang out a greeting. He was in his Rifles uniform. "It's Saturday!"

"Oh, I forgot. . . ."

"Will you come by later, Brother Johnny?"

"I will."

"Are you sure?"

"Sure."

He must miss Tom terribly, Morgan thought. Why hadn't I realized? At sixteen, he was still very much the baby of the family. "Did you hear the news?" Key was saying through a bite of biscuit as he wheeled into a chair and propped his elbows on the table. "The Yankee soldiers are coming to town today."

"How do you know?"

"To get another shipment of Lincoln guns."

"How do you know?" Aunt Hannah echoed.

"Mr. Duncan, the stationmaster, told me."

"You been hangin' aroun' dat dee-po agin? Chile, don' let Ole Miss heah you." Aunt Hannah sent a worried look toward the back entry. "An' git yo' elbows off'n de table."

"Mama's still in bed."

"Bed?"

"Now don' you go wirrin' yo'seff, Massa John. Ain't dat lady got a right to res' onc't in a while? A weddin' an' fo' soljuh boys off to wah." She shook her head and offered Key another biscuit. He jumped up and poured himself another cup of coffee. Even though it was August, there was a breeze here. And in winter the warming room, with its big fireplace, was always cozy. It was John Morgan's favorite room in the house. When they were little and used to visit from Shadeland, they had their suppers here. He leaned back and watched them. Kitty's words came back. Hopemont may never be the same.

"Don't look so glum, Brother Johnny." Key's face came into focus, his neat hair close-cropped, his grandmother's delicate nose, his soft mouth that could have been a girl's.

"Do I look glum? I'm sorry. Tell you what. I'll come by drill and then we can ride out to the farm."

"Splendid!"

"Meet me at the armory. . . . What time is it?"

Key looked at the watch Kitty had given him for Christmas. "Ten past nine."

"I'll be there in thirty minutes. Have to go by the factory first. Has Charl gone?"

"Yes."

"Tell him I want spit and polish."

Adam saddled two horses and he and Key separated at the corner of Mill and Second. He watched his young brother trot off, his back as straight as a pencil, his lower body one with the horse. Key was a rider, too.

He crossed Broadway and kept on West Third to Newtown Pike, where the Georgetown Road entered. Even from here, before the street curved back to Main Street, he could see his Confederate flag atop the factory standing out in a brisk southwest breeze. Richard's competence was still in evidence. A neat stack of orders, skewered by an upright spike, sat at Cal's right elbow. In a basket at the corner of the desk the morning mail waited for the Kentucky Central to Cincinnati. Cal reported everything going well —the Federals needed rope, and they were having a hard time filling all the orders for the navy. As for jeans, they couldn't make enough fast enough.

"But it's not any lack of Yankee orders that worries me, Johnny." He kept a map of the southern half of the country tacked to a board on the wall. He took it down and laid it on his desk. His finger jabbed at Missouri. "Booneville. Carthage. Wilson's Creek. Then retreat. We're winning the battles and losing the war."

"Why?"

"Squabbles between generals. Price wants this, McCullough wants that. While the Federals know what they want. Fremont has declared martial law in the whole state of Missouri, and anyone caught north of the Union Army with arms will be court-martialed and shot. Now rumor has it that Hardee may give up the assault on St. Louis entirely."

"What good would that do?"

"That's what I say."

"Unless . . ." John Morgan's eyes narrowed. "Unless there's something brewing in Kentucky . . ."

They looked at each other.

"And they plan a concentration of troops?"

"I wish we could help."

"Maybe we can." Cal winked and unlocked the bottom right-hand drawer of his desk. Two small boxes of gold caught the light. He closed the drawer, turned the key, sat down and leaned forward on the map, looking more earnest than his brother had ever seen him.

"I've been in touch with T.H. Shhh! Don't ask how."

"You know I've got to ask how."

"Well, he just may be in Kentucky," Cal whispered like a conspirator. "Colonel Trabue has gone to Louisville with Ben Monroe to recruit. There and around Frankfort. They're trying to raise a regiment. . . ."

Amos Jackson appeared at the door with a question. He looked expectantly toward John Morgan and dipped his head politely.

"How are you, Amos?"

"Fine, Mistah John."

"And Moses?"

"Jes' fine."

Cal excused himself and followed Amos to the supply room. When he came back he resumed his secretive air, whispering, "I won't be surprised if T.H. comes home before he goes back to Tennessee. Do you know what they call him down there?"

"Now, Cal, how would I know? And where do you get your information?"

Cal ignored the questions.

"Uncle Tom." He grinned. "Can't you see him?"

"Mother hen."

"Right."

"But do you think—?"

Cal held a finger to his lips. "Who knows? In the meantime, I accept only cash for orders, and little by little I'm withdrawing from the bank and accepting from them only gold. If old Bench-leg Hanson comes this way, the Feds may just close the banks—or worse, confiscate everything. We've got to be prepared."

Such precautions were so unlike Cal that Morgan chuckled. "When did you—?" he began.

"Did I begin? Even before the wedding. When Richard decided to leave. And Charlton is doing the same."

"How many men do you think are at Camp Boone now?"

"Who knows? Thousands."

"I've also heard they don't have ammunition, and some have had to be sent home because they don't have guns."

"Don't believe it. Have you ever met a Southern boy without a gun?"

"Which reminds me—if you don't need me I've promised Key to be early at the armory."

"Everything"—Cal grinned—"is in excellent hands."

On Main Street Morgan had to wait for a long line of men in a column of fours to march by. They were carrying a Rebel banner and singing at the tops of their voices. He was not surprised to see James Clay in the lead. He had resigned from the Rifles, then the State Guard. Now Morgan knew why. Clay dropped from the line and came over to stand by Morgan's horse.

"Yes, we're headed south," he said, his face beaming. How like his father, the fox of the old days, he looked! "Enough of this despotism," he almost shouted. "Have you heard that they've arrested old Governor Morehead— took him in the middle of the night from his home and sent him to prison?"

"Whatever for?"

"Do they need a reason?"

Morgan quickly searched in his jacket for a pencil and paper.

"Would you take a note to Tom? He'll be at Camp Boone." He scribbled quickly. "If you get there . . ."

"There is no *if*," James Clay looked at him squarely and grinned. "Remember that. No *if*." Deftly he slipped the note inside his jacket and shifted his musket. His blue eyes shone as he waved and stepped into the last line of the column, his haversack a misshapen hump across his shoulders. Morgan watched them march down the wide dirt street, keeping to the right near the brick sidewalk and the crowds that cheered them on. From the armory at Main and Upper a loud cheer came from the Rifles.

He would always remember the next few hours. As he tied his horse at the post on the Upper Street side of the armory he heard the whistle of a train coming into the station. Almost as soon as that sound died away another took its place. By the time he rounded the corner to go in the Main Street entrance he saw a column of two hundred cavalrymen, with a Federal colonel at its head, turn from Limestone into Main, a block away. They were coming from the Nicholasville Road, from Camp Dick Robinson. "What . . . ?" he said to himself, and an old man he knew answered from the sidewalk, "They've come for another shipment of them Lincoln guns, John. Must've arrived on the train." The man spit and glanced away. "Don't mind tellin' you, they think you're a Secesh with plans to seize them guns."

"That's ridiculous."

But his eyes were on the horses, which had all rounded the corner by now. Even from here he could see a crowd in front of the Phoenix Hotel as the Federals trotted smartly by. A man yelled something and a soldier pointed his rifle at the crowd. Women screamed, and over Morgan's head a bugle blasted from the roof of the armory. It was the Rifles' signal for assembly.

Just at that moment the Colonel halted his company at the head of Short Street by Beard's stable, and the crowd began converging in that direction. Morgan was about to go in when a loud tocsin rang out from the steeple of the courthouse. Immediately the streets were filled with Home Guards. They must have taken the bugle as a call to arms! As he ran inside he met Key and John Castleman dragging out the old brass cannon used on the Fourth of July.

"What are you doing?"

"We're taking a stand, sir." Smartly, quietly, John Castleman, twenty, swung the piece about. "Lieutenant's orders."

Morgan bit back a grin. Lieutenant James West. Yes, that was like him. But to Castleman he frowned. "Don't touch that piece without further orders."

He ran up the steps to find his Rifles taking their positions at the windows, others buttoning on jackets and shouldering arms for a foray into the streets. His heart couldn't help but swell with pride as he watched them. More arrived, quietly but quickly assembling. They had barely completed a hurried roll call when the sentry admitted John C. Breckinridge, out of breath from running up from the Phoenix.

"See here, Morgan. This is ridiculous. Let's not lose our heads."

John C. Breckinridge was only four years his senior, but he had already been the Vice-President of the United States and, but for a split party, might have been President. With his large head, plump face and dark-shadowed eyes, he had the look of heaviness peculiar to statesmen. He was still panting.

"It's your fault."

"Mine?" Puzzlement clouded Breckinridge's eyes.

"If you'd won the presidency last year, none of this would be happening."

"Oh. Well! But seriously, John. Please . . ." Breckinridge looked exactly like the man he was: a father whose young son, against his orders, had gone south to enlist; a loyal Unionist still trying for neutrality in the face of daily violence by the government he wanted to support.

"My men receive their orders from me," Morgan said easily. "And I can assure you I'll give no foolish order before its time."

"But you would give one in its time?" Breckinridge smiled at his own feeble attempt at humor. They could still hear the crowd.

"I've sent scouts to investigate. We'll act accordingly. If any citizen of Lexington is hurt, it is still the responsibility of the State Guard to maintain the peace."

"I know. I know you will, John." Breckinridge tucked his chin and cleared his throat. "And I hope to God you don't have to." He reached out and drew Morgan aside. "Let me say this now." He was breathing hastily, like a man with a bad heart. His eyes wandered to the motto of the Rifles printed in large letters and framed on the wall: OUR LAWS THE COMMANDS OF OUR CAPTAIN. "This is not the proper time," he said to the sign. "Wait. Your time will come." He looked back at Morgan with those piercing eyes that had pinioned adversaries on the floor of the Senate. "Your time will come," he repeated, as his fingers relaxed their grip on Morgan's sleeve. "Things are happening right now—I can't say—which will give us all an opportunity soon."

Morgan's heart leaped with a sudden thrill. Were the Confederates planning a massive offensive in Kentucky? Breckinridge knew something.

When he left, Morgan received news from his scout that all had gone peaceably at the station: Colonel Bramlette had ordered the guns onto wagons and was in the process of escorting them back to camp. Some of the Rifles wanted to practice at Cheapside, just to make a "show," but Morgan persuaded them to wait. "It's our job to keep the peace, not to encourage panic." But he couldn't keep appreciation from his voice. Nor could he help repeating Breckinridge's promise: "Your time will come." Then he added, "It would be a good idea for four or five of you to stay here another hour, just in case."

Six volunteers jumped in line.

"I thought you wanted to ride out to the farm."

"Not now, Brother Johnny!" Key's face was shining.

"Then I'll go back to the office. I can hear your bugle from there."

Cal was surprised to see him back so soon.

"I thought you might be worried," Morgan explained.

"What was that all about?"

"Just a detachment from Camp Robinson to pick up a shipment of guns."

The sound of looms and a steady, contented bustle came from the back. Cal shut the door and sat down.

"I've got a little news of my own," he said. "Judge Gratz is looking for you."

"Judge Gratz?"

"I think it's about the flag. He's getting jittery. I think he'll do anything to keep the peace, Johnny." He leaned back. "The Federals at Camp Robinson number about ten thousand now. They're getting recruits from Ohio, and some Union boys from Tennessee. Judge Monroe has just 'defected' and made a scorching statement in Nashville. Renounced a government that would enslave him. I think maybe the arrest of Morehead triggered it."

He surprised himself with the vehemence of his own voice: "Ben Gratz can keep his advice to himself."

"Judge Gratz is only trying to help, Johnny."

Another cheer came from the direction of the armory.

"Besides—Charl just brought in the latest list of Union casualties. Cary Gratz was killed in Missouri."

"Damn! I'll see him this afternoon."

"Yes, I would if I were you. Just to settle him. Nothing to worry about. Can you tend store for a while? I need to go to the bank."

"Another withdrawal?"

"What else?" Cal grinned. He reached for his hat and left, whistling between his teeth.

The office was hot and the muffled sound of the treadles made the air seem thicker. He walked back among the workers, busy measuring, cutting, pinning. The machines stood like fetishes, served by bowed heads. Packing cases and tables covered by rolls of cloth crowded the aisles. Three seamstresses near him stopped work and looked up. Morgan went back to the office to find Amanda sitting behind his desk.

"Do you always look so serious?"

"Are you always so sneaky?" he smiled back.

"When I have to be."

It was the first time he had seen her since Becky's death.

"May I do anything for you?"

"Yes." It came after a pause, but there was nothing indecisive about it. "Yes."

She got up and walked around his desk. He was still between two small chairs, used for clients. She took one, and swung her foot under the hem of her skirt. Her green eyes were on his, her soft mouth serious. She drew the lightest of summer shawls across her shoulders.

"Yes, as a matter of fact there is."

He waited. He was strangely embarrassed with her, and walked around the desk and sat down, folding his hands out in front of him as if she were a customer. "What?" he prompted.

"I've got to warn you, Johnny . . ."

Her look was so serious he laughed, half to calm her. "Warn?"

"Jake is hiring hands to the Federals," she said, as if changing the subject.

"Well, he must be doing quite well, since the Federals are doing quite well."

"You don't have to be cautious with me, Johnny."

Her smile brought it all back.

"I never have, have I?"

She laughed. "No. What I want to say is, that . . . Jake and the Feds are like that." She held up two fingers. "I've heard them talking . . ."

"If you've come to warn me about the flag, you're late. I'm seeing Judge Gratz about it this afternoon."

"It's not the flag. Something worse, but I don't know what. I just thought I would warn you."

"I'm glad you did."

She rose, and he was on his feet in an instant, waiting. The desk was between them.

"I'm sorry about Becky."

"Yes. It's still unreal."

Her eyes held his for the slightest moment. "Maybe we're all dead already, Johnny, and life's the dream."

At Hopemont he unsaddled himself, since Adam was busy painting the *calèche*, and walked through the garden to the Gratz house. He found the Judge in his study. The day had clouded over and the smell of rain made the humid August air seem cool.

"Come, come in!" Ben Gratz opened his arms affably. "So glad to see you, John. You are looking well."

"And you, Judge Gratz. I'm sorry about Cary."

There was an awkward moment. The Judge looked off, then met his eyes again and nodded.

"Cal tells me you want to see me?"

"Yes. Have a seat. Have a seat. Yes. Nothing much."

Ben Gratz had never been good at small talk. Morgan knew he was worried, and waited.

"It's just that—" He coughed slightly.

"Cal said it might concern the flag."

"Yes. Yes, it does. I don't think you realize the significance of that flag, John. Since the Federals are at Camp Robinson, and a Union force has occupied Paducah—"

"Kentucky is no longer neutral, is it? But it's still a free country?"

"You were always one to run off after rainbows, John. I'm not talking about a principle, or an abstraction. I'm talking about a piece of cloth that is a banner of rebellion."

"But a piece of cloth—surely it couldn't cause such an uproar as you fear if it didn't represent . . . one of those rainbows?" His own breath was coming short and his hands had begun to tremble. "The flag I ran up is a mark of sympathy for our neighbor states who are bold enough to stand up for their own beliefs," he said as calmly as he could. In respect for the old man's grief he added, "You always told us to do that, sir. Remember?"

Judge Gratz was an old man who suffered, occasionally, from bouts of gout. He sighed heavily. "I'm only asking you to take it down, John. I learned a long time ago how stubborn you are. I just want you to know they are arresting people in Louisville for less than that."

"Louisville was always a Yankee town." He grinned, trying to make a joke of it.

Ben Gratz refused to be amused. "You may not know . . ." he said quietly, as if to stop, then thought better of it and went on: "They tried to arrest John Breckinridge and failed."

"But he's—"

"For the Union and neutrality? I'm afraid the time is fast approaching when neutrality will no longer be tolerated."

It was a strong statement, coming from a pro-Union man. "If it will make you feel better, Judge, I won't do anything rash."

"You have your family to think of."

"That's precisely what I was going to say."

That's precisely why I may just do something, he said to himself as he walked down the Judge's steps. *Or may not do anything at all*, he added when he looked up at the lovely façade of Hopemont. How could he endanger that, for anything in the world? As he turned the knob on the garden door and let himself in under the spiral stairs, he had the chilling feeling that it might be endangered already, in spite of anything he did.

Just after midnight Cal woke him. T.H. Hunt was downstairs.

27

"I can't stay," T.H. said, after his nephews were through hugging him and pounding him on the back. "I've already seen Mary. I'm on my way now."

Henrietta, pulling her robe closer, dropped the drapes across the window and motioned to Bouviette for coffee. They were in the warming room. With its single window and two exits, it made a logical meeting place. Cal had indeed been in touch with T.H. He mentioned Becky's death and Morgan met his eyes. "I was so sorry, Johnny."

"I know."

"These things . . . happen. We don't know why."

"No. . . ."

Bouviette served the coffee. T.H. sat at the table and held them spellbound.

"Yes! Tom's fine. He's on my staff and sends his love. I thought it too dangerous to take him with me this time."

Henrietta nodded, afraid for the first time in her life to interrupt. When she was satisfied that Tom was safe and well, she sat back to listen.

"It's quite a place," he said again. "Wide, flat fields for drilling. Plenty of water and firewood. Two miles west of the L&N tracks and about seven from Clarksville. Temp Withers has done a good job. By the time I got there fifty companies had applied for service—and he was only ordered to form twenty-six! They are coming by scores. Scores! Before the summer is over we should have at least ten thousand. Did you know young Bob Breckinridge, John C.'s cousin, is there? And his son Joe? So many Kentuckians— no wonder they named it Camp Boone."

He answered their questions as best he could. Was the food good? How were they sleeping? Did he have enough clothing? What did he need? T.H. sipped coffee and smiled. "Your prayers, my dear sister, your prayers."

"You know you have them."

"And ours, too," Tommie put in, between Charlton and Key in the doorway.

T.H. became earnest. "You ought to know Trabue. Marvelous man. Comes from Columbia, Kentucky. Saw service in Mexico. A lawyer. Old Trib, they call him. And Eddie Byrne. Edward Byrne." He said the name in wonder.

"What about Eddie Byrne?" Henrietta asked. She was as eager as her sons.

"You may not believe this, Henrietta, but Ed Byrne raised and equipped a battery of artillery for the Confederate service out of his own pocket. The finest horses and harnesses he could find. He contracted with a foundry in

Memphis to make four bronze six-pounder fieldpieces. He'd planned to take them personally to Charleston when he heard that Sumter surrendered. Then he decided to find a Kentucky outfit to attach himself to. I wasn't there when he arrived, but they tell me his entry into Camp Boone was memorable! He came with tents, wagons, blankets . . . everything. When he saw how many boys were without blankets, he sent back to Mississippi, and the ladies of Greenville sent five hundred quilts—taken from their own beds—so that every man in the Second Kentucky had one! Did you know Doctor Wible?"

The talk turned to measles.

Two hours later he was gone, and they went back upstairs. Hopemont was very quiet after he left.

"What do you think, Johnny?" It was Cal, in the dark, calling him as he used to when they were children. Cal would know he couldn't sleep.

"I don't know."

"All those quilts. Just think of all those quilts. And those brass six-pounders. Imagine." Even across the room, Cal couldn't conceal the longing in his voice. "I hope Tom stays warm."

On September 4, Leonidas Polk, the Episcopal Bishop of Louisiana, now a Confederate general, occupied the Mississippi River town of Columbus, Kentucky, as a countermeasure against the Federal presence at Paducah. Ten days later, to block a threatened Federal invasion of East Tennessee through Kentucky, Confederate General Zollicoffer brought several thousand men from Knoxville to guard the Cumberland Gap. So Kentucky had been invaded by both sides.

"We will withdraw if the Federals do likewise," said Polk.

"We cannot sit idly by and see Kentucky become a Yankee invasion route for the lower South," insisted Zollicoffer.

On September 6, Jefferson Davis, ill upstairs in the presidential house in Richmond, heard a familiar step on the stairs. "It's Al Johnston!" he cried out. "I'd know that step anywhere!"

And it was.

Even before Sumter, Albert Sidney Johnston, commandant of the Department of the Pacific, resigned his commission with the U.S. Army and went to Los Angeles as a private citizen. In June, warned of possible arrest if he tried to return East by ship, he set out on horseback across the desert. Orders for his arrest followed. With little food and water—once he went seventy miles without water for his horse—his optimism never flagged. He made it to Galveston and by boat to New Orleans, then to Richmond. Davis had heard of his arrival in New Orleans by telegraph, and was half-expecting him. He gave him immediate command of all the troops in the West.

Cal was ecstatic. "Now you'll see some action!" he laughed.

But on the 11th of September the Kentucky legislature passed a resolution ordering all Confederate troops out of the state.

The implications were clear, and nobody was surprised when Simon Bolivar Buckner wired the Confederate War Department that "no political necessity now exists for withholding a commission, if one is intended for me." Two days later Albert Sidney Johnston made him a brigadier-general.

Before he left, Buckner issued a call for all Kentuckians to defend their homeland from northern invasion, and overnight schoolrooms were emptied, lawyers left clients, young boys tall for their age began lying about birthdays and parental permission.

"*Now* you'll see things happen!" Cal kept repeating, until Tommie, in mockery, would run to the window, draw back the curtain, and look down Mill Street in a pantomime of expectation.

But underneath they were all excited. Almost as soon as he had arrived in Nashville, Sidney Johnston enrolled all available Tennessee troops, plus a regiment of cavalry under Nathan Bedford Forrest, and rushed into Kentucky. Buckner, with thirteen hundred men, took the lead; "Ole Bench-leg" Roger Hanson followed with the Second Kentucky Infantry, Byrne's battery, and a company of Tennessee cavalry. Two or three thousand Tennesseans joined them before they reached Bowling Green. Hardee arrived from Columbus, and Forrest was sent to scout the country between the Green River and the Cumberland.

Charlton couldn't keep still, walking back and forth across the parlor. "I've ridden that country," he said.

"I know you have," John Morgan grinned at him.

"Excellent roads," Charlton went on, as if not hearing him. "And the railroad to Memphis. But even if these were lost, there's the rail line to Nashville directly south, with the Cumberland making a great, sweeping semicircle to flank their rear."

Morgan laughed out loud. "Charl! You're a regular general! You've really been studying Cal's map!"

"You bet I have! No wonder Lincoln said what he did!"

"And what was that?"

"To win this war he needed either God or Kentucky, but if he had to choose, he'd take Kentucky."

"The L&N," Morgan said.

Cal took it up. "No! The rivers. Remember what Basil said? Regular avenues for gunboats! The Tennessee all the way down into Alabama, the Cumberland past Nashville." He stopped in front of his mother's writing table. He sat down and found a piece of Tommie's blue writing paper and made blunt, quick strokes, crosshatched to represent railroads, with thicker, curving lines for the rivers.

Tommie looked over his shoulder. "But what if the Yankees come down here?" Her finger swooped from the left.

"Hah! That's where Fort Henry on the Tennessee and Fort Donelson on the Cumberland do their jobs."

"It looks foolproof," admitted Morgan.

"It is. The man's a genius. Do you remember him, riding down that street in Mexico? My God, I'd follow him anywhere!"

Morgan picked up Cal's scribble and frowned. In his mind he could see the rivers, as Cal said, like two avenues cutting into the heart of the South, the Cumberland dipping down to Nashville and up again to Mill Springs, near the Gap. The Tennessee would be even more inviting for a Union invasion, dropping due south from Paducah into Alabama. "I hope they hold," he said.

"Who?" asked Charlton, distracted.

"Not *who*. *What*. Those forts. Henry and Donelson."

Henrietta came in then, and the talk turned to other things. She *was* beginning to look like Queen Victoria, with a deepening line between her brows. *We don't want to worry her* was in the glance the brothers shot across Tommie's head when their mother entered. *Oh, but don't you wish we could be there?* flashed even through the caution.

Who would take care of them? Morgan asked himself that night. He couldn't sleep, and scenes of a depopulated Hopemont spread before his eyes. Charlton and Cal, of course, would want to go. That would leave only Key and Adam, the stableboy, with Randolph to help. Ah, but his mother had brothers, and influential ones at that. Uncle Frank and Robert would undoubtedly stay. And Dick Curd was one of the staunchest Union men in the county. She could rely on them. Still, the thought of a lone woman, with a daughter and a sixteen-year-old son in a town held by hostile troops . . . He would have to talk to Cal. In case. He fell to daydreaming campaigns of his own. If he had only been . . . No, it was all silly. His place was here. But what could he do?

He could send shipments of jeans south. Why hadn't he thought of that before? Delicious! To supply the Confederacy from West Main Street, right under the eyes of the Yankees! He slept like a baby.

Sunday. Services at Christ Church, in the old Hunt pew where his grandparents and uncles and aunts had sat. Tommie sang in the choir, but Morgan kept hearing Tom's high, clear tenor sounding like an angel. God, take care of him. His mother in her bonnet, praying for her sons, for Kitty, for the baby, and for A.P. because Kitty loved him. For T.H., her gentle brother. Charlton, with his blond Calvin Morgan good looks. Cal's honest face. And next to him, Key being very proper, keeping his place in the prayer book, aware of a young girl's eyes.

"Why didn't he pray for the Confederacy?" Tommie asked peevishly, once they were home.

"He prayed for peace, dear."

"But Mama, just because Lexington is full of those nasty Federals . . ."

"Tom Crittenden is a Federal, and you always thought him a gentleman."

"Well, he's not. How can you even think such a thing? I know what. I'll have a Confederate party this afternoon. It's a nice day. We'll have it in the garden. I'll have Aunt Hannah bake a Confederate cake."

"Looks like a good day to ride out to the farm." Cal winked. "Get out of the way. How about it, Charlton? Johnny?"

"May I come, Brother?"

"How could I keep you away?" Cal laughed, roughing up Key's hair.

"I'll show you my pony's faster'n yours!"

"You will not!"

It was noon by the time they passed the cemetery and turned into Main Street, coming home. Key, riding in front, was the first to see it. He kicked his pony and galloped ahead of his brothers, yelling.

Morgan smelled it. Then, as he followed Key, with Charlton and Cal behind, they all spurred their horses into a gallop, not stopping until they reached the factory. A cart, piled high with wood, was parked against the side door. Bright orange-red, furious flames were outlining the office window, and the stifling, resinous smell of burning tar told them the fire had already reached the roof. Charlton dashed for the fire department, which had already received the alarm and met him halfway down Main Street, the engine careening behind its running horses. Hoses were dragged out. A bucket brigade was formed. Key brought their horses beyond range of the smoke and noise and held the bridles, watching the factory send up great shafts of flame. Charlton ran up, out of breath. Cal, busy with buckets, saw Johnny go into the office.

The desk was gone.

"We might be able to save the storage room," a fireman tipped his hat and informed Morgan. "We've made a fire break through the back. . . ."

From where they stood they could hear the axes.

"Yes, thank you . . ." Morgan answered vaguely.

"Now you'd better get outside, Mr. Morgan."

"Yes."

You'll do well, Johnny. Why, we'll make a new sign. Hunt-Morgan. What do you think of that, eh?

The sun set red behind them.

"Well, it's gone," Cal managed to say as they trotted into Broadway.

"Not entirely, Cally," said Charlton behind them. "I checked the machinery. Most of it's intact. I think we could . . ."

They hardly heard him. They walked through the back entry, a column of weary, smoke-blackened figures. Aunt Betty and Aunt Hannah, with Annie serving, had hot coffee ready. Tommie pulled her brothers into the parlor and Henrietta poured her older sons stiff drinks of whiskey, then took one herself. The dinner table was set, and a moist night breeze stirred the curtains. On the sideboard sat Tommie's Confederate cake.

"I wonder how Amanda knew?" Morgan asked Cal upstairs, as they were washing off.

"What did she say? Tell me everything she said."

"She just warned me."

"Did she say anything about Jake?"

"Only that he was hiring out hands to the Federals for their construction down at Camp Robinson."

Cal thought a long minute, rubbing the back of his neck with a towel. His sandy hair was rumpled and wet, and stuck to his forehead. He brushed it away and bent to the mirror over the washbasin. "My, you're handsome," he told himself.

"Be serious, Cal!"

"I am. Have you ever seen such a handsome fella?"

But his eyes narrowed, as if he were trying to get something clear to himself. "I think we ought to get legal advice. Let's see Uncle Frank."

"Round up all your factory hands," Key Hunt said. "I know it will look like an inquisition. Send word by your foreman—that free man. What's his name?"

"Amos Jackson."

"Are you absolutely *sure* you didn't tell anyone about the money?"

Neither Amos nor his son Moses, nor any of the Jackson family could be found. Neighbors said they moved away yesterday.

"But why would Amos do it? Besides, how did he know about the money?"

When the hands assembled, Cal discovered that four workers from the ropewalk had disappeared also.

"My guess is they've gone to the Federal camp," Key Hunt said.

"But why?"

"As a haven. Union soldiers have been advertising it as such. Who knows what those poor souls believe? The Federals pay free hands fifty cents a day. Slaves get nothing. The Ohio River has moved south," he said grimly.

"It's already a little late for a ride down there and back today," said Cal.

"That shouldn't be your next move anyway."

"What then?" asked Morgan.

"Let's see if we can get a warrant from the sheriff," his uncle said. "We'll tell him about those partially burned bolts that were soaked in coal oil."

Morgan nodded. He was already pulling on his coat to go out the door.

The sheriff, a large, affable man, lost his smile when he learned why they were there. He addressed his remarks to Key Hunt, avoiding John Morgan's eyes. "Circumstantial evidence," he drawled.

"Circumstantial?" Cal burst out. "Why, the firemen saw those bolts. Clear evidence of arson."

"And we've got a list of missing workers," Morgan said meaningfully.

"I'm sorry." The sheriff looked at Morgan for the first time. "Under the circumstances, with feelings running high—" He stopped abruptly and asked a little pleadingly, "Now why did you have to go and put up that Rebel flag, John?"

Morgan tilted his head and smiled. As softly and as evenly as he could, he asked, "Do you know a law against it, sheriff?"

Outside, he determined to ask Robert Hunt to go with him to the Union camp. Robert had doctored most of his hands and could vouch for their identities. They could saddle up within the hour and be there before sundown. Why wait? He had to enlist Charlton's help in persuading Key to stay home. When they went by Robert's house the doctor was just driving up. It was almost four o'clock before they started, and almost dark by the time they were admitted to General Nelson's tent. Riding through camp at a walk, Morgan couldn't help remembering Mexico. This camp was much better organized than Camargo. Rows of Sibley tents pointed sharp white pyramids, like so many fingers, skyward. Neatly swept gravel walks defined the areas, and small, carefully lettered signs identified regiments, brigades, companies. Groups of soldiers were sitting about, polishing their buckles and spurs with ashes from potbellied stoves or from clay ovens used to bake bread. A sutler's wagon was doing a brisk business.

William "Bull" Nelson, from an old Kentucky family, had been a lieutenant in the U.S. Navy before the war. Lincoln had sent him to organize the Home Guards and then made him a brigadier-general. His three-hundred-pound, six-foot frame, plus his blustering, profane manner had earned him his nickname. He gathered himself up in his chair when the Morgans entered and dismissed his orderly with a curt nod, not taking his eyes from his visitors' faces nor his cigar from his mouth. When he noticed Robert Hunt he half rose, then decided not to exert himself, and moved the cigar from one corner of his mouth to the other.

Morgan stated the reason for the visit. Never, Nelson thought, had he seen a man so furious.

"Yes," he admitted. "I do recollect the Jacksons. Father and son. We drafted them this morning and sent them to Cincinnati for outfitting and assignment."

"Drafted?"

"They are free men—free to choose." Nelson lifted the cigar away from his face and drew his lips back over his teeth.

"And our four factory hands?" Morgan gave their names.

"I know nothing about them," Nelson said casually. "But I can tell you that it is not beyond possibility that they have been confiscated."

"Confiscated?"

"They are property of Southern sympathizers."

Robert's hand shot out toward Morgan's arm. "The Federal government, General Nelson," the doctor said evenly, "has stated unequivocally that property in this state would be inviolate."

"Not for traitors."

"What does that mean?" Cal got out.

"James Clay was arrested on his way south. Even now he is on his way to prison, near Boston. On his person was a letter from you, Mr. Morgan. Need I quote some damaging lines?"

"I was merely telling my brother of my wife's death, sir." Yes, he thought. Anger can be a pain, a rapier thrust in the middle, straight to the heart.

"And promising to help him," he heard Nelson say.

"I spoke of our uncle's—T.H. Hunt's—family in Lexington," Morgan said with emphatic slowness, to quiet the rage that threatened to shake his voice.

"That may be. Then again, it may not." Nelson stood up and his flat, broad face reddened. Fat bulged in front of his ears and made a greasy indention in his cheek. He had all the unthinking determination of a man who believes he is serving the public good, and the insolence of a man who has the means to do so.

Strangely, Morgan couldn't dislike him. Nelson was a machine, vain from wielding a power he thought was his own.

"I'll bet he never fought a duel," Charlton muttered to his uncle outside the tent. The *clink-clang* of a farrier's anvil came to them.

"That's an odd thing to say at a time like this," Robert remarked. "You aren't thinking of challenging him, are you?"

The idea was so grotesque that Morgan laughed out loud and two privates cleaning their guns nearby stopped and stared. But the laughter cleared the rage, and he breathed easier.

"Well, the money's gone," said Cal as they mounted. "Charl may be right. There may be enough undamaged machinery to crank up again."

Morgan untied his reins and flung them over the withers. He placed his left foot in the stirrup and swung up, fishing for the other iron. When he found it he settled back and looked at his brothers. Their worried faces waited. "We'll see if we can salvage the machines. If not . . . In the meantime we can use one end of the ropewalk. . . . And all hands can pitch in to clean up the place."

Already his mind was full of plans. He had lost four hands. All right. Money. Cal estimated eighteen thousand dollars in gold. He had to accept that. Pawns. But he still had a board full of knights and queens and bishops. He still had some faithful workers and—he smiled at them—the best brothers in the world. He trotted back to Lexington in good spirits.

The idea of making Confederate uniforms under the eyes of the Federals at Lexington and smuggling them south intrigued him. Why hadn't he thought of that before? He looked back at Cal and grinned.

"What the hell are you smiling about?" Cal called out.

Charlton, yes. Charlton. He would get Charlton to take the first shipment south. To Camp Boone. Wouldn't Tom die to see him?

For the next two days they worked like demons, clearing, cleaning, ordering hands about, and burning what could not be salvaged. In the middle of a cloud of dust, with his coat off and his sleeves rolled up, Morgan heard the news: Albert Sidney Johnston was on the move, and at the head of his column was Simon Bolivar Buckner!

Charlton breathlessly repeated the rumor: Buckner's advance had already seized the bridge over the Green River at Munfordville, and another detachment had burned a bridge at the Rolling Fork, only thirty-three miles from Louisville.

Key, his arms loaded with record books, dropped them and yelled, "Hurrah! Hurrah!"

"Do you know what this means?" Cal exploded. "With Polk at Columbus and Zollicoffer at the Gap, the Confederate line of defense runs from the Mississippi to the mountains—with Buckner threatening Louisville!" He searched a cupboard, uncorked a bottle of whiskey and they did a jig, right there among broken glass and charred, water-soaked wool.

On Wednesday the state legislature asked for Federal aid. Federal aid came quickly. The next day fifteen hundred Union soldiers set up camp at the fairgrounds a mile from town.

"Lexington's been invaded!" cried Henrietta. She became more belliger-
ent, not less so. When a servant appeared that night at the door from the
Gratz house, she said huffily to her sons, "Judge Gratz is a *Union* man. What
in the world can he want with John? Be careful . . ."

He crossed the garden and entered the familiar study. A candle gave out
a yellow, moving light. Ben Gratz was at his desk and turned abruptly at his
name.

"Yes, yes, John. Do sit down. How is your mother?"

"Fine, sir."

"Have a drink? A cigar?" When his guest declined the old man cleared his
throat. He seemed strangely ill at ease, but when Morgan made a joke about
Confederate flags he got up and shut the door. When he took his seat again
Morgan saw how pale he was.

Ben Gratz leaned forward and peered at his neighbor. "There's to be an
exodus." He stressed the word. "It has been determined by the Lincoln
government to make examples of those remaining in Kentucky who profess
sympathy for the South, and *to arrest at once* every public and influential man
in the state known to be critical of the Administration."

He stopped abruptly and turned his swivel chair on its steel screw to the
giant rolltop desk that filled one wall of the small room. From a cubbyhole
he pulled a folded paper and held it with a trembling hand toward the
candlelight. The paper shook.

"John C. Breckinridge. Colonel G. W. Johnson. William Preston. He was
our minister to Mexico."

"I know."

"Judge Monroe, of course." The old man looked over his spectacles.

"He's already left."

"No matter. I am reading you the names of those who will be declared
traitors. Any person on this list still present will be arrested at the same hour
and *consigned to prison*. Even"—he paused—"the former Vice-President of
the United States."

"Why are you telling me?"

"You are in good company, John."

The realization, like a chill, passed over him.

"For a *flag?*" he almost shouted.

"For having an uncle and two brothers in the Confederate service and for
expressing Southern sympathies."

"But everybody in town has relatives in that service. And name me a man
who hasn't expressed . . ."

Ben Gratz made no answer.

"I see."

"I hope you do, John."

"When?"

"As a loyal Union man, one who has taken the oath, I am not obliged to say."

"I see."

"But I could not issue a warrant for a neighbor's arrest without warning
him."

John Morgan looked up to honest suffering in the old man's eyes.

"Of course not."

By Friday a regiment of Federal cavalry under Colonel Frank Wolford was camped on the outskirts of town. Dick Curd came around with the news.

"Frank?"

"The world has changed, John."

Morgan looked back at Dick's worried face. His cheeks had turned pink above his porkchops.

"But that's not all I've come to tell you." In a lowered voice he said: "The order has been issued to disarm the State Guard."

At first he thought he hadn't heard clearly.

"You will surrender your guns to the Home Guard, or to the Federal troops. Tomorrow."

They were in his grandfather's office. On the desk lay an onyx-handled letter opener, a gift to John Hunt from Henry Clay. Morgan picked it up and turned it in his fingers.

"Thank you, Dick. I know how much it meant to you—to your principles —to warn me."

His nephew's sincerity was embarrassing. Dick Curd took the hand that was offered to him, shook it quickly, and left.

There wasn't a minute to lose. He had to think. He closed his eyes. *I've sold the factory. If I don't, they will take it anyway.* T.H. was right. And I've waited too long. They intend to take everything. No, by God, no!

In the dining room he found Cal, not yet gone to the factory. Trying to keep his voice calm, he asked him if he could step into the study for a minute.

"Who was that in the front entry, dear?" Henrietta asked.

"Uncle Frank," he lied. "Just wanted to know our latest news from Kitty." Once the door was closed he turned to Cal.

"They're disarming the Guard," he got out.

"Damn!"

"Finishing it off was a logical move, wasn't it? We should have foreseen that. And much more."

Cal's uplifted brows asked a silent question.

"Confiscation of property."

"Then I'll mortgage everything I can. Up to the hilt. What's left of the factory. The machinery—that should get several thousand, at least. I'll take only cash—hide it in Aunt Betty's skirts if I have to!"

Morgan's worried eyes turned up at the corners with his smile.

"I'm glad to hear you say that, Cally. Because I'm going south, and I want you to stay here and protect our interests." He had told nobody of the threat of arrest. Maybe Cal, who did not belong to the Guard, could escape harassment.

"I'll be damned if I'll let you go without me!" Cal exploded.

"And leave Ma here alone, with Key and Tommie?"

The picture was sobering.

"You know how much I want to go," Cal said needlessly.

Mexico and Alexander Gibson Morgan. Tommy Cunningham at Camargo. Zach Taylor at Buena Vista. "And you must know how much I'll need you," said Morgan hoarsely. He cleared his throat. "But Ma will need you more." He waited a long minute.

"What do you want me to do?"

"I want you to get two wagons ready," he said quickly. "Have Randolph send them from the farm to the armory, around back. Loaded *half full* with hay."

"Why would you need hay?"

Morgan didn't hear him, but kept rubbing his top lip with a forefinger, holding his jaw with his thumb. Then he threw his hand out with a laugh. "Make up a reason, if anybody asks. You were always good at making up reasons. Tell them you intend to spread it on the floor of the factory to soak up some of that mud." He scribbled quickly a list of twelve names. "Have these men behind the armory at exactly nine o'clock tonight. Ask West to call a special Friday-night drill meeting. We sometimes meet on Fridays, so there'll be nothing suspicious about that. Have everybody upstairs at the armory for a marching drill. Everybody except the twelve."

"I think I understand," grinned Cal.

"This morning I'll ride out to Shryock's Ferry and make arrangements. Yes," he said louder, as Henrietta knocked briefly and came in, "I think I'll ride out to Warren's about that new horse of his. Oh, hello, Ma. Would you like to go? It's a lovely day."

"No, thank you, John. You know how uncertain this late September weather is. Why, just last week we had that hailstorm. Came from nowhere."

"Well, I've got to be going," said Cal.

"Without finishing your breakfast? I've never known you not to finish your breakfast."

"That's right, Cal. Finish your breakfast. We'll need all the energy we can get."

"Now, what—" Henrietta began, but her eldest son kissed her so soundly on the cheek that she almost lost her balance.

To make his movements less conspicuous, Morgan did go to Warren Viley's farm, which was on the way to the ferry. He found a surprise.

"I know your intentions, John."

"You do?"

"It's in your eye. And I've been expecting it for weeks. I was frankly surprised that it hasn't come sooner. Now I have something to show you."

They walked back to the stables and stopped in front of a stall. Viley had a groom lead out a black mare.

"She's sired by Drennan," Viley said in his noncommittal way.

She was the most perfect beauty Morgan had ever seen, even in Kentucky. She was small—not fifteen hands high—but there was immense power in her short barrel, those broad loins and muscled thighs. Her head almost took his breath away. Wide-set eyes, and a nose that tapered down to a muzzle delicate enough, as Uncle Simon would have said, "to pick a lady's pocket."

Her superb neck was set deep into a pair of shoulders that gleamed like satin. As the groom walked her away and back, there was no mistaking the clean legs, with tendons like steel wires. Her hooves, like the rest of her, were deceptively small, but perfectly rounded, and as hard as flint.

"You've heard the old saying," Warren Viley said behind him. "A good horse should look like a lion and ride like a lamb. Well, this one looks like a lamb, but I'll guarantee you, John, she'll ride like a lion."

"You can't mean . . ."

"Now, you don't want to ride a horse with a blaze into battle, do you?" Viley said, careless of the groom, who stood flashing a smile. "That blaze can be seen a hundred yards away, a perfect target. I know Bess here has a bit of a star between her eyes, and two white hind pasterns. But the rest of her is pure night."

Morgan was still stunned. "Are you—?"

"Her name's Black Bess. She's yours," Warren Viley said.

The seven miles to Shyrock's Ferry, on the Kentucky River, was joy. She was sturdy, and held his hundred and eighty pounds, his six-foot-one frame, as if he were a feather. Her canter was a rocking chair, and her gallop a flowing line. But more amazing than her gaits was the feel of her heart, her spirit under and in him. Her responses were more than automatic—they were instinctual. It was almost as if she read his mind. She rode, as Uncle Simon would have said, "in the wind of the boot." The old man who ran the ferry watched them trot up with a gleam in his eye.

"Quite a hoss yew got there," he said.

Morgan dismounted and rubbed her neck. "Just got her this morning."

"Yew look like yew've been together always."

Nonchalantly, as if he had nothing better to do, Morgan rode with him across the river. On the way he admired the view and sounded the man on his political sympathies. He was a Southern man down to his toes. Once ashore, Morgan had little trouble finding a dozen men to play their parts later that night.

On the way back he stopped to thank the planter again, but Viley had gone into Versailles on business. He hadn't the time to stop by Amanda's on the way out, but now, with this much of his business done, he couldn't resist the temptation to turn into her drive.

"I didn't recognize you. In that blue overcoat and with a different horse, I thought . . ."

"I was one of your Federal friends?"

"May I get you something?"

"Yes."

She waited. "What, Johnny?"

"Freedom."

She read his mind. "Of course. Anything. Jake is having some Union officers to dinner. I could keep them awhile, if you like." She grinned.

"That would be convenient."

"Now. Anything else?"

"I may let you know."

She gave him a long look with her green eyes. "I'll miss you, Johnny," she whispered. "Take care of yourself."

By the time he got back to town he had word from Cal that his orders of the morning had been carried out. He rode Bess down Main Street to the factory, but he had missed Randolph by minutes. He had already returned to the farm.

"He left something for you," said Cal.

It was Jesse.

In the back room off the ropewalk the boy was waiting. "Pa sez to kum wif you, Marse John," he said uncertainly.

Morgan reached out and held his shoulder with a firm hand. "Of course. And welcome, Jesse. You'll be the best lieutenant I have."

The boy beamed.

So did the Rifles, when they learned the plan. They assembled after supper at the armory and even welcomed several Federal soldiers from Camp Dick Robinson who had stopped by to watch the drill. They drilled exceedingly well, tramping noisily across the boards on the second floor. Downstairs, they knew, quieter but more important work was going on. Morgan was not there, but since his wife's death, that was not unusual. The Federals had come to expect his absence. But, as duly ordered, packing cases were lined against the walls, heavy enough to contain the guns these same Union men were to pick up the next day. They contained rocks.

Downstairs and behind the armory James West was quietly urging the loading of the two hay wagons when a shadowy figure appeared from the alley. The boys stopped, frozen, for an instant. The man walked out of the shadows. Upstairs the histrionic stamping grew louder. Had the Rifles overdone their act? From here, the man's overcoat looked blue. Lieutenant West drew a revolver from his belt and waited. The round face and blond head of Cripps Wickliffe emerged from the darkness.

"Whew! You gave me a turn!" West breathed. "I thought you lived in Bardstown."

Wickliffe ignored the remark. "What are you doing?" he asked. When he understood, he laughed so loud West threw a hand over his face.

"Delighted! Delighted!" Wickliffe got out. "When . . . ?"

"As soon as we are ready. Captain Morgan will go with us across the river, then return to town to get more men tomorrow," West whispered.

Wickliffe nodded, and scribbled a note. "Here, give him this."

Jesse, ambling along in his shuffling way, passed by the alley behind the armory, then walked as slowly to Hopemont. Once inside the back door, he burst forth with the news: The guns had been loaded in the hay and the men were ready to ride to the ferry. In the carriage yard, Adam had Black Bess ready. Morgan would ride with them, at least until they were out of danger, then return to Lexington. "My guess is," he told Cal, "they won't arrest me until they find the guns have gone. By then"—he winked—"it will be too late."

The night, luckily, had clouded over. There was no moon, and a rain that fell earlier that day had disappeared. The ground was just moist enough to absorb sound. As quietly as possible, the men behind the armory pulled off. They had had no notice of their plans, no chance to pack extra clothes. But without a word of protest they belted on cartridge boxes and shouldered loaded rifles. There was Tom Quirk, shrewd as an Irish peasant and quick as a fox; already Morgan, in his mind, had pegged him as a future scout. There was Pleasant Whitlow, a sweet boy with a stammer who could be trusted completely. Ralph Sheldon—who could describe the way that boy could ride? The others—Tom Logwood, Henry Elder, Jim Howe, and Xenophon Hawkins—were good solid sorts who knew when to keep their mouths shut and their heads down, but were dead shots when they needed to be. Five more made their number seventeen, and Morgan met them outside of town, where the Versailles Road met Parker's Mill.

"I didn't see you!" Pleasant Whitlow called out softly. "Where'd you get that black horse?"

"That's the purpose," Morgan smiled back.

Tomorrow he would gather more men. And by tomorrow night he would meet these boys, God willing, in the barn across the Kentucky River, and they would be on their way south.

South! It was on all their minds, and had taken on all the glories of a Promised Land. It was all they could do to keep from singing. He left them just as the lights of Amanda's Italianate house came into view, and watched them safely past, knowing that Union officers were inside having a good time. He trotted back to Hopemont, patting Black Bess on the neck as he went. "Don't want to tire you, ole girl. We've got many a mile ahead of us, I hope." Around him the night was as black as his horse. Good.

Jesse, unknown in the town as a Hopemont servant, was busy with verbal messages. By midnight, besides the seventeen, Morgan had twenty committed men, with horses and arms, ready to move immediately. Jesse would go with them. Unlike the men with the wagons, the rest of his force was fully prepared. By morning, he knew, the Federals would discover their loss, and an order for his arrest would be immediate. He rose before sunup and left his brothers still eating breakfast to follow his mother into the study. She stood before him, a plump little figure of a woman. Like Bess, he thought. Inside, all iron. He lifted her hand to his mouth and kissed her fingers.

"I knew you'd go," she whispered, her eyes lingering on a wisp of his hair at the back of his neck. "You are a Hunt, and the Hunts are honorable men."

He brushed her fingers against his cheek. "And the Morgans," he murmured.

"And the Morgans." Her hand touched his head in light, hesitant strokes. Then, impulsively, she let her upper body fall on his and buried her face against him. But it was only for a moment. When he straightened to look at her she was standing bolt upright with a smile on her face.

"May the Good Lord bless and keep you," she said brightly. Her hand in his was firm. "Now call Charlton."

"You know?"

"Of course. How could he help not?" She became intense, and frowned. "Key—he stays."

"Of course."

"He's only a boy."

"Of course . . ."

"He'll try to run after you, but you must promise to send him home."

"I will, Ma."

"And Tom. When you meet. You must take care of him."

"I will." He smiled then at her intensity. "And me? Who will take care of me?"

"My prayers."

He watched her standing there, receiving her sons, admitting them, extracting motherly promises. She might have been Boadicea or, as his father had said so often, a Roman matron.

They would leave an hour apart. Charlton would go first, down Main Street directly west, as if he were going out to the farm or to the factory, then cut across a lane behind the trotting track to the Frankfort Pike. Another back road would take him across Elkhorn Creek to the rendezvous halfway between Amanda's and the Viley plantation. Morgan would ride north, down Newtown Pike as if headed toward Ironworks Road and another party with the Castlemans at Castleton, then swing back west behind the Leestown farm to the Versailles Road. It would be longer, but more elusive, with a half-dozen side roads to use in case he was followed.

Charlton had already left when he came down the back stairs into the warming room.

"What you doin' heah, Marse John?"

He thought Aunt Hannah would have a fit. What did she think? That he could hide upstairs indefinitely?

"To tell you good-bye. Where's Key?"

Before she could answer they heard firing from Main Street.

"I'll go!" said Adam from the corner. They hadn't noticed he was there. When Morgan nodded, he slipped out the back door.

"Well, I smell pancakes!"

"You dooz?"

But when Annie set them on the table he cocked his head to listen.

"Better eat hearty, Marse John."

"Sounds like a warning."

Aunt Hannah sucked in her breath. "It is."

When Adam came back with the news that four of the Rifles and some of the Federals had a shootout at the armory, Aunt Hannah dropped her spoon and sank down by the hearth, watching them all with round eyes. A sound from the hall made them jump. It was Tommie, sobbing and wiping her face with a handkerchief. Johnny kissed her and held her against his coat. His mother had told him good-bye earlier, and superstitiously refused to see him again. Key came in and stood to one side, still numbed by the proceedings. "I'll send for you as soon as I can," Morgan said again, but saw that the boy didn't believe him. Cal shot him a grin and he shook Cal's hand, then impulsively gave him a bear hug. They stood silently for a long minute pounding each other's backs. Then Morgan found himself standing by the back door looking past them at Aunt Betty, coming down the stairs. She said nothing, only looked at him with her coon-dog's eyes, swollen with tears and loss of sleep. They would always be among his most beautiful memories of Kentucky.

Part III

September 1861-July 1862

28

There was not a moment to lose. By the time he reached the rendezvous the horses were fidgeting and some of the men had dismounted to take strategic positions with their pistols, just in case. A horizontal glow lit the fields. Without a word, James West and the others remounted and set out at a soft canter, careful to stay on the grass wherever the stone fences allowed. When they did use the road they dropped back to a trot. Amanda's house was quiet as a sleeping cat. Just past the Viley plantation a flock of birds bunched and circled, spread and bunched again, slicing the air, heading south. For the first time since he left Lexington John Morgan relaxed. He watched them, a black cloud leveling out like a shelf to catch the rising sun. It seemed an omen, although, he kept telling himself, they are only migrating, as they've done every September for a hundred thousand years. This year, though, seemed special. Unconsciously, he was holding his breath.

They were just descending to the ferry when they heard the staccato hoofbeats of a galloping horse behind them. They took cover, pistols cocked. The horse sped by, then stopped and returned at a walk, the rider studying the ground like an Indian. Bill Kennett, nearest the road, shifted slightly and the rider looked up. Charlton yelled out before Kennett could shoot. The rider was Key.

"What are you doing here?"

The boy had never seen his brother look so stern. He almost broke into tears.

"And in a *blue* overcoat. Don't you know you're likely to get yourself killed?"

"Cally . . . Cally's been arrested!" the boy got out. He turned his eyes from Charlton's red face to Johnny in the shade of a tree behind him.

"Get down," Morgan said softly. "Come over here. No. Keep your horse's head to me. That white blaze can be seen at thirty yards." He tried to keep his voice even. Cal. "When?"

"About an hour ago. And they say they'll take Aunt Hannah and Aunt Bet. . . ." Key turned horrified eyes up to his brother's face. "I've *got* to come with you, Brother Johnny! For the Cause! You said so yourself, that if we don't all do—"

Two hands held his shoulders. "Cal's arrested? Well, don't you see? With Cal gone, you're the man of the house now. You've got to stay. . . ." Morgan's eyes searched the boy's face. Finally Key looked down and nodded.

Something in the shaking shoulders made Morgan add: "Later. Maybe later I can send for you. If I promise to send for you when the time is right?"

Key looked up. "Promise?"

"Promise. Gentleman's honor. In the meantime you have a big job to do at home. You have two helpless women and a houseful of servants to care for. You understand?"

When he nodded Morgan let go his shoulders and went on in a fatherly voice. "Remember what I told you. If there's any trouble, see Uncle Dick. He's a Union man, and they trust him. He'll know what to do."

If they take the farm . . . no, I can't tell him that. He has enough to think about. "Now go back as fast as you can. Avoid Versailles. Take the old cut-off behind Aman . . . behind Stonewall. Then go north to the farm. Have some breakfast with Randolph. They'll think you've just been out there hunting or something. . . ."

His conspiratorial tone did the trick. Key's face brightened. It was a glorious adventure, after all.

They watched him trot back toward Versailles and turned briskly to their own business, aware that minutes had been lost which might prove precious. Luckily, the ferry was on their side of the river, and large enough to accommodate fifteen men and horses in one trip. Still, the loading, crossing, and unloading took the best part of an hour. Once on the other side, under the great hanging curtain of limestone cliffs, the men mounted, noisily calling out and waving to the ferryman, who stood, hands on hips, grinning at their exuberance. When their horses scrambled up the narrow ascent to rolling fields they threw out their chests and sang at the tops of their voices. Leading them, not singing himself but allowing his face to spread in a smile, John Hunt Morgan went to war.

He let them finish one good round of "Cheer, Boys, Cheer" before holding up his hand, palm flat, toward them. No sense in asking for trouble. And Cal, dear Cal, was gone.

It was almost sundown by the time they reached the barn where Tom Quirk greeted them with a high tale of capturing a Federal soldier, scaring him with threats of scalping, then letting him go twenty miles out of town. So that caused the little affair at the armory? No, in any case they would have come for the guns and found them gone. The flick of a frown left his face, and Morgan shared his men's elation at getting away so cleanly.

But night was coming on, and wagons meant they had to stay with the roads. He unfolded and read again the smudged note in his pocket. "Meet me at a place about two miles west of Bloomfield on the Bardstown Road. We call it Camp Charity and you'll know why when you see it. My *ex*-State Guard company will be there waiting for you. There's strength in numbers. Don't go south without us. Wick."

In the dim light of the barn the farmer, with his family, arrived in a wake of servants bearing a good supper. With the Federals just across the Kentucky River, they heard with relief that their guests would be leaving before sunup. The men had time for only a few hours' sleep. They left their horses saddled. Tom Logwood woke them with the smell of coffee, and they drank deep before swinging up.

It was almost sundown before they heard a firm yet cautious "Who goes there?" ring out on a rise of land beyond Bloomfield.

"Recruits for the Confederate Army," Morgan answered stoutly, barely able to suppress a grin from his grimy face.

At the main camp they were challenged again, but this time it was a mere formality, for the guard on duty recognized the Rifles uniforms and led them to "headquarters," a tent on a rise at the southeast edge of a field. Inside, John Cripps Wickliffe rose from behind a rough board table and held out his hand. "It's about time. I've been worried sick. Expected you yesterday."

"Camp Charity" was lush Nelson County pastureland, with shelves of grass-covered limestone overlooking a stream that provided water for the hundred or so men already gathered in tents or under blankets drawn over fence rails to simulate shelter.

Ben Bruce rode in two hours later with the latest news from Lexington. The little affair at the armory had brought from the fairgrounds two pieces of Federal artillery, which were planted to sweep Main Street.

"It was good you left when you did."

"And you?"

"It's time we all left."

From Bardstown, Boston, Springfield and a dozen little towns, more recruits came to swell the ranks, most without horses, some without guns. A week later, two hundred would-be soldiers started south for Bowling Green. Elected their leader by common consent, John Morgan rode at the head of the column. It was evening, since a night march was safer: Saturday the 28th of September. With the supply wagons and the men on foot, the going would be slow. And cautious: They knew that the country between Nelson County and the Green River, where Buckner's advance guard held Munfordville on the Louisville & Nashville Railroad, would be thick with Home Guards and bushwhackers. When scouts reported two separate groups, Morgan gave the signal to close up and pass between them at the double-quick. The maneuver scared both and gave the new Rebels something to joke about. By the last day of September they reached the south side of the Green, opposite Munfordville. They'd marched over a hundred miles in thirty-six hours. The welcome was thunderous.

How could he know, then, how intimate each hill and valley of that Green River country would become for him? Hollows hid between sudden ridges, and soft valleys sent mists through cedars. Now, in this first week of October, turning leaves promised an early autumn. The Green River had the clearest, greenest water he had ever seen. On its southern bank "Camp Woodsonville" spread out for a quarter of a mile, with upturned drums and powder kegs serving as recruiting tables, around which the latest influx of volunteers swarmed, his own men now jostling and joking among them. Did they realize the significance of what they were doing?

Roger Hanson's pickets here at Munfordville were the outermost advance of the Confederate center. With Buckner in Bowling Green, the total line extended from the Cumberland Gap to the Mississippi—over three hundred miles long.

Albert Sidney Johnston watched this thin line from his headquarters in

Nashville. From there, on his maps, it must have looked like the fringe of a shawl thrown across Kentucky. Could they hold back the fifty thousand—some rumors said one hundred thousand—Yankees under Sherman, who had already started pushing down from Louisville along the railroad as far as Elizabethtown and Nolin Creek, just north of Munfordville? Johnston's army couldn't boast six thousand men, a good number of them armed with nothing but old smoothbore flintlocks, and some not armed at all.

Morgan was not unaware of the risks they were taking. But all worry faded when he noticed a man in a gray coat and the high soft boots of a Confederate officer talking with a younger man, who was listening intently. From the blue facing of the collar he knew the officer was Infantry. From the slightly rounded shoulders, the leg thrust out, the gesturing hands and bent head, he knew it must be T.H.

"Wait! Wait!"

He had never felt a hug like that.

"Johnny! I knew you'd come. I didn't know when, of course, but I knew . . . Where's Cal?"

He told him.

T.H. sobered, then looked up. "Cal can take care of himself. Don't worry, Johnny. These civilian arrests are never for long. Looks like a case of simple retaliation to me. Cal will talk his way out of it. You know Cal!"

Once inside his tent T.H. bubbled with news. Basil Duke was with General Hindman at Bell's Tavern, just thirteen miles away, between this camp and Bowling Green. Young Sam Morgan was with him. "Came back with me from Nashville."

"Nashville?"

"I went down there to see about munitions. You didn't know your uncle Sam is turning out over a ton of gunpowder a day, and has a new gun factory going up on South Cherry Street?"

"So that's where you got the uniform."

"I thought you'd notice."

"Charlton is with me."

"I could have guessed."

"And your aide?"

"You mean my best aide? Gone to Colonel Hanson's tent with a message. Won't he be surprised to see you!"

"Brother Johnny!"

They thought Tom would burst. But he was full of his own news, a cavalry fight just reported to headquarters. "Brother Johnny, you should have heard!"

Forrest . . . Forrest. The name ran like a fire through the camp.

"Who is he?"

"Businessman from Memphis," said T.H. "You wouldn't want him for an enemy. Smoother than a snake. Not like your usual cavalry leader." He shook his head.

"How are they?"

"Oh . . . I suppose it's not their fault. They follow orders."

"Which are?"

"To patrol the countryside. Each with a designated area."

"Sounds dull."

"Just a little more exhilarating than drill, I should say."

Tom, looking thinner but fit, was still gawking at his brother as if he had dropped from the moon.

"Charlton is here," he said, grinning.

"He *is?* Where?"

"Out there, somewhere. We brought two wagonloads of guns. And Jesse . . ."

"Jesse?"

Tom ran ahead, and they followed him to the wagons. Jesse was perched on a box at the back of the second wagon.

"How are you, boy?" T.H. asked kindly, after Tom stopped bubbling and walked off to find Charlton. "Can you make ash cake?"

"Nawsah."

"You'll learn soon enough. What's in that box you're sitting on?"

Jesse grew nervous, sprung back the hasp and looked in. "Well, I'll be!" Morgan laughed. Randolph had sent horseshoes.

"Don't laugh," his uncle said grimly. "Just pray you keep enough horses fit to use them."

It was true. Three had already become spavined on the hard march down, and another had a bad splint on the near fore. Good mounts were scarce. Some of his dismounted men, disappointed, joined infantry outfits. Within an hour, Cripps had decided to sign on with the infantry regiment T.H. was trying to form.

"No cheating at cards, now!"

They shook hands, each wondering when or if they would meet again.

Colonel Roger "Bench-leg" Hanson was delighted to see Morgan again. He lumbered up out of his chair and reached across his desk, pumping his hand. The days at the trotting track came back, when Hanson "commanded" the Lexington drill teams.

"I've got a new nickname," Hanson growled. "It's 'Ole Flintlock' now. I don't mind the name, just the adjective. . . ." Hanson's van Dyke had spread into a soft bush under his chin, but his mouth was still firm, his eyes as piercing. "I'll find plenty for your boys to do, you may be sure." He searched his cluttered desk for a clean sheet of paper, gave up, found an envelope and scribbled.

Once outside, Morgan pulled it from his pocket and read Hanson's scrawl: "Captain John H. Morgan is directed to take all the mounted force he can procure and proceed up Green River and scout along the railroad this side of Nolin and the Powder Mills." He walked over, checked Bess, then saw to the setting up of his "headquarters" in an old church at the edge of the camp.

When T.H. saw the orders he drew his mouth back and shrugged. Morgan waited. "Scout along the railroad, is it? That's all they ever do." He turned to his nephew with sudden energy. "See here, Johnny, if you want to see some real action, you'll need men of experience. I have to go to Bowling Green. On the way we could stop and see Basil. . . ."

Morgan jumped at the chance.

At Bell's Tavern the train stopped long enough for them to run across the tracks to General Hindman's headquarters. They saw Basil almost immediately, skipping down the steps, tucking orders into his jacket. He turned on his heels and introduced them to Hindman, a burly, impatient man who had seen action in Missouri. The General stood, his legs apart on the wide boards of the porch. Behind him a tall young officer named Shaver reached past his commander to shake hands.

Hindman began insisting that they stay the night, but T.H. kept to his plan of going on to Bowling Green that day. As if to echo him the engine blew its whistle.

"I have a favor to ask," said T.H.

"Certainly."

"May Lieutenant Duke accompany us?"

"As a matter of fact, I have some dispatches he can take with him. So you see you will do *me* a favor," Hindman smiled.

"He'd be a great man to work for," Morgan told Basil, as they waited for the railroad crew to take on more water and firewood.

"I'm hoping, now you're here, we can work together," Basil said over another whistle.

Morgan said nothing. He looked off across the October fields and the curve of double iron tracks stretching between. A hawk flew overhead, his *skree, skree* trailing away, a disappointed sound. A gray colt bounding. Already it seemed so long ago. And so unimportant. As he was now. He had no "command"—only a handful of boys and scribbled orders to play hide-and-seek. Basil had an official commission, with a legitimate assignment. He felt the volunteer's inadequacy before the usefulness of those already "mustered in."

As they mounted the steps Sam Morgan, Jr., ran up and there was another "family reunion." "Now we'll win, by golly!" Not yet twenty, Sam reminded Morgan of Tom. With sandy hair where Tom's was dark, and pudgy cheeks where Tom's were thin, Sam had that same contagious enthusiasm. How could he let them down?

They left Sam on the platform and watched through the train windows, smudged thick with smoke, the "knobs" north of the Barren River, hills heavy with beech, oak, poplar, walnut, sugar maples and pawpaws. The pastures here, Basil explained, were called barrens—hence the name of the river.

His voice was suddenly drowned out by a sound like thunder. Morgan instinctively reached for his pistol: It sounded like distant artillery. Ahead of them and on both sides of the tracks horsemen and wagons were spread for a quarter of a mile.

"What?"

Basil laughed, then pointed to a grove of timber that extended several miles over one of the knobs. Out of it millions of birds swelled like a giant blanket flung in the wind. Their fluttering wings created a booming squabble like nothing Morgan had ever heard. Some of the horsemen raised their guns and hundreds fell.

"Pigeon roost!" Basil called out over the din. "Smith's Grove. They've just started. Wait till the real migration gets here!" The hunters made way for the train. It was a strange war.

Bowling Green, however, was all business. He had never seen a town so tense, so full of bustle. Brass twelve-pounders glistened from a bluff on the river. Buckner had set up headquarters in a house at Adams and Plain streets. Downstairs, on the ground floor, there were enough rooms for the family to continue living there—Sam Blackburn, a Mexican War veteran with six daughters.

"Yes," laughed Basil. "There's Jeanie, Kate, Amanda, Juliette, Minnie, and Josephine . . . and young ladies from Nashville who give concerts for hospital funds. . . ."

"Sounds as if this town is busy with more than war."

They were passing the hospital, where deaths from measles were mounting daily. "Oh, it is," murmured T.H.

Buckner was delighted. That same determination, those same snapping eyes, that commanding presence. Morgan had forgotten just how much this man meant to him.

"So you've brought your Rifles." Buckner motioned them into seats and pulled at his mustache. His chin was clean-shaven, as if he refused to conceal the strength of his jaw. A muscle in it twitched. He accepted Basil's dispatches, tore their seals and read quickly, pursing his lips. "Yes, that's fine. Tell General Hindman I concur fully." He wrote quickly and handed them back. "How many men have you now?" he shot out at Morgan. When Morgan told him, Buckner grinned as if at a secret joke. "They'll be more, and shortly, Captain Morgan. You're at the Green?"

"Woodsonville, sir."

Buckner nodded and would have said more, but an aide, anxious with apologies, stepped in and said from the doorway, "Those gentlemen from Nashville, sir."

"Yes, oh yes. Well!" He rose and extended his hand to each of them. "I won't forget you," he said firmly. His handshake was as quick and as decisive as his eyes.

Ben Helm was there with a cavalry regiment, which he drilled and inspected with West Point alacrity. At the depot recruits were arriving from Camp Boone. Couriers dashed up and down the stone steps of Buckner's headquarters. Buggies, wagons, gigs and fancy carriages crowded the streets. But underneath the carnival was the grim knowledge that Johnston, down in Nashville, was trying to make an army out of ragged, raw volunteers, and Buckner, up here on the Barren at Bowling Green, was holding a tenuous position. The Union troops they would face were Western men— frontier-bred and as at home with an eye down a rifle as any. There were no New England Yankees here. They would have their hands full and knew it, under all those boasts that "One Reb could take on ten Yankees and still be back for supper." Down on the riverbank infantry sergeants were drilling barefoot recruits.

Basil, standing beside Morgan, looked on with amusement.

"I don't laugh, though," he said, after a minute. He shook his head and gazed off. "No, I don't laugh." Basil was twenty-three, just a year older than Charlton, and had already seen enough action to make him cautious. Always quiet, with a dry wit, he had, in these dark moods, a remoteness akin to premonition. He turned his broad, handsome face, which could, when he was intense, look like a bulldog's, to his brother-in-law and smiled. "I want to join you. We've got to win this war."

"I can't let you, Basil. I'm nothing. Just a volunteer among a thousand. I have a handful of boys . . . no command."

"You will have. Give yourself time."

Morgan felt a grim little smile tug at the corner of his mouth. "Among these West Point types?"

Two days later T.H. Hunt had a colonel's commission in his pocket and permission to set up a separate camp for his infantry regiment just outside Bowling Green. In the same dispatch Basil received permission from Buckner, with General Hindman's agreement to be confirmed, to transfer to "Morgan's company."

"Now," he said, suppressing a grin, "we'll start fighting this war in earnest!"

He stood there, dear, dependable Basil. Morgan took his hand and felt a warmth of gratitude flood his chest.

"You're damned right we will."

For three weeks, every night, they set out on their "excursions," not returning for twenty-four hours, just in time to set out again. They drove in Yankee pickets and chased some all the way to Nolin Creek, in full view of the Federal advance position. They learned to sleep in their saddles and could smell a bushwhacker in a thicket faster than a dog could flush a bird. Twice their captain, in a blue overcoat, passed himself off as a Federal officer, and they joked all the way back to camp.

Once, with fifteen of his own men and twenty-five Tennesseans, Morgan almost got too close. Not four hundred yards off his men could see rows of bayonets glistening, just visible above a little rise in the road. Their own horses were steaming and restless, threatening to snort. Morgan ordered a dismount, every fourth man a horse-holder. Some of the men looked at him quizzically. Who knows, he thought. They may end up calling me Mad John Morgan. But it worked for Will. . . . Once the horses were led away, his men, settled in bushes on both sides of the road, waited breathlessly. Morgan again held up his hand for silence. The bayonets had stopped just beyond the rise. What were they doing?

Alone, he walked about a hundred and fifty yards to an empty house. From the parlor window he could see them clearly, a body of about seventy

Yankee infantrymen walking toward the front porch. He slipped out the kitchen door before he could determine whether this was merely a scout or an advance for a heavier force down the road.

Once back with his men he intended to order a remount, but before he could reach Bess, he heard a voice from behind. He was discovered! He stepped into the road in full view of a Federal officer. Here it was. His men were watching. With no emotion at all he raised his pistol and fired. The man fell. The war had begun.

His shot was answered by a volley from the house, now fully occupied. If they had been just a little sooner, or a little rasher, they could be in that house now, with its commanding position. Only the thicket and the trees saved them from a fatal mistake. Morgan saw the reproach on Basil's face. With James West, Tom Quirk and Tom, he crept forward, working his way to a spot within good range of the front porch. But these antics did little good: A breathless horse-holder ran up with the news that they were being outflanked by a Federal reinforcement, just arrived.

"He's read too many newspapers," James West moaned the next day when they learned from their scouts that no reinforcements had come after all, and that the infantry had started retreating about the same time Morgan's company did.

But it whetted their spirits. If they could get that close and come away with only one man slightly wounded and several more just shot through their clothes . . . well! They breathed easier, became braver, and belonging to "Morgan's company" was something to brag about.

Hanson, delighted, ordered some condemned artillery horses assigned to the outfit. Morgan accepted gladly; with a little care, they could replace some badly exhausted mounts and allow rotation. After that, one scout was accomplished with most of the men riding these rejected horses: They covered sixty-eight miles in twenty hours.

It was good, he thought, that they had something to brag about. The Confederate Army paid its infantry privates eleven dollars a month. It paid its cavalry exactly nothing. "I guess they think our kind can live off the land," some of the men grumbled good-naturedly, but it was a grumble just the same. How could they expect respect from loyal Southerners if they became scavengers? And when they invaded Federally-held territory, how could they expect to win converts to the Cause if they stole supplies? And how could they refrain from pilfering if they were kept hungry and ill-clad by their own government?

Hanson realized the problem. "The cavalry—somehow they think all you need is glory. I'll see what can be done."

The infantry, too, was giving Hanson headaches. Outside his tent men would look at each other and grin as that voice rose: "Sick, sick! Why, sir, I was twelve months with the Army in Mexico and wasn't sick a day! A furlough, sir? Why, I was twelve months with the Army in Mexico and didn't know what a furlough meant!"

"That's why they call him Ole Flintlock," whispered Basil, chuckling.

But they loved him, and laughed with rather than at him the day he tried his "Mexican veteran" routine with a drunken soldier. "Drunk, sir, drunk? Why, I was with the Army in Mexico for twelve months and . . . and . . ."

To their laughter, without a word, he walked away.

After the little "turn" Morgan's boys had with the Yankees at the empty house, Hanson determined to send a larger detail to the Federal outposts, drive them in and cause a real alarm. "They're getting entirely too uppity, sirs," he said, hunching his shoulders.

"Yes, sir."

This time it would be a real force. Hanson ordered a Tennessee major with two hundred and forty cavalrymen to be conducted by Morgan, with his twenty, to attack the Union advance at Nolin Creek. "Lord," said Tom Logwood, when they assembled, "I ain't seen so menny hosses in one place in my life. Nobody kin beat us now."

But five miles from Nolin Creek the Tennesseans turned back.

"Turned back!" Morgan spurred Bess and caught up with the Major. The man was utterly cowed.

"They've heard the alarm, Captain. We'd be walking into an ambush!"

Morgan looked at the Major's watery blue eyes and determined to go on by himself. To a man, his company agreed. They rode to the point where the enemy pickets usually operated. The place was deserted. Nothing but dry leaves and the sound of a nearby creek made a noise. He ordered a halt, not a dismount, and looked around at their faces. They would need to scout. Private Sisson caught his eye. Silently, he motioned him to follow.

Duke, left in command, was surprised to see Captain Biffel, of the Tennessee battalion, coming up with about twenty men. Disgusted at the Major's behavior, he had decided to help Morgan. No sooner had his men ridden into the thicket across the road than a column of Federal cavalry appeared not a hundred yards away. Basil signaled absolute quiet. If they fired, Morgan and Sisson were certain prisoners, for this was a large detachment, and they would be no match for it, even with Biffel's reinforcement.

The men held their breaths. October leaves drifted down. A bird called, breaking the silence. The Yankees stopped in the road and just stayed there for about twenty minutes, consulting. Then they turned and galloped off. Morgan and Sisson returned, out of breath. They had had a close call, running, lying in the brush.

"I was afraid they would attack you. There must have been a hundred and twenty of them!" Morgan said, out of breath.

"And what would you have done, on foot as you were?" Basil frowned. His captain took too many chances.

Nothing, Morgan answered to himself. They had done nothing during these weeks but spook around in the woods and play tag with Yankee pickets. His men had learned to handle fatigue, to ride hard and to let their stomachs be satisfied with cornmeal wrapped in corn shucks stuck on a stick into campfires—the "ash cakes" T.H. had joked about—and to tolerate inadequate clothing and downpours. On the worst nights they crowded into the little church at Woodsonville and slept bunched in corners. This was his "army." Audacious they might be, but how much could twenty men accomplish?

Then, to his utter astonishment an order came from Buckner's adjutant: "I am directed by General Buckner to say that if you can buy horses in your neighborhood, the Quartermaster can be ordered to purchase them. Can you arm yourselves with shotguns? Sabers will be furnished as soon as they can be provided."

"Hurrah!" shouted Charlton.

"Not so hurrah yet," cautioned Basil. "You haven't had to deal with the Confederate quartermaster. They'll take weeks, and then squabble."

"Then I'll buy them myself, and hope to be reimbursed later," Morgan said quietly. "Those artillery horses have done good service, but we can't expect more. Get the word out."

They did. Farmers around began coming in, and Charlton wrote out the receipts for them: "Rec'd of Capt. John H. Morgan one hundred and twenty-five dollars for one sorrel mare I warrant sound. . . . Rec'd of Jno. Morgan one hundred and twenty dollars for a bay horse and rifle."

"It's not enough, not if we're to increase our strength," Morgan said.

"What will you do?"

"Go to Nashville." He grinned at his brother's mournful look. "All right, Charl. You can come along. You, too, Tom. Basil will have to hold the fort."

"What about me?" asked Sam, who had transferred into "Morgan's company" at Woodsonville. "I know Nashville like the palm of my hand. And maybe Paw will throw in some bargains."

Morgan laughed outright. "All right, all right. You Tennessee Morgans are all alike. Yankees under the skin . . ." At his cousin's stricken look he added: "Good traders, that is."

They went by train, and brought back enough caps, shirts, pants, and gloves for hard-riding cavalry service. "After this, we'll let the other Uncle Sam supply us," Morgan joked.

He enjoyed that week in Nashville. Charlton ticked off the receipts:

13 overcoats at $10 each	$130
9 overcoats at $7	$ 63
9 doz. gauntlets @ $9	$ 81
1 pr. silk hdkfs	$ 5
box and drayage	$ 1
Total	$280

"*Silk handkerchiefs?*" blurted Sam Morgan, Sr., indignantly. "You're fighting a war, John."

"But in style." His nephew grinned. "I forgot scented soap. Can you find me some? Just to set your fears at rest, Uncle, here's an order for guns. . . ."

Albert Sidney Johnston had his headquarters at Edgefield, across the Cumberland. The day before they left, Morgan and his brothers and cousin waited in an anteroom, hats in hand turning slowly across their knees, for two hours. Tired of watching polished boots march across the red flowered carpet, Morgan was about to leave when a young lieutenant stepped purposefully toward them, his body bent in a polite bow. "The General will see you now."

That same high forehead, the sandy-brown hair streaked with gray now, its single lock making a point, as if to say: This is the face, this is the man. Those same drawn-in brows, only drawn in a bit more now, to make two vertical lines above the nose. Morgan had forgotten how intense those eyes could be. There was a certain sense of tragedy about them, as if Albert Sidney Johnston were looking into your soul and determined to accept with utter resignation whatever he found there. It was a look that made men do their best. It was a look that John Morgan remembered from Monterrey and, reinforced now, would take to his grave. It was the look of honor.

Johnston broke the spell by flashing his brilliant smile, white teeth against tanned face below his corsair's mustache, and holding out his hand. He rose to his full height, his broad shoulders and massive chest denying his fifty-eight years.

"I've heard of your exploits," he surprised them by saying. "Colonel Hanson in his reports has often mentioned 'Morgan's company.' When do you intend to muster in officially?"

"As soon as possible," said Morgan. Charlton, Sam and Tom echoed his words with nods.

"We need every good man we can get." Johnston paused, this magnificent man who could inspire instant love. The image of a torn red shirt and cool courage in that eternity of walking beside Davis down that street in Monterrey . . . that moment from the past seemed to hold them as their eyes met. "I'm sorry the capital has been moved to Richmond," Johnston confided, and would have said more, but a knock made him look up, and he accepted a dispatch from an aide.

"Well, I see you are busy, General. Thank you for seeing us."

"Are you leaving today?"

"Yes."

"Hmm. Would the twenty-seventh do?"

"Yes, sir!"

"Tell your men."

Once back at Woodsonville, the news spread: Morgan's company would be officially mustered into the service of the Confederacy. Colonel William Preston Johnston, the General's son, came up for the ceremony. It was held at the old church on October 27, 1861. The oath was administered to eighty-four men. Basil Duke, Greenberry Roberts and James Smith were elected First Lieutenants; James West, Sam McKee, A. Z. Boyer, Van Buren Sellers, Charlton and Sam Morgan, Second Lieutenants. The Sergeants were all good men: Houston, Lewis, Bethard, Morris, Stanhope, Berry, Elder. Tom Logwood and John Sprague made Corporal. Some of his best men were among the Privates: Xenophon Hawkins, Walter Ferguson, Ben Drake, Tom Quirk, Winder Monroe, and Tom Morgan. The elections took on the mood of a picnic, with many questionable remarks about marksmanship and courage. Colonel Johnston, obviously amused but attentive to duty, spent some time in Colonel Hanson's tent before taking the train for Bowling Green. After he left, Hanson announced to them that Albert Sidney Johnston had just sent word that his Army of Kentucky was officially organized, and that he would move headquarters from Nashville to Bowling Green tomorrow. A great cheer went up. The Army of Kentucky! Of course. What else could he call it? They were on their way.

"Yes . . . on our way backwards," Charlton announced an hour later. Orders were that when the Confederates consolidated at Bowling Green, Hanson and his cavalry would leave Woodsonville.

"In other words, retreat," someone said.

"Not necessarily," John Morgan replied.

He spoke firmly, to give them courage. Behind his words he could see the Union forces accumulating, all across the North, pouring down from Louisville into central Kentucky. But he said, "With General Johnston moving his headquarters to Bowling Green, he is obviously adjusting his line. Bell's Tavern is still intact. That's only a little bit down the road. That doesn't sound like a retreat, does it?"

Yet they knew they were abandoning the Green River and Munfordville. A week later, the Federals were in their camp at Woodsonville.

"Woodsonville," Charlton groaned. "They can't do that!"

Morgan saw his frustration. "You're right," he said softly. "Get James West. And get your coat. It may be cold out there."

"Johnny?"

With two men and no orders, John Morgan set out from Bell's Tavern to do what he could. The night was cold, with no moon but not dark, either. The Kentucky sky was covered with stars, and they made their way by that light past their own sentries and out the Munfordville Road. To their left the railroad bed rose like a dam. Bess snorted and he scratched her withers to quiet her. That had been a trick that Uncle Simon had taught him. Would she learn it? It could save his life. Ahead the gray road lay between drying weeds and heads of foxgrass dipping under night wind. Against the sky they could see the outline of the depot at Rowlett's Station. His scouts had reported Federal pickets just beyond this place.

He raised his hand and they dismounted, Charlton holding the horses while James West followed him around the corner of the depot. From the shelter of the shadows they could see in the distance, perhaps two hundred yards away, the campfire of the Yankee pickets. They slipped around the corner of the building again, West with a can of turpentine. Morgan took matches from his jacket, struck and dropped four in a row. They put more on the cordwood stacked by the track, then ran for the horses. Without looking back they cantered about a quarter of a mile, then turned to see the flames engulf the depot. Charlton let out a Rebel yell, but before the pickets could chase them, they set out at a dead run for home.

The whole camp talked of the exploit, but Morgan wasn't satisfied. The little episode only whetted his appetite for more. With one side of his mind he realized how little they were doing: a stretch of rail easily repaired here, an insignificant depot there. Johnston's intensity had worried him. *I'm sorry the capital has been moved to Richmond.* Did he feel abandoned? He was trying to build an army out of enthusiastic plowboys who called themselves "The Estill County Dead-Shots," or "Hell's Rangers." Johnston's look said it all: What would they do when they had to confront twelve-pounder howitzers manned by experienced artillery? Most had never fired those old smoothbore shotguns in anger. Killing a squirrel or a deer wasn't loading and reloading under fire.

The generals surrounding Johnston at Bowling Green seemed oblivious of that tension. Old General Hardee—he was only forty-six but his Georgia drawl gave him a grandfatherly air—looked blissfully encased in his impeccable uniform. Buckner, of course, was more aware, but he was a rarity. More characteristic of headquarters were the politician-soldiers like John Breckinridge, who, although he might have some untapped military qualities, was still a politician, strolling about the Blackburn house as if he were greeting ambassadors from foreign countries. It was not that they didn't work hard—they all worked hard. But measles and pneumonia were still the enemy in hastily organized hospitals. What would happen, Johnston's look said to those old-timers from the Mexican War days, when they needed morphine for amputations, quinine for malaria?

The contrast between those who understood and those who didn't always made Morgan's trips to headquarters frustrating. And strangely enough, even more frustrating because of the ladies. It wasn't long before they discovered Tom's tenor voice, and he was in great demand. Charlton, twenty-two and handsome in his cavalry uniform, was in his glory. As for himself, he was fully conscious, as he buttoned his jacket with its captain's bars, that such outward symbols of virility might be all he could ever offer them. He gave them burning depots and night rides to talk about as they looked up at him with their expectant, shining eyes. How could they know their slender shoulders and tilting heads left a hollow at the pit of his stomach? Becky. He had killed her with neglect and misunderstanding. Didn't these girls know what a high risk he was? He found himself strutting around in front of them like a peacock. With one side of his mind he said, *For the Cause.* With the other—Aunt Betty would have washed his mouth out.

The other group that seemed to have no understanding of that precarious Confederate line supported by lonely, scared pickets was, oddly enough, the West Pointers. Or was he being merely jealous of Ben Helm's smart drill teams?

"You could do that," Tom said one Sunday as they watched Helm's cavalry rally by fours. "The Rifles made turns a lot tighter than that."

"Turns don't get you down the road," his brother said, with that little grin which had become habitual when he was thinking. "Or fight a battle when you get there."

Their next orders seemed to confirm his sense of insignificance.

"Cattle!" Tom almost yelled.

"That's right." Basil's voice was unusually quiet. "Grayson County.

North side of the Green. To collect and bring down to Bowling Green a herd that's just been purchased."

"That's not war!"

"You'll think it is when you get there. That country's crawling with Home Guards. And they're a very determined bunch up there, I hear. They'll try every trick."

They did. And the cattle proved less than cooperative, milling in bunches, threatening to stampede. By the time they returned to Bowling Green the cowboy jokes had worn thin.

But they were greeted with a welcome surprise. New recruits, wanting to join Morgan's outfit, had come by the score. By Buckner's order, fresh horses, new saddles, bridles and tents were issued to Morgan's company— which, with the addition of two companies, Company B, captained by Tom Allen, a doctor from Shelbyville, Kentucky, and Company C, assigned to Captain James Bowles of Louisville, who had just arrived from Virginia, brought the total strength to 160. It was "Morgan's squadron" now, one of the best-equipped units in the Confederate service, its lieutenants brilliant riders and popular with the men. Private ("Colonel") Frank Leathers, an ex-Kentucky legislator who had once led a militia company, quickly became like a father to them all.

Their camp was called Burnham, but despite the fact that more recruits arrived and were sworn in, it never became home for them, as the little church at Woodsonville had been. For one thing, Morgan was spending more time at headquarters and less time with his men. And the November rains had set in. Despite the tents, which were the envy of other outfits, and captured Yankee weatherproof "shebangs," the damp, chilly nights were depressing. The lieutenants began "playing soldier"—demanding drills and inspections.

At Johnston's headquarters things moved faster. John C. Breckinridge left for Richmond. When he came back it was as a brigadier-general, with orders to take the brigade from Hanson. Buckner, Morgan knew, wanted it— rightly expected it. Johnston's regret about the removal of the capital took on new meaning. An ex-Vice-President of the enemy took precedent over a soldier whose military ability had caused even Lincoln to offer him the rank of general. Morgan was at headquarters when Breckinridge returned from Virginia. But Breckinridge stayed only long enough to confer with Buckner and Hanson before leaving for Russellville, where he hoped to use his political charm on a state convention and vote Kentucky out of the Union.

Politically, it was right. Militarily, it might be all wrong. By mid-November, when Breckinridge took over the brigade, he had, technically, a force of 5,000. In reality, because of measles, typhoid and a number of causes, he could count only 3,400 infantry, 120 artillerymen in Byrne's batteries, and 160 cavalry under John Hunt Morgan. During those weeks of the Russellville convention the joke going around was that the Yankees had taken Woodsonville, and the politicians had taken Bowling Green.

They needed something to joke about. Autumn rains turned to sleet.

Snow lay on the ground for weeks. Some of the troops were freezing, with no axes to cut firewood. Morgan's squadron was better off than many, with crude sod fireplaces in their tents, until two burned in the middle of an icy night.

In the meantime, news from the scouts was not good. The Bacon Creek railroad bridge they'd burned on the retreat was now rebuilt and ready to receive the rails. In another day or two the line would be open to Buell's mighty army, rumored to be more than 100,000. Morgan asked permission of General Breckinridge to destroy the bridge again, immediately. Permission was granted, and he started out that night with his entire command.

"I've never seen such a cold night." Charlton shivered.

Morgan said nothing. Jesse, beside him, was jogging on a little roan, and Morgan reached in his jacket and pulled out a piece of lightbread and handed it over. The boy's face, so like Randolph's, grinned. Morgan looked ahead again, down the road past the pigeon roost, quiet now with its thousands of birds asleep in the trees. The night was as black as Bess's mane. He knew his breath was sending out a cloud in front of his face, for he felt the moisture, but he couldn't see it. The creak of leather and the *shh-shh* of horses' hooves on fresh snow were the only sounds. They had long ago traded the sabers Buckner had issued for more ammunition and an occasional pistol. He thought of Will, and William Henry Harrison, and those impossible treks through sleet and rain up around the Maumee. You'd be proud of me, you old cuss.

They rode all night, halting at daybreak just south of the Green, and made camp in the woods. The orders were sent out: absolutely no noise, no fires. Luckily, it was a sunny day, and toward afternoon actually turned a little warm.

Luckily, too, when night came and the chill resumed, so did the march. It was easier to keep warm on horseback. Fingers could be tucked inside pockets by turns. Toes were another matter, but the men had learned the trick of wrapping their feet in newspapers. Now, if he could just keep them from singing . . .

The ford at Woodsonville was not guarded, and a party of Home Guards, stationed in Munfordville, were quickly routed. Morgan's companies passed on and reached the bridge at Bacon Creek about midnight. It, too, had no guard. What were the Yankees thinking of?

"Maybe they just don't know how crazy the Rebels are," Greenberry Roberts answered with a grin.

The men knew what to do. In three hours the railroad bridge at Bacon Creek was effectively destroyed, and another fire lit the night sky. Where were the Yankees? Morgan's men met no resistance, and they grumbled at some good sport missed.

It was a trifling victory, easily remedied in a few days by a good railroad crew. But it gave his men the experience of a long night march, of handling themselves under pressure, and above all, of discipline. He knew that Ben Helm, with his horsemen "rallying by fours," thought his tactics crude. Let him. A name had implanted itself in his mind. Tom's excitement still gave his little exploits meaning. Forrest. That name, Forrest. The first cavalry fight in the West. Ben could drill from now until the Mississippi went dry, but he wanted to win a war.

29

Buckner, Hanson, Breckinridge, Johnston—all seemed pleased with the destruction of the bridge at Bacon Creek. T.H., in Bowling Green with Cripps Wickliffe, now on his staff, hailed Morgan as a hero. He knew better, but he was pleased. The next day General Hindman requested that Morgan's squadron come to Bell's Tavern for "special duty." The men hurrahed. Somebody, at last, was noticing.

There was good reason for the special duty at Bell's Tavern: The Yankees were moving on Bowling Green in three columns of twenty thousand each. Bell's Tavern lay in their path, Johnston's outpost facing the advancing Union Army. Just a few days before, General Hindman had sent Colonel Terry with a regiment of Texas Rangers to challenge that advance. The Federal force he met proved to be a scouting party not much larger than his own. Maybe it was that relief which triggered Terry's exuberant charge. That and a chance, finally, after months of monotony, to do something. The Federal regiment, deployed in a skirmish line, was taken completely by surprise. The Confederates swarmed forward, Terry leading the charge. He fell with six of his men as the enemy sent one last volley before they fled.

"Ardor be damned!" Hindman fumed when he heard of Terry's death, not realizing that he was always bragging about his own reputation for dash and fury. No one could convince him that Terry's impatience had done anything but foil a vaster Confederate plan that might have given Buell and Sherman something to think about. News of Morgan's exploit at the Bacon Creek bridge reached him an hour later. "Send for him," Hindman called out to his adjutant. When the squadron arrived, Hindman sent Basil Duke with a flag of truce to bring back Terry's dead and wounded.

The next month would have been torture for the squadron if Hindman had not been the energetic, restless man he was. Morgan knew his men, and he knew inactivity was the worst possible situation for them. Hindman was always for an enterprise, however foolhardy, and gave them a free rein, which boosted morale more than some of the little successes that resulted. Bit by bit the squadron was becoming harder, leaner, more fit. Hours in the saddle could be extended with less fatigue; meals could be missed. Sisson and Tribble became experts at napping while their horses walked, catching themselves off balance, waking, shifting, and sleeping again. More recruits came in, one of them a boy who couldn't have been more than fourteen. "Billy Milton, sir," he said, trying to keep his voice from breaking. He was squeezing a cap in his hands. "I brought my horse with me, sir."

When Morgan looked into that face, how could he turn him down? "Can you beat a drum, boy?"

"I can learn, sir!"

"Then go find Lieutenant Duke. Tell him to put you on the rolls. Company A."

It was Christmas Eve. He watched the boy run off, slapping his thigh with his cap.

During this time at Bell's Tavern he heard from Kitty. Another baby had been born, named Frances. The delay in writing was explained by the death of little Henrietta, who did not survive the trip East.

The idea that he would never see that impish little face again . . . that flash of intelligence, that sudden, silent laugh, that little body filled with joy. Kitty had been with A.P.'s relatives in Culpeper, but the baby was born in Richmond, where A.P. was organizing a division he had already decided to call the Light, after the famous Light Brigade at Balaclava . . . the ink of her letter blurred again. Kitty, Kitty, in your blond loveliness, keeping his spirits up. God bless you both. May little Frances survive. Richard was well.

Under Hindman's encouragement, his boys felt at home. "Hunting Yankees" became a sport. The forays became more adventuresome, the groups smaller. Audaciously, sometimes five or ten men would start out on a "scout." They could slip into the Federal camps, learn more information— or, if they were lucky, destroy more supplies—than a larger force could have done. The old Rifles' slogan, "Our laws, the commands of our captain," became Scripture. Morgan could trust his life to any man in the outfit.

He came to look forward to those nights by the fire after supper, a whiskey in his hand, and the warm friendship of General Hindman and his second-in-command, Colonel Shaver. The others—Colonel Dan Govan of the Second Arkansas, Colonel Alexander Hawthorn of the Sixth, and Colonel John Dean and Major James Martin of the Seventh—were Western men down to their boots, who had seen action in Missouri and with the Indians, who understood bravery but, more importantly, cowardice and the catalyst of enthusiasm. They were all aware as they talked that the Federals were in force at Lebanon, only sixty miles away. When Tom Quirk reported that they were breaking camp and heading east toward Columbia, Hindman knew the Yankees were making their move.

"They're after the Gap," Hindman growled.

"If those mountain passes go, East Tennessee could go, Bowling Green could be outflanked," Shaver said.

"And Nashville . . ." Morgan added. Hindman looked up, unable to keep astonishment from his face. Losing Nashville was unthinkable. He dispatched his adjutant to Johnston's headquarters and asked permission to move out immediately. The adjutant returned, with permission refused.

"What are they thinking of?" Hindman fumed. "You don't win sitting on your tail" was Hindman's favorite expression, delivered with his peculiar drawl, and he used it now. He gave Morgan a free hand, to use as many men as he needed, to do what he could . . . anywhere he could.

Those were the sort of orders John Morgan had been waiting for. On the morning of January 20, with five picked men, he left for the Green River.

They crossed the Green at an unguarded ferry. "Ain't they sure of themselves?" Ben Drake said in mock wonder. The next day they rode all the way into Lebanon, where several hundred Federals were left behind to guard a large storehouse between the town and their bivouac. The Yankees strolled leisurely between their camp, the storehouse, and town. Toward sundown, when the messes were busy at their campfires and the smell of good food was overpowering, Morgan's men fired the storehouse and captured the guard and a few stragglers walking back from town. They kept the guard as prisoners; the stragglers handed over their overcoats in exchange for freedom —how could six men control over twenty prisoners in enemy territory and make it back to their own lines anyway? They settled for nine prisoners, donned the overcoats, and were given a merry chase by two companies of Yankee cavalry who couldn't catch them. They splashed into the river, yelling, Tom Quirk first, with a captured Yankee flag. The next day they marched into Yankee-held Glasgow with their nine prisoners in column, and the United States flag flying in front. Back at Bell's Tavern it made a good story, and Hindman, delighted, opened a bottle of shuck and toasted another "victory."

Morgan did not send these prisoners to the guardhouse, but placed them with different messes, one man to each tent, with the occupants of that tent responsible for his charge. As a joke, James West had the idea of sending around a bottle of wine to each tent—sparkling catawba, local but good— and assuring the prisoners that this was the usual Confederate fare. The next morning five of them, with tears in their eyes, begged to be taken into the Confederate service. "That'll make a dandy tale at Bowling Green!" grinned a Texas Ranger, one of Terry's men. They had so little to cling to, this little army playing cat and mouse.

If Morgan and his five men had known, as they rode away from Lebanon congratulating themselves with their handful of prisoners, that that same day in Bowling Green General Johnston was reading a telegram telling him of George Crittenden's loss of the Gap, they might not have been so sanguine. Bowling Green—the whole Confederate effort in the West—was now in jeopardy, with the right end of the line gone. Worse was to come.

The Tennessee River, flowing into the Ohio at Paducah, could carry an invading army into northern Alabama as far as Florence, where the Memphis & Charleston Railroad crossed the middle South like an artery. The Cumberland, emptying into the Ohio only twelve miles upstream from Paducah, led straight to Nashville, the depot of supplies and the railroad hub for Louisville, Chattanooga and Atlanta. Fort Henry, on the Tennessee just south of the Kentucky state line, was a closed fieldwork on low ground near the river's edge. Another fort was planned for the opposite, west bank. Twelve miles to the east, on the Cumberland, Fort Donelson sat on a high bluff a mile below the village of Dover, only forty miles from where the river joined the Ohio and seventy-five miles from Nashville, to the southeast. Work had started in early May but neither fort was complete by the time Johnston took command at Nashville in September. Early in October he had asked Richmond for a competent commander, but got a civil engineer named Tilghman who delayed approval of construction plans for six weeks. Mean-

while, Federal Generals Halleck and Grant were gathering a flotilla of gunboats at Louisville and Cincinnati. As early as the middle of October the
gunboat *Conestoga* had made its way up the Tennessee and threw shells at
Fort Henry just to develop the range of its guns.

Nashville was completely unfortified. Bowling Green, if the rivers were
taken, would be untenable.

Johnston had to move fast. The rivers would soon be swollen from winter
rains, capable of carrying those Federal gunboats far inland. On the same
day that he received the news of Crittenden's loss of the Gap, he sent
Buckner and Hanson with eight thousand men under Brigadier-General
John Floyd to Clarksville to reinforce the forts. The men left behind at
Bowling Green, irritated at not being chosen, called the Second Kentucky
"Buckner's pets." Floyd arrived with his own Virginia brigade and insisted
that Buckner wait at Russellville with his Kentuckians while Floyd "rode to
the rescue."

Johnston wasn't fast enough. By the time he sent his own chief engineer,
Major Gilmer, to encourage Tilghman, Grant arrived from Paducah with a
flotilla and twelve thousand men: Fort Henry fell. Johnston had no alternative but to order the immediate evacuation of Bowling Green and to send
Buckner's men, languishing at Russellville, to Fort Donelson on the Cumberland, which had to be held at all costs. Hindman, when he called his
captains around him at Bell's Tavern, was out of breath with excitement.
Breckinridge was to be ready to evacuate Bowling Green the next morning,
with Trabue's Fourth Kentucky and Morgan's cavalry as rear guard.

Morgan's squadron bivouacked that night in the huts left by Hanson in
Bowling Green. The Federals shelled the town before the last Confederate
soldier crossed the river.

A few miles north of Franklin Johnston's army stopped again. Morgan
had been riding back and forth all day, encouraging stragglers, closing up
ranks, looking out for bushwhackers. The wind was bone-cutting cold, but
bearable until a determined rain turned to sleet. Slush congealed to ice.
They bedded down beside the road, and despite Breckinridge's orders, a
quarter-mile of rail fence disappeared into campfires. They awoke that next
morning, Valentine's Day, to snow-covered ground. Rumor that they were
actually pursuing Thomas, the Federal general who had defeated Crittenden
at Cumberland Gap, had sustained them on the march to Franklin. But on
this cold morning, with the sky like a leaden weight and their sodden shoes
sending shafts of pain through their toes, the truth became apparent. "We're
retreating, boys!" Ben Drake joked. As if in answer, Tom Berry reversed
his captured blue overcoat. "Ah ain't carrin' no Yankee coat button-first inta
Tennessee."

The closer they got to the line the more silent the rows of men became.
James Bowles rode at the head of his Company C like a statue. Some of the
boys, leaving home for the first time, fought back tears. The veterans—
those who had come out of Lexington with Morgan in Rifles uniforms—set
their faces in grim smiles, silent, past joking. Frank Leathers, mounted on

one of the artillery horses, sagged visibly with fatigue. As if on cue, they stopped when a small sign by the side of the road announced that they were indeed leaving Kentucky. They dismounted and laid down their guns. Shivering and blowing into their hands, flapping their arms across their chests, they avoided each other's eyes. They were instinctively waiting for something, no one knew what, until General Breckinridge, who had been riding a little ahead with his staff, returned. He dismounted, and as if by silent, contagious consent, each member of his staff did so also. With his men, on foot and leading his horse, the former Vice-President of the United States crossed the line in solemn procession.

Silently, they trudged on. John Morgan led Bess, with his lieutenants, sergeants, and privates all secretly vowing, as they walked out of Kentucky, to return.

That night, as if nature herself were taunting them with defeat, the temperature dropped to zero. The next day they trudged twenty-seven miles through snow, urged into double-quick by a rumor that the Yankees were just behind them. They were not, but marching faster kept them warm and created a sense of purpose. As Morgan rode the lines he saw brighter, more determined faces. Some even cheered him as Bess trotted by. With the hills getting steeper on the road to Nashville, they would need all the determination they could muster.

"And we thought Anderson County was rough!" Charlton laughed before he spurred his horse to check the rear guard.

It wasn't until the next morning, Sunday, that Breckinridge's brigade caught sight of the Cumberland and Nashville beyond. General Johnston reestablished his headquarters at Edgefield Junction, and they bivouacked there for the night, pending orders.

Albert Sidney Johnston had gone to bed Saturday night with the words "a victory complete and glorious" still ringing in his ears: Fort Donelson had held, after all! By the time he awoke that Sunday morning, another telegram trembled in the hands of his adjutant: The fort had fallen, with the surrender of more than seven thousand Confederate troops. Generals Floyd and Pillow had escaped; Buckner and Hanson were prisoners. There was no question now: Unfortified Nashville, the "warehouse of the Confederacy," would have to be abandoned.

Morgan did not report to headquarters. He was too busy getting the troops across the bridge into town. By the time they entered the streets, the earlier exhilaration of the citizens had turned to gloom, then panic. By ten o'clock rumor fed terror: Buell, with thirty-five thousand troops, was already at Springfield, twenty-five miles away. Federal gunboats had already left Clarksville and would reach Nashville by three P.M., when the shelling would begin. By noon, carriages, buggies, gigs, and carts piled high with household goods made passage almost impossible. Railroad cars at the depot filled, then overflowed and rolled south covered with refugees. All that day Confederate troops kept pouring through, hungry, wet, worn out. Some stopped to help old ladies load boxes; others joined the looters who were already entering abandoned houses. In a lull, Sam offered the hospitality of his father's house. It was a haven of calm in chaos. Sam Morgan, Sr., insisted that his nephews use it as headquarters. Three hours later they collapsed between clean sheets and thought they were in paradise. They had been in the saddle for more than twenty hours.

Just after sunup, after a night of drumming rain, orders from General Breckinridge, delivered by a breathless aide, sent them to Johnston's headquarters for further instructions.

The crowd at Edgefield milled about the closed double doors of the parlor in the house that Johnston was using. Orderlies, couriers, civilians and officers spilled over onto the muddy lawn, too excited to notice the rain that had settled into a determined drizzle. Polk had already left Columbus; Kentucky was lost. General Floyd, with his four Virginia regiments, and General Pillow had just arrived from Fort Donelson on two small steamboats. Information was scarce. Only two things seemed certain: Buckner had surrendered and Forrest had cut his way out, with five hundred cavalrymen and two hundred others mounted on artillery horses, across a frozen road just before the surrender, swearing he could have gotten the whole damned Confederate Army away if they'd let him.

The crowd was so thick at the bottom of the steps that Morgan, with Basil Duke and three of his lieutenants, had to wait at one side and strain to hear the speeches that General Floyd, General Hardee and Major Munford, Johnston's aide-de-camp, felt compelled to make. The usual "gallant defense in the face of overwhelming numbers" fell, with the drizzle, on skeptical ears. John Morgan wondered at the safe escape of those Virginia regiments, and sent a look to Breckinridge on the porch, who motioned him inside.

"Remember, John, that day at the armory in Lexington, when I said your time would come?" Breckinridge drawled, his eyes on a blank wall. He swung them slowly and met Morgan's. "Well," he said harshly, "it's here."

Johnston had the saving of his own army now to think of. When he left Bowling Green it numbered 14,000. Before he reached Nashville, 5,400 were either sick or unfit for duty. Halleck's Union forces at Louisville numbered well over 100,000, with Buell's 50–60,000 as his advance guard already across the Barren River at Bowling Green.

"General Johnston sent me to find you, Captain Morgan. And General Breckinridge? The General is about to give orders. . . ." The young man with wide-set brown eyes who spoke introduced himself as Adam Johnson, a scout with Forrest. His slow way of smiling through the hurried words made Morgan like him immediately.

They followed him through the doors. Anxious men were waiting attentively around the walls. Forrest's scout withdrew to a place against the wall by a window and listened with the others as Johnston gave his orders in a smooth, clear voice. They were precise. General Floyd he put in charge of the evacuation of Nashville and the maintenance of order. The First Missouri Infantry would constitute a military police force, aided by Morgan's cavalry, which would patrol the streets and suburbs and assist in rounding up any available wagons or other conveyances for the transportation of quartermaster stores to the depot. Once the stores—particularly the munitions—were safely away, the bridges would be fired.

With that word "fired," Johnston stopped. "The army will move on to Murfreesboro, where further orders will be issued," he said quietly. "Now, gentlemen, we all have a job to do." He nodded toward each of them with that brisk courtesy which refused, even in haste, to abandon dignity, his eyes looking beyond them in that way he had, a muscle in his jaw working. This time he did not smile.

Outside, Adam Johnson mounted and rode with Morgan, Basil and the others across the suspension bridge to Nashville, stopping at Sam Morgan's house. Basil left them to ride on with Charlton to begin the patrols. Adam Johnson, obviously upset and exhausted, accepted Morgan's invitation to come in. When Sam, Sr., came home he insisted that Johnson stay with them until Colonel Forrest arrived. After a good meal and four cups of coffee—he hadn't tasted any in two weeks—Adam answered the old man's questions.

His soft voice made the room seem even quieter.

"Yes, sir. It was Colonel Forrest's opinion that two-thirds of the troops could have gotten out. On a scout that afternoon we had discovered a road —a frozen swamp. The enemy, even then, had not completely occupied their old line, having to camp on a field full of their own dead and dying. Colonel Forrest believed if we had fought them the next day we could have whipped them. Or at least effected a retreat, ten thousand by road and the rest by boats across the river. The road was open as late as eight o'clock Sunday morning. Not a Federal was in sight when we went through, just after daylight."

Telling it seemed to exhaust him.

"When do you expect Colonel Forrest?" Morgan said.

"As fast as that horse of his can travel." Adam Johnson smiled.

A servant interrupted. Someone was at the door to see Captain Morgan.

It was a wide-eyed boy not much older than Key.

"Captain Morgan? You see, Maw. I tole you he wuz here. . . ."

It was then Morgan noticed the frail little woman behind the boy. She pulled her shawl closer and shivered.

"Here, come inside out of the cold."

"No, thank you, sir," the woman said, but allowed his hand on her elbow to draw her into the warmth of the hall. She cast a frightened look at the slender mirror in the hall tree. Whatever she saw there seemed to reassure her, for she looked from the mirror to Morgan's face with new courage. Her son was talking, squaring his shoulders and lifting his chin and forcing his eyes, under their soft lashes, to look aggressive.

"Ah ain't got no hoss. . . ."

"His pa took it to Fort Donelson," the mother finished.

"But Ah kin fight's as good as enny."

"He so wanted to join your company, Captain Morgan."

"I think we can find you a horse."

"You see, Jim? I told you he was a gentleman. He will take care of you. . . ."

Morgan for the first time noticed her purple lips. The woman was still shivering with cold. "Here, Mrs. . . ."

"Geslin."

"Mrs. Geslin, come into the parlor."

"Oh, no, sir. We'll be going . . . as soon as you say James here . . . can join. You see, my husband went to the fort, and George went to Columbus with General Polk. . . ." The uncertain fates of both washed her face with fear.

"Of course we can use him, Mrs. Geslin. You look like a stout lad, James. Report to Lieutenant Duke. Lieutenant Basil Duke. You'll find him bivouacked down near the square. Tell him you're to be assigned to Company A. That's my favorite company." He smiled at the mother.

"You will take care of him, Captain? We will win this horrible war . . . ?"

He watched them walking away into that raw night, the thin little woman wrapped in her shawl, the boy striding out a little ahead, as if he couldn't wait to find Company A.

When Albert Sidney Johnston left Nashville the next morning he seemed to take all order with him. Floyd was obviously pleased with power. Without the presence of Johnston and his staff, Pillow, too, assumed the hauteur of the veteran soldier. Just after first light Morgan found the colonel of the First Missouri and they worked out a schedule. The cavalry would locate, the infantry would convey every available wheel in the city toward the quartermaster storehouses; they would accept the aid of any willing citizen in loading the cars at the depot.

Once the news of Johnston's departure was out, the crowds were worse than yesterday. Fetlock-deep mud and screaming women made Bess fidget. Arrogant men in carriages refused to move, and one almost hit her head with a buggy whip. Morgan drew his pistol and the man moved on. The infantry squad behind him unloaded three wagons and headed back toward the warehouse. The crowd, too, surged in that direction. "Make way, make way!" Charlton yelled, brandishing his "wrist breaker," a Federal saber captured on one of their Green River raids. They had two blocks to go when Basil Duke appeared at Morgan's side.

"Floyd has ordered the distribution of public stores to the citizens."

"What?"

It was true. By the time they reached the warehouse, sides of smoked meat, sacks of meal, blankets and shoes—even bales of clothing—were being carried out the front doors or tossed from upstairs windows. Morgan's men sat their horses in disbelief. Basil sped back to headquarters to check, returned in a half-hour to say yes, it was true. The rumor that the Federals were in the outskirts had sent a fresh wave of panic into Edgefield; Floyd moved his headquarters to City Hall. . . .

Basil had barely finished when a young major of Floyd's staff sidled his horse through to them. The orders were rescinded! Morgan's cavalry and the First Missouri were now charged with the duty of stopping the pilfering. . . .

The mood of the crowd turned ugly. One woman in a big blue apron filled with bacon bunched it into a club and swung expertly at a young infantryman, who sprawled in the mud, much to the laughter of the crowd. That little incident served to trigger more effort, and a half-dozen men made a dash for the warehouse door. Bess, in the middle of that mob, hardly had room to plant her feet. Morgan was about to give the order to charge when a man with graying side-whiskers climbed on a wagon and waved his arms at the crowd. Mayor Cheatham assured them that a fair distribution would resume as soon as some Nashville citizens, appointed by him, could arrive on the scene. A small cheer went up. Incredulous, Charlton, Basil, and James West waited on their horses. Saving anything was obviously hopeless. Morgan sent Tom and Winder Monroe to Captain Allen and Captain Bowles, whose companies patrolled the suburbs, for a council at Front Street and the Public Square. The "peaceable evacuation of Nashville" had turned into a joke.

That afternoon Pillow issued a handbill: He would speak at the Public Square at seven P.M. The crowd dispersed, but sporadic looting continued.

Adam Johnson went with Morgan to hear the Great Address at the Public Square. It proved to be an announcement that no stand against the invading Federal Army was planned.

"The officers who will come among you are gentlemen," Pillow said in his whining voice, "and, of course, will behave as such toward you." Then Brigadier-General Gideon J. Pillow, of Columbia, Tennessee, boarded a train for home.

"Captain Morgan?"

He looked around to see a slight young man of twenty with ice-blue eyes, a square-cut chin and thick, black curly hair. The thin lips under a wisp of mustache seemed reluctant to smile.

"Yes?"

The young man handed him a paper. "Lieutenant Tom Hines, Buckner's Raiders, detailed to your squadron by General Johnston, sir."

Morgan studied the paper and looked up. "Buckner's Raiders?" He had to suppress a smile. The boy saw it and stiffened, controlling a frown which threatened to shatter the carefully kept calm on his face.

"Oldham County, Kentucky." The boy bent his head to clear his throat, touching his mouth with a raised fist. "I was a professor there—foreign languages."

He spoke so softly that Morgan had to bend to hear. He couldn't have weighed more than a hundred pounds, and yet Tom Hines had the same quiet toughness that had fooled him before. He looked at the orders again. Hines was to serve in the capacity of scout and "special aide." The crowd, breaking up after Pillow's speech, jostled around them. "Follow me," Morgan said.

In Sam Morgan's house Tom Hines seemed to relax. Morgan offered him wine and he accepted.

"Tell me about your service."

"Not much to tell, sir."

"Well, what there is, tell it," Morgan invited, with a lift of his glass.

"Fifteen of us—mostly my students and the fencing master—rode down to Lexington the day after Sumter. . . ." Hines's voice trailed off; then, almost offhandedly, he reached into his pocket and drew out a folded paper, which he handed to Morgan. On it were orders, over General Johnston's signature, to fire two boats which were being converted into Confederate gunboats. Hines waited until he was certain Morgan had finished reading, then said in his quiet way, as if they were being overheard, "A dozen men should do it."

Charlton came in just as he spoke, and Hines's eyes immediately became those of a boy out for a lark.

"I think we'll have time for a little supper first," Morgan smiled. "This is my uncle's house, Lieutenant Hines, and I am sure if he were here—he is out trying to save what he can of his warehouse—he would agree. I'll see if I can arouse the servants."

When he returned and they waited for the table to be set, Hines talked with Charlton about Greek philosophy as if the Yankees didn't exist.

"My father liked the Greeks," Morgan said. "In school, I had a teacher who claimed they thought of themselves as gods. In a way, they remind me of my men."

Tom Hines drew in his square chin and watched a servant bring in food. "It's a damned foolish way to think, if you'll pardon my saying so, sir," he got out. But his eyes were vacuous, completely empty of emotion.

After they ate Charlton went out to order the horses readied. In the hall, pulling on his coat, he had a chance to whisper to his brother, "I don't trust him. What are his convictions?"

"Johnston recommends him."

"And that settles it for you."

Morgan smiled. "To tell you the truth, I'm not sure he has any. He could be, no doubt, a dangerous man."

"Then why . . . ?"

"But we pride ourselves on being dangerous men, too, don't we, Charl?" He laughed. "Come on, it's time to light that fire."

True to the confusion that had reigned all day, someone gave out the alarm, and as the fire bell pealed and the fire-engine horses careened through the streets, Walter Ferguson and Xenophon Hawkins and a dozen other Morgan men drank shuck and watched the burning boats melt the icy edges of the Cumberland River.

Tuesday morning dawned cloudy and damp. But there was no rain, nor Federal gunboats. Tom Quirk, reporting about eight o'clock, had seen no Yankees within twenty miles. "But we did see something else." The Irishman grinned. "If you come on outside now, Capt'n, you'll see for yourself. But better hurry. They'll be at the Public Square by now."

Sam Morgan's house, fortunately, was not too far from the heart of town. John Morgan rode between his brothers Charlton and Tom, whose little bay mare pricked up her ears at the sight. Bedraggled, wet, muddy but upright cavalrymen rode their horses as if in knightly procession . . . all five hundred of them, with two hundred others mounted on broad-backed artillery horses. At their head a dark, rawboned man sat straighter than the rest, the angle of his head and the tilt of his chin a dare. Nathan Bedford Forrest had come to town.

There was no bluster, but a thin-lipped grin and a sudden extended hand. Forrest turned and gave orders for the care of his men and horses, then asked the way to headquarters. Morgan introduced himself. "I'll rest later," Forrest waved away one of his aides. "City Hall, is it? Very well, meet me there in half an hour. Now, Morgan, tell me the situation."

When Forrest learned about the distribution of government stores he fairly exploded. Without waiting for the orderly to announce him, he strode through the doors to Floyd's desk. Applicants for favors scattered. Morgan, just outside, couldn't hear everything that was said, but did catch snatches. "Suspension bridge . . . open for supplies . . ." came Forrest's growl, and Floyd's "No, military necessity. Military necessity." Floyd seemed to like the phrase, and Forrest came out fuming.

"Just like them, the damned fools!" he said under his breath. Morgan followed him down the steps and swung up on Bess. Forrest was already trotting a little ahead before he calmed down enough to speak: "Burn the railroad bridge tonight, cut the cables of the suspension bridge. Now does that make sense, with supplies still across the river? My God, how much longer can this Confederacy last?" He spurred his horse and almost ran down a dozen civilians. Morgan squeezed Bess and followed.

That night, while their men put torches to the L&N drawbridge and Morgan and Forrest watched from their horses the smoking timbers send tall pillars of smoke skyward, Forrest seemed to have forgotten his irritation and was, for him, in a mellow mood. He leaned on his saddle and told Morgan a story. He was young, and trying to break up a dogfight.

"Damn fool, I was. Rode an unbroke colt right inta the middle uv 'em. Got pitched off!" He laughed. "Wal, don't you know my flailin' around scairt those dogs off? I learned a valuable lesson then, sir, a lesson your boys oughter heed. A tight fix can sometimes be your best opportunity, if you'll jest let the other feller believe you can make more ruckus than he can. They should've known that at Donelson," he added glumly. "Come on, Cap, let's git thet suspension bridge. . . ."

The men scrambled like cats, cut the cables, and the great bridge, 700 feet long and 110 feet high, the pride of Nashville, buckled, tilted, and crashed into the icy Cumberland as they watched from shore.

On Wednesday Floyd changed his orders again. The Federals were not as near as he thought. The remaining supplies in the warehouses were to be shipped off for the use of the Confederate Army. But by now it was almost impossible to keep the crowds away. At one point Forrest's men charged the mob, sabers drawn. At another, Mayor Cheatham called out the fire engine and drenched the mob with water. The next morning Floyd and his staff climbed aboard a train for Chattanooga, leaving Forrest in charge of Nashville.

For three days the work went on. Seven hundred boxes of clothing. Eight hundred wagonloads of meat. Several hundred bales of osnaburg. The river rose to flood stage and the sullen crowds glared at the line of Forrest's horses, a solid wall of resistance even the most adventurous looter dared not challenge. On Saturday the bridge of the Nashville & Chattanooga Railroad gave way to the surging Cumberland. Nashville was gone.

Sam Morgan moved his family to Alabama, where his wife had relatives, late Saturday afternoon. The first of Federal General Buell's men appeared across the river at Edgefield Sunday morning. Forrest ordered Morgan to act as a rear guard that night, and some of the men from Company A watched from side streets as the Yankees landed by boat and marched into the square.

"We always seem to be the last to leave," Charlton quipped. "First Bowling Green, now this. How many towns do you think we'll conquer in this fashion?"

It was a bitter joke, not needing an answer.

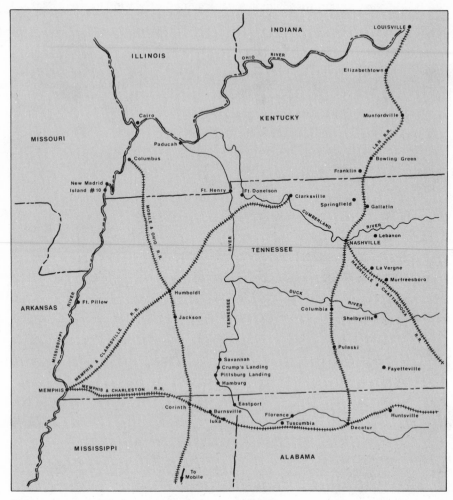

Western Front, Spring 1862

30

For a week Morgan's men camped at a little town called La Vergne, about halfway between Nashville and Murfreesboro, on the railroad. With Johnston regrouping at Murfreesboro, Morgan's job was to disrupt any Union move by rail. Hines, Adam Johnson and Forrest's command rode on to Johnston's headquarters. Morgan would always remember Forrest riding off. Under his jokes and rough ways was a man who refused to be killed. Caution, once a battle started, was not in his vocabulary. It was the only way to fight.

About eight miles from Nashville and seven from La Vergne a lunatic asylum on the Murfreesboro Pike—much to the amusement of Rebel pickets —housed the Fourth Ohio Cavalry, commanded by General Mitchell. The vedettes of both sides stood in clear view of each other by day and often swapped jokes at night, but Morgan's scouts were another matter. Tom Quirk and his men soon learned to infiltrate the Federal picket lines, get in their rear and "create some action."

After several of Quirk's forays, the enemy pickets were withdrawn at night, some miles toward the asylum. If he could outflank them, thought Morgan, maybe he could capture their General Mitchell and exchange him for Buckner! When he ordered a detail of nine men to attempt the mission, Basil objected.

"We'll be like a thrown rider in a bunch of dogs," Morgan grinned.

"What?"

"We can try!"

They were armed with shotguns loaded with buckshot. They easily got behind the Federal vedettes, then dismounted quietly. After the horses were led away, Morgan lay behind a low fence with four of the men to wait. They knew what to do: hold fire until the whole party—about thirty—had passed. Then up, fire, drive them toward their own camp.

It didn't work that way. The Yankee officer stopped to talk with his guides, then sent half a dozen men to reconnoiter on each side of the road. They came right up to the fence. A stab of exhilaration shot through Morgan's chest. He stood up and shouted "Now!"

His men let go a volley. The officer fell, the others ran. The men reloaded, fired again, and two more dropped, sprawling, wounded. The Yankees ran all the way back to their own camp, and James West, one of those who had waited by the fence, was left to watch the road while Morgan returned to get more men. He ordered a chain picket established from that point to La Vergne. The Confederacy had recovered a few miles, on this front, at least. But they had failed to capture an exchange for Buckner.

"What did you mean, a thrown rider in a bunch of dogs?"

"Something Forrest told me, Basil. A tight spot can be an opportunity—
if that's the last place the enemy expects you to be. . . . And if you make so
much noise they think you're stronger than you are."

"In other words, you make yourself a tight spot."

"That's right. Wasn't it fun?"

Basil's look suspected his captain's sanity.

"Why don't we do it in Nashville?"

"*Nashville?*"

"You'll have to admit *that* would be a tight spot."

"There's no argument there."

"It would be the very thing they'd least expect."

Basil thought a minute. "Yes, it would, wouldn't it?"

So the expedition to burn the steamboat *Minnetonka* was born.

It was the 26th of February. The weather, at last, had turned; a blue
Tennessee sky promised a clear night. There would be no moon, but the
men who had patrolled the suburbs during the evacuation knew the neigh-
borhoods. If they left by noon they could reach the outskirts before sundown.

"Isn't that dangerous?" James West asked.

"We have no idea what situations we'll have to . . . alter." Morgan
grinned, but with a little frown pulling at his eyes. "I'll need twelve good
men."

Lieutenant James West was the first to volunteer. Tom Quirk, Charlton,
Jack Wilson, Ambrose Young, Van Buren Sellers and a half-dozen others
who knew the streets, including Sam Morgan and James Geslin. Private
Tom Morgan, to his chagrin but with a promise of "next time," was left
behind. In Federal overcoats they rode cross-country to the northeast and
picked up the Lebanon Pike so they could enter Nashville from the east.
The road for a long stretch was flooded with backwater from the river and
the tollgate had been abandoned. At first the horses splashed leisurely
through the pastern-high muddy water, until it became stirrup-deep. Little
waves, picked up by the wind, made the fields a lake. If they were to make
it into Nashville before dark, another way had to be found. Quirk, riding
ahead, reported a farmer on the porch of a cabin who professed Federal
sympathy and agreed to guide them.

It was a shortcut only a native could have known, and there were two
good hours of daylight left by the time they rode into town. They hadn't
gone four blocks along Front Street before they heard hoofbeats approaching
from an intersection. Morgan held his hand up, a signal to wait. In the
shadows, with hearts beating, they watched a Federal cavalry squad trot by.
Morgan's hand came down, and they fell in behind, in smooth fours. It was
beautiful, their blue coats joining the others, dispelling any doubt concerning their "identity." They were on the colt. Now to find a place to get
thrown.

After half a dozen blocks they dropped away from their "formation,"
dismounted and led their horses along the river bank. Through the thickets
they could see the *Minnetonka* pulling against the chains that held her fore

and aft to trees. If she were fired and cut loose she would drift directly into Federal gunboats and transports moored not more than five hundred yards downstream. From here you could see the Yankees lining the decks of the transports and strolling around. Yes, definitely, this was the place.

Luckily, as if it had been waiting for them, an overturned skiff bobbed against a plank fence not five feet away. The fence, torn down by the flood, drifted out into the river for about seventy-five feet. Warfield, Garrett and little Sam Buckner volunteered. They tore away two of the planks as paddles. Breathlessly, Morgan watched them make their way across the water toward the boat. Twenty interminable minutes passed. A crowd gathered and instinctively realized these were not Federals in the blue coats. One old man, his tobacco-stained beard flopping against his neck, held out a shaking, nervous hand and begged them to leave. Others in the crowd took up the whispered refrain: "Leave! Leave!" The Federal cavalry were scouring the city—a large body had just passed up the street. . . . Then orange flames broke out on the *Minnetonka*. But she remained moored to the trees.

They watched the skiff appear again, then catch in the current, turn like a top and head downstream, where the Yankee soldiers sat on the decks watching everything that was going on. In another minute they could be shot!

Just before the skiff left the little eddy which, like a whirlpool, had spun them, Sam Buckner caught one end of the drifting fence and held on. With Warfield grabbing him around the waist and Garrett guiding the boat with his "oar" they hauled themselves, plank by plank, ashore.

Instead of cheering, the crowd became angry in its concern now for its own safety. Morgan looked around. Yes, the colt had bucked and he was definitely on the ground, but the dogs hadn't scattered. Not at all. Getting out would be decidedly more difficult than getting in.

"When did that cavalry squad pass by?"

"Fifteen minutes, sir," Private Petticord answered.

"There's a cemetery near the Murfreesboro Pike," James Geslin offered. "We could meet there. . . ."

With a nod, Morgan sent all but five of his men in that direction, with orders to wait. The skiff, at last, was secured, held by a dozen willing hands helping the boys ashore. Overhead, the clatter of cavalry brought mute stares of terror into the faces of the crowd. The sun had now touched the river. In the swift February twilight, they would have no more than an hour of good visibility to make it across those flooded roads.

At the cemetery, in the half-light, seven tombstones suddenly sprouted grimy faces: All the men there were safe, their horses tied nearby. But bad news: The tollgate on the Murfreesboro Pike was operating—and operating efficiently. They had met a man who had been refused passage because he was without a pass. Morgan turned Bess to the pike and stationed himself about two hundred yards from the tollgate. It was almost a half-hour before his quarry appeared: a businessman in a fine tweed overcoat. "Why, I didn't notice you in that bush there," the man said nervously. "Are you a picket?"

"If you mean a Federal picket—yes, I am."

"Of course I mean a Federal picket! What other kind are there?"

"Do you have a pass, sir?" Morgan called out.

"Yes. yes, I do. From General Mitchell. Here it is."

Morgan studied the paper and pursed his lips. He took so much time examining it that the man became indignant.

"See here, it's a perfectly good pass . . ."

"How do I know? It may be a forgery. I'll need to take this in. . . ." He tucked it inside his Federal overcoat and legged Bess into a trot with the precision of a man reporting to his superiors.

At the tollgate they had to wait for a group of Yankee officers to pass through. As the Federals rode past, Morgan snapped them a smart salute and the officer in charge, on a large gray horse, returned the courtesy.

"Who are they?" Van Buren Sellers asked the tollkeeper, to divert him from too close a scrutiny of the pass.

"Just some officers looking for a place to camp," he said too glibly, folding the paper and handing it back. He motioned them on.

They rode through, but the man's lie worried James West, who insisted they stop in a clump of cedars. By this time full night had descended. They dismounted and waited. The damp ground was cold and the cedar boughs prickly. They couldn't see more than fifty feet ahead. Then, just beyond that point, a clink of sabers told them the officers had returned.

Silently, Morgan motioned his men toward a rail fence. The Federals left the pike and rode into the trees. Henry Elder tripped on a vine and fell against the fence. One of the rails dropped off. Morgan slipped a shotgun to his shoulder and raised it to fire. Before he could, the Federals sent a volley into the fence and fled. Peter Atherton yelled out. He was shot in the thigh. Morgan helped him to his horse and they reached camp at La Vergne, after crossing and recrossing the pike to avoid Mitchell's pickets, about midnight.

The news of the daring expedition against the steamboat at Nashville reached Johnston's headquarters at Murfreesboro before the army resumed its retreat. Three cheers. The Bonnie Blue Flag. Dixie. Morgan the New Marion. How could he tell them the expedition had been a failure? Another "almost." If the *Minnetonka* had been released from her moorings . . . If those gunboats had exploded . . . If those transports, loaded with troops, had sunk! Why hadn't they expected steel cables? He accepted his men's toasts and cheers, but as he left the bulk of his command at La Vergne and rode toward Murfreesboro with forty of his own and some fifty cavalrymen under the command of a Lieutenant-Colonel Wood from Wirt Adams's Mississippi regiment, he wondered if he would ever deserve their total trust.

He couldn't know, then, that he was riding toward a pair of blue eyes that would make him believe anything.

Murfreesboro was a lovely little city, with a cupola-topped red brick courthouse on a knoll overlooking a countryside that could have been Kentucky, with the smooth surface of Stones River cutting through a valley of woodland pastures. Clean sheets and civilization! Even Bess seemed to grow lighter in her trot as the spires of churches and the rooflines of houses came into sight.

General Breckinridge had left the day before, after a review and the rousing cadence of a brass band. Morgan was sorry to have missed T.H. and Wick—he hadn't seen the Fifth Kentucky since Bowling Green. Did they have letters from home? Where was Cal? What was happening at Hopemont?

General Hardee's camp on the north side of town was already deserted, with the exception of a few tents and captured Yankee shebangs left for Morgan's use by Hardee's order. The main Confederate force was already on its way toward Shelbyville, the last troops leaving just that morning. A farmer came from a nearby house and told them that the General might still be in town. Colonel Wood sent him a salute and turned in his saddle to Morgan. "I think I know where he is. Colonel Ready's. Let's go!"

The Ready house, on Main Street within sight of the courthouse, was reached through a garden. An old light-skinned Negro named Albert let them in. Wood, who had been here before, made a joke as he let him take his cape. Morgan stood in the entry hall in his full dress uniform. It was thus he saw her, and he was glad he had let his mustache grow out to meet his beard, and that his beard had softened and met his collar. Behind that, maybe she wouldn't notice the effect she made.

"Colonel" Charles Ready, a short round man with florid cheeks and side-whiskers, was a civilian who had picked up his "rank," like so many Southerners, from some vague militia service. In reality he was a Southern-sympathizing Whig Congressman who had predictably lost his seat in the last election and returned to Tennessee with his two daughters and ailing wife to do what he could for the Cause. During these past two weeks he had become the confidant of the Confederate generals, particularly Hardee, who had accepted so many dinner invitations that his staff had come to think of the Ready house as a second headquarters. Colonel Ready played the affable host, recounting for the girls' amusement the *Minnetonka* incident as he glibly passed the introductions around: General Hardee; young Vertner, his aide; and Colonel Wharton, of the famous Texas Rangers.

The younger girl, Alice, had thick brown hair and freckles, with a straight nose and full little mouth and an overbite that made her lisp in a way that kept the General in a state of gentle laughter. She might have been sixteen. The other girl, who sat at the spinet and had just finished playing, turned her blue-eyed gaze on the newcomers. Morgan had never seen hair that black, or eyes that blue. He stammered at the introductions. Her name was Mattie.

"Martha," her father said. "But we call her Mattie," he added fondly. "Now, Mattie, give the gentlemen one more song."

If Morgan had been offered a thousand dollars, he couldn't have named it. It might have been "The Yellow Rose of Texas"—in honor of Wharton —or it could have been "The Long, Long, Dreary Day" that the Nashville girls loved to sing so plaintively. He stood against the wall, unmoving, until the girls, obedient to Colonel Ready's admonition that the gentlemen had some hasty business before the General had to leave, walked his way. With a flippant toss of her hair, Alice, who was everybody's pet, gave Wood a little curtsy. Wood stiffened his knees and bent from the waist in a mock bow. Mattie, behind her, waited her turn, then held out her hand, her eyes on Wood's face before she moved them to his. "Captain Morgan," she said in her soft voice, "we're so glad you could come." He held her gaze before he bent his lips to her fingers. She slipped her hand from his and turned in some confusion to Alice. "We've been sad to say good-bye this morning to our only brother and Alice's friend, Hugh Gwyn."

"Escaped from Donelson," added Alice.

"The only boy she ever let read her diary," Mattie teased, but she was looking at him again.

"Yes, yes," her father beamed behind her. "Now that Morgan's here we'll be safe from the Yankees a while longer. Right, William?"

General Hardee, conferring with Colonel Wharton about leaving some of his Rangers to help Morgan, nodded a broad smile in their direction. To Hardee's opposition to another visit to the asylum Morgan said, conscious of those blue eyes on him, "Sir, it would be an impossibility for them to catch me." None of them, busy with their own thoughts, had noticed the chasm that had opened under his feet.

On the way back to camp, under Wood's jokes, he moaned out something about the silliness of women and their coquetries. To his surprise Wood became instantly serious. "Ah, yes, John, but they are why we do all this, aren't they? In their silliness, as you call it, lies all the wisdom and comfort and meaning of the world." Then, to erase the sadness, Wood called back: "You've been sleeping too much in tents!"

"Will you come in to church?" Wood's scrubbed face asked him the next morning.

"When you know me better, you'll know I'm not religious."

"Well, neither am I. But one takes one's life where one finds it. I've shared the Readys' pew for the past few weeks, and I'm still trying to make some headway with their older daughter."

"Mattie?" Her name sounded strange on his lips. It was the first time he had said it.

Wood, busy with his boots, blew into the shine and rubbed them. "I wish my boy polished boots like your Jesse. Where did you find him?"

"Home." It was another word that felt strange. "He's also good with the horses," he added quickly, to cover the sound of nostalgia.

But Wood hadn't noticed. He was buttoning his coat, looking into his mirror and smoothing his hair. "Alice, of course, got religion at a school near Baltimore, as she will tell you if you give her half a chance. But Alice catches things like that as easily as measles. Now it's the Cause."

"Are you being cynical?"

"Not at all. I'm just glad I'm on the right side." He winked. "Suppose I'd been born a Damn Yankee?"

"What about . . . the older girl?"

"Actually there's another older daughter—married to a doctor in Nashville."

"Nashville?"

"Oh, don't worry. I've heard Alice deride her often enough for kindness to the enemy. It seems the good doctor is having it both ways."

"And Mattie?"

"You know, that girl is strange. I heard when the Colonel was in Congress that she was the belle of Washington. Engaged to some chap from Illinois, until the war. Or almost so. With her, you're never sure. She's one who doesn't talk about her feelings much. Maybe it's because the mother is so often ill, and she's become the mistress of the house. Just wait till spring, Alice says, when Sis turns the place upside down for cleaning."

"I wish we could be here for that," Morgan said so glumly that the retreat of Johnston's army loomed before them like a bad dream.

"Well, I'm off," said Wood, before he could feel depressed.

There was much to do. Despite a good staff and the excellent cooperation already existing between Wood's men and his own, the physical comfort of the troops demanded the care of a hundred details. He regretted leaving Basil at La Vergne. Basil had become his right-hand man. Wharton's Texas Rangers, promised by Hardee, should arrive by Tuesday. Perhaps then he could make some changes, let Captain Bowles take Basil's place, and get the steady, dependable Duke to help him in Murfreesboro. With ninety men, plus the twenty or so from Wharton, he had the job of holding back Buell's whole Federal Army. It was awesome. He almost regretted the *Minnetonka* incident, which had given Hardee the impression that he was invincible. And he had foolishly, in a moment of vanity, added to it with that remark about not getting caught.

Wood, when he came in at sundown, was ecstatic.

"They want you to come for supper."

"Who?"

"Not 'who'—when. Eight o'clock. So you've just time to get ready."

Wood was busy sending his servant for hot water and peeling off his clothes. "Where is my basin? Oh, the pleasures of camp life! May I borrow some of that soap? Morgan, you should have been there. The minister made such a touching appeal, as Alice said. Spoke of the need to care for the wounded. So, after church, the girls would have it that I help them deliver some chicken broth, and we spent the next two hours comforting the sick and dying at the hospital. Then Alice got sick, poor girl. She'd never smelt blood before. . . . Thanks! This *does* perfume the old armpits. And"—Wood spit out a flick of foam from the corner of his mouth—"and you'll never know what the Colonel said to Mattie when we got back."

Morgan laughed and looked down at his legs stretched out on the goods box they used for a desk. "What?" He reached down to pull off a boot.

"That he was inviting us because Captain Morgan is a widower and a little sad. He wants her to sing for you!"

He was glad his face was turned away. "He does, does he? Say, Wood, can you give me a hand?"

Ducks with olives, chicken in jelly, pheasant, ham, chocolate cream, fruit-cake, claret. Under the warmth of food and the hospitality of the Colonel and his ladies, cold marches and wet socks seemed unreal. Mrs. Ready was a little gray-haired woman who must have looked like Alice when she was young: that same straight little nose, an almond shape to the brown eyes which gave to her face a mischievousness, even when she was most serious. She was serious now as she spoke of the war. "We joined them freely. Why can't we leave freely? There's nothing in their Constitution to prevent . . ." Then she turned her level gaze on Morgan as if he alone in the room could give her an answer. "If they hate us so much, Captain Morgan, why do they want to keep us?" It was a question so hard-rock simple that it was charming. The fine bones of her face under its paper-thin skin, her little fluttery hands, reminded him of his grandmother.

"I liked them well enough, in Washington City!" she said, still in that bewildered tone. She had loved it, she went on, had been friends with the McLanes, the Emorys, all the best families. Now Washington was a ghost town. Did he know only three "good" families had gone to the Inaugural Ball? As for herself, she had come back to Tennessee and turned herself into a pillar of salt.

"Oh, not quite, Mama." Mattie smiled. She nodded to Albert, hovering by her, as a signal to clear. "But isn't it good to be home?"

Morgan learned that the ducks had come from their river farm north of town.

"Do you ride?" he asked Mattie suddenly—too suddenly, Wood's eyes told him, but it was an honest question. He would need to know every road and lane around this town as quickly as he could.

"Yes! I love to ride." She looked at her father. "May I, Papa?"

"Of course! Now when have you ever asked my permission before, Daughter?"

After dessert they drifted to the parlor. This time he did hear what she sang. And the way she sang it. "My Old Kentucky Home" sounded as if she had written it for him. When she reached "Weep no more, my lady," her blue eyes seemed to promise that she would never, if she could help it, let him be sad again.

He was standing near the piano, a glass of wine in his hand. Wood had just asked him a question, which he'd answered automatically, and then, not to appear impolite, he nodded toward Colonel Ready, who took the point up, something about Federal strength in Nashville. When his eyes went back to her she was playing again. He watched her fingers slipping between the black keys, her arms lingering, her wrists lifted languidly as the phrases ended, then began again. With another nod to Wood and her father he stepped closer and leaned on the polished wood, careful to avoid her face, to keep from embarrassing her. Not only her arms and wrists and fingers played that sadly hopeful music, but her whole body.

"That's lovely," he all but whispered, and waited. "What is it?"

"One of the waltzes—the A-flat. Do you like Chopin?"

"He's got the ear of a donkey! Don't ask him!" Wood called out with a grin, and the spell was broken. She rose and he followed her as casually as he could across the room, where Alice was holding court on the sofa, her father and Wood on either side of her.

Morgan asked how their visit to the hospital had gone. Alice answered with such an outburst of passion that he couldn't control the tug of a smile behind his mustache. He pulled at one end and bent his head in simulated sympathy. For such a professed Christian, she could certainly hate her enemies generously enough. But something she said about Donelson made him perk up his ears.

"I'll visit them soon. One of my men . . ."

"May we come with you?"

Mattie, as soon as she uttered those words, looked down at the brooch that held little silk tucks across her breast. A light flush lay on her cheeks. Then she looked at him, determined but at the same time strangely vulnerable. He had an almost irrepressible desire to take her in his arms, but instead he cleared his throat and said, "Of course! Perhaps you can direct me to the men from Donelson. . . ."

Colonel Ready refused to let Alice go, but Captain Morgan was welcome to accompany Mattie if she wished to. He found himself the next morning following her into the two houses on Church Street that were used as a temporary hospital. What would happen to them when the Federals came? So many were too ill to be moved. Although the surgeons were trying, the shortage of morphine and anesthesia was shocking. Mattie carried in a basket over her arm a supply of homemade bandages—cut-up linen sheets—and some peach preserves and blackberry jam. Most of the less seriously wounded had gone south with the army. Those left behind brought home the horror.

Morgan found Peter Atherton first. His thigh had developed gangrene and his leg would be amputated that afternoon. The boy was strangely calm and resigned. His head rolled on the pillow, and when he recognized his captain he reached out a pleading hand and caught Morgan's arm. "Capt'n . . . if I die, will you show my folks my grave?"

The boy noticed Mattie then and said more quietly, "Well, maybe it don't matter. But will you take down a letter to my father back home in Alabama if I tell you?"

Mattie's eyes stung under tears but she said as easily as she could: "Of course. I'll get a paper. . . ."

When she was gone the hand on his arm tightened and Atherton's face paled. With a finger he motioned Morgan closer. "I know I'm gonna die, sir."

"No, no . . ."

"Yes. Don't you smell it? It's the stink of death. Be sure that letter gits home. . . ."

Mattie was back and he left them, to find the man from Donelson. "Buckner's pets," the man said hoarsely, but the grin was bitter. "Wonder what they'd call me now?" With a bandage covering half his face, the man declared through twisted lips that he knew for a fact that Buckner was in solitary confinement.

"No, no, that can't be . . ."

"It is, Capt'n. I swear. There's been no word, has there? Ain't that queer?"

He assured him that under the circumstances . . . but he wasn't sure himself. Buckner in confinement!

Mattie was still clutching the letter and crying openly by the time he got back to her. "Oh, it's so heart-rending! And he was so grateful for the help! Asking his father to visit his grave. Oh, John . . ." Her blue eyes had gone violet with tears.

"Come, let's go home."

The eyes of the men haunted him. The stench. But above all, that grip on his arm. He could still feel it as they walked into open air again.

Peter Atherton died that night.

"Damn this war!"

"Mattie!"

"Well, I don't care, Father. Damn it anyway. Damn the politicians who squabbled and started it. It was easy for them—fighting with words. The old fools."

Colonel Ready turned incredulous eyes from his daughter's face and avoided looking at Captain Morgan and Colonel Wood, who had just arrived with the news. He had been one of those politicians, and didn't feel up to finding excuses.

The truth was, the Yankees could come any day. His wife had already ordered the linens packed, directing operations like a general from her bedroom. She came downstairs and sent courtly, swallow-tailed Albert into the back yard with the silver and instructions to hide it so the devil himself couldn't find it. Then she turned to her young warrior, as she called him, whose fondness for Mattie she in no way discouraged, and confided some surprising opinions for a recluse. The uncomfortable hotels in Montgomery had *really* moved the Congress to Richmond; her husband's idea to buy up old steamers in Europe so the South could ship its cotton to England was humbug.

"And when you fight, don't believe all this talk of luck, my boy," the lady wobbled her head. "It's *pluck* that will see you through." Then, before she left him she touched his sleeve and looked at him with those glittering brown eyes: "The Yankees may kill us—if they think they can make any *money* by it—they'll take our land and everything we've got—but they'll never conquer us!" She walked away leaving him wondering at her "decline." The family blamed those Washington winters. After all, they said, the Colonel had been in Congress for seven years—long enough for the Yankee climate to do anybody in. Morgan doubted it, and said something flattering to Mattie about her mother's patriotism.

"Mattie was not exactly a peace commissioner herself in Nashville." Colonel Ready cleared his throat and sent his daughter a look of mock disapproval.

Mattie made a face.

"When that Yankee officer was slandering Captain Morgan and you stopped him dead with that remark," her father insisted.

"What remark?"

"It was nothing . . ." But her eyes held his.

"No, what remark?" She was actually blushing.

"When he asked your name, Daughter, and you said, 'Write Mattie Ready now, but by the grace of God one day I hope to call myself the wife of John Morgan.' Surely you remember?"

"Father! That was merely to stop his abuse. . . ." She dipped her head in confusion, then raised it defiantly. "So what if I did? It stopped him, didn't it? And we got our passes, didn't we?"

"You were in Nashville after the occupation?"

"We went up to escort Cousin Kate and Puss Ready back," the Colonel answered. "And Kate's little boy, Charley. They were in Nashville visiting Mary. They are at the farm. I hope you meet them."

"I don't." Alice, who had been silent all this time, laughed. "Watch out for your shins."

But his eyes were on Mattie. *Write Mattie Ready now, but . . .*

The next day she agreed to ride with him. His excuse, although genuine, was repeated for her parents' benefit; he needed to learn more about the back roads in the surrounding countryside. Hers was to get out of the house, where her mother's packing had reached a pitch of frenzy.

"I'm not afraid of them in the least," she said. "My only fear is that they may arrest Papa. He'll never take their oath."

It was the first time she had spoken of her feelings. Why, she's as vehement as Alice, he thought. Maybe more so. Wood was right: Alice had caught the Cause as she had caught religion, or might catch measles. Mattie's determination was as quiet and as resistant as a stone. He could feel sorry for that Yankee officer in Nashville.

They rode to the south of town, where the land lay flat and the river crossed the road about a mile and a half from the last houses. Then they cut across, avoiding limestone boulders in the fields, until they came to a little lane that connected with the Nashville Pike. She was an excellent rider, almost as good as Amanda, and might have been better, if she had been astride. But there was something so elegant about the way her skirts fell away when she cantered, he couldn't have wished her different. He followed her like a magnet. When they reached her house again she stopped before he could dismount and said softly, "Let's go on to Oaklands. It's not far."

"All right."

It wasn't. Just a few blocks down from the courthouse and to the left, a great plantation with enormous trees opened out under the sky. The house, a soft pink brick with long windows looking through the white wooden arches of a graceful gallery, sat like some haven from his dreams.

"It's Italianate," she said.

He laughed out loud, and she frowned.

He couldn't stop laughing. "Where are the crenelated towers?"

"Italianate architecture doesn't have crenelated towers, silly."

"Oh?"

"No. It's . . . light, and . . . graceful and . . . charming."

For a moment he didn't take his eyes from hers. She was saying those words as he helped her down, and for the briefest instant their bodies touched. The weight of her against him shot a pain of delight through his whole body and blurred the small, plump little woman who was walking down the steps greeting "her Mattie" and inviting them inside. Rachel Maney, whose husband was a colonel in Polk's corps, Cheatham's division, was full of news.

"You know General Polk?" she interrupted to ask him.

"No, ma'am."

"Episcopal Bishop of Louisiana," she said. "Proves we have God on our side."

He couldn't tell, from her tone or look, if she was joking.

They walked into the lovely entrance hall with its graceful curving stairs, its drawing room with chandeliers and pier mirrors and sixteen-foot ceilings and Sheraton tables and carved cornices and warmth and hospitality, and Wood's words came back: *They are why we do all this, aren't they?* When Mrs. Maney discovered that he had a sister married to one of Lee's generals, her appreciation turned into an embarrassing awe.

Mattie accepted her teacup and gazed past him through the long windows across the lawn and suppressed a smile. He inquired about the acreage, the number of hands, and was surprised to learn that they processed their own cotton and had, in fact, quite a textile operation. When he spoke of his factory in Kentucky, Rachel Maney proved to be more than a plump housewife. She knew the intricacies of the business almost as well as T.H. "It's too bad," she stopped short. "Your factory . . . But never mind. We'll get it back, won't we, Mattie? With these young warriors, *sans peur, sans reproche.*" She patted the girl's hand, and for an instant Martha Ready sat a little straighter and looked across at him, the smile gone.

"Yes we will, won't we?"

The next day, Tuesday, the contingent of Wharton's Rangers arrived, and he was busy all day. He sent two men with a message to Basil to come to Murfreesboro no later than Thursday. From his rides over the countryside with Mattie he had developed a plan. Quirk, ever the faithful scout, had kept him posted. There was little activity from Mitchell's Fourth Ohio at the asylum, other than the usual picket skirmish. Buell was still too busy regrouping in Nashville. If he could surprise the Fourth Ohio and capture Mitchell before Buell gave the word to move, maybe he would be able to exchange Mitchell for Buckner after all. The words "solitary confinement" still rang in his brain.

"What do you think?"

"A capital idea." Basil grinned over at young Tom Morgan. "When do we start?" They had ridden in a day early, guessing something was up. "It's dull as rain up there."

"La Vergne was never one of my favorite places, either." He grinned back, but so broadly Charlton looked suspicious.

"What makes Murfreesboro so interesting?"

"As a matter of fact, I've just received a note from a young lady . . ."

"Ahhh—ha!"

"No. It's not what you think." He handed it to Charlton. It was from Alice.

> As you know, Captain Morgan, since the army was here so much was damaged when they used our farm as a camp that Papa had a little corn brought into town and put in our icehouse. Well, yesterday Cap went to the stable to get the horse and discovered some *soldiers* in the icehouse! I was afraid they were Yankees and sent him to find Papa, but he had gone to the farm. Mama was sick and Mattie was at the hospital so I flew out there—without a bonnet—out of breath, I can tell you. They were from Texas but I called them gentlemen just the same and asked that they not take the corn. They scampered away—all *perfectly* respectful of me. But I'm afraid they will return and our corn, like so much at the farm, will be gone. Papa doesn't know I'm writing this, but will you please tell them to stay away?
>
> Alice

"Who's Alice?" asked Tom.

"You'll find out soon enough, you young rascal! I've asked the Rangers to write apologies. And sent, as a courtesy, a guard to be placed around the house. If you like, we can deliver the apologies in person."

Wood laughed so long and hard Morgan thought he would choke. "And get some more of that good pheasant and ham and wild duck and Madeira?" Wood asked when he could catch his breath. "Of course. We wouldn't be gentlemen if we didn't deliver the apologies in person, would we? Besides, we have to check that guard."

Basil, Charlton and Tom came, too, and could attest to the hospitality of Murfreesboro. Alice turned her charms on Basil, but learning he was married, settled for Charlton, who grinned all evening, much to Tom's distress. In a weak moment Charlton confided to her that they planned an expedition, and Alice, who had come to think of herself as a kind of confidant of General Hardee—he had left Murfreesboro wearing a blue comfort she had given him—pressed him for details. "Well, I suppose there's no harm in telling that we intend no less than an assault on the asylum to capture General Mitchell," Charlton said, then looked at his brother for forgiveness.

"General Mitchell!" Alice clapped her hands. "I hear he's a vulgar old Yankee . . ."

"We intend to exchange him for Buckner," Morgan said, with a smile to Charlton. "I guess our secret is safe with you."

"That'll set him!" Colonel Ready beamed. "Mattie, sing us a song!"

She went to the spinet, and both girls let loose with *"Hurrah! Hurrah! For Southern rights, hurrah! Hurrah for The Bonnie Blue Flag That bears a single star!"*

We are a band of brothers
And native to the soil,
Fighting for our liberty,
With treasure, blood, and toil.
And when our rights were threaten'd
The cry rose near and far,
Hurrah for The Bonnie Blue Flag
That bears a single star!

Tom joined in with his high ringing tenor, and the whole room, including old Albert, who was standing at the door of the dining room, a silver tray with drinks trembling in his hand, sang the chorus, and Alice began dancing around the room between the chairs, her hands raised above her head, her skirts catching at their guests' spurs:

HURRAH! HURRAH! For Southern rights, HURRAH!
Hurrah for The Bonnie Blue Flag
That bears a single star!

How could they, he thought, do anything else but win this war, with such enthusiasm behind them? Young and innocent as she was, he believed Alice when she said, "I would shoot them if they came into my room if Papa would let me have a pistol." When he told her that many of them were gentlemen, she spit out like some fierce little animal, "I would shoot them, gentlemen or not, the dogs."

"Oh, then maybe I'd better not bring you any prisoners."

"Would you! Oh, would you, Captain Morgan?" She looked so pleadingly at them that Wood's grin broke into a laugh.

"Suppose I promise you some?"

"I should treat them according to the usages of modern warfare," Alice answered primly, with a giggle.

The next day, Thursday, it snowed, one of those wet, big-flaked March snows which wouldn't last but which would prevent a track-free expedition. By afternoon they knew it would be gone—at this time of year the temperature could turn to springtime within hours—but all chance of a surprise attack would be gone also, and with Mitchell's whole brigade now stationed at the asylum, surprise was essential. They waited, cleaned their guns, counted out their rations of ammunition and food, and set out just after midnight. Since they knew the road to La Vergne like the back of their hands, and since this territory was, with the exception of an occasional Yankee picket, in Confederate control, they joked and sang as if they were out for a coon hunt. Once past their camp, however, they became different men. The seven miles to the asylum seemed endless. Finally, Morgan gave the signal to spread out and hide in thickets along the road about a mile from Mitchell's headquarters. The Federals had so many men that their bivouacs were scattered, and there was much passing back and forth between them. Morgan hoped to capture some couriers or guards, raise a ruckus that would bring out officers, with the chance of getting Mitchell.

They were lucky. In the course of an hour Wood had twenty-eight prisoners and Basil another sixty. A number of wagons loaded with supplies were burned, the teams used as mounts for the prisoners, who seemed terrified at the name "Morgan," and were docile enough. But only one staff officer, a captain, was among them. The big game was yet to be caught. Morgan sent the sixty off under a guard of ten men, Charlton in charge. Wood marched his twenty-eight off smartly.

Morgan stayed behind with one man, his faithful James West. He loved this sort of antic, wearing a Federal overcoat, passing himself off casually. He rode down the road directly toward Mitchell's headquarters with West, who was also in a blue overcoat. They met a guard of ten men, whose sergeant hailed them brusquely. Morgan hadn't failed to notice that their guns were stacked by a fence, and placed himself between the men and that fence and began berating the Sergeant for neglect of duty. "Don't you know it's just such neglect as this that enables that horse thief Morgan to play all his tricks?" He motioned West to place a pistol at the Sergeant's head. "Men have been court-martialed for less," he growled. "I have half a mind to march you to headquarters. In fact," he said, as if the idea had just occurred to him, "you are all under arrest."

Regretfully, for they were good Enfields, he left the guns stacked where they were—two men could hardly have carried them—and marched the men in the direction of La Vergne.

"Hey," the Sergeant blurted. "This ain't the way to camp."

"It is to ours," grinned West.

But capturing these ten men meant abandoning any hope of taking Mitchell. And there was no time to lose. The smoke from the burning wagons would, in another minute, attract attention, as it did. Morgan would never forget that mad chase back to La Vergne, over fences and ditches, down gullies and through woods. Only his knowledge of the countryside saved them. When Charlton returned to camp at Murfreesboro Saturday night, he had a similar experience to report—only his sixty prisoners had gotten away. Looking back, it had been madness to expect ten Confederates to escort sixty men on horses with enemy cavalry in pursuit. Basil was so upset he begged to do more, and immediately. He asked for permission to push as close to Nashville as possible, to find out what was going on. "They could move on Johnston any day," he said. "Besides, maybe I can get a general for you."

Morgan agreed, sent the ten prisoners to join Wood's twenty-eight and then collapsed on his bunk. It had been a hard two days, and no exchange for Buckner. Bess had lost a shoe. He looked over at Jesse, sleeping peacefully, and dreamt that night of home. God, if only Cal were here.

At the blacksmith's tent the next day he waited, coffee in hand, for another shoe to be fashioned and nailed on. "I've never seen you so impatient," Wood said, grinning.

"We promised the young ladies prisoners, didn't we?"

"They'll be in church now."

"Capital."

At the church door Private Tom Morgan found the sexton and gave him an elegantly penned note from his captain. Colonel Wood and Captain Morgan would present the ladies, in about an hour, with thirty-eight Yankee prisoners. "Give them time to get excited," Wood grinned. They washed up carefully, as anxious as schoolboys.

The procession into town was medieval, lacking only banners. Morgan and Wood wore their dress uniforms, yellow fringed sashes, sabers, wide hats with the single, turned-up brim, fully conscious of the impression they made. Ahead rode a number of Texas boys, who could not contain their exuberance. They galloped across Main Street and around the square, with Morgan's column following. By the time they reached the Ready house a crowd had gathered, surrounding them with cheers and waving handkerchiefs—and taunts for the well-dressed Federals. Morgan and Wood waited until the middle of the column marched opposite the front door, then gave the order to halt, and rode back to the stepping stone. Without dismounting they swept off their hats, and Morgan said to Mattie and Alice, standing in the walk by the gate, "Ladies, I present you with your prisoners. What disposal shall be made of them?"

Alice could only giggle, but Mattie, formally and as loud as she could so the crowd could hear, said, "You have performed your part so well, we are willing to entrust it all to you."

They sat chatting atop their horses for another fifteen minutes, drinking in the adulation. In the festive atmosphere, one old German actually stepped out of the ranks of the prisoners to ask the ladies for a glass of water, then, with a little begging speech, he protested his detainment: He was a teamster, not a soldier, only trying to keep his family in Cincinnata from starving . . . "Well, here's helt tuh de ladies in water." Colonel Ready came out and invited the two braves back to dine, then stood on the sidewalk watching them file away to the courthouse, where the prisoners were placed in cells in the basement.

Morgan rode back, leaving Wood to question a prisoner. He tied Bess at the hitching post and walked up the semicircular brick steps and stood a moment before the Ready door watching the porch swing, the trees and some early bulbs pushing through the flower beds. Spring! Once it had meant horse races and foals. Had Miss Lexington foaled? She was due this month! Now an early spring meant only that armies would move. His days, perhaps his hours, in Murfreesboro were numbered. He had left four of his own men as prisoners up at the asylum. He had failed to get an exchange for Buckner, despite all this pageantry. Because of the pageantry, he felt empty as he lifted the knocker. Mattie let him in.

"You are sad," she said simply.

"I left four men of my own up there."

"Oh, how horrible! What will you do?"

That's my girl, he thought. Not what can you do, but what will you do. "Go get them, of course. Quirk's already scouting the situation," he said jauntily, and felt better.

And you will, too, her eyes said.

"I'll . . ."

She drank in his earnest face, the gaze from his gray eyes, the shape of his
mustache, the softness of his lips in the even softer beard that had lost its
point and merely wandered down to his collar in a helpless, little-boy way.
His uniform was, as usual, impeccable, and from it emanated the faintest
scent of tobacco, so masculine, so mysterious, so forbidden. "I'll . . ." she
tried again, but this time her eyes dropped to his mouth and she longed to
melt into the comfort, the strength of him. He was like some strange god
who had come to her with a secret neither of them could understand. She
only knew she wanted to cling to him, to hold him and be held by him. The
circle of his arms . . . oh, that would be a universe all its own. He was
sweetness and light when so much around was misery.

She had never been kissed like that. His chest against hers made her own
press against him, the breath rise in her throat until, behind her closed eyes,
her whole body seemed to float, to become soft with longing. When his lips
left hers they returned in little seeking, sucking kisses down her neck, under
her ear. So this is what it's like, she thought. So this . . . no wonder they
talk about it so. He clasped her to him, rocked her to and fro. She never
wanted to leave those arms. Oh, Morgan, my Morgan . . .

"I love you, Mattie," he was whispering in her hair. "I've loved you from
that first time I saw you. Do you remember? When I walked into that room
and you were singing? I saw . . ."

"What did you see?"

He was so tall! *You'll love those Kentuckians* her father had said. Could he
have known how much?

He was looking down into her face and said quite simply, "Will you wait
for me, Mattie?"

Behind them they could hear Albert mumbling to the other servants in
the dining room.

"I'd wait for you, John Morgan, until the sky falls in and the earth crum-
bles and the sea dries up. I'll—"

His hand reached out to her hair and stopped her. "That's quite long
enough."

31

Cousin Kate was a wide-bosomed woman with a fat, flat face. The day her little boy, Charley, came in from the farm with Puss Ready, Mattie's mother murmured, "At a time like this," but never for the world would she have admitted that the presence of Yankees in Nashville could change one slice of baked ham in her hospitality. She chatted with no mention of Mary, her Nashville daughter, who had actually entertained Yankee officers in her house. When the Confederate guests arrived, the gentlemen in uniform were "friends of the Colonel's."

Puss Ready was tall and slim, with a hawk's nose and eyes that didn't miss much. Morgan wondered how in the world she had ever attained that nickname. He never learned her real one. Cousin Kate did the talking, when she could stop Little Charley from interrupting. He raced around, letting out yells from his round blond head. Involuntarily, Morgan drew in his shins.

"We came to see the Yankees," Cousin Kate called out over the uproar. "Do you think that's possible, Captain?"

"I . . ."

"I hardly think that's proper, on a Sabbath afternoon, Kate," Mattie answered for him.

"But Colonel Wood told Alice . . ."

"I'm afraid Colonel Wood is sometimes enthusiastic."

"Well, Captain, Ah nevah! And why shouldn't he be? Just think, this town with Yankee prisonahs for a change. Ah remembah the day the Yankees marched into Nashville, strutting around, pistols drawn. You may be sure *Ah* didn't notice them. Wouldn't give the satisfaction."

"We were packing to leave," Mattie reminded her.

"Nevah-the-*less*," Puss put in, her beady black eyes on the Captain as if she would flirt with him, "we seem to remembah you were pretty pert with that one who came into the pawlah . . ."

"Were they quartered in your house?" he asked, and received a glance of gratitude from Mattie.

"In *Mary's* house," Cousin Kate answered for her. She turned to Mattie. "Ah heah your sister's a right propah Yankee by now." Before she could get an answer she swung her head to Morgan. "Ah wouldn't live in Nashville if you gave it to me. We were just visitin'—from *Knoxville*. Ah nevah saw such wishy-washy folks in mah life! Let the Yankees take ovah, mind you, helpin' themselves to everything. When Colonel Ready drove up with that carriage Ah was nevah so glad to see anybody . . . *Charley stop that!*"

"They're all cowards," Puss squeezed out between drawn lips. "Every one."

Morgan couldn't help chuckling, and almost said, I wish that were so, but thought better of it. He would rather face the Yankees than these two, with their little Viking. They were interrupted by Albert. The old German from Cincinnati was at the door, with Sam Buckner, his guard, asking for a quilt.

"The nerve!" the ladies chorused.

"I'll see to it," said Mattie, and he followed her into the hall, where Albert was keeping an uneasy vigil at the door, and answering, as best he could, the stream of talk the old fellow sent out. He lost his tongue when he saw Morgan.

"Is Colonel Wood coming to dine?" Morgan asked Sam.

"He's still interrogating, sir. He sent you a message that he would be by in a little." His eyes wandered past Morgan's shoulder to Alice, who had returned with Mattie and an old quilt. The German, subdued and satisfied, mumbled and bowed.

"Why don't you come with him?" Alice asked.

Sam's eyes lit up. "Would you . . . could I . . . sir!"

"You have the lady's invitation, soldier. The relief guard should be here soon from camp."

"Bring Tom Morgan, too," Mattie said, to cover her sister's impertinence. "We love the way he sings."

"Little Tom? Sure, ma'am!"

There was magic in the Ready parlor that night, with Tom's sweet tenor floating above the girls' soft voices. "*Somewhere my love lies dreaming . . . Sweetly dreaming . . . The happy hours away . . .*" And then all the color of a rousing, rollicking "Camptown Races." After dinner, in a moment of good-bye in the hall, Mattie smiled up at him.

"So you gave him a Yankee pistol."

"Who?"

"Private Buckner."

"It was nothing . . ."

"He loves you. He was worried sick that you wouldn't return. All your men love you. I've never seen such devotion in my life."

Her straightforwardness embarrassed him, and he fell silent.

"So what will you do about the four?"

"Go get them." *As soon as I know Basil is safe from Nashville*, he said to himself.

Basil returned the next morning full of high jinks and tales of ambush. They had gotten to within four miles of Nashville and McCook's division, but then were nearly surrounded and had to run for it. So, despite the high jinks, another fruitless effort.

Before noon Morgan set out with Wood and half a dozen men and a flag of truce to get his prisoners. He brought four Yankees as exchange. When they got to the picket line they met Mitchell's whole brigade, cavalry, artillery, and infantry riding in wagons, on their way to Murfreesboro to capture him. General Mitchell almost burst with indignation. Morgan had never seen a man so enraged. "This is against the usages of war, sir. Outrage . . . trick. You knew I was about to capture you. . . ."

In broad daylight, in a countryside full of Confederate sympathizers, oh, yes, thought Morgan. Wood's frown wiped the grin from his face. Mitchell, under the usages of war, had every right, in spite of the flag, to continue his little expedition, and a glance could tell them, once they reached La Vergne, that they outnumbered the Confederates ten to one. But General Mitchell was so furious that the main object of his expedition stood before him safe and calmly requesting an exchange of prisoners that he put out of his mind what would have been a more practical victory at the moment, the capture of Morgan's whole squadron. Both sides pulled up and dismounted, and conducted their business under a large oak.

One of Mitchell's majors pulled Wood aside.

"How many . . . how many men does Morgan have?"

Wood shifted his eyes, deliberately looking secretive. "I'll tell you *in confidence*, Major . . ."

"Yes?"

"You've seen the mischief he is capable of."

"Yes."

"Such activity could only be accomplished by a *large force*." Wood was whispering now, but his words hissed between their bent heads. The Yankee major said nothing. Wood went on: "I tell you, he hears from people I never *heard* of. He controls the motions of men even *he* rarely sees. . . . I, Major, who am cognizant of almost everything that goes on in his camp, am often surprised to receive news of enterprises accomplished by his orders in quarters very *remote* from where he is personally operating. . . ."

The Major was nodding, chin on chest, eyes closed. He opened them with a flash of fear that made Wood almost burst out laughing.

Mitchell, however, was no fool, and Morgan and Wood knew their days were numbered. When they had made their exchange and reached camp again, Morgan confided to Colonel Wood that he must make one last impression before they left. Impression on whom? Wood almost asked, but didn't. He agreed that the Yankees must be kept in a constant state of uncertainty. It was a little like tweaking the toe of a sleeping giant, with all the titillation of schoolboys stealing apples. They both knew how insignificant it was, but how significant they must make it seem.

Morgan was studying a map, his finger moving through the yellow light of a coal oil lantern along an old road from the Lebanon Pike north. It crossed the Cumberland and stopped at Gallatin, on the main line of the L&N. "Not far from here there's a railroad tunnel. If we could destroy that . . . that would be a parting shot, eh?"

"How long do you think it would take?"

"How long do we have?"

"Let's try it and see!"

"For such an expedition, we'll have to get permission."

Morgan's caution surprised him. At Wood's look Morgan added, "We could leave at first light for Shelbyville."

Hardee was glad to see them, although reluctant to agree. His own plans were for an imminent move directly south, through Fayetteville, Tennessee, to Huntsville, Alabama. In fact, the camp was in the turmoil of packing when they arrived. Some of the regiments had already left for Fayetteville, but luckily the Fifth Kentucky was not one of them. It was the first time Morgan had had a chance to see T.H. and Wick since Bowling Green. T.H. was glum. The loss of Pea Ridge was on all their minds: That meant the loss of Missouri. Even the news from Hampton Roads, that the *Virginia* had blocked, in her duel with the *Monitor*, a Federal move up the James against Richmond, did little to encourage him. "Oh, it was grand, but it only proves our need for more ironclads. If we had only gone on to Washington after Manassas," T.H. said. "For four whole days we could have. That victory will be our undoing."

"But I've news from home," Cripps Wickliffe said brightly. "It appears that the Yankees are courting Kentucky, hoping to win her to their side. The Leestown farm is intact. But everybody is holding his breath."

"There's still a chance, then," Morgan said softly.

"Where? What?"

"At home. If we could get Kentucky . . ."

"Yes!" T.H. caught the implication. "If we could only get Kentucky . . ."

They stayed overnight, catching the train back to Murfreesboro on Wednesday. The next day, the 13th of March, the last of Johnston's army left for Alabama. "You may play your little trick at Gallatin," Hardee had said, "but you must leave immediately for Huntsville. You will know why when you get there."

There was mail, as always, at headquarters, to be received or delivered, letters pressed into hands with last-minute entreaties. Mattie and Alice had sent three with them for their brother Horace, on Hardee's staff. He was already in Fayetteville, but he had left one of his own behind at Shelbyville, to be delivered by the first persons going to Murfreesboro. There was one for Alice from Hugh Gwyn.

"He must be an extraordinary young man," said Wood, acting jealous.

"Oh, he is!" Alice answered, tilting her head so that her full little mouth could show to its best advantage. Mattie, who had gone to the corner window to read the letter from Horace, lifted her eyes to Morgan under worried brows.

"What does it mean?"

"It means the army will concentrate at Huntsville, Alabama."

"And . . . ?"

"And, more than that, I can't say."

You won't say, her eyes said. But that's all right. Maybe one day there will be no secrets between us. She gave him her most engaging smile. "Can you stay for dinner?"

Alice couldn't stop talking. Horace was their only brother. He was a lieutenant in Colonel Palmer's Twenty-third Tennessee Infantry. And Private Hugh Gwyn the only true, noble friend she had ever known, the only one she would have forever. She liked that word, *forever*. "Many dear loved ones may be severed forever—not merely for weeks, but *forever*. Oh, Captain Morgan, don't you see? All in this world should be happiness and love.

Lent started last Wednesday. How can we call ourselves Christians when we are caught in so much . . . Oh, for one gleam of light in the darkness . . . But we will be successful," she caught herself up. "God will yet smile on us. Everything will turn right in the end."

"There's only one thing more dangerous than a scared Yankee—and that's a Southern woman turned religious," whispered Wood to him as they mounted again on their way back to camp.

"I hope you're right." Morgan laughed. "Then we *are* invincible!"

In a private moment, he had told Mattie of his expedition to Gallatin. She had given him a little New Testament, in Morocco leather and gilt-edged India paper. He could feel it now, in the inside pocket of his uniform, pressed against his chest. The feel of her body against his came back. *I hope you are right*, he said again to himself as he headed Bess down Main Street. *Then we are invincible.*

"What's that you're humming?"

"Was I humming?"

Just about eight miles on the north side of the Cumberland River, the little town of Gallatin slept beside the main line of the L&N tracks, thirty miles northeast of Nashville and fifty almost due north from Murfreesboro. Overlooked by the Federals as a place of little importance, it controlled, if one looked at the map, the direct communication by train between Louisville —where Halleck commanded the whole Western operation—and Nashville, where Buell waited to move on Johnston. Besides, there was that tunnel.

"If I could destroy that tunnel," Morgan mused, "the Federal line to Louisville might be out of commission for months."

Wood looked up from his candle. It flickered from the sudden gust made by Morgan's waving hand. He looked over at Basil Duke, deep in a book. "What do you think?" he asked Duke.

"I always wait and see the situation at first hand," Basil answered with a grin, then sobered. "We may not have time. The Rangers left us this morning. I need not remind you that they are never overcautious."

"Then we'd best start at once," his captain answered. "If we can't destroy the tunnel, the least we can do is tear up a little track and listen in on their telegraph . . ."

"And send some messages ourselves!" Wood chuckled.

It wasn't until midday on Saturday that they finally trotted out of town. All day Friday was spent in final preparations for the evacuation from the camp at La Vergne and the smaller one at Murfreesboro. That night, under the pretense of needing some information concerning the back roads, Morgan rode with Wood to the Ready house to see the Colonel. He was at the farm, but, as Wood jokingly said, the girls would do.

Indeed, they would. The night took on all the aspects of a farewell, and as the hours passed, Morgan kept telling little stories of his time in the Green River country, of close calls around Nashville. Wood countered with stories of his own, until it was well after midnight when they left. Alice had been suppressing a yawn through at least three tales of valor. When she worried about the flagstaff at the courthouse, which had flown the Bonnie Blue Flag these past weeks, Morgan promised to send Sam Buckner around the next morning before they left to cut it down for her. She was ecstatic, jumping up, suddenly wide awake, clapping her hands.

"But keep it," he warned. "We'll need it again . . ."

He would never forget the look Mattie gave him. Was this really good-bye? He lingered another hour, so long that Wood had to clear his throat in the darkness of the front porch and protest the chill. "It's not June yet," he warned. "Miss Mattie will catch a cold."

"Not in the warmth of such good company," she stoutly answered. When Morgan turned to look at her she added, to cover her embarrassment, "It's actually balmy tonight."

"That's right," he murmured. "The weather is with us. We shall be successful this time."

"Aren't you always?"

They were very close. Alice had walked on with Colonel Wood and they were alone. She looked up, and before he knew what he was doing he had her in his arms, his mouth drinking from hers all the warmth he had missed so long. Her hands, caressing the back of his neck, pressed him back to her when he started to draw away. Their message, the total acceptance, the need, sent hot chills down his spine. They heard Wood clear his throat again and propriety pulled them apart. It had been only a few seconds, but it was enough to feed their memories for a long time.

Before noon, he sent young Sam Buckner around with the flagpole, gleefully cut down, which Sam presented as a knight might some trophy. Morgan bowed formally when they passed the house on their way out of town. It might be, a voice in the back of his head kept saying, the last time I see her. Colonel Ready rode with them until they crossed the river. "Tell the young ladies," Morgan said as he waved his good-bye, "that I will bring them a victory."

"Oh, for a thousand Morgans!" Alice exclaimed when her father told her.

"I wouldn't be getting too enthusiastic now, Daughter. Buell is about to move from Nashville . . ."

"They'll never catch him! Not in a million years! He will come back, our Marion, crowned with fresh and never-fading laurels. What a bright, thrilling page his adventures will make in the future history of the Confederacy, when it is written! Then should I be living, how I shall love to say, I knew him quite well. . . . God bless him and spare him till the end of this awful war. . . ."

"Alice!"

"Well, it's true, Papa. We all love him. You do, too, don't you, Papa?"

"I . . . I admire all our gallant fighting men. . . ." Colonel Ready, used to his wife's reticence, was a little taken aback by this explosion of feminine feeling. Mattie said nothing.

Alice had Albert and Cap carry the flagpole into her bedroom, where she proposed to hide it until the Confederate Army came back. "And they will come back!"

"Of course they will, dear."

"You don't think so, do you, Mama?"

"I think your pole might serve the Confederacy just as well if you chopped it up and burned it for firewood," Cousin Kate said with her usual emphasis.

No wonder Charley was such a brat. Alice couldn't help asking, "Why?"

"They seem to be making a habit of that, don't they? Burning everything behind them? That crazy General Johnston! It will be the first time in history that a war will be won by retreating!"

"Are you ladies ready?" the Colonel called from the foot of the stairs. "The buggy is out front."

"Be with you in a minute, Papa! Are you sure it's out of the way enough?"

"Of course. We'll just arrange this rug so."

"Thank you, Mama. You're the best mama in the world."

"Alice, are you coming?" Mattie, halfway down the stairs, with Little Charley in tow, had only agreed to this overnight visit to the farm because she knew her father was worried about the Yankees coming. She couldn't for the life of her see the difference . . . she could handle a dozen Yankees better than Cousin Kate's offspring. She handed Charley up to Albert, whose battered stovepipe, in the process, slipped rakishly over his wool head. Charley begged to sit on the coachman's seat, and Albert, with one arm around him, flicked the horse into a trot.

Alice, after six hours of Little Charley and Cousin Kate's nonstop talk, called out in the middle of the night, "*I can't stand this!*"

Worried about Morgan, the Yankees, her nerves frayed by Cousin Kate, Mattie threw back the covers and walked to the window. She laid her forehead against the cold pane, then stood very straight. "Very well. We'll ask Papa if we can go home in the morning. Now, get some sleep!"

Colonel Ready complained, but agreed to let the girls return to town, Puss with them. Kate would stay at the farm with Charley. He, too, would stay, but he did not want to tell them why: He had determined just this morning to conceal the livestock—the work horses and milk cows—in two isolated barns on the far side of the cornfield.

Mattie, Alice and Puss were in Murfreesboro before noon. Two hours later the first Federals rode into town.

Alice was in her room writing in her diary when the servants rushed upstairs calling, "The Yankees has come!" Mattie ran down and ordered all the downstairs windows bolted. Behind closed blinds in their room again, the girls watched the Yankees ride by, wary-eyed, their fingers on their pistols.

"My, they are a good-looking lot, aren't they?" said Puss, her long pointed nose brushing the drape. "And well dressed, too."

"And why shouldn't they be!" said Alice indignantly. "They have all the factories, all the guns, all the everything. . . . I think they are from that silly Ohio regiment, the one Captain Morgan took prisoners from."

"Colonel Wood, too," Mattie reminded her.

They didn't stay long. Evidently the main force was camped by the river, and this reconnaissance satisfied them that the town was quiet.

Quiet! If they had known! Alice and Mattie had Cap hitch the horse and took the buggy back to the farm to warn their father. They found him in deep consultation with one of Morgan's men, who had made it through the lines in Federal clothes.

"Don't you know they brag they'll hang you for guerrillas if they catch—" The Colonel stopped when he saw his daughters.

"Is he safe?" Mattie asked.

"He is safe, ma'am. If his horse don't give out. They ride like the wind. . . ."

"You've ridden pretty hard yourself, young man," Colonel Ready said appreciatively. "Here, let's get you a good meal before you collapse."

They did not, as it turned out, have much more information than the young cavalryman could see for himself: Mitchell's Fourth Ohio bivouacked at the river just outside town, Buell's army on the move from Nashville. The woods were full of bluecoats.

"But not all legally worn, ma'am." He winked at Mattie.

He was so tall and blond, so young, so optimistic and so thin in a raw-boned, tanned way. His voice was soft, his manner gentle. He couldn't have been eighteen. Exhausted, he slept for two hours, begging them to wake him no later. He must report . . . They loaded his pockets with ham sandwiches and gave him a fresh horse. Even Little Charley stood in silent awe as he galloped off.

They had the news the next morning, after they went home. He had been caught three miles from the river, just east of the railroad tracks, at the edge of a cotton field. They gave him a military trial and hanged him from an oak tree just north of town.

"Now girls, now girls." It was the tenth time he had said that, and Colonel Ready caught himself. "It must have been that Federal overcoat. Technically, it made him a spy . . ."

"Ohhh!" His words brought forth a fresh wailing.

"He will come back, you wait and see!" Alice almost screamed at him, her chin trembling. "Flaunting his banner, driving the . . . enemy . . . before him! What a glorious day . . . No, let me finish! What a glorious day we have to . . . look forward . . . to. God is with us! We will succeed! I do not feel the least fear . . ."

She slumped in Mattie's arms and the servants carried her upstairs, where Mattie sat by her bed all night, unsleeping, staring straight ahead, the memory of that gentle smile, that sweet boy, so shy, so shy. She couldn't shake it, even after her mother came in and insisted she go to her own room and try to sleep. Did his neck snap when the rope slipped? Did they mount him on a horse, or build a platform? Papa wouldn't talk about it. *John Hunt Morgan might be in one of those blue overcoats* . . . she couldn't think of it.

Colonel Ready sat in his room staring at his hands, not seeing them. His wife, in bed from all the excitement, asked him weakly to come rest.

"You've done all you can. You went out there. . . ."

"I couldn't believe it," he kept saying. "I thought they were gentlemen. Even General Mitchell was ready to listen when I explained that they are regular cavalry troops, mustered into the Confederate Army and worthy of the civilized ways of war . . . the usages of war. . . . That Major! That Major!"

"I know, dear."

" 'A little bloodletting will be good for my digestion,' he said."

"I know, dear."

"And the General didn't argue! I can't . . . I can't . . . I'm too old for all this. My God, Mary, what's to become of us?"

No one had ever seen this sturdy little man so at a loss. It was her turn to be strong. "We will do what we can, Charles. We *will* do what we can."

She said it so fiercely he looked up. "Yes," he said. "Yes. What we can. Whatever that is."

Two days passed. No news. Kate, with Little Charley, ventured back to town. Colonel Ready returned to the farm. Then late Wednesday night a solitary horseman rang the doorbell and Alice ran to Mattie's room to find her sister. She found Kate and Puss leaning out, talking to a man on the sidewalk who needed to see Colonel Ready. "He's not here!" Mattie called out, already pulling on her robe. She ran downstairs, Alice behind her. It was Sam Murrill, Morgan's courier. Face covered with dust, hair matted to his head, his voice came in spurts as he handed her a note. She recognized that round handwriting with its eloquent loops. Would it be safe for him to pass through town? He was at Lascassas.

"That's about ten miles from here!" she hissed.

"Yes, ma'am."

"He wants to know where the Federals are camped."

"Yes, ma'am."

She borrowed his pencil and scribbled: "They are eight miles from here, come in haste . . ."

They watched the boy remount and gallop off.

"Who was that, dear?"

"A courier from Captain Morgan," Alice burst out. "Oh, Mama . . ."

"And what did he want?" As smooth as if she were passing pudding.

"Oh, Mama, to know how far the Yankees are . . ."

"And what did you tell him?" The voice grew louder as the lady appeared at her door.

"That they are about eight miles from here," answered Mattie.

The frail lady at the top of the stairs displayed an amazing amount of energy at the news. "They are closer than that, and you know it! You'll get him killed, just like that boy who came Sunday night . . ."

"You *know* about that?"

"Of course. Your father . . ."

"He *talked* to them?"

"He arranged for his . . . burial. I tell you, Mattie, you'll get us all killed. . . . You are sacrificing some of our best men, and Lord knows we need every one! Now you'll get the town shelled. . . . They are just at the river, not three miles from here, and you know it. Whatever possessed you?"

"Yes, whatever did?" asked Kate, beside Mrs. Ready at the top of the stairs. "Now nobody can go back to sleep until this business is over. . . ."

Cousin Kate did sleep, though, on the day sofa in Mattie's room, and snored. Puss curled beside her, staring at the fire, which Alice and Mattie took turns poking, until Alice, too, nodded and closed her eyes. The only sound was the hiss of the fire, and Cousin Kate, and Alice's kitten, purring in Mattie's lap. Thank God Charley was in the old nursery, at the back of the house. Mattie occasionally looked up, told Alice to go to bed, then stared at the fire again, her hand stroking the cat. She turned him over and cradled him against her arm.

"What if the Yankees reach town before he does?" Alice whispered. "We might get Papa's pistols and station ourselves at the square . . . behind the columns at the courthouse. Oh, if Papa were here! Maybe we should send Albert to the farm for him."

"We should have thought of that an hour ago," Mattie said. The kitten stretched. He was gray, with four white feet and golden eyes. Mattie picked up one front paw, then the other, caressing them with her thumb. "It may already be too late," she almost whispered.

"Don't say that!"

"What are you doing?"

"Getting my shawl. And my boots."

"Whatever for?"

"If they come, I'm going to get the fleetest horse I can find and warn Captain Morgan . . ."

"How will you know where to find him?"

"He said he was at Lascassas . . ."

"You know as well as I do there are three different ways to get there . . . I showed them to him myself." Mattie's tone was so reproachful that Alice fell back, twisting her hands. Immediately Mattie regretted the harshness in her voice. The kitten jumped down. "Why don't you try to get some sleep, honey bun? Crawl in my bed. I'll wake you if anyone comes. . . ."

It didn't take much persuasion, and Alice, refusing to undress, pulled the covers over her, her shawl and boots within reach. The only sound now was the snap of the fire. It sent little wavering flashes of light across the walls. From somewhere a dog barked, and then all was quiet. But Mattie couldn't doze. Did he know of the hanging? She hadn't told the courier last night. Last night—yes, it was, for now the first light of another day was already shining on the edges of the sky. She drew her shawl closer and moved her feet together. Why did it always seem so much colder just before the sun came up? Why hadn't she thought before how it must be for the soldiers marching, sleeping on the ground, without a tent or even a blanket or even one of those Yankee waterproofs—why did they call them shebangs? They must have a language all their own in camp. Oh, how she wanted to share everything with him, not just her prayers for his safety! He had come to Murfreesboro just two short weeks ago, when they were feeling sad about Johnston's army leaving . . . and now she couldn't remember her life without him. *I never want to be without him.* The fire took it up, and danced it on the walls. She didn't care, she didn't care if it was unladylike or not, if she ever saw him again she would tell him. She had never felt such a longing, such a terror in her life. Suppose Mama was right, and they had put him in danger?

A rock on the window clattered like ice. She pushed up the sash and saw two horsemen below, one on a jet-black horse with a star.

"Mattie?"

She flew downstairs, Alice behind. By the time they reached the front door the horsemen had dismounted and, witness or not, she found herself in his arms.

Confusedly, pushing her hair back with a shaking hand, she heard Colonel Wood, beside them, thanking her for the note.

"Yes, yes." Morgan grinned. "It saved us a long ride and an immense deal of trouble . . . we knew nothing except what we could learn from some country people, and they told us the town was infested with Federals. One of my scouts didn't return . . ."

So he didn't know. Of course, how could he?

"What are we standing here for? Come in. Papa is at the farm. Mama is still asleep." Mattie shut the door behind them and they sat on the double benches in the hall. "Your scout . . ."

"Was hanged, Captain Morgan," Alice finished for her, wringing her hands. "Oh, you mustn't stay here!" Her eyes ran frighteningly over the blue overcoats, then to their faces again.

"We'll be fine, Alice," Morgan leaned forward, but he was visibly shaken.

"Mitchell and his troops are camped on the other side of the river . . ."

"On the Nashville Pike?"

"Yes."

"And they haven't bivouacked in the town?"

"No . . . they received such a snub Sunday when they came in here and paraded around on their horses. Just after church . . ." Alice stopped.

Morgan leaned back, and for the first time they guessed how weary he must be. Without waking the servants, Mattie stoked the stove, made coffee and scrambled eggs.

"What will you do?" Mattie asked, with a glance through the kitchen window toward the street.

"Join Johnston at Huntsville."

"No—I mean—now?"

"Gather my boys, waiting in that little wood just west of the square . . ."

They hung on his words so eagerly. He told them of Gallatin, of some fun they'd had with a telegraph operator, who was bragging about what he would do if Morgan came. Morgan demanded his pistol and Wood said, "Sir, may I introduce you to Captain John Morgan?" Wood added his own vivid description of a ride on a locomotive up to the tunnel, the destruction of which, unfortunately, would take more time than they had . . .

So they hadn't destroyed the tunnel after all. A rooster crowed. Yes, time. Their eyes met.

"We ran the locomotive off the track and over a steep bank," Wood was saying. "They won't use that one again."

Their eyes met again and she didn't care if the others saw what she was saying with them. The good-byes began, and when they walked outside the sky was already pale with another day. They hung back, deliberately allowing the others to get ahead. He took both her hands in his and let his eyes drink in her hair, the shape of her face, as if he would store her in his memory.

"When they come, your father has addresses in Huntsville."

"We'll stay. We'll be safe."

She said it with such assurance that he had to believe her. "If things were different . . ."

"If things were different I might never have met you, John Morgan."

Still he stood there, his head bent, his gray eyes on hers. The catch in her voice tore at his heart.

"Mattie . . . oh, Mattie, will you marry me? You don't have to answer now . . ."

"Why not?" she whispered. "We both know we may not have . . ." She hesitated, shook her head and let her eyes travel to his. "Much time. I will marry you, John Morgan. With all my heart! Just be safe . . . I'll pray every minute. . . ."

"John!" Wood had already mounted and Alice was holding Bess's reins. Morgan swung up and waved. The two women waited by the gate until they could see his men forming by the courthouse at the end of the street. Tom Morgan started up "Cheer, Boys, Cheer! Away with Idle Sorrow!" and the others joined in. How brave they were! Alice swore afterwards that the clearest voice was the Captain's.

"Oh, Alice."

"Well, it's true. How brave they are to stand there singing with the Yankees at their heels! God bless them!"

They stood watching the riders until they could see no more.

When Mattie turned toward the house she saw Alice's face, red and trembling, swollen with tears. "Oh, darlin' . . ."

Alice flung out an arm and swept her hand away. "He's *your* beau! *Any*body can see that! He never once noticed me, and I . . . I prayed for him so!"

"We all love him, Alice."

"But not like *that*," Alice said. "Not like that!"

Before she could stop her, Alice ran upstairs and Mattie heard the tearing of paper behind the door of her room.

"Whatever is Alice doing?" Cousin Kate, yawning, asked in the hallway.

"I suspect she's . . . rearranging her diary."

"At a time like this? I do declaih in Nashville we had bettah things to do with the Yankees comin'!"

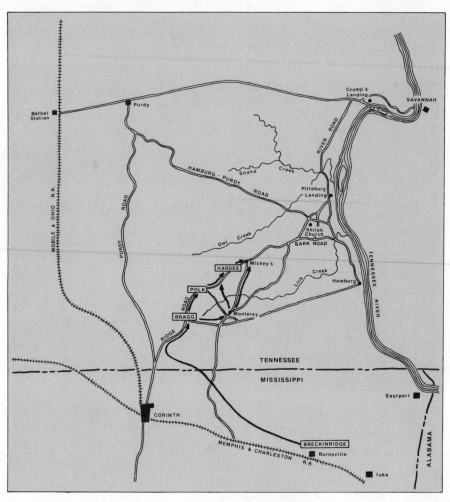

Confederate Advance at Shiloh
April 3–6, 1862

32

SHILOH! *Shiloh*. The sound of that name, like the vibrato of a chill wind, would blow everything, everything before it. A silent, sacred, secret place for tabernacles to wait, as in the days of Samuel: *And the whole congregation of the children of Israel assembled. . . . And the land was subdued before them.*

Shiloh.

A little log church in Tennessee.

An insignificant country meeting place surrounded by a tumbled, up-ended land of vine-choked woods and ravines with sheer drops of a hundred feet or more, of forests and fields where more than a hundred thousand men would struggle and scream and leave more Americans dead in two days than the Revolution, the War of 1812 and the Mexican War combined. Where the thunder of cannon, like a mad giant hammering the sky, his feet mired in blood-soaked mud, would annihilate valor, however brave, however individual.

From the river and across trembling peach blossoms and peaceful ponds and the dark, haunted mounds of dead Indians the roar would deafen and drown and finally silence the groans of the wounded and dying, and the giant would laugh at those onrushing lines with their flags fluttering and their notion of honor and wait for the fear that would numb and the pain that would blind all human hope. Like a monster lifting his head above the clouds, War would watch the miscalculation and error, the orders received too late or sent too soon, nameless boys dying and a general with steel-blue eyes and a square jaw, under vines and in the shade of April leaves, laughing at the wound that would kill him.

No grave, however deep, can bury you, O Shiloh.

No wind, however strong, can blow the memory of you away.

Pierre Gustave Toutant Beauregard lit a cigar. He blew the smoke from him and tilted back in his chair, letting his fingers wander down the tiny triangle of hair that tapered to a point below his lower lip. He tucked his chin and rolled his expressive Gallic eyes to the ceiling. On it he saw the telegram he was about to send to Richmond: FOR A WEEK ISLAND #10 HAS WITHSTOOD BOMBARDMENT. THE ENEMY HAS THROWN 3,000 SHELLS, EXPENDED 100,000 POUNDS OF GUNPOWDER, WITH THE RESULT THAT WE HAVE SUFFERED ONE MAN KILLED AND NONE SERIOUSLY WOUNDED. OUR BATTERIES ARE ENTIRELY INTACT.

More numbers. The War Department loved numbers. In his mind he added: *We haf dishabled one enemy gunboat, another iz reported to be sunk.*

His frown deepened. That sounded weak. "How to end it?" he asked aloud. Ah, *oui*. "Ze fantasee of invincible Yankee power iz at las' dispelled."

Splahndeed! He pulled at the cigar and sent out another ring. His optimism was genuine. True, New Madrid had been abandoned, but Island Number Ten held: Downriver, Fort Pillow and Memphis were safe. And farther down, his beloved New Orleans. Hadn't one lady, when asked in whom she trusted, answered, "God and Beauregard"? He blew his nose.

The lady was right. His career had been brilliant. Mexico with Scott, Superintendent at the Point, then, luckily, in charge at Charleston, to direct the bombardment of Sumter! After that, tactical commander at Bull Run and Manassas, where they began calling him "Old Bory"—although he did not look his forty-three years!—and, even more to his liking, "the Southern Napoleon." He swiveled his chair, stuck his feet up and studied his nails.

He was the South's fifth-ranking general. And why not? At least Davis had agreed that he deserved an independent command, out from under Joe Johnston, and sent him west. In spite of chronic bronchitis, hadn't he pushed on to Bowling Green and agreed to take command at Columbus, with that fuddy-duddy Bishop Polk under him? No one could argue with his astonishment when he learned of the pitiably small garrison there—he, the hero of Manassas! Only with much reluctance—and because he was dedicated to the Cause—did he agree to remain, to help Sidney Johnston defend the Mississippi Valley.

And defend it he would! He got up and strode across the room, fully conscious of his resemblance to Bonaparte. (His hair, his hair he absolutely refused to brush forward—hadn't his mother always admired his forehead, the sign of character?) He walked to the window and pulled back the drape, his finely chiseled hand clinging to the folds. Outside the ugly little town of Corinth, Mississippi, lay encased in March mud. Ah, but it held the key to the Memphis & Charleston Railroad. And its name had a classical ring. Could it be here, he thought, yes here as well as anywhere—whoever heard of Waterloo before 1815?—that he, P. G. T. Beauregard, would go down in history as the greatest general on the North American continent?

He could be proud of the way he had moved swiftly after the fall of Donelson. Within a week he had arranged for all available troops in West Tennessee to gather here, not only because of the railroad, but because the Tennessee River, where the Yankees were gathering, was only twenty miles away. If Halleck planned to assault anywhere, it would be here. That upstart Grant had been removed from his command since Donelson—the Yankees had their squabbles too. Now Old Charlie Smith was in command. Commandant of cadets at the Point—would he ever forget? Another fuddy-duddy.

But there was Buell in Nashville with his thirty-five thousand—maybe more! If Buell ever sent reinforcements to Smith's forty thousand—aye, that would be a rub indeed. *Diable à quatre! Oui*, but he, Pierre Gustave Toutant, would be more than a match for them—if he could get Sidney Johnston to move.

Those letters to the governors—that had been absolutely masterly. He had risked Johnston's ire, but, as usual, when a thing went well, all was forgiven. And it had gone well. Alabama had sent twelve regiments, Louisiana all its troops for ninety days, Tennessee every able-bodied man! And Braxton Bragg—*mon Dieu*, there was a man of action! Even before Johnston left Shelbyville, Bragg sent four regiments up from the Gulf Coast, arriving himself ahead of his men to take charge of the rest of his regulars from Mobile and Pensacola that first week of March. Within ten days all ten thousand were there, and he, Beauregard, could now count twenty-one thousand men under his command at Corinth. No wonder he could advise Johnston to hurry! If only Johnston would *move. Fait à peindre, Dieu sait!* He would send Johnston a telegram, too!

He stepped to his desk, rang his bell, and when the orderly didn't show his head, bounded to the door himself and called loudly. He was like a bottle of bubbly wine about to explode.

At Decatur, Alabama, Albert Sidney Johnston was thinking of Texas. About this time of year the blue lupin and wild phlox would be moving under prairie wind. Overhead, ducks and geese would be circling before they settled. From the porch of his farmhouse he used to watch them. Suddenly he laughed out loud at the memory of a wild goose he'd shot through the liver with a half-ounce ball. The goose rose and flew several hundred yards before he fell again. When they cleaned him they found in a healed wound several long slugs—Canadian—that he'd carried around goodness knew how long.

Now why in tarnation, Johnston thought, am I thinking about that goose now? Because you see the Federals still flying high, with the healed wounds of Bull Run and Manassas, and the factories and the guns and the men to heal more wounds. What you need is a half-ounce ball to bring that eagle down. Turn him into a goose.

He looked at the map spread before him. The great river, the Mississippi, with Memphis and New Orleans—the heart of the South. Virginia and the coast. We could lose everything east of the mountains, but there would be no Confederacy without the Mississippi Valley. New Orleans, Mobile were vital. In that, he agreed with the Little Frenchman. He hadn't objected, basically, with those confidential letters to the governors, asking for troops. What he had objected to was the half-veiled promise—no, an outright proposal—to move against Paducah, seize the mouths of the Tennessee and Cumberland rivers, then take Cairo, St. Louis. . . . It was a grand, mad plan and he wished it could work. But Buell sat in Nashville and Halleck held St. Louis; Missouri as well as Kentucky were in Federal hands, and Admiral Foote's flotilla, not to mention "Unconditional Surrender" Grant's troops from Donelson, were on the Tennessee. If Buell chose to move, they were done for. It was imperative, absolutely imperative, that he get to Corinth, combine forces with Beauregard and Bragg before Buell had a chance to reinforce Sherman on the river. He thought not of Grant or Prentiss or Hurlbut or Charlie Smith, but of Sherman, the only man among them who realized that the North would need a quarter of a million men to put down this rebellion—and who had been considered insane because he'd said so! He'd lost a command over that. But he was the only man among them who sensed the truth.

Yet even Sherman, if the cards were played right, could be surprised.

His eyes swung east. For eight months after Bull Run, George McClellan hadn't moved. But dispatches indicated that things in Virginia would change. Just a week ago the Federals began ferrying troops from Fortress Monroe onto the peninsula between the York and the James rivers. Little Mac—they called him a Napoleon, too (so now each side had one!)—had been busy, ever since Lincoln called him east from Ohio, building a formidable army—some estimates were as high as three hundred thousand—drilled and organized and sustained by a sizable fleet. It was ironic that Lincoln hampered McClellan with his "military" meddling. Almost as ironic as the fact that Jeff Davis, when he was Secretary of War under Pierce, had sent Mac to the Crimea to learn all the latest arts of war. Well, that saddle of Mac's was, as the Southern cavalrymen found out when they'd captured some, definitely made for the comfort of the *horse*.

The grin faded from Johnston's face as he looked at the map again. For months now McClellan had faced the Confederates across the Potomac, outnumbering them three to one. Now, with this move of 112,000 troops to the peninsula, Johnston began to divine the oblique plan that was in the Federal mind: nothing less than an assault on Richmond.

Yet there was, since Bull Run, much unrest in the North, if not downright panic. One of the reasons Lincoln held back McDowell's forty thousand troops from joining Mac was the excuse that the capital needed defending. The eagle was scared. Perhaps he could turn him into a goose after all.

His eyes went back to Tennessee. Yes, the Yankees were on the river, camped at Pittsburg Landing—tens of thousands of them—his scouts estimated more than forty thousand. . . . But he had tricked them, with the oldest Indian ruse in the book. On the way through those muddy roads from Shelbyville to Huntsville, which had slowed him to twelve miles an hour, he had diverted mail and as many supply trains as he could spare—to Chattanooga. Luckily, he had ordered Floyd there, and Floyd's Virginians were already en route. The Federals were biting the bait. Tapped telegraph wires told him that Grant was reporting the Confederates falling back to Chattanooga. Two days later Sherman agreed, and the next day Buell advised McClellan that the main Rebel force was headed east. Instead, by March 10 that force was in Decatur, with John Scott's shotgun-toting Louisiana cavalrymen and now Morgan's Kentuckians keeping up a steady diversion, with Wharton's Texans fanning out to protect the rear, and with Hindman and the vanguard on their way to Tuscumbia, despite the rain.

He agreed with Beauregard's telegram, received just that morning, that Sherman's recent raid on Eastport, Mississippi, might be the beginning of a battle. "But let them set their own trap," he said aloud. Twenty short miles from the Federal camps, Corinth controlled the railroad. Vulnerable? You could look at it that way . . . if you were weak-kneed. Corinth was also a link to the whole lower South, a cornucopia through which Southern manpower and all available materiel could pour down on those—as yet—unsuspecting Yankees on the river.

To himself, he asked if he dared fail. Criticism, since the loss of Nashville, had caused all but one of the Tennessee congressmen to call for his resignation. To his dying day he would always remember Jeff Davis's answer: "If Sidney Johnston is not a general, sir, we had best give up this war, for we have no general to send you."

He looked down at his unfinished letter to his old friend. He knew Davis needed reassurance, if for nothing but to pass on to others. He had been, perhaps, too silent, because the facts of Donelson were not fully known, and he refused to defame a man on rumor. Buckner, he felt, was beyond reproach. His own opinion of Pillow and Floyd was, after all, opinion. He finished his letter quickly: "Leaving this place today to meet Bragg and Beauregard at Corinth. As for your request for an explanation of the recent disasters, I can only say, the test of merit in my profession with the people is success. It is a hard rule, but I think it right. . . ."

He signed his name with a quick flourish, gave the letter to an orderly and picked up his hat. Before he reached the depot he was handed a telegram just received from Beauregard, asking for another brigade. Beauregard expected a battle.

"So do I, Bory," Johnston said under his breath. "So do I."

The Tennessee was an odd river. Beginning in the Cumberland Mountains, it dipped south into Alabama, then made a sudden bend and rushed north for two hundred miles to join the Ohio at Paducah. Almost as erratic was the Cumberland, which emptied into the Ohio only twelve miles upriver from Paducah, after wandering from eastern Kentucky down to Nashville before turning north.

But nothing matched the Tennessee. At the great 90-degree bend there was a stretch known as the Narrows, where the water, constricted by a rocky channel, became a labyrinth of jagged reefs and drowned boulders that churned into a forty-mile froth of rapids. No wonder the land there had lagged in development. It was still, just twenty years ago, Indian country—and barely settled yet. If the railroad hadn't come through, Chattanooga would be just another landing on that forbidding river. It was the railroad which had finally conquered the Tennessee, bypassing it with its narrow-gauge tracks.

Albert Sidney Johnston dozed, listening to the *pat-tah-tuh-pah-tah-tuh* of the wheels. A frown deepened the vertical line between his eyes. Yes, it was wild, that country. And virtually unknown. He hoped Beauregard had scouted it properly.

Pale March sunshine turned mauve through the black funnel from the engine; luckily, the day was still cool enough so that the sooty window could remain closed. The ninety-three miles from Decatur to Corinth were long enough without choking on woodsmoke.

Corinth. In his mind Johnston could see it: the great gathering of an army. Would Van Dorn arrive in time? Time, the wheels said, may be running out. *Pah-tah-tuh.* For six months he had maintained a Confederate boundary from East Tennessee to Kansas. Even the loss of Missouri at Pea Ridge, although a blow, would not have spelled disaster if the forts had held. His troops had performed magnificently—their line so thin at places it was practically nonexistent. After the fall of Fort Henry there were so few men available that this same Memphis & Charleston Railroad was virtually undefended along the Tennessee—only the eight companies of Colonel Chalmers's Ninth Mississippi and a portion of the Thirty-eighth Tennessee under Colonel Looney were in North Mississippi to patrol the whole region. No wonder Union gunboats steamed up the Tennessee all the way to Florence, Alabama, captured two steamers—one with iron bound for Richmond —and seized the half-completed gunboat *Eastport.* Confederate sympathizers set fire to six other steamers to prevent their capture, and only the impassable river beyond Muscle Shoals stopped further invasion. Colonel Helm had orders to burn the Florence bridge if the Federals passed Eastport. Those frantic dispatches from Beauregard. Beauregard was an engineer, and had been on the ground there for six weeks; he knew as well as anybody the nature of the river. Why would he need another brigade so desperately?

Ah, but you know Beauregard. Yes, yes, I know Beauregard. And Bragg? And Bragg, unfortunately.

His mind went to Braxton Bragg, and he sighed. He of the long face, morose, massive eyebrows, and childish jealousy of his reputation. That blow-up with Colonel Gates in Mexico was still talked of. A good disciplinarian, they said. Ah, yes. But how much is stiff discipline a sadistic outlet for one's frustration with one's colleagues? As punctiliousness might be an equally veiled aggression against one's superiors? All that careful, to a point, minute observance of the rules. All that promptness. There was not an ounce of enthusiasm in it, but a kind of miserly deposit, as one might save away pennies, tidbits of a "clean" record. The I-did-nots outweighing the I-dids. With a reputation that stood on that one glorious moment at Buena Vista when Old Zach had called out, "Give 'em hell, Mister Bragg!" and Braxton, then a young artilleryman of thirty, stood by his gun while the grape showered around him. Like a child starved for attention, he had basked in that approval, but like a child expecting too much reward, he'd left the army in a huff when he received orders for the Indian Territory—as if they all hadn't served time on that front—and blamed Jeff Davis, as Secretary of War, for sending him "to chase Indians with six-pounders."

Johnston could just imagine the look on that hangdog face when Davis sent, not for him, but for Beauregard to come to Montgomery when the war started.

His mind went back to Beauregard. North Mississippi and Tennessee— this was Beauregard's district, and he certainly had no intention of intruding on another man's territory. He trusted the Little Frenchman with maps, roads, methods of putting an army into action. But he knew that once in the presence of the enemy, the chief, the only, the saving strategy of battle was in the decision to fight. *That is where I shall be,* he said to himself, *in the thick of it, to see that all goes right.* If Beauregard wants glory, let him have it . . .

it's a small price to pay for victory. With Buell in Nashville and Lew Wallace at Crump's Landing with an additional seven thousand reinforcements, time is running out. Each hour, each hour is crucial.

Johnston looked out the train window. The track here passed close to the river before it swept, swollen from spring rain, north to Eastport. That's my Rubicon, he thought. And then, as quickly, the soft, broad face of Polk came to him. Dear Leonidas. Could either of them have guessed, when they'd been roommates at the Point, that he would be a bishop one day? Polk, too, was at Corinth. Yes, together they would win. Leonidas and he, and all those brave boys gathering by rail and mule cart and barefoot. . . . There would be no lack of enthusiasm, after all.

He would give Leonidas the left, Bragg the center, Hardee the right, and George Crittenden the reserve. He could see his message to Davis already forming in his mind: HOPE ENGAGEMENT BEFORE BUELL CAN FORM JUNCTION. They had to! He smiled across at his son and aide, William Preston, whose own head had begun to bob. *Pah-tah-tuh*. He'd better take advantage of this lull in the storm. There would be just time enough for a nap before the bustle of Beauregard and the braggadocio of Braxton. . . .

John Morgan dismounted and tied Bess to a post by the sidewalk in front of the dusty railroad hotel. From here, as he looped the leather, he could see the sign on the depot—DECATUR—and the pile of plantation bells by the baggage wagon, those bells and assorted metals that he'd noticed beside railroad tracks all the way from Huntsville, as the call for metal brought donations of everything from old plows to brass candlesticks—anything that could make a cannon. There was also the usual lethargy after a major departure, as if the baggage boys, the telegraph operators, and even the little Negro hired to sweep the waiting room were caught up in the wake of an unseen sea, as the main action swept away from them.

He turned from a quip of Charlton's, tying next to him, to glance down the track. General Johnston's train had just left. Good. His pickets were posted, quarters were secured for the night before the march resumed. His men deserved a rest. The countryside here was solid Confederate; they expected little trouble, and indeed, since leaving Shelbyville their main enemy had been the thick, fathomless, everlasting red clay mud. They expected the ninety-odd miles to Corinth—actually, since Breckinridge was at Burnsville, closer to seventy miles—to be leisurely enough, following the river before striking out for Tuscumbia and Iuka, just over the Mississippi line. But this was North Alabama, and nothing came easy in these hills. Or in this mud. Better horses than Bess had broken down. He patted her neck and made sure she had enough rein to reach the watering trough before he smiled back at Tom and Basil and James West, just striding across the street toward him with a report from the scouts: all clear; they could bask in a hot bath, unfreeze their bones and warm their insides.

Eleven days later Morgan's squadron rode into the little town of Burnsville, early on the morning of April 3, in time to learn that Buell had made his move from Nashville the day before.

In the camp of Colonel Thomas H. Hunt's Fifth Kentucky the tents were already coming down. "We march this afternoon," said T.H., after getting over the surprise of seeing his nephews again. After ten minutes of greetings, T.H. reached over and handed Morgan a packet of letters. "Here. These came just before we left Shelbyville." T.H.'s kind eyes roved his nephew's face for the expected astonishment.

Morgan accepted the letters gingerly, as if they would break.

"Came through *channels*," T.H. joked. "Courtesy of Cripps's uncle Charlie, on Polk's staff."

But he wasn't listening. Hopemont! Home. The garden and the smells and the fireplaces and clean sheets. Aunt Betty and Tommie and Ma . . . Ma! Was she all right? Key . . . Randolph and Uncle Robert and Uncle Frank. The news was insignificant and world-shattering, trite and tremendous. Tommie missed Basil. Cal was still in prison . . . they were all praying for an exchange. The farm was fine . . . none of her slaves had been declared "fugitive"—a trick the Yankees used to get free labor. They wouldn't dare! The word was underscored with double wavy lines, and he could almost hear his mother's little gasp of contempt. Key wanted to join. That worried her. When was he invading Kentucky, to rescue them? Sanders Bruce was with Nelson's division, Buell's army. Miss Lexington had a filly. What should they name her?

He came up like a swimmer from water, to find Cripps Wickliffe grinning broadly.

"Such concentration!" Cripps laughed. "Here. Warm your insides!" He poured cups of steamy, mud-brown liquid and handed them around.

"My God!" T.H., who had just accepted one, spurted and pitched it out. "How do you expect a man to win a war on scorched sweet potato peelings? Johnny! Basil! Charlton! You boys will have time to ride over to Corinth. Maybe Gibson or Pond or some of those Louisiana troops will have some decent coffee! It will be worth a king's ransom on the battlefield!"

"But it's twelve . . . maybe fifteen miles . . . that would be . . . and we've . . ." sighed Charlton.

"Now don't tell me your Kentucky horses can't be back before our supply wagons are loaded!"

His enthusiasm was contagious. They were, as he kept telling them, about to fight the biggest battle ever witnessed on the North American continent. "Over in Corinth, you should see them! Two days ago one Texas outfit arrived barefoot, with no guns at all! But they'll do it!" T.H. beamed. "If valor will do it, they'll do it! Did you know Breckinridge has the Reserve Corps now?"

"I thought George . . ."

"Unfortunately General Bragg removed Crittenden from his command three days ago."

Basil mimed a tilted bottle, and T.H. nodded.

"But don't blame Crit. He's had bad luck—under indictment for losing the Gap—not his fault. . . . And now Bragg, heavy on temperance, with no

patience for anybody who enjoys his whiskey. . . . Speaking of which.
. . . . Get the taste of that bad coffee out of your mouths?"

They nodded, and were supplied. Salt, sugar, flour, beef or coffee might
be short or nonexistent, but the Confederate Army managed to find its
shuck.

"So now Breckinridge has the reserve . . ." Basil studied his glass.

"I know what you think . . . Breckinridge the politician. But he's a real
mover. I've just come back from Atlanta, where he sent me to round up
anything with two legs . . . sick or not. And he loves his boys. When he
found out the condition of our guns, he sent over a thousand to Corinth for
repair and gave me an order for six hundred new rifles for my regiment . . .
from a shipment just received off a blockade runner."

At corps headquarters, Breckinridge was delighted to see them. He rose
from his desk and walked around it, extending his hand. "Just in time," he
said. "Charlie Smith skinned his shins on a rowboat, and Grant's in charge
at Pittsburg Landing—or rather, Savannah, where he's set up headquarters.
Maybe now we can pay him back for Donelson."

"Have you news of Buckner?"

Breckinridge shook his head. He returned to his chair and leaned forward
with sudden energy. "Here's the river." His pencil made a sweep. "Here on
the south, Lick Creek. On the north, Snake Creek, with Owl Creek coming
up from the southwest to join Snake Creek here. We approach from the
southwest, our lines across the base of a triangle roughly three miles wide.
In that triangle: the Yankees. Now here's the plan. Hardee in advance from
Corinth on the Ridge Road. Followed by Polk. Bragg's Second Corps, the
largest, will go to Monterey—a crossroads—where we will concentrate after
Bragg has moved on."

"And the assault?" asked Basil.

Breckinridge lifted the dome of his forehead and gave them an intent look
from his slightly protuberant eyes. "Saturday morning. We're to take three
days' rations and forty rounds each. If we need more"—his grin broadened
his massive, clean-shaven chin—"our good friends at the Landing can supply
us. By the way, have you rested? Enough for a ride on to headquarters? I
have some dispatches for General Johnston. Besides, I think he has something for you."

"We've got a grocery list from Uncle Tom," Charlton blurted, then sobered into a salute. After all, this was a brigadier-general, and the ex-Vice-
President of the United States.

Corinth was a whirlwind. Breckinridge's camp at Burnsville was calm
compared to this confusion. The massing of an army—raw recruits and
leather-faced farmers, schoolteachers and storekeepers—spread before their
eyes. At every corner enlistment tables—cotton bales laid sideways, upturned kegs. Ex-state senators signing on as privates. Brothers, sometimes
four or five in a wagon, with their squirrel rifles—hadn't the call come for
every able-bodied man in Tennessee? There was something touching in their
volunteer shyness—boys who had never been in the presence of such overt

enthusiasm before. But they soon relaxed, and joined the shouting. There was no ignorance in their innocence: They had seen death before, had watched their sisters die in childbirth and their little brothers succumb to swamp fever; they had delivered death themselves to deer in oak woods and bears in canebrakes. Shoddy, lean and sharp-eyed, they carried themselves with the quiet assurance of frontiersmen, stubborn, independent, tough. They stood aside for overloaded baggage wagons, teamsters yelling at mules, artillery horses pulling caissons, squads of soldiers moving at the double-quick. A kind of mad envy, a breathless, blood-pulsing, thought-stopping ardor of high adventure shone from all their faces. It was as if they all knew, even the soldier's dog wagging his tail as he trotted behind his marching master, that they were living a moment in history. Buell was marching with his Yankees from Nashville, but they would hightail it to the river and whip Grant before reinforcements could get there. Won't them Yankees be surprised! Sitting in their camps eating good beef and biscuits, making their Yankee tea. Sitting like ducks on a pond . . . YEAOW! After months of discouragement, retreat and self-doubt, oh, the glory of really, at last, *moving*. Never mind that their single-shot pistols and .69 caliber muskets were good only at short range and their lieutenants kept telling them they would have to take enemy fire until they were close enough to shoot. "Jest let me at 'em . . . we'll find fancy carbines and Enfields enough once we git there!"

Blond, good-looking Charlton was not unconscious of the stares of some of the Mississippi girls as they walked to headquarters. James West threw his head back and enjoyed a good laugh when they turned their attention to some Louisiana Zouaves flashing by in their bright uniforms. "Well, don't worry, Lieutenant," West drawled. "All it takes to make a Zouave is an Irishman and two yards of red flannel. Maybe we can find a bolt for you!"

"Too bad we sent Quirk scouting," Morgan called back, then nodded to a staff colonel rushing past, his businesslike salute as crisp as the points of his mustache.

"Isn't the smell of *excitement* in the air, Brother Johnny?" Tom whispered, and James West, behind him, smiled, but was no less impressed.

Johnston had his headquarters in a house called "the Rose Cottage." Since ten-thirty last night his world had changed. Cheatham sent word from Bethel Station that Lew Wallace had started a move from Crump's Landing—possibly against Memphis. As Cheatham's scouts explored, two brigades of bluecoats stood in line of battle to meet them. Another telegram, delivered just after midnight, told Johnston that the rest of Lew Wallace's division now faced Cheatham. So it was more than just a skirmish. With Beauregard's "Now is the time to advance and strike" ringing in his ears, Johnston had crossed the street and awakened Bragg, who agreed. Colonel Jordan, Beauregard's chief of staff and acting adjutant-general of the army, was aroused also, and wrote orders to dictation in a corner of Bragg's bedroom. Buell had crossed the Duck River; Van Dorn had not yet arrived to help. They couldn't wait. Johnston's telegram to Davis had been brief: Polk, left; Hardee, center; Bragg, right wing; Breckinridge, reserve. When his generals

—all except Breckinridge—met him at ten o'clock that morning, he could scarcely conceal his shock at Beauregard's idea that the whole operation should be a "reconnaissance in force"—to strike a sudden blow and return to Corinth. Little more than a raid! To appease the Little Frenchman, who had stayed up all night scribbling tactics, Johnston had set aside his own plan and agreed to Pierre's "three waves": Hardee in the advance, Bragg, Polk, then Breckinridge. It was, Johnston reminded himself, just such a deployment Napoleon had used at Waterloo, a thought he pushed to the back of his mind. After all, he would be there, to lead them. That was the important thing. That, and enthusiasm, and the will to win.

It was with genuine pleasure that he interrupted a stream of orders to see Morgan again. His blue eyes sparkled as he rose and extended his hand. The urgency of the day had tired, but not wearied him—he had been closeted with Beauregard caring for a thousand details since noon—and the sight of those Kentucky boys acted on him like a tonic. He introduced them to Beauregard and called his adjutant.

"Colonel Jordan, have you those dispatches for General Hardee? Fine. Send William in." He looked back at Morgan. "He did it before. I thought you might appreciate . . . Come in, come in! Have we Colonel Morgan's stars?"

At eight o'clock that morning Brigadier-General Tom Hindman received verbal orders from General Hardee to march "as soon as practicable." Some of his men, hearing the news earlier, had been ready and waiting since dawn. Hardee's first brigade, Hindman's Arkansas boys, with their Tennessee battery, would be in the van. But some of Polk's men—at least two brigades—had camped in town and clogged the narrow streets with their wagons and artillery pieces. So Hindman's troops milled about for hours, stacked their arms, and finally ate some of the rations scheduled for the march.

Hindman could do nothing but swear. He sent Colonel Shaver to headquarters with another protest against the delay and a request for further orders. Shaver saw the familiar black horse tied at the fence and met Morgan halfway down the walk.

"John!" Shaver sent a rangy arm out for a handshake, which ended in a bear hug. "Some different from those scouts at Bell's Tavern, eh? Aren't you with the reserve? Isn't this something? We should have been gone hours ago," he worried.

"It's *Colonel* Morgan," Charlton beamed.

"That so? Congratulations! Hope we'll have even more to congratulate ourselves about day after tomorrow! If we ever get there. . . ." Impatience had soured much of the excitement of his men, and Shaver was suffering from the same malady now. Although in a hurry to see Beauregard and get Polk moving, he was delighted with the diversion of seeing the "Green River boys" again. Some of the enthusiasm he had felt earlier in the day returned. "Coffee, is it? Your Colonel Hunt must be as bad as General Johnston. I've never seen him without a cup in his hand, or on his desk. Yes, right over there, beyond that church spire. Take the next street to the left. It's about four blocks. Colonel Pond's brigade, Ruggles's First Division. If *they* don't have coffee, nobody does."

Morgan watched him take the porch steps two at a time and almost run down an orderly with a sheaf of papers. His own copy of Special Orders No. 8 was folded inside his coat, and he had already committed it to memory: Hardee in the lead, from Corinth down the Ridge Road to the Landing. Followed by Polk. Bragg, leaving the Ridge Road to follow the lower road to Monterey. Breckinridge at Monterey "by the shortest and best routes" after Bragg had moved on—which, at the rate things were going, would mean tomorrow morning. Tom Quirk and the other scouts were now busy confirming those shortest and best routes, and a sudden stab of excitement sent a hot pain to Morgan's throat. The day had been sunny, but now a cloudy sky promised rain. They had to get back. He mounted Bess and followed Shaver's directions, was stopped half a dozen times by the crowds, until he found an alley between houses and motioned Charlton to follow. Tom, with James West in the rear, became separated by a squad of marching artillerymen, but caught up.

Colonel Preston Pond's Louisiana brigade was certainly colorful, in dress uniforms with enough gold braid to decorate a dance hall. "But aren't you" —West ventured to ask Major Mouton of the Eighteenth Louisiana—"just a bit worried about the color of your coat?"

"*Moi?* So it iz blue! Once we are on the field, *monsieur*, no one, I assure you, will mistake us for Yanquis!" When he heard they wanted coffee, he was delighted. He invited them to his headquarters, a small frame house on the corner, and sent for some. "Will twenty pounds be eenuff?"

An officer near the window, whose curly black head bent over his moving pencil, looked up. It was Etienne Villard.

"*Mon ami!* How are you? Olivier is here . . . with General Gladden's First Louisiana."

"Julien?" Morgan grinned at Etienne's hands flying in the air.

"Julien is with Colonel Gibson's brigade, the Fourth Louisiana Regiment . . . Colonel Henry Allen. Edouard, *alors!* The only one of us who does not wear a blue collar . . . he is with the Washington Artillery, Captain Hodgson, in General Anderson's Second Brigade. But we are all with General Ruggles's First Division, Bragg's Corps."

"Your mother?"

"*Maman . . . elle est morte*," he murmured.

"I am so sorry." He hesitated. "And your sister?"

"*Bien!* Well! Her husband is a cotton broker—or will be again, once we can ship anything. . . ." He stopped to hand a list to Major Mouton, who left to oversee personally the loading of ammunition. When the door closed Etienne found them chairs and passed cigars around. Morgan and West drew on theirs luxuriously. Tom choked a little, and grinned. Charlton declined.

"So . . ."

After the initial introductions, they found little to talk about. Through the excitement the first faint tug of fatigue was building. They speculated about Yankee strength and their own duty, but their wonder at the unreal day smothered thought. The coffee arrived. They shook Etienne's hand and, cigars still smoking, mounted and threaded their way through the crowd back to the Burnsville Road. Eugenie's four brothers were here! They passed a row of redbuds, bright pink against green-black cedars. In deep woods, white shelves of dogwood caught shadows. The air was soft, moist with a hint of rain. They left the town and headed east. It was true: The whole South was here.

John Morgan would never forget that march. When they reached Burnsville it was almost sundown. The orders he carried directed Breckinridge to start at first light. During their absence more precious Enfields had arrived, and the men were in good spirits, cooking three days' rations.

"This will be the beginning." Cripps winked. "The first step back to Kentucky."

We can't lose. It was on Wick's face, in his eyes. All day Morgan, too, had felt it. We can't lose. Like a talisman to cling to.

They believed it. They had to. And didn't they have good cause? The Yankees might have better equipment, but if determination meant anything, the men under Breckinridge would win. Colonel Robert Trabue's First Brigade, with the exception of two Alabama battalions and one from Tennessee, was Kentucky to the core. Two Kentucky batteries under Byrne and Cobb made up their artillery, with Morgan's squadron providing cavalry. As for the other two brigades under Breckinridge's command, Bowen's had a Kentucky cavalry company under Phil Thompson, and Stratham's, although without cavalry, had two crack regiments from Mississippi. Free-lancing with the whole army, unattached and available for all were Forrest's Tennessee regiment, Wharton's Texans and Wirt Adams's Mississippi cavalry— with Colonel Wood from the Murfreesboro days. Two batteries were also unattached: McClung's Tennessee and Roberts's Arkansas.

Breckinridge, the last to march, would have the longest route. That evening T.H. assembled his regiment in front of his tent and read General Johnston's battle orders. "I have put you in motion to offer battle to the invaders of your country," T.H. read. "You can but march to a decisive victory . . ."

T.H. looked around and caught Morgan's eye, and continuing, no longer looking at the paper in his hands, but at his nephew and beyond, as if the words were written against the sky: " . . . remembering the fair, broad, abounding land, the happy homes, and the ties that would be desolated by your defeat."

33

The bugle sounded through pelting rain. By daylight they stood in the muddy road. Trabue's baggage, loaded into wagons the day before, started for Corinth, where it would follow Bragg's trains along the Ridge Road, a shorter distance, and one that would avoid the swamps between Burnsville and Monterey. Morgan's squadron went with it, with orders to double back cross-country and bivouac with the troops that night.

Basil Duke had never seen so many wagons. His Missouri experience, which set him apart from Charlton and James West and even James Bowles as a veteran, contained nothing of this massive, endless line of supply. It seemed as if they had enough ammunition to fight all the wars on earth. Where had it come from? Miraculously, it had gathered, through blockade and capture, to arrive here at Corinth by train and mulepack and wagon, in a last-ditch effort to stop the Yankee tide.

They had to win!

It was almost noon—and still raining—when Breckinridge's trains joined Bragg's on the muddy Ridge Road, growing hourly more impassable. The wheels of overloaded wagons and caissons sank axle-deep in ooze. Men swore and sweated, despite the bone-chilling drizzle that ran down the horses' forelocks and spun off hats. As Morgan and Tom were riding down the long files of Bragg's troops they heard a cracked voice whine, "I'll tell yuh! She commenct-ta *prizin'* an' *prizin'*, and 'fore long thet loada rock jumped outa thet ditch. . . ."

"Aw, now, Grandpa, tell us anuthah!"

"You lie worse'n the Yankees, ole man. . . . Betcha hafta get somebody else tuh call yore dog!"

"Ah tell yuh, that lil' mare squatted, commenct-ta prize agin'st thet collar an' . . . heah, lemme show yuh! Ah'll betcha yore ration this lil' Kentucky hoss I got cheer kin outdo them lazy artillery hosses enny day. . . ."

"WILL!" Tom shouted.

He looked up, rain dripping from his nose. He pushed back his hat and grinned. "Wal, blamed be! Tom! Johnee! Yew tell these here fellers a Kentucky hoss kin outrun, outpull, outdo enny of them Mississippi nags enny day of thuh week!"

They stood aside on their horses and watched two massive workhorses wait passively in the matted grass while the artillery boys jokingly rigged Will's little bay mare to the mired caisson. "There's no way in the world . . . he's crazy . . ." came to Morgan as he sat Bess and watched. One little mare in place of two artillery horses . . . impossible.

"Yes, yes. Watch, now." Will was talking as if to himself: "Take a lesson cheer. She'll honker down an' wait. See her take a feel? Now . . . come on, honey."

"Watch it!" one of the gunners yelled as the ammunition boxes jumped. The mare's haunches bunched hard, her hinds bent hock-deep in mud. The wheels of the caisson spit clods of clay. One wedged under Bess's throat latch and Morgan bent down to flip it away.

"Well, you proved your point!" he called out as they watched the caisson, rehitched to its limber and pulling away, find a place in line.

"How come they nivver believe a feller, when we tell 'em about our hosses? Johnee! Johnee!"

He had to dismount. They embraced right there in the mud, in the middle of the road, a back-pounding, arm-crushing hug.

"How's about I jine you, Johnee?"

"Who are you with?"

"Hell, I jest started follering these here fellers yestiddy at Corinth, heard they'd be a fight. Don't even know *who* they belong to. But jest think! We could . . ." The old eyes looked at him and finished: *Maybe get home again.*

It rained again that night. Mud turned to glue and added to the frustration of the next two days' confusion.

Maybe it was inevitable: forty thousand unseasoned volunteers on narrow country roads trying to maneuver à la Bonaparte. First, Hardee's advance turned off from the Ridge (Corinth-Pittsburg Landing) Road into a side lane to camp near a spring, while Polk's troops marched past the lane only to find, about midnight, not Hardee's main column, but his advance pickets, and themselves not behind, but ahead of Hardee. The next morning, Friday April 4, Hardee's men, returning to the main road, discovered their route clogged with Polk's wagons. After literally lifting them aside, Hardee's corps moved on; then Polk stopped again, to await one of Bragg's divisions, since Polk, as the "third wave," would deploy behind and to the left of Bragg on the battlefield. But Bragg, who had split his force at Monterey to march down two separate roads (to converge at the Ridge Road not later than sunset Thursday), found that his first division under Ruggles, through a misinterpretation of "tomorrow morning," would not reach the rendezvous until almost noon Friday. The baggage wagons of Bragg's Second Division, under Withers, had bogged down in the thick clay so badly that Withers's troops did not arrive until late Thursday night.

The comedy continued. Bragg, realizing the miserable condition of the Monterey Road, changed his plan, and ordered Ruggles to follow Withers to Mickey's, a farmhouse where the Bark Road (to Lick Creek and the river) met the Ridge Road. But Polk, scheduled to march behind Ruggles, had already arrived, and Ruggles's changed route—plus more rain—caused a delay that ended in Polk's bivouacking along the Ridge Road at sundown Friday. Withers reached Mickey's twenty-four hours behind schedule. Even worse, the troops with Breckinridge had slogged through twenty-three miles of boot-sucking glue, but their artillery had not arrived by sundown Friday, with battle order for dawn Saturday.

"I need that artillery! Find it!"

Morgan had never seen Breckinridge so furious.

With a half-dozen picked men, he rode down the quagmire toward Corinth. Jesse, beside him, was half asleep with fatigue. He would order him to stay in camp tomorrow, if possible. No need to expose him to battle. As eager as he was to help, Jesse was often in the way. "He's better at cleaning tack," Charlton joked, but it was true. Faithful and eager, a boy who carried his heart in his eyes, Jesse . . . was home. He was Hopemont and the Leestown farm and Miss Lexington, whose filly was now running across fields of bluegrass. *April in Kentucky . . . will break your heart with joy.* His father at Shadeland. Now, just remembering, it came close. Calvin Morgan, in his grave. With his grandfather, and grandmother, and Aunt Catherine and Uncle Johnny, and T.H.'s babies, and Uncle Ben and Uncle Simon. And Alexander Gibson, his hat with a plume. Suddenly the mud disappeared, and Bess's slow, sucking trudge, which made her neck arch like a plow horse, became his own straining, urging longing for HOME. The letter said Sanders was with Nelson, marching from Nashville. Strange if they should meet. He wondered if Sanders was encountering the same Tennessee mud. If he was, he could only feel sorry for him.

Eight miles later he found the artillery mired down, long lines of tipped wagons, straining horses and swearing men in the dark. Captain Byrne himself had dismounted to help lift a wagon from a ditch. He looked up, mud shining in his beard. "Tell the General we'll get there before daylight." Byrne looked again at his beloved six-pounders, those guns he'd brought from Memphis to Camp Boone, paid for from his own pocket. They were, his troops joked, like his own children.

"The next two miles are the worst," Morgan told him. "After that the roadbed is higher."

"Then we'll get there. In time." Byrne gave a boyish, sloppy salute, but turned back to his work without looking at Morgan again.

He hated to wake Breckinridge. He found his adjutant and left him with the news: The artillery and baggage wagons would be there by daylight. That would be, with reveille at three A.M., none too soon.

The Confederate forces were camped in a semicircular band one mile thick, with Breckinridge's three brigades in the rear, Polk's four brigades next in line behind Bragg's corps, the largest with six brigades. Hardee's three brigades were out in front: Hindman's Arkansas boys, the Irishman Pat Cleburne's Mississippi and Tennessee regiments, and Sterling Wood's mixed group of Arkansas, Alabama and Tennessee troops, their pickets less than a mile from Shiloh Church, where Sherman slept. Tomorrow morning those men would begin the battle.

"Begin the battle." What did it mean? Charge across a field, rout Prentiss in his camp—and then? It all looked so neat on paper, and the reclining forms Morgan passed as Bess stepped softly over wet leaves and sank her pasterns in mud had, very few of them, ever shot a gun in anger. But there was no worry. The air was electric with anticipation; the real problem, in spite of the fatigue of the march and the confusion from Corinth, was whether they could relax enough to sleep. Nobody talked about dying. Everybody wanted to "see the elephant." To prove himself. This wasn't Mexico.

About midnight the rain became a raging storm, and the troops, without tents and sleeping on their guns or beside their horses, were soaked. At three A.M. Saturday, with troops in line under a torrential downpour, movement was postponed until sunup. About five A.M. the rain stopped, but the roads were now swollen streams. Johnston, at Monterey with Beauregard, determined to form his lines at seven o'clock and attack at eight. Hardee's men, in the advance, did not form until ten A.M.—without their ammunition wagons, still stuck on the Ridge Road. Polk's First Division, ready since before dawn, had to wait five hours for Bragg's men to pass the crossroads known as Mickey's. Then, because Bragg had decided Friday night to shift Gladden's brigade of Wither's division to Hardee's right, and Gladden, down the Monterey Road, had to pass Chalmers's and Jackson's brigades of Wither's division, a maneuver which in turn caused these troops to halt and only delay Ruggles, whose division of Bragg's corps was not yet in the second line, where it was to form the entire left wing. . . . A human chessboard had gone insane.

The attack could not begin without Ruggles's six thousand men. Johnston sent to Bragg for an explanation; Bragg sent to the rear for the same. Four hours passed. Amazement surpassed anger as Johnston sent to Bragg, who would "forward the information." It was now after noon. Johnston exploded: "This is perfectly puerile! This is not war! Let us have our horses."

He found Ruggles's troops standing in an open field, blocked by Polk.

Not until four P.M. Saturday did Ruggles's Louisiana brigades form behind Hardee's first line. Ahead of them—not two miles away from Hardee's impatient troops—the Federals sat in their Sibley tents. Hardee's men were so close that when Beauregard, whose strict order for silence had been disregarded, heard drumming, he ordered it stopped—only to discover that the drums were Federal. Early on Friday, Confederate soldiers had blundered into Federal pickets within three-quarters of a mile of Sherman's headquarters. Once, Captain Avery's Georgia Dragoons got within two hundred yards of a Yankee infantry column and watched the drill—until they were fired on, but not before they learned the position of the enemy camps.

Beauregard, in his headquarters in Mickey's farmhouse at the Ridge–Bark Road intersection, waited for Polk. Beauregard was worried. Bragg, whose troops were at last in the second line, had lost all hope of surprise. Too many men had fired their guns to see if their powder was dry; when a deer bounded from the woods they cheered. Some even blew bugles. Clanton's Alabama cavalry had a skirmish with the Fifth Ohio yesterday afternoon, and when Clanton was chased back, four hundred Ohio troops blundered into Cleburne's infantry and artillery—Hardee's advance line—which opened up and drove them back toward Sherman's camp at Shiloh Church.

If the Yankees didn't know they were here, they were dumb as well as deaf. When Polk rode up, Beauregard blamed him for the delays, and agreed with Bragg that the army should return to Corinth. It was about five o'clock.

Johnston reined his thoroughbred bay, Fire-eater. He dismounted and stood at the edge of the road, drawing his gray cape around him. Beauregard, so full of Napoleon's tactics, paced up and down, arguing for withdrawal. Bragg, whose changed orders had orchestrated the confusion, concurred. Polk sat on a stump, held his head in his hands and said nothing.

"Zey will be entrenched to zee eyes," Beauregard blurted, in his excitement losing his usually precise English. "All hope of zurprise—gone. Bezides, Braxton's men have eaten all zaire rations. . . ."

Johnston turned to Bragg. "Is this true?"

Before Bragg could reply, Polk spoke up. "My men are in fine shape, sir, ready for battle. It is my opinion we should attack." His head went down again.

Johnston glanced toward his staff, shifting on their mounts in fetlock-deep mud. He was about to send for Breckinridge when he rode up.

"My men, General, have ample provisions," Breckinridge offered. "If General Bragg's troops need any, we can supply them."

John Morgan took his eyes from Johnston's face to look in disbelief at Breckinridge. By pure chance they had ridden this way, and he scratched Bess's withers to keep her from fidgeting. She stood to one side, her rider within earshot of what might be the most momentous council of the whole war. Johnston kept his face still, but his blue eyes had turned a steel gray. As he remounted, he looked at his generals. "Gentlemen, we shall attack at daylight tomorrow." It was a full day late. Maybe a full day too late, but he looked beyond them to the dripping trees. They said nothing.

As they were riding off, Morgan heard Johnston call back to a member of his staff, "I would fight them if they were a million!"

Johnston! My God, how he loved him! *The more they crowd in there between those two creeks, the worse we can make it for them.* . . . It was something Forrest would have said. Damn to hell Beauregard's tactics, Bragg's whining. . . .

My God, how I love him! Standing there like Ezekiel between that little Frenchman jumping around like a puppet and gloomy, long-faced Bragg. Only Polk, Johnston's old roommate, had stood by him. And Breckinridge. Yes, Breckinridge. With his round eyes and round head and slow politician's ways, which when he smiled betrayed enormous energy underneath that quiet exterior. He had come to love him, too.

They rode back to "camp" under a clearing sky. Breckinridge's job as commander of the reserve was to wait for the battle to begin and be needed. But Breckinridge was not a man content to wait. He knew by heart Johnston's plan to turn the Federal left away from the river, drive it back onto Owl Creek and away from the gunboats, their base of supply. In order to do that, a good ford across Lick Creek on the river road coming up from the south was essential. Confederate sympathizers in the area had been helpful; they had their information from Sherman's picket details, who often spent overnight at convenient farmhouses. But had Beauregard, for all his tactics, done his homework? Breckinridge suspected a lot of those fancy ideas came from the army's adjutant. It was all right for a man to be ambitous, but there came a point when unsolicited advice, if pressed too far, became fawning. Tom Jordan might be still rankling because Beauregard had left him in the rear at Bull Run! There was a time when reputation became ridiculous.

What about those fords across Lick Creek? Would they be heavily guarded? Did the Yankees realize that their Ohio cavalry had, completely by chance Friday afternoon, uncovered the advance force of the whole Confederate Army?

As they walked their horses in the cool air and watched forbidden campfires make long lines in the woods, Breckinridge motioned to Morgan to dismount with him and let the others go on. He had no fire himself, but a blanket spread under a tree, and lowered his bulky body with some discomfort to the ground. He unbuttoned his coat and leaned back. "Owl Creek," he said, and sighed. His boots, wet since morning, stuck to his socks.

"Here, let me, sir."

"Thanks."

"Owl Creek?"

"The General's got to turn the Union forces back onto Owl Creek, away from the river. And the only way to do that is up the river road from Hamburg, from the south, across Lick Creek. Get behind Stuart's camp. But what's that country really like? I talked with Colonel Clanton. There's a backwoods road leading from the main Corinth road across the creek. One of Clanton's vedettes, captured by the Fifth Ohio, escaped during the night and we have his description. If we could find out more . . . Beauregard, I'm afraid, hasn't done a thorough scouting job. Now we know Stuart has advanced his pickets. The General may be walking into a hornet's nest for all we know."

"A few good riders could find out."

Breckinridge looked up.

"A few good men could get between Stuart's camp and his pickets . . ." Morgan said softly. "You said they were advanced?"

"Yes, but . . . into that hive of Yankees? They're as thick as the hairs on a pig's back. Besides, they wouldn't give you permission . . . Bragg has been calling Clanton 'gallant to rashness' ever since that skirmish. If he didn't have a battle on his hands he might even consider a court-martial. . . ."

"They'd believe one of their West Point engineers."

Breckinridge sat up and stretched his long legs.

"They would, wouldn't they?"

They looked at each other and grinned in the dark. Breckinridge found a stub of candle and lit it. He scribbled a note on the back of an envelope. "Take this to General Bragg," he said as he wrote, biting his tongue. "There. That should do it. And good luck!"

Will went with him. Will and James West, John Sisson, Tom Quirk and Charlton. To Basil he gave the job of explaining to Tom Morgan why he would be left behind again: His time would come. Secretly, he wished he had left Charlton, too. What if? No, he couldn't think that way. Not tonight.

He had seen Braxton Bragg only once, at Mickey's, just before sundown when the generals met in the middle of the road. He had argued with zeal then, his black eyes under that shelf of brow glinting with inspiration and contempt by turns. It was plain Bragg disliked Johnston, but then, whom did he like? His men feared and dreaded him. Tales of discipline pushed too far—sixteen men hanged on a single tree for some infringement—were surely exaggerated, but looking at that cadaverous face, Morgan didn't doubt that, if it weren't true, it could be. Now, in his tent, the General smacked his purple lips in their nest of salt-and-pepper beard and leaned back to hear Morgan's proposal with the undisguised distrust of a West Pointer for a volunteer. Only Morgan's reputation as a well-connected Kentucky gentleman persuaded Braxton Bragg to listen, watching the steeple his fingers made before him.

"So you wish to explore the Federal left, Colonel Morgan?"

"General Breckinridge thinks another reconnaissance by one of your engineers might be well, given the importance of that terrain to General Johnston's plan, sir."

There must have been something in the tone of that reply—a polite dare, the faintest implied challenge to the General's vanity as a man who "left no stone unturned," combined with a gentlemanly offer to help him turn the last one—and perhaps gain the admiration of Richmond—that caused Bragg to fall forward suddenly and rise to his feet. In a voice cracking with arrogance not quite covering his excitement, he told his orderly to summon Captain Lockett, a member of his staff and assistant engineer of the army. "He can . . . assess the situation." But they would not, Bragg added emphatically, do so before four A.M. "Plenty of time." He wagged his eyebrows and cleared his throat. "Report here then. I'll inform Captain Lockett myself."

"Wal, whaddya ekspect?" Will consoled as they mounted. "Now . . . Genr'l Harrison woulda scouted the situation *now*. . . . But we'll wait till his four A.M. jes' ta keep thuh peace. Wouldn't wanta miss a good fight cuz some blamed genr'l tied me up fur court-martial . . . er worse."

"So you've heard those stories, too, you old goat!"

"Ah, Johnee, but ain't it grand?"

The night was cool and clear, and low on the horizon a sliver of moon lay turned up to hold rain.

"But look over yonder . . . the Big Dipper's standin' on its handle to spill it! It'll be dry as powder tamorry, yew wait an' see!"

Morgan's squadron camped in thick woods, the almost impassable underbrush becoming, jokingly, a "good box mattress" after some shebangs were spread and trampled on. After a three-hour rest, Jesse saddled Bess and waited while Morgan changed his roster, substituting Sam McKee for Charlton, who had specific instructions to keep Tom under his wing until they got back. "And if I don't get back before you start out . . . well, just don't let him get too impetuous."

———

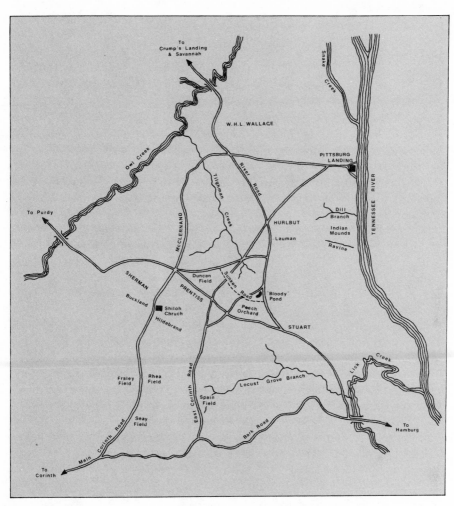

Federal Camps at Pittsburg Landing

"Gentlemen."

William Tecumseh Sherman watched Brigadier-General W. H. L. Wallace and Lieutenant-Colonel McPherson of Grant's staff mount their horses and start off down the road to the Landing. The moon had set, but the spring stars were out. In this fickle, tumbled-up land along this crazy river, you'd better enjoy good weather when you had it. Before daylight it could be storming again. Sherman rubbed his hand over his stubby hair and yawned. That fool Worthington, wanting axes to build an abatis. Why, this whole damned land was an abatis. He yawned again and let his hand drift down over his eyes, pinching the top of his nose with his thumb and forefinger. It had been a long day.

He lifted the flap of his tent and sank back on his cot. He pulled off his boots before blowing out the candle, then undressed in the dark. He was damned tired.

If Worthington were the only one he had to worry about! There was Hildebrand, another old fool. Maybe worse than Worthington. Past sixty, with no tactics, not even a staff! What could you expect from a brigade commander like that? No wonder he kept getting reports from the Seventy-seventh Ohio of an "enemy in our front in full force." Full force. Those fools had never seen full force in their lives. He'd ordered the sergeant arrested. And Jesse Appler, one of Hildebrand's colonels—another senile Ohio volunteer who saw Confederates in the bushes. Would he ever forget the day Appler arrived—with "troops" who had never drilled? Tired as he was, Sherman grinned. He would have given a fistful of greenbacks to have seen Appler's face when his message reached him: "Take your damned regiment back to Ohio. There is no enemy nearer than Corinth!"

What did Grant expect him to do with this handful of fools? Ah, his "generals." McClernand, whose presidential appointment was a paid political debt. Only "military" experience: three months' service as a volunteer private in the Black Hawk War, where his benefactor also served for a few weeks, until he lost his horse and had to walk back to Illinois. So much for a "military" President!

Sherman set aside the bushy face of McClernand and ticked off the others. Hurlbut, another friend of Lincoln. Could hold his liquor, but his South Carolina drawl was too sugary, and he parted his hair too low. If a man was bald, let him admit it, and not slosh what hair he had over his head like a wet rag. W. H. L. Wallace. Another Illinois lawyer who seemed surprised enough at his meteoric rise to brigadier. Probably attributed it to Divine Intervention. His religion was almost as sugary as Hurlbut's drawl. God, was there a man among them?

Lew Wallace, at Crump's Landing? No, another uneasy customer. "The enemy can, I am told, throw a bridge across the creek in three hours, and by good roads get into my rear." I'll get into your rear. Sherman turned over and thumped the camp bag, stuffed with extra shirts, that he used as a pillow. Still, he couldn't sleep.

Prentiss? Another God-damned Illinois lawyer. Four months ago the elected captain of an infantry company. Today a brigadier-general. My God.

Night sounds came: sounds that should have given him ease. Nearby, not fifty feet from his tent, the old log church sat in fitful moonlight.

Well, at least he had the confidence of Grant. Comfortable (and enjoying his whiskey) at the Cherry house in Savannah, where Charlie Smith was dying of that leg infection, Grant had at least left him alone to his own devices. They both agreed the Rebels would sit tight on that railroad at Corinth. Why should they risk abandoning it, to be outflanked by a superior Union force? The five divisions he had at the Landing, plus Lew Wallace's at Crump's, would be more than enough to deter that ragtag "army." Even fools, well-fed and well-armed, were better than those grits-fed butternuts. He deliberately pushed into the back of his mind his own warnings, which had lost him a command, that this would be a long war.

For that matter, this had been a long two days. Aside from arresting that sergeant with his story of Confederates eating breakfast in the woods bordering Seay field Friday morning, there was, he had to admit (give a point to Appler), Buckland's loss of a lieutenant and six men that same afternoon, not three-quarters of a mile from camp. But Buckland—another lawyer and politician—had panicked, when he knew Grant's orders were emphatic: They were to avoid any major contact before Buell came up. Buckland had sent one company forward, and when they didn't return damned if he didn't send another. "That's when I had to order out Ricker's cavalry," Sherman mumbled aloud, and jammed his "pillow" under his cheek. But damned if, before Ricker got there, Buckland didn't send out three more companies—stopped not by the Rebels but by more rain.

Ricker. Well. Major Ricker. Excellent battalion commander, Fifth Ohio. But even he had succumbed to the jitters. Found Buckland's men engaged with a Rebel cavalry unit in a strip of fallen timber. Ricker made a dash, and the grays disappeared. Sherman frowned and sat up, still angry. When a man like Ricker . . . He had ridden out there himself, with his staff in pouring rain, to put a stop to the nonsense. When Ricker returned with ten prisoners, a Rebel saddle, and a tall tale about Confederate artillery, he'd had enough. Once back in his tent he sent his adjutant with orders that "in no event should a brigadier go beyond his advance pickets without orders of the division commander." Furthermore, the Seventy-second Ohio—Buckland's brigade—"were to cease wearing those damned gray flannel shirts." Then he ate supper, smoked a cigar and was in fairly good spirits to meet Grant.

That's when McPherson and Wallace rode up. Grant's horse had slipped in the mud and had fallen on him; his ankle was so swollen his boot had to be cut off, and he'd gone back to the Landing. God, this Tennessee mud would kill more of them than the Secessionists! He threw back his blanket, found his coat and stepped outside in the cool spring air. How beautiful it was, though, he thought. The ghostly white of the dogwoods, and those peach blossoms in the orchard behind Prentiss's camps. Why couldn't they have found a political solution?

Brigadier-General Benjamin Mayberry Prentiss allowed his thin lips to relax. He knew his men called him, behind his back, "Preacher Ben." But he had grown his Mennonite beard deliberately, to give himself more stature. His camp, on Sherman's left, occupied some good level ground in a triangle between the Purdy and East Corinth roads, and he had no intention of incurring the General's wrath with false alarms. Besides, Sherman's camp at the church was in the advance position, and the Confederate cavalry his pickets reported seeing for the past two days were surely known to Sherman. When Major Powell and Colonel Graves came in after the review that afternoon with tales of seeing some Rebels watching them drill, he had allowed Colonel Moore, with three companies of the Twenty-first Missouri, to conduct a reconnaissance. About seven P.M., just before Sherman's courier arrived, Moore reported no enemy in sight. But Graves came again, with a story from Company H of the Twelfth Michigan, about campfires and drums.

Prentiss showed Graves the order from Sherman. "I think you can safely tell Captain Johnson to bring his company back. There's nothing to worry about. In fact there may be something to worry about if we stir around out there too much. The General doesn't like it." Prentiss was about to go to bed when Graves returned, this time with Johnson in tow. Prentiss rose to his full height, conscious that the candlelight played over his broad brow. "I want no more tales of Confederates in bushes." They looked at his beard and the thin line of his lips and left.

"Preacher Ben," he said aloud to himself, "you're getting more military every day."

John Morgan waited a full half-hour outside Bragg's headquarters before Captain Lockett and Lieutenant Steel, another engineer, came out. With silent salutes they mounted and fell in beside their cavalry escort. Lieutenant Steel proved invaluable: He had surveyed this Tennessee River country before the war, and his mind was a map of back roads and wagon trails. They rode directly east on the Bark Road and met no outposts from Prentiss's camp. Beyond, they entered almost impassable underbrush. "Don't worry," Steel whispered. "Locust Grove Branch starts down there. We can use the ravine for cover. It leads to the river road. But we'll avoid the road. We'll cut up a swag that will take us between Stuart's pickets and his camp." Lockett, as the senior engineer, trotted ahead, and a half-hour later, after the horses struggled up the mud-slippery sides of the ravine to Will's "Be blamed if this ain't straight up" and Quirk's "Shh!" Steel gave the signal to halt.

Silently they dismounted, and Morgan's men waited in the woods at the mouth of the swag while the two engineers crept forward. They were gone almost an hour. A gray light had begun to filter through the trees; from here you could hear the faint swish of the river in flood. Down there to the right the Tennessee rushed past its cliffs and Grant's gunboats at the Landing, north to Kentucky. If you were a ship you might travel that river and be home in a few days. Would be a good river "for a tall nigger to be baptized in." Sins all the way to the sea. Uncle Isaac would like that.

He was thinking these crazy thoughts and scratching Bess's withers when he heard it: the first faint spatter of musketry. Almost like woodpeckers tapping on trees. Somewhere back there, almost two miles away and across those fields that lay on either side of the road in front of the church, Hardee's boys were firing. The battle had started. It must be just past five o'clock. His mind flew to Hindman and Shaver and his fingers closed on the reins. Breckinridge would not be needed till later. The information Steel and Lockett were gathering might be the most important service they could do for Johnston: It was here that Stuart's camps—Sherman's Second Brigade —occupied the critical Federal left, which had to be turned. They had to know the lay of the land between Stuart and the river. The sound of cannon now joined the *rat-tat* of muskets and lit the sky to the west. At last, through the underbrush and the mist drifting in from the river, the white staff collars of the two engineers, like flitting birds, came into view as they jerked forward at a full run. The way back might not be as free of Yankees as the way in had been.

But miraculously, it was. Then, full realization dawned as the long roll was heard through the Union camps: The Yankees had been surprised! In his mind Morgan could see it: those fields bordered by rail fences and thick woods, but now covered even thicker with Confederates, their bayonets bristling in the sunlight that was growing brighter by the minute. It must have been a staggering sight. How he envied Hindman! And Shaver, his Arkansas boys with their bowie knives tucked in their belts! It was no coincidence that Hardee's corps—Sidney Johnston's Army of Kentucky— had started the battle. Hardee, who had been a major in Johnston's old Second Cavalry. Those men from Bowling Green and the Green River days. . . .

Bragg's corps had the job of initiating the movement against Prentiss, in the center. Morgan's little detail met Gladden's and Chalmers's brigades, of Bragg's Second Division, runing toward them on the Bark Road before they reached Bragg's headquarters. Where was Bragg? Lockett and Steel rode off to find him, and Morgan led his men in a swing through some woods south to Breckinridge's camp.

The Kentucky boys were beside themselves. When the sun came up, a bright orange world against the sky, they yelled out in joy, "The sun of Austerlitz!" and laughed like madmen. Even Breckinridge, normally in control of himself, was pacing wildly. "We'll do it!" he yelled at Morgan's men when they rode up. "We'll do it brilliantly!" And he hit the palm of his hand with his fist so loudly under her nose that Bess jumped.

"I saw General Johnston just before sunup. He was in magnificent spirits. I've never seen him look so animated. When he heard the firing he turned to Beauregard, who was still urging him to retreat to Corinth—can you believe it?—and said, 'The battle has opened, gentlemen. Tonight we will water our horses in the Tennessee.' "

"That's like him."

"Now dismount. I have a good breakfast for you—or what passes for one."

"Who can . . ."

"Who can eat at a time like this? You had better, my boy. You had better." Besides dried beef, hardtack and coffee, Breckinridge insisted he have a good stiff drink of whiskey. "To victory." Breckinridge lifted his glass and frowned at it. "To Kentucky," he added.

It was the last good food or drink John Morgan would have for two days.

It was almost seven o'clock before he found the squadron, who had also eaten and now stood around after roll call listening, as everybody was, to the sounds of rifle fire coming from the direction of Seay field and the woods in front of Sherman's camps. "If we don't hurry up they'll finish them off before we can fire a shot!" Charlton moaned.

"Tom, what are you doing?"

"Picking a violet, Brother Johnny! If I wear it in my cap, maybe the Yankees won't shoot me! It's a sign of peace, isn't it?"

It was as soft, and as smoky-blue, as her eyes. Oh, God, he had to live to see her again! He started to say something to Tom, but the long roll stopped the words in his mouth. It was time to move.

To the stirring sounds of a brass band, Breckinridge, riding down the lines with his son Joseph by his side, deployed his men in columns along the intersection of the Corinth and Bark roads. Here they would wait for orders. It was a balmy morning, with the smell of grass and the flash of red-winged blackbirds on rail fences. At eight-thirty orders came: Sherman's infantry was engaged west of Shiloh Church. Breckinridge would move to the left. Morgan's cavalry, scouting ahead, met some of Polk's corps still in the road. T.H. Hunt's Fifth Kentucky regiment, tired of waiting, had unslung their knapsacks and set a guard on the pile. A familiar golden head towered over the others, and Morgan called out to Cripps: "Wick! We'll beat 'em today!"

"Yes, we will! Yessir, we will!"

T.H. stood proudly by and nodded. His men would be one of the first reserve regiments to march, and he was ready. Morgan looked around for Tom, who was riding gaily beside Charlton. Yes, they had to win. If only Cal were here! The long lines of Breckinridge's three brigades had started.

Morgan, who had stayed in front of Trabue's First Brigade, was startled to see a general officer on a big bay ride up with part of his staff and confer with Brigadier-General Stewart, whose Second Brigade of Polk's corps was just ahead. It was Albert Sidney Johnston. He dashed off to the right, to the sound of firing, then reined up and trotted back to Morgan. "Divide your command. Come with me."

Within seconds it was done. He left James Bowles with Company C and the Texas Rangers to stay with Trabue and took Company A and Tom Allen's Company B to the right. Johnston, galloping ahead, was already out of sight. Morgan, with a glance at Basil, pushed Bess into a gallop. The fresh morning wind in his face, the blur of trees. Pounding, pumping legs under him. The rhythm of her black shoulders, the dip of her head. God, how she loved to run. Delilah. Monterrey. No, this was bigger than that. This was bigger than anything.

The shambles of Prentiss's camps slowed them. They were stepping over dead men, in every conceivable position, folded over, sprawled apart. They turned their heads from the mutilations, then stared again, as if pulled by some ghastly need to see, to record this desolation. It was a nightmare out of hell. Some of the forms groaned, rolled, lay still. The smell of baked chicken, biscuits, coffee still hot—they must have been surprised eating breakfast. Stacks of good hay stood between the Sibley tents. A disemboweled horse, trailing intestines, weaved ahead of them. Another, blood spurting from his throat, with the saddle of his colonel still strapped to his back, sank to his knees. One of Hardee's men, stumbling over corpses and clutching a bloody arm, looked at them with wild eyes.

"You'd better go to the rear," Basil yelled out.

"Cap, this here fight ain't got no rear!" The man seemed to wake up, looked around, found a good Yankee rifle and cartridges, and marched off in the direction of the firing, still bent, still stumbling.

Prentiss's main battle line rested along the north edge of Spain field, where Stuart's troops had held a parade just yesterday. Facing them, Gladden's First Brigade of Wither's Second Division, Bragg's corps, had been under withering fire for more than an hour. A thin haze of smoke obscured the long blue line of Yankees waiting in the trees.

Olivier is here, too, said Etienne. Gladden's First Louisiana. . . .

When Stewart's brigade came up, Johnston gave the order to charge. The Rebel yell became one blood-chilling shriek as the Pelican flag of Gladden's brigade, with its four Alabama regiments, disappeared into the smoke, Stewart's Arkansas and Tennessee troops close behind. Gladden, galloping ahead, could be seen, sword raised and waving. Then an earth-splitting roar of Federal cannon raked the lines. Morgan looked at Johnston. Hardee had just ridden up. They were watching the action with their staffs. Over their heads Johnston called out to Morgan: "I'm saving you. You may have to outflank that battery, if it's not taken."

Just to the right of Munch's Minnesota battery, Hickenlooper's Ohio Light Artillery was pouring double charges of canister from a line of six-pounders into the onrushing Confederates as fast as the gunners could give orders. But now Robertson's Florida battery, which had come up with Gladden, wheeled its twelve-pounder Napoleons into position. Morgan had never seen men move so fast or so smoothly: sponge barrel, ram bag and ball, thumb vent, hook lanyard to primer, stand at attention while the gunner, at his sight, gave the signal: Fire! Clockwork, four a minute. The sound was deafening. The ground shook. Bess trembled in every hair and he had to press her sides to steady her shifting legs. Suddenly, miraculously, the sounds slowed. As the smoke lifted, they could see what was left of Hickenlooper's battery—all twenty-four horses in one section lay in a heap. Others, with their gunners, made a wild dash into the woods. Hickenlooper, who waited as long as he could on his own bleeding mount, fell as the horse went down and ran off behind the last of his retreating guns. To his left as he went, one of Munch's six-pounders, stuck between two trees, suddenly bounded out, men hanging onto its limber as its horses careened through the underbrush. Gladden's brigade and Stewart's troops poured after them.

But something was wrong. They were carrying Gladden back from the field, his left arm almost torn off. A group of bending forms stood around him, and Dr. Yandell, Johnston's physician, sent a message to the staff which spread like wildfire: He would amputate right there, no time to lose. The forms made a respectful circle and Morgan squeezed his eyes shut at the scream: oh, for a few grams of that morphine Kitty had in her hem! But Hardee and Johnston were now galloping off to the right, and Morgan's two companies followed.

By now all semblance of the grand three-wave Napoleonic plan was gone. Troops from Hardee, Bragg, Polk and Breckinridge were mixed, obeying orders on the spot. Across almost vertical, boggy ravines and impassable blackjack woods some got lost, but joined the first command they met. Chalmers's Mississippi brigade had swung in to the right of Gladden through an oak forest east of Spain field. An attack here would turn Prentiss's left flank and perhaps surround him. Morgan, in the wake of Johnston's staff, arrived just in time to see Chalmers give the signal for a bayonet charge. But only the 360 men of the Tenth Mississippi heard him, and sprang forward yelling their heads off. It was as if the ground had suddenly sprouted spikes of steel. Over a thousand Federals—the last of Prentiss's resistance—didn't wait for them to gain the woods, but got up and ran.

"Well!" Johnston said. "That 'mates them."

It was just after nine P.M., and already the camps of Sherman and Prentiss were in Confederate hands. Clockwork . . . it had all gone like clockwork! Some of Gladden's troops were already bringing back Federal prisoners, mostly wounded. Captain Lockett rode up very agitated. Morgan saw Johnston nod, say something to Dr. Yandell, who began protesting. Johnston calmed the doctor with a gesture of his hand, that half-raised, almost Indian sign he had that could be reassuring but imperious at the same time. Johnston rode off to the right, Hardee following, leaving the doctor with the Federal wounded. Morgan put Bess into a canter. They were winning, by God, they were winning! He could hear Charlton and Tom singing behind him. He would follow Albert Sidney Johnston through hell.

Only Johnston knew how critical a delay now would be. He needed troops desperately on the right. Luckily, he had sent for Breckinridge over an hour ago. But Beauregard had ordered him to countermarch toward Prentiss's abandoned camps, and Johnston's reserve was now more than two hours away. They were giving Hurlbut entirely too much time to re-form! Johnston rode so fast Hardee could hardly keep up.

Beauregard rode with them. On a ridge bordering Locust Branch and moving obliquely northeast, Beauregard with two brigades had entered the abandoned camp of the Seventy-first Ohio, Stuart's brigade, and almost marched head-on into Hurlbut's whole Fourth Division, spread out in a long semicircle from the river road on the east through a peach orchard and field to some brush on the west. Three Union batteries stood strategically placed, one just east of the road, another just west of the orchard, and the third at the far west of the line. A gentle knoll, barely a swell of land, traveled through the orchard to the west, paralleling a fence bristling with Yankee bayonets. East of the road McArthur's three Illinois regiments faced Jackson's brigade of Bragg's Second Division. Breckinridge sat on his big bay in a small clump of trees, his eyes trained on his troops. This would be his boys' first fight of the day and they were excited. His own breath was coming short and he glanced at Joseph, by his side. Only seventeen, and holding himself like a man. Breckinridge let his breath out and saw Statham's Fifteenth Mississippi move up at the double-quick, then, after some desultory firing, stop to re-form in the woods. Johnston came riding up, a tin cup in his hand.

Breckinridge explained his dilemma, and Johnston sent immediately for reinforcements from Polk.

A tense hour passed. Heavy fighting from the east—Chalmers's brigade was confronting Stuart's camp on the far right. And worse: Beauregard's "roving staff," Colonel Jordan, had been wandering the battlefield all day giving orders. Jordan had sent Stephens's Sixth Tennessee of Cheatham's division into a senseless charge against a Union battery in Duncan field. With banners flying, Stephens's three regiments fled toward an angle of the Federal lines where the battery had unlimbered. At the double-quick, over three hundred yards of open ground, with several thousand Federals watching, they ran headlong into the waiting volleys of artillery and musketry. They made it to mid-field before a murderous crossfire from McClernand's Eighth Illinois opened up. The carnage was appalling. Stephens, thrown from his wounded horse, followed his men from the field, with Hurlbut's men close behind. Colonel Tom Jordan had given the Federals their first countercharge of the day.

It didn't last. The Confederates stood their ground, and the blue lines faded into the thickets and to the safety of a sunken road beyond. Still disgruntled, General Cheatham, his bushy mustache and long curly hair matted with sweat, relieved his frustration in a string of curses. Johnston's smile was sympathetic. Making little circles with the tin cup, he promised Cheatham that he would now have a chance to "make it up." Deploying Stephens in the cotton field, with Statham of Breckinridge's corps and Bowen's brigade, also of the reserve, to the right of the road, Johnston called up Jackson's troops from Bragg's corps to take the advance on the right. All this consumed almost an hour. The sun was high. Stephens's men, having faced that murderous assault in Duncan field, were near exhaustion. Breckinridge had little to worry about from Bowen, just east of the road between Statham and Jackson. A regular West Point officer who had served on the frontier, Bowen commanded troops who came, for the most part, west of the Mississippi—men who could handle the deep ravines and overgrown ridges between their line and the waiting Federals. It was Statham's inexperienced troops he was worried about.

As it turned out, his faith in Bowen and his fears for Statham were justified.

Almost before Johnston gave the order, Bowen's infantry charged through the woods. Johnston rode with them, directing the charges. General Withers rode up. Earlier, he had sent two regiments from Jackson's brigade over here to help. He wanted to see how his boys were doing. When he appeared they cheered, rushed out of the underbrush, and the Federal left flank gave way. Within minutes, Jackson's regiments poured nearly all of their fifty rounds of ammunition after the retreating Federals.

To the left, straddling the road and at the end of the orchard, Statham's troops were another matter. In a shallow ravine the Twentieth Tennessee came under withering fire, and watched spellbound as a small herd of goats were annihilated before their eyes. Would Morgan, at the edge of the ravine, ever forget the image of that aged billy running between those two battle lines? Johnston, with Bowen, was dangerously exposed to the hail of bullets, but from where Johnston stood he could see most of Statham's line. Governor Harris of Tennessee had come up with Withers, and they sat their horses watching Statham's efforts. Morgan, with Basil and James West, was a little to the left, behind the group, within earshot of orders. Breckinridge rode up, out of breath.

"General, I have a Tennessee regiment that won't fight."

Governor Harris bristled. "General Breckinridge, I would like to see that regiment!"

"The Forty-fifth Volunteer Tennessee Infantry," Breckinridge said, still unsettled.

Johnston, sensing Harris's embarrassment, waved the cup and said, "Let the Governor go to them."

The Forty-fifth Tennessee was stationed on the right, next to the Twentieth Tennessee. The Twentieth had pushed forward into a small fenced mule lot. Mistaking them for Yankees, the Forty-fifth had poured a volley into their ranks and were now, in the aftermath of that shock, almost demoralized. When Johnston called for a bayonet charge, they froze. Breckinridge again rode back to the General.

"Then I will help you," said Johnston. "We can get them to make a charge."

Without a word he rode to the line, where the men were waiting. He rode up and down it slowly, with no hat on his head, his saber in its scabbard, and only the little tin cup in his hand, twirling it as he talked. Then he began touching it to an occasional bayonet as he encouraged them. His voice, even from where Morgan sat on Bess, was soft and steady. He was pleading with these men to die, and suddenly, catching their growing enthusiasm, Johnston turned his face toward the enemy and shouted, "I will lead you!" An officer of the Twentieth Tennessee pulled off his cap, stuck it on his bayonet, and raised it high in the air. With that screaming, screeching yell, they poured out of the ravine toward Hurlbut. It was a few minutes before two P.M.

The whole orchard trembled. Nothing John Morgan had seen—not even Gladden's gallant charge—could match those ranks. On and on they marched in quick-step, without firing a gun, the crossed stars of the Confederate battle flag floating overhead. Statham's inexperienced Fifteenth Mississippi leveled their bayonets to within a hundred yards of Hurlbut's line. Then, as the Federals opened fire, the shattered peach blossoms exploded into the air to drift down on the wounded and dying.

The Forty-first Illinois ran. Statham's mangled brigade swarmed under the trees and onto the knoll, to find that the Federals had regrouped. The Mississippians took cover behind the little roll of land, but it was over for Hurlbut and he knew it. Johnston, sitting on Fire-eater, stood on a field covered with dead and still showered with Minié balls. Morgan, on the road and just behind the Forty-fifth Tennessee, saw Governor Harris ride over to him. Johnston lifted his foot and laughed, showing Harris the sole of his shoe. Hardee, who had joined them, trotted toward the road and shouted to Morgan: "The General says to take that battery" and pointed to Willard's guns, attached to McArthur's Eighty-first Ohio, to the right of the road and threatening a crossfire into the orchard.

But the cannoneers were hurrying to limber up and get away. Amazingly, even while Morgan watched, they managed to wheel around and pull off four six-pounders and two twelve-pounders. How fast fear can move a man! One gun was left. On it, still struggling in their harnesses, dying horses flailed: All had been shot except one. Just as Morgan was lifting his hand for the charge, a ball hit the horse in the root of his tail, and he took off, dragging gun, dead horses, harness and all.

Hardee trotted up, all grins. "We've got 'em, my boy!" His aide, red-headed little Vertner, who had been so many times to the Ready house in Murfreesboro, laughed out loud.

"We got em!" he echoed.

All the ground surrounding the peach orchard was lost to the Union troops. The Confederates were streaming beyond the orchard, past a pond, into more woods. Some of the men stopped to drink, their tongues on fire from biting cartridges. They flung themselves on the ground, ignoring the dead who lay half out of the water, turning it red with blood. A gap of nearly a half-mile separated what was left of McArthur's turned flank from Stuart, who was still contesting ground with Chalmers closer to the river. Morgan fully expected to be sent there when Colonel Munford of Breckinridge's staff rode up breathless, tears standing in his eyes.

"General Johnston is dead."

It couldn't be! Johnston! Not Johnston! He had seen him . . . seen him send his doctor back. To enemy wounded! Tears stung his eyes. He whirled Bess and looked for Basil. Charlton, Tom and the rest of Company A were a little way away, down a slope into some woods. He gave a familiar whistle, and they rode up.

"We are to report immediately—to the left—find General Bragg," he got out.

Unknown to them, at that moment, Stuart's Illinois and Ohio regiments finally gave way before Chalmers's hard-fighting Mississippi troops—some of Bragg's finest. Stuart, wounded in the shoulder, turned toward the Landing, his men with less than two rounds of ammunition apiece. From the

Tennessee River to Sarah Bell's peach orchard, a corridor lay open all the way to Pittsburg Landing and victory. Sidney Johnston's plan, to turn the Federal left, had succeeded. It had been the key, and it had been turned. Victory was within their grasp. They marched, instead, to the northeast, to the sound of the hardest firing, as Beauregard had commanded. It was an old Napoleonic axiom.

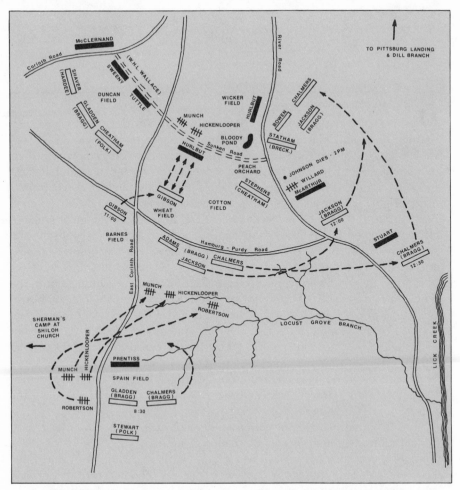

Surrender of Prentiss and the Formation of
Hornets' Nest
8:30 AM–3 PM Sunday, April 6, 1862

34

Beauregard was two miles to the rear, and Breckinridge rode like a man without direction. Hardee learned the news in a state of shock. There was no one to lead those troops on the Confederate right. Bragg now was their only hope. Morgan rode wildly, over dead and dying men and horses, headless, armless, legless corpses twisted like dolls pitched down from a great height, splattered, crushed into the blood-soaked mud. With so much death around, it seemed indecent to be alive, to be breathing great gulps of air, with a good horse under your hands, the blue sky. How could the sky spread overhead, or the sun shine on this madness? He was numb from fear and senseless with fatigue, past thinking. In the wheat field behind Prentiss's old camps he saw a company of young boys marching in columns of fours. They turned smartly at the corners, shoulders in line, their color bearer holding aloft a snapping banner. Around and around they went in a perfect square. When Morgan rode past, their captain smiled grimly. "They're out of ammunition," he said quietly. "This is all I can do to keep them from panic." Morgan rode on. The faces of those children—some couldn't have been sixteen—if he lived, he would never forget. If he lived. That seemed so unimportant now. To get to Bragg burned in his mind. To save the victory Johnston had won.

Hurlbut in retreat had not been idle. West of the pond behind the orchard he had regrouped along a sunken road, linking his 4,500 troops with 1,000 from Prentiss and 5,800 from W. H. L. Wallace, who commanded the Federal right flank into some thick woods across the main road to Corinth. More than eleven thousand men, with seven batteries totaling thirty-eight guns, now faced Bragg's exhausted men. Since noon, across a cotton field, toward a split-rail fence and underbrush so thick it seemed impossible for even a rabbit to get through, Gibson's four Louisiana regiments made charge after charge against the Federals in the sunken road. When Morgan found Bragg and before he could give him his news the General lifted his arm in a gesture that clearly indicated he would speak to no one, no matter what the message. Bragg was furious. Ahead, on the field, a struggle was going on over a flag. Bragg had just sent Captain Lockett to take the colors of the Fourth Louisiana and carry them forward. Colonel Allen, with a bullet hole in each cheek and blood streaming from his mouth, rushed toward Lockett and jerked the staff from him. Bragg, with his hand still up, rode up to Allen. Even from where Morgan waited, he could hear that insufferable, schoolmaster voice: "Colonel Allen, I want no faltering now."

Allen, blood still gushing, whirled his horse and gave his men the order for still another attack. Gibson, on the right with no artillery cover, personally led an Arkansas regiment all the way to the fence. The Union line suddenly broke into one sheet of flame. The sound was deafening, one solid roar—Hickenlooper had regrouped to unlimber behind Hurlbut, Munch to his right. Morgan's breath came short. What was it like, to run across that field, lumpy with the dead, and hold your fire until you got to that fence, to be met by canister and close-range rifle fire? The brush, crushed by projectiles, was still a matted, impregnable wall—it was, indeed, as Bragg's staff started calling it, a nest of hornets. Now, to his horror, Morgan saw the woods catch fire. The wounded in there, unable to escape, began screaming. Smoke obliterated the sun. Through that hell Gibson's men, for the third time, led by Colonel Allen with his mouth foaming blood, rushed on. Then, as quickly as it started, the firing stopped, and Gibson's men fell back. A lone Confederate ran between the brush and Allen's advance line. Around his waist he had wrapped a captured Federal flag.

"There's your Yankee, boys!" came a yell, and a hundred guns were leveled at the running form, which split apart and fell, rolled a little, and lay still. It was Julien Villard.

Would he go mad? Braxton Bragg, still not satisfied, turned his long face to a staff member and raged, "Gibson is an arrant coward. Send him in again." It was then he noticed Morgan and received the news of Sidney Johnston's death.

Gibson withdrew, to regroup and find ammunition. Hardee arrived, to take charge of the Nest while Bragg found Breckinridge. "Now, as for you," Hardee told Morgan grimly, "I am sending you around the left of this mess. Go toward the river, if you can, and charge the first enemy you see."

The Nest would be taken more than two hours later, but only after Brigadier-General Ruggles, commanding Bragg's First Division, to which Gibson and his unlucky Louisiana troops belonged, at last used the artillery Bragg refused to employ earlier. Never before had the North American continent borne such a barrage. In front of Duncan field sixty-two field guns were annihilating the Nest before five P.M., while Breckinridge, marching northwest, was unwittingly and without plan outflanking it.

As he left Hardee, John Morgan began forming a plan of his own. For hours now he had felt useless, an errand boy. This was no place for cavalry! Now, just maybe, it could be. The vision of so many men marching so coolly into death. . . . He had to justify them, redeem himself. His two companies had to find Polk's corps on the Confederate left—Trabue's brigade and T.H.—and scout the Fifth Kentucky north to the river. Maybe he could outflank what was left of Sherman, meet the troops under Breckinridge, and encircle the whole damned Yankee Army!

The day was hot. Not a breeze stirred through thick woods. They found a lane running south, and from the map he carried in his mind, they were sure to cross Tilghman Creek soon. Yes, there it was. It must join Owl Creek not far from here. He let his sweating men dismount. They divided the bits of hardtack left in their pockets and scooped water in their hands. A private from Company B ran up, white as a sheet. "Colonel, I . . . I . . . in the woods . . . there he was, a dead Yankee, and I almost . . . I almost!"

"Ain't yo' Mammy taught yew better outhouse manners than thet?" Some-one laughed.

But the boy was shaken, and burst into tears. Others looked away. Morgan gave the order to remount. They were barely settled in their saddles when, quick as wild animals, the mood changed. In a field to the left a regiment of bluecoats were marching past, apparently unconcerned and un-aware the Rebels were there. Basil Duke shot his colonel a quizzical look. How could the Yankees be *here*, unless, on this crazy battlefield, things were even more mixed up than they knew?

Morgan ordered a platoon of Company A to dismount and approach cau-tiously. From the trees they could see one of the bluecoats, a little man with a saber almost as big as he was, cutting his orders in the air with an offhand abandon. There was a touch of Gallic eloquence in the gesture that made Morgan signal Basil. It was Colonel Mouton's Eighteenth Louisiana, in their dress blues! "Goddamn!" James West whispered, before he let his breath out. "We almost . . ."

"Another almost!"

It relieved the tension.

But what was Mouton's regiment doing? They were part of Pond's bri-gade, Bragg's corps. "Maybe we aren't as far left as we thought," James West said. "Shouldn't we be seeing Polk?"

A volley of musketry from the left, followed by a roar of artillery stopped the reply in Basil's mouth. The Eighteenth Louisiana had disappeared into a ravine and now headed up a slope, still in column. The Federals held the timber at the edge of the field. As Mouton's men rushed over the slope into open ground in front of the timber, two twenty-four-pounders raked their lines. Miraculously, and still in column, they made a right-face. Like tin soldiers in tempo they withdrew, so aligned that one shell took off four left thighs at once before it cut a sergeant in two.

Why didn't the Federals come out and chase them?

A din, as of screeching crows in a wind, gave them the answer: To the right, the first swarming mass of Yankee refugees were running from the Nest to the river with the rest of Trabue's brigade after them. It was Bull Run all over again!

Mouton was moving north and Morgan spurred Bess and gave the signal to follow.

It was past five o'clock and growing cloudy when he finally found Polk. He was sitting under a tree, on a blanket, peeling an apple. From the direc-tion of the river, over a mile away, the relentless, measured boom of big guns began. "It's the Federals' gunboats," Bishop Polk said easily. "But don't worry, my boy. Look." Morgan followed his raised hand and saw trees to the rear take flame. "They'll overshoot us. Beauregard's in more trouble than we are. What we've got to do now is drive those Yankees into the river and get control of Owl Creek before Lew Wallace comes down from Crump's Landing. That area is vital. I've already directed the Fifth Kentucky up there."

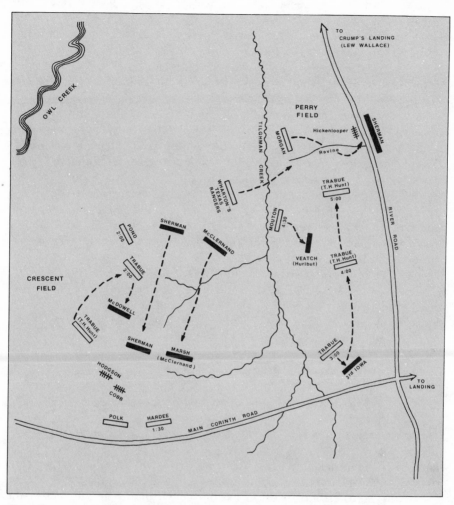

Action on Confederate Left—North of Nest
Noon–5 PM April 6, 1862

Morgan's heart jumped. T.H. Was he still alive? And the rest of the squadron?

"Your men have acquitted themselves well today. They're not half a mile from here, if you hurry. . . ."

They saw the Texas Rangers first, then Captain Bowles. Ralph Sheldon galloped up, red-faced and sweaty, with a grin from ear to ear. His look said it all. They were together again.

As they rode past an infantry column, some of the Fifth Kentucky cheered. In a field just beyond a ravine Federal skirmishers ran out from some woods not eight yards away, their object T.H.'s marching columns. Morgan gave the signal to charge, and his three companies thundered across open ground and dashed, full gallop, into the trees. The skirmishers disappeared, and the squadron floundered in a mass of tangled underbrush. But they pushed on, until suddenly they found themselves confronted by a full infantry regiment of Sherman's army. There was a flash of musketry, almost in their faces, but they kept on, running down and over the men on the ground—little Sam Buckner, of *Minnetonka* fame, slashing away with a captured saber and yelling at the top of his voice.

It was a trap. Why had they bit the bait? Spoiling for a fight. The worst kind of motive. Before they got away, three saddles were empty: They lost Lieutenant James West, Sam Buckner, and James Geslin. Gone. Their bodies lying back there in the woods. West, dear old West. And young Sam, and Geslin. *You see? I told you he was a gentleman. He will take care. . . .*

When they reached the Rangers, the Texans asked what they would do next.

"Go in," Charlton shouted. "By God, go in!"

"Then we will too!" the Texans yelled. "Come on with us!" They galloped down the rear of Morgan's line, turned short to the left, and charged into the woods, Charlton with them. They found the rest of the Yankee brigade and drove them back until a high fence stopped them. Some of their riderless horses galloped back past the squadron, waiting in the field.

To his horror, Morgan saw Charlton clutch his thigh and reel in the saddle. Ben Drake was on him at once; while Greenberry Roberts steadied his horse, Ben slipped Charlton to the ground.

"I'm all right!" Charlton moaned.

"Get over here and let me see."

"I'm all right, I tell you!"

Tom Quirk dropped from his horse and with his big Irish hands lifted Charlton to ride double behind his saddle. "If he can hang on, I'll get him back to the rear," Quirk said.

"Find Doctor Yandell. Come back at once."

Morgan could say no more. Ahead, from an excellent position on the top of a ravine across Perry field, and protected by the sharpshooters of the Twenty-ninth Illinois, Hickenlooper's battery had unlimbered to annihilate the Fifth Kentucky. Morgan felt his blood turn to ice. The booming from the river split the air. James West. Sam Buckner. Jim Geslin. Now maybe Charlton. Or T.H.! No. NO! Like a madman, he led his men across the ravine, almost straight down, slipping through thick vines, through "impassable" terrain that vanished under the flashing feet of their horses. They came up and out like fire spewed from a geyser, so close to the battery that the gunner fled over the top of a hill at a full run.

"CHARGE!"

He bent double, his head close to Bess's mane. As they cleared the top of the hill they met the rest of Sherman's army drawn up in line, taking aim.

The Federals fired wildly, and not too well. Minié balls singed the air and left holes in their clothes as they whirled and ran. Miraculously, they lost no one. They galloped back to their own lines, where Colonel Hunt was about to call for reinforcements to press the attack, when a member of Beauregard's staff rode up with a message.

It was an order to withdraw.

The Nest, which had anchored the Federal center, was gone. Preacher Ben Prentiss, with his whole division, was captured. The Federal left, according to Johnston's plan, had been turned since early afternoon.

If Beauregard had known, the battle now hung in the balance at a murderous ravine called Dills Branch, south of the Landing.

Choked with trees, vines and underbrush, its slippery sides rose like canyon walls. Bragg's brigades under Chalmers and Jackson regrouped under fire from a line of Federal siege guns against the sky. Jackson, out of ammunition, gave the signal, and his men made their advance without cartridges. At the top of the ridge they met a flaming rifle volley that sent them reeling. But General Ruggles, fresh from his artillery success at Duncan field, had already promised help, and Withers, the division commander of Jackson and Chalmers, was busily sending for ammunition. Bragg himself, not easily moved, allowed himself some emotion. "There is every prospect of success," he told Jackson as he watched him leave to see Withers about more troops. Within the hour, they could have the Landing.

On his way, Jackson was stopped by Beauregard's aide-de-camp with orders to retire.

When the man reached Bragg he was incredulous, and asked if he had given those orders to anyone else. The aide pointed to Jackson's troops, already withdrawing from the ravine. "My God," Bragg shouted, "it's too late!"

Only Mouton's Eighteenth Louisiana regiment, in their dress blues, remained in line of battle, four hundred yards in front of Sherman. Nobody had told them to retreat.

Pierre Gustave Toutant Beauregard retired that night fully convinced that the day was won. Only a little skirmishing after breakfast, and they could return to Corinth and hot baths and a good meal. He wheezed and mixed a powder in a glass of water. Damn this bronchial infection. The infernal Tennessee rain didn't help. The faces of his generals—Hardee, Breckinridge, Cheatham, Polk—came back. They had certainly been cheerful enough, and left in good humor. Even Bragg. Yes, that telegram from Helm's scouts was reassuring—Buell moving toward Decatur, still a hundred miles away! They had beaten Grant before Buell could come up, after all! There was nothing for the Federals to do but retire. Even Lew Wallace's seven thousand at Crump's Landing would be useless to them now. If he did march south it would be into a Confederate trap. *Alors* . . .

Colonel Gilmer had come in about nine P.M. and confirmed his feelings. For two hours, since seven o'clock, a Federal band played "Hail, Columbia!" down at the Landing. When they heard it, the Confederate troops cheered. It was a sure sign of debarkation. The battle was over and the enemy was leaving. Beauregard's dream of fame had come true: Corinth and Waterloo. One a victory, the other a defeat. He would be greater than Napoleon! He turned from his chief engineer and dispatched some of his staff to Corinth as an escort for Johnston's body. Only then, after reading Helm's telegram again, did he allow himself a sigh.

Prentiss had been cocky, with his story of Buell arriving tonight. It was all bluff, the bravado of a captured man.

Morgan left Wharton's Texas Rangers to cover Mouton's regiment and rode to find Breckinridge. He was worried about Charlton. He had seen these "minor" wounds before: They were deceptive.

Everywhere on the way soldiers were throwing down their guns and looting the Federal camps. Haversacks bulged with food, pistols, even daguerreotypes, if they were framed in silver. Some were already on their way to getting drunk on Yankee brandy found in the officers' tents. Fresh beef, sugar, coffee, rice, flour, crackers, hams, cornmeal, apples, cheese, candy . . . Yankee butter . . . it was all there, with blankets, overcoats, oilcloths . . . even a new blue civilian suit! Gilt-edged paper, steel writing pens, envelopes, love letters. First-class Enfields, with cartridges. In one of Sherman's camps, as Morgan passed, one of the Confederate boys had already started a fire in an abandoned oven. There would be good fresh bread there in a few hours! They acted as if the battle were over. Maybe it was! They had broken the Nest, pushed the Yankees all the way to the river . . . Good God, maybe it *was* over. Maybe, by morning, they would wake to find the gunboats and the transports gone, carrying Sherman and his runaways downriver, back to Paducah and St. Louis, where they belonged. Then Sidney Johnston's dream, of ridding Middle Tennessee of the invader, would come true. Maybe then the South could take the offensive, before the Northern juggernaut of factories and unlimited manpower overwhelmed them. All they asked for was to be left alone. Was that too much? Maybe, by God, at Shiloh, they had gotten their message across. The Confederate Army certainly slept, that night, closer to the Tennessee River than it had the day before. If only . . .

Last light, under gathering clouds, was going. It was nine o'clock and pitch-dark by the time he found Breckinridge, with Hardee in one of the tents in Prentiss's old camp. The Yankee gunboats had changed their tempo. One of them fired at five-, ten-, and fifteen-second intervals, while the other kept up its ten-minute pounding.

"What a waste of ammunition," said Breckinridge between gulps of a whiskey he held in his hand. He raised it in a silent invitation to Morgan, who nodded. An orderly stepped forward with an empty glass and Breckinridge poured his friend a drink. "If they think, after today, that a little bombardment can scare us . . ."

Before Morgan could ask for orders—he needed to find Colonel Trabue —Nathan Bedford Forrest filled the tent flap with his large frame, the candlelight quivering as a gust of wind swept past. He was out of breath and frowning like some Old Testament prophet. A detachment of his scouts under Lieutenant Sheridan, dressed in Federal overcoats, reported Buell's troops disembarking at the Landing.

General Hardee, who had been sitting on a camp cot, unbuttoned his coat and pulled off his shoes.

"It's been a long day, Colonel Forrest."

Morgan hadn't realized before how much Hardee looked like a sack of laundry. His paunch sagged through his shirt and his van Dyke, gone shaggy, had trapped a piece of hardtack that bounced when he talked. He wondered what Alice Ready would think of her general now, minus his pomade. His tone to Forrest was so condescending that the cavalryman addressed himself to Breckinridge.

"Buell has arrived," Forrest clipped out. "We should either attack immediately or abandon the field."

"Come now, Colonel Forrest," Hardee said, before Breckinridge could answer. "Even you must know such a decision has to be made by the commanding officer. If you really think drastic measures are necessary, I suggest you find General Beauregard immediately, and relate your news to him."

"Will you come with me?"

Forrest wheeled toward Morgan, as if the others were not there.

You know I will his look answered, and he followed Forrest from the tent. Silently they mounted. Morgan found his men and gave them the necessary instructions: They were to find Trabue and send a detail back to Breckinridge's tent to await further orders. Basil, his dark eyes worried, protested: "You're not a scout. You're too valuable to us. Suppose . . ."

"I'll hear none of it. If Buell is landing, we should know."

They rode in a circle, through sleeping soldiers, dying campfires, their horses stumbling over lumpy forms on the ground. Already the stench of decaying horseflesh emanated from those piles of harness-tangled masses that had been cut away from abandoned cannon.

Beauregard. Beauregard was the word that burned in their brains. A major from Colonel Govan's Second Arkansas thought he was at the church. But the church was now a hospital. There was no time to look for Charlton, and they rode on. A young lieutenant with the Georgia Dragoons had seen Beauregard near Barnes field just off the Ridge Road. A gunner with Captain Gage's Alabama Battery, just an hour ago, heard that headquarters had been moved back to Mickey's. . . . They stopped asking after a while, and rode in circles. Where, dammit, was Beauregard? Forrest, without a word, spurred his horse, and Morgan followed him to his outpost, near Chalmers's line facing Dill Branch down by the river. The closer they got the louder the gunboats boomed, until it seemed as if their heads would blow off.

Forrest motioned impatiently toward the Confederate line, now quiet with exhausted troops. "They picked the worst direction for their assault," he growled. "Even a crow could see how impossible that approach is. . . ."

He dismounted, conferred with his men, and found two fresh Federal overcoats, handed one up to Morgan, then mounted again. They poked their arms through, retraced their steps, and followed a ravine to the right of Dill Branch. Their horses dug at the sheer sides, slippery now from rain which had started again, until they climbed to level ground in deep trees, an ancient grove of oaks and beeches that tossed in the growing wind. It must be past midnight. Between flashes of lightning—the rain was a storm in earnest now —and the fire from the gunboats, Morgan could make out the dark forms of buildings in front, scattered in the trees.

"What?"

Forrest flashed his white, even teeth in the greenish-yellow light from a gunblast. "Indian mounds," he said softly. "Tall enough to hide a regiment."

Indian mounds! Between the steep ravine that curved away behind them and Dill Branch just ahead, this grove of great trees and Indian burial mounds—some twenty feet high—had been completely bypassed by the swirl of battle. Forrest dismounted and walked to the edge of the hundred-foot-plus drop to the river. Across the water, in flashes of fire and lightning, the land leveled out in farm fields. Earlier his scout had watched the *Minnehaha* almost swamp under swarms of Yankee refugees from the Landing, some pushed into the water to drown by Nelson's men, crossing from the other side. The rest of Nelson's division—the Ohio brigades of Ammen and Hazen, and Sanders Bruce's Twentieth Kentucky—had sloshed their way inland even before sundown. Now, in this storm, McCook's division with three brigades and Tom Crittenden's with two more were completing the crossing. The Federal Army of the Ohio had arrived.

"How many?" Forrest heard Morgan ask behind him.

"I figure about fifteen thousand. Maybe eighteen. Or twenty."

"With Wallace's seven thousand that would be . . ."

"At least twenty-five thousand fresh troops," Forrest finished.

"I see your point."

"But they aren't organized yet. That crowd of cowards at the Landing will delay their artillery. If we attack now, we have 'em."

The longing in Forrest's voice was like a cry.

"Let's do it. Let's find Beauregard . . ."

Overhead the trees roiled in the wind. Thunder crashed, then rolled off, like caissons being dragged across the sky. Morgan mounted. They left the security of the mounds, but the Union soldiers were so busy no pickets saw them as they vanished down the ravine to the left. They shed their Federal overcoats before Chalmers's vedettes could make a mistake.

In Stuart's old camps, past Bloody Pond and through the orchard, lightning lit up the ground lumpy with corpses. Morgan watched Forrest's drenched back ahead. They crossed the cotton field, mushy with mud and worse—every step Bess took he prayed was in mud.

There was no organization. Confederate troops slept where they had stopped in battle at sundown. There was no effort to bring up ammunition wagons, distribute cartridges. Empty guns and spent soldiers collapsed together in mixed regiments with an officer close enough to take command. An occasional picket challenged them in the dark. They made their way to the Hamburg-Purdy Road, cross-country almost to the church, then turned toward the main Corinth Road and Duncan field, where Ruggles's batteries had finally broken the Nest that afternoon. Trotting well ahead, Forrest leaned into a canter and Morgan kept up, despite the curses of sleeping soldiers trying to stay dry in fence rows. They were almost to Tilghman Creek, at the point where Wharton's Rangers and Ketchum's Alabama battery were covering for Mouton, when Forrest raised his hand and brought his horse up abruptly. They dismounted and walked into some trees. Not a hundred yards beyond them Lew Wallace's troops were already settled in between the creek and the river road.

The squadron! Had the Federals outflanked the squadron? But there was no time to think. If they couldn't find Beauregard, they at least knew where Hardee was. They raced back to Hardee's headquarters. The General came out, rubbing his beard. He listened politely. Morgan, on Bess, had not dismounted but waited in the shadows. Although Hardee answered quietly enough, he could hear him plainly. His slow Georgia drawl might have been that of a father admonishing a child. "Now, Colonel Forrest, Ah advise you to return to yo' regiment and maintain a vigilunt watch. Repo't any hostile movements." Even Hardee didn't know where Beauregard was. Forrest gave up. It was two A.M.

"Get some sleep, Morgan," he said in that be-damned way of his. "You'll need it."

Major-General Lew Wallace's Third Division of Grant's Army of the Tennessee crossed the bridge at Snake Creek on the Confederate left about an hour after Beauregard gave his order to cease firing. As first light disclosed Ketchum's Alabama battery among some trees, Wallace gave the command to attack. Thompson's Ninth Indiana artillery opened up, taking Ketchum by surprise. But the Confederates rallied, manned their guns and answered. Taking advantage of a rise in the ground to his right, Wallace posted Thurber's Missouri battery to start a crossfire.

Morgan's squadron had camped in the mud near Duncan field. By daylight, as the men roused themselves from the most miserable, rain-soaked night they could remember, the firing picked up. Ketchum, with some of his best horses dead, managed to limber up his cannon and withdraw about a hundred yards to re-form. Behind him Preston Pond's brigade, with Mouton's Eighteenth Louisiana nearest the Yankee line, realized their peril and started running toward the Corinth Road. Only Wharton's Texas Rangers, with Ketchum's hard-pressed battery, covered their retreat as Wallace's troops, five thousand strong, burst over the field.

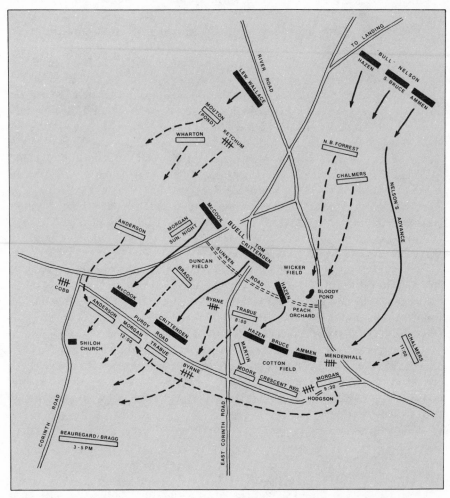

Federal Offensive—Wallace, Buell, Nelson
Monday, April 7, 1862

Brigadier-General William "Bull" Nelson had come a long way since his recruiting days at Camp Dick Robinson near Lexington. After successfully chasing the Confederates through Pound Gap in eastern Kentucky, he was given the Fourth Division at Louisville, and last night he had been proud of them. The debarkation had gone like clockwork, in spite of those thousands of craven cowards crowding the landing. Ammen's brigade got ashore first, then Hazen, followed by Sanders Bruce's Twentieth Kentucky. In all there were four Kentucky regiments, three Ohio and two Indiana. By ten-thirty some of Ammen's men were in battle line. At three A.M. "Bull" Nelson gave the orders to his troops: As soon as you can see, start firing.

As the sun came up, Nelson's division, Hazen to the right, Bruce at center, Ammen on the left, was ready. To their right, Union General Tom Crittenden's Fifth Division was in position astride a road to the river, with McCook's Second Division, the largest of Buell's command, in the rear.

Nathan Bedford Forrest had settled his men for what remained of the night in Hurlbut's old headquarters, a level clearing with some Yankee hay left conveniently for his horses. They were awakened at first light by firing in the direction of Tilghman Creek, toward the river. Forrest ordered his men to mount up just in time to greet Colonel William B. Hazen's Forty-first Ohio as they marched out of the woods, and to cover the retreat of Chalmers's exhausted brigade.

Hazen marched on, joined by Bruce. Less than a half-mile beyond Hurlbut's headquarters, across Wicker field, the Federals discovered a Confederate battery at the edge of a woods near a pond. They charged and captured the guns, only to be met by Chalmers's regrouped and waiting men, who drove them back. There the eager Union soldiers skirmished for more than an hour, receiving orders from Nelson that they had gone too far and were in danger of being outflanked on their right, until Crittenden's troops could catch up. Ahead they could see a dozen bodies floating in the pond, swollen, humped backs like stuffed turtles bobbing. Beyond, a tattered peach orchard caught the rising sun and birds sang overhead between the *zing-tat* of rifle fire.

Nelson could do no more at this point without artillery support but hold the Confederates at bay. Artillery was coming, however: Mendenhall's battery, diverted from Crittenden, soon had its rifled Rodman guns in place and was firing case shot at two hundred yards, splitting apart the trees around the hidden Rebel cannon. Still Nelson waited for Crittenden. It was now just after seven o'clock. In another hour Buell would have nearly eighteen thousand fresh troops on the field, with Tom Wood's Sixth Division expected before noon. Nelson's men were deployed in a front almost a mile long, from Ammen's brigade on high ground just east of the river road, with Bruce through the old Hornet's Nest and Hazen to the edge of Duncan field. Beyond, the rest of Buell's army extended west of the road to Corinth.

Chalmers's ammunition wagons couldn't be found. He had no choice but to retreat through the peach orchard and cotton field to Stuart's old camps beyond. Relief was in sight: Diagonally across the cotton field, with Morgan's squadron as a screen, Hodgson's New Orleans Washington Artillery had unlimbered, and Generals Hardee and Breckinridge stood nearby. At ten A.M. Beauregard sent the order: Charge.

With Martin's Seventh Arkansas from Hardee's First Brigade leading, the Confederates broke across a corner of the cotton field toward a log cabin just to the left of the peach trees. Mendenhall's battery switched from case to canister, but still the gray line came on, shouting "Bull Run! Bull Run!" Hazen's Federal Kentucky regiment broke and ran. Morgan, held back by Hardee to protect the New Orleans battery on the south edge of the field, saw the big bulk of Bull Nelson riding back and forth among his panicked troops. On Hazen's left, however, another group of Kentuckians—Sanders's brigade—met the onrushing Confederates in a terrible, hand-to-hand contest in the underbrush. Hazen's Forty-first Ohio now turned the stalemate into a counterattack, loading and firing as they ran forward, and it was the turn of Bruce's Kentuckians to yell, "They run! See, they can run, too!"

It was a wild stumble over rough terrain. Morgan's squadron, still under orders to hold fire at the battery, watched the oncoming regiments and prayed Hodgson's men could hold. Edouard Villard was one of Hodgson's captains, in charge of a twenty-four-pounder howitzer. Stunned, Morgan saw the Federals swarm over three guns—two twelve-pounders and Edouard's howitzer—saw Edouard fall and try desperately to fight off his attackers. Even more incredulously, Morgan watched a Federal colonel rush out of a knot of men and shove aside one of his soldiers who was about to run the unarmed Edouard through with his bayonet. On they came, but not for long: The Crescent Regiment, running at the double-quick, poured onto the field. Morgan's men saw their chance and swarmed over the captured cannon while the Louisiana infantry drove the Federals back. There, in the confusion, some of the Yankee troops fired into their own men.

Hardee was beside himself. His black thoroughbred had been shot from under him at the fight for Hodgson's guns. His coat was full of holes. Now he saw, at about the time that the Crescent Regiment drove back Bruce's Kentuckians, John Moore's Second Texas, the troops that had marched barefoot from Houston to Corinth. Cautioning the Texans that Martin's Seventh Arkansas might be in their line of fire, Hardee led them personally across the field toward the orchard. When the Texans saw some troops in the woods just beyond and to the left of the orchard—the old sunken road line—they stopped, unsure if they were Confederates. Hardee was furious. They were so close now that a short-range volley exploded into the line, and the Texans ran. "Stop those men!" Hardee yelled. "Pack of cowards!" Nothing pleased him, not even the fact that Chalmers, relinquishing his own command to lead the Fifth Tennessee and Twenty-sixth Alabama from Stuart's camps, was on his way to bolster Hardee's right, where Ammen was forming for a fresh attack east of the orchard.

For one thing, Hardee was worried about the Confederate left near Shiloh Church, where Bragg had been holding off McCook's Second Division for almost four hours. He ordered Morgan to the left.

Morgan found Trabue's brigade—T.H.'s Fifth Kentucky and Byrne's battery—facing Tom Crittenden's fresh troops. Morgan's squadron was deployed to Trabue's left. They hardly had time to take position before the order came to charge. They dashed headlong at Boyle's "Louisville Yankees," hoping to flank a battery to the left of Boyle in the woods past Duncan field. The volley they received staggered them; in the fight back Basil caught a Minié ball in his shoulder. Another grazed his face.

"It's nothing!" he yelled, angry tears diluting blood. He wiped his eyes with the sleeve of his good arm and tried a grin, but in ten more minutes his face was white, and Morgan, noticing for the first time the blood spreading across his torn coat, sent him to the rear.

"Cheer, Boys, Cheer!" rang out, little Tom Morgan's voice rising above the chatter of musketry. James West. Geslin, Sam Buckner. Charlton. Now Basil. Where would it end? Then he saw Jack Green, not eighteen years old, who had joined them at Camp Charity, lying dead with a hole in his head, his horse trotting around aimlessly. Ben Drake caught up the bridle and led it to the nearby woods, where Jesse and the reserve waited for orders.

It was predictable: With Crittenden's two Federal brigades descending on the depleted Confederate line and Hazen now able to turn his troops from the fight at the orchard to face Trabue from the right, the Kentuckians withdrew. Luckily, Trabue made his way down to the Purdy Road to march west—only to face a new threat: McCook's three fresh brigades approaching from the river. There Trabue's men met their divided command again, Cobb's battery and the Fourth Kentucky and Fourth Alabama—which were almost single-handedly holding the Confederate left. General Patton Anderson's Florida battalion swung around to line up on the Purdy Road to help. Morgan looked for Tom and motioned him to stay close. They would make a stand now across Sherman's old headquarters and astride the road to Corinth that led, just to the south of them, past Shiloh Church, where Charlton lay wounded. God willing, they would make it. . . .

Only one of McCook's three brigades was in the front line—Rousseau's mixed Indiana-Kentucky-Ohio troops. They were so cautious (one battery was out of ammunition, the other had been sent to help Nelson at the orchard) that one of Tom Crittenden's brigades—Sooy Smith's—had time to strike Trabue first. Morgan's squadron, back to full strength, was now on Trabue's right facing Lauman's veteran troops from Hurlbut's division.

Along the edge of Sherman's old review field, Cobb had unlimbered. Federal infantry from Boyle and Smith captured two guns, with their dead and dying horses still struggling in their harnesses. Cobb re-formed, was overcome again, and had to stop. Morgan, in horror, saw a shell kill two gunners in Cobb's battery and cut the hands from a third. The boy looked down, unbelieving. Only Stanford's Mississippi battery, an old reliable from Polk's corps, stood in the Purdy Road pouring shot into the oncoming troops of McCook. Stanford swore to hold on, but his supporting infantry—Anderson and Trabue—were forced back, and his guns were engulfed. The Federal advance was not stopped until it met a regrouped Anderson with some of Cheatham's troops who had retreated from McClernand's old camps.

The scattered Yankees under Rousseau were almost out of ammunition. They withdrew for more, but fresh troops stepped forward to fill their places, and Mendenhall's guns moved up. The Confederates attacked again, yelling like madmen, their flag fluttering, to get those cannon. The Sixth Indiana stopped them, but a new threat for the Yankees appeared to their left: Morgan's squadron at full gallop.

He gave the signal for the "accordion," a formation of four horsemen spread apart, then together again, then apart again, so that the whole column became a moving shuttle, hard to hit. It was a maneuver his Lexington Rifles had invented. The Federals watched the spectacle with open mouths. Mendenhall struggled to wheel his guns, and Morgan was within thirty yards of the battery when a high fence stopped the horses. They galloped to the left, but not before the Yankee infantry found its target, bunched together now, and emptied half a dozen saddles. Morgan turned to see John Sisson slump forward. He wheeled Bess, caught the bridle, and galloped off, praying John could hold on.

How many men had he lost? He was afraid to think. He saw Will and Tom Logwood riding ahead. Little J. W. DeWitt, who'd joined them at Camp Charity, cantered past, intent on keeping up. The retreating Confederates were giving way across an open field, and the main line had withdrawn a quarter of a mile south to Sherman's tents. Most of them were out of ammunition. Morgan's squadron rode past bent, sweat-soaked backs searching the dead for cartridges. General officers worked like privates. General Cheatham dismounted and served a Confederate cannon while a staff officer carried a battle flag under a volley of fire to steady the troops. General Patton Anderson walked a battalion through Sherman's tents to find ammunition. One section of artillery stood idle, the gunners staring at their empty twelve-pounder Napoleons and dead horses. On the Confederate right Hardee's Irish general Pat Cleburne was retreating before McClernand's infantry; on the left, still fighting Lew Wallace's fresh troops, Ketchum's Alabama battery, with Gibson's exhausted men and Wharton's Rangers, were nearly insane with fatigue. Preston Pond's brigade, which had marched and countermarched all day, from Owl Creek to the orchard and halfway back, were ordered to the vicinity of the Main Corinth Road. About two P.M. the order came through Colonel Jordan from headquarters: All were to withdraw to Shiloh Church.

By the time Morgan reached the church most of the wounded had been moved farther down the Main Corinth Road. But he had another surprise: Tom Morgan came trotting up with Wharton's Texans, his young, sweaty face dead-tired but grinning. Colonel Wood, with his detachment from Wirt Adams's Mississippi cavalry, was with him.

Then grimly, from nowhere, Beauregard appeared. Mounted, he seemed almost larger than life, with his big round head and high brow. He flashed his eyes and almost dropped his reins as he gestured. Federal rifle fire sprayed the air. Through the noise he yelled: Pond would attack, aided by all available troops. Then the little Frenchman turned his neck, turtlelike, over the crowd. When he saw the Fifth Kentucky, and without addressing T.H., he ordered it forward. "Forward!" he shouted.

Forward could be anywhere. When T.H. asked for directions, Beauregard swore, but added, "Put them in right here." Other regiments were ordered into line near the church, but collapsing with fatigue, they showed little enthusiasm. Beauregard, in exasperation, bent down from his horse, grabbed a flag and spurred forward, yelling, "Fix bayonets! Charge!"

The Fifth Kentucky ran ahead, with Mouton's Eighteenth Louisiana and the rest of Pond's brigade close behind. The Thirty-fourth Illinois received the brunt of the Rebel attack. When its colonel grabbed his flag and rushed forward, he was wounded also. A sheet of flame from the rear told that Lew Wallace, too, was in trouble.

Here, by the church, among these men sinking with exhaustion, occurred some of the fiercest fighting of the day. Colonel Alfred Mouton was shot in the head and reeled, whirling, before he fell. The Thirty-eighth Tennessee, another of Pond's regiments, was decimated, raked by Federal howitzers at close range. Yet somehow on they ran, charging over McClernand's drill ground until they met Lauman's troops and Rousseau's men, back from Buell with replenished cartridge boxes. Behind them Willard's Illinois Light Artillery greeted the oncoming, yelling gray lines with a murderous fire, the cannoneers jumping like demons in the blinding smoke. Now another battery opened up, and as the Confederates ran back across the open field some tripped, pitched headlong, crept or lay still. To quick-step was to risk instant death; to stop meant certain capture. The time was three-thirty P.M.

Morgan never heard the order to withdraw; it seemed to happen instinctively, by unanimous consent. Ketchum's Alabama battery, with one gun from Byrne, took a stand on the left. In front of a house on the Main Corinth Road, where the Confederate wounded were now gathered, Beauregard set another battery.

But the day wasn't over. Desultory firing went on all afternoon. In a wheat field across the Purdy Road, the Fifth United States Light Artillery, supported by a regiment of Sanders Bruce's brigade, dueled with Harper's Mississippi battery. Suddenly Buell ordered Bruce to attack. With part of the Ninth Indiana, he charged with fixed bayonets. The Mississippians, out of canister and without sufficient infantry support, fell back. Returning from a search of Prentiss's camps for ammunition, Martin's Second Confederate regiment routed Bruce in a quick countercharge. Other soldiers from Breckinridge's corps, just to Martin's left, joined in the chase. Cripps's uncle, Colonel Charles Wickliffe, brought his Seventh Kentucky across a creek, up a hill in underbrush near the Ridge Road, and ran into a fresh brigade of Nelson's division just arrived at the Landing, two thousand strong. Wickliffe died instantly from a shot in the head and Martin, fearing capture, fell back. It was just after three o'clock. As they were regrouping, looking for cover, a messenger arrived from Bragg with orders to retreat.

By chance, Martin's men became the rear guard, with Joe Wheeler's cavalry as cover and Moore's Second Texas watching the Bark Road to Mickey's.

At the church, long lines began the miserable march to Corinth, burning Federal camps as they went, and loading captured arms with the wounded in wagons. Lew Wallace, with fresh ammunition, pursued them all the way to the new "hospital," where, at the sight of Confederate wounded—and the growing pile of amputated legs and arms by the side porch—he called off his men.

No fires were allowed that night. Men slept where they fell, some even standing; to keep away from the wet ground, they leaned against trees. Morgan's men were stiff and sore to the bone, but uncomplaining when he told them they would scout the Bark Road to Mickey's. Within an hour he had located Charlton, resting on a blanket, the edge of a parked wagon providing makeshift shelter.

He was feverish and shivering, the wound still not attended to. His blond hair was matted with sweat, his face red.

"S-s-stop worrying about me, Johnny. The doctor'll get to me in time. Tom?"

"I'm here, Charlton." Tom's voice broke.

The blue eyes came back around and Charlton ran his tongue over cracked lips. "Quirk?"

"He's with the men," Morgan said. "Do you want some water?"

Charlton moved his head slowly and motioned him closer with a lifted finger. "Don't tell her."

"I'm the soul of tact. You know that."

"If we could get Ma down here you'd get well in no time." Tom tried to chuckle.

"Heah, now," a voice wheezed behind them. "On a night like this, Ah don't cotton to a lack of fires. This boy needs to stay *wawm*." Will disappeared.

"Now you rest. Tom will stay with you. I'm going to find Doctor Yandell."

"Johnny?"

"Yes?"

"We woulda got 'em, Johnny, if that fence . . ."

Morgan turned away as Charlton's face crumpled in tears.

Will came back, with news of a forbidden fire. "Ain't you nevah heard of Nature's Chimney? Won't no Yankees see thet fire, and this boy kin stay wawm. Ain't you had enuf wild onion smell, boy?" he asked Charlton as he helped Morgan lift him. "Whew! Ain't we had our noses close to the ground long enuf?"

They settled Charlton as comfortably as they could near the fire Will had started in a hollow tree. All around, squads of "grandfather privates" and Negro servants were trying to make some order among the groans and clutter. Federal shebangs did little to keep the cold away as night fell, but there were few complaints. That was what was so remarkable. Any little act of kindness was appreciated. Even Will had to wipe his eyes after one boy, with an amputated right arm, thanked him for a drink of water. Dr. Yandell, in the crowded front room of the farmhouse, assured Morgan that his brother would get the best available care. Haggard, dead-eyed, the doctor was on the verge of collapse himself. "In the morning," he said. "Perhaps in the morning," in answer to Morgan's question about moving the wounded back to Corinth.

A boy in the corner kept groaning "My God, my God," over and over.

"Is there anything we can do for him?" Morgan asked a sergeant who sat huddled near the door.

"He's dyin', Cap," the Sergeant said. "You kin pray he won't last long like that."

It was then Morgan saw the massive hole in the stomach, and the intestines escaping the bandage. When he found Charlton again he spoke firmly to keep his voice from shaking. "I'm leaving Jesse with you."

"No, you don't. You need him. Tom, where's your hand?"

"Here."

"Make Johnny treat you right, you hear?"

"I'll stay with the boy," Will's gruff voice announced behind them. "Meet you in Corinth. Now I vote we all git some sleep, while we kin. Yew wawm enuf, boy?" As he said it he peeled off his jacket and covered Charlton. Tom, exhausted, was already dozing. "We'll all be sick if'n we don't look out," Will grumbled. "Ah don't know about yew, but Ah'm gittin' me some shut-eye."

Morgan leaned against the nearby rail fence and closed his eyes. *Where was Basil?* He hadn't found Basil. The sound of pelting rain woke him, but Will had already pulled Charlton closer to the fire and Tom had crawled under a blanket stretched across a low-hanging limb. Morgan returned to the fence and pulled his hat over his eyes. He was too exhausted to sleep. He was waiting for first light.

He must have slept, for he jumped at the sound of firing. Some of the boys, without ball screws to draw wet loads from their muskets, must have given up and cleaned them the easy way. For fifteen minutes the Yankees answered, with drum rolls, bugle calls and spattered volleys.

"Them crazy fools must think we're startin' all over agin." Will swore, got up and stretched, rubbing his chin.

As a muddy sky reflected daylight, rag-dirty clouds drifted from the river, ballooning with rain. In an effort to get up, Morgan laid his hand on the ground, and it sank in wet clay. He pulled it out, found the lower fence rail, and pushed himself up. He wondered if the Yankees were as tired as he was. When he walked toward the tree Will stopped him. "They're restin'. Leave 'em be. I'll scrounge some breakfast. Where's thet boy of yours?"

They found Jesse, and Will sent him to collect rain water. From his pockets Will produced enough coffee to brew a thin drink, but it revived them. "Wonder if them Yankees stampeded?" he asked companionably. It was as if he were speculating about a coon up a tree.

They had become callous at the sight of so much death. The guilt John Morgan felt yesterday turned into a deep sense of nameless gratitude that he was alive. Just to breathe, to draw in one breath after another, was a miracle. Then his mind flashed to James West and the thousands of others lying in that mud. As he helped Will and Tom half-carry Charlton into the house, Dr. Yandell avoided his eyes.

"Bury the dead?" the doctor asked, as if it were a word he couldn't understand.

"Surely, in civilized warfare . . ." Morgan began.

The doctor turned on him with more energy than he thought he had left. *"War isn't civilized,"* he said viciously. He had been working all night.

About ten o'clock the march began. Where the Main Corinth Road met the Bark Road, just beyond Mickey's, Sherman's pickets watched cautiously. "Why don't they come out?" Tom Quirk whispered. "Maybe they're scared," Ben Drake clucked with mock concern. They had been posted here since daylight, smelling Yankee bacon. "I'd start a war myself for a hunk of that and a fresh egg," Xenophon Hawkins sighed. Behind a ridge that almost paralleled the road they were watching an open field through which the Bark Road passed, where the road to Monterey branched off. Near here Breckinridge's troops had bivouacked Saturday night, a million years ago.

Ahead of them, providing additional cover, a band of fallen timber lay diagonally from the woods almost to the road. The combined Confederate cavalry detachment, posted since midnight and under Forrest's command, consisted of about 350 men—Colonel Wood's Mississippians, Terry's Texas Rangers, two companies from Morgan and the rest from Forrest. Forrest, who had spent the night here, saw Morgan join his men about eight o'clock and rode over to meet him.

"They're anxious," he said in his abrupt way. His eyes turned hard as he sent a look toward Sherman's camps. "When a coward's anxious he can be dangerous."

Morgan followed his gaze, but the trees looked innocent enough, and the Bark Road, turned into fresh mud from last night's rain, tucked itself into the trampled grass like a lumpy tan quilt leading nowhere. His first reaction, to discount Forrest's warning, was immediately replaced by another: Forrest had been right before. If Hardee had only listened! If Chalmers and Jackson had swung around Dill's Branch and attacked anywhere but from the southeast! Forrest was like a fox, with a sixth sense about the lay of a land and an insight about his enemy's intentions that was uncanny. It followed no bookish analysis, no tactical plan, but it was right. No wonder Bragg and Beauregard disliked him. Furthermore, he had the bluntness of the businessman with no need for the reputation of officer and gentleman. But he was more of a gentleman than any of them, Morgan thought, watching that square jaw.

Forrest nodded toward the trees. And there they were: 240 men of Hildebrand's brigade, sent by Sherman to clean out stragglers. Forrest legged his horse into a trot and his men, Morgan among them, followed. When they reached the fallen timber the Yankees hesitated, and Forrest said quietly to his aide, Major Anderson: "Well, Anderson, shall we give 'em a daar?" Without waiting for an answer he lifted his hand for the charge. Forrest's, Morgan's and Wood's troops broke over the ridge with leveled shotguns. Forrest, with more than a score of men, dashed into the fallen timber, slashing sabers, firing pistols.

The Federals, with no time to reload, fixed bayonets and prepared for the worst. Forrest's men rode into them with deadly aim. One Federal officer, shot in the head, still had his hand on the hilt of his sword, stuck in the ground. When he fell back the sword flipped high in the air, end over end, like a toy. A second later the Yankee infantrymen broke and fled, some firing wildly. Terry's veteran Rangers poured down the Bark Road in pursuit, and were in hand-to-hand combat with a cavalry unit less than a hundred yards behind the infantry when Morgan rode up, Tom Quirk by his side. It was madness: a mixture of unhorsed cavalry and infantry running everywhere. Yankee officers, on foot, shouting and cursing. Riderless horses, reins flying, missing trees by inches. That's when they saw Sherman.

He had ridden forward with his staff to observe and report to Grant that all was quiet on the perimeter. What he saw was Nathan Bedford Forrest riding like a madman into his ranks. His staff fled through the mud, but not before James McCoy, his young aide-de-camp, sprawled beside his fallen horse.

Forrest raced ahead of his men, his pistol exploding. Sherman ran to cover behind his reserve line, re-forming in a cotton field. They made a short, thick, solid front. When the Confederates saw that wall, they turned back. Forrest galloped headlong to within fifty yards of the Federal brigade before he reined his horse. To shouts of "Kill him! Kill him and his horse!" Sherman's infantry swarmed forward, trying to drag him from his horse. Forrest slashed out with his saber. One Yankee soldier stuck a pistol against his hip and pulled: The blast lifted Forrest from the saddle but did not unhorse him. He became a wounded beast. Whirling his horse, he grabbed the soldier by the collar, swung him up, used him as a shield and then, out of range, flung him to the ground before he galloped up to his astonished command.

The ball had struck his left side above the hip and cut nearly into his spine. With his leg dangling out of his stirrup, his horse shot twice, Forrest trotted into the woods, the last casualty on the battlefield of Shiloh.

35

The retreating lines stretched for almost ten miles, long lines of wagons loaded with wounded, piled like sacks, groaning and cursing the lurching wheels that stuck in axle-deep mud. Exhausted horses and mules strained forward, some sinking in their harnesses, which were removed, in some cases carefully placed in other wagons, or on the limbers of gun carriages. Behind the wagons came the infantry, too tired to curse, staggering, supporting each other or a dangling, broken arm. About nightfall a cold, drizzling rain became a pitiless hail, as if the sky itself were bombarding them with vindictiveness.

In Corinth the ghastly trains arrived, dripping blood on the streets as the wounded were carried up the steps of houses, onto sidewalks, or laid out at the depot platform, where shocked ladies received, made comfortable, nursed and by daylight slumped, exhausted themselves, in a nightmare of dead and dying. For two weeks mothers appeared, from little towns like Bolivar and Middleburg and Hickory Valley and Rogers Springs, to gather their wounded, to take their boys home, in most cases to die. Chest and stomach wounds were the worst; mercifully, the pain would not last long. Amputees had, the doctors knew, a 10 percent chance. As for the others, they managed, and a slow exodus began.

The generals made proclamations. The Battle of Shiloh was a Confederate success. Braxton Bragg's first act was to assemble his troops, the brave men of Shiloh and Elkhorn (for by now Van Dorn's troops had arrived from Arkansas), to tell them that "A few more days of needful preparation and organization and I shall give your banners to the breeze." He would lead them "to additional honors to those you have already won on other fields." Then he added: "But be prepared to undergo privations and labor with cheerfulness and alacrity." Strangely, insanely, they cheered.

Underneath, Morgan knew why. Something had happened. After Shiloh, nothing, not even the well-intentioned speeches of its own generals, could have told the Confederate soldier what he knew in his bowels, in his soul: that a gut-deep determination to survive had been born.

For three days Breckinridge, with the rear guard, camped on the Corinth Road, burying the dead from the "hospital," collecting straggling wounded and sending on to Beauregard scavanged Yankee guns. Morgan's squadron remained in the vicinity of the battlefield for more than a week. But the Federals were quiet, busy burning dead horses and burying their dead. An acrid, incredible stench blew in with the smoke. Before dawn Tuesday Morgan received an order from Beauregard's headquarters to send a courier for permission to gather the Confederate dead and wounded from the battlefield.

Sam Morgan and Gus Magee volunteered to go. Morgan watched them leave just as daylight began lifting mist in the woods. Sam carried the white flag and galloped forward, his body bent in a V. Three hours later they returned. When Magee dismounted, Morgan saw the answer written on his face.

"They're burying their own. Neat rows. Separate graves. The Confederates . . ."

"The Confederates?"

"General Grant refuses," Sam spoke up, "to release them. Claims the climate . . . health reasons." He looked down at his boots, scuffing the trampled grass under his feet.

Magee cleared his throat. "The Confederates are being buried seven deep in open trenches. Or where they fell, where convenient."

So. James, beloved West. Standing so straight when he took the oath at Woodsonville. And Jim Geslin. Behind his mother, so full of trust, in the terror of retreat through Nashville. And Buckner, just a boy. They were all just boys. Buckner chopping down that flagpole for Alice. They should be courting somewhere. Flung down like dogs in a common grave. He would never know where. He prayed they were dead.

It rained constantly, threatening to wash away the mud from shallow graves. Mounted Confederate vedettes, shifting on their horses, watched the reeking, mud-running, corpse-strewn battlefield in disbelief. For four days the smoke kept rising from those mounds of horseflesh. In the distance squads of bent forms, carrying dead and wounded, looked like giant, misshapen ants against the underbrush. Morgan, late one afternoon, rode near Fraley field with Tom. They heard voices, and Morgan held up his hand for silence. Two Yankee infantrymen were laughing and talking not fifty feet away. They soon saw what their joke was: A hand and half an arm had escaped a grave, and one of the soldiers had stuck a piece of hardtack between the fingers.

"Wouldn't want this feller to go to the next world empty-handed, now would we? Might get a mite hongry before he gets thar!"

Tom sank back in his saddle, his face white. Tears cut through rage: The sleeve on the arm was gray.

This was no way to win. The bungled massing of men to die like cattle, to be blown apart by twelve-pounders and thrown into open ditches like dogs—while the other side had unlimited numbers, unlimited resources. Not yet cranked up. Not yet. So now was the time to try.

An independent command. A tough, tightly organized, fiercely loyal group of men who could strike behind enemy lines, disrupt supplies and communications, cause enough havoc, capture by surprise enough ammunition and prisoners to bolster the doubt already prevalent in the Northern press that the North just might not be invincible.

Before the Fifth Kentucky moved on to Corinth, Morgan sought out T.H. But before he could tell his uncle his plan, T.H. had his own news.

"Island Number Ten is gone. Fell Monday."

"That means . . ."

"That means Memphis. It's only a matter of time."

"Not if we win Kentucky!"

"Kentucky?" T.H. looked at him as if he were insane.

"It's the key to this war. Even Lincoln said that."

"Pardon me, Johnny, but here we sit in Mississippi. We've just lost a major battle—in spite of what our generals say. The enemy control the Cumberland and Nashville, and now the Tennessee. The Ohio and half the Mississippi."

"Ah, but do they? Do they control the people? You know Kentucky. Give them a victory, give them soldiers they can believe in . . . You know where their hearts are."

"So what do you propose to do?"

"A small force could turn the tables on this invasion. Do a little invading itself. Get behind the 'lines'—after all, there are no lines, but towns held here, camps there—and prove that the South intends to win."

Something of the old T.H. grinned, the young businessman with the tucked-up sleeves. "I just heard that Charlton has been lucky enough to have been sent to the hospital at Huntsville," he told his nephew. "Too bad he'll miss this new invasion. By the way, who did you say would lead it?"

Colonel T.H. Hunt, with the Fifth Kentucky, moved on to Corinth the next day. On April 11, 1862, Huntsville, Alabama, with its Memphis-to-Chattanooga Railroad, fell.

Grant lost his command because of Shiloh. His successor made no move to pursue Beauregard, and the scouts reported no activity indicating that he intended to do so. By the 15th of April Morgan had orders for Corinth. When he got there he learned that T.H., with Breckinridge's corps, were at their old camp at Burnsville.

He had to see Beauregard! He had to get an independent command before the Yankees made their move!

Beauregard was ill. Braxton Bragg sat in his headquarters at the courthouse, leaning into a mound of papers, his long face all but hidden by the shadow of a deep-set window and his own overhanging, shaggy brows. He looked up at Morgan's name and waved his aide away.

"So?" he said. He allowed a sour smile to turn his mouth down and extended his arm. Morgan accepted the limp handshake and took the indicated seat. He was dressed in full uniform for this interview. The cadaverous face of Braxton Bragg was waiting. He knew, from rumor, that Bragg was worried about this wife, left alone on his Louisiana plantation.

The afternoon sun, shining through the fly-specked window, lay across the General's folded hands. He listened to Morgan's proposal.

Morgan cleared his throat. "Now that Halleck has replaced Grant, they're sure to move . . ."

"No, no, no." Bragg waved his hand. "I will need you in my own . . . uh . . . withdrawal."

"I thought"—Morgan tried to erase insistence from his words—"since Halleck can get reinforcements from Island Number Ten, they'll surely move. And when they do, I'll be there to disrupt their communications with

Nashville." There was still that tunnel at Gallatin. He knew Bragg disliked cavalrymen, especially volunteer, non-West Point cavalrymen, and for some reason, Kentuckians. Impertinence might not set well. He saw from Bragg's face that he had overstepped himself with that "I'll be there."

"My men know that country," he defended. "There are none more inventive, more audacious . . ."

"Oh, I know, Colonel, how audacious you are," Bragg almost sneered, then leaned forward toward his aide who, with apologies for the interruption, admitted John C. Breckinridge into the room.

"Excuse me, General." Breckinridge looked toward Morgan. "When I learned the identity of your visitor, I took it upon myself . . ."

The General rose. In the presence of Breckinridge, Bragg became a different man. With an unctiousness just short of fawning, he begged his visitor to make himself comfortable.

"Well, I might as well," Breckinridge sighed and chuckled, including Morgan in his humor. "Since I might not have too much time for rest. Halleck, my friends, has started to move toward Corinth with a hundred and twenty thousand men."

"Mattie! MATTIE!"

Alice slammed the door, her palms behind her pressed against the wood. Mattie looked up. She had spread three dresses across her bed, with the idea of cutting off the worn places and combining them into one. But it would take some doing. One was a deep red, the other a pale green, and the third a little print with blue triangles. She held the scissors in her hand, a frown still on her face.

"Mattie, you've got to come downstairs!" Alice left the door and tugged at her sister's sleeve. "They've arrested Mr. Winship for hoisting the Southern flag . . ." Her lips were white.

Mattie set the shears down and reached one hand out to hold Alice's arm. "Alice look at me. Really look at me. Didn't we expect it? Didn't we expect much worse, really? You have to hold onto—"

"And two of them are downstairs this minute asking about the flagstaff. They say they know it's here. Maybe Mr. Winship told them. . . . We can't let them have it, Mattie! Just because their own stupid flag fell off the courthouse in that wind. Remember how we laughed? Why can't they make their own flagpole? Why do they want ours? It's sacred, I tell you. . . . Before I let them get their horrid hands on it, I'll—"

"Let's ask Papa."

"Papa's still out at their dreadful camp. He's so polite to them it makes me sick!"

"You know very well why he's polite to them, my pet. If he hadn't gone out there Puss and Cousin Kate would never have gotten passes to go home. Weren't you the one so relieved to get rid of Charley?"

Changing the subject seemed to calm her. She plopped down on one of the dresses, almost sitting on the scissors.

"Here . . . don't cut yourself."

"But what are we to do? Let's ask Mama!"

Mattie looked away. Didn't Alice know what was happening? Ever since Morgan left and the Yankees came, and Colonel Ready refused to leave, her mother had closed herself in her room. She refused to eat. Brandy had taken the place of meals. Mattie kept Alice away, hoping to bring her around. But food sent up was left on the tray. The scissors in her hand shook as she laid them on the dresser. "I'll ask Mama." She tried to keep her voice even. "Yes, that's a good idea. I'll ask her now."

"I'll come with you . . ."

"No! Are they still downstairs?"

"Yes."

"Then too much movement up here might arouse suspicion. They may have heard you already. . . ."

The suggestion seemed to work. Alice bent her head on her chest and clutched her fists against her stomach. "I'll wait here."

"Good." Mattie slipped across the hall to their mother's room. Mary Ready was sitting in a chair by the window, staring out at the bare March trees. A cold wind blew against the pane.

"Mama?"

The woman turned hollow eyes on her daughter. Purple circles puffed the skin beneath them. There was something almost too soft—decayed—about that face with its wild halo of disheveled hair. In this unguarded moment she had removed her upper plate, and her lips had disappeared in pleats of skin. The girl before her seemed to come into focus. "Mattie?"

An uneaten breakfast congealed in a plate on the little table beside her. Mattie ignored it. She longed to bend down, take her in her arms, and if that didn't work, shake her into some sense. *You can't go on like this, Mama* was on her lips, but she said instead, "Some Yankee soldiers are downstairs wanting the flagpole. Papa is still out at their camp. Alice wants to know what to do. It's still under her bed."

A smile broke the lips. The watery eyes came alive. "Why not have Cap put it out in the back yard? That way they won't bother the house."

"Yes . . . I'll tell Alice."

The question, the pretense of coming here for an answer to keep Alice upstairs and out of trouble, no longer seemed important. *He* was gone . . . she would never see him again! She would never feel his arms, his lips . . . and what did it matter, she thought bitterly, beside her problems now. She cleared the tray, tucked a quilt around her mother's lap. "Are you warm enough? Do you want me to send Eliza up with a cup of tea? A nice warm cup of tea?"

"Yes . . ." her mother said vaguely. "That would be nice." But the eyes, like the lips, had already retreated, and as if in answer the wind sent a gust against the window like the blow of a fist.

From the head of the stairs Mattie could hear her father's voice, controlled, dignified, polite, as he came through the front door and chatted with the soldiers. She had lied to Alice. It wasn't just for passes that he'd gone to General Mitchell. He had actually invited Colonel Marr to make their house his headquarters! *Why, I knew him in Washington City, Daughter. An old friend from Washington* . . . "How could you?" she had screamed, and his smile and shrugged shoulders cut her to the bone. She could still see him walking away. *He's made his compromise* sank into her, and now the fact that they might need that compromise was making her furious. When she returned to Alice she was shaking with rage.

"Oh, don't *you* be afraid of them, Sister! They are nothing but dogs. . . ."

She let Alice think she was afraid. Alice was a child, and would be no more help than her mother. She took a deep breath and heard her father climb the stairs.

"We'll have to burn it," he said flatly. "We should have done it before. I've sent for Cap to cut it into pieces for the fireplaces."

Alice wailed and kicked her feet. "No! No! To desecrate that sacred wood, which held to the breeze the only—"

"All right, *all right!*" Colonel Ready held up his hands. "We'll burn it in *your* fireplace. It can be an offering to the gods!"

Alice, who was reading *The Days of Bruce*, brightened. Cap cut the pole into convenient lengths, and Alice stayed up all night watching them blaze on the grate in her bedroom . . . a fire, she said, hot enough to burn a whole Yankee.

The coals were still glowing the next morning when Eliza brought up a card. Colonel Ready went down, his daughters following. A Captain Prentice was waiting in the parlor with a letter from Mary Cheatham in Nashville.

"Your kind sister . . ." the man addressed Mattie, "said I should tell you that since you've seen a good many Confederate captains, she supposed you would have no objection to seeing some Federals."

Before their father could answer, Alice shot out: "We've seen so many Confederates, that's just the reason we can't stand the sight of Yankees! Our sister and her traitor husband can keep their invitations to themselves!"

Colonel Ready, behind her, reddened. "Captain Prentice is on General Mitchell's staff, dear. I knew him in Washington City."

"I don't care where you knew him, Papa! I . . ." She ran upstairs crying, Mattie after.

"See here. Now, see here," her father stammered in fury after the man left. He stood in the middle of the rug before the smoldering fire. "I know how you feel. But I am trying to save this house, young lady. This house which puts a roof over your head and food in your stomach and provides someplace for your mother . . ." His eyes wandered to Mattie and stopped. *Yes*, hers answered. *I see what you are doing. I'll help all I can.*

But it would be harder than she thought. The next morning Albert did not return from a trip to the farm.

"They're stealing our people!" Alice whined. "I know! Haven't you heard about Mr. Carney's yard man? They took him right out of the vegetables."

"Come, now, Alice," her father mumbled. "Albert's just been de-layed . . ."

"We sent him for a *ham*, Papa. And it's almost suppah time."

Colonel Ready went upstairs.

Albert came in about midnight. He had worn an old gray coat. As he passed the Union camp, cries of "Secesh nigger!" rang out and he was surrounded. When they sent him for water he ran through some woods and escaped.

"And Uriah and the buggy?" Mattie asked. When he didn't answer she said, "Never mind. We'll get the horse and buggy."

"Yes . . ." said Alice. "Maybe some of Papa's new Yankee friends will return it."

It will mean another trip to camp, Mattie thought, secretly agreeing with Alice. Papa will like that. He won't mind at all.

"And that Yankee dandy captain! I feel as if I could spit on them and never call them anything but dogs! I think sometimes the only relief from them will be death . . . I pray for it! I feel suffocated . . . tramped on and strangled . . ."

"Oh, come now, Alice, it wasn't his fault. It was Mary who put us in a position of being insulted."

"Then I'll never speak to Mary again, either!"

General Mitchell was evidently intrigued by his young captain's report. "I'd like to see the little lioness myself!" he chuckled. "What do you say we all go?" he said to his son, standing behind his chair. After all, he thought, the Ready house was Morgan's hangout when he was here. It's time I found out why. When Colonel Ready came by about the horse and buggy Mitchell was most gracious, and extracted the invitation easily.

Two days later General Mitchell and his staff waited on the Ready front porch for Albert to fetch his master. The old man ran up the stairs, sweat beading the furrows of his forehead. "Dey's heah, Massa. Miss Mattie . . . dey's heah!"

"You girls will come to the parlor," Colonel Ready said, and cleared his throat. He pulled at his lapels and walked stiffly down the stairs, the tails of his frock coat swinging.

The vain old fool! thought Alice as Mitchell bowed. If he thinks I'm going to open my mouth he has another think coming. She stuck her chin out.

Mattie was hardly more civil, although she tried. The nerve, to bring his whole staff, and then stand there inviting himself again—and adding insult to injury by asking if he could give "the young ladies"—he seemed fascinated by Alice—a "serenade." Watching him now she could believe the rumor that when her Morgan was here he had cut the rank from his collar. No wonder his stupid Ohio troops had quartered in an asylum. Then she saw her father's eyes.

"We thank you very much for your offer, sir," she said sweetly, holding out her hand. "But our mother has not been well. . . ."

"Perhaps just a little music might cheer her," her father put in quickly. Alice ran upstairs in tears.

That night a small brass band stood in the rainy street. From four houses, heads appeared.

"I won't look at them, the dogs!" Alice fumed. But as they played she wrote in her diary:

> *Thursday, March 27.* I do not want to see any of them, gentlemen or not, the dogs. But the music is so fine I am obliged to listen. Much against my will I must confess.

The next day, when Cap disappeared, she scratched out the page, then tore it up.

"No . . . we'll not get him back," Colonel Ready said wearily, keeping his eyes from his wife's face. "I understand they have about fifty now."

"Nigger thieves!"

"Now, Mary . . ."

For the first time her condition frightened him. All that week houses had been searched. Mr. Carney had refused to take the oath, and was sent to Fort Warren, near Boston. Colonel Ready stared at the wallpaper behind her head. This was his. He would not give it up. He would not leave it to be confiscated as property of a Southern sympathizer. He would take their damned oath if he had to. He could not tell her of the note he had received that morning from Colonel Parkhurst, the military governor of Murfrees-boro, saying, with the imminent move of the army, it had become necessary for him to take the oath. Although the troops were scheduled to leave at two P.M., Captain Rounds would wait upon him to administer it.

Colonel Ready left his wife and went to headquarters, fully intending to take their oath, to save his house. But once there, with his hand on a Bible, the words stuck in his throat. He could not. He was taken to the depot and not allowed to return home. Three other men, arrested that morning, were waiting. The train for Nashville was about to leave. He sent a note for his clothes.

"You see . . . *you see?*" Alice screamed. "It did no good to be nice to them! The PEN . . . i . . . tentiary!"

"Hush, Alice. We don't know that." But Mattie was trembling.

"We have to tell Mama!"

"Yes . . ."

They left her, collapsed, with Eliza holding smelling salts. They packed as many clothes as they could into one small valise and ran onto the platform just as the whistle blew. A cloud of steam enveloped their father as he took the bag from them. It was as if he were disappearing into a mist. Alice cried for three days.

"Come, honey, it's Sunday."

"Sunday . . ." Alice looked at the sky, fitful with clouds. Through the open window she could smell the jasmine. "Yes. Sunday."

That afternoon they heard a strange rumbling. A chill passed over Mattie. "Come, Alice," she said suddenly. "Let's see if we can sew those dresses." She stuck thread in a needle and punched it through the cloth, pulled it out, then punched again.

The sound came from the sky, close to the ground, from the northwest. It came from Shiloh.

Toward sundown on the 28th of April, Morgan, his squadron quartered in Breckinridge's old camp at Burnsville, found T.H. Hunt's Fifth Kentucky Infantry, the Colonel himself busy with an aide. When he looked up, T.H. folded the message he was reading and turned to his nephew with those kind eyes that reminded John Morgan so much of his grandmother.

"I've had news of Basil," T.H. said quietly. "He's been captured. He's in Nashville."

"Nashville?"

"Don't worry. He's in good hands."

Something in the way he said it made Morgan cautious.

"How do you know he's in good hands?"

"Seems as if it's handy to have a Union man in the family."

"What . . . ?"

T.H. lowered his voice. "It seems the people he's with got word to Lexington and Dick Curd came down. I have it from *reliable sources* that your brother-in-law may be crossing into our territory any day." At his nephew's astonishment he added with a grin: "To join this invasion of yours."

They were interrupted by a courier from Corinth. New Orleans had fallen.

Outside, the April night was soft against their faces. The waning moon had risen early and golden through the trees. Now as they crossed a field toward Morgan's bivouac it rode high in the sky, on its way to setting.

"I wonder how Charl is?" Morgan asked, not expecting an answer. "Just his luck to be sent to Huntsville before the Yankees took it. Damn!"

"But you got Bragg to agree to this expedition into Tennessee," T.H. said, to break the silence. "I'm glad he let you have Wood. He's a good man."

"We might just not stop with Tennessee." Morgan surprised himself with the fury in his own words.

"That's what I expected you to say!" T.H. Hunt held out his hand. "Good luck."

The squadron moved out at daylight. They camped that night six miles from the Tennessee, and reached it the next morning. The river was still high, broad and rolling in flood. At the ferry one small boat, capable of carrying only a dozen horses at a time, bobbed like a stick near shore. Squads were sent to look for a better crossing, or another boat, but none could be found. Two days and nights were spent loading, unloading, coaxing horses, watching always at the sides of eyes for that bulky shadow looming on the horizon that they had all come to fear, ever since the booming at Shiloh. The Yankees were surely patrolling. But "gunboat fever" subsided as fatigue took over.

That night one of the men played a harmonica, and the sound floated across the water like a balm. On the north bank of the river Morgan heard it over the message to Beauregard that was already composing itself in his mind: *Last of command just crossed river . . . will go to Lawrenceburg, have cut wires on Savannah Road. . . .* He moved closer to the campfire and scribbled. Then, with a stab of expectation and elation he hadn't felt since Shiloh, he wrote: *Determined to reach Lexington.*

They left the river and headed northeast, Jesse, now a bugler with Company A, riding in the van. The next day, about midmorning, a scout reported four hundred Federals on the road to Columbia. "Mostly convalescents, sir," the boy said, saluting. "Putting up telegraph line to Huntsville."

"Did you find out who's in charge?"

"General Mitchell's son, sir. Old friend from the asylum." The boy grinned.

Mitchell had captured Huntsville—and Charlton. A plan formed in Morgan's mind. "Well, it would be only gentlemanly to pay an old friend a visit, wouldn't it?"

He wasn't interested in convalescents. But Mitchell's son, if he could catch and parole him, would make good bait for Charlton.

Still, he had to be careful. His squadron was outnumbered two to one. He had to convince them he had them surrounded—and by a superior force. He called Jesse.

"How loud can you holler, Jess?" Bess shifted as he waited.

"Holler, Massa?"

"And blow that bugle."

Jesse's face spread in a smile.

"Tell you what. You run your horse as fast as you can through those woods over there, blow that bugle and holler up a regiment, then ride again, blow again, till the Yankees think we're an army."

"How menny regiments, Massa?"

"At least five."

"Yassuh!"

It worked. From the woods, at intervals, "regiments" were called up and a truce flag was sent in with a demand for surrender. Young Captain Mitchell, given the choice of a Southern prison or parole, promised to get an exchange for Charlton Morgan if he could. He had admired Morgan's antics, and his taste in ladies in Murfreesboro. He had gone to the Ready house with his father, to see for himself. He meant it when he said, "I'll do all I can." A brother of Morgan's, he knew, would do as much for him.

As soon as the paroles were written they rode on. Southern Tennessee was fertile country, with forage and rations and hospitable farmers spiking the rations, more often than not, with a generous lacing of moonshine. By the time they crossed the Duck River and entered the lush, broad valley that lay between Shelbyville and Murfreesboro, they had the loose, ragtag camaraderie of a band of veterans very sure of themselves. Where were the Yankees?

"In Murfreesboro."

"Ah, yes. Murfreesboro." Morgan looked at Greenberry Roberts, one of his best lieutenants, who still wore his Lexington Rifles jacket.

"Colonel?" Lieutenant Roberts grinned.

I will marry you, John Morgan. With all my heart!

How could he stay away? The thought of her in his arms almost took his breath. Then another face came: Xen Hawkins, reporting last night. "Murfreesboro is crawling with Union troops, sir! At least five thousand. . . ." He couldn't put her in danger, even if he were rash enough to risk his own men. He had endangered her enough already. He had to be reasonable.

"Sir?"

Morgan couldn't meet Roberts's eyes. His breath came short.

"Sir?"

"The answer is no."

The column reached Lebanon, northeast of La Vergne, just after sunset on the 5th of May. He posted companies A, B, and C at the college, with their horses tied to trees on the campus. Colonel Wood's men, with Captain Brown's understrength company and Leathers's mule train, were quartered at the livery stables near the town square. Wood, who had been left in the vicinity of Murfreesboro with a small party to watch for enemy activity, came in after midnight and reported all quiet. Morgan, with his staff, had headquarters at the hotel, but Wood insisted on sleeping with his men down at the stables.

Ten miles from Lebanon the Cumberland River swung north toward Kentucky. Morgan posted pickets on all the main roads, left orders for saddling-up at four o'clock. They would cross early; Kentucky lay beyond the river. He had more than three hundred loyal, brave, gallant men. Nothing could stop him now. *Determined to reach Lexington. . . .* They were 170 miles into Yankee territory in pouring rain. They were on their own.

On the Murfreesboro Pike the pickets were soaked. A few went into a farmhouse to dry their clothes, then the whole detail followed. Dead-tired from riding, and a little groggy from too much shuck donated by admirers along the way, they built a fire and slept. Before they woke, one whole regiment of Federal cavalry had passed.

Pleasant Whitlow jumped up, aghast. Without a word, he mounted bareback and passed the Federal column at a run. The Yankees were so surprised they didn't fire: Whitlow reached the hotel just as the first of the Union troopers turned the corner. He was yelling at the top of his voice when a Yankee bullet found him. His head snapped back and he was dead before he hit the ground.

At the college, the three companies were just saddling up when the first bluecoats came into view. Company C, nearest town, was struck first, and scattered. A. Z. Boyer, Second Lieutenant with Company A, rallied his men and fell back toward Lebanon, where he formed across the road. Roused by Whitlow's yell, Morgan rode up with his staff just as the Federals arrived. He ordered a dismount. "Reserve your fire! Drive them back when you do open!"

The Yankees posted their horses smartly. Still under orders, Company A waited.

"Now!"

A volley opened up from the Confederate line, and several Yankee horses panicked and ran toward them. One, carrying General Dumont, swerved and avoided capture. Another took Colonel Frank Wolford straight through the butternuts.

"Frank!"

"Johnny!"

Morgan offered his hand. They might have been meeting on the streets of Lexington.

The prisoners were quickly herded and a retreat began. The men at the college and at the livery stable were hopelessly cut off: The Federals would have their share of prisoners that day, among them Colonel Wood and Tom Logwood and Lieutenant Sellers. And Jesse. Luckily, Tom had been at the hotel. Only later would Morgan learn of the death of Captain Brown.

With about a hundred men, he galloped headlong down the Rome-Carthage Road to the northeast. Suddenly the rear was attacked, the Yankees sabering where they could. A dash, screams. The men around him opened their horses into a dead run. Bess, jumping with excitement, pulled hard. When he tried to collect her, the reins jerked back slack in his hands: She had broken leather! Quirk, Drake, young Tom Morgan dashed up—a half-dozen tried to catch her bridle, but she pulled away, a raging tornado.

Behind them, all resistance gave way. Prisoners were abandoned. A few shots were fired, then the riders concentrated on getting away. Just behind him a horse fell—whose, he couldn't say—and at least four more piled up, causing an awful rout, to right and left. He waved his free arm to the woods, as a signal that they should go there to re-form. Beneath him Bess was a thousand pounds of fear. There was no stopping her. Tom Quirk passed, then fell back, his horse obviously winded. Morgan recognized it as General Dumont's mount, but was too busy with Bess to yell questions. Twenty minutes later Quirk passed again, on another horse. Before they got to Rome, thirteen miles away, Quirk had changed mounts three times. By then Bess finally decided that her own fatigue was cause enough to drop back to a canter. Not a hundred yards behind them, Wolford's Kentucky Yankees, on fresh thoroughbreds, were catching up. Morgan yelled to push the men forward. They still had eight more miles before they could reach the ferry. Bess now was entirely between his legs and his voice; there was no control on her head whatever. His life depended on her responses. He would have given ten thousand dollars for a yard of leather and two minutes to hitch her up. But she pumped on, following the other horses, obedient to his weight, the steadiness of his balance. God bless that horse, and Warren Viley's training!

Ahead, he saw the boat—luckily, on this side of the river. She stopped when the other horses were pulled up, and he slid off and onto the little ferry with his men, crowding on the boards until the Cumberland lapped at their boots. They looked back at their horses. Bess was trotting aimlessly back and forth on the bank, sniffing the ground. Then she looked up and whinnied. By his own orders they had left their mounts.

"I'll get her!" Quirk yelled, and jumped into a canoe attached to the ferry as a lifeboat. He paddled wildly, but the Yankees were on the bank now, firing as fast as they could. In two minutes the canoe was riddled with holes. Miraculously unhurt, Quirk turned and reached the ferry again just before they moored on the other side, his Irish face crumpled with rage and disappointment. Morgan's eyes went to that black form across the water. Against the fresh green of spring fields he saw her for the last time. She stood obediently when a Federal soldier walked up, as he had taught her to.

When he camped that night he had less than twenty men. Less than when he'd left Lexington last fall. Six, he knew, were killed; how many were wounded he couldn't know. He guessed at least a hundred and twenty were captured. James Bowles. Ralph Sheldon. Sellers. Young Henry Magruder, who had just joined him at Burnsville after Shiloh. Tom Logwood, who, like Sheldon and Sellers, had been with him from the beginning. The squadron was gone.

Colonel Wood, he learned later, held out for hours, until the Federals threatened to burn the town.

Unabashedly, he gave way to tears. They were camped in a woods. The rain had stopped, but low thunder in the distance grumbled ominously. His "career" was ended. What in hell did he think he was doing? They were two hundred miles from Confederate help. His dream of harassing Halleck— what a joke! Or of going into Kentucky! Basil was right. He was too lax with discipline. There was no excuse for those pickets. It amounted to abandoning their posts. . . . He looked up to see the worried eyes of Tom.

"We'll make it right, Brother Johnny. Just you wait and see."

"Of course. Of course we will!"

"Some of the boys are out right now trying to get you another horse."

"That's . . ." But Morgan couldn't finish. Tom, to hide emotion, turned away.

They marched into the mountainous country southeast to Sparta, fifty miles east of Murfreesboro. For two days they rested, shoeing horses and equipping themselves as best they could, mostly from the generosity of the townspeople. Two local companies, unarmed raw recruits of Tennessee boys under Captains Bledsoe and Hamilton, joined him. Some of the men from what they now called "the Lebanon Races" came straggling in, until Morgan could count almost a hundred and fifty, for the most part badly armed, but even more determined now to go on. Jesse was not among them. But their faith renewed his own. Just after dawn on the 9th of May he assembled his men and told them his secret: They were going to Kentucky.

36

L eaving the Tennesseans behind, he didn't have fifty men. The night before they left a man named Champe Ferguson appeared with five mountaineers, offering themselves as guides.

"Can you trust him?" Tom Quirk whispered to Ben Drake after Ferguson and his men walked away.

"I heard a' him. He's a rough 'un," Ben said soberly. "Let's tell the Colonel."

Morgan listened. Three of his best lieutenants, waiting for last-minute orders, watched Ben.

"He's in this here war for revenge, pure an' simple. Wife an' daughter roughed up . . . to put it somewhat . . . by some Yankee soljurs an' Home Guards. When he found 'em he killed all the parties concerned and became what you might call an outlaw . . . takes no prisoners, does Champe Ferguson."

"He'll take prisoners if he works for me."

"I told him that, and he agrees," Quirk spoke up. "With two exceptions."

"And those?"

"His brother, who went Union. And Tinker Dave Beattie. Some kinda feud," Ben answered.

"The likelihood of his meeting either one on this trip is slim, don't you think?" Lieutenant Messick offered. Good guides, until they reached Bowling Green, were absolutely essential. Their eyes went to Morgan.

"I'll see him."

Morgan's headquarters were in an abandoned farmhouse at the edge of the town of Sparta. Behind it a steep cliff provided good protection, and below the rambling front porch the land tumbled away in boulders. The man who loomed now in the doorway looked at home in the half-light of that bare room. His large head, covered by tight black curls, formed a helmet above the hooded eyes. The irises and pupils were of the same muddy color, like a falcon's. They had the look some blind people have, until you realized how piercingly he was watching you.

"I understand you want to scout for us."

Champe Ferguson lowered his massive head and spit. The action wrinkled the stubby cheeks. He shifted his feet and looked up.

"And that you've agreed to take prisoners."

"All except that renegade brother and Beattie." The eyes withdrew, then found focus again. The chin jutted at the last word in a defiance that might have been boyish except for the clenched fists at his sides.

Morgan, too, pretended to hesitate. He had known a few of these mountain men. Their lack of formal schooling was more than outweighed by an intense will and energy, but also by a strange gentleness, a loyalty freely and immediately given to friends, matched only by a ferocity equally and as quickly given to enemies. A dangerous man stood before him, but one who had chosen sides. If they were anything, these mountain men, it was stubborn—perhaps the most dependable part of loyalty. If Champe agreed to leave his own prisoners alone—with the exception of that brother and Tinker Dave—he could believe him. Such men might murder or steal, might hunt or be hunted, but they never lied. To another man Morgan might have offered his hand. To Ferguson he nodded, looked stern and grinned.

Ferguson spat again, a surprisingly delicate gesture, done with his tongue through a gap in his front teeth. It made a hissing sound, like a snake.

"Ah've got twenty men. No need fer rations. We take kar uv ourselves. Jest tell us your route: We'll keep it clar."

And he did. His scouts became a moving net thrown out for miles, reporting like clockwork before sunup and just after sunset, sometimes with a captured informant in tow.

"The South could use some generals like that," Quirk said admiringly.

They reached the ferry over the Cumberland, sixty miles from Sparta, by forced march that night. Tired as they were, there was no complaint. They seemed determined to undo the blunder at Lebanon. When they spoke, it was of Yankee horses and the guns they would capture. Some of them knew this country from the Bowling Green days, and as they rode on, they eased into some degree of confidence.

They marched by back roads, lanes known only to Ferguson and his scouts, some tortuous and straight up cliffs, some not more than cattle trails, some disappearing into creek bottoms. They could have kept the whole operation secret if the Home Guards, once they entered Kentucky, hadn't been, as Drake growled, so long-winded. Their conch shells could be heard all along the route. It was a sound that traveled faster than the horses. "Bushwhacker" became a name hated even more than Yankee. "At least a Federal shows himself," Ben grumbled. "These snakes're behind every tree."

The next day they were in sight of Glasgow. It was a beautiful May morning. Who could feel unhappy on a day like this? They had crossed into Kentucky during the night. The very ground felt different under their feet. Morgan sent a scout to Bowling Green, to verify Ferguson's report. If he could, he would capture as many Yankees as possible and burn their supplies. Cotton was the prize. U.S. Treasury Secretary Chase was encouraging speculators to send South for bales—often bought with false promises to field hands who didn't own the crop. These "purchases" were often stored near Federal garrisons for protection, and Morgan's orders specifically mentioned destroying them. He could just imagine the inventory at Bowling Green.

The scout came back. Ferguson's information was correct: Over five hundred rested Yankees were entrenched in Bowling Green. Reluctantly, Morgan agreed with the scout: An attack by fifty men would be suicide. He was the mouse now, playing games with the cat. Caution could save them. Daring would come in its own time. They moved on.

There was the L&N between Bowling Green and the Green River. He knew that country like the back of his hand. He would waylay the first train that passed. They trotted their horses through Glasgow, pressed on toward Cave City, traveling all night. Early the next day, when they were about twelve miles shy of Cave City, Morgan left the command and rode forward, beyond his vedettes, with five picked men.

Another unbelievably beautiful morning. May in Kentucky! He couldn't believe he was here again. The railbed rose like a levee across the valley. Deep in the distance they heard it: the sure chortle and puff of an engine from the direction of Bowling Green. Suppose it contained the men he'd lost at Lebanon? It wasn't unlikely! He raised his arm and they hid in a little clump of trees by the road. What luck! It was a long train! They could see it swaying behind the little engine, the funnel of woodsmoke touching ground, spewing sparks. But he couldn't take it with five men! It grew larger as it approached. Morgan would take it with five men, by God, if he had to! Tom shot him a look. He was about to raise his hand for the charge when they saw the rest of the command coming up. As soon as they were in earshot he shouted, and they swarmed forward.

It was over in minutes. They whooped like Indians, fifty galloping circles back and forth across the track. The engine came to a steaming stop, and the engineer and fireman climbed down, hands up. There were forty-eight cars. All freight, no prisoners. But a Federal payroll of eight thousand dollars in the mail car, which took a little sting from their disappointment. Champe Ferguson, returning from a scout up the line, reported a train coming from the opposite direction, down the track from Louisville. They had to make a quick business of this one! With the energy of schoolboys turned loose, they had a good blaze going and all forty-eight cars, plus the engineer's prize engine, turned to smoke.

"I just hope that Louisville train doesn't see it."

"They won't," drawled Ferguson. "There's a bend just up yondah. They'll be a-comin' at sech a speed, they won't see till hit's too late." Then he offered to take a few men, tear up some ties and place them upright in a cow-gap. "So's they cain't back up." He grinned.

They waited, in ambush, for a good half-hour. Then they saw it: a passenger train puffing leisurely, its cowcatcher fanning out over the tracks. When the burning freight cars came into view, the engine of the passenger train slowed, then ground to a halt. Morgan let his men handle the engineer. He went to the passenger cars, where one Federal major, on the platform, had opened up with a pair of Colts. Ben Biggerstaff dismounted and took a shot at him with his rifle. The bullet struck within an inch of the Major's head, and the Colts, out of ammunition, were lowered.

"I'll take those," Ben said graciously, "sir."

Morgan strolled into the cars, crowded with Federal officers and their ladies. The Major with the pistols was named Coffee. After surrendering his guns, he introduced himself and Major Helveti, of Wolford's regiment.

"Ah, Frank! Dear Frank!"

"You know him, sir?"

"A childhood friend. I am John Morgan."

One of the ladies, who had been clinging to the arm of her husband, took courage. "We heard you had been killed! All your men captured!"

Morgan grinned. "Hardly, ma'am."

The lining up and paroling of prisoners began. When they came to a blond young captain, his wife, red-faced with weeping, rushed to Morgan with her mouth open. "You won't kill my husband, will you, sir? You won't kill him?"

"My dear madam." He bowed—he hoped debonairly—and gave her that smile that tugged one side of his mouth. "I had no idea you had a husband!"

"Why, of course, sir. Here he is. Don't kill him!"

Morgan looked at the young captain, his blond hair curling down to his stiff blue collar. His pink cheeks were brushed with down. Morgan wondered if he shaved yet. "Do you think I should?" he asked, as if seriously considering it.

"Oh, no . . . !"

The wail was so genuine that he almost laughed out loud. "Then he is no longer my prisoner, ma'am. He is yours."

His men protested, but he released the officer unconditionally, advising him to console his wife. After all, he thought secretly, if Yankee women had no more backbone than this one, the poor fellows needed all the help they could get.

He felt . . . expansive. He wasn't here to kill Yankees, anyway, but to win a war. He could do that by disrupting their railroads, destroying their supplies, taking the war to them, wherever they least expected. Making them so nervous they would start making mistakes. . . . It was May, and he was in Kentucky again.

But he knew that with only fifty men, he couldn't hope to make it to Lexington. Once the news of these trains reached Bowling Green every road would be swarming with Federals. Yet he was in Kentucky, and he breathed deep. He looked at these tired, hoop-skirted, beribboned women and their pale, untried men in their fresh, pressed uniforms, and the smile he gave them had more than a little contempt in it. He had proved he could survive. And survive he would. Never again would he risk losing everything for a little lack of discipline, a little planning. He would return to Tennessee, regroup, get permission for a real command, and return to Kentucky in style, not like some bushwhacker with a band of thieves. To the surprise of his men he ordered the train released, and begged the ladies to accept it "as a small token" of his esteem. As he passed Major Coffee, the Federal officer lifted one eyebrow in appreciation and sent Morgan a brief salute. A half-hour ago he would have killed him with one of his Colts. Now he stepped forward and suggested, in the light of things, that they all repair, while the paroles were being written, to the Cave City Hotel where the passengers could dine before resuming their journey. Almost in a holiday mood, Morgan on behalf of his men accepted, and the proprietor, completely confused, rushed to accommodate his odd mixture of Yankee and Rebel clientele.

Before they left Major Coffee promised to try, to the best of his ability, to use his parole as an exchange for Colonel Wood, and if not Wood, Charlton.

With a good meal under their belts, Company A trotted down a side road away from the railroad, Tom Morgan's "Cheer, Boys, Cheer!" leading the way. They were leaving Kentucky, but they had saved face. They could go south with a new heart. Champe Ferguson was sent to bring in the scouts, and they marched steadily, by back roads, until they came to within fifteen miles of Glasgow. There a Southern sympathizer offered his farm, and Morgan gladly accepted. Jesse was gone, and without thinking, Morgan handed Ben Drake his horse, asking him to unsaddle and feed. Ben, weary from twelve hours of scouting, looked sour, but said nothing. By the time he came back to the house, his colonel had reserved a place for him by the fire, and the next morning, when Morgan woke him, Ben was angry and confused. "Why didn't you wake me sooner, Colonel? My horse ain't been fed!"

"I wanted you to sleep a little longer, Ben. Your horse is fed and curried . . . I've saddled him myself. Now get some breakfast." Discipline was one thing. Loyalty like Drake's was something that would get him to Lexington and back again. If he could just get Beauregard to agree!

He would need guns. Supplies. Uniforms . . . or just pants. Anything. Shoes, above all, shoes. Some of his men were already barefoot. And horse-shoes. Grimly, he remembered how he'd deprecated Randolph's box at Woodsonville. He's give a double eagle for it now.

Once across the Cumberland the march to Sparta was without incident. As soon as the men were quartered and in camp, he set out for Corinth with one thing in mind. He would see Beauregard. He had all but lost a command, but he had put together the skeleton of another, and had kept the Federals guessing all the way to Bowling Green and beyond. If he had had just a hundred more men, with arms, he might have made it to Louisville. No. Caution, remember? But Beauregard, of all the generals, would know what he was talking about.

The first man he met in Corinth was Adam Johnson.

"Morgan, I'm so glad you've come!" The brown eyes warmed. "Colonel Forrest . . ."

"He's here?"

There was something in Johnson's face that hesitated. "Yes. Came back from Memphis a little over two weeks ago . . ."

Morgan waited for him to go on. Instead, Johnson smiled again. "Why don't you join me at the hotel? Get out of this dust." He waved an arm at the busy street.

Morgan laughed. "Sounds like a good idea to me!"

As they walked through the doors, fresh handshakes with some of Forrest's scouts renewed memories of his uncle Sam's house in Nashville, and the retreat, when he'd first met Adam. Johnson must have remembered, too, because he asked suddenly: "And how is Mr. Morgan? Did he get away?"

"He moved to Huntsville. When that fell, he went to Talladega."

"You Morgans are survivors, I see."

"And Colonel Forrest?" Morgan couldn't help asking. Again, Johnson seemed to avoid the question, busy with pulling out chairs and ordering whiskey. "He's here, you say?" he prompted.

"Yes. We leave day after tomorrow for Chattanooga to recruit and arm a command for operations in West Tennessee and Kentucky. His old command—I must tell you General Bragg gave it . . . to someone else. As much as he wants to go, I don't think he's up to it."

"His wound?"

Johnson nodded. "He came back to us too soon. But you know him! He had an operation in Memphis—unsuccessful—to remove that ball. Then after he got here his horse jumped a log . . . the wound became swollen, reopened . . . he had a second operation. . . ."

"Successful, I hope?"

"The doctor says so. He's been in bed for two weeks, but insists on going. Beauregard gave him *carte blanche*."

Morgan's heart leaped. Yes, for a man like Forrest that would be the only way! Turn him loose. He could recruit a brigade in no time. "Is he receiving visitors?"

"I've got some business to finish, but he would shoot me on the spot if he knew you were here and I didn't deliver you to him within the hour."

Forrest was sitting at a small desk in his room. His cheeks were sunken, his face drawn. He looked up when they entered and Morgan had to consciously change the expression on his face when he saw Forrest's appearance. That tall, broad-shouldered frame was obviously weakened. But the eyes were still like steel, and glinted now as he recognized his visitor.

"I hear you've been testing your horse's ability over logs, sir."

"Damned fool. You knew that horse I had at Shiloh died? Best horse I ever had. It's hell to lose a good horse."

"I know."

"Well. But we must look to ourselves, eh? And I've lost more than a horse. I've lost my whole damned command. Or rather—it's been 'reassigned.' " He looked at the dead end of a pencil and threw it into a wastebasket.

"Why?" Morgan asked, but Forrest misunderstood.

"By Bragg," Forrest shot out. "Braxton Bragg. Here. Have some whiskey. Good Tennessee stuff." Unlike almost everybody else in Confederate service, Forrest never drank, but he found a glass, upended it to shake the dust out, and poured. "So I'm going to Chattanooga to organize a new command."

"So Adam tells me. Here's to it."

"Yore damned right."

When Morgan smiled at Forrest's celebrated impatience, he frowned. "It's already the last of May, John. And it's not just Halleck I'm thinking of. There's a strong rumor going the rounds that Beauregard will be replaced by the end of this month." He shut his mouth in a grim line.

"By?"

"Bragg," Forrest growled the word. "And God help us then. He'll be miserly with the cavalry, you wait and see. Or rather don't wait. When he takes over, there'll be enough dispatches flying back and forth to Richmond to outflank all the excuses at Shiloh." Forrest broke off to enjoy a silent laugh. When he stopped shaking he leaned forward. "A military *savant* who has 'marched by interior lines, striking the fragments of the enemy's force with his own,' " he mimicked. " 'Oh,' said I, 'you mean you took a shortcut and got there first, General?' " Forrest laughed again. "I thought he would die." He leaned back, allowing the old eager look to come into his eyes again. "But we'll lick 'em yet, won't we, Morgan? Yankees and West Pointers."

Forrest, in that fallen timber at Shiloh. *Well, Anderson, shall we give 'em a daar?* Morgan determined to go to headquarters at once.

Beauregard was expansive. His natural Gallic optimism had not allowed the news of his removal to interfere with the saving of his army. They would have to abandon Corinth; he had no taste for a siege. He would go to Tupelo, but Halleck wouldn't know it. Breckinridge with the rear guard could make enough noise: The Yankees would be hoodwinked again. The idea gave him so much pleasure he forgot he was ill. He sent his orderly for another bottle of wine.

He was just opening it when Morgan was announced. The sight of the cavalryman, with his energetic step and ready salute, cheered him even more. "So you want a command?" he said, with a grin behind his mustache. "Have a seat, have a seat."

"Yes, sir."

"So you need guns?" Beauregard asked in the same tone.

"Yes, sir."

"And supplies, and clothing, and ammunition, and wagons, I suppose? Well, see here, Colonel, so does everyone else. I received your message. *Determined to reach Lexington*, was it?"

Morgan sat a little stiffer. "I still am, sir."

"*Alors.* In spite of your . . . horse race?"

"It will take more than a little bad luck to stop me from gaining Kentucky for the Confederacy, sir."

Beauregard's eyes widened. He liked Morgan's style.

"Well, then." He cleared his throat. "It seems to me a man who intends to take Kentucky will need at least a brigade, eh?" He pulled a pad of paper toward him and began writing with a flourish. He set the pen down. "Here," he said, with a grin that disappeared as he watched Morgan read the orders and fold the paper slowly.

"Thank you, General."

"Eh. *Alors.* I am sorry it cannot be more . . ."

"It is more than adequate, sir."

"For some men, no. For you, yes." Beauregard rose and extended his hand. "Oh, and Morgan . . ."

"Sir?"

"We all make mistakes, eh?" It was a plea for understanding as well as a question. A plea with the sound of farewell. So the rumors were true.

Outside Adam Johnson showered him with questions.

"Fifteen thousand dollars, and orders to raise a brigade . . . independent command . . . expedition for Kentucky!"

"YEAOW!"

A week before, two fine companies of Texas cavalry, commanded by native Kentuckians, had arrived in Corinth, and their captains, hearing that Morgan was in town, approached Beauregard with the request for assignment. His adjutant passed it on to Morgan, who made out the necessary papers on the spot.

Thus Richard Gano and John Huffman joined the squadron "to see service in Kentucky." Morgan would leave immediately for Chattanooga, a three-day ride. Gano and Huffman would follow as soon as their horses could be reshod.

To be mustering in, buying horses, gathering supplies for a trip home—all the way home this time—so soon after losing the squadron—and Bess—and watching a mere handful of men escape across the Cumberland. It was a trust he determined to be worthy of. He had to succeed!

He had never been so busy. There were horses to buy, and good mounts were going as high as two hundred dollars around Chattanooga. Many of their horses had suffered from hard riding—spavins and cracked hoofs—including his own. He walked through the blacksmith area and watched with satisfaction as toe clips were welded on. "Do you have enough borax?" He looked into a barrel. "If not, I'll get some." But the smith grinned, pointing to a fresh supply. A farmer brought in some mildewed tack that anyone else would have rejected, but Frank Leathers traded at once. "When a saddle's got mildew, that's a sign there's life in it. Dry leather don't hold mold—only cracks!" He loaded his wagon and left at once for camp.

Within a week Gano and Huffman arrived from Corinth with a surprise. Basil was with them.

"How are you? Are you all right? How did you get to Corinth?"

"It's a long story."

"Uncle Dick?"

Basil nodded.

"Are you actually all right?"

Their elation turned to sadness as they asked about those captured or wounded or killed. They sat silently puffing cigars, each locked in his own memory as a name was thought of. "And Quirk?"

"Tom's indestructible. Quirk and Drake—fine. Pleasant Whitlow . . ." Morgan cleared his throat. Whitlow that night at the armory loading guns in hay. He had a slight stutter that the Rifles used to tease him about. There had been no stuttering that morning he'd galloped, shouting, down that street in Lebanon. . . .

"Don't blame yourself, John."

"They are my boys," he said stubbornly.

At headquarters the talk was of Butler's infamous General Order No. 28.

Imagine ordering that any lady showing contempt for a Union soldier be "treated as a woman of the town!" "Those New Orleans women," they chuckled through their outrage, "must have given the Yankees a scare!"

As for Virginia, McClellan had advanced a magnificent army of 156,000 to the banks of the Chickahominy and crossed on the last day of May—the day after Morgan arrived in Chattanooga—to fight the bloody but indecisive Battle of Seven Pines. Joseph E. Johnston was wounded in that battle, and now Robert E. Lee took command. Everyone wondered what he would do.

"One thing is certain," Gano murmured. "They'll concentrate on protecting Richmond and forget about us."

"Haven't they always?" Basil asked, the memory of Shiloh still bitter.

Yet when they read captured Northern papers lauding the fact that the commands of Fremont, Banks and McDowell would concentrate under Pope to cooperate with McClellan against Richmond, they fumed.

But Jackson was coming down the Shenandoah Valley, victorious at Winchester and Front Royal, and those who knew the Chickahominy, how it meandered in a circle around Richmond before emptying into the James, knew also that McClellan had divided his forces in a dangerous crescent, advantageous to the Confederates.

"If I were there . . ."

"If you were there, sir?" Morgan watched the face of Kirby Smith, about his own age. Breveted captain for bravery in Mexico, an Indian fighter in Texas, a mathematics professor at the Point before the war and now a lieutenant-general, Smith had that same unflinching energy, that same intensity that Morgan had thought could belong to only one man. They had been drinking whiskey in the General's hotel room and discussing the Virginia situation. Now, as Smith leaned forward, Morgan was surprised and delighted at just how much he reminded him of Sidney Johnston.

"If I were there I'd get Jackson to join as quickly as possible with A.P. Hill," Smith said. "Clean out the Federals on the south bank of that river . . . which would allow Longstreet to cross—"

"And chase the Yankees back to Washington," Morgan finished for him. Smith beamed. "General Hill is my brother-in-law." Morgan smiled. "And my brother Richard is on his staff."

"Let's wish them luck! In the meantime . . . I'm glad you saw Beauregard. When you come back from this expedition, let me recommend you to General Bragg personally, if you don't mind. He's the sort of man . . . well! . . . let's say, who needs persuading?" He wiped a handkerchief across his broad, balding brow and tucked it in his pocket again. In spite of his full beard, his face had a clean-cut, chiseled look, like a Spanish don. He leaned a little forward and studied Morgan, then said seriously: "I want to win this war. I don't mind telling you I hope to use this little trip of yours into Kentucky as a proof to Bragg that Federal territory *can* be invaded successfully. I've got to go to Knoxville tomorrow. If I can be of help to you in any way, just let me know."

When Morgan walked down the stairs to the lobby a broad-shouldered, short man in a green civilian suit, his head dipped into a newspaper, looked vaguely familiar. As Morgan approached, the man turned. For an awkward moment, Morgan hesitated.

"You don't remember me, Colonel? Those drinks at the Phoenix?"

It was Gordon Niles, the New York newspaperman.

"Of course! Of course! Sorry about your *Journey into the South*."

"I've come to enlist in your new outfit, sir. I'm determined. So you'd better play it safe and accept me in the lowest rank you have."

"Why, I'll place you in my favorite company, Mr. Niles! Only after you allow me to let you test the liquor of Chattanooga, the way we did in Lexington!"

Private Gordon Niles, of Company A, agreed to become his adjutant over their third whiskey.

Morgan, with his new adjutant and staff, plunged into the work of getting a command together. The three original companies were quickly brought up to full strength—and beyond. Men came from all around, on foot, some with their horses. News of the expedition spread. Morgan had to smile at one of the letters he received from Camp Mercer, Georgia.

> We whose names are hereto affixed . . . long for a more active field of duty. . . . One of our number E. W. Maulding has served as a Comanche hunter in Texas, is A #1 with the lasso and if you can not immediately supply us with horses will soon rope in enough of them from the Yankees to mount us. . . . We are now armed with Miss. Rifles and would like to have our guns transferred with us. Hoping that you will give our request. . . .

Camp Mercer, near Savannah, was too far away for G. W. Wartlow, T. Ireland, R. Campbell, A. Dicks and the others to make it to Chattanooga in time. He let his eyes run over the list of signatures before he handed it to Niles for a reply. He wished he could take them all.

Three hundred men of the First Kentucky Infantry who had disbanded in Virginia because of expired service came to Chattanooga to join Morgan. Men filtered back from "the Races" . . . but not Jesse. Billy Milton escaped, and James Bowles, captain of Company C again. Company A was given to Captain Jacob Cassell, a private who had enlisted in March and who had proved so popular with the men that his election was unanimously approved. Company B stayed with John Allen, Tom's brother, and Tom became the brigade surgeon.

One of the new privates in Company A, a Canadian named George Ellsworth, was, he said, an excellent telegraph operator, and offered his services in that capacity. Fighting as he came, twenty-one-year-old John Breckinridge Castleman arrived from Kentucky with a company recruited around Lexington. It became Company D, at last completing the roster started by Brown. In his memory many of the "old" Morgan men enlisted on the spot —among them Breck Castleman's young brother Humphreys, who had left

Lexington last September as one of the original "Camp Charity" outfit. Company E, mostly First Kentucky infantrymen, were sworn in under tall, handsome Captain John Hutchinson, one of the most popular officers in the command. Tom Webber, from Mississippi, who had been with Bragg at Pensacola, had Company F, and the nucleus of another company, mustered in in Alabama by Captain McFarland, would be Company G when it came up to strength.

Meanwhile, letters started coming in from Kentucky pleading for an invasion. "To be rescued from the Bluebellies!" one "Secesh" wrote from Anderson County. "And the sooner the better!" One paper had a petition with more than five hundred names.

"Evidently your fame is spreading." Castleman smiled as he admitted a dark-haired, slight young man into Morgan's headquarters. Morgan looked up into the waiting contemplation of Tom Hines. He hadn't seen him since the retreat through Nashville.

"I've been in Richmond, sir," Hines answered his question. He kept his slim boy's face absolutely still, then held Morgan with his ice-blue eyes. "You're all the talk there, sir. I've come back to serve with you, if you need me."

"Need you? We certainly do!"

"I'd like to enlist immediately, sir," Hines said stubbornly, as if they would change the subject. "Company D."

"Company D, is it? With Castleman and Eastin? The cavaliers?" Morgan chuckled. "Company D it is, Private Hines."

Company D had become known as a kind of "gentleman's company," and the joke was that the valiant were in A, the cautious in B, the serious in C, and the ladies would be in D if they could.

On his birthday he got the surprise of his life. Major George Washington Morgan stood before him, fresh from the Third Tennessee Infantry. "Thought Ah'd ride a hoss fer a change," Wash drawled, his wide-eyed, tanned face breaking into a grin before bear hugs and back-poundings made him cough and plead for air. "Hey, don't kill me yet! Leave some for the Yankees!"

Beauregard surrendered Corinth on May 30. A week later Memphis fell. The news only made Morgan's men more determined.

When they drilled and he called out fours and young Tom Morgan's voice rose in song—good God, it was great to be alive. Basil was second-in-command. Wash became known simply as "Major Wash." Niles was Adjutant, Llewellyn Quartermaster, Hiram Reese Commissary. Tom Hines's extraordinary evidence of leadership earned him a captaincy of scouts. There were six companies, with the beginning of a seventh, and the regiment numbered almost four hundred men. The Second Kentucky Cavalry, Colonel John Hunt Morgan, commanding, was born.

A letter from Richard brought news of Kitty and A.P. Jeb Stuart's cavalry had made a brilliant raid encircling McClellan's lines. A.P.'s division was the largest in the army. After the battle at Seven Pines, Lee assembled all divisions and brigades and announced there would be no further retreat toward Richmond, that the mission of the newly named Army of Northern Virginia would be aggressive.

"You would like him," Richard wrote, and a glob of ink told he was having trouble with his pen. "Lee's a fighter—our kind of man. You'll see some fireworks before the summer's over. Kitty's fine. Can you believe little Frances is seven months old? We all mourn little Henrietta, but this baby has brought such joy at a time when it's sorely needed. . . ."

He would write again. Could Morgan let him know where he was? He'd had to telegraph Bragg's headquarters at Tupelo to find out the Second Kentucky was at Chattanooga. There was no news from home.

After scrubbing off, Morgan set the letter aside and was about to dress for dinner when Niles came in, apologetic and breathless. "I thought you'd like to see this immediately, Colonel. A message from General Bragg."

Morgan unfolded the paper. Bragg was rescinding Beauregard's orders, withdrawing permission for an expedition. The regiment would train and recruit at Chattanooga until further notice. Damned pompous ass!

Without a word, Morgan put the paper in his pocket and walked to the telegraph office. As quickly as he could, he scribbled a reply and watched the operator tap it out: REQUEST IMMEDIATE TRANSFER TO THE COMMAND OF GENERAL KIRBY SMITH, KNOXVILLE.

And if he doesn't give it to me, I'm going anyway . . .

To his surprise, an affirmative answer came within the hour, General Smith confirming.

37

Knoxville was, as Basil Duke admitted later, "something more like it." And Kirby Smith also.

Morgan looked from Basil to the General. "If I'm successful, I'll send you a report from Kentucky."

"If you're successful, Colonel Morgan, we'll plan a *much larger expedition* before the snow flies," General Smith said, holding out his hand. "And your success will be all the justification I'll need to talk General Bragg into agreement. Yes, send me that report from Kentucky. The minute I get it, I'll wire Richmond for orders. . . ."

Within two weeks most of the men were mounted. Drill, after being without horses for so long, brought no complaint from men with fresh mounts. It was too good to ride again. Morgan went daily to camp to watch.

"Don't yew know yew cain't back a hoss before yew gather him up first?"

Morgan turned around, unbelieving.

"Will! Where in hell did you come from?"

"Exactly. Hell it wuz, among them Yankees. Ah went with Charl to Huntsville, worked in thet hospittle. . . ."

"Has he been exchanged? Have you heard?"

"Not a word. Last thing I knowed, they'd shipped him nawth. Whar, Ah don't know. . . ."

Morgan's heart sank. "How did you get here?"

"Rubbed lye soap in mah armpits." Will grinned. "Honest, Johnny!" he said to Morgan's look. "Hit raises yore temperture. Don't yew know thet? Then Ah had a 'pain' in mah neck, commencta roll aroun'. . . . Them fellers thot Ah had brain fever, shore enuf. Pshaw, hit wuz easy."

The boy whose horse wouldn't back was still having trouble. The more he jerked the reins, the higher the horse's head went.

"Hey, there!" Will yelled. "Yew'll git him ta rear an' dump yew!" Will ran over, took the reins and pulled the boy off. "Here, let me show yew! Durn fool!"

Morgan reached out to the boy's shoulder before he hit him. "It's all right," he said. "He knows what he's doing. Just watch." Will gathered the leathers, hands low, tucked his seat and waited. The horse's nose went down and he stepped back in even, straight strides.

"Thet's how yew do it, boy." Will looked over, then jumped down. "Don't mean to . . ."

"Thanks," the boy said. "Now watch, and see if I can do it."

Morgan left them with a wave, but Will was too busy to notice. Within a week he became a kind of unofficial drill master, teaching maneuvers he remembered from those days up on the Maumee, and even talked Frank Leathers into using his mules for practice, for those soldiers without horses.

When they weren't drilling, the men were arguing over the merits of the Enfield vs. the Sharps, the Springfield vs. the Spencer.

"If a man will stop to load, he'll stay cool enough to take aim," the "muzzle-loaders" argued.

"But if a man *don't* stay cool"—someone laughed—"he can stuff his gun with balls and never shoot it." The danger of multiple shots rammed in haste had made many a gun useless. They had found enough of them on the ground that first day at Shiloh.

"Ah, only Yankees are dumb enough to do that," one of the "muzzle-loaders" said.

"Well, give me a gun I can load lying down . . . I've seen too many boys sit up to ram a charge home and get shot for all their cool," a breech-loading advocate insisted. "For all their cool," he repeated, and stared ahead of him.

"Hell, a man with a good pistol can put both underground," a third soldier laughed. The other two nodded. There was no argument to that.

It was good the men had something to feel confident about. The news from Virginia was not good. A Union army was camped just eight miles from Richmond, bogged down after being stopped at Fair Oaks. Eight miles. Turner Ashby, one of the great Virginia cavalrymen, was dead. But as fear choked the East, the West felt more than ever that the war had to be won here . . . or nowhere. Morgan knew men expressed fear in many ways. There was, in this talk of guns, a kind of inward settling: If his men could dare the guns, they could dare the Yankees behind them. As he passed, he threw out a remark to help: "Too many of our men have an unreasonable fear of the Spencer."

"That's right! That's right!"

He looked around and grinned. "But you boys can keep them guessing!"

More laughter. Yes, if men like this could survive, they already had a victory.

When he stepped into his tent Gordon Niles rose to introduce a visitor. It was Major Coffee.

The Federal officer rose at once and extended his hand. "I'm awfully sorry, Colonel. I was unable to effect an exchange," he said in his husky voice.

The shock in Morgan's face made him grin.

"About all I did was convince them that I am your prisoner, and that a parole is a word of honor. So here I am. Sorry about Colonel Wood, though." After receiving a parole from Morgan at Cave City, Coffee had gone to Nashville, where Robert Wood was held prisoner, but General Dumont refused to release him. Then Coffee went to Washington, to the Secretary of War. Rebuffed with indignation—and, Morgan guessed, with some official shock and confusion on the part of Yankee bureaucrats hearing such an outlandish request—Coffee traveled, via Kentucky, where his wife was ill, back to Nashville, then through Huntsville to Chattanooga. At

Chattanooga he hired a carriage for the trip to Knoxville. By the time he arrived he had preserved his honor but not his money: He was stone broke.

It was almost as good as seeing an old friend. The conviviality of that hour at the hotel in Cave City, the release of the train to the ladies, the jokes—all returned. Morgan was staying at the Bell House and took a room for Coffee at his own expense. For a week the Major had complete freedom of his camp and often dined with the staff, overhearing plans . . . until Kirby Smith got wind of it. Morgan was called to headquarters and curtly ordered to send Coffee to Richmond as a prisoner.

Morgan was shocked. "He's my prisoner, General. I have a right to dispose of him as I think best."

"See here, Morgan, you are not some Border Chieftain. You are a colonel in the Confederate Army. Major Coffee is a prisoner of that army. He will go to Richmond."

"I had hoped to exchange him for Colonel Wood."

"So I heard. And the exchange failed."

"Perhaps, if I get him back to Kentucky under an armed escort . . ."

The look on Kirby Smith's face stopped him.

When Coffee heard of it he refused to let Morgan endanger his career. "It could result in a court-martial. . . . No. I'd never let a friend get into trouble on my account, if I could help it. I believe I will be exchanged. Besides, I'd like to go to Richmond and see the sights."

There was nothing for it: Morgan paid his room and board and saw him off.

When he returned to the hotel with Basil, he was stopped by a man with shoulder-length white hair framing a lean, sunburned face and two flaming blue eyes.

"Pardon me, sir," the man said in a clipped accent, "I should like to introduce myself. Colonel George St. Leger Grenfel, late of Her Majesty's service—and also the service of the good French Republic, and that excellent Moorish gentleman, Abd-el-Kader."

"Weren't those last two enemies?" Basil blurted.

"Merely the fortunes of war. The fortunes of war." St. Leger stuck out a gnarled hand with impeccably clean nails and said, "See here, Morgan, I'm awfully glad to be here. I hope you don't mind the intrusion. When I landed in Richmond I asked President Davis where I could see some action in a cavalier group, and he sent me to you. If it's not convenient . . . Beastly of me not to have telegraphed. . . ."

"No, no, not at all. . . ."

Thus one of the most memorable friendships of Morgan's life began.

Over whiskey and cigars, late at night and at dawn—the man seemed indefatigable—St. Leger regaled them with stories. At seventeen he had run away to join the Chasseurs d'Afrique. For five years he fought with the French against the Moors, then with the Moors against the French, then for the Governor of Gibraltar against the Riff pirates. He had been in Uruguay with Garibaldi, in the Crimea and in India during the Sepoy Rebellion.

When the American war started he was raising sheep in South America and couldn't stand it.

"Isn't there something bloody humiliating about being human?" St. Leger mused, biting his pipe. "All this *getting,* you know, lads—that goes. Simply goes on a horse. And especially when another chap is shooting at you. Marvelous! Exhilarating! No, there's nothing like it. And you learn from your enemies, gentlemen. In the war with Abd-el-Kader . . . now *there* was a noble Moor. . . ."

"I still don't see how you can switch loyalties so easily." Basil frowned.

The Englishman pulled his pipe from his mouth and gripped the bowl with his fingers. If I did that, Morgan thought, I would burn my hand.

"It wasn't loyalty I switched," St. Leger said gruffly, looking off. "Kader was betrayed by the bloody French, then by his own people. It was the French who abandoned the last bastion of a soldier. . . ."

"And that . . . ?" began Basil.

The circle of listeners seemed to come into focus. St. Leger relaxed, rubbed his hand on his pants and laughed. "Honor, gentlemen. She's the only mistress who will stay by you. But I'm getting too beastly serious. The only loyalty I have is to life, my only enemy boredom. It's boredom that starts wars. And marriages, I might add."

When the laughter died, St. Leger leaned back. "Keep 'em busy, I say. The best thing a man can do is to make love to as many of 'em as you safely can. The next best thing is to shoot at somebody or be shot at. Jolly good solution, either one. Sometimes, depending on circumstances, one can do both. . . ."

The next day Wash proudly escorted him to the drill field. Afterwards, over breakfast, Morgan asked St. Leger how he liked it.

"Splendid, splendid! But if you will pardon me, gentlemen, your force has now outgrown Maury's skirmish tactics for cavalry, I believe you call it?" The blue eyes below the white hair danced.

"How so?" Far from being indignant, as St. Leger had feared, Morgan offered his guest pen and paper. The Englishman, with quick, nervous movements, soon had it covered with half-circles and slashes.

"Here, old boy. See. The usual method of counting off in sets, dismounting, deploying to the flanks, to the rear . . . there are just too many movements for a quick change of front, with as many men as you can now employ . . . and over the uncertain terrain you will most probably encounter."

"What would you suggest?" Basil swallowed his coffee, attentive as a schoolboy.

St. Leger tilted his head. "Imagine, sirs, a regiment drawn up in single rank. The flank companies are skirmishing, sometimes on horseback. The enemy approaches. You throw out those skirmishers on foot, so deployed as to cover the whole front of the regiment (where they have arrived in quick order via fleet mounts). While they are so employed, the rest of your men dismount, arrange themselves (horse-holders to the nearest cover) as terrain permits, in files two yards apart, but the whole in a long flexible line curving

forward at each extremity, to be thrown about, at will, like a rope. . . .
Then imagine this line sent forward at the double-quick, at the run . . .
with always a small body of mounted men kept in reserve to act on the
flanks, to cover a retreat, or press a victory. . . ."

"I see it!" said Captain Bowles, who had been silent until now.

"Fancy mounted footwork is jolly fine in camp, but you may not always
have the same, well-trained horses. There may come a day when you will
be riding anything with four legs that you can get. But your men will always
—let us hope—have their own legs, and if they know exactly what is expected of them in any emergency . . . a whole regiment, sir, could be
brought into line within thirty minutes from the first alarm."

"Welcome to the Second Kentucky." Morgan held out his hand.

They tried St. Leger's tactics, and the new drill made the men forget their
recent boredom. It was amazing how quickly mounted skirmishers could
become foot soldiers, how quickly and with utter precision mounted troops
could form that invincible, in-curving infantry "rope," with a mounted reserve covering the flanks. Each day's practice gave the men fresh confidence.

In a staff blue coat and red silk cap with cord and tassels, St. Leger taught
some of the men how to shoot from the saddle, front, side, and rear. He
would take fine aim by half-rising in his stirrups, his arm half-extended, his
body leaning toward the target. When Tom Logwood, who had lost his
horse at "the Lebanon Races," complained that "it was one thing to do fancy
shooting from a trained horse, and another from a green colt afraid of fire,"
St. Leger offered to repeat his feat if Tom Quirk and Ben Drake, riding
experienced mounts, would flank him.

"Yu'v got to treat a horse like the girls, lads. Soooothe 'em when they're
excited, and put the timid with the more experienced."

Off they went, St. Leger firing his .44 caliber Adams six-shooter as fast
as he could change targets, Logwood's sorrel, untrained colt under him as
calm as a veteran. That settled it. From that moment on, St. Leger Grenfel
took his place beside Mad Anthony Wayne, George Rogers Clark and William Henry Harrison in Will's pantheon, and if a recruit unused to "Morgan's ways" complained, Will turned into a drill sergeant worthy of the
British "Line."

Will wasn't St. Leger's only admirer. Tom Morgan dogged his steps,
listening to every word.

"How would you like to be assigned to Grenfel?" Morgan asked his brother
one morning, knowing the answer.

"Do you mean it, Brother Johnny? Really?"

"I'll see what I can do."

"Oh, could you?"

What Tom didn't know was that the evening before he had already talked
with St. Leger, who reluctantly agreed.

"Do I detect some hesitation?"

"Oh, the boy's got mettle—he wouldn't be your brother otherwise. But
he's impulsive. That's good, when combined with experience. . . ."

"That's precisely why—"

"Why I'm to play nanny?" The Englishman's eyes drifted from Morgan's face to the horizon. There was a sudden sadness.

Before Morgan could protest, St. Leger surprised him by smiling beneath his mustache. "Very well, my American friend. I can promise you—with one qualification—that no harm shall come to him while he is in my charge."

"And the qualification?"

"That he obeys me implicitly."

"Agreed."

"Now." Grenfel's eyes, which had drifted to the last light, turned from the sunset to focus on Morgan again. "How do you intend to use your vedettes, Colonel?"

"Scouts several miles out for information, vedettes on the roads immediately around . . ."

"Why not . . ."

And an elaborate plan was worked out, with suggestions thrown in from all sides, by Basil, the young lieutenants, and the company commanders at a council that night. St. Leger sat in the middle of the circle like a hard-muscled Santa Claus with his elves. There would be twenty-five picked men in an advance guard—a guard of honor, four hundred yards in front of the column, to receive and send orders to the vedettes. As for the vedettes, there would be six, with a spearhead pair scouting side roads and an automatic replacement system as each pair moved forward. Morgan could see that such a plan was nearly foolproof. Basil appreciated St. Leger's cautious attention to detail. This was one Englishman who did not intend to be surprised.

The next morning Morgan looked up from his desk to see Captain John Hutchinson of Company E saluting smartly. He motioned him at ease.

"Who, sir, is your Fairy Godmother?"

"What?"

"Beauregard? General Smith? President Davis?"

"What in the name of the devil are you talking about, Hutch?" He followed him outside to see two mountain howitzers in the street.

"Sent from Richmond, for Colonel Morgan's use." Hutchinson handed him a note.

> I must say Colonel that the execution of this order for arms gave me more satisfaction than any shipment I have ever made. I felt that they are going into the best of hands.
>
> > Capt. Childs
> > Charleston Arsenal

"So he really meant it! He wants nothing to stop us!" *We'll plan a much larger expedition—*

"Sir?"

"Before the snow flies, Hutch." He grinned.

"Sir?"

He knew the gun. These two would be invaluable. Small enough to go wherever a horse could, they delivered shells with accuracy at eight hundred yards, canister and grape at two or three hundred. Only one horse was needed to pull one, and over rough terrain the whole thing—tube, shafts, carriage and wheels—could be disassembled and transported on two pack mules, with a third mule for ammunition. Even better, it could be reassembled and ready to fire in less than a minute. Two men could maneuver one of those guns in line, with little noise, quite close to the enemy. Even their carriages were sturdy and simply made—and therefore easily repaired. The men immediately nicknamed them "the Bull Pups."

"We're not a regiment," Jake Cassell beamed. "We're an army!"

It was true. Everyone seemed to want to "join Morgan." With the promised expedition, the name took on an aura of excitement. Private R. A. Alston, a South Carolina cavalryman in Company A, requested permission to raise a company when they reached Kentucky, in order to earn a captaincy.

Captain Thomas Henry Hines had his own reasons.

Morgan would remember later, with the deepest bitterness of his life, the beginnings of a dark labyrinth into which he stepped so casually that morning Hines came to see him. Hines kept his slim boy's face absolutely still, but there was the steady, alert readiness in his eyes of the sharpshooter taking aim.

"Don't look so worried," Morgan laughed. "I've heard from Breck Castleman that you want to take a detail into Kentucky on special duty. . . ."

"Did I look worried?" Hines dipped his chin and stifled a yawn. When he raised his head Morgan could swear the boy looked as if he were about to doze. What a consummate spy he would make, he thought.

"Breck also tells me you are interested in meeting Chief Justice Bullitt. I didn't know you wore an Indian-head penny in your lapel."

Captain Hines shook his head in silent laughter. "You're too modest, sir. Why do you think I joined you? You were all they talked of in Richmond. Morgan. They started comparing you to the Swamp Fox of the Revolution."

"They are in need of heroes."

"They talked of something else . . . a Northwest Conspiracy. . . ."

Morgan looked at him in disbelief. His own upbringing put the work of spies in the same category as thieves and liars, and made the clandestine loyalties of the Southern-sympathizing Yankee "Copperheads"—self-styled "Knights of the Golden Circle"—dishonorable. Such men—Judge Bullitt of Kentucky included—waited, as far as he was concerned, to join the winning side. To Morgan they weren't worth wooing. To Hines, as Hines had so often said, nothing done in the name of the Cause was dishonorable.

Morgan had to admit that the boy's enthusiasm was contagious. Breck Castleman and his handsome lieutenant, George Eastin, listened to every scheme with wonder, and since Hines had joined them, followed him around, mesmerized. Ah, well, it was playing at war. If Hines wanted to make contact with Judge Bullitt, what harm could there be, if he would recruit sympathetic guides, find out which bridges were unprotected, which supply depots were weakly garrisoned, which steamboats could be burned . . . it would be good training. He needed all the excellent scouts he could get. Almost offhandedly he agreed.

"You won't regret this, sir."

"Meet me in Kentucky." Morgan smiled and held out his hand.

"I'll keep in touch!" Hines saluted smartly, turned on his heel and almost ran back to his men.

News of Morgan's raid spread. A Colonel Hunt, from Georgia, arrived in Knoxville with a "Partisan Ranger" regiment to join. With Hunt's 350, his own 370 and Gano's 156, Morgan had 876 men, some 200 without arms. "Never mind," he told Niles. "We'll get guns and good horses where we're going."

Now if Major Coffee could manage an exchange for Charlton . . . "Do you think he's well? Is there any way of knowing where they sent him?"

Tom frowned at the question and sent his brother a hesitant look. "I had a feeling about Coffee, standing there in that train waving his Colts, then inviting us all to dinner. He's a man to trust, I think. He'll try, if anybody can." Then something struck him and Tom collapsed in laughter.

"What the devil?"

"*I* know why you're worried, Brother Johnny! When we get to Lexington, you don't want to face Ma."

When we get to Lexington. That lovely word put everything else out of his mind. In his pocket he carried a letter from T.H., now in Vicksburg, to be delivered to Aunt Mary. At the bottom T.H. had scrawled: "If anybody can get this through the lines I know you will. Good luck."

The command left Knoxville on July 4 to the strains of "The Hunters of Kentucky":

> *And now if danger e'er annoys,*
> *Remember what our trade is;*
> *Just send for us Kentucky boys,*
> *And we'll protect you, ladies!*

They were truly, truly going home. Nothing could stop them now.

They reached Sparta, 104 miles away, on the evening of the third day. The march had been rough. The recruits, unused to eight or ten hours in the saddle over rugged terrain, dared not lag behind. Bushwhackers, shooting from ledges forty feet overhead, disappeared before the men could find a path to outflank them. They killed one of Gano's Texans and sent one of the scouts back with his tongue cut out.

The only man not surprised was St. Leger. "Amateurs," he mumbled, and asked permission to pursue.

"You will take me, won't you, sir?" Tom Morgan begged.

St. Leger, looking off, seemed not to have heard.

"You will allow me to go?" Tom repeated.

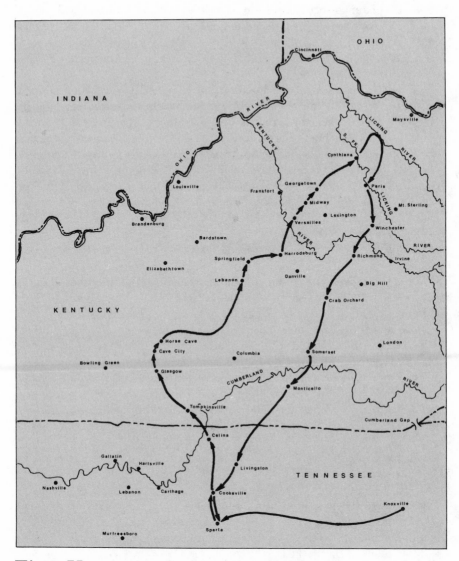

First Kentucky Raid, July 1862

The Englishman seemed to be looking inward, in that sudden sad way he had. He looked up with a jerk of his head, as if seeing the boy for the first time. "If you obey me . . . implicitly," he bit out, not waiting for an answer. Tom fell in behind, with four other men St. Leger chose quickly, with a wave of his hand.

The horses hunched upward over a mud-slippery bank. Tom could feel the ballooning of his horse's haunches under him as the hinds dug forward for a hold. He ducked through a tangle of vines on an overhanging branch and saw St. Leger's horse ahead, already scrambling up the last of the rocks. One slipped and came bounding down past the other riders, but the Englishman, now on flatter ground above them, rode on without waiting. Morning fog still lingered in the trees. Tom had never ridden in woods as thick as this. For an instant he was back at Shiloh, the same breathtaking expectation making a pain in his ribs. Ahead, St. Leger's silk cap lost color; only the tassels were visible through the gray air, like the tail feathers of a jaunty bird. The men with him—all seasoned scouts—kept a maddeningly slow pace. Why didn't they ride forward? Suddenly a shot rang out, and as if St. Leger had given the command, they crashed through the trees, Tom at their heels. His horse caught a foreleg in a thick vine and stopped. Tom had to back him out, hearing all the time shouts and thrashing in the bushes not thirty feet away, over a little rise out of sight. By the time he arrived it was all over and a bushwhacker, a knife in his chest, lay in that strange, twisted attitude of death, his left leg in its muddy tan homespun still jerking. One of the men dismounted, retrieved his knife, and they turned their horses in the short radius allowed by the trees for the trip back. St. Leger said nothing. He merely nodded, but as he rode up Tom saw, under the Englishman's mustache, that he was grinning from ear to ear.

The town of Sparta never looked so good to them, for there Champe Ferguson waited, offering his services again. He spit through the space in his teeth. Morgan nodded, and smiled.

By noon of the fourth day they reached a ford on the Cumberland at a village called Celina, where a forward vedette reported a Federal garrison at Tompkinsville, across the state line in Kentucky, eighteen miles away.

"How many?" Basil asked.

"About three hundred and fifty, sir. A Major Jordan commanding."

"Well, Duke, shall we give 'em a daar?" Morgan grinned at St. Leger's uncomprehending look.

The men were dead-tired. The Cumberland, on that humid July evening, was cool and inviting. He let his boys have a frolic, a good swim for themselves in a pool near shore. Morgan was standing with a coffee cup in his hand looking out over the river when Will came up.

"The river's up a little," Will said, and spit.

"It's wide here. And shallow. Didn't you always tell me that was the sign of a good rock bottom?"

"It's up," Will said, and looked off.

It was his old way, and Morgan waited. "What would you do?"

"Me?" Will looked at the expanse of water, more than a hundred feet across, with an occasional fist of foam where the tip of a rock broke the surface. "I'd slow thet current with a string of hosses."

Morgan looked at the picket line, where in the shade groups of horses were already nodding into each other's noses, their backsides fanned out in semicircles, their hind pasterns cocked in rest. Well, maybe. He drained his cup and threw the dregs away. "You're in charge tomorrow."

At sundown the vedettes escorted in a Major Hamilton, with a company of Tennessee Rangers, who joined them. Around a campfire St. Leger grew expansive, with tales of the Crimea and the siege of Jhansi. Tom Morgan listened with new respect.

"There were eleven thousand Sepoys in the garrison, reinforced by twenty thousand. Sir Hugh Rose, with fifteen hundred men, completely routed them!"

"And how did he do that?" Breck Castleman, almost as spellbound as Tom, waited for St. Leger to draw on his pipe.

"With a boldness that was . . . remarkable! Divided his force, but kept hammering at that fort . . . outflank, then assault. It was a hundred and ten in the shade." He shook his head and puffed.

"Let's try it!" said Gano, with a look at Morgan. "My men could outflank, Colonel Hunt's regiment and yours, Colonel, could carry the assault. . . ."

"I could join you on the flanking operation." Major Harrison grinned. "My boys know these roads. There's one to the right of Tompkinsville. By that we could get on the Yankees' line of retreat toward Glasgow. . . ."

"Yeaow!" yelled Tom, then blushed. "Only practicing my Rebel yell, sirs!"

St. Leger's "flank and assault" became the pattern of the raid, and time after time it was successful. Gano's men, especially, took pride in their part. "It makes us feel like Injuns. . . ." No outfit could let out the blood-chilling Rebel yell as loud or as long as the Texans. That alone, Morgan joked, could kill Yankees.

"Well, it'll at least make 'em turn their heads, so you can go to work in the front," Gano growled in his quiet, husky way.

Before dawn on that ninth day of July, saddle blankets were shaken out and cinches tightened in the dark. As if he were conducting a Napoleonic siege, Will ordered mounted troopers to stand their horses stirrup-to-stirrup as a living dam, belly-deep in the river. The water built up against their flanks, then flowed toward the banks: It worked.

As the rocky bottom of the ford became more visible, the other horses waded through and the Bull Pups made it across with ease. They were on their way! With yelps and yells, the equine "dam" broke apart and galloped over the far bank toward Kentucky.

It was five o'clock and broad daylight by the time they reached Tompkinsville. With the sun up, there would be no surprise now. Colonel Hunt's Georgians formed to the left, Duke on the right, with the howitzers in the center. There was no reserve; the Yankees in this case were outnumbered, and St. Leger, delighted, rode back and forth, his white hair catching the sun that was just gilding the early morning fog, his red skullcap looking, as Tom quipped, "damned jolly" on his head. The Federals were posted on a wooded hill, and to reach them the Confederates would have to cross an open field. This prospect only made St. Leger smile more, and he kept admonishing the troops, "Now don't fire until you are within sixty yards of them, do you hear? Sixty yards. Then one volley from us will bloody well be enough." The boys of Company A looked at one another: What if the Yankees fired first?

They did, three or four volleys, while the Second Kentucky ran on, with St. Leger ahead of them, jumping his horse over a fence and slashing with his saber like a Moor. When Morgan's men sent a single line of flame from the much maligned muzzle-loaders, they set to rest forever any fear they might have had of the Spencer. The fight lasted only ten minutes, but a wagon train of twenty wagons and fifty mules, besides a number of cavalry horses, were captured. Gordon Niles got a good horse and found a print shop where he ran off recruiting posters. Morgan laughed out loud at the theatrics:

> Kentuckians! I have come to liberate you
> from the hands of your oppressors! We need
> the willing hands of 50,000 of Kentucky's
> bravest sons!
> Strike—for your altars and your fires!
> Strike—for the green graves of your sires!
> God—and your native land!

Abundant supplies of coffee and sugar rewarded a search of the enemy camp, causing some to murmur, "Them Yankees live well, don't they?"— but others, veterans of Shiloh, paid more attention to the prisoners. Gano, with his flanking operation, rounded up the lion's share, including the Federal commander, Major Jordan. But portly, quiet Colonel Hunt, with his soft Georgia drawl, lay with a shattered leg.

"Don't be foolish, Morgan. I'm not . . ." Hunt groaned as he shifted his shoulders on the bed. They had moved him into a house of Southern sympathizers, who stood in awe against the walls watching the scene.

Tom Allen snapped his black bag shut and looked at his commander. "He can't be moved. Oh, I know how you want to take your wounded with you, but this time, no, John. . . ."

Morgan knew he would never see the kindly Georgian again. The leg festered like some crushed piece of meat under the bandages. Wounds like that were doomed to gangrene. He drew Tom aside.

"I trust your judgment, Tom. Have you talked with him about amputation?"

Tom Allen ducked his chin and looked sidewise at his patient, who had thrust his head back and closed his eyes.

"Ordinarily I would, but he hasn't the strength for an operation. He's already lost too much blood. I'll leave morphine, some antiseptic. There's a chance. These ladies will do all that is possible."

They left him behind, to learn from their scouts that he died a few days later.

The tents, stores and anything not worth taking were destroyed. As for the feared breech-loading Yankee carbines, the surplus were thrown away.

By three o'clock that afternoon all the prisoners were paroled and Morgan's men were on the road to Glasgow—unoccupied by the enemy and the home of Company C. They rode into town just past midnight and rested until nine o'clock the next morning, after the ladies and relatives in the town served them a huge breakfast in the square. One of the diners was a Yankee straggler, caught the night before. Between big bites of biscuit he boasted that McClellan was in Richmond. He posed as an officer until Lieutenant Boyer picked him up by the collar and held him, feet dangling in the air. It turned out that he was a bugler with the Ninth Pennsylvania, and quickly changed his story: McClellan was in Richmond, all right, but as a prisoner.

They knew that Lee had started his Peninsula Campaign at Mechanicsville on June 23, and that on July 2, just before they left, he had been engaged at Malvern Hill, but they left Knoxville before dispatches arrived to tell the outcome. "Maybe it's time to use the telegraph," Morgan said to George Ellsworth, who was more than anxious to prove his prowess. At Bear Wallow, Ellsworth tapped the line between Louisville and Nashville to get the latest information on Virginia and the strength of Federal garrisons in Kentucky. He carried a pocket instrument that could cut into the circuit without breaking the current. Under his high forehead his heavy eyelids drooped over an aquiline nose; he could have been a surgeon about to make an incision. Carefully connecting his own instrument to the line, he began to take the dispatches. Usually he just listened, but they were coming slowly, and with Morgan making signs to hurry, Ellsworth got into a casual conversation, the best way, he had often found, to learn news. They were calling the battles around Richmond the Seven Days. As it turned out, the Federal operator in Louisville reluctantly admitted that Lee had driven McClellan back eighteen miles to the James River: Richmond was saved. Morgan scribbled a note and handed it to Ellsworth: Tell him that Morgan has arrived with ten thousand cavalry and that Nathan Bedford Forrest has captured Murfreesboro! George tapped it out.

A tremendous bolt of lightning interrupted the communications. "Even the Man Upstairs had to put a stop to it." Morgan laughed. "Come on, George, pack up your box of tricks. We've got an all-night march ahead of us." When the men heard this story they started calling Ellsworth "Lightning."

They were drenched and waited for the worst of the storm to pass, then started out in the blackest night they could remember. "One advantage," breathed Tom. "Nobody else will be out here looking for us!"

They marched to a farm within fifteen miles of Lebanon before noon. Morgan was determined that Lebanon, Kentucky, would not be another Lebanon, Tennessee. Pickets were on each road, vedettes beyond them, scouts in a vast circle across the countryside. He ordered a halt and sent John Allen with Company B to destroy the railroad between Lebanon and

Lebanon Junction, on the way to Louisville, to prevent Federal movement from that direction and to make the enemy think his main force was headed west. While they waited for Allen's men to do their work, a detail captured the staunchest Union man in town for interrogation. As it turned out, it was the provost marshal.

"Why don't you just make a prisoner of him?" Captain Hutchinson asked.

"Hutch, you know as well as I do, that we would only have to come to terms with a fresh supply next time. This way, we leave a trail of 'understandings' behind."

"Next time! Atta boy! Did you see his face when he hesitated? I thought I would burst!"

Morgan chuckled. "They believe we kill prisoners."

"And even our own wounded. What monsters they think we are."

"That's because we don't leave our wounded behind."

"Whenever we can," said Basil soberly.

"Whenever we can."

It was midafternoon before they were on their way again, and almost sundown when they reached the Rolling Fork, six miles from Lebanon.

"God, have you ever seen a more beautiful valley?" asked Gano. He was riding with Morgan and his staff in front of the advance guard. Suddenly shots rang out just as they entered a covered bridge. Morgan's hat flew off.

"They're at the other end of the bridge!" hissed Basil.

Morgan ordered one of the howitzers brought up. A platoon of the leading company dismounted and brought it at the double-quick. One shell cleared the Federals at the other end, but also tore up a portion of the bridge, which had to be repaired—there was no ford for five or six miles. Another delay. And adding to the anxiety, on the other side of the river and commanding the bridge stood a bluff covered with timber. They fully expected a rain of bullets, but amazingly, when they crossed, the Federals were gone.

The enemy had regrouped within a mile of town, and St. Leger's "rope" was thrown out, in the form of Hutchinson's Company E and Bowles's Company C dashing headlong on foot, E Company's young lieutenants Gabe Alexander, W. S. Rogers and James Sale in the lead. The town, with two hundred prisoners, surrendered about ten o'clock.

There could be no relaxation of vigilance now; they were in the heart of Federal Kentucky, just east of Elizabethtown and south of Louisville. The excellent railroads that Morgan's grandfather had helped finance could move troops too quickly. Pickets were posted on every road and the whole command slept in line, ready for instant battle. For the second night in a row the sky was black. Lieutenant Bill Kennett from Company B returned with the news that they had just started to destroy the tracks when a troop train appeared from Louisville. There was a skirmish, but the train turned back.

"And the tracks?"

"They won't travel over that line for a few days."

Daylight revealed just how much they had captured in the Lebanon warehouses. There were enough guns to arm every man. One building was piled to the rafters with ammunition—cartridges, and even a supply for the howitzers. They destroyed what they couldn't carry and completely emptied a stone magazine, throwing the powder into the river. In a commissary large quantities of meat, flour, coffee and sugar were turned over to the people in the town. As for clothes, they found so much that whole platoons took turns going inside, stripping to the skin and returning completely outfitted. While they were busy, Gordon Niles distributed the flaming proclamation he had printed at Glasgow. But there was no need: News of Morgan had spread, and recruits came, and were hurriedly mustered in. One boy walked twenty miles. By early afternoon they were on the march again.

Overhead high cirrus clouds raced across a blue sky. Could it be true? Was he actually in Kentucky again, and getting closer by the mile to Lexington? To home? Red clover, blue chicory and the creamy-white Queen Anne's lace of July—yes, his heart sang, it was true!

And best of all, Kentucky knew he was home. All along the way the news had been the same: If an arc of flame traced the path of a torch flying end-over-end into a depot or a warehouse—it was Morgan. If a shot rang out, followed by a blood-chilling Rebel yell and thundering hoofbeats trailing off into the night—it was Morgan. If at a remote trestle a Yankee guard was silenced by an arm thrown around his neck and a soft whisper at his ear admonishing him not to move while he heard the heavy crack of crowbars breaking up the rails—it was Morgan. Sometimes it wasn't, but more often than not it was. The name took on magic as he passed through those towns, and his men knew it, in a kind of wild, inner pride that shone even through dust and fatigue. Southern sympathizers along the way gladly traded horses, even though compensation came in Confederate currency. "Don't worry. It'll be good soon. . . ."

They marched through Springfield without stopping. A few miles from Harrodsburg he called a halt. The sun was setting, and they would need rest and food for a night march. As high, scudding clouds caught the last light, first gold, then crimson and purple in the paling sky, the men built fires and roasted long strips of bacon on sharp sticks. Stale cornbread, hardtack and biscuits caught the dripping grease. He saw St. Leger accept some from Will and attack it with relish. The light faded, and still he did not give the order to move. The men were exhausted, and it seemed that this was as good a place as any for an hour's respite. The night was balmy, but he knew a heavy dew would soon be gathering, which would wet the ground but clear the air and make the night ride refreshing. They carried no tents. They were truly a "light" cavalry unit. Some captured shebangs appeared and were spread on the ground, but for the most part the men rolled back where they lay, arms over eyes, near their horses.

He ate his own soggy cornbread and thought he had never tasted anything so good. For the first time in his life he seemed to know himself, to have found himself, to be content with what he found and what he knew. For the first time in his life he ate because he was hungry and slept like a dead man because he was tired. But at the same time he had never felt as alert, so inwardly happy. And now Mattie was waiting in Murfreesboro! As he watched the angelic face of his brother Tom and, across the way, Basil slouched against a fence, he thought about his life. He had searched for this peace in so many things—in marriage with Becky, in playing paterfamilias for his mother's family, in business, in horse-racing, with Amanda. Nothing had worked, until now. It wasn't just the Cause, although he believed as fervently as T.H. that the Lincoln government was a tyranny. He would be here because these men were here, these his friends were here, because this was his country. These fields. It was as simple as that. And down that road in the now uncertain light of a half-moon lay Harrodsburg. Harrodsburg! It was only twenty-eight miles from home! Excitement choked him. He got up and walked to the fence where Basil had been leaning, pulling on a pipe.

"So you feel it, too?" said Basil, not turning. He blew a puff of smoke from him and it became a silver plume. "Will you try to get there?"

"Will you?" Morgan felt, rather than saw, his brother-in-law's grin. "Tommie will be surprised."

"Yes, she would, wouldn't she?" Basil knocked out his pipe and pushed against the top rail, bent his head and turned his face to Morgan. "That's why I won't go . . ."

"Won't?"

"Can you imagine how many damned Federals will be in that town? I wouldn't put your sister in such danger for anything . . . even the Cause."

"But a little night reconnaissance?"

"You sound like Tom! No, Johnny. Not this time. This is a little excursion to prove to Braxton Bragg that something bigger is feasible later, remember? Remember what General Smith—"

"Then let's be about it!" He laid a hand on Basil's shoulder. "Give the order to move."

They stopped again, just after sunup, to wash off in a creek. It was Sunday morning, and Harrodsburg was Southern to the hilt. Churchgoers would be on the street. "I want to march into town with a presentable little army—good for recruiting, you know!"

Basil said nothing, but St. Leger Grenfel winked. *"Morituri te salutamus,"* he said pompously, and bowed.

"Not if I have anything to do about it!" Morgan laughed, and found it hard not to giggle.

It was nine o'clock before the outskirts of town were reached. As the fours marched down the street women threw flowers. One rushed toward Morgan holding up a baby. "His name's Beauregard!" she exulted. "He's better-looking than the General, ma'am," Morgan said sincerely.

Their entry took on the aspect of a Roman triumph. There was an impromptu picnic; every house became a cornucopia flooding the astonished, laughing men with food. "Speech! Speech!" they yelled when they saw Morgan in the center. He climbed up on a parked wagon and looked out over their heads. "If the men of Kentucky had but the spirit of her women she would have long since been free!"

He descended to cheers. There was plenty of forage for the horses. Between gorging themselves, his men took naps under the trees, on porches, and in some cases even in houses, invited by admiring sympathizers. Re-

cruiting was brisk. When Morgan saw one boy, barely fifteen, riding double
behind a trooper, he lifted him from the horse and sent him home.

"Wait till I come again," he said kindly, to lessen the boy's disappointment.

Beyond Harrodsburg lay the heart of enemy territory, and St. Leger's
constant reminder of vigilance did not go unheeded. All bases were covered:
Gano was sent to circle to the north of Lexington and burn the bridges of
the Kentucky Central Railroad, to stop Federal reinforcements from Cincinnati. Will went with him. To keep the Yankees guessing, Morgan ordered
the column to march west toward Frankfort. Just after midnight, camp was
made at Lawrenceburg, where another Union provost marshal was captured
and lectured on the advisability of cooperation. At daybreak a scouting party
was sent to drive in the pickets on the Frankfort Pike, with orders to double
back and meet Morgan in Versailles.

Before the sun came up the men were saddled and ready, and the abrupt
swing to the right brought that burst of joy to his throat again. They were
bound for Shyrock's Ferry. And then, and then! They had marched more
than three hundred miles in eight days, but to watch the fours as they fell in
that morning you would never have known it. Blue sky overhead and a
skirmish with some Home Guards the night before only made the advance
guard trot out more jauntily than ever.

At the ferry they had a surprise. Maybe the Home Guards did it. The
boat was sunk. There was nothing to do but to raise and repair it. As he
waited, Morgan couldn't help remembering the night he had crossed here
with Bess. He wondered if the same old man ran things. There was no one
in sight. On the hill overlooking the river he could see his own pickets on
duty against the sky.

They didn't reach Versailles until almost sundown. But what a glorious
sundown! The great orange ball seemed to linger lovingly over the land.
They would, from this point on, have to maintain an iron discipline: Lexington was just over a dozen miles away. Already, he knew where they would
camp.

38

Warren Viley welcomed them with delight, although his face fell when he saw the horse Morgan tied to the fence.

"Where's Black Bess?"

A pang of guilt cut through Morgan's joy at seeing Warren's kind face. He told him the story as painlessly as he could.

"I'd planned on seeing her again," Viley murmured, fell silent, then looked up with a wan smile. "But . . . who knows, maybe one day we will get her back. Strange things happen in war!"

He couldn't tell him it was hopeless. Instead, he asked if his men could camp, and for an hour the preparations and introductions took Viley's mind off his loss.

"And the news from town?" Morgan asked, when they returned to the house.

"I don't get into town much."

He had to press him, and it came out: The factory had been confiscated, and was running again "under new management." Well, he'd expected that. "And the Leestown farm?"

"They haven't touched that. I imagine your uncle Dick was a help there. Although . . ."

"Although?"

Warren Viley took a deep breath and looked past Morgan's head. Without letting his eyes waver he said evenly: "The Federals have ignored all efforts to release Cal."

"You know where he is?"

Viley shook his head. He looked again at Morgan. "They've rounded up all the best horses in the Bluegrass. They've taken Miss Lexington. And her filly."

Morgan was silent. "Ma?"

Viley smiled wanly. "Your mother is more than a match for any Yankee. But I imagine . . . if you really want news . . ." He motioned to a servant to replenish the gentlemen's glasses, and John Morgan caught his meaning. Yes, it would be possible to ride over to Amanda's tonight.

"As a matter of fact, I do have a spare Federal overcoat." He smiled as he raised his glass to Viley's toast.

The crenelated towers of Amanda's "Italianate" house shone in the light of the half-moon. He wondered what it would be like to see her again or, indeed, if he could see her. It was late by the time he tied his horse to the post in the drive. He fully intended to go to the back door, but now that he was here something in him made that seem indecent, almost cowardly. He strode up the front steps as if it were broad daylight and he was merely paying a call. The elderly manservant met him and without a word motioned him into the "ballroom." He sat in one of the wing chairs flanking the little marble table. The servant lit a candle and left it on the mantel. When Morgan heard someone coming he snuffed it and stood close to the curtain by the window, letting his eyes get used to the dark.

Across a shaft of moonlight he saw her before she noticed him. She was in a long, filmy dressing gown, her red hair tumbling across her shoulders. From her agitation—she must have guessed who the visitor was—he knew Jake must be upstairs.

"Johnny! You—"

"I know. I shouldn't be here. Thought you might enjoy a neighborly visit."

In the thin light she could see his grin. "Is Paw with you? I got a note from Huntsville. . . ."

"Yes. He is fine. On his way north of here, with some Texans, to burn bridges."

"He'll like that." She giggled nervously. "And you?"

"Fine."

A mixture of regret and wonder, not untinged with nostalgia, overcame him. The warmth of her had once been such a refuge. Now caution, that alert--but-dead-center calm that sent all his senses to his nerve ends, intervened.

There must have been something in his answer that told her of Mattie. She became formal, giving him information, as if knowing that was why he came. She told him that Lexington was swarming with Yankees, a regular garrison, at least four thousand stationed out by the trotting track, just north of the Versailles Road. His factory was gone, his horses. Jake, in the role of labor quartermaster for the Feds, had started "recruiting" slaves of Southern sympathizers—not exactly confiscation (they still don't want to stir up Kentucky)—but to get free labor at their camps.

There was no bitterness in her voice, only acceptance. As she had, by now, accepted Jake? She took the two steps to the window and laid a hand on the drape. As she held it her knuckles made four little knobs on the back of her hand, like a child's. He had watched those hands, once so red and cracked from washing. Everybody had a right to try.

"And you? Are you fine?"

The knuckles turned white; then, as she let go, the fingers reached for his hand. She laid her cheek against his. There was no kiss; just that pressure of her cheek against his. It was the saddest gesture of his life.

He collapsed into Warren Viley's soft bed. Warren himself woke him the next morning. It was after seven. He jumped up as if he had been shot.

"It's all right," Viley laughed. "Everything's under control. Your men are in excellent hands—and I might say spirits. Colonel Duke and Major Wash thought they needed a rest. They're out there now. Major Niles also. Meanwhile, I want you to enjoy a good breakfast."

As if to confirm Viley's enthusiasm a delegation from Versailles rode up, prominent Southern sympathizers of the town. Basil and Niles came back from the barn, and the Viley servants served coffee on the deep porch facing the front lawn. The spokesman was a man Morgan had done business with before the war. He had pale red hair and freckles to match, which gave his face a mottled look. His suit was freshly pressed, and his polished shoes caught the light as he crossed his legs and balanced a cup on his knee.

"Yessir, Colonel Morgan, we are pleased to see you," he said vaguely.

"I imagine, sir, you have brought recruits?" Morgan asked affably.

The man cleared his throat and looked at one of his companions through heavy eyebrows. The other man sat straighter and pulled at one porkchop whisker. The third man, standing, stepped forward and said nervously, "It's about the election in August, sir."

"What about it?" Morgan looked back at the first man, who uncrossed his legs and carefully set his cup down. "Well, sir?"

"The plain fact is, Colonel Morgan, we have come to beg you to leave the state. . . ."

"Wh—"

"As rapidly as possible," the man standing went on in a rush. "Your presence now will utterly ruin our chances in the election, if it has not already done so. . . . The fear and panic this raid has . . ."

Morgan took his time getting to his feet. He felt the pull on his spine as he stretched himself to his full height. Now he knew what the first man's hair reminded him of: Tennessee dust. The dust that rose from a line of horses on the march, that stung your eyes and stuck your tongue to the roof of your mouth. The dust that turned to mud and covered graves.

"Gentlemen, I came into this state on your invitation—from hundreds of men such as yourselves. You promised me that the flower of the state would join me to save this country from tyranny. Now you ask me to leave. Gentlemen, you may represent the 'Secesh' of Woodford County, but you are not Kentucky! You are not the brave men who will save their homes from the invader. They are here, I tell you, and they will find me! They will find my presence welcome enough, I assure you! And you may thank the rules of hospitality that I cannot give you the exit you deserve!"

After they left, fumbling and embarrassed, a scout rode up, saluting his colonel smartly. "Pickets report complete confusion, sir! The Federals think you are on your way to Frankfort, or Lexington, or both! Home Guards running in both directions!" The boy was out of breath, and Morgan smiled.

"You see, Basil? We'll do it! We'll win Kentucky for Kirby Smith. And Sidney Johnston! By God, we'll do it!" He looked past Gordon Niles at the long shadows on the grass.

But he knew his time was short. The scouting parties dispatched toward Frankfort returned; now the Federals would know no concentration was being made in that direction. Enemy communication with Lexington was still open and clear; the possibility of a joint attack was real. His only hope was that Company B had put enough scare into Louisville to keep Jerry Boyle's Yankees from venturing out. Tom Quirk reported the Feds were "in a state of terror . . . Begorra!"

It was ten o'clock before the column moved toward Georgetown. Their immediate destination was the little town of Midway, called so because it stood equidistant between Lexington and Frankfort. It was on the railroad, but safe enough, with a network of roads leading in four directions. Most important, it had a telegraph office, and he needed desperately to know what the Yankees were doing, and to interfere with that communication. When they arrived he walked toward the depot with George Ellsworth. In the July heat the operator was lounging on the platform in front of his office. George, somewhat abruptly, asked him to call Lexington for the exact time.

"The time?" The man reached for his pocket watch. "I . . ."

"I need to know the *exact* time," George growled, with those scowling eyebrows.

"We hear that the horse thief, Morgan, is in the vicinity, and it's important," added Morgan.

"Yes, sir!"

They followed the little man into his office, where George studied his style of handling the key. When the time was duly given, Morgan put a pistol to the man's head and introduced himself.

George rummaged through the man's desk and found what he was looking for, a little signal book, with the calls for all the offices. The wire was fairly jumping with dispatches going back and forth from Louisville, Lexington, Georgetown, Paris and Frankfort, all containing references to Morgan. General Jeremiah Boyle at Louisville had increased his force from five thousand to ten thousand and asked Mayor Hatch of Cincinnati for artillery and men "by special train without delay." But Cincinnati, too, was by this time in a panic, and Lincoln telegraphed Halleck in Corinth: "They are having a stampede in Kentucky. Please look to it."

"This is it!" Ellsworth came as close to exulting as Morgan had ever seen him. He flipped through the book, then discovered that there were two wires on the line. One was a "through" wire, from Lexington to Frankfort; the other connected the smaller stations. It was soon obvious that all military messages were going over the first, which did not enter the Midway office.

"What are you doing?"

"I'm sending a man to cut that line." Ellsworth shot his colonel a look that passed for a grin. "Be back in a minute."

When he returned he announced quietly, "Now Lexington has to come through Midway." He sat down and manipulated some wires. "There!" he breathed. "I thought as much. When I apply the ground wire it makes no difference with the circuit—I can cut Frankfort off! We, *mon capitain*, will be Frankfort!"

Almost before he stopped chuckling, Lexington came on the line.

LEXINGTON, JULY 15, 1862

TO J. W. WOOLUMS, OPERATOR, MIDWAY:

WILL THERE BE ANY DANGER IN COMING TO MIDWAY? IS EVERYTHING RIGHT?

TAYLOR

The Cincinnati operator then called Frankfort. Ellsworth answered with a tall tale that Morgan, with ten thousand men, was already crossing the Ohio and a move against Cincinnati was imminent. Just as he signed off, Lexington sent a message to Frankfort which wiped the smile from their faces.

> LEXINGTON, JULY 15, 1862
> TO GENERAL FINNELL, FRANKFORT:
>   I WISH YOU TO MOVE THE FORCES AT FRANKFORT, ON THE LINE OF THE LEXINGTON RAILROAD, IMMEDIATELY, AND HAVE THE CARS FOLLOW AND TAKE THEM UP AS SOON AS POSSIBLE. FURTHER ORDERS WILL AWAIT THEM AT MIDWAY. I WILL, IN THREE OR FOUR HOURS, MOVE FORWARD ON THE GEORGETOWN PIKE; WILL HAVE MOST OF MY MEN MOUNTED. MORGAN LEFT VERSAILLES THIS MORNING WITH EIGHT HUNDRED AND FIFTY MEN, ON THE MIDWAY ROAD, MOVING IN THE DIRECTION OF GEORGETOWN.
>   BRIGADIER-GENERAL WARD

"Damn!" yelled Ellsworth. "They know everything!"

Morgan handed him the pistol and leaned over the table, scribbling. Without a word he exchanged the paper for the gun and resumed his vigil over the operator. Ellsworth grinned. "This should do it," he said.

> MIDWAY, JULY 15, 1862
> TO BRIGADIER-GENERAL WARD, LEXINGTON:
>   MORGAN, WITH UPWARD OF ONE THOUSAND MEN, CAME WITHIN A MILE OF HERE, AND TOOK THE OLD FRANKFORT ROAD, MARCHING, WE SUPPOSE, FOR FRANKFORT. THIS IS RELIABLE.
>   WOOLUMS—OPERATOR

They lounged, lit cigars, and waited. Then minutes later the instrument started jumping again.

> LEXINGTON, JULY 15, 1862
> TO GENERAL FINNELL, FRANKFORT:
>   MORGAN, WITH MORE THAN ONE THOUSAND MEN, CAME WITHIN A MILE OF MIDWAY AND TOOK THE OLD FRANKFORT ROAD. THIS DISPATCH RECEIVED FROM MIDWAY, AND IS RELIABLE. THE REGIMENT FROM FRANKFORT HAD BETTER BE RECALLED.
>   BRIGADIER-GENERAL WARD

"Whew!" Ellsworth took out a handkerchief and wiped his eyes. "That was too close for comfort!"

"Now Frankfort needs to be attacked," grinned Morgan.

Ellsworth groaned. "I don't know the operator's name in Frankfort! They're sure to be onto me if I . . ." He snapped his fingers. "I think I have it!"

He waited until the lines were busy, then broke in as if he were in Frankfort and greatly agitated—agitated enough to forgo signing his name.

FRANKFORT TO LEXINGTON:

TELL GENERAL WARD OUR PICKETS ARE JUST DRIVEN IN. GREAT EXCITE-
MENT. PICKETS SAY THE FORCE OF ENEMY MUST BE TWO THOUSAND.

OPERATOR

Morgan looked at the wall clock. It was almost two in the afternoon; if
they were to make Georgetown by sundown they had to move. He waited
while Ellsworth went outside to make a ground connection, leaving the
circuit open on the Lexington end.

"That will let them believe that the Frankfort operator has skedaddled
. . . that the infamous Morgan has destroyed the telegraph," he said when
he came back. "And we won't tell them differently, will we, now?" he asked
the operator, still cowering under Morgan's pistol. "Or we'll come back and
make a proper Yankee of you!"

On the way to Georgetown scouts were sent to destroy any trains from
Lexington or Frankfort, but the tracks were quiet: Ellsworth's trick had
worked. Morgan settled down with his staff at the head of the column to
enjoy the countryside. This spring's crop of foals were nursing in the fields,
their dams' heads nuzzling and cropping grass. Miss Lexington's filly would
be about that size. He hoped they wouldn't wean her too soon. . . .

Georgetown would be ideal. He could give his men a rest there. Twelve
miles north of Lexington, twenty east of Frankfort, with Southern sympathizers and good roads in all directions, it was made to order. Only a small
force of Home Guards occupied the town, and these were, as Wash said,
"easily cared for." As they rode down the last long hill toward the courthouse, they saw a figure leaning halfway out a window and calling at the top
of his voice: "See here, yew yeller bellies! See yore flag yonder? Air you
gonna desert it? Ain't yew got no disCIPlin'?"

Then the man waxed poetical, in a good imitation of a politician at
a barbecue: "Remain, an' perform thuh pleasin' dooty of dyin' under its
GLORious folds, an' afford us the AGREEable spectacle that you will thus
PREsent!"

Morgan looked at Basil, Basil at Wash, Wash at Gordon Niles, Niles at
St. Leger, and St. Leger back at Will, who was now leaning so far into the
air that he almost fell.

"Captured by them homely guards!" Will spit in disgust. When he saw
the last of the "homespun Yankees" chased up the street, his head disappeared and emerged, a little frayed but none the worse for wear, on the
sidewalk.

"Colonel Gano?"

"Oh, I think he cut thet railroad off, all right. At least, he wuz headed in
thet direction when . . . yew shoulda heerd those Kentucky Yankees, tryin'
to whup up fear! Tole them wimmen an' chillun thet Morgan's men left a
trail of smokin' towns an' wailin' widders. But," he added with a grin and
poked Johnny Morgan in the ribs as he used to after a good horse story,
"they think you've got ten er twelve thousand men with yew, all armed with
long beards an' butcher knives!"

Even before the men fell at ease Ellsworth was busy at the telegraph and ran out of the office yelling like a madman. Forrest *had* taken Murfreesboro! They had been downright prophetic!

Mattie. Mattie was free! His heart lifted. He would take every precaution. This raid had to be a success. He sent Captain Hamilton's Tennesseans to Stamping Ground, thirteen miles northwest, to scatter a Home Guard unit, and more detachments back to Midway to disrupt troop movements from Frankfort. John Castleman's Company D would destroy the bridges on the Kentucky Central between Lexington and Paris, then return to Georgetown for further orders. As an added precaution, and to keep St. Leger happy, he had the men remain in line of battle day and night.

And Lexington? he asked himself, looking at the map he had spread on the long hall table. He was in the house of a Georgetown citizen who had gone through the motions of having his smokehouse "impressed"—so he could say, afterwards, that he had given nothing of his own free will. His wife, less cautious, sent servants scurrying, until all the staff were not only comfortable but stuffing themselves. All afternoon Gordon Niles had been busy printing recruiting posters. A dozen miles away Lexington lay behind its stockade, a veritable garrison. Morgan looked up at a small white cloud drifting over the town. It was drifting south.

"You can't be serious." Basil Duke's square jaw twitched.

"I am. Some of the men are 'delivering' recruiting posters. Don't you want to come with me?"

"It would be bad enough if the command lost one leader. Why risk two? It's insane."

"That's precisely my point. It's so insane they'll never suspect. . . ."

"Promise me one thing."

"Anything. Almost."

"You'll give that little sister of yours the biggest kiss east of the Mississippi."

"Why not west also?"

"And be damned careful."

If he could take Lexington, Basil could kiss his bride himself. The need and the hope of that meeting was in Basil's handclasp as he left him. He dressed hurriedly, thankful for the hot water and fresh towels his host sent up. He took his last clean shirt from his saddlebag and spread it on the bed. He'd been so long on a horse he felt like a centaur. As he scrubbed down, dipping and squeezing the sponge, his excitement grew. To see Hopemont again! It would be too good to be true. . . .

To avoid suspicion, he separated from the handful of men making their way into Lexington to deliver the posters—in reality, to see relatives and girlfriends. He let them go ahead, then trotted down the Georgetown Road, aglow in the moonlight. To avoid the tollgate he took Iron Works Pike east at Donerail. Ahead, Iron Works crossed Newtown Pike, and just beyond lay the great lawns of Castleton. Now young Breck Castleman, who had left all this to join him, was on his way to destroy a railroad. That world, the trees said as they leaned overhead, is gone. That world, the stone fences echoed, is deep beneath your feet and in your soul and cannot die.

Did he dare turn down Newtown Pike, one of the main roads into town? He continued on Iron Works, past Castleton to Russell Cave. Heavy heads of phlox waved purple-pink blooms at the edge of fields and the shadows of trees lay thick across the road, the candle-like moonlight dusting the limestone with a pale glow. When he turned south onto Russell Cave he was four miles from home.

He strained to hear any gunshots from his left, where the Paris Pike swung northeast, and where Castleman and Company D would be busy burning bridges. He bowed gallantly to an elderly couple in a carriage, then stopped his horse to look back. On the horizon two orange lights billowed smoke. Company D had done its work well.

He legged his horse into a trot, then sat deep, gave it its head and cantered to within a mile of Broadway. There he lapsed into a casual walk; a lathered animal would draw attention. As nonchalantly as he could, with his breath short, he let the horse amble left into Third Street toward Transy, the picture of a Federal officer paying a social visit.

With a beating heart he turned into North Mill. Just before he got to the Gratz house he heard it: the unmistakable, collective hoofbeat of a column of cavalry behind him. He kicked his horse into a gallop, but not before he heard the shout, the clank of sabers. He sped past Hopemont and turned the corner into Second Street so fast the horse almost slipped. Into the carriage yard, over the low hedge—he had no idea of his destination until he stopped in front of the garden door that led into the stairwell. He slid off, prayed it wouldn't be locked, and it wasn't. He led the horse through the door and sank breathless on the bottom step of the curving stairs. He hardly had time to catch his breath before he heard a pounding on the front door. Quickly, he closed the door to the entry hall and stood paralyzed while he heard Tommie sincerely and then his mother imperiously assure the Federal officer that her son was not in Lexington to her knowledge and certainly not in this house. He could search if he liked. . . .

The horse shifted, swinging its hind hooves smartly against the floor boards. A nervous gelding, he might neigh! Morgan caught up the bridle and gave it a jerk, then patted the horse's neck in long, smooth strokes, holding his breath until his throat hurt. The Federals, not satisfied, had walked into the hall; he could hear their swords against their leather boots. There was a moment of hesitation, and a voice he recognized as Key's asking a question, and then his mother's again, only this time more strident, and the closing of the door, the shuffling sound of men mounting, and the movement of horses away. He cracked the door and whispered: "Ma!"

They were on him in an instant, until the little stairwell was full of horse, crinolines, servants, and a sixteen-year-old boy holding up a candle in disbelief. "A horse!"

"Well, it's not an elephant," Tommie said emphatically. "Put out that candle! Do you want the Yankees coming back?"

Henrietta took charge. "Adam, stay here with the horse. Keep him quiet at all costs. I'll send some corn. Let's go through the parlor. Keep to the garden windows. To the warming room."

"Why are you whispering, Mama?" Tommie giggled. "They aren't back yet!" Her brown curls stood like upright springs on either side of her round, shining cheeks. She hadn't let go her brother's hand since she first saw him. And Basil? her eyes asked.

"Lieutenant-Colonel Duke is fine."

"A colonel!"

"And you, Brother Johnny?" Key mopped his head with one hand, to smooth his hair.

"A colonel, too." Morgan grinned.

He followed them through the parlor, downstairs bedroom and back hall to the warming room, where Aunt Betty waited with hot coffee.

"Cal?" His eyes went to his mother. "Tell me about Cal, Ma."

"They arrested him right away after you left," Tommie answered for her. "Of course he wouldn't take their oath! Or give bond!"

Morgan kept his eyes on his mother's face.

"What did they expect?" she said with pride. "To buy a Morgan's loyalty?"

"The going price is five hundred dollars," Tommie ran on. "One man in Louisville actually gave them ten thousand! Can you imagine? You don't even have to sign anything—they have the papers already made out. . . ."

"No oath required," Key put in. "If you're willing to pay."

"Oh, they're doing a brisk business," his mother said bitterly. "They call it 'the patriotic office.' When Cal refused, they kept him three days in the county jail, then sent him to Cincinnati. For a while we didn't know . . . now, just this week, we've learned he's in a hotel in New York, where they keep 'political' prisoners." *I wish we could tell you more*, her eyes ended. She lifted her shoulders. "We have a lot to thank Dick Curd for. He maneuvered the transfer."

"Seems as if Uncle Dick has been busy lately. You know about Basil?"

"I do." Then his mother flashed her dazzling smile. "Who do you think sent Dick down there?"

Aunt Betty, Annie and Aunt Hannah brought fresh bread, cheese, cold turkey, ham and wine. Morgan wolfed them down under a shower of questions. When he had satisfied them that he was fine, that Tom was fine, that he'd heard from Richard and Kitty and that the baby was well, the question he feared came.

"And Charlton?"

"You didn't get my letter?"

Tommie laughed harshly. "They let no letters through. The damned Yankees!"

"Henrietta! Such language!"

"Well, it's true, Mama. . . ."

He told them.

"Do you know where he is? Is there hope of exchange?"

"We suspect he's at Fort Warren."

"And the exchange?"

"There is hope." Then he told Annie about Jesse. Which led to a full account of the "Races," Colonel Wood and Major Coffee.

"Imagine a Federal coming back to you through the lines because his commanding officer wouldn't honor his parole!" murmured Key.

A high, trembling neigh interrupted him. "I'll get that corn," he said. When he returned he began at once to beg to go back with Johnny. "If Tom can go, I can," he pouted. "I'm as good a shot. . . ."

Morgan reached out to the boy's shoulder. "I'll get you next time," he said. "That's a promise."

"Next time?"

"Yes, Tommie. And next time will be the big time. I can't tell you more. . . ."

"You can't be too soon," his sister said.

"What does that mean?"

They told him about Lexington, Tommie, Key, his mother, Aunt Betty each adding a word. Martial law . . . passes required. No people on the streets after four o'clock . . . taverns closed.

"Taverns closed! I'll bet Uncle Robert doesn't like that!"

"And you've been indicted for treason!" Key announced proudly.

His mother gave him a look but Tommie took it up like a litany. The Yankee traders who swarmed after their army like the locusts of Egypt. The empty stores, and even houses, sold at auction . . . or awarded to favorites under the Abandoned Property Act. Young Richard Curd had joined the Confederate Army in Virginia.

"How did Uncle Dick take it?"

"Dick is . . . philosophical," his mother answered.

"And Uncle Robert . . . without those taverns to keep him busy?"

"Still up to his ole tricks, yo' uncle Robert is," Aunt Hannah put in. She had been standing behind Tommie's chair and dipped her head in a chuckle.

"Robert has devised a method of sending quinine South," Henrietta clipped out, barely able to suppress the smile that tugged at her mouth.

". . . In the bellies of daid cows an' sech, sewed up agin. . . ." Annie ventured.

"And Randolph?"

"The farm is fine."

Something in her son's look made Henrietta add: "Now I won't have you even thinking about going near the place. There is no sense tempting fate. There are five thousand Federals camped at the trotting track . . . they crowd the streets, the roads. They are watching every house. . . ."

"And Randolph?" he insisted.

"Randolph bes fine, Massa," Aunt Betty answered softly.

"They—or rather their Union-sympathizing Kentucky henchmen—tried to confiscate his family as free labor, until Dick stepped in. He's on to all their tricks. . . ."

The unmistakable sound of horses' hooves from the direction of the carriage yard stopped her.

"Them! It's them!" Key hissed.

Like a general, Henrietta took charge. There would be no chance, now, of returning through the parlor. They could see him through the garden windows. He would have to go up the back stairs, cross through the bedrooms, then down the spiral stairs to reach the horse. Even as his mother hesitated, the sound of Yankee voices rose sharply, impudently. Without a word she motioned her son to the back entry, and he understood. For a second, she stood in the doorway of the warming room, her dress filling the space, her eyes, brilliant with worry, on his. He stepped toward her to take her in his arms but she took him instead, pushing his head onto her shoulder, like a child. No words came, but a soft groan as she made a little rocking motion with her body before she let him go. Immediately, even before he reached the landing and ran through the upper hall past the bedroom, he heard her calling brightly to her visitors, inviting them to search the house if they needed to, but to please spare her flower beds unnecessary trampling. He spun down the stairs, took the reins from a thoroughly frightened Adam, who opened the garden door and watched his master leap the fence into North Mill and race up the hill toward Transy just as the Yankees in the carriage yard jumped back on their horses and galloped after him.

They were fast, but he had a two-block lead, and once across Broadway he knew too many back lanes to allow capture. Still, he heard them behind him, and didn't lose them entirely until he crossed Newtown Pike and cut cross-country. The moon was gone but he could have found his way blindfolded. When he reached Cane Run he led the horse directly into the creek, and followed its course to the east of Donerail until it crossed the Georgetown Road. Just before the road, which he had left well served by pickets, he let the horse have a leisurely drink, then rode the rest of the way into Georgetown in safety.

Reluctantly, now, he knew it would be impossible to take Lexington with the force he had. It was well past midnight—he guessed about two o'clock—when his host let him in and he pulled off his boots and lay back on the bed. Too tired to undress and too excited to sleep, he lay on top of the covers with his head cupped in his hands and stared at the ceiling flickering in the light of a single candle. On the plaster he began drawing with his mind a map of Kentucky.

He knew he would be safe in Georgetown—as long as the Yankees believed he had ten thousand men. A little artistry from Ellsworth could keep that up for a while longer. Gano to the north, Company B toward Frankfort, Captain Hamilton northwest at Stamping Ground, and now Castleman's Company D east to Paris—that would keep them guessing. Only a force of at least ten thousand would risk splitting apart like that in enemy territory. Little did they know his main column was now dangerously depleted. Tomorrow—tomorrow serious recruiting. All day. He could see it: Alston would get his company! They were in the Southern-sympathizing Bluegrass. He would prove to Braxton Bragg that Kentucky could rally. He wouldn't let Kirby Smith down.

The candle wavered and the map emerged again. So now, if not Lexington? His eyes drifted northeast. Cynthiana, on the Kentucky Central, thirty-two miles north of Lexington and only about twenty-two from Georgetown. If he moved against Cynthiana, the Yankees would think he was preparing to attack Cincinnati; at the same time, if he sent a small force to drive in the Lexington pickets they would think he was moving there . . . meanwhile, Cynthiana would afford him at least three escape routes, the best due south, then southeast to Paris and Winchester. From there he could cross the Kentucky River, march to Richmond and . . . He blew out the candle and went to sleep.

St. Leger was delighted with the plan. Georgetown that day was a bee-hive. At the college the whole ground floor of Giddings Hall was converted into a recruiting center. By noon W. C. P. Breckinridge, a young lawyer from Lexington, ran the blockade with twenty followers, and within an hour a full company was raised, with Breckinridge elected captain. Before sun-down men came from the surrounding counties, and Alston had his company and his captaincy. Gordon Niles and the staff were busy all day with muster rolls. Company A was still the favorite, but it was already, since the recruiting in Chattanooga, past capacity. Companies B and D were away, so it became a rivalry between James Bowles's Company C and John Hutchinson's Company E, which added fifty-four names. Webber's Company F, formed in May and mostly Mississippian, and McFarland's "Alabama" Company G (also "old-timers" with two months' service) were less popular. It seemed, joked St. Leger, that States' Rights was carried down to the barracks. But it was a friendly rivalry, and the men were in good spirits.

Gano and Allen came in just after dark, their missions completed. Morgan called in Dick McCann. "Get the best three advance guards you know and give them each this message, to be delivered to General Smith at Knoxville by different routes." There was such elation in his voice that McCann laughed out loud. He had been a captain in the infantry, but found it too slow for him, and had joined the squadron that summer. He was a crack scout, famous for his moonlight exploits around Nashville, where not a few Federals and Union sympathizers found themselves escorted into Confederate camps with their information. He stood respectfully to one side as Morgan penned his message to Kirby Smith in the circle made by a coal oil lamp. Morgan didn't even try to keep the grin from his face as he wrote the words: *Expedition successful. Kentucky is with us. 25,000 to 30,000 men will join you at once. I have taken eleven towns with heavy army stores.*

Then, as an afterthought he added, letting his pen sweep with a flourish: *Arrange that meeting. Col. Jno. H. Morgan, 2nd Ky. Cav., Commanding. July 16, 1862.*

Gordon Niles came in just as Dick was leaving. He returned McCann's salute and took a chair by the table. At forty-four his hair had turned salt-and-pepper, and he'd grown some side-whiskers that made him look like a distracted schoolteacher. But his eyes were as bright and as inquisitive as

ever, and his enthusiasm for writing broadsides and recruiting posters was
endless. Niles was gratified to see his colonel in such a good mood, but kept
his surprise to himself as Morgan repeated the message. Twenty-five thousand recruits were a bit much to hope for. It was one thing to exaggerate in
a broadside; it was another to promise a general thousands of men you had
no means of delivering! Still, maybe Morgan was right. Maybe he could.
His colonel wanted so damned much to believe, to will this war won. The
garden at Hopemont came back, that hospitality he would never forget. He
had shared Morgan's love for this land the first time he'd seen it. But he had
also seen those politicians at Viley's farm. They had been sent away like
whipped pups, and everybody had chuckled. But their words stuck with
him. They had asked Morgan to leave the state, and they were Secesh! He'd
talked to Basil about it, and found to his surprise that Basil felt protective,
too. Were they protecting Morgan from himself? Then he remembered why
he had come.

"There's someone to see you."

"Another recruit? You'll recruit the whole state if you're not careful!"

Niles walked to the door and said quietly, "You can come in now."

It was Randolph. Behind him a boy of thirteen rolled his eyes at the high
ceilings and unfamiliar surroundings of such a big schoolhouse. When he
saw Morgan watching him, he looked down and shuffled his feet.

"Well, sit down, sit down!"

But Randolph declined. Instead, he shifted his cap in his hands and said
how glad they all were to see him.

"You've been to town?"

"Yassuh."

"Then you know about Jesse. I believe they'll let him go. He's not in
uniform. They've probably released him in the Murfreesboro area. And
since it's in Confederate hands again, we'll find him."

Randolph was watching him carefully, as if from a long way away. That
handsome Masai head, those same thoughtful eyes. For an instant they were
boys again in the springhouse, on horseback across the fields, or watching
the shives sending long streamers of flame into an October sky. In that look
he knew the loss of Jesse was forgiven, and now the big brown hand maneuvered the reluctant shoulders of another boy forward, who looked exactly
like James at the same age. "Do you ride, too, Billy?" Morgan asked kindly.
When the boy shuffled his feet and didn't answer he added, "Your big
brother rode Miss Lexington in a race once. Did he tell you about that?"

"Yassuh." While the three men waited, grinning, he took courage and
looked at them. "I rode her too . . . all 'roun' de pashtuh. She kin go."

"Where is she going now?" he asked Randolph. "And James?"

Randolph let his eyes drop, then brought them back to Morgan's face.
"Dey put James on dere labuh force. But Marse Dick, he got him off. We
not been bothered since. De fahm iz fine."

"Do you know who took Miss Lexington?"

"Some Yankee cap'n out at de trottin' track got her."

"That would be Frank Wolford's outfit."

"Yassuh."

"Well, if he's from Kentucky she'll get good treatment. And the foal?"

"Ah dunno, Massa. . . ."

In the silence Morgan cleared his throat. He asked, as easily as he could, "Well, so you want to ride with the cavalry, do you, Billy? We'll have to see about getting you a uniform."

The boy ducked his head and sucked in his upper lip.

"I'll take care of him." Morgan turned to Randolph, who nodded instructions about being good. When he was offered a place for the night Randolph declined. He climbed aboard the mule he and Billy had ridden double on, waved once and swayed off, his broad shoulders as level as ever, his thighs and legs glued to the mule's sides. Faithful servant. Good friend. I'll see you again, and when I do it will be to free James forever of the fear of a labor gang, and you of losing any more sons to my stupidity, which you forgive and I cannot.

The Tennesseans at Stamping Ground and Castleman toward Paris were the only pieces of the net out now, but it was critical that their activity still draw attention. That next morning Tom Hines appeared, enthusiastic about his Copperheads, who had kept him informed about Morgan's progress across the state. He explained in detail to his colonel, Basil, and St. Leger over coffee and sandwiches that Chief Justice Bullitt, Grand Commander of the Knights of the Golden Circle, was ready to join in a conspiracy that would bring Kentucky into the Confederacy. On his way from Knoxville Hines had been bushwhacked, losing a horse shot from under him. He entertained them for a good two hours with tales of narrow escapes. Like the others Morgan was amused by all this cloak and dagger, but said nothing.

"They still believe in you, sir!" Tom Hines's blue eyes were blazing. "All this month, while you were marching north, they knew it! The Knights rode through towns in southern Illinois, cheering Jeff Davis and John Hunt Morgan! Everywhere I went I found people willing to help. . . ."

"Like those bushwhackers?" Basil joked, but nothing could dampen Hines's enthusiasm.

"I understand you had a little help from the ladies," Morgan said, referring to one narrow escape. "I am truly sorry about your parents."

"Well, we'll soon set things right." And again, there was that almost miraculous change in Hines's face. He became a sorrowful little boy again. It was a familiar enough story by now: the father of a Morgan man arrested, his mother left ill to be cared for by neighbors. When Hines tried to visit her a Union informer told the provost marshal and a Federal patrol almost caught him. Well, he was back, and in good spirits, and that was all that mattered. If he wanted to play spy, Morgan wouldn't interfere; there were many ways of fighting wars, he reminded himself. He was a little surprised at St. Leger, though; he would have thought intrigue would have been the last cup of tea for a man who loved cavalry charges. "He'll go far," the Englishman beamed. "If any of us survive this war, he will."

Just after dawn the scouts reported increased Federal activity in the direction of Lexington and Frankfort. "They are onto us," worried Basil.

"Not yet," Ellsworth grinned. "Do you realize you have just been joined by another two thousand men?"

"I wish that were so." Morgan looked past him at the recruits lining up for breakfast. Eager they might be, but armed they were not. "But I hope they believe it."

"They do."

"How much time do you figure?"

"You'll have the rest of today, and with vigilance, we can start in the morning."

"We'll need the rest of today to get Harrison and Castleman back."

"You'll do it."

Morgan looked at the slight Canadian, with his winning smile. He wished he had a thousand "Lightnings."

Will and Frank Leathers were in charge of the horses. Throughout the day some brisk trading went on with farmers who brought stock in from the surrounding counties—some as gifts, some to be exchanged. Rations for the rest of the march were cooked. By early afternoon Harrison's company returned from Stamping Ground, and Breck Castleman reported smartly, with that energetic salute and grin of his, that "all was well" at the railroad bridges near Paris.

"Are you tired?"

"Do I look it?"

"Your men?"

"Ready to go again!"

Morgan had never known a more competent soldier than young Castleman. He had a quiet, aristocratic manner about him that made attending to the slightest detail seem a favor asked rather than a command given. His men adored him. They were all his friends, boys who had fought their way out of Kentucky to "join Morgan" at Chattanooga.

"How would you like to make a scout into Lexington tonight, see how things are, and keep the Yankees busy, meet me in two or three days at Winchester?"

He needn't have asked.

"You will have to prevent a whole brigade of the United States Army from attacking us."

"I understand, sir."

Castleman had exactly eighty-two men. He would be completely isolated, and he would have to avoid taking prisoners while harassing the Federal garrison into thinking Morgan's whole command was involved. Without hesitation Castleman saluted, turned on his heel and marched off as if he had five thousand. He was Company D's captain, its senior officer. He was twenty-two.

God, how he loved them. God, how he couldn't fail. Before Castleman left he sent Tom Hines with him as a special scout. They would need all the sharpshooters they could get.

With Company D and one other detachment thrown out as bait, the main column left Georgetown the next morning for the twenty-two-mile march to Cynthiana. Scouts and sympathizers reported four hundred Federals of Metcalfe's cavalry regiment, with the same number of Home Guards, Lieutenant-Colonel Landrum, commanding, in the town. There was also a twelve-pounder howitzer manned by firemen from Cincinnati. "Firemen?" Hutch joked. "We'll give them a fire to put out!"

It was a lovely summer morning, the 18th of July. The road from Georgetown to Cynthiana swept by some of the best farmland in the state—woodland pastures and fields of an incredible green. Roadside trees rustled in the breeze. Just a short year ago he might have been riding with T.H. or his uncle Robert. Just a year ago, three days from now, Becky died.

The sun was strong, but a southwest wind kept enough cloud cover moving to prevent the heat exhaustion the horses had felt on the way to Glasgow. The strictest precautions, concerning scouting and picketing, were observed. A mile or two from Cynthiana the hills smoothed into a long plateau, then dropped into the broad floodplain of the Licking River. In the distance the level tops of trees marked the valley. The advance guard drove in the Federal pickets and captured four. The men had their orders; each squad knew what to do. A covered bridge over the river would meet them on this road, with the town of Cynthiana just on the other side. He knew that, beside the bridge, there was a ford waist-deep. Above and below the bridge, about a mile, other fords made an outflanking maneuver attractive. Just before the advance guard drove in the pickets he sent Gano above, the Georgians from Colonel Hunt's old regiment to the ford below, for encirclement. The brunt of the frontal attack would fall to the Second Kentucky.

As they crossed the open plain toward the bridge Companies A and B were deployed to the right of the road, E and F to the left, with C held in reserve, mounted: It was St. Leger's classic plan. The unarmed recruits were in the rear, promised captured arms once the town was taken. The howitzers were placed about three hundred and fifty yards from the bridge, and near the road.

Even before the "Bull Pups" were positioned, rifle fire began from the houses lining the river on the opposite bank. The Cincinnati firemen soon had the bridge, the road and the two howitzers in range of their twelve-pounder and began, as Basil remarked, some "pretty good target practice." On the left, Companies E and F ran to the river's edge and poured enough volleys across the narrow stretch of water to make the enemy on the opposite bank surrender, gladly obeying the orders shouted down by Hutch and Webber that their prisoners throw down their guns and swim over to be captured.

Company A, the veterans from Shiloh, were given the more difficult job of taking the covered bridge for a direct assault. On the town side a long warehouse provided excellent cover for Federal sharpshooters and Home Guards picking off the men as they approached. After three attempts Jake Cassell, leading A Company, abandoned the bridge altogether and ordered his men into the water. They plunged in, holding their guns high over their heads. The first man to reach the bank—Private William Craig, one of the "Woodsonville originals"—was killed instantly. The men behind him managed to crawl up the bank and use the warehouse as cover. But not for long: Now more Federals and Home Guardsmen appeared by the hundreds in adjacent yards and upstairs windows, pouring a murderous crossfire in a forty-yard range.

Morgan ordered the howitzers brought up, but the close fire drove the gunners back—all but a boy named Talbot, who loaded and fired alone, with balls striking his gun. The horse with the other gun, wounded and terrorized, ran into the river and up the opposite bank into a crowd of Home Guards. In the confusion, with Company A pinned down, Morgan raised his arm, and James Bowles with Company C charged across the bridge and up the main street on horseback. Company B, now entrenched on the river bank, were in a good position to clean out the sharpshooters whose fire had paralyzed Company A. Once Company A saw they were free, they made a dash. Little Private James Moore from Louisiana, not sixteen, fell with two wounds. Sergeant Tom Quirk, out of ammunition, saw in horror his buddy Ben Drake about to be shot and struck down the Union soldier with a stone.

Just now Gano appeared on one side and the Georgians on the other. Everybody swarmed over the twelve-pounder. The enemy were by now running as fast as they could, turning to fire and running again. St. Leger led a cavalry charge on the depot and picked up eleven bullets in his horse, his body and his clothes—but emerged laughing, twirling his little scarlet skullcap, perforated by balls. Company C chased the Federals for eight or ten miles on the road to Maysville and missed capturing Colonel Landrum only because he was riding a fast horse. Little Billy Peyton, Morgan's orderly, was the last to give up the chase, and "almost got him, sir." George Arnold, a member of the advance guard who had volunteered to make the charge with Company C, was not so lucky. He dropped from his horse, his thigh and arm broken, and would die of gangrene within the week. A boy named Clarke, eager, sweet-faced, who had jumped at the chance to deliver a message to Colonel Gano, was felled with five balls through his body. Company A lost so many officers that the command fell to one of its third lieutenants, Sam Morgan.

Four hundred and twenty prisoners were taken, and it wasn't until afternoon that the march could be resumed. About five miles outside Paris the advance was surprised by a delegation of citizens from the town offering surrender. Morgan's exhausted men reached the Paris town square about sundown and camped on the Winchester Road by a stream that ran over flat rocks in a beautiful, softly rising pasture. Here, before midnight, the scouts found them, with news that a force of three thousand Federals had left Lexington to intercept them. Against St. Leger's advice, Morgan left orders for saddling up at seven o'clock, after breakfast. "They've got to rest, Colonel," he said, ignoring the Englishman's grunts.

Just as St. Leger feared, as the sun traced first light across the pastures and before they could finish their coffee, three thousand Federals rode into Paris. Encumbered with wagons of wounded, Morgan's command—with less than eight hundred armed men—would have had a fight. But the Yankees moved cautiously and missed their chance. By noon the command was in Winchester, met by Castleman and Company D, with their own cavalry charge to tell.

"A skirmish at Mount Horeb Church, sir," Breck said breathlessly. "My horse astride my father's grave. Six of our dismounted sharpshooters across the road—Captain Hines—behind a fence. We didn't have to wait long."

"And?" Morgan suppressed a smile.

"We beat 'em, sir! Chased them back! Then cut telegraph poles and burned two bridges on the Kentucky Central. . . ."

As Castleman told his story Morgan couldn't help thinking how like some latter-day Sir Philip Sidney this gallant, handsome boy was. He represented for him everything he loved about the South—its manners, its breeding, and underneath its gentility, its guts. For such men he would go to hell and back. For such men the least he could do was win this war.

But there was, now, no time to lose. From what Castleman said, the Yankees had at last guessed his true strength. Not only were Federals from Lexington under General Clay Smith following him, but the scouts brought in reports that Frank Wolford was collecting forces to the south to form a "reception committee." From Paris, through Winchester and across the Kentucky River to Richmond—would they ever forget that march? The horses captured with the twelve-pounder at Cynthiana died of exhaustion before they reached the ferry, just before dark. As the sun set across the water, with a pink afterglow that lit the sky, they looked back as if they were leaving the Promised Land. "Never mind," Morgan whispered to himself as he saw their faces. "You'll come again." They reached Richmond, completely exhausted, at four in the morning.

"They have to rest," Basil insisted, and he reluctantly agreed. "They don't have your . . . drive."

"My insanity?" Morgan gave his brother-in-law that enigmatic half-smile. "Maybe they don't know Frank as well as I do. He's a damned fine soldier, and he'll bend every effort to intercept us. Besides, I've just had news that a force has left Louisville. . . ."

"That's convenient."

But Basil was already yawning, and Richmond was a thoroughly Southern town. They took their time the next day, recruiting a whole new company under Captain Jennings as Company K. "Enjoy your rest while you can," Morgan told his men. "When we start, we're going."

They left Richmond at four that afternoon, marched all night and reached Crab Orchard, by winding back roads, before daylight. All along the way, through the blackest night any of them could remember, bushwhackers made every step a nightmare. The scouts reported that they were led by a "Captain King," and Ellsworth, in a sudden fit of nervous reaction, vowed to capture him. With one of the scouts, he took Grenfel's horse, with his highly prized English saddle, and even more highly prized overcoat tied behind, containing the gold that St. Leger had arrived with from Virginia.

They located, soon enough, "Captain King's" house: a shanty perched on a slate-slippery hillside anchored by chained coon-dog houses and saturated with urine. They dismounted, marched through the stench and demanded

King's surrender. That worthy man answered with volleys, and in the retreat the scout was wounded and Ellsworth lost Grenfel's horse, English saddle, gold-laden overcoat and all. St. Leger would have killed him, and Morgan had to keep George concealed for the next three days of the march, listening to the old man's high-voiced accusations and denunciations of lax discipline all the way to Somerset, which they reached by sundown. St. Leger momentarily got his mind off his loss when he led a raiding party into a Federal commissary. With something of his old vigor and optimism he directed the loading of blankets, shoes, saddles, hams, coffee, flour and sugar onto captured wagons and the destruction of the rest. Ammunition for empty guns—even powder for the howitzers—was an added prize. While the men were busy, Ellsworth took possession of the telegraph office and wired Louisville, countermanding all of General Boyle's orders for pursuit. Morgan, on his way back to Tennessee and convinced that he had at least proved that an invasion—and more important, recruiting—was possible, felt festive enough to send some complimentary dispatches of his own to George Prentice, his adversary at *The Louisville Journal,* and to General Clay Smith, the Federal commander at Lexington. Ellsworth ended with an inspired flair:

> HEADQUARTERS, TELEGRAPH DEPT. OF KY.
> CONFEDERATE STATES OF AMERICA
> GENERAL ORDER NO. I
>   WHEN AN OPERATOR IS POSITIVELY INFORMED THAT THE ENEMY IS MARCHING ON HIS STATION, HE WILL IMMEDIATELY PROCEED TO DESTROY THE TELEGRAPHIC INSTRUMENTS AND ALL MATERIAL IN HIS CHARGE. SUCH INSTANCES OF CARELESSNESS, AS WERE EXHIBITED ON THE PART OF THE OPERATORS AT LEBANON, MIDWAY, AND GEORGETOWN, WILL BE SEVERELY DEALT WITH. BY ORDER OF
>
> G. A. ELLSWORTH,
> GENERAL MILITARY SUPT., C.S. TELEGRAPHIC DEPT.

Once across the Cumberland they felt safer, but their pace did not slow; counting detours to put bushwhackers off track, they made the last ninety miles into Sparta, Tennessee, in twenty-four hours. Morgan sent for Niles and handed him two telegrams, one to Braxton Bragg, the other to Kirby Smith. Niles saluted and went to find Ellsworth. In the telegraph office he leaned back wearily in a chair and watched the keys tick out under George's fingers:

> I LEFT KNOXVILLE ON THE 4TH DAY OF THIS MONTH, WITH ABOUT NINE HUNDRED MEN, AND RETURNED TO LIVINGSTON ON THE 28TH INST. WITH NEARLY TWELVE HUNDRED, HAVING BEEN ABSENT JUST TWENTY-FOUR DAYS, DURING WHICH TIME I HAVE TRAVELED OVER A THOUSAND MILES, CAPTURED SEVENTEEN TOWNS, DESTROYED ALL THE GOVERNMENT SUPPLIES AND ARMS IN THEM, DISPERSED ABOUT FIFTEEN HUNDRED HOME GUARDS AND PAROLED NEARLY TWELVE HUNDRED REGULAR TROOPS. I LOST

IN KILLED, WOUNDED AND MISSING OF THE NUMBER THAT I CARRIED INTO
KENTUCKY, ABOUT NINETY.

Niles looked past Ellsworth's bent head at first light misting with fog
against the window. It was true, every word of it. And that was the trouble.
They had recruited about three hundred men—not the thousands Morgan
had promised—and lost ninety. Kentucky had *not* arisen, like some sleeping
beauty waiting to be kissed. Three hundred recruits were hardly justification
for a larger invasion. Niles wondered what Kirby Smith would say. He
could just imagine Bragg's reaction. His orders were to wait for an answer.

He must have dozed, because the full sun shone through the window as
Ellsworth shook him. He looked down at the paper.

REPORT IMMEDIATELY MY HDQ. WE ARE READY TO MOVE. E. KIRBY SMITH.

He looked up at Ellsworth's noncommittal face. "He's as crazy as the
Colonel!" Niles blurted.

The Canadian lifted his eyebrows. "Who knows, this Kentucky may be
just crazy enough for both of them!"

———————————Part IV———————————

August 1862–May 1863

39

"**M**organ! Morgan, I knew you'd get here in time." Kirby Smith reached a long arm across his desk and nodded his visitor toward a chair. "The minute I got your report from Georgetown I telegraphed Richmond—also Bragg. By God, the time is ripe! I'm leaving tomorrow to meet Bragg at Chattanooga and it's imperative you be there . . . only this time you're traveling by train. After a good night's sleep, I'm sure that will be a welcome change."

"I've had no news. . . ."

"We know Buell's asked permission to abandon the railroad around Corinth for a move into East Tennessee. Bragg has got to move out of Tupelo before that happens. We've got to make him see that your ride into Kentucky can change everything. That it is possible to cut Buell off from his supply base. To cut him off from Louisville."

The implications of that "cut him off from Louisville" made Morgan's breath short. That meant nothing less than taking Kentucky! He forced himself to wait. Smith wasn't through.

"With Grant at Corinth, and Federal divisions west of the Mississippi, and with Buell still playing with that railroad—the Federals are divided. Now's the time to strike, before Buell can concentrate at Nashville. To talk Bragg into moving . . ." At Morgan's raised eyebrows Smith answered the silent question: "Forty-five thousand. Bragg has forty-five thousand. He could leave a mask at Tupelo, and from Chattanooga drive a wedge between Buell and the Gap. Then . . ."

In his excitement, Smith leaned forward. "Bragg could dash across the Cumberland, break through those scattered forces and take Nashville." He handed a paper across the desk. "I sent that to him four days ago, by special courier. He telegraphed this morning. He's willing to talk."

Smith's words sent a thrill of excitement through Morgan's fatigue.

"I've even offered to place my command under his, if that will help."

Morgan looked up from the paper.

"What are commands, after all?" Smith breathed. "If feeding one man's vanity will win this war . . . We've got to convince Bragg that we can gain Kentucky." He stopped, as if he were taking a plunge: "Take the war into Ohio and force a peace . . ."

Smith laughed out loud at the shock on Morgan's face. "Listen to me! My wife said I was always good at getting the cart before the horse. By the way, I forgot. Have you made arrangements for tonight?"

"No, sir."

"Use my rooms at the Bell House. If I get through here in time I'll meet you for dinner. . . . We can get an early start tomorrow."

Before he left headquarters Morgan stopped by the bulletin board, which posted the latest casualty lists. His eyes went first to Virginia. Richard, thank God, was all right, and A.P. Then as he was about to turn a name leaped out at him: Richard Curd, killed at the battle at Frazier's Farm.

Young Dick Curd. With that "Buena Vista hat" after Mexico. Tears misted his eyes.

The clerk at the desk of the Bell House recognized him, and he ordered hot water and towels. He shut the door of Smith's room and smoothed his uniform as best he could, stripped to the waist and scrubbed, promising himself a nap before supper. Young Dick Curd. He couldn't rest, but sat on the side of the bed feeling the excitement of his role in Kirby Smith's plans become a vindication for Dick's death. He flipped out a clean shirt and went downstairs.

The dining room was crowded and a waiter showed him to a small table by a window. As he weaved his way among the diners, nods and grins from people he didn't know told him that his raid had been a success, and he was recognized. As General Smith said before he left him, what other action was there in the West? Since Shiloh, there had been nothing but loss. Memphis, New Orleans. So, if the newspapers gave him undue notice, it was because they had no other success to print. The Yankee press used its own form of compliment: "the pimp of Southern chivalry."

He was looking at the menu card when a young girl, accompanied by a thin, dark man he took to be her husband, came over to the table.

"You are Colonel Morgan, aren't you?" She looked at him through a blond fringe of bang that parted in the middle to reveal a smooth forehead and provocative gray eyes. Her mouth wore a little line near one corner, as if she were used to drawing it back in a mocking smile. The way she tilted her sharp little chin and held her arms close to her sides—everything about her was provocative. She was the kind of girl, just short of brazen, who could invite without being improper. He felt a stab of desire. No wonder the poor fellow with her looked nervous.

"All the talk is of you, Colonel Morgan! They're calling you 'The Thunderbolt of the Confederacy!' "

"They are too flattering. . . ."

"How long will you be here? Are you staying at the Bell House?"

"Come, now, Lucy," the man with her said. "Can't you see . . ." He tugged at the lapels of his civilian suit and watched the ceiling in embarrassment.

It was unusual to see a man of his age out of uniform. Perhaps his health . . . Morgan was amused as Lucy chattered on, then took her companion in tow and flounced across the room. She was fully conscious of the impression she made. Several artillery officers at a nearby table winked as she passed. For such, he reminded himself soberly, is your fame.

The little train to Chattanooga, not to ruin the reputation of Southern railroads, broke down for a delay of two hours. It was almost ten o'clock that next night before General Kirby Smith and Colonel John Morgan were admitted into General Bragg's room in Chattanooga.

Bragg had already gone to bed and received them in his robe. It was cut too small at the bottom and he kept pulling it over his knobby knees. The hair above his ears stuck straight out, like his eyebrows. He was obviously sleepy, but he listened politely to Smith's description of Morgan's success. Bragg seemed impressed, although reluctantly.

Smith leaned forward. "If you'd rather not move your command into my department, I could use the mountain passes in East Tennessee, meet you in Kentucky, General. Before Buell can concentrate and move, you could make a triumphant march, cut him off from Louisville. Kentucky can be ours!"

The words Kirby Smith did not use, but implied, rang clear: *Glory. Reputation*. The campaign would be Bragg's, and the triumph.

"If Kentucky were in the Confederacy . . . well, I don't have to tell you what that would mean," Smith added.

"And you are certain they are with us?"

"Recruits came in almost faster than we could write the muster rolls," Morgan intruded. "Victorious, you could raise fifty thousand, General. The Ohio River could be ours."

"Cincinnati . . ." Smith murmured. Bragg's brown eyes, like plums, gleamed under his heavy brows.

"It's certainly possible," Bragg admitted with a tinge of hope.

"With Forrest in Middle Tennessee, your rear would be safe," Smith added. "He reports nothing but anti-Union feeling down there."

"Victory in the West," Bragg murmured.

Kirby Smith nodded, fearing to say more.

Morgan caught his eye. Yes! It wasn't too late! It was entirely possible! Those long night marches. Those bone-breaking hours in the saddle—his men had proved it, and here they were, two generals of the Confederate Army, listening to his hopes. If Bragg only had the guts! He saw timidity fight with greed for fame on the long face, its mouth flanked by two parallel furrows from nose to chin.

"I could move into Central Kentucky," Bragg mused. "To the Green, then toward Louisville. No, toward Lexington. Consolidate forces with you, General Smith—then Louisville . . . Cincinnati. . . ."

Morgan started to interrupt, to say that a move directly to Louisville would be best, to get between the Federal forces at Frankfort and at the same time block Buell's escape route, but he held his tongue and let Bragg dream on. From the suppressed elation on Smith's face, he knew they had won.

Braxton Bragg called his adjutant and dictated a message to Adjutant-General Cooper in Richmond:

The feeling in Middle Tenn. and Ky. is represented by Forrest and Morgan to have become intensely hostile to the enemy, and nothing is wanted but arms and support to bring the people into our ranks, for they have found neutrality has afforded them no protection. A move into Ky. to cut Buell's supply lines has every prospect of success.

"Is that what you want, gentlemen?"

"That will do just fine." Kirby Smith grinned. It wasn't everything, but it was a start.

They returned to Knoxville none too soon; within two days Buell received permission to move.

"We've got to strike before he can concentrate at Nashville," Kirby Smith said. "I'll need you to make things hot for him."

"Gallatin again," Morgan grinned.

"Yes . . . and I've sent Colonel Scott with orders to ride with me to Kentucky."

John Scott! Another brilliant cavalryman who had served under Forrest. If Bragg would move his army out of Mississippi, by God, they could avenge Sidney Johnston!

Again, he could not resist the temptation to stop by the casualty lists. This time his eyes sought Vicksburg, where T.H. was with Breckinridge. Their assault against Baton Rouge had failed. Dreading what he might find he ran his finger down the list and stopped at Hunt, Col. T.H., wounded.

Behind him a familiar voice sent a thrill of disbelief through his chest.

"I know it, I know it: Don't say it! I look like hell." It was Charlton.

Their eyes met before they fell against each other in a swaying hug.

"What else are you supposed to look like after a visit to our good Yankee friends up North?" Morgan said when he could catch his breath. With a grin he added: "Just wait a bit and Ma will fix you up."

"Ma?"

He could hardly keep from shouting. "We're going home, Charl!" Protocol and Charlton's wound, still on the mend, kept them from dancing around Kirby Smith's office.

But it was Sunday August 10 before he had his marching orders. Delays with supplies, the wounded. Gano's fears were confirmed: The howitzers were not yet repaired. He would have to leave them, with instructions for Charlton to accompany them later. That will give him a while longer to gain his strength, Morgan said to himself.

"Let's hope it won't be too long," Gano growled as he left.

The plain fact was, Bragg had delayed at Chattanooga. Not much, but enough; within those few days Buell, with an alacrity almost unbelievable, had concentrated at Nashville. "Your job will be tougher," Kirby Smith said grimly.

"Maybe not." Morgan smiled at Charlton, who already, in this last week, seemed to have gotten some color back in his cheeks. "Maybe not. The horse has just thrown us, that's all."

"What?"

"Something General Forrest said once, sir. If Buell is in Nashville, maybe that's an opportunity. . . ."

General Smith looked past Morgan at a map on the wall, then let his eyes drift back to that lopsided smile. "You mean . . . ?"

"There's more than one way to take a town, General. I know those people of Middle Tennessee. They've given the Yankees damned little help. Yes, he's concentrated in Nashville, but he's *in* Nashville . . . and once his supply line to Louisville is cut, he'll have to run for it or risk a siege. When he does . . ."

"When he does, by God, I'll have a reception committee waiting for him."

"If General Bragg moves," Morgan couldn't help saying. He remembered Bragg's *Is that what you want, gentlemen?* Was Bragg one of those men who could follow orders brilliantly—he had done so in Mexico and at Shiloh—but vacillated on his own? If that were the case, they would have to provide him with no excuses. "If General Bragg moves," he repeated.

He left Charlton to see to the Bull Pups and took the morning train for Sparta. By the 12th of August the Second Kentucky had routed a Union force at Hartsville and were watching the Gallatin tunnel burn. Dick McCann had volunteered for "engineer." To cheers and jeers he blew the whistle. With a good head of steam it must have reached forty miles an hour. A hundred feet from the entrance he bailed out and the locomotive chugged on. Everyone ran. The noise was awful: explosions as the boiler tore apart and the loose rock overhead collapsed.

"With those veins of coal in it," Basil said triumphantly, "it should burn for a week!"

Ellsworth was not through having fun at the telegraph office. He wired Bowling Green: MORGAN IS HEADED YOUR WAY WITH 4,000 MEN. Then he sent dispatches to several well-known Federal officers, telling of imaginary commands under Morgan, using names they all knew. Before he left he telegraphed Prentice at his newspaper in Louisville: WASH MORGAN IS AT GALLATIN WITH FOUR HUNDRED INDIANS, RAISED ESPECIALLY TO GET YOUR SCALP.

"Let him print that!" he called over to McCann as he mounted. "Those Louisville Yankees will believe anything!"

Toward midnight, with Lieutenant Manly and a few men left at Gallatin to burn the amphitheater at the fairgrounds, the command returned to Hartsville.

Just as they reached town a scout came in with the news that Manly had been killed.

"*After* he surrendered," the man let out breathlessly.

A Federal force of twelve hundred, with four pieces of artillery, had taken Gallatin, leaving three hundred infantry in the town. Basil was not surprised at Morgan's order. Before daylight they were on their way to retake the town. The Federals were gone.

Morgan rode with a detail and Gordon Niles to get Manly's body, which had been carried to the livery stable. A boy ran up.

"Yew see him, don't yew, mister? Yew see him?" He led them to an alley between two houses.

It was the corpse of one of Manly's men, lying face down, his clothes torn and muddy.

"They beat him up, kicked him all over."

"Yeah, yeah. Afta he wuz dead," a smaller boy added.

Morgan cleared his throat and looked away. When he'd heard that Lieutenant Manly was shot after he'd surrendered he hadn't believed it. He believed it now.

The sun had already topped the trees. Quickly, with more energy than Niles could remember, John Morgan ordered a burial party, then mounted and pointed. Most of the men had not seen the corpse, but as they passed and the word spread, the fours increased their pace. Down the Nashville Pike, the bridge where Manly died still showed, soaked into the boards, the stain of his blood. When they saw it their anger mounted. Basil tried to keep order, but some of the men spurred their horses in a silent fury unlike any Morgan had ever seen, even at Shiloh. They might run headlong into the Federals. He kicked his own horse and the whole column raced like madmen.

The Yankees had stockades all along this railroad. But the fury had to be spent. Morgan had always avoided these stockades before. Twelve feet high, of heavy upright timbers surrounded by ditches, they were virtually impregnable. A squad of men at their base would be no closer to taking them than at a hundred yards. But this time he didn't try to stop them. He doubted if he could have, anyway. St. Leger was in awe—the first time Morgan had seen that look of total admiration on his face. It was quickly followed by a scowl.

"See here, Morgan. This is a rout!"

"They've got to work it out, Grenfel."

The Englishman said nothing, but Morgan knew what he was thinking: Such lax discipline in the British Line would have erupted in a string of courts-martial.

Hutchinson caught the first garrison by surprise, the Yankees just returning from a reconnaissance. Some broke and ran, jumped on handcars and pumped for all they were worth. The young officers and the privates from Company E—even Private Tom Henry, a blacksmith who had joined the command just five days ago—poured into the stockade. Forty Yankees fell. It was over in minutes. The second stockade, about five miles down the road, surrendered without a shot. The third was another matter.

Morgan's men were still rushing down the road, their horses bunched and wet with sweat. They ran all the way to Edgefield Junction, where Albert Sidney Johnston had had his headquarters before the fall of Nashville.

First Lieutenant James Smith, one of Morgan's favorites at Shiloh and wounded at Cynthiana, reached the stockade yelling, "This one belongs to Company A!" He ran toward the logs, pierced for musketry, and fell back, shot in the head. Two more men fell before Castleman, with Company D, came to their support. Morgan rode up. Basil, his face smeared with dust, yelled over, "It's madness!" Just then Niles, who had rushed forward with Castleman, fell with six balls through his chest.

"Order them back!" Basil screamed.

He might have, but now the fury caught his own body, and for the first time since he had put on a uniform John Morgan fought in the exhilaration of rage. Yes! They had kicked that poor corpse in Gallatin, and killed Manly

after he'd surrendered . . . and now Gordon, with his boyish enthusiasm
. . . they were demons deserving to die. He spurred his horse and yelled at
the top of his voice until tears closed his eyes. It was Basil who gave the
order to withdraw.

"If only we'd had the howitzers!" he kept saying afterwards.

"My dear Colonel, you surprise me." St. Leger's cool voice came to him.
"Fight a battle while it's fought, not after. Regret . . . the Arabs have a
saying . . ."

Morgan didn't listen. He touched his horse into a lope and the column
followed. Somewhere back there, lying like sacks across their saddles, Smith
and Niles were riding with him for the last time, Smith with his quiet laugh,
and Niles with his *Vedette*, the Second Kentucky's own newspaper. How
proud he had been of its first issue, printed just a few days ago! The garden
at Hopemont, those talks about slavery. So far away, and so pointless now
in the face of this tyranny. His mother's worried face. "If only you could
take him fox-hunting. . . . He is a gentleman, but your father . . ." The bar
at the Phoenix. *We'll go there again, Gordon. You'll see. Kentucky is with us.*

God willing.

Before sundown, four fresh graves were dug in the cemetery at Gallatin.
He left money for monuments, and rode away, Randolph's Billy by his side.
He wondered how many people, fifty or a hundred years from now, would
see those graves—Gordon Niles, C.S.A., Lieutenant James Smith, C.S.A.
And remember. But at least they had monuments. Not like Shiloh.

In the morning the scouts reported twenty-four companies of Federal
cavalry under General Richard W. Johnson, picked troops from Mc-
Minnville, advancing rapidly through Hartsville. Their infantry and artillery had not yet come up. Why were the Yankee cavalry so anxious? It
wasn't like them to attack without cover. Morgan didn't like it. His men,
already alerted, were forming fours. Morgan greeted St. Leger, stepping
toward him with the alacrity of a schoolboy.

"Well, Morgan! We're at 'em this time!"

"We are . . . but cautiously."

He outlined his plan: He was not out for a fight until he could determine
the enemy's strength. No more rage.

"It's my opinion that we should form and fight, right here," Basil said
softly. "We could whip them."

Gordon Niles running, falling. Colonel Wood, holding out until the end
at Lebanon. Manly . . . "We'll get fights enough, Basil. I can't find such a
command again."

He hardly got the words from his mouth when the Yankees came dashing
down the road. With that half-smile he turned to Duke. "Looks as if we'll
have to whip these fellows sure enough, after all." He turned in his saddle.
"Form formation! Attack!"

When the Yankees rode to within thirty yards of the road, they opened.
Every Morgan man had elbow room; every man took aim at a single target
and two-thirds of the Yankee force, man and horse, fell. The rest of the

bluecoats ran, to form a V. St. Leger marveled at their stupidity. "Why, they can't crossfire at the wide end without hitting their own men. . . . Poor blokes! They want drill, they do!" It was over in minutes.

Their Colonel Johnson had boasted that he would capture Morgan, and had ordered dinner at the hotel in Hartsville for his return. Now an embarrassed and subdued Federal officer looked up pleadingly. "You don't suppose, do you, Colonel, that you could arrange my parole before we get to town?"

Morgan watched him, a middle-aged man with a paunch. It was he, Morgan, who had been the victor. *Noblesse oblige.* He halted about three miles from Hartsville, made out the papers, and ate the dinner himself.

The next morning he found out why the Yankee cavalry did not wait for its infantry and artillery support. Nathan Bedford Forrest rode into town with part of his command.

"I thought they were all after you," he said with a grin that sent a glint into those gray eyes under their level brows. "Infantry, artillery, as well as Johnson's boys. Thought I'd better help."

"As you see, we're in fine shape."

"Then I'll be going again," Forrest growled. He remounted, leaned down with his big paw and shook Morgan's hand. "Take care of yourself. Looks like everything here is under control."

Recruits rode in the next day, compliments of Colonel Adam Johnson of Forrest's command, enough to fill two companies. "Where does he find them?" Basil asked the air above his head. "That man . . . !" Admiration turned to awe.

While they waited at Hartsville for the signal from Kirby Smith that would start their race into Kentucky, the tension and the August heat took its toll on tempers and tolerance. Two recruits deserted after St. Leger ordered them to polish his "accoutrements." St. Leger scowled at Morgan's abrupt tone.

"You pamper them, sir," he said, the memory of Ellsworth and his lost gold still rankling. "There can never be effective service in a democratic army."

"There can never be effective service in a tyrannical one, either."

The Englishman, politely, and with a stoic effort, waited for him to finish before he saluted and left.

Within a week, Morgan would have to eat his words. The deserters, who had actually joined the Yankees, were caught and stood court-martial. The armed man was sentenced to death, the first and only execution in the history of Morgan's command. The unarmed soldier was sentenced to be flogged. That, too, was the only time in the history of Morgan's command that such punishment was used. Joe Desha was O.D. But man after man refused to pick up the whip. Then a second lieutenant from Desha's company walked up to help his captain "out of the difficulty." He spoke of his "duty," but it was soon obvious that he was enjoying every stroke. When he raised his arm for number forty a roar of anger came from Desha, who dashed forward on his horse and threatened to shoot the man if he didn't drop the whip that second. Basil Duke dismissed the lieutenant from the Confederate service on the spot.

"You have no right. This is highly irregular. . . ."

"You are probably correct," seethed Basil between his teeth, "but I meant what I said. Your conduct unbecoming . . . any court-martial would convict . . ."

St. Leger through it all was silent, but Morgan noticed that he spoke to Basil with a note of affection in his voice that night. Discipline was one thing, a gentleman was another.

The Second Kentucky's work at Hartsville was done. The railroad—Buell's main supply line from the North—was cut between Gallatin and Nashville. The twenty-four picked companies of General Johnson's Union cavalry, sent to take Morgan, were now running somewhere on the other side of the Cumberland. Scouts reported that Forrest was sweeping everything clean around Nashville. It only remained for Buell to run like a rabbit north, and for Bragg and Kirby Smith to set the trap.

On the morning of August 28 the long wait was over: orders from Kirby Smith. *Meet me in Lexington on the 2nd of September.*

Morgan threw the paper in the air and gave out a whoop.

Kirby Smith's advance troops were already through the Cumberland passes, and Bragg's long wagon trains had started crossing the Tennessee. Tonight, Morgan's command would sleep under Kentucky stars.

Charlton, with the Bull Pups, caught up with them at Columbia.

"You can be very proud of your brother." Dr. Tom Allen stretched his legs luxuriously. "He took care of those guns like babies. At night we'd camp by woods, no fire, always in line, with the Bull Pups trained on the road."

"A regular Napoleon," joked Wash.

"Once the Yankees passed not twenty yards from us!"

"That's too close," Morgan grumbled, feeling like an irate father. But he couldn't conceal his pride for long. "You'd better get a good meal and a night's rest. We leave at sunup."

"I'll settle for a bath and a clean shirt," Charlton yawned.

"Better be on yer toes tamarrah," Tom Quirk warned. "Casey County's full of 'whackers."

He was right. The advance guard had gone on toward Liberty and they were passing through a cut in the hills when a shot rang out and Billy, who had been trotting next to Morgan, fell forward.

The bushwhacker was not fifty yards away, scrambling through the brush. Two men immediately galloped after him and Tom Franks, his horse running at full speed, killed him instantly, hitting him in the head. The man's body jumped in the air, made two complete end-over-end flips and came to rest against a cedar tree.

"Can you hold on?" Morgan asked Billy.

"Yassuh."

Once out of the cut, Morgan halted the column, lifted Billy down, and sent for Tom Allen.

"Ah'll bes all right, Massa."

"You're just like your daddy," growled Morgan. "Won't tell when it hurts. Here." He handed Billy his flask and the boy took a hesitant gulp, squinting back tears.

The ball was lodged in the upper arm. Captain Allen peeled back the torn homespun and looked glum. "Now this will hurt, boy. Here."

Billy bit the bullet while Allen cut into the wound and found the ball.

"Well, lucky it didn't hit bone. But we've got to get a better dressing for this when we reach Liberty."

They marched into the night, Billy wearing his sling like a trophy. "Ah'm a real soljuh now, ain't Ah, Massa?"

"Yes, you are."

"Papa will be proud uv me. When you think we gits home, Massa?"

"Tonight we'll make Hustonville."

"Where dat, Massa?"

"Fourteen miles from Danville—about a good morning's ride."

"Danville bes almost home?"

"Almost."

That night at Hustonville they learned of Kirby Smith's great victory at Richmond.

"Beat 'em! Beat 'em, by God!" the man yelled. "And ole Bull Nelson wounded! Smith's probably in Lexington by now. Yessir, Lexington's Confederate, sir, I'll bet my horse on it!"

The word spread and fatigue vanished. Some of the men wanted to push on to Danville that night, but Morgan ordered a halt and a good night's sleep. He intended to reach Nicholasville that next day. They would be twelve miles from home. Kirby Smith, cresting the Cumberlands and crossing the rivers, had done what he set out to do. The plan that had lain in penciled lines on pieces of paper was alive.

Where was Bragg? Had he taken Nashville? Or pushed into Kentucky, blocking Buell from Louisville? The column trotted into Nicholasville just as the sun was going down, and Ellsworth immediately took charge of the telegraph office. The Yankee operator at Louisville was immediately suspicious:

> YOU ARE ELLSWORTH—I CAN TELL. YOU DAMNED BLOKE, YOU CAN'T MAKE
> A FOOL OF ME.

Ellsworth clicked back:

> THE ALMIGHTY HAS SPARED ME THAT TROUBLE. DON'T YOU KNOW, YOU ASS,
> ELLSWORTH IS SICK AT KNOXVILLE?

But they got no news. Bivouacked twelve miles from Lexington, Morgan couldn't sleep. The staff had accepted the hospitality of a farmer near the edge of town, and when he got up and walked out into the road, he found Tom and Wash leaning against a fence, watching a pasture in the moonlight.

"Where do you think they are?" asked Wash, not needing to explain.

Bragg . . . Bragg. He had to move! "Surely they've crossed the Cumberland by now," Tom spoke up. "Don't you think so, Brother Johnny? At those fords we used coming up from Sparta?"

Morgan looked over the fields toward a row of trees moving in night wind. All effort now must be given to victory. There could be no slip-ups, no room for mistakes. They had to win Kentucky. The thought made him breathless.

"The people are with us," he said to the trees.

"England is on our side. Did you see those newspapers Major Alston found in Glasgow?" Wash pulled on his pipe, an affectation acquired since he'd known St. Leger. "It's rumored, any day she'll give the Confederacy recognition."

If Kentucky fell away from the Union, the rivers would be theirs: the Cumberland, the Tennessee, the Mississippi. They could retake Memphis, Baton Rouge, New Orleans. If the North didn't sue for peace first.

On they dreamed, leaning on the fence, puffing smoke at the stars: Lee, on August 26, had whipped them again at Second Manassas and was invading Maryland. It was, the joy and hope in their voices said, the floodtide of the Confederacy: The Yankees would feel war on both fronts. The Southern people in the border states would rise up; Southern sympathizers in the North would join them. The Yankees would get a taste of invasion. . . .

Morgan listened to their short, in-taken breath, their sudden laughter, and let his own hope soar. The spirits of his men had never been better, and the friendliness of the people in the towns they had passed told it all: Kentucky was theirs. It only remained to avoid mistakes.

The next morning he took extra care dressing, in spite of Charlton's jokes.

"You're looking pretty smooth yourself," Morgan told him.

"Well, I thought I would give the ladies a treat. Besides, I have to keep up with big brother."

They turned into Tate's Creek Pike and rode past Shadeland. The morning was fresh, the sky blue. If he lived a thousand years, he would never forget.

40

Ten A.M., the 4th of September. They walked their horses deliberately and ceremoniously down Main Street. Banners from Kirby Smith's tumultuous welcome two days ago were still fluttering above doorways, and now from almost every window handkerchiefs were waving. Confederate flags were everywhere. A crowd at the Phoenix let out a cheer, and his men, proud as peacocks, sat tall in their saddles. Even the horses seemed to catch the mood: heads high, action-prancing, shining chestnuts and satin-smooth bays. A young boy broke through the crowd and ran up, catching Morgan's bridle. "Brother Johnny! I told them you would come! I told them!"

"Key! Key!" Tom yelled. "Over here!"

"This time I'm going with you if you leave again! I've made Mama promise . . ."

"We're not going anywhere!" Morgan laughed deep. "We're here to stay!"

Just saying it made all things possible.

They dismounted at Cheapside. From the crowd at the Phoenix Hotel, it was easy to tell where Kirby Smith had set up headquarters. Morgan moved through the excited, admiring people past the doors. The cheer that went up behind him made him stop and turn. There they were—his own men, mounted and still in lines of fours in the street, and Kirby Smith's ragtag army, the heroes of the battle of Richmond. Tattered clothing and sore feet couldn't dampen their enthusiasm.

Kirby Smith rose when he entered. Sunlight made an arc on his high forehead. His whole body radiated that peculiar energy that only success can bring. *We've done it* was in every gesture, every intonation. "Any trouble?"

"We took care of it."

Smith nodded and laughed. "You're here just in time. Bragg is on his way. I've sent General Heth toward Cincinnati, to keep them occupied, but that's only a momentary diversion. Bragg will be sending any day for reinforcements, and I expect to withdraw Heth to help."

"How many men does Heth have?"

"Six thousand infantry."

"Six hundred cavalry could do the job." Morgan grinned.

"That's precisely what I had in mind." Smith was still standing. He turned to his orderly and asked not to be disturbed. Then he motioned Morgan into a chair and sat down. It was clear the flush on his face was not only from success but from the anticipation of more success, and he couldn't wait to get started. He offered his guest a cigar, and when he declined, cut and lit one himself, tearing at the air with his match until it went out.

"I tell you we've got 'em. Got 'em, by George. We've gotten between

Buell and Louisville—his source of supply! Bragg has merely to march north, and with every mile he marches, Buell will follow. And every mile he follows, the closer to *us* he will get. Bragg can choose his spot to fight, and we'll be there to help. . . . The only Federals we have to watch are those at the Gap, but Stephenson, with nine thousand men, and Humphrey Marshall, with five thousand more in eastern Kentucky, can handle them." He took a pull and blew smoke from him.

A sudden yell and the striking up of a brass band brought a bawling, raucous "Cheer, Boys, Cheer!" through the windows. From where he sat Morgan couldn't see the street, but in his mind it stretched through waving banners east to Ashland and west past the factory. A sudden idea made him smile.

"Where is your quartermaster, General?"

"At the armory."

"Ah! I know the building well. I also know where there might be enough clothes to freshen up those heroes of yours."

"Good, good! One of our boys had to hold his hat across his backside when we marched in for fear the ladies would laugh. By the way—I've had a request for you, from Colonel T.H. Hunt. He wants you to arrange for his wife and daughter to go to Augusta, Georgia. To stay with his wife's relatives."

Morgan nodded. "About Cincinnati. I can give that assignment to Colonel Duke. Just say the word."

"I will, I will. In the meantime . . ."

In the meantime, Hopemont was waiting, just blocks away.

Billy, his arm still in a sling, was holding his colonel's horse in the milling crowd. Before Morgan mounted he dispatched Breck Castleman with Company D to the jeans factory, to deliver any clothes and cloth he found to the armory. His men could camp at the trotting track, where barns for the horses were available. Riding up Mill Street with Basil, Sam Morgan, Charlton and St. Leger Grenfel by his side—Tom had gone ahead with Key—he moved as in a dream, the lateral side-to-side sway of his horse's walk measuring with its age-old rhythm the pulsing, processional joy in his veins. There it was, with its fan window and fence and garden.

"I told you I'd take care of him, Ma. He doesn't look the worse for wear!"

Henrietta was holding the blond head of Charlton in her hands. Aunt Betty was sobbing openly, and Basil, ignoring everybody, already had Tommie in his arms. Sam Morgan, who had last visited here at Morgan's wedding as a boy of seven, was again welcomed into the family. Wash, with the men at the trotting track, would come by later. Morgan introduced St. Leger, and Henrietta, recovering herself, became a hostess again. In half an hour Eleanor and Dick Curd, with Henry, now twenty-one, came over.

"I was so sorry to hear . . ." began Morgan.

Eleanor Curd pinched back tears, but her husband looked steadily at him with dry, kind eyes. "How did you know about Richard? Oh . . . those casualty lists, of course."

"And T.H.? Have you heard from T.H.?" Henrietta asked. Her eyes had a new, searching way about them.

"He's been wounded, Ma."

Her hand flew to her mouth and she squeezed her eyes against the news. Tommie leaned against Basil and moaned. "How . . ."

"I have no idea. And Helm, too. They're at Port Hudson, Mississippi, which I understand is defensible. He's asked me to arrange for Aunt Mary and Anna Frances to go to her relatives in Georgia."

"Ah, but that won't be necessary now! He can come here, where we can look after him."

"That's right, Mama!" Tommie smiled. "So much will be possible now, now that Kentucky is Confederate!"

"Cal?"

"Still in New York."

"And?"

"He seems fine. I've had two letters . . ."

"The farm?"

She was quiet so long he had to ask again.

"After your raid in July the Yankees became quite nasty," she said stiffly. She seldom used that term—it was usually "the Federals," spoken with a tightening of her upper lip. He waited. "Randolph's been drafted." Her voice almost broke.

"Drafted?"

That night, after everyone had gone to bed, he sat in his old bedroom upstairs and read Cal's letters. He was bragging about "Johnny's reputation" and sending Cousin Sallie love advice. Then a sentence at the end jumped out at him:

> The manner in which John's men were treated in Lexington only goes to illustrate that of all infamous and cowardly tyrants that this war has produced, Kentucky bears off the palm, such an act of cowardice and barbarity has not been enacted any place else, not even in Massachusetts has there been such—and proves that Kentucky Yankees excel their masters in all their mean and cowardly traits.

He sent his love to Tommie and Key and Aunt Betty.

Act of cowardice and barbarity? To his men in Lexington? Had anything reached the New York papers that even he did not know? But the only men who had entered Lexington on the July raid were Castleman's detail, sent to harass and give the main column time to reach Winchester . . . the little skirmish at Mount Horeb Church. He would have to see Castleman in the morning. Cowardice and barbarity . . . ? And his mother: *The Yankees became quite nasty*. She wasn't telling him everything.

Castleman knew nothing. All his men, fortunately, had returned from that foray into town. "There were a few boys who rode in earlier, sir," Breck reminded him. "With recruiting posters." Morgan went to Key Hunt.

"They were hanged, both of them. One was ill, the other stayed behind

to help him. . . . They were turned in after your fight at Cynthiana. By one
of our kind neighbors pretending to get a doctor. . . ."

"But why . . . ?"

"It wasn't in the papers . . . they cover their own evil deeds. The fact is
that after your visit to us in July there were so many arrests, here and in
Louisville, the jails were full of 'sympathizers.' Some were transferred to
Camp Chase and points north. Cal probably met someone . . ."

"Cal also spoke of Ma's having trouble, Uncle Frank."

"Yes, well. It seems our lords demanded that Southern sympathizers
indemnify any loss 'suffered from Jack Morgan's bandits.' Henrietta has had
to pay for a barn burned—probably by some stableboy's carelessness and
having nothing to do with you. I naturally protested, but . . . I'm afraid we
will continue to pay as long as they refuse to recognize your troops as
legitimate."

"Legitimate!"

"Guerrillas . . . out of uniform. You know their excuses!"

They had to keep Kentucky. They had to. Guerrillas!

He made Hopemont his headquarters, with his grandfather's little office
the hub of activity. He wanted to set up at the trotting track, but Henrietta
would have none of it. "I want to see you every minute," she said fiercely.

"But Ma, I'll be here a while."

She wouldn't listen. How could he know the chill which had settled in
her soul since Shiloh? She wanted to see no more casualty lists. She kept
Aunt Betty and Aunt Hannah busy around the clock making cakes and
biscuits and keeping a river of coffee flowing. Recruiting was brisk. Alston,
who was adjutant since the death of Niles, had a hard time keeping up. One
of the recruits was Courtland Prentice, son of the Louisville newspaper
editor. "Come to join those Indians," he joked to Wash.

William C. P. Breckinridge, the young lawyer who had joined them in
July, now had permission from Kirby Smith to raise a battalion, and Gano
to recruit enough men for a regiment. Sam Morgan, not to be outdone, got
his own company, admitted into the Second Kentucky as Company I, Tom
Franks second in command, with Private Tom Morgan and Second Lieutenant Winder Monroe transferred and promoted from Companies A and G to
first lieutenants. Into Sam's company, young Key Morgan, much to his joy,
was signed on as a private.

Meanwhile, Morgan received some permission of his own: to capture a
stockade on the Salt River, and to burn the L&N bridge between Lexington
and Frankfort. He gave the job to John Hutchinson. When Hutchinson
walked into the little office that morning Morgan thought he had seldom
seen a man so perfectly answering his idea of a soldier. Darkly handsome,
standing six feet four, he had a dimpled chin below that expansive smile
which couldn't quite hide its boyishness under a carefully trimmed mustache. There was a happiness about him—almost a gaiety—playing across
his face when he heard the orders. He raised one eyebrow. "Yes, sir!" His
voice cracked a little, like a boy's.

"Yes, sir, I understand, sir." The mouth was unsmiling, the eyes inward and thoughtful. Morgan watched him walk away with an animal, almost careless grace that defied defeat.

Charlton insisted on going. "They're my babies, after all," he said when he heard the Bull Pups were assigned.

"You're not an artilleryman."

"I can think of nobody better to handle them," Hutch put in. And that was that.

Two colonels appeared the next morning with permission from Kirby Smith to join Morgan's command. So different, the quiet Roy Cluke and the outgoing, aggressive D. W. Chenault, they were the kind of men, like Gano, who could increase his effectiveness. He immediately reassigned some of his best recruits into their regiments, among them Sid Cunningham, Tommy's younger brother, who was made a lieutenant the next day. It was not just in numbers that the brigade was gaining in strength.

As if to underscore the fact that Kentucky was Confederate, a telegram arrived from Richard.

> HARPER'S FERRY SEPT. 18, 1862
> DEAR MA,
>   GENL. HILL, KITTY, BABY AND MYSELF ALL WELL. MUCH LOVE TO ALL.
>   AFFY,
>   R.C. MORGAN

"You see?" Morgan smiled as he watched his mother's face. "Everything will come right now, Ma. Now all we have to do is get T.H. back so you can fuss over him." He held his arms wide. "What are you crying for?"

Her voice, muffled against his shirt, trembled with relief. She drew back and looked at him. "We'll get Aunt Hannah to bake one of Tommie's 'Confederate cakes,' " she giggled.

They were interrupted by Aunt Betty announcing a visitor. At the curb stood Keene Richards, stroking the long sloping shoulder of a gleaming chestnut gelding. "He's yours," Richards said. "With a little spiffing up he might match the gleam in your eye!" Before Morgan could answer he handed over the reins. "Name's Glencoe."

As if that weren't enough, that afternoon the ladies of Lexington sent a delegation to Hopemont bearing an embroidered silk flag. He accepted it graciously, watching their faces. Their dresses were bright and unmended; their eyes brazen with the knowledge of their own charm, their mouths soft, with no grim lines at the corners. To them this was all pageantry, the excitement of a possible flirtation. He was Colonel John Hunt Morgan, a gray uniform with polished boots and buttons, and he stood six feet one, one hundred and eighty pounds of gentleman before them and unknown to them longing for the quiet courage, the inner grace of a blue-eyed "brick of a girl" in Tennessee. He had seen the empty brandy bottles being carried by a servant from her mother's room. He had guessed at her mother's "nervous condition"—and he had seen her father's preoccupation with politics which, over the years, could have caused that retreat. Mattie was the real strength of that family. The memory of her, with her hair mussed and tumbling around her shoulders as she ran downstairs that night they'd talked till dawn, with Colonel Wood and Alice on the lookout as they'd lingered over good-byes. And he had asked her to marry him, and she had said yes! If they could secure Kentucky he could bring her home to Hopemont! . . .

The women came into focus, women who didn't know war—or Yankees. Would they have believed Lieutenant Manly's broken body or the scout with his tongue cut out? Or the fact that, because so many of his men lacked uniforms, they were being convicted as spies and hanged? Had they watched the execution of those two boys just a month ago?

No, that wasn't pretty. These same ladies might have fluttered the Federal flag from their windows while those boys died. Part of the game. Part of being in the fortunate position of living in a border state, wooed by both sides. He accepted their gift graciously and asked his men to elect a color bearer. They chose Private John Cooper from Company A, and as they watched him proudly carry the flag at the trotting track on parade, Henrietta Morgan turned to her son and said, "Who is she?"

"Who? What, Ma?"

"I saw you accepting that flag from those girls. I think I know my son well enough to know when his mind's not on his business."

He smiled to himself.

"I could have told you in July, but there wasn't time. . . ."

She waited, not reminding him that he'd been home two weeks and hadn't said a word.

"Her name's Martha Ready. Her friends call her Mattie. Her father was a Congressman from Tennessee."

"Murfreesboro?"

"How did you know?"

"You seem to have a catch in your voice when you pronounce that name." She looked away, then pinched her eyes against tears. "Oh, if this war!" She caught herself up. "You couldn't remember . . . you were just a child. But your Aunt Catherine was betrothed. Her fiancé, too, died of the cholera. When he knew the end must come, he sent me the ring she . . . would have worn. Remind me to give it to you before you go away."

She said it all so matter-of-factly, he smiled. She would ignore gratitude and he knew it. Instead of saying "thank you" he asked in genuine puzzlement, "How do you know I'm going away?"

"You always do."

Hutchinson made a tremendous march. The Yankees surrendered; the L&N bridge to Frankfort—four hundred and fifty feet of it—was burned, and Hutch reported smartly, every hair in place, looking as if he had come from the drawing room rather than the saddle.

They were doing it! They were protecting their base, while Bragg, with Hardee, Polk, Cheatham—all those men who had been at Shiloh, and now with Buckner, too, who had been exchanged—marched across Kentucky. He could see it: long lines of wagon trains, artillery pieces, infantry, cavalry . . . through the Sequatchie Valley, past the Cumberland . . . and Breckinridge had been ordered to Knoxville, to be prepared to follow. Breckin-ridge and maybe, if his wound allowed, T.H.! It was already the 10th; in two days Bragg could be in Glasgow, within striking distance of Bowling Green, the only depot of supplies for the Yankees between Nashville and Louisville. Nothing, nothing should allow reinforcements to come to Buell's aid. Heth, across the river from Cincinnati, might be needed at any minute, when Bragg gave the word. Morgan looked up at Hutch.

"Are your men ready to go again?"

"Fit as cigar box fiddles."

"Then let me confer with General Smith. I think you might have a chance to play a tune up by the Ohio."

Before they left, Joe Desha, wanting service with the infantry—"I'm get-ting too old to ride that hard!"—resigned his captaincy in order to enlist in T.H. Hunt's Fifth Kentucky, due any day. To Dick Curd's chagrin young Henry enlisted for the same purpose.

"Well, nothing surprises me any more." Henrietta twitched her nose. "Family loyalties split apart. Dick's been a gem, but at least Henry, like his brother, has had enough sense to choose the right side." Tommie rushed to her mother and gave her a hug.

After they went to bed Morgan stayed behind in the parlor, enjoying a breeze from the garden. A knock on the front door surprised him. It was late, almost midnight. Margaret Bruce, whose son had fought him at Shiloh, had come over to inquire after Ben.

"Now that it seems . . ." She stopped, as if the words were hurting her throat. "Now that Kentucky might join the Confederacy," she started again, but this time finished, "perhaps Ben could arrange a transfer here?"

It was a plea from an aging, frightened woman.

"I'm sure it could be arranged."

"Have you seen him?"

"We travel around a bit too much in the cavalry, I'm afraid," said Morgan. "Some of the boys saw him at Corinth." When her face fell, he quickly added: "But perhaps he's serving at one of the big hospitals. Atlanta . . ."

"Surely he'll write, now that he can."

"I'll wager you'll hear from him as soon as he learns we're here." He said it too brightly. She looked at him, her eyes suddenly veiled with distrust: Yes, Sanders had always been her favorite. And he was marching north with Buell even while they were talking, to meet Bragg in the battle they were all waiting for.

"Now that he can, surely Ben will write," she said, retreating onto safe ground again. Inexplicably, her old habit of repetition endeared her to him in that moment. He wanted to take her in his arms, to comfort, to atone . . . then instinctively she drew up her shoulders, apologized for taking his time, and left.

Private John Cooper, the color bearer from Company A, was elected captain of Desha's Company L and almost strutted when Morgan assigned his company, with Jones's Company M, to go with Hutchinson to the Ohio

River. That would leave him with six companies, besides Gano's squadron and Bill Breckinridge's regiment, the Ninth Kentucky.

"Tense as peacocks," joked St. Leger, who seemed in no hurry to reenter the fray. He was thoroughly enjoying himself, accepting the attentions of Aunt Hannah and Aunt Betty and Tommie and all the visiting ladies with the delight of a schoolboy on holiday. He held Key and Tom spellbound with his tales of emirs and sultans.

September 17. Bragg reached Munfordville. Buell was at Bowling Green.

"Excellent! Excellent!" murmured St. Leger, biting his pipe and studying the map. "Now he's got him. He's within a hundred and thirty miles of help —from us. He can either march west and force a decisive battle or better still play General Rose's old game in India, divide his forces, flank Buell, take Nashville and still keep the Yanks from Louisville. Smith could . . ."

Headquarters at the Phoenix was electric with anticipation. Every telegram, every courier—this could be the one. Regiments were held at the ready, guns cleaned, ammunition packed, wagons loaded. Kirby Smith was Sidney Johnston before Shiloh; nothing could stop them now.

Except Braxton Bragg.

The faces at headquarters confirmed Morgan's fear. Unbelievably, Bragg's army had left the Green and marched northeast toward Bardstown, leaving the way to Louisville clear. Forrest's cavalry was the only hindrance the Yankees encountered. It only remained now for Buell to regroup, turn, and take everything Kirby Smith had fought for.

Morgan stopped just long enough for the solid wave of regret to overwhelm him. Bardstown, of all places. When they could have had Louisville. And Nashville.

"Yes, he said it." Kirby Smith nodded for the eighth time. "At a council held before they left Munfordville. He told Buckner, 'This campaign must be won by marching, not by fighting.' "

"He said that?"

Morgan realized he was merely repeating himself, stirring his own disappointment with a growing contempt. Outside General Smith's office he found St. Leger in a corner chatting with an artillery major. The Major threw back his head at a joke and sent a peal of laughter to the ceiling. When the Englishman saw Morgan, he excused himself.

"I want you to go to Bardstown. Immediately. See Buckner. Find out what the chances are for permission to take my brigade to Cincinnati. . . ."

"Cincinnati?" The round eyes sparkled.

"Well, not Cincinnati, but around it. . . . Threaten the hell out of them, draw them away from Louisville. That will allow Smith to join Bragg and take Louisville. . . ."

Even as he spoke, he knew the scheme was wild. But the idea of invading Ohio had been in the back of his mind ever since Smith had talked of relieving Heth.

"A good cavalry outfit could do it," Morgan went on, calmer now as he saw agreement—almost glee—on Grenfel's face. "I'd almost do it without orders, but a coordinated attack on Louisville would have to be contingent on my success. . . ."

"I'll leave within the hour. How far is it?"

"A good fifty miles. You don't want to . . ."

"My dear boy, Allah couldn't stop me."

That night Henrietta had invited General Kirby Smith and some of his staff to dinner. An uncertain gaiety was evident among the young officers who were enjoying the company of some of Tommie's friends, invited for the occasion. When the General and two of his colonels retired to the study with Morgan and Wash, their polite optimism faded. At Glasgow Bragg had executed two Confederate soldiers for stealing a few apples—and then complained about the lack of recruits.

"What can you expect?" Their faces reflected the unspoken question. The spoken ones were more specific: *If* Bragg's idea had been to make the Federals leave Tennessee, they could understand his march north to Glasgow without giving battle. But once there, they couldn't understand why he didn't send part of his force back to the by now partially evacuated Nashville and establish himself in Tennessee. *If* Bragg intended offering battle between Buell and Louisville, why had he abandoned that intention? Bragg had 27,320 men, Buell 30,000. An even figure, given the veterans of Shiloh on Bragg's side and the raw troops on Buell's. For that matter, when he was at Munfordville, he could have held Buell on the Green. Kirby Smith was only a six-day march away. With ten thousand additional troops from Smith, Bragg's numerical advantage would have been enough for even the most timid commander. In preparation for that expected order, Smith had recalled Heth from northern Kentucky, and Hutchinson was holding there until more troops could be sent. Kirby Smith raised his head and looked at Morgan through cigar smoke. He knew Morgan was waiting for orders from Bragg for a thrust into Ohio. Light from a lamp on John Hunt's old desk chiseled lines around the General's eyes.

"Now may be the time to reinforce Captain Hutchinson," Smith said. "With your most trusted commander. They may have tough going up there on the river."

Morgan looked at Wash; Wash nodded, got up and left. A minute later he returned with Basil Duke, whose quiet, catlike face grew thoughtful when he heard the news.

They were all desperately waiting for Buckner's answer to St. Leger. The servants could not be kept out of the secret. Aunt Betty upstairs, Aunt Hannah in the warming room, Annie folding linens—all kept a nervous lookout, until just after daylight on the third day they heard Annie screaming at the top of her lungs from the servant's quarters: "Dere dey is! Dere dey is! Dey's heah, Massa Johnny! Dey's heah!"

Morgan walked into the carriage yard and held onto St. Leger's bridle. As the sky grew brighter he read the message. Buckner wrote:

> I need not say how flattering to me is your proposition and how agreeable to me would be the relation you propose. I saw General Bragg

on the subject at once. He desired me to say that the movement of the
two armies (Smith's and his own) would probably be in such direction
that it would very soon enable him to place you in a position in every
way gratifying to you.

"What the hell!" he broke out. There was something too politely vague
about that "in every way gratifying." Was this Buckner, Simon Bolivar
Buckner, his old friend from State Guard and Bowling Green days? Exchanged, finally, after months in prison. Could he have changed that much?
Only then did he notice St. Leger watching him.

"Well, what do you think?"

"The man's got no humor."

Morgan thought of Bragg's bushy brows and laughed out loud.

"But worse, he's not overburdened with brains, either. And Buckner . . .
Buckner's hands are tied."

"So what do you propose?"

"Under the circumstances, lad, we can only wait and see. Maybe England
will recognize the Confederacy."

Morgan looked up quickly to see if Grenfel were joking, but he had
already turned away.

Word never came from Bragg. Instead, orders arrived splitting Morgan's
command. He was to march as fast as possible into eastern Kentucky and
intercept a Union force on its way from the Cumberland Gap to the Ohio.
He would join the troops under Stephenson and Humphrey Marshall and
stop the Yankees altogether if he could, delay them if he could not. Basil
and the rest of the brigade would go to the aid of Hutchinson whenever
General Smith gave the word.

"Take Company A," Morgan said, pulling on his gloves. "And Kennett,
Bowles."

"The old regulars?"

"The old regulars. And Company I." Morgan grinned toward his cousin
Sam. "You'll see enough action with Basil, I promise you."

Henrietta, when she heard, marched her oldest son into her bedroom and
closed the door.

"You can't do it," she said, as if there would be no argument.

He waited.

"Oh, you know perfectly well what I'm talking about! Sending Tom *and*
Key up there to the Ohio River! It's madness!"

He cleared his throat and looked through the window at the garden.

"Basil is in command. He'll take care of them."

"In battle?" Her tone killed his argument.

"St. Leger has promised to look after Tom."

"St. Leger," she said in the same deadly tone.

He turned from the window. "We've sat on Tom as much as we dare to.
He's a lot like Key, Ma."

"Key? He's just a baby!"

"I . . ." Morgan started. "I can always use another orderly."

"To go with you into eastern Kentucky? You told me yourself you'll be felling trees across mountain roads, riding all night up and down merciless ridges. And the weather this time of year in those hills . . ."

"I can . . . assign him to the quartermaster. Gather supplies in Lexington. . . ."

"That's an idea," she said, quieter.

"Promote him. Promote him to sergeant. Temporary duty until Basil gets back with Sam's company." He didn't say "back with Tom."

Henrietta was satisfied and went to supervise dinner. When she left, Morgan muttered under his breath, as if she were still in the room: "What makes you think Basil will get back before we do?"

Even St. Leger was worried about the eastern Kentucky assignment. "You'll have mostly recruits. I could be of more use . . ."

"I'll make up for experience with numbers," Morgan grinned. "Besides, I'll have Gano. Take care of that young lieutenant of ours," he said as he shook St. Leger's hand.

They learned from the scouts the next morning that the Federals from the Gap were moving toward Mount Sterling. That could mean only one of two things: that they intended to threaten Lexington from the east or they were making a run back North. He had to head them off in the rugged hills northeast of Irvine. This was Union country; the bushwhackers around Sparta could take lessons from these mountain men. And Marshall? Would he cooperate? The memory of a bloated, drunken face in Memphis and the sweating, swearing commander of a handful of Kentucky boys in the Mexican heat came back; Morgan hoped the mountain air would be brisk enough to keep that head clear.

The Yankees beat them to Hazel Green. His men were now behind the Federals, not in front of them. The day was humid-hot. Where the hell was Marshall? Alston rode down the road with Jennings, who came back with the news that a creek crossed the road down there, with mighty fine drinking for the horses. The boys of Company H gladly followed.

It was a beautiful creek, below a short, steep, wooded hill. The clear water as it fell across smooth rocks, the white bark of sycamores against cedars: Morgan could understand, suddenly, how the early settlers might have mistaken these hollows for the glens of Scotland. Yet there was a gloom here, a sadness, a sense of waiting tragedy. Well, that, too, might have touched something in the Gaelic soul.

A dozen men dismounted to drink from the deeper pools near the bank. The horses, their ears working rhythmically, sucked daintily, then luxuriously. It was then that Wash, his hand on lax reins, looked up to see a Yankee regiment in line of battle on the crest of the hill.

"My God . . ." he got out just before the first volley hit.

The hill was too steep, and the Yankees overfired. Morgan took a quick look behind him: a long lane with high fences on either side. It looked like death or capture. He felt a cold, dead calm spreading at the pit of his stomach. "Major Breckinridge," he clipped out, "advance. Captain Jennings, prepare to fire."

God bless those thoroughbreds! They scrambled like cats up that ridge. The Yankees, thinking the Rebs were safe enough in the trap, had made camp over the hill, out of sight. It was a close call.

That night it rained. A blessed delay.

A worse job was yet to come. There had been no report of Marshall or of Stephenson. Morgan's own force—about a thousand men—was too small to halt the Federal Army. Harassing them, killing a few, taking prisoners would not do. They had to be delayed, brought to a stop if possible. He looked up at the dark, forbidding hills, with their dead-end "hollers" and pointless ridges running nowhere. Wash had expressed more than once his contempt for such a country, and the men complained about the sharp flints and slippery shale that made even trotting a hell for the horses. Well, if they got lost, so might the Yankees. If the roads were narrow and precipitous, he would turn that into an advantage, too.

Not again! Wash's look said, but he passed the order down the line: another forced march.

Morgan pulled his gum cloth closer and watched Wash's horse slip down the wet hillside through the muck of rotten leaves, feeling Glencoe's haunches bunch and balance under him as he followed. He knew what Wash must be thinking: It had been six days since they'd tasted a piece of bread, and although pawpaws kept them from starving and the occasional rabbit was filling enough, it was decidedly not the kind of service one bragged about to the girls back home. Even privation could be borne if the inhabitants were cooperative—which they were not. It was a poor country—isolated cabins with dried-out garden patches watched over by tight-lipped women with shotguns. Where were the men? He didn't have to ask. They had already met enough bushwhackers to answer that question.

But bushwhackers or not, they had to get in front of the Yankees, fell trees, barricade roads, burn bridges, and make every inch cost a skirmish, do everything possible to delay that march until Stephenson and Marshall could strike. So far, in the last five days, the Federals had not marched over thirty miles—less than six miles a day. They were doing their job. *If Marshall would do his.* Distant thunder answered him, and the low moan of wind through the trees. Glencoe pricked his ears. Around him, in soaking rain, the men were waiting. It was time to go again.

Three hours and twenty tortuous miles later, when the scouts reported that they were well in advance of the enemy column, Morgan ordered the ax crews out to block the road with trees and allowed a few campfires to be built in a ravine. He looked up to see one of the men from Company H with a big grin on his face. Two of his buddies stood nodding behind him.

"Yessir, Colonel. A weddin'. A regular dance—fiddles an' all—in a barn over yonder, just over that hill in a holler. The folks seem real friendly, said we could come over if we liked. . . ."

"They've got some mighty good grub over there, Colonel. Don't seem to be no harm. . . ."

Will Webb, not far away, came over and said, "Shore would be a treat. Wonder if they have enny bread?" he asked dreamily.

Reluctantly, Morgan agreed to let about thirty of the men go, Will in "command." When almost two hours passed, he rode over himself, with Alston. At the head of the hollow, past a miserable cabin, a barn was fairly exploding with the sound of fiddles and stomping feet. They stopped just outside the range of light and listened.

> *Hunt thet fox an' chase thet coon!*
> *Dance yore gal in the light of the moon. . . .*
> *Do-se-do an' circle right*
> *Make a star that shines so bright!*
>
> *Swing yore partner roun' an' roun'*
> *Now take yore corner inta town.*
> *Find your partner, promenade*
> *Don't tell me that yore too tir'd!*

Even from where they sat their horses, they could tell which girl was the bride, which boy the groom. The bride's blue-flowered dress swung out like the thick mane of red hair on her shoulders, and the groom, a thin young man with suspenders marking a damp X across his back, danced as if they were the only ones there.

Amanda could have been like that, he thought. Could have married some young man and had his children, milked the cow and gone to the spring for water. Spent her life here in these hills, in peace. Listened to the birds. And the memory came of that overstuffed, overostentatious house with its ridiculous "ballroom"—of Jake's fat-lipped grin. Yes, you should have been that girl down there, Amanda.

A wedding. He had asked Mattie to marry him. God, this was the only thing worth having, after all. Wars came, wars went. Win, lose. Governments, emperors, kings. What did it matter? He took a deep breath of night air, washed clean by rain. With sudden impatience, he sent Alston down to tell the men it was time to leave.

The last day of September dawned clear and beautiful. Still no Marshall, or Stephenson. Toward sundown it started to rain again.

"Colonel!"

It was Alston.

"The scouts report some mountaineers with guns approaching."

Morgan left the fire and walked with him to the top of the ravine, mounted and rode in the direction Alston indicated, sending about twenty men around the hill to outflank their visitors, in case. With a sudden smile he whispered in the dark: "I'll pass for Colonel De Courcey. Don't you say a word. That South Carolina accent will give us away!"

No sooner had he said it than six men approached. Luckily their gum cloths covered their uniforms.

"Yew thar. Who are yew?" a boy in front called out. His shotgun dipped only slightly in front of him. Morgan recognized the bridegroom and wondered how he could be so sharp-eyed after last night.

Alston spoke up without thinking, "That's Colonel De Courcey."

"Why, Ah thot Colonel De Courcey's brigade wuz behind. We're mighty glad to see yew."

"Would you like to join us?" Morgan asked, hoping he sounded like a Yankee.

"Ah wouldn't kar if Ah did," the boy breathed, lowering his gun. "This here, boys, iz Colonel De Courcey. Ah tole yew Ah knowed him."

But evidently he was not the leader, for another man, an older, shorter, squarer farmer with heavy shoulders rode up on a squat mountain mule and eyed the two officers suspiciously. The stub of a cigar sent drifting smoke into his squinting eyes. Glencoe shifted, revealing a gray pants leg. The man glanced down, then up at Morgan's face. It was, fortunately, dark in the woods.

"Yew'r a fool, Ben. We cain't jine up with no regulars." He turned toward Morgan and Alston and said stoutly, "We kin do yew more good right heah at home, killin' the damned Secesh." He spit.

Even in the half-light, Alston could see Morgan's sweet, approving smile as he said, "Oh, you've killed Secesh, have you?"

"Ah reckon we have," Ben spoke up. "Ain't we? Why, jest las' week, we made ole Bill kill his brother."

Alston blurted, "Kill his brother?"

The man on the mule ignored the question. He had never taken his eyes from Morgan. He crossed his arms, leaned forward on his saddle, spit the cigar out and said companionably, "Yew see, Bill went South. When he kum back, we said we wuz goin' tuh hang him fer a spy. . . ."

"Yew shoulda seen him squirm!" Ben put in, but shut his mouth when the older man turned around to look at him.

"And did you?" Morgan asked, just as companionably.

The older man looked back and spat again, took a minute and said, "He said he'd do anything if we let him off, thet his family would starve if'n we hung him."

"And did you?"

"Naw. We made him kill his brother Jack instid. He didn't want to do it, but we tole him we'd kill 'em both if'n he didn't. We nivver liked Jack noway, did we, Ben?" He looked over at the boy.

Morgan's smile set like ice on his face, but his voice remained unchanged. Still friendly, still encouraging, he asked them about the roads, the politics of different people, where they lived, how many of his own men (Federals) they had seen, why they were Union men.

"Whut truck do we have with slavers?" Ben said, then added viciously, "Ain't we been slaves enuf, clearin' this here land?"

When Morgan asked how many Confederates were in the area and they told him the exact number of his own command, it was too much. He leaned forward slightly. "I am John Morgan," he said quietly, at the same time lifting his hand as a signal to his men who had come up behind the trees, "and I am going to hang you at daylight."

Before they could react, a dozen scouts overpowered them. Morgan and Alston let their horses pick their way back down the ravine to the campfire.

Something was wrong. Although he had delighted in holding the upper hand, now as they rode back he was sick at himself. He could shoot a man in a fair fight. Could he really kill a man for his convictions? *Whut truck do we have with slavers?* He had seen those boulders under cliffs, which weren't boulders at all but piles of rocks, rocks that had been pulled from fields by back-breaking labor. Yes, it was true. What truck did Ben have? He would be his own slave, as his father had been before him, and his sons after . . . as his bride who could have been Amanda not so long ago.

And what truck did he have, hanging him? Ben could have been Champe Ferguson, on the other side. Given different circumstances, John Morgan might have been Colonel De Courcey and this man his guide. He dismounted, let Billy Peyton, his orderly, take his horse, and bedded down for what remained of the night.

"You can't mean it?" Alston was puzzled. Reveille had sounded, and first light was showing through the trees.

"I do," Morgan said between bites of fatback. If he ever got back to civilization, he would never look at white bacon again. "Let them go."

"But . . ."

Morgan looked off. He didn't join the Confederate service to imitate his enemies. Wordlessly, shrugging his shoulders, Alston rescinded the order.

It was the 1st of October. Bragg had allowed Buell to get to Louisville, to regroup, and had refused St. Leger permission to draw the Federals off at Cincinnati. And here he was, cutting down trees and threatening to hang some poor bastard who had probably used a family fued as an excuse for his politics. Where the hell was Marshall?

Bushwhackers were becoming braver, picking their targets at will. Billy Peyton, infuriated at the wounding of a friend, chased one waving an empty pistol, demanding surrender. But the man had two guns, one not yet fired. As he took aim Billy threw himself sideways on his horse, Indian fashion, and escaped with a slight wound across his arm. His exploit encouraged the raw recruits to get braver in the woods; they knew now that the extra vedettes the Federal infantry sent out only increased Yankee chances of being surrounded by enterprising Kentucky cavalrymen. Twenty-five more prisoners were taken that morning, and Alston had just finished making out their paroles when, about noon, a courier arrived from Kirby Smith. Now what? Morgan opened the message and read through fatigue and bitterness: He was to withdraw from Federal General George Morgan's front, not to attempt further to impede his progress. He was to rejoin the main army at Lexington, *or wherever it might be.*

We've lost Kentucky, he thought, tears stinging his eyes. We've lost Kentucky. He looked at his men, weary, wet, hungry. For what? *Wherever it might be.* A new fear rose through the sense of betrayal: He must save Basil

and the rest of his men, effect a retreat in good order, assess the situation
. . . act independently as soon as he could. In any way he could. If only he
had gone to Ohio!

As Morgan's worn-out men marched down the Winchester Road into
Lexington, the outskirts of town took on every appearance of a place preparing for evacuation. At the depot wagonloads of food and clothing were being
tied down, mule and horse teams standing patiently in their harnesses under
the long overhang of the baggage platform. He rode directly to the hotel.
Through a crowd of anxious, chattering officers and civilians he reached the
General's orderly, who admitted him immediately.

"Disaster," Smith said, without preliminaries. His normally placid, cheerful face seemed to have tightened, like leather, across his cheekbones. "As
soon as I learned of Buell's move from Louisville, I sent for you. Bragg's
been playing politician at Frankfort, installing a Provisional Governor!" He
stopped to blow breath from him. "We've just received word that the 'inauguration' was broken up by uninvited Northern guests." As he spoke he
folded and packed away papers in a valise, nodding silent instructions to his
adjutant, who lifted various objects—orders, telegrams, maps—in a comic
sign language, his eyebrows working questions and answers as he did so.
Some Smith frowned at, which were immediately dropped into a wastebasket, to be burned.

"Right after Buell left Louisville," Smith went on, a little calmer, "Bragg
ordered Polk to Frankfort, thinking the whole Federal force was moving that
way, although our scouts told us differently. Polk refused the order and
moved instead to Camp Breckinridge. . . ."

"South of Nicholasville," Morgan said, to cover his own confusion. The
vision of Leonidas Polk, West Point–trained, refusing an order . . . things
had come to a pass indeed.

Smith seemed not to hear. "Polk realized the main columns of Buell's
army—the real force we'll have to fight—could be in Bardstown by this
afternoon." He stopped, looked up suddenly and asked, "How many men
can you spare? To help Buford or Wharton? I intend to defend that road to
Harrodsburg at any cost."

The true gentlemen among the generals he had known had always given
to their orders the hint of a request. Kentuckians, because of the status of
their state, were exempt from the Confederate draft; they were all volunteers. Only a gentleman like Kirby Smith would remember something like
that under stress. Yes, a request, not an order. No wonder it was said Bragg
hated Kentuckians.

"I can send Major Breckinridge's regiment immediately."

"Good. How many men do you have?"

"Total, fifteen hundred effectives. About five hundred of those with Colonel Duke."

A frown drew Smith's eyebrows together. "Then you don't know about
Augusta? Another disaster. Colonel Duke is at Cynthiana."

Morgan's heart jumped. Basil! What had happened?

Kirby Smith snapped the valise shut, handed it to the orderly and said kindly, "I believe we reached that place in good order."

"I'll send for him immediately. Where . . . ?"

"I'd like you on the Versailles Road, in the direction of Frankfort. We expect some action."

"We'll be there."

Suddenly, like a balloon that had just lost air, Kirby Smith's body seemed to relax for the first time. He had sent all his dispatches, done all he could. His horse was waiting.

"He has, with my troops, more men than we had at Shiloh! Not counting six thousand cavalry and artillery! And he's allowing Buell to split his army with the oldest trick in the book!" Anxiety gave way to awe. "Why would Buell march east? Why would he want Lexington when he's got Louisville? No. He'll march south, back to Nashville. I know that. Polk knows that— that's why he disobeyed orders. It's the oldest trick in the book. . . ."

Incompetence will kill us yet. . . . Forrest's face came back, that tanned, hard-set Injun jaw. And almost immediately, Bragg's hairy wrists showing under his cuffs, that mirthless laugh. Little Joe Wheeler, whose shirts never fit, was his favorite cavalryman. Ironically, the same day—September 27— that Basil was fighting for his life in Augusta, Bragg reassigned Forrest's command and sent Forrest back to Tennessee to recruit another. Surely men like Polk and Buckner knew Bragg was a fool. If only Buckner hadn't been so modest, there at the beginning . . . he could have been in Bragg's place now. Then another face came: a young colonel with a hard-rock determination on the redoubt at La Teneria. No, Jeff Davis wouldn't remove Bragg; he wouldn't abandon a friend. They could only hope he wouldn't allow personal loyalty to lose a war.

Smith had been talking and he had been answering all the while the faces swelled and faded. Now, the General held out his hand.

"I'll leave all that to your discretion," he continued a point. "My men at Versailles will cooperate with you. My main force will be only eight or ten miles to the southwest, in the vicinity of Lawrenceburg."

"Until further notice."

"Until further notice," Smith repeated grimly. They both knew that the bulk of the Confederate Army would have to drop farther south to block Buell's march from Bardstown. Polk at Camp Breckinridge was vulnerable. Nothing could have told him more of Smith's pessimism than his last remark: "Give your mother my regrets. I would have enjoyed another evening at Hopemont."

He found Alston, gave Bill Breckinridge his orders, and sent a courier to Cynthiana, with instructions for Basil to keep a careful lookout, and if cut off, to swing south by way of Richmond and Lancaster. If he knew Basil, the implications of those words, more than anything he could have said, would tell him how bad things were. And if he knew Basil, he would come at once. In the meantime, his men could stand a day's rest. He only hoped they would have a day.

Wash had already ridden around to Hopemont and was full of news when he got there. Lee, stopped at Antietam, had given up his Maryland offensive and had crossed the Potomac back into Virginia. And Lincoln had issued what he called an "Emancipation Proclamation."

Tommie ran into the room with a face red from crying. "I know something horrible. Has happened to Basil. We've had a note from . . ." Her fist flew against her mouth to stop a sob.

"We've sent for them. They'll be here as soon as possible."

"As possible?" Her shoulders were shaking. He went to her and held them with his hands, then tilted her face to his.

"Tomorrow, if I know that anxious husband of yours."

"But it's . . ."

"He'll march all night, if he has to. He'll be here."

Dinner that night was unusually silent.

Wash offered to ride out to the trotting track to see how the men were doing. Morgan sent to the Leestown farm for Billy, home "on leave." Now was the time to gather in all forces.

Including your own, he yawned to himself. He was dead-tired, and Tommie, worn out with worry, was already nodding on the sofa.

But he couldn't sleep. Kirby Smith had used the word disaster. Basil. Charlton. Tom. Charlton was safe—he'd sent the note from Cynthiana. And Smith said they had made a retreat in good order. Retreat, retreat. *Or wherever it might be.* Goddamn Bragg!

When he'd sent Hutch to northern Kentucky, Cincinnati was defended by shopkeepers. Even before Basil reached him, Hutchinson was facing a force of twelve to fifteen thousand Federals across the river and in Covington. What had happened? Disaster . . .

They heard Tom first, just after sunup. He was calling from the warming room, and there they were: Charlton and St. Leger Grenfel and Basil, looking harried. "Sam's dead," Charlton blurted. "And Greenberry Roberts, and Lieutenant Rogers. And Kennett and King and White . . . and Courtland Prentice."

"Sam . . . ?" Tommie's eyes went to Basil and she shivered.

"Come, you're starved and cold," said Henrietta, twitching her nose. "Tom, get some dry clothes on before you catch—" She started to say "your death" and stopped. "Some brandy. In the parlor. Bouviette! Fire in the parlor!"

Bill Kennett had been one of the old originals; and Greenberry, that handsome, courageous boy, at nineteen in command of the advance guard. Courtland Prentice, joining "the horse thieves" less than a month ago. But above all, Sam.

He heard it all later, with Basil turning his brandy glass in his hand and staring at the fire.

"It's not your fault. You did all you could," Morgan said for the tenth time.

"No, it is my fault. I should never have let them go into that street, knowing those Home Guards were in the houses. Then the fires broke out. Rogers was shot trying to save some people in an upstairs bedroom."

He let him talk it out.

St. Leger, who had been sitting across the room, cleared his throat and blinked at the memory. He started to say something, then bit his pipe and bowed his head. In the silence, so low the sputter of the fire almost covered his voice, he murmured: "We die of our virtues, not our vices."

Basil looked at him in surprise. "Maybe we do." The remark seemed to calm him. He looked at Morgan and finished, in a matter-of-fact tone now: "Kennett and White died later. Some of the women, while the shells were still falling, came out of side streets to help the wounded." He stopped, seeing it all again. "I've made Tom Franks captain of Company I, pending your approval. He's a good man."

The mention of Company I, formed not a month ago in Lexington . . . how enthusiastic Sam had been! Without using his name, as if using it would somehow defile his memory, Morgan said quietly, "Yes . . . a worthy successor. He would have liked that."

"William Messick I've made first lieutenant in Company A. I've already told Privates Parks and Ashbrook they are first and second lieutenants in Company E, to take Rogers's and King's places. . . ."

Morgan nodded. The business of going on moved in. Without knowing it, they were burying their dead.

"And Sergeant Hays. I've offered him his choice. Captaincy of Company B, since Kennett's death, or the command of the advance guard. I guess you know which one he chose."

"He'll have to move some to beat Greenberry," Tom blurted.

"He will."

"I approve all your promotions, of course. You've done a good job, Basil."

The memory of that horrible march to Cynthiana faded at that "good job." Basically an optimist, Basil brightened. He said, "We've got a bigger job ahead of us. This retreat will be only temporary—you'll see. We'll maneuver them into a fight, then take Louisville, and keep Kentucky."

He stopped short when he heard Morgan's laugh.

"Dear Basil, we are going to give up the stakes without an effort to win. Can't you see this is consistent with Bragg's policy all along? He came into Kentucky to escape a fight—he said so—and now he's going out of it for the same reason. And he's perfectly right. He does well to avoid a battle, even when his troops are willing. Any commander does well to avoid a battle when he's demoralized himself. He's the best general the North ever had."

The sarcasm of Morgan's tone made Basil's heart sink. He had such a stricken look on his face that Morgan laughed again, this time without bitterness. "Come. General Smith wants us out on the Versailles Road, to meet any force from Frankfort. He will concentrate around Lawrenceburg."

"And for right now I want you in the dining room, to meet any hunger. We will concentrate on Aunt Hannah's ham and biscuits," Henrietta ordered from the doorway. It was full daylight, with the blazing trees of October sending shafts of orange through the windows. Tomorrow morning, when that sun came up again, they would be gone. It was too much. At least she could make them eat.

St. Leger, who was catching a cold, was thankful enough to enjoy the comforts of Hopemont one more time. From the sofa he watched the flurry of Aunt Hannah and Bouviette rushing around preparing a feast, and tried to cheer the ladies.

"Have you seen a copy of Mr. Lincoln's silly paper?" Henrietta asked. She wanted to get the talk away from Moors. Tommie was nervous enough. While St. Leger read the newspaper, Dick Curd came by. "Do stay," she insisted. Dick always brought a note of calm. And he may need a little cheering himself, she thought. He had watched Henry march off just this morning.

"For a little."

"Well!" St. Leger snapped the paper and folded it neatly on the table beside him. "Did I ever tell you how the Sepoy Rebellion started? Over cartridges."

"That's not unusual, is it?" Tommie put in. Sometimes she resented this once-upon-a-time way of his. He was always telling Key about prisoners with tongues cut out, lips split, men without hands or feet or eyelids. It made her shiver, and she didn't like it at all when Key's eyes lit up.

"Ah, but we are speaking of India," St. Leger said mysteriously. "When Minié balls were first delivered. They require, as you know, a heavily greased patch at the end. Now, to load a muzzle-loader, you have to bite the cartridge. Rumor spread that the grease used had defiled the soldiers. . . ."

"Why?" asked Key.

"They can touch nothing made from the cow, lad. So, in spite of the fact that clarified butter was to be the future ingredient, and the men were allowed to prepare their own grease, Bengals at Berhampur refused to receive their percussion caps . . ."

Henrietta, disappointed that they were talking about shooting again, said, "I can't see what this has to do with Mr. Lincoln's foolish paper."

"England is about to recognize the Confederacy," Dick Curd put in. "I think I know what Colonel Grenfel is getting at."

"And England is in a rather self-righteous mood, although the Almighty only knows why, with Ireland on her conscience," St. Leger growled.

"It's always been my observation that a little guilt makes the self-righteous only more insufferable." Henrietta raised her eyebrows.

How like the Queen she looks, St. Leger thought. But at least they had stopped being so jittery. "Quite right, quite right, dear lady. And to the very point. A little grease, shall we say? A little defilement—in this case, slavery—to clean up? And presto! They have turned their war into a *jihad*. Instead of 'Allah' they chant 'Union'—and that is supposed to mean something holy."

"It's nothing," sniffed Henrietta. "If you read it, you'll realize he's 'freed' nobody. All slaves in Federally-held territory are exempt, and he doesn't have jurisdiction over the rest, anyway. He's just trying to start a rebellion. . . ."

"Don't underrate it." Dick Curd frowned. "It's a brilliant move, in fact. It does a number of things. First, it will prevent foreign intervention. It *may* cause a rebellion, although I think Mr. Lincoln forgets the loyalty of the Southern slave—or his illiteracy. Most of them may never hear of it! But the cleverest move it makes is the appeasement of the Northern Abolitionist —and the forcing, through conscience, of the moderates into the Abolitionists' camp. It is certainly unconstitutional. There is nothing in the Constitution that gives him that power. That's why he had to leave slavery intact in the border states and in those areas occupied by Federal troops . . . the Constitution promises to protect property—"

Henrietta stopped him with "The hypocrite! Why should he bother with the Constitution? He's ignored it ever since he took office. No, I'll tell you what it is—the Yankees are so used to having their 'rights' taken from them that they don't know the difference!"

"That reminds me . . ." began St. Leger.

Tommie had had enough. All day long her nerves had been frayed. Basil, Basil. He was going away again, maybe to be killed! "All this talk of Yankee freedom," she cried out. "A dirty blanket for military trials . . . The prevention . . . the prevention of justice. And the killing!" She ran from the room.

St. Leger tried to apologize and Henrietta expressed confusion over Tommie's behavior. Silence fell. He looked out the window and let his mind drift to England, where his own daughter—the offspring of a childhood marriage —had perhaps been as worried as Tommie when one of those infrequent letters of his came from far-flung places. That lovely countryside rose up, soft hills, silent clouds. He had thought of it watching similar hills, riding back from Bardstown. He had done what he could for Morgan, and he'd liked Buckner awfully. But he had seen official indifference break men and campaigns before. Trotting over those fields . . . and here in the warmth of this house. . . . Yes, he could feel how sacred this Kentucky was for them, and he suddenly felt excluded, homeless, alone.

"*Jihad,*" he said again, he didn't know why.

41

"I can't do anything with him! And you know how delicate he is! It's amazing I kept him home when you left the last time!"

He's a sworn-in soldier of the Confederate Army, he wanted to say. You agreed to his mustering in when you thought we had Kentucky. Now that . . .

"Key is the quartermaster sergeant for Company I, Ma."

"Oh, come now, Johnny! You know that was just convenient! He's only just turned seventeen. . . ."

"We have plenty of men seventeen. George Castleman's fifteen."

"That's no argument! What must the Castlemans be thinking of! Little boys . . ." She shut her eyes against tears, and her mouth started trembling. "He's so like his father. Those chills he gets. His chest . . ."

Morgan felt the pressure of Kirby Smith's orders in his breast pocket, sent from Versailles: *Ascertain enemy in Frankfort. Come at once.* Basil had already left.

He took her shoulders in his hands. "If I promise to take care of him? If I promise that, once in Murfreesboro, I won't let him into combat?"

"And how will you do that?"

"If Mattie will still have me, I'm getting married as soon as we get back. He can stay with the Readys. It looks, from the sound of things, that he's determined to go. Better with me than another outfit, don't you think? He'll be a great help, in case . . ."

But she didn't hear the "in case" and he couldn't have explained it if she'd asked. They were interrupted by Tommie, breathless from running downstairs with her announcement: She was going south with Kirby Smith's army.

"The General has promised us an escort."

"Us?"

"Ten ladies. We'll have two carriages . . ."

"It's too dangerous! I won't have it . . ."

"Mama—oh, Mama. If Mrs. Breckinridge and Mrs. Hanson can go, I see no reason . . . these ladies have an invitation to stay with friends in Atlanta . . . kind people . . ." She had told Basil good-bye the night before, and he had agreed. "And to be with Basil, when I can," she said more quietly.

"How do you know you'll see Basil?"

"Johnny will give him leave, won't you, Johnny?" she asked archly, to ease the tension. More seriously she said, "We've discussed it."

Morgan, standing by the garden window in the parlor, watched these two women—Tommie the courageous, loyal tomboy; his mother, who would now be alone in this big house surrounded by Yankees. She had her brothers and Dick Curd, but she would be alone.

"Cal will be back soon." He tried to make his voice sound convincing.

She looked at him across the chairs and tables. Outlined by the light behind her from the dining room, Henrietta Morgan stood in the arched doorway and threw her head back and smiled.

"Yes. Of course he will, won't he?"

Her cheeks were wet with tears but her eyes were shining. After Tommie went upstairs, she turned to him. "I know you'll do what's best, Johnny." She looked around at the sound of voices from the entry hall as Charlton came in with Tom. "You'll take care of them, won't you?" But in case he should interpret her question as fear she reached into a pocket of her apron and drew out a small box. "You forgot this."

"Thank you, Ma. Now I've got . . ."

"I know. You've got to go."

Most of the command had pushed past Versailles and were awaiting orders in a field six miles from Frankfort by the time Morgan rode up. A scout had just reported no enemy troops in the capital. Morgan called for him and the man was positive: The Yankees left for Lawrenceburg at one last night. The man was Walter Ferguson, who had been with him since Camp Boone. The report was reliable.

That could mean only one thing. The Federals were dropping south of Kirby Smith to join Buell in Bragg's front. Bragg, now at Harrodsburg and separated from Polk and Smith, would be completely cut off. Morgan could see it: They would eliminate Polk, then encircle Bragg, and defeat Smith. It would all be over.

He ordered more scouts into Frankfort, sent other details down the Georgetown and Owenton roads, then scrawled a note to Kirby Smith. Never had he felt such impatience. His hand was shaking as he dipped the pen and went on:

> One of *My Scouts* in this *moment* entered the town found no troops the citizens say they crossed the river last night and are on thier way as fast as possible to join Gen. Buell—who they report in rear of Gen. Bragg.

He read it over, ignoring the misspelling of "their," then added:

> This is I think reliable
>
> Very Truly
> JnoHMorgan

In his hurry he had run his name together as one word. He looked up at Basil's grin. "Hell, John, will you have time . . . ?"

"You're right."

Morgan waved aside the courier and mounted, Basil behind. He might as well see Smith himself.

It was afternoon by the time they reached Versailles. Smith greeted them with that peculiarly formal haste that imminent danger brings to a brave man. He read the note in silence, pursing his lips and shaking his high balding forehead from side to side, as if he would cure a headache. "The good general wants us to wait. Can you imagine? *Wait!*" He lifted those fine eyes to his visitors and then, with sudden vigor, reached for a pen and wrote quickly under Morgan's name: "I shall make no change in my plan—if the enemy is routed in my front, I shall push out towards Taylorsville on Buell's line of communications unless otherwise directed. I hope to be in Lawrenceburg tomorrow morning." As an afterthought he wrote: VERSAILLES. 3:10 P.M. OCT. 8, 1862.

He looked up, his eyes still on his visitors, Basil Duke leaning against the wall, his arms crossed, John Morgan sitting bolt upright in a chair to one side of the desk. Without taking his eyes from them he said in his quiet voice: "Colonel Pegram, please make this urgent. For General Bragg. Colonel Taylor or any commanding officer. Will forward by a fresh horse to General Bragg at or near Harrodsburg."

"Covering fire," he added to Morgan when Pegram left.

"Covering ass," Morgan murmured thankfully, in his agitated relief too loud. The gentlemanly Floridian raised his eyebrows and straightened his shoulders as he held out his hand.

"Covering whatever needs protecting," General Smith corrected. The hand was slender and warm.

The date, as General Smith had reported, was October 8. Leonidas Polk, Episcopal Bishop of Louisiana, was rushing south with three divisions to get in Buell's front. That morning, while Morgan's scouts were in Frankfort, the two armies—fifteen thousand Confederates and nine divisions of forty-five thousand Federals—blundered together looking for water at a place called Perryville. Nowhere, ever, had there been more merciless hand-to-hand fighting. When it was over the Confederates knew they had thrown away another hard-won fight. Bragg sat in Harrodsburg with the rest of his army—some said with as many as thirty thousand men—and did nothing. Worse, maybe, was the Yankee General Buell, less than five miles away, who claimed not to have heard the guns, and threw away his chance to entrap Bragg. Afterwards, the old spa at Graham Springs became a hospital, where amputated arms and legs rose to the second-story gallery.

Morgan's cavalry, with Scott's and Ashby's, was now ordered to screen Kirby Smith's left as he moved, with the rest of Bragg's army, from Harrodsburg southeast to Camp Breckinridge. "This is where it'll be!" they called out on all sides. "This is where we'll lick the Yankees!" The camp lay in an acute angle of the Kentucky and Dix rivers, with impassable cliffs and few crossings, and commanding hills for artillery. "This is where it will be!" they exulted. "This place could only be taken by famine, and we don't intend to starve!" It was Friday, the 10th of October. Not even a cold, persistent rain could dampen their spirits. Not since that first day at Shiloh had these troops been so sure of victory.

Then Braxton Bragg, with less cause than Beauregard had at Shiloh, ordered a retreat.

Buell did not follow, and for that, lost his command. For twenty miles the Confederate lines spread across the countryside. A brigade of cavalry led the way, followed by the infantry and great herds of cattle, sheep and hogs, driven along the road by some of the Texas "cowboys" from Wharton's outfit. Then came the artillery, and caravans of refugees—stagecoaches, carriages, and farm wagons piled with furniture. Trains of captured provisions, ammunition—four thousand shiny new wagons, with U.S. brands on their canvas, which Kirby Smith had captured at the battle of Richmond.

On October 10, fifty thousand Confederates stood ready to fight for Kentucky. By the 1st of November they had disappeared from the landscape like a mist.

Humphrey Marshall was sent to Virginia through Pound Gap, Kirby Smith to Knoxville, and Bragg headed back to Murfreesboro. Even while Bragg's men were marching, while they were leading long trains of ammo wagons, cursing cowboys and frightened ladies south, John C. Breckinridge's Orphan Brigade, with Roger Hanson (exchanged in August) and Colonel T.H. Hunt's Fifth Kentucky, broke camp within twenty miles of the Cumberland Gap on their way into Kentucky. It was a glorious, Indian summer morning. Only a cloud of dust told of a courier, with the news that they would't go home after all.

On the night of the 10th, with the army gathering at Camp Breckinridge for the battle that would win Kentucky, Morgan moved into position about six miles from Harrodsburg on the Danville Pike to picket the extreme left flank. He sent a courier to Brown's Lock, near Bowling Green, where Hines was enjoying leave, with two words: *Harrodsburg. Quick.* Then he pulled his gum cloth over his holster and leaned Glencoe into a walk. Just before midnight the rain eased, and he could see a great semicircle of enemy campfires stretching in front of Harrodsburg. He had ordered no fires, to the halfhearted grumbling of the men. He sent Jacob Cassell to scout the situation directly in front. Cassell returned just before daylight and reported a cavalry picket about a mile and a quarter away, with infantry—maybe a regiment —a few hundred yards beyond the pickets.

"It was too dark to see, Colonel, but I satisfied myself that they've got at least one piece of artillery."

"How . . . ?"

"The mud. From the depth of the tracks, I'd say they could only have been made by a gun. . . ."

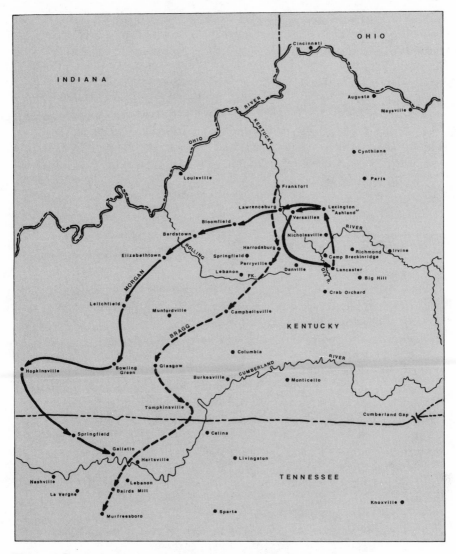

The Confederate Retreat, Oct., 1863

He should have listened. They wasted time with a useless skirmish, but worse: By early afternoon they heard of Bragg's retreat. The Federals entered Harrodsburg and moved into Danville, four miles away. With Yankees on three sides, Morgan had to do exactly what they would never think he would do: head north.

St. Leger was delighted. It was just the kind of game he enjoyed. "That's it, lads! That's it!"

They struck out across country, no enemy in sight. About sundown Tom Hines rode in with a vedette, dead-tired but eager. "Why didn't you tell me the *Yankees* were in Harrodsburg?" He whistled.

"We thought we'd go out for a little ride," Breck Castleman drawled, grinned, and stuck out his hand. "Now, with you back, we can retreat in style."

"Retreat?"

They told him.

Before dawn a courier arrived with orders to follow the army toward Lancaster.

Until that order came, Morgan really didn't believe they were leaving. He had neglected one thing. T.H. expected that he would get Aunt Mary and Anna Frances through the lines. How foolish now his mother's idea seemed, that T.H. would come home! He sent Hines with a flag to Frank Wolford, asking permission that they be allowed to leave. Before sunset the answer arrived: "It's done. Frank."

Morgan took the paper from the boy and folded it into a pocket. To Basil's lifted eyebrows he said "Aunt Mary," and Basil nodded.

Ahead, the way south lay relatively clear. They reached Lancaster about noon, and were greeted by the artillery of one of Buell's divisions which had been skirmishing with Joe Wheeler's cavalry all day.

"Some reception!" growled Wash.

"How far away is General Smith's rear guard?" Basil asked a scout, still out of breath.

"Not an hour's good ride, sir."

Basil scribbled a note. Smith's artillery, which always followed the infantry, might be closer than that. If he could get them. . . .

Forty-five minutes later two guns belonging to Rain's brigade, Kirby Smith's rear guard, were brought back and ended the argument in Lancaster. The fire lasted until dark, but the men bedded down in line of battle that night.

W. C. P. Breckinridge, whose regiment had been detached to Ashby, came in about midnight; Ashby's command was camped just outside town. "Looks as if this is it, Colonel," Breckinridge said quietly. He had found a sleepless Morgan watching a campfire. "Tomorrow morning we'll move on. The scouts report, after that artillery duel, the Yankees have withdrawn."

St. Leger, sleepless also, came into the circle of light. He leaned forward, emptied his pipe and tucked it in his jacket. As he did so the tassel on his skullcap flopped forward. He must have been, Morgan reflected, a handsome man in his youth.

"A miserable war," Breckinridge said.

"Ah, but it's the only one we've got!" The Englishman tried a laugh. None of them enjoyed a retreat. "It's so . . . methodical," St. Leger added, and they knew what he meant.

Morgan looked at the night sky. The sounds of a sleeping camp came to him: the soft shifting of horses, the sputter of wood burning low. Yes, tomorrow they would head south. Defeat. He turned to St. Leger. "Would you ride to General Smith with a request?"

He didn't have to explain.

"I've been thinking the same thing, myself," Grenfel grinned. Oh, he did like John Morgan's style.

"Be my liaison to General Bragg," Morgan said, looking up. "And meet me in Murfreesboro. . . ."

Permission from Kirby Smith to select his own line of retreat from Kentucky, with the understanding that he would protect the rear of the infantry until all danger was over. What harm could there be in that? Not in a million years would the Yankees be suspecting a move on Lexington. Not in a million years. They would think every Confederate within a hundred miles was racing as fast as he could to leave the state. And a move now could draw them off from those long lines of tired men moving south.

"You're not fooling me." Basil smiled. "You're mad as hell and you want another chance."

"Tell him," Morgan said to St. Leger, "we can feed our men and horses, have them in good condition at the end of the retreat by taking a different route from the army, which will consume all forage in its path. . . ."

"Good excuse."

"Basil . . ."

"All right, all right."

"Tell him that, in the route we propose to take, we can cross Buell's rear, take prisoners, capture trains, and seriously annoy the enemy. Tell him I'll establish myself in the neighborhood of Gallatin, do a little more 'railroading' to upset the Federals in Nashville. At Gallatin we'll be able to guard Bragg's flank at Murfreesboro. Tell General Smith I'll move on to Gum Springs and wait for his reply there.

"And," Morgan added, "just so he won't think we're abandoning him, tell him I am sending Colonel Cluke's and Colonel Chenault's regiments to join his rear guard . . . within the hour."

St. Leger mounted smartly and tossed his tassel. It was precisely the kind of plan he loved. "I see you're becoming a diplomat as well, lad." He touched his horse and was gone.

But Smith's permission was reluctantly given, in spite of the two regiments. Morgan could "remain where he was twenty-four hours longer; then he might take the course his judgment directed." The message arrived at four P.M. on the 16th of October, a Thursday. By early afternoon Friday camp was broken and the command was ready to go. If no Federals appeared, or if Smith's permission was not withdrawn, by this time tomorrow they could be in Lexington. . . .

Morgan stood with his watch in his hand. It was three-thirty. With his watch still in his hand, he swung up on Glencoe. A faint smile broke across his face as the minutes ticked off. He pocketed his watch and raised his hand. Eighteen hundred Morgan men were on their way. . . .

Never had they accomplished a forced march in better spirits. Strict silence was cheerfully obeyed. "I'd cut my tongue out if it meant fooling those S.O.B.'s."

"Hesh up," Will Webb told the soldier, "er Ah'll do it fer yew."

That morning the scouts reported a body of Federal cavalry at Lexington a day or so before—the Fourth Ohio, their old friends from La Vergne days. The main camp was at Henry Clay's Ashland, about two miles from town on the Richmond Road. One or two Federal companies were quartered in town, at the courthouse. As a double check, Morgan sent Tom Quirk to do his own investigation. He returned about sundown, verifying the presence of the Fouth Ohio, and also a force under General Granger at Paris. "In fact," Quirk said, "it wouldn't surprise me if he hasn't already started marching toward Lexington within the past hour. I'd add him into my calculations, Colonel."

"Do you think it's wise to split your forces?" Basil worried.

"It's St. Leger's old trick. We won with it in July," Morgan answered. He would send Gano's Third and Bill Breckinridge's Ninth Kentucky regiments by way of the Richmond Road to approach Lexington from the east. The rest of the column would move by Tate's Creek Pike, to enter town from the south. A simultaneous attack at Ashland was planned for daylight. "Don't worry," Morgan said softly. "We'll send a detail into town to take care of the courthouse, and another halfway between town and Ashland, to take care of any retreat."

It was pitch-dark by the time the column crossed the river and a little after midnight when they reached Tate's Creek Pike. They passed Shadeland, ghostly under a paling moon and passing clouds. Morgan sent word back down the column: There was a church just ahead where they could camp; beyond that, the tollgate stood exactly one mile from town. If they camped in the churchyard and surrounding fields they would have good water and be just over two miles, cross-country, from the Yankee camp at Ashland. He tied Glencoe to the locust tree by the churchyard fence and looked across the graves to the church, white in the moonlight.

"What a night!" beamed Wash behind him. He was standing in almost the same spot where they had had their "dool." The trees were bigger now, and some graves had been added. He looked around. "We'll git 'em this time," he chuckled. "Won't they be surprised?"

There were no fires, no food, no sleep except for fitful dozing against fences or in their saddles. The ground, from the rains, was still soaked. Those who had them spread Yankee shebangs on the grass and tried to get comfortable. Pickets were thrown out on all sides, toward the tollgate, back beyond Shadeland, down country lanes cutting east-west. As daylight brought the outlines of the hills into focus, the Second Kentucky mounted.

Two companies under Captain Cassell were sent into Lexington to capture the provost marshal, the Federals at the courthouse, and to picket the road to Paris. Captain Bowles, with two companies, was stationed on the Richmond Road between town and Ashland, to intercept any retreat once the attack began. The Federal camp was in the woods just east of Henry Clay's house, and Basil had the job of starting the action.

Just as Basil's men entered the woods they heard firing from the Richmond Road, where Gano—although they couldn't know it—was merely sending a volley at a stray picket. That sound was their prearranged signal for starting the attack, and they galloped in. According to plan, Breckinridge would start in on foot, Gano supporting him, mounted, on the Richmond Road; Basil with the rest of the Second Kentucky would approach from the east, having swung across the fields from Tate's Creek.

As it turned out, Breckinridge was in line and advancing when this first firing was heard, just as Basil's companies approached from the opposite direction. Both columns—foot soldiers and mounted troops—were on elevated ground, the Yankees in a bowl of land between; the Confederates were firing at each other. When Basil saw a wall of white smoke slashed by flame he wheeled his horse and gave the order to re-form farther back. From this new position they watched Breckinridge's dismounted riflemen swarm into the enemy camp—only to be blown away by the Bull Pups, set up to the right and in charge of Sergeant Corbett with the strictest orders that he fire only if the enemy offered stubborn resistance.

As it turned out, the Yankees were just as confused. Surrounded, they surrendered. It was all over in twenty minutes. Basil's men sat their horses parallel to the Richmond Road guarding prisoners. Now, it was Gano's turn to make a mistake: His regiment opened on Duke. One prisoner was shot. Morgan rushed in, riding in front of the prisoners to stop the firing, and took a dozen bullets through his clothes. Down the line, Basil's adjutant, Captain Pat Thorpe, whose trademark was a Zouave jacket studded with red buttons, was waving his arms like a mad puppet: Gano, he claimed, had aimed personally at him. "He knows this coat!" Thorpe yelled. "He could have killed me!"

It had been too easy. In spite of the mixups, their losses were slight. Then, as the prisoners were rounded up and Gano learned his error, a Federal officer broke loose on a galloping horse, turned and fired point-blank at Wash Morgan. Wash fell forward on his saddle as Will Webb, yelling like a banshee, kicked his bay into a run and killed the man with one shot from his pistol.

As the men were helping themselves to Yankee Colts, carbines and good saddles, and as Basil and Alston were forming the prisoners for the march into town, Morgan, with his brothers, followed the wagon that brought Wash to Hopemont. Charlton and Tom took a detour to Robert Hunt's house. They had just carried Wash into the parlor when Henrietta appeared and directed them to the downstairs bedroom, to Calvin's big bed that overlooked the garden. The bullet had entered squarely in the middle of the chest: The look on everyone's face told Wash that they, too, knew it was fatal. Wash turned his tanned face to his cousin and tried a grin.

"Prop me up, Johnny," he whispered. "Give me a cigar."

"A cigar?"

Wash tried an even broader grin and pain made it a grimace. He looked from Johnny to Aunt Betty and back again, then at Henrietta Morgan. She was holding back sobs with a frown that he misinterpreted as disapproval. You never liked me, his eyes said. He closed them. He felt the cigar between his fingers and opened his eyes to Johnny's worried face. "We . . ."

Morgan leaned forward. The match flared.

"I'll show you how a Morgan can die," Wash said loud enough for all to hear. They waited, an agonizingly long half-hour, professing faith nobody believed. Aunt Betty plumped pillows, sent Annie scurrying for another blanket. Wash watched them through the veil of his smoke, a gentle, quizzical look of irony on his face. Before they knew what had happened, the hand with the cigar slipped and his head rolled to one side.

He was dead before Robert Hunt could get there. Morgan walked to the fireplace and watched the flames take the cigar. Behind him he heard deep sobbing.

Basil came in to report that Cassell, Bowles, Hutchinson and a dozen lieutenants were at the courthouse writing paroles. Then he went to find Tommie.

"Why don't you rest an hour, Johnny?" Henrietta said suddenly. "Until the paroles are written? It will be a grueling march back . . . hours in the saddle . . . don't tell me I'm not right. . . ."

He smiled weakly at this woman who was sending her sons to war. "You are right, Ma." He climbed the back stairs and sank into his old bed. Wash . . . Wash at his wedding, giving him the gun he'd won in Mexico. *Honor to the brave. For gallantry and high military bearing.* Oh, you had it today, Wash! Honor . . . but had it been worth it? He couldn't allow himself to think.

Aunt Betty, in the parlor, was the only one in the shock after Wash's death to hear the front doorbell. She opened it onto a panting Confederate soldier who asked to see the Colonel. Behind her Basil sensed her confusion and said, "I am Colonel Morgan's second-in-command."

He took the message. It was from Kirby Smith, rescinding permission to leave the state by their own route. Instead, General Bragg had ordered Morgan to guard the salt works in Virginia.

Basil held his face very steady before he folded the paper and nodded to the courier. "There will be no answer," he said. When the man had gone he slipped it in a pocket and closed his eyes. The salt mines! What was the matter with Humphrey Marshall, already in the mountains? With the Yankees in Nashville, and Morgan's men experts at wrecking railroads? That's where they should be . . . where they would be. "Where is Colonel Morgan?" he asked Annie, on her way upstairs.

"Ah thinks Ole Miss done made him take a res'."

"Good," said Basil. He walked back into the bedroom where Wash lay and laid the paper gently on the cigar, not yet completely consumed.

By early afternoon they were on their way again. They were headed toward Shyrock's Ferry. Just as on that first leavetaking, their route would take them down the Versailles Road. Will asked permission to stop at Amanda's, and Morgan waited, mounted, under one of the ash trees that lined her drive. He saw her briefly at the door, and she him: Even from this distance he could see the anguish on her face. Glencoe shifted; he laid one gloved hand on the horse's neck, never taking his eyes from hers. She broke the connection at last, to kiss her father on both cheeks, and then, in one spontaneous spasm of love, they embraced. Will turned, mounted. She waved at Will, then toward him. Morgan bowed and lifted his hand. It might be the last time.

At the ferry Gano and Breckinridge crossed to the western side. With the river in front of him and the road to Lexington closed behind him, and the fatigue of a forced march of over sixty miles telling on the troops, Morgan reluctantly set up camp on the east side with the rest of the column. It wasn't long before Dumont's Federal artillery swung into action from the hills overlooking the ferry, on Morgan's side of the river. He jumped to his feet and sent an orderly to Gano and Breckinridge with orders to occupy Lawrenceburg and hold the Frankfort Road. The river in autumn was at low water. The howitzers were sent over first, then the brigade. Pickets on the Versailles Road were withdrawn. They abandoned the Bluegrass.

They couldn't know, as they marched into Gallatin on the 4th of November, how anxiously their arrival had been awaited.

Nathan Bedford Forrest, in Murfreesboro recruiting and trying to equip —with shotguns and old flintlocks—his new outfit, heard the news first. Immediately, he sent word to General John C. Breckinridge, Colonel "Bench-leg" Hanson and Colonel T.H. Hunt, who had arrived from Knoxville with what was left of the "Orphan Brigade" after Louisiana and reassignments. Maybe now, thought Forrest, we can crank this war up again.

They had two artillery units—Graves's and Cobb's—to withstand an offensive expected any day from Nashville. Rosecrans, who had taken Buell's place, came to his new command fresh from victories over Van Dorn and Sterling Price in Mississippi and, with the supplies at Nashville which would make him independent of the railroads, he intended to take Murfreesboro and East Tennessee before the Confederates could regroup. If he had known that Breckinridge and Forrest's incomplete command was the sole force holding him off, he might have moved sooner. Breckinridge's Kentuckians, even with the recent addition of the Forty-first Alabama Infantry, numbered just over twenty-five hundred men. The Federal force at Nashville, by a conservative estimate, stood at forty-five thousand.

Every day for the past two weeks, Breckinridge had expected Morgan. "When he gets here," he told Hanson, "we'll do it."

Hanson passed the idea to Forrest: "When he gets here, we'll do it." And to Colonel Hunt: "Why doesn't that nephew of yours turn up?"

What they planned to do was nothing less than the destruction of Rosecrans's supplies, which would delay—and if they could keep it up, might delay indefinitely—a move against Murfreesboro.

When Morgan's scout came in with the news that the Second Kentucky had arrived in Gallatin, he was sent back on a fresh horse with orders for Morgan to strike the railroad yards at Edgefield, across the Cumberland from Nashville.

"Here, wait a minute." Cripps Wickliffe stopped T.H. Hunt. "May I, Colonel?" T.H. handed him the paper. Cripps scribbled quickly, an invitation to "play poker in your Uncle Sam's house."

"He'll know what that means." Cripps grinned.

The plan was masterly, if it worked. Forrest, with about a thousand cavalry, would move up the Murfreesboro Road, supported closely by Hanson, and reach the garrisoned lunatic asylum, six miles from the heart of Nashville, by daylight. Morgan would dash into Edgefield and burn the cars while Forrest, south of the river, would make all the racket he could, with Hanson's troops to encourage the opinion that a real invasion by a large force was taking place from that direction.

There was only one flaw, as far as Cripps could see it: Morgan would have to get close enough to Edgefield to make his move before first light or else all surprise would be gone, and not only Union artillery from Capitol Hill but gunboats in the river would open up. This meant that Forrest would have to start his commotion before Morgan made his move. Even if they attacked simultaneously, Morgan, being as close to the cars as he would have to be, would be vulnerable. He only hoped Forrest would start whooping it up before first light.

Even as Cripps worried, Breckinridge opened a dispatch from Bragg: The operation was canceled. There would be no time now to send a message to Forrest. Nor to warn Morgan. As for Hanson's infantry, they had marched all night and were watching the outlines of the Cumberland in the first faint light before sunup when Breckinridge's courier stopped them: Colonel Hanson would countermarch his troops to La Vergne. Forrest and Morgan were abandoned.

"He'll survive," T.H. breathed. "He'll come out all right."

"Of course he will." Cripps smiled wanly.

But it wasn't until they heard that he had made it back to Gallatin that they breathed easier. If they had known that Gallatin, too, was in Federal hands even before Morgan got there, they might not have felt so relieved.

The retreat from Nashville was one running fight. In an attempt to evade his pursuers, Morgan had left most of his men in a woods and rode at the head of a small group of prisoners when a Federal cavalry outfit galloped down the road and chased the detachment back into the trees. Morgan found himself isolated, with Lieutenant Quirk. There was only one way back: right through the Federal regiment. With a nod which Quirk immediately understood, they put their horses into a brisk trot. A Yankee sergeant yelled out. There was nothing to do but stop.

"I am Colonel Quincy," Morgan said gruffly. "We are on our way to my regiment. These men"—he indicated the prisoners—"I have arrested for straggling. Traitorous, treacherous habit—must be stopped."

"That's a strange-looking uniform for a Federal officer," said the Sergeant. "I ain't never seen one wearing gray."

The prisoners listened silently, grinning, enjoying the show. Any minute the shoe would be on the other foot.

John Morgan drew himself to his full height. Glencoe swiveled his ears. "Your commander shall hear of this insubordination! I'll bring my men here, and show you how insults are dealt with!"

One of the prisoners stepped forward, but before he could open his mouth Morgan, with Quirk just behind him, jumped a fence and struck full speed across country. After an hour's dead run they saw Duke and the men waiting for them. Basil shook his head. "Full Confederate uniform," he kept mumbling. "And Yankee prisoners standing around who could have told on you any second!"

They evaded the Yankees at Gallatin by crossing the river and went into camp four miles beyond Lebanon on the Murfreesboro Pike. But their work wasn't done. Just as they were getting settled scouts reported a Federal force coming down the Nashville-Lebanon Pike to Silver Springs, seven miles from Lebanon. Morgan sent them back to find out if the enemy would halt or continue. They returned with the news that the Federals showed no signs of moving—and right behind them came the Yankees!

Determined to avoid another "Races," Morgan sent Bill Breckinridge's entire battalion, the dependable Ninth Kentucky, to counterattack; with Bennett's Ninth Tennessee they occupied Lebanon that night. Morgan and the Second Kentucky rode on to Baird's Mill, eight miles from Lebanon and eleven from Murfreesboro. It was four miles closer to Mattie.

Mattie. And John C. Breckinridge. And T.H., and Hanson! He dressed carefully, and the next morning trotted toward Murfreesboro as if Glencoe were stepping on clouds. Most of the leaves were gone in Kentucky by now; here in Tennessee enough were left to give color to the woods against a sky sliced by thin clouds. Breckinridge's camp was just across Stones River. He dismounted in front of the headquarters tent and found the General expecting him. Roger Hanson, with his broad, frank face, was there, too. Breckinridge immediately sent for Colonel Hunt and Forrest, who had made brigadier after the capture of Murfreesboro in July.

"General Forrest," said Morgan, holding out his hand. "This is the first time I've had a chance to congratulate you on your promotion. It seems," he added with a grin, "we haven't been able to get close enough to shake hands."

Forrest pumped his hand and laughed out loud. "That business at Nashville! If we'd had Hanson we could have . . ."

He was interrupted by the entrance of T.H., who stood against the light a moment before he accustomed himself to the dimness of the tent and limped toward them. The day was warm, and Breckinridge invited them outside into an area covered by a large rectangular canvas supported by poles. An orderly brought coffee, and Morgan turned to his uncle. T.H. had grown thin, and looked small and old. His wound had been in the hip, and he lowered himself into a chair with difficulty. He had lost so much weight that his uniform hung from his shoulders. But the same gentle look was there when he heard that Mary and his daughter would receive passage through the lines.

"He'll do it," Morgan assured him. "Frank's a gentleman. They'll get through."

"I know they will."

Morgan asked about Cripps, and Henry Curd.

"Cripps is out on a scout, or he would be here to welcome you!" T.H. laughed. "As for young Henry, I was never so surprised, the day he arrived. He's on my staff. A fine boy . . ."

"It was the bloodiest day of the war," Breckinridge mumbled to a remark Forrest made about Antietam. "But A.P. Hill"—he turned to Morgan— "saved the day."

"But Lee left Maryland," Morgan prompted.

"Lee left Maryland," Breckinridge conceded.

"Lord, I wished I'd been there!" Hanson laughed till tears came. He wiped them with a handkerchief and blew his nose. "When Jeb Stuart ran around McClellan's whole army . . . for the second time! That must have been something to see!"

T.H. Hunt said thoughtfully, "But now McClellan's been replaced by Burnside."

"They're sure now to move on Richmond," Forrest grumbled. "We've got to make it hot for them out here."

"General Bragg has gone to Richmond . . . also General Polk. . . ." Breckinridge put in.

Breckinridge was too much of a gentleman to say, but Morgan guessed: to complain in person to President Davis against Polk for the debacle in Kentucky. And Polk, to defend himself, had gone to make his own case. Morgan looked at Forrest, who shrugged and frowned.

"And Buckner?" Morgan asked Hanson. "What about Buckner? Will he be coming with Bragg?"

"He's made major-general. He may come with Bragg."

"It's more likely he'll be assigned to East Tennessee to help Kirby Smith." Breckinridge leaned the bulk of his upper body forward and crossed his legs.

Yes, the thought traveled from face to face, Bragg might just pigeonhole Buckner in Knoxville when he's needed here.

"We'll make it hot for 'em," Forrest growled again.

"Where is your camp?" Breckinridge asked Morgan with sudden energy.

"Baird's Mill, sir. With orders to keep our Nashville friends busy at Lebanon."

"And I know you will." Breckinridge turned to the scowling man beside him. "Cheer up, General. With two cavalry units such as yours and Morgan's, we're in good shape here at Murfreesboro. And now," he glanced around at Morgan, "since it looks as if your brigade has everything well in hand, I suggest you take a little rest and well-needed recreation, Colonel. If your scouts report any news, I'll send it on." The grin was unmistakable: Everyone there knew where they could find him.

42

A November drizzle sent shivers of rain down the window. Mattie looked out at the bare trees and watched a soggy leaf make its way to the ground. Behind her her mother was sneezing. She turned and pulled a quilt over her bony knees. Why was unhappiness so sad? If it could be just simple unhappiness. But it had to have this weight of sadness with it. Worry over food. Worry over the servants, and not enough money. Her father acting as if nothing had happened. A dinner tonight for General Forrest and General Breckinridge and Colonel Hanson. And of course they'd accepted. Of course. The Confederates had come, and everything was supposed to be rosy again.

"Mattie, will you . . . ?" The vague eyes turned to her.

"Of course, Mama."

She went to the basin, dipped a cloth, wrung it out, flipped it in the air and spread it across her mother's forehead. No sooner had she sat on the side of the bed than Mary Ready moaned, leaned over and spewed vomit on the floor. "I'm so sick, Mattie," she whimpered.

Mattie went to the door and called out. Eliza came running. Mattie pointed wordlessly, and the girl began cleaning up the mess. *Why do you do this?* she wanted to shout. What good do you think you are doing yourself? Running away? Forbidding brandy had done no good. She only found new places to hide it, in the armoire, in the cabinet behind the chamberpot.

Oh, how I hate this! And then Mattie saw the pleading eyes, the trembling mouth, the bewildered hands, and she suddenly wanted to take her mother in her arms and say *It's all right. It will be all right, Mama. You will see.* Instead, she bustled about, acting grumpy.

"I'm . . ." the woman looked up, the whites of her eyes a mustard yellow. "I'm . . ."

The look stopped Mattie's hand in midair, smoothing the quilt. She folded the frail shoulders in her arms and felt the fear.

"That's all right, Mama. Rest now."

She went to her own room, to watch the rain.

She lay on her bed, one arm across her eyes. Alice's cat jumped up and sat on her chest, kneading her and purring. She stuck her chin up and felt the tears run back across her cheek. The Confederates had come. But where was *he?* And what did it matter, even if he came again? What could she do? No, she was glad she hadn't told her father of their "engagement." It seemed so silly now. All her longing. All her prayers . . . Her father, half-insane. All he could talk about was those three months in the penitentiary and his hatred of Lincoln. Her mother sinking away in brandy and self-pity. It was better if he never came again. Her chin trembled. If she never saw him again.

Eight months ago she would have given anything . . . Now, what difference could it make? Brother was gone, somewhere in Bragg's army. Alice was a child. There was no one. No one . . . The tear trickled into her ear and she moved her hand to wipe it. The cat shifted his weight and dug deeper.

She brought her mind back: The Confederates had come. But they had come before. They had lost Murfreesboro before, and they could lose it again. Then what? Papa had been arrested before. Next time he could be executed. She saw before that you couldn't trust the Yankees, that she couldn't trust Papa. Look how he had invited that hateful Mitchell and his staff, had asked her to be nice to them! Be fair, he was only trying to save the house. Yes, in the penitentiary.

Alice came dancing in.

"Guess what? Albert says there's enough molasses for a pie tonight and . . ."

Mattie reached up and threw the cat against the wall. He hit a chair with his head and almost immediately his eye began to swell.

"How could you?" Alice cried. "How could you be so mean? Look at him! Look at my Mittens!"

Murfreesboro hadn't changed. The courthouse on the hill at the top of the square stood like a *grande dame* in the sunlight, with the streets, like the folds of a skirt, falling away in four directions. As Morgan turned into Main a swirl of leaves showered across his shoulders. The Ready house never looked better. The same narrow walk, the same small gate in the fence, the chairs on the porch. His heart pounded in his ears as he turned the bell. He felt like a schoolboy again. Mattie! Mattie!

Alice, with a cup of lard in her hand for the cat's cut, almost dropped it when she opened the door and saw him. She threw her arms around his neck, squealing with delight. "Mama! Mattie! Colonel Morgan's here!"

She came in then, looking smaller, somehow, than he remembered. The mystery cleared when he noticed the hall carpet gone.

"We've made slippers from it," Alice piped up. "Wasn't that clever? It was Mattie's idea. For the soldiers. Then we said, why not for us? We have to save our shoes, and these slippers are perfectly good for house . . ."

It seemed insane to be standing here talking about a carpet. He stole a glance at Mattie's flushed face, which she had dipped away from him but held now for his inspection, as if no embarrassment could be important enough to keep her from drinking in every line of him. Yet something was wrong. It was a gaze from a distance, sad and waiting. And she had been crying. He said something innocuous about Confederate uniforms and she didn't smile. Finally, to cover his own embarrassment, he gave her a little bow and held out his hand. When she offered hers, he took her fingers to his lips in a mock eighteenth-century courtesy, and the shock of touching her again took his breath. She smiled then and as if by magic a glimpse of the old Mattie crossed her face. That's my girl, he wanted to say, but the reception, in spite of Alice's bubbling, had been so formal he was wary. Alice went upstairs, leaving a wake of silence. He cleared his throat and followed Mattie into the parlor.

Colonel Ready sat behind a mound of newspapers. His face was thinner, even drawn; his eyes seemed slightly out of focus, as if he were concentrating on something far removed from the topic of conversation. They brightened only when Alice returned. Alice shook her curls.

"What a day! I never thought to see Papa in the *penitentiary!* What will the dirty Yankees do next, I asked. They grind us closer and closer, until we don't dare call even our house our own. Imagine, Colonel Morgan, to tear a man of Papa's age from his family, on twenty minutes' warning without even allowing him to get his clothes!"

"It must have been—"

"Mama cried and screamed. . . . None of us knew what to do, except to keep *absolutely* quiet. We certainly didn't want those Yankees to think we were afraid! There they were, standing all around. Armed from head to foot. I was sorry Papa's pistol was at home! He told me where the cartridges were, said it was loaded, all I had to do was to cock it and fire. I wished . . ."

"My dear," chuckled the Colonel, "the looks you gave them were enough to bury them on the spot!"

"Then they started playing that detestable dirge of theirs . . . making a saint out of that Brown. The murderer! As if he had a soul that could *march* anywhere!"

"Now, Alice . . ." The old man leaned forward and tried to pat her arm, but she was out of reach.

She jumped up, her skirt flouncing. "You should have been here when General Forrest took our town! It happened right on Mrs. Maney's front yard at Oaklands. The surrender was right there in her dining room. And after you left . . . will we ever forget the day they marched Colonel Wood and your men to the depot to send them to prison? But just before they boarded the train all of them gave a shout for Morgan! It was glorious! Then, after they left there was a grand search of the town . . . two hundred stands of arms were found, loaded. . . . So you see they will never defeat us, never . . ."

"How is your mother?" he asked Mattie.

Before she could answer Alice piped up again: "Mama held up when she needed to!"

"Yes, she was marvelous when she had to be," Mattie said.

"*You* are marvelous, my dear," the Colonel insisted. "Alice, why don't you go get us some tea?" He watched his daughter leave the room and turned to his favorite employment since his imprisonment, gathering evidence against Lincoln. He picked up one of the newspapers and waved it at his visitor.

"In July their Congress passed an act freeing slaves in the hands of their army. Then they appropriated half a million dollars for their deportation to Central America. That's how they would treat them! Can you believe that?"

"Papa. I don't believe . . ."

"Listen to this . . ." The old man leaned forward and thumped the paper. "A speech he made to free Negroes—published in Greeley's *Tribune* in August—just a month before his so-called Proclamation. He told them they'd never be equal, even if freed, that their only hope was to emigrate! They don't want the niggers themselves! Here, read it yourself!"

He pushed the folded paper at Morgan, who was conscious only of the rustling of Mattie's skirt as she took a chair next to his. He pretended to read and the words slid together under his fingers: *"not a single man of your race equal . . . but for you there would not be war . . . unwillingness on the part of our people . . . for you free colored people to remain . . . Central America . . . climate similar to their native land . . . for the good of mankind."* Only the blatant hypocrisy of those words at last stirred his interest and sent to his mind a plausible remark as he handed the paper back.

Colonel Ready, quick to sense any interest on his side of the argument, stuffed another clipping in his hand. "Look at the date. Look at the date!" he chuckled, as if Lincoln himself had conceded a point. "The Executive Mansion, Washington, August twenty-second. A month to the day before his so-called Proclamation! This is a letter to Horace Greeley," the old man said needlessly, for Morgan was already reading. "Look there! He says flat out that if he could save the Union without freeing the first slave he would do it!"

" '. . . and if I could do it by freeing some and leaving others alone, I would do that,' " Morgan quoted, only to prove to the old man that he was reading.

"Which is exactly what his so-called Proclamation did," Ready growled cheerfully, aware that he had an appreciative audience. Mattie, who had waited for that lull in the conversation, wondered what had happened to Alice.

"Now that girl would make two soldiers!" Colonel Ready grunted. "If she were a boy . . ."

"And your brother?" Morgan looked at Mattie again.

"With General Bragg's army . . ."

And so they talked of General Bragg's army, due any day, of Perryville, of the war in Virginia, of General Pemberton defending Vicksburg.

Why are you so cold? his eyes asked, and hers refused to answer. But where is my brave girl? his mind carried on the conversation. Remember when you said you would shoot them all, and how we laughed when we realized you sounded just like Alice? You said . . . I said too many things, her eyes said. She looked away from him for a second but he was determined to make her look back. When she did he gazed with a new tenderness into her eyes, as if to tell her that whatever had happened, he would understand.

"Take Nashville!" her father was almost shouting, in that way old people have who are going deaf. "That's what we should do! No sense them Yankees in Nashville!"

You see how he rambles, her look said. That's not what I want to talk to you alone about, his smile answered.

Alice returned with a tray laden with whiskey, wine and little sandwiches, soft cheese on lightbread.

"Where's Albert?" the old man exploded.

"Now, don't scold." Alice laughed. "Albert's busy. It's a festive day, you said so yourself. We've invited all your favorite people to dinner. And remember how you—we all—looked forward to Colonel Morgan's return?"

"Alice, where are you going?"

"To fetch Mama. I can't stand it. Here it is, Colonel Morgan is here, and she doesn't know! Oh, don't fret, she'll be all right. You'll see!"

They watched her leave, and the cloak of awkward silence which Morgan was getting used to fell over them again. This was his reception! He felt the little ring box in his pocket dig into his ribs. He looked at the old man again, deriding a Washington acquaintance now busy taking bribes from Union contractors. He hadn't mentioned . . . surely he knew?

It was hours later—after they had had lunch and the afternoon had grown warm enough for a stroll in the garden—that he managed to get her alone. Her mother had come down, finally, frailer than ever, her face white with powder, her eyes two hollows in her face. She held out a shaking hand. The hairbrush had scraped lines of powder into her neck. He found himself talking to her as he would talk to a child. The change in her was embarrassing.

The crisp air seemed a blessing after the stuffy parlor, when both parents decided that they must have a rest before dinner, to which General Breckinridge and Colonel Hanson and Colonel Morgan's uncle, Colonel Hunt, were invited. "And of course, General Forrest." Mrs. Ready tried a smile.

"You know we've asked him a thousand times before, Mama," said Alice. "And he always refuses."

"Not this time," Colonel Ready said confidently. "You'll see, my girl, you'll see."

So it was in this interlude, with the mother again upstairs and Alice sent to make sure about the table linens and the Colonel napping luxuriously in his chair, that Morgan and Mattie Ready took their stroll among the dead and dying November flowers. He hadn't, in those scenes that had run so often through his head, ever imagined a hesitancy on his part, unless it had been a deliberate pausing, a strategy aimed at overwhelming her with his passion. Now there was this abyss between them, and he didn't know why.

"What does your father say?"

"I haven't told him. Can't you see?"

"No. Why?"

"Why? Can't you see *why?*"

Her blue eyes were blazing, her hands trembling. When he tried to take one of them she pulled away.

"When you were gone . . . I missed you so!" she made herself finish, and bit her lip, but kept a distance between them, walking on a little ahead. "But Mama is helpless. Absolutely, completely helpless. And you saw Father." She watched her slippers swing against the leaves. The sound seemed to give her comfort. "Since he's come back from those months away, he's a changed man. He can do nothing but spread those Yankee newspapers around him and 'fight the war.' " She stopped and turned then. He held up his hand to say something, but she stopped him.

"And there's Brother. With Bragg's army. But is he alive?"

"You would have . . ."

"And Alice. What am I to do with Alice?" she said, working herself up again. "She's so impetuous! When the Yankees were here it was all I could do to keep her from taking Papa's pistol and shooting some officers who came to call!"

"The Yankees aren't here any more," he reminded her. In that tone, a little reproachful but at the same time encouraging, he was telling her so much more.

"No, and Bragg's army isn't either," she shot out harshly.

For the first time fear that he might lose her gripped his heart. She was right. Forty-five thousand Yankees were in Nashville, and the men he'd left around Lebanon could hold them off only so long without real reinforcements. But he couldn't—he wouldn't think about that now. They were passing a bench and he bent down and swept it clean of leaves with his hand. She sat beside him, her eyes brimming. In the physical act of allowing their bodies to touch, all verbal arguments were suddenly—magically—overcome. His arms went around her. Her cheek, damp from crying, broke his heart. Her mouth, when his own had traced a line down the tears to her lips, was warm and trembling. "My darling," he whispered. "My own Mattie darling." Gone was the high intensity that had sent his heart pounding into his throat when he saw her again. Now he sank, like a man gladly surrendering his freedom, into the nearness of her. He took her in his arms again and kissed her until he felt her sadness fade.

Still, they had not spoken of marriage.

"You will come tonight?" She pulled away, suddenly too formal.

"Of course." Then he saw Albert at the side door.

"Ole Miss wants to know if'n you kin come in now, Miss Mattie. De chill . . ." The role of chaperone evidently embarrassed him, and he raised his woolly eyebrows.

"Yes, of course, Albert. And I'll need to check the kitchen for tonight. Will there be time for you to go out to the farm if we need anything?"

"Yassum." The old man sighed, relieved at her businesslike tone.

"Oh, I hate them so!" Alice squealed, squirming into her dress. "I hate them almost as much as Papa does!"

Ordinarily, Mattie would have corrected her little sister on her un-Christian attitudes, but she let her ramble on, the best disguise now for her own confusion. Mittens sat on the hearth, stretching himself. He humped his back and shivered with pleasure, then reached out with one paw, then the other. The swollen eye made his face lopsided. He yawned.

"I'm sorry about Mittens. . . ."

In her elation, Alice giggled. "He does *dig* at you so. I've often been tempted to pitch him away myself!"

To emphasize her forgiveness, Alice reached out and gave her sister a squeeze.

All the preparations had been taken care of, all the invitations sent. With two generals and three colonels and any of Morgan's staff who could come, it promised to be a regular gala, and yet a sadness had settled in Mattie's stomach that refused to move. Was she really rejecting him? After that kiss?

"Wasn't he marvelous? Don't you just love him?" Alice sighed, and there was no need to question her lightning-quick change of subject, or who "him" meant. "That gay, kind, frank look . . . so handsome! I'd forgotten just how handsome he is! And so quiet, so grave. So modest! It only makes him more adorable. Yes, he is our Marion, our own special Marion! Our knight in shining armor! When he's around I'm not afraid of anything. I'd—"

"You've told us all many times what you would do, Little One. Have you told Albert that General Forrest is coming after all? And Eliza to get more pecans for the pies?"

"Will Mama wear her blue?" Alice asked her reflection in the mirror, fluffing up her hair.

That night after dinner, when the gentlemen asked for music, she was almost afraid that Mattie would refuse. But she didn't, and Alice sang with her sister thumping out the melodies behind her, thankful that, after all that chilly propriety at the table, Mattie was cheerful again.

Morgan watched them from his chair across the room, and the cold fear he felt in the garden returned. "Dixie." "The Bonnie Blue Flag." With a set, sad little smile on her face, Mattie kept her eyes on the music. It was as if she were trying to say that, if nothing were possible, at least she would make this moment last. He looked from her to her parents and saw in a flash what she had so desperately tried to tell him: Yes, she *was* the family now.

On the sofa Colonel Ready sat with his fat thighs spread apart, his head thrust forward, a silly smile of simple delight on his face, his frail wife next to him, her bony shoulders making two points in the lace of her dress. Yes, the brick had become the whole house. And you wouldn't want her to be any other way, he kept telling himself, although he didn't for a minute believe it.

The whole night had been unreal. A sudden rainstorm swept across the river just after sundown, then disappeared as quickly as it came. Basil rode in from camp wet to the bone and sat drying out by the fire listening to Colonel Hanson making light of Yankee prisons since his exchange. He had meant to introduce Mattie to T.H. as his betrothed. . . . Nothing seemed more absurd now. Across the room General Breckinridge was laughing so hard at one of Colonel Ready's makeshift jokes that his face turned beet-red, and T.H., with his sweet, fatherly smile, played the flirt with Alice, while Key Morgan and young Henry Curd, invited as a member of T.H.'s staff, vied for her attention. Morgan watched them all from his seat opposite Basil by the fire, turning a whiskey in his hand. It seemed incredible that thirty miles away, as the crow flew, Tom and Charlton and his whole command faced a major Yankee army assembled for their destruction. Mattie was right. Where was Bragg?

Forrest crossed the room and sat beside him. Mattie had started "Lorena," and as Alice picked up its maudlin phrases, Forrest growled under his drooping mustache, "That song will do us in quicker than the Yankees."

They continued to sit side by side, two aging businessmen caught up in spit and polish. For the first time Morgan felt the futility and the fatigue of that Kentucky campaign. They had all hoped for so much, and lost. What was a thirty-seven-year-old widower thinking about a young girl for, anyway? He stared at her shoulders, smooth and shining above the green velvet. Against her throat a string of pearls gleamed softly. A vague, nagging dissatisfaction settled. What had he expected? And then she sang "Think on Me," pinning him with her eyes, as if she were saying good-bye. The boy in him wanted to rush over and take her in his arms; the man in him saw her life fresh and unencumbered, youth facing an untraveled road of untouched years. She deserved more than he could give.

He excused himself early, and rode back to Breckinridge's headquarters with Forrest.

"Nice horse you've got there. Looks tireless."

"He is."

"Like some women," Forrest said, clucking to his horse and settling his heels in his stirrups. Morgan put Glencoe into a trot and they rode side by side silently until they came to the river. After they crossed the bridge Forrest swung suddenly around in his saddle and shot back: "A woman without loyalty ain't worth a damn."

So he knew, all along.

Bad news was waiting. A scout had ridden in from Baird's Mill: Yankees had driven Bill Breckinridge's Ninth Kentucky and Colonel Bennett's Ninth Tennessee from Lebanon. "But Colonel Gano . . . Colonel Gano checked them later, sir," the scout got out. "Saved the day."

"I've got to go."

Behind him Forrest cleared his throat. "Things sound pretty well taken care of out there for tonight. Ah've got some extra horses. Maybe General Breckinridge can scare up some artillery for first light. Better get some rest."

Morgan felt that big paw on his shoulder. Forrest had been right too often before.

But the Yankees returned before he could get there with Forrest's detail, generously given. Gano, who had remained at Lebanon, was forced to retreat. The whole command was at Baird's Mill by the time Morgan rode into camp.

When he arrived Gano was preparing for a last-ditch stand. It was on all their faces: the knowledge that they alone had to hold off the Yankees from Murfreesboro. "Bragg had better hurry," Gano grunted. He had just received word that the Federals were now in strong force at Jefferson, seven miles away.

Something had to be done. Morgan and Basil rode back to headquarters to get permission for General Breckinridge's battery to be sent immediately, and discovered that it had already left. An invitation from the Readys to dine that night was waiting. Morgan took a minute to scribble a note of regret, then swung up on Glencoe again with a new fear: My God, I may not live to see her again. In the face of that, his caution seemed stupid. If she would have him, he would ask her again. He prayed he would have the chance.

The reinforcements arrived none too soon. By the time he and Duke got back to the Mill they found everything gone—including the battery. Gano, Bennett and the Second Kentucky had wasted no time, but had set out to attack the Yankees at Lebanon. Basil and Morgan followed. Gano was just taking his position to fight and the artillery had been planted to shell the Federal camp, a semicircle of fires. "Hope they enjoy their suppers," growled Gano. "This might be their last."

Basil looked at Morgan. Neither wanted a major fight at Lebanon, where the Federals at Jefferson could outflank them, take Baird's Mill and cut them off from Murfreesboro. Gano had left so hurriedly that he hadn't received reports from his scouts—something the wily Texan had never done before. Luckily, the shelling made the Yankees retreat, but not until Gano was satisfied that they were gone did he allow his men to follow the rest of the command back to the Mill. The saddles were kept on the horses all night, and the men slept in line of battle. But the Federals did not attack, and for the next two days things were quiet.

Morgan stayed on at camp. He sent Hutchinson to watch the Nashville Road and Major Steele to Hartsville, but just as Steele's men crossed the Cumberland, Frank Wolford's regiment attacked, and Steele was forced to recross.

"So Frank's down here now." Basil grinned. "Can't get rid of your friends, can you, Johnny?"

"Doesn't look like it," Tom Quirk called from the door of Morgan's tent. Behind him were the men of the "Old Squadron," captured at the Lebanon Races in May. Sisson, Sellers, Sam McKee, Tom Logwood, and a crowd beyond the door. Jesse was not with them.

It was a joyous reunion, and Morgan wanted to do something special. Basil suggested an elite company of scouts. Morgan agreed, and appointed Lieutenant Tom Quirk to command them, with Lieutenant Owens, who had been captured and exchanged, as First Lieutenant. Sellers would go to a company in Bennett's regiment. There were sixty of them—at once armed and mounted. They had left the outfit seven months before when it was less than half a regiment. Now they returned to a brigade of five regiments and two battalions. Their surprise and pleasure gave the rest of the men new confidence in themselves, as if they had forgotten just how strong they were. "Now in the old days . . ." became a joke that covered up unabashed pride.

They needed all the confidence they could get. It was already past the middle of November and still no Bragg. Morgan longed to ride into Murfreesboro, and a dozen times he could have, but sent Basil or Bowles or Alston to headquarters instead, on the pretext that his presence was needed in camp. Her blue eyes haunted him, that strange new anger, that one moment of wanting. She needed time. And he, so used to physical risk and even the real possibility of instant death, needed a new kind of courage.

They were all waiting—his men for the Army of Tennessee to come up from Chattanooga and all points south, he for an inner reinforcement against rejection. When he looked up to see his adjutant, Major Pendleton, walk in puzzled at another rebuff from Richmond, he welcomed the diversion.

"They say the brigade is 'unknown in the records of this office.' How do you ever get commissions verified, Colonel?"

Pendleton was on temporary duty from Bennett's regiment. He couldn't know how often the Second Kentucky had ignored protocol. They were too busy fighting a war to send in fancy reports or accurate muster rolls. Theoretically, but in truth only sporadically, and as Basil joked, only "in fits and pieces," the Confederate government had started paying its cavalry. But as a cavalry commander more or less independent, except for having to report to General Breckinridge, Morgan had become in the eyes of the military pundits in Richmond an unpardonable upstart. This wasn't the first time the outfit was "unknown."

"I have an idea." Basil chuckled from across the room. "Why not send them a report they won't be able to ignore?"

With the help of some of the men who had artistic talent, Basil directed the creation of a muster roll that measured not in inches but in feet, showing the date of organization for each regiment, the men originally on each roll, all the changes, how they occurred, up to the date the document was sent by courier. It took four days, and once rolled up looked more like a rug than a scroll.

"If St. Leger were here he'd accuse you of having a harem girl in there," Basil joked as the man left for Chattanooga.

"With orders to ride on as far as Richmond if he has to," Tom Morgan piped up proudly.

"This is one time they can't ignore us," Gano laughed as they watched the man trot away. "Damn fools."

They had not turned yet to go back inside when a scout rode up out of breath. Bragg's Army of Tennessee had arrived.

Down country roads, across rivers, along the slopes of mountains they came, the veterans of Shiloh and Perryville and a hundred other battles nobody heard of. Withers and Chalmers, Cheatham and Cleburne, and Randall Gibson, whose Louisiana troops had faced the Sunken Road. Murfreesboro was now humming, and still Morgan stayed in camp. Bragg, Hardee, Polk. With the exception of Buckner and Kirby Smith, most of the field officers of the Western front were there. Since the Federals held Nashville, all northbound trains of the Nashville & Chattanooga Railroad stopped at Murfreesboro. The spur line from Tullahoma to McMinnville and another from Dechard to Fayetteville made Murfreesboro a hub in the heart of Tennessee's "breadbasket."

"Why not ride in?" Basil asked the next morning.

"We've got a job to do here," Morgan said evasively. "I'm sending Hutch to Gallatin . . . news of Yankee reinforcements up there."

Basil said nothing, and Alston shrugged his shoulders.

"Cluke and Chenault should be reporting in any day," Morgan said to the papers on his desk. "When they come—and by that time maybe Bragg can send us some help—that will be time enough to relax. Not until."

It didn't take long for good news to travel: Hutchinson, with Company A of Bill Breckinridge's battalion and a small detail from his own Company E, attacked the Federals at Gallatin and drove them across the river toward Nashville. Morgan was so pleased that he admitted, at last, with Bragg's whole army in Murfreesboro, it was time some of his men and horses could get the rest they deserved. He sent Hutch with the Second Kentucky and Breckinridge's Ninth Kentucky southwest to Lincoln County for forage. "And recreation," he added, to the warwhoop Hutch let out. Tom, Key and Charlton would go with him. There was a lot of bustle and good humor at the depot as men and horses were loaded onto the cars for the trip to Dechard, where they would transfer to the spur line for Fayetteville. As Morgan watched them leave he had the first sense of satisfaction in months. For the time being, the rest of the men in camp at Baird's Mill would be safe enough: Scouts reported Cluke's and Chenault's regiments, sent to join Kirby Smith's rear guard on the retreat from Kentucky, were on their way. His men had done their job. With Forrest's ragtag recruits and John C. Breckinridge's determination, a slim Confederate force had held off Rosecrans's army. It was in a mood of celebration that Morgan turned from the depot for the short ride to headquarters.

He found Breckinridge fuming. "Little Joe" Wheeler, Bragg's pet and now Chief of Cavalry, had been ordered to reorganize Forrest's latest command. Forrest would recruit another, to harass Grant in Mississippi. This, for Forrest, was the final blow. "He'll do it," Morgan murmured, blinking back sudden emotion. How many times would he watch that great hulk of a man swing up on a horse, defeated by West Point "savants," perhaps the only genius among them?

Forrest had already gone by the time he reached headquarters. When he asked for General Hardee, the answer brought a stab of excitement to his throat. "I expect he's around at Colonel Ready's, sir."

Colonel Ready sat by his fireplace beaming. Lieutenant Horace Ready was home. A year older than Mattie, he was a tall, blond, good-looking young man with a winning smile under the tan that lay like a sheen across his square jaw. He inspired confidence and sent out waves of optimism with each easy smile.

"*Of course* we'll win!" he laughed, and turned to Mattie. "And I hear you've captured a most important prize yourself, young lady."

It was an old joke from their childhood and she no longer reminded him that she wasn't that much younger than he was.

In a private moment earlier that afternoon she had told him.

"That's crazy!" The smile faded from her brother's face.

She jumped up and went to the window of her room and pulled back the curtain. It was a gray, cold, drizzly day.

"But can't you see I can't?" she asked the dripping trees. "Look at Mama. Just look at her. You saw . . . and Papa. Somebody . . ."

"I'm home now, Matt."

He took her shoulders in his slim tan hands and turned her to him. "I'm here. . . ." He lifted his chin to accommodate the curve of her head as she threw herself against him. She sobbed into his shirt.

"We'll make everything *all right*," he whispered against her hair. "Just you wait. If you love him . . . that's all that matters."

"Oh, I do," she sniffed into his chest, moving her head.

"Then it's settled." He held her out and sought her eyes. "You'll tell him the minute you see him." He threw his head back in sudden laughter.

"What is it?"

"You won't need to say a word, Little Sister. It will be in your eyes."

As soon as Morgan could—he was stopped by General Cheatham, Colonel Burks of the Eleventh Texas Cavalry and then Randall Gibson—he rode Glencoe around to Main Street and tied him at the Ready gate. Snowflakes had begun to fall, drifting softly across the porch steps as he walked up. Albert let him in.

"Early snow," he said casually enough, allowing Albert to take his cloak.

"Yassuh. But dey bes big flakes. Won' las'."

"Is the Colonel in?"

"Yassuh. Wif Genr'l Hardee. In de pawlah."

A fire blazed in the grate, and the General, in his favorite place on the sofa, was holding forth to the full attention of the Colonel and his daughters on the horrors of forced marches. When he saw Morgan he stopped in midsentence. Alice squealed and the Colonel rose, dropping a dozen newspapers from his lap. Mattie, too, got up, and stood waiting behind the others. Morgan made his pleasantries and dared a smile.

"I'm glad to see you looking well."

"We are all well since we know dear Brother is safe," she said softly, but kindly enough. "General Hardee has just told us he might give him permission to stay here for a few days."

"I've got a wager he'll come today!" Alice sang out behind him.

He kept his eyes on Mattie's face. "Every day is precious now," he said.

"Yes, isn't it?" Hardee, in good form, beamed. He had obviously just enjoyed a good meal and was not bashful about the adulation he was receiving again from his "favorite little scout." It was hard, under the circumstances, to believe the General spoke of forced marches from experience.

But his good humor proved timely. When, in a lull in the conversation Morgan mentioned Forrest's lost command, Hardee became expansive. "You know of course that this very day—November twenty-fourth—General Joe Johnston takes over his duties as the supreme commander in the West. That means that the armies of Bragg, Kirby Smith and Pemberton are under him."

Morgan waited for the General to enjoy the lighting of a cigar.

"And"—Hardee puffed—"Bragg made sure that one of his last orders as supreme commander was another blow to Forrest."

"Damn!" Colonel Ready exploded, then caught Mattie's eye and subsided. "What can be done?"

"I imagine General Forrest can take care of himself. He's probably already on his way."

"He is," Morgan confirmed. "I've just come from headquarters."

At that, Mattie sent him a look of compassion.

"They won't hear the last of Forrest yet," her father said with emotion. "Nor of Morgan," he said suddenly, with a chuckle.

"What will you do?" Hardee asked through his smoke.

"Request permission, through General Breckinridge, to strike at Hartsville, sir," Morgan answered without thinking. Mattie was looking up at him with shining eyes. For that, he could conjure a thousand dreams.

"A logical target. Quite logical," Hardee murmured, as if he were choosing between slices of ham on a plate.

"I'll see you out. Must you go so soon?"

She had risen, and pinned him with her blue eyes.

"Yes—I had only a few minutes. I hope I didn't interrupt . . . ."

"Nonsense, my boy," Colonel Ready called out. "Any time. You don't mind . . . ?" He indicated his lap full of papers and his comfortable position.

"Don't disturb yourself, sir. Thank you, sir," he bowed to Hardee and then to Alice. "I hope you win your wager."

In the hall Mattie stopped by the door. Albert was nowhere in sight. She found his cloak among others on the hall tree and their hands brushed momentarily as they both reached for it. She blushed, dropped her eyes and looked up again with some of the old boldness, but with a new hint of contrition. "You've been well?" she said, asking so much more.

"Now that the army is here . . ." He didn't finish.

"Perhaps you can come to town more often?" She smiled at his nod. "I . . . we all hope so. You must meet Brother. I'm sure you'd like him."

"I'm sure I would." He had buttoned his cloak and was standing by the door, his hand on the knob. Her "Be careful . . ." lingered in his ears all the way to the river.

When the denial came for the Hartsville raid he went immediately to Bragg's headquarters. As he strode up the steps orderlies stepped aside, and as Bragg's aide let him into the room the General must have known he had a very determined Kentuckian facing him.

Bragg's bulldog brows were even shaggier, his eyes set deeper in their sockets than Morgan remembered. He was thinner and looked even more cadaverous. His short hair refused to stay brushed back but stuck out from his part, like wires. His upper lip, sunk behind a graying mustache, gave his mouth a sour expression as it wagged open over his beard. He was marking a paper with a pencil and had not looked up. When he did he leaned back and nodded in a slack way that was intended to negate his visitor. His uniform was impeccable.

"Colonel Morgan," he said in a tone he considered cheerful beneath those scowling eyes. "I haven't seen you in a while."

Morgan said nothing. He'd have to handle the old fool with kid gloves, and make him feel that the idea was his.

Bragg paused, as if to say something, then thought better of it. Uncomfortable with small talk, he frowned and got on with it: "I understand, through General Breckinridge, that you wish to attack the Federal garrison at Hartsville."

"There's a big warehouse there, and my men need shoes." He tried to make his voice light. If Bragg knew how much he wanted this, his refusal would be automatic.

Braxton Bragg's dislike of Kentuckians had become a joke by now among Breckinridge's staff. Most blamed it on his bad luck in September, when his recruiting schemes backfired. Basil had other ideas. "Look at him," he'd said. "How would you feel if you were a younger son in a family of twelve, with a brother on the Supreme Court and another who's been governor of North Carolina? And you'd resigned from the army to make a fortune, and then lost it all?"

"He's just one of those perfectionists afraid of taking risks, Basil."

"That's my point. He's the pea under your mattress, Princess. Watch out for him."

He was watching. But Rosecrans was in Nashville with Buell's veterans and his men at Lebanon couldn't hold them back indefinitely. Any destruction of supplies that could delay a Yankee move would buy time. He began regretting that he had sent Hutch and the others to rest horses, with a Union Army less than a good day's ride away from Mattie. Two days could see their infantry facing Murfreesboro.

Now, as he watched Bragg, he made the mistake of saying, "My command has been lucky enough to hold the enemy back, thus far, just south of Lebanon. That's too close for comfort."

"Let that be my decision, Colonel. What makes you think you would be any more successful at Hartsville?"

"My request included permission to use the Orphan Brigade as infantry support."

The second he said it, Morgan realized that the nickname was unfortunate. It would remind Braxton Bragg that Hanson's and T.H. Hunt's outfits were almost exclusively Kentuckian. But he couldn't stop now. "With the Second Kentucky and the Ninth Kentucky Infantry, we could do it," he insisted.

"Colonel Hunt is your uncle, is he not? I seem to remember the connection."

"Colonel Hunt is, as General Breckinridge has known for a long time, an excellent officer. . . ."

"You don't have to lecture me on the qualifications of my officers, Colonel," Bragg said with that venomous acridity which he mistook for a "voice of authority." But it was no mere affectation; even if he had wanted to, the General could not have disguised the scorn born of a defensive sense of inferiority. He refused to admit he was jealous of these wealthy, easy-mannered Kentuckians, and the more he refused the truth, the more it infuriated him. And fed his hate. He added with querulous indignation: "Colonel Hunt, too, you remember, was at Shiloh." It may have been offered as proof that he "knew his officers," but it was said as if T.H. had lost the battle.

With that rebuff stinging his ears, Morgan received his refusal, turned on his heels and left.

"So I wait!" he fumed, but Basil, who had been waiting for him outside, grinned.

"Maybe we should sic an ex-Vice-President on him."

It was just the remark to break the tension.

"You're right—he may hate volunteers and Kentuckians—but not when they are politicians. Then he becomes a fawning fool." As they walked past a group of officers Morgan burst out laughing. "I'd almost forgotten! You won't believe! It was volunteers . . . and I, goddammit, was with them . . . who saved his ass at Buena Vista!"

"That calls for a drink. Let's find T.H."

They both knew the real reason, and they both shied away from it: Braxton Bragg was not about to allow those cavalry commanders not in his favor to see any more action than was absolutely necessary.

"I wonder what kind of soldier Joe Johnston is?" Morgan mused.

"Another paper general, I hear. Extremely touchy about his date of rank. Secretary of State Benjamin was against his appointment. . . ."

"He's our kind of man, lad!" said a voice behind them. It was St. Leger Grenfel, just arrived from Knoxville. "And due here in a few days! I saw him at Chat-ta-nooga. Imagine, these American names!"

They swarmed over him, asking for news.

Lee was at Fredericksburg behind fortifications facing 147 Union guns. Already, before St. Leger left Chattanooga, he'd heard that the first refugees were arriving in Richmond.

Kitty! Kitty and her baby . . . and no word from Richard or A.P. St. Leger saw his look. "Those lads have been busy. They'll be fine! I think we have more to worry about out here in the West. With Grant moving from Corinth to Holly Springs. That can mean only one thing: Vicksburg."

"You said Johnston is our kind," Morgan reminded him. "How?"

"Just this, lad: He wants our troops from Arkansas to cross the Mississippi, join Pemberton at Vicksburg. Wants Bragg to catch Grant from behind, then our combined forces can chase up to Nashville and make Tennessee unhealthy for Rosecrans. Oh, it's a plan that will work! And he's coming here. Within the week. You'll like him. But in the meantime . . ." The Englishman rubbed his hands and blew through his mustache. "Where can I find a good, hot bath?"

Before they could answer he shot out another question.

"Where are my boys?"

"I sent Tom and Key down to Lincoln County—that's near the Alabama line—with the horses. Charlton also."

"Oh, yes, the Morgan clan are alive and well," Basil smiled. "Unless you count the Colonel here, who is suffering, if I'm not mistaken, from a certain pair of blue eyes."

"Well, well, is that so? Let me meet her lad, let me meet her! Only after that bath . . ."

Murfreesboro was bustling, a miniature Confederate capital of the West. Mary Breckinridge had made it through the lines, and Virginia Hanson, too. The ladies set up housekeeping and gave dinners. "Ole Flintlock" Hanson started daily inspections and evening dress parades, much to the disgust of Major Cripps Wickliffe. Morgan introduced St. Leger to Breckinridge's staff, and he was in his element with these professionals of the line. As soon as he could, Morgan rode Glencoe around to Main Street and tied him at the Ready gate.

Albert beamed as he opened the door. To his amazement it was a changed house. The girls were busy tacking up Christmas greenery. "It's not too soon!" Mattie laughed, her eyes dancing, her shoulders curving invitingly under her dress as she reached up. She was standing on a stool. When she stepped down her hem caught and she almost fell, but his arms found her and they both rolled back, laughing.

Alice, on a pillow by the window cutting ribbons, looked even more like a darling child. When she saw him her face turned red and she jumped up on the window seat and leaned on her elbows against the sill, looking out. "Oh, don't you just love the cold! I love the cold." She pressed her nose against the glass. "It makes everything seem so alive!"

All was warmth and sun. When their mother came in, instead of scolding or feeling faint, she laughed too. What had happened? Everything that had been glum before was now light; everything that had seemed impossible before now seemed not only possible but inevitable. In a flash he knew that Mattie would marry him, that all obstacles had disappeared, and he didn't know why.

He soon learned, when their brother walked in. He was the light of his mother's eye, the pet of his father. . . . They didn't even use his name, but called him Brother, or more often Darling Brother, as if he were the only one in the world.

Lieutenant Horace Ready was a delightful young man, one of those dashing officers Morgan had seen so often in Confederate service—tough but gentle, with a wiry determination to live at any cost but that of honor. He reminded him of Hutchinson, and there could be no higher compliment. He would have recruited him in a minute if his loyalty to General Hardee had not been so obvious.

Brother saw no reason, Mattie told him later that night, why they couldn't . . . He folded her in his arms and rocked her in the warmth of acceptance and relief. They kissed, searchingly . . . until he had to stop before he embarrassed her with his own need.

"They are calling you 'The Thunderbolt of the Confederacy.' " She smiled into his collar.

"So I've heard." He squeezed her to him.

He showed her his Aunt Catherine's ring, and told her more of his family, of the days at Hopemont; now that the fever of indecision was over they talked like newlyweds until past midnight. As he walked down the steps in the flush of personal victory, he determined to ask permission to attack Hartsville again.

The mood at Breckinridge's camp the next day matched his own. St. Leger had quickly made friends, joining Hanson in his passion for inspections. "What makes a good soldier?" he'd asked one of Bench-leg's men, and when the soldier answered "a man that kin sleep on a fence rail and cover with a shoestring," Grenfel laughed until his tasseled cap fell off. He repeated the story so often Cripps Wickliffe presented him with a shoestring and called it "Grenfel's blanket."

T.H., too, had lost his glum look. He had a letter from his wife, settled with her relatives in Augusta. He went about his duties as if he were at some military school and not about to face one of the biggest battles of the war.

"Do you think so?" Cripps asked his colonel as they walked their horses back to camp from the latest inspection. Morgan and his staff rode with them.

"It's only a matter of time," T.H. said quietly. "We've been lucky so far." But it was said matter-of-factly, as they said everything these days. With a new commander due any day and the army together again, they felt they could face anything Rosecrans could send.

Now's the time, thought Morgan. He asked again. This time he received not only permission to attack Hartsville but infantry support as well. Hanson, with the Fourth and Sixth regiments, plus Graves's battery, would march to Baird's Mill and wait as reinforcements while Colonel T.H. Hunt, with Cobb's battery and a detachment of the Second Kentucky and his old Fifth (renamed the Ninth Kentucky Infantry), would follow Morgan's cavalry to Hartsville, forty miles north of Murfreesboro, to take one of the strongest Federal garrisons on the Cumberland.

Everything he wanted! He couldn't believe it. With Cripps and Bench-leg and T.H., and even young Henry Curd, it would be Old Home Week— practically a Kentucky expedition! Not until he saw St. Leger's face did he suspect it was the wily Englishman who had smoothed the way with Bragg.

"Well, lad, you wanted me to act as liaison, remember?"

"Something more must be in the wind," Morgan said slowly, stepping on a burned-out cigar. When he looked up, he saw the mock disappointment on Grenfel's face.

"Well, it is true, General Johnston is expected tomorrow."

"I see."

"So do it," Alston spoke up. "Don't you agree, Duke?"

"I do," grinned Basil. "What difference can it make? We got what we wanted, didn't we?"

"He either wants to get us out of the way for the grand reception, or he wants to prove to his new commander that he is fighting a war. . . . We'll be the only force out," Breck Castleman growled, but it was said with a suppressed smile that broke into an open laugh when another thought came to him. "But I guess we can't go anywhere until our colonel brings the news to headquarters."

"That's right," Morgan answered, so happy nothing could spoil the day.

"To headquarters it is!" And he mounted Glencoe and turned, not to the Mill, but back to town.

Breathlessly, in the downstairs hall, holding her hands, he asked, "When I come back?"

"Oh, yes, darling. When you come back. God bless and keep . . ."

"Don't worry."

She looked at him. "That's like telling the sun not to come up."

"How could I not come back to you?"

He would forever and always, to the day he died, remember the look on her face. He could still feel her kiss as he whistled all the way back to Breckinridge's camp. T.H. had already issued his men forty rounds each, with orders to move out at dawn. A heavy snowstorm was passing. "It'll be clear tomorrow, you wait and see," he heard Cripps say.

"Do you want to wager that?"

Cripps smiled back. "You know I never bet with a friend on a sure thing."

"You just want to go up there to get out of dress parade," Morgan said easily.

"You know me too well."

"You'll be staying in camp tonight?" T.H. asked.

"I'm riding back to the Mill," Morgan said. "It will save three hours tomorrow. Especially if it snows," he joked, and dodged Hardee's infantry manual that Cripps threw at him.

The land lay in white mounds under the brittle light of a December moon. Ahead, the icy waters of the Cumberland would provide the best element of surprise. Nobody in his right mind would attack in weather like this. Just as nobody in his right mind would have turned back to Lexington. . . .

Private Henry Magruder was on picket duty and stopped him sharply, then grinned recognition. A tireless boy who found energy when everybody else sank with exhaustion, he had joined them just after Shiloh. Morgan returned the salute and passed on. They were his men. He drew a deep breath and the cold air stung his nose. They were his men and his command was now a real brigade, full strength and confident. And with Mattie waiting, they would take Hartsville.

Early the next morning the snow began to fall again, small sticky flakes that crowded leisurely onto themselves as they drifted, then slanted as the wind picked up. St. Leger's shoestring blanket lost its humor. Before dawn "Gary Owen" rang out and the cavalry saddled up. Hanson's troops arrived, with T.H. Hunt's not far behind. Morgan placed the main force under Basil —Gano's Third Kentucky (now under Colonel Huffman since Gano, with a heart problem, had gone on leave), Bennett's, Cluke's and Chenault's regiments, with Stoner's battalion, which had joined them in Murfreesboro—a total of fifteen hundred men. T.H. brought seven hundred. Quirk's scouts and other details had been sent during the night to reconnoiter in the direction of Hartsville, to watch the enemy camp at Castalian Springs, to report on the fords, and to picket the Nashville-Lebanon Pike. Basil was reluctant to leave before all the reports came in. The weather grew colder. Will took advantage of the extra time to go around cutting off the horses' tails.

"What in the world?" asked Basil. Alston absolutely refused to have his horse touched.

"See thet slush? Do yew want tuh wait till half their tails become boards of ice and bang against their hocks and bloody up their hinds? It'll be rough enuf goin' as it is, boys."

When St. Leger agreed, and stood his shiny thoroughbred to have its creamy tail cropped, Alston relented. They left camp about eleven A.M., the 7th of December, a Sunday, Hunt's infantry just behind. Lieutenant Henry Curd saluted and called out as Morgan galloped up the line. The infantry, marching through mud, trudged now on freezing feet. Some of the cavalry exchanged places with them and let the foot soldiers ride in order to rest. That was a mistake: Wet shoes and boots became even colder in stirrups, and the men begged to get down. By this time the cavalry had wet feet, and it was their turn to feel their toes turn to stone. It was now dark, and finding a horse's rightful owner became a problem that brought out the best cavalry curses, with no trace of humor.

Morgan couldn't blame them. It had been a miserable march. When they reached the ford about ten o'clock that night the infantry and Cobb's battery were scheduled to cross first. But only two small leaky boats were available, and it took seven hours—until five o'clock the next morning—for the crossing to be complete.

The cavalry had an even worse time. The river had risen since the last reconnaissance report, and past fording. They had to find a crossing farther down, and the only one proved to be a narrow bridle path which could admit only one horse at a time. But that ended in a little bluff four feet high. There was nothing for it but to leap the horses into that icy water—both man and horse taking a plunging bath, to come up sputtering. The bank on the far side was almost as bad. By the time a dozen horses had crossed, the path was a quagmire. The first men across built fires to thaw themselves, but eleven horses died and fifteen men had to be left behind with frostbite.

All this took most of the day, and by three o'clock Basil was so frustrated that he decided to take the men already across—with most of his command still on the southern side of the river—and march on to Hartsville.

Morgan, with the advance, was within three miles of the town at their designated meeting place and waiting by the time Duke got there.

The danger now was real: Surely the Federals at Castalian Springs, where six thousand Union troops were camped, were alerted to the action. That morning Morgan's advance guards had come upon a strong Yankee picket force about a half-mile from the main camp. The Federals fired and retreated. There would be no surprise. The attack was on.

St. Leger Grenfel was in his glory. The Yankee camp lay in thick woods on a rise of ground with their guns ready to rake anybody foolish enough to advance. In front of those guns lay a large meadow with a depression which deepened to the south into a ravine as it approached the river. Morgan's first plan, to form his infantry in this ravine, had to be abandoned: The Federal line was too close.

"I thought the scouts said fifteen hundred." Alex Tribble spat as they watched them form.

"Add a thousand to that, Captain," Basil murmured. He turned to Morgan. "Looks as if you have more than you bargained for, Colonel."

Morgan's mouth set in a grin. "You gentlemen must whip and catch these fellows, and cross the river in two hours and a half, or we'll have six thousand more on our backs."

Deducting horse-holders, the two regiments under Cluke and Chenault numbered four hundred and fifty men. They formed at a gallop, dismounted and formed again, as the horse-holders led away their mounts. Morgan ordered Cobb's battery to face the enemy left. Even before the men dismounted the Yankee Parrot guns opened an artillery duel with Cobb. Morgan would have given a month's leave for Gano now: Except for a slight skirmish, Cluke's men had never been under fire, Chenault's never. But they moved without pausing over that meadow, halting only long enough to send a volley before the little hollow of land allowed them to reload. Then, as they came up and out, they broke into a run. The enemy fire was high; after sending one volley the Federals fell back about twenty steps, trying to reload. Cluke's and Chenault's men ran on, and the Yankee line broke into a rout. By now T.H. Hunt's infantry scrambled out of the ravine, the Second Kentucky in the advance.

To his horror Basil saw them stop. Somebody had given the order to halt! But they soon rushed on again, practically overswept by the oncoming Ninth Kentucky, swarming over the ground. To their right Cobb still kept up a deadly fire, until a Yankee shell exploded one of his caissons and a Confederate private who had been sitting on top of it. They unlimbered and formed again. By now the Yankees, completely surrounded by T.H. Hunt's infantry and Morgan's regiments, took refuge behind a hill close to the river. Just as they retreated Morgan was reinforced by seventy-five men from Huffman. The Yankees behind their hill were dropping with each volley. A white flag appeared, and it was over. A. G. Montgomery, who had carried Buckner's truce to Grant at the surrender of Donelson, conducted the Yankee commander to Colonel Hunt for the surrender of almost two thousand Federals.

St. Leger, on his big gray, his red tassel flying, leaned forward so far shaking Breck Castleman's hand that he almost fell off his horse. The whole fight had lasted less than an hour. Morgan had never seen his men so elated. As soon as he could he found a piece of paper and, without dismounting and using his knee as a writing board, scribbled a note to Mattie: *Complete victory, my darling. Get your wedding dress ready.* He handed it to Sam Murrill, his chief of couriers, and watched him gallop off.

Still, they licked their wounds. The Confederate loss was 125, 65 from the Second Kentucky, 18 from the Ninth, ten from Cobb's battery and 32 from T.H.'s command. The more gravely wounded had to be left behind. As for the Yankees, the number of killed and wounded was over four hundred, and 2,004 prisoners were marched back to Murfreesboro—plus wagons of boots, shoes and ammunition.

They had no time to lose. The prisoners were gotten across the river first, then the cavalry, with an infantryman riding double on each horse. Six thousand Federals from Castalian Springs were already on the road behind, stopped by Quirk's elite guard, but not for long. Morgan sent Cluke, then Gano's men to hold them back just long enough for the river crossing. No sooner had Cobb unlimbered on the southern side than the Yankee guns answered on the opposite shore. Another ten minutes and it might have been a different story. It was a close call.

But a brilliant one, and as they marched through Lebanon and back to camp they knew they had a victory on their hands. In his congratulatory order, Braxton Bragg spoke of intelligence, zeal and gallantry, of cordial thanks and congratulations.

It was Tuesday before Morgan rode into Murfreesboro. He reached Mattie as soon as he could.

"So you did it," she said, her eyes shining.

"Now it's time for you to keep your side of the bargain."

43

"**M**y side?"

"Don't pretend." He took her hand and kissed it, taking a little longer to release it than General Hardee, who stood to one side of the Ready parlor with General Breckinridge and other officers of their staffs, thought, with envy, quite proper. General Johnston had arrived, and the whole town was abuzz with the news that President Davis himself would come to confer with his generals in a few days.

Behind her a half-circle of Confederate uniforms waited. Morgan let his eyes drift to General Hardee's face before he brought them back to hers. The moment was becoming awkward. They were waiting to congratulate him.

"What about Sunday?" she whispered.

"Everything good always happens to me on Sunday."

Hardee had overheard. "That's right, John Morgan! The Battle of Hartsville will go down as one of our outstanding victories! Now, come. I don't think you've met General Johnston. He leaves in the morning. . . ."

Joseph Eggleston Johnston was a wiry man of fifty-five with dark eyes, olive complexion, a dome of a forehead and the beard of a Spanish grandee. His father was of Scottish descent, his mother a niece of Patrick Henry. Johnston had graduated from the Point in the same class as Robert E. Lee. Like so many army professionals of his generation, he had served in the so-called Black Hawk and Seminole Wars, left the army for economic reasons, then went with Scott to Veracruz, fought at Churubusco, Molino del Rey, and Mexico City, was wounded and received three brevets for gallantry. And like so many of his fellow Virginians, he resigned immediately from the U.S. Army to enter Confederate service after Sumter. It was to Joe Johnston, rushing to Beauregard's aid at Bull Run, that the credit for that victory was given, but also the blame for not taking Washington. As Morgan shook his hand, he thought he understood: Here was a man whose energy, so dynamic you could almost feel it, was above all controlled. And in that instant, Morgan trusted him.

But the talk was light, and of the ladies. Hardee came up and reminisced about their last days in Murfreesboro, when Wood and Morgan covered Sidney Johnston's retreat. Alice was apparently just as much "in love" with her "dear old General" as ever, and he basked in her attentions. General Cheatham was there, and the Maneys from Oaklands, and General-Bishop Polk, a great bear of a man with a lock of gray hair that refused to stay out of his eyes. It was then, with talk of the fight at Hartsville at full tilt, that Mattie left her father by the fireplace and he raised his arms for silence. The buzzing stopped. All heads turned to him as Colonel Ready cleared his throat in anticipation of their reception of his news.

"Ladies and gentlemen . . ." He cleared again, and tried to control the smile that was pushing his side-whiskers out past his ears.

"Ladies and gentlemen! This is a most momentous occasion. Besides the arrival of General Johnston, in whose honor this dinner is given, we have two other reasons for rejoicing." He paused and looked around. The attention of his audience shifted to Morgan, then back again. When the chatter subsided, Colonel Ready tucked his hand in his vest and threw back his head. "The great victory at Hartsville . . ." Applause. Hurrahs. "And . . ." He lifted his arms again and brought them back to his sides slowly. "The betrothal of our daughter Mattie to the hero of Hartsville, Colonel John Morgan."

Colonel Ready didn't notice that Alice, her hand to her mouth, flew from the room. To their applause and exclamations the old man lifted his hands and wagged his fingers for silence. "And in these stirring times, which seem to demand that we live as fully as we can while still preserving our lovely customs"—*Hear, hear!*—"our Mattie and her hero have set the lucky date for next Sunday, here in this parlor, and you all are forthwith invited."

Mattie, in her blue-eyed, black-shining-silk-hair glory, was surrounded and allowed each to kiss her hand in turn. Rachel Maney marched toward her through the crowd with open arms, hugged her and led her away to a circle of ladies on the sofa. From the froth of their crinolines and scented heads she looked for Alice. "I think she went upstairs," her mother said with a frown. Mattie excused herself and found Alice face-down across her bed. When she entered her sister jumped up and ran to her, burying her face in her shoulder.

"Oh, Mattie, Mattie, forgive me! I've had such wicked thoughts lately! Then, when I heard Papa actually announce . . ." She caught her breath and blew her nose. "I've been miserable, un-Christian . . . oh, but I . . ." And she screwed up her face and wailed again. Mattie drew her to her, one hand patting her shoulder.

"We all love him. That's not un-Christian!" She pushed her sister away and held her at arm's length until Alice looked up. "You will be his sister, too, and I'm sure, if you had been a little older, he would have chosen you above me. . . ."

"Oh, do you think so?"

"Of course! You're much prettier. Everybody says so. There are a dozen boys downstairs this minute just holding their breaths waiting to ask for your hand."

"Well, I won't have them!" Alice exploded, but through a sudden smile.

Oh, to be that young and innocent, thought Mattie, feeling the weight of her family responsibilities, forgetting she was not yet twenty herself.

"Just think, Alice! If God made one John Morgan, maybe he's made another! He has five brothers! Don't you remember how you loved to hear young Tom sing 'Cheer, Boys, Cheer' when they were here before? I saw him watching you. . . . Then there's Henry Curd, his cousin. So handsome . . ."

"None of them," said Alice firmly, "can hold a candle to Hugh Gwyn. Do you remember how sweet he was, apologizing for reading my diary?" She ran to her dresser and brought back a handkerchief. When she untied the knot a gold ring lay in her hand. "It has his initials on the inside. He sent it to his mother to give to me, before the battle at Perryville. And I've neglected him so!"

"There, you see? And here we are, fishing around for another beau when poor Hugh is pining away at Knoxville."

"I'll write him! I'll write him tonight! This very minute!"

Not even her sister's reminder that, from the sound of things downstairs, the food was being served, could prevent Alice from unhinging the lap desk she had brought back from Washington City and using the last of her good stationery, saved for momentous occasions.

Morgan saw Mattie leave the parlor from a whirlpool of congratulations that confirmed his own feelings: He must be the luckiest man in the world. General Polk was offering to perform the ceremony, if they wished, and was of course accepted . . . a fact that St. Leger Grenfel found absolutely delightful. "A wedding, lad, officiated by an Anglican bishop in a soldier's uniform—what more could one wish for?"

General Bragg was late, but when he arrived the congratulations began all over again, and the reason for his tardiness Colonel Ready soon forgave: He had just come from the depot where he met Mrs. Bragg, who had fled their Louisiana plantation and was given safe conduct through the lines.

"She's had a frightful trip," Braxton Bragg said. "But when I told her I was invited here, and that my generals would be here, she insisted on coming."

And indeed, Morgan thought when he saw her, she would. A plump woman with nothing soft about her, from the bun of her drawn-back hair to the bulb of her chin, he could well imagine how she had gotten that safe conduct through the lines. She looked more like a general than her husband.

"Sir," she moaned to Breckinridge, "you have no idea how horrible it was. The house ruined and pillaged, the furniture destroyed, the carpets and featherbeds cut to pieces in their foolish search for hidden gold by those unrestrained vandals! Then, when nothing was left, they confiscated the plantation and sold it. . . ."

"My dear Madam," moaned St. Leger, stepping up in his best British-Officer-of-the-Line style, "how horrible!" When Mrs. Ready captured her and led her off, he followed. Morgan saw him from across the room, tilting his head, sticking out one leg as he stood on the other, and the ladies' upturned faces, fascinated by his accent.

General Polk, too, had found an audience. To smooth over, perhaps, a reference to Perryville—and his recent altercation with General Bragg in Richmond on that subject—he recounted, with his down-home laugh that exploded his face into wrinkles, two mistakes, one Yankee, one his own. Morgan, his eyes on the door for Mattie, hardly heard him.

"A close call," they all agreed, and each began adding his own tall tale. Braxton Bragg scowled under the shelf of his forehead in what he must have considered a pleasant expression. He looked across the room where his wife had St. Leger Grenfel pinned to the wall. Morgan followed his gaze and caught Grenfel's look, which said *Rescue me!* Morgan answered with lifted eyebrows that answered: *You asked for it, old boy*, then excused himself and strolled over. After St. Leger's chuckle—he had just laughed at something she'd said—died down, the lady congratulated Morgan on the news of his marriage.

"Thank—"

"I was just telling Mr. Grenfel here," she went on, "about a letter I wrote Braxton before Shiloh. 'Don't trust those Tennessee troops,' I told him. 'Put the Tennesseans where your batteries can fire on them if they attempt to run.' Now I'm here in the midst of them, where I never thought I'd be."

"The fortunes of war are strange," Morgan murmured.

"Fortunes, indeed!" And she was off again about the loss of her plantation, which they had bought with their hard-earned money, and not inherited, "like some folks."

Mattie, at the door, overheard, and lifted her eyebrows, then smiled. He excused himself and to a medley of female exclamations led her into the dining room. They pretended for a few seconds to be examining the food already being brought to the sideboard.

"How is Alice?" he murmured, then looked at her.

"She's writing a letter to Hugh Gwyn," Mattie answered as softly, and reached for his hand. *He's clever*, her father had said, when he heard that she wanted to marry him. *But he's Napoleon, not Caesar*, her father had said. *A little boy trying to be a man.*

"Wasn't Caesar, too, a little boy?" she'd asked then. "Aren't all men? Don't they need all the comfort they can get, all the love . . . especially when they're Napoleons? I can't help what he is, Papa. I can't help what I am. I love him."

It was then she knew, as she knew now standing beside his tall form, so magnificent in his uniform, as she felt his presence so near, so modest, so disturbing, that even if her parents had objected, she would marry him anyway. Even if the whole world objected. And she giggled, remembering her answer to the Yankee in Nashville: . . . *by the grace of God one day I hope to call myself* . . .

"Mrs. John Hunt Morgan," she said out loud, squeezing his arm.

"Horrible thought, isn't it?"

"Silly. I'm just trying it out, that's all. Don't you like the ring of it?"

If a dozen eyes hadn't followed them, he might have loved her right there, and not waited for their wedding night.

As if the Fates were adding to his happiness, the next day Adam Johnson reached Murfreesboro with a regiment he had raised in western Kentucky and promptly, with the good wishes and blessing of Forrest, who had sent him, joined the command.

"It's a fine body of men," Basil beamed. "And splendidly officered." He especially liked Robert Martin, the regiment's lieutenant-colonel, and Major Owens, with a reputation for discipline.

"Sorry we're a little under strength." Adam Johnson watched Morgan with soft brown eyes. "Lost some to capture, but we've got almost four hundred effectives, if you can use them."

"If!" Morgan beamed, then told him his good news.

"So the ladies finally captured you," Johnson laughed. "I thought you were the confirmed bachelor in the Confederate service!"

"I saw General Forrest just before he left," Morgan said then, and they commiserated over Forrest's ill luck.

"Oh, he's already recruited another command," Adam Johnson smiled. "And giving 'em hell all over West Tennessee! Remember what I told you in Nashville? God, the man's a genius, escaping from Donelson like that . . . seems like a million years."

Jefferson Davis arrived by special train from Chattanooga on Friday and made his headquarters at Oaklands. Morgan and Mattie, with Basil and St. Leger, rode over in Colonel Ready's carriage, remembering that day they'd had tea in the front parlor. The house now had a historical air about it. It was on the front lawn, Mattie told St. Leger, that Forrest had won Murfreesboro; at the dining room table that he had presented the terms of surrender to Tom Crittenden, and in the little study off the dining room that a Federal officer from the Ninth Michigan Infantry lay wounded.

"Yes, the yard boys are still raking up Minié balls in the grass," Rachel Maney smiled. It was evident Forrest was her hero of all time. That he wasn't here now seemed such a shame.

"Ah, but the cavalry is well represented," President Davis said graciously as he held out his hand to Morgan, who had just stepped into the sunny front room. He bowed low to Mattie and raised the glance of his thin, worn face, so often doing its own battle with neuralgia, to the smooth glow of her plump young cheeks.

The contrast between those two sent a stab to Morgan's heart. He had aged so. The last time he'd seen him was at the ball in New Orleans, after Mexico. He remembered running to the levee and watching the wake of the steamer as it rounded the bend. Little did he ever suspect that he would be seeing him again, but not like this. He seemed to be deliberately cheerful. Were the rumors true that he'd had some differences with Joe Johnston? With the Federals facing Fredericksburg and Richmond in danger, he had enough to worry about.

As if to remind himself that he must keep up his spirits at all costs, Davis prolonged his chat with them in spite of the fact that his generals waited in the dining room with maps spread on the table. This was, his look seemed to say, a drifting moment in time that he intended to catch and savor. "And do you still have a black hawk's feather, Colonel Morgan?"

"You do have a memory, sir! That must have been . . ."

"Don't remind me of my age! But come! It wasn't to congratulate you on your victory at Hartsville that I sent for you this morning . . . although I do that with deep gratitude as you might guess. I've just learned that I have another reason. . . ." He bowed to Mattie. "I'm most pleased to meet your young lady. Come . . ."

It was then Morgan noticed how the officers around the table were watching them and grinning. John C. Breckinridge and Roger Hanson reached out to shake his hand as he entered.

"Now," said the President of the Confederacy, and paused. "Now I wish to present to you, Colonel Morgan, the commission of brigadier-general . . . promotion will be formally announced at the review tomorrow. But since I learned of your wedding, I thought I would see you personally . . . and find out whether I'm invited or not!"

Hanson, too, was brigadier, Duke a full colonel, Hutchinson a lieutenant-colonel. Promotions would move down the line of his command.

"You will be our most honored guest," Morgan answered. "And there are no words to thank you, Mister President. . . ."

"Then don't try!" Davis said graciously, as he returned the salute and watched them leave.

Morgan later found out, from St. Leger, that Hardee had urged the commission be that of major-general, but that Davis had said, "I don't want to give my boys all their sugar plums at once."

"Brigadier is quite good enough." Morgan smiled when he heard it. Tomorrow Davis would review his troops, and Mattie was anxious to sew on his new rank that night.

When they crossed the deep gallery of Oaklands and settled again for the short trip home, St. Leger was unusually quiet. Sitting opposite them, he let his eyes drift from Albert's worn top hat to the "lucky couple," and hoped they would be. But with Basil Duke, as he dressed for the parade the next morning, the Englishman couldn't keep quiet. Of all the men he knew who loved Morgan, Duke had the deepest feeling. If anyone could dispel his fears, Basil could.

"What do you think of Miss Ready?" Grenfel ventured.

"A lovely girl. John couldn't have found a better. She'll be a real soldier's wife."

"I hope so."

"Do I detect a note of doubt?" Basil tried a chuckle but was having trouble with his buttons.

"In my opinion, and mind, lad, I've seen lots of ladies . . . she reminds me of some English girls I've known. Entirely too conscious of their charm. Became regular religious reformers in their old age—if they didn't reform their husbands first."

"Oh, Mattie's not like that," Basil said, biting his tongue. He got the last button to lie flat and twisted his head. His collar was too tight.

"Well, lad," St. Leger puffed out, slapping his knee, "I hope you're right. But a man with a wife, to my way of thinking, is less likely to risk death, for all their talk of protecting the ladies. A man like your Morgan, a cavalier, is especially vulnerable. And a soldier not willing to die . . . is no soldier.

This young lady is an extremely capable young woman; the more capable she is the more he admires her; the more he admires her the less risk he will take. The story of Samson is a myth; all his strength wasn't in his hair!"

At that Basil fell back laughing. "He'll be fine, Grenfel. You wait and see!"

I've seen enough now, Grenfel said to himself. Fascination he could understand—hadn't he been victim often enough himself? But passion—nothing but a good fight was worth a man losing his head over. Still grumbling, he followed Duke to the waiting horses.

All of Murfreesboro turned out. They couldn't know, as they watched the troops smartly coming to attention and their President reviewing them from his horse as he passed slowly down the line, that at Fredericksburg Lee was driving back six Union assaults. When the telegram arrived they had added reason to rejoice: Lee had saved Richmond and they had another Confederate victory. Morgan had just finished changing from his full-dress uniform when an orderly from the President's staff summoned him to Oaklands. He assumed it was to relay some message from Richard, since A.P. Hill was at Fredericksburg, but instead Davis, pacing nervously back and forth over Rachel Maney's parlor carpet, had something even more immediate in mind.

"The North has reached its nadir of depression with this defeat at Fredericksburg," he said in jerks, with each step. "They have, after almost two years of trying, failed to take Virginia. If we can stop them in the West . . ." and he stopped himself and looked meaningfully at Morgan. "If we can stop those supplies from reaching Rosecrans in Nashville. . . ."

Morgan had heard rumors, through Basil and St. Leger, of heavy discussions yesterday and last night between Davis and his generals. The President's description now, in broad outline, of a campaign was exactly opposite to one which Grenfel had reported as Joe Johnston's plan. Johnston had left yesterday—in a huff? St. Leger thought so. So they wouldn't be outflanking Grant and attacking Nashville, after all. They would, as Davis explained, send Stevenson's division of Kirby Smith's force—eight thousand men—to aid Pemberton at Vicksburg while Bragg, with thirty thousand, would remain at Murfreesboro to hold Middle Tennessee against seventy thousand Federals at Nashville . . . and Morgan's cavalry would tear up the railroad north of Bowling Green and destroy important trestles south of Louisville.

"Besides," said Davis, "Rosecrans won't move until the Cumberland rises in the spring, to afford him the aid of his gunboats . . ."

Morgan said nothing, remembering the Cumberland was already high enough.

"A Christmas raid," Davis was saying enthusiastically, sitting down at last and crossing his legs and staring at the fire. "They'll never suspect . . ."

Grenfel had already told him that Bragg had opposed another raid—in spite of the victory at Hartsville—saying that Morgan was dangerous because he wanted to act independently. "This is not your decision, sir," Grenfel reported Davis as saying, "but my own." The Englishman had chuckled at this weary, soft-spoken scarecrow of a President arguing with the ghoul-like Bragg, but Morgan, watching his President now, his face flushed with enthusiasm, was touched. Here was another man who wanted to win the war, hogtied by timid generals, his own loyalties, and squabbles over states' rights. Still, he thought Johnston's plan was better. He didn't like Bragg dividing his forces like that. But a raid!

"You have sent part of your command to Fayetteville, I understand."

"Yes, sir. To rest the horses."

"How soon can you get them here?"

Morgan calculated. "If I send today, they could possibly be here by Thursday."

Davis gave him his slow smile. "And in the meantime . . ."

"Yes, sir! You will be there tonight?"

"With bells on."

Because their President would leave just after the wedding tomorrow, the Readys had invited him to a dinner that night—a gala, as Alice, clapping her hands, described it. Thinking of Mattie now, Morgan mounted and rode toward Main Street, wondering if he dared tell her about this raid. If Hutch did indeed arrive by Thursday, they would leave Murfreesboro by Sunday at the latest, exactly a week to the day after the wedding. Hardly news one presented to a new bride the night before she married. He rode past the Ready house and straight to Breckinridge's camp to find Basil and Bill Breckinridge.

"I knew it was coming," said Basil.

"You don't approve?"

"The scouts report too much activity at Nashville for comfort."

"They won't move," said Morgan, flushed with the confidence of Davis. "We'll be too fast for them. Now, if you'll excuse me, I need a haircut."

St. Leger, when he saw the grin, let out a laugh. "Of course! To the young lady's house tonight, then our little party, your last evening of bachelor bliss! I say, old man, do you have another bar of that scented soap?"

The sun set behind a bank of red clouds. "It should be a good day tomorrow for Hutch," Basil said brightly. They were dismounting and handing their horses to the Ready groom, who led them to the carriage yard. Morgan unbuttoned his left glove and grinned.

"You're a good soldier, Basil, but sometimes your mind is too much on your work."

"Not with a raid coming up."

If he thought he could escape war talk in the Ready parlor, Morgan was disappointed.

"The hypocrites!" Colonel Ready was calling out from across the room. "Can you imagine . . . they want to form a new state, split off from Virginia. In effect, to secede . . . and their Congress will vote for it!"

Several guests had arrived, and one of them said something that Morgan didn't hear. He had caught Mattie's eye and message: When will all this be over so we can be alone? Tomorrow night . . .

"But seriously, General Hardee." Colonel Ready leaned forward and shot a look at his wife as if to say, *I will talk about it, in spite of you. I know it's her wedding supper and all that, but I must talk . . . I must say my piece.* His cigar, in a dish on a little table beside him, was dying a slow death. "The planter in this country—on this continent—is done for. The Yankees will ruin the planters in Confederate territory, over which they have no power, by 'freeing' the slaves in the hope of a rebellion, and ruin the planters in Yankee-held territory by *refusing* to free them—so we go bankrupt either way!"

"Come, now, dear," his wife piped up, "I fail to see how the Yankee planter will go bankrupt." Her daughter's wedding had given her new strength. She wanted to enjoy herself, and she wished he would hush up.

"All I know is," the old man said, picking up the dead cigar and pulling on it, "all I know is that if I could only hire the labor I need instead of taking care of a man's mother and father and wife and twelve children and paying all their medical bills. . . ."

"I think you're missing the point, dear," Mrs. Ready dared to say, and cleared her throat. "They don't want them in their own territories, slave or free. Didn't you tell me Lincoln's own state of Illinois passed that law prohibiting *any* nigra from crosssing its borders? They just don't want them on their hands—"

"But they're on somebody's hands," Horace Ready put in, with some awe at his mother's entrance into the discussion.

"Yes! That's my point, son!" Colonel Ready frowned. "Their owners' hands, who will go bankrupt and the Yankees will be there, conveniently, for the kill, as Mrs. Bragg says. They'll confiscate and sell—as they did the Braggs' plantation." He spoke to Horace but looked at his wife.

"General Bragg left his land," General Hardee reminded him, "and they took it under the Abandoned Property Act."

"But *Mrs.* Bragg was there!"

All eyes turned to Mattie, her blue eyes blazing.

"Ah, well, as Mrs. Bragg says, you have to have the *shopkeeper's* mentality to understand them," her father sputtered, aghast at his daughter's audacity. "They only fool with things that *pay*. . . ." At that moment the President arrived. As he passed his wife to greet him, Colonel Ready bent down. "This wedding . . . it's made you feverish!"

The talk turned to the victory in Virginia, and supper was served.

"I'm sorry."

"Don't be. Why?"

"Father . . ."

"Isn't used to your opinions?"

"Oh, yes . . ."

"But not in company?"

"Yes. But tonight . . ."

"Your mother spoke up. I thought that was delightful."

"You did? Father didn't."

"The women in my family are all outspoken, I'm afraid. You would feel right at home at Hopemont. My mother will love you."

"John Morgan, you'd turn anything into a compliment."

You make it easy was on his lips, but President Davis was striding across the room, his arm cocked.

"You do remember you promised?" The thin face broke into a wrinkled smile.

Do you mind? her eyes asked as her hand slipped onto Davis's arm. Morgan relinquished her with an old-world bow and looked up to see St. Leger watching him. Then the Englishman broke into a hearty laugh and shook his head. "Come along, lad. Let two old bachelors go in together."

Mattie, next to the President, tried to keep the talk light; then her mother made a small joke about Colonel Ready's newspapers, and someone mentioned *The Richmond Examiner*. The criticism Davis received from the Southern press was embarrassing. General Polk started a story to deflect it, but Davis leaned forward over his plate. "Yes, yes . . ." he said whimsically, nodding toward his wine as if considering the idea for the first time. "I live on the horns of a double dilemma. I consider myself a Jeffersonian, and as you may remember, he thought of Congress as a creature of the states— spawned by them and subject to their judgment. And here I am," he tried to chuckle, "with a Constitution committed to states' rights. . . . There is nothing in *our* Constitution that gives me the broad powers Lincoln has . . . or has taken."

"You wouldn't want to be such a tyrant," Colonel Ready fumed.

"Ah, there are times." Davis smiled in what he hoped was a joking way. "But, come! A toast to the young couple! How fortunate, to be here for this momentous occasion. I knew this young man in Mexico. . . ."

Afterwards, when the last guest had left, Mattie said quickly, "I'll see you out." He had to duck to avoid a garland of cedar boughs at the door. Once in the hall she swung around to face him.

"You're going somewhere, aren't you? *When?* You didn't tell me!"

"It's not certain yet . . . it was discussed only this afternoon . . ."

"*When?*"

"Not until Hutch can get back."

"How long will that take?"

"How did you know?"

"Never mind. How long?"

"If I send for him tomorrow . . . by Thursday."

"Look at me, John Morgan! Look at me! You've sent for him today!"

He raised a hand to push back a strand of her hair but she caught his arm and pushed it away.

"It was decided only this afternoon. I meant to tell you. . . ."

"*When?*"

He couldn't tell her they were going almost to Louisville, to destroy the tallest, largest trestles on the L&N, nor that it would be a hell of a lot easier getting a whole division of Confederate cavalry into Kentucky than out, once the Yankees knew they were there.

He took a deep breath. "We're leaving Sunday, Mattie. A week from tomorrow. I didn't want to worry you. . . ."

To his amazement a look of adoration and acceptance came over her face.

"Oh, how I love you, John Hunt Morgan! You wouldn't be you if you didn't want to go. You need to learn, though, that you'll soon have another recruit in this independent command of yours. Don't you think the latest soldier to join should know what's going on?"

By the time he got back to camp the boys had been celebrating over an hour. "Here is our guest of honor!" Henry Curd called out as Morgan stepped into the tent General Breckinridge had assigned them.

"Where is the General?"

"He'll be along," said T.H. "He's upset about something."

"A deserter," Basil put in. "Have a whiskey!"

"Now, boys!" Cripps shouted, climbing on a chair. "I'll give a toast!"

Their warmth and good wishes almost made him late the next morning. With St. Leger's Moorish songs still ringing in his ears, he stood in the Ready parlor with Bishop Polk and Basil looking over the rows of chairs toward the hall door. Cheatham, Hardee, Bragg. T.H. and Cripps, the blond head of young Henry Curd looking even more boyish next to the thin face of the President. The Hansons, the Breckinridges, St. Leger. They were turning in that expectant, half-amused, half-solemn way people at weddings assume as they wait for the bride. With a pang of guilt he missed Tom and Key and Charl—everything had happened so fast. He hadn't mentioned his wedding in that dispatch to Hutch. They were at this moment, right now, getting their horses ready for loading onto the cars.

Just as he thought that, the first yellow glow of candles and rustle of skirts signaled the appearance of the bridesmaids, their candles, in lieu of flowers, held so delicately, the soft light sending an upward glow across their faces, and Alice's the prettiest. Then Mattie in a lace gown looking lovelier than he had ever seen her and more radiant. His own weak knees gained some strength as she stopped and turned beside him. He took a shallow breath and slipped his eyes toward her as Bishop Polk began the service. "Dearly beloved, we are gathered . . . reverently, discreetly, advisedly, soberly, and in the fear of God . . . I require and charge . . . Wilt thou have this woman to be thy wedded wife, to live together after God's ordinance . . . ? Wilt thou love her, comfort her, honor her, and keep her in sickness and in health; and, forsaking all others, keep thee only unto her, so long as ye both shall live? . . .

"Who giveth this woman to be married to this man?"

"I, Martha Ready, take thee, John Hunt Morgan, to . . ."

All he remembered were her eyes, so earnest, so sincere, so deeply blue. She looked up with such frankness, without fear or affectation. And more passionate, because of that lack, than any eyes he had ever looked into in his whole life. His heart turned over.

". . . I give thee my troth."

Then his own voice, coming in from someplace far away: "With this ring I thee wed, and with all my worldly goods I thee endow: In the Name of the Father, and of the Son, and of the Holy Ghost. Amen."

Bishop Polk closed the manual. Mattie lifted her veil, and there was the kiss, the outstretched arms of friends and well-wishers as they moved away from the little improvised altar . . . the reception, the mounds of food, the regimental bands—two in the street, the third finally gaining entrance at

President Davis's command that no wedding was complete without dancing. As he waltzed Mattie around, smiling faces swirled: T.H., so gravely kind, Cripps still mischievous, a beaming Adam Johnson, and Basil, his rock. Even Braxton Bragg, his morose features trying to look festive. Albert atop the Ready carriage, and the ride to the farm, where they would spend three glorious, hidden days captured from reality. Of course you can do it, General Breckinridge had said. We'll handle things here. But just to make sure, Basil sent another message to Hutch and alerted the camp at Baird's Mill. In the meantime . . .

There might not have been a war. Snow fell again that night, with a hesitant, uneven sound, like birds picking at the tin roof of the farmhouse. Two servants had been imported from town the day before, and friendly fires turned the walls into rosy shadows as daylight faded. They sat on a small sofa which had been drawn up before the front parlor fire and luxuriated in their privacy. There was no need now to hesitate about his arm around her shoulders, or on her part to rest her head and snuggle against him. For a while light banter about the wedding and some of the guests stayed with them, but when that fell away they were left in a circle of firelight in a world of their own. That was when the snow began to fall, a sleepy, and yet exciting sound. My God, he thought, she's so young, and for the first time he worried. But he needn't have. As he took their candle and lighted her way to the bedroom and set it on the dresser, she turned to his arms as naturally as if they had lived together always.

Slowly, without taking his lips from hers, he slipped her shawl away and let it drop on a chair. He carried her to the bed and laid her lightly, as a child, against the pillows. She had, to his delight, dressed without stays, and the row of buttons down her bodice turned easily under his fingers. She watched his face as he maneuvered them, with that same trust she had sent to him at the altar. When he reached the bottom she sat up and pulled off her skirts, her head bent to his kisses on her neck. When she turned her cloud of silk-black, tumbled hair and her round face to him there was no teasing, only honest need. It was as if, although a virgin, she had waited for this night all her life.

"You're quite a lady," he said at last.

"You're quite a general."

"I've never heard you giggle like that."

"I've never been this happy before. Kiss me again."

He obliged. "How are you happy?" he persisted.

"Oh . . . like a little girl."

"You"—he traced a hair back from her cheek—"don't act like one."

"And you? What about you?"

There was so little time. So little luxury, that other couples must have known, without a war, to discover the mysteries of themselves, to sort out each other and discover a new being, the two of them, resonances passing back and forth and seeking and getting answers. The candle was sputtering and he blew it out and they listened to the tinny sound of the snow—half sleet as the wind picked up—and he told her about Uncle Simon and Uncle

Ben and Sard dying in the log barn and about Black Bess and Delilah and Randolph.

"And is Billy still your groom?"

"Yes, but I let him go with my brothers to Lincoln County."

"Is he a good groom?"

He told her about raising hemp, about firing the shives and about his grandfather and Hopemont and his mother and Aunt Bet, his father and the Morgans and Shadeland.

"We had a horse named Shadeland, too."

He sounded so serious she leaned up over him and rested against his chest. She followed his eyebrow with her finger and promised softly, "You'll go back to Shadeland one day. And I'll go with you." She bit her lip to keep a tear from falling and he pulled her down to him and held her head in both hands as he drank from her mouth again.

"Unless you . . . abandon me the way you did Black Bess, running back and forth on the other side of a river?"

But he saw now that his kiss had done its work and the question was frivolous. "I wouldn't have to," he laughed. "I can just see you, if you were a horse with those Yankees trying to catch you. You'd give them such a time they'd come flying over the water and we'd have them all for prisoners!"

But when, in bed the next morning, they listened to a cold rain dripping from the gutters and he told her that Uncle Ben used to call it "daid hosses eatin' grain," she put her fingers to his mouth with such a serious look that he would have laughed if she hadn't held his eyes with her own.

"Don't use that word," she said firmly. "Don't ever. There's so much . . . death . . . around." She was honestly trembling and he pulled the covers over her.

"You'll catch your . . ."

"See?"

The moment passed; she was smiling again. She was his Mattie, his brick of a girl, and rain or shine, he would win this war for her if he could.

Their three days melted into one. They bundled, ate, bundled some more, drank the last of her father's good Madeira, slept, awoke with the same amazement that they were together, that no messages had come to tear them apart. A passing farmer on a mule was enough to send her scurrying to the window, to draw the curtain. To his laugh and warning that General Breckinridge knew where he was if he wanted him, she would retort that General Breckinridge could get somebody else to ride around for him just this week, please and thank you! Her efforts at dressing for their last dinner together tore at his heart, for he had seen her mended skirts and the shoes she had saved for best. This was the girl who had set the pace of fashion in Washington when her father was a Congressman, his flirty, witty Mattie.

"Don't fuss at me too badly," he told her the morning they packed for the trip back to town. "We can do some railroading, divert the Yankees from moving out of Nashville . . ." When he saw she wasn't convinced he added: "And I can bring back a dress for you. What color do you want?"

Hutch arrived, as planned, on Thursday. Tom, as Basil predicted, was mad as hell at him for not knowing about the wedding, but excited about the raid. They were to leave as soon as possible. When Morgan walked into Breckinridge's headquarters he knew how much depended on their success.

"The British Parliament meets in January," Breckinridge began, without preliminaries. Before Morgan could ask what this had to do with the Confederate Army in Tennessee, the General leaned forward earnestly. "It won't be Mr. Lincoln's 'Freedom Paper' which will get them on our side," he said quickly, shaking his hair back and striking a match, which he stretched across his desk to Morgan's waiting cigar. He lit his own and flicked the flame into a dish. "No. It will be their own starving mill workers in Manchester who will force England to join France in intervention. If the Confederacy can hold onto Middle Tennessee. . . ."

When Morgan started to speak Breckinridge stopped him with another explosion. "It's significant . . ." He waved the cigar. ". . . It's extremely significant that Lincoln didn't deliver his December first speech in person. Have you read it? No . . ." The tall Kentuckian grinned. "I suppose not. Been too busy with other things? But it's important to remember that there was no mention of the pursuit of the war in that speech. And he suggested compensated emancipation. Of course . . . the Republicans have turned a cold shoulder."

"That's not surprising, is it, sir? How they would hate to pay us the first cent! I'm amazed he even considered such a thing."

"Maybe he's just sorry he started this war. Or we'll make him sorry. Have you heard the latest about Forrest?"

He could have expected it. With a depleted brigade and a four-gun battery, Forrest was roaming West Tennessee checking Grant's advance into Mississippi. It was a tale of hot pursuits and skirmishes, of all-night marches through snow and ice and a complete rout of the Federals down by the Tennessee River.

"Happened yesterday. The news just reached us," Breckinridge said.

That was so like him. Forrest, who had harassed Buell on Bragg's march into Kentucky and for thanks lost his command to Wharton; who raised another at Murfreesboro and saw it assigned to Wheeler, and now, with untrained recruits armed with shotguns fending off the Yankees and delaying Grant . . . Morgan could almost smell those railroad trestles burning, rejoice at those close escapes. The memory of that tall form leaning casually in his saddle, the light in his eyes: *Shall we give 'em a daar?*

His excitement must have affected his own eyes, for the General stood up and looked at him affectionately as he offered his hand. "Yours will be the first Confederate entry into Kentucky since we abandoned it," he said in somewhat oratorical tones. "It cannot fail."

"It will not."

"Make no mistake," Basil said as they rode away. "This is Bragg's plan, not the President's."

Morgan shook his head.

"You don't think so? Look at it this way. Bragg gets to sit at Murfreesboro

. . . he didn't want to attack Grant anyway. So now his cavalry . . . Forrest in West Tennessee, you up on the L&N in Kentucky . . . will do his work for him."

"At least it will prevent Rosecrans from moving, if those supplies can't travel."

Duke shrugged. There's always the river, he wanted to remind him, but didn't. He thought of St. Leger. *Your John Morgan is Don Quixote tilting windmills,* the Englishman had said. *But I like that, lad. I like that.* Yet who, Basil asked himself as he watched his brother-in-law, is Sancho Panza?

"Tracks can be repaired," Basil said after a minute.

"Not those trestles at Muldraugh's Hill," Morgan parried brightly. "Not so easily. You'll have to agree to that."

"I'll have to agree."

If we get there, Basil added to himself. Or back. Forty men can run into the woods, but not four thousand. And every Fed from the Cumberlands to the Ohio will know we're there. And they were moving now without Gano, still on leave.

"We've got Chenault, Cluke and Adam Johnson," Morgan smiled, reading his mind. "And this bridegroom expects to get back to his bride in one piece."

But he knew Basil was right.

The command, with the Second Kentucky and Bill Breckinridge's regiment back from their rest, numbered just under four thousand men, with some two hundred unarmed but mounted. It was entirely too unwieldy. On a raid, especially, communication was critical. All day Thursday, as Hutchinson's men came in, Morgan was busy at headquarters. By Friday morning he realized something must be done, and called a staff meeting. He proposed that they divide the command in two, one brigade under Duke, the other under Adam Johnson, the senior colonel there. For some reason Adam declined—perhaps because he did not consider himself enough of a "Morgan man."

After consulting the records, St. Leger, as adjutant-general, stepped forward with three names: Colonel Roy Cluke, Colonel W. C. P. Breckinridge, and his own. In awkward silence Morgan fingered the paper. St. Leger was not, legitimately, in the Confederate service, but merely on attached duty. There followed some discussion about Cluke's date of rank counting from the day he was authorized to raise a regiment and the day the regiment rolls were filled. If the first date were accepted, Cluke would outrank Bill Breckinridge; if the latter, Breck would outrank him. As for Grenfel, Morgan shrugged his shoulders. Nobody, with the exception of Johnson, had received his commission from Richmond, although rank was recognized. The decision would be, then, entirely up to the commander, and Morgan knew there was no love lost between the wiry Englishman and the soft-spoken, seemingly effeminate Breckinridge. But he had seen Bill in battle, and knew his abilities: He had made his Ninth Kentucky a regiment to be proud of. As for Cluke, Roy had joined him, with Chenault, in Lexington in September, about the same time that Kirby Smith had given Breckinridge authority to raise a battalion and Gano had raised his regiment. The decision came down in favor of Breckinridge.

St. Leger fumed, but as adjutant, did his job. The first brigade, Duke's, was composed of the Second Kentucky, Lieutenant-Colonel Hutchinson, commanding; the Third Kentucky (Gano's regiment), Lieutenant-Colonel Huffman commanding (Gano being on furlough); the Eighth Kentucky, Colonel Leroy S. Cluke commanding, with Palmer's battery of four pieces (two twelve-pounder howitzers and two six-pounder guns). The second brigade, now Breckinridge's, would contain the Ninth Kentucky, Lieutenant-Colonel Stoner commanding; the Tenth Kentucky, Colonel Adam Johnson commanding, and the Fourteenth Tennessee, Colonel Bennett commanding. The second brigade would have one three-inch Parrot, commanded by Captain White, and the two mountain howitzers—the Bull Pups—under Lieutenant Corbett. The troops were to leave Murfreesboro immediately, for camp at Alexandria, some thirty miles by winding roads to the northeast. Departure: Monday morning.

"It's a regular army, Brother Johnny!" Key exulted.

Morgan looked at him, so full of news. It had been a good rest down there, for both men and horses. He had never seen Hutchinson, or his men, look so fit. And he had kept his promise to his mother, that Key would stay out of battle. So far. Charlton, on his staff, was busy with details at camp, and Lieutenant Tom Morgan he had sent with a detail from Company A, Second Kentucky, to help Castleman's Company D reload their gear for the march. He mounted Glencoe and motioned Key to come with him. As they rode away from the river into town he half turned in his saddle and grinned. "How would you like to stay in Murfreesboro? Alice has lots of pretty girlfriends."

"Brother Johnny! And let you have all the fun chasing Yankees? I joined you to fight, didn't I? When am I going to have the chance?"

Morgan looked off and waited for Key's horse to catch up. He slowed Glencoe and they walked side by side. "Do you remember what I told you when I sent you back to Lexington?"

The boy frowned. "I remember you said it would be only temporary."

"But also that you had a job to do."

"Some job!"

"It has to be done. And this time"—he tried to make his voice sound grim—"this time you may have a bigger battle on your hands than any of us bargain for."

Again, as he had done before, he sensed that he had touched some chord of response, and quickly built on it. "Look," he said, slowing to a stop and speaking even softer. "Rosecrans is sitting in Nashville just waiting to make a move on Murfreesboro. General Breckinridge is sending us to divert them, but everybody knows that the real battle will be here."

"They do?"

"Ask Uncle T.H."

When the boy thought a moment Morgan added: "Only this time you've got two girls and a sick lady . . . and . . ."

When Key reluctantly asked, "Their father isn't in the best of health, either, is he?" he knew he had won.

If he could have known, also, that he would never see Murfreesboro, Tennessee, again, he might not have felt so satisfied.

44

It was his last night with Mattie before they left.

"How many 'last nights' will we have before this is all over?" she asked, her eyes roaming his face.

His hand reached out and smoothed her hair. It lay across the pillow like a black fan, the light of the candle by their bed catching little golden lights. "With Forrest in West Tennessee and Van Dorn between Grant and Vicksburg . . . things will begin popping soon."

"Soon? Then why don't they start? Why do we sit here waiting for those Yankees in Nash—"

"That's exactly what we're doing." He watched the little pinched circles at the corners of her mouth and tried to sound convincing. "Forrest will keep them busy on his side, I'll hit the railroad in Kentucky. Besides, they won't move until spring. . . ."

"That's what they think about you. Suppose they start playing your game?"

"You would have made a good general." He grinned. "Can the general take an order?"

"What?" she said, still distracted.

"Kiss me."

When he walked into Breckinridge's headquarters the next morning to say good-bye, he could have cut the gloom with a dull knife. He found T.H. and learned the story.

"The General's at a court-martial, Johnny."

That wasn't unusual, for a Saturday morning. Morgan told him so.

"I know. But this one's different. Two weeks ago one of Bragg's bounty hunters brought in three men from the Sixth Kentucky."

Morgan could have said again that there was nothing unusual about that, either, but the look on his uncle's face stopped him.

"One of those men—he's just a boy—is Private Asa Lewis. Some of my best men know him. He'd enlisted for twelve months, and when his outfit was reorganized for three years or the period of the war, Lewis naturally thought the reorganization of his regiment didn't bind those soldiers who hadn't personally reenlisted. You know the problem."

"That seems reasonable."

"It would be, anywhere else. But you know as well as I do Bragg's policy of drafting Kentucky exiles, and how some of his Kentucky officers threatened to resign . . ."

"I don't . . ."

T.H. walked to the window and looked out across the camp toward Stones River. The cupola on the courthouse at Murfreesboro was just visible beyond the trees. He talked slowly, as if to himself. "So, not feeling that he was obligated to stay with the regiment, Lewis went home. His father had died, his mother with three children was alone. Lewis requested a furlough to go home and lay in a crop, and the request was denied. You see," said T.H., "he'd gone home before without permission and come back, with only a reprimand. That won't be the case now. General Breckinridge has spoken in his behalf."

Another Southern farmboy called home by harvest time. If they didn't do it, who would? Hundreds had, to return to their units with few questions asked. Then his own *why* stuck in his throat. Yes, Bragg could use this boy as his scapegoat, his example to the Kentuckians. *But surely he wouldn't* was smothered by *Oh, yes he would.*

Cripps came in a second later, his face white. "Guilty as charged," he said, and sat down. "The sentence is death."

T.H. looked down. "When?"

"The day after Christmas."

"Damn!"

"That's six days from now," Morgan said evenly. "That's enough time for a . . ."

"He won't change his mind. I wish I could think so." T.H., at his desk again, rested his head in his hands and looked up. "He's said too many times Kentucky blood is too feverish for the health of the army. Well, now, he's been subordinated to Joe Johnston and has another chip on his shoulder. He'll use it to do a little bloodletting. Just as he got rid of Forrest, and is now . . ."

But T.H. stopped. For the first time Morgan admitted to himself his own half-buried suspicion, that this raid into Kentucky was just another move on the chessboard of Braxton Bragg's ego. *As he is now getting rid of Morgan?* his smile said as he watched T.H. leave. But it was the President's idea, he reminded himself.

He didn't see Breckinridge. He waited another half-hour. Henry Curd came in with coffee and they drank in silence. Hanson stopped by, looking grim, but only for a moment. With his usual determination to cling to every vestige of optimism around, he swore things would come right. He had gained some weight, and his breath came short when he was excited, but Roger Hanson was still one of the most handsome men in Confederate uniform, and for all his love of drill, one of the most adored by his men. He stuck out his hand now.

"I know you'll do well, John."

"Will you be at the review?"

"I wouldn't miss it."

Well, maybe T.H. was wrong about the death sentence, Morgan thought as he put on his hat and walked out into the sunshine. Breckinridge still carried a lot of weight, and six days might see Braxton Bragg's mood change. As for his own, it had never been better, and he couldn't let his doubts about Bragg's intentions worry him. The idea that a general, even an egotistical one, would deliberately misuse his cavalry as some kind of punishment was downright insane. . . . Still, you did tell him Kentucky recruits would come swarming. That loss is in his craw and he won't forget it.

Long before he reached the square his mind swung to his work. He knew that his men in bivouac at Alexandria had been busy around the clock. The regiments were being carefully inspected by the surgeons and horse doctors, and every sick soldier and disabled horse ordered replaced. Only stout men and serviceable mounts would be permitted to come this time. Even those left behind in Murfreesboro seemed to partake of the excitement as they broke camp for the move—including jokes about Will Webb's short-tailed horses.

"Nivver yew mind," Will spit. "Ain't summertime yit. Y'all wull be choppin' off yourn—er wisht yew had!"

Lunch at the Readys' was hurried, but blessedly so—his schedule gave them no time for lengthy good-byes. Tomorrow the Readys and Key would drive the thirty miles to Alexandria in their carriage. Lieutenant Ready, his good humor bubbling over, had received permission to live at home for a few days and would come with them. So, Morgan sighed as he mounted Glencoe and looked back at them lined up by the walk, the breeze moving Mattie's skirt as she waved her hand, it has been easier than I thought. Now if I can make coming back as happy an occasion. . . .

Sunday was a gorgeous day. Blue sky, bright sun. Who could be unhappy on a day like this? Everything would go well. The first man he saw as he approached his bivouac was Breck Castleman, mounted on his Kentucky thoroughbred, a gray mare. Brushed and polished in a fresh uniform, Captain Castleman's young face was a sun itself. Of course. There was no doubt. The commander of the finest cavalry division in the Southern army sat straighter in his stirrups.

And it was. As they formed, their regimental colors fluttering in the breeze, their horses' flanks shining in the sun, he knew it was. Mattie and Alice, with Key between them, were sitting in the Ready carriage, their father and brother watching behind a grinning Albert. T.H., God bless him, and Roger Hanson, with Henry Curd and Major Cripps Wickliffe had taken the time to ride out. From where he sat Glencoe, Morgan saw Henry chatting with Alice, and the imposing form of Hanson mounted beside him.

Morgan had never commanded so many men. Almost four thousand troops. He had never been so proud. The most gallant, dashing, skillful men in the full flush of their youth moved forward into line, their horses prancing, their firearms shining, their bugles blowing, their officers ramrod-straight. The command was given, and the whole division came to a halt, facing their general. As adjutant, St. Leger rode over to take his place, on the other side of Duke, with a plume in his hat. Bill Breckinridge was on Morgan's left. Their horses shifted; their arms, held in rigid, reverent salutes, remained like four triangles in the glinting sunlight.

The visitors were watching from a little knoll overlooking the shallow valley where company after company stood their horses in line. Morgan's eyes moved from the Ready carriage to the men before him. Bowles, Sheldon, Quirk; Adam Johnson, Cluke and Chenault, Bennett with his antic

Tennesseans, Captain White and the Parrots, Lieutenant Corbett with the howitzers. He tried to swallow back the lump in his throat as he watched blond, handsome Charlton and young Tom Morgan trot by, saluting. On the right flank the artillery wheeled into position. Ah, it was a spectacle right out of Agincourt! It must be doing Grenfel's heart good. To be off on another jolly lark with St. Leger, to have Charl back from prison and Basil with a whole brigade. What more under the stars could a man hope for?

For three miles in fours they passed before him. Then the regimental bands struck up Duke's "Morgan's War Song" sung to the "Marseillaise":

> *Ye sons of the South, take your weapons in hand,*
> *For the foot of the foe hath insulted your land.*
> *Sound! Sound the loud alarm!*
> *Arise! Arise and arm!*

Almost simultaneously they broke into "Here's health to Duke and Morgan, drink it down. . . . Here's health to Duke and Morgan. . . . Down, boys, drink it down!" before they swung into the soul-catching chorus of "My Old Kentucky Home."

As the last of the column passed, with a last look at the little rise of ground where the visitors still watched, Morgan galloped down the line to the cheers that increased in volume and gathered like a wave to overwhelm him while Glencoe, sensing the elation, swiveled his ears.

After the review, after he had told Mattie good-bye again and received best wishes from T.H., Cripps, Henry and Hanson, Basil rode up with the news that St. Leger had resigned. To avoid explanation, Grenfel had ridden back to town.

His own happiness must have blinded him to the Englishman's state of mind.

"Haven't you noticed?" Basil worried. "He's been going around in a pique ever since Bill Breckinridge got the second brigade. Like an English nanny." A sudden thought made him laugh. "He's joining the nannies in a way. . . . He's going to be Bragg's Inspector-General of Cavalry."

Who . . . ? he started to ask, then stopped himself. It was one of the duties of a commander to make these decisions; he couldn't put that burden on Duke.

"Captain Maginis," Basil offered, "has seen as much service as any soldier here. And he was ordnance officer for General Walthall."

"In Hindman's division?"

"The same."

"I've heard General Walthall is very demanding."

Basil, who had personally asked for Maginis to be assigned to his staff with the first brigade, waited a minute before adding, "I think he'd make an excellent A-G."

Morgan looked at his brother-in-law and smiled.

"Done."

The next morning, Monday, December 22, the division took up its march for Kentucky. The weather held: It was another beautiful day, clear, cloudless, a bright sun filtering through dark green cedars as they swung up. Again, as they had done at the review, the men cheered their leader and his staff as they galloped forward to the advance. They reached the ford at Sand Shoals without incident just before dark. Duke's brigade crossed, but nightfall found the two commands separated, with the cold waters of the Cumberland flowing between.

By daylight Tuesday the first companies of Bill Breckinridge's brigade were in the water, and in spite of the delay, the command made thirty miles before bivouac. That night in camp, while some of the men baked ash cakes in the embers of their campfires, Will Webb and Frank Leathers saw to the horses and mules. Much to his chagrin, Will's own horse had lost a shoe, and in the process had torn a gap below a nail hole. "I'll fix it," said Leathers, who had already started his forge. But when he trimmed, he sliced into the sole and blood spurted.

"Durn, durn, durn!" Will sputtered. They stuffed the area with oakum and tar, but his horse limped back to the picket line. Will walked over to a campfire where some of the men were already peeling back their corn shucks. The warm smell of fresh cornbread eased him somewhat. When he saw the open, cheerful face of Tom Morgan making the best of his meal, he felt better. "Yew want to come along," he whispered, "if Ah kin find a hoss tuh trade?"

They both knew Morgan's strict rule about horse-pressing. At Tom's shocked look Will added: "Don't yew worry none, sonny. Ah won't cause no ruckus. If Ah find a good'un, Ah'll fancy-talk. A man cain't be blamed if a feller wants tuh trade, now kin he?"

Toward midmorning, after they had crossed the Kentucky line, Will saw a man turn into the road from a side lane just as the second brigade passed. He dropped back from his place in the column and motioned Tom to fall in beside him. They kept their horses at a walk and found the man ambling along on his horse in the grass beside the road, filled with Morgan's men. Will pulled up beside him, tipped his hat and spit. They rode side by side for a hundred yards, Tom following. Will soon learned the man was a preacher.

"Yew reckon it'll be a hard winter?" Will called out companionably.

"Yessir, Ah do," said the stranger, whose black broadcloth coat seemed ill-equipped to handle too much cold weather. "Heard a katydid holler on the Fourth of Joo-ly. Yew kin count ninety days, and yew'll git yore first frost. An' we had it . . . early."

"Why, that's right, we did," Will said, as if the preacher's remark were an unexpected treasure of wisdom. He waited a few paces, sitting slightly heavier on his right seat bone, to keep his weight off that bad left hind. "Seen enny woolly worms?"

"Ah don't hold no truck with woolly worms," the preacher grumbled, but his irritation at this tomfoolery made him look sidewise at Will for the first time, then back at the road again.

Will waited awhile, then said, "That's a mighty likely hoss yew're ridin', sir—a mighty likely animal."

The preacher straightened. "Yes, he's a right pert nag."

"Smart, too, ain't he? Nothin' thuh matter with him?" Will winked at Tom, who was now abreast of him on the other side.

"He's sound from his ears to his hocks. Thar ain't a soft spot in him," the preacher said, as if he'd been insulted, and looked Will full in the face.

"This here's a good chunk o' hoss, too," said Will. "He's by Denmark. His dam was by Drennon out of a Whip mare. He can go all the gaits when he's right, but a fool of a blacksmith pricked him this mornin'."

"Pull his shoes," said the preacher, "an' let him stand a week in wet grass."

"Ah ain't got thuh time. As yew kin see, Ah'm engaged in public service."

They had fallen about fifty yards behind the column. Even the Bull Pups were rattling along ahead of them across the crusted ground. With another wink at Tom, Will went on in the same companionable tone: "As yew see, Ah'm travelin' a piece, an' Ah'm compelled to ask yew to swap hosses. Yew sound like a man who kin doctor this hoss."

"The hell you say," the preacher exploded. "Yew're the drunkenest man to hide it so well I ever see."

"Yore gettin' the best of the trade, stranger," said Will, looking hurt. "Thar ain't sech a fox-trotter an' single-foot-racker as my hoss—or rather yore hoss," he said, as he pulled a pistol from his belt. "Fer he's yourn now—in Kentucky. Don't multiply words, now, but climb down. Yore hoss thar needs attention; take him an' tend to him."

They exchanged, Tom aghast.

"That's how yew swap hosses in the army, boy," laughed Will, when they regained the column. Tom noticed, however, that Will avoided riding near the staff officers for the rest of the day. In enemy country you needed written permission from your captain, with the owner paid in Confederate currency; in loyal country, in the presence of an officer and with the consent of the owner, you could trade. Will was off-limits and he knew it, and tried unsuccessfully to pretend to Major Bowles, when he rode past Company C, that his horse had always been chestnut, and not a bay.

That night they went into camp five miles from Glasgow. Breckinridge sent Captain Jones, Company A of the second brigade to reconnoiter. When Morgan learned that Breckinridge intended entering the town, he sent Major Steele with two companies of Duke's brigade as support . . . and insurance. "It's Christmas Eve," he joked. "I know my boys. If there's a tavern open, they could stop for too much cheer." Will Webb, and to Morgan's chagrin, Tom Morgan went with them. "Ah'll take kar of thuh boy," Will promised.

There was a tavern open. Just as Jones entered Glasgow, a Michigan battalion came into town from the opposite side to give it some business. The night was dark. The two columns met in the town square and the flash of pistols and shotguns and reeling horses obscured for a time the fact that Jones was down, mortally wounded in the chest. As the first company of Major Steele's detail rounded the corner, Will saw Jones and dismounted, in spite of the fact that the Federals still held the square and were sending volleys down the street. Tom, just behind him, saw with horror a Yankee soldier raise his rifle and fire. Will grabbed his neck and fell back, his face a blur of blood. Tom, yelling at the top of his voice, dashed up, but Lieutenant Sam Peyton was after him.

"No use!" Peyton was yelling, when two bullets found him, one in the arm, the other in the thigh. His horse, crazed with fear, ran headlong toward the enemy. With his good hand Peyton propped his carbine on the other arm and fired at a stray Yankee trying to capture him, but another came from behind and he went down, tumbling to the ground with the second man, who jammed a pistol in his chest. Before the man could fire Sam reached up with his knife and slit his throat.

By the time Tom Morgan reached him, Sam Peyton was weak from loss of blood. "You tried to save me," Tom choked.

"Don't tell anybody," Peyton tried a grin. "Just . . ." But he passed out before the words could come.

"Damn Yankees!" yelled Tom. Will's body, up the street, blurred in tears. "Damn, damn!" Under his arm Peyton's heavy body sank back. *I've got to get him across my saddle, I've got to . . .* A sound of rushing hoofbeats. The Yankees were gone.

That next morning—Christmas—the division followed the Federals down the road toward Louisville. Peyton and Jones, unable to be moved, were left in Glasgow. As a cold rain started, Will was buried in the cemetery.

Morgan stood bareheaded, stunned. A gray, roiling sky hung low, with distant thunder. Will was gone. He stood a moment before remounting, unable to believe that under that muddy mound Will was still at last. No more stories of Genrul Harrison or those rainy times up on the Maumee . . . how many more would he see gone? West, Niles, Wash. He left money for a headstone and his grief came out in a stern rebuke to his brother: "I don't ever want to see you do such a damn fool thing again!"

The news of the raid would spread. Every Federal outfit in Kentucky would be on their trail now. He sent Quirk with Lieutenants Peddicord, Hays, Hawkins and the advance guard of Duke's brigade—fifty men—to clear the road ahead of any Yankee cavalry they met. The guard ran into— and through—a whole battalion, and when Quirk dashed back, doubled over his saddle, he caught two balls on the top of his head. When he saw his general a bloody bandage swathed his head, but a big Irish grin sat on his mouth.

"You mean you haven't reported to the surgeon?"

"Begorra, General, a head built in County Kerry an' used to the shillelagh can't be done in by a little Yankee bullet!"

Just before sunset, as they were starting to cross the Green, the men found "the biggest wagon in Kentucky"—loaded with Christmas goodies for the market at Glasgow, but abandoned by the sudden military activity. There was enough food—cakes, pies, cured hams, smoked fowl—to give each regiment a Christmas banquet that night and make their river crossing, even in pouring rain, something of a picnic. Morgan had sent Adam Johnson, veteran of Forrest's quick marches, toward Munfordville to throw the Yankees off track. Maybe he could. The command stopped for a few hours on the north bank of the Green—their first rest since leaving Tennessee.

Just after daybreak they were on their way again, with men and horses slashing through icy rain and mud. They were getting closer to their old stomping grounds. Morgan rode with Ellsworth and the advance guard into the little town of Upton to cut the wires and tell tall tales over the telegraph.

"They may be on to us," Lightning worried. "There's only one reason why we'd be this far north, and they know it."

"Then let's visit the Bacon Creek bridge again," Morgan smiled. "They may think that will satisfy us. . . ."

"And if we don't make it to the Muldraugh trestles," Ellsworth started, then saw his general's face. "But we'll make it," he ended, and turned back to his wires.

"This is getting to be a habit," Basil joked. They had burned the bridge at Bacon Creek twice before, in the old Woodsonville days.

"But this time there's a stockade, close enough to cover you with fire."

"Then give us a gun to answer them."

Hutchinson was in command, Basil relinquishing that prerogative as a courtesy. They took Webber's Company F, Company B and Castleman's Company D, plus some details from Gano's Third Kentucky—and the Parrot. "I want you to have enough men to withstand any force they might send up from Munfordville. It's only eight miles away."

"I know exactly how far it is," Castleman grinned, and followed George Eastin and his other lieutenants to their horses. They were all "old" Morgan men now, and besides, they would have the aid of the Parrot, a prize from Hartsville.

Morgan, Charlton, Tom and the others waited at Upton. Three hours went by. Surrounded by burned-out cigars and the remnants of his supper, Morgan could stand it no longer. He mounted, and taking Charlton and Captain Maginis with him, rode the six miles to the bridge.

"Well," he breathed. "Things have changed."

There was a large stockade less than a hundred yards from the bridge. Hutch had brought the Parrot within range and they were shelling as fast as the gunners could load, but the garrison stood intact.

"Where's Castleman?" Morgan yelled at Webber.

"Took Companies B and D down the Munfordville road . . . Federal cavalry," he got out between shells. Morgan's eyes went back to the bridge, where Hutch, in his impatience, had ordered a dozen men with torches. But they were within rifle range from the stockade—and in rain, which put out their fires as quickly as they were started. More men—perhaps a half-dozen —had gotten behind the abutment and were throwing lighted pieces of wood onto the flooring, but the Federals quickly shot them away. Just before Morgan arrived Captain Wolfe of the Third Kentucky was shot in the head and lay across the bridge, too far from the end to be safely carried off. Two shells from the Parrot now found their mark, setting on fire an old barn that had been included within the walls of the garrison. Morgan quickly scribbled a note and sent it in under a flag. He demanded immediate surrender. By this time the flames from the barn were shooting fifty feet against the sky. The word came back: terms accepted. Captain Wolfe, after two hours on the bridge, rose to his knees and shook his head. The beating rain had revived him; the wound was luckily just a graze.

"Now Basil, it's your turn," Hutch joked from his big gray as he leaned a sweaty face toward Duke. "The General wants you to burn the bridge at Nolin Creek. Take the Bull Pups."

Charlton insisted on going with the howitzers, and Morgan consented. Shortly after they left, Castleman came back with word that the road to Munfordville was clear. They waited to sign paroles, then rode back to Upton. Exhaustion was taking its toll.

At Upton they caught an hour's rest until Duke's detail returned from Nolin Creek with the news that the railroad bridge and culverts and cow-gaps for four miles on either side were gone.

"We can't wait here," said Morgan. In spite of a numbing fatigue, they had to move on. The Federal garrisons at Glasgow and Munfordville were alerted; in spite of Ellsworth's efforts, Morgan was sure the one at Elizabeth-town would be waiting for them.

Thirty miles away stood the prizes: the great trestles rising ninety feet from the floor of the Ohio River Valley, each five hundred feet long. But between the invaders and the trestles lay Elizabethtown. They could circle the town, but that meant being caught between that garrison and Mul-draugh's Hill, with no retreat except down its steep sides into the river.

Adam Johnson, back from his feint, met them at Hammondsville, and they camped that night within six miles of Elizabethtown. Quirk's scouts reported six hundred Federals, commanded by Lieutenant-Colonel Smith. As Morgan's command trotted in fours toward the town the next morning a courier with a flag stopped them with a message for General Morgan. Colo-nel Smith knew his strength, could surround him, could compel his surren-der. Colonel Smith trusted a prompt capitulation would spare him the disagreeable necessity of using force. As tired as he was, Morgan let out a belly laugh which completely confused the Union corporal, a German im-migrant who hardly spoke English. One thing the Corporal knew: His colo-nel wanted the Rebs to surrender.

"Tell him," smiled Morgan, "I admire his spirit—unusual in my experi-ence—but tell him also that I know *his* strength, that I have *him* surrounded, and, on the contrary, I have the honor to demand *his* surrender."

They watched the short little man remount his horse and scamper away, still confused, but convinced, by the laughter that followed him, that his colonel's offer had been refused.

During the parley the men had not been idle. Breckinridge's brigade formed on the left of the road, Duke's on the right. Cluke's Eighth Kentucky dismounted and approached the town, its left flank cautiously close to the road. Both brigades, on Morgan's orders, kept the bulk of their men in reserve. The Parrot was placed in the road. As soon as another message from Colonel Smith was received, with the news that Morgan's terms were re-fused, the Parrot opened. Morgan rode with Tom to the town's cemetery, on a high hill left of the road. Here the Bull Pups and the other Parrot had been set up.

They could see Cluke's men—who had nicknamed themselves "The War Dogs"—moving warily. The enemy had entrenched themselves in houses, and although there were only six hundred Yankee soldiers, memories of Augusta made the gunners keep up a steady fire of grape and canister. Rifles opened from the houses. Cluke's men took whatever meager cover doorways offered. Then Colonel Stoner, Bill Breckinridge's second-in-command, burst into town from the left with the Ninth Kentucky and occupied the houses at the edge of town. Duke sent for one of the howitzers, and Morgan ordered Lieutenant Corbett to place it on the railroad embankment, where it crossed the road.

From the hill Morgan and Tom watched the drama. All the gunners were driven away from the howitzers except Lieutenant Corbett, who sat on his carriage while bullets hopped from his gun. He yelled at the top of his voice and his men returned and started their regular shelling again. Not ten minutes later the first white flag waved from a house—presumably Smith's headquarters—and it was all over. Ironically, Smith was not ready to surrender, but his men were, and when a Federal major came galloping down the street waving a white handkerchief they poured out of the houses and threw down their guns. Six hundred fine rifles, more than enough to arm those Morgan men without guns, were taken. Elizabethtown was theirs. After the paroles they enjoyed a good supper and the prospect of the first night's rest since they left Tennessee. The trestles waited. But Morgan's business wasn't finished.

"Whatever for?" Basil frowned, then grinned. "I see . . ."

"I promised her, and I thought we could go shopping together. I trust your judgment . . ." They had to wake a shopkeeper, but Morgan found what he wanted. Mattie would be pleased.

"It's a bit—risqué, don't you think?" Basil worried.

"It's for a risqué lady," Morgan smiled.

Anxiety returned with daylight. He sent for Ellsworth. "Are you sure Louisville isn't alerted?"

"General Jerry Boyle thinks you're on your way to Lexington," the Canadian said solemnly, then let his eyes disappear in silent laughter, his shoulders shaking. "Remember Midway?"

They followed the railroad for fifteen miles to the trestles. With a bitter wind whipping off the river, the men were busy all the way tearing up track. Breckinridge's brigade would take the stockade at the lower trestle, defended by six hundred Union troops; Duke's would attack the garrison at the upper trestle, two hundred strong. Again, the Federals refused to surrender, and the shelling began. It took two hours, but the white flags finally appeared— and six hundred and fifty prisoners of the Seventy-first Indiana Infantry. Morgan set up headquarters in a farmhouse, and Captain Maginis joked that he'd done more paperwork for Morgan as adjutant than he'd done as an ordnance officer for a whole division.

But at least they were out of the wind. From the upstairs windows,

Morgan could see one corner of the nearer trestle, and watched it catch, the smoke billowing black against the sky. The rain had stopped, and the wind would help. It did. It took the flames and whipped them across the crisscrossed beams and even from here he could hear the great crackling. Then, finally, the first great crash, out of sight, and then the second, and his view from the window gave him nothing but smoke. That much was done. He had successfully broken Rosecrans's line to Louisville. The great span of open sky between the cliffs of Muldraugh and the Ohio Valley were again free for the birds. It would take the Yankees some time to repair this souvenir of a Morgan visit.

"The Thunderbolt strikes again," Adam Johnson drawled behind him. "Wonder what the other boys are doing."

They learned quickly enough. One scouting party, under Hines, destroyed a bridge only twenty-eight miles from Louisville; another burned two more on the Lebanon branch line. The same scouts who burned the bridges reported a Federal force of five thousand infantry, two thousand cavalry and several pieces of artillery already on their trail. It was time to get four thousand men back to Tennessee. It would be the hardest job, and the closest call, of their lives.

They made it that night to the bank of the Rolling Fork and camped along the Elizabethtown-Bardstown Road, the advance bivouac beside the swollen river, with Quirk's scouts as outposts on the other side. The wind had died, but had blown in colder air, with no chance to dry wet clothes—and worse, wet cartridges. They spread soggy blankets and freezing shebangs in the mud and tried to sleep.

It was not just the sound of rushing water that kept them awake: The valley spread around them, a level plain four miles wide ringed by hills to the north and west, where the road from Elizabethtown dropped four hundred feet to the valley floor. From there any pursuing force would have a splendid view. A piece of artillery planted on that road was unthinkable. Thank God the rear guard—three hundred picked men—were up there guarding it.

Before daylight they fumbled for their saddles and warmed the horses' bits with their breath and hands before putting on bridles. The horses had eaten at Elizabethtown; not since, and now there would be no time for salvaging even the driest corncob from winter fields. "Let's go, ole Sally," Randolph's Billy spoke to his mare. In spite of his general's orders that he get some sleep he had been up since midnight helping Frank Leathers get the artillery horses ready. "Them Yankees is after us."

In first light of the 29th, a week to the day since they left Tennessee, they started crossing the Rolling Fork, still foaming and twisting across its valley. By eleven o'clock most of the men had sloshed over a ford a mile or two upstream from the road. The rear guard, with their pickets and vedettes, were now collecting at two fords, deeper and more difficult, to the right of a brick house which had served as headquarters. Major Bullock, with Cluke's regiment and the Bull Pups, was busy burning a railroad bridge five miles farther downstream. Morgan, with Duke, Breckinridge and three regimental commanders, Cluke, Stoner and Hutchinson, stayed in the house and for two hours had tried to finish a court-martial that had begun shortly after breaking camp at Upton. It was well known that, in Gano's absence, some of his Texans resented Colonel Huffman's taking command, and some had brought charges that Huffman had violated terms negotiated for prisoners at Bacon Creek. What began as an accusation concerning the theft of a Federal officer's watch had blossomed into doubt about Huffman's integrity. Roy Cluke, with a bad cold, blew his nose and looked at the impassive, hawklike face of Huffman, who listened intently to a summary of the charges as Captain Maginis read them. Basil pursed his lips and caught a doze, and Bill Breckinridge gazed past his general with those heavy-lidded eyes of his. They were all dead-tired and edgy, but this was the sort of thing that couldn't wait, and the sooner they had done with it the better.

A rattle of musketry in the direction of the rear guard made Basil jump. Maginis, without changing the tone of his voice, doubled the pace of his information, and they voted to acquit Huffman. As Morgan got his hat and walked onto the porch a breathless vedette from the rear guard rode up.

"They've captured some of us, General!"

Morgan looked at the troops across the river and a familiar stab of healthy fear made him suddenly alert as an animal. Somewhere in the hills behind him the Federals were already taking position—seven thousand, with artillery. The sun was high, and the chill on the back of his neck returned. He turned to Stoner and Hutchinson. "Come with me across the river." To Basil he said, "We'll wait for you there. Hold the fords at all costs, until Cluke's regiment can get back from that railroad bridge." He didn't have to say what they all knew in an instant: If they left that regiment on this side of the river, the Yankees would capture them. He left Basil in command, shook his hand, then each in turn. "Thank you for settling this. How fast can you ride?" he asked an orderly, but didn't wait for an answer. "Tell Major Bullock—you'll find him about five miles downstream—to get here as soon as he can." He watched the boy fly and turned to his officers, already mounting. "If necessary, we can recross to help, or cover you. . . ."

Basil watched his general trot through the woods to the ford upstream and looked at scudding clouds. They were racing across the sky, and growing darker. A band of yellow light edged the hills. "Cold weather ahead, gentlemen," Roy Cluke was saying behind him as he buttoned his coat. "I hope Bullock gets my regiment back before—"

He hadn't finished when a shell burst not two hundred yards to the rear, and their nightmare began.

Basil let his eyes drift over the terrain. What he saw was a meadow about three hundred yards wide, with a sudden rise across the middle, like a terrace. Surrounding the meadow deep woods stood like a curtain. On the fourth side, the swollen river. Then, a sound he dreaded: the uneven, thunderous hoofbeats of the rear guard, driven back by the enemy.

Quickly, Basil sent skirmishers into the woods and deployed men behind the terrace, then sent again for Bullock. Tom Hines, now a captain in Breckinridge's brigade, stepped forward and volunteered to go. There was little cover for the horses; Basil sent the horse-holders to the left, where the terrain offered a small gully—better than nothing, but not adequate. Then he turned to face his foe.

His blood turned cold. The scouts had counted accurately. Coming slowly toward them, five thousand Federal infantry, two thousand cavalry and several pieces of artillery emerged from the woods and entered the meadow with the relentlessness of a machine. Duke's skirmishers fell back past the brick house, where the Union artillery pieces—five guns—had unlimbered. Just as the first shells thundered over, the Bull Pups, sent with Bullock, came galloping out of the woods on the downstream side, followed by the yells of the War Dogs, Tom Hines in the forefront.

"Don't fire?" At first Cluke was incensed; then he saw Duke's reasoning. They were in no position to start an artillery duel with Yankee Parrots, which had already raked the horses, four going down with one shell. Instead, the Pups were sent as fast as their horses could take them to the upper ford. They got across. Now Cluke, rejoined with his regiment, immediately put five companies in line, and sent the rest over with the Pups. But eight hundred men of Morgan's command faced annihilation.

It was then that a courier arrived from across the river with instructions from General Morgan to Colonel Duke to withdraw. Basil threw back his head in frustration. "Tell the General I devoutly wished I could!"

The Yankees were now closing in for the kill, deployed in a long line, with a skirmish line in front, their bayonets glistening. The Federal Parrots by the house now opened up again, and for the first time the Yankee cavalry appeared in the woods to the left, beyond the horses.

I never thought it would end like this, Duke thought. If that gallant rear guard gives way, we'll be bayoneted right here, on the bank of the Rolling Fork. He looked around at the beautiful flat valley, with its fringe of hills, remembering how Gano had admired it. Well Gano wasn't here. . . . Then, unbelievably, he heard the Rebel yell. He looked in astonishment at his men. The harder they were pressed, the more defiant they became. They actually looked happy! He had ordered Captains Pendleton and Hines to charge on the left with three companies and take a battery on that side. "While you do so," he said as they left him, "we'll begin our with-drawal. . . ."

As if he could! He was talking like a madman! And did he intend to leave Pendleton and three companies as a pawn while they ran? It was madness . . .

Then pain stopped all thought.

A shell had landed in the little group of officers conferring by the river: Lieutenant Moreland, Basil's acting aide-de-camp, lost his horse, killed under him, and Basil was wounded in the head by a fragment. Bill Breckinridge took command and watched Pendleton and Hines silence the Yankee battery, killing and driving away the gunners.

"Colonel!"

Breckinridge whirled to find one of Cluke's men almost speechless with hurry.

"A ford—behind our position over there . . ."

The men were thrown into columns and crossed the ford at the last minute. It was luck, luck. The Yankee commander Harlan chose not to pursue. Luck.

"And courage," Basil moaned to Morgan once they set him down on the other side. "You should have seen Logan and Page, and Austin, and Tom Hines . . . Cluke, as always. . . ."

"Hush, now." Morgan was appalled at Basil's loss of color. "We're going home!"

That night they camped at Bardstown, where Dr. John Scott, surgeon of the Second Kentucky, cared for Duke, now in delirium. Chenault came back from destroying a stockade at Boston. Adam Johnson was already moving as fast as he could to attack the pickets in front of Lebanon, where the scouts reported a concentration of Federal troops, eight thousand strong, with artillery, to block Morgan's route south. If Adam could keep them busy, the rest of the command could skirt Lebanon to the west. But Harlan was in their rear; delay meant disaster.

"Do you think he can travel?"

Dr. Scott looked at the haggard face of his commander and shook his head. "A piece of bone behind the ear is gone. But I know you won't mind me," he said, and tried a smile. "I'll make him as comfortable as I can. Find a buggy. . . ." They did.

At Springfield the scouts reported a large force marching from Glasgow to intercept them at Columbia. It was necessary now to get beyond Lebanon and cross the Cumberland before the Federals could get within striking distance.

"Frank Wolford's with that force," Charlton called over. They had just dismounted for a stretch and a cup of coffee.

"If Johnson can draw off that regiment of cavalry from New Market, that will give us a clear way around Lebanon."

"Begging your pardon, General," Hutch put in, "but calling it clear might be a little optimistic. Some of my boys who live around here say the only road they know of will bring us within two and a half miles of Lebanon . . . too close for much comfort."

"Then it will be absolutely necessary to draw their attention elsewhere."

"We could try Will's old Injun trick," Charlton said as he pitched the dregs from his cup.

"Which one?"

"Campfires."

"You're right! It might just work!" It was remarkable, how coffee could cut through fatigue. And stretching your legs. How many hours had they been in the saddle? He preferred not to count. The horses were showing more wear than the men. But they were Kentucky horses, most of them, and their stamina had never let him down. "I feel better already," he said to

Hutchinson, who was still frowning. "A few campfires on the north side of Lebanon could fool Harlan, too, and do double duty."

Hutch said: "It will have to be a night march."

"Excuse me, sirs." Breck Castleman saluted. "We've had an invitation . . . dinner . . . just down the road."

Morgan could feel bone-breaking fatigue pull him into his saddle. He looked off. An all-night march. "All right, Breck, since it will be our last one for a while. Two hours."

"Yes, sir!"

"I'd almost forgotten what a square meal tastes like," Charlton murmured as they took their places at the white linen-spread table, where Eastin and Castleman were obviously enjoying the company of young ladies almost as much as their ham and biscuits. The conversation had stalled on the petty tyrannies of Colonel Halisey and his Yankee cavalry, quartered in Lebanon, but now, luckily, off chasing Morgan. One of the prettier girls swore that she would marry the man who would kill him. Eastin immediately, with his usual courtesy, rose and promised to do so, to general laughter. Morgan, who had left the table momentarily to check on Basil, returned just in time to toast his effort. It was all so light, so foolish. How could the ladies know those tight stabs of fear, the hard-rock gut determination that kept a man going when everything was against him? But here they were, his men smiling in their muddy uniforms, their eyes meeting soft promises across candlelight. Yet sometimes a bright pair of eyes was all a man had. He looked at his handsome young officers and the scented, smiling girls and let them enjoy the warmth of this house another hour. Before midnight—and the wind had picked up—they would be on the march again.

The night had turned bitter cold, and the little road between Lebanon and St. Mary's was little more than a lumpy, frozen lane. The "natives" in Hutch's outfit soon lost their way in the dark and the column floundered along not knowing if they kept to the road or not. Wind blew freezing rain like a weapon. Mustaches and beards turned to white wool. Eyebrows and lashes matted. Rain turned to sleet and stung their faces. Morgan's fingers were ten points of stabbing pain, and his toes turned to balls of aching steel in his boots. Each breath hurt, and he could no longer feel his reins through wet, frozen gloves. Frost crusted the horses' bits to their mouths, and those horses with tails left trails of blood from hind legs torn raw by foot-long blocks of ice. Worst of all the energy the animals needed to keep warm subtracted from their ability to move, and the frozen edges of mud, sharp as knives, cut their frogs with each step. Morgan rode back and forth down the line, encouraging, prodding, taunting: They must not stop. Spurs dug and whips torn from naked trees came out and kept them going for a while. Then the stumbling began.

Now Morgan knew what pitch-black meant: They moved as into a tunnel of black cotton. The two horses pulling one of the ten-pounder Parrots bogged down in mud axle-deep and a dozen men got down and flogged them forward. It was no use: The wheels of the gun carriage were out of sight.

The horses were on their knees, and when Morgan rode up he thought they were at a peculiar angle. The men tried again, but the horses didn't move. "Get those horses moving there," a sergeant called out. Some of the men had taken advantage of the halt to dismount and stamp their frozen feet and flail themselves to get the blood back into their fingers.

"Can't, sir," a boy with blue lips answered. "They've broken their front legs . . . both of them."

One of them was the chestnut Will had traded for.

"We need two horses here!" the Sergeant called out again.

"Let me give him mine," Tom said behind his brother. "I can ride double with you."

His voice sounded so choked that his brother couldn't refuse.

"Here, that's warmer, anyway," Morgan said quietly, as Tom settled behind him. Only then did he realize his legs were rubbed raw from crotch to knee: His frozen pants were hard as boards.

They heard the shots, then the two replacements were hitched up, and the Parrot pulled onto the road again.

Some of Quirk's scouts came back just as first light revealed the naked, frozen countryside. After all that marching, they were only eight miles from Springfield and just over two from Lebanon. But Quirk and Peddicord, with details from the Second and Eleventh regiments, had done their job well: Lebanon was in turmoil and preparing to attack Morgan's "camp" on the north side of town.

With the sun, spirits rose. The sleet had stopped and the trees shone like cut crystal: The ice didn't melt for hours, and after their grueling night they watched the sparkling landscape with awe until, just south of New Market, they picked up the main road again.

Castleman had drawn field duty officer. Lieutenant Eastin, still taking jokes about the night before, asked permission to go with Captain Tribble a mile off the road to a shoe shop.

"Why, George," another field lieutenant from Company D called over, "aren't those old boots good enough for the ladies?"

George answered by lifting one foot, to show the sole half gone.

"All right, all right," said Castleman. "But be back before the rear guard passes. After that, you may be Yankee bait."

"We promise!" But the shoe shop was almost all the way into the town of New Market, and by the time they made the road again the rear guard had passed. As they turned into the road they were chased by three Federal officers riding in advance of their pursuing column. Eastin quickly turned into a side lane. Two of the three Yankees chased Tribble, the third fired at Eastin, missed, and they fell from their horses grappling in the mud. Eastin, younger and stronger, had the better of it and forced the Federal to the ground, his pistol at his head. The man surrendered, and as Eastin lifted his knee from the man's chest, the Federal pulled his own pistol and fired, grazing Eastin's cheek. Eastin killed him, point-blank, and kept his sword. It was Colonel Halisey.

Alex Tribble got his men, too, forcing one to surrender with his head under water. When they brought their prisoners back to the column, Eastin's proposal of marriage passed down the line.

Of such shenanigans, thought Quirk as he looked for the General, is morale made.

But Quirk had more on his mind: His scouts had discovered some of Frank Wolford's officers in the farmhouse of James Sanders, on top of a hill. More importantly, the Yankees had placed cannon in a church opposite the Sanders house to shell Morgan as he came down the road. If Quirk had known that his general was at that moment entering the house in the disguise of a Federal officer to check on the whereabouts of Wolford, he might have fallen off his horse.

How strange, Morgan thought to himself, are the fortunes of war indeed. He did not know James Sanders, a prosperous farmer, but his daughter brought back vague memories of an afternoon at Hopemont. When her father called her name it all fell into place: She was a friend of Tommie's, had visited Lexington . . . summer, a mist of muslin, giggles in the parlor. He was "Major Cunningham," on special service to General Grant, traveling from Mississippi to Louisville. "Major Cunningham" told them the latest news from Holly Springs.

"Holly Springs, sir? But surely you know that the Confederate Van Dorn captured that town on the twentieth of December and destroyed General Grant's supply base?"

"Yes, yes!" Morgan caught himself, and frowned. "Precisely why I must get to Louisville. General Grant has a plan. . . ."

Their faces eased.

"Can you tell me where Colonel Wolford is at this moment?" Morgan turned to the younger of the two Federal officers, a redheaded captain with freckles across his nose.

"With the main column," the boy said importantly. "Gone to Lebanon to catch Morgan."

"But what if he skirts Lebanon and comes through here?"

"Then we have a reception committee of another sort waiting for him," said the Yankee major from across the room. He interrupted a conversation with Mrs. Sanders to nod toward the window. "Across the road, in the church there on the hill . . . a cannon, all set to shell Morgan if he comes this way."

"I'll toast that!" Morgan laughed. "What a shrewd bit of strategy!"

"We thought so."

"Now, if you'll excuse me, gentlemen, I must get an hour's rest before moving on . . ." He looked enquiringly toward the daughter.

"Of course, Major," James Sanders said. "Carey Anne, can you show the Major to our guest bedroom? Are you sure you cannot spend the night?"

"No, no. What I have to say to General Boyle at Louisville cannot wait. An hour's rest will do, sir, and I'm much obliged."

They watched him follow the girl upstairs.

When she closed the door of the bedroom, Morgan threw back his Federal overcoat. Her hand flew to her mouth.

"Why, Miss Carey, don't you know me?"

"Johnny Morgan! If they find you they'll—"

"But they won't, will they, Miss Carey? Not if you'll show me a way out. I still remember that afternoon at Hopemont, when you visited Tommie. My, you are as pretty as ever!"

Steps on the stairs made her turn pale.

"Is everything all right, dear? Does the Major need hot water? I can send some up!" her mother was calling from the landing.

She cracked the door and said in an even voice: "Everything is fine, Mama. I was just checking to see if the Major wanted a fire."

"And does he?"

"He says no, he'll only be staying long enough for a short rest."

"Then come right down"—the *what will people think!* ringing under her words.

"Right now, Mama!" She closed the door and turned to Morgan. "We'll have to wait till she goes. There's stairs at the end of the hall."

They waited until the lady's footsteps faded, followed by voices near the front door. Their guests were leaving.

"Quick!" the girl whispered. "They'll be going to the church . . ."

"Can you delay them?"

"I'll try!"

"Good girl!"

As he slipped down the back stairs he heard her calling to them that they musn't leave before they tasted a special cake her mother had made. Coffee would keep them warm on their night vigil. . . .

As soon as he could, he let Glencoe pick up a gallop. The head of his column was less than two miles from the church, which also, the girl told him, served as a storehouse for ammunition. Lieutenant Peddicord, with Tom Logwood, rode in the advance guard.

"Whew!" Logwood let his breath out in a soft whistle. "If I hadn't known your horse, I might have shot you!"

They were delighted by the news. When the detachment with orders to fire the church arrived at the hill, the Federals were still standing about the farmer's parlor across the road. As quietly as possible, two Yankee guards were silenced by strong arms across their throats and pistols in their chests. While they were being gagged and bound to trees some distance off and told that Morgan was heading north, not south, Lieutenant Hays and his men lifted window sashes, opened doors and stood their horses well back as the first torches were thrown. The church exploded in flame, but they were gone before the Federals ran out of the house to see what was happening. Even after they regained the column, sounds of splintering timber and flashes of exploding cartridges lit the sky.

By nightfall they made Campbellsville, a worn-out, weary, wet band of refugees. Unbelievably, a Federal commissary stood full for the taking, and dry blankets, boots and beef were distributed to the men. But most of all, with the Yankees fleeing north to catch them, they could rest. Early Wednes-

day, the last day of 1862, they saddled up and marched south. They had
another bitter night ahead of them before they reached the Cumberland.

All that day, before halting at Columbia in the afternoon, they heard a
sound that brought chills down their spines. Morgan had been riding in the
van, but dropped back now beside Basil's buggy as it stopped on the crest of
a hill. Thunder, the men said, but Morgan and Duke looked at each other;
they knew better.

The sound of cannonading came from the direction of Murfreesboro, more
than a hundred miles away.

45

Mattie Ready was upstairs Sunday afternoon with Alice getting ready for the New Year's Eve party they planned for Wednesday night when a knock at the front door made them fly down the stairs. Maybe Morgan was back! Instead, a soldier from their brother's outfit asked for Horace Ready. He was to return to camp immediately. To the girls' worried look, the boy's veil of discipline fell away. "The Yankees, the Yankees are marching from Nashville!"

Colonel Ready, who heard him from the parlor, threw on his coat and went out. It was raining—had been raining for two days, a cold, numbing rain. The girls, watching their brother leave, stood speechless in the hall. He jumped a puddle, missed, laughed, then caught up with the serious soldier, who had marched on ahead, not waiting for him.

"Well," said Mattie, "there's no use in our standing here. Let's see how many sheets and towels are left, so we can make bandages."

But they couldn't. Curiosity drew them to the sidewalk, where they stood under a dripping umbrella and watched line after line of glittering bayonets pass through town on their way to the river.

They forgot their hatred of General Bragg, the main topic of conversation all week, ever since, the day after Christmas, the public execution of Private Lewis at the Court House Square. Their father would not allow them to attend, but they leaned out an upstairs window anyway and saw the wagon bearing Lewis turn the corner, and a wagon carrying a coffin follow. The execution would happen on the other side, out of sight, but they heard later from their brother how the condemned man asked for the handkerchief only so he couldn't recognize his fellow Kentuckians who would kill him. General Breckinridge, Horace said, tried until the last to get Bragg to rescind the order, then dismounted and talked to Lewis, then remounted and took his place, but when the rifles cracked the General fell forward on his saddle. . . . The boy was buried in the Murfreesboro cemetery the next day, next to a cousin who had died in Confederate service a year before.

Now, with Federal troops in front of Murfreesboro, the girls prayed that Bragg would be as inflexible with the Yankees, and said so, under the umbrella and shivering, more from emotion than from the cold.

"He's mean," Alice said with a new kind of grimness, and pushed back her hair. "But that's what we need . . . meanness."

Key Morgan, who had come up behind them said, "No . . . what we need is Brother Johnny!"

Mattie, to their surprise, broke into sobs, gathered up her skirts and ran into the house.

"Breckinridge is well placed," their father said to their urgent questions, when he came home at noon. "With Hunt's regiments, Cobb's battery and the Forty-first Alabama on a hill in his front overlooking the river."

"Colonel T.H. Hunt's regiments?" Alice asked, and Mattie caught her look.

"Henry Curd is a smart boy," Mattie smiled. "I'm sure he'll be all right."

"They're all good, splendid, glorious men!" Alice beamed through sudden tears. "God can't help but give them a victory!"

Only their pleas, plus their mother's round-eyed reminder from her sickbed to Key that he had promised to protect them, kept him from joining the troops still marching outside. She looked so frail, this old lady! Oh, why had he promised?

Monday dawned cold, with more rain. The streets churned with mud and wagons. Colonel Ready gave them strict orders: They were to stay indoors. By nightfall all the extra towels and sheets—and even some spare petticoats —had disappeared into bandages. Before noon Tuesday they heard cannon, and ran out in the freezing drizzle to watch the empty streets. A sky the color of mustard hung in the direction of the river, and there was a sting in the air.

"Saltpeter," said Key authoritatively.

Soon they were busy cooking rations, beef and cornmeal, and sending Albert to the river with a wagon loaded with boxes.

"How do we know what they need?" worried Alice.

"Don't worry," said Key. "They'll need everything." When he insisted on going, they knew they couldn't keep him this time. He came back about midnight, pale and dirty and completely soaked, professing hunger, but when they set a supper in front of him he couldn't eat. Henry Curd was dead—a cannonball passed straight through him—but he didn't tell them.

"Where is Albert?" Mattie finally asked.

"I came back on a borrowed horse," Key said. "Albert stayed . . ." Again he couldn't finish: *to help bury the dead.* "To help," he added.

A stab of fear shot blood to Alice's face.

"I haven't seen him," Key answered the unspoken question.

"He's with the Twenty-third Tennessee, General Cleburne's Third Brigade," Mattie said evenly.

He couldn't tell her that General Hardee's corps was stretched out for three miles from the Nashville Road to the Lebanon Pike, that it was impossible to find their brother.

"Lieutenant-Colonel Keeble's Twenty-third Tennessee," Alice said too brightly, her eyes shining.

Mattie, listening to the rain, said nothing. When Alice left the room, Key told her. She sat numbed, staring. "Poor Henry," she managed to say, and then jumped nervously. No, we won't tell her, she said to herself. Not till we have to. She's . . . too much like Mama.

The next morning a bright sun lifted the fog. "Mattie?" Alice called from her bed through the door when she saw her sister in the hall tying her robe.

Before she could answer, Mattie felt the house shake. The artillery had started again.

All morning, they sat in the parlor, unable to speak.

"I can't stand it!" Key almost bawled out. "I've got to go out there."

Colonel Ready, who had persuaded his wife to dress and come downstairs, jumped up too in a fit of manly pride.

"You're right, son! Our boys need us!"

His wife, this time, didn't argue.

Mattie tried to see "out there." The river, where it crossed the Nashville Road, was shallow. Many a time she'd ridden her horse across . . . and the morning of a day last spring, when *they* had ridden over together, his horse splashing as they trotted, his lovely, fresh, handsome face frowning in concern lest her mare slip on the stones. She couldn't bear to think of it now or she would miss him too much. She concentrated on the river: Was it swollen much from the rains? It had to be. Would that be in favor of, or against the Confederate cause? Then her mind went to those thick groves of cedars, their prickly branches so low to the ground nobody could get through. And hills. Was that where the artillery had been set up? Whose artillery? Morning faded into a dreary afternoon, afternoon into night.

"Mattie, do get some sleep, darlin'. Why, you're dozing right off the chair!"

She opened her eyes to see her mother's usually pale face flushed with worry. "Oh, Mama, I'm—"

Before she could finish, her father and Key came back, shaking off rain like two fuzzy dogs.

"You should have seen them! Magnificent boys! Why, they surprised the Yankees this morning . . . bad as Shiloh!"

"Like a pivot," Key whistled. "We turned them right back onto the road . . ."

"Who is we?" asked Alice from the doorway. From the tone of his voice she knew the news must be good, and she sent them a smile that crinkled the corners of her eyes.

"A victory, my girl!" her father laughed. "A complete victory!"

"I hear General Bragg is going to send Richmond a wire," said Key, "telling them he has a New Year's present for President Davis!"

Our advance . . . enemy driven . . . crash upon crash of musketry . . . our boys . . . through fields, over fences. Such a charge was never witnessed! Puts Marshal Ney to shame!

"And you say it's a victory?" prompted Mattie, only to hear it again.

"A victory." Her father sat down, out of breath.

Mattie jumped up. Her shawl dropped from her shoulders. "Eliza! Eliza! Get everybody some coffee!" She turned to them. "The wounded will be coming . . ." And then, to their shocked, sad faces: "But won't the General be pleased!"

"Which one?" teased Key.

"The one who isn't here," she said, picking up the shawl to keep her face away.

Superstitiously, she was afraid of joy. *Not till I know*, she said to herself. She went to the window. A brilliant winter moon had turned Murfreesboro into a silver city: The cupola of the courthouse could have been a minaret. But across the street the bare arms of a maple fell in black shadows across the walk, the fence, and into the Ready yard almost to the porch. She shivered. And what was it like, *out there?* The abandoned cannon and scattered caissons, the wounded artillery horses still writhing. Dead soldiers lying in those wild attitudes in which they fell, congealed by the bitter cold. And those cedar groves, so pretty in the springtime . . . what blood and gore did they shade now from the moonlight?

The mutilated wounded—shivering and shuddering by some campfire. There was no need to ask again. They had already said they hadn't seen Brother. They were so full of victory! Key had managed to become a courier, and was proud of his exploits under fire. But the wounded . . . She squeezed her eyes.

Yet the next day, New Year's, all was quiet. Murfreesboro received its wounded, Federal as well as Confederate. Churches, warehouses and the Academy filled, and the bandages disappeared. Toward sundown Alice, giving a soldier a drink of water, noticed his insignia.

"The Twenty-third Tennessee!" she squealed.

"Yes, ma'am."

"Do you know Brother?"

"We were all brothers out there," the boy answered.

"I mean . . . Lieutenant Horace . . . Ready."

The boy's face brightened. "Oh, yes, ma'am! He's well an' fit. Seen him just before"—his eyes went to his arm—"*this* happened. Yes, ma'am, he's fine!"

Alice put the pail of water she was carrying into the hands of the nearest lady and ran home with the news.

"Now all we have to do is get some good news from that cavalry man of yours," Colonel Ready said to Mattie, "and things can get back to normal."

"Won't Sister Mary be surprised?" Alice gloated. "With her Yankee friends in Nashville!"

"Shh, Alice!" Mrs. Ready looked up weakly. "Your sister Mary is merely being kind. After all, Yankees are people, too, and since her husband is a doct—"

"Oh, Mama, how can you say that! Those miserable Yankees! You said yourself . . ."

Her father surprised them all by chuckling. "It seems to me the victors can afford to be a little charitable. They've failed and we've won. Isn't that what we wanted, Pet?"

An hour later Colonel T.H. Hunt, weary but gracious, tapped at the front door. They had brought Lieutenant Curd's body into town for burial.

Alice ran upstairs, Mattie after her.

"I can't! I can't! Don't tell me to! How can I . . . accept it? So . . . so . . . !" Alice buried her red, tear-stained face into a twisted handkerchief. Mattie moved from the door to the bed and took her sister in her arms and was shocked by the depth of her sobs. She was still holding her when their mother came in. Mattie's look signaled silence, the best medicine.

"I'll see that he is moved back home after this war is over," T.H. promised grimly, with such conviction they had to believe him.

Or have I really come to think, the horrible thought came to Mattie Morgan, *that it will never end?*

Braxton Bragg sent his telegram, expecting Rosecrans to withdraw. Instead, Rosecrans massed fifty-seven field pieces on the west bank of Stones River, crossed a whole division to the east side during the night and occupied a strategic hill directly in Breckinridge's front, almost at right angles with Hanson's troops, who had formed, with three other brigades, beyond an open field. The Confederates knew that to retake the hill would mean crossing that field in full view of the Federal guns across the river, if the artillery on the hill didn't get them first.

"It's a trap," Roger Hanson told Brigadier-General William Preston, whose brigade was formed on his right. "What does Palmer think?"

"The same."

"And Adams?"

"It would be suicide to take it."

"They're holding out that hill like a carrot to a rabbit."

"And yet we may have to."

"What?"

"Their infantry have penetrated a thousand yards beyond the east bank, where the river makes a bend downstream on your right."

"Pegram's cavalry can take care of them," Hanson said gruffly. "I'll see what The Chief thinks."

But General John C. Breckinridge had already been called for a parley with Bragg. They met upstream, well within Confederate lines, on the west side of the river near a ford below the bridge.

"I want artillery on that hill," Bragg said without preliminaries. The tuft of hair that joined his eyebrows disappeared in a frown.

Breckinridge looked at the river flowing under the bridge and thought how incredibly peaceful it looks. He turned back to the piercing eyes, but Bragg didn't give him a chance to speak.

"Your command has been spared thus far in this battle," Bragg said peevishly. "Now . . ."

"With all due respect," Breckinridge bowed to his commanding general, and picked up a stick. "Look." He sketched the situation in the soft mud by his feet. "If we cross that field . . . eight hundred yards . . . it will be suicide. It is in full view, not only from the artillery on the hill, but the batteries across the river, on this ridge."

"Sir, my information is different. I have given the order to attack the enemy in your front at four P.M. and expect it to be obeyed."

Breckinridge stood to his full height.

"Four o'clock," his commanding general repeated.

Without a word, Breckinridge broke the stick and mounted.

"By the way," Bragg called up happily, his frown gone. "I've given Palmer's brigade to General Pillow."

Pillow, the coward of Donelson. It was the last straw. Maybe the rumors were right. Maybe Braxton Bragg did want to annihilate the Kentuckians. Breckinridge spurred his horse and galloped off.

Roger Hanson threatened to go to Bragg's tent and kill him. They had to restrain him. Only when Randall Gibson, whose Thirteenth Louisiana was now under Adams's First Brigade, reminded him that he had led a few useless attacks himself at Shiloh, did Hanson subside. It was the last time Gibson saw him alive.

"Mother, you can't! You'll catch your death!"

Mrs. Ready looked at her daughter and smiled. Tragedy had given her strength. She hadn't tasted brandy in three days. "Just get me my cloak, dear. The thick wool one."

"But what good can you do? What earthly good?"

"It is not earthly good I am thinking of," Mattie's mother answered, and then let her face tense in a grim smile. "Or maybe it is—if I can help Virginia Hanson through this ordeal."

"Let Key go with you."

"I'll send him back as soon as I arrive," Mrs. Ready said, looking toward her husband, slumped in a chair by the fire. He had given her strict orders that the girls should have as much protection as possible, in case of an evacuation, in case . . . But she closed her eyes against visions of Yankees tearing into her trunks, breaking up the house. The sudden surge of strength she had felt when she heard that the battle was not going well was remarkable—almost miraculous—and she clung to it stubbornly. Her daughters, with orders to hide everything of value, watched with awe this woman they hardly recognized.

Virginia Hanson and Mary Breckinridge had rented rooms in crowded Murfreesboro in the same house. When they heard the news they hired a wagon and drove with a servant to the battlefield. Mrs. Ready and Key went with them. Dr. Yandell came out of his hospital tent to tell them he did not think Hanson could live. Rice Graves, too, who had supported with his artillery Pillow's advance (Pillow himself hiding behind a tree), was severely wounded.

All that day the rain continued to fall, then turned to sleet. Hanson and Graves were brought to town, where Roger Hanson took a long time to die. Out on the battlefield the men shivered, waiting for Rosecrans to retire. They didn't know that before noon that morning Wheeler's scouts had arrived at Bragg's headquarters with captured papers of Major-General McCook giving the news of reinforcements and numbering the Federal force at seventy thousand. At ten the next morning Bragg called a meeting of his staff. It would be the Confederates, not the Federals, who would withdraw.

After the meeting Breckinridge got away and came to town to tell his old friend good-bye. Before Hanson died that night, the Confederate Army was streaming south, Bragg to Tullahoma, Hardee's corps on to Winchester, on the Dechard-Fayetteville spur line. Middle Tennessee, for all practical purposes, was gone.

Alice watched them all day from an upstairs window with dry eyes wild with shame.

"I'm not afraid of them! Let them come, the dogs! As long as I have Papa's pistol . . ."

Mattie was in her room with one of the servants, packing. She looked up, a skirt half folded over her arm, and watched the squared, small shoulders of her sister framed by the window. *You really should be leaving now, little lady*, he had said, in his clipped English voice. *As a member of the General's staff, perhaps I can get you a conveyance . . . something comfortable.* St. Leger's eyes had gone to Key. But how could she leave Alice? So all day Saturday they watched them stagger through the streets, half-ragged, mostly barefoot, bone-tired, wet to the skin from sleeping out in the merciless cold—Braxton Bragg's Army of Tennessee. She ordered the coffee, kept for company, to be made as long as it lasted, then went to the dried skins of sweet potatoes, their everyday fare. "It seems you could have done just the opposite," her father said. "They won't know the difference." But as each grateful boy set his rifle down and cupped dirty hands around the tin cup that Mattie handed him, she felt that she was giving *him* a warm drink in their stead. Oh, where was he! Was he even alive? She had to know. Didn't her father or Alice realize that? Key was the only one who seemed to understand.

"You'd better hurry, Miss Mattie. De las' of de soljuhs is leavin'."

"How do you know?" Alice turned, but Albert stood there stubbornly.

"Artillery passin'. Dey's always de las'."

Her father had wanted to go. Some deep male fury churned at the bottom of his stomach. Could he stand here and see those brave boys marching away without helping? But his wife, to his surprise, became adamant. "Remember Mrs. Bragg," she said. "Do you want to lose everything . . . do you want to give them the satisfaction? They can take the slaves—good riddance, most of them. But the house? And the farm?"

The farm, he could have reminded her, was gone anyway—the farmhouse shelled by Byrne's battery as Breckinridge's sharpshooters raced across the field toward the hill and into the river to be slaughtered by the artillery on the ridge. This house was all they had left. All of a long political career, all of those family gatherings, where their children had been born. This house . . . the Yankees almost got it when he was sent to the penitentiary. It was an old trick of theirs, to arrest a man and then take his house under the Abandoned Property Act—even when, as his wife reminded him, a man's family still lived there. His Washington connections had saved it before. With a daughter married to John Morgan, he could no longer count on help from them. Very well, then, this house would be his battlefield. The best revenge, after all, would be to keep it from falling prey to their high-handed greed. They wouldn't free his slaves, he knew, because they would be in Federal territory now. Maybe they had less to lose than his wife thought. Yes, in her female wisdom, she was right. He would stay.

His daughters were another matter. He closed his eyes at the thought. The Yankees had been polite enough before, but since Bragg's retreat from

Kentucky reports of ill treatment multiplied. They had declared Morgan a guerrilla; his wife could hardly expect preferential treatment. And Alice! Her Confederate sympathies drove her to indiscretion. She would definitely be safer. . . .

"Where *are* you going?" he heard his older daughter call out.

"De Yankees is comin', Miss Mattie!" the high wail of Eliza shrieked. "De Yankees is comin'!"

Mattie looked at the girl, her kerchief sidewise on her head.

"Go out back and help Albert!"

"Dat ole man! He's diggin' up de—"

"I know what he's doing! Go help him!"

But when Mattie looked out the back door the yard looked like a cemetery. Mounds of dirt dotted every open space between the rose bushes.

"Albert!"

The old man bowed and wiped his brow.

"Ole Miss say tuh burry de silvuh. . . ."

"I know, but do you have to dig up the whole county?"

"Ah figured if'n we's have lots'a holes, de Yankees won't know which't one is de right one."

"And do you?"

But she had to turn from him to stifle her laugh. They were all going crazy!

Supper was a grim affair. Boiled cabbage, leftover pieces of ham. "If Mama stays, I stay" had come so often from Alice that they had all given up. Mattie's valise had been packed for hours. *They'll take the horse, first thing —they always do* ran through her mind. Then what will I do? She looked pleadingly at Key Morgan, who in turn looked at Alice. Then the doorbell rang.

It was Colonel Hunt.

"My brigade has been given rear guard duty," he said without preliminaries, after refusing, with a slight wave of his hand, their invitation to eat. "I strongly suggest, if any of you want to leave, it would be best to do so now. Key, are you going with the ladies?"

"I'm not going!" Alice piped up.

T.H. turned his head sideways, his kind eyes on the girl. "Well, now, I know how you feel, Miss Alice . . ."

"Mama's not going, so I can't. . . ."

"We will need all the nurses we can possibly get," the man in the rumpled Confederate uniform said wearily.

"He's right, Alice," said Key. His voice cracked and he cleared his throat. "You saw them. . . ."

"Tullahoma is forty miles away," Colonel Hunt began. He was interrupted by the crack of musketry in the distance. It reminded them how quiet the town had become since the last caissons had lumbered through. Eliza ran to the door yelling, "De Yankees! It's de Yankees!" She stood there wringing her hands and making faces. When Mattie saw her sister's lips go white, she knew she must somehow change her mind.

"The last train leaves within the hour," T.H. said evenly. "If you like, I can ask General Hardee to send a member of his staff to escort you . . ."

"We would be most grateful, Colonel."

He looked at Mattie's face a long moment, bowed and left them.

A flurry of packing, punctuated by Mrs. Ready's stout insistence that she would be fine. Mattie would always remember her hands working the edge of her handkerchief and that brave, thin smile. Her father gave gruff advice and went downstairs when he heard voices in the hall. Albert had admitted a young major from Hardee's staff. Mattie, just behind her father, was still on the stairs.

"Beg your pardon, sir . . . ma'am. General Hardee sends his respects, and requests the presence of your family on his car . . . the train is ready to leave in twenty minutes." His worried eyes, under their smooth brows, looked at each of them in turn.

"I'll go!" Alice cried from the top of the stairs, surprising them all. She ran into her room.

"I can't understand that girl!" mumbled her father, but Mattie smiled to herself. Why hadn't she thought of it? If anybody could get Alice to move, her favorite general could. When Alice came downstairs she was wearing three dresses.

"You've gained thirty pounds!"

Alice tossed her head. "You just wait. You'll wish you had more clothes!"

The little depot was ablaze with a mist of spurting steam in the bone-chilling drizzle. The young major had waited for them and handed them up now into the last car of the train. Key Morgan spread a quilt across their knees, as solicitous as a brother. The noise in the car was almost as suffocating as the wood smoke from the engine and the potbellied stove at the far end. Ahead was a "ladies' car," but with the train about to start they had no time to find it; almost as soon as they settled and stuffed their bags under their seats a jolt started the creaking wheels on their way.

General Hardee was nowhere to be seen. "He must be in another car conferring with his staff," Alice whispered. The engine gave a brisk whistle and then a long wail. Mattie looked through the smudged window at Murfreesboro sliding past: the muddy streets, mules and wagons and straggling soldiers in the half light of sundown. There on its hill the courthouse, and beyond, out of sight, her house, her dear house . . . she was beginning to feel sorry for herself when she noticed a line of soldiers marching near the train as it slowed for a crossing. There was something peculiar about the one nearest the tracks, the way he stumbled. Then she saw his left arm was entirely gone. His face, turned dumbly ahead, was white as a sheet. The breast and sleeve of his coat had been torn away, and the shredded cloth seemed to have been sucked into his wound. The train stopped entirely, its engine puffing, and the line of soldiers, too, halted. She saw to her horror . . . his heart move under the clotting blood. He took a few steps when the column began walking again, then slumped forward and fell. A cloud of steam covered him as his buddies picked him up and carried him toward the steps of a house. The train moved on.

The young major from Hardee's staff had gone to the back of the car, where the potbellied stove glowed red through its black iron sides. Around it half a dozen soldiers held out their hands, stamped their feet and joked. The next time Alice saw him, the young major was sitting in the last seat dead-asleep, his head back and his mouth open.

Night was coming on outside. Rain streamed down the panes like tears. A lantern was lit at each end of the car and the smell of coal oil, with the sidewise lurching of the rails, made Alice sleepy, then sick. She took off her bonnet and rested her head against the seat and wiggled under her three dresses into something she tried to tell herself was a more comfortable position. Mattie, across from her, was studying the muddy hem of her own best velvet dress and her ruined shoes. She yawned and crossed her arms, and in another half-hour was dead-asleep herself.

The real worry, where they would stay, what would happen to them, came later when she woke in the stuffy car full of cigar smoke. Key, anxious for news, had joined the circle around the stove. Mattie watched his sandy head and ready smile, her own face feeling oily with fatigue. Never, never in her whole life had she been so tired or felt so dirty. For him it was a lark. He basked in the reflected glory of having a brother who was a general, and spoke constantly of his courage and his coolness. It was his warmth Mattie longed for.

She looked up to see the fatherly figure of General Hardee bending slightly from the waist, his gray goatee wagging with the indulgent smile he sent the sleeping Alice.

"I see our young lady is taking the trip well," he whispered.

Mattie gathered her skirts to make room for him. The soggy soles of her shoes left two puddles of mud as she moved over. For a few seconds they watched the blissful child's face of the girl on the opposite seat. The General spoke in low tones about the town of Winchester. "You'll be pleased to know Miss Rose and Miss Sally Baker are in the second car ahead. They have relatives there, I understand. I took the opportunity . . . I hope you do not find me impertinent . . . of mentioning your presence with us. Perhaps they can help you obtain lodgings once we arrive." Two vertical lines drew his eyebrows together.

"Why, that's very kind, General Hardee. Very kind, indeed." She turned her eyes on him. "Now shall we wake this little staff member of yours?"

Winchester was an uproar, with wagonloads of wounded, tents and lean-tos. Miss Baker did find a room for them in the house of a cousin—shared by five other ladies. Key, with a son of the family, slept in the pantry on feed sacks, all the blankets having gone to the makeshift hospitals. The next morning the sun came out and Alice, lighter by twelve pounds, started making the rounds looking for Horace. When she came back at nightfall she hadn't found him, but she was full of talk about a Scottish lady from Alabama who had been at the Battle of Corinth and had supervised a hospital at Tupelo.

"She's a member of the Women's Relief Society. They collect money to help the sick and wounded. Mattie, what are you doing?"

"We may have a member of the wounded here with us." She stopped just long enough to set a pail down and rearrange the cloth wrapped around the wire handle. "Key. He's got a raging fever."

"Have you sent for a doctor?"

"They're too busy—I've been putting cold water . . . What are you doing?"

Alice swung her shawl wide, then hugged it to her. "I'm going back to the hospital . . . It could be brain fever. I've heard them talk of it. Pain . . . in the back of the neck. Has he had pain in the back of the neck?"

"No, no, Alice. He's been soaked with rain, up for two nights, and when he did sleep it was on the floor. Isn't that enough?"

But the round, gold-brown eyes were shining. Alice Ready had found her "profession." All her fury against the Yankees, all her energies would go now into nursing the wounded.

"All right. But only after you eat. Here, here's a piece of bread. I'll wager you haven't eaten all day."

Alice folded it and wolfed a bite. "If you'll . . . get a little supper. Maybe I can talk a doctor into coming by."

"Yes. We'll do that." Mattie watched Alice leave and gave Bessie, the maid, an order for soup, then carried the pail upstairs. Two hours later the doctor came. She had dozed by the bed, Key's heavy, fitful breathing growing shallower, but steady. She had wiped his matted hair with a towel so often the sandy curls lay plastered black against his head.

The doctor lifted his ear from the boy's chest and sighed. "I wish all my patients were this well," he said. "The boy needs rest . . . and nourishment. A little broth. He should have a little bath when he wakes."

"I am awake, doctor," mumbled Key, his flushed face trying a smile. "I'm all right. Tell them . . . I'm . . ."

"Absolute rest! A week. A week's rest. What a sentence!" Alice tried to make light of it, but in fact her own fatigue was making her silly, and she cleared her throat so the doctor wouldn't notice. He snapped his bag shut, then blew his nose, balled up his handkerchief and wiped his eyes, then replaced his glasses and stifled a yawn. "I envy you, my son. And now, young ladies, your promise . . . ?"

"Will he be all right, doctor?" Mattie asked anxiously as they walked downstairs.

"Keep him warm. Plenty of liquid. Yes."

To her utter chagrin Mattie discovered the kitchen deserted, and no soup. "That girl!" she said, shaking.

"Never mind, ma'am. I'm too tired to eat anyway." The doctor smiled graciously. "What we all need is the nourishment of sleep."

After he left, Alice watched her sister with the kettle. "At least we can have some tea," Mattie was saying, relieved. All the servants had gone to bed and the kitchen was quiet. They brought their cups into the dining room.

"I heard some news today."

Mattie's cup shook.

"No . . . no, it's not about Brother. Still no news from him. But I heard the cavalry headquarters will be at McMinnville."

"The cavalry . . . ?"

Alice took a deep breath. "The cavalry forces have been divided in two: Forrest in the West, Wheeler in the East. Yes, yes, I'm sure he'll be there!"

Mattie threw her head back and yelped, then stifled her giggles, for fear she would wake Key. Her fatigue vanished, the hours of watching and worry. Impatience almost as sharp as pain took its place. "I've got to go. Don't you see? You'll be perfectly safe here. Miss Sally and the others—the Scottish lady . . . what's her name?"

"Mrs. Endicott."

"Mrs. Endicott. The, the . . ." Mattie walked to the door and back. "The . . ."

"Women's Relief Society," Alice finished.

"Yes, yes, that's it. The Women's . . . you do see I have to go?" She stopped and saw Alice as if for the first time and bit her lip. "General Hardee. He'll know what to do! Yes, that's it. I'll ask . . . oh, Alice, Alice! Do you suppose he'll be there?"

"General Hardee?"

The question and the look Alice shot her woke Mattie at last. "Oh, but Alice, will you, can you . . . ?"

"You said it yourself. I'll be fine." Alice closed her eyes and nodded. "Go. Of course, you have to. I would!" The hug her sister gave her almost took her breath.

The next morning Mattie put on her best dress and waited patiently outside General Hardee's door. When a number of officers emerged, she was called in by an aide.

"Ah wouldn't." The General ran fingers through his thick graying hair. "Ah know how much you want to go, Miss Mattie. But this is no time for a young lady to be traveling alone. The cars are still occupied with troops . . ."

"It's not that far!"

"You would have to change trains at Decherd, and again at Tullahoma, Miss Mattie. Goodness knows how long you would have to wait," he said in his soft Georgia drawl. He sounded like a mammy, and the more her distress affected him the more like a mammy he sounded.

"I'm . . ."

"Of coh'us! You ah a puhfuctly capable young wommin, Miss Mattie. We all know that!" When he saw her face fall he added with a tug at his goatee: "Ah can send a courier to General Wheeler's headquahtahs with instructions that General Morgan know yoah wheah-a-bouts the minute he arrives."

Disappointed, she could see the wisdom of it. Could his smile also be an indulgent warning not to be too anxious? A tinge of shame colored her cheeks. Didn't men ever understand?

"I'll send a letter!"

"Excellent ideah." He motioned her to a small table and she spread the paper and dipped the pen, her hand shaking. Could it be possible that *he* would hold this in his hands?

> *My Dearest Darling*—Come to me My own Darling quickly. I was wretched but now I am almost happy and will be quite when my precious husband is with me again. . . .

She didn't care if she sounded desperate! She didn't care if she threw away all those dainty admonitions about holding back, about "being a lady." She was cold and lonely, her body in need of warmth and reassurance, and she didn't care. She took a breath and tried to see him reading this.

> *I had some dark days dearest*—and when the battle was raging around me in such fury, and everybody from the commander-in-chief to the privates were praying for "Morgan to come," I thanked God in the anguish of my heart that it was not for me to say where you should be.
> I am all right here, my Darling. I reached here with Alice and Key and although an entire stranger to the people, they received me, as the saying is, with open arms because I am your wife. I am with Mrs. Ransom on Main Street, not far from headquarters. Tell Glencoe not to gallop too fast, or break a leg. I want you well and whole—
>
> Love,
Mattie

She folded the paper twice and took a breath and saw the General smiling behind her. His aide let her out.

"So I won't be going," she said disconsolately to Alice as she busied herself hanging up her dress. In the armoire her best green velvet, with the lace collar, hung like a promise waiting. She had dreamed of meeting him in that dress. She suddenly threw herself into the rich soft folds and cried like a baby.

"Oh, Mattie . . ."

She drew back and sniffed. "I'm sorry. I suppose you think I'm awful, with all those boys so badly wounded." She felt her face crumpling again. "But I did want to be so beautiful for him, Alice!"

"I know, I know . . . And you are, you are!"

"And I have helped Key, haven't I?"

"Of course . . . you're just tired, Sister. . . ."

"No, no! That's not it! Nobody understands!"

Alice reached her hands out and Mattie caught them and felt the rough knuckles. She looked up at the puffs of fatigue under her little sister's eyes. Why, she looks like an old woman . . . her dear, cheerful Alice. This war will make us all into old women . . . and she wanted more than ever to keep the ribbons, the lace, what was left of everything that could make her desirable for *him*—that seemed the only firm, unchanged thing in the world.

"I *do* understand," Alice was murmuring, her head bowed. "I do."

Suddenly the memory of those burned diary pages came back. Poor Alice
. . . how serious had her attachment been? Mattie had been so in love herself
she had ignored . . . "When I do go," she said firmly, "you and Key go with
me."

Alice shook her head. "No. I can be of use here, and Key, when he's well.
This may be the only time you'll ever have with him, Sister . . ."

The letter came, dated January 17. Captain Dick McCann appeared the
morning of the 18th with instructions to accompany her to McMinnville on
the afternoon train.

> My Own Darling,
> Reached this place from Smithville on the 14th. When I heard from
> General Hardee of your presence in Winchester I was overjoyed. If you
> will come to me, my dearest, we can have the family together again. I
> have obtained quarters in the home of Dr. Armstrong, large enough for
> Alice and Key also. God Bless and protect you till we meet . . .

"I can't."

"But Alice, you must."

"No . . . I thought we'd talked it all out before. I can be of much better
use here, and Key can't travel yet. You go, Mattie, it's your duty . . . and
give him all our love!"

The engine was stoked and steaming when they reached the station. Mattie watched Alice grow smaller, then disappear altogether as the train pulled
away. Dick McCann was talking, full of stories of exploits around Gallatin
last summer, before the September raid.

"Once, Doc Williams and I went on one of those 'visits' around Nashville
. . . met some Yankee vedettes, sent two men to get between them and the
Federal camp. The moon was out, and we'd intended to charge them but
they saw us first and fired. . . ."

She looked out the window at the hills going by and thought, Johnny!
Johnny! She could almost feel his arms around her, his lips . . .

"Well, ma'am, one ball struck me on the brass buckle of my saber belt
. . . the blow sent me off my horse and I thought I'd been sent to The Next
World right there . . ."

. . . his lips. His eyes. What would he think of her? Had she changed?
She was tired, and anxious, and how many times had Alice told her if she
didn't watch out she would suffer as their mother had from nerves? No, she
was strong . . . hadn't the family always called her strong? Still, he had
been to Kentucky, where the girls were pretty . . .

" 'Dick,' said the Doc, 'are you hurt?' " 'Yes,' I sez, 'killed deader'n a
corpse, Doc. Shot right through the bowels'—pardon me, ma'am. . . .
'Quick,' I sez, 'pass me the bottle before I die . . .' "

The Captain laughed good-naturedly and she joined him politely.

"Well, I guess you don't want to hear no more soldier's tales, ma'am."

"I do, I do! I want to know everything about my husband's men."

"They worship him, ma'am," McCann said simply. "It's like that: They
worship him."

I do too, her eyes said, but she turned quickly to the window before he could see just how much. They were coming into Tullahoma and the bustle of getting off and making connection with the little train which would take them on the spur line through Manchester and on to McMinnville made the talk turn to what they would eat while they waited. She looked up to see a familiar figure walking toward them, his shoulders slightly bent.

"Colonel Hunt!"

"Mattie, my dear. Johnny sent me a message that you would be coming through. I've had a scout posted, who only now sent a message to my headquarters, around the corner, that the most beautiful girl he had ever seen just stepped off the train . . ."

But through the flattery he looked weary and distracted.

"Have you eaten?" He turned to McCann.

"We were just wondering about that, sir."

"Well, then . . . there's a hotel across the street. I can't promise you much, but it's clean . . ."

His Ninth Kentucky, he told McCann as they walked toward the hotel, with the Forty-first Alabama and Cobb's battery had drawn rear guard duty after the battle of Murfreesboro. But army talk seemed to pain him and he turned to Mattie as he opened the door. "My wife is in Augusta now. I hope to join her soon."

"Leave, sir?" McCann asked behind them.

"Perhaps," T.H. said evasively. He waited until they were seated at a table and the waiter had taken their order before he spoke again. "I have some news for Colonel Duke. A letter . . . from his wife. He will be a father, it seems, next summer."

"Oh, that's wonderful. . . ."

"Colonel Duke was wounded on our last raid, sir," McCann said quickly. "He's been sent to Atlanta."

"That's where his wife is!" T.H. caught himself up. "Then it's serious."

"A head wound, sir."

Mattie gasped.

"Not too serious, ma'am. We expect him back in a month or so. We joked that he has the head of an Irishman!"

The food was warm and T.H. talked of Augusta again. He had never been there. Mary liked it. They did not speak of the war again. Why do we try so hard, she thought. He looks so tired, so worn out. A shrill whistle from the depot made her jump. It was time to go.

T.H. graciously kissed her on both cheeks and sent his love to his nephews. "Tell Tom to behave!" As she watched him waving from behind the smudged window of her car in his crumpled uniform, Mattie suddenly saw the family resemblance: a kindness, a graciousness, rather than a physical likeness. The stab of impatience, that almost took her breath, returned.

He was there, waiting, in a chill drizzle at sundown, when the little train pulled into the station at McMinnville. There was chatter, bustle over her two bags, jokes about the weather. McCann excused himself and left them. He helped her into the buggy he'd hired and they drove to Dr. Armstrong's house. She told him Basil's news. He talked about the house, arrangements, the fact that he hoped she would be comfortable . . . all chatter that faded once they met the Armstrongs in the parlor and passed up the stairs to their rooms. Then heaven began.

46

"**A**re you warm?" His lips traced the hairline behind her ear.

As answer, she rubbed the plump backside of her calf across his thigh and snuggled against his chest.

"You'll spoil me."

She lifted her head back to look at his chin. "How?"

"All this . . . rest."

She smiled and slipped one arm under him and hugged him to her. "I wouldn't say you've been resting, exactly."

He stretched his long legs past hers and sighed at the feel of cool sheets. Little pink roses strayed across the wallpaper and walnut furniture gleamed in the faint light of a January afternoon. Lace curtains, drawn at the window, gave the gray sky a pearly look. Outside it was raining, that eternal, infernal cold Tennessee winter rain. "The fire's gone out," he said.

"Of course! They didn't want to disturb us. What can they be thinking?"

He looked down at the clean part in her black hair and grinned. "Do you care?"

"You know I don't, John Morgan."

"Are you hungry?"

"Ravenous."

"Do you want to get something to eat?"

"Not if I have to move."

He closed his eyes and smiled. "You are so warm. You will never know how warm you are."

A frozen bird, in the mouth of that dog following one of the men when they'd marched around Lebanon, after Basil was wounded. My God, even the birds froze on that trip. He squeezed her to him. He hadn't lied about her being warm. If only his men could be half as comfortable. Even here at McMinnville, things weren't much better. He thought of them: worn out, ragged, sick. Colonel Bennett, who had come to him with his Tennesseans in the Gallatin days, who had been with him at Hartsville and in Kentucky. Dead of pneumonia. As for rations, it was all Alston and Maginis could do to get bad pork and wormy cornmeal. And they were expected to patrol a line from Murfreesboro to Kentucky!

Their horses were worse. The South was supporting two armies now: Forage for man and beast had become so scarce that one third of his men stood picket on foot, and one fourth of the horses in Bill Breckinridge's brigade lay dead. Every time a patrol came back they carried tied to their saddles, like gruesome trophies, the legs of dead horses cut off at the ankle —shoes were too valuable to leave. Worse, confined to "camp"—those lean-tos and makeshift tents—the cavalry couldn't supply themselves, as they were expected to do. Corn had to be hauled thirty miles, in competition with other units in the area, and already they were down to two ears per day for each horse, if they were lucky. Thank God he'd sent Chenault into Kentucky to rest what horses his regiment had left, and to collect more. How that order had enraged Little Joe Wheeler! "You are under my command, General Morgan," the sanctimonious little son of a bitch had said. While his boys starved and his horses died. He would send another expedition as soon as possible . . . with or without permission.

"You're frowning."

"Am I?"

"You're even more handsome when you frown."

"Then I'll scowl all the time."

"Impossible, John Morgan. I would die if I never saw you smiling. . . ."

He kissed that mouth that spoke of death and the wanting overcame everything. When she opened her eyes again he was standing near the wash stand, buttoning his shirt. She watched his dear face bent down.

"Where did you learn to make love? No . . . don't answer that."

He looked up, his face serious in surprise. Then that little-boy smile traveled to his eyes and he came over to her and kissed her lightly.

"Last night," he answered. "And this morning. And just about a half-hour ago."

"I'm so afraid I won't make you happy."

"My darling. My own dear darling." He grinned to make her smile, but she did not smile. She took his hand and caressed it, held it against her cheek. "If you never . . . had to go away!"

"You'd get completely tired of me. Besides, half the fun is in the coming back. Now, I'll have a starved little girl if I don't get downstairs and send up hot water, a fire and some food. . . . Oh, and I forgot." He went to the armoire and drew out a brown paper package. "This is from Kentucky."

"John, you didn't?"

"Open it."

She sat up and fumbled with the heavy string, and he took out a penknife and cut it. The paper, laid back, revealed rose silk. She took it out and shook it across the bed. "Hand me my robe!" He did so, and she stood holding the dress against her. "Oh, John! It's so elegant! But isn't it cut rather low?"

"Of course! Why not?"

"Isn't it . . . rather . . . naughty?"

He laughed out loud. "I tell you what. Doctor Armstrong has invited General Wheeler and his staff to a dinner tomorrow night in your honor. If Wheeler blushes, it's too much . . . for him."

"And you?"

"Nothing about you, Mattie Ready, would ever be too much for me."

"Do you have to go?"

"Only to headquarters, just down the street. Be back within the hour."

"Promise?"

"Promise. I'll send a servant with breakfast and a fire."

She saw the frown return even before he closed the door.

The rain poured in sheets as he walked the short two blocks to Wheeler's headquarters: Out at camp his men must be chilled to the bone. And tomorrow they would look up at those bleak skies as the bugle sounded, stir their numbed bodies, wrap rags around their feet for shoes and mount their half-starved, stumbling horses, themselves no less faint and hungry, to go out and hold back a foe outnumbering them ten to one. Wheeler had to agree to recruit mounts in Kentucky. He had to!

At twenty-six, Brigadier-General Joseph "Little Joe" Wheeler, in his too-big shirts, had the look of an anxious altar boy, as if he were trying to make up in innocent hauteur what he lacked in height. But there was for Morgan something too precise about his little ears, high-domed forehead, neat plastered hair and impassive eyebrows that looked painted on above the heavy-lidded eyes. He had a straight-bridged nose that came to a point and a no-nonsense, dense black beard and mustache, trimmed to a hair, that smothered his mouth. His love of protocol was a standing joke, but it had evidently impressed Braxton Bragg, who made him Commander-in-Chief over Wharton, himself—and Forrest. Wheeler held out his hand now (the cuffs fell halfway down his fingers) and bowed slightly from the waist.

"Congratulations, General. I hear your bride has arrived."

"Yes, yes, thank you."

There was an awkward pause. An aide made a sign, the meaning of which completely escaped Morgan. He waited, then said, "I've been thinking about the state of the men and horses, sir. That cotton homespun passing for wool uniforms the ordnance department sent to Murfreesboro has completely given way . . ."

"Cavalry units are lucky to get that much from ordnance, as you well know, General."

It was said with such irritation that for a moment Morgan wondered if Wheeler regretted leaving the infantry. Yet he couldn't keep impatience from his voice as he persisted: "Forage for the horses is approaching the disaster mark. If I could send an expedition into Kentucky to replenish the stock. . . ."

General Wheeler sat down. He had not invited Morgan to do so. He had the habit of smacking his lips between words, as if he were tasting them.

"Under the circumstances, that will be entirely impossible, General Morgan, and you know it," he bit out. "Your picket lines run from Woodbury into eastern Kentucky. We must hold that country south of the Cumberland at all costs." He shook his head.

"We shall do our duty, sir."

"With the help of the Almighty, sir, we shall all do our duty."

He truly forgot to convey Dr. Armstrong's invitation. Well, it could be sent around later. When he reached the anteroom he learned the reason for the General's strange behavior . . . for him, almost rude. He had just received news of his promotion to major-general, and expected a congratulation in return.

Mattie giggled when he told her. "That serves you right for staying in bed all day!"

"What did they expect a red-blooded man to do?"

"He's mad at you."

"No. He's madder than hell at me. And when he meets you, he'll be jealous, too."

"Maybe I shouldn't wear your dress after all," she teased. "We don't want an enemy."

"We'll have one anyway," Morgan murmured, for he had already decided to send an expedition for horses as soon as he could, with or without Wheeler's permission. He went downstairs to the little room he used as an office. All his orders, all his plans were forgotten fifteen minutes later. Cal walked in.

When he could find his voice he yelled, "Cally! You son of a gun! Cal! Where the hell . . . ?"

They laughed insanely at each other for a full two minutes. They were boys again at Shadeland; on the plains of Texas. Morgan poured two whiskies and they touched glasses.

"So how . . . ?"

"When the news reached New York that Bragg lost Kentucky I changed my tune." Cal laughed when he could catch his breath. "I started writing home 'I have no intention of joining the Rebel army' . . . and somebody believed it. So . . . they let me go!" Worn out from his trip, he sank his head back on the chair and tilted his hat forward, balancing the brim on the bridge of his nose.

"Cal! I still can't believe."

"Believe, Brother."

Morgan turned his own chair around and straddled it, facing him.

"I said nothing about the Rebel cavalry," Cal grinned under the hat.

"Tell me everything!"

Cal sat up. "That's a big order! I left Yankeeland in November, made it to Vicksburg for Christmas, where I was much surprised to read in a newspaper that my big brother was married. And why didn't you wait for me before you burned those trestles at Muldraugh Hill?"

Morgan watched him sip his whiskey and told him what he knew of Stones River.

"Roger Hanson. And little Henry," Cal murmured, shaking his head. "It's hard to believe. What will Uncle Dick say? I saw in a New York paper that Basil was wounded at Shiloh."

"He was wounded again on the Christmas raid. Head. Near the ear. He's in Atlanta."

"With Tommie, then . . ."

"The rascal's going to be a father. We just heard." To Cal's raised eyebrows he added: "It wasn't a bad wound, Cal. He should be back to duty soon. And home?"

"From her letters, Ma's lonesome, but being brave about it. You remember how Uncle Frank used to josh her about keeping the lame, the halt and the blind? As things turned out, it may have been a very wise choice. They'll never confiscate Adam. . . . Oh, how good it is to be here!"

Morgan heard the catch in his brother's voice.

"God knows . . ." His own emotion took his breath. He reached for Cal's hand and blinked back sudden tears. "Glad you made it," he said quietly.

At the Armstrongs' dinner General Wheeler was cordial, and Mattie the belle of the evening. Tom rode in from the outpost at Woodbury. Charlton arrived late, and it became a family reunion, a second wedding party. Under the influence of the Armstrongs' best and last bottles of wine, Wheeler warmed to the atmosphere. He told a story of Rosecrans complaining that the Rebs did not wear uniforms, and Bragg's reply, that when the Yankees saw fit to supply them with the proper attire they would be glad to oblige. That rare streak of humor in his general made even Little Joe collapse in laughter. Morgan caught Cal's eye. God, it was good to have him here!

"I want to know everything," Mattie said afterwards, when they were in their room again and he had blown out the lamp. "I want to know every single thing that's worrying you."

He could never fool her. It was no longer a joke, in spite of Bragg's quip, that his men were in constant danger of being hanged. He pushed the thought aside. "Well, there is one thing that is an awful concern."

"Tell me."

"General Wheeler didn't blush . . . once!"

She slipped off the rose silk and hung it carefully in the armoire. As she closed the door the mirror caught his image on the bed watching her. "I'm so glad Cal's back," she said to the image, then turned to him.

"I am, too."

She let her nightgown fall over her head and unhitched her camisole under its folds, then pulled off her pantalettes. She lifted the covers and snuggled next to him. His arm went around her shoulders and held her close. "Tell me about Cal," she said.

"Cal?" He looked at the ceiling and sighed. "He's just about the best brother alive. He'd do anything for you. He's got the best heart. You can depend on him."

"Sounds like somebody I know."

"Who?"

She rolled over, her face above his.

"Guess."

Having her with him made all things possible. And now Cal!

The next morning she had a long letter from Alice. Key was fine and their brother Horace was at Wartrace, with Hardee's corps. "We've written, asking if he can come down to Winchester on leave," Alice's plump little-girl handwriting said. Morgan bent over as he handed the page back. "Send her our love, and tell her she and Key must come here, if all goes well."

If. Rosecrans in Nashville and Bragg at Tullahoma glared at each other across a range of high foothills, where roads connecting Murfreesboro and

Tullahoma crossed at three gaps: Hoover's, Guy's, and at the little town of Liberty. Polk held Guy's; Hardee watched Hoover's. Morgan's men were at Liberty, through which the Yankees could approach McMinnville and Bragg's right flank. It was the Confederate base closest to Nashville, a salient.

"It's wide open," Morgan worried. "They're sitting ducks."

"Then reinforce them—with or without Wheeler's permission," said Cal.

Morgan looked at that round, good-natured face, those sincere eyes.

"Woodbury's not much better. If that falls, the men at Liberty will be cut off from McMinnville and the railroad to Tullahoma . . . in fact, a Federal force could get between Bragg's army and his cavalry."

"Who's at Woodbury?"

"Hutch. Lieutenant-Colonel Hutchinson."

"You said he is a good man?"

"The best. And he's got John Castleman as second-in-command."

"Breck? Then you have nothing to worry about!"

Morgan wrote the orders: Bill Breckinridge would reinforce Quirk at Liberty with three regiments. As for Hutchinson, it seemed he could, for the moment, take care of himself: With less than a hundred men, he attacked a Federal force, and although outnumbered, took two hundred prisoners and fifty wagons of supplies. For this he was complimented by general orders from Bragg himself. As it turned out, however, that little victory brought disaster.

Because of Hutch's success, Rosecrans determined to whip any Confederate cavalry his troops might meet. He began sending out units of cavalry stronger than any they expected to encounter, backed up by infantry to finish any fight their cavalry couldn't win. This stepped-up activity occurred even before Quirk went to Liberty, and now that Breckinridge's three regiments were there, it was even more imperative that Hutch hold Woodbury. And that they get those horses from Kentucky.

Then disaster struck. On January 24, three thousand Federals approached Woodbury, mostly infantry, with artillery, and Hutch decided not to give up without a fight. He formed behind a stone wall, but sent Captain John Cooper with his men to parade around on the top of a hill to make the enemy think reinforcements were coming. All through that shelling, with no artillery to answer, Hutch suffered patiently until the stone wall was taken. Then he watched as Captain Tribble and Lieutenant Lea, charging at the head of their companies, retook it. Only then, outnumbered and with the artillery still pounding, did he order a retreat. Aided by Cooper's fresh troops, they were dropping back in good form when one part of the line faltered. Hutch immediately rode forward to encourage it. He was trotting back, laughing gleefully at their successful retreat, when a ball found him on the temple. He fell dead instantly.

"Captain Castleman is in command, sir," the boy with the message said. "Sir?"

Hutch. Yes, he would be laughing. Slapping his horse with his hat as he came. A Western man, as free as prairie air. "Born to be a soldier," St. Leger had said when he first saw him. Just twenty-four. In spite of his boyish ways, he had always seemed older. God, if he had only reinforced him. . . .

"I feel as if my right hand has been cut off," he told Mattie when he could speak of it.

She had missed a period. She had been so happy . . . beyond anything she had ever dreamed. What if she were carrying part of him inside, part of which could become . . . it made her breathless. Now she saw his face. *I feel as if my right hand has been cut off*. The grief of that. And John Hutchinson, that dashing, magnetic man. She could have fallen in love with him herself, if she had not met her Morgan first. She felt her body stiffen in fear.

"And Woodbury?"

"Castleman held."

For how long? he thought. They all knew, even Bragg at Tullahoma, that Rosecrans was getting braver.

"Then why, in all tarnation, is Bragg doing this to us?" Captain Maginis waved a sheet of paper at his general an hour later.

Morgan took it. It was a telegram ordering all unmounted cavalry transferred to the infantry. "It's the last straw," Maginis was saying behind his back. "Absolutely the last. Our men won't stand for it! They've watched their horses die; they've fought with empty stomachs themselves, in this infernal sleet and cold. . . ."

"Send for Colonel Alston," Morgan said quietly. The time to appeal to Richmond had come. Then, a stroke of luck: The next morning Wheeler received orders to retake Fort Donelson, with Forrest's help. Morgan would be left in command at McMinnville.

The first thing he needed to do was save morale. There was only one cure for that: action. Gano returned from leave. Morgan immediately put him in charge at Woodbury. An hour after he left, he called a staff meeting. James Bowles, now a lieutenant-colonel, watched him expectantly.

"Rosecrans needs a good scare," Morgan said.

Cal caught on at once. "With Forrest and Wheeler at Donelson, and you . . ."

"Into Nashville . . ."

"I wonder how much damage we could do?" Cal asked wistfully.

"More than if we sit here."

"Can you get Wheeler to agree?" Bowles asked.

"I won't even try."

With fifty men. That's all he needed. It would be like old times. He knew the territory.

"Some things have changed," Alston warned.

"Oh?"

"New garrisons. Outposts. I met a man just yesterday who may help us, though."

"Send him to me."

The man was a shrewd, clear-eyed boy about Tom's age, a Nashville native who knew every street and latest picket line. His mother lived near the depot. After meeting him Morgan dictated a letter to Maginis. "From General Rosecrans to Captain Johnson, Fifth Kentucky Union Cavalry. Orders to proceed from Murfreesboro to Lebanon, thence to Nashville, for the purpose of arresting all stragglers, make all discoveries, etc."

"Do you think that sounds official enough?" he asked Cal. "We'll form at Liberty," he said to Maginis.

He would take Major Steele, Captain Cassell, and Quirk, with fifty picked men. Tom, left behind, pouted. "Cal's going," he said disconsolately.

"Cal's a—" he almost said *veteran*, then stopped.

"And Charl's going with Cluke to Kentucky to rest horses. I heard you say so to the Colonel just yesterday."

"Charl's on Cluke's staff."

"And I'm not on yours, am I?"

The anger hurt. How could he tell Tom that he feared his little brother's dash and daring? That hadn't helped Hutch. "You'll get your turn," he said.

"That's what you always . . ."

"That's an order."

"Yes, *sir!*"

Wheeler, busy planning his Donelson trip, was preoccupied; Morgan in any case would have to make his "visit" before assuming the duties of command. He blew out his candle and walked upstairs by the light of a winter moon through a hall window.

Telling Mattie he had to inspect the condition of the camp, he rode out to Liberty that next morning. Toward sundown the sky clouded over: They could expect no help from the moon. They rode to Stewart's ferry on Stones River. About twenty Federals rode up to the other side. Morgan immediately legged Glencoe into a brisk trot, touched his hat and asked brightly, "Captain, what is the news in Nashville?"

"Who are you?"

"Captain Johnson, Fifth Kentucky Cavalry, just from Murfreesboro, by way of Lebanon, going to Nashville by General Rosecrans's order—who are you?" he hoped he asked in the same demanding tone.

It was a Michigan regiment, new to the territory. Morgan sat straighter in his saddle. "Are you going far?" he asked more companionably. "If so . . ."

"We're headed back to Nashville. Have you any news of Morgan?"

"His cavalry are at Liberty," Morgan said truthfully, and then added, a little less truthfully: "none closer. Well, Sergeant," he said, turning to Quirk, "carry as many men over as possible and we'll swim the horses." When he saw the Michigan officer move as if to go, he couldn't help having some fun. "Wait up, sir, and I'll ride with you into Nashville."

In this atmosphere of camaraderie the officer waited, and even handed "Captain Johnson" the latest Nashville paper. Most of the Federals dismounted and began stamping their feet and flailing their arms to keep warm while a dozen Nashville-bound "Yankees" crossed on the little ferry, the "Sergeant" in charge. On the return trip, as more men scrambled down the bank toward the ferry their gray pants showed under the blue overcoats and half a dozen Yankee soldiers yelled out. There was nothing for it but to surround them; luckily the horses hadn't started to cross yet. The Captain and fifteen Federals surrendered, but the rest escaped to give the alarm.

Useless child's play. Another lost chance. His "Yankees" recrossed the river and rode silently back to camp.

"What good would a few destroyed supplies have been, anyway?" Cal asked to console him.

Yes, what good? Never in his life had he felt so helpless. Sick men, dying horses. And a commanding general who would turn his cavalry into infantry if he would let him! About his abortive Nashville raid he felt a mixture of relief and guilt: relief that Mattie didn't know, and guilt that he had kept it from her. Guilt overcame relief when he saw her at the Armstrong door.

"John!" She was trembling. "John, I've been so . . . a telegram came . . . they couldn't find Captain Maginis, and came around here . . ."

He fumbled it open with his heavy cavalry gloves.

"Good news! Richard's coming! Transferring from A.P.'s staff to mine! He's the only Morgan brother you haven't met. You'll like him. . . ."

The telegram was sent from Tullahoma. That could mean Richard might arrive any time—as soon as tomorrow. After he had a good bath and supper Morgan settled into a quiet evening with Mattie mending by the fire. He flipped open the Nashville paper and read the comforting news that the Yankees were having their troubles, too. Desertions. And Rosecrans had paraded fifty paroled men in Nashville as an "example"—in nightcaps. So much for paroles. Grant mustered out of service two captains for dereliction of duty—present during pillaging. Well, that was better. Maybe Grant was a gentleman. This was followed, in the same column, with the news that Grant was putting slaves to work picking cotton in Mississippi, people who had followed his army, paying them a "wage sufficient to buy food" and shipping the cotton north. Ah, but always a Yankee gentleman. His eye drifted to a box in the lower lefthand corner: A NOTICE. TO ALL WHO HAVE LOST FRIENDS IN THE ARMY.

"When do you suppose he'll come?"

> The undersigned—having passed within all the military lines, is now prepared to receive orders to disinter, embalm or disinfect—metallic or wood coffins—the remains of those who have fallen. . . .

"Who?"

"Richard." She bit off a thread, pulled it through her needle, her arm gracefully out.

> Having agents and embalmers on the different fields of battle—we guarantee—utmost expedition—warrant perfect success—refer to the friends of all whom he has embalmed.

"He'll be so full of news! I wonder what it's like in Richmond. . . ."

> For full particulars, apply to WILLIAM H. COOKE, 140 Broadway, New York.

He leaned back. The date of the advertisement was November 30. Before Murfreesboro. Were Mr. Cooke's "agents" waiting by Stones River to pick up the "remains"? The smell of money . . . He looked at the fire. Dear Hutch. And Wash. And those open Confederate trenches at Shiloh. No chance of money there. The ghouls.

"I declare, John Morgan, I do believe you haven't heard a word I've said."

"I'm sorry."

"I said I don't know how much more I can mend this old green dress."

Home. Would he ever see it again? Not with stupid little Nashville "raids." Something bigger. Bigger . . . She came into focus. "You look good in green. I'll get you another. . . ."

Something in his face made her heart break. She threw down the mending and rushed to him. "Oh, my darling . . ." The feel of his chest against her made their bodies one. She buried her head against him and almost told him then. But he was so worried, so torn with fears himself. How could she add to them?

Richard arrived the next day.

"You might have given me fair warning!"

"You might have refused!"

Cal was still pumping his hand. "Let's send word to Tom. Charl's in Kentucky recruiting horses."

"Where's Key? Your last letter said something about his leaving Lexington . . ."

"Winchester, with Mattie's sister. We hope to have them here next month if . . ."

"If?"

"Sometimes it doesn't do to think of too many damned 'ifs.' "

"But now that I'm here . . ."

"You're right."

They settled down to learn the latest news.

"And A.P.?"

"Powell hasn't been well since Antietam. Fatigue and . . ."

"And?"

"Jackson. Did you know that Jackson filed formal charges . . . neglect of duty?"

"Ridiculous!"

"Agree. Stonewall got his nose out of joint because A.P. told a subordinate to obey orders from corps headquarters only if they came through his division. A.P. has demanded a court of inquiry . . . I hear General Lee has filed the whole mess in his desk drawer. As a result, Longstreet and Jackson are made lieutenant-generals, but Powell's Light Division is still the largest in the army . . ."

"How many men?" Cal, puzzled at the protocol, asked the obvious question.

"Almost twelve thousand."

Cal whistled. "That's not a division."

"And Kitty?" Morgan asked. "She is well?"

"You'll be an uncle again this spring. You didn't know?"

"How could I? You write so often. . . ."

"We had a lull back in October. She went with A.P. to Culpeper, out of Federal hands for a change, to visit his relatives. She's a camp follower now, she jokes. Little Frances is over a year old. You should see her! A.P. returned from leave just in time to make it to Fredericksburg. . . ."

"That was quite a fight."

"It was more than that, Cal! It was the first time Uncle Robert used entrenchments, and the Yankees thought they had him, but he forced Burnside to attack just where he wanted him to. . . . More than half of Lee's casualties were in A.P.'s division. That brother-in-law of ours is magnificent."

"Saturday, December the thirteenth."

"Yes. Why do you remember?"

"The day before my wedding, Little Brother. The news of Fredericksburg came as President Davis was reviewing the troops. . . ."

Richard, accepting a whiskey, spilled some and waved the glass at them. "And just after Davis left Murfreesboro he went down to Jackson, Mississippi, made a speech. Said the *next good news for the Confederacy* would come from *the Northwest*. Now what do you suppose he meant by that?"

He stopped and looked at them so suspiciously that Cal laughed. Morgan said, "I can't imagine."

Richard was waiting like a lawyer. Then he offered, offhandedly, "Since then I've had a very interesting talk with Judah Benjamin, the Secretary of State."

"Well?"

"Surely you've heard of the Knights of the Golden Circle?" Richard leaned forward, his arms on his knees, turning his glass in his hands. "The Sons of Liberty?"

"Oh, I have, I have." Morgan was amused. "The next thing we know you'll be asking us to join—what did McGregor call it—the Knights of the Silver Sword?" This was Richard, the boy going to Cuba. Still chasing rainbows.

"I tell you there may be as many as a quarter of a million Copperheads in Indiana, Illinois and Ohio who don't want this war, and who are willing to do something about it," Richard said so soberly his brother feared he had hurt his feelings.

"You'll have to meet Captain Hines. He's our cloak-and-dagger man." Morgan let the smile drift to his eyes so Richard wouldn't think he was being cynical. "But my feeling still is, that if these Sons of Liberty or Knights— or whatever they want to call themselves—really want to do something about this war, let them. They're big boys. They don't need any prodding from Confederates, risking their lives playing spy."

"I know you think I'm the dreamer, Johnny, but there's a lot of talk in Richmond. A Northwest Conspiracy . . ."

"It's time to eat," laughed Cal. "Mattie's expecting us. I hear she's borrowed the Armstrong's kitchen for a real feast. Don't want to be late!"

Mattie was charmed. She had baked her favorite dishes, and lit the last of the hoarded candles at the sideboard. Beaming, she greeted them in the rose silk dress. It might have been an evening at Hopemont. Richard regaled them with an imitation of Heros von Borcke, a Prussian on Jeb Stuart's staff. After the laughter died down the talk turned to Kitty and A.P. and the stalemate at the Rappahannock.

"A.P. saved Lee up on Antietam Creek . . . did you know that?"

Richmond. It all seemed so far away from hungry horses and hunted men.

"The only man in the Cabinet with half a grain of sense is Benjamin. Judah Benjamin," Richard said with relish. "Now there's a Confederate for you! Gave up everything! Maybe only the Jews know how to do that.

"Even he is interested in a Northwest Conspiracy," Richard persisted. "One of your men was recommended to him, in fact. . . ."

"It had to be Tom Hines." Morgan chuckled. "By all means. Captain of scouts, and a good one. Slick as a snake. Has had contact with Judge Bullitt, our Kentucky Copperhead, last summer. But I'm not in the spy business, Richard. You know how I feel about that."

"There may come a time when we'll want to win this war any way we can," Richard said solemnly.

"With honor," Morgan added grimly.

"Of course! I didn't say otherwise, did I?"

Before they finished eating Maginis sent word that two regiments, under Colonels D. H. Smith and Warren Grigsby, would join the command, by order of General Bragg. The telegram was from St. Leger.

It was past midnight by the time they got to bed, but Morgan knew now what he must do. Gano back, rested and fit; two new regiments; and now Richard. They gave him strength. For something more than outpost duty. Something bigger. As Richard told tall stories and young Tom watched, sending them all his sweet smile, the "something" solidified—his old dream of invading Ohio, of giving the Yankees a taste of their own medicine. They were all so young, so brilliantly, shiningly young. Now if Basil would only get well and come back.

Ohio. Why not? Before all the horses collapsed, and his men starved to death. Buckner would do it! Kirby Smith! Sidney Johnston—*I would fight them if they were a million*—would do it! Let them know what being invaded is all about. Do more good than all these little "raids" into Nashville, and certainly more than this talk of conspiracy. Cowards' talk. The scheme of desperate men. Well, they weren't that desperate yet. Ohio! Wheeler had left this morning for his rendezvous with Forrest against Donelson, and he was in command. In command he would be.

As if to confirm his determination, Colonel D. Howard Smith, a big man with a massive red beard, and Colonel Warren Grigsby arrived with their regiments, the Fifth and Sixth Kentucky. Morgan sent Alston to Richmond to see St. Leger. He had to have supplies. Elation almost took his breath. He couldn't even speak of it to Mattie. Not yet. Not until he could hope . . . Ohio!

The Federals had learned their lesson. They no longer depended on the railroads. Very well then. He would hit the rivers. And scout north while doing so. Richard's enthusiasm over Hines made him realize how right he would be for the job. An independent invasion would need thorough reconnaissance by a master scout. Early the next morning he sent for him. Those ice-blue eyes and that solemn look told him Hines was ready.

"A small detail."

Hines said nothing, his gaze still steady.

"No more than a dozen men."

Hines let his head dip in a nod and waited.

"Federal transports on the Green River, up to Evansville, Indiana."

Hines's look said: This can't be everything. If you'd wanted boats burned you could have done that on the Cumberland . . . might better have done that on the Cumberland, upstream from Nashville.

"Evansville's on the Ohio, sir," Hines murmured. His eyes had never left his general's face.

Morgan returned that gaze. "That's right. If you happen to meet any friends up there, find out everything you can." He watched the slow grin under Hines's mustache spread into a smile. How appropriate, he thought, that Tom Hines should be the first to know.

But he would need to impress Bragg, if he hoped for permission for an invasion. He turned to Captain Maginis, busy at his desk across the room. With the addition of Smith's and Grigsby's regiments the command was back to strength. "Send word to Colonel Cluke that I'd like to see him."

Before Hines left, Richard came in with Cal. Morgan introduced Hines.

"Captain Hines," Richard said, and held out his hand.

"Colonel Morgan."

While they chatted, word came in that Roy Cluke would be delayed. In the meantime, Morgan could confer with Smith and Grigsby. He sent for them, then turned to Richard in explanation.

"Colonel Chenault is scouting and picketing the roads around Monticello and across the Cumberland, in Kentucky. Forage and rest for the horses. I'm sending Cluke up there, too. When Cluke passes through, Chenault can supply him with two fresh companies."

"Where will Cluke be going?" Richard asked.

Morgan took a breath, then grinned.

"You don't mean?" Cal whooped.

"All the way home." Morgan said it with closed eyes, and felt the pounding they gave him in their joy.

Cluke left on the 4th of February, the day they learned of Wheeler's failure at Donelson. He left with seven hundred and fifty effectives, among them Company A of the Second Kentucky, with artillery.

"That means . . ." Cal didn't finish.

"Right. I'm sending Corbett with the Bull Pups, and you know Charl wouldn't be left behind without them."

"And if Company A goes, that means Tom . . ."

"We couldn't keep him, could we?"

"Then I hereby apply for permission to accompany this expedition," Cal announced stoutly. "Staff officer from the General's staff, specially attached."

His brother surprised him. "Agreed. Roy will need all the help he can get. If I promise you a regiment, Richard, will you brighten up?"

"There aren't many things I'd pass up a trip home for. A regiment of cavalry is one of them," Richard grinned.

"Well, I know one thing." Cal laughed. "It'll be the best-organized regiment in the Confederacy! Do you remember those neat books he kept at the factory?"

"What are we standing around here for? Let's get going!"

Tom Hines set out on the 7th of February and did not return until the 3rd of March.

Napoleon, after crossing the Alps, could not have been more proud than Captain Thomas Henry Hines when he came back to McMinnville with his fourteen troopers asleep in their saddles. Hines's slim, almost hesitant little-boy's mustache had blossomed into a regular corsair's badge of daring.

This success had given Hines mettle. He was ready for anything. Those wide-set blue eyes, that barely audible voice and the sadness of his mouth encouraged confidences. Some people said he was a dead ringer for John Wilkes Booth, the actor. And an actor he was, but with a determination behind those eyes that looked straight through you. He could be a Southern gentleman quoting Rabelais, an innocent youth needing directions . . . or a horse trader. He was obviously having the time of his life. His men worshiped him, and they were delighted when Burnside in Louisville, after Hines's visit, issued his General Order No. 38, ordering the death penalty for "persons found concealed in lines belonging to the service of the enemy." *He means us*, they beamed.

"Congratulations," said Morgan, when Hines reported. "If you keep this up, you might even have a price on your head."

The blue eyes danced, then turned empty again.

As for Cluke, after almost a month of constant fighting, but stronger by eighteen hundred recruits and fresh horses, he rejoined Chenault in southern Kentucky before the end of February. Both expeditions were successful and should prove something to Bragg . . . and to Richmond. *For something bigger later*. Yet there was a price: Charlton didn't come back.

"How many times will that little brother of ours be captured before this war is over?"

Richard tried to make a joke of it, but Morgan murmured: "Not too many, if we can end it soon."

Richard got his regiment, the Fourteenth Kentucky. D. Howard Smith and Warren Grigsby were first-rate officers, and reports from Chenault were of fat men and rested horses. Wheeler came back, Donelson lost, another case of West Point brass not listening to Forrest. Morgan broke out in laughter when he heard that Forrest told Bragg he would be in his coffin before he served under Little Joe again.

Alston arrived from Richmond with no money for supplies but plenty of gossip. Bragg had written Joe Johnston, whose aide told Alston that Bragg feared "Morgan is overcome with too large a command. With a regiment or small brigade he did more and better service than with a division. Wheeler will correct this."

Just when I'd hoped for more troops, Morgan moaned to himself. And then the fear: The bastard's planning to reduce, not increase, my command!

Alston saw his look. "Never mind, sir. There are forces at work. Senator Simms asked me to deliver this." He handed over a letter.

Morgan scanned the even handwriting. His heart warmed at Simms's denunciation of Bragg's gossip. "To overshadow your future efforts is contemptible beyond degree. . . . Bragg, in my opinion, is a grand military abortion. When this struggle is over he will pass from public notice as one whose military course was a tragedy of errors."

Still, no supplies. His men couldn't fight with good will, however official. He heard Alston saying behind him, "You should have been there, sir, when Senator Orr, from South Carolina, said Kentucky was just a bystander! I've never seen a man madder than Simms was that day! 'John Morgan with a little squad of two thousand men has captured and killed more Yankees than South Carolina has troops in the field,' he said. 'He has taken and destroyed more public property belonging to the enemy than half the state of South Carolina would sell for under the hammer at any country auction!'

"You should have been there, sir," Alston said again.

Alston brought other letters, three for Richard and a long one for Morgan from Kitty. A.P. was optimistic about the war, although not yet in the best of health. How was Basil? Had he heard about Maxie Gregg, killed at Fredericksburg? He had been Powell's right hand. Food was getting to be ridiculous—butter twenty dollars a pound! In Richmond they tried to keep up their spirits with "starvation balls"—no food and septuagenarian fiddlers. Little Frances was well . . . Kitty sent her love to Mattie. She knew she must be a real soldier's wife. "My brother couldn't have chosen otherwise. . . ."

But no supplies. And then, better than any mail or political support in Richmond, Basil came back.

"I know your news," Morgan grinned.

"You do? How?"

"Oh, we have ways. . . . When's the big date?"

"August . . ."

"That calls for a cigar!" Morgan called out. Still, Basil was pale, and he didn't tell him about Ohio.

So much "called for cigars" as he strengthened his command and waited for spring. Adam Johnson left in February on leave for Texas. "I'll expect you in May," Morgan told him. "No later." Lieutenant-Colonel Robert Martin, handsome, young and efficient, would take over the Tenth Kentucky while Johnson was gone.

"When the bloom is on the sage," Adam nodded, "I'll see you."

"Get lots of rest. I'll work the pants off you when you get back."

He succeeded in getting Ed Byrne and his six-pounders assigned to the command. Shiloh. God, the memories. Through the bleak winter days he invited his staff and field officers to the house, and the Armstrong parlor became a second headquarters. Webber and Alston, Bowles and Messick and Sisson. Castleman, Grigsby, Smith, Bill Breckinridge. And Gano. Mattie, meeting Gano for the first time, charmed him completely.

"But you will excuse me, sir?" she said as she slipped from the circle of gray uniforms. She had caught Morgan's eye and message that the Nashville man was waiting to take her letter to Mary. She still had some doubts.

"Are you sure he can get it through?"

"For you, darling, yes, anything. This man can take it, and deliver an answer safely."

"How can he do that?"

"How do you suppose we know anything?" He smiled softly. "Don't worry. He's perfectly reliable."

With the buzz around her, Mattie sat at a little writing table in the corner and wrote by the light of one of Mrs. Armstrong's "Confederate candles"— a piece of rope dipped in wax and stuck in a bottle.

His beautiful eyes caught hers above a dozen heads. She dipped her pen again.

> Dearest Sis,
> My life is all a joyous dream now from which I fear to awaken. . . .

She looked across the room at his tall, straight form. He had turned back to the others. Even his gestures were gracious. If she sounded a little smug, she didn't care. Mary as the oldest girl had always looked down a little on her sisters. But thread is four dollars a spool, a voice in the corner of her mind reminded. And Mary is in Nashville with all those shops full of Yankee goods. Near the door she saw the Nashville man, Charles Mason, waiting.

> . . . This man can bring out anything, Sis, you wish to send, and I shall be so very much obliged to you if you will send me two pairs of slippers No. 4 or 4½, and some pins large and small. If you cannot get the green dress the General sent for, get the lilac one—I have a gray riding habit Sis and can get nothing to trim it with. I should like blue velvet.

It was getting to sound like a shopping list. She must have had a frown on her face because Morgan came over then and leaned over her. He slipped his hand over hers and took the pen, adding a P.S.: "I had hoped to see you in Nashville but an accident prevented. Kiss your sweet little girl for her new uncle—it would be folly for me to tell you how happy I am, knowing Mattie as you do."

"Have you told her about your new dress?" he whispered, smiling, and left her.

Mattie added a P.S. of her own:

I came near forgetting Sis a very important thing I want to tell you of. It is this. I have me an elegant evening dress, cut to a low waist and it fits me so stylishly that the General is so proud of it he will not consent to let my letter go without this postscript. He brought the dress for me from Kentucky—it is a beautiful rose color—

Then she couldn't resist adding more to her list and wrote:

Please send me some large hooks and eyes and a corset . . . if possible, No. 21. Sis, please send me some black stick pomatum. I want it for my husband.

When the reply came back she could have screamed. Mary Cheatham did not send the corset or the hooks and eyes or the pomatum. Instead, she asked: *Dear Mattie, you think the honeymoon will never pass, don't you?*

"She's a damned Yankee!" she said through tears, and tore up the letter before he could see it.

He had enough to worry about. Rosecrans had sent his Yankee wounded to the rear, tightened up on passes. General Bragg thought . . . hoped? . . . it meant retreat. *Her* general was convinced it meant the Yankees intended to advance, and he must stop them. Only Mattie Morgan knew the cause of his excitement, the reason he took another brandy, and excused himself to go to bed early.

The next morning he told her good-bye at the door, as cordially and as easily if he were just going out to check on his men, as he said he was.

She knew differently. Something in his voice. Again, last night, she almost told him about the baby. Now she couldn't.

An Ohio raid. If he didn't hurry, he would lose his chance. If Rosecrans moved . . . Already his troops at Liberty, barely six hundred strong, were in danger of a Federal force that had already advanced and bivouacked at Milton, just eighteen miles away. Bill Breckinridge, with a section of Byrne's battery, had posted his command across the Murfreesboro Pike and had sent for Gano to help with his whole regiment. He would never have done that if things weren't serious. Rosecrans might be trying to get between Bragg and his cavalry. . . .

It was almost dark by the time Morgan saw Byrne's guns, unlimbered and in position. Shortly after, Gano arrived. The scouts reported from two to four thousand infantry moving on the pike, with two hundred cavalry and one section of artillery. When Morgan trotted toward his vedettes on the Milton Road the Federals were within five miles of Liberty. Quirk reported they had gone into bivouac in a strong position.

"Good. While they sleep, we move." He ordered Breckinridge, Byrne and Gano to form within four miles of that bivouac and wait for first light. In the meantime the scouts could report any sign of reinforcements. It was rough country. He had, in a way, time on his side, if no help came for the Federals from Murfreesboro. The enemy position was too strong; he must watch until they marched beyond a cut in the mountains. Otherwise, it would be impossible to dislodge them. There was nothing to do but wait.

Just after daylight scouts reported movement. Quirk was ordered to attack their rear when they passed the mountain, to delay them until the whole column could arrive. Within a mile of Milton, Quirk attacked. The Yankees halted and brought their artillery up. When Morgan heard the guns he raised his arm and his men broke fours into a long, stretching gallop down the road. It was too much for some of the horses, who fell or dropped out. Regiments became divided, and there was some confusion when they arrived. Quirk's scouts were undergoing heavy shelling. The main Yankee infantry column began falling back, probably for a better position. Their cavalry was nowhere in sight. Minus the horse-holders, Morgan had a thousand men. He decided to attack at once, capture the column and artillery before the Federal cavalry came up.

Lieutenant-Colonel Robert Martin, with the Tenth Kentucky, dismounted to the left; Breckinridge's Ninth to the right. With the two artillery pieces, the rest of the column mounted and approached in fours as reserve.

But the Federal artillery had been placed on a steep hill covered by cedars, and to reach it, the men would have to cross a cedar woods, rough and broken. Enemy skirmishers were already in the trees. Morgan ordered Byrne's battery to the left of the road within four hundred yards of their guns. From there they might silence them.

He watched his men go forward gallantly. As they moved, Morgan ordered Martin to the right to help Breckinridge, Quirk to harass the rear. Gano would now dismount and attack the front.

Byrne's guns unlimbered and Martin charged. Gano's troops had by now dismounted within a hundred yards of the Yankee guns. Breckinridge's men, the dependable Ninth Kentucky, on the right, now made their move, but one of the enemy guns swung around to meet them dead center. Horses and men were falling. Colonel Grigsby was within fifty yards of the Federal battery when he had to halt. Sporadic, scattering shots told why. It was a sound they all dreaded. They were out of ammunition. Colonel Napier, of Grigsby's regiment, incensed by the lack of cartridges, led a bayonet charge and was severely wounded. Grigsby caught a ball while encouraging his men. Two more rounds would have brought them victory, and two thousand Federals would have been captured.

Would have. With ammunition gone, Morgan could do nothing but order a retreat. His columns fell back to Milton, where they found an ordnance train and four pieces of artillery sent from McMinnville. "We'll try again, sir!" Martin yelled, and they galloped back, to find the Yankees across the road, but in much the same position. An artillery duel followed, until Quirk was driven from the rear by Federal reinforcements. As the Confederate line fell back some wavered and Morgan watched Martin, to encourage them, halt and wait until his men formed again in good order. Still under fire, Martin waited a minute longer. He was now all alone. Then, at a slow walk, he took off his hat and rode his horse out of the bullets. Even the Yankees cheered. It was foolish and glorious, and the hat had a long black plume.

Inside, Morgan was furious. What if he had lost Martin, as he'd lost Hutch? They would have to learn to fight like Yankees. But deeper inside he loved them all, plumed hats, arrogant slowness under shells, insolent laughter in the face of death. Who couldn't love them? Let the Yankees fight like Yankees, their cavalry riding on pillows and hiding behind infantry.

But back at Liberty his column, like a wounded beast, licked its wounds. The loss in officers was staggering. Four young captains were dead, among them John Cooper, who as a private had carried the silk banner at Lexington. Young Captain Sales, under arrest for drunkenness in McMinnville, was fighting with his musket as a volunteer when he was shot. Morgan's own clothing was torn by bullets. He made the rounds to the wounded and talked with one boy who had his hand blown off by the premature discharge of his gun.

"I'll be back as soon as possible, sir."

That night he died.

As for the Yankees, he didn't like it. This mission had been to ascertain if Rosecrans was retreating from Nashville. The fight at Milton gave him the answer. At Liberty he wrote Mattie:

March 19, 1863

My Darling,

   I enclose a note to Col. Duke. Send it to him at once. You will see upon reading it that the Federals are not retreating. I have scarcely a moment to write. Must end. God bless and protect "My Own Beautiful" is the prayer of your devoted husband.

The note ordered Duke to take the whole command to Liberty, where they expected a concentrated attack. Mattie handed it to Basil and then fainted. He carried her to her room, where Dr. Armstrong examined her. Downstairs, in the parlor, Basil sent word to his men to break camp and waited, with the memory of her tear-streaked face haunting him. The doctor came down, his brow contracted in a worried frown. Words like "hysterical" and "depression" flew past Basil in the air.

"I would advise," said the doctor, "that the General come here if he can, if only for a few hours."

But she's . . . Basil started to say. But she's always seemed so strong. Maybe under that strength was the nervous frailty of her mother? A mental breakdown now . . . ? "Yes, perhaps it could be arranged," he mumbled, stunned. Just when they needed him.

Morgan cut cross-country to Blue Hill: It was quicker. When he got back he found her upstairs resting, the blinds drawn. She woke when he opened the door and half-rose against the pillows.

"Oh, my darling . . . my precious darling . . ." He took her in his arms and to his surprise she drew away, her body stiff in anger.

"I'm so ashamed of myself! So ashamed!" She turned from him. "How could I be so stupid?"

"Stupid, darling? Ashamed?" He reached out and turned her face to his. She kept her eyes away. "You needed me and I came. What's wrong with that?"

"I took you away from your men . . . they need you more. I realized it the minute Basil left. I'm so selfish . . . ! If anything should ever . . . !"

She looked up, then dipped her head so he couldn't see the tears. She had to press her lips together. She was determined to keep her secret as long as possible. He had enough trouble! Thank God the doctor had gone and he hadn't talked with him! He lifted her chin with a finger and tipped her face up until she looked at him. He found her mouth with his and when the wanting and the asking came, and he had answered, and she rested in the hollow of his shoulder, his arms around her, she slept like a child. She is a child, he thought. Nineteen. When you were nineteen you hadn't even gone to Mexico. When Tommie was nineteen she went up to Blue Lick to watch the Rifles that summer. If this war had never come, this girl sleeping beside you would be worried about nothing more than the next cotillion. . . .

He watched her lashes resting on her cheek, her straight little nose in the air, her mouth soft in sleep. He reached out and traced her cheek with his finger lightly; afraid to wake her but needing to feel the softness, the nearness, the warmth. "Mattie, Mattie," he whispered. "Mattie . . ." She had followed him, traveled with a retreating army, left Alice and Key and had come alone to be with him. His brave girl. Impulsive, headstrong, completely dependable; she was a Morgan down to her toes. One lovely, smooth shoulder had escaped the covers; he pulled them up and tucked them around her back and slipped out of bed. The sun had already gone down. It was time to go.

47

It was full night by the time he reached the Smithville Road. In the distance he heard horses, and instinctively closed his fingers on his reins and led Glencoe into the woods. What he saw astounded him. Morgan men ambling their horses in an unhurried, almost casual retreat! There was no panic. The road was filled with riders quietly talking to each other about "just not gonna be made to fight." In their lax, tobacco-spitting faces was a brick-wall determination close to mutiny.

He called out, identified himself, and one man sheepishly admitted, "Well General . . . I'm scattered."

What the hell was going on? He had never been one to threaten court-martial, and anyway, in the mood these men were in, it would have rolled off their backs like water. The closer to Liberty the more jammed the road became. The oncoming riders could have been on their way to town on a Saturday afternoon. They had made their decision, and nobody was going to change it.

Morgan didn't try. He found Basil.

"God, I'm glad you're here! When I rode out with Colonel Smith we met Breck's regiment in full retreat . . . then Gano's. Gano'd been forced to make a stand at 'Snow's Hill.' When we rode up Huffman was under attack, but Gano and Quirk with about eighty men had just dashed forward. . . ."

"And?"

Basil calmed. "I ordered Martin to watch the Smithville Road, where our wagons had been sent earlier. . . ."

Morgan could see it, through Basil's words: the command riding through Smithville, the teamsters looking up to see bluecoats blocking the road. Some turned their teams around; others scrambled through thickets, down runoffs where only a pony could pass. Wagons smashing, mules neighing in terror.

"It was the worst mess I've ever seen," Colonel Smith swore. He spewed tobacco over his long red beard and almost swallowed his quid.

That night they camped fourteen miles from McMinnville, where Morgan found them.

Around the campfires, the retreat was forgotten. The talk was of dash and daring, this time told even more stoutly, to mask disappointment. The best, the one he would always remember, was of John Castleman's sitting erect on his gray Kentucky mare about forty feet in the rear of his men, with the whole Yankee aim on him. Castleman kept sitting there, drawing their fire, until his horse was shot, his clothes were shot, and until every leg of that beautiful mare was broken. Lieutenant Ashbrook, trying to come to his relief, caught a ball and went down reeling. Tom Jordan ran to help and fell wounded. Finally Castleman gave the order to his men to "commence firing."

"When I left my tree, sir," C. Y. Wilson told Morgan, "I passed Captain Castleman with tears in his eyes looking at the dying struggles of that beautiful Kentucky thoroughbred that had carried him safely in so many . . . so many . . ." Private Wilson's eyes were wet with memory. "He had ordered his staff to the rear and was the only mounted soldier visible to the enemy, sir."

Another foolish, glorious, stupid, gallant episode. Where in hell . . . good God, where in hell could he replace a man like Breck? Then Basil, looking especially tired, reported more bad news: Gano had decided to resign.

"He means it," Basil told his general. "He's had a bad heart. That's why he took leave. All this constant exposure. And you know Gano. He'll give the last drop of his energy. I don't blame him."

Neither one of them spoke of the fiasco at Snow's Hill. Could that have been Gano's final straw?

"And Mattie?"

Morgan didn't know whether to frown in vexation at being away when his men needed him or smile at the memory of his visit. "Fine." He cleared his throat. "As for the Yankees, we'll take care of them in due time."

His note to Mattie the next day didn't sound so sure.

> Here I am My precious Angel, still thinking of my own Mattie, and cursing the fate that separates us. If possible I may go to McMinnville tonight, as I have just received a dispatch from Gen. Wheeler, stating that a large force of Feds. are moving on Woodbury. This may mean that they will try to come to McMinnville. If anything should occur while I am absent, take the wagon and horses and move to Sparta—also remember Cal's trunk and have it placed with ours.

She didn't know that a false bottom in Cal's trunk contained enough Yankee greenbacks to equip a regiment, but an hour after the courier left with the letter he regretted writing it. She would only worry. That afternoon the scouts reported no activity from the enemy. He decided to ride back to town the next morning to reassure her. He left Basil in charge, and met a brigade sent by Wheeler to reinforce them. They would be safe for a while. Three days later a disgruntled Basil wrote Morgan hoping that "Mr. Wheeler's people" would leave. . . . Wheeler himself had come out to "visit the camp." While he was there they had a "Yankee scare." Wheeler became very excited. Duke found out it was a false alarm; no Federals had crossed Stones River. "When they do come, expect us to give a good account of ourselves . . ." Morgan read aloud to Mattie. He didn't finish Basil's sentence: ". . . in McMinnville."

Outside, spring sunshine flooded the hills. Each day, each hour was stolen time. Wheeler took his command, with Wharton's, to Alexandria and fanned out east of Nashville from La Vergne to Lebanon, even onto the grounds of

Andrew Jackson's "Hermitage" on the Nashville-Lebanon Road. Once or twice there was enemy movement from Murfreesboro, but no skirmishing to speak of. His own troops, with the exception of Colonel Smith's regiment at Alexandria, stayed on at Liberty. And he, with a mounted escort of fifty men, waited in McMinnville for Cluke and Chenault and the fat horses from Kentucky. Waited to consolidate his forces. Waited for Ohio.

In the meantime, McMinnville was a sitting target. When T.H., at Manchester, heard of his situation he immediately dispatched Major Cripps Wickliffe with ninety troopers from the Ninth Kentucky Infantry.

" 'To help that crazy nephew.' " Cripps grinned. "I think he's really more concerned about Mattie."

Robert Martin, the handsome young lieutenant-colonel from Adam Johnson's regiment, was there with Dick McCann when Cripps walked in. "We can have a card game," Morgan said casually, but he was grateful just the same.

He deliberately kept bad news from Mattie. When they heard that the new Federal cavalry commander at Murfreesboro, Colonel Wilder, hanged four Morgan men fifteen miles north of town, he was careful that no remark should escape one of his young captains gathering in the Armstrong parlor after supper. Or that Gano had left permanently. Instead he implied that it would be temporary. He did tell her about Castleman's bravery, then damned himself for doing so. "He could have been killed!" she shuddered, and he knew she was seeing him on that horse with the broken legs. Every night she read from her prayer book and he listened, to comfort her. At first it was an indulgence. Then he realized how much she needed to cling to something.

Cluke returned on the 8th of April from Kentucky, and Cal bubbled with all the details of the raid, the brilliant action at Mt. Sterling, the escape from encircling Yankees.

"And Charl?"

Cal shook his head. "You know as well as I do, Johnny, they won't let him go this time." He blew his nose; he had a miserable cold.

"Well maybe they won't keep him long in any case!" Richard called over from the window. He had ridden in from his regiment just that morning, and after a much-appreciated bath, had been watching a robin picking in the grass of the Armstrongs' lawn. "I tell you things are going to break soon! The mood in Richmond is good. The North is sick of this war! Draft riots everywhere . . . And Lee . . ."

"What about Lee?" Cal asked.

"He's a fighter, pure and simple. Some people still call him a book soldier, but he's got enough sense to restrain himself from those gallant antics that lost us Sidney Johnston."

Morgan straightened, and Cal cleared his throat. Richard seemed not to notice. "They blame him in Richmond for building entrenchments," he went on, "but Richmond is still Confederate, and those entrenchments saved us at Fredericksburg. What I'm worried about, I tell you frankly, is the

West." *You're sounding like one of those insufferable Richmond savants* was on Morgan's face. This time Richard noticed but finished: "Joseph Eggleston Johnston, for all your faith in him, Johnny. What's he done? He may be worse than Bragg . . ."

Richard smiled at their groans. "I met a lady in Richmond who knew him. Forget her name . . ."

"Now, Richard!"

"Honestly. She was married, anyway."

"When has that stopped you?"

"Come on, you talk as if . . ."

"We know what you are," Cal said with a slow smile. "Tell us about Joe Johnston."

"I met a lady in Richmond who knew him in his younger days. He was one of those 'great hunters,' one of those 'crack shots' who never brought back a bird. Conditions just never seemed right—dogs too far or too near, birds too high or too low. I think he hasn't changed. He's waiting for that never perfect moment. He could have taken Washington after First Bull Run. Now answer me this: What has he done since he replaced Bragg?"

"He's been sick," Cal answered through his stopped-up nose. "I can sympathize with that!" He looked up as Roy Cluke walked in with Cripps Wickliffe, who was still halfway in the hall hanging up his coat.

"They'll never take Vicksburg, if that's what you're driving at," Cripps, who had heard Richard's question, said firmly as he came in. "Those batteries on the bluffs. And to the north, the Yazoo swamps. Sherman should have known better. That Yankee canal . . ."

Roy Cluke, still riding the wave of his own success, caught his mood. "Imagine! Trying to divert the Mississippi River! I didn't think even Sam Grant was that crazy!"

They're fighting the Mississippi River, they concluded. No, Vicksburg would not fall. Still, Sam Grant had crossed an army from Memphis into Louisiana and had marched south of Vicksburg on the west bank. What was he up to?

"I'm more worried about Nashville," Cal put in.

Suddenly the threat of Rosecrans and the galling memory of Bragg's incompetence entered the room. "You know what Polk says," Cluke frowned, as if reading their minds. "We have more to fear from Tullahoma than from Murfreesboro."

"How about a card game?" Cripps asked.

As the cards were passed around, with the talk of Vicksburg still fresh, someone mentioned Sherman again, and the vandalism in Mississippi.

"What is Sherman's army?" Cal insisted. "Mostly new recruits. What can you expect?"

"I should hope our men will act better when they invade the North, recruits or not," Morgan answered almost absently, as if to himself.

"There's no fear of that, is there?" Cluke grumbled as he picked up his cards.

Morgan looked up and Cal, who had caught something in his brother's face, turned to Cluke and said too quickly: "That's right! We have no recruits. Only veterans."

"Mistah John?"

It was one of the Armstrongs' servants.

"Miss Mattie, she . . ."

"Excuse me, gentlemen."

He took the stairs two at a time and found her sitting in a rocking chair by the window. Her face matched the pallor of the curtains, and his heart jumped, but when she turned her eyes to him he could see she was more angry than ill.

She laid aside a letter from Mary and handed him a clipping from *The Nashville Daily Union:* "Morgan seems to have been losing his character for enterprise and daring; many of his rivals, ladies particularly, are unkind enough to attribute his present inefficiency to the fact that he is married. The fair Delilah, they assume, has shorn him of his locks."

"That's unfair!" she cried out when she saw he had finished. "It's Bragg, not me, who is holding back his cavalry!"

"Don't let those Tennessee Yankees worry you, Mattie. They're just pandering to their Federal overlords. If we were there, they'd be sneering at Frank Wolford."

"But it's unfair! Un . . . gentlemanly!"

She looked so woebegone he sat on his heels to be on her level. "Look here, Mattie Ready Morgan. Nothing they say should . . . can . . . harm you! Why, it's a compliment! And anybody who knows a bullet from a bluebird knows my command has been anything other than inactive. They haven't said a word about Cluke's raid into Kentucky. They only print what they want their jailors to hear. Just wait till we retake Nashville. I'll make that editor eat his words. Promise me one thing: you'll keep this clipping, so I can do it!"

He must have looked as ridiculous as his threat. She smiled weakly and reached out with a trembling hand to smooth back his hair. "Yes, my darling. Yes, of course you will. . . ."

He didn't tell her of his own letter, from one of his men at Manchester, since Bragg had transferred his dismounted troops to the infantry. *I am convinced, sir, that if some power is not interposed your division will be deprived permanently of true men who voluntarily enlisted in the Confederate service . . .*

"Why are you frowning?"

"Was I?" He rose and bent over the back of her chair, crossing her arms with his and kissing the part in her hair.

"It's General Wheeler, isn't it? He doesn't like you . . . you're too efficient for him!"

He laughed and kissed her hair again, pressing his nose into the faint scent of soap. "No," he said into her hair, "he just follows orders."

The nearness of him made her forget her anger. She pressed her cheek against his collar and reminded him that he had guests downstairs. "I'm sorry I interrupted you."

"Won't you come down? They all love your company . . ."

"I'm a mess! I haven't combed—"

"You're lovely."

"No, really, John. In fact I've just finished an answer to Mary. Is your Nashville man still here?" At his nod she handed him the letter. She couldn't tell him of her dizziness! "Just let me sit here for a while. I may be down later."

"If that Yankee editor knew you, he wouldn't be blaming me for staying home whenever I can," he said as he took her letter. But immediately he saw he had reopened the wound and added quickly: "The best defense against their slander is to ignore it. Such lies are not worth bothering about. Did you know they're saying I'm under arrest for disobeying orders? And that my men are threatening to disband? They'll say anything to undermine morale. I just laugh at them, and so should you, my darling. Mrs. Armstrong has made some ice cream—with molasses, but it's pretty good. Shall I send some up?"

"Yes, do that. . . . Yes, do. And before you leave, could you open that window a little? I've tried, but it's stuck."

He pulled so violently that the window flew up. Without metal weights, donated to the Cause, it wouldn't stay, and he had to prop it with a book.

"I like to hear the birds," she said in sudden, meek apology as he kissed her.

Before sundown they had the news: The first Federal gunboats had slipped by the batteries at Vicksburg on the 16th. "So that's what he's up to," Robert Martin grumbled, and the others nodded. Sam Grant would recross the Mississippi and attack Vicksburg from the rear.

"Not if Pemberton has anything to do with it," said Cripps. "Or Joe Johnston." He had addressed Martin, but he looked toward Morgan. "You may have to send your wife away soon."

"I know," Morgan answered in the hall as he saw Cripps off. He would ride back to Liberty that night, with dispatches for Basil. "I've just been waiting for her health . . . I'll make the arrangements. . . ."

Was the Nashville paper right, after all? These past three weeks had been as close to normal living as he had had since he'd left home. He knew they couldn't last. There was no guarantee Grant's destination was Vicksburg; he might divert part of his army to reinforce Rosecrans at Nashville . . . Cripps was right. Mattie would have to leave.

He waited until the next evening to tell her.

"It will be best," he kept repeating. "And here. Here is something for you."

"A pistol?"

He pressed it in her hand.

"John, you know . . ."

"I want to show you how to use it. Things are . . . too uncertain." He made himself say, in spite of the danger of alarming her: "We've waited perhaps too long now. If anything happens, take the wagon, and Cal's trunk.

Try to make it to Sparta. Here's an address. These people . . . were kind to me when we camped there last summer." He stopped long enough to write. "You may have to defend yourself. . . . Here, let me show you . . . and tomorrow . . ."

Her fingers flew to his mouth.

"Don't . . . don't use that word!"

"Why, you're shivering . . . darling! Here, Mattie, don't be cold. . . ."

"I'm not. I'm . . ." She couldn't use that word *afraid*. "Tell you what! You teach me to use it in the morning. *Tomorrow* morning," she added, with a smile.

At dawn, rapid knocking at their door and a thoroughly scared Billy woke them.

"Massa John . . . dey's heah . . . de Yankees!"

Morgan was on his feet and pulling on his clothes. "Saddle . . ."

"He bes all reddy an' waitin'," Billy said breathlessly, rolling his eyes from his general to the lady and back again.

"Then come with me," Morgan said impatiently. He bent for Mattie's kiss. "Remember . . ."

"I will! Now go . . ."

A Federal cavalry brigade, supported by infantry and artillery, broke through the McMinnville picket line at first light and charged into town eight abreast. Martin and McCann, who were staying at the Armstrong house, reached their horses first. Morgan ran out the side door and jumped on Glencoe just as the others turned toward the Sparta Road. Billy was just behind. The Yankee cavalrymen caught up with them and shots spun through the air. Martin turned and charged, his reins in his teeth and both pistols blazing, until he took a ball in one lung. He fell back and the reins, luckily still in his mouth, held the horse on course until he could regain his balance, spin around and follow Morgan. McCann's horse was shot and fell, bringing him to the ground. Morgan galloped on, hearing only later that McCann, to delay them, stood in the middle of the street yelling, "Come on, you Yankee sons-a-bitches! So you've got the old chief at last!" But they soon discovered their mistake. McCann was run over, sabered, and captured. Just behind Morgan, Martin managed to cling to his saddle and ride on. Once into some woods they stopped and sent a volley. For some reason —maybe at that point the Yankees were believing McCann—the enemy turned and went back to town.

But they were badly separated. Would Cripps escape . . . and his infantry, sent to help? He could only pray that Mattie got away.

They cut cross-country toward Liberty.

The valley road to Sparta was still in the deep shade of early morning when Mattie turned the horse away from the last houses of McMinnville. Dr. Armstrong himself had helped her hitch up; they were very kind and spoke in hurried whispers as he directed the servant who loaded Cal's trunk. She sat on the box and tucked the pistol under her skirt. Her hands were shaking on the reins when she clucked the horse back and straightened out the wheels before she waved good-bye. Once past the last house, in open country, she began to relax.

It was thirty-six miles to Sparta, but the road went over rough country. With luck, she would be there by sundown. She watched the horse's ears swivel and fell to watching the rhythmic rise and fall of his back. Just listening to the solid *slop-slop* of hooves in mud gave her a sense of competence. He had told her to go to Sparta, and she would. She would wait for him there. She took a deep breath of the fresh April morning, flipped the reins and smiled to herself. How many times had she wished she could share his life? Well, at last she was. . . .

She hadn't gone a hundred yards when she heard it: the unmistakable sound of horses approaching. Her first instinct was to turn off the road, but unluckily she was approaching a long hill with no side lanes and steep gullies. She struck out with the whip, but the horse only plunged ahead without gaining speed. She didn't dare turn her head. They were coming closer. She sat straighter and sent the whip flying. As if to mock her, it tangled in the traces. She half stood up to undo it and looked around to see the wagon surrounded by Federal uniforms.

She sat down quickly, to cover the pistol. She would use it if she had to! She looked with what she hoped was obvious disdain at a Yankee sergeant grinning at her.

"Where is your infantry?" she almost shouted, and then, in chagrin, lowered her voice: Above all she would be a lady and teach them a lesson. "Or your pillows? I hear you need both to operate as cavalry . . . what has your great army come to, catching ladies. . . ."

The man just kept grinning. "May I see your papers, ma'am?"

Palefaces! He was completely blond, with white eyelashes. How she hated them all! "I have no papers," she said haughtily. "I'm going to Sparta, as any fool can see, since this road goes nowhere else. To visit relatives," she said, somewhat more subdued, and gave him a questioning glance when he wasn't looking.

He had been diverted for good reason: His captain was trotting up smartly. The Sergeant saluted. "I think we've got her, sir."

The Captain returned the salute in a negligent manner and leaned forward against his saddle. "I see, I see. And how are you today, ma'am?"

Something in his manner made her swallow a retort and she said as calmly as she could, "Fine, thank you."

"You are the wife of General John Morgan, I understand." His horse shifted and he drew his elbows back, his leather gloves closing on the reins. The sight of them more than anything else made her blush to the roots of her hair. When Confederate soldiers didn't have shoes . . . they could sit here in their wool uniforms, with their Yankee factories, their immigrant slaves . . .

The man asked his question a second time.

"Yes . . . yes. I don't deny it! If he were here . . ."

"If he were here . . . !" the Sergeant began, then stopped at a look from his captain.

"Since he is not," the Captain said carefully, replacing his hat that he had taken off in deference, "we have no further business here. We are not fighting this war against women, ma'am."

Before she could answer he touched his horse and was gone, the others following.

That first week in May Morgan made a big circle, leaving Smithville on the 4th.

From a captured Yankee newspaper he learned of Grierson's cavalry raid into Louisiana and the boast that he had "proved the South a shell." "Shell indeed," he muttered to himself. Then anger gave way to rage: Here he was, ordered to protect Wheeler's commissary supplies . . . it was a job for a nanny goat.

His mind turned to Forrest, busy all that spring. How he had just chased Streight all the way through Alabama to Georgia, and after a ten-day running battle captured the whole lot . . . seventeen hundred Yankees with only six hundred tired Confederates. "Forrest fire" people were calling him, and his own men, when they heard, chafing in relative idleness, longed for something big. He was just finishing supper when Richard came in with the news of Chancellorsville.

"Hooker with ninety thousand . . . and another forty-two thousand opposite Fredericksburg, and Lee with a total of sixty thousand, and half of those in the Shenandoah! Can you believe that man? That masterful outflanking move on Saturday night . . . can you believe it? He's got the North on the run. Now's the time to strike. You watch. He won't let much grass grow under his feet. He'll do it. I know he'll do it!"

A victory . . . but Stonewall Jackson severely wounded. Lee, from this distance, seemed a statue standing alone.

"A.P. is wounded too," Richard added hesitantly. "The message didn't say how seriously. Have you heard from Mattie?"

"She's in Sparta." You hope! He pushed away the fear and said, "She hasn't had time to know of our move yet."

"I hope she doesn't learn of this little tidbit," Cal said glumly. He handed his brother a clipping from a captured Nashville paper. Morgan scanned it, then looked up quickly.

"So that's why . . ."

Cal nodded. "It all fits, doesn't it? Mason must have tipped them off about our small force at McMinnville. Otherwise they would never have dashed in like that. . . ."

"But to arrest her sister, and Doctor Cheatham! Sent to prison!"

"They probably figured that was the least they could do for a guerrilla's relative."

Morgan balled up the paper and dashed it to the floor. "Goddamn them! Goddamn them all to hell!" And goddamn himself, for hiring a Yankee spy to carry Mattie's letters!

"A useful idea. But I think you threw away the paper too soon." Cal bent to pick it up, smoothed it on the table, and shoved it across. "There's more news in that little boxed-in notice at the bottom."

Morgan couldn't believe it: Van Dorn had been murdered on the 8th by a jealous husband. Cal smiled whimsically. "What a waste."

More waste was to come. The men stood at silent attention when Morgan read to them a dispatch from Tullahoma: Stonewall Jackson was dead. Now Lee really seemed alone.

They weren't done with news. On the 14th Grant passed through Jackson, Mississippi. On the 18th Natchez fell.

"So we're losing the Delta," Alston murmured. "The merry month of May."

"Let's see if we can find some good in this," Richard, the optimist, grinned. "At least Grant will be too busy to help Rosecrans!"

"That's right!"

"And Burnside hasn't moved yet!"

"He hasn't."

They fell silent. Burnside, in charge at Louisville after his failure at Fredericksburg, had thirty thousand men in Kentucky by the latest report. Kirby Smith and Buckner would be no match for him if he chose to attack Knoxville. And there were the twelve thousand Yankee troops across southern Kentucky, north of the Cumberland—among them five thousand excellent cavalry under General Judah. Not to mention Rosecrans, with a rumored sixty thousand in Nashville. The Feds were divided. Still, Bragg waited.

The last day of May they received an unexpected visitor. John Morgan had seen T.H. last in Murfreesboro, before the December raid. He couldn't believe how much he had aged. His beard was almost completely white and that gentle face, so reminiscent of his grandmother's, was pale with fatigue. He had ridden in posthaste from Shelbyville, where Bragg was conferring with Polk.

"I've turned the Orphans over to Joe Lewis," T.H. said without preliminaries. "They're on their way to Vicksburg. Orders came a week ago. When Joe Johnston needed troops, General Bragg saw his chance to get rid of General Breckinridge and those 'damned Kentuckians' . . . they're probably somewhere around Jackson by now." At his nephew's look he added quickly: "Ever since Stones River . . . the army has become nothing but a squabble over reputation and promotions . . . Trabue died in Richmond—brain fever —trying to get one."

"Cripps?"

"Says when they whip Grant at Vicksburg he'll travel on downriver to check out those ladies you told him about in New Orleans."

"So he made it. I didn't get a chance to thank him for helping me in McMinnville last month. That was a hot time! And you?"

"After Stones River, Breckinridge tried to make me a brigadier—twenty-five officers sent a petition to President Davis. That was a mistake! The fact that they went over Bragg's head made him pull another tantrum. I'm beginning to wonder if even the President is hesitant to cross him."

"That may be ending soon," Richard said brightly. "It can't last forever!"

"Yes. Well." T.H. accepted a whiskey and looked away. When he turned his face back to them, they saw tears in his eyes.

"Razor blades in a monkey's paw . . . you remember what Uncle Simon used to say." Morgan smiled, to try to cheer him.

"Yes, but Uncle Simon is dead and Bragg thinks he's a horseman," T.H. shot back. "Good God! He lost Kentucky for a few pounds of beef, a few lost breakfasts! When my men have gone days at a time living on dry corn shucks and dandelion greens. . . . Damn their tactics! Generals who couldn't find their way to an outhouse without an engineer to show the way! Brave enough when somebody else is doing the charging . . ."

The old T.H. had emerged through that sagging fatigue. He looked at Richard. "Now." T.H. stood up and rubbed his hands together. "What's for supper? I'm starved!"

"How about a rest first? Give us a chance to devour that mail you brought."

"Good idea . . ."

Cal and Richard each had letters, not only from Kitty, but from A.P. Morgan had a letter and a package from Kitty. The package was Calvin Morgan's old copy of Xenophon.

"It was the only thing I took with me from home," Kitty wrote. "But you should have it. I meant to send it by Richard."

Even Tom had some mail . . . from a girl in Lexington, smuggled through the lines. Morgan sent for him, and also for an extra good meal. They would have a family reunion that night.

He read Kitty's letter with his brothers' voices in the air around him.

> Dearest Johnny:
>   Her name is Lucy Lee, named after the General. She has little wisps of red hair, just like her father! She is beautiful, Johnny, I wish you could see her. We asked General Lee to be the godfather and he agreed, but the christening was interrupted—the General had to leave—Powell and Ewell were made lieutenant-generals the same day! The old Light Division is now part of a new Third Corps. . . .

A.P.'s wound at Chancellorsville was only superficial: the flat side of a shell fragment against the calf of his leg. Not enough to prevent him, after his promotion, to ride in General Lee's review of Stonewall's old corps.

> You should have seen it, Johnny! Three divisions drawn up one behind the other. Lee riding Traveller, with his full staff. Powell and Jube Early, etc. swept around the entire corps at a full gallop. Without breaking pace, Lee led his entourage around each division separately. Oh, you should have seen them! The course of the review covered over nine miles and the pace was such that all fell out except one young cavalry staff officer and Powell. Traveller was breathless. So was I!

A.P. had a new horse, a black stallion named Prince. His old gray Champ was worn out. He had a new field uniform and soft black hat . . . and he was carrying that hambone again, and a pipe made for him by one of his men. . . .

Richard, by the window, folded his own letters carefully and stuffed them into his pocket. "Great news, isn't it?" he said so cautiously that Morgan looked up at him.

"A.P.'s new corps? Yes."

Richard nodded and left the room without another word. Cal looked at his brother. "Now, what do you make of that?"

"Something in his mail must have upset him."

"I must tell you, Johnny, if you haven't noticed . . . how much time Richard spends with Ellsworth at the telegraph office."

"Maybe he's learning the Morse code," Morgan answered lightly.

"Maybe."

Tom came in, scrubbed clean with his curly hair still damp and unruly. There was something so direct about him, so buoyant in his butternut uniform—poor cotton masquerading as wool—that radiated the eternal optimism of youth. Morgan was constantly amazed by the sweetness of his smile, even after grueling hours in the saddle. And that voice, clear as a flute, singing as they rode. A toughness. A spiritual toughness in the body of a child. But most of all—and this endeared Lieutenant Thomas Hunt Morgan to his troops—was the honest modesty that he wore with all the innocence of an angel. He was, in a way, awesomely, an angel . . . no wonder their mother unashamedly loved him more than the other children, and nobody minded . . . and she had made her oldest son promise to take care of him.

"Where is Uncle Tom?"

"Resting. How is our Romeo? Imagine, letters from Lexington!"

"Just one wishing me a happy birthday . . . a little late," Tom murmured.

"An old man of nineteen."

"You're just jealous, Brother Cally."

"Tell you what. Suppose you answer the young lady and make a date to see her sometime soon?" Morgan said as he poured himself a whiskey.

"You can't mean it?" Tom asked, to cover embarrassment.

Cal broke out laughing. "You never quit, do you, Johnny?"

"Let's hope not." It was Richard at the door, returned and in a good humor again. T.H. came in with him, a different man after a brief rest. He shook Johnny's hand, then Cal's, and hugged Tom.

"Little T.H.," he said. It was his joke, because the "H" in his own name stood for Hart, not Hunt. "I'm ready for one of those," he said and waited, smiling, while Cal handed him a glass. He took it and held it like an ablution, before tipping it to his mouth and smacking his lips. "Pretty good shuck. My, but it's good to see you all. Johnny! Cal! Richard! Tom! Do you still sing?"

"Yes, sir!"

"You'll have to give me a rendition of "The Bonnie Blue Flag" after supper."

"Yes, sir!"

"And Mattie?"

"Fine. In Sparta, I hope."

"Good. I'm glad Mattie's fine. I don't think I had the chance to thank you properly for helping my family get through the lines."

"How are they?"

"Mary's fine. And Nanny." He cleared his throat, and they both thought of all those little graves.

"She must be quite a lady by now."

"Seventeen." He waited, evidently thinking of something else. "Do you remember when Joe Nuckols made his men give back their guns to the Guard when they left Kentucky? Because the state had paid for them and he didn't want to leave with anything not belonging to him?" He chuckled hollowly and shook his head in disbelief. "Imagine . . ."

"Those days died at Shiloh."

"So much died at Shiloh."

But something else was bothering him. Something bigger than Shiloh. He spoke again of Stones River, of Breckinridge's foolish charge, the loss of Hanson. Morgan let him talk on, as if he hadn't heard. "And Henry. A cannonball went straight through him, Johnny. Do you remember how he used to laugh and joke? Do you remember how we joshed him about drinking too much at your wedding? Thank God he died on Wednesday."

"Wednesday?"

"At Stones River, those who fell on Friday were . . . Well. It was Shiloh over again."

"But they didn't even have the excuse of hot weather . . ."

"When you're winning, you don't need excuses."

Winning! He looked at T.H. in horror. He couldn't think that! Or he wouldn't, with every drop of his blood, let it happen.

"If we mean to play at war," moaned T.H., "as we play chess, by some tactical manual, we are sure to lose the game. They have every advantage. They can lose pawns till the end of time, and never feel it. We will be throwing away all we have—the only thing we can put all our hopes in— Southern dash, that reckless gallantry. . . . That could have won in '61. Now . . ." He stopped, his eyes watering.

"Now?"

"I came to tell you boys good-bye. I'm resigning."

In a chorus of protests, he raised both hands and almost spilled his drink.

"Whoa! Not so fast!" He sniffed and wiped his face with a handkerchief. "That doesn't mean I'm quitting! But let's be practical, as you know I have always been. I'm not a young man any more, and since that wound in Louisiana, less of one. Now, with Mary and Anna Frances in Augusta . . . financially, I've lost everything. The factory's gone. All my money. I have Mary and Nanny to think of."

His voice drifted away from Morgan. In its place a roaring came: *The Cause! Kentucky! Honor! The code d'honneur*. . . . No, T.H. couldn't . . .

". . . My service was purely voluntary," T.H. was saying. "You might say ironic, since my state has chosen to stay with the Union. . . ."

Yes, goddammit, Kentucky stayed with the Union. But had it? Couldn't it be persuaded? This was no time to quit! Wouldn't an invasion of the North prove . . .

"I'm going to join Mary at Augusta," T.H. said more calmly. "If you have need to send Mattie over there, don't hesitate, Johnny. She will always have a home with us."

Morgan nodded, stunned and angry, but T.H. seemed satisfied.

Tom had to leave early; his bivouac was on the other side of town and his captain had given him permission to leave for only a few hours. "I think I'll ride out that way with him," said Cal. "It's a nice night. Smell that honeysuckle! Check on things. You'll be around a few days?" he asked T.H.

"I may leave tomorrow. I'd rather you'd stay, Cal. I have something . . ." Then, afraid he sounded too serious, T.H. added: "That is, if I can tear myself away from this good food. I thought you were deprived in camp, Johnny?"

"That's why we're at Alexandria, Uncle." Cal grinned and took his seat again. "Within a good day's ride of Chenault and Cluke's men up by the Cumberland. They keep us supplied."

"I might have guessed you got your meat and flour from somewhere. Middle Tennessee is bare . . ."

"Skinned might be the better word."

"Richmond's not much better. Bread riots. While our President begs his people to plant food instead of cotton!" T.H. got up suddenly and paced back and forth. "Do you remember—from the beginning? How they held back their cotton thinking they would raise the price overseas? Overseas! And then the blockade, and the cotton piled up—unless both armies missed burning it! And they think they're winning!"

Richard started to say something and thought better of it.

"Well, so does the North!" T.H. stopped and faced them. "The North is sick of this war. Thousands of desertions after their so-called 'Emancipation' Proclamation. They've lost four of the six major battles in Virginia, and the other two were draws. Now riots in New York resisting the draft . . . I tell you there is a time in every game when a man has to lay his cards on the table."

T.H. took a breath, looked at Morgan and went on: "General Lee had a choice. He could either send troops to help Bragg and Pendleton at Vicksburg or invade Pennsylvania and outflank Washington . . ."

"You said 'had.' "

"That's right."

"Then he's made his decision."

"If an enterprising cavalry outfit could invade the North and keep the Yankees busy west of the mountains. . . . This may be our last chance," T.H. said slowly.

"They'd flock after him like bees after honey," Richard put in, avoiding his brother's eyes. "A raid like that could draw off a hundred thousand Feds."

"Such a man might lose his command," said Cal. "Too far from help. Isolated . . ."

"But if he moved fast enough," said Richard, "he might just manage to cross over into Pennsylvania and join Lee. . . ."

"He wouldn't necessarily have to be alone," said T.H. quietly.

"What do you mean?"

"Vallandigham. Congressman from Ohio. Has been protesting the Lincoln administration from the beginning. He was arrested, given a military trial, sentenced to prison, then banished."

"I don't understand. . . ."

"He has an enormous following of Copperheads. Maybe Lincoln didn't want to give them a martyr."

T.H. sat down, leaned forward on his knees and rubbed his hands together, staring at his nephews.

"He was given permission to pass through the Confederacy if we promised to send him to a neutral country. . . . Well, he's in Shelbyville this minute." In a softer tone he said: "So is General Bragg." Almost inaudibly: "So is Colonel Fremantle, of the Coldstream Guards." Then finally: "That's no coincidence."

In their silence he continued in the same monotone: "Our agents in London first alerted us—or rather someone very high in the Richmond command." He stopped and looked at Cal and Johnny in turn. "Do I have your absolute promise, oath of honor, you will keep this to yourselves?"

"Why not Richard?" Morgan smiled.

"Richard's already in on this," his uncle answered seriously. "Tell him."

"Why do you think A.P. sent me from Richmond?" Richard asked through cigar smoke.

"Vallandigham, through our London agents, has offered an uprising . . . of the whole Northwest, which will sue for peace . . . in exchange for a double invasion . . ." The thought made even T.H. catch his breath. "It is estimated there are two hundred fifty thousand Sons of Liberty and Knights of the Golden Circle waiting to take state arsenals in Ohio, Illinois, Indiana . . . release Confederate prisoners and arm them. . . ."

"Double . . . ?"

"Don't you see, Johnny?" Richard jumped up and pulled his folded letters from his pocket. "What did Kitty say?"

"She has another little girl . . ."

"Don't you see? General Lee was to be her godfather. Why do you suppose a christening was interrupted? A *christening?* I tell you Lee's up to something. He intends to invade Pennsylvania . . . look at the date of Kitty's letter. Written on the twenty-fourth. Arrived in Shelbyville the night of the thirtieth—last night. Have you ever heard of a letter traveling so fast? I'll bet that's the fastest delivery of a personal letter in the history of the Confederacy . . . or anywhere else for that matter! It had to come in with dispatches straight from Richmond. It's not just a sisterly note . . . and A.P.'s letter to me confirms it." He waved the paper.

Kitty, with morphine in her hem. Yes, she would be capable of a little conspiracy for the Cause.

"A.P. has a new horse. And he's carrying that hambone again. Why do you suppose she mentioned that? She's trying to tell you something."

"But a double invasion?"

"One in the West, don't you see?" Richard asked impatiently. "Your own idea, to go into Ohio, only now in conjunction with Lee."

"Who is the contact in Richmond?"

"None other than Secretary of State Judah Benjamin, who was once a British subject."

"Then am I guessing correctly who the contact at Bragg's headquarters might be?"

"I daresay you are," Richard clipped, in a fair imitation of St. Leger.

"I suppose you met him in Richmond?"

"Everybody met him. He's a man not easy to forget."

"The old rascal."

"Where is Basil?" T.H. asked suddenly.

"Livingston. To see about forage."

"Don't you see, then, Johnny?" T.H. took it up. "Think about your men, your horses. The Southern cavalry can't go on much longer. How much longer? A summer campaign is shaping up. Can your men last till winter again? And then what? I saw your horses . . ."

Something was wrong. Sons of Liberty. Knights of the Golden Circle. He had wanted to go to Ohio, but not like this . . . "Why not Forrest? God, the man is lightning . . ."

"He doesn't have your connections."

"You mean A.P.?" When T.H. shook his head he asked: "Grenfel?"

"He means Captain Hines," Richard said quietly.

So, Richard had known him in Richmond after all. Why hadn't he guessed?

T.H. Hunt leaned forward again and ran the tip of his tongue across his lips. "There are two gentlemen right now at Shelbyville at Bragg's headquarters. Confederate officers. One General Lee's kin. Waiting for orders to pass through the lines for special duty in Cincinnati, Chicago. . . . Vallandigham is due to leave for Chattanooga, then Wilmington . . . and Canada . . . day after tomorrow."

"Bragg would never give permission. He's refused before."

"His refusal is precisely why I am here, and why Vallandigham is interested in you," T.H. said quickly. "You are the only one in the Confederate service who could do it . . . who knows Kentucky like the back of his hand, who has done it before and has the nerve to do it again! Don't tell me you don't want to!"

They looked at him and he could say nothing for the sudden pounding of his heart. It had been his dream, and they knew it. But a dream of an independent invasion. Not like this, with closet connections. What was it

Richard said when he'd first reported? It took on new meaning now: *There may come a time when we'll want to win this war any way we can.*

"Such a man, if he fails, will be branded a fool," T.H. was saying evenly. "Nobody will know. He will act—ostensibly—without orders. And even if he manages, by a miracle, to survive, I doubt seriously whether all those bright young men would ever follow such a man again. So I want you to think about this, Johnny. It will mean, as Cal here quite rightly realizes, the loss of your command. And your reputation . . . even, and it may come to that, your honor. . . ."

The vision of a young colonel disobeying orders as he scrambled up a fort under the blazing Mexican sun. "Does President Davis know?"

"If he does, he's not saying. He can't, for political reasons," Richard answered.

T.H.'s voice came to him as if from far off: "Even if you keep them away from Bragg a little while—you're buying time."

Those boys fighting barefoot at Perryville, retreating, retreating. Forrest's miserable face at Shiloh when nobody believed him. Davis knew something about disobeying orders! Damn their tactics!

"All we need to do is get Bragg's permission for a Kentucky raid," T.H. went on. "If you just happen to go too far, just happen to cross the Ohio— your orders are from the President."

"Verbal, of course," added Richard.

So if he failed, Bragg could blame him for insubordination.

"He won't," said Richard, reading his mind. "In the first place, you won't fail. In the second, I have Jeff Davis's promise, through A.P., that Bragg will never say anything about it."

"So Davis does know. Then he must have changed."

"We all have," said T.H. "Will you do it?"

"Is Grenfel still at headquarters?"

"Yes. I saw him yesterday."

"Does he still think my marriage has affected my daring?"

"Why, I . . ."

"Tell him he was wrong."

Part V

June 1863 – September 1864

48

T.H. said in his soft way: "There is only one problem."

"I thought you said Davis would make sure Bragg would never say anything about it."

"If you fail. But Bragg could prevent you from trying. . . ."

Morgan looked quickly at Richard.

"Bragg really doesn't know anything about this. He could court-martial you—and he would in a minute—if you cross him before your real orders come . . . and you are on your way."

"And when will that be?"

"When Lee makes his move. You'll get a message—direct from Virginia."

"Cat and mouse."

"That's about it. Only for a while. And in the meantime, you could legitimately get your command into Kentucky, collect supplies. . . ."

"And send a detail North, to make connections, with instructions from the two gentlemen now at Shelbyville," T.H. added.

Morgan didn't tell them he had already sent Hines into Indiana in February, and that he already had those connections. He didn't need to tell them, Richard's look said: They already knew. And now, to cross into Ohio, to meet Lee! It was the kind of thing Sidney Johnston would have given his reputation for. Or Kirby Smith. Or Buckner!

"I was wrong, T.H." He smiled. "The real cat and mouse might just be Bragg and Rosecrans."

"You'll need to go through channels, ask for permission. . . ."

"Maybe if you sent a present. I hear Mrs. Bragg is without a horse," Richard tried to add more evenly.

"A bribe?" He almost collapsed with laughter.

"A bribe. Pure and simple. Or call it an expedient expenditure in an emergency. It's worth a try."

The next morning Morgan set out for Tullahoma.

Braxton Bragg was taken off balance by Morgan's entrance into headquarters. He rose and held out his hand, a scowl fighting with the half-smile that, out of politeness, he tried to spread across his mouth. Morgan had come by rail, and all the way on the little train he rehearsed his entrance, what he would say, his arguments. To his surprise Bragg was conciliatory, expecting an explosion about the dismounted troops assigned to the infantry.

That was an unexpected advantage: With his opponent on the defensive, Morgan gave his proposal as a concession. What a stroke of luck!

"An expedition into Kentucky?" Bragg pursed his lips.

"If I could go now—or within the month, General, I could draw off Judah and keep him busy for any maneuvers you might have in mind," he heard himself say quietly.

Bragg cleared his throat and made a steeple of his fingers and leaned back.

"If Burnside should move against Knoxville—it would be very useful to draw off Judah," Morgan offered again, risking saying too much, and then, because he feared the risking, risked more: "Gierson brags he proved the South a shell. We could prove the North an even emptier one! If I could take a force into Ohio. . . ."

It was the old game of asking for too much and then getting more than you hoped for. The forehead slanting back from the shelf of brow drew together in a deep vertical line. It was clear the General was preparing a refusal. How he must love wielding that power! But it was a refusal with more permission than Morgan thought possible.

"If you could capture Louisville, General Morgan, disrupt the rail lines up there, you could keep Burnside permanently busy."

Maybe he's more scared than I thought.

"That is true, General." He deliberately kept elation from his voice. A second later he didn't have to. Bragg's next words made the effort unnecessary.

"It would be best if the Ninth Kentucky—W. C. P. Breckinridge's regiment—stay here."

Bill Breckinridge's Ninth! Some of the best men he had! Captain Dortch, short, gutsy, broad-faced Dortch facing that Federal gun at Liberty and fighting until he gave out of ammunition. So this was the price of permission. He might have known. He took a deep breath and nodded.

"Well!" Bragg leaned forward suddenly, as a man does who is busy and dismissing a subordinate. "You have *carte blanche*, then, General Morgan, *when the time comes*, to go anywhere in Kentucky." He watched his visitor. "But *not* Ohio," he glowered, and smacked his lips. "You are not to cross that river."

No, I am supposed to leave a regiment hostage to your whims, risk the rest of my command in Kentucky, to watch it cut up by Burnside and Judah, while you dilly-dally with Rosecrans in Tennessee. His own voice surprised him. With the firmest, almost sweetest tones he could muster, he snapped to his feet, flashed his Morgan smile and said, "Excellent, sir! I shall . . . do my duty by the country, sir! You won't be disappointed!"

Once outside, he remembered bitterly Alston's report. Bragg had got what he wanted, after all: *Morgan is overcome with too large a command . . . Wheeler will correct this.* So the Ninth would, in effect, be under Wheeler. Then he reminded himself that he hadn't promised *not* to cross the Ohio. By God, he hadn't! To appease his conscience, and to Richard's delight, he sent Mrs. Bragg a horse when he got back to McMinnville. A splendid mare, just arrived via Chenault from Kentucky, was on its way to Tullahoma.

"I knew you'd learn to be a politician one of these days," Richard grinned. He went out just as a courier came in with a note from Mattie. Cal was still in the room when Morgan read it. His eyes misted.

"What's wrong?"

"She's in Sparta, and has been invited to Atlanta by a family her father knew . . ." If she could go, if he could get leave to accompany her, they could meet Alice and Key in Chattanooga . . . There was something desperate in that *Just to Chattanooga, my Darling, where we can all get a train for Atlanta. Then you can return to your men* . . .

That, too, was denied.

But Hines was delighted. He would report to Shelbyville immediately, to the two Confederate officers, Colonel Lawrence Anton Williams, the kinsman of General Lee, and Lieutenant Walter Peters. From there the elusive Thomas Henry Hines could handle it. Officially he would be setting up a "convalescent horse camp somewhere in Kentucky." He would also be checking out the fords at Maysville—and points east—on the Ohio.

"Why?" Richard asked after Hines left.

"Just a precaution. In case I have to reenter Kentucky."

"You wait! You'll meet Lee in Pennsylvania and end this damned war."

"I hope you're right."

"You know I'm right! Now go. If you want to make Sparta by sundown."

She wasn't expecting him. There had been no time to send a note. He took Billy and four men and trotted down the road to Liberty, then picked up the pike to Smithville. It was their old "territory"—although infested with Yankees. They crossed the Caney Fork and rode into Sparta before dark. He knew the house: The servants there recognized Billy and called out. Morgan threw him the reins and took the steps two at a time.

"Joh—"

He picked her up and whirled her around, then buried his face in her neck.

"Joh—"

"Don't say anything. Just let me look at you. Oh, Mattie! If you only knew how much I wanted to come down here. I had to. . . ."

"I know. Your place is with them." She looked down, then let her blue eyes meet his. He got up, walked around, told her all the latest news, while all the time feeling the slow, delicious excitement of being near her wash over him. She listened, laughed, followed his every move. He sat down again.

"And you?"

"There's nothing much to tell," she said evasively. "Alice writes once in a while. Key is well . . . these people here are kind. I . . . miss you."

"It won't be long. I promise you it won't be long. One more expedition, and then I can come back to you. You'll see. One more!" A stab of sexual need and his hopes almost took his breath. "We'll win this time!"

To his utter surprise she broke into tears. Before he could say anything she got out quickly: "I'm . . . I'm . . ." She bit her lip. "Oh, it's all so wrong now for you! It's bad enough having to worry about me. . . ." Her fingers tore into the palm of her hand and she squeezed it into a fist.

He took her hands in his as her news dawned on him. "If what you're trying to tell me is what I think it is, you've made me the happiest man in the world."

A knock at the door and a voice through the panel: Would General Morgan like some supper sent up? Mattie looked up. He motioned with a shake of his head.

"No, Nellie. We'll go down."

" 'Bout an hour, ma'am."

"Fine!"

She smiled and he kissed her, and he was suddenly home again. When they could talk she said in the smallest, far-off voice: "I felt so guilty, not telling you! I almost told you a couple of times. . . ."

So that's why she wanted to go to Atlanta, why her note sounded desperate. Now, with the biggest raid of his life about to happen, with all the chips in place—Lee, Davis, the invasion into Ohio at last, which might end the war. . . . He could let nothing alter that. He had to arrange for her safety. It was easy enough for a man without a family to be reckless. His quick condemnation of T.H. came back to haunt him as he pulled her to him and squeezed her shoulders. Now he knew T.H. was still fighting, maybe in a more effective way.

"I love you so much," she murmured into his chest, then pushed herself away. "Don't think I'm sorry, John Morgan! I have the best part of you with me, something even the Yankees can't—"

A sob stopped her. When she raised her eyes to his all his need returned, not to be denied this time. Outside the air moved in the stained-glass light of a summer sunset. Birds were chattering. It was June.

"Happy birthday, darling," she sighed. "Are you happy?"

"Deliciously. I'd forgotten my birthday."

"When were you the most happy?"

"Silly girl." He shifted his legs under the quilt and touched her toes with his.

"No, I want to know. Can you remember a day when you were completely happy all day?"

"You're cooking something up."

"No, I'm not. Honest."

He thought a minute. "My wedding day. No. The day I met you."

"Before that."

"Before that? Oh, maybe one of those days at Shadeland, when I rode over to Will's and listened to Injun stories."

"Who was Will?"

He told her.

"What happened to him?"

"He died Christmas Eve, at Glasgow . . ." In the silence he added: "And you? When were you happy? Mattie?"

"When I met you."

"Before that." He watched the flat coin of the lamp flame and pulled her closer.

"There was no before that. My life started with you."

She turned and nestled into him. He covered her shoulders and held her close. Within this slender girl's body, the mystery of life. He caught his breath at the pride and the responsibility of it.

"It's time to go. They'll be waiting supper," she whispered.

"I suppose they will. I never want to move." He groaned. "It's so good to lie here like this!"

"We can come back."

He lifted a strand of her black hair, like silk, to his lips, then cupped one hand over her breast and drew her to him. He knew now he couldn't tell her everything. A Northwest Conspiracy? A raid into Ohio to meet Lee? It was too preposterous. Maybe he didn't believe it himself.

In the end he did tell her his intentions to cross the river. That much she deserved to know.

"I don't like it," she said. She had been watching a line of sun on the windowsill the next morning. Their coffee cups, with the dregs congealed, tilted precariously on a table by the bed.

"You can trust T.H. Orders from the top."

"Can you trust Davis? Suppose it's a plot? Then General Bragg can blame you . . . haven't people been court-martialed for a lot less?"

He told her about Davis at La Teneria. "He knows what 'disobeying' orders is all about," he said firmly.

"He's just too timid to stand up to Bragg . . . I've heard Basil say it a thousand times. Now you're being the pawn for his prudence . . . that famous prudence of his."

"Will you be happy with T.H. and Aunt Mary in Augusta?"

She nodded against him.

"Rather than Atlanta?"

She nodded again.

"I'll send a message to Bragg today, asking for leave."

"I thought he refused?"

"That was only once. I think he's gotten used to my persistence. He's probably sitting at his desk right now waiting for another message from his favorite cavalryman. We can meet Alice and Key in Chattanooga, as you'd planned. Would you like that? Hey, what are you doing?" She had rolled over on top of him and was planting little kisses across his face. He found her mouth and the line of sun fell across the covers before they stirred again.

To Colonel H. W. Walter, Adj. Gen., Hdq. Army of Tennessee, Gen'l. Bragg, Commanding.

"Sounds very formal."

"It is!" He dipped the pen again. *Hdq., Morgan's Division, Sparta, June 2nd., 1863.*

"Is this your headquarters?"

He felt her finger slip down his neck as he wrote.

> Colonel: I have the honor to apply for leave of absence for twenty days, in order to proceed South with my family and make arrangements for them during my anticipated absence.

I am, Colonel, Very Respectfully Your Obt Servant, Jno. H. Morgan, Brig.-Genl.

"Now we have the rest of the day to ourselves," he said after the man left.

"How long will it take him?"

"Posthaste and double-quick, we should have an answer day after tomorrow."

"Then we have two whole days."

"It looks like it."

On the 4th of June the answer came, scribbled on the back of his letter: *Hdq. Army of Tennessee, June 3rd., 1863. Respectfully refused. It is impossible to spare a good officer from the Army at this time. By commission Genl. Bragg, Approved and Respectfully forwarded, H. W. Walter, Adj.*

Her face went white. "Maybe . . . maybe he refused because you didn't go through channels . . ."

"I'll ask Wheeler to intercede for me." He didn't tell her he would use her pregnancy as his excuse. It might be the only thing that could move Wheeler to act. Little Joe wrote Bragg from McMinnville, June 5th: *I beg you will pardon my making this personal application, General Morgan's peculiar circumstances being the only apology I have to offer.*

"Are you satisfied?" he smiled. "My men will soon wish they'd stayed in camp, with all this courier service!"

"But it's worth it."

"Yes, it's worth it."

"Now . . . Happy Birthday! A little late. I had trouble finding sugar . . ." She had a cake and a prayer book. Morning sickness had started in earnest and she was miserable. To make her happy he knelt by their bed at night and said the familiar lines he hadn't used since he'd mumbled them beside his mother in Elisha Pratt's little country church. *Hallowed be Thy Name. . . . Thy kingdom come.* There was a rhythm to it that seemed to give her peace.

"You will keep it with you?"

"Always."

Wheeler had his answer from Bragg on the 7th:

> Respectfully returned. The Genl. Commanding regrets exceedingly the interest of the service will not permit him to grant Genl. Morgan's leave at this time. Genl. Morgan cannot be spared now. A change of circumstances may occur in a few days that will allow the indulgence to be granted. The Genl. will willingly grant the leave when it can be done without injury to the service.

Little Joe dictated his own orders to Morgan immediately: He was to pull his patrols out of Kentucky and away from the Cumberland and to concentrate at Liberty, Tennessee.

Morgan was furious. They had held that country around the Cumberland all these months, with no help from "headquarters." It was all he could do to keep his handwriting on a straight line: *I would like to be informed as to what length of time my command will remain at Liberty.*

The next day, the 8th, President Davis sent two telegrams, one to General Lee, the other to A.P. Hill. Morgan would never know about them, but T.H. sent him a message that Morgan received at sundown:

> Shelbyville, Tenn. The Genl. Commanding countermands his previous order and sends you against the Federal garrison at Carthage. This move to be effected immediately. V. left here on the second, the two gentlemen I spoke of leave here shortly to make arrangements.

Carthage. On the Cumberland. Effected immediately. "That's my cue."

"You can't be . . ."

"We knew it had to happen."

She said nothing.

"You're my little general, remember? Now let me help you pack. Here's the money." He pulled a leather bag from his valise. He loosened the string and showed her the gold. "It's all I've got. But this should be enough. What are you doing?"

She was undoing her hair.

"Just seeing if Cousin Kate's trick works. When she left Nashville she wore her money in her bun!"

"Was Puss with her?"

"Yes."

"Then she was safe enough!" he laughed. Then, soberly: "Promise you'll go to Augusta as soon as you can. I'll feel a lot better if you're with T.H. His wife and daughter . . . you'll love them, and be part of the family. It'll be almost as good as going home to Hopemont . . ."

She reached up and brushed his cheek with a kiss. "I know it will. Now don't worry!"

He saw her off on the Kingston stage. It would be a long ride to Knoxville. "But you can rest a few days, then take the train to Chattanooga and meet Alice and Key. From there the line to Atlanta is fairly dependable."

"It's you I'm worried about."

"I'll be fine. I have your prayer book, haven't I?" He looked so much like a little boy standing there, for all his six-plus feet and his flawless uniform. She found his arms one more time.

As John Morgan rode toward Alexandria that morning of the 9th of June, the two Confederate officers, Colonel Williams and Lieutenant Peters, were at that moment refused their request by James A. Garfield, Rosecrans's Chief of Staff, to be shot rather than hanged. The day before, posing as Union officers who had lost their passes, they had been arrested. The colonel on duty when the arrests were made, out of sorts with his liver, downed a brandy and declared, "My bile is stirred! Some hanging would do me good."

Morgan arrived at camp the morning of the 10th to find that Bragg had recalled the Bull Pups.

"What in thunder . . . ?"

Basil shrugged his shoulders. "We could have expected it, couldn't we?"

"Not now! He knows I'll need . . . damn him!"

"Well, we've got Ed Byrne."

"Yes, thank God." Still, the Bull Pups . . . there was nothing like them for the kind of work that lay ahead. Damn him!

Although Basil's first brigade made headquarters at Alexandria, the rest of the command, with Adam Johnson, now back from leave, camped on the Lebanon Pike.

"How is Major Webber?"

"Not good. The doctors say it's his stomach. He has to be lifted into his saddle."

"He may not be able to come on this trip."

Basil laughed outright. "You know Webber! You couldn't hold him back with wild horses."

"Good. I'm riding back to McMinnville. We'll need more supplies."

"You've been edgy since you came back from Sparta. Do you have anything to tell me?"

"Well . . . aside from being a father. . . ."

When Basil's congratulations stopped, Morgan smiled. "And we're not just going into Kentucky. We're crossing the Ohio, Basil. To meet Lee in Pennsylvania!"

Basil turned white, then red, frowned, and threw his head back and howled.

"Mum's the word."

"Mum. Absolutely! Be sure and bring a heap of ammunition back with you!"

"I'll meet you in Monticello. As soon as I can. Don't expect me for a few days. I've got some things to work out through channels."

"Do you seriously think you can get Bragg to issue such orders?"

Morgan shook his head, then held out his hand before he called Billy to saddle up. "All I need from him is enough time to gather that ammunition."

"That shouldn't be hard to do. Delay is his middle name."

It was June 12th by the time he reached McMinnville, the 14th when he received a brief order from Wheeler scrawled on a scrap of paper: *Prepare fifteen hundred men to move as you propose as soon as possible.*

His palms sweat as he set the note aside. *Prepare fifteen hundred men!* Fifteen hundred men were hardly enough to cross Ohio and meet Lee. The courier was waiting. "I'll send for you. Please wait outside," he said. He drew some paper to him and wrote a request for two thousand additional troops.

Wheeler's adjutant sent him a note three days later:

> The Maj.-Genl. Comd'g directs me to write you in reply to your last dispatch that he will make every endeavor to have your force increased to the extent you call for. He will see Gen'l Bragg tomorrow morning and induce him to give his consent to the plan you propose.

The Major-General would be Breckinridge. Did he know? Had T.H. told him? Then his mind went back to Wheeler. So like him to avoid offending

Bragg with a request—and then do nothing, while at the same time take credit for doing everything. But could Breckinridge pull it off? Would Bragg really give him another two thousand men? Delay now was a two-edged sword: He needed time to hear from Richmond, but each day spent fed the nagging fear that he might be missing his chance: *Lee!* Yet he had to get supplies. Without those his command faced annihilation. Where were his real orders? He hadn't heard a word from T.H. since that message.

And Mattie? She could at least send a note from Knoxville! Before he went to bed he walked over to Ellsworth's quarters, woke him, and watched as he tapped out a message: HOW ARE YOU? WHEN DID YOU ARRIVE? ALL WELL HERE. ANSWER. Then he repacked some shirts in a small trunk, scheduled to go with the ammo wagon, and found Kitty's copy of *Xenophon* among them. He picked it up and dropped it on the bed, intending to read it later. It fell open on a marked page. Kitty had underlined a passage and he brought it closer to the candle to read:

> . . . let us not, in the name of the gods, wait for others to come to us and summon us to the noblest deeds, but let us take the lead ourselves, and arouse the rest to valour. Show yourselves the best of the captains, and more worthy to be generals than the generals themselves.

She had underlined that last sentence twice, and he read it again. He grinned. He would give Bragg and Davis exactly two more days. Then he would go it alone.

The next morning he had his answer: Bragg's Yes to the two thousand. Then Ellsworth walked in with his owl's eyes and big smile and a telegram from A.P. Hill. Ewell had won the Second Battle of Winchester, capturing 3,358 Federals and twenty-three cannon. The Confederate loss was 269. He was on his way! Lee was on his way!

"Lee's on his way!" Morgan shouted, waving the telegram and stomping around the room.

"Yes, sir! If you say so, sir!" Ellsworth had never seen his general so elated about news from Virginia.

It was already the 18th. They had wasted two weeks. Maybe he should have gone sooner? If he were at the Cumberland now, with this ammunition, instead of a five days' ride away . . . but he couldn't think of that now.

After he started, he wished it had been a five days' ride. The roads were quagmires. Summer rains had turned mountain streams into white water rivers. Morgan instructed his men to take the wagons apart and stow them, with their contents, in canoes, and reassemble the whole lot on the far shore. The mules—obedient, dependable animals—were made to swim. Once across one river they had to do it all again at the next. It took Morgan a week to get to Monticello, and another five days to gather his command and march to the Cumberland near Burkesville. It was the first of July. That night he called a staff meeting. His men deserved to know.

"We have orders to capture Louisville," he told them. Adam Johnson watched him with his wide brown eyes. Webber and Steele broke out in war whoops; Colonel D. Howard Smith pulled his long red beard straight out and let it flop against his stomach. Warren Grigsby and Roy Cluke said nothing, but watched him warily. Colonel Chenault, at his elbow, grinned.

"But we're not going to Louisville."

Another, deeper silence.

"If we go to Louisville, we'll just be cut up in Kentucky. If we cross the river downstream from Louisville and take the chase across Indiana and Ohio, we'll sick the whole pack after us. . . ."

"Ohio?" someone said, and then a fresher, wilder whooping began. His officers acted like boys on a school holiday. Fatigue from days of marching fed pent-up energy anxious for action. Basil was watching him intently. Besides Richard and Cal, he was the only one there who knew about Lee.

On the 2nd of July the crossing of the Cumberland began.

It was out of its banks and running like a mill race. Lieutenant Bennett Young, who had crossed the river with Quirk's scouts, reported Judah only twelve miles away; they had to get over as quickly as possible.

As the bugles sounded that morning and the men fell out even before first light, he knew he had to tell them what they could expect. It was the only honest thing to do. He asked for an informal "dress" parade in the half light and rode Glencoe back and forth, with the waters of the Cumberland at his back.

"You are Morgan men," he called out, and they cheered. "But you will be more than that on this expedition: Each of you, to make this effort succeed, will have to be his own general. There may be times when you and you alone will have to make a decision. We are going where there will be much hard fighting, much hard riding. Long marches and little sleep. I want you to know that I will not think less of a man if he chooses not to go. I do not want obedience unless it is freely given."

There was complete silence, except for the river lapping its brown water.

"The man giving such obedience freely has a right to know why it is given."

Again, total silence, except for the occasional blowing of a horse.

"And, in case some of you haven't heard yet, we are not just going into Kentucky. We are crossing the Ohio and . . ." A cheer went up so that he had to wait two full minutes for the tumult to die down. "We are crossing the Ohio and bringing this war to the Yankees!"

The cheer became a roar. He laid his reins across the pommel and held up both hands. When the men subsided he said: "Our objective is to meet General Lee in Pennsylvania."

Absolute, shocked silence. He continued in a ringing challenge: "Any man among you who does not want to come with us should stay this side of the Cumberland. Any man among you who decides, even after we start, that he does not want to partake of this expedition is free to leave. I want no privates, no sergeants, no lieutenants. I want only generals."

Why had he worried? Those fresh faces turned up to him. Duke, behind, with a foolish plume in his hat. Smiles all around. They broke out with "Here's health to Duke and Morgan, Drink it down; Here's health to Duke and Morgan, Drink it down, boys, drink it down!" Tom Morgan's sweet tenor started "My Old Kentucky Home" and a thousand voices joined in. A little thing like a flooded river or a hundred thousand Yankees couldn't stop them now.

But the river tried its damndest. They battled with two little flatboats that seemed ready to sink under the weight of six men much less a Parrot gun. They had to take the wagons apart, maneuver the ammunition across in canoes, and reassemble the wagons on the far shore.

Things went wrong from the beginning. Judah was alerted. In the first skirmish after crossing, although they chased the Yankees back, Quirk was so severely wounded in the arm that he had to be treated in the home of a local physician. Morgan saw the big Irishman's head draw back in pain. That head which had wagged so insolently, so many times, at danger. Quirk —his eyes and ears, ever since that night when they'd first left Lexington. Now, just when he was needed.

"You'll do fine," Quirk got out with his County Kerry accent. "You've got Drake an' Franks . . . an' Peddicord an' Xen Hawkins an' Bennett Young. I kud still come, mind ya," he said when he saw Morgan's look. "But even me ole mare wouldn't know what ta do with the kinda signals I kud give with one arm."

If he received good care, perhaps gangrene could be avoided. Morgan shook Quirk's good hand and left. The command was already moving toward Columbia.

They camped that night ten miles from the river. Scouts reported that Bragg had already moved from Tullahoma to Cowan, where his army lay in line of battle.

"What do you make of it?" worried Cal.

"That we started none too soon."

More bad luck at Columbia: a little victory over a detachment of Frank Wolford's troops, but the price was Captain Cassell wounded. And an activity which was to haunt Morgan for the rest of the raid: looting. When he heard of it he arrested the marauders, ordered punishment and appointed Major Steele as provost marshal to see to restitution.

"We are not here to pillage."

"I must tell you, General," said Steele quietly, "not all of these boys are your old 'regulars.' "

"They'll soon learn that if they want to stay with me they will be . . . or at least act the part."

Steele said nothing.

Morgan had another complaint, which worried him more. Richard came in fuming. "I'll prefer charges. I'll do it, so help me God I will."

"Who? Against who?"

To his astonishment his brother answered: "Tom."

"Tom?"

"He's entirely too reckless. Against orders. You can ask Colonel Duke."

"Send him here."

Lieutenant Tom Morgan came in five minutes later, saluted smartly and underwent the severest tongue-lashing Morgan had ever given one of his officers. Tom took it, then waited for him to calm down before he asked, "May I talk to you like a brother, General?"

"I have nothing more to say in the official capacity. Yes, I suppose so."

"You're always talking about dash and daring . . . admiring it. That's all I ever heard in connection with Lieutenant-Colonel Hutchinson . . ."

"Hutch is dead! That's precisely why he died!"

"Or Breck Castleman," Tom insisted. "How brave he was when he sat his mare at Snow's Hill."

"Castleman is damned lucky he's alive. If by a brotherly talk you mean to argue, I have no more to say. Except this: I promised Ma I would take care of you, and take care of you, goddammit, I will!"

Tom let his eyes go bland again. "Is that all, sir?"

"That is all."

That wasn't quite all. He found Basil Duke. "I'd like that little brother of mine transferred from Company I to your staff. As a personal favor."

Basil nodded solemnly. He had seen Tom take too many risks himself. "First thing."

Basil rode beside him until just before sundown, when they went into camp about six miles from Columbia. Morgan went to the wounded wagon to check on Jake Cassell. Around ten o'clock Captain Franks came in to report a Federal regiment at Green River bridge, directly in their path toward Campbellsville and Lebanon. "Not again!" the men joked. But with the river up, there was no hope of finding a ford in the dark. Morgan sent Franks back with instructions to return before sunup. They would have to take this one.

Tom Franks came back about four o'clock with the news that there had been the ringing of axes and the crash of falling timber all night. When they reached the bridge at first light they were surprised to find that the Yankees had left the stockade at the bridge and had moved into some woods where the river almost bent to meet itself and formed a narrow neck of land. Protected by steep river banks, a rifle pit and a ravine, the place was impregnable. Basil Duke stood in awe at the man's skill. "He could defend himself against an army in there! Even when we clear the pit, that field puffs up like a pillow. Any gun planted there wouldn't last ten minutes. And there's no other way to take it. . . ."

"Except by frontal attack," Morgan said beside him. Still, he left no stone unturned: He sent Cluke's Eighth Kentucky to look for a ford. Then Byrne set up his Parrot about six hundred yards from the bridge and a flag was sent in, demanding surrender. To Morgan's surprise, Colonel Moore answered that, because it was the Fourth of July, he'd rather not. When the flag came back Byrne opened up the Parrot and soon knocked sections of a rail fence into splinters. The Yankee riflemen retired. Adam Johnson with two regiments would make the attack across open ground. He moved in at a run, dashed across the field and into the woods, only to find a barricade of felled trees with their branches facing the field—and more logs and underbrush in front of that. The first rush carried Johnson's men too close. Stopped by the timber, and with inadequate ammunition, they were helpless targets under fire from the woods. Colonel Chenault had his brains blown out at close range as he was firing his pistol into the abatis and calling his men to follow. Alex Tribble, who had just transferred to Chenault's regiment from the Second Kentucky, fell next.

"Duke!" Morgan yelled, but he didn't have to say more. Basil sent in the Fifth Kentucky. Colonel Smith with his beard flying led his men at the double-quick, but they were stopped by the timber as the others had been, and added to the disaster by crowding in that narrow bottleneck of land.

The Yankee fire was not heavy; it didn't have to be. Almost every shot found its mark. Major Brent, Lieutenant Cowan, Lieutenant Holloway . . . in less than a half-hour, thirty-six priceless, irreplaceable men lay dead beside more than forty-five wounded. Morgan sent in a flag to bury the dead and Moore agreed, sending back the bodies. In the meantime Cluke found a ford. The command fell back, crossed the Green and marched without stopping through Campbellsville. They made camp five miles from Lebanon, after driving in enemy pickets. Morgan ate his supper in silence.

"Don't blame yourself," Basil said quietly across the campfire. "It always worked before. The Twenty-fifth Michigan Infantry has a better officer than most, that's all."

"I should have known. And we had to ford anyway. What good did it do?"

"You can't win them all."

"But Chenault . . . and Tribble."

"Sir?"

It was Captain Maginis, the adjutant.

"Have you eaten, Captain?"

"Yes, yes, sir, thank you. I've come on a very unpleasant mission, General. Captain Murphy was in charge of holding a citizen of Lebanon, to prevent his going into town and possibly giving the alarm . . ."

"And he wants to join our merry band?"

"No, sir. Captain Murphy let him go after he promised to spend the night at a farm nearby and refrain from going into town."

"Wise man." Morgan waited.

"But before the man left, sir, Captain Murphy stole his watch."

"What?"

"He was bragging about it to me."

"Place him under arrest. Pending court-martial. We have enough trouble."

"Yes, sir."

As he walked away, Morgan turned to Duke. "Do you remember when you recommended Maginis? When St. Leger left. I've never been sorry."

The camp was quiet, the night dark. Except for cook fires, no light was allowed. From somewhere a harmonica wailed "Lorena." An hour later, just as he was about to settle under the tent-half Billy had spread for him, Morgan was startled by a shot. "What in the . . . ?"

The guard had not disarmed Murphy. When he learned it was Maginis who had turned him in, he broke away and killed him instantly. There would be another grave to mark the march.

After that, he couldn't sleep. What were they doing? Now killing each other? He remembered Steele's look, his words: They weren't all the old regulars. He walked to a worm fence and leaned on the top rail. Across the unseen hills in the dark night, clouded over with threatening rain, lay Lexington and home. As the crow flew, sixty miles? A hard day's ride. An easy two. Could it be possible, that somewhere out there was Hopemont . . . and Shadeland . . . and his mother, and Aunt Bet and Aunt Hannah and Uncle Robert and Randolph? No, Randolph was in the Union Army. Somewhere in the Union Army. He looked up and in the swirl of dark one tiny light shone, then disappeared, then shone again. It was incredible to think that nothing but space separated him from that star. Just as nothing but space separated him from Hopemont. No, more than space. A thousand years. Well, it would all come right once they crossed the Ohio. A form rose in the triangle of the fence rails next to him. "General?"

It always amazed him how accurate his scouts were. Lebanon was garrisoned by Colonel Charles Hanson's Twentieth Kentucky, plus detachments from three other Kentucky regiments, a total of five hundred. "The Twentieth?"

"Yes, sir."

Sanders Bruce had been with that regiment at Shiloh. And Charles Hanson, incredibly, the brother of Bench-leg. The unreal night closed in.

"There's more, sir."

Two Michigan regiments were not far off, on the road to Harrodsburg.

"Thank you, Sergeant."

"Sir."

He felt, rather than saw, the man's salute. Horses shifting. A dog barking somewhere. Before he knew it the cocks would be crowing. Better get some sleep. Sleep? Last night Chenault, Tribble, Maginis were alive . . . But there was the Ohio to cross, and Lee.

The sun came up on a torrid July day. The men moved out silently, like tired but determined professionals, their horses' heads swinging, their own arms, whose hands by now seemed to have sprouted reins, scrubbing their horses' necks with the motion. The creak of leather and the clink of saber or canteen. Next stop: Lebanon, Kentucky. At the first houses almost automatically Duke's brigade formed on the right of the road with two regiments as reserve, Johnson's brigade on the left, Byrne's battery in the road in the center. Before a shot was fired the Federal skirmishers, posted at the edge of town, fled. Lieutenant-Colonel Robert Alston carried the flag with a request for surrender. When he was fired on from one of the houses a dozen Morgan men threatened to return the shots and only swiftly shouted orders held the negotiations together.

"Those are Kentucky troops down there, sir," Adam Johnson reminded his general. "We'll play hell budging Bench-leg's brother."

As expected, Colonel Hanson's reply was negative. Alston then, following instructions, advised the removal of women and children. Thirty minutes later the shelling began.

Hanson had withdrawn to the brick depot, set low, where the Parrots could do little damage except to the roof. Morgan sent scouts around Lebanon to cut the telegraph wire to Louisville—but not before the news of an attack reached Burnside, who told Hanson to hold out; reinforcements would be on their way. Down in the town Roy Cluke's Eighth Kentucky prepared for the assault. Captain Franks with a detail of the advance guard had orders to set fire to the south end of the depot, and they did so almost at the moment Cluke moved. From where he sat Glencoe Morgan could see those gray, bent backs, their legs moving like spiders as they met the Yankee rifle fire. Grigsby's regiment and the Ninth Tennessee, since Bennett's death now under Colonel Ward, ran toward the houses on the right; Cluke's and Chenault's, commanded now by Lieutenant-Colonel Tucker, to the left. Lieutenant Lawrence moved a Parrot to a hill overlooking the depot and swung into action. But he was exposed, and Yankee sharpshooters kept up a running duel for almost three hours. The Michigan troops, out on the Harrodsburg Road, would not delay forever; Cluke's men were pinned in the weeds close to the depot. What he needed were men experienced in street fighting. He turned to Duke, and without a word, Basil nodded. The Second Kentucky, the Old Regulars, the veterans of Cynthiana and Augusta. They could do it. Major Webber, his face ashen with illness and determination, formed his men and moved. Morgan would never forget those men. Somewhere down there Cal was in the middle of it. Thank God, Basil had put Tom on his staff. Maybe that would keep him out of trouble for a while. Some final, sporadic shooting from the houses now came to him before the white flags appeared.

Then Cal rode up, his face sodden with tears, his voice shaking so he could hardly get the words out.

"Tom . . . Tom. He's dead, Johnny! Shot through the heart! He was standing right by me, firing his pistol in the windows of the depot, when they hit him . . . in the heart! He's dead, Johnny!"

"I don't believe it! He was on the staff . . . he wasn't even supposed to be . . ."

"He died in my arms, Johnny! He said, 'Cally, I'm dying!' He knew he was dying! That was the only place they could have killed him, the bastards!"

Without a word, Morgan spurred Glencoe into a run. So that was what the crowd at the depot door was all about. When he reached the spot a dozen men had Colonel Hanson, his arms pinned, marching him roughly about. Somehow Morgan found his voice.

"Let that man go! Let him go, I say! He is our prisoner . . . it won't change anything!" He had to dismount and wrestle one man to the ground. When he looked up they were all crying. Behind them, in the dim light of the waiting room and in the acrid smell of smoke, Sanders Bruce stood watching him.

Ammunition, rifles, medicine . . . a fine supply was loaded from the warehouse in Lebanon. But nothing mattered. Sanders sent a note of condolence, which wavered through tears. Cal stood with him in the garden of the Reverend T. H. Cleland, watching the fresh mound of earth. Basil and Richard waited near the gate.

"We'll move him home after this," said Cal fiercely.

"I'll notify your mother right away," the Reverend said.

Morgan looked at him with dead eyes; he saw nothing. There were others; he should think about the others: Lieutenant Gardner, Private Worsham, Sergeant Franklin, who talked to him just last night. And Franks was wounded . . . also Sergeant Jones, Lieutenant Xen Hawkins and good old Tom Logwood—saved by Walter Ferguson under galling fire from the depot windows as he lay helpless in the street. He should think of them, priceless, every one. But Tom's sweet face, his disappointed, puzzled look when he'd given him that dressing down about rashness, blurred all else: blurred the thick summer grass and the smell of roses and the knowledge that Judah from the south and Burnside from the north were on to him. Blurred even Cal's worried face. From somewhere he felt a hand on his arm. It was time to go.

The prisoners were double-quicked eight miles to Springfield, where Colonel Alston would issue paroles, Sanders Bruce's among them. Had Sanders spoken to him? It no longer mattered.

At Springfield Basil Duke sent Captain Gabe Alexander with Company H to watch the road to Harrodsburg, then ordered an all-night march for Bardstown. They crossed Beech Creek, which ran into the Rolling Fork, and went—fell—into camp just outside Bardstown about four o'clock. "They have to rest," Adam Johnson murmured. He was more worried about Morgan, whose ashen face saw nothing.

"Six hours will be the best we can do," Basil answered. "Even then, we may regret it."

Captain Ralph Sheldon, Company C, Second Kentucky, reported from a scout to Muldraugh Hill, just south of Louisville. But where was Alston? They learned later that after finishing the paroles at Springfield he had let Captain Davis and the others ride on and caught a nap on a porch. When Alston woke up he was surrounded by Yankees.

Quirk, Tom, Chenault, Tribble, Alston. . . .

Part of the halt was spent waiting for Johnson's second brigade to march through Bardstown and take the advance. This morning's reveille found one whole company deserted. Gone. Gone completely. The first time in the history of his command. Oh, he had had stragglers before. But hadn't he told them that anyone not wanting to go should stay? He wanted no obedience not freely given. "One day they'll regret it!" Cal broke out.

"Dear old Cal, this isn't Agincourt."

Deliberately, he pushed all feeling to the bottom of his mind. Lee . . . Lee. It became an obsession. He sent for Captains Sam Taylor and Clay Merriwether, in Johnson's brigade. Sam was a little gamecock, a nephew of

General Zachary Taylor. If anybody could do the job he had in mind, Taylor could. "You'll need a detail of at least forty men," Morgan told him.

"Boats? Capture boats? Yes, sir!"

"Meet me at Brandenburg."

At Bardstown Junction just south of Shepherdsville—and thirty miles from Louisville—they stopped just long enough for Ellsworth to "work his magic" with the L&N operator. While he was tapping out his messages, Morgan called in Captain William Davis of Company D, Second Kentucky, and Colonel Cluke.

"We need some good men to make them think our main column is headed for Louisville. Cross the river at Twelve Mile Island. Meet the column in Salem, Indiana. Davis, I'd like to see Company D take the job. Castleman . . . do you think Lieutenant Eastin can ride with that Yankee sword? Now Roy, which of your companies can you spare to go with them?"

"Company A, sir," Cluke answered.

"Good. Then we'll see you boys in . . . three days."

"Three days?"

Their shock cut into his grief. Something of his old humor came back. "Do you think we should make it two?"

"General Morgan!" Ellsworth saluted in his civilian way. "You are now ten thousand strong and headed for Louisville. But," he added, "you have a strong Federal force behind you . . . and that's the truth."

"How far?"

"Twenty-four hours."

They crossed the Salt and marched all night. That next afternoon they halted at the little town of Garnettsville, ten miles from the Ohio. They could rest here until just after midnight, when they would be on their way again. "Now?" Captain Hart Gibson, who had taken Maginis's job as adjutant, asked hesitantly.

"Now. Yes, call them in now. We may not have time once we cross that water."

But there would be no court-martial. Captain Murphy was nowhere to be found.

It was an omen. A murder and the murderer gone. No, that was foolish. That was fear talking. And underneath, a festering wound: grief for Tom.

Ten miles away the little town of Brandenburg sat on a high bank with the muddy Ohio lapping at its only street, which fell like a child's slide toward a small wharf where a boat bobbed at its mooring. Sam Taylor and Clay Merriwether had had quite a day. A half-dozen Morgan men drifted innocently enough toward the skipper of the boat and inquired about the steamer from Louisville.

"The *John B. Combs?*" the old man said. "Yessiree, sonny. Due in about noon. Allus a little late, though, and with the river high like this, she's gotta watch out fer them logs."

Taylor, standing by, looked out at the drifting branches of trees turning on themselves. The current was swift; ropes of brown water, like giant braids, joining and breaking apart. He judged the river here to be almost a thousand yards across. He strolled up, as if interested in the conversation. "Any other boats due by?"

"Why, yes, the mailboat—a fast paddle-wheeler, but she don't have no scheduled stop. Might not even come by here unless some folks got mail."

Sam Taylor took off his hat and scratched his head, the prearranged signal. Four men boarded the boat, pistols ready. The skipper, sputtering but willing, obeyed orders. More Morgan men gathered and waited on the wharf until the *John B. Combs* came into sight. Just as the gangplank came down but before the first passenger or crewman could step off, thirty-six "passengers" swarmed aboard.

"See here, I'm Captain Ballard . . ." The man stopped at the sight of guns.

"I'm afraid we'll have to borrow your ship here for a little Confederate service," Merriwether grinned. Behind him women were screaming and gentlemen were cowering. "How many passengers?"

"Fifty."

"We have . . . we have personal belongings in the ship's safe," a thin-faced man with watery eyes choked. "You aren't going to burn this boat are you?"

"Not till we're through with it, sir," Merriwether laughed, but the captain paled. Taylor expertly ordered the ten thousand dollars in the ship's safe distributed to the rightful owners, ordered the passengers ashore with a warning that they were not to leave town, and kept the crew.

No sooner had the last passenger left than the mailboat *Alice Dean*, like a swift filly, spewed foam from her paddles. Merriwether ordered Ballard to set out at once. In midstream he ordered Ballard to stop. The bows were about to touch. "We'll be smashed!" the captain yelled.

Like pirates they boarded the *Alice Dean* and introduced themselves to Captain Pepper. Both boats were waiting for Morgan when he rode Glencoe into town the next morning.

Morgan waited just outside Brandenburg. Toward dawn, Lieutenant Peddicord of Quirk's scouts reported a large white house on a high bluff just downriver from the wharf. "Would make an excellent headquarters, sir."

Morgan started to write a message, when Peddicord cleared his throat.

"No need, if you'll excuse me, sir. Colonel Robert Buckner lives there. Cousin of the General's, I believe. Veteran of '12."

Morgan set his pencil aside. "Sympathetic?"

Peddicord suppressed a grin. "The Colonel says his back yard would make an excellent artillery position. And there's a porch where you can watch the action. And, the Colonel says, have some hot food."

The river was still a gray shimmer under morning fog when the Colonel led his guest across the clipped grass of his back lawn to "reconnoiter" the situation.

It couldn't have been better. Upstream the Ohio made an S, with the

Buckner house occupying the flat side of the bottom curve, giving full view of any boat which might venture down from Louisville. To the left the river straightened again. Morgan walked to the bank and realized that the house stood on a diagonal line almost directly above the little wharf, out of sight because of some bushes. Across the water an unobstructed view spread for miles of the Indiana shore. He thanked Colonel Buckner for his hospitality, left instructions with his men and rode around to the wharf, where he spotted a youth leaning against a post picking his teeth. It was such an unconscious, casual pose . . . too unconscious. He felt a smile tug at the corner of his mouth as he raised an arm and the young man walked over.

"They are with you, General," Tom Hines said languidly, closing his eyes to slits and looking away, as if they were talking about the weather, the piece of straw still in his mouth. He took it out and rolled it in his fingers, studying it. "Bullitt in Louisville. I have it straight from Colonel Harney. And in Indiana Bowles says he can raise twenty thousand overnight. . . ."

Morgan leaned his head to the left. "We're at a white house on the bluff. See you there." He turned Glencoe for the steep climb up the little street.

His men had already set up their batteries by the time he got there. The Colonel's household had hot food on tables, but he was not hungry. He sat on the back porch looking across the river feeling suddenly overcome. It was strange how the grief which had ridden with him, as if waiting for him to stop, came full force now.

We'll make it right, Brother Johnny. Just you wait and see.

Tom at "the Races," when he'd lost everything. Now he was in a garden in another Lebanon. . . .

Cheer, boys, cheer! Away with idle sorrow!

God, how that boy could sing.

"Gryllus is dead," the messenger said. The wind under the oak caught Calvin Morgan's hair and he brushed it from his eyes and looked across the pond.

And Xenophon took off the garland.

"What happened then?"

Then the messenger said, "His death was noble." And Xenophon put the garland on his head again. It is said he had tears, but he refused to shed them. Instead, he said for all to hear: "I knew that I begat him mortal."

His father looking away, as he was looking off at this river now. *I knew I begat him mortal.* He was like a son more than a brother, the son I never had. *Cally I'm dying.* . . . In the heart. Yes, Cal. The only place they could have killed him.

"Twenty thousand, General," Hines was saying in that soft, offhand way of his. He had come up silently and was leaning on the porch rail watching him. He had scouted Indiana for Copperhead contacts and lost most of his men to capture by a Federal gunboat. With ten men he swam the Ohio and stopped an L&N train for a meeting with Colonel Harney, editor of a Louisville paper and a prominent Southern sympathizer. When Burnside heard of this meeting he put a price of a thousand dollars on Hines's head.

"Twenty thousand will rise up to help you. I have their word."

Morgan looked at the wide-set eyes, the round head looking too wobbly for the little neck, the swashbuckler's mustache. Who was this talking about Copperheads? He would have nothing to do with spies! He had almost court-martialed one of his own officers for taking a prisoner's watch! His stomach turned over. Was this what Hutch and James West, Niles and Chenault and Tom had died for? What he was fighting for? Where is Mattie? Had she even reached Knoxville?

"I'll have nothing to do with your Copperheads," Morgan told the astonished Hines. Down at the river the mist was lifting. A hard day's work lay ahead.

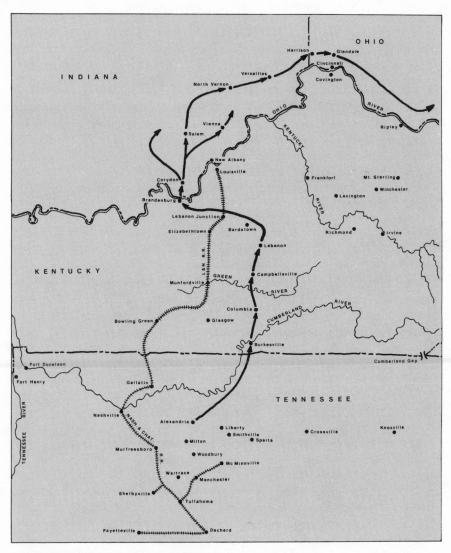

Ohio Raid, July 1863

49

Before Hines could answer an unexpected shelling sounded from the Indiana shore. Morgan looked through a field glass but couldn't see much, then focused on a farm wagon. The bed had been removed and an old cannon placed on the cross pieces. The first shell managed by a miracle to reach the wharf at Brandenburg and wound Captain Wilson, quartermaster of Basil's brigade. The rest fell short.

By now the sun was burning off the fog and Morgan could see through the glass a mixture of blue uniforms and civilian clothes—Indiana militia with Federal regulars—posted behind two small houses and a clump of haystacks. He turned to give the order but it was unnecessary: Lieutenant Lawrence had already opened with his Parrots, and Morgan watched the little drama through the glass: the troops on the other side trying desperately to remove their "artillery" under the shells falling all too accurately from the Parrots—and finally abandoning the wagon and running to a wooded ridge about five hundred yards from the river. Basil immediately put the Second Kentucky and Ninth Tennessee across the river in pursuit, the horses remaining on the Bradenburg side. Webber and Ward led their men, almost ignoring a volley from the ridge, across the open fields inland. The boats, returning for the horses, had not reached the wharf when a Federal gunboat appeared.

Snub-nosed and oak-planked, she looked top-heavy, but when she opened up three twelve-pounder howitzers and demonstrated how nimbly she could swing about, the horse-handlers ran with their charges out of sight. Byrne, standing on the cliff by the Buckner house, immediately ordered the two Parrots to answer. Most of his shots missed, but it was hard to tell when she was hit, with the oak planking, and the way she could sidle in the current. The men at the wharf crowded together to watch.

Morgan watched also, from the Buckner porch. His two best regiments were now separated from him by that river, and they were dismounted. Cal was over there. And Ralph Sheldon and R. G. Marriner . . . and Webber and Ward and a hundred irreplaceable men. They might be attacked at any minute by overwhelming forces—the scouts had reported that when they landed in Indiana they could be expected to be outnumbered twenty to one. The element of surprise was gone. Behind him, less than a day's ride: Judah's cavalry. From Louisville: Burnside, who must know by now the telegrams were false.

He could see it. All across Indiana and Illinois and Ohio. Telegraph lines buzzing with a Rebel invasion. Rail cars loading troops. They would have to run the gauntlet day and night until they met Lee. The brown waters of the swollen Ohio, lapping shore. What lay across it? An opulent, arrogant land, determined on destruction. Very well, let them try.

The artillery duel between the little gunboat and Byrne's Parrots lasted almost an hour before the boat steamed back up the river. Immediately, the *John B. Combs* and the *Alice Dean* were put into service again, loading and delivering horses to the regiments pinned down on the other shore. Then as soon as they returned they were busy ferrying the rest of the command. No time was lost, but the sun was setting by the time the first brigade was safely across.

Then the snub-nosed little gunboat reappeared, this time with an escort. But the Parrots encouraged them to change their travel plans, and they steamed upriver again. By midnight Adam Johnson's second brigade and the artillery were over. They burned the government mailboat, but let Captain Ballard's *John B. Combs* go free. As they watched the *Alice Dean* burn, Adam Johnson spoke to his general: "I could go downriver, cross back into Kentucky and keep them busy for you."

Morgan looked into those sincere brown eyes. "Thank you, Colonel. But we'll need every good man we have."

The first brigade bedded down that night six miles from the river. Some of the men had champagne taken from the *John B. Combs* and drank it in the kitchen of an empty farmhouse. All the farmhouses were empty, the doors left open, suppers still warm on the tables. It was as if all the inhabitants had vanished into thin air. The hills and fields lay quiet. It was an unnerving experience. Where were the Yankees? Morgan and Basil slept that night in a house near the road and found, by two freshly baked pies, a note begging the invaders not to burn their home. "Who do they think we are . . . vandals?" asked Duke indignantly. They could hear the boys with the champagne. It was the only sound in that deserted countryside. The great raid had begun.

A few miles from Corydon the column was fired on from a house, which was promptly burned, and the troopers who burned it were as promptly arrested by Major Steele. The orders were strict: There would be no unnecessary destruction. "How long do you think that order can last?" Steele asked Cal in a moment of candor, not expecting an answer.

They soon had more to think about. About a mile from Corydon the Indiana Home Guards who had made their unsuccessful stand at the river waited behind a barricade of logs and piled-up fence rails. Richard ordered a charge, but their tired horses failed to clear the rails and fell. Riders who did manage to land clear received a volley at close range and eight men dropped—among them Lieutenant Thorpe of Company A. More than thirty men lay wounded. Adam Johnson, just behind, sent a regiment around to flank the militia, put the howitzers into action and ordered the rest of his men, now dismounted, to fire. It was over in minutes, and in Corydon 345 Home Guards were paroled at Kintner's Hotel, where Morgan and his staff ate lunch.

"It's true, General."

Morgan held his face still.

"Here, I'll send my daughter." The man motioned for his daughter, a pretty girl of eighteen. "She'll get the paper."

Gettysburg. While they were fighting at the Green, at that bridge where Chenault had his brains blown out, Lee was turning back to Virginia. That same day, Vicksburg surrendered. *So we won't be meeting him.* He cleared his throat and handed the paper to Duke.

Without a word, Basil rose. Ten minutes later, in a room off the dining room, his staff waited. With the wide Ohio at their backs and thousands of Federal regulars and Indiana Home Guards after them, there was only one way out of this mess: those fords Hines had found east of Cincinnati.

"We'll have to get around Cincinnati first," Major Webber drawled.

"True."

"What the hell!" Cal said almost too loudly. "We'll give 'em a run for their money . . ."

"And draw the Yankees away from Buckner in Knoxville and maybe even from Bragg in Tennessee," Colonel Smith put in.

"Let's at 'em!" Adam Johnson growled, in a fair imitation of Forrest.

At Brandenburg Morgan had let some known Union sympathizers "overhear" plans that the Rebels were on their way to Indianapolis to release the six thousand Confederate prisoners at Camp Morton. Now it was time to add to the scare. Before the column left Corydon, Morgan went with Lightning to the telegraph office, where they learned that sixty-five thousand troops—mostly Indiana Home Guards, but also some Michigan regulars— had crowded into Indianapolis. Good. "How many men do I have?"

"Twenty thousand," Ellsworth grinned.

"Now tell them . . . tell them Forrest is coming . . . with ten thousand more! And Buckner. Buckner is moving out of Knoxville. . . ."

They left the frightened operator tied to his chair and rode back to the hotel. Most of the stores displayed the lone star flag of the Knights of the Golden Circle. Some even had pictures of Morgan and Jeff Davis in their windows. A commotion at the blacksmith's shed stopped them.

"But it's all I've got!" a boy Morgan recognized from Company C, Second Kentucky, was saying.

"What's the trouble here, Private?"

"This man won't take Confederate money for his horse. I've given him my Kentucky mare in trade . . ."

Morgan's eyes drifted from the Copperhead flag nailed above the blacksmith's head to the boy, his hair plastered with sweat, his voice breaking in fatigue and resentment. Tom. Tom. He could have been Tom. Morgan pointed to the flag. "If you're so interested in supporting us, sir, you surely won't mind donating a horse to the Confederate cause, will you, now?" He smiled sweetly, then turned to the boy. "Keep both horses, Private." He touched Glencoe and rode on.

Split. One column to swing west, another north to Salem, the third to Vienna to the east. Then, together again, northeast to Harrison, just over the Ohio line and north of Cincinnati. Horses, men collapsing. Even before they got to Salem they had to leave eleven men too badly wounded to be moved. And they learned at the telegraph office that General Hobson, with the Thirteenth Federal Kentucky, headquartered at Louisville under Brigadier-General Jeremiah Boyle, had crossed the Ohio at Brandenburg without his supply train.

"That means he intends to move," Ellsworth said as he packed away his instrument.

"Not fast enough," Morgan answered grimly.

Another wish? They had wasted precious time at Salem waiting for Davis and Castleman and the two companies sent to Louisville. Probably captured? In the lull some of Tom Webber's boys had a holiday looting.

"I'll be damned . . ."

"Let them do it," said Morgan, weary of Steele's warnings. "It's harmless." This was the countryside where Sherman had recruited those troops who had vandalized Mississippi. He watched Webber's Mississippians coming out of stores with bolts of calico, ladies' hats, lengths of veil. One had seven pairs of ice skates tied together dangling from his neck, another a chafing dish strapped to his saddle. The prize for eccentricity went to the boy balancing a bird cage with three canaries flopping around inside.

But no Davis or Castleman. They rode on. Ten thousand Home Guards to the southeast, three thousand more troops to the west. Federal orders were to fell timber and obstruct all roads in Morgan's path. Tired as horses and men were, Morgan ordered another forced march. They were traveling on animals that had seen hard use in Tennessee even before they left Kentucky, and now in another day they would be on a line due west of Cincinnati. Some were stumbling, their ribs showing, and worse: that tell-tale "hatrack" on the backside. The Indiana farm horses some of the men had traded for, although fat, were soft, and began falling in their tracks. When the Second Kentucky, at the head of the column, came upon three hundred well-mounted Home Guards led by an aging captain, Cal had had enough. He introduced himself as a staff officer of Colonel Wolford's cavalry. "And this is Colonel Wolford," he said, pointing to Morgan.

"Oh, really? Glad to meet you, Colonel."

"Would you like to see the Colonel's famous horse drill?"

"I would, I would!"

"Our horses are entirely too tired, sir. Unfortunately, we have been chasing that horse thief Morgan." Cal turned to go.

"Take mine," the old man offered. "I'd shore like to see you fellers ride. It's not often we git excitement around these parts."

"Well, if you insist." Cal answered so fast his brother gave him a look. "Tell you what. We'll exchange horses, and if you'll line up on either side of the road, we'll show you an execution you won't soon forget. Isn't that right, Colonel Wolford?"

"Colonel Wolford" grinned. The exchange was made—except for Glencoe —and the Indiana Home Guards arranged themselves on their exchanged mounts on the grass by the road. When Morgan raised his hand, his men galloped off in a cloud of dust. Cal, when they finally pulled up, couldn't stop laughing.

The sun was setting over the Indiana fields when Ellsworth delivered his latest news: Governor Morton had called General Lew Wallace to Indianapolis, where a network of railroads could transport troops anywhere in the state. *We're in for it* was the message on Ellsworth's usually impassive face.

About midnight General Wallace rode into Vernon, but by that time Morgan's exhausted horse thieves were throwing themselves down to catch what rest they could, enjoying a report that Colonel Adam Johnson had bluffed a Yankee detachment by using a stovepipe as a "cannon." "Stovepipe Johnson" passed around the campfires, but most were too weary to laugh. It had been another fifteen-mile, horse-lathering gallop to get here, and to lie down felt too good.

How long could men and horses last at this pace? Morgan left a call for three A.M. "Three hours sleep again!" Cal groaned, then sobered at his brother's frown. They were averaging twenty-one hours in the saddle. To answer his own question, Morgan murmured silently to himself: *As long as we can.*

In the eerie half-light before dawn they were in stirrups again. It took another hour for the fours to form; they were waiting for the details to come in from burning another bridge, cutting telegraph wires and destroying another water tower at another depot. Finally, just as they were ready to move, the screams of a girl made Morgan stop and ride up. Some of his men were protesting two Union flags flying from her porch, each, she said, to celebrate Gettysburg and Vicksburg. With Hobson on their tails, thirty thousand troops at Cincinnati, another sixty-five thousand at Indianapolis, his men were defending the Confederacy by arguing with a girl about two flags! He ordered them to leave, posted a guard to see that the flags stayed. The fact that stores were being looted no longer interested him, but this silliness was ridiculous. They had to get around Cincinnati to the river.

The wealth of the land was amazing. People. So many people. And crops. The tall corn of July, and fat cows and chickens everywhere. It had been so long. Only now did it dawn on them how poor the South had become. Twenty-five miles from the Ohio line three hundred Home Guards were captured and paroled. But Lew Wallace and his Yankee regulars were just five miles away. Colonel Grigsby with the Sixth Kentucky was sent to burn bridges and destroy tracks in that direction. In the process he came across a herd of horses destined for the Union cavalry and rode back like a knight from some fairy tale, a fancy white circus mare in tow as a special present for the General. Morgan gave her to Billy, whose old sorrel was worn out.

"They'll see me, Massa!"

"Not if you ride in the middle."

"Then Ah'se be boxed in!"

The troopers who heard him laughed and called him "Box." The name stuck, but the mare was a first-class animal, and the boy wasn't Uncle Simon's grandson for nothing.

"You've got to keep her groomed."

"On them dusty roads, Massa?" He was a beautiful child, Randolph's Billy, with a thick wool cap of hair, darker than Jesse, as if his skin had been dusted with bronze powder. He had the habit of sucking in his upper lip as if biting it with his lower.

"Your daddy would."

"Do you s'pose we'll meet up wif him, Massa?"

It would be too strange to skirmish with Randolph!

"He's probably, at this minute, grooming some nice white horse, just like this one, for some Yankee general."

"Ah hopes he leaves a burr on her back an' she throws him."

He was so serious, and frowned just like his father, that Morgan enjoyed the first good laugh he'd had since he'd crossed the Cumberland. It was so good to laugh. He'd almost forgotten how.

He sent Sam Taylor to scout the situation in Cincinnati, and to move faster he divided the command again, this time into four sections, one south toward Kentucky on a feint. All the rest of that day they marched, and most of the night. Some of the men were so tired they slept in their saddles, asking their buddies to hold the reins as the horses walked along. Others actually fell off or slipped away into fields to lie down. Officers and sergeants were kept busy prodding, waking, threatening. Horses collapsed, and riding double until another mount could be found became common.

"That feint must've worked, sir," Hines reported. "They think you're headed for the river and a retreat into Kentucky."

"Not with that water rising," Morgan frowned. "And if they had an ounce of sense they'd know it."

To get around Cincinnati and find a decent ford: That was his next mountain. But to make a great, nonstop semicircle around the city to the river they would have to march more than ninety miles. His men were bone-tired, their horses worse. They had been marching almost constantly since they'd crossed the Cumberland eleven days ago. Only determination of inhuman proportions would keep them from collapsing. With the loss of the company that had deserted in Kentucky and the two companies sent with Davis and Castleman to Twelve Mile Island—probably captured by now—plus stragglers, the wounded and dead, he had less than two thousand men left. Lee, Gettysburg—it all seemed unreal. The only thing that mattered now was saving the command.

He avoided reminding himself that once across the Ohio and into Kentucky again he would face that Yankee gauntlet waiting for him, would have to work his way through Rosecrans. . . . No. The Ohio. If he could cross that river. If he could stand on its southern bank, he would be in heaven.

And they would. Nothing could stop them! He rode down the lines that morning conscious that his back was straighter, his smile steadier, than it had been since Lebanon. Oh, Tom, Tom, we're coming home.

Judah and Hobson, with the worn-out "remounts" Morgan had cordially left across the countryside, could not catch him from the rear if he kept moving; Burnside in Cincinnati could not move troops by rail fast enough before they reached the river . . . if they kept moving. *They must keep moving.*

About one o'clock Sam Taylor met them. His scout to Cincinnati revealed a city under martial law with police and firemen on twenty-four-hour duty. The town was in a state of panic. But behind the column the scouts reported Yankee cavalry less than a half-day's ride away.

They had to rest. He ordered a halt of two hours, and sent a feint to Hamilton, on the Dayton railroad, with a wild telegram via Ellsworth that Morgan's band was headed for Columbus to capture the governor.

"If we can just get around Cincinnati," Cal worried. "If not, we may have to fight our way through Burnside."

"Old Mutton Chops? His troops will be in one of two places: the center of town drinking German beer or riding the train."

They both knew it was a lie and Cal didn't smile. Morgan sent for Sam Taylor again, for precise details of the suburbs. Yes, if they could just get past Burnside they could make it to the river, and the worst would be over.

They crossed the Miami River and burned the bridges behind them. It was after sundown by the time they reached Glendale. The night, luckily, was intensely dark. Morgan rode ahead, in the advance, with Hines and the scouts and Adam Johnson's second brigade.

Basil's first brigade brought up the rear, with Cluke in its advance, just behind the last of Adam's men. For the first time on a long march, Morgan did not ride back and forth himself, prodding the men.

"What's he humming?" one of Johnson's men asked. "He rides up there humming to himself, with that smile on his face. As if he's mesmerized."

Cal and the rest of the staff took on the job of "riding herd." But even so, the lax and careless discipline, which Morgan had always depended on to encourage devotion, was no match for fatigue. The rear companies of Johnson's brigade halted, straggled and delayed Cluke's men, leading the first brigade in the rear. A gap developed and Cluke realized in a panic the plain fact that they were lost in the dark. He ordered the bolts of calico lit as torches. Long experience had taught him that dust raised by horses drifts in the direction of movement; when the dust settled too far away to be seen, they followed "soap suds" dropped from the horses' mouths. At every delay men almost mad from loss of sleep crept off to lie down; some fell from their saddles and had to be propped back again like sacks of grain. Some, who strapped themselves in, were sorry when their horses collapsed under them, pinning them to the ground. The buggies carrying the wounded tipped and lurched over the ruts. Grigsby's Sixth Kentucky followed, and only the Colonel's extreme efforts kept his column from going to pieces. Major Steele kept up a running fight against enemy pickets, scouts and parties of militia all night.

At daylight they had passed by the principal suburbs and were near the Little Miami Railroad. As expected, Yankee pickets at the crossing peppered the air with musket shot, but were soon driven back, and several good horses were taken. The whistle of a train with recruits bound for Camp Dennison was a signal for the "railroad crews" to swing into action. Within minutes,

Lieutenant Peddicord in charge, the scouts tore up track, stacked cross ties in a cattle gap, and waited. The train whizzed past, steam and sparks flying. Cal, riding back with Duke at the time, would never forget that breathless second of waiting before the crash of metal and splintering timbers exploded the air. When the dust cleared the engine was on its side and the cars, still on the track, spewed forth raw recruits tumbling out to be sent under guard to Morgan.

By the time the last of Duke's brigade left the railroad the Federal soldiers at Camp Dennison had been alerted and were in pursuit. Throughout the rest of the morning their occasional rifle fire kept the men awake, then sputtered to silence.

"I'd give a thousand dollars for an hour's sleep," moaned Cluke, and Basil held his horse while the Colonel dozed.

In the advance, far ahead of Morgan and Johnson riding with the leading brigade, the vedettes began playing games with the local militia. Privates Warfield and Burks became experts at riding into parties of them, presenting themselves as the advance guard of a detail of Federal cavalry, holding them in conversation until the main column appeared. Hundreds were captured and paroled. In the dust and heat and fatigue of that July day contempt for the Ohio militia fed jokes that could keep a man awake.

By four o'clock they halted at Williamsburg, twenty-eight miles east of Cincinnati, after thirty-five hours in the saddle. They had covered more than ninety miles since the last halt.

They collapsed rather than dismounted, and slept like dead men. Toward sundown Morgan walked over to Cal and Adam Johnson. The foragers had just brought in some corn, which they could roast over campfires, and pies and fresh milk left in the deserted houses. He sank down to the ground on crossed legs and reached a thankful hand out to Richard handing him a cup of coffee. It was then that Morgan turned to Johnson.

"All our troubles are over, Stovepipe. The river is twenty-five miles away. Tomorrow we'll be on Southern soil."

Nobody made a sound.

"You don't believe me?"

"The river's up," said Cal.

"You aren't thinking about abandoning your original plan, to cross at Buffington Island?" Johnson asked. There had been a council about that before the long swing around Cincinnati.

"That's another hundred miles of marching." Morgan looked off.

"But it's upstream from where the Kanawha enters the Ohio . . . the water should be better there," Johnson argued.

"Couldn't be worse—I'll agree with that!" Cal said, seeing his brother's indecision.

"I could go with Hines down to Ripley tonight," Richard offered. "We could be there by sunup. Check on the river."

"That's precisely where they'll look for us," said Morgan with a sigh. "You're right, Stovepipe. Buffington it is. But Richard's idea would make a good feint. Why don't you do it, and meet the column at Locust Grove or

Jasper? We'll be crossing the Scioto somewhere between Jasper and Pike-ton." He was so tired he had to force the words out.

"You keep that map in your head, don't you?"

The sun sent long shafts of shadows across the fields. The cool of night would be welcome after the dust and heat and grit of that day.

"Only as far as the river, Cal. From there I can follow my nose." But he rescinded Richard's night ride: They were too exhausted.

At first light Richard, Hines and the scouts were off for the fast march twenty miles south to Ripley. The main column moved away in semblance of fours toward the rising sun, following the railroad through Sardinia and Macon into Winchester: again that eerie, deserted countryside with pies and milk in houses with half-opened doors. Once in a while, at some street corner, a small group gathered to watch the bedraggled, worn-out band of Rebels pass by. Something to tell their grandchildren.

Richard came back with Hines and rejoined the column at Locust Grove with the news that a crossing, as Cal had suspected, would be impossible. Behind them, Michigan and Kentucky Union cavalry units were gaining ground. Ahead, home-grown militia were ripping up bridges and felling trees in their path. More than a dozen halts had to be made with the cry of "Ho! Axes forward here!" Big Tom Boss of C Company, Second Kentucky, who carried an ax and bowie knife stuck in his belt as a matter of course, led the clearing crews. Near Jasper Ellsworth tapped the wires and learned that Judah's forces were now on the Ohio River in a flotilla following Morgan's movements on land. Ellsworth sent the news that Morgan was headed for Chillicothe, to the northwest; then the column crossed the Scioto and headed east, ransacking Jasper and looting Piketon for food and shoes. By midnight they had marched almost eighty miles and camped on the fairgrounds at Jackson, where the latest newspaper, found in the depot, declared Morgan's men to be bandits, murderers and guerrillas deserving death on capture. After three hours' sleep, and before dawn, they burned the depot and for good measure the newspaper office before dividing into two columns again, Duke's first brigade marching toward Wilkesville, Johnson's second toward Vinton. Hobson rode into Jackson about noon.

Before sundown Duke was in Wilkesville and called a halt for rest until three A.M. Johnson joined him the next morning just west of Pomeroy, a town on the river near Buffington Island. The roads were covered with fallen timber; Union troops under Hobson and Shackleford were only five hours behind the column and Judah's troops, now on shore, were on parallel roads to the rear. On the river gunboats patrolled all crossings.

Passing around Pomeroy was one running fight, not with militia now but with regulars. At each crossroad they appeared; the woods sprouted blue-coats. The road to the river ran for nearly five miles through a ravine, with the enemy posted above. A gauntlet. Grigsby took the lead with the Sixth Kentucky and dashed through at a gallop. Major Webber brought up the rear. At Chester, at one o'clock, a halt was called to let the column close up and find a guide. By the time they started again an hour and a half had been wasted.

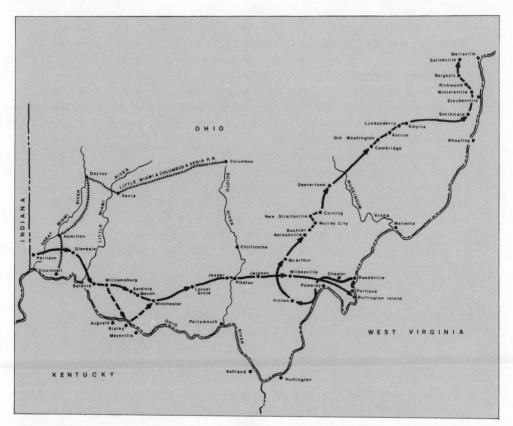

Ohio Raid to the Surrender, July 1863

About eight that night they reached Portland, a village on the Ohio just above Buffington Island. They bivouacked in a narrow valley between a ridge and the river. The night was solid black. An earthwork, built to guard the ford, housed some three hundred Federal infantry, with two field guns. "If we're to cross at all, General," said Duke, "we should do so tonight. If we wait till morning those guns—not to mention Hobson and Judah—will prevent us."

"He's right," said Johnson. "Our artillery ammunition is nearly exhausted —not more than three rounds each."

Below them in the night they could hear the river rushing by. It had risen several feet in the last twenty-four hours. Gunboats could now approach the island, the same gunboats which had delivered Judah to their rear. In broad daylight, three bursts from Byrne's Parrots wouldn't hold them back long. But there was the earthwork commanding the ford, with its three hundred defenders. Morgan had absolutely no knowledge of the ground, or even the direction an attack should take. If unsuccessful, even a repulse could turn into a rout, with troops almost crazed by fatigue.

"We could double-quick to a ford upstream, and let the wagons and buggies follow," Basil offered.

Morgan looked bewildered. Leave the wounded?

"They could be moved later," Webber said.

Were they insane? With Hobson and Judah a half-day's ride behind?

"I'll risk everything before I leave them," Morgan said in a tone not to be argued with.

Basil stopped short, shocked. *We die of our virtues*, St. Leger had said. God love his general, but God help him, too. Basil watched him order scouting parties to search for fords and received his own order to place two regiments in position as close to the earthwork as possible for an attack at first light, if no fords were found. Basil selected Colonel Smith's Fifth Kentucky and Warren Grigsby's Sixth, and formed them about four hundred yards from the earthwork. The troops collapsed that night with the running Ohio in their ears.

Before full dawn Lieutenant Lawrence had arranged his Parrots on a tongue of land jutting north from a range of hills running parallel with the river. As soon as Duke's men could see, they moved. The silence from the mound of logs and dirt was unreal. Were the Yankees waiting to annihilate them with one volley? The two regiments belly-crept, then knelt, then stood up and crawled over. The stockade had been abandoned during the night, its two field pieces dismantled and dumped into the river! They could have crossed last night! They could be, this morning, on Kentucky soil!

Morgan immediately put Smith in charge of the two regiments and sent them to guard the road to Pomeroy. They hadn't ridden out of sight when the sound of musketry sent Basil Duke following with reinforcements. By the time Basil got there he met Smith's men holding their own against the advance of Judah's cavalry, eight to ten thousand strong. The valley where the road crossed was only a mile long, with a ridge to the west paralleling the river, which ran almost due north and south. At the northern end of the valley the ridge and river almost met. Basil returned to Morgan for instructions, but when he rode up the valley again he met Smith's dismounted men in full retreat. "Rally to horses" was called, but before they could, three regiments of enemy cavalry charged. The dismounted men managed to drive them back, but part of Smith's Fifth Kentucky was cut off. Some who had reached their horses dismounted again and formed across the road. Someone brought the news that the Parrots were captured. Duke sent word to Morgan to send the Second Kentucky. With them, he intended to clear and hold the ridge.

Before they could arrive, Johnson's rear vedettes, posted on the Chester road overnight, were driven in by Hobson's three thousand cavalry, and Johnson formed his brigade to meet the threat from that direction. Morgan's command, less than nineteen hundred men, with not more than five cartridges per man and no artillery, would have to face the combined force of Judah and Hobson.

At the time the attack began—from both directions—gunboats steamed toward shore and began shelling with five or six guns. Hobson joined in with his two, Judah with his five or six. Shells soared from three sides. Caught in the valley between the ridge, now occupied by Michigan skirmishers, and the river, Duke's men and Smith's two regiments lay exposed to a murderous crossfire. Morgan, at the southern and wider end of the valley, began drawing off, moving in almost perfect order, but mounted stragglers galloped off with each shell that burst near them. Panic spread to the ambulance teams and the long train of wagons was soon locked, overturned, their terrified horses breaking loose and plunging through the troops. A few teams ran north toward the narrow end of the valley, straight into a section of howitzers still attached to the second brigade, and wagons and guns, wounded men and horses rolled headlong into the ravine.

Duke looked around. His left flank was completely turned, and Grigsby's Sixth Kentucky, under the command now of Major Bullitt, was almost surrounded. Johnson and Duke, with less than four hundred men, had held off the assault for more than half an hour. It was time to go.

At first their withdrawal was in good order. Until they saw, at the end of the valley, only two avenues of retreat. Then the men broke into a gallop. In the rush that followed, both exits were blocked and under pounding from the gunboats. Now the Michigan cavalry struck from the rear; Duke and Johnson became separated. When Duke learned that Johnson had made it back to Morgan, he surrendered.

Part of the Ninth Tennessee and Richard's Fourteenth Kentucky were captured. But thirty men from Grigsby's and Smith's regiments swam the river *sans* clothes or guns, and George Ellsworth, Grigsby and Byrne swam over on their horses. Upstream fifty men from the Ninth Tennessee, under Captains Kirkpatrick and Sisson, on a leaky flatboat, made it to the other side. Seven hundred Confederates were captured, another 120 killed or wounded, and within forty-eight hours, another hundred made prisoner by the Ohio militia.

But where was Morgan? General Shackleford, in command of all forces in pursuit, was furious. He called for a thousand volunteers, and five regular regiments assembled—Frank Wolford's among them—to join the chase.

Fourteen hundred Morgan men rode east, two hundred fifty from the old Second Kentucky. Fifteen miles upstream, at Reedsville, the river narrowed. The water would be deep, but you could almost throw a stone into West Virginia. A strong horse could make it, and indomitable men. Adam Johnson led his brigade into the water. Some of the horses floundered, went under. Before the first men reached the opposite shore the gunboat appeared around the bend and began lobbing shells at the swimmers. Morgan, on Glencoe, was in midstream when the first shells exploded the water. Billy, near him, was screaming. "Come on, Billy, we'll make it!" The boy had long ago traded the prancing circus mare for an Ohio plow horse, and sat now on the broad back bent double, his face buried in mane.

They were almost there. Glencoe was amazing, that thoroughbred, pumping shoulders shining bronze-wet in water. Swimming horses were all around. The river ran deep and fast, but they were making it. Then he looked back and his heart sank.

On the Ohio shore his men, his command, the remnants of those "generals" who had come with him so far, so long. Surrounded. He couldn't do it. He closed his left hand and Glencoe obeyed.

The gelding turned and began beating his forelegs, his powerful chest cresting the muddy water.

"Mass' John!"

"Go on, Billy!" he yelled.

"Mass' John!" The boy, slipping sideways, almost slid off. To save himself, he grabbed rein, and turned the horse.

"*No!*"

"Ah cain't . . ." He didn't finish, busy with the current.

"Go on!"

Wind took the words. Billy, now downstream, was still aboard, but drifting toward the island. As Morgan scrambled up the bank on the Ohio side, he looked across the river. Maybe as many as three hundred, or more, of his men made it. Adam Johnson on his Texas roan, and Sid Cunningham, Kirkpatrick, Sisson. . . . Billy's plow horse was nowhere in sight.

His men must be surrendered with dignity. They must go as far as they could, and find decent surrender terms. . . . It was no longer a case of saving the command, but of saving it from abuse. And giving the Yankees a last run for their money.

As he saw Tom Webber's dusty, startled face switch from pain to astonishment, he knew he had made the right decision.

Cal on the white circus mare was desperately trying to rally the men. When he looked around and saw his brother he relaxed his face into a grim smile. "I told these boys we'd get out of this!"

Inland. Northwest, where the Yankees least expected a move. That was it. By nightfall, of course, they had picked up Morgan's trail, but he wasn't out of tricks yet. He pulled one of Will's oldest. The men built a circle of campfires, then walked their horses as quietly as they could before they broke into a dead run. The Yankee cavalry—Hobson's command, with Frank Wolford's outfit as the advance—quickly surrounded the "camp" and settled down for the night, fully expecting to make a wholesale capture when the sun came up.

Five miles away he called for a two-hour rest to assess the situation. He reorganized his "brigades"—now only about four hundred men each—and gave Webber the first, Cluke the second. There was no need to tell them what to expect. In unfamiliar country with worn-out men and exhausted horses, pursued by an enemy who would try to surround them with faster animals and troops from every source, they were in a lion's den.

But as they rode off, you would never have known it. He had never seen such cheerful determination, such sheer nerve and resolution in his life. Where it came from he would never know. Webber, still suffering from dysentery, was so weak now he had to be helped into his saddle. His young captains begged him to be captured and get a doctor's treatment, but the thought of dropping out made him even more adamant about staying. He was leading "his boys" and no pain could bend that erect form. They nick-named him "The Iron Man."

As for Cluke, his energy, like his hope, never faded. When the scouts reported a ford six miles downstream from Pomeroy he spoke up in favor of trying it, even though they knew the water would be even worse than at Buffington—and the Yankees watching every move.

"We'll make it this time!" The words kept spinning in Morgan's brain. They were Cal's, dear Cal's. On the way their horses lifted a telltale cloud of dust, but so did Wolford's. Each knew the exact position of the other. If they could reach the river first. . . .

The ford was guarded by Ohio militia who had commandeered an old boat used to tow coal barges from Pittsburg. Its only gun was an old cannon, but from where they were the advance vedettes had no way of knowing it wasn't the Union gunboat with more powerful field guns. When Cluke reported the situation, Morgan reluctantly agreed that only one course lay before them: inland again, with another try at a ford upstream . . . as far upstream from Pomeroy as possible. The wagons with their wounded lurched behind their plodding mules. The vedettes were skirmishing now almost constantly. About three o'clock Shackleford's regulars finally caught up with them; Morgan lost ten men. He had no intention of doing battle with exhausted troops. And to ask his wounded to travel one more mile would be brutality. He offered to negotiate. While Lieutenant-Colonel Cole-man, in charge of the wounded—almost two hundred men—conferred about a surrender, Morgan got away.

They followed creeks into the hills, marching all night. If the horses didn't eat soon they would be totally dismounted. A cornfield at sunrise looked like heaven, and a halt was called to forage. They were near Vinton, a town ten miles from the river. Both men and horses ate the corn—and afterwards, for blessed minutes, the men sprawled like sacks in the sun. Down Raccoon Creek, which entered the field from the south, Hines and his scouts came yelling, followed closely by two hundred fifty Ohio militia, who stopped abruptly when they saw the quickly forming fours. Morgan sent in a flag of truce demanding surrender, with the information that he had two thousand men with him, with more in the rear.

The trick worked: The Ohio major surrendered his whole command, and two hundred fifty Morgan men, after a quick parole, had fresh guns.

They looked up to see another company of Ohio Home Guards marching in from Vinton. They tried the same trick again, and it worked! Another parole, and another stack of arms. It was time to leave.

They followed the creek upstream almost due north, then swung west and camped for what remained of the night about four miles north of McArthur. By this time, although Morgan did not know it—how he missed Ellsworth! —sixty-five thousand Ohio militia were after him, plus the regulars.

They didn't even bother to tear up the tracks of the Marietta & Cincinnati Railroad, but pushed on another twenty miles that next morning to Nelsonville. They begged food now, and pilfered stores, and "traded" horses when they could. It was the 22nd of July, exactly twenty days since they had crossed the Cumberland.

Buchtel, Murray City, New Straitsville, Corning. An almost savage determination turned into mesmerized motion. Like puppets in a dumb show, silent, glum, with fatigue staining their eyes red and amber, falling forward in their saddles, they made another twenty miles into Deavertown; over forty miles that day on horses whose legs were trembling with the desire to collapse.

Before daylight the next morning they had the news from the scouts: Wolford and Runkle's Ohio militia were closing in. Morgan ordered an immediate move. The Muskingum lay ahead. Once across the river, he knew what he had to do: march straight northeast toward Steubenville. There had to be a ford there. As the crow flew, another seventy-eight miles.

Skirmish at Blue Rock, a delay which allowed Wolford to close the gap even more. Afternoon, a divided column, a hundred men lost in skirmishing. Yankee patrols at every crossroad, behind every hill. Hobson had left Buffington and had crossed the Muskingum: For the first time the Federals were in front of them.

What trick could he pull now? An Indian backtrack. Toward the Ohio. Might just work.

But the clouds of dust which told him where Wolford and Hobson were also announced his own line of march. By sundown what was left of his command found themselves trapped by a high bluff and Federals on three sides.

The hill behind them rose at least a thousand feet, almost straight up. But it was the only way out. Morgan's keen eye noticed a little runoff cut in the slate, with outcroppings on either side. In the spring it must be a waterfall. When he showed it to Webber, even the Iron Man paled at the idea. "If we lead our horses single file, we could just do it," Morgan insisted. Cal was the only one to believe him, then Cluke agreed. After nightfall the campfire ruse was used again. Once they were blazing, the trek began.

Cinches were tightened, and everything that could make a noise was tied down—canteens, tin pots, axes. Anything that stuck out too far and might bang against a rock was either left behind or rearranged. Commands and advice were whispered. Once a horse slipped, rolled over and a man yelled; the horse limped off and the man scrambled on. Some men were on all fours, reins caught under armpits. Others, bent double and mounted, hissed encouragement to their animals. Then the miracle happened: Fear drove out just enough exhaustion to get them to the top.

It must have been just after midnight. Morgan had led the way, Cluke in the rear. Long before first light they were up and over and riding hard toward the north. No more pies in deserted houses; they were not expected. Surprise, then awe in the towns. But they were moving slower now. They made less than twenty miles that day, and camped in Cumberland that night.

The town surrendered to the weary men without a shot. Morgan slept in the hotel, after a hot bath and a meal, but during the night sixty men deserted.

Daylight saw the depleted command heading toward the National Road. "Let's see where all that tariff money went," Cal joked.

They crossed the Baltimore & Ohio east of Cambridge at a place called Campbell's Station, burned the depot and bridge, and found ten thousand dollars in greenbacks in the company safe. Once on the National Road, a mild cheer went up. By noon, Old Washington and lunch at the American Hotel. They were less than thirty-five miles from the ford near Mingo Junction, downstream from Steubenville. Just as they were folding their napkins Shackleford's advance rode into town. A skirmish, then the Road again. Six hours east found them in Hendrysburg, toward the river.

But something was wrong. A cloud of dust in the distance. Morgan ordered the column away from the river, north again, toward Antrim, where they rested two hours. Then on again: Londonderry, Smyrna, Moorefield, Smithfield. Five miles from the river on the road to Wintersville he ordered scouts to look for a ford, found a farmhouse and collapsed on a bed. An hour later squeals from the women downstairs told him troops were coming, but Cal at the doorway was whispering: only militia. He slept again.

Not for long. About twenty minutes later news of Federal regulars had him pulling on his boots and mounting. They made it through Wintersville, after charging the militia, then Richmond, and ten miles more to Bergholz. They camped by a creek. They were headed away from the river again.

"But we're not much more than ten miles from the Ohio, even here. Right down this creek." It was Cal, but Morgan was too tired to answer.

There had been, in most cases, not even unsaddling. A loose cinch, a hobble to allow grazing, and the men fell asleep where they dismounted. It was the 25th of July. In the morning, he knew, there would be more desertions, out of fear or sheer exhaustion. He got out his tattered map and studied it by the stub of a candle. They were ninety miles from Lake Erie. Two days' ride in the old days, three—with luck—on jaded horses. Three days. He had no idea where the Feds were. He would give his right arm for Ellsworth. Maybe he had concentrated too much on the river. Maybe, if they could get to the lake they could get over on boats . . . the men were too exhausted to do more. He would tell Webber in the morning. Yes, the lake . . . Canada. . . .

They had discussed surrender. But after Gettysburg they knew all exchanges had been suspended. To a man, in the last staff meeting, they agreed to fight to the end. But Lake Erie. Why hadn't he thought of that before? He dozed with a vision of its water catching sun. Sunday. Tomorrow was Sunday. Hadn't everything big always happened to him on Sunday? Wouldn't Mattie be surprised to find out he was in Canada? Webber the Iron Man, and Cluke and good old Cal. Yes, they could make it.

He told them so the next morning over breakfast. They had taken only two bites of cornpone and hardboiled eggs when two regiments of Michigan cavalry burst out of the woods. With a speed that had become instinctive his men mounted and dashed down the road toward Salineville. It proved to be one savage, running fight; he was amazed that his men had so much fight left. On their ungainly farm horses, their ammunition all but gone. Their loss was terrible: He looked back to see half a dozen jerk as the balls hit and fall from their saddles into the path of oncoming horses. How many dropped back and were captured he had no way of knowing. He decided to make a stand.

The Yankees saw their quarry halting to form and found a worm fence, where they dismounted, rifles ready. Then something happened that every Morgan man left with the command would remember: Ralph Sheldon with Company C of the veteran Second Kentucky charged. His tired horses breasted the fence, knocking down the top rails, some falling and taking their riders with them. But most, miraculously, made it, Sheldon's men flying through the air, pistols blazing. Morgan, with the remnants of his command, broke away.

Cal and Cluke estimated that they had lost as many as two hundred eighty men. How many were killed or wounded? Or captured? As they rode north they watched a telltale column of dust rise parallel with their own. Only then did the myth of escape become clear to John Morgan. Canada, indeed. His worn-out little band of men, half of whom were either sick or wounded. His eyes went back to the column of dust hanging horizontally over the trees. If it were Wolford he could expect some courtesy, maybe even generosity. If it were not . . . his best bet would be to find some militia company and make a deal. He rode forward and alerted the scouts.

About noon they saw what they wanted: a small company of Ohio Home Guards commanded by a Captain James Burbeck, a native of Lisbon, not far away. Morgan sent a flag of truce and asked for negotiations. When the Captain himself rode up saluting, Morgan knew he had his man.

"Good day, sir." Morgan held out his hand and the man took it, nodding solemnly.

"I understand you are General Morgan."

"You understand correctly."

The man looked around at the bedraggled but determined-looking men. His own company did not outnumber them, but they were in terrible shape.

"I understand you wish to discuss negotiations."

"I do, sir. If we could dismount . . ."

They did so, and walked to a tree. Oh, God, it was good to rest. Another sleepless night of worry had done little for the pain in his lower back. Sometimes he thought his skin would sprout saddle leather. "A drink, sir?" He pulled out a flask with about an inch of whiskey left.

"Thank you." Burbeck tilted his head, then listened. Morgan was promising to ride through his district without further destruction of property in exchange for a guide to a ford on the Ohio. They were about ten miles from the river, from a town called Wellsville, across from Pennsylvania, Burbeck explained. There was a ford there.

"We will need a guide," the weary Morgan repeated, almost inaudibly.

"I will be most happy to be your guide, sir," Burbeck got out, unable to conceal his sympathy.

Morgan looked up and grinned his crooked smile. "You are a gentleman sir, and I thank you for it."

They mounted, and closer now, the cloud of dust. Made by fresher horses. The Michigan cavalry? Shackleford? Hobson? Judah? Or Frank Wolford? He chatted with Burbeck. Another mile, and the column of dust advanced. Burbeck was talking away when Morgan interrupted him with a sudden apology: "Pardon me, Captain. How would you, after all, like to receive my surrender?"

"Why, General, it would be an honor to do so."

"But perhaps you could not give me such terms as I would wish."

"General Morgan," said Burbeck expansively, "you could write your own terms, and I would grant them."

"Very well, then, it's a bargain. I will surrender to you."

They stopped, the staff riding up. Officially, Morgan surrendered his command, upon condition that the officers and men were to be paroled, the men to keep their horses, the officers their horses and side arms. They had barely finished when the column of dust closed in.

It was two o'clock, a hot Sunday afternoon, July 26, 1863. They stood under a spreading oak on the farm of David Crubaugh, six miles southeast of Lisbon. Three hundred eighty-four men, four hundred horses, all the arms and equipment. They remounted and rode less than half a mile down the road when Major Rue of the Ninth Union Kentucky Cavalry appeared. Morgan immediately sent Major Steele with a flag of truce.

"Who the hell is this Burbeck?" Rue stammered. "You tell Morgan to surrender to me or prepare to fight."

Major Steele, bone tired, discouraged, and hoping that the surrender to the Ohio militia would stick, heard himself say, "Morgan surrenders."

Shackleford, eating a late lunch at a farmhouse not three miles away, scraped back his chair and motioned to Frank Wolford to follow. They arrived about two-thirty and peremptorily took charge of the prisoners. Major Rue, a Kentuckian and Mexican War veteran, introduced Morgan to the other Federal officers as they rode up. Wolford nodded, watching Morgan intently.

"You have met?" Rue asked.

"Oh, yes," said Morgan. "Yes, we have met."

Relief flooded over him. All around, men sliding off horses, dropping to the ground. It was over. Whatever he had done, how much time he had gained for Bragg or the Cause, it was over.

Shackleford was furious. He refused to accept the original surrender; the Ohio militia had no authority. Burbeck was a mere civilian. And he certainly had no intention of honoring any parole. Frank Wolford, who had once been Morgan's prisoner, remembered small kindnesses and made a plea for the paroles to be honored. While he was doing so Morgan, standing off under the tree, gave Captain Burbeck the Arabian circus mare, and Major Rue a sorrel. When he walked over, General Shackleford ran a cold eye over both horses and took both for his own use, announcing that he would ship Glencoe as a gift to General Winfield Scott. Wolford caught Morgan's eye. Without a flicker Morgan reached down and undid his silver spurs and handed them to him. "A personal gift to an old friend. You don't object, General?" To Major Rue he gave his Colt and holster, and to a nice-looking young Yankee lieutenant a fancy bridle Will Webb had made. Shackleford walked away.

The captives were marched that afternoon down to the little town of Wellsville on the Ohio for transport by rail to Cincinnati. Frank Wolford, in charge of the officers, invited them to the Whittaker House for chicken and dumplings. Once inside, he turned to them with a graciousness that stung through their fatigue. "Gentlemen, you are my guests. This establishment, with its bar, cigar stand, and anything else it has to offer, is at your service and my expense. Just don't leave town."

It was the pity in his smile, more than the rudeness of Shackleford, that brought them close to tears.

Richard was wounded. In the thigh, low, near the knee. The ball had passed through the flesh only, but it was an ugly wound. Basil, too, was lame. His horse had bolted in that final dash from the valley at Buffington, fallen down and rolled on his leg before he could kick the stirrup loose. When he saw Richard he tried to be jovial, with remarks about veterans. Richard grunted. It was a ten-mile march to the river, where the transports waited to take the prisoners to Cincinnati. It was no joke.

As it turned out, Captain Day, General Judah's inspector, was a professional soldier, and although he was careful to guard his captives, he showed them every courtesy, including finding them space on a wagon. The five little steamboats—the *Henry Logan*, the *Imperial*, the *Starlight*, the *Tariscon* and the *Ingomar*—were lined up at the Buffington wharf when they arrived. Soon every inch of deck was covered by Confederates—mostly clad in farm clothes, very few uniforms. Basil wore a pair of blue jeans and a white shirt, with a black hat; Richard sported gray trousers, the only remnant of his Virginia splendor, and now torn and bloody. Captain Day had his hands full that night: In a cloudburst and the hours of drizzle until dawn, scores of Morgan men slid overboard and made for the West Virginia shore. Captain Tom Berry, one of the Lexington Rifles who had loaded the hay wagon with guns the night they left home for war, wore like a badge of honor a handkerchief over a head wound behind his left ear. Once underway, he sat below decks for a haircut. "Take it all," he said almost too cheerfully. The next morning they learned why: *Sans* long hair and mustache, Berry, in a dark civilian suit he had acquired from one of the looted stores, strolled off the gangplank with some passengers when the *Tariscon* stopped at a landing between Gallipolis and Portsmouth.

It took three days to reach Cincinnati. Hard biscuits, fat bacon and more rain. The enlisted men were kept on board overnight at the Fifth Street dock, the officers marched immediately to City Prison on Ninth Street. Rumor had it the enlisted men were to be sent to Camp Morton, near Indianapolis, and to Camp Douglas at Chicago. Where the officers would go was anybody's guess.

They were formed in two lines, with guards four deep on each side, and marched through jeering crowds who crowed for their execution. Basil, because of his rank, and Richard, because of his wound, were given a buggy and an overview of the mob pushing against the protecting Federal soldiers, who became more contemptuous at this show of boldness by those same citizens who had hid indoors so short a time before.

"Brave, ain't they?" a Yankee private called up to Basil.

Once inside the jail all soldierly camaraderie ceased. They were no longer celebrities or even oddities, but prisoners neither getting more nor deserving less than the laws of war proscribed. They were told the next day that their destination was Johnson's Island, near Sandusky, in Lake Erie. The loss of their freedom was no less painful than the worry over the rest of the command. Had they made it across the river? The day they left Cincinnati they had their answer when the news reached them of Morgan's capture.

At Johnson's Island the prisoners from Gettysburg were coming in, and the barracks were crowded. Basil learned from an artillery captain that Charlton Morgan was at Camp Douglas. "The hellhole of the North," someone said. "When was he captured?"

"February."

"They don't issue blankets at Douglas either. Pest house. Die like flies. Even the Yankee soldiers almost mutinied. The Sanitary Commission closed it in April, but with Gettysburg, they've opened their hotel again."

"Don't worry," said the artillery captain. "It's easy to escape from Douglas."

Four days later Basil and Richard were on the move again. Forty Morgan officers were told they were to entrain, destination unknown. Their worst fears were realized when they pulled into Columbus. A Federal officer stepped briskly into the car and raised his voice over the noise of the baggage platform and the spewing steam which poured through the windows. "The State of Ohio," he yelled, "has claimed Morgan and his officers."

Basil looked at Richard, whose leg was propped on a seat. The State of Ohio?

"You are to be sent to the Ohio State Penitentiary," the officer proclaimed with satisfaction. "Colonel Streight, an Ohio officer captured by Forrest, has been sent to the penitentiary in Georgia. That's about the correct ratio, don't you think? One Ohio colonel for forty horse thieves. . . . Come along, now."

So Burnside, Basil fumed, a man prepared to flee a city full of his own troops upon the approach of two thousand weary men, has turned us over to the Governor of Ohio who claimed capture of Morgan when in reality— if he could believe the papers—it was a surrender freely given and then nullified by a Yankee general, whose Michigan and Kentucky troops had finally outnumbered him.

Fury and resentment gave way to despair when they marched under the heavy stone doorway of the Ohio State Penitentiary. All attempts at jocularity, which had kept up a semblance of spirit, disappeared in that gloom. They were standing in a building four hundred feet long, some forty feet wide, with a ceiling almost fifty feet high. On one side tall windows looked out onto a prison yard. It was a room within a room, for the cell blocks, stacked back-to-back five high with catwalks across their fronts, faced alleys eleven feet wide that ran the full length of the building and opened at each end into a hall about twenty feet square. It was in one of these halls that Basil and the men stood waiting.

Richard and the others too looked up at the cells, the knuckles of hands that held onto bars, shadowy faces. Their attention was drawn to a potbel-

lied man marching in with a no-nonsense step that he must have thought
was military. He strutted back and forth, hitched up his pants and surveyed
them with a greasy face and an uneasy eye. But there was nothing uneasy
about the brutality in his voice. His name was Merion. He was the warden,
and he made it clear they were here to be treated as felons. Behind him a
red-faced trusty with little pig's eyes who had been introduced as "Scotty"
nodded at each pause and looked his new charges over as if he couldn't wait
to "treat" them.

After a weary half-hour of this tirade Merion left, and there was an interval before the trusty and a kindly old man who was, from his uniform, a
kind of subwarden, began moving them forward toward their cells. As Duke
passed an iron-barred door a convict spoke with a low voice through the
grating. Basil, with a whiff of sour sweat in his nose, started to make a
remark about familiarity on such short acquaintance when he heard, under
the man's shorn head and through the stubble of a grimy beard, an unfor-
gettable, bitter laugh. The convict was John Morgan.

The stage was stifling. Mattie held down the hot knot of morning sickness
and closed her eyes. If she looked at the lurching countryside it was worse;
her fellow passengers were three men, two octogenarians and the third a fat
sutler of some kind. The only thing that kept her sane was the occasional
fresh air when they stopped and the men—the old ones laboriously—dismounted. And the fact that the first major stop from Sparta, Crossville, was
only twenty-five miles away. Still, it took four hours to get there.

She stepped down, helped by a boy with elastic bands holding back his
sleeves who had run over from the hotel on the corner. "I don't need a room
. . . just a little rest," she got out.

"Yes, ma'am!" Without asking, he reached up for her valise, which the
driver handed down.

"You don't understand . . . I'm not staying. I'm going on to Kingston.
Just some tea . . . a little tea. . . ."

Looking hurt, the boy handed back her valise. The driver, a man with
small eyes and a face like leather, stuck his whip in its holder and leaned
toward her. "Yew in a might hurry fer jest tea, ain't yew, ma'am?"

"I thought . . ."

He dropped down beside her, and the smell of him made her almost recoil.
The man noticed, and scowled. "If yer gonna git enny dinner terday, yew'd
better git in thar and grub up. Don't want no faintin' females on this run."

As she turned, her chin unconsciously in the air, he called after her, "Be
right smart about it, too!"

Be right smart? Did he know who he was talking to? She swished her
skirts. She was Mrs. John Hunt Morgan. And beyond that, she was a
Southern Lady. She hoped her look told him as much! If he only knew that
her husband was this minute traveling under secret, direct orders from the
President himself! That he was on his way to win this war, to invade the
hateful North! While she was on a secret mission of her own, too—to take
care of his unborn child. The insolence! The idea! You couldn't talk to *trash*.

That was just it. You couldn't talk to them because they wouldn't *listen*. The boy with the pushed-up sleeves was still skipping along beside her. Something in the driver's look told her he wouldn't wait if she were late.

"Will I have time?" she asked the hotel boy.

"Oh, yes, ma'am. They take a full hour here at Crossville."

As they entered the lobby he looked over at the desk clerk, waiting with even wider elastic bands at the counter.

"A little tea," she repeated.

"They change teams here, ma'am. You sure you don't want a room? You'll have plenty of time."

"Where do they start?"

"Right out front, ma'am. Starts out front. But if I wuz you, ma'am, I'd git myself a dinner before loadin'. Unless you want to rest."

She found one empty table in the crowded dining room, sat down and let her shawl slip back. A food-spotted card lay in the middle, on the soiled cloth. She picked it up and read:

> We have made considerable improvement in our House of late, and those who wish to remain over at Crossville will find, with us, airy rooms, clean beds, with abundance of fires, FRESH FOWL in season, and EVERY LUXURY money can buy. If our guests do not find everything here as represented, they can publish us to THE WORLD as imposters, and the ignominy will be OURS.

She looked up to see a skinny Negro girl waiting patiently for her order. "I'll have . . ."

"We got nuthin' but sweet potatoes, ma'am." The girl rolled her eyes and let the thick end of a pink tongue wet one corner of her mouth.

"Very well, then. Some sweet potatoes. Can you fix some tea?"

"Yessum, Ah'll try."

She watched her leave and tried to avoid the eyes of the other guests. With one foot she shoved her chair an inch closer to the wall. Every luxury money can buy! She looked at the noisy clientele, busy eating or talking with mouths full, gesturing with upraised forks, and stared at the broad back of a farmer, the oval of sweat between his shoulder blades darkening his homespun shirt, the thick red neck above that and the greasy black hair above that. The wallpaper beyond him was a muddy red splotched with what once might have been flowers. A sour smell of stale cabbage and fatback hung like a memory in the air. She was wondering when the windows were opened last when the potatoes came—cold. But at least the tea was warm. She ate as fast as she could without choking, paid the proprietor, who was waiting by the door into the "lobby," and walked outside to find the stage gone.

"Gone? Why, yes, ma'am, it's gone," said the clerk at the desk, astonished at her question. "Left . . . oh, ten minutes ago. Yew wuz inta dinner, wuz yew—pity! Yew'll have ter stay over till tamarry now, won't yew—pity!"

Mattie stifled her rage and asked as quietly as she could: "Which road does the stage take?"

"Why, the only one, ma'am. Carried yore bag off, too, did he? Suppose he fergot yew. Pity!"

She whirled from him and almost ran into a young soldier just coming in the door.

"Are you all right, ma'am?" He reached out a hand to steady her, and to her surprise, she found she was close to tears. She spilled her story out with a rush of sobs.

"I'll find you a wagon, ma'am. I'm goin' to Kingston myself. Here, you sit right here. Are you sure you're all right? That is"—he blushed—"if you'll permit me to escort you, ma'am."

For the first time she saw how young he was.

"Yes . . . that would be fine. Do you really think you could? I've got money. . . ."

He raised his hand and shook his head. "Just wait in there, ma'am. I'll be back as soon as I can . . ."

She turned back into the lobby and sat under the eyes of the desk clerk, who still expected her to ask for a room. When the soldier came back she felt as if she were welcoming an old friend. He had sandy hair like Key's. A wagon waited, with a gray farm horse hitched to it.

"How far is it to Kingston?" she asked as he handed her up and took his own seat beside her on the buckboard.

"Thirty miles as the crow flies. Only sometimes the crow don't fly too straight."

He flipped the reins so unconcernedly she almost giggled. "My clothes . . . have gone ahead on the stage."

"Oh, in that case maybe we can catch up! Yes, we'll . . ." And the horse plunged forward. She caught her bonnet and shawl to her and leaned into the momentum. The day had suddenly taken on all the aspects of adventure. The boy beside her had that quiet toughness her Morgan had tried to explain so many times. The gift of turning disaster into opportunity. She actually laughed, and forgot all about being sick. It was June. The sky was blue. She was on her way to Knoxville, and then to Chattanooga to meet Alice and Key, and carrying *his* baby. And he was leading his men on a glorious mission. What more could she want?

Three miles out of town, in the mud of a steep hill, they found the stage bogged down, its wheels sunk below the hubs, the passengers standing around waiting for something to be done. The driver, as nonchalant as ever, shifted his quid when he saw her drive up.

"Hallo, ma'am. That yew?"

"You know it is! Why didn't you wait for me?"

At her tone the man straightened. "Well, now. Reckoned yew wuz inside —mustn't blame me! Shouldn't take so long swallerin' yer dinner . . ." For the first time he saw the soldier and swung his head away to spit. When his face came back around again it wore a sly grin. "This gentleman here"—he pointed to a passenger—"tole me yew had changed yer mind, and wouldn't be comin.' 'Yes,' he sez, 'it's all right,' and Ah reckoned it wuz. . . ."

"Just give me my valise," Mattie sighed, with a look at the boy beside her.

"And the trunk—the small one." The young soldier tied the reins, jumped down, reached up for Cal's trunk and her bag, and tucked them in behind the seat. Only when they topped the hill and started down the other side did they burst out laughing.

The horse trotted on. If they kept this pace they could be in Kingston before full night. But the sky had clouded over and a wind promising rain flattened their clothes against their bodies. She caught at her bonnet.

"Are you warm enough, ma'am?"

His concern made her relax for the first time since she'd left McMinnville. "What is your name?

"Ward, ma'am. Ward Burnette. From Fulton."

"Where is that?"

"Kentucky. Just over the line, ma'am." He flipped the reins and whistled softly. "My granddaddy collects horses for General Forrest. Donated, for miles around. Has a big barn. I've seen a hundred horses in that barn."

"What do you do with them?"

"We wait for General Forrest to send for them; sometimes we ride them to another meeting place. My brother Raymond . . . went down this summer, didn't come back."

"Were you surprised?"

He looked off, trying to suppress a grin. "No, ma'am. He's the sixth brother I've had to leave for the cav'lry."

"All in the cavalry?"

"Ain't no other service worth joinin', is there, ma'am?"

"I guess not. My husband . . ."

"Oh, I know who your husband is, ma'am. You're Mrs. Morgan."

"How did you know?"

He grinned sheepishly. "You don't suppose the General didn't send out a few scouts to see you to Kingston, now did you, ma'am?"

"You're . . ."

"And we'll meet another at the ferry."

She leaned back, feeling suddenly taken care of. The darling . . .

"This here sure is rough country," Ward Burnette said. "Nothing like back home."

"Tell me about home."

The word sounded like a prayer. The boy thought a minute, his eyes going soft. "Good land. River bottom . . ." It was as if he saw it, and forgot to say more.

"What will you do at Kingston?"

"Oh, I'm not stopping there. Going on to Knoxville to ride with Colonel Scott. He's with General Buckner at Knoxville."

"General Buckner is a favorite of my husband's."

"We Kentucky men got to stick together," Ward Burnette said stoutly, then laughed at his own audacity. "You know . . ."

"I know." She watched his hands on the reins, his worn-out shoes. Her own weren't much better.

"General Forrest, he's the greatest general of them all, Pa says. Why, when—"

He didn't finish. A bullet found him between the shoulder blades, and he fell forward. Other shots rang out from the overhanging cliffs on either side: They were in one of the narrow hollows that seemed to get deeper and narrower as the road slipped downhill. The horse reared at the shot and bucked against the traces. The boy's body fell sideways and off, the reins flying. Mattie clung to the side with both hands, the mud from the sloshing hooves plastering her face. Suddenly a wheel gave way and she was flung against a bank, the horse and wagon careening on until it caught on a stump and pulled the horse to a stop. She looked up into the faces of two Yankee soldiers.

"Well, lookee whut we got here," the taller one said. He grinned broadly as he pulled her to her feet. He might have been handsome, in a dark, farmboy way, if he hadn't had such cold eyes. She had never seen such eyes. The other one, shorter and fat, said nervously, "Come on, Clem, let's git outta here. The hoss . . ."

"Yew git her hoss," the tall one said, never taking his eyes from the girl, who had begun to shiver. He shifted his rifle and pulled her up the bank.

"Where . . . ?" she got out.

Without answering, he kept on. The land slipped, tipping. She had to support herself with her hands and knees. Thorn vines tore at her skirt and dug through her gloves. The Yankee had never let go, and a circle of pain just above her elbow threatened to cut off her circulation. "Ow!"

He stopped just long enough to slap her across the face and catch her before she fell back down the bank toward the road. He dragged her fifty feet through brush and cedars into the mouth of a doorway. It was some kind of hut—a pigsty. The roof was low, the ground dry, with an animal stench that took her breath. The man said not a word, but settled himself opposite her and picked his teeth in the dark. She could hear the *click, click, suck, suck.* Then the rustle of damp leaves outside. He clamped a hand across her mouth until his buddy whispered. He immediately relaxed and let out a soft chuckle. "Whut took yew so long?"

She saw now a kind of canvas, or deerskin—it was too dark to tell—flap at the opening. Sweat had started running down her neck and between her breasts. She heard the shorter man tie the horse and step through, dragging something behind him. It was her valise.

"What?" the tall soldier let out angrily.

"Now wait, now wait a bit, Clem. Yore allus tellin' me I'm dumb, but look here. Whut if we put on dresses?"

"Dresses?"

The fat boy brought out the stub of a candle and lit it.

"Yeah . . . ain't you allus been tellin' me how you done everythin' bounty jumpin'? How you enlisted in one county, then skedaddled to another, changed yore name an' looks, enlisted agin . . . least till the last time . . . Ain't yew?"

"Yew bet. I wuzn't dumb, like yew. Sell yourself fer a substitute!"

The younger one suddenly lost his good humor and leaned forward, gritting his teeth. "I done tole you, Clem, I got thet money fer my folks . . . least I didn't *lie!*"

Mattie thought the tall soldier would kill him just then. He reached for his rifle. To her utter surprise he changed his mind and laughed. "Why, shore. Let's see them dresses." He pulled her rose silk from the valise and shook it out in front of him. The skirt snagged on a knot of dirt by his shoe and he kicked it out. "I'll take this one!"

"An . . . I'll try this one!" The fat boy unfolded her green velvet. When he saw her cringe he turned to her kindly and said, "I won't do it no harm, ma'am. And it just might git me back . . ."

She shook with fury. "I wasn't shivering from fear, you . . . you deserters!"

"Hey, watch yore tongue, yew Southern whore!" the older one called over.

Outside, a horse neighed. The fat boy, unable to get his dress buttoned, gave up and grabbed his gun. Voices! Before she knew what happened the older one made a run for it. She heard the horse snap the rope and scamper away. She ran out then, waving her arms. The gray head of the farm horse disappeared as it shambled through the trees. Behind her, the fat boy had come out of the hut and was running toward the woods when a gun from somewhere fired. By the time she turned he lay in a heap, her green velvet soaking up the blood from his chest.

"Well, lady, whut the hell you doin' in my pigpen?"

Bushwhacker. The word sent a chill down her spine. The man loomed larger than life, leaning over her. They would kill you first and ask questions later. They had no mercy. The man squinted and spit. She saw he had no teeth, and a long ugly scar ran down one cheek. "Ho, there, Sam!" he called out. No answer. "Durned fool," he murmured.

"Durned fool," he said to her. "Tole him thet hoss warn't up here. Nevah mind! Now we got two hosses!" He threw back his head and laughed and as he came toward her she noticed he had a limp.

"Nevah yew fear, young lady," he said, his breath too close. "Ah ain't gonna eat yew. Come on home with me. The old lady'll fix yew up." He tried a toothless, fatherly smile, and she brushed down her skirt and walked toward the hut.

"Whut're yew goin' in thar fer?"

"My bag . . ."

He waited while she stuffed the rose silk in, then he slung the valise over his shoulder and walked ahead. She followed the lurching shapeless black hat down the hill to his house.

A woman sat on the porch washing her face and arms in a basin. She, like her husband, was barefoot. "Well, Ah never!" she said when she saw Mattie. "Ah thought yew wuz out lookin' fer a hoss?"

"Shet up," the man said genially. "This here's company. She done brung us a hoss. Sam back yit?" When she shook her head he said, "Then I'll send thuh niggah. He's twic't as fas' as Sam anyhow." He went into the house and slammed the door without another word.

The woman surveyed her visitor.

"Whew, ain't it hot?"

Mattie nodded.

"Kum. Take yoreseff a seat. . . . We don't git much company these parts."

Mattie noticed a small log building on the side of the house, and a girl of about twelve coming toward them.

"Thet's mah kitchen," the woman said proudly, and dashed the water from the basin. It hit the grassless yard with a plop and ran down the hard clay toward two chickens rooting in some bushes. "We cooked in the fire here—" she jerked her thumb toward the house. "Till we got thet kitchen." All the while she talked the girl came on at an even pace, slapping the ground with her feet. "This here's company," the woman said. "Say howdy."

"Howdy." The girl let her eyes drift up, then away.

"I'm glad . . ." Mattie reached her hand out to thin air, then brought it back.

"She's shy," the woman said. Which wasn't, Mattie quickly decided, a problem the lady of the house shared. "My ole man . . . he'll tell yew he got his leg frum thuh Mexican War, fightin' down in the Texies. Don' yew believe hit! He got thet laig frum a feud with his uncle. But he's a worker, he is! Ain't a man in the county works harder than—"

"There's a Confederate boy dead down by the road," Mattie said in a sudden fit of nerves and remorse.

"They is?" The woman put down the towel and got up. "Whyn't yew say so? Bessie! Bessie!" The timid daughter reappeared. "Tell yore Paw tuh git down thar an' see whut thet soljur feller has on him. Might have some money," she said to Mattie as the girl ran back into the house.

"Ah done took keer of thet," the man called out from somewhere inside. "Done sent Sam down."

"He back?"

No answer. The woman smiled sweetly and conspiratorially at Mattie, as if to say *We women must tolerate them*. "Kum on," she said as she pulled herself up heavily. "We'll see whut's fer supper."

Dead bodies being picked . . . the eroded fields and bare yard and dirty towel, which the woman was now offering, if she cared to "warsh up"—the whole day crashed around her.

"Wal, I nevver."

She looked up into the woman's fat, worried, slightly amused face. "Ain't this a sight, now? Whut this gurl needs is some nurrishment."

She felt sturdy hands under her armpits hauling her into a chair, opened her eyes into the watery, colorless eyes of the woman, who was waving the dirty towel limply. With each pass stale sweat, as acrid as urine, stung her nose.

"I'm . . . fine. Thank you." She sat up to avoid more mothering.

Dinner was served in the kitchen: Indian peas and fat bacon, with cornbread slowly soaking up the pot liquor and grease. Although two little Negro girls stood in a corner, it was the daughter who served, and went back to the fire while they ate. The man said nothing, intent on his food. After a while the son came in, a thin boy of about fifteen. He, too, ate silently, his fingernails caked with mud.

"So whut did yew find?" the man said.

"Nuthin', Paw. An ole trunk with some dandified clothes. But them fellers wuz empty."

The man nodded with satisfaction, the stubble on his cheeks working as he chewed. He swallowed and said, "Ain't I done tole yew before? Ain't I now?"

"Yes, Paw." A Negro woman came in, who had evidently been working in the fields. She went to the fire and stirred the pot, and the daughter of the house took her place at the table.

"All soljurs is paupers," the man announced. "An' this here war . . . ain't nobody kumin' in here an' take mah hard-earned propurty frum me! Free the niggers? As hard as Ah've worked? Nosirree."

"Then you're for the Confederates?" It was Mattie's first try at conversation since she sat down. Maybe they wouldn't notice how little she ate.

"Ah ain't fer neither side!" The man swallowed, took a drink of coffee and swilled it around his mouth. "Durned fools!"

Buried behind his wife's tired, worn-out face lingered a shred of gentility which must have told her she should act the hostess. She looked at her company and smiled, revealing a row of yellow teeth and a space in front where two should have been. She addressed herself to her son, in semblance of politeness to their guest. "I done tole yore Paw menny a time Ah wisht we kud git rid of our niggers . . . vile, nasty, worthless things. But free 'em an' they'd think they's as good as white folks!"

Mattie looked at the Negro woman, whose face was as placid as a sphinx. From childhood she had been taught to mind her manners in front of servants . . . she remembered dear old Albert. "If you don't mind," she got out, and pushed back her chair.

"Don't feel well?" The man was suddenly solicitous. "Ah ain't even had a chanc't to ask yew where yore headed."

"Kingston . . ."

"Kingston, is it now?"

"Knoxville, actually . . ."

"Knoxville?" It was a chorus. Even the boy Sam looked up from his plate.

"How're yew gonna git acrost thuh Clinch?" the boy said.

"Shet up, boy," his father shot back, never letting his eyes leave Mattie, who seemed to have for him a new interest. "They's a ferry. Well, now. Kingston."

"If I could get a wagon . . . I've got money . . . I could get . . . There's a railroad. A train . . . for Knoxville."

"Well, now, thet's a might lot to ask," the man said. "Hit's a right smart piece to Kingston."

"I'll pay."

"How much?"

She had no idea. The leather pouch in her bun felt heavy against the back of her neck. "I'll give you five dollars," she said stoutly.

The man leaned back, laughing.

"Gold," she said.

He sobered. Propriety made him wait a minute. Then he patted his bare feet on the floorboards as a sign of satiety and pushed his plate aside. "Ah reckon we kin git yew to thuh ferry fer thet."

The square clapboard house had three rooms and a loft; a bed in a corner of the "parlor" told where the man and his wife slept. The outhouse was down a path to a cedar brake. On the way back from the kitchen Mattie excused herself and walked down to it. The moon had come out, throwing shadows in a moving breeze. The fat Yankee and Ward Burnette were still out there. The stench from the hole under her stung her nose and turned her fear to anger. Was this what her Morgan and his gallant men and Forrest and all the others were fighting for? Fighting and dying for? So this man with his stupid wife and dim-witted son could till these barren fields and brag about their niggers? But once outside the fresh air revived reality: just make it through this night, to Kingston tomorrow. The train, and Cousin Kate's. She climbed the stairs to the loft and lay down on a shuck mattress —a dirty sheet and a greasy pillowcase. She spread a handkerchief across the pillow and felt the bun again. She wouldn't take down her hair tonight.

When she came downstairs the next morning the woman was already on the porch fully dressed and fanning herself. The smell of coffee from the kitchen made the day seem brighter. "Red in thuh mawnin'," the woman said, pointing. "Rain later. Mebbe yew should stay another day."

A little Negro boy wearing himself out on the triangle interrupted her answer. She followed the woman into the kitchen, where pancakes were cooking on an iron griddle at the fire. The daughter was dipping more batter from the same basin the woman had used the day before. The Negro woman was presumably in the fields.

"Ah fergot tuh ask yew if'n yew wanted tuh warsh. up first," the woman said kindly when she saw Mattie look at the basin.

"No . . . that's quite all right. Where is Sam?"

"Hitchin' up," the man said. He came in and piled fatback and molasses on his cakes, cut them crosswise and talked with his mouth full. "If'n yew start now, Ah reckon yew'll git thar before sundown. Hit's well nigh thirty mile."

"Ah tole her she should stay another day," the woman said. "She ain't no trouble."

Her husband, at the head of the table, stopped chewing and grinned. "Kum on, now, woman. Cain't yew see this here little lady's got herseff a Rebel boyfriend? Else why would a lone woman be a-runnin' around thuh countryside like that?"

Mattie had had enough. In another half-hour she would be shed of this place, as the woman beside her would say. "I have a husband, sir."

The man laughed out loud, his eyes crinkling shut. "Hey, don't matter tuh me none, little lady." His breath came short. "Husband er boyfriend. Confederate er Yankee. In a hundert years, won't matter no more'n a rabbit's print in last year's snow."

She paid him before she left. He pocketed the money and stood spread-eagled in the road watching them until they were out of sight.

It was almost midnight before they reached the ferry. She had never seen such mountains, such roads. The horse lost a shoe and they stopped to find a smith. Then it stormed, and rivers of mud slithered down the ridges. The boy didn't talk much, only clucked at the horse now and then. She couldn't make out if he were sullen or shy, and after a while it didn't matter. Soaked to the skin, tired and hungry by the time they reached the river, she was feeling a little sullen herself.

The ferry had stopped running, of course. It was full night and the river was high. She would have to wait until morning. A small hotel for travelers squatted halfway up the nearest hill. She paid for Sam's room and her own, and forgot to notice if the sheets were clean that night. He was gone by the time she dressed, and the ferry was already making its second run. Once over, she bought a box lunch in Kingston and took the stage for Concord, where she could catch the train. When it rolled in on its cushion of steam she heaved a long sigh and groaned with relief when she took a seat. Then three miles out of Campbell's Station it broke down and the passengers found themselves trying to find shade to sit in by the track while they waited for another. The horseflies and bees were unmerciful, and a kindly mail agent invited her into the mail car. A young wounded soldier sat cross-legged in the corner, his shoulder in a bloody sling. She opened her box lunch and he in his turn took out a dirty rag and unfolded it to reveal two hardtack biscuits. He looked timidly toward her box and offered to swap her one or both for a bite of soft food. It was then she noticed the lower part of his face was swollen so badly she wondered how he could eat at all.

"Here," she said. "Take it all . . . no, I couldn't take yours. I'm not hungry, really. . . ."

He insisted that she take the biscuits, and to be kind she did, but couldn't force herself to touch one. He tenderly, almost lovingly tasted the light bread, but had to break off thin slabs of the chicken breast to get it past his broken teeth. How he could smile when he caught her watching him was more than she could understand. That toughness again. . . .

They waited five hours. She thought of Ward Burnette and the farm family, "Cinderella" as she had come to think of the daughter. It all seemed so far away. She had forgotten to look for a scout at the ferry, then remembered a young man waiting to one side on his horse who nodded to her when she got on. She had seen no sign of anyone since. She was entirely alone. The faint wail of the relief train in the distance stopped all thought. The passengers scrambled on. She didn't see the wounded soldier again, and let his biscuits drop by the track as she climbed up.

Cousin Kate was overjoyed, awed at the adventures and determined that she should have no more. "You'll stay with us," she said firmly.

There was Puss, the same hawk-faced Puss, looking and walking more mannish than ever. But she, too, was solicitous. Before the day was over they talked her into telegraphing Alice and Key to come to Knoxville. "Rather than travel down to Chattanooga . . . Atlanta . . . Augusta! Why it's out of the question," Puss said. Mentally, she was rolling up her sleeves, taking charge. Even little Charley, in her presence, seemed subdued. At seven he had lost—or had learned to control—a lot of his steam. He was, indeed, a beautiful child. He watched their visitor with his round blue eyes.

"Maybe I will have Alice come here," Mattie said.

The news of Morgan's capture reached Knoxville on the 28th of July, two days after Alice and Key arrived. Mattie fainted and Puss called the doctor. Alice and Kate took turns staying up all night.

"She can't go on like this without hurting the baby," said Kate. The doctor prescribed a sedative, and Mattie slept twenty-four hours.

She woke hollow-eyed and weak but determined to see General Buckner.

"I'll go!" said Key. "I should have been with them!" he reproached himself for the hundredth time.

"You've got a bigger job here," Alice reminded him, but watched him leave with a sigh: Mattie wasn't up to a visit to headquarters. They waited on the back porch. The white heads of a hydrangea nodded heavily in the heat. Charley was pumping a rope swing under a big tree, his turned-back toes scraping the grass. Prison. What did it mean? The penitentiary. Like a felon. The fiends! But rage only made Mattie's head throb, and with an effort she watched Charley. Back and forth, his blond head catching the sun. She twisted a handkerchief into a knot to keep from crying.

Key came back with no news. No news at all. "They seem to be waiting," he said, and didn't add: braced for anything. "General Buckner did say he would send a courier around with the first news he might have."

"Did you thank him?"

"Profusely."

But they all knew that Burnside, without Morgan to hold him back, was like a dog let loose from his leash—it was only a matter of time. Rosecrans now had the breadbasket of Middle Tennessee, as well as Nashville, and Bragg had retreated across the Tennessee River. If Chattanooga fell the whole lower South would be open. . . . Knoxville, a hundred miles northeast, would become an island.

"But Knoxville will be safe! You wait and see!" Puss kept saying.

The messenger from General Buckner—she would always be grateful for his remembering—came early on the morning of the 2nd of September. The Yankees were approaching Knoxville! Buckner had ordered an evacuation! So Burnside had made his move at last: twenty-five thousand Yankees against Buckner's five thousand.

"I don't know why you have to go!" Puss Ready whined.

Mattie brushed her cheek with her fingers. Dear Puss, under all that bluster. "We'll be fine. We're only doing what John had planned for us from the beginning—to go to his uncle T.H. in Augusta. That's where he will be looking for us when he returns."

"It's best to go now while the railroad to Chattanooga is still open," Key, trying to shut Alice's valise, reminded.

It was Murfreesboro all over again. The train was crowded with soldiers, whole families fleeing the Yankees. Kate and Puss had obstinately refused to leave. Kate's husband Ed came home that morning from his job on the railroad to drive them to the station. He was a kind man with a fringe of beard tracing his jawbone. He tried to bring his smile into his gray eyes under their bushy brows, but it wouldn't come. It lingered on his mouth, which kissed each of them in turn. "It hasn't been long enough," he said. "I didn't . . ."

"It won't be long!" Alice lied. "We'll all get together soon!"

They watched him from the train window, a small pudgy man lost in the thronging crowd. A cloud of steam from the engine obscured him totally, and then the wheels began to move. All the way into Chattanooga the car was bustling, some men standing up. When they pulled into the station they changed from the Virginia & Tennessee Railroad to the Western & Atlantic, with just enough time to go into a nearby hotel and get a quick meal. Again, the soldiers, many wounded, crowded on, headed for the hospitals in Atlanta. By this time the fatigue and stale air seemed normal, and Mattie almost dozed, with Alice's head on her shoulder.

All the windows were open to the heat and smoke. Three seats down a young woman in a green bonnet flirted with a Confederate major. There was something too new about his uniform, too indoor-pale about his face for the yellow cavalry facing on his collar. They bent their heads to a folded newspaper and threw themselves back in laughter. The girl's bonnet was straw . . . good straw, not Confederate plaited willow bark. Mattie hated her instantly! Then just before Atlanta two Confederate officers boarded the train, spoke quietly with the Major and escorted him off.

"Yankee spy!" whispered Alice.

"I thought you were asleep! Do you think so? Really?"

Atlanta! They were pulling into Atlanta, the citadel of the South! She wished she could see Tommie, and said so.

"For all we know . . ." Alice said, looking out the window as casually as she could, to cover her anxiety. She *had* to get Mattie settled in Augusta before the baby came! She cleared her throat. "For all we know," she said more firmly, "she may have moved. . . ."

They spent overnight in a miserable railroad hotel near the tracks and caught the first train out the next morning. Mattie would always remember the smell of stale bodies and the roll of the wheels. Before they left they wired T.H. and settled back to watch purple-red Georgia cotton fields pass their window.

Augusta was bustling. T.H. met them with a hired carriage, and they had a view of the Savannah River before they turned a corner into his street. The fresh air was delicious, and his words came in fitfully. His wife was looking forward to their visit. And Anna Frances. When they met Mary Hunt and "Nannie" and had settled into their rooms, T.H. told them quietly: Young Tom Morgan was dead. Just before John crossed the Ohio.

"Oh, my God . . . !"

"Alice! Alice, darling!" Mattie looked wildly to Mary Hunt. "Get some . . ."

Without a word, smelling salts appeared. Alice, on the window seat, her head in Mattie's lap, gasped at the sting, opened her eyes and turned her head into her sister's skirt. Mattie cradled the shaking shoulders and only then allowed herself to cry. Oh, what must he have felt, trying to hold his men together, fighting the damned Yankees, dealing with his grief! How he loved Tom! That sweet, happy face. "Cheer, Boys, Cheer . . ." She squeezed her eyes and opened them to see Key staring past her like a madman.

"Oh, Key! Oh, Key!"

T.H. stepped forward and took the boy in his arms.

Thank God they were in Augusta! It was, for Key, like being home. T.H. and Mary and Nannie helped him over the rough spots. Hopemont came back—Christ Church—Tom in the choir, Tom riding with him at the Leestown farm. After a week Key could tell Alice about those times without breaking into tears.

T.H. was a kind old man. The family loved him so, admired him for his loyalty, his devotion. His bravery at Stones River. Above all his gentle ways, his love of his men . . . the Orphan Brigade. Her Morgan had told her how T.H. had become his second father, and she could understand it. Yet, as the weeks went by a strange resentment set in, in spite of his kindness. He'd told John he'd lost everything, but his wife had taken enough with her from Lexington to set them up in Augusta. And even his devotion to the Cause had been exposed when he'd resigned. If he had been some poor private he would have been hanged for his "resignation"—like Asa Lewis at Murfreesboro. They had another word for it when you were a private. Underneath it all Mattie suspected he was just plain tired . . . or scared.

Or spoiled. His wife catered to his every whim, and his daughter wasn't much better. As for financial arrangements, she and Alice insisted on paying board, and her money was dwindling. Augusta had one of the big hospitals, and Key and Alice offered their services and were busy. But she stayed home, nervous and pregnant, listening to all the glories of Hopemont as if it were some Valhalla somewhere. The fact that she had thought of it exactly in the same way for so long didn't help, but only exposed that dream for what it was. Her Morgan was in a penitentiary, treated like a criminal, and all these people could do was brag about the old days. And Kitty. How brave she was, to be following A.P. around. Well, what about Mattie Ready? Nobody, it seemed, who wasn't a Hunt or a Morgan, mattered. She was bitterly disappointed, and more alone than ever. When Alice came in from a good day, satisfied that she had helped some poor soul write a letter or die or get through another twenty-four hours, Mattie could have screamed. What about *her* soldier? She had a letter from him, finally. He knew she was taking care of herself. Taking care! If only he knew how miserable she was! She went to church as her only solace, and met a kind lady from Danville, Virginia, a Mrs. Withers, who invited her to come live with her. "We have an absolutely huge house," Tassie Withers said. "My husband and sons are away fighting this dreadful war. It would do me good to have some company for a change. Oh, do come. . . ."

She accepted, Alice reluctantly. Key refused to leave. He had found work at the hospital, and when Uncle T.H. and Aunt Mary agreed that he should stay, it was settled. The Ready girls, after appropriate apologies, used the excuse that Danville would be closer to Richmond, where the General would probably report when they released him. Yes, it would be better. Mattie sighed a secret relief the day they boarded the train.

It was another of those Southern railroad trips: Branchville, where they would catch the South Carolina Railroad into Columbia, then the Charlotte & South Carolina line into Charlotte, where the North Carolina Railroad would take them to Greensboro and into Danville. Through all these changes Alice was her bright, cheerful self. Under the charm of Tassie Withers, who was an independent Southern lady down to her toenails, Mattie relaxed. It was almost in a holiday mood that they arrived at the Withers's substantial house on a high bank overlooking the Dan River. Danville was just across the North Carolina border, only a little more than a hundred and twenty-five miles from Richmond.

Mattie felt immediately at home. Mrs. Withers gave a dinner for her guests. Partridges and claret, ducks and olives, oysters. "There's life in the old country yet!" Mrs. Withers smiled.

Alice was less happy. "You have the baby to think of. Taking care of yourself. I've become so used to the wounded . . . I miss my hospital. Key writes that he's so useful. . . ."

"If you want to go back to Augusta . . ."

Alice bent her head and bit her lip.

"No, I can't leave you. Mrs. Withers is kind, but she is not kin. No. I'm staying."

Chickamauga. Alice rushed to the depot, looked on the lists of dead and wounded posted. *Lieutenant Horace Ready*. Dear Brother! No! She rushed home. "Wounded. Name with the wounded. I've got to go. Got to go . . ."

"How do you know where he will be sent?"

"He'll go to the big hospital in Atlanta. There's no doubt."

"Maybe T.H. can get him transferred to Augusta. Didn't you say he knew all the doctors?"

"Yes, yes. We can try." Then she squared her shoulders. "But I absolutely refuse to go and leave you alone."

"But I'm not . . ."

"We've talked about all this before. You need somebody. . . ."

"All right! But where in heaven's name am I going to find money for a servant?" At Alice's stricken face she added: "All right. I'll find it."

She had heard talk among the ladies about the sales of clothes. You couldn't get shoes now except from local Negro cobblers—bunions and corns! Mourning clothes brought outrageous prices, as much as five hundred

Confederate dollars for a dress with bonnet and gloves. Her mind went to the rose silk.

She sold it for six hundred dollars, payable in installments, and bought a young girl named Abby. She was simple, but willing.

"She smacks her mouth too much when she talks."

"Now Alice, nobody's perfect. She will do fine. Besides, her last mistress —a lady I met at church—told me she has helped with births before. She will be fine."

The need to be with Horace, if he could possibly be transferred to Augusta, overcame Alice's doubts, and Mattie and Mrs. Withers, with the Withers's old manservant carrying her valise, saw Alice off on the train.

"Wire me when you get there."

"I will! Take care of yourself!"

"I will!"

Mattie saw the train pull out with something like fear choking her chest. She went straight home and wrote another letter to Richmond. Because of pressure from the North since Gettysburg, a limited exchange had been started. Maybe, since it had been established that their Colonel Streight wasn't in the Georgia Penitentiary after all—but she had heard that, running out of the Streight excuse, they were using the capture of the Yankee General Neal Dow as the reason for new delay. The Northern press reported that Dow, in a Southern penitentiary, was being held as hostage for Morgan. Mattie besieged Richmond. She wrote to Secretary of War James Seddon and Colonel Robert Ould, the Prisoner Exchange Commissioner. Was it true that Dow was being held hostage for her husband? "I am confident," Ould answered, "that they would never agree to exchange your noble husband for any general of theirs whom we now have or may hereafter capture. They think him too great a prize and dread him too much in his liberated future. *The only hope seems to be for the Confederate authorities to refuse to make any special exchanges.*"

Mattie read the words over and over. Damn them! Did they mean to do nothing? But he doesn't say the Yankees will refuse to make special exchanges, she told herself. When it suits them, she thought bitterly. And now Brother was wounded, and nobody cared! The Cause! A bunch of selfish people, each with his own ax to grind, as her father would say. And her father, her mother . . . what of them? She was totally, utterly alone. In spite of the kindness of Tassie Withers, alone.

Except for Abby. Alice had been right, of course. She did need someone. But it was purchased caring. What could it amount to? She took to spending days in her room, not even going down for meals, and to avoid more solicitous chiding, started redoing her wardrobe.

"Lordy goodness, yes." Tassie Withers smiled as she offered her a piece of lace to replace a torn bodice. "Why, I've turned all my poor old dresses inside out, upside down and sideways! If this war doesn't end soon we'll all be sewing them together and not caring if the colors match!"

Tactfully, she left the lace and her guest alone. Abby began carrying trays back as full as they came. Whole mornings were spent in tears, the needle in midair. Ould's letter was in shreds from reading and rereading. No, they didn't care . . . he could rot in prison for all they cared! And Brother wounded and Alice gone! Should she go back to Augusta? But the memory of T.H., so contentedly defeated, and his meek little wife and Anna Frances always talking about Lexington, Lexington as if they regretted leaving that hypocritical Kentucky that couldn't make up its mind until it was too late . . . that two-faced Kentucky talking out of both sides of its mouth. John Morgan had been a fool to think he could get support there! It was nothing but a Yankee puppet pretending to be "honorable"! Anger broke into more tears and then real depression set in. She saw no one and even the girl Abby was afraid, finally, to ask her mistress a question. She tugged at the knot in her red kerchief and let her lower lip hang like a horse's. Sometimes she would stand in the corner of the room—the shades were more often drawn now—watching this strange white woman and scratching herself under her armpits.

Finally Tassie Withers in desperation called the doctor, who came in dripping from a November rain. When he saw Mattie he prescribed Dover's Powders. "They will allow her to rest. I'm a firm believer in the body's rejuvenative powers," he said. "Let it rest and it will start its own rebuilding process." He turned to Abby. "The directions are written on this paper. Show them to your mistress and put in a glass of water what she tells you to. Do you understand?"

"Yassuh."

"That's fine." He turned to Mrs. Withers. "I'll call in tomorrow. Keep her warm. She doesn't need the croup on top of everything else."

After he left, Abby tore open the envelope and dumped the powder into a wine glass, filled it with water and handed it to her mistress. "Heah is dis medicine de doctah done lef'. Swallah it down, Missus, and you bes all well agin."

In the half-light of the bedroom, with rain drumming on the roof, Mattie sat up in bed and held the glass.

"Go on, now, Missus, drinks it down!"

Four hours later, when Mattie started tossing and screaming, the girl ran from the room and bumped into Mrs. Withers on the stairs.

"She done started screamin', Missus!"

"I can hear, girl, I can hear!" By the time Tassie Withers reached the bed Mattie's head was bathed in sweat and her distended stomach was rolling under the covers. Mrs. Withers's face turned white as she whirled to the girl. "Where is that medicine the doctor left?"

"She done took it all, Missus!"

"All? My God, where are the directions?"

"D'rections? I nevah seen no . . ."

Mrs. Withers flung on a shawl and ran the two blocks to the doctor's house herself. It was not quite dawn. He arrived wiping his face and pulling at his nose. "You say she must have taken it all?" he asked as they walked up the stairs.

Just inside the door, the girl Abby crouched. He pulled her into the hall and demanded: "How much of that medicine did you give your mistress?"

"Ah dunno, Mista. De powdah whut wuz in dat papah. . . ."

"My God!" The doctor threw up his hands. "There was enough opium in that package to kill a mule! You . . . here, you'd better get out of my way, girl, before I forget I have promised to save human life." He turned to Mrs. Withers. "I'm afraid we're in for a siege of it, my lady." He took off his coat, closed the door and went to work.

Her body fought, then resigned itself to a vise of pain. At first she waited in dread for the next contraction which slammed in from all sides and held. Admonitions to relax between, or breath with your mouth, or try to keep from bearing down . . . none did any good, until the overwhelming need to press, press, press, to rid herself of the weight and the burden . . . the heads by the bed blurred, her own feet, strapped to the bedposts, the light at the window, the wet cloth across her eyes . . . blurred, blurred into one great scream, one great opening of her body which at last, at last obeyed. . . .

For ten hours she fought. Tassie Withers sent a message to the telegraph office for Alice to come immediately. In Augusta T.H. found her at the hospital and they went directly to the depot. Alice boarded the train and sat wringing her hands, staring round-eyed at the countryside, seeing nothing. Mattie, Mattie. Dearest. I should never have left you, my dear, darling, sweet Sister! Never, never . . . The train was choked with soldiers and the air was stifling, but she noticed none of it. Merciful Father be with her and sustain her. . . .

It was the 14th of November. Mattie Morgan's stillborn baby girl lay cold and unmoving, awaiting burial.

51

There was no time for anything other than that brief glance, that bitter laugh. Basil, with the others, was marched to the first steel stairs that led to the upper cells. One by one they were halted in front of a heavy door that slammed with a bang. Basil was stopped on the third level, and as he faced that bare space with its iron bunk and night bucket—the whole cell couldn't have been more than three and a half by seven feet—the stone weight of the Ohio Penitentiary came down on him.

The windows to the prison yard ended at the second level. From here he looked out on a blank brick wall and the alley below. He half-expected some whispered greeting, but the guards were close by, on special duty, perhaps, for the newcomers, and the rule was that talking or communication of any kind was strictly forbidden. The stench of stale urine, dusty concrete and damp brick invaded. No food was served on that first day, of any kind.

This end of the building must have been reserved for Morgan's men, whose cells were as closed as tombs. At the other end, about seven o'clock, he heard a steady, rolling tramp of feet. A military step, and then a scrambling trot; a military step and then a scramble: You could tell when they reached the stairs. When each one entered his cell, that banging, clanging, slide and thump of bolts. Then silence, total silence, except for the occasional bark of a dog somewhere. Basil turned on his bunk, a hard pad, one blanket. He curled up like a fetus, intent on hearing one human sound. A cough, then nothing again. He had just dozed when a lantern was swung close to the bars and into his face. It swung away, with absolutely no sound. He watched the brick wall and saw the lantern's reflection move, then descend. The man must either wear slippers, or be a cat! Every two hours he came, until Basil, no longer caring, fell asleep.

The next morning the newcomers were marched into the prison yard where two big hogsheads stood filled with water, each with its attendant, a big Negro convict. Against a far wall a man in a chair sat watching the proceedings. The men were stripped and one by one made to stand in the hogsheads, where they were scrubbed down with stiff horse brushes. Any sound of protest only made the bristles dig deeper. After the fifth man the water was black, and Colonel Smith remarked wryly that he thought it had done quite enough for health and deserved a change. But he stepped in, Richard Morgan into the other. Richard gave a cry when the bristles hit his wound, and the man eased the scrubbing a little, for which Richard sent him a look of thanks.

Then the man in the chair rose. He was the barber.

Heads bare as spittoons. Delicately cared-for mustaches, gone. Colonel Smith's patriarchal beard, which had swept to his waist, now lay about his feet in shreds. As they pulled on their clothes, Basil tried to make light of it by expressing surprise at the features of Smith's face never seen before, but the answer that greeted this remark sent him back into the hall like a reprimanded schoolboy.

There, there they were, waiting for the trip to "breakfast." There they were! What a reunion they had, under the eyes of the guards who watched over them night and day . . . Cal and Roy Cluke and John Morgan . . . Hart Gibson, who had taken Maginis's place after the murder, and Major Steele and Sam Taylor, Tom Hines, Ben Drake. They caught up on news, pumping Drake's hand and slapping Sam Taylor on the back. The Cincinnati jail—only Morgan and the men captured in Salineville were given the more choice quarters in the cellar.

"Compared to those," grumbled Hines, "the Augean stables were French boudoirs."

Morgan was strangely silent. After he asked Richard about his wound he stood aside and watched the others. So many brave young men. Supporting each other with jokes. He had seen them watch the last fifteen Kentucky thoroughbreds auctioned off in front of Merion's stable. That was the only time, since the capture, that the mask of humor fell away.

Basil walked up and his general suddenly became animated. But he didn't talk about the capture, or Burnside, or exchange. Instead, he told him this was the East Hall. There were sixty-eight officers from the command here. The top tiers of the East Hall and the whole of the West Hall were reserved for convicts . . . that the noises Basil had heard last night were the convicts returning to their cells. That they ate twice a day and were allowed to exercise in the alleyway. Yesterday afternoon, when news of more Morgan men reached the warden, all the military prisoners were confined without benefit of exercise.

"Yes . . . we exercise in the alley—the doors are left open, and only closed at night. About seven o'clock you'll hear the tap of a key on the stove there at the end of the alley. That's the signal for the doors. To be closed."

Basil looked at him in wonder. Nothing about what had happened. Nothing about the outside world. Only these details about exercise, going to meals, the tap of a key. From a man with a bald, shaved head he hardly recognized.

"But we can read at night . . . till lights out. Candles are allowed for an hour after the gas is turned off. . . ."

To keep his sanity as much as to keep track of time, Basil scratched that day two marks in the brick of his cell wall.

The next morning Colonel Leroy Cluke was sent to McLean barracks on a trumped-up charge about violating an oath taken before he entered Confederate service. They heard later he was transferred to Johnson's Island.

"He'll like it," said Duke brightly, to cheer Morgan. "When we were there . . ." Then he stopped, under the eyes of the others, who knew about the lack of blankets.

"Ah, well, it's not so bad here." Cal, who seemed to keep a cold, coughed. "We can have candles for an hour after lights out . . ."

"Yes. I know."

It did seem, after the first ten days, that the rules relaxed. Mail was allowed, and then packages from home. When he finished reading his letter Basil handed it to his general. Tommie had a baby girl, named . . . Morgan's eyes blurred. Thomas Morgan Duke. "We'll call her Tommie," Tommie scribbled at the bottom of the letter. "But not for me. For Tom." Henrietta Morgan had forwarded the letter from Lexington.

"She came here, you know," Morgan said, clearing his throat.

"Who?"

"Ma. Three days after the surrender. Old man Hevay, the subwarden, told me she had traveled to Cincinnati to see Burnside and demanded to see us. Demand denied, of course." He looked up, and some of the old Morgan humor lit his eyes. "Can't you just see her? Queen Victoria glaring at Old Mutton Chops!" He stopped, then looked away. The love and fury that had sent her flying silenced him. Even though they hadn't seen her, even though her mission failed, they felt better just knowing she had tried.

Basil, too, settled into the routine. Food. Food from home! Pound cake— they had forgotten!—jams, jellies. A ham! Finally, so much flooded in from Kentucky that Merion stopped it, then used the packages piling on his desk for his own table.

They were, however, permitted to buy books. With his last silver Hines managed to get a copy of *Les Miserables*, not yet printed in English. Every evening, in the hall before the key tapped, some of the men asked for the latest translation. Hevay passed by, fascinated that Hines could read French. "All them words in his head . . . and him no bigger'n a fence post!"

Somebody obtained marbles and brisk games were held in the alley. Even better, Sam Taylor talked Hevay into letting him drag in a ladder from the prison yard to use for exercise. They ran up and down, did chin-ups, even handstands. But an underlying restlessness and nervousness, and sudden irritability grew.

"Chess . . . that's the answer! You don't know? I'll teach you!"

Crude handmade chessboards, with chips of wood to represent knights, queens, pawns balanced on knees. Someone bought a chess book, and it was soon dog-eared. Admiring audiences crowded around the antagonists, and the news would spread down the alley how Cicero Coleman had just checkmated Hart Gibson by a flank movement with his knight. . . . Foster Cheatham, one of Morgan's bright young captains, vowed to toast the winner. The next day, pleading ill health, he tried to bribe a guard for some whiskey. Scott heard of it, then Merion, and Cheatham was sent to the dungeon for twenty-four hours.

The dungeon. It had been a rumor until now. When Cheatham came back pale and shaken, and so bent he couldn't walk, they sobered.

Major Higley was next. A guard had shoved him. "Disrespectful" language was not permitted . . . and Higley spent a day in the "devil's hole."

An anonymous letter, picked up in the hall, ridiculed the guards. Cheatham, protesting innocence, was blamed, and spent another forty-eight hours in that slimy room green with mold, where a man could barely stand. The stench of the night bucket came back with him to linger for days.

Any of a dozen men could have written it. "A gentleman would confess," Morgan said softly to Basil as they walked to breakfast. They had just washed up—thrown water over their faces from basins on a board in the prison yard.

"We both know two or three—maybe four who wouldn't."

Morgan said nothing.

Days. The unreality, and then the accepted reality of the slop that passed for food, the alley, the iron-hard beds. Basil began to see how the outside world could disappear. You no longer smelled the stale sweat or the stench from the kitchen. You dipped your bread into greasy "soup" and forgot how to taste. The nights were worse. Time could pass at "exercise," reading or chess, but once the key tapped on the stove and doors clanged shut, time really began.

Once, in the prison yard, Morgan sent him that half smile, and Basil knew his general was surviving in the only way a man could: day by day, minute by minute.

Morgan could have told him not to wish too much for sleep. When nightmares didn't wake you screaming, daylight brought a reality you'd rather forget.

So much refused to go away. Shadeland came back. So much. And the boys who were gone. Hutch, and Manly, and Wash. And above all, above and beyond them all singing his sweet tenor, Tom. He wrote Mattie: *August 10, 1863. My Dearest. That day two months ago I parted from you . . . little did I think, My Dearest, that the separation would be for such a length of time, but My Darling you must bear up under it, like a soldier's wife and rest assured that as soon as I am released, I shall hasten to you. . . . Rec'd a box of clothing from Mother yesterday . . .*

I was surprised they let me have it. No, he couldn't say that.

. . . and a long letter, a great portion of it being devoted to you, My Sweet Wife. I know you are taking care of yourself. Know also how much I love you.

It all sounded so stilted. Frighteningly, when he admitted it, she already seemed unreal. He began reading her prayer book every night before the gas lights were ordered out, and then by candle when he could find one. The rhythm of the liturgy more than the meaning evoked her face.

August 12, 1863. If I only knew that you were in good health I would be much better reconciled. . . .

August 17, 1863: Mother sent an elegant pound cake and fine baked ham. So you see My Precious One we are getting along bravely.

He couldn't tell her Merion confiscated everything.

. . . Get a great number of letters from our friends in Kentucky, but would sacrifice every pleasure and comfort to get a single line from My Lovely Mattie. It would be a treasure.

Did that reveal exasperation? He hadn't heard a word from her! Surely she could write! Or had his own letters gotten through?

That afternoon, in the middle of their antics on the ladder, Scott bellowed abruptly. They had visitors.

They filed out of their cells to watch a contingent of prisoners who had just come into the hall. Scotty was there, and old Hevay, and for the occasion Merion made his appearance. It was a scene from a day they would all remember. Morgan, who had come up almost last, stood by Cal and looked past a dozen shoulders at Tom Webber.

"Dick McCann!" Cal whispered out of the corner of his mouth. "I'll be . . . and Ralph Sheldon! And Jacob Bennett . . . Merriwether . . ."

"And Charlton," Morgan said so quietly Cal had to look again.

"By God it is! Charl! Charl!"

Merion turned his sour face toward them and Cal straightened and suddenly became a model prisoner. "Charl, I can't believe it," he said under his breath, his mouth still screwed sideways.

As soon as they could they gathered around in one great back-slapping reunion. "Charl! You look great! Why was Ma so worried?" He had been transferred from Douglas to Camp Chase. And immediately their elation at seeing him faded before the knowledge that coming from Chase to Columbus was close to moving from a mansion to a pigsty.

They had little time to talk: Scotty broke up their little gathering with orders for the "bath and haircut." The newcomers were assigned to the fourth range. Bennett, Sheldon and Merriwether had been transferred because they had tried to escape. As soon as they could, before the call to supper and lights out, they answered a hundred hurried questions.

"Chase wasn't that well guarded," Sheldon said matter-of-factly. "And we would have made it, except for those dogs. If we'd have waited for a rainy night, they would've never found our scent. . . ."

He winked over at Morgan. A stab of hope: why not here?

"When they asked me why I did it," Sheldon said with a grin, "I told them it was their business to keep me, but my business to get away."

"From what I can see," Smith mumbled hoarsely—he was still angry at losing his beard—"we've got enough Morgan men to do a good job of it here."

It was almost unbelievable. McCann, Bennett, Sheldon, Charlton, Richard, Cal, Basil . . . together again. And together, if they could keep up their spirits, they could survive.

The next day, September 1, the Morgans were called into the hall, then ushered into another room with a wire grating at one end.

"Your mother . . . and your sister," Scotty mumbled, and stood against a wall.

Sister! But Tommie was in Atlanta, and Kitty . . . The visitors were not allowed to speak. They stood on the other side of the screen. He had forgotten she was so small. He would never forget her eyes. Cal came over first, to stand beside him, then Richard, then Charlton. She lifted a white-gloved hand to her face when she saw Richard limp. Then the hand went down. The girl beside her was Delphine O'Brien.

In the silence, a shifting of feet, but from Henrietta Morgan not a sound.

"That's enough," the guard called out.

"What do you suppose . . . ?" Charlton whispered when they were back in the alley.

"They're up to something." Cal looked at Charlton and winked, then bent to his cough.

The next day Morgan requested some medicine for Cal. He was refused.

Newspapers were strictly forbidden, but once in a while, if the news was bad for the South, Merion allowed one to be brought by the cells. Scotty, who usually delivered, was delighted whenever he could announce disaster. Burnside took Knoxville on September 2, and some of Buckner's troops, cut off, surrendered Cumberland Gap on the 9th without a fight.

Gloom settled on the faint hope Henrietta's visit had stirred. East Tennessee, that wedge into the whole lower South—lost! Bragg had to hold now at Chattanooga! He had to! Morgan folded the paper before handing it on to the next man. Well, you kept the Yankees busy as long as you could.

If he could only just get out of this hell hole and do something! And Mattie! Nothing from Mattie! Thank God she had gone to T.H., who would take care of her!

The men grumbled, then argued. Anything to irritate, as if irritation made them feel alive. Napoleon's mistakes at Waterloo, the height of General Joe Johnston, the number of Yankees killed at Bull Run. Boredom won.

> September 13: Another week has passed, my darling wife, without anything from you. I look eagerly forward to each day to bring a sweet missive but it is almost hoping against hope, for I am aware of the great difficulty of getting letters through. I have written you fourteen.

Peevish! Blaming! With a swift pen he dashed words across the page:

> It would be useless for me to attempt My Darling Mattie to describe the great pain that this lengthened separation from you gives me, and but for the consolation that hope affords, I would indeed be most miserable. But you know, My Beautiful One, that by nature I am blessed with good spirits and look at the bright side of everything. But for the uncertainty of your condition, I could bear this incarceration with a much greater degree of stoicism. Farewell my darling. 10,000 blessings accompany this. Think of me often and know that my entire devotion and love are all yours.

> September 16: Colonel Duke is in good health and brags a great deal on his fine "boy." But he had better look out. I think his superiority over all others will be short-lived.

"Why doesn't she write?" he broke out to Cal the next day. An hour later, to his joy, an envelope was delivered to him. When he saw the handwriting he almost tore it from the man's hand. The guard waited, then guffawed. It was empty.

"Damn Merion!"

"What did you say?"

"Nothing," said Cal, who had no taste for the dungeon.

Cal would, as it turned out, be a guest there soon enough. It was Hevay, a kind old man who was trying to cheer them, and a Confederate victory which cast Cal's caution away. After mail call one day Hevay stopped him and offered him an old newspaper. It was dated Sunday, July 5, just after Gettysburg.

"Maybe you can find something interestin' in it," Hevay said softly.

Cal thanked him and returned to his cell, wondering why he had bothered to give him this paper—he had seen it before. THE MIGHTY BATTLE AT GETTYSBURG LEAVES 51,000 CASUALTIES; WHAT NEXT, LEE? STACK ARMS AT VICKSBURG. PEMBERTON WINS PAROLE FOR MEN. . . . He let it drop to the floor and lay down on his bunk. The cough cut into his chest and he doubled up, then let his body ease out again. God, if he could ever feel warm! He dozed, and woke to the sound of the jailor's key, the slamming of doors. Only a few minutes now until lights out. He used his bucket, then returned to the bed. He sat down, pulled off his boots—the soles were almost gone—then stood up to take off his clothes. One of the boots had pushed aside the front page of the paper. Another date, with a September heading, lay underneath. Cal reached down, picked up the paper to find, sandwiched in the middle section, a paper dated Sunday, September 20.

FEDERAL ARMY IS FORCED BACK: DIGGING IN AT CHATTANOOGA.

Chattanooga? What was this?

> Chattanooga, Tenn.—With the retreat of Gen. W. S. Rosecrans' federal army to this town, the Battle of Chickamauga Creek was concluded on Sunday last as a Confederate victory.

Confederate victory? CONFEDERATE VICTORY??? He suppressed a yelp and read on. The gas went out and he lit the stub of a candle.

> The tide of battle turned late last Sunday afternoon, when Gen. James Longstreet, commanding Bragg's left wing, broke through a gap created in the federal line by a confusion of orders. The federal right was held staunchly by Gen. G. H. Thomas, aided by men under Gen. Gordon Granger. . . .

He swallowed a whoop, his hands shaking.

> Though Confederates were dropped as flies, they continued to overwhelm Union positions. Federal units collapsed, despite all that generals such as Philip Sheridan could do to stem the furious assaults. . . .

He didn't hear the signal they sent down the cells to tell of the approach of the "Cat Man," the detested night guard, who was shining a lantern through the bars.

"What have you got there? What paper is that?"

"Come in and see."

"No. You must pass it to me."

"I'll do nothing of the kind. If you think I have a paper that was smuggled in, why not unlock the door, come in, and get it?"

Even with his chest cold, Calvin Morgan was no man to grapple with, and the guard left for reinforcements. Cal quickly stepped to the rear wall, which did not, as they first supposed, back up to the other row of cells, but to a ventilator shaft that ran from floor to ceiling, with openings to each cell. He rolled the September paper and stuffed it up the shaft as far as his arm could reach.

The guard came back with Scotty. They found Cal casually reading the July paper in exactly the same position as before. "Now give me that paper," the guard blurted, obviously for the benefit of his superior, who spread his legs and glared.

"There it is," said Cal casually. "Old man Hevay gave it to me today."

The guard looked at it by the light of his lantern.

"Why didn't you give it to me before?" he whined, with a glance at Scotty.

"Because I thought you had no right to ask for it, and I had no assurance that you would give it back."

But Scotty, unconvinced, moved to the back of the cell and ran his arm up the ventilator shaft. His belly bumped the wall. He strained, pinching his face. The hand came down empty.

"Well, see that you give me what I ask for in the future," the guard was saying, again for his superior's benefit, "or the dungeon will reveal to you some secrets that will never get into print." He reached over and blew out Cal's candle. Except for the lantern, bouncing light down the alley, darkness moved in.

Cal waited until their footsteps faded. Then, against all regulations, which strictly forbade talking after lights out, he called to the next cell: "Chickamauga Creek! We beat the Yankees at Chattanooga! Breakthrough . . . bloody repulse . . . Pass it on!"

It ran like wildfire. Up and down the tiers, through bars, hands reached out, voices rose, even night jars banged on floors. A wild clamor seized East Hall. For fifteen minutes Mardi Gras, Christmas, the Fourth of July—it was all there, one glorious yelping, yelling sound.

The guardhouse emptied and uniformed men ran everywhere. Up the narrow metal stairs, over the balconies, their sticks striking the barred doors and adding to the din.

A half-hour later Cal, Basil Duke, Captain Jacob Bennett and little Lieutenant John Bowles, who had been particularly exuberant, were marched to the warden's office. Merion, sour from being disturbed, nodded toward Scotty, who marched them off to another office where, one by one, they stood before him as he fondled a paperweight on his desk.

Cal was first. To a question about the newspaper, which he answered truthfully—it was dated July 5 and given him by Hevay—Scotty nodded to a guard who twisted his arm behind him. When he was asked again and gave the same answer, the guard kicked him in the groin. As Cal came up with a gasp the question was asked again, and again the same answer, and again the kick. "Strip the damned horse thief," said Scotty, and stood up and paced the room until it was done. "Now examine him."

"No!"

The word was barely out of his mouth when a knee was planted, low, in his back. He sank in a half-faint, and after the examination felt himself dragged from the room. "Next!"

Then Cal saw the dungeon, and knew what the others were talking about. On a lower level, on the stairs, before they reached the heavy iron door, he heard a high cry. They must have John Bowles, he thought. Goddamn their souls! The door banged and he sank in the stench, coughing.

They had shoved his clothes at him in a bundle and he pulled them on now, to avoid having to lay them on the wet stones. It was pitch-black, and the sheet iron nailed to the door on the outside extended at least six inches on either side: There was not a breath of air. He bumped his head and remembered that the room had been designed so that a man couldn't stand up. Or lie down, evidently, for when he groped for the dimensions, his hand struck the night bucket, which tilted and spilled some of its contents across his arm. He went back to the door again and tried to crouch, but the pain in his lower back and across his groin was excruciating. Don't faint. Cough, cry, do anything, but don't faint.

When they were released the next afternoon exercise at the ladder stopped and the others watched silently as they stumbled toward their cells. Lieutenant Bowles, as he passed his general, stopped briefly. "They'll never . . ." He almost choked and went on: "They'll never . . . do that to me again!"

He was close to tears. He couldn't be twenty, Morgan thought. He had joined Company C to be with his brother James, but Lieutenant-Colonel Bowles had been left behind in Tennessee, with a wound picked up skirmishing near McMinnville. Young Johnny had his brother's spirit. His words still cut the air: They'll never do that to me again. Morgan nodded an unblinking agreement and watched the boy's shoulders straighten.

Things did seem—they all agreed as they washed up at the basins in the prison yard—worse since Chickamauga. There was no mail at all now, censored or otherwise. The next day, as a test, Tom Webber tried to get a letter out. It was confiscated, and Webber, still weak from dysentery, was sent to the dungeon. When he came out twenty-four hours later, the "Iron Man" was as limp as a rag. Silently, they watched him being helped to his cell.

They marched off to supper. Besides bedcheck at night, the only time roll was taken was at meals. If a man failed to appear his cell was searched. Morgan stared down at his bowl and then up at the rows of his men seated at the two-foot-wide tables. A few ate. Most stared ahead. Where was Johnny Bowles? The barking of dogs. A shot rang out.

They heard later. Scotty bragging in the hall, the guards nervously nodding and grinning. Lieutenant Bowles had made it over the first low wall, but was shot running across the yard toward the outer one. What did he think? He could scale a wall twenty-five feet high?

Lieutenant John Bowles. That day in Hartsville, when he walked up wanting to join. In August, a year ago. One of so many . . . gallant, brave. He took for granted.

"Did you hear what he said?" Tom Hines whispered as Morgan passed on his way to his cell. "Outer wall twenty-five feet. . . ."

He went to bed that night seeing it all: the low wall in the yard toward the town side, then another prison yard, then the high wall with its sentry boxes and dogs. And John Bowles. Running. Then . . . the shot. *They'll never do that to me again.* Where would they bury him? In their prison cemetery? Exchange was a joke. And escape hopeless. Unless . . . no, hopeless.

The next morning, as a precaution, Morgan was moved from the ground floor to the second tier.

"Do they think I'll escape?" he said wearily.

Old man Hevay looked at him with a trace of pity. Then he told him Colonel Roy Cluke had died on Johnson's Island. Diphtheria.

Alone, and shivering. Without a blanket and the wind whipping off Lake Erie. Dear Cluke! Dear old dependable Cluke. *There had to be a way.*

"There is," said Hines over chess in his cell that afternoon. In the alley some of the boys were pretending to exercise on the ladder—none of them had the heart for it—and Morgan wondered why Tom had insisted on this chess game. Hines studied the board and lifted his eyebrows and looked at Morgan without moving his head. "I found out something very interesting yesterday."

"What?"

"I was reading . . . for a change I sat on the floor by the door. Then I noticed how dry the floor was. It's on the same level as the ground, and yet it's dry! That means *it's not on the ground,*" Hines hissed.

Morgan shook his head as if rejecting a move.

"Where do you suppose that ventilator shaft gets its air?" Hines asked softly, but the excitement made his hand tremble.

"You've been reading too much Hugo," Morgan smiled.

"Precisely! That air has to come from somewhere. Suppose there were an air chamber running under these cells?" His eyes drifted to old Hevay lounging on a chair in the alley. "Let's ask him." They slipped the board from their knees, got up and walked over.

"The General here won't believe me," Hines pretended an argument.

"About what? Don't you Rebs have ennythin' to do except fight?"

"I told him you would know. I told him if there was anything about this building, you would know."

"Well, now I do fancy I know a little about this place."

"We were just sitting in there playing chess . . ."

"That's right. I saw you. Who won? Did you let him beat you again, General?"

"We noticed how dry the floor was, and I kept telling him it must be dry for some reason."

"Why, that's true! A regular tunnel runs under the cells."

"But why?" Morgan pretended to be patiently waiting for wisdom.

"Why, for the air that goes to the ceiling. Now you boys see how the State of Ohio cares for the health of its inmates? I tell you this is the best penitentiary east of the Mississippi."

"Can't be too many west of it," Hines grinned, and the old man guffawed. They had their answer.

"We've only got to dig to it. Don't you see?"

Hines was hanging upside down on the ladder, his head away from the guards. Morgan, pretending to chin himself, looked down at Hines's upside-down face and almost laughed. He dropped to his feet and Hines rolled over, springing up like a cat. He brushed himself off and said out of the corner of his mouth: "Under my bunk. Just big enough for a man to slip through."

But they would need tools. The floor was concrete over brick. How thick it was they didn't know. And the cells were swept out every day by guards. It seemed hopeless. "Wait a few days," Morgan said.

On the last day of October he wrote a letter to General Mason, commandant of the district, complaining of the lethargy of his men, the lack of exercise which contributed to their depression. He mustered the most courteous phrases, reminding the General that his men were gentlemen, professionals deserving the status of prisoners of war, and not felons.

The guard he entrusted the note to was a boy who had looked sorrowfully at some of the inmates when they were returned from the dungeon. Morgan held him in conversation a few minutes more, and gained a quasi-promise that he would also get a letter out to the General's mother in Lexington. He had just been drafted and was due to be sent South to the front and asked the General, in turn, if he could give him a note saying that Morgan's men had been treated well in Ohio. "In case I need it," the boy said, blushing.

"Tomorrow. You shall have both," Morgan promised.

He had his answer from General Mason on November 3: "It is not a part of my military duty to require more than your safe confinement in the Ohio Penitentiary, giving you as far as practicable all the privileges of prisoners of war."

That same day a Sergeant Moon was assigned as their "prison steward." An Indiana farmboy a little in awe of his charges, Moon let it be known his orders were to keep his prisoners, not punish them. Morgan, in turn, expressed his gratitude, and asked politely if the Sergeant had received any instructions concerning the cells. "Then you won't mind if we clean our own? Give us a little exercise."

"Fine with me, sir."

And mail? When the Sergeant said mail would be allowed, Morgan wrote another quick note to Henrietta, brief and not too explicit, but with a reference to the need of money. How much good it would do, or how she would get any to him, he had no way of knowing.

Tools. Those cutoff iron knives they ate with—made deliberately blunt to keep them from being used as weapons. Perfect chisels. But how to get them from the dining room? Impossible. Unless . . . yes. They were brought to the cells. Cal was sick, and truly not much better. And Webber.

If he could raise a ruckus with Merion, using the same arguments he had in the letter . . . military prisoners of war, not criminals . . . and now with Sergeant Moon's presence to reinforce that position . . . maybe, just maybe they could get food sent to their cells.

It worked. With Hines reading near the door, Jim Hockersmith and Sam Taylor played chess in the back of Hines's cell—when they weren't digging. Hines became a model prisoner, sweeping his cell often.

But the floor was harder than granite. After two hours Taylor's hands were raw from the square handle of the knife, and Hockersmith, a big man who had been a stonemason, had only a handful of concrete chips in his pocket to show for their labor. Besides, the prison guards were used to seeing all the faces in the alley: Any absence, even with the excuse of chess, might draw suspicion. Hines came up with a schedule: two men to dig for an hour, relieved by two more. They could get in, he figured, five hours a day. Hockersmith shrugged his massive shoulders. Sam Taylor, to cure his hands, was given the next day off. Hines, finished with *Les Miserables*, started reading *The Decline and Fall*.

Cal Morgan and Tom Webber were still ill, and knives were replaced. As a precaution, Morgan became chummy with Scotty. Proud of being a trusty, Scotty described the promotion system in the prison. Morgan hinted that if one day he were released he would certainly attest to Scotty's devotion to duty. The chess game in Hines's cell went on.

The wonders of the Roman Empire absorbed Hines so much that he seldom exercised on the ladder. He had worked out a system of signaling: one tap to start work, two to stop, three imminent danger. When he saw a guard coming toward Cell Number 20, three taps would send the men back to chess. If there was no time to tap Hines would start humming. "The Old Crow Crossed the Road" was a favorite. If a guard came up and lingered too long asking what that story was all about anyway, Hines's old training as a teacher came in handy. He overwhelmed the man with details of the Roman Constitution in the age of the Antonines, or the virtues of Alexander Severus, or the state of Persia after the restoration of the monarchy by Artaxerxes . . . and drove the man away with boredom. By the end of the reign of Claudius the place in the chipped-out floor measured fourteen inches across, and Hines swapped a pair of socks with a convict for an old black carpetbag, which he kept casually under his bed to hide their "excavation." The next afternoon Hockersmith mouthed silently as he passed him: *We're through the concrete.*

The six layers of brick, which formed the arch of the air chamber, although eighteen inches thick, were held together by old mortar soft enough to be worked loose. Jacob Bennett and Ralph Sheldon had the first shift, Sam Taylor and Gus Magee the second. Knives wore out, snapped off. Hines looked toward his mattress, where concrete chips humped and poked like some Asian torture. Tonight wouldn't be exactly the sleep of the gods. Hockersmith and Ben Drake's turn was next. It must have been in the reign of Diocletian that it happened.

It was about two o'clock in the afternoon, November 5. Hockersmith was digging, Ben Drake at the chess board. Hockersmith's knife suddenly found a weak spot in the mortar and slipped. He worked it back and forth and felt through the blade. At the blunt end: nothing! He had reached the chamber! Quickly he worked the knife sideways, the old remembered muscles in his stonemason's arm coming into play. As softly as he could, he lifted the first brick away. Then the second. Holding his breath for fear they would make too much noise, he let them slip through the hole. Two dull thumps on damp earth told him the chamber must be at least high enough for a man to stand in—or almost. Too excited to do more, he replaced the carpetbag and passed Hines in the doorway. "You can get rid of your lumpy mattress tonight," he mumbled, pointing to Gibbon as if they had been talking about the Romans.

That night Hines, after lights out and between visits of the Cat, slipped back the carpetbag and noiselessly moved his bunk. With the chess board he pushed against a row of crumbling bricks, and they fell away. Again: two more. With his heart in his throat he tied one end of his blanket to a leg of the bed and let the rest drop into the hole. Then he stuffed the stub of a candle in his pocket and thanked his mother for making him small. He lowered his bare feet into the cold air of the chamber and dropped. Overhead the blanket dangled. He struck a match and lit the candle. Its flame blinded him at first until he held it away from him and peered into the dark. He walked to the end one way: a stone wall. Then the other: a grating! But no light shone through. Was it an old opening bricked or stoned over? He walked back, this time measuring his stride. The chamber must be twenty feet long, but the building was forty feet wide, which meant only the grating end led outdoors; the other end was under the building. That grating puzzled him. He would have to show it to Hockersmith.

He had lost all sense of time. A sound upstairs made his heart almost stop. The Cat? He blew out the candle, grabbed the blanket and pulled. The bed gave a little, scraping against the floor, then hung onto a rough place in the chipped concrete. He pulled himself through and quickly replaced everything. Oh, Lord! He forgot to get rid of the Asian torture!

In quick whispers on the way to breakfast Hines told Hockersmith about the grating. "We'll see," Big Jim answered evenly. "At that end?" Hines nodded yes.

Luckily, it was wash day. As they were wringing out their drawers and shirts in the prison yard and hanging them up to dry, Hockersmith took extra trouble with his, choosing a place on the clothesline at the corner of the yard near the wall. As he peered up to hang a shirt straight he saw the reason no light came through that grating: A pile of coal had been dumped against the building on that side! When he went back to the kettle and dipped up another pair of drawers from the boiling suds, Hockersmith shook his head. "It'll have to be the wall," he whispered to Hines as he waved the hot drawers back and forth on the end of a stick to cool. Hines followed him over to a trough, where they spent some extra minutes rinsing and wringing.

"Hey, you there! Speed it up, will ya?" But before they could answer, the guard turned back to his buddies lounging against the sunny warmth of the wall.

An hour later Hines expressed no interest in exercise, complaining of a chill and saying he might even take a nap. "But you boys can play chess," he remarked casually to Bennett and Hockersmith, who made their way to Number 20. They passed the General in another conversation with Scotty, who hardly noticed their passing.

Once in the cell, with Bennett on the lookout and a blanket rolled up on the bunk to represent Hines, Hockersmith, followed by Hines, dropped through the hole. Hines lit his candle and led Hockersmith to the wall at the end of the tunnel. "Those stones must be three feet thick!" he whispered, his breath waving the flame as Hockersmith ran an expert hand over the mortar.

"This stone," Big Jim said. "Sharp point. Maybe we can work this one out first."

Hines looked at the massive blocks in despair. With those knives? It had been work enough chipping up a floor! Hockersmith shrugged, and they walked back to the hole just in time to hear Bennett's three taps. When the guard looked in, they were intent on chess and a nap.

Two days went by. They were at a stalemate. Hines began dreaming of that massive foundation wall. Even after they got through that—an impossibility—there would be solid ground to dig through. And they had no idea exactly how far over that coal pile lay. They would have to see that prison yard.

Morgan, well aware of the problem—he had taken a sudden interest in Gibbon—and enjoying the new cordiality shown him by Scotty, who was pleased that the arrangement under Sergeant Moon actually relieved his boys of some duty, found out quickly that one of the trusty's pretentions to glory was his knowledge of attempted escapes.

"You do say?" said Morgan, with a wink toward Hines. "And what was your most successful escape attempt, Scotty?" Hines drew Sam Taylor closer, as if to hear a good story.

"Why, I suppose that time them fool fellers tried to get outta them skylights." Scotty lifted his face to the smutty glass rectangles almost fifty feet overhead.

"That must have been incredible!" whistled Hines, looking up.

"It was!" Scotty looked at them expansively. "Why, them two fellers crawled up them catwalks like squirrels. I don't allow there's another set of durned fools as agile as them two in the whole country."

"Did they make it?"

"Got out onto the roof before we got 'em. But nobody has ever got out of here. Nossir. And that's not likely to be attempted ever again, ever. Unless a man's a monkey."

With a look toward Taylor and a lifted eyebrow Morgan said, "Why, I'll wager my prayer book that Captain Taylor, small as he is, can do it."

The look caught, and held. *They had to know in which direction to dig that tunnel. Here was a chance.*

Sam jumped forward. "Why, if you'll let me, sir, I'll show you I can climb up to that ceiling in nothing flat!"

"You'll break your durned fool neck!"

"No, I won't!" Sam begged. The others joined in. It became a point of honor that Scotty let him, or else they threatened not to believe his story.

"All right, all right. But I've got my eye on you every second. No funny business."

Sam with a grin sprang up the first two flights of stairs, stopped at the second railing to wave at them, then scrambled up the fifth and topmost tier. From there his slight body took on the antics of a spider. Cautiously, with one foot feeling after the other, he balanced on the last rail and took a breath-stopping jump over three feet of empty space to grab a crossbar. Then he pulled himself onto the sill of the skylight, looked out, and waved back. They cheered, then held their breaths again as he dropped back over that empty space to the rail and made his way leisurely down to them.

So now they knew the direction. But with what?

Then a miracle happened. The next morning as they were washing up before breakfast, Hockersmith spied a rusty spade, its handle broken in two, lying near the wall of the yard. Why it was there, how it got there he would never know, but he didn't waste much time wondering. Immediately he began a game of rough-and-tumble with Bennett. The guards, used to this little romp, turned to a small fire they had built to keep warm. With a look from Hockersmith, Sheldon joined in. Soon they were rolling on the ground; then Big Jim got up, sealed off the view while Bennett slipped the shovel down one pants leg. When Bennett walked into chow nobody remarked on his sudden improvement in posture: The broken handle was sharp, and the blade was pointed.

Bennett was the first one at the chess board in Cell 20. As soon as they could, they lowered Hockersmith and passed the shovel down. Bennett followed. "Candles!" he said when he came up. "Candles, lots of them! We're going to do it!"

Cold. The damp of an Ohio autumn moving into winter. Rain drizzled, then cleared. "The leaves must be gone from the trees by now," someone said. They hadn't seen a blade of grass since July. Morgan took his turn with the others, although he couldn't be gone as long; they watched him too closely. Sam Taylor's hands were blistered again, and the work went slowly. Less than a dozen men knew of the plot. When Morgan spoke of expanding their work force Hines would have none of it.

"Major Steele, Colonel Smith, Dick McCann, Ralph Sheldon, and the crew. That's enough. There are four men on the third range ready to take the oath. One is a potential traitor."

How could he be so sure? His little spy was amazing.

A letter from Mattie brought the urgency of escape to a pitch. From here, she might as well be on the moon. The rounded schoolgirl handwriting, the scent of her paper. Danville? What about T.H.? He thought she was in Augusta!

November 11. In my last to you, My Love, advised you to go to
Augusta if you preferred that place. It is so important you should be
comfortably situated and it shall make but a small difference in the time
of my joining you. If your present place pleases, then remain. I wish in
this matter you would consult your health and comfort entirely. You
are aware of the importance.

Know dearest, you are first and last in all the prayers of your devoted
husband.

That pretense again of exchange. That "my joining you." Well, it just
might happen . . . and sooner than anybody knew.

It took three days to loosen the first big rock. More than two men would
be needed to budge it. Four went down, praying they wouldn't be missed.
Or the poker borrowed from the stove at the far end of the alley, doing
double duty as a crowbar. It bent, to the disgust of Hockersmith, who threw
it aside and shouldered the stone away. Behind it, another stone, but that
was soon dug out. Behind that: a solid wall of earth. They quit work for
that day.

With a map of the yard in their heads, tunneling began. Shirts came off
to carry dirt, hauled to the far end of the air chamber. Sweating in the dark,
with sputtering candles, they found the digging painfully slow. The first
crumbly earth gave way to clay, as solid as brick.

"Those knives will have to be a little sharper," said Hockersmith. With
the poker, as if playing some new game, the men at the far end of the alley
could be seen hitting something on the floor. When the guard walked up the
knives disappeared, and a game of ticktacktoe resumed. The guard walked
away, his head shaking. These Rebs were crazy.

The trick worked: Serrated edges appeared. With these, and a razor the
barber had traded to Richard for his watch, the digging went on.

The work stopped for a whole day when Major James McCreary was
caught with a knife in the prison yard. He was sent to "the hole" for five
days, and came out barely able to stand up, his feet swollen and blood oozing
from his fingernails. There was only one question he had for them when he
could speak: How was the tunnel?

That afternoon Sergeant Moon delivered a package to John Morgan and
stood by while he opened it. It was a Bible.

"Your sister sent it, sir."

"My sister?"

"Yes . . . I believe she was here before, with your mother."

"Oh. Thank you, Sergeant. I need all the divine help I can get."

His hands were shaking when he climbed the stairs to his cell. He sat on
his bunk and opened the pages to the one where the marking ribbon lay.
Would there be a clue here? He ran his eyes down the edge of the paper,
then saw it: a tiny ink dot. The verse read: The last shall be first and the
first shall be last. What could it mean? He closed the book, then examined
the spine, the back cover. It did seem a little thick! With a glance through
the bars to make sure no guards were in sight, he slipped a knife intended

for Hines from his pocket and slit the inside cover. In the back he found five hundred dollars in Federal greenbacks; in the front another. A thousand dollars! God bless Ma, and Delphine. They were out there. He wasn't alone. Scotty, happening by, nodded approval.

"I see you got religion, General."

"This seems to be a place that makes another world rather appealing."

The sarcasm was beyond Scotty's intelligence, but assuming that something amusing had been said, Scotty allowed his pig's eyes to grin shut with a chuckle as he walked off. Morgan turned from the Bible to a letter he had started to Washington, a request that they be transferred to a military prison. Cal said it was useless, and he agreed, but an attempted transfer might just be another grain of sand to throw in their eyes. Men trying to get out legally would surely not be trying to escape otherwise. Suddenly he heard Scotty calling loudly on the ground floor. He walked out onto the balcony. It was Hockersmith's turn in the tunnel. Maybe he was down there! Maybe he hadn't heard the signal from the lookouts! Scotty didn't usually come by at this time of day. With a sixth sense for danger, Morgan stepped lightly down the stairs and called the trusty over.

"Where's Hockersmith?" Scotty grumbled.

"He's not feeling well . . . in fact, he's in my cell." He said it loud enough, he hoped, for Ralph Sheldon, standing nearby, to hear. "By the way, Scotty, I have here a letter I am penning to Washington, proposing that we be removed . . . to a military prison. I am wondering, with your knowledge of incarceration and the language used, if you could give me some advice? I've had a little trouble with the wording here at the end. . . ."

Scotty, obviously flattered, straightened. "I'll see what I can do."

"The light's so bad here. Why don't we walk down to the hall, where it's better?"

Behind them, as they strolled, Sheldon gave the signal. Hockersmith scrambled out of the tunnel and into Morgan's cell. When Scotty turned back and climbed the stairs he found the big stonemason lying on Morgan's bunk, groaning. "Must've been somethin' I et," he got out, and pretended such pain that he could hardly make it to his own bunk.

"About my letter," Morgan said in the doorway.

"Oh, it'll do first rate," Scotty said.

Oh, it already has.

The next day was Thanksgiving. Hockersmith stayed "sick" for two days, just to play safe. Morgan, pretending to visit his ailing friend, was stopped by Scotty as he was leaving Big Jim's cell. "Finish thet letter yet?"

"Why, yes I have, as a matter of fact. Would you mail it for me, please?"

The tunnel was almost completed. Cal, to scale the walls, had started a rope from torn strips of mattress ticking. Lying on his side so much of the time now, as he did during the day—his cough wasn't much better—he could easily conceal his work between his knees under the covers. They would need a grappling iron; then McCann remembered the bent poker.

Civilian clothes, some sent from home, were hoarded. The digging, inch by inch, went on. It was the 22nd of November.

Hines, over chess the next morning, confessed a new anxiety. He needed accurate measurements of the cells. His plan was to dig under each bunk from the tunnel side a hole large enough for a man to slip through, leaving only a thin crust of cement, which could be kicked in when the time came. Over his shoulder, Morgan saw old Hevay. "I'll fix it," he said.

Again, that talk about the marvelous architectural wonders of the Ohio Penitentiary. "I judge this alley to be ten feet wide," said Morgan offhandedly. "That would make this space to the ceiling, let's see . . . four hundred and forty. No, that's square feet. What is the formula for a cube? I've forgotten."

"Don't know myself," said Hevay, "but this here hallway is eleven feet across."

"Can't be," Hines picked it up.

"Well, here, I'll prove it," said Hevay, and sent for a ruler. Gus Magee spaced the ruler across the floor.

"You're right!" Gus said.

"And the cells? I'll bet they're no more than three feet wide!" insisted Hines.

"No, sir, they're three and a half exactly," the old man said with satisfaction. "You measure and see! With another foot for the walls!"

So Hines knew exactly where to make his holes.

Who should go? They had discussed it often enough, in whispers. And how many? Morgan's cell was on the second tier. Richard was still lame. Cal was weak from this long bout with the croup. Webber had lost much of his stamina. There was general agreement that little Sam Taylor should go, as a badge of honor. Hines, of course, the mastermind. And Hockersmith, who had done so much of the digging. They could leave fluffed-up dummies to gain a little time. To that end a dozen men started sleeping with their blankets drawn up over their faces, as if to shade them from the Cat's lantern.

But how many? The general consensus was: seven. The lots fell on Sheldon, Bennett, and Magee. Ben Drake, who had hoped to make it back to Quirk and do some "first-rate scouting," was disappointed. So was Cal. And Basil. And Charlton.

"I'll take care of these boys for you while you're gone," Basil said.

Morgan corrected him: "Till we meet again."

The men held their breaths in bed at night as the bed checks went by. Every two hours, the Cat with his lantern. Still, still the nights. Cal's rope got longer. From a young private, one of the military guard, Morgan bought for fifteen dollars the train schedule for the Little Miami Railroad. All they needed now was a night of rain. Sheldon insisted on that: He remembered those dogs at Camp Chase.

Morgan's breath came short. Mattie. Mattie in Danville, Virginia. Why? Was she comfortable? *From this distance cannot give you advice. Take a good deal of exercise in the open air and keep the rose on your cheeks* . . . Had he sounded too stern? He had not had another word. If he ever got out of this godforsaken place he would head straight for Virginia. A night of rain. That's all they needed.

On the 27th of November, by pure chance, Morgan learned from Sergeant Moon that there would be a change of command: General Mason was being transferred.

"That will mean an inspection," he told Richard and Charlton as they emptied their night buckets in the open ditch that ran along one side of the prison yard. He straightened and looked up at a cold but clear November sky. Rain or not, it would have to be. . . . "Tomorrow night," he whispered, a stab of excitement almost closing his throat. Richard nodded. Because of his lameness, he was still on the ground floor, in Cell 21, next to Hines. Long ago they had decided, because of their resemblance, they would change cells. Tomorrow, his eyes said.

They hoped, by now, the guards were used to seeing men sleep with blankets over their heads; maybe they wouldn't look too hard for faces. When Hines heard the news he had an added reason for choosing tomorrow night: The traitor on the third range, who had been in the prison hospital for a week ("probably taking their oath"), was not back yet. That day, the 27th of November, dragged on.

Richard made the switch about ten minutes before the key sounded against the stove. Four men had been assigned the duty of sprinkling bits of coal from the stove along the alley: The Cat would have a hard time creeping up on them tonight.

The plan. Sam Taylor would descend into the air chamber ten minutes after the midnight bed check. The train left Columbus at one-twenty, and it was calculated they would need an hour to get to the depot. That would give them ten minutes to spare. Nobody slept that night.

Twelve o'clock struck. The Cat crunched the coal, swung his lantern into the General's cell, saw Richard's bulk turned away from him, and left satisfied. Ten minutes dragged. No sound. Sam Taylor slipped from bed, fluffed up a dummy under his blanket, stamped through the crust of the hole in his cell and jumped through. He bumped into Hines, and they signaled the others.

They passed one by one through the tunnel, then Hockersmith took his knife and cut through the last of the sod. The night sky shone through. He pulled himself up, then the others, and they were in the open air.

All but Hines. The temptation had been too great. This had been his idea, his baby all along. Hines crept back to his cell. He couldn't resist the final defiance of danger: a candle. Carefully, he wrote:

Castle Merion Cell No. 20
Nov. 27th, 1863
Commencement—Nov. 4th, 1863
Conclusion—Nov. 20th, 1863
No. of hours for labor per day—3
Tools—two small knives.

Well, it isn't completely truthful, he said to himself. Then flippantly, because he knew Merion couldn't read French:

> *La patience est amère, mais son fruit est doux.*
> By order of my six honorable Confederates.
>
> Th. H. Hines
Capt., CSA

"What the hell?"

Hines grinned at the head through the floor. It was Magee. "Be right with you!" he rasped as he pinned the note to his blanket. "Forgot my scrapbook!"

They scrambled toward the hole. The others had already crossed the yard to the short wall where, in the half-light, Hines and Magee could see the poker dug in for a hold, the rope taut as the third man climbed up and dropped into the larger yard beyond.

The beginning of the night had been clear; now it was drizzling, with a gusty wind. The gods are with us, Sheldon whispered to himself. They crossed the second yard and faced the high wall. They stayed in the shadows from the windows of a building housing female inmates. The drizzle turned to rain. The dogs were evidently in their kennels, and a sputtering campfire at the far end of the yard in the lee of the wall indicated that the guards had left their boxes on the top of the wall and were trying to stay warm.

Hockersmith threw the poker up again, with Cal's rope. It caught the coping and held. Morgan went first. That sixth sense penetrating: Something was wrong. Tentatively, he felt the ledge, and there it was: a tripping device, a small rope leading to an alarm at the sentry box. He took out a knife and cut it, gently easing the tension. Then he motioned the others. When the last man was up, Cal's rope was hauled up and the hook placed into the inner shelf of the coping on the other side. One by one they slid down, their hands burning. At the bottom, tug and sway as he might, Hockersmith, then Magee, then Sheldon could not flip it loose: There was nothing for it, they would have to leave that telltale rope hanging there.

Hines and Morgan went straight to the depot. Morgan lounged in the shadows while Hines bought two tickets for Cincinnati. He came back with the news that the train was ten minutes late. Ten minutes, and that rope left on the wall! With daylight, the news would spread like wildfire.

The train, spewing sparks, rolled in at last. Morgan mounted, then Hines. They hadn't the first scrap of identification on them; if passes of any kind were asked for they were doomed. Morgan spotted a Federal major who looked like a congenial fellow and asked if he could share his seat. Hines walked on down the aisle and found a seat by a window. The Major, pleased with the newcomer's manners, pulled out a flask and Morgan accepted, and they were chatting along when the conductor passed and tipped his hat. Outside, the gray stone mass of the Ohio Penitentiary could be seen through the rain.

"I hear the horse thief Morgan is residing there," the Major said affably.

"So I hear," Morgan said, and lifted the flask. "May he always be as confined as he is at this moment!"

But he was worried. That rope. He looked up at the swaying, varnished ceiling, then over at Hockersmith and Bennett, who sat at the far end of the car. They had decided to go off in pairs, except Magee, who would travel alone. Sheldon and Taylor had taken seats in the car ahead. Once out of Columbus, the night took over the windows, and drops of rain skidded down the dirty glass to puddle at the bottom. The Federal major was talking about the Art of War, about Past Campaigns, about Generals I Have Known. Morgan looked up to see Hines watching him. As if he recognized an old friend, he excused himself, jumped up and walked over, and followed Hines into the doorway, where the sway of the train almost took them off their feet. Hines grabbed at the wall and whispered, with a punctuating laugh as if he were reminiscing about their past acquaintance: "We'll have to get off before Cincinnati—HA! HA!—you know that."

"Yes, yes, I remember well!" Then: "Check at Xenia."

Morgan went back to his major. When the train pulled into Xenia, Hines got off with the pretext of checking the schedule into Dayton and followed the conductor into the telegraph office, as if by mistake. When he reboarded the train and strolled down the aisle, he shook his head slightly. Morgan relaxed: They had no news yet by telegraph. The Major got off at Dayton and Morgan dozed.

A grinding jolt woke him. The conductor walked through.

"Something on the tracks, folks."

The train was due in Cincinnati at 7:05, plenty of time for the sun to come up and reveal that dangling rope. Hines and the two "drovers"—Hockersmith and Bennett—went out to help. Morgan followed. A farm wagon, loaded with sacks of grain, had jammed on the rough crossing in the mud and slipped a wheel. The team had to be unhitched, the grain unloaded. The "drovers" at once sprang forward and lent their shoulders to the job of heaving the wagon loose. The delay was costly. Morgan felt every minute beating in his brain. They would never make Cincinnati now before the telegraph carried the news. It was hopeless. By the time he reached his seat they had lost almost an hour.

At Hamilton, it was Bennett's turn to visit the depot. When he walked down the aisle the barest shake of his head told the others that there had been no news yet. In order to avoid talking to anyone, Morgan pretended to sleep. Forty-five minutes later he felt a hand on his shoulder.

"Don't you think it's time?"

It was Hines, with that almost inaudible voice. Morgan got up and followed him through the door. They stood over the coupling between cars, balancing as the floor rose and fell. The first houses were passing. As the train slowed they straddled the opening. Hines, then Morgan jumped off. They landed squarely in front of three Union soldiers sitting on a wagon.

52

"Whut the hell you jumpin' off the train for?" one of the soldiers said.

"What the devil is the use of a man going on to town when he lives out here?" asked Morgan in the same tone. "Besides, what's it matter to you?"

The man turned away.

They reached the river and hired a boy to take them across in a skiff. At a house near the ferry they pretended to be in need of a doctor, and the woman there sent her son with them to a doctor's house four miles away. There, once the boy had gone, they pretended to have heard that the doctor wanted to sell two of his horses. His wife gave them breakfast. One of her daughters noticed that Morgan's hands were raw and red and he quickly made up a story about a runaway stallion. "You see why I am in need of a good horse."

By Saturday night they were near Union, in Boone County, at the home of Henry Corwin, a Southern sympathizer who had helped Hines before. They were given fresh horses and blue jeans for the cold nights. They were hog dealers or government contractors buying cattle for the Union Army; sometimes Morgan was a quartermaster, Hines a sutler. Once, they found themselves in a house of uncertain sympathies, until Hines noticed a copy of *The Cincinnati Enquirer*, a Democratic paper. Hines said casually: "I see that General Morgan, Captain Hines and other officers have escaped the penitentiary."

"Yes," said the man, "and you are Captain Hines."

Hines bowed, and took his chance: "Permit me to introduce General Morgan."

They traveled at night, concealed themselves by day. Although Boyle's scouts were out from Louisville, Morgan was not well known in northern Kentucky. Once into Scott County, he had friends.

"I know what you're thinking," said Hines. "We can't do it."

"How did you know that's what I'm thinking?"

"It would be a dashing thing to do . . . I can see you now! But Lexington is the first place they'll look. It will be crawling with troops."

They rode southwest away from Lexington through Anderson to Nelson County, and down to the Cumberland; they crossed the river near Burkesville, where they had started their raid into Ohio five months ago, when Quirk was wounded.

"I wish we had him now!"

"So I'm not scout enough?"

In two weeks they stood by the bank of the Little Tennessee. They were in Yankee territory, and the river was heavily guarded. Morgan was walking his horse to keep him from getting a chill and waiting for Hines when he felt that sixth sense again; he motioned to Hines to mount at once, and they rode straight up a mountain just as a detail of Federals dashed up. It started to rain, and he knew they would be taken in the morning: They were surrounded. They decided to run the gauntlet—as quietly as they could. As they came down, leading their horses, the first picket they met was asleep!

At the next house Morgan was a Federal quartermaster again needing a guide, with the promise that the man should have sugar and coffee if he could get them to Athens. They were headed for Bragg's army at Chattanooga, until at Athens they learned of Missionary Ridge and Lookout Mountain.

"Them Rebs ain't there no mo'—hee! hee!" a toothless old man said. Then he looked at them closely. "Where you two fellers been, anyhow?"

They spurred their horses and were gone.

They had to travel back roads. One night Morgan sent Hines to a house to ask directions. As he waited, shots rang out, then the sound of galloping horses. He knew Hines must be cut off; he was alone. He waited as long as he could.

He made it over the mountains into Franklin, North Carolina. There Lieutenant Gathright of Adam Johnson's Tenth Kentucky was at a hotel getting his boots repaired. A man walked up and said General Morgan was there. "I don't believe it . . ." Then there he was, surrounded by ladies, chatting as if he had never left Dixie.

They talked all night. They went to Gathright's room and Morgan sipped whiskey while Gathright talked.

He had been with Company D—Castleman's outfit—sent to Twelve Mile Island at Louisville on the Ohio raid. Morgan listened intently. Now he could find out how they were captured.

Gathright told his story, turning his glass in his hand, taking quick little gulps of whiskey and looking at the fire. It was a case of fifty men pinned down on the island by three approaching steamboats. "The rest made it to Indiana. I had a flatboat—got to the island twice—almost didn't make it that second time . . . but we got thirty-four men off before the boats closed in. So there were forty-two of us, only eight mounted. By the time we reached Knoxville we all had horses!"

"Castleman?"

"Got away."

"And the others?"

"Captured. Davis. Eastin. Henry Magruder, we heard, was executed as a guerrilla near Louisville."

Morgan looked down.

"But Eastin escaped from Douglas . . ."

"The devil you say? And Davis?"

"Still in prison."

The fire in the grate crackled and Gathright, who had lit a pipe, leaned forward and replenished it with a coal.

Chickamauga. The men who swam the Ohio at Buffington had been collected by Adam Johnson and Warren Grigsby and marched down to Georgia.

"Just in time, too. We were ordered to report to General Forrest, already on the field." It was about ten o'clock, September 18. "We were deployed as skirmishers . . . mounted . . . in front of Hood's division, Longstreet's corps, just come from Virginia. . . ."

Through the warmth of the whiskey Morgan could see it, the lines of troops, the hills, the morning mist. But he wasn't ready for something the Lieutenant said next.

"General Forrest rode past us . . . you know how he can gallop and yell at the same time! He told us to do our duty. And then he spoke of you, said we were Morgan men. Gave us your name as our battle cry. . . ."

Morgan looked away and Gathright cleared his throat, pulled on his pipe and gazed at the fire.

"And Forrest? What about Forrest?"

Gathright spilled some live ashes on the floor and stomped them with his boot. "Goddamn! There he was, after the battle, in a tree with his spyglass . . ."

"*Forrest?*"

"Can't you see him? Dictating to Major Anderson a dispatch to Polk. 'Have been on the point of Missionary Ridge and can see Chattanooga and everything around. The enemy's trains are leaving, going around the point of Lookout Mountain . . . I think they are evacuating as hard as they can go. I think we ought to push forward as rapidly as possible.' I'll never forget those words."

"Did they believe him?"

"Yes and no. Longstreet interpreted that to mean we should encircle Chattanooga, coop them up. . . ."

"But he said push forward . . ."

"You and I know that when General Forrest says push he means push. But Bragg wouldn't listen. He did nothing. Nothing. Except squabble with his generals and give the Yankees time to dig in."

"So he threw away another victory." He didn't have to explain.

"Yes." Gathright knocked out his pipe and stood up, pushing on the mantel with his hands and staring down at the fire. "Bragg tried to break us up. He sent Kirkpatrick with Wheeler against Murfreesboro. But before the good general could scatter Dortch, too, Forrest took that battalion with him up the Knoxville Railroad. To get them, he said, 'as far as possible from the Old Man's clutches.' But everybody knew it was just a matter of time before another big battle would shape up. By this time—mid-November—Bragg needed infantry. That's when he ordered your men dismounted and Forrest refused. . . ."

Morgan drained his glass and set it down. "Refused?"

"And lost his command."

"*Lost his command?*"

"That's not all," Gathright raised both hands, then took his seat again and leaned forward. He rubbed his thumbs back and forth. "He really told Bragg off this time. Can you believe while we were on the Ridge he received orders from Bragg to turn his command over to Wheeler?"

"I can believe it."

"Only this time Forrest really gave it to him. Told him he had stood his meanness long enough. Called him a damned scoundrel and a coward . . . dared him to arrest him. Told him if he ever again tried to interfere with him or cross his path it would be at the peril of his life!"

Morgan rolled back in helpless laughter. Only Forrest would do that. Could do that. "What happened next?"

"Exactly what he predicted. Nothing."

"But he lost his command?"

"Yes. He had to go back to West Tennessee and raise another. But as a major-general. Davis promoted him over Bragg's protests the next day."

The fire blurred from tears of disbelief and joy. "That's the best story I've ever heard . . ."

Gathright sobered again. "They say one out of every three Confederates died at Chickamauga. General Helm was killed."

The fire blazed.

"You see how serious it is."

"Yes, I see. Is Kirkpatrick still with Wheeler?"

"The two battalions are now under Colonel Grigsby," the Lieutenant said matter-of-factly. "Barely brigade strength."

They need you came through the quiet voice of Gathright.

As if reading his mind the Lieutenant said: "They will petition immediately to be assigned to you the minute they hear you're back. They'll set up a yell that'll end the war! They've waited. . . ."

And he needed them. How he needed them! He needed to gather them into a coherent whole again, his generals. He could see them now, with Forrest galloping back and forth: "Let 'Morgan' be your battle cry!" Hungry, half-clad, ill-fed, they were men to be proud of. He would get them together again. A surge of energy joined his longing for Mattie. He would lead them again! Sixteen thousand Confederates died or were wounded at Chickamauga, and among the dead Ben Helm. They couldn't afford many more victories like that! He had to get back, find his men, find his command. . . .

Gathright, talked out, went to bed. Morgan sat by the fire and dozed. At daylight he took a stage to Spartanburg and caught a train for Columbia, South Carolina, where he telegraphed Mattie: JUST ARRIVED. WILL MAKE NO STOP UNTIL I REACH YOU.

"How could he?"

For the tenth time Mattie crushed the hateful newsprint and let it fall. And for the tenth time Alice picked it up and smoothed it out, this time on her skirt, for she was sitting at the foot of her sister's bed.

"How could he?" Mattie repeated, turning her violet-blue eyes, welling with tears, on Alice. "After all . . ." She didn't have to finish. Hadn't she said it enough, since this morning, when the newspaper came? After all she

had been through, after the hours of fear and terror and the loss of the baby.
. . . Her lip trembled. "To be in North Carolina when he could have wired
me. 'In a bevy of ladies,' indeed! a bev—y of . . ." She threw back her head
to control the tears and bit her lip.

"He had no way of knowing, Mattie," Alice begged. "He probably wants
to surprise . . ." But Mattie was staring at the ceiling. "Here, let me brush
your hair. Mrs. Withers is having a dinner tonight, remember? It's Christmas Eve, Mattie. Christmas Eve! Oh, don't you feel a magic about it? Maybe
it's the smell of cedar in the house. All that fresh . . . evergreen. . . ." She
maneuvered her sister to the dressing table and let the brush sink into the
thick, shining hair.

"He escaped in November," Mattie said, pinching her eyes shut at the tug
of the brush but also to squeeze back tears. Christmas. Didn't Alice realize
the smell of cedar brought back her wedding day? Murfreesboro and Mama
. . . Didn't any of them know what all that meant now? How her little girl
would never know the joys of a Christmas morning. Never see a toy, or a
robin, or the blue sky or the green grass. Never know how much she was
loved. A dead baby, with her father in prison. Never knowing.

"The twenty-seventh," Alice was saying.

"Almost a month ago," Mattie replied to the pull of the brush, clinging to
her resentment to fend off grief. The nerve of that Methodist preacher saying
it was God's will. God's will indeed! And some of the others, implying the
baby's death might be a punishment of some sort. What had she ever done?
Or John Morgan? Her silence they took as acquiescence, when really she
considered their speculations so insulting she refused to give them the benefit
of an answer. Punishment, indeed! Then she'd rather not believe in such a
God. Oh, how she had defended him in her secret answers to them! How
she had remembered his dear face, his lovely eyes. . . . Just because he was
so handsome the nasty Northern press had called him a womanizer. . . .
And just because she had defended him so, to read in this morning's paper
that he was in a hotel *in a bevy of ladies.* . . . He had betrayed her defense,
all those letters to Commissioner Ould in Richmond begging for an exchange!

"A month ago," she said into her chest, her head bent, the tears stinging
her eyelids.

"I'm sure it took days to get through the lines. Imagine the danger."

"Of course it was marvelous!" Mattie ducked her head sideways to look
out the window, where the sight of another gray day confirmed her mood.
Alice waited behind her, the brush raised. Mattie straightened and tried to
keep her chin from trembling as she said to her sister in the mirror: "It's
always marvelous . . . for them! It gives them something to talk about over
cigars . . . how they outflanked somebody or tricked a picket. It's a game
with them!"

What about her own pain, the blood and soreness of her own body, the
panic, the fear? The more she thought of that scene described in the Richmond paper the more she could see that straight back, so self-assured, hear
that laugh that could be so musical, see his eyes that could flash so easily

into amusement . . . surrounded by a *bevy of ladies!* "Why do they call them that?" she asked angrily, and Alice, from the sound, didn't have to ask who "them" were. "Like a flock of geese!"

"Oh, you know how they try to dramatize everything," Alice said with just the right inflection to tell her sister she agreed with her perfectly, but now it was time to get ready for Mattie's first trip—the momentous first trip —downstairs. Behind them and around them, like a cocoon, Tassie Withers's ordered household had become more than a refuge: It was like a well-oiled machine in which they were working parts. Alice went with Mrs. Withers and her aged coachman every Monday into Danville "shopping"— a word used lightly because of the lack of goods to be bought; Tuesday was given to making bandages, Wednesday to visiting, Thursday to bandages again. . . .

"Would you like to help me finish hanging the decorations?" Alice asked, but as soon as she said it she realized she was moving too fast.

"No, you do that sort of thing so well." There was no hint of sadness but the effort at small talk failed. "I think I'll stay up here a bit. I can finish myself." And to make sure Alice realized she loved her, Mattie held up her face for her sister's kiss. Alice surrendered the brush and left.

Mattie picked it up and turned it automatically in her hand. Poor girl. She's worried about Brother and now her beau, who sounds like such a kind person. And wasn't it just like Alice to fall in love with a man who'd lost an arm? She could just see it, the empty sleeve, the grateful eyes, and Alice doing all she could—with a pang Mattie knew her sister wanted to marry him.

She pulled the brush through her hair again and looked in the mirror. Her blue eyes with their thick lashes looked back in the pale face. She laid the brush down and drew her fingers slowly down her cheeks. *He* was coming! She rested her elbows and cradled her chin in her palm and stared at the face of this stranger. He was coming!

Ever since she'd heard of the escape—two of them, Sheldon and Taylor, were recaptured almost immediately and returned to the penitentiary—she had gone through a series of phases. First there was the utter thrill of knowing that he had *dared* to defy them—and succeeded! Then there was the fear, the trembling terror in the middle of the night . . . she remembered she was still bleeding then, and crampy and sore, and how she had lain awake for two whole nights until Alice sent for the doctor—she could see him caught, shot, tortured. . . . They would have no mercy.

Then good health rebelled, and her twenty-year-old body, with a life and needs of its own, thrust itself between Mattie and her fear. Her blood was no longer red but stringy with mucus, a clotted brown, salty smell that dwindled finally until she dropped the last napkin, folded and sticky, in the pail of water to soak. That much was over, and now the soreness was almost entirely gone, and with the aroma of coffee and newly baked bread coming up the stairs she allowed a small smile to come into the image in the mirror and agreed with Alice: It was time to start living again. She walked unsteadily to the bed and lifted her arms, letting her dress fall down around her, then bent her head to button the front. The action made her dizzy and she sat on the edge of the bed to steady herself, and the old specter of *You might never see him again* came back, with all those frantic letters to T.H., who knew no more than she did. Not until this morning, when the bevy of ladies. . . . Surely he could make it now from North Carolina!

If only she had her rose silk dress! Or money! That fool Abby. . . . And Mrs. Withers couldn't get but three hundred dollars for her . . . Confederate money, too, and worth a Yankee nickel to the dollar! But there were no dresses to buy anyway. . . . She looked across at the mirror again trying to adjust the let-out gathers around the waist. She hadn't pulled on the second stocking when Alice returned, breathless, with a telegram in her hand.

Will make no stop until I reach you.

Even afterwards, Alice marveled at the quickness of the change. Choking excitement replaced resentment; the cad of a moment before became a god of light and deliverance. The news sent Tassie Withers's household into a whirlwind of expectation: Christmas, the long-planned-for dinner took a back seat. Every footstep on the sidewalk, every passing horseman became suspect. Mattie, so nervous she had to be helped downstairs—her legs after so much confinement were stabbing needles of pain—begged their forgiveness and was helped back to her room even before dessert. Yet she didn't undress, but sat by the fire waiting. How could she sleep? She dozed in the rocker and about midnight she heard it—the front door. She found a candle and stood in the upstairs hall. There he was—unbelievably, there he was! Standing still in a dark civilian suit under the light of the hall gaslight, his head slightly inclined to Mrs. Withers, his hat in the angle of his arm, held there with an impatience that sent a stab of satisfaction and joy into Mattie's throat. She was about to call out when he looked up in that good-natured, confident way he had—and her heart melted. He bounded up the stairs, hat flung in a corner, all propriety gone and smothered her with kisses as the whole house, awakened, gathered in the hall to watch.

Home, home, home and safe. What it meant for him she could only guess: She knew he would never tell her everything, to spare her feelings, as she now too would never tell him everything. He held her from him and waited.

"The baby . . . oh, John, she was so beautiful—" A sob caught her words. His eyes roved her face. With her chin still trembling, she said in a rush, "Mrs. Withers was so kind. It wasn't that. Or the travel. I was fine at first! Then it all seemed so hopeless, all those letters to Richmond . . . Then . . . oh, my God!"

He drew her to him then, his cheek on the top of her head as she cried into his chest. "That's . . . that's all right, my darling. Everything will be fine now. You'll see. All you've got to do now is gain your strength." When she looked at him he tried a smile. "And be my brave girl again."

That night, as he talked of the prison and the escape and his hope of convincing Richmond to work for an exchange for his men—as he talked and hoped and shared his thoughts of helping Basil and Cal and the others, she listened with a new sense of understanding, for she had been in a kind of prison, too, and had run some gauntlets herself. She told him, as lightly as she could, of her trip from Sparta.

"He said that, did he?"

"Yes. He was a horrible man, and his wife was horrible, and his son and his farm. The whole thing was horrible."

"A rabbit's print in snow."

"I didn't think there was anything so special about that. He was cynical and selfish."

"I suppose. And Cal's trunk?"

"His son brought it to the house the next morning, but it was so damaged I couldn't use it. I was never so glad to get anywhere as I was Knoxville, and then it had to fall. . . ."

After a moment he said, "Tell me about T.H. How is Key? And Alice has a beau?"

"I know she wants to marry him."

"Then she shall marry him." He pulled her to him. "That is, if he asks her," he teased. At her look he said: "We'll see that he asks her."

She was still frowning and biting one corner of her lip. "But Papa and Mama? How can we let them know?"

"We'll get a letter through the lines," he said confidently, moving his legs under the sheet. "Now, get some sleep."

Outside Christmas morning was dawning. Unbelievably, a new day meant something besides running. Just to lie here was enough. To sink into the smells, the sounds. The little things that told you you were safe. Life. They had never meant so much before. Mattie stirred. He whispered in her hair: "Rest, my darling, rest . . ."

But he could hardly do so himself. Long after her head grew heavy again against his shoulder he watched the gathering light beyond the window. His command—his command. To get those boys back again! Gathright had told him Adam Johnson was gathering the men at Decatur, Georgia. He would go there as soon as he could! To lead them again, to be with them again . . . dear old Bowles, and Cassell, and Martin. . . . He drifted to sleep.

Mattie the next day became ill with a fever. "The excitement has been too much," the doctor pronounced, clipping his bag shut. "Rest for a few days. . . ."

The front door was kept busy with well-wishers, telegrams and then letters and notes from his old squadron. Alston, in Holly Springs, Mississippi, sent him a letter written in early December by R. G. Matthews. Morgan held the words in his hand:

> When I heard of his escape from prison, it was the proudest moment of my life, and if he can only reach Dixie safe again I want to clasp him in my arms. If I survive this war I want no prouder record than to say, I followed Morgan. And if I fall on my tomb I would have written, He died with Morgan.

It was almost too much. Matthews had been one of those quiet boys; who would have thought? Alston added a note: He was waiting for orders, and would move at once.

"What are you smiling about?"

"Some of these boys make me almost believe in myself."

"You don't fool me," she smiled. "You believe in yourself. Here, let me see it."

Reluctantly, he handed it over, then opened another. D. H. Llewellyn had been with Bragg at Dalton when they heard of his escape. "It sent a thrill of joy through the whole army," Llewellyn wrote. "All are looking for you to come here and your presence will be equal to a large reinforcement. Dortch has already petitioned to be assigned to your command. His battalion has men from several regiments of the old division." Then Llewellyn went on in a more sober mood: He hinted that there might be some trouble getting the command again.

> Colonel Grigsby has been commanding your men since Chicka-mauga. He told Captain Kirkpatrick that he must drop the name of Morgan in his command as there is no such name in the army now.

"You see? You see I told you they love you!" Mattie called from the bed.

Llewellyn had scribbled a P.S.: "I have a case of French brandy and shall save it until you come."

He got up and moved restlessly to the window, where a light snow had begun to fall lazily past the panes. *No such name in the army*. Grigsby, holding the rear together on that awful march around Cincinnati. That startled look he always sent you above that bushy mustache. Grigsby, swimming the Ohio with Byrne and Kirkpatrick . . . What did he mean, no such name? Wasn't surviving prison the worst kind of warfare? The face of young John Bowles as he came out of the dungeon . . . gunned down trying to escape. Webber, weak as a kitten, being helped to his bunk. . . . What had happened?

Llewellyn wrote that Grigsby commanded two battalions: W. C. P. Breckinridge's Ninth and the First Kentucky. Even if the First—the gathered remnants Adam Johnson had collected—could not be called his, surely Breck's Ninth, left behind by Bragg's order when he went to Ohio, was still officially in the command? He had to get to Richmond! He had to get his men back! He looked at Mattie propped on her pillows, a little color in her cheeks. She wet her lips and smiled at him. He grinned and straightened his shoulders. He couldn't go. Not just yet.

The next day a letter Adam Johnson sent from Decatur added to the anxiety:

> It is rumored with some appearance of truth that a court of inquiry will be called as to why you crossed the Ohio River and that General Wheeler has preferred charges against you. I write this for the purpose

of putting you on your guard, believing that if true it is only for the purpose of delaying you in obtaining your command. There is no doubt that there are parties who would injure you if possible, and I would advise you to be prepared. I am willing to share any part of the blame attached to crossing the river. I approved it then and will do so again if the opportunity offers.

Parties who would injure? Blame for crossing . . . delay in getting the command? Rage gave way to fear. He had to talk to Davis . . . and only in Richmond could he hope to start some kind of exchange. But surely, the more reasonable side of his mind whispered, Davis would acknowledge those unwritten secret orders, would exonerate him?

Then, no sooner had he relaxed than a letter arrived from Representative E. M. Bruce of the Kentucky delegation urging him to come to the capital, implying, as Adam had, that there was opposition: "Your friends desire to extend to you a public reception on your arrival, and thusly say to the despicable foe that in their futile efforts to degrade you before the world they have only elevated you in the estimation of all Confederate citizens, and the whole civilized world."

He folded the letter and tucked it away with the rest, but when Mattie found it she faced him with blazing eyes. "What does he mean, *despicable foe . . . efforts to degrade you before the world?*"

The doctor said she shouldn't be excited. "Yankees, darlin' . . . who else?"

"Then we'll show them!" She was sitting by the fire with a quilt across her lap, her feet on a footstool. He watched the eagerness in her face, but also the thinness of her arms under the shawl as she twisted her needle through another endless loop.

"I'll have enough socks to supply the army!"

She knew how discouraged he must be. And could see, from the letters, how he was loved. With that peculiar love and closeness of men who have faced death together. It was a closeness women could never know. She knew he was watching the needle, and to keep him from guessing her thoughts she made a face. "It looks as if you'll have them if your wife has anything to do with it." She suddenly flung aside her knitting. The ball of wool spun across the floor. She was in his arms sobbing.

"Of course," the doctor said in his kind but firm way. "I realize, General, that they are expecting you. But I would advise postponing your trip a week. At least a week. And . . ." He raised his eyebrows.

"No, I haven't," said Morgan gruffly.

"That's good. A little while, my son. A little while, and all these things come about in their own good time."

He left the doctor and walked back upstairs. The day had turned sunny and clear, with fresh snow sparkling. Mattie was dressed and standing by the window. "It's so gorgeous out," she said. "Let's go for a walk, even if it's just around the block. He did say I could, didn't he?"

"He said you could do what you felt up to," he answered.

"Well," she arched an eyebrow, "in that case . . ."

"No, no, now . . ." He crossed the room and encircled her with his arms. "A little while, he said."

"Doesn't he know how warm-blooded we Tennessee ladies are?"

"I think he's got a good idea."

When they came back there was a telegram from John C. Breckinridge: IMPERATIVE I SEE YOU. HAVE BOOKED ROOMS AT THE BALLARD HOUSE.

"No, we can't," he answered her unspoken question after she read it. "A week. I promised the doctor a week."

Alice, after much discussion, decided to return to Augusta, where she could continue her work at the hospital . . . and see her artillery captain. Morgan sent a long letter to T.H., who was handling his finances, and a note to Key. A week later Mattie, in spite of her frailty, looked radiant as they drove to the station and waved good-bye to Mrs. Withers. They settled in their seats like newlyweds, holding hands under the shawl he spread over her knees.

"There was quite a crowd at the Richmond depot last week. They were expecting you." The conductor grinned as he took their tickets.

"Maybe we can make a quieter entry this time," Morgan said.

"I wouldn't bet on it."

The conductor was right. Even in his plain civilian suit, Morgan was recognized. They took a carriage to the Ballard House, but by the time they arrived a crowd had assembled near the doors. Visitors came up to their rooms almost immediately . . . Morgan was glad Breckinridge had engaged a suite with a separate sitting room. Almost as soon as the porter left and before they could open their bags, Breckinridge with his wife Mary appeared at the door.

"We're so glad you're here!" The General held out both hands and took Morgan's in his, pumping the air. "And Mrs. Morgan. This is my wife, Mary."

Mattie smiled. "We've met . . . Murfreesboro."

Breckinridge ushered his wife to a loveseat next to Mattie. After some pleasantries, and while the ladies bent their heads in polite chatter, he took Morgan's arm. Still portly and square-jawed, with those light gray eyes that blazed at you under deep brows, Breckinridge had let his corsair's mustache grow past his shaven cheeks. He pulled at it now as Morgan offered him a brandy from a traveling case.

"I'm so glad you've come," the General said for the third time. "I heard about Tom. I'm sorry."

The sincerity of the sympathy caught at Morgan's throat. He nodded in silence.

"We've got to make it right for him."

"I received your telegram," Morgan said needlessly.

"After the army went into winter quarters at Dalton . . ." Breckinridge sat down and crossed his legs, "I asked for leave. Buckner was with Longstreet—cut off in East Tennessee."

"He's here?"

"Not only is he here but he's been given the Cavalry Corps, Army of the Tennessee . . . with you as second in command!"

He couldn't believe it! After all those warnings about opposition! Maybe the "foes" had been taken care of. What he heard next brought a stab of joy.

"We're lobbying for another Kentucky campaign."

He knew it! With Buckner in charge, what else? But Breckinridge looked so intense he dared not interrupt.

"Tennessee's gone. The morale of the Orphans has never been worse. The only way they'll ever see home again is to desert—and some of them are taking the Federal oath. Buck and I are confident—and we know you believe this too—that if we could go into Kentucky, thousands would rally to our cause. But the best way to get them is to send the Kentucky brigade in mounted. As soon as we arrived in Richmond we presented a petition to Seddon. . . ."

Breckinridge took an appreciative draught and Morgan waited. "And?"

"You might guess."

Morgan said nothing.

"The Secretary of War 'did not favor the plan,' but would ask Joe Johnston."

"And?"

"And Johnston 'did not favor the plan' either. It seems, in his words, he doesn't want to make 'bad cavalry' out of good infantry. So that's where we stand now. Johnston flatters us—says he wouldn't give up our paltry fourteen hundred infantry for all the mounted men we could recruit. . . ."

"So what do you intend to do?"

Breckinridge shifted to the edge of his chair and leaned toward Morgan, pinning him with his eyes. "We intend to petition the President. Ask that *all Kentucky troops in the service be combined and mounted.*"

The ladies from their side of the room sent across a peal of laughter. Morgan looked at Mattie and smiled. "You'll have my support, General, and you know it!" he said, still smiling across at her. "As soon as I can get to Decatur."

"Don't go just yet. Our first skirmish is here in Richmond. I've just received my new assignment—the Department of Southwestern Virginia."

"Just the place to launch a Kentucky campaign!"

"It would be. Now I expect Mrs. Morgan is tired from her journey. You're having a big day tomorrow . . . City Hall and all that. A.P. Hill will be down from the front. Stuart will be there. Will you dine with us after a rest?"

Mattie, obviously delighted with Mary Breckinridge, accepted with a laugh that was almost a giggle. He hadn't seen her so happy in a long time. He was about to follow her into the bedroom to unpack when a knock at the door admitted St. Leger Grenfel.

After that first explosive, mock-dance step that took him to Morgan and a bear hug, St. Leger looked at her and came to attention. "My dear lady. I haven't seen you since Murfreesboro."

There was something so pathetically amusing in his appearance that she summoned the last of her energy to tease him a little. "Where, I understand, you thought my marriage to the General would ruin his career."

Grenfel actually blushed, bowed, and kissed her hand. Morgan burst out laughing. It was the first time he had ever seen the Englishman speechless. They watched her close the bedroom door with a remark about dressing for dinner.

"So?" said Morgan, pouring him some brandy without asking. St. Leger accepted and raised his glass in a toast.

The prospect of seeing A.P., and maybe Kitty—of joining Buckner and a combined Kentucky force . . . he had already made up his mind to ask for Southwestern Virginia—the idea of an expedition. . . . It was unbelievable. And now St. Leger again. The urgency of Breckinridge's words were still with him: Tennessee's lost. The whole Mississippi Valley. Stalemate in Georgia, and now in Virginia. *If we could get this thing moving before spring* . . .

"If we could get this thing moving before spring," he echoed. "You know about Buckner's new assignment?"

"My dear boy, who do you think maneuvered it?" Grenfel grinned, then as quickly frowned. "There's been a massive enemy build-up," he said in that clipped way of his. "You know, of course."

"I know nothing!"

"For the past six months . . . some say by seven hundred thousand, with another hundred thousand three-months' men from places like Ohio, to allow the veterans to fight . . . Worse, they're sending recruiting agents to the jails of Europe, promising bounties, homesteads—four hundred acres of Southern land . . ." He pulled a clipping from his pocket. "And read this."

It was an ad from a New York paper promising "acceptable *alien* substitutes for men who are enrolled, and men who are not enrolled, for the coming Draft, and also for men who have already been drafted."

"Yankee version of slavery," St. Leger said behind him.

"Already drafted? How can they do that? And 'without the inconvenience of leaving their places of business!' " Morgan let his eyes linger on the paper before he handed it back. "And you say they're promising immigrants Southern land?"

"This spring should be interesting," St. Leger said in his dry way.

"Have you seen A.P.?"

"Things are stalled up at the Rapidan. He gets into town once in a while." Grenfel cleared his throat. "Don't be surprised when you see him." In the silence that followed he added: "There was some talk of his being removed from active service. Fatigue. But your sister's a wonder, my dear boy, a wonder. Has stamina for them both. He'll be all right. This visit to you will perk him up."

"And you?"

St. Leger gave his friend a long look. "I could never fool you, could I? The truth is, lad, I've tired of Stuart's banjo-playing . . . tired, really, of Richmond." His face exploded with a laugh. "A desert of inertia, full of the worst kind of mirage . . . bureaucratic incompetence. And now, since our friend Braxton has become chief military advisor to the President . . . well, it's hopeless. He has Davis's ear, and you know me . . . I speak frankly. Bragg wants you court-martialed for crossing the Ohio."

So that was it. "I could have guessed."

"You knew?"

"I knew somebody was trying, but I didn't know who."

"He's mad as hell at being replaced by Joe Johnston. After losing Missionary Ridge, what could he expect? He threw away Chattanooga, and now blames Breckinridge for being drunk. . . ."

"John *C.* Breckinridge?" Morgan laughed at Grenfel's nod.

"He's even mad at Longstreet, who rushed west to save him. But let's not talk of all this, lad. Tell me about your escape. Jolly good the reports we had of it."

"Have you heard from Hines?"

"As a matter of fact, I have."

"I knew it! I knew he would get away!"

"I haven't seen him, but I hear talk . . . something secret. Mission in Canada, or some such. Have no doubt, lad, you'll see him the minute he knows you're here."

It was well past midnight before he got to bed. Buckner came by just as they were walking down to dinner. He held out his expansive hand for a grip, patting Morgan's arm with the other. "It's so *damned* good to have you back!" he whispered hoarsely with emotion. "Now we'll get started!" His thick brown hair still looked uncombed as it tumbled back from that broad brow, and the eyes, so direct and earnest, hadn't changed since those days in Kentucky. It was he, and not Bragg, who should have been in command all this time.

"Congratulations, sir, on your new assignment."

"And you. Have you seen John?"

"Yes. I'd like to be assigned . . ."

Buckner stopped him with that quiet smile. "I thought you would. But there's time enough to talk about all this tomorrow. I see your young lady's waiting."

"Thank you, sir."

Buckner dipped his upper body in a courtly bow. It was the first time Mattie had met him, and Morgan delighted in her obvious reaction. "Quite a knight in armor, isn't he?" he whispered after Buckner left. "All us Kentucky boys exude charm. You sure you want to come home after the war?"

She blushed and kissed him on the cheek. They were standing by the closed door, listening to Buckner's retreating steps on the carpet outside. She rubbed the tip of her nose against his ear, her mouth open. He caught her to him. "If we didn't have to go to dinner. . . ."

"But we do," she whispered against him. "All sorts of people are waiting to see you."

"But . . ."

She pressed his mouth with her little gloved hand. "There's tomorrow. I'll be here tomorrow."

"I thought you didn't like that word."

Dinner was a series of interruptions. Jeb Stuart introduced himself, with Heros von Borcke, his Prussian aide, still having trouble talking because of a wound in his throat. Before they left the table A.P. Hill walked in, his eyes lighting up his thin face.

"May I introduce you to Mattie?" said Morgan, rising and trying to hide his surprise at the change.

"Dolly will be delighted to meet her new sister," Hill smiled as he took a chair next to her. "And introduce you both to your new niece."

"Lucy Lee," said Morgan quietly.

"You know her name!"

"Yes. Just before the Ohio raid. . . ." Evidently A.P. knew nothing of Kitty's letter. "Good news always travels fast through channels."

A.P.'s haggard face lit with sudden joy. "And little Frances plays 'Mama' with her already. . . ."

"How . . . ?" Mattie asked, but didn't finish.

"Two. Walking, trying to talk. You should see her, Johnny! Dolly said she reminds her of Tom. . . . Tommie has a little girl, too. We heard through T.H."

"Yes. Born last August. She named her Tom . . . another Tommie in the family," Morgan added, at the sudden sadness in A.P.'s face. "Where is Kitty?"

"Milford, just south of Fredericksburg. Culpeper is in Federal hands . . ."

"And Jackson? Richard told me something of Jackson . . ."

The minute he said it he regretted it, remembering Jackson's charges. A.P.'s face turned red.

"You knew about Frazier's Farm. Where Dick Curd died? McClellan should have been outflanked, and wasn't. The plain fact was, Stonewall wouldn't *move*. That's where he got his nickname, not because he is impregnable. In fact, he's insufferable. Like some Old Testament Prophet. Refusing to fight on Sunday . . ."

"Let's go up to the room afterwards, where we can have a good visit," suggested Mattie, sensing the fury and fatigue behind that vast red beard.

"No, thank you, really." Still Powell Hill sat, almost too tired to move. General Breckinridge was keeping up a steady stream of chatter, to be kind, and Hill rested back in his chair, toying with a spoon. He closed his eyes and the General's words came to him as from a great distance: *The famous Light Brigade, you know, Mrs. Morgan. General Lee's right hand . . .*

Heth. Jube Early. Ewell. Ewell wasn't well; his wooden leg gave him infinite trouble. John Hood—everybody called him Sam—had lost a leg, too. Chickamauga. He's here.

"You can't help but meet him," Mrs. Breckinridge put in. "He's every-where . . . and head over heels in love with Buck . . . Sally Buchanan Campbell . . . Mary Chestnut's sister. . . ."

"Buckner slept with him the night before," Breckinridge nodded. "Said that once before he'd slept with a man who lost his leg the next day . . ."

The talk went back to the rivers: the Rappahannock, the Rapidan, the North Anna, the South Anna, the Pamunkey, the James. Like stepping-stones. Mattie gathered that the front was at the Rappahannock, or was it the Rapidan? Finally the map in her mind faded under the stress of trying to be pleasant without yawning. Yes, if Uncle Robert can keep the Yankees from digging in, can keep them guessing . . . her Morgan was right. She should have rested. . . .

That night Richmond had its first snow of the season, and they awoke to find mounds of diamonds where trash cans had been: a clean fairyland, with the air so cold it hurt. About nine o'clock Generals Stuart, Buckner, Breckinridge, and Mayor Mayo of Richmond called to escort them to City Hall for a formal reception. A bone-chilling wind blew from the river but crowds of well-wishers stood ankle deep in snow on the sidewalks as the carriage rolled past. Morgan, holding Mattie's hand, tried to bow gracefully at the calls, but said sidewise to her. "I'm not good at this regal stuff."

"You don't have to be." She squeezed his fingers. "They know a king when they see one."

The ceremony was staged on the south portico, where the wind almost took their breath. They hoped—in vain—that it would shorten the mayor's speech. It didn't.

He was reminded, he ballooned his breath in front of him, he was brought back . . . his thoughts were brought back. To '76, when we were at war with a civilized nation. When it pleased Providence to raise up to us a Southern Marion.

"Now we are engaged in a far deadlier war—if the savage crusade against our lives, our laws and our institutions can be called such—and it has pleased God to raise up another Marion. . . ." He stopped until the crowd subsided. "Another Marion . . . in the person of General John H. Morgan, who stands before you."

More cheers, and the crowd was looking expectantly toward him. He rose, conscious that his civilian suit contrasted with Stuart's brilliant uniform, complete with sweeping plume, next to him.

"I hope my future career will not prove unworthy of the honor you have done me," he blurted, blushed, and sat down to thunderous applause.

Stuart spoke next. "I am grateful." Stuart raised both arms for quiet and grinned. "I am grateful to see Virginia paying honor to the heroic son of Kentucky." Cheers. Stuart looked around, his plume swooping. "Some of our friends have said we are rivals. Now I'm not denying this. We are rivals . . . in a glorious Cause which I hope we both win!"

They went from City Hall to a reception at the President's house. There the Davises formally received them—the Kentucky delegation, Davis joked, since Buckner and Breckinridge flanked Morgan.

He was appalled at the change in Davis. His sunken cheeks, prominent cheekbones and wisping gray hair gave his face a skeletal look that was frightening. It was like looking at some rigid statue that had been left out in the rain too long. Where this frail body found the stamina and energy to run a war was, from any visible evidence, a mystery. Davis was accused often in the Richmond press of being too haughty, too austere. Morgan wondered how much that reticent aloofness could be pain from the facial neuralgia from which he suffered and which must be excruciating. In this social situation there was no chance to talk. The President stood stiffly formal, while at the same time trying to be casual.

His Secretary of State, Judah Benjamin, the Jewish lawyer from New Orleans, had no such problem: Salon chatter fell from him as easily as his smiles. Morgan remembered Richard's admiration, but the man was a little too unctuous for his own taste. Mattie had known him in Washington when he had been a senator, and he charmed her now by remembering. Next came Secretary of War Seddon, his hair falling lank and limp from a bald brow on either side of a face that should have belonged to a ghoul. Then Adjutant-General Cooper, a sour-faced old man whose lower lip curled up as if he were smelling something. . . . These were the men he would have to ask favors from! Bragg was there, acting as if a court-martial would be the last thing on his mind, recalling loudly how his early faith in Morgan and Forrest after Shiloh had contributed to their careers.

Taking credit where there is none Mattie's eyes flashed, but before his wife could make a *faux pas* Morgan steered her toward Mrs. Davis, who, after the reception line had broken up, stood chatting with Buckner and Breckinridge.

"My, how the town lights up with these tall Kentuckians!" Varina Davis, in pearls and black velvet, smiled. She was a small woman tending to plumpness, with marble-clear skin, drawn-back hair framing a pair of eyes remarkable for their intelligence. She came from a plantation near Natchez. Morgan, watching her expert handling of introductions and small talk, remembered that delta country, those big houses he had seen from the riverboat coming home from Mexico. Varina Davis's eyes met his and seemed to receive his thoughts. She smiled again. "I suppose you will want to gather your old command about you immediately, General," she said. She was the first person in the room who had mentioned the one thing that had been on his mind.

"If not sooner," he grinned. Then, more soberly: "And take care of my comrades still in Ohio."

"As for the first . . ." She deftly reached out and touched the sleeve of a passing guest. "I should like to introduce you to Colonel Chestnut. He is our wizard of supply, as you are of the saddle . . ."

"I'm afraid that's what they call Forrest, ma'am."

"Three wizards, then. James has imported arms through the Trenholm firm, laid the foundations of a niter-bed . . . repaired all our old guns, built ships, imported clothes, shoes. In spite of the blockade. He has imported cotton cards, and has set all the idle hands of Richmond weaving. I tell you all of Virginia is set to spinning cotton. If you visit Mrs. Lee, you'll find her daughters . . . all working. . . . virtually a cottage industry." While Morgan talked with James Chestnut, Varina Davis led Mattie aside, strolling with her toward a wall of uniforms, the brightest of them Stuart's. Before they arrived she invited Mattie to her next "Luncheon for Ladies Only."

Lee walked in late from the front, flawless in his gray wool uniform, smelling of hastily splashed cologne. In spite of his spit-and-polish, there was something shaggy about his beard and soft about his eyes which explained his troopers' love, and his nickname. Only beloved family servants or dear relatives were ever called "Uncle" in the South. Yet there was an awesomeness about the man, a stature that went beyond his physical body and made you want to look up, even when it wasn't necessary. . . . Morgan wondered how many of the men who called him "Uncle Robert" had ever met him.

Yet Lee, too, deftly switched to small talk when Morgan wanted to ask serious questions. At every turn, it seemed more important to remember some prank or quirk of the promotion lists than to speak of dismounted cavalrymen desperate to get back into the fight. In the end, the names of quartermaster clerks and the address of the ordnance offices he learned from James Chestnut proved to be the most valuable things Morgan took away with him that evening.

A.P. rode back with them to the hotel. He would return to his division the next morning, and the prospect made him seem less tired, more rested, as he walked into the lobby on one side of Mattie, her hand in his arm. "You don't fool me," Morgan grinned. "It's the thought of seeing Kitty that's perked you up."

"I will admit." A.P. smiled. "Your sister does encourage me."

"I should love to meet her."

"You will, my dear. She's promised to come to Richmond to see her hero brother as soon as she can."

At the Richmond Theater the bill was quickly altered to *Nick of the Woods —a Kentucky Tragedy*. *The Richmond Inquirer* wanted his biography. One woman requested a lock of his hair, since she was making a wreath of all the generals' hair. A young South Carolina soldier stopped him in the lobby one morning asking for an autograph for his sister. A professor at the Columbia Female College wanted him to attend a reception so his young ladies "could show appreciation to a hero." A Georgia poet wanted permission to dedicate a canto to him. A cobbler wanted to make him a new pair of boots.

"Now that last offer is the one that counts," he joked to Mattie. They were dressing for church, where they would sit with Buckner and Breckinridge, and President Davis. The next day he was scheduled to visit the two houses of the Virginia Assembly, and Tuesday they would make a formal call on the President.

He did not intend to make it completely social. He was desperately worried about his men in Columbus. What had they done to Richard when they'd discovered the switch? And Charl and Basil? And Cal? And Sheldon and Taylor? Before he met with Davis he wanted to see for himself the condition of Yankee prisoners at Libby Prison. He intended to protest through Federal diplomatic channels and to ask that Union officers with rank comparable to his men in Ohio be housed in the South's penitentiaries. Maybe an eye for an eye would work.

"They won't care," Davis said. "Unfortunately," he added to be kind, "they can afford to refuse exchange—they don't need their men the way we do ours." To his question about the command Davis said, "We will arrange a meeting with General Cooper and Secretary Seddon." To his repeated

concern for the prisoners the President murmured, "Commissioner Ould—
his office handles those matters. Have you seen him?"

This was no longer the young colonel defying orders and storming La
Teneria. This was an aging, thin-shouldered politician, intellectually withdrawn but trying to be polite, and veiling with offhand remarks the real
concern on his face: *We mustn't keep the ladies waiting.* Did he really believe
Bragg's charges? Not a word had been mentioned. Nor about those "orders
direct from the President" which had sent him to Ohio in the first place . . .
and Morgan was too much the gentleman to bring it up. The Northwest
Conspiracy was a joke now . . . or was it? He remembered St. Leger's talk
of a mission for Hines in Canada. Whatever it was, he wanted no part of it,
and wanted to tell Davis as much. But he had no chance.

Mattie seemed to be enjoying herself. Then the Davis chiildren came in.
Evidently, thought Morgan, this was to be no usual "call": By admitting the
children Davis was saying, in some symbolic way, that he considered his
guests to be closer than the ordinary obligatory visitors.

They were delightful children: Nine-year-old Pollie—also called Maggie
—was a real charmer, with her black eyes and floating brown hair, while
her brothers, seven-year-old Jefferson, Jr., four-year-old Joe and the toddler
Billie swarmed over Morgan, asking for Injun stories. "But Papa sez you ah
frum Kentucky," little Joe sulked.

"Joseph! Leave General Morgan alone!" Yet it was plain to see Varina
Davis was enjoying every minute of it.

"I'll tell you one if your Mama and Papa will let me come again to do so."
Morgan grinned, seeing now that their mother really would prefer that they
practice their manners.

"We'll surely have General Morgan again." Mrs. Davis was picking up
her cue. "Now tell our guests good night, and thank them for coming."

The President of the Confederacy watched his children leave with a softened look on his face. Yes, nobody wants this war to be over more than he
does, Morgan thought. Maybe his stiffness is a substitute for stamina. Or
the result of it. If Davis had one fault it was that fierce loyalty to old friends:
It was the only way Morgan could explain the persistent presence of Braxton
Bragg, now in the guise of an advisor as he had been in the guise of a general.
"He's an old nanny," Mattie half-whispered as they left, for Bragg had
intruded before the call was over.

"But a goat who can devour everything in sight."

"I don't much like your President more," she said seriously. "Cold . . .
cold. His wife is nice, though. She speaks French beautifully. Did you hear
her chatting with St. Leger? And Judah Benjamin. I knew him when Papa
was in Washington. . . . Did I tell you?"

"Yes. You told me." His mind was on his men in prison, and the ones
who wanted into his command again.

He worked on first things first. His tour of Libby Prison had convinced
him that conditions there were decidedly better than those in the Ohio State
Penitentiary. The next day he wrote down a full list of the barbarities
suffered—even thinking of them brought it all back—and it was with the

stench of the dungeon in his nostrils and the foul cold of the cells in his bones that he placed before Secretary of War Seddon his accusations. Seddon listened politely, turning in his chair to hand papers to clerks. When Morgan brought up the problem of his command, Seddon sent a tremor of practiced concern across that dome of a balding head and took up his surprised-professor look. Why, he would certainly . . . Yes, this was a matter needing . . . Between the two curtains of his gray, lank hair he looked at Morgan. Colonel Breckinridge's Ninth Kentucky? See Major Melford.

Morgan thanked him, negotiated a regiment of secretaries and found Melford, then went to Commissioner Ould, in charge of exchanges, the blandest of the lot. Ould didn't even try to disguise his indifference.

"My men," Morgan said evenly, "have the right to be treated fairly. They have captured thousands of Yankee prisoners and in all cases have treated them well. . . . In return they have suffered. . . ."

Ould nodded and implied that the General's complaint was no worse than a hundred others. That he, Ould, was resigned to hear all. Was, by the grace of God, the Cause, the President and his own bottomless patience, a martyr behind this mountain of requests.

"I must remind you, sir . . ." Morgan tried to keep his voice from shaking. "That the Confederate authorities have the power to obtain better treatment for these men . . ." Then he suggested the reciprocal penitentiary treatment.

"We shall see what we can do." Ould all but yawned. "I will be in touch with the different governors soon." He looked through Morgan to thoughts of his own. He rose to shake his visitor's hand, still distracted, his mind on his afternoon off.

He'll do nothing ran through Morgan's brain. I'll give him a week, then I'll see Davis.

He made the rounds: Adjutant-General Cooper, looking as sour as ever. Then to the Office of Provision and Clothing, where T. C. De Leon, a pleasant clerk, and John De Bree, chief of the bureau, gave him promises. Next he went to the quartermaster-general, Colonel A. C. Myers, with about as much luck.

"It would seem that your requests should cause us no undue problems. If you will leave your list I will see that it gets to Mr. B. . . ."

Or Captain M or Major L. . . .

Outside the rain matched his mood. The fresh, clean snow of four days ago puddled now into dirty pillows against the sidewalks. Would spring ever come? And yet he clung to this cold, for it meant the armies were still mired down, the North could not move.

As he stepped off the curb he felt a tug on his sleeve.

"Alston! Alston, you old dog! I thought you were in Mississippi!"

"I couldn't stay away," Alston said simply.

"How are you?" Morgan was still squeezing his arm, unable to believe. "I understand you didn't stay captured long."

Alston chuckled. "I fell asleep on a porch . . . but the boys who captured me, it turned out, were some I'd just paroled, and their officer was a real Yankee gentleman. 'Honor those paroles!' he said. So here I am . . ." More seriously he added, "I've been with Colonel Johnson. Went to Decatur as soon as I heard you were here. Eastin and Castleman are coming to Richmond. Said they couldn't stay away, either. And Hines."

"Hines?"

"They'll be here any day."

Alston. That same grin, that same laugh, that same South Carolina drawl. That morning in Knoxville when a fresh private in Company A asked permission to recruit a company and get a captaincy on their first raid into Kentucky. "Do you remember," Morgan said suddenly, "when we were in the mountains and you pretended I was Colonel DeCourcey?"

"Or that time near Gallatin when Hutch and Bill Breckinridge. . . ."

"Let's get out of this rain."

In the nearest bar they sat in a corner and talked like conspirators, punctuating stories with laughter. Then, with the past reestablished, the present moved in.

"Your troops are in a deplorable condition, General. Shoes, overcoats, saddles, blankets . . . everything. Horses starving. Absolutely no ammunition. Colonel Johnson has done a remarkable job, but he's not God."

Morgan looked away. "All that will be changed, if I have anything to do with it."

"If you could go to Georgia we could supply that command and get the men together again . . . you could, General! I've never known you to let military protocol stop you before!"

"And it won't this time." He tried to smile. "Will you be my A-G?"

"You know I will."

"Come around to the Ballard House in about an hour."

What Alston didn't know, Morgan thought to himself as he left him, was that before he could go to Decatur he had to get that prison exchange. Webber and the others had followed him into the great gamble, and it was his fault they lay rotting and freezing. It was only in Richmond that he could help them. Once that was done . . .

Back at the hotel, letters and telegrams were already piling up at the desk. Requests for transfer: ". . . our proudest ambition being to serve our country with you as a leader." Six inmates of the Richmond jail felt that they "would be of far more benefit to our suffering country in this her hour of need in the field contending against an insolent foe than in being held here in prison." B. Mordecai of Columbia, South Carolina, sent six English saddles and trappings "as a slight token of his high appreciation." And $475 came from Chester, South Carolina.

His heart swelled. They were out there, just as Alston said. All those people. And his men. Adam, dear Adam. And Robert Martin, and Kirkpatrick, and Sisson, and Ellsworth, and Byrne. Lightning working his magic at Midway, on their first big raid into Kentucky, that July. Byrne with his battery at Shiloh, mud shining in his beard, looking up. *Tell the General we'll get there before daylight.* Colonel Martin on his horse in that slow walk under fire in the fight at Milton. With that long black plume. Would he ever forget! We'll get you more guns, Ed! If he could just get Bill Breckinridge's Ninth

Kentucky back again! He would see Adjutant-General Cooper again, first thing. Issue a proclamation! He went back to the rooms. Mattie had gone to Mrs. Davis's luncheon. He found a pen and paper at the little table. He would ask them all to assemble in Georgia. Then . . .

Jan. 13, 1864

SOLDIERS!

I am once more among you, after a long and painful imprisonment. I am anxious to be again in the field. I, therefore, call on soldiers of my command to assemble—Your country needs your service; the field of operation is wide, and the future glorious, if we only deserve it.

He stopped. They owed so much to those who had gone before. To dear old Cluke, dead in prison, to Chenault, with his brains blown out. To Pleasant Whitlow and Greenberry Roberts and Sam Morgan. To Tom. To those still in Chase and Douglas and that damned penitentiary. His brothers, and Basil . . . to those boys captured on Twelve Mile Island. And Quirk. God, he would give an arm for Quirk! Was he alive? He picked up the pen again:

Remember how many of your true comrades are still pining in a felon's cell. They call loudly on you for help. They expect it. Will you disappoint them? The work before us will be arduous, and will require brave hearts and willing hands. Let no man falter or delay.

He read it over, then added: "for no time is to be lost. Every one must bring his horse and gun who can." He signed it "John H. Morgan, Brigadier-General, Provisional Army, Confederate Service." In the left-hand corner, at the bottom: "Official. R. A. Alston, Lieutenant-Colonel and Acting A.A. General."

He delivered it to Alston, waiting in the lobby, and met Mattie as he walked toward the stairs. She was just undoing the tassels of her cloak. Her face was pink from the cold and her eyes were sparkling.

"Had a good luncheon, darling?"

"Gumbo . . . all sorts of strange things! I met the most fascinating lady . . . a Mrs. Putnam. And Mary Chestnut . . ."

"So you're having a good time?"

"As Mrs. Chestnut would say, it was a day equal to one of Stonewall's marches!"

"You went to the Webbses' for breakfast," he said, smiling, and followed her up the stairs, careful not to step on her skirt.

"Yes! And from there to General Lawton's, then to the Chestnuts' . . . Hood was there, and General Stuart in his cavalry jacket and high boots. Oh, how I wished you could have been there to hold up your reputation!"

She stopped on the landing to get her breath and he laughed out loud.

"My dear, darling Mattie, if it needs holding up then let it fall!"

To his surprise she turned blazing blue eyes on him and said in a shaky voice: "You can make a joke of it, John Morgan, but it seems you forget . . . how much these contacts can mean. . . . You don't suppose I go because I enjoy them, do you?"

He said in perplexed honesty, "Why I thought you did! I've been so busy . . ."

They had reached their door and he fumbled with the key.

"Yes. Busy and I know what you're trying to do! But it's just like Papa used to say about Washington . . ." He let her in and she dropped her cloak on a chair. "Decisions aren't made from logic, but from connections . . ."

"Did he now?"

"We've been invited to a charade at the Iveses'. Tomorrow night. Colonel Ives is the President's aide. His wife is the niece of Admiral Semmes. I hear General Buckner's been practicing all day at the Carys'. You will come, won't you? I can't expect these wobbly old Kentucky senators to escort me everywhere! I know how you hate that sort of thing."

"Who told you?" He poked the fire and pulled the drapes against the cold. Seeing Alston had given him such a lift. And sending out his proclamation. Maybe Ould would do something! Maybe Mattie was right. He should get on a first-name basis with these people. It would take time to contact the governors. And if Ould didn't act, there was Davis. "I'd love to go to a charade," he grinned, turning from the window. "A charade would do me good."

But she missed the irony in his voice. "It would!"

"And you? You must be exhausted, holding up that flagging reputation of mine!" He said it with a chuckle, his arms open wide to receive her. Wait six weeks, the doctor had said. Well, it was two months since the baby. . . .

Afterwards she lay against the soft padding between his chest and his shoulder staring up at him, her hair spread down his arm. His hand rested lightly across her waist, his eyes closed against the sweet smell of her. She was chatting on about a lady who made her chignon with a satin slipper.

"You just can't find false hair any more."

"You don't need any." He snuggled her.

He stuck his chin up. The action made the firelight travel across his cheek to his mouth.

"And do you know the ladies are actually saving their night jars for niter? Can you imagine that?"

"I can," he said drowsily.

"Mrs. Putnam tells some frightful tales of draft dodgers. Flashy young men who hang about on street corners . . . why, they're not gamblers, but young men studying for the ministry! And those brawny boys mixing liquor in barrooms? Why, they're consumptive invalids from the other side of the Potomac who are merely obeying the Surgeon-General's advice that they keep cheerful company and take gentle exercise!"

Unconsciously, she had taken on Sallie Putnam's tone, and barely able to keep his eyes open, he murmured, "The other side of the Potomac? Don't tell me we're getting Yankee spies in barrooms. Although on second thought that would be a good place . . ."

"Maryland refugees," she said emphatically, her eyes on the ceiling, watching the little fire snakes wriggle against the dark. Above her, against her hair, she could feel his regular breathing get heavier. He always went to sleep so fast afterwards, while it only seemed to rejuvenate her so! She would help him! She couldn't bear seeing those others . . . that simpering Hood and that braggart Stuart . . . getting all the glory! Mrs. Ould had been positively flattering about her redone dress, and she knew he was trying to help his men in prison! Yes, she decided, her eyes large and shining as she watched the flickering ceiling. Yes, she would help . . .

53

B efore noon he had a note from Breckinridge asking him to come by.

"I think we're on our way," Breckinridge said, trying to keep elation down. "Although not mounted." Then he told him that even Davis disapproved of giving his men horses. But Seddon did argue for the Kentuckians to be together. And more: The hope should be held out to them that they might return to Kentucky most speedily.

"He said that? Maybe I've underestimated him. . . ."

"Exactly. Now we've got to wait for Johnston's reply. The President has asked him to release your men in Georgia."

"This is good news!"

Breckinridge, the politician, gave him a look. "It may be a start," he said cautiously, but then allowed his own hope to explode in a belly laugh. "Have you had any luck?"

He had to admit that he had not.

"Never mind. The government is not the country, John. The country is those young men out there willing to fight for it. And the women. . . ."

A porter from the clerk's desk interrupted them. General Morgan had visitors downstairs.

He excused himself and found George Eastin, Breck Castleman and Tom Hines waiting in the lobby.

"Breck! And George, you dandy! And Tom!" When the first surprise was over—"You can't mean to tell us you didn't expect us," Hines said—they found themselves in a private room in the bar, leaning over their whiskies and laughing like schoolboys.

Hines's face tightened. "I'm here," he said so low it was as if he cherished his information and exposed it reluctantly, "to outline a plan to the President for *help* from *some friends*. . . ."

Morgan waited. He might have guessed. Something turned in his stomach. Hadn't he had enough of all that? But as Hines went on in that presumptuous way of his, the plan made sense. A Captain Longuemare from Missouri was actually the architect: He had seen Davis even before contacting Hines. Morgan didn't have to ask who in Richmond put him in touch with his little spy. But he had to agree with the analysis Hines was outlining now: With Northern discontent and weariness ever since Gettysburg, and now with the stalemate in Georgia and Virginia, the iron seemed hot for a strike.

Strike, yes, he wanted to say. A raid into Kentucky, not this business, but he kept quiet and let Hines go on.

"Capture state arsenals," Hines said in that low voice. "Release and arm Confederate prisoners. There are as many Confederate prisoners in the

North right now as Lee has in his whole army. And do you know what Davis's final reaction was?" Hines turned his wide-set sheep's eyes in that cold face toward him.

"Horror, I suspect."

"No! He jumped up and started pacing in front of me. 'It's a great plan,' he said. 'In the West you have men. Here, only puppets. If you can get good leaders, Captain Hines—military men—West Point–trained . . .' "—Hines took on Davis's masklike look—" 'If you can do that' "—Hines peered at his audience and sucked in his cheeks—" 'I'll have utter confidence in it.' " Hines let a laugh relax his face.

"He wants another Albert Sidney Johnston. . . ."

"No. He wants you! You and Forrest! Neither one West Point!" Hines let a smile move his mouth under that precise mustache, then became intense again. "We know General Breckinridge's plans and he's right: Southwestern Virginia is the place to launch the campaign."

"You say *the* campaign. Do you link such a move with a conspiracy?"

"Why not?"

"And we know that Breckinridge has asked that you, General, be assigned there," added Castleman.

Hines waved his hand loosely, his eyes closed.

Morgan watched him. "You know my opinion of all that?"

"Things have changed." It was Eastin, smiling darkly. He had caught some of Hines's penchant for drama. "The Mississippi is gone . . . now Tennessee. Once the spring push begins . . . or when it does . . . we've got to be ready."

His words were so close to Breckinridge's and to his own thoughts that Morgan frowned to conceal his agreement. The frown deepened when Eastin described a favorite diversion of the guards at Douglas: making naked prisoners ride "Morgan's mule," a sawhorse suspended six feet off the floor by ropes attached to the ceiling. When the "mule" did not move fast enough, blocks of wood were tied to feet to "spur" the "mule" onward . . .

As Eastin spoke, Hines watched his general. "From all sides," Hines said, when arming the prisoners was mentioned again. "From the Ohio . . ."

"But how do you propose to release those prisoners at Douglas? Chicago is a long way from the Ohio."

"By way of Canada," Hines said evenly, without moving his lips.

So St. Leger was right.

"You're not rejoining the command?"

"With your permission, General, I remain in Richmond for further orders from the President." He didn't tell him he already had them, and more: permission to recruit a cavalry force that could act in conjunction with his efforts.

And do you have anyone in mind? Davis had asked in that woebegone way of his.

"Yes, sir, I do."

Davis asked the obvious: "Morgan?"

"No, sir, but one of Morgan's best . . . and trained by Forrest." To Davis's raised eyebrows Hines answered: "Colonel Adam Johnson, sir."

"Well!" The President smiled. "Tell me when you'll need him and we'll see about it."

"I will, sir, I will." *And Morgan, too, if I can get him, when the time comes,* Hines said to himself.

To that purpose he had started recruiting others. Castleman and George Eastin were the first.

"I'm rejoining you, sir," said Castleman. "And so is George. We saw Major Alston this morning. I'm going with you to Decatur."

"So you know about that, too?"

When Eastin saw his general's grin, he refilled the glasses for a toast.

By the time Morgan got back to his room Mattie was fully dressed and close to tears. "I can't wear this old thing! Just look at it!"

"It looks fine to me."

"Fine! Fine? This is a hand-me-down, John Morgan. A dress Tassie Withers gave me. It must have had every inch turned upside down and sideways. And I'll never cover up this spot. . . ." She tugged viciously at a gather to camouflage a mended tear. "Besides, I can't wear something twice. . . ."

"Why don't you wear the green velvet?" he said absent-mindedly. "You always looked . . ."

"The *green velvet?* You don't remember anything, do you?" And the vague dissatisfaction with herself that had been growing all day while he gadded around with his men friends . . . she could just see those fashionable women clustering about her at the Iveses' charade tonight . . . condescending . . . rose to choke her into silence.

My God, he thought, twisting his head as he unbuttoned the stiff collar of his uniform. I'm worried about mistreated prisoners and Northwest Conspiracies and shoes for the feet of my men and food for their stomachs and this girl is crying about wearing something twice! He took off his coat, rolled up his sleeves and splashed water on his face from the basin. Behind him Mattie was whimpering. He scrubbed his head viciously with a towel and turned to her. "Castleman is here. And Eastin, escaped from Douglas. And Tom Hines. Seddon told General Breckinridge today his Kentucky troops could be together. That means an expedition just might be possible . . . I'm sorry if I've neglected you, Mattie. I'll wire T.H. for some money and we'll get you the best new dress in Virginia. Just give me . . ."

All her arguments, that she was trying to help him and he didn't understand, faded when she saw his look. But because she had made the issue, pride kept her from capitulating too easily. She had to recover gracefully, and came out of the skirmish satisfied with the promise of a new outfit.

"Here!" she said, pinning a silk rose at her waist. "This will cover it . . ." She stood back to look at herself in the mirror so he couldn't see how still really irritated—with herself, now, and not with him—she was.

"That's lovely," he said behind her. He turned her to him and waited for her to relax into the kiss. He had to see Seddon tomorrow. Or Benjamin or

Ould. He had to lodge a formal protest. Eastin's stories of men without blankets dying of pneumonia, men hanged by their thumbs with a doctor present, who said they could take more . . .

". . . Now if we don't hurry we'll be late." He held her away, catching his breath at the violet blue of her eyes.

At the Iveses' a woolly-haired butler let them in. Mattie allowed him to take her cloak. Behind him Cora Ives, resplendent in family diamonds and black lace, lifted her arms in welcome. Mattie's eyes went from the table set with silver to the old butler now making his way in the background.

"Marvelous, isn't he?" the lady whispered. "One of those noiseless darkies who would consider themselves complete failures if you ever had to ask for anything." She sighed. "A dying race, I'm afraid." She guided them into her parlor, glittering with candles.

Mattie's Washington memories came back with every gleam of linen and whiff of perfume. How she had shone there, the belle of soirées! She remembered that silly little Congressman from Illinois—no match for her Morgan —how devoted he was! She had been so long away from the center of things she had forgotten . . . and how tired she was of worrying about money and being drab! Wasn't this the real world, after all, and not that grubbing farmer with his wife washing in the pancake basin? Wasn't this—and she could hardly define "this," unless it was a stubborn determination to float somewhere above, if even an inch or two, above the muck—wasn't this what distinguished men from animals? To be civilized! Yes! *This* was what her husband, John Hunt Morgan, and the others were fighting for—civilization —and she would help him, as Cora Ives surely helped her husband, by being witty and charming and ever so fashionable. Hadn't she seen it working in Washington? It was so often not what one was, but one's presence. . . . She squared her shoulders, feeling suddenly comfortable as she walked into the room under everybody's gaze, even while she calculated how she could get material for a new dress, or find out who the best seamstress was.

The ladies were already banked against the walls. A regular flower bed, Morgan started to say, but Mattie was waving to Mrs. Chestnut. Mrs. Preston, whose husband had the conscription, came over, and Mrs. Ould. Mrs. Ould's dyed black hair looked like a block of wood against the deadly white of her face—some *poudre de riz* had stuck in the wrinkles of her neck —and her dress was strips of green and blue paper. Mattie could have laughed out loud at Morgan's look. "She told me," she whispered to him behind her fan, "she's supposed to be the River Nile. But don't say a word! It's a secret."

Opened arms and greetings led him away from her to a place—opened up for him generously by Buckner—in the group of men, clad in black and gray, like so many barn swallows. On a sofa in front of the men sat the President and Mrs. Davis, with black-eyed little Maggie Davis on one end. "Wait till you see Burty," someone said.

"Why?"

"It's supposed to be a secret—but he had to shave his mustache for the part!"

"Shh!"

Under the buzz and chatter, like an organ continuo, the voice of the President droned a melancholy cadence as he spoke with General Lawton. Across the room St. Leger Grenfel, as a Moor, dipped his turban in greeting. It was pinned by a brooch holding down a spray of chicken feathers. On a sofa against the far wall John Hood was spread like a willing sacrifice on the altar of a dozen young girls' admiration. Jeb Stuart, with that magnificent waved beard, not a hair out of place, walked quickly across the floor in his high boots, wrinkled fashionably above the ankles, and said something to General Breckinridge, who laughed out loud as if he hadn't a care in the world. A peal of giggles came from Hood's sofa, "Buck" Campbell's the loudest.

Mrs. Semmes stepped forward and announced in a high tremulo that the charade was about to begin. Her husband, senator from Louisiana, watched fondly from a chair set close to the President's sofa. Mattie, across the room between Mary Breckinridge and Mrs. Putnam, sent Morgan a smile. From a side door Hetty Cary sallied forth in a gray wig and a high choker of pearls. Her trailing dress, the train improvised from a tablecloth, swept grandly past, turned, and made a circle at her feet. Then she puffed out her cheeks and raised a stick over John Morgan as if she would confer knighthood. Everybody clapped. After her Queen Victoria, easily guessed, came Maggie Davis as a Fair Penitent, then Burton Harrison, the President's secretary, *sans* mustache, as an Indian brave, followed by a half dozen others —Buckner, it turned out, was "Beast" Butler issuing his famous Order 38 in New Orleans (and strangely enough, the only reference to the war)— until the floodtide of Mrs. Ould overwhelmed them all as the River Nile.

Buckner grinned. "May I?" he asked, with a glance toward Mattie.

"Yes, of course! She would be delighted!" Morgan watched Buckner's long-legged stride take him to Mattie, saw him bend briefly from the waist, and the crook of his arm accept her hand as he escorted her into supper. One by one the men around him peeled away, and he found himself paired with Mrs. Ould.

Well, you did want to get on a first-name basis, didn't you?

All through dinner he remembered this lady's husband, the yawn, the indifference. He decided to see Davis first thing.

"I'll wait for you," Mattie said mischievously, as he dressed the next morning.

"Yes. I won't be long. Plenty of time. Eleven o'clock?"

"Yes."

She watched him leave, then jumped from the bed and opened the drawer of the night stand. She pulled out a scissors from her leather case and sat before the mirror. She saw Buck Campbell flirting with John Hood. And Hetty Cary looking at her Morgan. Hetty Cary had *bangs*. Curled bangs, at that. She lifted her chin, studied her hairline, and lifted the scissors. The long strands of black hair fell in her lap. She looked at what was left: shaggy spikes pointing past her eyebrows. She tore a page of stationery, wet the pieces and made papers, twisting them around the ends of her hair. Four knots stood out over her eyes. She looked at herself and smiled. *Won't he be surprised?*

An hour later, dressed in her fur-trimmed cape, she sat in the lobby by a potted palm with a good view of the front door. Ahead of her, in a diagonal line, the "ladies' wall"—to prevent male eyes from glancing at ankles—separated her from the rest of the room. On the other side of the palm two girls were giggling.

"Who is going to Europe for General Hood's leg?" one whispered.

"Doctor Darby," the other said.

"Suppose the ship is wrecked?"

"Never mind . . . half a dozen are ordered."

"No wonder the General says they call him a centipede—his leg is in everybody's mouth!"

Mattie was shocked. She saw the tip of the nearest girl's skirt, and her shoe. The very idea of making a joke of a man's leg . . . Then their next words pinned her to the chair.

"I'll tell you who's in everybody's mouth." The first girl giggled, and waited.

"You don't have to tell *me*," the first girl emphasized, and sighed.

"That wife of his . . . ugh! How can he *stand* her?"

"I wasn't thinking of *her*," the first one said. "Have you ever seen a pair of eyes like that? The way he looked back at me when I saw him leave the lobby this morning!"

"The Thunderbolt of the Confederacy," the first one whispered. "I'd like to be struck by him! Did you read that account, when he came back from prison? Surrounded by a bevy of ladies. I'll bet he was! Can you—"

Mattie got up and ran to the stairs, tripping on her skirt on the first step. She stopped, leaned on the rail to get her breath. *Have you ever seen a pair of eyes like that? Surrounded by a bevy. . . .* And she had so wanted to help him! Had even cut her hair for their wedding picture, and was waiting for him to return, as a surprise! Maybe the Yankee paper was right! Maybe he was a womanizer, *or would be, if he had the chance!*

He went straight to Seddon's office. He would ask for nothing less than permission to assemble his men in Southwest Virginia for a raid into Kentucky. Before he reached the door he met St. Leger in the hall. "Wait for me here," he said.

"You're up to something!"

"I am."

"In that case, I'll wait."

The Secretary of War motioned Morgan into a chair. "I hear you have conferred with General Breckinridge," he said. The long hair which fell from either side of his balding head framed a long nose. In spite of his efforts at geniality, Seddon still looked like a ghoul.

Morgan waited a minute. "You must understand then, Mr. Secretary, how anxious I am to gather my command. . . ."

Seddon turned his mouth down in an effort to suppress a smile. "We have heard." He handed him a letter.

It was from Joe Johnston, angrily protesting recruiting by Morgan's and Forrest's agents in Georgia. *They are breaking up our infantry, enticing them to desert, and shielding deserters, as well as conscripts and volunteers out of the infantry where alone we want them.* Morgan looked up.

"However, there is a situation graver than that," Seddon whined.

Adam Johnson, dear Adam, was sending agents throughout the South to solicit funds and equipment. Through the first flush of gratitude Morgan heard himself say to the waiting man before him: "Kentuckians do not beg, sir. I will send Colonel Johnson a telegram immediately."

"I should hope that will correct the situation, General." Then, condescendingly: "Independent cavalry commanders sometimes do not understand the necessities of the regular army." He didn't bother to rise when Morgan left.

In the hall, St. Leger had news. A clerk from Adjutant-General Cooper's office had just told him of a telegram from General Joe Johnston refusing any cavalry transfers. Including the Ninth Kentucky or Dortch, whose petition was denied.

"Damn!"

"Don't waste your energies swearing, lad."

"That comes as strange advice from you."

The Englishman grunted. "Play on their vanity, lad, their vanity. Make what you want what they need. Have you read any Yankee papers lately?"

"What, have you another clipping for me?"

St. Leger ignored the remark. "They say the Confederate cavalry has lost its nerve. Why not pick up that little gauntlet? Just tell me what you want to do, and we'll convince this Confederacy of yours it's in their best interest to let you do it."

Within a half-hour, on a little desk in the hall outside Seddon's office, the masterpiece was written: Morgan suggesting that he could invade Kentucky by crossing the Cumberlands at Pound Gap, recruit, get horses, draw off the Federal cavalry threatening Joe Johnston in North Georgia. St. Leger, playing on Richmond's love of reputation, dictated: "Give me, sir, only the assistance I now claim, and the enemy will no longer vaunt themselves that the vigor of our cavalry is diminished. . . ."

Morgan left the letter with Seddon's secretary and watched Grenfel stroll jauntily off. One more, he said to himself. It had been a long day. Ordnance. He spoke with A. B. Upshur, Chief Clerk. Captain Brooke, the man said in a high thin whine, was out of town.

Why was it every time he left them he felt up to his armpits in manure?

It wasn't that they were hostile; he could have dealt with that. It was that they were so unconsciously incompetent . . . totally unaware of the fact that all their energies were directed at paper, and not the problem at hand. It might have been ludicrous if it hadn't been so sad, if it hadn't involved the lives of his men. He wondered how these flunkies faced their wives at night.

He was looking forward to a good stiff drink when he got back to the hotel.

Mattie faced him, furious.

"What have you done to your hair?"

"You don't like it? You seemed to like it well enough on Hetty Cary."

"What are you talking about?"

"We had an appointment with the photographer, remember? Where have you been for the last three hours? I've been waiting . . . in the lobby. . . ."

It was to be their *wedding* picture . . . the idea took her breath. Now she had ruined her looks! And for him! It was too much! And he didn't care!

"You deliberately stayed away . . ."

"Mattie, I . . . I forgot."

His plea was the last straw. She picked up her hand mirror and flung it at him. To infuriate her even more he caught the mirror and laid it back on the dresser. He stood there, so tall, so polite, in that quiet way waiting. His eyes sought hers, then roved her face.

He didn't say a word. He only stood there, waiting. *Have you ever seen a pair of eyes like that?* The girl was right. And they were hers, hers. . . .

She turned from him, sobbing. Brother wounded, and Alice didn't know where he was. Who would be next, when the fighting started again? She couldn't think about it! Didn't he know how much this picture meant to her? Then she felt his hands on her shoulders.

"We'll go tomorrow, first thing," he said between kisses down her neck.

Kitty Hill arrived at noon, just after the session with the photographer. When they came back to the hotel there she was, Kitty Hill with little Frances and baby Lucy.

Brother and sister swirled in an embrace that almost caused them to stumble over little Frances, sucking her thumb. Celina, looking up from the baby in her arms, beamed from a low chair by the window.

"This is Lucy Lee," Kitty said simply, her face radiant. "Isn't she beautiful!"

"Looks like her father," Morgan teased. "May I take her, Celina?"

"Be careful!"

A corner of the blanket caught in the chair arm and in the instant it took to free it he felt Celina's fingers brush the back of his hand. Celina— home—the warmth of it came crashing down.

"How are you, Celina?" She was an old woman now, and the years came back.

"Fine, Massa, jes' fine . . ."

He held out his arms as she handed the baby over.

She was beautiful, with the pertest of noses, like her mother's. She was so light! She closed her eyes against the glare of the window and a delicate fringe of eyelash rested against her cheek. He looked up at Mattie and smiled.

Kitty bent to little Frances and looked up to her brother. "This is your Uncle Johnny, Francey. Say 'Pleased to meet you!' "

The little girl looked at the floor and up again, and crooked her forefinger over her nose. Morgan gave the baby back to Celina and dropped to his heels and rocked back and forth, trying to make Francey look at him. When she did he held out his arms. "Come, let's ride! Would you like to ride a horsey?" he asked, and when the thumb came out to reveal a smile, he swung her onto his shoulders and began galloping around the room until the pictures on the wall shook. Francey, squealing delight, pleaded to stop. When her "horsey" did, she yelled again, pretending to kick with spurs. The "horse" began again, to more squeals; then Morgan, really beginning to tire, swung her around and hugged her to his heart, the fine blond hair mingling with his beard. Mattie watched them with a softened delight. She had feared a little this meeting with his celebrated sister. Now she could feel only pride. She was so proud, so proud to be his wife! He was so sweet, so utterly sweet! And the feeling that she *would help him* almost choked her as he bent down to kiss her cheek.

"How long can you stay?" he asked Kitty across the top of Mattie's head.

"Well," she laughed, "Powell wants me in Richmond . . ."

"Oh, do stay with us!" Mattie begged, but Kitty smiled in a way her brother would always remember. "I have to go back," she said simply. "A.P. . . ." But she didn't finish.

It was a lovely interlude. They had supper sent up, and Hopemont, all the old days, came back. It was over too soon. Kitty left the next afternoon, and permission to raid Kentucky was refused an hour later.

Could Richmond be so fickle? One day acclaiming him, the next guarding its prerogatives? Seddon saying one thing, Cooper another. He had no time to waste on their nonsense.

"You'd better, lad." St. Leger pulled at his pipe and studied the smoke. They had just seen Kitty off, and some of the old days came back for him too. But his American friend was, the Englishman thought irritably and at the same time affectionately, for all his gentility and connections, provincial. The tobacco was good; first-rate stuff just arrived via blockade. He settled himself in one of the chairs in the lobby and couldn't resist the temptation to sound pedantic—an inclination which always measured, in direct ratio, his expectation that he would be misunderstood.

"As Lord Chesterfield wrote his son, a man of the world must, like the chameleon, be able to take every hue. Now that's not dishonest—only, as Chesterfield said, a necessary compliance, for it relates to manners, not to morals." He bowed to some people walking by.

"And how do you separate the two?" Morgan frowned, momentarily distracted. Mattie, after seeing Kitty off, pleaded a headache and stayed upstairs. He sat with Grenfel in a corner of the lobby by one of the potted palms. The Englishman leaned forward and dumped his ashes in the dirt, then relit his pipe.

"Oh, I know," Grenfel pulled his smoke, then watched it leave him, smacking his lips. "You want the whole world to be of a piece. Because you, lad, are too much of a piece. No, let me finish. You've got to realize that these people—Seddon, Cooper, Ould—especially Ould!"—he laughed— "are protecting their little windmills."

"Well, if being a chameleon's so important, and you say I've no talent for it, how about being my liaison in Richmond?"

"Why, where are you going?"

"To Georgia. As if you didn't know."

"I see. I really . . ." St. Leger studied his pipe, and then the people passing in the lobby before him. "This Confederacy of yours, if you don't mind my saying so, my friend, is like a man clinging to the face of a mountain in a storm. He no longer thinks about getting to the top, but surviving on his ledge. To go back down is unthinkable—impossible, since he has sacrificed so much to get here. To go on with an avalanche coming down on him is equally impossible, so he turns inward on himself, like some animal devouring its own entrails. That's what your government is now. Your women are smarter. They go to their 'starvation balls'—as they call them—and watch this *danse macabre*, without hope, with a kind of shameless despair that is really remarkable. But it's too sad, too sad, and I've had enough sadness, my friend . . ." Grenfel looked up into those expectant eyes, stopped, then laughed. "Ah, well! *Il faut savoir s'ennuyer*, eh? All right, lad. For you . . ."

"Decatur, Georgia. I should have gone two weeks ago. To my men."

To my men. Shoeless and hungry, waiting . . .

Grenfel's voice came back: "You've made quite an impression here in Richmond, lad."

"Impression. Taffy pulls and charades. This whole town is a joke! What will come of it?"

"*Imshi besselema*, as the Arabs say." Grenfel smiled.

"And what is that supposed to mean?"

"It's what they say when they can't think of anything else. It's almost untranslatable, but it means something like 'Go in peace.' "

"I wish I could."

"The Arabs have another saying. That no wish is given to you that you haven't the power to fulfill."

"I wish," Morgan said even more slowly, "that were so."

"Ah, sometimes we have to work a little harder for some than for others, my boy. . . ." But it was a false optimism and Grenfel dropped it and asked bluntly: "When do you leave?"

"Tomorrow morning. At last. And I've had no word . . . not a word . . . about the Ninth. What is that?"

"Another petition. Wanting a transfer," St. Leger breathed, then shook his head. "I'll see Melford tomorrow."

"Keep in touch."

"I will, lad. Oh, and Morgan . . ." Grenfel dipped his head sideways in that quick way he had, a boyish gesture that had so endeared him to the men. "Be careful, eh?"

As he walked away, Morgan felt the Englishman's eyes on him. He started to turn and look, but superstition kept him from it. To turn and look meant that you expected never to see that person again.

54

"**B**urn *Chicago and New York?*" Even Castleman was a bit awed. He looked at Eastin.

"That's what Hines said. If they can do it, we can do it. This war's come down to that." They were talking about Ulric Dahlgren's unsuccessful raid on Richmond—with the help of two thousand cavalrymen under General George Custer—and of his orders to assassinate President Davis and his Cabinet. Dahlgren, killed in the raid, was the youngest colonel in the U.S. Army and the son of an admiral. He had lost a leg at Gettysburg and was called by the Richmond papers "a polite young man." When the assassination orders were revealed he became "Ulric the Hun." Within a week Hines had his orders for Toronto.

"And the General?"

"Oh, Hines'll get the General in on it, you wait and see," Eastin said. "Just as he's gotten St. Leger."

"How?"

"I don't know, but you wait and see. Will you help us?"

Castleman blanched. He had always considered himself a Kentucky gentleman.

"Nothing underhanded, Breck. But you know how much the General wants to go back to Kentucky. If his Kentucky raid could be coordinated with an uprising in Ohio . . . there wouldn't be anything wrong with that, now would there?" Especially, Eastin wanted to add but didn't, if Adam Johnson is helping with the uprising?

If Castleman ever had any doubts about Hines's influence, they were dispelled when Eastin showed him orders signed by Seddon for the purchase of two hundred bales of cotton in North Mississippi, with Hines himself to arrange their disposal. On March 18 Hines asked that Major Wintersmith, of Colonel Bayne's Bureau of Ordnance, Richmond, be assigned as his agent, with the money to be deposited in Hines's account in a Montreal bank. When the Major, resenting orders sent him "by hand"—and by a mere captain—protested, Hines went to the top. Seddon's orders to Ordnance were clear: "Captain Hines wishes to depart on his mission as soon as possible." The next day, with an issued Navy Colt and orders to allow him to pass through the Confederate lines, Hines was off.

"When I go through Washington I'll shake hands with the President—the other President, that is, with a fistful of Confederate bonds to finance the Great Conspiracy." He winked at Eastin.

"How will you do that?"

"I look enough like John Wilkes Booth. It saved me before! See you in Canada!"

Morgan just missed him. He came back from Georgia depressed about the condition of his men. At each depot along the way, in each little town the shabbiness of the countryside was appalling. The women and children— barefoot in the cold—the old men. One woman came on board timidly begging. Her husband had been killed at Chickamauga. . . . He reached into his pocket and gave her two Confederate ten-dollar bills. He knew they wouldn't buy much. Her gratitude was embarrassing.

By the time he reached Decatur he realized the South was exhausted. He regretted now that swift telegram to Johnson. Kentuckians don't beg? When Adam was trying to outfit his regiments from an economy on its knees? He arrived humbled and apologetic.

"No, don't apologize," said Adam as they toured the camp. "We're doing better than we have been."

He saw men barefoot, their toes blue with cold, some with rags for shoes and thin blankets for saddles. Some had made bridles from the bark of pawpaw trees. At Byrne's battery a boy without hands, who wore some artificial ones made from old leather, was grooming the artillery horses—in the old days they would have been rejected as unsound and winded.

"Lost 'em at Shiloh, sir!" the boy said, holding his arms up. "But they do right well, an' ole Red Man here don't mind." Red Man, sway-backed and concave above the eyes, quivered his lower lip. Johnson made a friendly remark and they moved on.

"You see how it is."

Yes, he saw. And he returned more determined than ever to do something about it. As if to support his determination, orders were waiting in Richmond for the Department of Southwestern Virginia. And a full-strength regiment had been assigned to him, the Fourth Kentucky Cavalry under Henry Giltner.

"Congratulations!" John C. Breckinridge leaned across the map spread on his desk to shake his hand. "I'm sorry I didn't see you before you left. How are things in Decatur?"

"I'm still waiting for some word about the Ninth Kentucky, General. They're still refusing to let Dortch's battalion transfer. But I'll have the men under Adam Johnson."

"Have a drink? No?" Breckinridge poured himself a whiskey. "We've had exciting times while you've been away."

"So I've heard."

"Grant has been put in charge of the Army of the Potomac. Things are popping up there. From the minute he became lieutenant-general, he has taken charge. Left Sherman as his vice-regent in the West. Congress is giving him everything he wants. . . . Their intent this time is to crush the South. Some estimates as high as eight hundred thousand troops." Breckinridge squared his massive shoulders. "His plan, as I see it, is simple: He'll cross the Rapidan and march that seventy miles to Richmond from the north, while Butler moves out of Fortress Monroe, just one day's sail on the James from the south. Meanwhile, Sigel in the Valley will cut the railroad to Lynchburg, Lee's supply lifeline. This is where we come in. The Shenandoah must be held at all costs. I have heard General Lee say he fears hunger worse than Yankees. At all costs."

"Yes, sir."

Breckinridge glared. "Sigel will move down the Shenandoah to capture Lynchburg directly, if he can. It will be a concentrated effort, a three-pronged move. If Lee can hold on, we'll do our part. I suggest you head-quarter at Abingdon."

"Orders can be sent within the hour. My men have been waiting. I'll leave as soon as possible."

Breckinridge raised his eyebrows, then pulled one end of his long mus-tache and smiled his slow smile. "As soon as you get settled, see General Longstreet at Morristown. He's wintering there and around Greeneville, Tennessee. He may have some news for you."

"The Ninth?"

"You are forgetting our celebrated 'Reorganization,'" Breckinridge frowned. "Which is designed to completely wreck this army. I'll do all I can to get you back the Ninth Kentucky."

"Thank you, General." Morgan rose. He had to see St. Leger.

"He's . . . out of town," Bragg's orderly informed him.

"Where?"

"I . . . I don't know, sir. Probably out hunting," the orderly added, grin-ning.

Hunting what, the old dog?

"Abingdon?" Mattie asked, bewildered.

"I think you'll like it. I've heard it's a pretty little town. In the mountains. In the country. No more eggs at ten dollars a dozen, darling! Clear air, and the springtime there must be beautiful . . . look." He sat up and lumped the blanket across their knees. "Here's Virginia. The Tidewater, the Piedmont hills, and the mountains: the Blue Ridge, the Great Valley and the Alle-ghenies." He pulled up a fold and punched creases with the side of his hand. "The Great Valley—the Shenandoah—is drained by many rivers going in different directions. The Shenandoah River drains the whole northern third, and flows north to the Potomac."

"Harpers Ferry?"

"Yes! That's why that was important. The middle third is drained by the James and the Roanoke, which break through the Blue Ridge and flow east." He leaned closer, looking at her, his eyes glittering, his smile soft. "Now the southern third is drained by the New, which cuts through the Allegheny ridges to the west and flows"—his hand went up—"all the way into the Ohio. Then there's the Holston, which goes southwest into Tennessee near Knoxville."

"Over the edge of the bed," she teased.

"Now look. This line is the Virginia & Tennessee Railroad, coming up from Knoxville to Lynchburg and over to Petersburg, then straight north to Richmond. Lynchburg"—he tapped her knee—"is very important. It is not only on the railroad but it is also on the James River. It's Lee's supply depot."

"But why Abingdon . . . ?"

"It's on that railroad, too, down near the state line, and between the north and south forks of the Holston River. If the Federals come up from Knoxville through Bull's Gap, along that railroad . . . and look here, from Abingdon I can scout all that country along the railroad down into Tennessee. Protect the salt mines at Saltville and the lead mines at Wytheville. The whole southern third of the Valley. . . ."

"Closest to the Yankees."

"Yes."

"Like the advance?"

"Yes, I suppose you could call it that . . . but if that rail line to Lynchburg falls into their hands, or the lead. . . ."

She stopped him.

"Kiss me, John Morgan. You know I'll go with you anywhere."

He held her head in his hands, and the world went away. Lying beside him later, she raised herself on one elbow to watch his face. The eyelids of his closed eyes had blue shadows. His mouth, in sleep, was soft. She kissed it, and he stirred and held her against him. She rested her cheek against his chest.

"I've had a letter from Alice. She wants to come to Richmond."

"Just when we're leaving? She can come to Abingdon . . ."

"She wants to be near her beau."

"What outfit is he with?"

"Marye's battery, Pegram's battalion."

He was fully awake and opened his eyes. "Pegram? That's in A.P.'s command!"

"It is?"

"We'll ask A.P. to let him have leave. . . . But where will she stay?"

"Mrs. Breckinridge has already agreed . . ."

He held her from him. "Then you've already made arrangements?"

She nodded and he pulled her back to him, laughing. "Oh, my Mattie. My little general. Yes, you would, wouldn't you? And Key? Have you settled his fate, too?"

"I wrote that he could join your command when you got orders, if he wanted to."

"I surrender." He made a mock wave of his hand. "If Seddon or Ould or that fool Cooper could be half as efficient, we'd have nothing to worry about."

"Oh, yes we would."

Before he could stop her she was sobbing.

"Mattie?"

"Oh, it's so awful . . . all of this! So awful I can't think of it . . . I try!" She stopped and sniffed, and sat up. He held onto her arm. "I try, honestly I do!"

"Try just a little longer," he whispered. "I promise. Just a little longer. . . ."

From the Richmond pulpits the next day came the announcement: A boatload of returning prisoners . . . citizens were asked to send refreshments to the Capitol Square . . .

The town went wild. Hundreds crowded to see the lines of bewildered, grinning men trudge into the square. "Dixie" blared, and "Hurrah for the Graybacks." The President gave a stirring speech, then the Governor of Virginia. Beside Morgan Mattie was hopping up and down to see over the shoulders of a man in front. All at once Morgan recognized a face he knew.

"From the penitentiary!" he said, unbelieving. "See, Mattie, there . . . Colonel Smith! I'll be . . . and CAL!"

It was. It was, incredibly, Cal.

They stood on the sidewalk hugging, a circle of joy.

"Where's Key?" Cal shouted over the band.

"He's at Aug . . ." The band stopped. "He's at Augusta with T.H. Alice is there, too . . ."

But Cal worried him. His loss of weight and sallow color, a weakness in his walk, could not be covered up, even by the joy. "I'll be all right!"

"Of course you will."

"And A.P.?"

"Up at the front . . ." he said as they maneuvered through the edge of the crowd. "How's Webber? Steele? Basil? Charl? Richard? Did they make things hard on Richard when they found him in my bunk?"

"By that time they were so befuddled they didn't know what was going on."

They had to slow up for Smith, who was still suffering from a stomach ailment and limping.

"Webber was in solitary when we left," said Cal as they waited. "But maybe, just maybe, Duke and the others might be getting out. . . ."

It would be too much to hope for. He couldn't let himself think that far.

Shadeland. Every night he dreamed of Shadeland. He would wake to remember the hill behind the pond where they trained Sard; the long row of walnuts, the bluebirds, and how after a rain the sun shone golden across the fields; the mist in the hollows, the gray forms of stone fences, and then the overpowering smell of honeysuckle in spring. He would count the horses: Shadeland running after hawks, Delilah afraid of puddles, Miss Lexington racing against Sanders's stallion. And farther back: Tommy Cunningham and Theophile Parsons in the little brick schoolhouse, and McGregor and his cocks.

Cal brought it all back, he supposed. When they talked about their plans, when they outlined the future, the past came, unbidden, a continuity he clung to. Another, closer part of the past haunted him: his men in prison. He took Cal to Ould's office, as added evidence. Nothing happened.

"Never mind!" said Cal, smiling grimly. "We'll get them back. Besides, isn't it time to ride a horse again?"

Spring in the Southern mountains: the dreaded, looked-for time. Orders in his pocket to see Longstreet, and Mattie settled in a little rented house in Abingdon. Two days after they arrived he left for Tennessee.

Morristown, in the Holston Valley and on the Knoxville side of Bull's Gap, was really the advance. To Longstreet (West Point, Mexico, Bull Run, the Peninsula and Seven Days, Fredericksburg, Antietam, Gettysburg— and blamed for the delay at Cemetery Ridge) was given the job of holding the gaps and mountain passes northeast of Knoxville. If they fell, as Breckinridge had warned, the Shenandoah would go, and Richmond would be cut off from all supplies. But the minute Morgan met him, he knew Longstreet was the man for the job.

"I've kept in close touch with General Breckinridge, General Morgan," Longstreet said as he held out his hand and motioned his visitor to a chair. "And we both agree: A campaign into Kentucky is our first priority. Not only will it remount our troops, but provide a diversion to help Johnston in Georgia."

Morgan was elated, with the man, with his plans. The state of Longstreet's troops and horses was horrible, but he had gotten used to that. The will was there, that's what counted. On April 1, with orders for a Kentucky raid barely dry on the paper, he wired Mattie, waiting in Abingdon: AM DELIGHTED WITH GENL. LONGSTREET. WILL BE WITH YOU TONIGHT.

But instead of protecting the mountain passes, Longstreet was called back to Richmond, leaving Morgan to guard the whole southwest line with fewer than twenty-five hundred men . . . most not even there yet. A raid into Kentucky was postponed again.

Back in Abingdon, he realized his "camp" was ridiculously inadequate: log lean-tos barely able to keep out the chill mountain nights. Half-naked, disgruntled men sat around fires wondering if there would be enough food for the next meal. And an added, nagging worry: Too many of these men were recent recruits—stragglers from other outfits, with no loyalty to anybody. The Fourth Kentucky, recently assigned, was the worst. Its Colonel Giltner was a broad-faced, stocky officer of few words. When he returned Morgan's salute there was no smile nested in that salt-and-pepper beard. He made it clear he considered his regiment "attached" to Morgan.

"Of course, Colonel," Morgan said graciously. "Cigar?"

Giltner relaxed, and Morgan recognized, in the tense eyes and grim mouth, the months of fatigue they all felt. He waited to catch Giltner's glance as he held out a match. Over the flame their eyes met. They both knew their work was cut out for them, but in that instant they knew, too, they could trust one another. Still, Morgan would feel a lot better when Adam Johnson and Martin and Bowles and the veterans from Decatur arrived. He made a joke, Giltner laughed, and Cal came in.

Adam Johnson stepped off the train on April 2 without the men from Georgia, then asked permission to go to Richmond immediately. To get a separate command.

Morgan was incredulous. Adam, who had held his men together while he was in prison, who had so generously offered to defend the Ohio raid, who had been his mainstay, his hope. "Adam, Adam, how can I?" Morgan rubbed the heels of his palms against his temples and motioned him to a chair. "Sit down. I tell you, I've never needed you the way I need you now."

But Johnson evaded those searching eyes. He sat down reluctantly and studied Morgan's cigar, burning abandoned and forgotten in a brass tray near the corner of the desk. He knew himself to be a miserable liar, and wouldn't try any tall tales now. Besides, if he knew Morgan, they wouldn't work. But how could he tell him that he had been in communication with the Secretary of War and Hines? That it was his assignment to make the Copperhead connection in Kentucky and Ohio, until Morgan got there? His orders had been explicit: Morgan was not to know. He hoped the old excuses would work.

"You know I've never considered myself part of your force, sir." He cleared his throat. "When I brought the Tenth Kentucky to you in Murfreesboro it was of my own volition. Even when I worked under General Forrest, I acted independently."

Morgan missed the hesitancy; all he felt and sensed was something new, harsh and obdurate, about him. Those honest brown eyes looked up now with an almost hostile, dare-you glint, and a muscle in Johnson's jaw was working—a sure sign, in the old days, of anger. Morgan's first reaction was shock.

"I have no intention," he said softly, "of keeping an officer who does not want to work with me." He stopped, leaned over, crushed the cigar. The smoke drifted. "I do feel, however, you have given me no reason," he added stiffly, feeling resentment rise.

Johnson ignored the invitation. "I'm glad you feel like that, General. Colonel Alston will have my official resignation this afternoon." And he as stiffly left.

"Let him go," he heard Cal say behind him. "Martin will be here soon from Decatur. He's been Johnson's second-in-command from the beginning. He'll handle the Tenth Kentucky."

The Tenth Kentucky. What was it? Nobody had to tell him. And maybe that's why Adam was leaving. Understrength companies of dismounted or ill-mounted troops. Cal read his mind. "Martin can get them in shape," he said. "And you'll have Bowles, Kirkpatrick, Cassell. When they get here. In the meantime, Giltner's Fourth Kentucky . . . he's a good man."

The truth was he was cut to the heart. Adam's dear, dependable face turned arrogant . . . he was baffled. Nostalgia overcame bitterness. Adam in Nashville after that miserable retreat from Bowling Green. Adam speaking up at Sidney Johnston's headquarters to tell of Buckner at Donelson. The determination, the integrity. Adam in the dusty streets of Corinth greeting him after the Lebanon Races. And the joy at Murfreesboro that December when he and Martin joined the command. That had been high tide. Just after the victory at Hartsville, before his promotion, before his marriage. Adam with his bright young captains: Clay Merriwether, Jacob Bennett, little Sam Taylor. Johnson that night the command crossed the Green on the Christmas raid. Johnson swimming his horses over the Cumberland on their way to Ohio. Johnson's charge against the Green River abatis, where Chenault died. "Ole Stovepipe" escaping at Buffington, to lead

"Morgan's men" at Chickamauga. Now so suddenly distant. What had happened?

He blamed himself. He'd stayed in Richmond too long. Neglected the men, wasted time trying to talk those bureaucratic fools into supplies, into exchanges. He poured himself a whiskey. The warmth of it felt good. He belted another and waited for the familiar tingling to pass through his mind. Longstreet to Lee, and Adam God knew where. His men in Ohio lost and waiting. They might as well be on the moon. And his men here, holding the whole Valley against an army at Knoxville.

"What he can't know won't hurt him," Castleman almost murmured to Cal that afternoon, his voice soft.

"What do you mean by that?"

Castleman looked desperate. "I need somebody to confide in," he said.

Cal's good-natured look gave way to a frown.

"We both love him," Castleman said.

Cal waited.

"Can I trust you?"

"That's a stupid question."

"Can I?"

"You can."

"Hines recruited Colonel Johnson in Richmond. Johnson is on his way back to Secretary of War Seddon for orders, for a raid into western Kentucky, and more."

Cal shot him a look.

"A little trip north . . . Indiana, Ohio maybe. . . ."

"Does this have . . . ?"

"Yes. Colonel Johnson knows how much the General dislikes all that. But the effort—maybe our hope—lies in this conspiracy. You've seen the troops."

Oh, yes, Cal had seen them. And he knew the caliber of recruits coming in. A few veterans, but too many stragglers—if not downright deserters— and even criminals, the backwash of the South finding its way into the army now that people were starving. It had happened in other outfits, and now it was beginning to happen here: the scum of the South using army service as an excuse to eat—or rob or worse. Just that week Alston had received affidavits supporting charges of rape and thievery against some Morgan men. Cal was amazed when he read the complaints. Alston promised swift justice. Johnny would need every good officer he could get, and losing Johnson now was a terrible blow. Knowing that Johnson was involved in the conspiracy was for Cal a marginal satisfaction. He couldn't share Castleman's grim hope.

"Is anybody else in on this?"

"Eastin, and . . ." But he didn't finish. Colonel Giltner passed by, and they both saluted smartly.

The AWOL problem continued. On April 3, the day after Johnson left, Morgan instructed Alston as adjutant to dismount all guilty parties, send them to Castle Thunder at Richmond under charges and turn their horses

and equipment over to men of good reputation. When W. C. P. Breckinridge's Ninth Kentucky arrived, things would change.

Then the blow fell. A letter from St. Leger Grenfel, but Morgan as he
read couldn't be surprised:

March 30, 1864

General:

Sorry I missed you on your return to Richmond. Major Melford told
me that he regretted to say that nothing had been done, and that he
thought nothing would be done towards returning to you the regiments
of your old brigade. Whilst in conversation with the major in came
General Cooper stiff as a bayonet, with a face like a nutmeg grater. I
saw at a glance you had nothing to hope from him.

The way in which he spoke convinced me that it is Bragg's intention
to put "the meritorious officers" (his own tools) into all the posts of
responsibility and to turn out all those who do not swear by Jeff Davis
and himself.

Now General this will not do for me. Notwithstanding my great
regard for you and my desire to serve under you, I cannot stand this
senseless military despotism, and I have determined to renounce the
service altogether. You are a Son of the Soil, you are bound up by
feelings as a Southerner, as a Patriot, to put up with things I cannot
swallow—I had hoped to have remained until we had achieved our
independence, and to have participated in the honors won by you and
your Brigade. But the wood that I am made of is getting old and stiff
and no longer bends so readily as formerly. I shall sell off my horses
and leave the country.

You have uphill work before you, General! You have thousands of
friends, but unfortunately your enemies are those in power, mean men
whom nothing but jealousy of your reputation and popularity have set
against you. Let them not have any hold upon your Government. Keep
up discipline whatever you do! Put in a good A.G. who will take the
odium of a little necessary severity off your shoulders—and support
him. Do this and the present clouds will be driven away by your future
success—

George St. Leger Grenfel

P.S. I hear nothing of Hines.

So Grenfel was leaving. Then the thought moved in: The Ninth would
not be coming, after all. Bragg had won. If he couldn't court-martial, he
could deny. His eye fell on the P.S.: *I hear nothing of Hines.* A stab of
excitement: Hines was on the move! A sudden impatience gripped him.
Alston could handle things here. He had to get back to Richmond and get
orders. . . . And his men in prison. He would appeal directly to Davis if he
had to.

He found a bottle of whiskey in his desk and finished it. The redbuds
were out, and the dogwood. April in the mountains. As he walked toward
the little rented house and past neat picket fences he felt better. Captain
Charles Withers, Tassie Withers's son from Danville, twenty-one and eager,

had joined them. Although young, a no-nonsense sort. St. Leger's criticism about discipline rankled. Very well. He could make Alston second-in-command. Make Withers adjutant. Yes. That would be good. And the men were on their way from Georgia. Under Robert Martin. None braver. God, to see Bowles and Cassell and Ellsworth again!

As if to confirm his need of optimism, in the dining room candles were lit, and the table set with "best" (borrowed from neighbors) china. "In honor of the occasion," said Mattie quickly, and turned toward the kitchen. She left him with a letter from Captain Whiting, Alice's beau, and a note from Alice.

"So *that's* your reason." Morgan grinned as he put the letter down and took his place at the table. He opened a bottle of wine . . . their last. "Well, here's a toast to the bride. And since I have to go to Richmond . . ."

To his surprise she burst into tears.

"I . . . can't go with you!"

But Alice had set the date—why couldn't she go?

She closed her eyes so she wouldn't see his face. She was scared to death. She had entered that tunnel again, from which there was no return, through which there was only one escape—through terror and pain. She wondered if she could face it all again, and knew, her palms cold with sweat, she had to. At least, this time she could avoid the stupidity of servants. She wouldn't have Mrs. Withers, but she would have her Morgan with her . . . or would she? Would he be off on some "campaign" somewhere? Now Alice . . . and she wouldn't be able to go to her little sister's wedding! Then she opened her eyes and saw his face, so sad, so trying—what troubles he had she would never know, either. They were like two people adrift on boats in a storm. Suddenly she threw down her fork and fell in his arms and told him everything.

He grasped her to him and rocked her back and forth. "It will be all right this time," he murmured. He held her away from him to see her face. "And we'll have a beautiful baby, a Christmas present. . . ."

She sniffed, and smiled, and cuddled again. After five minutes he said "Do I smell biscuits?"

She jumped up and ran to the kitchen. Could she know how much this meant to him? That it gave him a future, something to believe in, to work for? So precious this girl was to him. To protect, to save, to keep and cherish . . . he felt humbled and grateful, and not a little awed. He was sorry now he'd had too much whiskey before supper, and then the wine. He must smell like a dead bear. After dinner, when they went upstairs, he walked to the washbasin and splashed water over his face and brushed his teeth. Behind him he could hear Mattie undressing for bed. He scrubbed himself down with a towel and put on a clean nightshirt. With child again, she suddenly seemed different, holy. Alice's news—and then Mattie's—had given the dinner an atmosphere of gaiety which translated now into all the expectation of a wedding night.

To his surprise she was trembling and uncertain. When he convinced her that it was all right, that everything would be all right, and just before he felt his body sink into sleep the thought came: I wonder how Richard and Charl and Basil and the others are sleeping tonight in Columbus . . . if I can get Davis to listen. . . .

Four days later he walked from the Richmond depot to the President's office with an official appeal for an exchange for his men in prison. He had worked it out on the train and copied it carefully the night before: I make this appeal to you, sir, as the Chief of the Republic . . . to whom we all look for protection from injustice, for relief from oppression, trusting that this solemn protest. . . .

Davis *had* to listen!

The President was busy and regretted, by way of an aide, that he could not see General Morgan.

Holding down what his father used to call his "Irish"—that rage that rose up like a pall to choke him—Morgan called on his Hunt "reasonableness." But by the time he reached Buckner's office rage got the better of him. Buckner's office was a small room off a hall, with the usual clutter. Buckner was delighted to see him. He pulled out a drawer. "Drink?"

He waved it aside.

"I've got to do something . . ." In the presence of this man who had suffered so much his anger at last subsided. He sat down. Buckner found glasses and poured, handed Morgan one and lifted his in a salute.

"Here's to Kentucky." After a minute he added: "That wasn't just a formality, John. There are rumors I'm to be sent to the Trans-Mississippi Department."

The rage returned. "So Bragg is getting rid of the competition," he said bitterly.

"To join Kirby Smith," Buckner went on.

"Wharton's out there too, isn't he?"

"Yes."

The Trans-Mississippi Department. A sense of helplessness descended. "When?"

"Oh, not until summer, probably. We still have time."

A warmth deeper than whiskey rose in his throat.

"When I give the word," Buckner was saying, "will you be ready?"

"If you'll pardon my impertinence, General, a foolish question."

"I'll leave the details to you."

Morgan said nothing.

"I'm just sorry I can't help you with supplies."

"That's why I'll be going, isn't it?" He tried to sound cheerful. "There are plenty of horses and men waiting across the mountains. . . ."

"And your old friend from Ohio, Hobson." Buckner laughed grimly. "He is concentrating at Mount Sterling . . . six regiments of cavalry. The minute he starts to join forces with the Federals in the Valley, you move."

"We'll be ready."

Buckner lifted those magnificent eyes and let the tension tugging at his mouth relax. "Of course. Of course you will. Where can I reach you?"

"I'm staying with General Breckinridge, sir. My wife's sister will be married tomorrow morning."

"Splendid! Wish them all the luck for me."

"I will."

Will you give me away, Johnny?

Alice's face, flushed and happy, the warmth of her hand in his. His kiss on her cheek as answer, her hug.

She was beautiful, her forehead under her lace veil clear and smooth, her eyes shining. Captain Whiting was a handsome, quiet young man with reddish-blond hair and a sweet smile. He couldn't have been twenty. My God, they were getting younger every day. Morgan gave Alice away, walking down the aisle of the Episcopal Church feeling the faint pressure of her hand on his sleeve. At the rail he stepped back into his place and thought of Mattie and the baby. *If only, if only death and destruction will hold off just a little longer . . . if only they can have their love as I love you. . . .*

Just before he boarded the train the news that Forrest had taken Fort Pillow came in on the wires. Stormed . . . thirty minutes . . . entire garrison . . . killed 500, took 100 horses. Lost 20 killed and 60 wounded. Morgan took his seat with something of his old swagger. If Forrest could . . . maybe he didn't need Richmond after all. Grenfel was wrong. There was a top to the mountain, and they would find it.

He spent overnight at Wytheville, where George Crittenden, now a colonel, had a cavalry detachment from General Jones's brigade. Seeing him brought the old days back, the beginning, when George had resigned his generalship after the fracas at Mill Springs, which had lost the Gap and cost Sidney Johnston his right flank—and Kentucky. *You couldn't stay out of the fight, could you, George?* was in Morgan's look, but he couldn't say it. Crit had thrown his career away for whiskey and the Confederacy had suffered his loss long enough. As Crittenden talked on, his long face growing longer, Morgan's thought went to Buckner, Bragg, the Yankees, St. Leger, the sour-faced bureaucrats in Richmond. "God love the boys who fell at Shiloh," Morgan said with sudden emotion.

"I'll drink to that."

He drank too much. Normally the warmth of whiskey soothed him. Didn't he have Buckner's verbal orders to move into Kentucky? But he knew, now that Buckner himself was a pawn, things might not be easy. His men were in miserable supply, and disheartened. And he had failed to get his prisoners back. Failed. That damned penitentiary. He wondered if Scotty was still as obnoxious as ever . . . who was in the dungeon tonight? And up at Chicago, in Camp Douglas, was anybody riding the "mule"?

When he reached Abingdon he had a headache which could have won the war if it could have been collected into cannon and aimed north. He tried to make a joke of it when he kissed Mattie.

"You smell like a dragon!"

He started to laugh, then saw she was really displeased. Something green in her hand—some sewing—she flung into a corner of the room and slammed the door. He winced, held his head, found the bed and sank down. But depression, not sleep, came. He had failed.

Mattie, downstairs in the garden, shook with rage and fought-back tears. Didn't he know she had just taken apart her last good petticoat to make him a vest? For good luck . . . her eyes went to their window. Hetty Cary! Had he seen Hetty Cary? And here she was cutting up her petticoat as a lining for a vest . . . a vest for good luck! And he didn't know, he didn't know, the doctor said she was not to get upset. . . . It was unfair, unfair! Here she was, getting sick all over again, as she would get big and shapeless as the summer went on. . . . Then she thought of Alice . . . and she had missed the wedding! She hadn't even been there! A bluejay swooped down in front of her, picking at the grass. She sat on a little bench in a corner by some bushes and felt the sun on her face. She took three deep breaths and only then allowed herself to cry.

The next morning Alston handed him the latest from Richmond: He was refused his request to send a recruiting party into Kentucky. "Skeleton organizations should be raised to full strength before new ones formed," the answer read. It must have come from Bragg, overruling Buckner.

"How in hell do they expect us to raise to full strength if we can't recruit?" Morgan stormed.

Alston sat down, put his feet up on another chair, stuck his hands in his pockets and watched his paunch. "Is there anybody you haven't asked?"

Morgan remembered kindly William Simms, the senator from Kentucky. "I'll write another letter."

"That's good." Alston stood up and sighed. "And I'll get busy with the ash cakes." He tried to smile as he left. "Oh, by the way, here's a captured Yankee paper. Breck Castleman just gave it to me."

Morgan heard Alston's "I'll never believe it" behind the headlines: FORT PILLOW MASSACRE . . . Union forces refuse to haul down flag . . . did not intend to surrender. Rebels scaled the walls . . . massacred Negro troops, burying some alive.

"What a pack of lies."

"There was some talk of the Yankees giving their nigra troops whiskey," Alston said. "Poor bastards must have been scared to death."

How far would the Yankees stoop? And to slander Forrest . . . Forrest. That man was still fighting a war. Not tied down, as he was, completely dependent on Richmond for supplies. Maligned by the North—you expected that. But hogtied by your own government? Alston left and Morgan pulled a sheet of paper to him and wrote in the heat of anger:

> I have nothing left but a disorganized body of men. The only organization I had—Breckinridge's Ninth Kentucky—has been taken from me to swell the ranks of another. Those men enlisted with the promise that they would remain in my command. That promise has been violated and I call upon you as one of the representatives to have this injustice repaired if possible.

Could Simms do anything? To encourage him, as well as to bolster his own hopes, he added: "Kentucky is more united in her feelings for the South than she has ever been, and . . . an army could be raised there if only one could occupy the state sixty days."

Two petitions from some of his men in Alabama trying to get back into the command lay under a paperweight. He enclosed them in the letter, asking Simms to return them: "I value them highly. The expressions of esteem contained in them for me I consider the very highest honor that can be conferred. Do all you can in this matter to best serve our common country. Save my brave boys and make me happy. My command leaves this place Monday for Wytheville."

He hadn't told Mattie. It was the end of April, the ground was thawing, and scouts reported Federal movement in the direction of the lead mines. They would attack Crit like a sitting duck. He had waited for his men from Georgia long enough. He gave orders for a move to Wytheville immediately.

Then, unbelievably, his men came in from Decatur the next day. Dick McCann, Martin . . . God, it was good to see them. All through the camp their arrival acted like a tonic. Horses were reshod, tack repaired, guns cleaned. Those units scheduled to go to Wytheville left; Morgan decided to stay with the new arrivals and supervise reorganization.

April ended. May began. Key arrived from Augusta and in his honor Mattie gave some of the young captains a special dinner. They left the house in good spirits. It was the 5th of May. That morning Grant crossed the Rapidan.

Just as that news came in, Ellsworth burst through the door with orders from Buckner: HOBSON ON THE MOVE. STOP HIM.

Almost as soon as Ellsworth brought this news from the telegraph office, scouts came in with a report of a double advance: a strong force under General Crook from the Kanawha Valley moving against the Virginia & Tennessee Railroad at the New River bridge, and a column of cavalry headed toward Saltville under General Averell. Averell, if he captured the salt works, could move on the lead mines at Wytheville; Crook, if he took that bridge, could cut off all communications with Richmond—and Lee's supplies. The spring had indeed begun.

He sent his dismounted cavalry to reinforce General Jenkins, defending the railroad and the New River bridge. With the mounted men of his old command under Kirkpatrick and Cassell—now called "Morgan's brigade" and under the command of Lieutenant-Colonel Alston—Morgan went after Averell.

The victory at Wytheville on May 11, 1864, which saved the lead mines, would be long talked about as Morgan's greatest victory. But too much else was happening, and fast: Lee was playing cat-and-mouse with Grant at Spotsylvania; Richmond was in real danger from a thrust on Petersburg; and on the same morning that Grant had crossed the Rapidan, Sherman, with three armies, made his move against Johnston and Hardee in Georgia. "On to Atlanta" joined "On to Richmond" in Northern headlines. Then, perhaps the worst dispatch of all: Buckner had his orders for Louisiana. Morgan felt his last prop had been taken away.

He walked with Ellsworth to the depot where a stack of wires told the story: a battle in the Wilderness, the bloodbath at Spotsylvania Courthouse, going on even now. Longstreet wounded. Powell Hill still Lee's right-hand man. Jeb Stuart killed at Yellow Tavern.

Morgan closed his eyes and leaned back. "They will kill us all," he murmured to the silvered tracks leading off into a descending fog.

"What? I couldn't hear you, sir."

"Nothing."

The heavy oak railroad chair creaked and the smells of the May night came. He looked through the half-opened window at the track shining away under a pale moon. A whippoorwill repeated itself incessantly. This would surely mean a move up the Valley by Sigel.

"And General Breckinridge?"

"Nothing."

That week they waited. Mattie came from Abingdon—a complete surprise.

"You sounded so successful, I thought this place must be perfectly secured . . ." She crinkled her nose.

"I'm . . . I'm so glad you came," he lied.

I couldn't live without you broke through the sob as she surrendered to his arms. He looked up at the top of the stairs where young Captain Withers, under house arrest for disobeying orders, stood watching them.

"Come on down," Morgan called to him. "I am no longer in command."

Her presence did complicate things. He knew he didn't dare move from Wytheville, and the danger was real. Crook had 6,000 infantry, Averell 2,500 cavalry. Sigel, reported to have 12,000, would undoubtedly try for a junction, then dash at Lynchburg. At least that's what he would do. Lee had to hold at Spotsylvania, Beauregard down on the James, and Breckinridge and his own meager force the Valley. In the meantime he could only hope that Hobson, across the mountains, was still consolidating, waiting for a signal to join Crook and Averell. Still, Hobson was no fool. And he was in Kentucky with those regiments of cavalry.

Then, things seemed to improve.

"You see, I bring you good luck," Mattie joked.

On the 15th Breckinridge stopped Sigel at Newmarket and drove him across the Shenandoah, capturing six batteries and a thousand stands of arms, plus Sigel's wagon trains. On the 16th Beauregard turned the Yankee flank just ten miles from Richmond, back to a place called the Bermuda Hundred, between the James and Appomattox rivers. On the 18th Grant tried to turn Lee's left, and failed.

But Grant now moved his whole army northeast, then east down the valley of the Rappahannock, forcing Lee to abandon his entrenchments. Breckinridge was ordered to help. The Shenandoah, without Breckinridge, was now fair game.

Morgan almost literally held his breath. Ellsworth and Alston were busy with incoming dispatches: Lee beat Grant by forced marches to a position between the North and South Anna rivers; Grant, cut loose from his supplies at Fredericksburg, pushed again, was stopped again, pushed again, was stopped again, on the 23rd and 25th.

"Grant'll swing around," George Crittenden said. "You watch."

"Do you think so?" Morgan heard Martin ask behind him.

"You watch."

Ellsworth walked up and handed him a paper. A name on the casualty lists from Spotsylvania made him jump: *Captain Richard Whiting.* Alice! Dear little Alice, and they hadn't known!

He found Mattie in their room holding up a green vest.

"See? It's all finished. Now don't fuss. It's for luck. And you've got to promise me . . ." then she saw his eyes.

"Oh, my God! What . . . I've got to go. . . ."

"You can't, darling. Impossible now. Richmond . . ." He stopped.

"Richmond?"

"No . . . it's just that with this new activity they've stopped all civilian travel on the trains. . . ."

"You can't tell me, John Morgan, you can't get a pass . . . ?" Her voice ended in a high squeal and he took her shaking shoulders in his hands and kissed her hair. He couldn't tell her that Alice, too, might be in danger.

In the front hall Key handed him a note from Captain Allen, at one of the camps on the Abingdon road.

> General: I would earnestly call your attention to the fact that hundreds of your men are absolutely naked. Some are in their shirts and drawers, while others are compelled to remain in camp and cover their nakedness with blankets. It is most shocking to what want and destitution these men are reduced.

He sent word to Alston to scour the countryside, write receipts for future payment on every piece of clothing available, every ear of corn or pound of flour he could find. Then the scouts brought in news of Hobson's plan to move his six regiments of cavalry out of Mount Sterling within the week to Louisa, on the West Virginia border, where he would join Burbridge and a Michigan cavalry force of twenty-five hundred for an invasion of the Valley.

"Is this reliable?"

The grimy trooper, still out of breath, panted a nod. "Sir, yes, sir. Reliable!"

Before Hobson and Burbridge could hook up with Crook and Averell for the kill, Morgan's instincts warned, the only thing that could save Southwest Virginia was a race for Mount Sterling. He knew he had to stop Hobson before he left for Louisa. Once reinforced by those twenty-five hundred Michigan troops and across the mountains—and with Breckinridge now busy with Lee and unable to help—no, it was unthinkable. He called a staff meeting.

Two days ago he had received a coded message from Seddon asking his opinion of an attempt by his men against Sherman's lines north of Atlanta. He had set it aside as another wild idea of bureaucratic daydreaming. Now he might just use it as an opportunity. . . . when he announced it to his officers, the idea sounded even wilder than it had in the dispatch. With Crook and Averell threatening the department with more than eight thousand men in the Valley, he saw the disbelief on his colonels' faces. But when he explained the danger from Hobson and the race for Mount Sterling, his young captains cheered.

"We'll just say we got lost—thought we were headed for Georgia," they laughed. "Haven't been home so long we forgot the way. . . ."

Even as he quieted them Morgan felt a stab of fear mixed with exhilaration —the unmistakable joy of a raid.

"And after we whip Hobson, sir, we might just draw the Yankees off from Atlanta," someone said.

"We might just draw them off all the way to Chicago," Castleman drawled to himself.

"It's not drawing off I'm thinking of. I intend to ask for permission to attack Sherman from the point of the compass he least expects an attack: the north. Instead of coming in from East Tennessee, we'll whip Hobson, then come down—"

"You've been waiting for this chance!" Robert Martin tried to suppress a grin. It was the Colonel Martin of the old days, taking a bullet in his lungs, cantering on. "Don't tell us you haven't! And my boys are ready, dismounted as most of them are. . . ."

Mention of the men's condition was sobering. Morgan was in the habit of letting his men express themselves, of listening, then giving his own opinion, which stuck.

"It may be our last chance," Castleman said slowly. "We can't fight Sherman without horses, sir. And nowhere else are you going to find them. Nowhere," Castleman added.

"The men are rotting here," Colonel Smith put in, and James Bowles, from his side of the room, nodded.

"I could hold the fort here at Wytheville," George Crittenden offered. "If you'll recommend me."

The plan had to work. But he hadn't heard from everybody. "I haven't heard any objections," he said, as if disappointed, and waited, looking around. Giltner, with those piercing eyes and grim mouth making a slash in his beard, lifted his head when Morgan's eyes went to him. "And you, Henry?"

"It's crazy, if you don't mind my saying so. If the Yankees gang up down this valley and march on Lynchburg they'll never bother to chase us. And even if we take care of Hobson, how many of them would come running after our little band, anyway?"

Morgan's courtesy went deeper, his men knew, than mere manners. He had a genuine sensitivity for the feelings of others, most of all when they disagreed with him. But those who knew him best were wary of his questions, especially when that little crooked smile warned of an intense self-conviction. The man he was listening to had better be brief and make sense.

"My grandfather told me that when you ride a horse you've got to think like the horse, Henry. Now it was crazy for a hundred thousand Yankees to chase us all over Ohio—but that's what they did. Still, you have a point, and I'd like you to expand it."

Like a lawyer, with that little half-smile, he listened to Colonel Giltner reduce with eloquence the command to a few ragged men.

"Then surely we can make little difference here," Morgan said. "Surely we can neither stop them nor get in their rear—which is everywhere." The little smile disappeared, and he became eager, excited, infectuous. "If we go to Kentucky we can get horses. And recruits, men willing to fight. Kentucky is sick—she is ready. We can find horses enough for all. Not your Georgia nags, but thoroughbreds. . . . Then we can cut down through Middle Tennessee and get at Sherman. . . ." *Give 'em a daar, Anderson, give 'em a daar* . . . Through his own voice he heard their cheers.

Joe Johnston wired back that he could hold Sherman until mid-August, but that Morgan must come with five thousand men. Five thousand! "Never mind," he told Cal. "We can do it." He found a paper and pencil, scribbled a response. Without quoting Johnston, he requested permission of Seddon to approach Sherman by way of Kentucky and Nashville, rather than through East Tennessee. He handed the paper to Cal.

We've got to stop Hobson and draw off Burbridge, Morgan told himself as he let himself into the front hall. The race to Mount Sterling had, in his mind, already begun. Mattie was just coming down the stairs. "I'll need that green vest," he said quietly. She moved to him and without a word held her face to his.

"He has no intention of moving against Sherman," Castleman said under his breath to Cal as they walked to the depot to find Ellsworth.

"What? Of course he does. . . ."

Castleman smiled. "We'll see."

He left Cal at the depot and rode out to camp to notify George Eastin, now Martin's adjutant with the Tenth Kentucky. They found Dr. Goode, a German surgeon—Hines's Richmond acquaintance—who had joined the command just two weeks ago. "Captain Hines iss in Torronto," Goode had hissed in his well-fed way when he arrived. "He asks me esspecially to contact you."

"And St. Leger?" Castleman had asked.

The German wagged his blond beard and glared. "There, too."

Castleman nodded. Maybe Morgan *thought* he was making a move against Sherman, but once successful in Kentucky he might just change his mind. All his officers knew an invasion of the North—that old dream and that bitter loss in Ohio—still rankled. They would gamble on that. Goode agreed. Castleman rode back to the depot with Eastin to send Seddon a message of their own. Adam Johnson was on his way to make connection with the eighty thousand Copperheads in Illinois, and another fifty thousand in Indiana, who now called themselves the Order of American Knights.

Vallandigham was in Ontario, and meeting with Hines. The membership totaled three hundred thousand, from Indiana, Illinois, across Ohio into New York, and of course Kentucky, with Judge Bullitt in charge at Louisville. Although exiled and condemned as a traitor because he dared criticize the Lincoln administration, Vallandigham had, even from Canada, almost won the Ohio gubernatorial election. He was still the Copperheads' driving force.

When Hines received Castleman's wire he arranged a meeting with Vallandigham for mid-June. The Knights would rise and release Confederate prisoners from Douglas, Morton, Chase and Rock Island. July 4 was the magic date, and the magic name of Morgan would inspire them. His entry into Kentucky would be the signal.

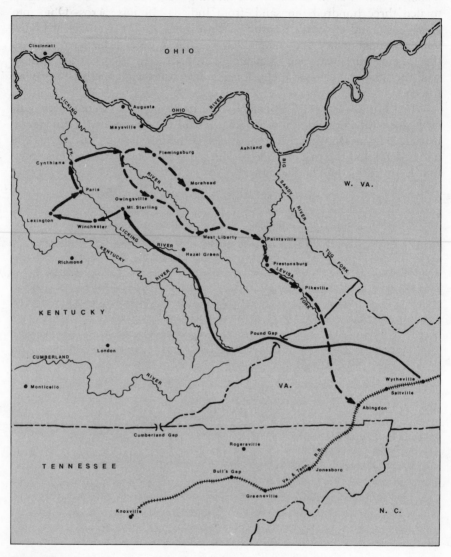

Morgan's Last Raid, June 1864

55

He sent Mattie back to Abingdon with an escort. He sat his horse and watched them until they were out of sight, then turned and cantered toward his men.

On the last day of May, at the courthouse in Russell County, Virginia, they stopped just long enough for Ellsworth to send his message, then they were on their way.

Morgan was rather pleased with his wire. After describing the Burbridge-Crook-Averell danger, he remembered that joke of Forrest's. He had Ellsworth tap out: THIS INFORMATION HAS DETERMINED ME TO MOVE AT ONCE INTO KENTUCKY, AND THUS DISTRACT THE PLANS OF THE ENEMY BY INITIATING A MOVEMENT WITHIN HIS LINES.

"That should please them! Sounds like Bragg!"

Ellsworth waited.

"My force will be about twenty-two hundred men," Morgan dictated, as Ellsworth tapped it out. "I expect to be pursued by the force at Louisa, which I will endeavor to avoid. There will be nothing in the state to retard my progress but a few scattered provost-guards."

Well, some of it was true, some of it wasn't. He had twenty-two hundred men, but six hundred had no horses, and Giltner was acting increasingly like a man doing him a favor by even being there. Giltner's men were hardy enough, but many were recruits from eastern Kentucky, notorious for its divided loyalties. In reality he had less than fourteen hundred of the old Morgan men, poorly armed, pitifully equipped, and even among them were some unused to the hardships of a mountain march.

He was riding between Alston and Cal in the advance; Key rode back with Castleman and what was left of "dashing Company D." Yes, some of it was true, some of it wasn't. What was true was that Burbridge, once he got wind of them, would bend every effort to pursue. Whether the old Second Kentucky could avoid him with almost a third of its men dismounted was another matter. And whether there would be only "a few scattered provost-guards" to impede their progress was still another. There was Hobson with six regiments at Mount Sterling, of whom the telegram had made no mention.

Giltner's muster rolls counted roughly seven hundred men. The rest of the command consisted of three brigades. Alston's hundred men had been divided into three small battalions under Lieutenant-Colonel Bowles, Major Cassell and Major Kirkpatrick. Lieutenant-Colonel Robert Martin had the second Morgan brigade, the poor bastards without horses. Martin volunteered for the job, determined to inspire them. The third Morgan brigade, about eight hundred strong, were veterans under Colonel Smith. There would be no artillery, not over the roads they expected to travel.

They reached the pass at Pound Gap on the 2nd of June, to find it blocked by one of Burbridge's mounted regiments from Louisa, three hundred strong.

"If they get away, we're in for it. They'll warn Burbridge. We've got to take them."

Alston was echoing his own thoughts. Morgan ordered Alston's brigade to make a detour and get behind them. He watched their horses gallop off, and in the distance could only guess their progress up those steep slopes covered with trees. They were too late. The Yankees got away.

To warn Burbridge. Well, it would have been only a matter of time, anyway. Burbridge, if Morgan knew anything about him, would want to take along artillery and that would slow him. Besides, it would take two days for the news to reach him. By that time . . .

But they had to hurry. Straining, slipping, sliding, gut-busting up and over those rock-sharp ridge roads, then down ravines, horses hobbling, lunging up again over boulders, the hell of eastern Kentucky. Footsore, many now without shoes, panting, swearing, the men by human will pushed on, some days as much as twenty-seven miles. The horses, long without forage enough to build stamina, had no such motivation. Their bony backsides, their skeletal heads with unknowing eyes obeyed and plodded on, their thin necks stretching, until a dozen, two dozen, finally two hundred from Giltner's brigade alone collapsed from exhaustion. There wasn't even time to hack at pasterns, and carry, like trophies, those precious shoes.

Ordering Walter Ferguson and some of Quirk's old scouts to find out the direction taken by the Federals from Pound Gap, Morgan pushed on, on, on. By the 7th, within a day of Mount Sterling, he sent the advance guard to patrol the road between Mount Sterling and Lexington, another company to guard the road between Mount Sterling and Paris, and a detail of fifty men to destroy the bridges of the Frankfort & Louisville Railroad in case reinforcements from Indiana were alerted to defend central Kentucky. Next he gave Major Chenoweth, a Gano veteran, the job of burning bridges on the Kentucky Central, the main rail line to Cincinnati. Then, as a final precaution, Captain Everett left with a hundred men to capture Maysville, on the Ohio. They all had orders to make as much excitement as possible, to spread the rumor that Morgan had arrived with thousands of men, to completely confuse as to the direction of his movements, and to report to him within three or four days at Lexington.

During the night of the 7th of June his men struggled through the last thicket, down the last ravine of the mountains; in the dark of that night they could feel the soft soil of the Bluegrass under their feet, and a cheer rose up which traveled back and back, squad to squad, company to company, even to the last man. They had covered two hundred and thirty torturous miles in ten days. They collapsed, those still with horses not unsaddling, to await first light.

It came, to give them their first sight in a long time of that lovely land.

Slanting over meadows and the undulating velvet of green hills, the sun picked up tossing purple heads of thistles waving over fields of daisies. Along stone fences the wasp shapes of honeysuckle hung, and in the hedgerows wild roses lay in masses of red and pink. The contrast to that dark, gloomy, rocky nether world of eastern Kentucky was magical: Even the birds were different, the meadow lark, the doves. It was human, it was kind, it was home. They laughed and cheered. They grieved for their dead horses, but as they looked out over that manicured prairie, they knew they could get more.

Before eight o'clock they reached Mount Sterling. They were a ragamuffin lot, but they had Adam Johnson's old Tenth, and Smith, and Bowles, and Giltner, looking vaguely like Ulysses Grant, with that hard mouth planted in that salt-and-pepper beard. But as they stood to horse it was Giltner's men who struck up "Cheer, Boys, Cheer." They had made it down what had become known as the "Rebel Trace," and they didn't intend to go home empty-handed.

The tents of Hobson's regiments stood out neatly white against the green of a broad plateau overlooking the town. Above, the porcelain-blue sky of a Kentucky June day. They halted, skirted the camp, listening to the lazy sounds of roosters. Morgan sent Captain Withers to ride forward and estimate the Federals' strength. As Withers rode off the Yankee vedettes opened fire. His horse bolted, carrying him straight through the edge of the tents. By a superhuman effort he got the animal under control and reported his estimate. Morgan, laughing and relieved, called over: "I didn't tell you to ride through and count them!"

But it was time to move: The whole camp would be alerted. He ordered Colonel Smith to take two battalions forward, with Giltner in reserve. Smith sent Cassell and Bowles to form mounted skirmish lines and charge.

It was over in minutes. Child's play. Hobson, the scourge of his Ohio raid, captured, with all their stores. While Smith's men guarded them, Giltner's brigade came into town at a canter. It was a holiday, and Giltner's troops, new to Morgan's brand of discipline, which depended on a man's honor rather than fear of punishment, started looting. Not a store, and in some cases private houses, escaped their efforts. Charles Withers, as adjutant, appealed to Alston, but Alston, half-ill from dysentery, could only refer him to the General, who was busy conferring with his scouts as to the whereabouts of Burbridge and making arrangements with Martin for the dismounted men, who would camp east of town. It would take Burbridge at least two or three days to get here. In the meantime . . .

In the meantime there was food at the hotel, and a score of houses opened by Southern sympathizers to his men. He seemed to ignore the reports of the looting. "Maybe he accepts it," Withers said.

"No, no . . . you don't know him," James Bowles countered. "He's preoccupied. Besides, he figures it's Giltner's business to control his own men." But by afternoon things had gotten worse. Much worse.

A delegation of townspeople found the General and told him that the Farmers' Bank of Mount Sterling had been robbed of $72,000. They demanded the return of the money, much of which were deposits by Confederate sympathizers. Then they produced a written order, signed by Captain Withers, demanding delivery of the money with a threat that, if not turned over, the town of Mount Sterling would be burned.

"It's not true!" Withers almost screamed. "That's not my signature. . . ."

Morgan, with Burbridge on his mind, was furious. He had just talked with a Mrs. Hamilton, who had come into town with food for his wounded . . . a Southern lady. . . . robbed of her jewels by some of Giltner's men. "What does this mean?" he thundered.

Withers was confused and dismayed at his general's attitude. He examined the signature. "This is not mine," was all he managed to get out.

"Not yours? Then whose?"

One of the bankers spoke up. "The paper was presented to us by a man with a blond beard and a German accent."

Dr. Goode. Morgan sent for him. He was nowhere to be found.

Burbridge was on his way. They still had to get horses, the key to any victory. Walter Ferguson had just come in with a report that 5,000 mounts were to be had in Lexington. Five thousand thoroughbreds! Enough to mount his entire command, with extra for recruits! The magic number that Joe Johnston was waiting for, down in Atlanta! It was four o'clock. He called Colonel Smith to prepare for a march to Lexington. Smith hesitated.

"I think we should take care of this bank robbery first, General."

"Do you want to walk back to Virginia, or do you want to get fresh horses?" Morgan asked impatiently, and then, ashamed of the sarcasm to his old friend, added more calmly: "I've only just heard of it. I have no time to take care of it now, but I will." Good God, to let looting ruin the raid, perhaps lose the command! "I will," he repeated. "We can't waste time now, Colonel, with Burbridge alerted. . . ."

Giltner would be left behind to distribute Yankee boots and saddles, destroy the rest and remount part of Martin's men with captured horses; Smith reluctantly agreed that it was more important to get to Lexington than to investigate a robbery which might, in the confusion, have nothing to do with Morgan. He started his fours down the Winchester Pike at a brisk trot.

"What's he doing?" Breck Castleman asked Cal anxiously.

"What, what?"

"Leaving Giltner and Martin . . . separated like that. Martin on the road east, with no horses, Giltner out of touch. If they are attacked . . ."

"They won't be," said Cal confidently. "The scouts just came in. Burbridge is moving toward Saltville. We're safe now. Don't worry."

Cal, too, had caught Bluegrass fever.

And why not? The cool air of sundown, the smell of ripe grass. The heat of the earth meeting the mists of the sky as first fog settled under the moon. It would be a lovely night, one of those dew-wet nights which promised a clear morning, once the fog lifted. It would be glorious. They would succeed. They might even go down to Georgia. Or up into Ohio. Anything could happen.

Night came. They bivouacked just outside Winchester, to march again toward Lexington the next morning. It was the first real rest they'd had since leaving Virginia. Yet Morgan couldn't sleep. He had been offered the hospitality of a farmhouse and walked out onto the porch. There it was in the stillness, with the dark mounds of trees against the pale silver-green land rolling away under the moon and alive with fireflies. His mother was sleeping now. Wouldn't she be surprised? A sudden joy close to pain caught his throat. Tomorrow . . .

The bugles sounded even before sunup. They had breakfast, much of it brought out by the townspeople, glad to have "their boys back again." but even before they finished, Sam Murrill's couriers came in, sent by Giltner. The worst had happened: Burbridge had come out of nowhere, at first light, overrun Martin's sleeping, dismounted troops, and cut through Giltner's brigade, which was now re-forming just west of Mount Sterling.

By the time Morgan got there he realized the enormity of the loss. Giltner, the unshakable, visibly shaken; George Eastin, grim as granite; Martin, twice wounded and refusing treatment, still trembling and white with shock. Troops scattered, most of the dismounted captured. The story came in pieces, through rage and disbelief, that aftermath of terror: Just past midnight Martin had sent Lieutenant-Colonel Brent, who had just joined the command, with fifty men as a rear guard to picket the road about a mile away. The night was so peaceful. It was so good to stop. Even if Burbridge turned, they thought, it would take him three days to get there. They would be safe enough while Giltner's Fourth Kentucky took what they needed from the Yankee warehouse, destroyed the rest and found horses. The men of that rear guard were as exhausted as the rest. No scouts rode in that night to tell them that Burbridge was making a forced march from Louisa, covering ninety miles in thirty hours, to scatter the vedettes and dash into Martin's camp. They rode over the men as they lay in their blankets. It was three in the morning. Martin, in a farmhouse, heard the shots and jumped on his horse, to find the Federals between himself and his men. Without a second thought he rode straight through the enemy, taking shots from both sides, to rejoin his troops. The Federals by now had brought up a piece of artillery, which was taken, then recaptured. Martin's men, on foot, fought desperately for more than an hour.

Morgan listened. He knew that desperation, a kind of madness that takes over and is called "unflinching courage" by armchair generals, but is known for what it is by the men who live it: self-preservation shorn of every cultural crutch, language, cause, bravado—just to catch that next breath, just to keep life. He let Martin go on, to get it out of his system, to get calm again. How they cut their way through town, held now by the Yankees, to join what was left of Giltner's force about two miles west. There, before Burbridge could re-form and add Hobson's fresh men as reinforcements, Martin proposed an attack, which Giltner agreed to. Martin moved around Mount Sterling again, to take the enemy in the rear—and find some of his scattered men if he could. Giltner would charge the front. They fought until Martin's ammunition gave out and he had to join Giltner again, for a retreat down the Winchester Road. The Yankees were evidently as tired as they were, and showed no signs of following. But fourteen officers and forty privates were dead. Eighty were so badly wounded they couldn't be moved; at least a hundred were captured and more than that scattered.

"Get those wounds taken care of now," Morgan told Martin quietly. One ball had gone through the calf of his left leg and his boot was cut half off.

Robert Martin looked from Morgan's face to Colonel Smith, then back again.

"I think you're right," Morgan continued in that same soothing tone. "The Yankee horses, after that march, are no good to anybody. They won't follow, at least not for twenty-four hours." Pain mixed with disappointment passed over Martin's face, in spite of his nod. His general knew what he must be feeling: Hobson, with most of his men, had gotten away. Where would he be waiting for them? And Burbridge, with a night's sleep under his belt, would be ready again. Not only ready, but astride the escape route east. That was the first time in his career Morgan had allowed that to happen —except in Ohio. George Eastin shot Breck Castleman a look and fell in beside him as the column turned toward Winchester. They would ride nonstop for Lexington, almost forty miles away. There was no time to lose.

The afternoon turned sultry. Sweat from men and horses mingled, became one aroma of nearly total exhaustion. Alston insisted on a brief halt at Winchester, to give any stragglers time to catch up. About twenty did, and they moved on. The sun set. There was no talking. The sound of trotting horses, the clank of a canteen. The night was completely black. But they knew the way, and tired as they were, their spirits picked up. About a mile from Lexington Morgan called another halt. Castleman walked his horse over, asking permission to approach the town under a flag of truce . . . actually to scout the situation. Key Morgan and Breck's younger brother Humphreys immediately stepped up.

"Tell him to take me, Cally," Key whispered.

Cal looked down at that eager face. "I'll ask."

"You know . . ." Morgan didn't finish.

"I know you've watched over him to the point that he feels inferior," Cal said.

Morgan's face clouded. "I . . . somehow didn't. They were so alike. Almost twins."

"You can't go on protecting him forever." *Tom's dead*, Cal wanted to say, but couldn't. Instead, he changed his tone, as if he were changing the subject. "It's so black out there, and they know the way. If they call out 'Flag of truce' often enough, they'll be safe."

Morgan looked past him for a second. "Key Morgan," he called out, "and Humphreys Castleman have just volunteered."

Key's face broke into a grin as he jumped on his horse.

"We're ready!" Breck Castleman called over, and they were gone.

On the left of the Winchester Road, as the three went into town, and before they reached Limestone Street, a woman from an upstairs window waved them down. "Are you Morgan?" When they nodded she whispered:

"Get close to the buildings . . . ride on the sidewalk! The Yankees have a cannon set up at the corner!"

Strangely enough, they had seen no pickets. The Yankees must have felt fairly secure. Castleman silently waved his thanks, and they pressed their horses close to the houses, then halted, and bawled out: "Bearer of flag of truce!" Finally a Yankee officer came to within hearing distance and ordered a halt, the flag-bearer to dismount and advance.

Breck, by a low wave of his hand, signaled the others to remain where they were. "My instructions are to demand the surrender of Lexington," he called out. "By orders of General John Hunt Morgan. You are surrounded," he added stoutly.

"I have no such authority," the officer answered, bewildered but cautious. He disappeared to consult his commander. In about twenty minutes he returned, declining to surrender.

With no orders beyond this rash boast, Castleman snapped out: "Then tell your commanding officer he has just assumed full responsibility for the destruction of Lexington! We have an overwhelming strength and intend to possess this town."

They were close enough now for Castleman to see that the man was a captain. He roared, but under the protection of the white flag, the three boys turned and cantered away. When the last house was passed, they let their horses reach for a gallop. Then minutes later they pulled up to their general, elated.

"Give me forty men, General," Breck panted, "and I'll convince them we *are* burning the town, without touching a private residence . . ."

The idea was so preposterous, the joy in the boy's voice so great, Morgan couldn't resist. "All right, all right! But you know this is highly irregular," he added, when he saw Giltner's frown. Even Colonel Smith was shaking his head. "They promise not to burn houses," he told them. "Let's not deny them a taste of glory!"

They found axes and Key leaned his horse into a dead run, the others following. Luckily these were the fresh mounts picked up at Mount Sterling . . . with the cool night air against their faces, they retraced their route to the end of Winchester Road, where a large corral, now taken over by the Yankees, held enough hay to start quite a blaze. A dozen of Castleman's forty led the horses out and the torch was thrown—inadvertently starting a fire in Wolff's brewery across the street. With horses galloping off in every direction, they cut their way across back yards to the old racecourse grounds. There they turned the horses out of the largest stable, owned, as Key knew, by kindly old Mr. Grimstead. But he threw the torch with glee and followed the others, opening the way through fences with axes to the Kentucky Central railroad yards, where the woodsheds were stacked high. "Must be a thousand cords in there," Humphreys whispered as the torches were thrown again.

Although only four buildings were burning, it looked as if a force had encircled half the town. As they rode up Short Street Castleman recognized a teller from David Sayre's bank. With the fires throwing up a red-gold glow against the sky, Breck kept his face away; the teller thought they were Federal cavalry and gave them all the information they needed. The Yankees were retreating toward Versailles.

Castleman, who would be twenty-three in exactly three days, sat his horse as dawn came up and sent three men, Phil Thompson, Henry Sampson and Howard McCann up Short to Limestone and out the Winchester Road to give General Morgan his compliments and say the town was evacuated. Key, who rode with them, was less official. He ran up and hugged his brother, yelling, "We whipped 'em, Brother Johnny! We whipped 'em!"

Morgan rode into town—into home and Hopemont—with the dawn of a June day behind him. Aunt Betty was overcome, then gathered herself like a general and marshaled breakfast for as many men as could be served in the carriage yard and garden. The others had splayed out over town looking for horses. Morgan, in a dream, sat in the warming room watching his mother's face, and listening to all the news. Charl and Richard . . . and Basil, Basil. If you could be here. He had to tell them that the penitentiary wasn't so bad, after all, although he knew they didn't believe him.

His mother. It had been a year and a half. Her hair, frosted across the top and temples, was still luxuriant, her eyes still luminous, with that old imperial look of the Hunts. She took her sons' faces in her hands, by the jowls, as she would a favorite dog's, and looked into their depths. First Cal's—she had worried over him so. Then Key, and last, Johnny. It was the first time he had seen her since that day in the prison, with Delphine. He read her thoughts: Charl and Dick.

"Richard will be fine, Ma. You know him. And Charl . . . nothing could ever keep Charl down!"

Tired as he was, the house with its smells and memories came in past the chatter, the giggles. He heard their voices, watched their faces. Aunt Hannah and Annie bustling back and forth. Aunt Betty urging coffee on everybody. "I'll have a brandy, if you have any," he told her as she passed.

"Honest Injun, Aunt Bet. I *tried* to get here for my birthday!"

With his mother all bases were touched: T.H., Uncle Robert, Uncle Frank. Dick Curd. They spoke of Henry, and Stones River, Mattie and the baby she had lost while he was in prison and the baby to come. "And Randolph?" he asked casually enough, then waited through an awkward silence. They were alone in the dining room.

"Maggie . . . had typhoid," Henrietta said quietly. She closed those honest eyes of hers, then looked at his squarely. "Randolph was stationed in Ohio. When he came home to take care of her he was . . . without leave. . . ."

"AWOL?" He tried to help her.

"Yes. They . . . they . . ." She stopped, took a breath. "They shot him as a deserter," she made herself finish.

In the silence his own heart seemed to stop. Then rage swept his body like a fever. When he opened his eyes he saw his own horror registered on her face. "I thought I might ride out there," he said insanely, forgetting Burbridge, knowing there would be no time. "And James?"

"Confiscated as property of a Southern sympathizer."

"But I thought . . ."

Through a grim smile that pulled back one corner of her mouth Henrietta Morgan said coldly: "Dick argued. How he argued! Used their 'Emancipation Paper' against them, in which they promise that, in Federally-held territory, property will be protected by the Constitution."

"But not for Southern sympathizers."

"Evidently not," she ended dully.

He couldn't stand it. Through all those hours in the saddle, the mountains, the tragedy at Mount Sterling, the loss of faith he saw on Giltner's face. Now his mother, indomitable and breaking, finally breaking.

"Well, James is the best horse trainer around. Maybe even the Bruces will hire him . . . paying the Yankees handsomely, of course," he added, thankful that sarcasm could still take the edge off grief. His mother blew her nose, and he waited for her to ball up the handkerchief, study the lace.

"Maybe so . . ." she said vaguely.

Randolph. My God. How much, how much. How much I took for granted. Took you all for granted. He looked back at his mother. Amanda. Did she know about Will?

"Will's dead, Ma."

"I know."

"You know?"

"T.H. wrote. His letters have a way of getting through."

"Have you told her?"

Something in the silence told him the old animosity was still there.

"It's out of the question," she said stiffly. "It's too dangerous. I'll not have you riding through that nest of Yankees. Besides . . ." she hunched her shoulders. "I've already told her." She lifted her eyes for understanding, as if she had betrayed her sense of class. He bent his head to kiss her hand, resting on the table. She lifted her other hand and caressed the back of his head. Cal and the others had come back and he could hear them laughing with Alston and Colonel Smith in the garden, where Aunt Hannah had sent Annie to serve his men.

"Has Billy come back?" he asked suddenly. Buffington, and Billy in the swift current of the river.

"No."

Only little Simon now, the fourth son. He would be eleven.

"And Simon?"

Henrietta Morgan looked away, embarrassed. "After James was taken, we couldn't find Simon anywhere. I even . . . I even sent Robert to that Bolton man, to see if he had been sold. . . ."

She looked up, suddenly angry at her helplessness, and at that stubborn devotion to honor which had taken Johnny from her, that she both hated and loved him for. Then she saw her mother looking down from the portrait, her morning cap in place, her eyes steady. Henrietta twitched her nose, straightened her shoulders and shut her eyes to keep from crying.

He wanted to hear nothing more. He walked through the dining room into the parlor, that proper parlor with its settees and spinet and portrait of Byron, and heard his hungry men still jostling and eager over bacon and biscuits in the garden. He looked through the archway to see his mother still standing by the dining room table. "Call Uncle Robert," he heard himself say. "Colonel Martin's been wounded. I'd like a good doctor to see him."

"It's done," Cal said behind him. "I sent for him ten minutes ago. He should be here shortly."

"In the meantime, all you men have to eat," Henrietta was saying. She bustled about, playing the hostess again, her face too bright. They had not talked of Tom. Her oldest son watched her. They gathered around the table, served by Annie and Aunt Hannah, and Adam, acting as butler. "Quite a change from Uncle Ben," Henrietta Morgan said when she could.

Robert Hunt came in, then Dick Curd, and Uncle Frank. It was, for an hour or two, a family reunion. They talked of Henry and T.H. while Robert Hunt went into the downstairs bedroom to look after Robert Martin. As the meal wound down, their obvious fatigue brought an invitation from Henrietta that her sons go upstairs and rest. "And any of you gentlemen," she added graciously. Cal and Key accepted, but Morgan, suddenly almost too tired to move, declined. "Then come with me," she said, swishing her skirts across the polished hall to the study. She closed the door behind him.

His grandfather's desk, his father's books . . . and across the street, Becky's house. He sat in a chair and watched his mother's face.

"Now tell me," she said.

There was a tension between them. She hadn't said a word before now. The fact that she hadn't asked Cal, but had waited until now . . . did she somehow blame him? *Take care of them, Johnny.*

"It was instantaneous," he said. "You know how impulsive he was. I'd warned him before . . . he was assigned to Basil's staff so . . . the fight was almost over . . . final charge . . . just before the enemy surrendered. He . . . died in Cal's arms."

"I thought you said it was instantaneous. Where is he buried?" Her voice was even, but her hand was shaking.

"In Reverend Cleland's garden in Lebanon."

"We'll have him moved," she bit out.

"We'll bring him home, Ma. . . ."

"Well!" She slapped her lap. "The others are waiting."

No moment of tenderness. No letting him put his arms around her. She did blame him, after all.

His officers had gone back to the men. His uncles were in the parlor. He found a chair by the empty fireplace and watched the long curtains billowing a breeze. If he could only stay here forever. He looked at their faces, heard their excited chatter. Burbridge lay across his line of retreat, and the scouts were reporting Hobson at Cynthiana. He would have to move out soon. And yet he sat there. Key Hunt stepped over and handed him a whiskey.

"Have you heard about Cold Harbor?"

"Cold Harbor?"

"Lee stopped Grant at Cold Harbor. On the third. A week ago." With the enthusiasm of a noncombatant, his uncle prided himself on his knowledge of military tactics. "Fourteen assaults in ten minutes. All repulsed, with the Yankee loss six to seven thousand! The first Confederate line was held by John Breckinridge. What do you think Grant will do now?"

Morgan closed his eyes and rested back. He felt the glass tip in his hand, then righted it. Without opening his eyes he said: "Go around. He'll go around. Amphibious . . ."

"But that would be . . . ridiculous!" His uncle blew his cheeks out. And then the civilian quickly gave deference to the man of experience: "Do you really think so?"

"Gunboats have saved him every time before," Morgan said, suddenly bored with a subject which had no meaning in this room, on this day. "At Shiloh, Vicksburg. He'll take to the water," he added in a softer tone to cover up the harshness of his original outburst.

"Want to wager?" Dr. Robert grinned from the doorway. "I have good news to report . . . Colonel Martin's wounds are superficial. How's Cripps?"

"With Johnston's army in Georgia. I haven't seen him since—" The memory of McMinnville, Pleasant Whitlow, before the Ohio raid. "In a while," he finished.

"How is Mattie?"

Robert's concern cut through his fatigue. T.H. had written them about the baby. Now he could tell them about the one they were expecting. Their faces were so bland, after all, so untouched by the war, as he told them. Worried, yes. But untouched, for all that. And then, with a pang, he remembered Tom, and Richard and Henry Curd. No, not all.

It started raining. "You'll have to wait for this shower to be over anyway," someone said. Through the window he could see his exhausted men standing in the rain, blessedly cooling off, not caring if they were wet to the skin. "You can't leave now," the voice—was it Uncle Frank's?—said again.

His universe had shifted. Even as he sat here, Hobson might be moving out of Cynthiana, and Burbridge was surely on his way from Mount Sterling —or waiting like a bird of prey to pick up the pieces. He had been dreaming, crazily in the back of his mind, of riding down the Versailles Road again. Would Amanda lend him a good mare? He hadn't had a good horse since Glencoe. He hadn't appreciated him.

"Tell Keene Richards his horse did a good job. When we surrendered in Ohio the Yankees gave him to General Winfield Scott."

"I hear from the papers he's planning to have his portrait done on him."

"Is that so?"

"I hope he bucks!" Cal shot out from the doorway, fresh from his rest.

Morgan laughed, but the effect of the brandy was gone, and he could hear Alston and Smith at the back of the house giving orders. Presently Captain Withers came in.

"The men are waiting, sir."

"Yes. Well."

"Where shall I tell Colonel Alston . . ."

"Georgetown."

"Georgetown, sir? But that's . . ."

"North? You haven't seen the Licking River at Cynthiana, have you, Captain? Pretty sight this time of year. We're going to give an old friend a visit." *If I can capture Hobson, if I can do that, maybe I can exchange him for Basil or Richard and Charl or both or all. . . .*

"I won't have you going!" his mother said in the hall as she fingered the buttons of his uniform. "I won't! You've hardly had a bite. . . ." She was trying for the old days, sensing he knew her blame, contrite through the half-feigned histrionics of the scold.

"I wasn't hungry. Besides, I'll be back," he lied. A weariness weighed down. They had gotten the horses, all right, enough to remount the whole command. But not one recruit. There would be no going to Atlanta or anywhere else now. Mattie's accusations about Kentucky came back. Maybe it did want it both ways, and would wind up with neither. . . . "Good-bye, Ma," he said suddenly, and went out the front door to avoid seeing Aunt Betty and the others again.

Before he reached the carriage yard Billy Milton ran up with a story of the scouts going out to Ashland, raiding the stables and leading out several thoroughbreds. The horse behind him looked vaguely familiar.

"Skedaddle!"

"Sir?"

"One of the best racers of all time. You took Skedaddle!" Ordinarily he would have sent him back. He threw the reins over and mounted. If John Clay could live in ease at Ashland, he would have to pay a price for it.

He skimmed along. It had been a long time. The feel of a good horse gave him a sense of acceptance that the deserted streets denied. He had a feeling, as he rode along, that faces behind curtains were watching them. Maybe the fires did it. Well, damn them in their comfort! Damn them all! Behind him the almost soundless rims of a spinning gig made him turn. A woman, bareheaded, her arms working the reins, pulled up, and he stopped. With a stab of delight and dismay he recognized Amanda. He dismounted and stood looking up at her.

"I'm sorry about Will. I should have written. But letters . . ."

"Your mother rode out one day."

"It happened Christmas Eve. Glasgow. He was a very brave man."

"Paw?" She looked off a moment, then down at her hands, then at him. "He would be proud to hear you say it."

"He's buried down there in the cemetery. There's a gravestone. We can move him after the war . . ."

"They're forming down on Versailles Road," she said quickly, harshly, impatient with his optimism. "You'd better, Johnny Mor—" She shook rain from her face, her green eyes wide.

"We'll be away before they can get to town," he said easily, suddenly feeling like his old competent self. He let go the side of the gig and re-mounted. As much to reassure himself as her he added: "We may be back," and grinned.

Already, the yellow dress across her shoulders was wet. The earthiness of her, in spite of her fine clothes, would always linger in the ample roundness of her breasts and arms. She was that other Kentucky, Will Webb's daugh-ter, the old pioneers who somehow survived. If they lost this war what would she and her kind become? Yankeefied, a little cruel with greed, maybe even vengeful against a race which had served their "betters." He suddenly felt the gulf that had always separated them deepen into a bottomless abyss. All her warmth, all her feline roundness would never overcome it. As he watched her he saw the blue eyes of another woman waiting for him and felt a mixture of nostalgia and regret. She noticed the change and straightened. She arranged the reins between her fingers, looked up, smiled, clucked and was gone. He watched the yellow dress move away. When he turned, the familiar tree-lined vista of the Georgetown Road was waiting.

At the factory, evidence of the fire was still there. If only he could have saved it. . . . It could have been a source of income. But his mother had investments Dick Curd's advice had provided. And she had her brothers, and Hopemont. He turned in his saddle and found the Presbyterian Church spire, then Old Morrison on the hill. Leaves rippled in the wind. Then there it was: the roof of home. Well, maybe it hadn't been an idle boast, after all. If they could whip Hobson, recruits would come, as they had in September of '62. Then . . . He let his eyes linger on the lines of Hopemont until Skedaddle, feeling pressure on one rein, thought he meant to turn. He faced front again, pressed his legs, and the trot lifted him into the old, ageless rhythm. It was ten miles to Georgetown as the crow flew, and twenty more to Cynthiana.

They could rest for two hours at the college, then push on, to cross the Licking River before daylight. Do a little surprising of their own. A hundred yards ahead his men were marching. He lifted his hand, waved his hat and leaned Skedaddle into a lope. As he passed down the line the rain, sporadic now, stopped completely and the freshened air and grassy smells came like a blessing. The men cheered as he passed. Hobson had chased him all over Ohio. He would return the favor!

Most of the men were bragging about their new mounts, comparing notes. They were in good spirits, but he recognized all the signs of a "second wind" before fatigue returned. Twelve miles to Georgetown would be enough.

Just after midnight Key, as orderly, woke him. It had been a good rest, needed down to their bootsoles. He had again accepted the hospitality of the college, sleeping in the president's house. He pulled on Mattie's vest and saw Key's face above the candle.

"Mighty hot for that, isn't it, Brother Johnny?"

"When a lady gives you good luck, my boy, never turn her down."

Before daylight they could hear the river. Beyond lay Cynthiana and those same buildings, those same streets they had fought through before, when

St. Leger made his dash to the depot. They were in the field again, facing the covered bridge. "I wonder where the old scoundrel is now," Cal said behind him, reading his thoughts.

Bowles and Kirkpatrick led the attack, dismounted, while Cassell's men crossed the ford and galloped around to the right to get behind the town. The sun had not yet come up; a heavy fog churned over itself in the air above the water, as if the river itself had risen like a curtain in front of them. The men entered the bridge, came out on the other side, and were in the streets before the Yankees, still asleep, knew they were there. Sporadic musketry, then a fire. "It's the livery stable!" Cal called out. The fire spread, and time was spent getting it under control. Then news came back that the garrison, four hundred strong, had surrendered.

"Four hundred? That's not Hobson!" Morgan ordered Giltner to take the Fourth Kentucky down the road to Augusta, and went with him. When they met Cassell's men behind the town Morgan galloped over and yelled that they should follow him. About ten minutes later they saw the unmistakable dust of horses ahead. Cassell's battalion, galloping ahead, gained Hobson's rear. With Giltner in front and nowhere to go, Hobson and thirteen hundred Yankees surrendered.

Morgan's first thought was parole and exchange. General Hobson was quite a prize. If he could arrange an exchange . . . Even while his men were marching their prisoners back to Cynthiana, Hobson told him in that dour way he had that the Federal War Department's orders forbade further paroles, under penalty of court-martial. "So you see, General, it's quite out of the question." Hobson restrained a smile.

Damn him, he's so self-assured. What does he know that I don't? That I can't be encumbered with over a thousand prisoners, who, without paroles, can turn and fight the minute they are released? To haul them back to Virginia would be impossible. He watched his men corral their charges, awaiting orders. He finally called a staff meeting.

"I see no way out," said Giltner glumly. "We'll have to let them go."

"Not without taking advantage of the situation first," Robert Martin, with a look to his superior, let go. Colonel Smith, to reinforce him, nodded.

"Seems a shame we can't return the favor of the prison experience," Smith growled through his beard.

Morgan hated this wrangling. In the old days he would have wasted no time. But Giltner, worried by Burbridge, was arguing for a march, without the prisoners, when the men were dead tired. Morgan knew that once the race for Virginia started there would be no chance to rest. Besides, he didn't want to throw away Hobson. Hobson, of all people! Permission from the Yankee War Department or not, he intended to parole him, send him to Cincinnati under an armed escort, with the idea that, to get him back, the Federals would have to let Basil and the others go. When Giltner finished, Morgan turned to Cal. "I want you to choose a dependable detail. Go to Cincinnati with General Hobson, effect an exchange. . . ."

When Cal came back ten minutes later and named Humphreys Castleman as one of his escort, Alston was furious.

"I saw myself—personally—Humphreys Castleman with money in Mount Sterling right after the robbery."

"You can't accuse a man for carrying money," Morgan said with that warning little smile tugging at one corner of his mouth. "I told you we would settle that matter in good time." He gave his permission and the men were gone with their charge within the hour. Then, making sure there were enough guards to watch the prisoners and wagon train, he sent half a dozen detachments in all directions to fire the bridges of the Kentucky Central and do any other damage to stop reinforcements from coming in. That left him with twelve hundred men.

"Now you'd better exchange those guns, Colonel Giltner. And take all the ammunition you can carry."

He returned to this little discussion almost as an afterthought. That morning, when they'd taken Cynthiana, Giltner had refused to exchange his men's guns for Yankee weapons, even though he was almost out of ammunition and the captured cartridges wouldn't fit. It was the old Enfield-Spencer controversy, the muzzle-loaders with their cool, steady aim-taking Rebels against the pull-lever, thumb-hammer-and-shoot breech-loaded Yankee. Foolishly and unbelievably, Giltner had argued that he would rather have an empty Enfield than a full Spencer. Morgan had dropped the argument, blaming fatigue, and took it up now expecting compliance. He got none. Giltner, still unwilling to abandon his better rifles, had provided his brigade with neither captured guns nor cartridges. Morgan bluntly asked him to do so now, and sent the Fourth Kentucky to camp on the Paris road. If he expects Burbridge, as he says he does, he'll be the first to greet him, he thought perversely. Anyway, he told himself, Burbridge won't move. He ate a good supper that night in a farmhouse on the Augusta Road and slept like a baby. It wasn't just the men who needed that rest.

But Burbridge did move. With the twenty-five hundred Michigan troops he had brought from Louisa, plus those left by Hobson at Mount Sterling— roughly thirteen hundred men—Burbridge could count almost four thousand against Morgan's twelve hundred. It was another predawn rout: Martin at Mount Sterling all over again; men being run over in their blankets, half-awake. Smith, with the Second Kentucky, quickly moved to Giltner's support, but the Fourth, many of whom were trapped before they could reach their horses and now completely out of ammunition, were reduced to swinging empty rifles like clubs. Giltner fought like a madman. To no avail. Morgan ordered the entire command to retreat along the Augusta Road and personally led a charge of the mounted reserve to cover the withdrawal. In spite of it all Giltner—or what was left of the Fourth Kentucky—was cut off from the Augusta Road and had to retreat south toward Leesburg. Smith, with Kirkpatrick severely wounded and Bowles driven from his position, fell back through Cynthiana to join Morgan, but found himself surrounded on three sides, with the river at their backs. The men crowded into the covered bridge. Horses panicked. Riders were thrown and trampled; some jumped in the river, to drown or be shot from shore. Others swam their horses Indian-style, leaning low to use their animals as shields. Afterwards there were stories of mounts jumping over stone fences into the river, of horses taking bullets but going on to jump the opposite bank, only to fall dead from loss of blood on the other side. When it was all over, most of the men escaped. But the command, reduced by two hundred fifty men killed, wounded and captured—among the prisoners was George Ellsworth—was badly scattered and totally without morale. Giltner, separated, continued south. Morgan moved northeast to Flemingsburg, then swung down through West Liberty, traveling by night, hiding in the hills by day.

Burbridge made no attempt to follow, thinking, almost rightly, that the mountains would finish them off. Besides, he was too busy rounding up "guerrillas." The scouts came in, Lieutenant Kelion Petticord holding back tears, to tell Morgan that Walter Ferguson had been executed. When he heard Morgan was in Kentucky again, Sherman declared all partisans of the Horse Thief to be "wild beasts." Burbridge was not slow to carry out the instructions of his superior: He ordered the execution of four guerrillas for every loyal citizen molested. When the supply of "guerrillas" did not match the quota, any Confederate prisoner would do.

Young Walter Ferguson, at Camp Boone. So eager. So long ago. No wonder those shutters were closed in Lexington. Burbridge's orders included the seizure of property of Rebel sympathizers "to indemnify the Government or loyal citizens for losses incurred by the acts of such lawless men . . ." He wondered now how safe his mother's income was—how strong Dick Curd's influence would be. And on what pretext four more of his prisoners would be marched foward, to be shot "near the scene of outrage."

"What's he doing?" Billy Milton whispered as they rode off. "Whistling softly like that . . . it's creepy, if you ask me. What's he whistling, anyway?"

John Morgan whistled to himself all the way over the mountains. *Come and laugh and dance with me.* They arrived at Abingdon on June 20, eight days after the debacle at Cynthiana, a ragtag band, completely worn-out.

In Louisville, the Kentucky Copperhead leader, Judge Bullitt, announced to his cohorts, "Morgan was too soon; we were not ready for him."

In Richmond, Secretary of War Seddon was already preparing to deny any knowledge of orders to Morgan for the raid.

Giltner, who had taken the easier route, was already at Abingdon, although he still had some junior officers rounding up stragglers in Kentucky. Giltner was understandably disgruntled, but something more than fatigue was bothering him. Morgan suspected it was the rebuff he received for refusing to use the captured guns and ammunition at Cynthiana, which might have made a difference. Maybe the man was worried that he would prefer charges of insubordination. If so, he tried to put him at his ease. The raid was over, and they had more important things to think about.

For one thing, there was discipline. The men seemed callous and reckless. He could understand the more recent recruits, with no loyalty to the command, but resistance to orders had spread even to the veterans, tired now from too much foraging, ignored by Richmond, impoverished, pushed to the brink of famine as the countryside, bent on survival, became less hospitable, became almost as wild and lawless as the men themselves.

But they were Confederate soldiers, not guerrillas, even though Richmond had condemned its cavalry to scavenging ever since the war started. They were Confederate soldiers, and they had to remember that. They would remember that. He ordered a roundup of all stragglers and the punishment of any members of his command who had used their Confederate status to rob or worse. He revoked all authority that had been granted independent scouts and directed every commanding officer to arrest and send to headquarters under guard every officer or soldier found absent from his command without regular leave in writing. When courts-martial and severe penalties failed, he appealed to Richmond for authority to reassign "a great many who are utterly worthless as cavalrymen" to the infantry.

Then as his first surge of indignation settled he realized that their intransigence was shared by too many of the officers. Something rotten was spreading throughout the command, some despair looking for a scapegoat. It wasn't just a loss of faith in Richmond—he had seen men cynical at government neglect and even corruption fight with awesome courage. No, this was deeper: maybe a loss of faith in themselves. He would do everything, anything, to restore that faith. That might be all they had now.

Looking back later, he wondered why it took him so long to learn who the scapegoat was. Alston asked that the Mount Sterling bank robbery be investigated immediately. He agreed, instructed Captain Allen, as inspector- general, to gather all evidence, and called a staff meeting.

Breck Castleman and Robert Martin did not appear. "Send for Lieutenant Eastin." Eastin, too, was gone.

What the hell was happening? Three of his best officers. He couldn't believe desertion. Not those three. Not Martin, who had ridden with Adam Johnson and Forrest, or Eastin, who had come from Kentucky with Castleman. Something was wrong.

He refused Allen's suggestion of a court-martial. There was undoubtedly an explanation. He turned to the defense of Southwest Virginia.

And to Mattie, who wanted him to send an escort for Alice.

"She's got to come! We're . . . all she has now!"

"I will, darling, as soon as I can. . . ."

Things had broken loose while he was away. On the 5th of June, while the command was struggling over the mountains toward Mount Sterling, Hunter swept down the Shenandoah and took Staunton. By the 13th Hunter had made a connection with Crook and Averell for an attack on Lynchburg. Sheridan, to help them, moved southwest to the rail line. But Sheridan met Wade Hampton's cavalry on the Gordonsville Road and was compelled to retreat across the North Anna. Then Jubal Early, with one leg, rode at the head of his column to drive Hunter back through the Kanawha Valley, with Hunter vandalizing as he went. That was the situation—tenuous and temporarily settled, when he arrived from Kentucky. Breckinridge was still with Lee.

George Crittenden had held onto Wytheville, but General Jones, who had succeeded Buckner, had been killed at Staunton. Morgan immediately asked that the men of Jones's brigade be transferred to him at Abingdon, and also those of General John Vaughn, who had at one time seven regiments, all mounted, from East Tennessee, plus one battalion of Georgia cavalry. If he could get these commands, with their artillery, he might build a decent defense. At the same time, to impress Richmond, he fudged a little, listing his four regiments as brigades, in the hope that they would classify as a division, even though his total strength, including Giltner, was less than three thousand. The survivors of the old Second Kentucky were now listed as the Second Battalion, under Major Cassell, in Colonel Smith's "brigade."

He had to get his department together. A sense of urgency, mixed with personal guilt, drove him now. Maybe that's why Castleman left? *If only I had won at Cynthiana. If only the recruits had come in.* He ignored the fact that none *had* come in, throughout the whole raid, in Lexington, or in George-town, or in Cynthiana when they *had* won, that night they sat with over a thousand Yankee prisoners. Where were Kentucky's boys then? He delib-erately forgot the looting in Mount Sterling, the fires in Lexington, those shuttered houses when he left home, and the feeling he'd had that his life no longer belonged there, but here, here with his men, holding onto what was left. And with his men at Chicago, and Columbus, Morton, Chase. . . . He reached for a letter, smuggled through the lines, from Private J. M. Lynn at Camp Douglas.

He closed his eyes. He had read this letter at least ten times—an abortive escape attempt at Chicago. He could see it: the commander of the prison ordering someone to step forward and tell the names of the men who had dug the tunnel. The long, silent wait, the Corporal reporting to the com-mander and returning, whispering to one of the guards. And the guard instantly cocking his musket, firing into the helpless mass of prisoners. . . .

"The bullet struck William Coles, killing him, and the buckshot wounded Henry Hutchins in the groin, passing through and tearing his hip fright-fully. His suffering was terrible and pitiful, and he did not die till morning . . . I would solemnly swear before any court, to the truthfulness of this account, if I ever get out of this accursed place. General, if you get this . . ."

The letter was broken off and unsigned, but he had no doubts about its authenticity. Smallpox was raging. Of the 5,750 prisoners at Douglas, 2,443 were sick, and the same story came from Morton and Chase and Rock Island in captured Yankee papers. Disease was bad enough. But to fire into helpless men.

Maybe he had been wrong about Hines.

He picked up another letter, just arrived that morning, from Senator Bruce. It warned that Seddon was already renouncing any responsibility for the Kentucky raid, saying that Morgan had no such orders. But Bruce had seen Ben Hill, the senator from Georgia, who told him that President Davis himself had admitted confidentially that he had "long ago ordered Morgan to make this movement upon Sherman's rear," that he had suggested moving directly through East Tennessee, but that Morgan had insisted on going by way of Kentucky, so he could get horses.

"Now I don't want to sound alarming," Bruce wrote, "but it has been my experience, in dealing with men even *in the highest places*, that what is said 'confidentially' is ancient history once the sound of their voices dies out. I must warn you that Seddon is already . . ."

He could fight Yankees. He couldn't fight this new enemy, deceit. He was not used to brooding and double-guessing. To lose Kentucky was bad enough. To lose the ability to act at all, to be hogtied by the hostility of superiors was monstrous. He had to go to Richmond. He began imaginary interviews. What he would say. What Davis or Bragg or Seddon would say. And then he realized that any absence now from the command could be judged as dereliction of duty and only add to the accusations.

"You don't look well, darling." Mattie, across the room, stopped knitting and looked over. "You've been back a whole week and all you've done is run out to the camps and worry with messages."

"I guess I haven't been good company lately."

She tried to tease him into good humor. "No, you certainly have not. In Richmond all the girls were hanging on you while you showered them with smiles. I hardly ever see one any more."

"How's this?" He made a face.

"Goodness! Enough to scare an unborn child."

"How are you?"

"Very fine, thank you, sir. I'll be fat soon and you won't love me." Her voice was only half-mocking now.

"That's not true, will never be true, and you know it. I've just had a lot on my mind. . . . Can you forgive me if I write one more letter tonight?"

He stood behind her, his hands massaging the back of her neck. She tilted her head to press his fingers. "Just one," she said, and he bent from the waist and kissed her.

Richmond, that pack of liars. There was only one man he could trust. He would write General Lee.

Lee, locked in siege at Petersburg. Should he worry him?

He had made the Yankees pay dearly ever since the Wilderness. . . . Grant's casualty lists reached fifty-five thousand for the month of May and that first week in June—almost as many men as Lee had in his whole army. But Grant had turned amphibious, and crossed the James as he had crossed the Mississippi, and laid siege to Petersburg. On June 14th, an assault. On the 16th. On the 17th. On the 18th he decided to take the town—where Kitty Morgan Hill, with her new baby and little Frances, was living to be near A.P. Three assaults on the 18th: at four in the morning, at noon, at four in the afternoon. Each repulsed. Night found the Confederates still in Petersburg, with a cost to Grant of another ten thousand. In the North he was now called "Butcher" and the Copperheads were clamoring for peace; in Washington, with a depleted treasury, Secretary Chase resigned. Lee, like a mole, held on.

"He's the only one," Morgan said to himself as he pulled the paper to him. How many men of integrity had he known? Albert Sidney Johnston, Buckner, Polk. But the good bishop had died on the 14th of June at Pine Moun-

tain, Georgia. Forrest! On the 10th—the day he rode into Lexington—
Forrest, outnumbered two to one, was stopping Sturgis on his way to help
Sherman, at Brice's Cross Roads in northern Mississippi, taking two thousand prisoners and chasing the Yankees back to Memphis. Forrest! Forrest
would never quit fighting, even if they tied both hands behind him. Joe
Johnston, with Kennesaw Mountain as the apex of his line, was still playing
chess with Sherman in front of Atlanta. And between the two fronts—
Georgia and Virginia—his own command sat half starved and straggling,
awaiting orders from a government bent on suicide. He picked up the pen
and wrote quickly:

> General: There are no troops menacing this department at the present
> time. Where must I strike the enemy? Would it be best to strike at the
> B&O Railroad or move to the rear of Knoxville and operate on the
> Nashville Road?

He ignored the thought that in the old days he would not have had to
ask—even Lee—where to fight. He would have been the one plotting, proposing . . . Lee would think him insane. Moving to the rear of Knoxville
over mountains with a worn-out command didn't even look possible on
paper. He folded the letter and started to tear it in half. He was reduced to
a man clutching at straws. Well, maybe he was. He laid the letter down and
reached for another whiskey.

The next day, another problem. His recruiting officer, Captain John Reynolds, had been captured near Knoxville and sentenced to be shot. He called
in his adjutant to request facts from the Federal commander and to declare
that "retaliation in kind shall be inflicted upon the first Federal officer of
equal rank who falls in my power." Vengeance, too, was new for him. This
was no longer the old days.

Lee wired him on June 30: COLLECT ALL AVAILABLE TROOPS IN YOUR REGION.
PROTECT SALT WORKS. WATCH MOVEMENTS OF THE ENEMY. RESTRAIN EXPEDI-
TION OF AVERELL'S CAVALRY.

Hell, what did he think he'd been doing? Collect . . . protect . . . watch
. . . restrain. Hell.

A headache throbbed behind his eyes. Outside the sky roiled with a
summer storm and distant thunder. Well, it would cool things off. As politely as he could, he answered Lee:

> I find there is much disorganization among the troops of this depart-
> ment since my return from Kentucky. But am organizing for the de-
> fense of the country as rapidly as possible and think I can hold it against
> any force that is threatening at present—I have 2,000 in the Dept. and
> will carry out your instructions.

Maybe promising to hold his department "against any force" with two thousand men might encourage the transfer of troops from Jones and Vaughn—
couldn't they see the bravado of such a promise? Surely they would say,

Let's send this man more troops. . . . And just to let them know that he had
ideas of his own he added:

> Don't you think a small body of men sent up toward Charlestown, to
> interfere with the supplies of Averell, would do more good than it could
> by remaining in his front?

Lee answered with characteristic patience: "Exert all your energies to
organize your troops and prepare for advance of the enemy. If you think
advantageous send part to cut off Averell's supplies."

A nothing answer. A pat on the head by the schoolmaster. To be fair, the
General was there, not here, and had his own problems. If only he still had
Adam Johnson, or St. Leger, or Basil! Dear Basil. Giltner, a little jealous,
would never be a support, and now he suspected that Giltner was contami-
nating Alston, who kept asking for an investigation of that damned bank
robbery. He'd sent Colonel Smith, his most dependable man, into Tennessee to watch Bull's Gap. He had Bowles, Cassell, Kirkpatrick. But what he
needed was a strategist. What he needed was Basil. Where the hell was Cal?
Had he succeeded with the exchange of Hobson?

He didn't have long to wonder. Cal came in the next day, his mission a
total failure. All exchanges cancelled. Cal gave his report, then stopped
abruptly. He was amazed at the change in Johnny. There was something
limp about him. How could he tell him that Humphreys Castleman had
admitted what Alston suspected was correct: that he and Breck had a connection with the Mount Sterling money—and Hines? Or that Breck Castleman and Eastin had recruited Martin—for what, he wasn't sure. When he
found out that Castleman and the others had gone, he fully intended to tell
his brother about the Hines connection. But now, with this dejected, distracted man in front of him, he dared not. After all, that might not be the
case at all, and Johnny looked as if he couldn't take any more bad news.

"Did you see any of the others?"

"Others?"

"Stragglers. Deserters. Convenient absentees. Too comfortable to find
their way back through the lines."

Cal looked up, shocked at the bitterness. "Why, no, I . . ."

"Here, have a drink, Cally. Would you like to go to Richmond for me?
Mattie's been after me to escort Alice here, but if I leave now it will only
feed—only cause more accusations of neglect."

"Neglect?"

"Never mind." He tried to make it light. "Besides, you could see that nice
young lady again . . . what was her name . . . Carrie Harrison? Will you
do it?"

But somebody in Richmond had listened. Maybe through Lee. Maybe
through Breckinridge or Senator Bruce. The day after Cal left, Colonel
Bradford, with a regiment from General Vaughn's brigade, reported for
duty. Bradford was a competent officer and his men were tough Tennessee
veterans.

He arrived none too soon. News of Federal activity at Bull's Gap caused Morgan to send not only Bradford but Giltner down there to help Smith if the Yankees moved out of Knoxville in force. They were hardly out of sight when he received orders that Bradford was being transferred to Breckinridge's command. He protested by telegraph to Adjutant-General Cooper: "The enemy are threatening us from the direction of Knoxville and these troops are needed in my front."

He had planned to leave for Bull's Gap the next day. Now he waited for a reply from Cooper. None came. Cal arrived on the afternoon train with Alice, and as it turned out, his life would never be the same again.

It started early. James Bowles, who had not yet left for Tennessee, came to him to warn him that Giltner and Alston—possibly even Colonel Smith —were planning to ask that he be relieved of his command. Bowles had not been gone ten minutes when Major Chenoweth, who had served with Gano and who, for valor at Mount Sterling Morgan had promoted, asked to be relieved of duty so he could join Adam Johnson.

Without a word, Morgan signed the order. *Sinking ship?* his eyes asked, but he wouldn't, couldn't say it. Then Cal walked in, and when Alice took off her bonnet in the hall, her lovely brown hair was white.

56

Tom Hines collected his wager about shaking Lincoln's hand. From Washington he went to Cincinnati, then to Detroit by train, by ferry to Windsor, Ontario. By the week of April 20 he was in Toronto and settled in a small boardinghouse run by a Mrs. Marsh, with room and meals for ten dollars a month. He soon learned that the center of Confederate activity was the Queen's Hotel bar. There he met a captain he recognized. Before another week passed he had rounded up fifty followers. They were in the bar pouring whiskies when the news of Morgan's victory at Wytheville came in. The papers said he had stopped the Federal effort to cut Lee's communications and capture the lead mine. They raised a toast at the Queen's and sang "The Raiders Ride Tonight."

It was a strange setup. Hines was in charge—or was he? Soon after arriving he was attached to a three-man Peace Commission: Thompson, Clay and Holcomb. Jacob Thompson of Mississippi, former Secretary of the Interior under President Buchanan, was a man with feverish, sore eyes and a brown spade beard. Clement Clay was a former U.S. Senator from Alabama, an invalid with an irritable voice who wanted to stay in Montreal with $95,000 in Federal greenbacks deposited in his name. James Holcomb, from Virginia, was scholarly but gullible. He had been in Montreal since December preparing and hoping for just such a mission.

Toward the end of May Thompson and Clay arrived in Toronto full of their adventure: they had run the blockade on a very fast—fourteen knots per hour—side-wheeler. Then there was a British mail ship, bound for Halifax . . .

Hines listened patiently enough at first. For a month, while the three "commissioners" conferred, he had rounded up escapees: Ben Drake and Henry Stone, who had served under Hines as a scout on the Ohio raid; Jack Trigg and John Ashbrook of Hutchinson's Company E; Bennet Young, one of Quirk's protégés. Then, as planned, Breck Castleman came in from Virginia with George Eastin and Robert Martin. And a real surprise: George Ellsworth, captured in Cynthiana in June.

Hines's first meeting with the Copperheads was with Thompson at the Clifton House, Niagara Falls. There was Fernando Wood, ex-mayor of New York City and owner of *The New York Daily News,* and Washington Hunt, ex-governor of New York. Vallandigham, too, was there, reporting that the North showed a definite fatigue after Lincoln's call for 500,000 more men. Vallandigham assured them that he could raise, in Indiana, Ohio and Illinois, at least 300,000 Copperheads willing to capture state arsenals, release Confederate prisoners. A plan was proposed: Castleman would be in charge of the assault at Rock Island, Hines at Camp Douglas. Simultaneously, attacks would be launched at Camp Morton, Indianapolis and Camp Chase at Columbus, Ohio. William Cleary, an Irish friend of Hines and acting secretary for the Commission, went to New York to buy thirty thousand dollars' worth of arms through a violin shop off Washington Square.

Another meeting of the Copperheads, this time at St. Catherine's, Ontario: Charles Walsh, Cook County, Illinois; Amos Green, commander of the Illinois Copperheads; James J. Barrett, "Adjutant-General" of the Sons of Liberty; H. H. Dodd from Indiana; T. C. Massie, Ohio; and Justice J. Bullitt, from Louisville, who had helped Hines before. The date for the uprising: July 4. Thompson wrote Secretary of State Judah Benjamin: Morgan's Kentucky raid would coincide. It would be their signal. But Morgan came too soon. July 4 was changed to July 16; July 16 to July 20.

In the meantime a tall, debonair, charismatic man neither Hines nor Castleman trusted joined the Commission. His name was George N. Sanders. He had once given a party for the future President of the United States in London when Buchanan was ambassador to the Court of St. James. In the early fifties Sanders had been the American consul in London, although mysteriously so, since the Senate refused to confirm his appointment.

Hines and Castleman soon found out he was a self-indulgent dreamer obsessed with his own plans. When he tried to persuade Hines to rob the banks in Niagara Falls, illogically assuming that such a loss of currency would cause the Yankees to resist the draft, Hines warned both Thompson and Clay, to no avail. As for the scholarly Holcomb, he was completely mesmerized.

Then St. Leger arrived, in his English tweeds with his dog and gun. He had come by way of Cuba and Washington, where he was quizzed about Confederate strength and given permission to travel, on an oath that he would not help the Rebels again. "And of course I won't, lads—just came along to see how you are doing. There's excellent pheasant shooting down in Illinois. Besides, they had no right to ask me all those questions!"

When Sanders, without Thompson's knowledge, sent for Horace Greeley and asked for safe conduct for himself and Clay to see Lincoln, Grenfel joined Hines and Castleman in warning Clay to avoid a man they considered a fool. Lincoln, as Hines and Grenfel predicted, refused to see anybody. But he did send Greeley to Canada to meet Sanders and Clay in Niagara Falls. Greeley's message: Union and no slavery. Thompson's answer: Independence. Precious time had been lost.

Hines swore. Delay with men of action would be fatal. They all knew it. "All I want to do is release Confederate prisoners, gentlemen, to fight this war, to end it. . . ."

At that fateful meeting Hines turned his slow eyes to the Copperheads and realized that their paths had parted: The "Sons of Liberty" would no longer be satisfied with peace; they wanted a separate empire of Northwestern states: another Confederacy, another secession. "We must look to bigger results than the mere release of prisoners," they said. Judge Bullitt would stage a big "barbecue" in Louisville. From there the crowd could take Cincinnati, then St. Louis . . . Sanders's crazy schemes were catching, like a disease.

August. Another "peace emissary" from Washington, this time Judge Jeremiah Black, former U.S. Attorney-General. On a casual suggestion from Secretary of War Stanton, he came saying the Secretary wanted peace terms, that everybody believed now Lincoln could never be reelected. The time was ripe, before the Democratic Convention in Chicago August 29, to conclude a peace. Hines and Castleman urged Thompson to communicate directly with Richmond, but Thompson, believing with Black that Lincoln's loss of the election would influence France and England to side with the Confederacy, sent Holcomb instead to London and Paris to see Mason and Slidell. . . .

If they could only get some real action now! Action that would push the Yankees into negotiations! With all the protests since Gettysburg and the casualty lists of "Butcher" Grant coming out of Virginia, the North was ready. *If they could only get Morgan back into Kentucky!*

"It's worth a try," Castleman moaned. "Anybody but these dreamers."

"Until we do," said Hines. "Until we do, we already have somebody in Kentucky."

Castleman looked at Eastin.

"Adam Johnson," Hines let out softly. "If Johnson can cross the Ohio and take Camp Morton . . ." Within the hour two couriers volunteered to take the message south.

Unbelievable luck. Adam Johnson had recruited a command and marched from Virginia to the Ohio River; he had been waiting for more than a week. Now he made his move. On the 14th of August he crossed to Shawneetown, Illinois, with the 16th as his target date at Camp Morton. Messengers from H. H. Dodd, the Indiana Copperhead leader, met him as he rode into Indiana with a promise of fifteen thousand stands of arms for the prisoners, and ten thousand armed men. Hobson, caught by Morgan at Cynthiana but released without parole, was chasing him, with orders from General Ewing to shoot Johnson on the spot—and his whole command.

Somebody talked. On a tip, 135,000 rounds of ammunition were seized in Dodd's office by Union spies. Johnson, when he heard of it, turned back.

On the evening of August 20, Hobson caught up with Johnson at a little place called Grubb's Crossroads. It was a black, starless night. Johnson decided to fight it out at dawn, a surprise attack. Even before the silhouettes of the Federal camp could be seen, with the sky paling to another day, Johnson led the charge. A bullet went into his right eye and through the left temple, taking both eyes with it. Even in total darkness now, Adam swung his horse around, calling to Chenoweth to save the men. When he surrendered, the Union troopers disobeyed orders: They treated him with kindness.

Hines, when he heard of it, knew they needed Morgan more than ever. "Get Ellsworth," he told Castleman. "Wire Richmond. Immediately. He's got to come. He's our only hope." God grant that lovely man enough luck to get into Kentucky on time. To hold them off, to draw attention. . . .

A new date was set: August 29, when the Democratic Convention met in Chicago.

The Mount Sterling bank robbery would not go away. His officers gossiped behind Morgan's back. Alston was getting his information from enlisted men of Company A, Second Battalion—Major Jacob Cassell's command. They said Dr. Goode ordered them to help rob the bank and named Humphreys Castleman as a participant. Alston passed the information on to Captain Allen who, as Inspector-General, should have investigated, but by a quirk of fate Allen, very ill, went on leave. Then affidavits in Alston's desk disappeared while Allen was gone.

When Allen got back he conferred with Colonel Smith, up from Tennessee. Bowles was at that meeting, and at the first opportunity approached his general.

"I don't know how to tell you this." James Bowles had been with him since Bowling Green, and Morgan waited. "Colonel Alston is writing Richmond, saying the conduct of your command in Kentucky was . . ."

"Was what, Colonel?"

"Enough to cause a man to blush at the name of Confederate soldier, sir," Bowles got out. "Furthermore, he is asking for a transfer . . ."

"So that's it."

"The bank robbery," Bowles nodded.

Morgan got up, walked to the window. "I don't for the life of me understand it. The Yankees rob banks as a matter of course—if they don't burn the town first. I've told Richmond I intend to investigate."

"That's . . . evidently not firm enough," Bowles said behind him. "Colonel Giltner . . . is asking for an investigation of his own."

"What do they want?" He turned, but the face of his friend held such pain and bewilderment that he didn't press the question. "I'll take care of it."

"Yes, sir."

But Bowles remained standing.

"Is that all?"

Bowles cleared his throat. "General, I have an open mind. I'm not here to pass judgment."

"Then don't."

Bowles shook his head in exasperation.

It was not like James Bowles to miss a cue to leave. Morgan looked up. Bowles started to say something, then thought better of it. In chagrin at his own brusqueness, Morgan walked to the door with him, his arm on Bowles's shoulder. "Take care of yourself, James. And close that damned mind of yours."

Morgan's thin smile had nothing of sarcasm in it. No, Bowles thought. Only sadness. He said nothing when his general added, sensing the sympathy, "It gets drafty. I ought to know."

Morgan watched the door close and asked himself, in genuine puzzlement: Why the bank? Could they really be all that concerned, when Giltner didn't

even try to control his men looting? Or was Giltner, feeling guilty, trying
to pass the guilt onto him? No, there had to be another reason.

Cal, who had been present during Bowles's visit, waited for the Colonel
to leave. Only an emergency could have forced him to say what he said now.

"There's a rumor going around Seddon's office that you might be replaced
because you can't be trusted. You went into Kentucky without orders. They
say. Now they're saying you've lost your nerve," he added, and breathed
out slowly.

"Damn to hell what they say!"

"They may be using this bank robbery as an excuse."

"But why would they want to ruin a dependable command?"

Cal shrugged. *Stupidity in high places*, his look said, but his brother hadn't
noticed.

"There's something rotten." Morgan let out a breath. "Something more.
Why did Breck and Martin and Eastin leave?"

Cal shook his head and looked kindly across at that bent head. "One thing
for sure. Those three have nothing to do with this loss of faith . . ." Then
Cal added cautiously: "Eastin was with Castleman and Company D from
the beginning. And Colonel Martin was Adam Johnson's second-in-command in the Tenth Kentucky. Doesn't that give you a clue?" He had been
watching that shattered face for days. An empty whiskey bottle, as too often
happened lately, sat by his brother's elbow.

"What? What?"

"Hines." Cal couldn't, on his honor, say more. Eastin and Castleman were
by this time in Canada to help Hines with a Copperhead uprising in Chicago, Martin with some wild scheme to burn New York. Not even Cal knew
all the details, nor just how much Adam Johnson was implicated.

"Who in that damned town can I trust?"

"The man who swore you into service," Cal said after a pause. "Colonel
Johnston."

"You're right! Why didn't I think of him before?"

Those Richmond faces came back: Ould, Cooper. He felt trapped. Even
though he had just written Cooper that he was being threatened from Knoxville, the idea that they thought he'd lost his nerve infuriated him. He shot
off a wire to Bragg:

> I DO NOT REGARD MY DEPARTMENT AS THREATENED AT PRESENT FROM ANY
> DIRECTION. I COULD ORGANIZE AN EXPEDITION OF FIVE HUNDRED OR SIX
> HUNDRED MEN TO MOVE THROUGH NORTH CAROLINA, VIA ASHEVILLE,
> FRANKLIN, ETC., AND OPERATE ON THE RAILROAD IN SHERMAN'S REAR, IF
> THE GOVERNMENT DEEMS IT ADVISABLE.

No answer. Never mind: there was William Preston Johnston, Sidney
Johnston's son on Davis's staff. Those same sincere eyes. As he composed
the letter, he chose his words carefully. For the first time in his life he was
dealing with a feeling new to him: resentment against one of his own officers,
tinged by fear.

Colonel: I wish it would meet the views of the President to send a good officer to take charge of the Kentucky troops that I found in the department. They were ordered to report to me by General Buckner and are under Colonel Giltner. It is important that an efficient officer be placed over the brigade, there is fine material in it. I am satisfied that any appointment made by the President will be entirely acceptable to the troops.

Just casual enough, without bluntly blaming Giltner for inefficiency. Now to end on a positive note: "Numbers of young men are coming out of Kentucky; seven reported yesterday."

It was a lie. They were stragglers roped in by Alston. But at least he had not accused Giltner openly, and mentioning the President would ask Johnston discreetly to pass the letter on. It was a little bit, he thought as he blew out the candle and watched moonlight on the floorboards, like scouting out the enemy before he found you. All's fair.

In the humid summer night the crickets cried for rain. He was worried about Kitty. The news of the Crater at Petersburg seemed at first unbelievable. Halted by Lee's earthworks, Grant decided to use some Pennsylvania coal miners to tunnel under the fortifications. They planted eight thousand pounds of powder and blasted a gap in the Confederate line. Men, guns, artillery horses and timbers shot into the air, then tumbled in a shapeless ruin. The explosion left a crater 30 feet deep and 170 feet long. A desperate, hand-to-hand battle followed, with Lee's men in a frenzy: Burnside's troops fell back, and Grant lost another four thousand men. The Crater had been a Union failure, but how long could Petersburg last? Kitty and little Frances and the baby . . .

The news had only added to Mattie's strange mood of apocalyptic doom. First, it was Alice's girlish religion that had turned sour; through fits of fear her husband's death at Spotsylvania became a judgment. That was understandable, and would pass with time, he thought. But it filtered into Mattie —his unshakable girl. Now she was saying that the death of her first baby must have been a judgment, too . . . With Alston and now Giltner this was almost more than he could take.

When she heard about the bank robbery and the accusation that he was delaying the investigation, she exploded.

"Why are you defending them?"

"I'm merely trying to establish evidence."

"I suppose you'll say they're friends."

He watched the drawn-back, bitter corner of her mouth.

"Well, just wait and see how those friends defend you in Richmond! They're just marking time for some excuse to ruin you . . . and you're too much a 'gentleman' to stop them!"

Her derision cut like a knife. He pushed the memory of it aside and sat in the parlor listening to summer insect sounds. He heard her go upstairs. He knew she was waiting for him. Outside a wind had picked up. He walked to the window. He had to face the fact that she was five months pregnant. Averell was in the Kanawha, Sheridan in the Shenandoah, and even if his troops could guard the Holston Valley and Bull's Gap from an invasion from Knoxville, Abingdon was not the place for a young girl—now two young girls—in what was becoming increasingly an unsafe situation. He had deliberately agreed to a visit from Alice with an idea of sending them both back to Augusta. But Sherman was on the move—he had crossed the Chattahoochie on July 17, and the next day Joe Johnston was replaced by John Hood, who was fighting for Atlanta on Peachtree Creek. So Georgia, too, might not be safe too much longer. The other alternative was to seek, through all the influence he could pull, safe passage through the lines back to Lexington, where her baby could be born at Hopemont. But even as he thought it, he knew it was impossible. That had been one of Cal's objectives, and he had failed.

He poured himself a whiskey by the moonlight shifting through moving leaves, and sat watching the wind jerk the shadows of trees against the night sky. And Cal had come back with Alice.

Won't you talk with her, John? She'll listen to you. She's always loved you. Please. For me.

What can I say that you haven't, Mattie?

You're a man. No, more: You're a soldier. You can tell her how it is. Even if you have to lie.

He had sought her eyes, those blue-violet entries into the softness of her, and found a new fear he had not seen before. *I'll try.*

And he did. He had. Alice, with a little gasp, had looked back and said: "Now I know why the Lord in His wisdom sent this war! It's to show us that this world is no good, that this life has no meaning . . . that our home is not here, but elsewhere . . . that the sooner we leave this vale of tears the better! Oh, to be with those who have crossed over, who are now where we all should be, where we were meant to be!"

He would always remember the look on her face under that straw-white hair, a peculiar mixture of rapture and wild despair. He realized now that her arguments were anchored in a rockbed resignation which no amount of love or reason could budge, because in that resignation Alice had found her own brand of sanity. So he watched her recede from him into a place he could not follow, where his own words rang echoes against the walls of her grief. If she had only been angry. He couldn't deal with this bottomless acceptance. If she had only cried, her shoulders shaking, or screamed. Anything. He could have dried her eyes, kissed her hands, rocked her. She became a ghost, stalking within earshot, haunting. They had given up surface remarks, meant to brighten. When she was there a heavy silence weighed like a stone.

And now Mattie. The weight had settled into her, too.

He looked from the sky into the yard across the street. Stars of another kind: fireflies. So many little lives. Yes, Cal had failed. Dear Cal, coming back from Richmond with Von Borcke's story about Bragg refusing to send Stuart infantry support. So Jeb Stuart died holding off eight thousand Yankees with eleven hundred men.

And Von Borcke?

He's going back to Europe.
Like St. Leger?
Cal had waited a minute before he answered.
Like St. Leger, he'd said.
St. Leger gone. And Hines, Castleman. Now Martin and Eastin. Something Cal said when he came back. Martin and Eastin gone . . . Eastin, Castleman, Company D. Hines. A connection began to emerge. He drained his glass and stood up. Cal said they were talking about a Board of Inquiry in Richmond, which might mean a court-martial. Well, if the Mount Sterling money could help release Confederate prisoners, more power to it. Or a conspiracy or whatever Hines might be up to. And damn their investigation.

To his surprise she was not in bed, but standing by the window.
"Aren't they wonderful?" she asked, not turning, but hearing him come in.
"What?" He pulled off his jacket and laid it on a chair.
"The lightning bugs," she said, too brightly. "I never knew how many there could be. Against the hills. Like a million blinking stars."
He stood beside her. "You'll catch cold here. The night air . . ."
" 'Consider the lilies of the field,' " she whispered, " 'how they grow; they toil not, neither do they spin. . . . Lay not up for yourselves treasures upon earth, where moth and rust doth corrupt, and where thieves break through and steal. . . .' " She squeezed her eyes shut. How she had railed at God when the baby died! He was punishing her for it now. He was punishing with the robbery, and these men like the "friends" of Job, who would bring him down if they could. Didn't he *see* that? He wouldn't listen. . . .
He turned her around, his hands on her shoulders. "Mattie. Darling. That's what I want to talk to you about. . . ."
"What?"
"The fireflies. It's already the third of August."
She would hear none of it. She went back to bed and watched him undress, get in beside her.
"We'll be perfectly all right here," she said, her voice breaking. "And Alice . . . how can she travel, poor thing?"
"I may have to go down into Tennessee any day now," he said to the ceiling.
She turned to him.
"I'll leave Cal in charge. But it would be better if you . . ."
"I'm not afraid!" She leaned back, straight, on her side of the bed.
"I know you aren't. My brave girl." His hand reached hers, but her fingers were cold. She drew her hand away.
Maybe all this business about Giltner would blow over after all.
Giltner wrote Secretary of War Seddon on August 21: "I regret the necessity which compels me to address you upon this subject, and beg leave to assure you that it is done only after every effort has been exhausted to induce General Morgan to take action."

Just to play it safe, Giltner sent another copy direct, "fearing the matter may be delayed in General Morgan's office."

When Morgan found out he exploded. He forwarded Giltner's letter at once, adding a note of his own to Seddon asking if he were to be arraigned by a subordinate officer. He admitted the bank was robbed, but denied any delay in an investigation: "The facts developed thus far are not sufficient to a full exposé of the matter, and I have delayed any public action in regard to it until the whole thing can be thoroughly sifted."

After all, it was Seddon who had sent Hines to Canada. If there really was any connection between this money and a conspiracy, Seddon would understand. And what he said in his defense was true. From the beginning, during that afternoon in Mount Sterling, he had ordered Captain Allen to investigate. So far Allen had uncovered only rumor. He wasn't lying when he said he did not have sufficient facts. "Captain Allen has been on leave with a surgeon's certificate of disability. I intend to investigate the charges fully once more facts are found. Colonel Giltner has been singularly lacking in soldierly respect and obedience in this matter." He sealed the letter and then forgot about the bank, and nearly everything else: A telegram from Hines, via Richmond, arrived.

HELP ADAM.

What could he mean? Had Adam joined the conspiracy? "Old Stovepipe," pretending to abandon him . . . even submitting to doubt . . . to help Hines and not saying so because he knew how he felt about all that. And Hines, if he knew his Copperheads, delayed by deceit and promises. Castleman, Eastin, Drake . . . Ellsworth. His hunch was right. He had to help them! He would help them!

Two hours later Lieutenant Xen Hawkins rode into camp with a message that the Federals had moved out of Bull's Gap: Smith, Giltner and Bradford were driven back to Carter's Station on the Watauga River, about thirty-five miles from Abingdon. There was no time to lose.

He shot off a wire to Seddon asking for orders for a Kentucky raid, sent a hurried note to Mattie, then ordered the fours to form. By the time he reached the Watauga the Yankees were retreating. Morgan gave orders immediately for pursuit, all the way to Greeneville, another thirty-seven miles away, and only eighteen from Bull's Gap. When he tied his reins in Greeneville he felt, for the first time since Ohio, close to collapsing. He had spent two hard days in the saddle. He set up temporary headquarters in the largest house in town, belonging to a Mrs. Williams, a professed Southern sympathizer, although her house, Withers reported, had been used by both armies. "She has two sons in the Confederacy, one in the Union Army, and her daughter-in-law, married to the Yankee, lives here."

"Are those all the statistics?" Morgan tried a smile. "Not a word about lightbread or ham?"

The Williams house with its large board-fenced garden and vineyard occupied a whole block. It faced east, overlooking its garden toward Main Street and a small frame Episcopal church at the corner. The Williams stables occupied the opposite, diagonal corner, at a point where the Rogersville, Bull's Gap, Warrensburg and Newport roads met. No wonder both armies had used this house: It was a veritable observation post. The boxwood hedge was neatly trimmed and there was a fragrance of late afternoon roses in carefully cultivated beds by the porch. With a weariness that was almost overpowering, Morgan accepted their hospitality.

The widow was a soft, broad-bosomed lady who made him feel immediately at home. "General Longstreet used the front corner bedroom overlooking the garden," she smiled. "I think you will find it comfortable, sir." She clapped fat little hands and sent a servant to make sure the room was ready.

"I'll wager the General slept well, as I will, too."

Then the lady reached out one arm to introduce him to Jenny Rumbaugh, visiting from Virginia, the sister of Mrs. Williams's daughter-in-law Lucy, married to her son Joe, and Mrs. Williams's youngest daughter, Fanny.

Jenny Rumbaugh, with the slightest trace of a very studied hauteur, declared herself delighted to meet him; young Fanny stood in awe. There was something vaguely familiar and disturbing about blond Lucy Williams, the wife of the Union soldier. Something provocative. The way she tilted her head to look at him, as if she dared him to remember. Her gray eyes met his, then slid away, and a line by one side of her mouth deepened into a small smile. Suddenly: Knoxville, and a brazen girl leading off a meek little civilian past grinning Confederate officers. She had let her bangs grow and wore her hair in the fashionable middle part, but that sharp little chin and the way she walked . . . she was the same. His eyes went to the picture of Joe Williams on the mantle. He was not the civilian gentleman Lucy Williams had in tow at the Bell House. "Sir?" She looked back at him again.

"I said—perhaps I have had the pleasure."

"I have never seen you before in my life, sir."

"Excuse me." Withers was motioning to him from the hall.

"There's a Federal officer here, sir. Upstairs. Assistant Adjutant-General to General Gillem. Wounded. Says he has a parole."

"Has he produced it?"

"Yes, sir."

"Well, there's nothing to worry about. I imagine the house is big enough for both of us!" The idea of hot water, a clean towel, warm supper and a bed made magnanimity easy. In the parlor doorway, on his way to thank Mrs. Williams for her hospitality, he brushed by Lucy on her way upstairs with her finger marking a place in her prayer book. "I'm glad to see we have God-fearing people here, ma'am. Will you say a prayer for me?"

She tossed her head and marched off, skirts swishing. By the time he reached his room hot water was in the pitcher and fresh towels were laid out. He peeled off his clothes and felt the lather caress his neck. He could do no more now and needed the rest: Bull's Gap lay less than twenty miles to the west. It was in that direction that he had sent Colonel Bradford's Tennesseans. They would cover not only the Bull's Gap Road but spread across the Warrensburg and Newport roads to the west and south, forming an arc. Giltner and Smith would watch the road northwest toward Rogersville, Smith about a mile and a half from town, Giltner farther out. Vedettes reported no activity this side of the Gap. Maybe Gillem, for now, had had enough. Cat and mouse.

He was glad he had come. His men needed the reassurance. Bothered by Richmond, he had left them too much on their own. Maybe that was part of the trouble: inaction. He would spend the night, ride back to Abingdon, apply again for a raid into Kentucky. He might still help Hines. . . .

The bed was inviting, but he was restless. He had to get back to Abingdon. Seddon's answer would surely be waiting. He would get the rest of his command, consolidate and head west, for Kentucky. What did Hines mean: Help Adam?

The bath revived him. He pulled on a clean shirt and decided to check on the pickets again. As he passed a door half-ajar at the head of the stairs he realized it was a smaller bedroom, a kind of inner room that had once been a cross hall to the other side of the house. He glanced in and saw, in the light of one small dormer window, a four-poster bed covered by a green brocade quilt. Propped against pillows in the bed sat the Federal officer. Their eyes met as Morgan passed, and the officer raised his hand in greeting. He had piercing blue eyes, ruddy cheeks and an expansive smile. "Won't you stop by?" he called out, and Morgan pushed the door fully open and entered.

"I want to thank you for your courtesy, General Morgan," the man said. "I've . . . just received this"—he pointed to his shoulder and right arm in a sling—". . . and the doctor says it will be a few days yet before I'm up and about."

"Nothing . . ." Morgan waved his hand.

The man folded a newspaper and reached it over to him. "I thought you might be interested."

MEMPHIS, Tenn.—Eluding Gen. A. J. Smith's 18,000 federals— sent into Mississippi to destroy him—Gen. N. B. Forrest set this federal city into an uproar early this morning by raiding it with 1,500 men.

Details are too confused, as we go to press, but it seems likely that Forrest and his lightning cavalry have clearly surprised the federal garrison here.

Morgan looked at the date: August 20. "It's so like him," he heard himself say.

"Yes, isn't it?" the man on the bed chuckled. "What a devil he is!"

Six days ago. Forrest in Memphis six days ago.

"But that's not the best of it," the man went on, leaning on his good elbow, then throwing himself back on the pillows in the enjoyment of what he had to tell. "He rode straight into the lobby of the Gayoso Hotel— without dismounting—to demand the capture of General Hurlbut. Fortunately for old Hurlbut, his notorious devotion to the ladies of the town had kept him from his room all night. . . ."

Yes, that too was like him. From the bed the Yankee captain was looking at him with those clear blue eyes and let his broad, soft mouth above a blond beard spread in a hearty laugh. He was the kind of man—rather short and stocky, with a steady, deep voice—that troops followed. Straightforward, he seemed to grip you with his integrity. Morgan's face relaxed. Here was a professional, like himself, who could admire a soldier like Forrest. The man waved a hand toward a chair by the bed and he took it.

"There's more. By the grapevine. Forgive my manners, General." With raised eyebrows directed to a nearby decanter, he invited Morgan to drink.

"Yes." Morgan crossed his ankles. "But allow me . . ." He poured for both of them and watched the man lift his glass with his left arm.

"To Forrest," he said.

"To Forrest." Morgan's eyes went back to the prayer book beside the decanter. It had a red spot near one corner—a dot of paint, perhaps, which he had noticed on the one Lucy Williams was carrying. It was an Episcopal Missal, the same kind his mother carried to Christ Church in Lexington.

"I haven't told you everything." The man, still in a fit of good humor, threw back the cover and swung his legs over the bed. "It seems that, when the Union prisoners were drawn up, General Washburne was minus his uniform, taken from his room by one of Forrest's men. Forrest ordered it to be found and returned to the General immediately. Well, not to be outdone, once Forrest was gone, Washburne sent through the lines under a flag of truce a full suit of Confederate gray made by Forrest's own Memphis tailor!"

Shades of Major Coffee. The whiskey was good.

"And that's not the end of the story. Forrest sent word back to Washburne that, since the Federals were refusing parole, Washburne should at least send something that night for his men to eat on the road to Hernando, where they could be found. So about daylight of the twenty-second here came Federal officers overtaking the Rebels with two wagons loaded with supplies!"

The man tilted his head and drained his glass with a shake of his head at the sting of pleasure. He was from Michigan, and had visited Charleston once, and even thought of moving there, but before the war his father died and he stayed home to take care of the family business. Then the talk drifted to horses, and to his surprise Morgan discovered the man knew all the Kentucky bloodlines. But for a quirk of birth and fate, this man might have been on his own staff, instead of Gillem's. He would trade him for Giltner in an instant.

"May I help you downstairs?"

"No, thank you, General. Mrs. Williams has provided me with a young orphan boy she has taken in—they've made him into a kind of orderly. He'll be up in a few minutes, I expect, with my supper. Parole honor, you know."

Morgan waved his hand.

"No, rules are rules. That's the least I can do."

"If you can walk, I insist."

"Very well." The man grinned. "I can see why you are a general. I'll be down in a few minutes."

Morgan sent Captain Withers with Lieutenant Hawkins to ride to the outposts. All was well. He could enjoy a good dinner, a good night's rest for the trip back to Abingdon in the morning. After he had it out with Giltner. But that could wait until he felt better. The throbbing headache that had plagued him since Jonesboro was still tightening a band of pain across his forehead. Giltner, Giltner. And Alston, and now maybe Smith. Like cholera, distrust of him was spreading among his own officers, who had always been the bulwark of his strength. Now, when he needed them most. He had to clear the air. He couldn't start a raid like this.

But for now there was the headache and the need to eat. When the Yankee captain came down, he greeted him as a friend. The Captain had the prayer book with him and laid it casually on Lucy Williams's sewing box. Then Captain Withers and Colonel Bowles, who were staying at the house also, walked in to tell him the report from the vedettes had not changed: All was well.

He took a chair by the parlor window thankful for the breeze which blew in from the porch. The moist, cooling air of an August mountain night invaded the room. Withers and Miss Rumbaugh were chatting gaily with the Union officer—the man had a talent for immediate rapport—and with Bowles, tired from the ride in, who was enjoying the soft sofa. Lucy Williams stepped into the room, followed by her mother-in-law and Fanny. A blond boy of about fourteen, whom Morgan took to be the orphan the Captain spoke of, hovered in the hall. Morgan passed pleasantries with Catherine Williams, who could talk of nothing but the gentility of General Longstreet. Lucy pointedly avoided him, giving her attention to Withers and the prisoner. When he looked at her sewing box, the prayer book was gone. He got up immediately, that sixth sense, like a leprechaun, pinching his brain. He walked swiftly into the hall and caught the orphan by the back door with the prayer book in his hand.

"Give me that, son," Morgan said quietly. The no-nonsense firmness in the soft voice made the boy relinquish the book immediately. Morgan shook it and a letter dropped out. By the dim hall gaslight he saw it was addressed to Gillem, with a complete report as to the numbers and placement of his men.

In spite of his promise to himself to handle this calmly, something snapped. He couldn't prove Lucy Williams was implicated, nor James Leddy, the orphan, now close to tears and in tow. But he could do something about the Yankee captain, that embodiment of integrity with all the wiles of a spy.

He had to admire the man. With the cool of Hutchinson under fire, he withstood the blast and allowed that soft mouth to purse its lips without a tremor. "Wouldn't you do the same, under similar circumstances, General?" he asked brazenly.

Morgan could only vent his anger in an order that this man be removed immediately to the prison at Lynchburg.

"Lynchburg?" Lucy Williams screamed. "He'll die on the way! He's in no condition to travel . . . !"

"And you, madam, are in no condition to argue."

Inadvertently, and by the merest circumstance, he had saved his command from an ambush. Giltner's treachery faded before this. He wouldn't bother to ride out to the bivouacs after all. What would he say to Giltner anyway? That he had forwarded his letter to Richmond, that he resented his suspicions, that he was as anxious as anybody now to investigate the damned bank robbery? Was Yankee money so important when Yankee treachery was everywhere? Giltner already knew how he felt about insubordination. It was action, not words, which could dispel distrust. A stab of impatience turned his mind to tomorrow. His job here was done: Gillem had retreated through the Gap back to Knoxville, and orders from Seddon might be waiting at Abingdon. When he told Withers and Bowles goodnight he dropped a strong hint that another Kentucky raid might be imminent.

But for now his head was throbbing. He would take advantage of General Longstreet's bedroom and start for Abingdon at first light.

When he arrived at Abingdon, Key and Cal rushed out with tremendous news. Richard and Basil were waiting for him! Released from prison, just in from Richmond. . . . He barely had time to hand Skedaddle's reins to an orderly when the homecoming began.

"I can't believe it."

"Believe it!" Richard laughed. His leg still gave him problems and he crossed it carefully. Basil, in his quiet way, nodded.

"We are released. And so is Steele, Webber. . . . In March we were sent to Fort Delaware. A rumor was making the rounds that fifty Federal officers had been exposed to the danger of our batteries. The Yankees issued an order that fifty Confederate officers of corresponding rank should be selected for the same privilege—so five generals and forty-five field officers were chosen from the different prisons. . . ."

"So who else?"

"From the penitentiary at Columbus there were seven. Colonel Ward, Richard here, Tucker, Webber, Steele, Higley and myself . . . in June we were put on a steamer for Hilton Head, where we stayed five weeks. . . ."

"Hot! Hot as hell!" Richard put in. "Portholes closed, in case we jumped ship . . . as if we would, with the sharks. . . ."

"We were taken to Morris Island," Basil went on, waving aside Cal's offer of a brandy, too intent on his story. "Subsequently six hundred Confederates arrived there, where they could enjoy the full benefit of our batteries on shore."

"But it wasn't the batteries that reduced us," Richard moaned. "It was scurvy and disease, and that awful food—"

"At last, on the first of August, it was announced that we were to be sent to Charleston for exchange—evidently we had survived their little scheme. . . ."

The guns at Charleston harbor thundering a welcome, the trip to Richmond . . . through it all Morgan heard other news: Tommie was coming to Richmond and a hundred of his horse-holders, plus two hundred others caught in the stampede at Cynthiana, had made their way to Forrest in Mississippi.

"Last month. At the battle of Harrisburg, near Tupelo. Yankees ran all the way back to Memphis! Then two weeks later the Feds sent out another "hunting party"—eighteen thousand this time—to get Forrest. But he fooled them. Took half his men and marched double-quick to Memphis. . . ." Basil took a breath. "But it's a damned shame, wasting him like that. He needs to be cutting Sherman's rail lines north of Atlanta, instead of fighting these raids."

"Why doesn't he, then?"

"Richmond's against it. Bragg won't even listen to General Lee, who said Forrest is their only chance to stop Sherman."

Morgan felt the resentment and irritation under Basil's words and tried to make his own light. "I've got good company, then. They won't listen to me, either."

"About that." Basil cleared his throat. "Seddon, they say, is about to order an investigation of the bank robbery. It's all over the War Department," Basil said reluctantly. "And moreover, they've made up their minds you're guilty. They won't hear a word in your defense. Senator Bruce—the whole Kentucky delegation—have spoken in your behalf. Nothing."

"There's even a rumor going around that you were sent into Kentucky in June for the express purpose of breaking you down." Richard shifted into a more comfortable position. "That damned arrogance of yours, they say. That damned Kentucky arrogance."

"They may not have seen anything yet," Morgan growled.

Basil said quietly: "I tried to explain to Seddon when I saw him (and I made a point to see him when I heard all this) that you would not have made such an expedition without the proper authority, that there must be some mistake . . . but Bragg's henchmen were there. It was impossible. I left in disgust. The best you can hope for is that they select good men for your Board of Inquiry. And it wouldn't hurt your cause if you insist on a court-martial, to clear the air. They plan to give you one anyway. Might as well beat them at their own game. . . ."

So a Board of Inquiry was being appointed. Morgan knew they would bring with them orders to suspend him from his command.

Basil could not deny it. "You're probably right."

"How immediate?"

"I've heard before the end of August."

"Today's the twenty-ninth."

His old friend looked so dejected that, to change the subject, Basil mentioned the Democratic Convention in Chicago. "Little Mac should win it. Even Seddon thinks McClellan's the man to beat Lincoln."

Morgan had not heard. He held up his glass. Forrest's Memphis raid. Like Brice's Crossroads and the rest. Not victories, after all. The Yankees were getting what they wanted—to keep Forrest in Mississippi and away from the railroad supplying Sherman. The L&N through Tennessee to Louisville.

That's where his own men should have gone. Not to Cynthiana or Lexington. They should have hit that railroad. . . .

The light caught the whiskey as he held it in his hand. In that instant, something happened. Without thought, but with a sensation undeniable and unalterable, he knew he would try again. He had men who knew the heart of Kentucky. He would tear up that railroad, from Louisville to Nashville if he had to. It could be done. It still could be done. He would do it for Forrest. For the Cause. He looked at the dear face of Duke. He started to tell him about Hines, but something held him back. Could he in honor ask for more sacrifice? Tommie would be in Richmond with Basil's baby. No, he had to do this one on his own. "I'm leaving for Tennessee in the morning."

"But you've just come back!" Cal blurted.

"Nevertheless, I'm going." They won't catch me, he thought. I'll gather the command and raid into Kentucky. Through Bull's Gap, taking my chances that Gillem has gone back to Knoxville. The scouts can tell. Bull's Gap to Rogersville, then across the Clinch up to Middlesboro, over to Monticello and Burkesville on the Cumberland. We can get horses there. When they see us in Clinton and Wayne counties again, they'll come running. Once there, it would be easy enough to contact Copperheads and find out what Hines was up to. He couldn't, wouldn't ask Basil or Richard to come. He excused himself. "I've got to see my wife, gentlemen."

There had been no orders. Adam Johnson and Hines were waiting. He would go to Kentucky this time without orders, as they were blaming him for doing anyway, and damn them all to hell.

Mattie was upstairs, her arms full of linen. She set the pile down on a chest in the hall and followed him into their bedroom.

"I've got to go back," he said bluntly.

"I know. Isn't it wonderful to have—"

"Tomorrow," he said.

"Tomorrow?"

"Back to Tennessee. Things are unsettled there."

"You didn't settle them? I thought I heard you say Gillem had been chased back through the Gap. . . ."

"You were listening?"

"How could I help it? You sounded so happy. I thought I would let you have some time with Basil and Richard before I came down. . . . Tomorrow?" She sat on the bed, her face white.

He couldn't, wouldn't tell her about Kentucky. Or Hines.

"It's just a move . . . to consolidate our positions."

"Poor Skedaddle will be worn out!"

"I'll take the train to Jonesboro. I'll wire Colonel Smith to have a detachment meet me there. It will only be for a few days. Then . . ." Then, if he did go to Kentucky, she would have some news indeed. It was the first time in his life he kept plans from her. "Where is Alice?"

"Resting," she said, without looking at him. "Basil said all they talked

about in Richmond was Early's ride up to Washington. You could do that!"
She threw it out like a challenge.

"So that's what you're worried about!" he chuckled, to cover irritation.
"My brave girl," he said, only half-joking. "With her notions of glory." But
it brought Richmond into the room. If she knew a Board of Inquiry was
probably on its way, she wouldn't be taunting him with "reputation." He
had to show them a victory. . . .

"I tell you what. I'll go down to Greeneville just one more time, to make
sure the bluecoats are cozy in Knoxville. If things are quiet, I promise you a
little vacation. It wouldn't be impossible to get away for a few days, escort
you and Alice down to Danville. You'd like to see Mrs. Withers again,
wouldn't you?"

Candy to a child. But he saw she pretended to believe. "Of course! That
would be delightful. Just what Alice needs."

"Then we'll do it. Now give me a quick kiss and let me wash up. Mustn't
keep our guests waiting . . ."

Richard's humorous account of the penitentiary after the escape: Scotty's
explosion, the confusion. Talk of the election. McClellan would win, there
was no doubt of it. Even Lincoln was conceding that he would not be
reelected, especially since the latest peace talk fiasco had broken down.
"Imagine, roping in Horace Greeley."

"He never intended to talk peace." Cal blew his nose.

"It will be different when McClellan is President," Richard persisted.

"Hines. I wonder what Hines is doing?" Morgan murmured.

Basil raised his head and looked steadily at the man who had been his
boyhood idol, now his brother-in-law, now his general. "I saw St. Leger
before he left. He asked me to tell you that in Africa there is a legend that
old lions, when they want to die, eat a porcupine." He spoke deliberately,
slowly, looked away, then back at Morgan.

"It seems they extract the spines, these old lions, eat the meat, and then
eat the spines also. It is their last meal. 'Well!' he said—and you know how
Grenfel can lean back and say 'Well!' " Basil stopped, then went on, and it
was as if Grenfel himself were in the room: " 'I have seen them in Africa
months afterwards at waterholes. So tell Morgan it takes an old experienced
lion to tackle a porcupine. The meat is sweet enough, and the spines don't
destroy, after all.' "

What does he mean? he almost said, and then he knew: St. Leger was
with Hines in Canada! He hadn't abandoned him after all! A well of sympathy, gratitude and love overwhelmed him. Before he could say anything
he felt Cal's hand on his arm.

"Come, let's go in to dinner. I think the ladies are waiting."

After the others had gone to bed, Morgan sat with Basil on the front
gallery in the dim light of a waning moon. He almost told him then, but
didn't. His raid, and St. Leger with Hines! Maybe he could connect with
Adam after all . . . and draw the Yankees away from Atlanta at the same
time! With the mood in the North, such an offensive might just . . . The

air was alive with evening and the scent of cut grass. They spoke then of Tom.

"Death is nothing," Basil said softly. "To live defeated and inglorious— that is to die daily."

"Very pretty," Morgan said after a long silence, and hoped the mockery in his voice covered the almost uncontrollable grief, and the rising excitement.

"Napoleon." Basil identified the quote.

"Do you think we're . . ."

"No. But sometimes close to it. Those idiots in Richmond."

For the third time he almost told him, and didn't. They were silent again, listening to night sounds. It had been an insufferably humid day; the air now was almost balmy with a slight breeze. Basil cleared his throat.

"Do you think much of Hopemont?"

"Actually, you know it's strange. I dream more of Shadeland."

Basil let the word hang in the air, and for a few minutes they were both riding over those fields again.

"Home!" Morgan paused. "I guess that word never loses meaning. I suppose that's the albatross that hangs from all our necks. We die for it, we fight wars over it, and some of us, like St. Leger, run from it all our lives, only to long for it, like lost children, in the end."

There was something so sad in his voice that Basil started to speak, but didn't. What was the Cause, anyway? Could it be that simple? Home. Basil watched his old friend's face in wonder. Something was changing in him, something beyond the knowledge of a court-martial. There was a stillness about him, behind the eyes, which contradicted this eager dreaming: *If only we had won at Cynthiana*. It was as if that last Kentucky raid had become a beast inside him, tearing him apart with guilt, and he had to keep his eyes on that beast, in a vain attempt to relive, to rectify. It was the stillness of a man without faith who turns to make-believe to keep from going insane, not realizing that make-believe has its own brand of insanity—the torture of what-if, I-should-have, might-have, could-have done.

But you didn't, Basil wanted to say. *You didn't, Johnny*.

From the light of the lamp shining through the parlor window Basil could see his face change as they talked of Tommie and the baby, of Kitty and A.P. and Petersburg. The more they talked the more—was it a trick of the light?—Johnny's tendency to have an underslung jaw became more pronounced, as if he were defying the world now with his chin, covered by that pear-shaped beard. His mustache had lost its Cavalier point and had become merely bushy, like two thick fingers pointing downward. The loss of hair that started in prison now made a high dome of his forehead. But most of all there was a change in his eyes. They had lost that sweet openness. They were pierced with a hard, almost defensive glitter, as if daring you to contradict him. Always deep-set, they never lost now a steady gaze that bored into, rather than looked at you. It was as if they were looking through his own disappointment and deep chagrin into your own soul, prepared—almost expecting—to find more that would disappoint him. Not begging for answers. Just certain he would find none. He had the look of a man always aiming a gun. Basil was glad when Mattie appeared at the door with the warning that if her general wanted to get an early start he had better get some rest.

"I thought you were in bed."

"I was. I couldn't sleep."

After Morgan went upstairs she stayed behind, to enjoy the night air. Basil chatted pleasantly enough, aware that they were forcing a kind of gaiety, insane in the light of the dejected man who had just left them.

"It's ironic," Basil said, "that they wanted to send him here before . . . only he never knew."

"Oh? When?"

"When Wash Morgan died at Hopemont, that October Bragg lost Kentucky. I was in the hall when Aunt Bet answered the door to a courier from General Smith. The orders were from Bragg. To defend the salt works in Virginia."

"What happened to them?"

"I burned them."

"Oh!"

"He wouldn't have gone anyway, if I know him. It would have ended his career."

"As it's doing now."

He looked up sharply, but said nothing. Then, to cheer her: "Fortunate, wasn't it? Instead, he went to Murfreesboro and got married."

She wouldn't be turned away. "So it was Bragg, even then."

"Maybe it was dishonorable. Narcissus couldn't see his shadow, and I helped him."

"You mean Bragg? Oh, John knows he's there, all right."

He couldn't tell her he didn't mean Bragg, but Johnny's own shortcomings . . . his belief in people, in the "code." It will kill him in the end, St. Leger had said when he left them at Murfreesboro. *I don't want to be around to see it.*

Basil looked at this girl, whose face was bitter before its time . . . gone sour trying to protect Johnny from himself. From all that belief. Then Johnny's face came back: *If we just hadn't lost at Cythiana. But they'll come to us yet!*

Oh, that faith in Kentucky.

"They're just like everybody else and he won't admit it," she surprised him by saying. Had they been sitting here reading each other's thoughts?

"Who?" he said, but smiled to let her know he knew who and she didn't have to answer.

"What are we to do? To help him, Basil?" She looked up, her chin trembling.

"My dear lady." He reached out and touched her shoulder. He fully intended to say *Have his child. Take care of yourself. Make him happy while you can.*

Instead, he heard himself murmur: "I wish I knew."

57

On August 29, when the Democratic Convention met in Chicago, the Sons of Liberty promised fifty thousand armed men for an assault against Camp Douglas. Hines listened. This was to be his last meeting with them in Canada before his Confederates . . . seventy-four men, armed with pistols, ammunition, railroad tickets to Chicago and a hundred dollars each . . . would board the train. They would travel in pairs, and meet in a room at the Richmond House marked "Missouri Delegation." Hines left them with that slightly swaggering step he had, and turned to St. Leger.

"Are you wearing that? You won't last twenty-four hours." And ruin our chances, his inner voice said. The uniform was of a soft gray wool.

"This is the uniform of my old battalion," Grenfel smiled as he swung up on the train. "Perfectly permissible, I assure you. Besides, I have my English papers, my gun and my dog, and if they ask me where I am going, I can tell them a fellow Englishman named Baxter has invited me to shoot prairie chickens at Carlyle, Illinois. . . ."

Hines shook his head and said nothing. He had gotten used to duplicity these last weeks. The Sons of Liberty were fools. He didn't believe a word they said, but they were his only allies, besides his faithful little band, who could accomplish nothing without them. He followed St. Leger's gray-clad back down the aisle.

By Saturday, the 27th of August, most of the men had arrived at Richmond House, on the corner of Lake Street and Michigan Avenue. Informers had already infiltrated Camp Douglas, to prepare the prisoners for the big day: Monday, August 29. Another meeting with Charles Walsh, Chicago politician and a leader of the Sons of Liberty, would iron out the details.

Walsh arrived late, a bad sign. Then the promises: too glib, too quickly given: "Thousands" of Copperheads, gathering in Chicago, would be ready. . . . But when details were asked for, Walsh became vague. He kept falling back on Hines's seventy-four Rebels: Somehow *they* would overthrow Camp Douglas, while "others" would "overthrow" the Illinois and Indiana state governments, capture the arsenals. . . .

That Saturday afternoon Hines rode out to Douglas on a trolley car to see for himself. What he saw was a well-fortified prison, incapable of being taken by less than a thousand men. He went back to the hotel and sent messages to his Copperhead cohorts for a final meeting Sunday morning.

Walsh nodded solemnly, pursing his lips. He was sure he could get many more than a thousand. Arms, in Chicago, would certainly be no problem. If they could get the guns into the right hands. . . . Walsh hesitated, then conferred with his associates, businessmen sitting around the hotel room as if they were at a sales conference.

Hines, with Castleman, Eastin, Drake, St. Leger and Martin, waited. Five minutes went by. Then ten. Finally, Walsh straightened his shoulders and offered a "counterproposal" to Hines's demand for a thousand men.

"If you can arrange for the Confederate government to guarantee an invasion of Kentucky and Missouri, we can guarantee an armed uprising in Ohio, Indiana and Illinois. Freeing all Confederate prisoners in those states," Walsh ended boastfully.

Tom Hines, superspy, seldom lost his temper. He always considered doing so a surrender, a reaction rather than an action. He lost it now. Still, he tried to keep his voice even, if for nothing but to convey his words clearly: "Gentlemen, what you propose will take months of planning. Colonel Johnson has already been captured and defeated in Indiana, as you know. I have alerted General Morgan, but he is in Virginia. Even if he left today, it would take him at least ten days to reach the Ohio River. I alerted him only on the assumption that our plans were in place: The Convention begins tomorrow, less than twenty-four hours from now. . . ."

Castleman caught his eye. Even though these men were fools, they were their only chance. "I've just been to Rock Island," Breck put in. "I believe we could take it easier than Douglas."

The Copperheads nodded among themselves.

"Give me five hundred men," Hines said, "and we'll take Rock Island."

The heads bent again, Walsh coming up like an otter for a breath of air: "I doubt if we can get five hundred armed men on such short notice, Captain Hines."

"Then give me two hundred!"

Another delay.

"That might be possible. Well. We'll try for five hundred," Walsh said when the meeting broke up, to console him. "We'll keep in touch."

That afternoon Hines paced the hotel room, waiting. Finally, just before sundown a message came: The Copperheads had secured the promises of twenty-five men.

"The game is up," he told Castleman. Eastin, who had dozed on the bed, got up. "We'll try later . . . southern Illinois."

"Is that where you're going?" Castleman asked. Hines nodded. "Then I'll go too."

Hines sent messages to the others, asking for volunteers. Of those, he selected twenty-two to go with him. The others he sent back to Canada to await orders. Before midnight, Hines and Breck Castleman and St. Leger Grenfel, on his way to shoot prairie chickens, were on an Illinois Central train bound for Mattoon.

"Ah, well, lads," said St. Leger philosophically, "I didn't like Chicago, really. Hovel of hogs and Hoosiers."

"That's Indiana." Hines grinned in spite of himself.

Grenfel would not be turned from his melancholy, which he seemed to be enjoying, as if to purge something. "It does not matter much which, does it? We've all got to live somewhere, sometime . . . and when the time comes, what difference will it make whether I lived in London or Illinois? Or whether I died in a four-poster with a nurse and phials on the bed table, or whether I died in a ditch? Not that I think it necessary to make myself uncomfortable, *bien au contraire*. . . ." He looked out the window. "Ah, what I need, lads, is a good pipe. . . ."

"What do you think?" Castleman whispered when he could.

"Election Day. Chicago again," Hines bit out. He might die in the effort, but he would see this out to the bitter end.

If he had known, as the wheels clipped the rails, that he would suffer treachery and avoid capture by hiding under a lady in her mattress, or that Castleman would be exiled, or that St. Leger, imprisoned on that Devil's Island called Fort Jefferson off Key West, would survive the torture of being thrown to sharks only to die escaping in a storm, Hines might not have been so sure.

Upstairs, Morgan could hear Basil's steady voice from the porch, and the soft murmur of Mattie as she answered. So Richmond planned a court-martial. A tight fist of resentment knotted the breath in his chest. And to relieve him of his command. He drew paper and pen toward him. The moist air of the night came in the open window. They could, the bastards. He saw Bragg's heavy, gloating face.

A bank had been robbed. Very well: Start there. Admit it. Admit even to negligence that it had been robbed. But then present the record. When we went into Ohio my men had strict orders: no looting. Yet in spite of everything Major Steele could do, pillaging did take place.

Did that sound too apologetic? He dipped the pen, scraped the excess ink off. Pillaging. But what was it: a few hams, a birdcage with three canaries, seven pairs of ice skates . . . in July! They wouldn't believe him. He wrote: "On the Ohio raid there was no wholesale ransacking or destruction of furniture or houses. One house was burned. One. And that one was occupied by the enemy using it as a fortress against our men. One house in a march of over a thousand miles, when our men were passing through that area of Indiana where Sherman had obtained recruits . . . those same recruits who had destroyed the homes of some of our Mississippi boys."

The raid into Kentucky in June: looting in Mount Sterling by Giltner's men (although don't mention him; just "attached troops"), the burning of barns and railroad firewood in Lexington, a livery stable in Cynthiana. . . .

A man should be judged by his good deeds as well as his bad. We never left our wounded—except in extreme cases, when moving might mean death. We took care of our own, without any expense to the Confederate government, who saw fit to let the cavalry forage for itself, while other branches received blankets, uniforms and regular pay. Our men supplied their own horses and in most cases their own arms. The wonder is, gentlemen, that they gave so selflessly to a Cause which has seen fit to ignore them. They are men who, having received nothing, should rightly feel that they owe nothing. And yet they have given everything. I make no excuses for them, and if the bank robbery of

$72,000 is indeed of their doing—and I have no proof of that—then let that, too, be laid to my charge, not theirs.

Something in that last phrase reminded him of Mattie. He had never told her. So much. He had hoped, when they came here from Richmond, that he could get his command together. *He's the pea under your mattress, Princess.* No, it was more than Bragg. Or his refusal to release the Ninth Kentucky and Dortch. He had many of the old regulars under Smith and Bowles. And there were Colonel Bradford's Tennessee troops and Giltner's regiment. A command was more than numbers. He had to face it: The spirit was gone out of them since . . . since Cynthiana. If he could inspire them again! He was about to dip the pen when a knock at the door made him look up.

Over the hot circle of light at the top of the lamp Cal's head appeared in the doorway. "Come on in . . ." He watched him move with a telltale shyness that seemed out of place in his big frame. "You always look like that when you want something," Morgan smiled.

"I want to go with you," Cal said bluntly. "No. Before you say anything, listen. Any number of men can hold things together here. Bowles. Jacob Cassell. Smith."

"Colonel Smith is going with me. And I'm sending Jake to bring back the men who were with Forrest in Mississippi."

"Oh, yes. I forgot," Cal said impatiently. "But any number. A dozen others." He stared at him across the light and the glow made the furrows deeper in his face.

"Have you written Carrie lately?"

Cal blushed, looked down at his hands and up again.

"That's the only thing worth having, Cal. I can't ask you to go with me."

Cal jumped up and walked across the room. "Good God, you talk as if you're not coming back. When you talk like that I've *got* to go . . ."

"Do I? I . . ."

"What's that you're writing?"

"Nothing. Something to Richmond."

Cal pulled the chair around to avoid the light, spread his legs and leaned forward on his elbows, scrubbing his bent head with his big hands. "The bank," he said to the floor.

"Yes."

"They're a bunch of politicians, Johnny. They've already made up their minds. You're grooming a dead horse."

"Maybe. But remember when we led old Sard out to bury him and he bucked?"

"Don't change the subject."

"I'm not."

"He had a hole in his chest. Yours is in your head. Only difference."

"I'll bring you a filly from Kentucky."

"I thought as much. Johnny, you've got to know something. You can't go. Giltner's sent documents . . ."

Morgan interrupted with that bone-cutting laugh.

"You mean those affidavits? What good . . ."

"For you to stay here? You could refute them. Let them have their inquiry. You could . . ."

"You've said it already, Cal. Grooming a dead horse. Remember what Sidney Johnston said before Shiloh?"

Cal waited, blinking down emotion.

"I'd fight them if they were a million," Morgan answered his own question through his teeth. Then, more kindly: "Good night, Cally. And remember Miss Harrison."

Cal saw it was useless. "Take care of yourself."

"I will."

He stared at the closed door. In the silence, Sidney Johnston's words came again. Yes, one man *could* turn the tide! He had seen it in Mexico with Zach Taylor. He had seen it on that muddy field at Shiloh. If only Johnston hadn't sent his surgeon to care for enemy wounded. Ah, there would always be an "if." You had to live with that. But *one man could do it.*

He realized now the letter was no good. Too . . . whining. He tore it up. What would they care about houses in Indiana or stables in Cynthiana, or wounded men or horses? They would laugh. They had "affidavits." Cal was right. They weren't interested in the truth. None of that fit into their political maneuverings. He would write another tomorrow, on the train to Jonesboro. A stiff one, full of high-sounding, official phrases. But no apologies. His men were gentlemen, every one.

He undressed and lay on the bed, covering only with a sheet. Seddon, with that lank hair hanging over those large ears, those ghoulish eyes. *He knew of the Kentucky raid.* By God, he'd ordered it, the bastard. In complete agreement . . . and now denying. What game was he playing?

Another face came: ice-blue eyes, a grim mouth that could soften into French phrases and get excited over the Roman Empire . . . Hines. Seddon had sent Hines, too, and would, when the time came, as easily deny that also. Was Hines being used, too, in some political chess game—like Horace Greeley and the "peace" talks that fizzled? Were Hines and Castleman and Eastin and Martin and Adam Johnson and his own command pawns on some kind of board that Seddon and Judah Benjamin . . . yes, and Davis, not above these games now . . . had set up to influence the growing desire in the North to end this war? He kicked the sheet off, turned on his side, felt no better and got up. There was a rocker near the window, Mattie's favorite place. He pulled it closer to the sill and leaned back. A piece of mending had caught on the cane seat and he fingered it, the neat stitches. Court-martial.

And his marriage, too—was that a failure? Maybe it was Basil's coming —his bringing with him so much of the past, and the contrast with what they now were, how they had changed. It had begun in Richmond before they moved to Abingdon, but in earnest since July, after the Kentucky raid. Her defense of Alice's Doomsday moods had become a solicitous caution, a careful toe-tipping consideration for him. At first, in his remorse and chagrin at the failure at Cynthiana, he had appreciated it; then, as her concern solidified into a kind of maternal patronizing, he resented, then resisted, because it helped him bury his guilt rather than face it.

And he did feel guilty—not only for Cynthiana but for all those who had suffered and died because of him. Hutch, Niles, Chenault, scores of boys like Walter Ferguson, and dear old Will. As if, all this time, he had been allowing others to pay his debt. To what? The Cause? But dying or lying wounded wouldn't help—only living and fighting. *Living well is the only revenge.* His father, one day at Shadeland, his eyes on the pond.

The idea that he might be feeling the South differently was shoved back in his mind, but would not go away. Pimps and dandies parading around Richmond. Davis had something of that in him, too. Even Davis. A little mincing. Something dry about the mouth.

No, no, his trouble was not the Cause, or Davis, or Bragg, but something closer. Mattie? Were the subtle changes in her a reflection of himself? Maybe all partners were mirrors. But in the background, overlooking both their shoulders, was Alice. Like a sibyl, a Cassandra, a Medusa who had turned herself to stone. She became, represented his worst fears: total depression pushed to madness.

Had some of her lostness rubbed off on him? Was that why Basil had looked so concerned when they met? Had he changed, physically, that much? Dear Basil had guessed at what he only now, watching the night, would admit: that he was clinging to a possible past, something that had never happened, and like a child he was beating his fists against reality: He had lost Kentucky at Cynthiana. If he could only feel rage. That was what he would have felt in the old days. He had had defeats before. Now, only a peculiar lethargy.

As he sat there with the cool mountain night coming in, he had the strange feeling of leaving his body, of watching himself from across the room. He saw a silhouette against the window, the fog in strands beyond. He felt powerless to move. Then Mattie broke the spell.

"He loves you almost as much as I do," she said softly, but there was tenseness underneath. She took off her clothes, keeping her back to him. She was six months' pregnant. He had never seen her like this. Her swollen body was for him more chaste, more dear and precious than it had ever been, a chalice holding new life. Yet he had not, lately, been able to tell her. So much . . . Alice, and now the Giltner thing . . . came between. A bitter woman came into focus in front of him.

She had slipped her gown over her head but made no move toward the bed. She stood with the absolute stillness of despair, her face vacant of emotion. Suddenly she burst out: "Yes . . . I love you, John Morgan! I've watched you spill out your insides—give your heart, your courage, every drop of your blood, every beat of your pulse—and for what? To be misunderstood, to be betrayed. By people like Braxton Bragg, and that sniveling Ould, and that . . . that Seddon! Cowards hiding behind desks. . . ." She stopped, out of breath.

"They have a job to do. . . ."

She would not be put off.

"You were doomed from the start. Basil knows it." The words seemed to hurt, but she forced herself to finish. "And now I know it. Only you won't admit it. You always think you can control everything, like you control a horse."

Basil! Had Basil lost faith in him? He covered confusion with flippancy: "I can't control you!"

"You like to see yourself alone, doing it all alone," she shot out to keep from crying.

Her words echoed his own *One man could do it*. Her contempt reduced that dream to the ridiculous.

He undressed and climbed into bed. To hold onto her composure, she turned down the lamp, watched it sputter, then got in beside him. They lay there, facing front, like two tin soldiers.

The truth of her statement cut to the bone. "I know." He reached for her hand, but she pulled her arm away.

"You think you're like that old horse of yours in the log barn, don't you?" She flung up her hand. "Fighting to the end." Her eyes filled with sudden tears as she stared at the ceiling.

"Sard?" He sat up and tried a laugh, but she refused to be diverted. She got up and walked to the window and shot back across the room:

"If a thousand Yankees had you cornered, you wouldn't give up." She sat, weak and bent, in the rocker. By the light of the moon he could see her hair part across her neck.

He started to get up too, then turned serious, to help her. "I wouldn't be so foolish," he said.

"It's not that!" she cried, waving her hand to nothing in particular. When he started to move she stopped him. "No . . . stay there. I can talk to you better there." She waited a minute. She stood up. He could hear her breathing. The outline of her body against the window, that bulging curve of pregnancy touched him as no other argument could. When she spoke again she lifted her head, her voice calmer.

"At first I believed in the Cause. Like Alice. All that indignation. And love for our soldiers defending us. Then you came along. I sometimes wish—!" She stopped, bent her head and shook it from side to side slowly, like a child trying to keep from crying. She rubbed her nose with the back of her hand before she could go on. Her voice was trembling but determined.

"You've seen what the war has done to Alice. Well, it's changed me, too. I don't mind telling you I've never been so afraid in my life. For you, I'm selfish. I've even prayed to God that if there were a bullet, let it hit somebody else . . . anybody else but you!"

He couldn't stand it. He walked to the window and took her in his arms.

She pushed him away. She lifted her chin and moonlight traced her cheekbone. Her eyes met his with a fierceness he had never seen before.

"I was wrong!" she almost shouted. "The bullet I should have feared is the one *inside*. It's already there, killing you. This belief . . . whatever it is.

I was wrong. It's not the Yankees that I'm fighting . . . it's this thing. . . . It's you!"

"Mattie . . ."

She squeezed her eyes shut and clenched her fists. "I'm so sick of your 'code' . . . your precious 'honor.' Can it feed babies, or stop boys from dying?"

He waited. Her confession, the putting into words, and his silence seemed to crush her resistance. He reached out and felt her shoulders soften under his hands, her breathing quieten. There were no words he could say, and he wouldn't have said them if he could have found them. He waited until she opened her eyes and moved against him.

"I don't mean to be unreasonable," she sniffed. "I didn't mean what I said about Sard."

"Of course you didn't, my darling." He suddenly realized how ignorant she must be of him, and of his own ignorance of her, this unfailing, brave girl of his fighting fear, blaming herself for wanting him to live. They were all, underneath, a little crazy, hoping for this damned war to end. They had all given so much. Mattie was right. He had forfeited his own life. So far. But she was wrong if she thought that beating oneself to death was his idea of fighting. Dash and courage—yes, she was right to distrust them. What were they, after all, but bluff? It was easy when a man had something to believe in . . . did he, like Mattie, believe in it any more? *If'n as long as you don' say it, mebbe it won' be so.* Uncle Ben's wisdom was no longer working. Had he "not been saying it" too long? No. He still believed in his men. And in himself. And in Hopemont, and Shadeland, and everything they stood for: in Kentucky. If he had to join a Northwest Conspiracy to save them, he would. And damn those Richmond Napoleons.

But he had to do it alone. He wished she could have been spared the squabble over Giltner. . . . but how could she? The whole command talked of it, and the investigation which was inevitable now. But how could he betray Castleman? And Eastin and Martin and Hines? They would give their lives for him. No, she didn't undertand. She was a woman surviving, she would never understand. . . .

"Let's go to bed now, darling. You've got to get your rest."

"Please . . . hold me one more time!"

"Many times. There will be many times."

"Those stupid men and their court-martial. How dare they?"

"It's only talk."

"How dare they?"

He led her across the room and tucked her in like a child.

"If I were in Richmond . . ."

He gave her a small smile across the pillows. "Go to sleep."

"You don't believe me? If I were in Rich—"

"If you were in Richmond we would win this war," he said, brushing her hair away from her cheek.

"You don't think we are?" It was her Judgment Day voice again.

He tried to sound convincing. "We will."

"I'm sorry about Skedaddle."

"It's just a sprained ankle. He'll be fine with rest."

"Have you got a good horse?"

"We'll use the train as far as Jonesboro. I'll get one there."

"Is that where the command is now?"

"Yes. Now you've got to get some sleep. It must be past midnight."

She sat up, hugging her knees, watching him, then suddenly jumped up. "I forgot. With all this excitement . . . Richard and Basil . . . I forgot. A letter." She went to her dresser, opened the top drawer and brought it to him. He lit the lamp and recognized the precise, tight handwriting.

It was from Dick Curd, passed through the lines, and dated July 10. A civil lawsuit had been filed on the 1st of July by the Farmers' Bank of Mount Sterling against one of Morgan's officers . . . Anderson Circuit Court File No. 310. . . . "As you see," Curd wrote, "it was brought out that you had issued strict orders vs. depredations, that you made your subordinate officers responsible for the good conduct of the men. This case will go to the Kentucky Court of Appeals. We will certainly try for a complete exoneration. . . . Use this letter and the enclosed information in any hearing you may have. . . ."

"What is it, darling? Good news?"

"Not bad." He folded the paper. "Not bad at all. A start." He felt better. He passed it to her and waited till she read it, then turned off the lamp.

"You see?" he said to the ceiling. "I told you everything will be all right."

Her hug was desperate, like a child's.

"It will, I promise," he repeated, to soothe her. "Now get some sleep," he whispered under the rising excitement about tomorrow, and now the good-will of Dick's news.

"Have you packed the green vest?"

"I wouldn't travel without it." His arm, around her shoulders, closed against her breasts. "Now . . . good night . . ."

Yes, it would be better now. With Curd's information to forward to Seddon, he could make a case for himself. Surely they would listen.

"You're not sleeping," she said against his ear. She began drifting her fingers across his face. He turned to her, and the warmth, the softness, overwhelmed him. For a moment it was the Mattie of the old days, of Murfreesboro.

"I'm sorry . . . I . . . must have too much on my mind." To be physically inept now was the last straw. He retreated behind a laugh he tried to keep light and ambiguous, but she raised her eyebrows and looked at him with those eyes that turned dark when she was worried.

The next morning his optimism was genuine. "See?" he called across the room as he slipped on the green vest. "I'm taking my *Meesawmi!*"

There was something so endearing in his smile that she rushed to him for one final kiss.

He purposely took a seat on the train apart from his men to pen a letter to Seddon. The sun slanting across the paper and the sway of the track reinforced his expectations: They had to listen. This time, no whining. This time, official.

Swiftly the pen moved across the page. His words came easy now, dry and flip. He dipped the pen in the shallow little well of the lap desk, steadying one corner with his lower arm.

> Allegations, the most vague and yet all tending to impeach my character, have obtained hearing and credence. I have not been called on, indeed I may say that an officer's reputation may suffer from such causes.

He stopped and reread the neat, round, looping hand. Should he tell them now just how much he knew? He decided they had better know he was no fool.

> I am informed that communications and documents of various kinds, relating to the alleged criminal transactions in Kentucky, have been addressed you by certain of my subordinates, and I have been profoundly ignorant of their existence, until after their receipt, and the intended impression had been produced.

He liked that "intended impression." In the same sarcastic tone he lashed out:

> I would respectfully ask if communications so furnished are not altogether irregular and prejudicial to good order and proper discipline?

Yes, yes. That was good. But it needed to be specific. Without naming names. That could come later.

> Indeed, sir, discipline and subordination have been impaired to such an extent in my command by proceedings, such as I have described, that an officer of high rank quitted a responsible post, without leave and in direct disobedience to my orders, and repaired to Richmond to urge in person his application for assignment to duty more consonant with his inclinations. It is, with all due respect, that I express my regret that his application was successful.

That was Alston, and God how he would miss him.

> Permit me again, sir, to urge earnestly—I have the honor to be, very respectfully,
>
>   Your obedient servant

He looked out the window, through the billowing engine smoke that obscured the sun. They rounded a curve and the smoke shifted to reveal a valley between hills, corn shocks standing like fat scarecrows in the golden stubble of harvested fields. He hated to mention Alston, even obliquely, but he had to make them see what they were doing. He folded the desk, put the letter in his pocket and walked over, swaying to the jerks of the train, to share a seat with Captain Withers. They chatted until the train pulled into Jonesboro.

Most of the men had come up from Greeneville to resupply from the rail line. He conferred with Smith and Bradford, and momentarily with Giltner, who seemed surprised at his good humor. Nothing, his manner seemed to say, is going to spoil this operation. He even dropped a hint to Giltner, as if taking him into a special confidence, that after they made sure Gillem was chased beyond the Gap, they might be on a little expedition of their own. He almost laughed out loud at the surprised look on Giltner's usually grim face. "Where is Captain Byrne?" he asked almost gaily. "I've got a little news for him." This time, by God, he would take artillery.

His men were badly armed and equipped, and discouraged, but if they could chase the Yankees through Bull's Gap, a dash into Kentucky to help Hines would be entirely possible. As he walked toward the hotel and bent to avoid a branch that hung out over the sidewalk, Morgan felt the letter in his pocket. Yes, well, they might as well court-martial him for two raids as well as one.

The fours would form early. He had a good horse. He went to bed feeling more confident than he had since he'd ridden out of Lexington.

He joined his waiting troops on the road south of town. Captain Cantrill, in command of the Second Battalion, saluted smartly as he rode up. With first light outlining the great line of the Smoky Mountains in the distance, they rode south toward Greeneville. Periodically, through the morning, the scouts came back, reporting no enemy. The day turned hot and humid. Thunderheads stacked up against the sun, rolling, it seemed, right out of the mountains. The creak of leather and the *clop-clop* of sweating horses; an occasional grumbling oath, the rush of a scout and his departure, the lumbering caissons in the rear: This was his life now. After ten miles, about a third of the way, he called a halt to rest the horses. His forage master, a young man with soft brown eyes and a Georgia drawl, asked if they could stop again at the grist mill this side of Greeneville: He could get some good meal and flour. At the permission, he saluted and loped away. When they reached the mill the rest of the command moved on to water and rest their horses under the trees at Tusculum College, outside the town.

That was when Lieutenant Xenophon Hawkins rode up, a dispatch in his hand. Atlanta had fallen.

Well, it had been only a matter of time and they'd all known it. But now the way was open all the way to the sea. . . . Sherman would have no mercy. Augusta, and T.H., and his idea of sending Mattie. . . .

Xen Hawkins watched his general's face. He had been one of those boys who had loaded the hay in the wagon behind the armory in Lexington that September night three years ago. In those three years his general had aged twenty, especially these last six months. An overwhelming longing came over him to help, any way he could.

The thunderheads continued to build, high giantheads looming. Behind one the sun peeked before disappearing altogether, like a bright eye suddenly gone. It would be a dark, possibly stormy night. Morgan dismounted and conferred with Captain Cantrill and Colonel Smith. Colonels Bowles and Giltner rode up, dismounted, and stood too under the shade of the trees.

They must take all precautions. He wanted no mistakes. Gillem was at the Gap, waiting. "I trust him, gentlemen, no farther than I can throw a six-pounder." The road, as they all knew, took a sharp turn just five hundred yards outside of Greeneville, with a flat-topped hill in the angle. The artillery would set up there, Captain Clark in command. A company of Cantrill's battalion under Lieutenant Xenophon Hawkins would accompany the guns.

The Jonesboro Road was the only one entering Greeneville from the north: That would be safe enough, with the artillery posted. Counterclockwise, the Rogersville Road was next: The rest of Smith's brigade would camp out there. Colonel Giltner's Fourth Kentucky would be stationed in that quarter also, with the two commands picketing all roads to the front and right flank. Colonel Bradford's Tennesseans would camp directly across the Bull's Gap Road, and would swing their pickets across the Warrensburg and Newport roads to the south. Thus every entrance into Greeneville would be secured. Headquarters would again be the Williams house, in direct line of sight from the artillery on the hill.

It sounded good. But if Basil or St. Leger had been there they would have reminded him that the heavy undergrowth on the hill prevented a view of the house, or even the roads south of town, by the men at the guns, and that the steep incline on the town side gave no field of fire in front: An enterprising enemy could scramble up and capture the battery without danger of one shell hitting them. But there would be no danger of that: All the roads were secured.

Mrs. Williams was pleased to see him. Even Lucy, recovered from his revocation of the Federal captain's parole, seemed not unhappy to make them comfortable, and offered to ride out with James Leddy in a wagon to the Williams farm for watermelons. The last of the crop. "But I promise they will be the sweetest." She let her laugh travel to her eyes, and the gentleman in Morgan relented. Perhaps he had been too harsh with her before. She was too silly, and too intent on swinging her hips as she walked away from him, to be a spy. A bugle sounded. He remounted, backed his horse and watched his fours file past. When the men saw him they sent up cheers for their leader. It was like the old days. They would prevail, after all.

The rain that had been threatening all afternoon fell in sudden torrents. He hoped his men could get settled before they and their guns were soaked. Mrs. Williams was prattling on. Wasn't it lucky she had already invited Major Arnold, commanding a Tennessee outfit in the vicinity, to dinner? Now they could make it a gala affair. They would bring out the blackberry wine and use her silver goblets.

She was interrupted by thunder. Morgan motioned to Major Gassett. They would have just time enough to ride to the telegraph office, then out to the pickets before dinner. He wanted to wire Mattie, and to make sure all was well. There was a little dissension, nothing more than friendly rivalry, he hoped, between Bradford's Tennesseans and the Kentucky troops. Bradford's men were already in place; the two roads they had been assigned to cover met within a mile of town at a V. Bradford had placed his pickets on the Warrensburg Road a mile and a half from town, and his first picket post on the Newport Road a little farther out, directly south. The scouts reported no activity.

His wire to Mattie was brief and, he hoped, reassuring: ARRIVED HERE TODAY. FIND THAT ENEMY HAVE NOT BEEN THIS SIDE OF BULL'S GAP AND NONE HERE.

The rain let up, but the flour the men had taken from the mill was soaked, as well as their guns. He rode back to the Williams house more than ready for that dinner. He saluted the sentinels, posted at intervals around the block, left his horse at the stable and walked across the garden to the side door.

Major Gassett had the room at the other end of the hall, Captain Withers the Federal officer's old room across from Morgan's. They washed up, and found a fire blazing in the parlor, the first of the season. Mrs. Williams, Miss Rumbaugh and young Fanny were in a festive mood: It would be a gala, indeed, although Mrs. Williams regretted Lucy's absence. "The rain probably caught her at the farm . . . I hope she got there before it came down."

"I'm sure she's safe and dry, Mama," Fanny said.

Morgan, in a corner by the fire, was suddenly tired. He had not yet recopied the letter in his pocket. What he wired to Mattie was true. There were no enemy this side of the Gap. But just how long that would remain the situation he had no way of knowing. The rain started again, this time lashing the windows, then settling into a steady drumming all through dinner. Some time afterwards a messenger arrived for Major Arnold with the news that some Federal movement from the Gap had been spotted, although to the north. Major Arnold ordered his horse, and Morgan decided to check on his own bivouacs again. Withers and Gassett ballooned their ponchos out behind them as they swung them over their shoulders. They walked across the soaked garden to the stables, where the orderlies and Headquarters company were quartered for the night. Their horses, by order still saddled, were waiting, Captain Withers's a little jumpy from the lightning. They made the complete round, from Smith's camp through Giltner's and Bradford's; all seemed well. They returned to the Williams house just in time to escape another downpour. They sat around the fire swapping jokes and drinking. Gassett had been with Pegram at Rich Mountain; Withers had a brother who had been with the Forty-second Virginia under Jackson at Antietam. Morgan heard their stories but the dread of what awaited him in Abingdon moved in. Would they really suspend him from his command? That question blazed up as he watched the fire. His early morning enthusiasm, his righteous resentment so carefully expressed in the letter, now seemed premature. They would do what they wanted. In spite of Dick Curd's evidence. Hadn't they proved it often enough before? Well, then, so would he. Hines was waiting! He wished he'd told Mattie. Suddenly he got up and ordered another check of the pickets; his boys might become careless in this rain. Arnold's scout might have been wrong about the direction Gillem had taken. Any movement on their part was dangerous. This raid must not fail.

Withers came back about midnight saying all was well. Morgan had gone to bed, but got up, pulled on his pants and jacket, and walked out onto the front gallery. Behind him the house was asleep, the ladies finally succumbing to silence. All around him fitful lightning threw out the sudden shapes of trees and hills.

Kentucky. How he longed for it and feared it; it was the ultimate victory, the ultimate defeat. Mattie had said once he had too much faith in its people —that all they really cared for was their comfort and their cattle. Another test of reality he was perhaps afraid of trying. Wanting the world all in one piece, St. Leger had said. Or was he using Kentucky as a way of justifying all those deaths, all that suffering? If so, that was a worse reason than any loss of faith. He looked out past the Williams garden.

Or had winning Kentucky become some kind of crazy penance for his childhood, a transfer of the old first-son obligation onto the Confederacy? There was the thorn of Cynthiana. That loss, more than the betrayal of Richmond, had made him powerless. . . .

He remembered the strange feeling he had that night at the window in Abingdon before Mattie came in, their last night together. He shivered and looked at the hills again. On one of them, Byrne's guns were keeping vigil. It was safe enough: How many times did he need to check? He went to bed.

He was tired. When he slept he sank into a deep mist. Before him, out of it, stepped a very short old man with a face the color and gleam of polished walnut. There was something reticent and refined in the old black eyes, so old they had a glaze of gray, and looking strangely like a dead bird's. There was a birdlike angle to his head, too, as he spoke in the familiar, cracked voice. *Dem beans is a-reddy fo' plantin', Massa John. Massa John, when youze gonna plant dem beans?* It was Uncle Ben.

Suddenly it seemed the most important thing in the world, the planting of the beans. He felt a handful bloom in his hand, and he dropped them, one by one, into a small trough that had opened at his feet. The trough became deeper and he had to lean forward. The beans began disappearing and he reached for them, feeling the soft earth crumble under his hand, then up his arms to the elbows, but they were gone.

"That's too deep," he heard himself say.

Ain't nuthin' too deep, Uncle Ben whispered above him.

When he looked up the old man was smiling. A torrent of rain broke around him; lightning flashed and the trench where he now sat knee-deep in mud began sinking, pulling him away. He threw both arms up but Uncle Ben seemed oblivious, remote in his own safety, secure and withdrawn beyond reach. He began beating at the sides of the trench, beating, beating. . . .

The knocks on the door became louder, until he sat up and called, "Come in."

It was Captain Withers. A glance at the window told him it was still dark.
"Is it still raining?"

"Yes, sir."

It would be miserable out there.

"Then let the men have time to dry their guns. Let's say seven o'clock."

"Yes, sir."

Withers closed the door and he listened: The roof of the Williams house drummed with rain. *Daid hosses eatin' grain.* Dear old Uncle Ben. Now why had he dreamt of him? He had been in such a deep sleep that, for a while, even with Withers pounding on the door, he'd forgotten where he was. He frowned, shaking his head. He must be worn out. He could already hear through the rain the roosters starting. Better catch ten minutes more. He dozed.

Withers walked through the dripping garden to the stables and woke the Headquarters clerk to write orders for Bradford, Giltner, Smith and the battery on the hill. He waited, with a cup of coffee, for the couriers to return with receipted slips that the orders were received. As he walked back to the house the rain slackened. Thunder was still rumbling off to the east, but the long night's storm was over.

Morgan, in his room, heard it too; it was a comforting sound. Another hour would give his boys time to dry their guns. There was nothing more miserable than waking up soaked to the bone, unless it was finding your cartridges soaked, too. He turned over and closed his eyes.

A burst of firing woke him. The unmistakable *tat-tat-tat* of rifle fire, and yells. Women calling: *"Yankees!"* A dream? Then again: *"Yankees!"*

He ran to the window and saw a bluecoat patrol galloping down Main Street and around to the stables. He pulled on his pants and boots just in time to join Major Gassett in the hall. They ran down the back stairs through the garden. It was too late: The Federals were circling the block. They ran then diagonally through the garden again, protected by the high board fence, to the basement of the church on the opposite corner. Rifle fire cut the trees, and shattered leaves fell through the arbor and rose bushes. The cellar of the church was damp and smelled of old mortar: a pool of uncertain sanctuary in the swirl of yelling outside. They crouched, thankful for no windows. In a few minutes, Withers came crawling through the flowers to join them. Morgan ordered him back to the house, to the upstairs windows, to signal the battery on the hill. And to see if there was a complete encirclement . . . any break at all, any possibility of getting out. Withers, breathless, begged them to return with him. "We can make a barricade . . . shoot from the windows. . . ." Morgan shook his head.

Withers left, and through the cellar door, held ajar, they watched his form dissolve in the mist. They waited ten minutes.

Next to Morgan, Gassett was breathing heavily. The damp of the dirt floor sent a chill that made the young major's teeth chatter. Through the crack in the door Morgan watched the garden and the dripping trees and arbor and the house. Sporadic firing, and the sound of voices. Fear, like ice, moved up his legs. His breath lingered in front of his face in a little cloud of fog. He sucked in and swallowed. Hines. What a dream. What was it Hines had said about courage? It comes from the French word for heart . . . and now the whole world had shrunk into that triangle between the stables, the church and the house, across that wet grass to the light in an upstairs window. And life had shrunk into his own body, into one single self. The final cause.

Withers came back with the news that the whole block was surrounded. "Thick as thieves . . . the streets solid blue." Then hesitantly, through the gloom of the cellar: "General, I think it would be best if you surrendered."

Morgan turned blazing eyes to this young man whose mother had been kind to his wife in Danville. He had never, outside of the last Kentucky raid, seen war. His own youth rose before him: He had once been like that. Believing in . . . so much. Now all that was left was to draw off their fire. To Major Gassett, who had joined his staff only last month, he said wearily, "It's useless. They've sworn never to take me prisoner. You've got to . . ."

"But General—"

Gassett was interrupted by a splintering of boards above their heads: The Yankees were breaking down the church doors.

"We've got to separate," Morgan heard himself say. "Through the garden . . . make for the house . . ."

His legs pumped under him. He hadn't had time to pull on his jacket . . . his nightshirt billowed white as he ran through the garden. A woman, awakened by the rifle fire, watched from her window across the street and screeched: "There's Morgan! Kill him! Kill him!"

He heard a yell, a dozen exploding rifles over the fence. He ran toward the grape arbor, the thorns of rose bushes tearing at him. Blinded by sweat, he knelt in the mud, hearing shouts on the other side of the boards: snorts, shouts, galloping, his own panting punctuating a fear that threatened to paralyze him. No, no, they were enemy but they were civilized. They were American, as he was. Usages of war. *Code d'honneur*. Even Grant. Withers right. They wouldn't shoot a man with his hands up.

Withers, racing to the house, heard a half-moan, half-cry: "Oh, God!" as he saw Morgan fall forward and the Yankees club a hole in the fence. Then, behind him, an exultant scream: "I've killed the damned horse thief!" just as his own arms were pinned to his sides, with the back porch steps within reach.

Withers stood with his captors just under the eave of the back porch and watched the Yankee troopers swarm over something white in the bushes. They were tearing his clothes off for souvenirs and dragging the body out through the hole in the fence. The two Yankees with Withers, drawn by curiosity, pulled their charge with them to the fence, and Withers saw, unbelieving, Morgan's body thrown over a mule to be paraded across town. Before they reached the corner the limp form fell from the saddle and dragged in the ditch. For one horrible instant Withers thought he detected life, the movement of an arm. But the grisly procession started up again, its leaders screaming in triumph. Withers struggled to break loose, did manage to get one shoulder away, but his captors gripped him again. "Where you think yore goin', sonny? Yew want similar treatment?"

Private Andrew Campbell of the Thirteenth Tennessee Union Cavalry claimed the honor of killing Morgan. He was thirty years old, a mountain boy who had enlisted at Nashville as a Confederate, switched in Arkansas to join the other side. He had already been threatened with court-martial for drunkenness, his captain intimating that Private Campbell, "having but few mental acquirements either to balance his splendid physical organization or to offset his failings," might resign or answer for certain irregularities. Now he was a hero. Gillem made him a lieutenant the next day.

It was still raining when Colonel Smith sent Lieutenant Schaffer into town for a brandy ration for his wet men. Lieutenant Schaffer met a horde of bluecoats rushing past him, firing from their saddles. He wheeled and returned to the bivouac, where Smith, and then Giltner, heard the firing.

Lieutenant Xenophon Hawkins heard it up on the hill with the battery. Without a second thought he charged down into town with twenty-five men. His dash through the Federals allowed Gassett and some of the men at the stables to escape. Gillem's men were already heading out the Jonesboro Road, and Captain White had unlimbered for a retreat. No effort was made by anyone except Hawkins to accomplish a rescue.

Gassett grabbed a horse and rode out to Colonel Smith, who had come around to the Jonesboro Road, the only road now not held by Gillem's troops. "What . . . ?"

"It must have been that gap betwen the pickets, south of town," Smith growled. "Damned Bradford."

But who could have known, thought Gassett . . . unless it was Lucy Williams. Somebody showed the Yankees a little-known lane between the Warrensburg and Newport roads. . . . "We've got to ride back in," Gassett got out.

"My ammunition is soaked. We're being flanked on the left. Do you think we're crazy, man?" The look on Gassett's face made Smith add: "Prudence and good sense tell me to fall back, Major, along this road to Jonesboro, since the artillery have already gone ahead. . . . Besides, I don't credit the rumor that the General has been killed. We have heard that too often before."

When Colonel Bradford heard the firing he immediately made a half-circle around the town to the Jonesboro Road to join Smith. Giltner was heading back to town about the same time, until a farmer told him the fight was now toward the north. On the way, shots parallel to him made Giltner swing wide. He did not reach Smith until he was seven miles past the town. The whole column, together again, began a cautious retreat and halted about fourteen miles out, sending a courier under a flag back for news.

"He can't be dead!" Xen Hawkins said softly, tears stinging his eyes. "He was everything we needed . . . he believed. He *believed!*"

The others looked up. At any moment they expected to see not the courier, but John Morgan, galloping up, his hat off, his face smiling.

Afterword

Mattie Morgan named her baby girl Johnny, after her father. She died of typhoid on her honeymoon. Mattie remarried and lived in Tennessee.

Cal made it through the war. Richard was captured on the Clinch River in November 1864, but he and Charlton returned to Kentucky from prison. Charlton lived at Hopemont, where his son, Thomas Hunt Morgan, was born—the last Morgan to be born there. Named for young Tom who died on the Ohio raid, he won the Nobel Prize for Physiology and Medicine in 1933 for his work in genetics. Key died in Lexington at the age of thirty-three in 1878, Henrietta in 1891, age eighty-six.

Basil Duke took over the command after Morgan died. The old regiments, reduced to 273 men, were armed, in Duke's words, with scarcely fifty serviceable guns. General John C. Breckinridge came to Abingdon with Colonel W. C. P. Breckinridge's Ninth Kentucky and Dortch's men, who had been refused so often to Morgan, and now arriving too late.

The guilt of Lucy Williams has never been proved. Joe Williams, her Union soldier husband, arrived in Greeneville September 5, the day after Morgan's death. Lucy left the same day for Knoxville. Her sister, Jenny Rumbaugh, stated that "she heard him tell her to go on to Knoxville with a flag of truce . . . that he was fearful if she remained here Morgan's men would arrest her and take her to Richmond." Joe and Lucy Williams were later divorced, Williams charging his wife with adultery and infanticide, "and what she did that September in Greeneville." Lucy countered with neglect and nonsupport.

Private Andrew Campbell, the Yankee soldier who shot Morgan and was made a lieutenant the next day by special order from then-Tennessee Governor Andrew Johnson, stayed in the army after the war. He became an alcoholic and a barroom brawler and, given the choice of resigning or answering at a court-martial for irregularities, he chose the former and resigned his commission. His command left Arkansas in 1869 without him.

After the war Basil Duke did write his *History of Morgan's Cavalry*. Of Morgan's death he wrote: "When he died, the glory and chivalry seemed gone from the struggle, and it became a tedious routine, enjoined by duty, and sustained only by sentiments of pride and hatred." He may have been more correct than he realized. Mrs. Thompson, the woman who signaled Morgan's presence in the garden at Greeneville, received a reward of one thousand dollars. In a newspaper account dated January 1, 1865, it was reported that Captain John Dowdy, C.S.A., recently escaped from an Ohio prison, traveled to Tennessee and shot Mrs. Thompson on Christmas Day, after refusing the thousand dollars if he would spare her.

A.P. Hill died just eight days before Appomattox. Morgan's command, under Duke, was at Danville, Virginia, when they learned of Lee's surrender, and Basil, now a brigadier-general, obtained permission to mount his men on mules taken from supply wagons for the march to North Carolina. They had few saddles now, and only rope halters. They were on their way to General Joe Johnston, who was negotiating an armistice with Sherman. President Davis and his Cabinet arrived at Charlotte, North Carolina, and Duke joined his cavalry escort. Davis wanted to march into Alabama, to join Forrest, believing that twenty-five hundred men could continue the war and form a nucleus for thousands of recruits. Basil stood respectfully at that last council, in the silence that followed those wild hopes. When Davis saw defeat he rose, bitter and faltering, and left the room. He was captured at Washington, Georgia. Nobody has ever ascertained what happened to the Confederate treasury. Secretary of State Judah Benjamin made his way via Florida to England, where he became a successful lawyer.

Tom Hines tried his coup again, on Election Day in November 1864. The plotters were arrested through treachery, but Hines escaped by hiding in a box mattress in the house of a Dr. Edwards in Chicago. On the bed above him Mrs. Edwards, ill and reputedly dying, received visitors in a house now surrounded by Federals. Among those visitors leaving the sickbed the next day was a slight young man who, under an autumn shower, held his umbrella across his face. Hines was almost taken again in Cincinnati, where he hid in a closet with a false back while Union troopers searched the house. Despite his belief that he would never live through the war, Hines returned to Kentucky, became a lawyer and, later, Chief Justice of the Kentucky Court of Appeals.

After the debacle at Chicago Castleman was exiled and St. Leger Grenfel was sent to Fort Jefferson off Key West, a hellhole surrounded by a shark-infested moat. There the aging Englishman had his hands tied and was thrown into twenty-five feet of water. When he surfaced, his feet were also tied, and he was sent down again. When he came up sputtering but still defiant, the lieutenant in charge ordered weights to be added to his feet. Three more times he was thrown in, and three more times he broke surface. Finally he was left on the wharf in disgust. Dr. Samuel Mudd, who had treated John Wilkes Booth, was sentenced there also, and Grenfel helped him fight a yellow fever epidemic. Mudd was pardoned; President Andrew Johnson denied clemency for the Englishman, in spite of protests from the British embassy. After almost three years in prison, in May 1868, St. Leger, with a companion, escaped in an open boat in a storm, never to be heard of again.

Colonel Robert Martin, with two young Morgan officers, John Headley and John Kennedy, did attempt to burn New York. Three hotels were burned and sixteen others damaged. Another fire was set at the Winter Garden Theater, where Edwin Booth, with his brothers Junius and John Wilkes, were appearing in *Julius Caesar*. Kennedy, who set fire to Barnum's Circus, was executed.

Shadeland still stands, reduced in acreage and surrounded by the suburbs of Lexington. It was, until her death in July 1984, occupied by Frances

"Tassie" Parker, a granddaughter of one of Morgan's men, G. A. Delong, captured with Company D at Twelve Mile Island on the Ohio raid.

It was not until January 1958 that the Warren Court dropped the case of the Mount Sterling bank robbery, proof, perhaps, that the controversy surrounding Morgan is still alive.

After the war Nathan Bedford Forrest, whose troops were the last to surrender east of the Mississippi, returned to Sunflower Landing, his plantation south of Memphis. Seven young Federal officers went with him, to lease land and raise crops. A new war awaited them: the semimilitary "Loyal Leagues," organized among the ex-slaves and sponsored by the Reconstruction Governor of Tennessee, "Parson" Brownlow, whose proclamation of martial law was seen as an invitation to violence. Disenfranchised ex-Confederates and their families, unprotected by law and fearing racial war, sought solace in societies of their own. It is generally believed (although not substantiated by a Congressional investigation in 1871) that Forrest was elected the first Grand Wizard of the original Ku Klux Klan. He ordered its dissolution in 1869, ten days after Brownlow's radical rule was overthrown by the gubernatorial election. Broken in health, bankrupt, Forrest saw his dream of building a railroad from Selma, Alabama, to Memphis shattered by the panic of 1873 and a yellow fever epidemic that same year. He died in 1877 at the age of fifty-six.

Cassius Marcellus Clay, the Kentucky abolitionist (and Henry Clay's cousin), became Ambassador to Russia (1861–1862; 1863–1869), where he educated the Cossacks in the use of the bowie knife and fathered a son by a ballet dancer.

Simon Bolivar Buckner returned to Kentucky to become its Governor (1887–1891) and a candidate for Vice-President in 1896; he was a pallbearer at Grant's funeral. Braxton Bragg worked as a civil engineer after the war in Mobile and later in Galveston, where he fell dead one day while crossing a street. The man he met there, and in whose arms he died, was Captain L. E. Trezevant, his dispatch bearer at Shiloh. Perhaps the strangest fact of all is that the young lieutenant sent to Lexington on recruiting duty during the cholera epidemic in 1833 was indeed Jefferson Davis.

Young Tom Morgan's body was sent from Lebanon, Kentucky, to Lexington the first week of April 1868, to await the reinterment of his brother John, in order that they might be buried in the same grave. On April 17, while the pallbearers waited under springtime trees—Tom Logwood, Henry Elder, Henry Beach, the boys who had left Lexington with a hay wagon a million years ago—John Morgan's funeral cortege, with a hundred of the Old Squadron, paused briefly in front of the Phoenix Hotel before making its way to Christ Church and the Lexington cemetery. The pallbearers were General E. Kirby Smith, General William Preston, Colonel James Bowles, Captains Tom Quirk, Ben Drake, Ben Biggerstaff, William Jones. One of the marshals: Captain T. H. Hines. Basil Duke, D. Howard Smith, Warren Grigsby, Breck Castleman, Trigg, Cantrell, Tom Berry . . . they stood in dappled sunshine where not many years later Aunt Betty, too, would lie, buried at the top of the long circle where, according to her last wish, she could "keep an eye on those boys."

They are there now under the big trees: Calvin and Henrietta, Johnny and Tom, Key, Charlton, Tommie and Basil Duke, and their daughter, Thomas Morgan Duke. In the last circle lie Captain Samuel Dold Morgan, Jr., C.S.A., killed at Augusta, Kentucky, in that hopeful September, and Major George Washington Morgan, who died at Hopemont after the skirmish at Ashland. To the left, overlooking them all, is a stone marked BOU-VIETTE JAMES, EVER FAITHFUL.

Some historical data have been altered for the story:

Morgan was not at the Battle of Monterrey. He and Cal, with their uncle Alexander Gibson Morgan, did not arrive at Camargo until November 19, 1846. They did see action at Buena Vista, where Alexander was killed.

The New York draft riots, in which Negroes were hanged from lampposts on Broadway, occurred in mid-July 1863, after Gettysburg. T.H. Hunt mentions them in May.

Shadeland, Morgan's boyhood home on Tates Creek Pike, Lexington, was built c. 1798 by Joshua Brown, not by the Bolton family, who are fictitious. John Hunt, Morgan's grandfather, purchased the property from the Brown heirs; Sanders Bruce, Becky Morgan's brother, did buy it from Hunt's heirs, in 1854, not 1849.

Alice Ready, Mattie's younger sister, wrote a diary, part of which is in the archives of the University of North Carolina at Chapel Hill and which inspired some descriptions, especially those of Cousin Kate, Puss and Charley and of the pre-Shiloh days in Murfreesboro. Her marriage, widowhood and depression are fictitious. Her diary entries end with Wednesday, April 30, 1862.

Mrs. Caroline Turner's aborted "trial" for cruelty to her slaves actually occurred in 1837, not 1852, and she was murdered in 1844, not 1854.

Cassius Clay had a confrontation with a hired gun named Brown at Mount Brilliant in 1843, not 1852, but did speak in Richmond, Kentucky, at a political rally on April 4, 1860.

Lewis Robards was the most notorious slave trader in Lexington in the 1840s, and I have quoted some of his advertisements from *The Lexington Observer and Reporter*. He did go bankrupt in 1856, but sold out to someone else, since Jake Bolton is a fictional character.

There was a Will Webb (called "Poor Will Webb" by Basil Duke in his *History of Morgan's Cavalry*). Like his fictional counterpart, Webb died at Glasgow on Morgan's Christmas raid, December 24, 1862.

KMI, the Kentucky Military Institute, was not operating in 1843, when, in the story, Johnny's grandfather wants him to go there. Colonel Allen bought the spa in 1845, although the deed is dated July 23, 1848. It was chartered as a school by the state legislature in 1847 and did provide facilities for the training of Buckner's State Guard before the war. Records show that Richard Morgan attended the school in 1851, when he was fifteen.

John Morgan was suspended from Transylvania University, but there is no record of the reason. One rumor told of trouble over "ungentlemanly language to passersby," and there is mention, in secondary sources, of "a more serious difficulty" with another student. Whatever the cause, it is true that a student named William Blanchard, also blamed in the affair, received a reprimand. Morgan did not accept the school's offer of reentry the next autumn. He entered the hemp business with his uncle T.H. Hunt.

Rebecca Bruce Morgan's birthday was June 18, 1830, not in September.

Horace Greeley's editorial in favor of letting the South go (December 17, 1860) could not have been received by mail in Lexington before December 20, the date of South Carolina's secession.

James Clay, Henry's son, was arrested in October 1861, not September.

The skirmish at Sacramento, Kentucky, in which Forrest routed a Federal force (and which was popularly called at the time the first cavalry fight in the West), occurred on December 28, 1861, not in September. And, although Lieutenant Gathright tells Morgan that Forrest became a major-general after Chickamauga, the promotion was not official until December 4, 1863.

There is no evidence that Dick Curd was the pro-Union member of Henrietta Morgan's family. Cal, however, while under arrest, did mention in a letter from New York (April 24, 1862) that Curd had been in Federally-held Nashville when Basil, wounded at Shiloh, found refuge with a Southern-sympathizing family. It may be correct to assume that Curd helped with Basil's release.

Although in the story Morgan hears of Walter Ferguson's death in June 1864, Ferguson was executed by Burbridge in Lexington not in June, but on November 15, 1864, after Morgan's death.

It is ironic to note that a repetition of Morgan's march north to the Ohio River to cross the mountains and join Lee in Virginia was contemplated by General John Hood after the fall of Atlanta. Hood's army met disaster at Franklin, Tennessee, and Nashville late in 1864. Again, as at Fort Donelson, Shiloh, and Chattanooga, Forrest's plan—this time to flank the Federals at Spring Hill, an action that would have avoided the slaughter at Franklin and the loss of Nashville—was ignored.

Although the execution of two Morgan men in Lexington is undocumented, the pro-Union *Louisville Daily Democrat* reported two of Morgan's men killed by angry citizens in Evansville, Indiana, in July 1862.

There was a Captain Charles Withers with Morgan in Greeneville when he was killed, but he was not the son of Tassie Withers of Danville, Virginia, since she is a fictitious character.

One mystery remains: a letter in the Rare Book Room of the University of Kentucky, in which a friend of the Morgan family wrote to Cal after the war concerning the mistreatment, for voting Democratic, of one William Morgan, who claimed to have been the body servant of the General. Although Randolph and Billy are created characters, one wonders if William Morgan could have been the servant nicknamed "Box" who turned back with Morgan in the Ohio River. It was common practice for slaves to take the last names of their masters.

Bibliography

BOOKS, LETTERS RELATED TO MORGAN

Adjutant General's Report, Kentucky Volunteers, Confederate States Army. Special Collections, University of Kentucky, Lexington.

Brown, Dee A. *The Bold Cavaliers.* Philadelphia and New York, 1959.

Davis, William C. *The Orphan Brigade.* Garden City, New York, 1980.

Duke, Basil. *A History of Morgan's Cavalry,* ed. Cecil F. Holland. Bloomington, Indiana, 1960. First published Cincinnati, 1867.

Holland, Cecil Fletcher. *Morgan and His Raiders.* New York, 1942.

Horan, James D. *Confederate Agent: A Discovery in History.* New York, 1954.

Horn, Stanley. *Tennessee's War.* Nashville, Tennessee, 1965.

Hunt, John Wesley. Letters. Rare Book Room. Transylvania University, Lexington, Kentucky.

Hunt-Morgan Papers. Special Collections. University of Kentucky, Lexington.

McDonough, James Lee. *Shiloh—in Hell Before Night.* Knoxville, Tennessee, 1977.

Metzler, William E. *Morgan and His Dixie Cavaliers.* Columbus, Ohio, 1976.

Morgan Letters. Hunt-Morgan House, Lexington, Kentucky.

Morgan, John Hunt. Letter. Archives, Western Kentucky University, Bowling Green, Kentucky.

Pollard, E. A. *Southern History of the War.* New York, 1886.

Ramage, James A. "John Hunt Morgan and the Kentucky Cavalry Volunteers in the Mexican War." *The Register of the Kentucky Historical Society.* Frankfort (Autumn 1983), pp. 343–365.

———. *John Wesley Hunt.* Lexington, Kentucky, 1974.

Swiggert, Howard. *The Rebel Raider: A Life of John H. Morgan.* Indianapolis, Indiana, 1934.

Sword, Wiley. *Shiloh: Bloody April.* New York, 1974.

Thomas, Edison H. *John Hunt Morgan and His Raiders.* Lexington, Kentucky, 1975.

DIARIES AND AUTOBIOGRAPHIES

Castleman, John Breckinridge. *Active Service.* Louisville, Kentucky, 1917.

Chestnut, Mary B. *A Diary from Dixie.* New York, 1929. First published New York, 1909.

Duke, Basil. *Reminiscences of Gen. B. W. Duke, C.S.A.* New York, 1911.

Fox, Gustavus V. *Confidential Correspondence of G. V. Fox, Ass't. Secretary of the Navy 1861–1865.* New York, 1918.

Hines, Thomas Henry. Papers and scrapbook. Special Collections. University of Kentucky, Lexington.

Ready, Alice. Diary, 1860–1862. Southern Historical Collection. University of North Carolina, Chapel Hill.

Von Borcke, Heros. *Memoirs of the Confederate War for Independence.* New York, 1938.

NEWSPAPERS

The Atlanta Century, March 1860–May 1865, ed. Norman Shavin. Atlanta, 1965.

The Lexington Observer and Reporter.

The Louisville Courier-Journal.

The Louisville Daily Democrat.

The New York Times.

The New York Tribune.

The Philadelphia Weekly Times.

The Spirit of the Times.

BIOGRAPHIES

Bodley, Temple. *George Rogers Clark: His Life and Public Services.* Boston, 1927.

Bowman, Col. S. M., and Lt. Col. R. B. Irwin. *Sherman and His Campaigns: A Military Biography.* New York, 1965.

Canfield, Cass. *The Iron Will of Jefferson Davis.* New York, 1978.

Cleaves, Freeman. *Old Tippecanoe: William Henry Harrison and His Time.* New York, 1939.

Davis, William C. *Breckinridge: Statesman, Soldier, Symbol.* Baton Rouge, Louisiana, 1974.

Durfee, David A., and H. F. Bremer. *William Henry Harrison, 1773–1841 and John Tyler, 1790–1862.* Dobbs Ferry, New York, 1970.

Green, James A. *William Henry Harrison, His Life and Times.* Richmond, Virginia, 1941.

Henry, Robert Selph. *"First with the Most" Forrest.* New York, 1944.

———(ed.). *As They Saw Forrest: Some Recollections and Comments of Contemporaries.* Jackson, Tennessee, 1956.

Johnston, William Preston. *Life of Albert Sidney Johnston.* New York, 1880.

Kirwan, Albert D. *John J. Crittenden: The Struggle for the Union.* Lexington, Kentucky, 1962.

Ludwig, Emil. *Lincoln.* Boston, 1930.

Ross, Ishbel. *The President's Wife: Mary Todd Lincoln.* New York, 1973.

Schenck, Martin. *Up Came Hill.* Harrisburg, Pennsylvania, 1958.

Seitz, Don C. *Braxton Bragg: General of the Confederacy.* Columbia, South Carolina, 1924.

Smiley, David L. *Lion of White Hall: The Life of Cassius M. Clay.* Gloucester, Massachusetts, 1969.

Strode, Hudson. *Jefferson Davis, American Patriot 1808–1861*. New York, 1955.
———. *Jefferson Davis: Confederate President*. New York, 1959.
———. *Jefferson Davis: Tragic Hero 1864–1889*. New York, 1964.
Townsend, W. Henry. *Lincoln and the Bluegrass*. Lexington, Kentucky, 1955.
Van Deusen, Glyndon G. *Life of Henry Clay*. Boston, 1937.
———. *William Henry Seward*. New York, 1967.
Wyeth, John Allan. *That Devil Forrest*. New York, 1959. First published New York, 1899.

GENERAL INFORMATION

Adams, James Truslow. *The March of Democracy: A History of the United States*. Vol. II: *A Half Century of Expansion;* Vol. III: *Civil War and Reconstruction*. New York, 1932.
American Historical Documents, ed. Charles W. Eliot. New York, 1969. First published New York, 1938.
Axton, W. F. *Tobacco and Kentucky*. Lexington, Kentucky, 1976.
Boles, John B. *Religion in Antebellum Kentucky*. Lexington, Kentucky, 1976.
Butler, Mann. *A History of the Commonwealth of Kentucky*. Berea, Kentucky, 1969. First published 1834.
Channing, Steven A. *Kentucky: A Bicentennial History*. New York, 1977.
Clark, T. D. "Trade Between Kentucky and the Cotton Kingdom in Livestock, Hemp, Slaves, 1840–1860." Unpublished thesis. University of Kentucky, Lexington, 1929.
Coggins, Jack. *Arms and Equipment of the Civil War*. New York, 1962.
Coleman, J. Winston. *Famous Kentucky Duels*. Frankfort, Kentucky, 1953.
———. *Kentucky: A Pictorial History*. Lexington, Kentucky, 1971.
———. *Lexington During the Civil War*. Lexington, Kentucky, 1938.
———. "Lexington's Slave Dealers and Their Southern Trade," *Filson Club Historical Quarterly*. Louisville, Kentucky (January 1938), pp. 1–23.
———. *Old Homes of the Blue Grass*. Lexington, Kentucky, 1950.
———. *Slavery Times in Kentucky*. Chapel Hill, North Carolina, 1940.
———. *The Springs of Kentucky: Watering Places 1800–1935*. Lexington, Kentucky, 1955.
———. *Stagecoach Days of the Bluegrass*. Louisville, Kentucky, 1935.
———. *Three Kentucky Artists*. Lexington, Kentucky, 1974.
Collins, Richard H. *History of Kentucky*. Frankfort, Kentucky, 1966.
The Confederate Soldier in the Civil War: Official Reports and Descriptions by Military and Government Leaders. New York, n.d.
Cotterill, Robert S. *History of Pioneer Kentucky*. Cincinnati, 1917.
Coulter, E. Merton. *The Civil War and Readjustment in Kentucky*. Chapel Hill, North Carolina, 1966.
Davis, Carl L. *Arming the Union: Small Arms in the Civil War*. Port Washington, New York, 1973.
The Divided Union, ed. J. G. Randall and David Donald. Boston, 1961.
Edwards, William B. *Civil War Guns*. Harrisburg, Pennsylvania, 1962.

Fuller, Claude E., and Richard D. Stuart. *Firearms of the Confederacy*. Huntington, West Virginia, 1944.

Hollingsworth, Kent. *The Great Ones*. Lexington, Kentucky, 1970.

———. *The Kentucky Thoroughbred*. Lexington, Kentucky, 1976.

Hopkins, James F. *History of the Hemp Industry in Kentucky*. Lexington, Kentucky, 1951.

Johnson, Rossiter. *Campfire and Battlefield*. New York, 1978. First published New York, 1894.

Jordan, Robert Paul. *The Civil War*. Kingsport, Tennessee, 1975.

Kane, Joseph Nathan. *Famous First Facts*. New York, 1964.

McBride, Robert M. "Oaklands." *Tennessee Historical Quarterly*. Nashville, Tennessee (December 1963), pp. 1–20.

McClellan, Elisabeth. *History of American Costume, 1607–1870*. New York, 1937.

Olmsted, Frederick Law. *The Slave States*. New York, 1959. First published 1861.

Parkman, Francis. *The Oregon Trail*. New York, 1950. First published 1849.

Peter, Robert. *History of Fayette County, Kentucky*. Chicago, 1882.

Ranck, George W. *History of Lexington, Kentucky*. Cincinnati, 1872.

Starobin, Robert S. *Industrial Slavery in the Old South*. New York, 1970.

Warren, Robert Penn. *The Legacy of the Civil War*. New York, 1961.

Wilson, Woodrow. *A History of the American People*, Vol. IV. New York, 1903.

Woodward, W. E. *A New American History*. New York, 1938.

Acknowledgments

It is with gratitude and humility that I acknowledge the generous help and sincere good wishes of those people who have contributed to the fulfillment of this story over the past six years. Without their sustaining interest, valuable information could not have been obtained. Although I wish to address individuals here who gave me direct assistance, my appreciation extends to the authors in the bibliography, many of whom provided me not only with facts but also with the ambience of the past. It is because of them, known personally or known only through the printed page, that this story came alive for me, as I hope it will for the reader.

Tassie Parker, whose grandfather rode with Morgan, lived at Shadeland and lent me rare books and family letters. She gave me much, much more, however. Her enthusiasm and vivacity, her faith in this book can only be described by the French word *élan*. It is to Tassie that I dedicate the story. She died at Shadeland in July 1984. How she would have loved seeing it completed. Words like "gratitude" and "acknowledgment" are useless here.

Stephen A. Oleksa, my son-in-law and mechanical engineer, graciously produced all the maps in this book. His professional dedication to accuracy will always be appreciated, as well as his tolerance of my perfectionism.

Raines Taylor, of the Blue Grass Trust for Historic Preservation, with offices housed at Hopemont, has been most helpful in providing me with Cal's letters from prison, genealogical data and other memorabilia of the Hunts and Morgans. Madie McIntosh, former hostess of Hopemont, searched out several portraits and shared with me her extensive knowledge of the family. Richard A. Shrader, Reference Archivist at the University of North Carolina, provided me with access to Alice Ready's diary, valuable for its descriptions of Mattie, Alice and the Ready household before and during the Battle of Shiloh. The personnel at Special Collections, University of Kentucky (Thomas Henry Hines Papers, Hunt-Morgan Papers, *Adjutant General's Report, Kentucky Volunteers, Confederate States Army*), and at the Rare Book Room at Transylvania University (John Wesley Hunt letters, some of which, from old John Hunt when he sold flour to the Spaniards in New Orleans in 1795, still had sealing wax) are remembered for their patience in finding material, as well as those librarians at the University of Western Kentucky, Bowling Green.

Other sources of information graciously given are the personnel at the Keeneland Library at the Keeneland Race Course (bloodlines and races), the Kentucky Horse Park (information on carriages), the Lexington Cemetery, the Kentucky Military History Museum, Frankfort, and Mr. Charles Layson, of Antique and Modern Firearms, Lexington.

Guides at the Shiloh National Military Park and the Stones River National Battlefield made those battles come alive, as well as a young man at "Oaklands," Murfreesboro, Tennessee, where Nathan Bedford Forrest accepted the surrender of the town after fighting on the grounds of that plantation.

Two authors from the bibliography must be mentioned. The first is, of course, Basil Duke, Morgan's brother-in-law and second-in-command, without whose *History of Morgan's Cavalry* and *Reminiscences* this story could not have been written. The second is the dashing John Breckinridge Castleman, whose autobiography, *Active Service*, provided me with some of the slave stories of Uncle Isaac and Uncle Ben, and the title.

The manuscript owes much to the special wisdom and sensitive criticism of Harvey Curtis Webster, now living in Las Cruces, New Mexico, whose careful reading and insightful comments encouraged a search for honesty and excellence. Ann La Farge of Ballantine Books became my second self, my artistic conscience; her untiring confidence became an impetus, almost an intoxication hard to resist. Dag Ryen of Lexington, author, horseman and Kentucky historian, was another source of inspiration and support.

The patience and understanding of my husband, Stanley, made this book possible. No words here can express my gratitude enough. The interest of our children, Catherine, Susan, Jim and Stan, Jr., has become a family tradition during this time of creation, and not to be taken for granted, or lightly. My mother's bardic Irish blood and the memory of my father, whose three uncles fought at Shiloh, whispered more than once ghostly comfort.

There are others, too, who cannot speak for themselves, except with a whinny or a neigh, who have taught me much about tact, rapport, and a generosity freely given—my horses. Without their lessons in tolerance and courage I would never have understood the triumphs and failures of those gray-clad horsemen who still travel, in the silence of a snowfall, through the drifting mist of an early morning fog, the back roads of Kentucky.

ABOUT THE AUTHOR

Four of Clara Rising's ancestors died in Confederate service. Her first piano teacher remembered "the Yankees marching into Nashville." For Mrs. Rising, as for many Southerners, the Civil War has never been far away.

A native of Mississippi who has traveled extensively with her Army husband (now retired) and their four children (now married), Clara Rising divides her year between Florida and a farm in Kentucky, and her time between writing and riding horses over some of the same roads Morgan used. Although her academic credits include a master's degree in Creative Writing from the University of Louisville and a Ph.D. from the University of Florida, this is her first published novel, seven years in the making.